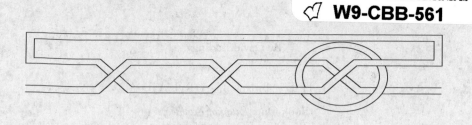

Praise for David Eddings

and *The Tamuli*

"Neatly blending simplicity and complexity, this tale of comradeship,
dastardly doings, multiple gods, strange races and noble and
ignoble humans is vintage Eddings."
—*Publishers Weekly*

"Outstanding reading entertainment . . .
fans will be more than pleased."
—*Romantic Times*

"Eddings continues to reward lovers of great,
sweeping fantasies with creative ingenuity in characterization,
world building, and magical effects."
—*Booklist*

"Another addictive fantasy from this expert in the genre."
—*Publishing News*

By David Eddings

THE BELGARIAD

Book One: *Pawn of Prophecy*
Book Two: *Queen of Sorcery*
Book Three: *Magician's Gambit*
Book Four: *Castle of Wizardry*
Book Five: *Enchanters' End Game*

THE MALLOREON

Book One: *Guardians of the West*
Book Two: *King of the Murgos*
Book Three: *Demon Lord of Karanda*
Book Four: *Sorceress of Darshiva*
Book Five: *The Seeress of Kell*

THE ELENIUM

Book One: *The Diamond Throne*
Book Two: *The Ruby Knight*
Book Three: *The Sapphire Rose*

THE TAMULI

Book One: *Domes of Fire*
Book Two: *The Shining Ones*
Book Three: *The Hidden City*

By David and Leigh Eddings

BELGARATH THE SORCERER

POLGARA THE SORCERESS

THE RIVAN CODEX

THE REDEMPTION OF ALTHALUS

REGINA'S SONG

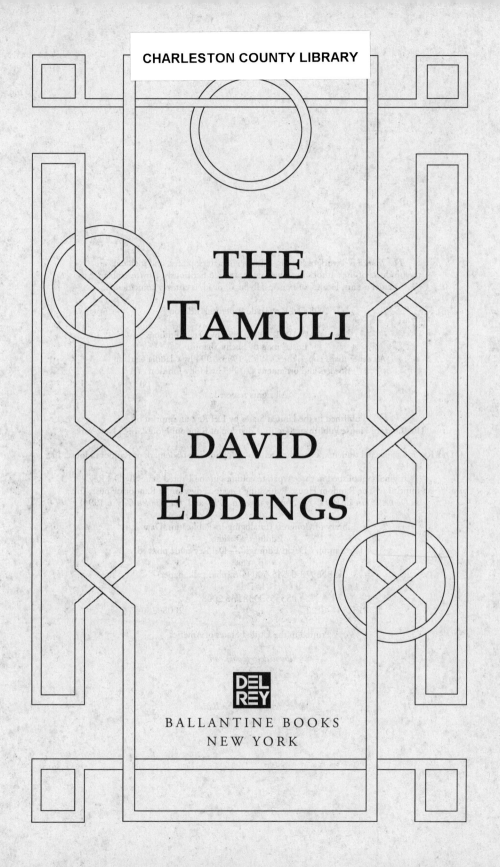

THE
TAMULI

DAVID
EDDINGS

DEL
REY

BALLANTINE BOOKS
NEW YORK

2008 Del Rey Trade Paperback Edition

Copyright © 1992, 1993, 1994 by David Eddings
"Eosia" map by Shelly Shapiro
All other maps copyright © 1992, 1993, 1994 by Claudia Carlson
Borders and ornament © 1993 by Holly Johnson

Originally published in three separate volumes in the United States by Del Rey,
an imprint of The Random House Publishing Group, a division of Random House, Inc.,
as *Domes of Fire* in 1992, *The Shining Ones* in 1993, and *The Hidden City* in 1994.

Library of Congress Cataloging-in-Publication Data
Eddings, David.
The Tamuli / David Eddings. — Del Rey trade pbk. ed.
p. cm.
ISBN 978-0-345-50094-6 (pbk. : alk. paper)
I. Title.
PS3555.D38T36 2008
813'.54—dc22   2008028947

Printed in the United States of America

www.delreybooks.com

6 8 9 7

Book design by Karin Batten

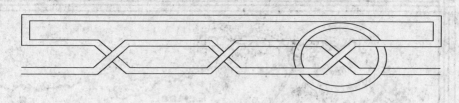

CONTENTS

Domes of Fire   3

The Shining Ones   339

The Hidden City   683

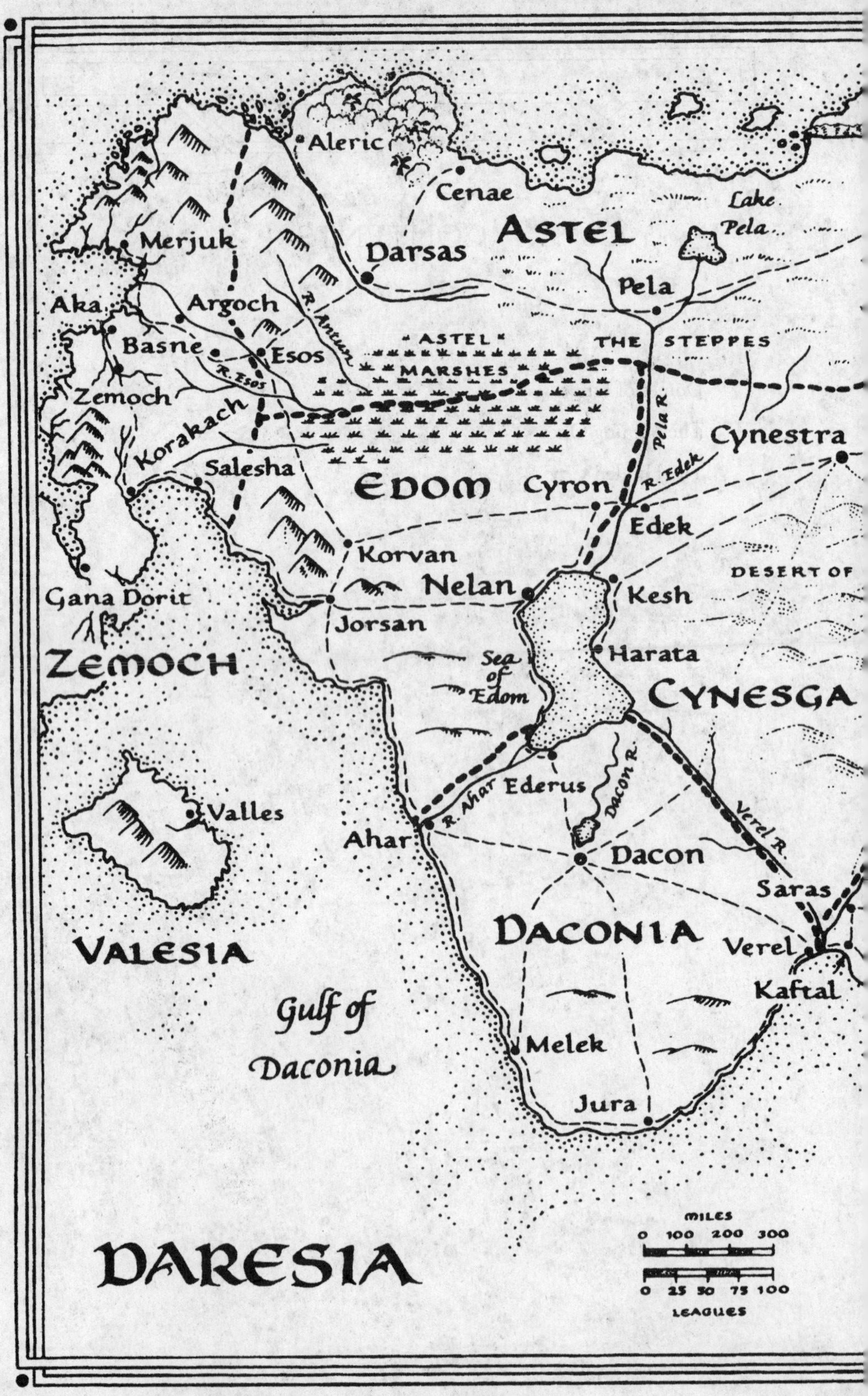

ASTEL

Aleric

Cenae

Darsas

Lake Pela

Pela

Merjuk

THE STEPPES

Aka

Argoch

R. Antua

Basne

Esos

R. Esos

ASTEL MARSHES

Cynestra

Zemoch

Korakach

EDOM

Cyron

R. Edek

Edek

Salesha

Pela R.

DESERT OF

Korvan

Nelan

Kesh

Gana Dorit

Jorsan

Harata

ZEMOCH

Sea of Edom

CYNESGA

Valles

R. Ahar

Ederus

Dacon R.

Verel R.

Ahar

Dacon

Saras

VALESIA

DACONIA

Verel

Kaftal

Gulf of Daconia

Melek

Jura

DARESIA

MILES

0   100   200   300

0   25 50 75 100

LEAGUES

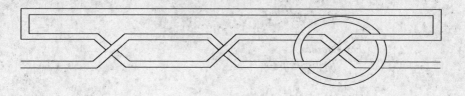

DOMES
OF FIRE

For Veronica,
for her help—

And for Maria,
for her enthusiasm—

Two very special ladies in our lives.

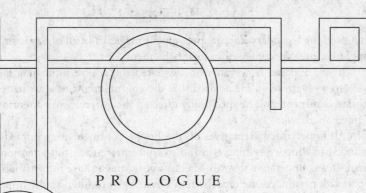

PROLOGUE

—Excerpted from Chapter Two of The Cyrga
Affair: An Examination of the Recent Crisis.
*Compiled by the Contemporary History
Department of the University of Matherion.*

I t was quite obvious to the Imperial Council at this point that
the empire was facing a threat of the gravest nature—a threat
that his Imperial Majesty's government was ill-prepared to
confront. The empire had long relied upon the armies of Atan
to defend her interests during the periodic outbreaks of incidental civic disorder
that are normal and to be expected in a disparate population ruled by a strong central authority. The situation facing his Majesty's government this time, however, did
not appear to arise from spontaneous demonstrations by a few malcontented hotheads spilling out into the streets from various university campuses during the traditional recess that follows final examinations. Those particular demonstrations can
be taken in stride, and order is usually restored with a minimum of bloodshed.

The government soon realized that this time, however, things were different.
The demonstrators were not high-spirited schoolboys, for one thing, and domestic
tranquility did not return when classes at the universities resumed. The authorities
might still have maintained order had the various disruptions been the result of ordinary revolutionary fervor. The mere presence of Atan warriors can dampen the
spirits of even the most enthusiastic under normal circumstances. This time, the
customary acts of vandalism accompanying the demonstrations were quite obviously of paranormal origin. Inevitably, the imperial government cast a questioning
eye at the Styrics in Sarsos. An investigation by Styric members of the Imperial
Council whose loyalty to the throne could not be questioned, however, quite clearly
indicated that Styricum had had no part in the disturbances. The paranormal incidents were obviously coming from some as-yet-to-be-determined sources and were
so widespread that they could not have emanated from the activities of a few Styric
renegades. The Styrics themselves were unable to identify the source of this activity,

and even the legendary Zalasta, preeminent magician in all of Styricum though he might be, ruefully confessed to total bafflement.

It was Zalasta, however, who suggested the course ultimately taken by his Majesty's government. He advised that the empire might seek assistance from the Eosian continent, and he specifically directed the government's attention to a man named Sparhawk.

All imperial representatives on the Eosian continent were immediately commanded to drop everything else and to concentrate their full attention upon this man. It was imperative that his Majesty's government have information about this Sparhawk person. As the reports from Eosia began to filter in, the Imperial Council began to develop a composite picture of Sparhawk: his appearance, his personality, and his history.

Sir Sparhawk, they discovered, was a member of one of the quasi-religious orders of the Elene Church. His particular order is referred to as the "Pandion Knights." He is a tall, lean man of early middle years with a battered face, a keen intelligence, and an abrupt, even abrasive manner. The Knights of the Elene Church are fearsome warriors, and Sir Sparhawk is in the forefront of their ranks of champions. At the time in the history of the Eosian continent when the four orders of the Church Knights were founded, the circumstances were so desperate that the Elenes set aside their customary prejudices and permitted the Militant Orders to receive instruction in the arcane practices of Styricum, and it was the proficiency of the Church Knights in those arts that helped them to prevail during the First Zemoch War some five centuries ago.

Sir Sparhawk held a position for which there is no equivalent in our empire. He was the hereditary "Champion" of the royal house of the kingdom of Elenia. Western Elenes have a chivalric culture replete with many archaisms. The "Challenge" (essentially an offer to engage in single combat) is the customary response of members of the nobility who feel that their honor has been somehow sullied. It is amazing to note that not even ruling monarchs are exempt from the necessity of answering these Challenges. In order to avoid the inconvenience of responding to the impertinences of assorted hotheads, the monarchs of Eosia customarily designate some highly skilled (and usually widely feared) warrior as a surrogate. Sir Sparhawk's nature and reputation are such that even the most quarrelsome nobles of the kingdom of Elenia find after careful consideration that they have not really been insulted. It is a credit to Sir Sparhawk's skill and cool judgment that he has seldom even been obliged to kill anyone during these affairs, since, by ancient custom, a severely incapacitated combatant may save his life by surrendering and withdrawing his Challenge.

After his father's death, Sir Sparhawk presented himself to King Aldreas, the father of the present queen, to take up his duties. King Aldreas, however, was a weak monarch, and he was dominated by his sister, Arissa, and by Annias, the Primate of Cimmura, who was also Princess Arissa's surreptitious lover and the father of her bastard son, Lycheas. The Primate of Cimmura, who was the de facto ruler of Elenia, had hopes of ascending the throne of the Archprelacy of the Elene Church in the Holy City of Chyrellos, and the presence of the stern and moralistic Church Knight at the court inconvenienced him. And so it was that he persuaded King Aldreas to send Sir Sparhawk into exile in the Kingdom of Rendor.

In time, King Aldreas also became inconvenient, and Primate Annias and the princess poisoned him, thus elevating Princess Ehlana, Aldreas' daughter, to the throne. Though she was young, Queen Ehlana had received some training from Sir Sparhawk as a child and she was a far stronger monarch than her father had been. She soon became more than a mere inconvenience to the primate. He poisoned her as well, but Sir Sparhawk's fellow Pandions, aided by their tutor in the arcane arts, a Styric woman named Sephrenia, cast an enchantment that sealed the queen up in crystal and sustained her life.

Thus it stood when Sir Sparhawk returned from exile. Since the Militant Orders had no wish to see the Primate of Cimmura on the Archprelate's throne, certain of the champions of the other three orders were sent to assist Sir Sparhawk in finding an antidote or a cure that could restore Queen Ehlana to health. Since the queen had denied Annias access to her treasury in the past, the Church Knights reasoned that should she be restored, she would once again deny Annias the funds he needed to pursue his candidacy.

Annias allied himself with a renegade Pandion named Martel, and this Martel person was, like all Pandions, skilled in the use of Styric magic. He cast obstacles, both physical and supernatural, in Sparhawk's path, but Sir Sparhawk and his companions were ultimately successful in discovering that Queen Ehlana could only be restored by a magical object known as the "Bhelliom."

Western Elenes are a peculiar people. They have a level of sophistication in worldly matters that sometimes surpasses our own, but at the same time, they have an almost childlike belief in the more lurid forms of magic. This "Bhelliom," we are told, is a very large sapphire that was laboriously carved into the shape of a rose at some time in the distant past. The Elenes here insist that the artisan who carved it was a *Troll*. We will not dwell on that absurdity.

At any rate, Sir Sparhawk and his friends overcame many obstacles and were ultimately able to obtain the peculiar talisman, and (they claim) it was successful in restoring Queen Ehlana—although one strongly suspects that their tutor, Sephrenia, accomplished the task unaided, and that the apparent use of the Bhelliom was little more than a subterfuge she used to protect her from the virulent bigotry of western Elenes.

When Archprelate Cluvonus died, the Hierocracy of the Elene Church journeyed to Chyrellos to participate in the "election" of his successor. (Election is a peculiar practice that involves the stating of preference. That candidate who receives the approval of a majority of his fellows is elevated to the office in question. This, of course, is an unnatural procedure, but since the Elene clergy is ostensibly celibate, there is no nonscandalous way the Archprelacy can be made hereditary.) The Primate of Cimmura had bribed a goodly number of high churchmen to state a preference for him during the deliberations of the Hierocracy, but he still fell short of the needed majority. It was at this point that his underling, the aforementioned Martel, led an assault on the Holy City, hoping thereby to stampede the Hierocracy into electing Primate Annias. Sir Sparhawk and a limited number of Church Knights were able to keep Martel away from the Basilica where the Hierocracy was deliberating. Most of the city of Chyrellos, however, was severely damaged or destroyed during the fighting.

As the situation reached crisis proportions, help arrived for the beleaguered defenders in the form of the armies of the western Elene kingdoms. (Elene politics, one notes, are quite robust.) The connection between the Primate of Cimmura and the renegade Martel came to light as well as the fact that the pair had a subterranean arrangement with Otha of Zemoch. Outraged by the perfidy of the man, the Hierocracy rejected his candidacy and elected instead one Dolmant, the Patriarch of Demos. This Dolmant appears to be competent, though it may be too early to say for certain.

Queen Ehlana of the Kingdom of Elenia was scarcely more than a child, but she appeared to be a strong-willed and spirited young woman. She had long had a secret preference for Sir Sparhawk, though he was more than twenty years her senior; and upon her recovery it had been announced that the two were betrothed. Following the election of Dolmant to the Archprelacy, they were wed. Peculiarly enough, the queen retained her authority, although we must suspect that Sir Sparhawk exerts considerable influence upon her in state as well as domestic matters.

The involvement of the Emperor of Zemoch in the internal affairs of the Elene Church was, of course, a *casus belli,* and the armies of western Eosia, led by the Church Knights, marched eastward across Lamorkand to meet the Zemoch hordes poised on the border. The long-dreaded Second Zemoch War had begun.

Sir Sparhawk and his companions, however, rode north to avoid the turmoil of the battlefield and then turned eastward, crossed the mountains of northern Zemoch, and surreptitiously made their way to Otha's capital at the city of Zemoch, evidently in pursuit of Annias and Martel.

The best efforts of the empire's agents in the west have failed to reveal precisely what took place at Zemoch. It is quite certain that Annias, Martel, and even Otha himself perished there, but they are of little note in the pageant of history. What is far more relevant is the incontrovertible fact that Azash, Elder God of Styricum and the driving force behind Otha and his Zemochs, *also* perished, and it is undeniably true that Sir Sparhawk was responsible. We must concede that the levels of magic unleashed at Zemoch were beyond our comprehension and that Sir Sparhawk has powers at his command such as no mortal has ever possessed. As evidence of the levels of violence unleashed in the confrontation, we need only point to the fact that the city of Zemoch was utterly destroyed during the discussions.

Clearly, Zalasta the Styric had been right. Sir Sparhawk, the Prince Consort of Queen Ehlana, was the one man in all the world capable of dealing with the crisis in Tamuli. Unfortunately, Sir Sparhawk was not a citizen of the Tamul Empire, and thus could not be summoned to the imperial capital at Matherion by the emperor. His Majesty's government was in a quandary. The emperor had no authority over this Sparhawk, and to have been obliged to appeal to a man who was essentially a private citizen would have been an unthinkable humiliation.

The situation in the empire was daily worsening, and our need for the intervention of Sir Sparhawk was growing more and more urgent. Of equal urgency was the absolute necessity of maintaining the empire's dignity. It was ultimately the Foreign Office's most brilliant diplomat, First Secretary Oscagne, who devised a solution to the dilemma. We will discuss his Excellency's brilliant diplomatic ploy at greater length in the following chapter.

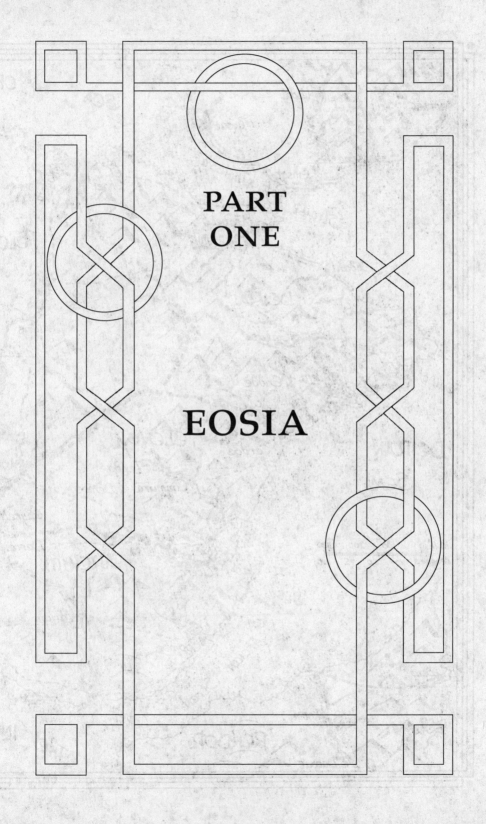

PART
ONE

EOSIA

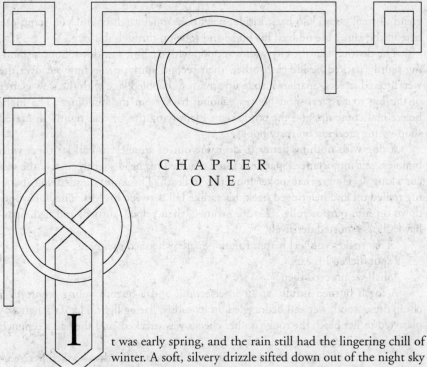

CHAPTER
ONE

I t was early spring, and the rain still had the lingering chill of winter. A soft, silvery drizzle sifted down out of the night sky and wreathed around the blocky watchtowers of Cimmura, hissing in the torches on each side of the broad gate and making the stones of the road leading up to the gate shiny and black. A lone rider approached the city. He was wrapped in a heavy traveller's cloak and rode a tall, shaggy roan horse with a long nose and flat, vicious eyes. The traveller was a big man, a bigness of large, heavy bone and ropy tendon rather than of flesh. His hair was coarse and black, and at some time his nose had been broken. He rode easily but with the peculiar alertness of the trained warrior.

The big roan shuddered absently, shaking the rain out of his shaggy coat as they approached the east gate of the city and stopped in the ruddy circle of torchlight just outside the wall.

An unshaven gate guard in a rust-splotched breastplate and helmet, his patched green cloak hanging negligently from one shoulder, came out of the gate house to look inquiringly at the traveller. He was swaying slightly on his feet.

"Just passing through, neighbor," the big man said in a quiet voice. He pushed back the hood of his cloak.

"Oh," the guard said, "it's you, Prince Sparhawk. I didn't recognize you. Welcome home."

"Thank you," Sparhawk replied. He could smell the cheap wine on the man's breath.

"Would you like to have me send word to the palace that you've arrived, your Highness?"

"No. Don't bother them. I can unsaddle my own horse." Sparhawk privately disliked ceremonies—particularly late at night. He leaned over and handed the guard a small coin. "Go back inside, neighbor. You'll catch cold if you stand out here in the rain." He nudged his horse and rode on through the gate.

The district near the city wall was poor, with shabby, run-down houses standing tightly packed beside each other, their second stories projecting out over the wet, littered streets. Sparhawk rode up a narrow, cobbled lane with the slow clatter of the big roan's steel-shod hooves echoing back from the buildings. The night breeze had come up, and the crude signs identifying this or that tightly shuttered shop swung creaking on rusty hooks.

A dog with nothing better to do came out of an alley to bark at them with brainless self-importance. Sparhawk's horse turned his head slightly to give the wet cur a long, level stare that spoke eloquently of death. The empty-headed dog's barking trailed off and he cringed back, his ratlike tail between his legs. The horse bore down on him purposefully. The dog whined, then yelped, turned, and fled. Sparhawk's horse snorted derisively.

"That makes you feel better, Faran?" Sparhawk asked the roan.

Faran flicked his ears.

"Shall we proceed then?"

A torch burned fitfully at an intersection, and a buxom young whore in a cheap dress stood, wet and bedraggled, in its ruddy, flaring light. Her dark hair was plastered to her head, the rouge on her cheeks was streaked, and she had a resigned expression on her face.

"What are you doing out here in the rain, Naween?" Sparhawk asked her, reining in his horse.

"I've been waiting for you, Sparhawk." Her tone was arch, and her dark eyes wicked.

"Or for anyone else?"

"Of course. I *am* a professional, Sparhawk, but I still owe you. Shouldn't we settle up one of these days?"

He ignored that. "What are you doing working the streets?"

"Shanda and I had a fight." She shrugged. "I decided to go into business for myself."

"You're not vicious enough to be a street-girl, Naween." He dipped his fingers into the pouch at his side, fished out several coins, and gave them to her. "Here," he instructed. "Get a room in an inn someplace and stay off the streets for a few days. I'll talk with Platime, and we'll see if we can make some arrangements for you."

Her eyes narrowed. "You don't have to do that, Sparhawk. I can take care of myself."

"Of *course* you can. That's why you're standing out here in the rain. Just do it, Naween. It's too late and too wet for arguments."

"This is two I owe you, Sparhawk. Are you absolutely sure . . ." She left it hanging.

"Quite sure, little sister. I'm married now, remember?"

"So?"

"Never mind. Get in out of the weather." Sparhawk rode on, shaking his head. He liked Naween, but she was hopelessly incapable of taking care of herself.

He passed through a quiet square where all the shops and booths were shut down. There were few people abroad tonight, and few business opportunities.

He let his mind drift back over the past month and a half. No one in Lamorkand had been willing to talk with him. Archprelate Dolmant was a wise man, learned in doctrine and Church politics, but he was woefully ignorant of the way the common people thought. Sparhawk had patiently tried to explain to him that sending a Church Knight out to gather information was a waste of time, but Dolmant had insisted, and Sparhawk's oath obliged him to obey. And so it was that he had wasted six weeks in the ugly cities of southern Lamorkand where no one had been willing to talk with him about anything more serious than the weather. To make matters even worse, Dolmant had quite obviously blamed the knight for his own blunder.

In a dark side street where the water dripped monotonously onto the cobblestones from the eaves of the houses, he felt Faran's muscles tense. "Sorry," he said quietly. "I wasn't paying attention." Someone was watching him, and he could clearly sense the animosity that had alerted his horse. Faran was a war-horse; he could probably sense antagonism in his veins. Sparhawk muttered a quick spell in the Styric tongue, concealing the gestures that accompanied it beneath his cloak. He released the spell slowly to avoid alerting whoever was watching him.

The watcher was not an Elene. Sparhawk sensed that immediately. He probed further. Then he frowned. There were more than one, and they were not Styrics either. He pulled his thought back, passively waiting for some clue as to their identity.

The realization came as a chilling shock. The watchers were not human. He shifted slightly in his saddle, sliding his hand toward his sword hilt.

Then the sense of the watchers was gone, and Faran shuddered with relief. He turned his ugly face to give his master a suspicious look.

"Don't ask me, Faran," Sparhawk told him. "I don't know either." But that was not entirely true. The touch of the minds in the darkness had been vaguely familiar, and that familiarity had raised questions in Sparhawk's mind, questions he did not want to face.

He paused at the palace gate long enough to firmly instruct the soldiers not to wake the whole house, then he dismounted in the courtyard.

A young man stepped out into the rain-swept yard from the stable. "Why didn't you send word that you were coming, Sparhawk?" he asked very quietly.

"Because I don't particularly like parades and wild celebrations in the middle of the night," Sparhawk told his squire, throwing back the hood of his cloak. "What are you doing up so late? I promised your mothers I'd make sure you got your rest. You're going to get me in trouble, Khalad."

"Are you trying to be funny?" Khalad's voice was gruff, abrasive. He took Faran's reins. "Come inside, Sparhawk. You'll rust if you stand out here in the rain."

"You're as bad as your father was."

"It's an old family trait." Khalad led the Prince Consort and his evil-tempered war-horse into the hay-smelling stable where a pair of lanterns gave off a golden light. Khalad was a husky young man with coarse black hair and a short-trimmed black beard. He wore tight-fitting black leather breeches, boots, and a sleeveless leather vest that left his arms and shoulders bare. A heavy dagger hung from his belt, and steel cuffs encircled his wrists. He looked and behaved so much like his father that Sparhawk felt again a pang of loss. "I thought Talen would be coming back with you," Sparhawk's squire said as he began unsaddling Faran.

"He's got a cold. His mother—and yours—decided that he shouldn't go out in the weather, and *I* certainly wasn't going to argue with them."

"Wise decision," Khalad said, absently slapping Faran on the nose as the big roan tried to bite him. "How are they?"

"Your mothers? Fine. Aslade's still trying to fatten Elys up, but she's not having too much luck. How did you find out I was in town?"

"One of Platime's cutthroats saw you coming through the gate. He sent word."

"I suppose I should have known. You didn't wake my wife, did you?"

"Not with Mirtai standing watch outside her door, I didn't. Give me that wet cloak, my Lord. I'll hang it in the kitchen to dry."

Sparhawk grunted and removed his sodden cloak.

"The mail shirt, too, Sparhawk," Khalad added, "before it rusts away entirely."

Sparhawk nodded, unbelted his sword, and began to struggle out of his chain-mail shirt. "How's your training going?"

Khalad made an indelicate sound. "I haven't learned anything I didn't already know. My father was a much better instructor than the ones at the chapterhouse. This idea of yours isn't going to work, Sparhawk. The other novices are all aristo-crats, and when my brothers and I outstrip them on the practice field, they resent it. We make enemies every time we turn around." He lifted the saddle from Faran's back and put it on the rail of a nearby stall. He briefly laid his hand on the big roan's back, then bent, picked up a handful of straw, and began to rub him down.

"Wake some groom and have him do that," Sparhawk told him. "Is anybody still awake in the kitchen?"

"The bakers are already up, I think."

"Have one of them throw something together for me to eat. It's been a long time since lunch."

"All right. What took you so long in Chyrellos?"

"I took a little side trip into Lamorkand. The civil war there's getting out of hand, and the Archprelate wanted me to nose around a bit."

"You should have gotten word to your wife. She was just about to send Mirtai out to find you." Khalad grinned at him. "I think you're going to get yelled at again, Sparhawk."

"There's nothing new about that. Is Kalten here in the palace?"

Khalad nodded. "The food's better here, and he isn't expected to pray three times a day. Besides, I think he's got his eye on one of the chambermaids."

"That wouldn't surprise me very much. Is Stragen here, too?"

"No. Something came up, and he had to go back to Emsat."

"Get Kalten up, then. Have him join us in the kitchen. I want to talk with him. I'll be along in a bit. I'm going to the bathhouse first."

"The water won't be warm. They let the fires go out at night."

"We're soldiers of God, Khalad. We're all supposed to be unspeakably brave."

"I'll try to remember that, my Lord."

The water in the bathhouse was definitely on the chilly side, so Sparhawk did not linger very long. He wrapped himself in a soft white robe and went through the dim corridors of the palace to the brightly lighted kitchens where Khalad waited with the sleepy-looking Kalten.

"Hail, noble Prince Consort," Kalten said dryly. Sir Kalten obviously didn't care much for the idea of being roused in the middle of the night.

"Hail, noble Boyhood Companion of the noble Prince Consort," Sparhawk replied.

"Now there's a cumbersome title," Kalten said sourly. "What's so important that it won't wait until morning?"

Sparhawk sat down at one of the worktables, and a white-smocked baker brought him a plate of roast beef and a steaming loaf still hot from the oven.

"Thanks, neighbor," Sparhawk said to him.

"Where have you been, Sparhawk?" Kalten demanded, sitting down across the table from his friend. Kalten had a wine flagon in one hand and a tin cup in the other.

"Sarathi sent me to Lamorkand," Sparhawk replied, tearing a chunk of bread from the loaf.

"Your wife's been making life miserable for everyone in the palace, you know."

"It's nice to know she cares."

"Not for the rest of us, it isn't. What did Dolmant need from Lamorkand?"

"Information. He didn't altogether believe some of the reports he's been getting."

"What's not to believe? The Lamorks are just engaging in their national pastime—civil war."

"There seems to be something a little different this time. Do you remember Count Gerrich?"

"The one who had us besieged in Baron Alstrom's castle? I never met him personally, but his name's sort of familiar."

"He seems to be coming out on top in the squabbles in western Lamorkand, and most everybody up there believes that he's got his eye on the throne."

"So?" Kalten helped himself to part of Sparhawk's loaf of bread. "Every baron in Lamorkand has his eyes on the throne. What's got Dolmant so concerned about it this time?"

"Gerrich's been making alliances beyond the borders of Lamorkand. Some of those border barons in Pelosia are more or less independent of King Soros."

"Everybody in Pelosia's independent of Soros. He isn't much of a king. He spends much too much time praying."

"That's a strange position for a soldier of God," Khalad murmured.

"You've got to keep these things in perspective, Khalad," Kalten told him. "Too much praying softens a man's brains."

"Anyway," Sparhawk went on, "if Gerrich succeeds in dragging those Pelosian barons into his bid for King Friedahl's throne, Friedahl's going to have to declare war on Pelosia. The Church already has a war going on in Rendor, and Dolmant's not very enthusiastic about a second front." He paused. "I ran across something else, though," he added. "I overheard a conversation I wasn't supposed to. The name Drychtnath came up. Do you know anything about him?"

Kalten shrugged. "He was the national hero of the Lamorks, way back. They say he was about twelve feet tall, ate an ox for breakfast every morning, and drank a hogshead of mead every evening. The story has it that he could shatter rocks by scowling at them and reach up and stop the sun with one hand. The stories might be just a little bit exaggerated, though."

"Very funny. The group I overheard were all telling each other that he's returned."

"That'd be a neat trick. I gather that his closest friend killed him. Stabbed him in the back and then ran a spear through his heart. You know how Lamorks are."

"That's a strange name," Khalad noted. "What does it mean?"

"Drychtnath?" Kalten scratched his head. " 'Dreadnought,' I think. Lamork mothers do that sort of thing to their children." He drained his cup and tipped his flagon over it. A few drops came out. "Are we going to be much longer at this?" he asked. "If we're going to sit up talking all night, I'll get more wine. To be honest with you though, Sparhawk, I'd really rather go back to my nice warm bed."

"And your nice warm chambermaid?" Khalad added.

"She gets lonesome." Kalten shrugged. His face grew serious. "If the Lamorks are talking about Drychtnath again, it means that they're starting to feel a little confined. Drychtnath wanted to rule the world, and anytime the Lamorks start invoking his name, it's a fair indication that they're beginning to look beyond their borders for elbow room."

Sparhawk pushed back his plate. "It's too late at night to start worrying about it now. Go back to bed, Kalten. You, too, Khalad. We can talk more about this tomorrow. I really ought to go pay a courtesy call on my wife." He stood up.

"That's all?" Kalten said. "A courtesy call?"

"There are many forms of courtesy, Kalten."

The corridors in the palace were dimly illuminated by widely spaced candles. Sparhawk went quietly past the throne room to the royal apartment. As usual, Mirtai dozed in a chair beside the door. Sparhawk stopped and considered the Tamul giantess. When her face was in repose, she was heart-stoppingly beautiful. Her skin was golden in the candlelight, and her eyelashes were so long that they touched her cheeks. Her sword lay in her lap with her hand lightly enclosing its hilt.

"Don't try to sneak up on me, Sparhawk." She said it without opening her eyes.

"How did you know it was me?"

"I could smell you. All you Elenes seem to forget that we have noses."

"How could you possibly smell me? I just took a bath."

"Yes. I noticed that, too. You should have taken the time to let the water heat up a little more."

"Sometimes you amaze me, do you know that?"

"You're easily amazed, Sparhawk." She opened her eyes. "Where have you been? Ehlana's been nearly frantic."

"How is she?"

"About the same. Aren't you ever going to let her grow up? I'm getting very tired of being owned by a child." In Mirtai's own eyes, she was a slave, the property of Queen Ehlana. This in no way hindered her in ruling the royal family of Elenia with an iron fist, arbitrarily deciding what was good for them and what was not. She had brusquely dismissed all the queen's attempts to emancipate her, pointing out that she was an Atan Tamul, and that her race was temperamentally unsuited for freedom. Sparhawk tended strongly to agree with her, since he was fairly certain that if she were left to follow her instincts, Mirtai could depopulate several fair-sized towns in short order.

She stood up, rising to her feet with exquisite grace. She was a good four inches taller than Sparhawk, and he felt again that odd sense of shrinking as he looked up at her. "What took you so long?" she asked him.

"I had to go to Lamorkand."

"Was that your idea or somebody else's?"

"Dolmant sent me."

"Make sure Ehlana understands that right from the start. If she thinks you went there on your own, the fight will last for weeks, and all that wrangling gets on my nerves." She produced the key to the royal apartment and gave Sparhawk a blunt, direct look. "Be very attentive, Sparhawk. She's missed you a great deal, and she needs some tangible evidence of your affection. And don't forget to bolt the bedroom door. Your daughter might be just a little young to be learning about certain things." She unlocked the door.

"Mirtai, do you *really* have to lock us all in every night?"

"Yes, I do. I can't get to sleep until I know that none of you is out wandering around the halls."

Sparhawk sighed. "Oh, by the way," he added. "Kring was in Chyrellos. I imagine he'll be along in a few days to propose marriage to you again."

"It's about time." She smiled. "It's been three months since his last proposal. I was beginning to think he didn't love me anymore."

"Are you ever going to accept him?"

"We'll see. Go wake up your wife, Sparhawk. I'll let you out in the morning." She gently pushed him through the doorway and locked the door behind him.

Sparhawk's daughter, Princess Danae, was curled up in a large chair by the fire. Danae was six years old now. Her hair was very dark, and her skin as white as milk. Her dark eyes were large, and her mouth a small pink bow. She was quite the little lady, her manner serious and very grown-up. Her constant companion, nonetheless, was a battered and disreputable-looking stuffed toy animal named Rollo. Rollo had descended to Princess Danae from her mother. As usual, Princess Danae's little feet had greenish grass stains on them. "You're late, Sparhawk," she said flatly to her father.

"Danae," he said to her, "you know you're not supposed to call me by name like that. If your mother hears you, she's going to start asking questions."

"She's asleep." Danae shrugged.

"Are you really sure about that?"

She gave him a withering look. "Of course I am. I'm not going to make any mistakes. I've done this many, many times before, you know. Where have you been?"

"I had to go to Lamorkand."

"Didn't it occur to you to send word to Mother? She's been absolutely unbearable for the last few weeks."

"I know. Any number of people have already told me about it. I didn't really think I'd be gone for so long. I'm glad you're awake. Maybe you can help me with something."

"I'll consider it—if you're nice to me."

"Stop that. What do you know about Drychtnath?"

"He was a barbarian, but he was an Elene, after all, so it was probably only natural."

"Your prejudices are showing."

"Nobody's perfect. Why this sudden interest in ancient history?"

"There's a wild story running through Lamorkand that Drychtnath's returned. They're all sitting around sharpening swords with exalted expressions on their faces. What's the real significance of that?"

"He was their king three or four thousand years ago. It was shortly after you Elenes discovered fire and came out of your caves."

"Be nice."

"Yes, Father. Anyway, Drychtnath hammered all the Lamorks into something that sort of resembled unity and then set out to conquer the world. The Lamorks were very impressed with him. He worshipped the old Lamork Gods, though, and your Elene Church was a little uncomfortable with the notion of a pagan sitting on the throne of the whole world, so she had him murdered."

"The Church wouldn't do that," he said flatly.

"Did you want to listen to the story or did you want to argue theology? After Drychtnath died, the Lamork priests disemboweled a few chickens and fondled their entrails in order to read the future. That's really a disgusting practice, Sparhawk. It's so messy." She shuddered.

"Don't blame me. I didn't think it up."

"The 'auguries,' as they called them, said that one day Drychtnath would return to take up where he'd left off and that he'd lead the Lamorks to world domination."

"You mean they actually believe that?"

"They did once."

"There are some rumors up there of backsliding—reversion to the worship of the old pagan Gods."

"It's the sort of thing you'd expect. When a Lamork starts thinking about Drychtnath, he automatically hauls the old Gods out of the closet. It's so foolish. Aren't there enough real Gods for them?"

"The old Lamork Gods aren't real, then?"

"Of course not. Where's your mind, Sparhawk?"

"The Troll-Gods are real. What's the difference?"

"There's all the difference in the world, Father. Any child can see that."

"Why don't I just take your word for it? And why don't you go back to bed?"

"Because you haven't kissed me yet."

"Oh. Sorry. I had my mind on something else."

"Keep your eye on the important things, Sparhawk. Do you want to have me wither away?"

"Of course not."

"Then give me a kiss."

He did that. As always she smelled of grass and trees. "Wash your feet," he told her.

"Oh, bother," she said.

"Do you want to spend a week explaining those grass stains to your mother?"

"That's all I get?" she protested. "One meager little kiss and bathing instructions?"

He laughed, picked her up, and kissed her again—several times. Then he put her down. "Now scoot."

She pouted a little and then sighed. She started back toward her bedroom, negligently carrying Rollo by one hind leg. "Don't keep Mother up all night," she said back over her shoulder. "And *please* try to be quiet. Why do you two always have to make so much noise?" She looked impishly back over her shoulder. "Why are you blushing, Father?" she asked innocently. Then she laughed and went on into her own room and closed the door.

He could never be sure if his daughter really understood the implications of such remarks, although he was certain that one level at least of her strangely layered personality understood quite well. He made sure that her door was latched and then went into the bedroom he shared with his wife. He closed and bolted the door behind him.

The fire had burned down to embers, but there was still sufficient light for him to be able to see the young woman who was the focus of his entire life. Her wealth of pale blond hair covered her pillow, and in sleep she looked very young and vulnerable. He stood at the foot of the bed looking at her. There were still traces in her face of the little girl he had trained and molded. He sighed. That train of thought always made him melancholy, because it brought home the fact that he was really too old for her. Ehlana should have a young husband—someone less battered, certainly someone handsome. He idly wondered where he had made the mistake that had so welded her affection to him that she had not even considered any other possible choice. It had probably been something minor—insignificant even. Who could ever know what kind of effect even the tiniest gesture might have on another?

"I know you're there, Sparhawk," she said without even opening her eyes. There was a slight edge to her voice.

"I was admiring the view." A light tone might head off the incipient unpleasantness, though he didn't really have much hope of that.

She opened her grey eyes. "Come over here," she commanded, holding her arms out to him.

"I was ever your Majesty's most obedient servant." He grinned at her, going to the side of the bed.

"Oh, *really*?" she replied, wrapping her arms about his neck and kissing him. He kissed her back, and that went on for quite some time.

"Do you suppose we could save the scolding until tomorrow morning, love?" he asked. "I'm a little tired tonight. Why don't we do the kissing and making up now, and you can scold me later?"

"And lose my edge? Don't be silly. I've been saving up all sorts of things to say to you."

"I can imagine. Dolmant sent me to Lamorkand to look into something. It took me a little longer than I expected."

"That's not fair, Sparhawk," she accused.

"I didn't follow that."

"You weren't supposed to say that yet. You're supposed to wait until after I've demanded an explanation before you give me one. Now you've gone and spoiled it."

"Can you ever forgive me?" He assumed an expression of exaggerated contrition and kissed her on the neck. His wife, he had discovered, loved these little games.

She laughed. "I'll think about it." She kissed him back. The women of his family were a very demonstrative little group, he decided. "All right then," she said. "You've gone and spoiled it anyway, so you might as well tell me what you were doing, and why you didn't send word that you'd be delayed."

"Politics, love. You know Dolmant. Lamorkand is right on the verge of exploding. Sarathi wanted a professional assessment, but he didn't want it generally known that I was going there at his instruction. He didn't want any messages explaining things floating around."

"I think it's time for me to have a little talk with our revered Archprelate," Ehlana said. "He seems to have a little trouble remembering just who I am."

"I don't recommend it, Ehlana."

"I'm not going to start a fight with him, my love. I'm just going to point out to him that he's ignoring the customary courtesies. He's supposed to *ask* before he commandeers my husband. I'm getting just a little weary of his Imperial Archprelacy, so I'm going to teach him some manners."

"Can I watch? That might just be a very interesting conversation."

"Sparhawk," she said, giving him a smoldering look, "if you want to avoid an official reprimand, you're going to have to start taking some significant steps to soften my displeasure."

"I was just getting to that," he told her, enfolding her in a tighter embrace.

"What took you so long?" she breathed.

It was quite a bit later, and the displeasure of the Queen of Elenia seemed to be definitely softening. "What did you find out in Lamorkand, Sparhawk?" she asked, stretching languorously. Politics were never really very far from the queen's mind.

"Western Lamorkand's in turmoil right now. There's a count up there—Gerrich, his name is. We ran across him when we were searching for Bhelliom. He was involved with Martel in one of those elaborate schemes devised to keep the Militant Orders out of Chyrellos during the election."

"That speaks volumes about this count's character."

"Perhaps, but Martel was very good at manipulating people. He stirred up a small war between Gerrich and Patriarch Ortzel's brother. Anyway, the campaign appears to have broadened the count's horizons a bit. He's begun to have some thoughts about the throne."

"Poor Freddie." Ehlana sighed. King Friedahl of Lamorkand was her distant cousin. "You couldn't *give* me that throne of his. Why should the Church be concerned, though? Freddie's got a large enough army to deal with one ambitious count."

"It's not quite so simple, love. Gerrich has been concluding alliances with other nobles in western Lamorkand. He's amassed an army nearly as big as the king's, and he's been talking with the Pelosian barons around Lake Venne."

"Those bandits," she said with a certain contempt. "*Anybody* can buy them."

"You're well versed in the politics of the region, Ehlana."

"I almost have to be, Sparhawk. Pelosia fronts my northeastern border. Does this current disturbance threaten us in any way?"

"Not at the moment. Gerrich has his eyes turned eastward—toward the capital."

"Maybe I should offer Freddie an alliance," she mused. "If general war breaks out in the region, I could snip off a nice piece of southwestern Pelosia."

"Are we developing territorial ambitions, your Majesty?"

"Not tonight, Sparhawk," she replied. "I've got other things on my mind tonight." And she reached out to him again.

It was quite a bit later, almost dawn. Ehlana's regular breathing told Sparhawk that she was asleep. He slipped from the bed and went to the window. His years of military training made it automatic for him to take a look at the weather just before daybreak.

The rain had abated, but the wind had picked up. It was early spring now, and there was little hope for decent weather for weeks. He was glad that he had reached home when he had, since the approaching day looked unpromising. He stared out at the torches flaring and tossing in the windy courtyard.

As they always did when the weather was bad, Sparhawk's thoughts drifted back to the years he had spent in the sun-blasted city of Jiroch on the arid north coast of Rendor, where the women, all veiled and robed in black, went to the well in the steely first light of day, and where the woman named Lillias had consumed his nights with what she chose to call love. He did not, however, remember that night in Cippria when Martel's assassins had quite nearly spilled out his life. He had settled that score with Martel in the Temple of Azash in Zemoch, so there was no real purpose in remembering the stockyard of Cippria, nor the sound of the monastery bells that had called to him out of the darkness.

That momentary sense of being watched, the sense that had come over him in the narrow street while he had been on his way to the palace, still nagged at him. Something he did not understand was going on, and he fervently wished that he could talk with Sephrenia about it.

CHAPTER TWO

"Your Majesty," the Earl of Lenda protested, "you can't address this kind of language to the Archprelate." Lenda was staring with chagrin at the piece of paper the queen had just handed him. "You've done everything but accuse him of being a thief and a scoundrel."

"Oh, did I leave those out?" she asked. "How careless of me." They were meeting in the blue-carpeted council chamber as they usually did at this time of the morning.

"Can't you do something with her, Sparhawk?" Lenda pleaded.

"Oh, Lenda," Ehlana laughed, smiling at the frail old man, "that's only a draft. I was a little irritated when I scribbled it down."

"A *little*?"

"I know we can't send the letter in its present form, my Lord. I just wanted you to know how I really felt about the matter before we rephrase it and couch it in diplomatic language. My whole point is that Dolmant's beginning to overstep his bounds. He's the Archprelate, not the emperor. The Church has too much authority over temporal affairs already, and, if someone doesn't bring Dolmant up short, every monarch in Eosia will become little more than his vassal. I'm sorry, gentlemen. I'm a true daughter of the Church, but I *won't* kneel to Dolmant and receive my crown back from him in some contrived little ceremony that has no purpose other than my humiliation."

Sparhawk was a bit surprised at his wife's political maturity. The power structure on the Eosian continent had always depended on a rather delicate balance between the authority of the Church and the power of the various kings. When that balance was disturbed, things went awry. "Her Majesty's point may be well taken, Lenda," he said thoughtfully. "The Eosian monarchies haven't been very strong for the last generation or so. Aldreas was . . ." He groped for a word.

"Inept," his wife coolly characterized her own father.

"I might not have gone quite *that* far," he murmured. "Wargun's erratic, Soros is a religious hysteric, Obler's old, and Friedahl reigns only at the sufferance of his barons. Dregos lets his relatives make all his decisions, King Brisant of Cammoria is a voluptuary, and I don't even know the name of the current King of Rendor."

"Ogyrin," Kalten supplied, "not that it really matters."

"Anyway," Sparhawk continued, sinking lower in his chair and rubbing the side of his face thoughtfully, "during this same period of time, we've had a number of very able churchmen in the Hierocracy. The incapacity of Cluvonus sort of encouraged the patriarchs to strike out on their own. If you had a vacant throne someplace, you could do a lot worse than put Emban on it—or Ortzel—or Bergsten, and even Annias had a very high degree of political skill. When kings grow weak, the Church grows strong—too strong, sometimes."

"Spit it out, Sparhawk," Platime growled. "Are you trying to say we should declare war on the Church?"

"Not today, Platime. We might want to keep the idea in reserve, though. Right now I think it's time to start sending some signals to Chyrellos, and our queen may be just the one to send them. After the way she stampeded the Hierocracy during Dolmant's election, I think they'll listen very carefully to just about anything she says. I don't know that I'd soften her letter all *that* much, Lenda. Let's see if we can get their attention."

Lenda's eyes were very bright. "*This* is the way the game's supposed to be played, my friends," he said enthusiastically.

"You *do* realize that it's altogether possible that Dolmant didn't realize that he was stepping over the line," Kalten noted. "Maybe he sent Sparhawk to Lamorkand as the interim Preceptor of the Pandion Order and completely overlooked the fact that he's also the Prince Consort. Sarathi's got a lot on his mind just now."

"If he's *that* absentminded, he's got no business occupying the Archprelate's throne," Ehlana asserted. Her eyes narrowed, always a dangerous sign. "Let's make it very clear to him that he's hurt my feelings. He'll go out of his way to smooth things over, and maybe I can take advantage of that to retrieve that duchy just north of Vardenais. Lenda, is there any way we can keep people from bequeathing their estates to the Church?"

"It's a long-standing custom, your Majesty."

"I know, but the land originally comes from the crown. Shouldn't we have *some* say in who inherits it? You'd think that if a nobleman dies without an heir, the estate would revert back to me, but every time there's a childless noble in Elenia, the churchmen flock around him like vultures trying to talk him into giving *them* the land."

"Jerk some titles," Platime suggested. "Make it a law that if a man doesn't have an heir, he doesn't keep his estate."

"The aristocracy would go up in flames," Lenda gasped.

"That's what the army's for," Platime said with a shrug, "to put out fires. I'll tell you what, Ehlana, you pass the law, and I'll arrange a few very public and very messy accidents for the ones who scream the loudest. Aristocrats aren't very bright, but they'll get the point. Eventually."

"Do you think I could get away with that?" Ehlana asked the Earl of Lenda.

"*Surely* your Majesty's not seriously considering it?"

"I have to do *something*, Lenda. The Church is eating up my kingdom acre by acre, and once she takes possession of an estate, the land's removed from the tax rolls forever." She paused. "This could just be a way to do what Sparhawk suggested—get the Church's attention. Why don't we draw up a draft of some outrageously repressive law and just 'accidentally' let a copy fall into the hands of some middle-level clergyman. It's probably safe to say that it'll be in Dolmant's hands before the ink's dry."

"That's really unscrupulous, my Queen," Lenda told her.

"I'm so glad you approve, my Lord." She looked around. "Have we got anything else this morning, gentlemen?"

"You've got some unauthorized bandits operating in the mountains near Cardos, Ehlana," Platime rumbled. The gross, black-bearded man sat with his feet upon the table. There was a wine flagon and goblet at his elbow. His doublet was wrinkled and food-spotted, and his shaggy hair hung down over his forehead, almost covering his eyes. Platime was constitutionally incapable of using formal titles, but the queen chose to overlook that.

"Unauthorized?" Kalten sounded amused.

"You know what I mean," Platime growled. "They don't have permission from the thieves' council to operate in that region, and they're breaking all the rules. I'm not positive, but I think they're some of the former henchmen of the Primate of Cimmura. You blundered there, Ehlana. You should have waited until you had them in custody before you declared them outlaws."

"Oh, well." She shrugged. "Nobody's perfect." Ehlana's relationship with Platime was peculiar. She realized that he was unable to mouth the polite formulas of the nobility, and so she accepted a bluntness from him that would have offended her had it come from anyone else. For all his faults, Platime was turning into a gifted, almost brilliant councillor, and Ehlana valued his advice greatly. "I'm not surprised to find out that Annias' old cronies have turned to highway robbery in their hour of need. They were all bandits to begin with anyway. There have always been outlaws in those mountains, though, so I doubt that another band will make all that much difference."

"Ehlana," he sighed, "you're the same as my very own baby sister, but sometimes you're terribly ignorant. An authorized bandit knows the rules. He knows which travellers can be robbed or killed and which ones have to be left alone. Nobody gets too excited if some overstuffed merchant gets his throat cut and his purse lifted, but if a government official or a high-ranking nobleman turns up dead in those mountains, the authorities have to take steps to at least make it *appear* that they're doing their jobs. That sort of official attention is very bad for business. Perfectly innocent criminals get rounded up and hanged. Highway robbery's not an occupation for amateurs.

"And there's another problem as well. These bandits are telling all the local peasantry that they're not really robbers, but patriots rebelling against a cruel tyrant—that's you, little sister. There's always enough discontent among the peasants to make some of them sympathetic toward that sort of thing. You aristocrats haven't any business getting involved in crime. You always try to mix politics in with it."

"But my dear Platime," she said winsomely, "I thought you knew. Politics *is* a crime."

The fat man roared with laughter. "I love this girl," he told the others. "Don't worry too much about it, Ehlana. I'll try to get some men inside their band, and when Stragen gets back, we'll put our heads together and work out some way to put those people out of business."

"I knew I could count on you," she said. She rose to her feet. "If that's all we have, gentlemen, I have an appointment with my dressmaker." She looked around. "Coming, Sparhawk?"

"In a moment," he replied. "I want to have a word with Platime."

She nodded and moved toward the door.

"What's on your mind, Sparhawk?" Platime asked.

"I saw Naween last night when I rode into town. She's working the streets."

"Naween? That's ridiculous! Half the time she even forgets to take the money."

"That's what I told her. She and Shanda had a falling-out, and she was standing on a street corner near the east gate. I sent her to an inn to get her out of the weather. Can we make some kind of arrangements for her?"

"I'll see what I can do," Platime promised.

Ehlana had not yet left the room, and Sparhawk sometimes forgot how sharp her ears were. "Who's this Naween?" she asked from the doorway with a slight edge to her voice.

"She's a whore." Platime shrugged. "A special friend of Sparhawk's."

"Platime!" Sparhawk gasped.

"Isn't she?"

"Well, I suppose so, but when you say it that way . . ." Sparhawk groped for the right words.

"Oh. I didn't mean it *that way*, Ehlana. So far as I know, your husband's completely faithful to you. Naween's a whore. That's her occupation, but it doesn't have anything to do with her friendship—not that she didn't make Sparhawk some offers—but she makes those offers to everybody. She's a very generous girl."

"Please, Platime," Sparhawk groaned, "don't be on my side anymore."

"Naween's a good girl," Platime continued to explain to Ehlana. "She works hard, she takes good care of her customers, and she pays her taxes."

"Taxes?" Ehlana exclaimed. "Are you telling me that my government encourages that sort of thing? Legitimizes it by taxing it?"

"Have you been living on the moon, Ehlana? Of course she pays taxes. We all do. Lenda sees to that. Naween helped Sparhawk once while you were sick. He was looking for that Krager fellow, and she helped him. Like I said, she offered him other services as well, but he turned her down—politely. She's always been a bit disappointed in him about that."

"You and I are going to have a long talk about this, Sparhawk," Ehlana said ominously.

"As your Majesty wishes." He sighed as she swept coolly from the room.

"She doesn't know very much about the real world, does she, Sparhawk?"

"It's her sheltered upbringing."

"I thought *you* were the one who brought her up."

"That's right."

"Then you've only got yourself to blame. I'll have Naween stop by and explain it all to her."

"Are you out of your mind?"

Talen came in from Demos the next day, riding into the courtyard with Sir Berit. Sparhawk and Khalad met them at the stable door. The Prince Consort was making some effort to be inconspicuous until such time as the queen's curiosity about Naween diminished.

Talen's nose was red, and his eyes looked puffy. "I thought you were going to stay at the farm until you got over that cold," Sparhawk said to him.

"I couldn't stand all that mothering," Talen said, slipping down from his saddle. "One mother is bad enough, but my brothers and I have two now. I don't think

I'll ever be able to look another bowl of chicken soup in the face again. Hello, Khalad."

"Talen." Sparhawk's burly young squire grunted. He looked critically at his half brother. "Your eyes look terrible."

"You ought to see them from in here." Talen was about fifteen now, and he was going through one of those "stages." Sparhawk was fairly certain that the young thief had grown three inches in the past month and a half. A goodly amount of forearm and wrist struck out of the sleeves of his doublet. "Do you think the cooks might have something to eat?" the boy asked. As a result of his rapid growth, Talen ate almost constantly now.

"I've got some papers for you to sign, Sparhawk," Berit said. "It's nothing very urgent, but I thought I'd ride in with Talen." Berit wore a mail shirt and he had a broadsword belted at his waist. His weapon of choice, however, was still the heavy war axe slung to his saddle.

"Are you going back to the chapterhouse?" Khalad asked him.

"Unless Sparhawk has something he wants me for here."

"I'll ride along with you, then. Sir Olart wants to give us more instruction with the lance this afternoon."

"Why don't you just unhorse him a few times?" Berit suggested. "Then he'll leave you alone. You could do it, you know. You're already better than he is."

Khalad shrugged. "It'd hurt his feelings."

"Not to mention his ribs, shoulders, and back." Berit laughed.

"It's a bit ostentatious to outperform your instructors," Khalad said. "The other novices are already a little sulky about the way my brothers and I are showing them up. We've tried to explain, but they're sensitive about the fact that we're peasants. You know how that goes." He looked inquiringly at Sparhawk. "Are you going to need me for anything this afternoon, my Lord?"

"No. Go ahead and dent Sir Olart's armor a bit. He's got an exaggerated notion of his own skill. Give him some instruction in the virtue of humility."

"I'm *really* hungry, Sparhawk," Talen complained.

"All right. Let's go to the kitchen." Sparhawk looked critically at his young friend. "Then I guess we'll have to send for the tailor again," he added. "You're growing like a weed."

"It's not my idea."

Khalad started to saddle his horse, and Sparhawk and Talen went into the palace in search of food. It was about an hour later when the two of them entered the royal apartment to find Ehlana, Mirtai, and Danae sitting by the fire. Ehlana was leafing through some documents. Danae was playing with Rollo, and Mirtai was sharpening one of her daggers.

"Well," Ehlana said, looking up from the documents, "if it isn't my noble Prince Consort and my wandering page."

Talen bowed. Then he sniffed loudly.

"Use your handkerchief," Mirtai told him.

"Yes, ma'am."

"How are your mothers?" Ehlana asked the young man. Everyone, perhaps unconsciously, used that phrasing when speaking to Talen and his half brothers. In a very real sense, though, the usage reflected reality. Aslade and Elys mothered Kurik's five sons excessively and impartially.

"Meddlesome, my Queen," Talen replied. "It's not really a good idea to get sick in that house. In the last week I think I've been dosed with every cold remedy known to man." A peculiar, squeaky noise came from somewhere in the general vicinity of the young man's midsection.

"Is that your stomach?" Mirtai asked him. "Are you hungry again?"

"No, I just ate. I probably won't get hungry again for at least fifteen minutes." Talen put one hand to the front of his doublet. "The little beast was being so quiet I almost forgot it was there." He went over to Danae, who was tying the strings of a little bonnet under the chin of her stuffed toy. "I've brought a present for you, Princess," he said.

Her eyes brightened. She set Rollo aside and sat waiting expectantly.

"But no kissing," he added. "Just a 'thank you' will do. I've got a cold, and you don't want to catch it."

"What did you bring me?" she asked eagerly.

"Oh, just a little something I found under a bush out on the road. It's a little wet and muddy, but you can dry it out and brush it off, I suppose. It's not much, but I thought you might like it—just a little." Talen was underplaying it for all he was worth.

"Could I see it, please?" she begged.

"Oh, I suppose so." He reached inside his doublet, took out a rather bedraggled grey kitten, and sat it on the floor in front of her. The kitten had mackerel stripes, a spiky tail, large ears, and an intently curious look in its blue eyes. It took a tentative step toward its new mistress.

Danae squealed with delight, picked up the kitten, and hugged it to her cheek. "I *love* it!" she exclaimed.

"There go the draperies," Mirtai said with resignation. "Kittens always want to climb the drapes."

Talen skillfully fended off Sparhawk's exuberant little daughter. "The cold, Danae," the boy warned. "I've got a cold, remember?" Sparhawk was certain that his daughter would grow more skilled with the passage of time and that it wouldn't be very long until Talen would no longer be able to evade her affection. The kitten had been no more than a gesture, Sparhawk was certain—some spur-of-the-moment impulse to which Talen had given no thought whatsoever. It rather effectively sealed the young man's fate, however. A few days before, Sparhawk had idly wondered where *he* had made the mistake that had permanently attached his wife's affection to him. He realized that this scruffy-looking kitten was Talen's mistake—or at least one of them. Sparhawk mentally shrugged. Talen would make an adequate son-in-law—once Danae had trained him.

"Is it all right, your Majesty?" Talen was asking the queen. "For her to have the kitten, I mean?"

"Isn't it just a little late to be asking that question, Talen?" Ehlana replied.

"Oh, I don't know," he said impudently. "I thought I'd timed it just about right."

Ehlana looked at her daughter, who was snuggling the kitten against her face.

All cats are born opportunists. The kitten patted the little girl's cheek with one soft paw and then nuzzled. Kittens are expert nuzzlers.

"How can I say no after you've already given it to her, Talen?"

"It *would* be a little difficult, wouldn't it, your Majesty?" The boy sniffed loudly.

Mirtai rose to her feet, put her dagger away, and crossed the room to Talen. She reached out her hand, and he flinched away.

"Oh, stop that," she told him. She laid her hand on his forehead. "You've got a fever."

"I didn't get it on purpose."

"We'd better get him to bed, Mirtai," Ehlana said, rising from her chair.

"We should sweat him first," the giantess said. "I'll take him to the bathhouse and steam him for a while." She took Talen's arm, firmly.

"You're not going into the bathhouse with me!" he protested, his face suddenly aflame.

"Be quiet," she commanded. "Send word to the cooks, Ehlana. Have them stir up a mustard plaster and boil up some chicken soup. When I bring him back from the bathhouse, we'll put the mustard plaster on his chest, pop him into bed, and spoon soup into him."

"Are you going to just stand there and let them do this to me, Sparhawk?" Talen appealed.

"I'd like to help you, my friend," Sparhawk replied, "but I've got my own health to consider, too, you know."

"I wish I was dead," Talen groaned as Mirtai pulled him from the room.

Stragen and Ulath arrived from Emsat a few days later and were immediately escorted to the royal apartment. "You're getting fat, Sparhawk," Ulath said bluntly, removing his Ogre-horned helmet.

"I've put on a few pounds," Sparhawk conceded.

"Soft living." Ulath grunted disapprovingly.

"How's Wargun?" Ehlana asked the huge blond Thalesian.

"His mind's gone," Ulath replied sadly. "They've got him locked up in the west wing of the palace. He spends most of his time raving."

Ehlana sighed. "I always rather liked him—when he was sober."

"I doubt that you'll feel the same way about his son, your Majesty," Stragen told her dryly. Like Platime, Stragen was a thief, but he had much better manners.

"I've never met him," Ehlana said.

"You might consider adding that to your next prayer of thanksgiving, your Majesty. His name's Avin—a short and insignificant name for a short and insignificant fellow. He doesn't show very much promise."

"Is he really that bad?" Ehlana asked Ulath.

"Avin Wargunsson? Stragen's being generous. Avin's a little man who spends all his time trying to make sure that people don't overlook him. When he found out that I was coming here, he called me to the palace and gave me a royal communication to bring to you. He spent two hours trying to impress me."

"Were you impressed?"

"Not particularly, no." Ulath reached inside his surcoat and drew out a folded and sealed sheet of parchment.

"What does it say?" she asked.

"I wouldn't know. I don't read other people's mail. My guess is that it's a serious discussion of the weather. Avin Wargunsson's desperately afraid that people might forget about him, so every traveller who leaves Emsat is loaded down with royal greetings."

"How was the trip?" Sparhawk asked them.

"I can't really say that I'd recommend sea travel at this time of year," Stragen replied. His icy blue eyes hardened. "I want to have a little talk with Platime. Ulath and I were set upon by some brigands in the mountains between here and Cardos. Bandits are supposed to know better than that."

"They aren't professionals," Sparhawk told him. "Platime knows about them, and he's going to take steps. Were there any problems?"

"Not for us." Ulath shrugged. "The amateurs out there didn't have a very good day, though. We left five of them in a ditch, and then the rest all remembered an important engagement somewhere else." He went to the door and looked out into the hall. Then he closed the door and looked around, his eyes wary. "Are there any servants or people like that in any of your rooms here, Sparhawk?" he asked.

"Mirtai and our daughter is all."

"That's all right. I think we can trust them. Komier sent me to let you know that Avin Wargunsson's been in contact with Count Gerrich down in Lamorkand. Gerrich's taking a run at King Friedahl's throne, and Avin's not quite bright. He doesn't know enough to stay out of the internal squabbles in Lamorkand. Komier thinks there might just possibly be some sort of secret arrangement between them. Patriarch Bergsten's taking the same message to Chyrellos."

"Count Gerrich's going to start to irritate Dolmant if he doesn't watch what he's doing," Ehlana said. "He's trying to make alliances every time he turns around, and he knows that's a violation of the rules. Lamork civil wars aren't supposed to involve other kingdoms."

"That's an actual rule?" Stragen asked her incredulously.

"Of course. It's been in place for a thousand years. If the Lamork barons were free to form alliances with nobles in other kingdoms, they'd plunge the continent into war every ten years. That used to happen until the Church stepped in and told them to stop."

"And you thought *our* society had peculiar rules." Stragen laughed to Platime.

"This is entirely different, Milord Stragen," Ehlana told him in a lofty tone. "*Our* peculiarities are matters of state policy. Yours are simply good common sense. There's a world of difference."

"So I gather."

Sparhawk was looking at all three of them when it happened, so there was no doubt that when *he* felt that peculiar chill and caught that faint flicker of darkness at the very outer edge of his vision, they did as well.

"Sparhawk!" Ehlana cried in alarm.

"Yes," he replied. "I know. I saw it, too."

Stragen had half drawn his rapier, his hand moving with catlike speed. "What is it?" he demanded, looking around the room.

"An impossibility," Ehlana said flatly. The look she gave her husband was a little less certain, however. "Isn't it, Sparhawk?" her voice trembled slightly.

"I certainly thought so," he replied.

"This isn't the time to be cryptic," Stragen said.

Then the chill and the shadow passed.

Ulath looked speculatively at Sparhawk. "Was that what I thought it was?" he asked.

"So it seems."

"Will someone please tell me what's going on here?" Stragen demanded.

"Do you remember that cloud that followed us up in Pelosia?" Ulath said.

"Of course. But that was Azash, wasn't it?"

"No. We thought so, but Aphrael told us that we were wrong. That was after you came back here, so you probably didn't hear about it. That shadow we just saw was the Troll-Gods. They're inside the Bhelliom."

"Inside?"

"They needed a place to hide after they'd lost a few arguments with the Younger Gods of Styricum."

Stragen looked at Sparhawk. "I thought you told me that you'd thrown Bhelliom into the sea."

"We did."

"And the Troll-Gods can't get out of it?"

"That's what we were led to believe."

"You should have found a deeper ocean."

"There aren't any deeper ones."

"That's too bad. It looks as if someone's managed to fish it out."

"It's logical, Sparhawk," Ulath said. "That box was lined with gold, and Aphrael told us that the gold would keep Bhelliom from getting out on its own. Since the Troll-Gods can't get out of Bhelliom, they were down there, too. Somebody's found that box."

"I've heard that the people who dive for pearls can go down quite deep," Stragen said.

"Not *that* deep," Sparhawk said. "Besides, there's something wrong."

"Are you just now realizing that?" Stragen asked him.

"That's not what I mean. When we were up in Pelosia, you could all see that cloud."

"Oh, yes," Ulath said fervently.

"But before that—when it was just a shadow—only Ehlana and I could see it, and that was because we were wearing the rings. This was definitely a shadow and not a cloud, wasn't it?"

"Yes," Stragen admitted.

"Then how is it that you and Ulath could see it, too?"

Stragen spread his hands helplessly.

"There's something else, as well," Sparhawk added. "The night I came home from Lamorkand, I felt something in the street watching me—several somethings.

They weren't Elene or Styric, and I don't think they were human. That shadow that just passed through here felt exactly the same."

"I wish there was some way we could talk with Sephrenia," Ulath muttered.

Sparhawk was fairly certain that there *was* a way, but he was not free to reveal it to any of them.

"Do we tell anybody else about this?" Stragen asked.

"Let's not start a panic until we find out more about it," Sparhawk decided.

"Right," Stragen agreed. "There's always plenty of time for panic later—plenty of reason, too, I think."

The weather cleared over the next few days, and that fact alone lifted spirits in the palace. Sparhawk spent some time closeted with Platime and Stragen, and then the two thieves sent men into Lamorkand to investigate the situation there. "That's what I should have done in the first place," Sparhawk said, "but Sarathi wouldn't give me the chance. Our revered Archprelate has a few blind spots. He can't seem to get it through his head that *official* investigators aren't going to ever really get to the bottom of things."

"Typical aristocratic ineptitude," Stragen drawled. "It's one of the things that makes life easier for people like Platime and me."

Sparhawk didn't argue with him about that. "Just tell your men to be careful," he cautioned them. "Lamorks tend to try to solve all their problems with daggers, and dead spies don't bring home very much useful information."

"Astonishing insight there, old boy," Stragen said, his rich voice dripping with irony. "It's absolutely amazing that Platime and I never thought of that."

"All right," Sparhawk admitted, "maybe I was being just a little obvious."

"We saw that, too, didn't we, Platime?"

Platime grunted. "Tell Ehlana that I'm going to be away from the palace for a few days, Sparhawk."

"Where are you going?"

"None of your business. There's something I want to take care of."

"All right, but keep in touch."

"You're being obvious again, Sparhawk." The fat man scratched his paunch. "I'll talk with Talen. He'll know how to get in touch with me if the queen really needs me for something." He groaned as he hauled himself to his feet. "I'm going to have to lose some weight," he said half to himself. Then he waddled to the door with that peculiarly spraddle-legged gait of the grossly obese.

"He's in a charming humor today," Sparhawk noted.

"He's got a lot on his mind just now." Stragen shrugged.

"How well connected are you in the palace at Emsat, Stragen?"

"I have some contacts there. What do you need?"

"I'd like to put some stumbling blocks in the way of this accommodation between Avin and Count Gerrich. Gerrich's beginning to get a little too much influence in northern Eosia. Maybe you ought to get word to Meland in Acie as well. Gerrich's making alliances in Pelosia and Thalesia already. It doesn't seem reasonable that he'd overlook Deira, and Deira's a little chaotic right now. Ask Meland to keep his eyes open."

"This Gerrich's really got you concerned, hasn't he?"

"There are some things going on in Lamorkand that I don't understand, Stragen, and I don't want Gerrich to get too far ahead of me while I'm trying to sort them out."

"That makes sense—I suppose."

Khalad came to his feet with his eyes slightly unfocused and with a thin dribble of blood coming out of his nose.

"You see? You overextended again," Mirtai told him.

"How did you do that?" Sparhawk's squire asked her.

"I'll show you. Kalten, come here."

"Not me." The blond Pandion refused, backing away.

"Don't be foolish. I'm not going to hurt you."

"Isn't that what you told Khalad before you bounced him off the flagstones?"

"You might as well do as I tell you, Kalten," she said. "You'll wind up doing it in the end anyway, and it won't be nearly as painful for you if you don't argue with me. Take out your sword and stab me in the heart with it."

"I don't want to hurt you, Mirtai."

"*You?* Hurt *me?*" Her laugh was sardonic.

"You don't have to be insulting about it," he said in an injured tone, drawing his sword.

It had all begun when Mirtai had passed through the palace courtyard while Kalten was giving Khalad some instruction in swordsmanship. She had made a couple of highly unflattering comments. One thing had led to another, and the end result had been this impromptu training session, during which Kalten and Khalad were learning humility, if nothing else.

"Stab me through the heart, Kalten," Mirtai said again.

In Kalten's defense it should be noted in passing that he really *did* try. He made a great deal of noise when he came down on his back on the flagstones.

"He made the same mistake you did," Mirtai pointed out to Khalad. "He straightened his arm too much. A straight arm is a locked arm. Always keep your elbow slightly bent."

"We're trained to thrust from the shoulder, Mirtai," Khalad explained.

"There are a lot of Elenes, I suppose." She shrugged. "It shouldn't be all that hard to replace you. The thing that makes me curious is why you all feel that it's necessary to stick your sword all the way through somebody. If you haven't hit the heart with the first six inches of the blade, another yard or so of steel going through the same hole won't make much difference, will it?"

"Maybe it's because it looks dramatic," Khalad said.

"You kill people for show? That's contemptible, and it's the sort of thinking that fills graveyards. Always keep your blade free so that you're ready for your next enemy. People fold up when you run swords through them, and then you have to kick the body off the blade before you can use it again."

"I'll try to remember that."

"I hope so. I rather like you, and I hate burying friends." She bent, professionally peeled Kalten's eyelid back, and glanced at his glazed eyeball. "You'd better throw a bucket of water on our friend here," she suggested, nodding to Sparhawk as he joined them. "He hasn't learned how to fall yet. We'll go into that next time."

"*Next* time?"

"Of course. If you're going to learn how to do this, you'd better learn how to do it right." She gave Sparhawk a challenging look. "Would you like to try?" she asked him.

"Ah—no, Mirtai, not right now. Thanks all the same, though."

She went on into the palace, looking just slightly pleased with herself.

"You know, I don't think I really want to be a knight after all, Sparhawk," Talen said from nearby. "It looks awfully painful."

"Where have you been? My wife's got people out looking for you."

"Yes. I saw them blundering around out in the streets. I had to go visit Platime in the cellar."

"Oh?"

"He picked up something he thought you ought to be aware of. You know those unauthorized bandits in the hills near Cardos?"

"Not personally, no."

"Funny, Sparhawk. Very funny. Platime's found out that somebody we know is sort of directing their activities."

"Oh? Who's that?"

"Can you believe that it's Krager? You should have killed him when you had the chance, Sparhawk."

CHAPTER THREE

The fog drifted in from the river not long after the sun went down that evening. The nights in Cimmura were always foggy in the spring when it wasn't raining. Sparhawk, Stragen, and Talen left the palace wearing plain clothing and heavy traveller's cloaks and rode to the southeast quarter of town.

"You don't necessarily have to tell your wife I said this, Sparhawk," Stragen noted, looking around with distaste, "but her capital's one of the least attractive cities in the world. You've got a truly miserable climate here."

"It's not so bad in the summertime," Sparhawk replied a little defensively.

"I missed last summer," the blond thief said. "I took a short nap one afternoon and slept right through it. Where are we going?"

"We want to see Platime."

"As I recall, his cellar's near the west gate of the city. You're taking us in the wrong direction."

"We have to go to a certain inn first." Sparhawk looked back over his shoulder. "Are we being followed, Talen?" he asked.

"Naturally."

Sparhawk grunted. "That's more or less what I expected."

They rode on with the thick mist swirling around the legs of their horses and making the fronts of the nearby houses dim and hazy-looking. They reached the inn on Rose Street, and a surly-appearing porter admitted them to the innyard and closed the gate behind them.

"Anything you find out about this place isn't for general dissemination," Sparhawk told Talen and Stragen as he dismounted. He handed Faran's reins to the porter. "You know about this horse, don't you, brother?" he warned the man.

"He's a legend, Sparhawk," the porter replied. "The things you wanted are in the room at the top of the stairs."

"How's the crowd in the tavern tonight?"

"Loud, smelly, and mostly drunk."

"There's nothing new about that. What I meant, though, was how many of them are there?"

"Fifteen or twenty. There are three of our men in there who know what to do."

"Good. Thank you, Sir Knight."

"You're welcome, Sir Knight."

Sparhawk led Talen and Stragen up the stairs.

"This inn, I gather, isn't altogether what it seems," Stragen observed.

"The Pandions own it," Talen told him. "They come here when they don't want to attract attention."

"There's a little more to it than that," Sparhawk told him. He opened the door at the top of the stairs, and the three of them entered.

Stragen looked at the workmen's smocks hanging on pegs near the door. "We're going to resort to subterfuge, I see."

"It's fairly standard practice." Sparhawk shrugged. "Let's get changed. I'd sort of like to get back to the palace before my wife sends out search parties."

The smocks were of blue canvas, worn and patched and with a few artfully placed smudges on them. There were woolen leggings as well and thick-soled workmen's boots. The caps were baggy affairs, designed more to keep off weather than they were for appearance.

"You're going to have to leave that here," Sparhawk said, pointing at Stragen's rapier. "It's a little obvious." The big Pandion tucked a heavy dagger under his belt.

"You know that there are people watching the gate of the inn, don't you, Sparhawk?" Talen said.

"I hope they enjoy their evening. We aren't going out through the gate, though." Sparhawk led them back down to the innyard, crossed to a narrow door in a side wall, and opened it. The warm air that boiled out through the doorway smelled of stale beer and unwashed bodies. The three of them went inside and closed the door behind them. They seemed to be in a small storeroom. The straw on the floor was moldy.

"Where are we?" Talen whispered.

"In a tavern," Sparhawk replied softly. "There's going to be a fight in just a few minutes. We'll slip out into the main room during the confusion." He went to the curtained doorway leading out into the tavern and twitched the curtain several times. "All right," he whispered. "We'll mingle with the crowd during the fight, and after a while, we'll leave. Behave as if you're slightly drunk, but don't overdo it."

"I'm impressed," Stragen said.

"I'm more than impressed," Talen added. "Not even Platime knows that there's more than one way out of that inn."

The fight began not long after that. It was noisy, involving a great deal of shouting and pushing and finally a few blows. Two totally uninvolved and evidently innocent bystanders were knocked senseless during the course of the altercation. Sparhawk and his friends smoothly insinuated themselves into the crowd and, after ten minutes or so, they reeled out through the door.

"A little unprofessional." Stragen sniffed. "A staged fight shouldn't involve the spectators that way."

"It should when the spectators might be looking for something other than a few tankards of ale," Sparhawk disagreed. "The two who fell asleep weren't regular patrons in the tavern. They might have been completely innocent, but then again, they might not. This way, we don't have to worry about them trailing along behind us."

"There's more to being a Pandion Knight than I thought," Talen noted. "I may like it after all."

They walked through the foggy streets toward the run-down quarter near the west gate, a maze of interconnecting lanes and unpaved alleys. They entered one of those alleys and went through it to a flight of muddy stone stairs leading down. A thick-bodied man lounged against the stone wall beside the stairs. "You're late," he said to Talen in a flat voice.

"We had to make sure we weren't being followed," the boy responded.

"Go on down," the man told them, "Platime's waiting."

The cellar hadn't changed. It was still smoky and dim, and it was filled with a babble of coarse voices coming from the thieves, whores, and cutthroats who lived there.

"I don't know how Platime can stand this place." Stragen shuddered.

Platime sat enthroned on a large chair on the other side of a smoky fire burning in an open pit. He heaved himself to his feet when he saw Sparhawk. "Where have you been?" he bellowed in a thunderous voice.

"Making sure that we weren't followed," Sparhawk replied.

The fat man grunted. "He's back here," he said, leading them toward the rear of the cellar. "He's very interested in his health at the moment, so I'm keeping him more or less out of sight." He pushed his way into a small, closetlike chamber where a man sat on a stool nursing a tankard of watery beer. The man was a small, nervous-looking fellow with thinning hair and a cringing manner.

"This is Pelk," Platime said. "He's a sneak thief. I sent him to Cardos to have a look around and to see what he could find out about some people we're interested in. Tell him what you found out, Pelk."

"Well, sir, good masters," the weedy man began, "it tuk me a goodly while to git close to them fellers, I'll tell the world, but I made myself useful, an' they finally sort of assepted me. They was all sorts of rigmarole I had to go thoo—swearin' oaths an' gettin' blindfolded the first couple times they tuk me to ther camp an' all, but after a while, they kinda let down ther guard, an' I come an' went purty much as I pleased. Like Platime prob'ly tole you, we figgered at first they wuz jist a buncha amachoors what didn't know nothin' about the way things is supposed to be did. We sees that sorta thing all the time, don't we, Platime? Them's the kind as gits therselves caught an' hung."

"And good riddance to them," Platime growled.

"Well, sir," Pelk continued, "like I say, me 'n' Platime, we figgered as how them fellers in the mountings was jist a buncha them amachoors I tole you about—fellers what'd took up cuttin' thoats fer fun an' profit, don't y'know. As she turns out, howsomever, they was more'n that. Ther leaders was six er seven noblemen as was real disappointed 'bout the way the big plans of the Primate Annias fell on ther faces, an' they was powerful unhappy 'bout what the queen had writ down on the warrants she put out fer 'em—nobles not bein' accustomed to bein' called them sorta names.

"Well, sir, t' short it up some, these here noblemen all run off into the mountings 'bout one jump ahead of the hangman, an' they tuk t' robbin' travellers t' make ends meet an' spent the resta ther time thinkin' up nasty names t' call the queen."

"Get to the point, Pelk," Platime told him wearily.

"Yessir, I wuz jist about to. Well now, it went on like that fer a spell, an' then this here Krager feller, he come into camp, an' some of them there nobles, they knowed him. He tole 'em as how he knowed some furriners as'd help 'em out iffn they'd raise enough fuss here in Elenia t' keep the queen an' her folks from gittin' too curious 'bout some stuff what's goin' on off in Lamorkand. This here Krager feller, he sez as how this stuff in Lamorkand might just could be a way fer 'em all t' change the way ther forchunes bin goin' since ol' Annias got hisself kilt. Well, sir, them dukes an' earls an' such got real innerested at that point, an' they told us all t' go talk t' the local peasants an' t' start runnin' down the tax collectors an' t' say as how it ain't natural fer no country t' be run by no woman an' the like. We wuz supposed t' stir up them peasants an' t' git 'em t' talkin' among therselves 'bout how the people oughtta all git together an' thow the queen out an' the like, an' then them nobles, they caught a few tax collectors an' hung 'em an' give the money back t' the folks it'd been stole from in the first place, an' them peasants, they wuz all happy as pigs in mud 'bout that." Pelk scratched at his head. "Well, sir, I guess I've said m' piece now. 'At's the way she stands in the mountings now. This here Krager feller, he's got some money with 'im, an' he's mighty free with it, so them nobles what's bin on short rations is gittin' downright fond of 'im."

"Pelk," Sparhawk told him, "you're a treasure." He gave the man several coins, and then he and his friends left the cubicle.

"What are we going to do about it, Sparhawk?" Platime asked.

"We're going to take steps," Sparhawk replied. "How many of these 'liberators' are there?"

"A hundred or so."

"I'll need a couple dozen of your men who know the country."

Platime nodded. "Are you going to bring in the army?"

"I don't think so. I think a troop of Pandions might make a more lasting impression on people who think they have grievances against our queen, don't you?"

"Isn't that just a bit extreme?" Stragen asked him.

"I want to make a statement, Stragen. I want everybody in Elenia to know just how much I disapprove of people who start plotting against my wife. I don't want to have to do it again, so I'm going to do it right the first time."

"He didn't *actually* talk like that, did he, Sparhawk?" Ehlana asked incredulously.

"That's fairly close," Sparhawk told her. "Stragen's got a very good ear for dialect."

"It's almost hypnotic, isn't it?" she marvelled. "And it goes on and on and on." She suddenly grinned impishly. "Write down 'happy as pigs in mud,' Lenda. I may want to find a way to work that into some official communication."

"As you wish, your Majesty," Lenda's tone was neutral, but Sparhawk knew that the old courtier disapproved.

"What are we going to do about this?" the queen asked.

"Sparhawk said that he was going to take steps, your Majesty," Talen told her. "You might not want to know too many details."

"Sparhawk and I don't keep secrets from each other, Talen."

"I'm not talking about secrets, your Majesty," the boy replied innocently. "I'm just talking about boring unimportant little things you shouldn't really waste your time on." He made it sound very plausible, but Ehlana looked more than a little suspicious.

"Don't embarrass me, Sparhawk," she warned.

"Of course not," he replied blandly.

The campaign was brief. Since Pelk knew the precise location of the camp of the dissidents, and Platime's men knew all the other hiding places in the surrounding mountains, there was no real place for the bandits to run, and they were certainly no match for the thirty black-armored Pandions Sparhawk, Kalten, and Ulath led against them. The surviving nobles were held for the queen's justice and the rest of the outlaws were turned over to the local sheriff for disposition.

"Well, my Lord of Belton," Sparhawk said to an earl crouched before him on a log, with a bloodstained bandage around his head and his hands bound behind him. "Things didn't turn out so well, did they?"

"Curse you, Sparhawk." Belton spat, squinting up against the afternoon's brightness. "How did you find out where we were?"

"My dear Belton," Sparhawk laughed, "you didn't *really* think you could hide from my wife, did you? She takes a very personal interest in her kingdom. She knows every tree, every town and village and all of the peasants. It's even rumored that she knows most of the deer by their first names."

"Why didn't you come after us earlier then?" Belton sneered.

"The queen was busy. She finally found the time to make some decisions about you and your friends. I don't imagine you'll care much for these decisions, old boy. What I'm really interested in is any information you might have about Krager. He and I haven't seen each other for quite some time, and I find myself yearning for his company again."

Belton's eyes grew frightened. "You won't get anything from me, Sparhawk," he blustered.

"How much would you care to wager on that?" Kalten asked him. "You'd save yourself a great deal of unpleasantness if you tell Sparhawk what he wants to know, and Krager's not so loveable that you'd really want to go through that in order to protect him."

"Just talk, Belton," Sparhawk insisted implacably.

"I—I *can't*!" Belton's sneering bravado crumbled. His face turned deathly pale, and he began to tremble violently. "Sparhawk, I beg of you. It means my life if I say anything."

"Your life isn't worth very much right now anyway," Ulath told him bluntly. "One way or another, you *are* going to talk."

"For God's sake, Sparhawk! You don't know what you're asking!"

"I'm not *asking*, Belton." Sparhawk's face was bleak.

Then, without any warning or reason, a deathly chill suddenly enveloped the woods, and the midafternoon sun darkened. Sparhawk glanced upward. The sky was very blue, but the sun appeared wan and sickly.

Belton screamed.

An inky cloud seemed to spring from the surrounding trees, coalescing around the shrieking prisoner. Sparhawk jumped back with a startled oath, his hand going to his sword hilt.

Belton's voice had risen to a screech, and there were horrible sounds coming from the now-impenetrable darkness surrounding him—sounds of breaking bones and tearing flesh. The shrieking broke off quite suddenly, but the sounds continued for several eternal-seeming minutes. Then, as quickly as it had come, the cloud vanished.

Sparhawk recoiled in revulsion. His prisoner had been torn to pieces.

"Good God!" Kalten gasped. "What happened?"

"We both know, Kalten," Sparhawk replied. "We've seen it before. Don't try to question any of the other prisoners. I'm almost positive they won't be allowed to answer."

There were five of them: Sparhawk, Ehlana, Kalten, Ulath, and Stragen. They had gathered in the royal apartment, and their mood was bleak.

"Was it the same cloud?" Stragen asked intently.

"There were some differences," Sparhawk replied, "more in the way it felt than anything I could really pin down."

"Why would the Troll-Gods be so interested in protecting Krager?" Ehlana asked, her face puzzled.

"I don't think it's Krager they're protecting," Sparhawk replied. "I think it has something to do with what's going on in Lamorkand." He slammed his fist down on the arm of his chair. "I *wish* Sephrenia were here!" he burst out with a sudden oath. "All we're doing is groping in the dark."

"Would you be opposed to logic at this point?" Stragen asked him.

"I wouldn't even be opposed to astrology just now," Sparhawk replied sourly.

"All right." The blond Thalesian thief rose to his feet and began to pace up and down, his eyes thoughtful. "First of all, we know that somehow the Troll-Gods have gotten out of that box."

"Actually, you haven't really proved that, Stragen," Ulath disagreed. "Not logically, anyway."

Stragen stopped pacing. "He's right, you know," he admitted. "We've been basing that conclusion on a guess. All we can say with any logical certainty is that we've encountered something that looks and feels like a manifestation of the Troll-Gods. Would you accept that, Sir Ulath?"

"I suppose I could go that far, Milord Stragen."

"I'm so happy. Do we know of anything else that does the same sort of things?"

"No," Ulath replied, "but that's not really relevant. We don't know about everything. There could be dozens of things we don't know about that take the form of shadows or clouds, tear people all to pieces, and give humans a chilly feeling when they're around."

"I'm not sure that logic is really getting us anywhere," Stragen conceded.

"There's nothing wrong with your logic, Stragen," Ehlana told him. "Your major premise is faulty, that's all."

"You, too, your Majesty?" Kalten groaned. "I thought there was at least one other person in the room who relied on common sense rather than all this tedious logic."

"All right, Sir Kalten," she said tartly, "what does your common sense tell you?"

"Well, first off, it tells me that you're all going at the problem backward. The question we should be asking is what makes Krager so special that something supernatural would go out of its way to protect him? Does it really matter *what* the supernatural thing is at the moment?"

"He might have something there, you know," Ulath said. "Krager's a cockroach, basically. His only real reason for existing is to be stepped on."

"I'm not so sure," Ehlana disagreed. "Krager worked for Martel, and Martel worked for Annias."

"Actually, dear, it was the other way around," Sparhawk corrected her.

She waved that distinction aside. "Belton and the others were all allied to Annias, and Krager used to carry messages between Annias and Martel. Belton and his cohorts would almost certainly have known Krager. Pelk's story more or less confirms that. That's what made Krager important in the first place." She paused, frowning. "But what made him important *after* the renegades were all in custody?"

"Backtracking." Ulath grunted.

"I beg your pardon?" The queen looked baffled.

"This whatever-it-is didn't want us to be able to trace Krager back to his present employer."

"Oh, that's obvious, Ulath." Kalten snorted. "His employer is Count Gerrich. Pelk told Sparhawk that there was somebody in Lamorkand who wanted to keep us so busy here in Elenia that we wouldn't have time to take any steps to put down all the turmoil over there. That *has* to be Gerrich."

"You're just guessing, Kalten," Ulath said. "You could very well be right, but it's still just a guess."

"Do you see what I mean about logic?" Kalten demanded of them. "What do you want, Ulath? A signed confession from Gerrich himself?"

"Do you have one handy? All I'm saying is that we ought to keep an open mind. I don't think we should close any doors yet, that's all."

There was a firm knock on the door, and it opened immediately afterward. Mirtai looked in. "Bevier and Tynian are here," she announced.

"They're supposed to be in Rendor," Sparhawk said. "What are they doing here?"

"Why don't you ask them?" Mirtai suggested pointedly. "They're right out here in the corridor."

The two knights entered the room. Sir Bevier was a slim, olive-skinned Arcian, and Sir Tynian a blond, burly Deiran. Both were in full armor.

"How are things in Rendor?" Kalten asked them.

"Hot, dry, dusty, hysterical," Tynian replied. "Rendor never changes. You know that."

Bevier dropped to one knee before Ehlana. Despite the best efforts of his friends, the young Cyrinic Knight was still painfully formal. "Your Majesty," he murmured respectfully.

"Oh, do stand up, my dear Bevier." She smiled at him. "We're friends, so there's no need for that. Besides, you creak like a rusty ironworks when you kneel."

"Overtrained, perhaps, your Majesty," he admitted.

"What are you two doing back here?" Sparhawk asked them.

"Carrying dispatches," Tynian replied. "Darellon's running things down there, and he wants the other preceptors kept abreast of things. We're also supposed to go on to Chyrellos and brief the Archprelate."

"How's the campaign going?" Kalten asked them.

"Badly." Tynian shrugged. "The Rendorish rebels aren't really organized, so there aren't any armies for us to meet. They hide amongst the population and come out at night to set fires and assassinate priests. Then they run back into their holes. We take reprisals the next day—burn villages, slaughter herds of sheep, and the like. None of it really proves anything."

"Do they have any kind of a leader as yet?" Sparhawk asked.

"They're still discussing that," Bevier said dryly. "The discussions are quite spirited. We usually find several dead candidates in the alleys every morning."

"Sarathi blundered," Tynian said.

Bevier gasped.

"I'm not trying to offend your religious sensibilities, my young friend," Tynian said, "but it's the truth. Most of the clergymen he sent to Rendor were much more interested in punishment than in reconciliation. We had a chance for real peace in Rendor, and it fell apart because Dolmant didn't send somebody down there to keep a leash on the missionaries." Tynian set his helmet on a table and unbuckled his sword belt. "I even saw one silly ass in a cassock tearing the veils off women in the street. After the crowd seized him, he tried to order me to protect him. *That's* the kind of priests the Church has been sending to Rendor."

"What did you do?" Stragen asked him.

"For some reason I couldn't quite hear what he was saying," Tynian replied. "All the noise the crowd was making, more than likely."

"What did they do to him?" Kalten grinned.

"They hanged him. Quite a neat job, actually."

"You didn't even go to his defense?" Bevier exclaimed.

"Our instructions were very explicit, Bevier. We were told to protect the clergy against unprovoked attacks. That idiot violated the modesty of about a dozen Rendorish women. That crowd had plenty of provocation. The silly ass had it coming. If that crowd hadn't hanged him, I probably would have. That's what Darellon wants us to suggest to Sarathi. He thinks the Church should pull all those fanatic missionaries out of Rendor until things quiet down. Then he suggests that we send in a new batch—a slightly less fervent one." The Alcione Knight laid his sword down beside his helmet and lowered himself into a chair. "What's been happening here?" he asked.

"Why don't the rest of you fill them in?" Sparhawk suggested. "There's someone I want to talk with for a few minutes." He turned and quietly went back into the royal apartment.

The person he wanted to talk with was not some court functionary, but rather his own daughter. He found her playing with her kitten. After some thought, her Royal little Highness had decided to name the small animal "Mmrr," a sound that, when she uttered it, sounded so much like the kitten's purr that Sparhawk usually couldn't tell for sure which of them was making it. Princess Danae had many gifts.

"We need to talk," Sparhawk told her, closing the door behind him as he entered.

"What is it now, Sparhawk?" she asked.

"Tynian and Bevier just arrived."

"Yes. I know."

"Are you playing with things again? Are you deliberately gathering all our friends here?"

"Of course I am, Father."

"Would you mind telling me why?"

"There's something we're going to need to do before long. I thought I'd save some time by getting everybody here in advance."

"You'd probably better tell me what it is that we have to do."

"I'm not supposed to do that."

"You never pay any attention to any of the *other* rules."

"This is different, Father. We're absolutely not supposed to talk about the future. If you think about it for a moment, I'm sure you'll see why. Ouch!" Mmrr had bitten her finger. Danae spoke sharply with the kitten—a series of little growls, a meow or two, and concluding with a forgiving purr. The kitten managed to look slightly ashamed of itself and proceeded to lick the injured finger.

"Please don't talk in cat, Danae," Sparhawk said in a pained tone. "If some chambermaid hears you, it'll take us both a month to explain."

"Nobody's going to hear me, Sparhawk. You've got something else on your mind, haven't you?"

"I want to talk with Sephrenia. There are some things I don't understand, and I need her help with them."

"I'll help you, Father."

He shook his head. "Your explanations always leave me with more questions than I had when we started. Can you get in touch with Sephrenia for me?"

She looked around. "It probably wouldn't be a good idea here in the palace, Father," she told him. "It involves something that might be hard to explain if someone overheard us."

"You're going to be in two places at the same time again?"

"Well—sort of." She picked up her kitten. "Why don't you find some excuse to take me out for a ride tomorrow morning? We'll go out of the city and I can take care of things there. Tell Mother that you want to give me a riding lesson."

"You don't have a pony, Danae."

She gave him an angelic smile. "My goodness," she said, "that sort of means that you're going to have to give me one, doesn't it?"

He gave her a long, steady look.

"You *were* going to give me a pony eventually, weren't you, Father?" She gave it a moment's thought. "A white one, Sparhawk," she added. "I definitely want a white one." Then she snuggled her kitten against her cheek, and they both started to purr.

Sparhawk and his daughter rode out of Cimmura not long after breakfast the following morning. The weather was blustery, and Mirtai had objected rather vociferously until Princess Danae told her not to be so fussy. For some reason, the word "fussy" absolutely enraged the Tamul giantess. She stormed away, swearing sulphurously in her own language.

It had taken Sparhawk hours to find a white pony for his daughter, and he was quite convinced after he had that it was the only white one in the whole town. When Danae greeted the stubby little creature like an old friend, he began to have a number of suspicions. Over the past couple of years, he and his daughter had painfully hammered out a list of the things she wasn't supposed to do. The process had begun rather abruptly in the palace garden one summer afternoon when he had come around a box hedge to find a small swarm of fairies pollinating flowers under Danae's supervision. Although she had probably been right when she had asserted that fairies were really much better at it than bees, he had firmly put his foot down. After a bit of thought this time, however, he decided not to make an issue of his daughter's obvious connivance in obtaining a specific pony. He needed her help right now, and she might point out with a certain amount of justification that to forbid one form of what they had come to call "tampering" while encouraging another was inconsistent.

"Is this going to involve anything spectacular?" he asked her when they were several miles out of town.

"How do you mean, spectacular?"

"You don't have to fly or anything, do you?"

"It's awkward that way, but I can if you'd like."

"No, that's all right, Danae. What I'm getting at is, would you be doing anything that would startle travellers if we went out into this meadow a ways and you did whatever it is there?"

"They won't see a thing, Father," she assured him. "I'll race you to that tree out there." She didn't even make a pretense of nudging her pony's flanks, and despite Faran's best efforts, the pony beat him to the tree by a good twenty yards. The big roan war-horse glowered suspiciously at the short-legged pony when Sparhawk reined him in.

"You cheated," Sparhawk accused his daughter.

"Only a little." She slid down from her pony and sat cross-legged under the tree. She lifted her small face and sang in a trilling, flutelike voice. Her song broke off, and for several moments she sat blank-faced and absolutely immobile. She did not even appear to be breathing, and Sparhawk had the chilling feeling that he was absolutely alone, although she clearly sat not two yards away from him.

"What is it, Sparhawk?" Danae's lips moved, but it was Sephrenia's voice that asked the question, and when Danae opened her eyes, they had changed. Danae's eyes were very dark; Sephrenia's were deep blue, almost lavender.

"We miss you, little mother," he told her, kneeling and kissing the palms of his daughter's hands.

"You called me from halfway round the world to tell me that? I'm touched, but—"

"It's something a little more, Sephrenia. We've been seeing that shadow again—the cloud, too."

"That's impossible."

"I sort of thought so myself, but we keep seeing them all the same. It's different, though. It feels different for one thing, and this time it's not just Ehlana and I who see it. Stragen and Ulath saw it, too."

"You'd better tell me exactly what's been happening, Sparhawk."

He went into greater detail about the shadow and then briefly described the incident in the mountains near Cardos. "Whatever this thing is," he concluded, "it seems very intent on keeping us from finding out what's going on in Lamorkand."

"Is there some kind of trouble there?"

"Count Gerrich is raising a rebellion. He seems to think that the crown might fit him. He's even going so far as to claim that Drychtnath's returned. That's ridiculous, isn't it?"

Her eyes grew distant. "Is this shadow you've been seeing exactly the same as the one you and Ehlana saw before?" she asked.

"It feels different somehow."

"Do you get that same sense that it has more than one consciousness in it?"

"That hasn't changed. It's a small group, but it's a group all the same, and the cloud that tore the Earl of Belton to pieces was definitely the same. Did the Troll-Gods manage to escape from Bhelliom somehow?"

"Let me think my way through it for a moment, Sparhawk," she replied. She considered it for a time. In a curious way she was impressing her own appearance on Danae's face. "I think we may have a problem, dear one," she said finally.

"I noticed that myself, little mother."

"Stop trying to be clever, Sparhawk. Do you remember the Dawn-men who came out of that cloud up in Pelosia?"

Sparhawk shuddered. "I've been making a special point of trying to forget that."

"Don't discount the possibility that the wild stories about Drychtnath may have some basis in fact. The Troll-Gods can reach back in time and bring creatures and people forward to where we are now. Drychtnath may very well indeed have returned."

Sparhawk groaned. "Then the Troll-Gods have managed to escape, haven't they?"

"I didn't say that, Sparhawk. Just because the Troll-Gods did this one time doesn't mean that they're the *only* ones who know how. For all I know, Aphrael could do it herself." She paused. "You could have asked *her* these questions, you know."

"Possibly, but I don't think I could have asked her *this* one, because I don't think she'd know the answer. She doesn't seem to be able to grasp the concept of limitations for some reason."

"You've noticed," she said dryly.

"Be nice. She's my daughter, after all."

"She was my sister first, so I have a certain amount of seniority in the matter. What is it that she wouldn't be able to answer?"

"Could a Styric magician—or any other magician—be behind all this? Could we be dealing with a human?"

"No, Sparhawk, I don't think so. In forty thousand years there have only been two Styric magicians who were able to reach back into time, and they could only do it imperfectly. For all practical purposes what we're talking about is beyond human capability."

"That's what I wanted to find out for sure. We're dealing with Gods then?"

"I'm afraid so, Sparhawk, almost certainly."

CHAPTER FOUR

Preceptor Sparhawk:

    It is our hope that this finds you and your family in good health.

    A matter of some delicacy has arisen, and we find that your presence is required here in Chyrellos. You are therefore commanded by the Church to proceed forthwith to the Basilica and to present yourself before our throne to receive our further instruction. We know that as a true son of the Church you will not delay. We shall expect your attendance upon us within the week.

                                            Dolmant, Archprelate

Sparhawk lowered the letter and looked around at the others.

"He gets right to the point, doesn't he?" Kalten observed. "Of course Dolmant never was one to beat around the bush."

Queen Ehlana gave a howl of absolute fury and began beating her fists on the council table and stamping her feet on the floor.

"You'll hurt your hands," Sparhawk cautioned.

"How *dare* he?" she exploded. "How *dare* he?"

"A bit abrupt, perhaps," Stragen noted cautiously.

"You will ignore this churlish command, Sparhawk!" Ehlana ordered.

"I can't do that."

"You are *my* husband and *my* subject! If Dolmant wants to see you, he'll ask *my* permission! This is outrageous!"

"The Archprelate *does* in fact have the authority to summon the preceptor of one of the Militant Orders to Chyrellos, your Majesty," the Earl of Lenda diffidently told the fuming queen.

"You're wearing too many hats, Sparhawk," Tynian told his friend. "You should resign from a few of these exalted positions you hold."

"It's that devastating personality of his," Kalten said to Ulath, "and all those unspeakable gifts. People just wither and die in his absence."

"I forbid it!" Ehlana said flatly.

"I have to obey him, Ehlana," Sparhawk explained. "I'm a Church Knight."

Her eyes narrowed. "Very well then," she decided, "since Dolmant's feeling so authoritarian, we'll *all* obey his stupid command. We'll go to Chyrellos and set up shop in the Basilica. I'll let him know that I expect him to provide me with adequate facilities and an administrative staff—at *his* expense. He and I are going to have this out once and for all."

"This promises to be one of the high points in the history of the Church," Stragen observed.

"I'll make that pompous ass wish he'd never been born," Ehlana declared ominously.

Nothing Sparhawk might say could in any way change his wife's mind. If the truth were to be known, however, he did not really try all that hard, because he could see her point. Dolmant was being high-handed. He tended at times to run roughshod over the kings of Eosia, and so the clash of wills between the Archprelate and the Queen of Elenia was probably inevitable. The unfortunate thing was that they were genuinely fond of each other, and neither of them was opposing the other out of petty vanity or pride. Dolmant was asserting the authority of the Church, and Ehlana that of the Elenian throne. They had become institutions instead of people. It was Sparhawk's misfortune to be caught in the middle.

He was absolutely certain that the arrogant tone of the Archprelate's letter had not come from his friend but from some half-drowsing scribe absentmindedly scribbling formula phrases. What Dolmant had most probably said was something on the order of "Send a letter to Sparhawk and tell him I'd like to see him." That was *not,* however, what had arrived in Cimmura. What had arrived had set Ehlana's teeth on edge, and she went out of her way to make the impending visit to Chyrellos as inconvenient for the Archprelate as she possibly could.

Her first step was to depopulate the palace. *Everybody* had to join her entourage. The queen needed ladies in waiting. The ladies in waiting needed maids. They all needed grooms and footmen. Lenda and Platime, who were to remain in Cimmura to maintain the government, were left almost unassisted.

"Looks almost like an army mobilizing, doesn't it?" Kalten said gaily as they came down the palace stairs on the morning of their departure.

"Let's hope the Archprelate doesn't misunderstand," Ulath murmured. "He wouldn't really believe your wife was planning to lay siege to the Basilica, would he, Sparhawk?"

Once they left Cimmura, the colorfully dressed Elenian court stretched out for miles under a blue spring sky. Had it not been for the steely glint in the queen's eyes, this might have been no more than one of those "outings" so loved by idle courtiers. Ehlana had "suggested" that Sparhawk, as acting Preceptor of the Pandion Order, should also be suitably accompanied. They had haggled about the number of Pandions he should take with him to Chyrellos. He had held out at first for Kalten, Berit, and perhaps one or two others, while the queen had been more in favor of bringing along the entire order. They had finally agreed upon a score of black-armored knights.

It was impossible to make any kind of time with so large an entourage. They seemed almost to creep across the face of Elenia, plodding easterly to Lenda and then southeasterly toward Demos and Chyrellos. The peasantry took the occasion of their passing as an excuse for a holiday, and the road was usually lined with crowds of country people who had come out to gawk. "It's a good thing we don't do this very often," Sparhawk observed to his wife not long after they had passed the city of Lenda.

"I rather enjoy getting out, Sparhawk." The queen and Princess Danae were riding in an ornate carriage drawn by six white horses.

"I'm sure you do, but this is the planting season. The peasants should be in the fields. Too many of these royal excursions could cause a famine."

"You really don't approve of what I'm doing, do you, Sparhawk?"

"I understand why you're doing it, Ehlana, and you're probably right. Dolmant needs to be reminded that his authority isn't absolute, but I think this particular approach is just a little frivolous."

"Of course it's frivolous, Sparhawk," she admitted quite calmly. "That's the whole point. In spite of all the evidence he's had to the contrary, Dolmant still thinks I'm a silly little girl. I'm going to rub his nose in 'silly' for a while. Then, when he's good and tired of it, I'll take him aside and suggest that it would be much easier on him if he took me seriously. That should get his attention. Then we'll be able to get down to business."

"Everything you do is politically motivated, isn't it?"

"Well, not quite *everything*, Sparhawk."

They stopped briefly in Demos, and Khalad and Talen took the royal couple, Kalten, Danae, and Mirtai to visit their mothers. Aslade and Elys mothered everyone impartially. Sparhawk strongly suspected that this was one of the main reasons his wife quite often found excuses to travel to Demos. Her childhood had been bleak and motherless, and anytime she felt insecure or uncertain, some reason seemed to come up why her presence in Demos was absolutely necessary. Aslade's kitchen was warm, and its walls were hung with burnished copper pots. It was a homey sort of place that seemed to answer some deep need in the Queen of Elenia. The smells alone were enough to banish most of the cares of all who entered it.

Elys, Talen's mother, was a radiant blond woman, and Aslade was a kind of monument to motherhood. They adored each other. Aslade had been Kurik's wife, and Elys his mistress, but there appeared to be no jealousy between them. They were practical women, and they both realized that jealousy was a useless kind of thing that never made anyone feel good. Sparhawk and Kalten were immediately banished from the kitchen, Khalad and Talen were sent to mend a fence, and the Queen of Elenia and her Tamul slave continued their intermittent education in the art of cooking while Aslade and Elys mothered Danae.

"I can't remember the last time I saw a queen kneading bread dough." Kalten grinned as he and Sparhawk strolled around the familiar dooryard.

"I think she's making pie crusts," Sparhawk corrected him.

"Dough is dough, Sparhawk."

"Remind me never to ask you to bake me a pie."

"No danger there." Kalten laughed. "Mirtai looks very natural, though. She's had lots of practice cutting things—and people—up. I just wish she wouldn't use her own daggers. You can never really be sure where they've been."

"She always cleans them after she stabs somebody."

"It's the idea of it, Sparhawk." Kalten shuddered. "The thought of it makes my blood run cold."

"Don't think about it then."

"You're going to be late, you know," Kalten reminded his friend. "Dolmant only gave you a week to get to Chyrellos."

"It couldn't be helped."

"Do you want me to ride on ahead and let him know you're coming?"

"And spoil the surprise my wife has planned for him? Don't be silly."

They were no more than a league southeast of Demos the next morning when the attack came. A hundred men—peculiarly dressed with strange weapons—burst over the top of a low knoll, bellowing war cries. They thundered forward on foot for the most part; the ones on horseback appeared to be their leaders.

The courtiers fled squealing in terror as Sparhawk barked commands to his Pandions. The twenty black-armored knights formed up around the queen's carriage and easily repelled the first assault. Men on foot are not really a match for mounted knights.

"What's that language?" Kalten shouted.

"Old Lamork, I think," Ulath replied. "It's a lot like Old Thalesian."

"Sparhawk!" Mirtai barked. "Don't give them time to regroup!" She pointed her blood-smeared sword at the attackers milling around at the top of the knoll.

"She's got a point," Tynian agreed.

Sparhawk quickly assessed the situation, deployed some of his knights to protect Ehlana, and formed up the remainder of his force.

"Charge!" he roared.

It is the lance that makes the armored knight so devastating against foot troops. The man on foot has no defense against it, and he cannot even flee. A third of the attackers had fallen in the initial assault, and a score fell victim to the lances during Sparhawk's charge. The knights then fell to work with swords and axes. Bevier's lochaber axe was particularly devastating, and he left wide tracks of the dead and dying through the tightly packed ranks of the now confused attackers.

It was Mirtai, however, who stunned them all with a shocking display of sheer ferocity. Her sword was lighter than the broadswords of the Church Knights, and she wielded it with almost the delicacy of Stragen's rapier. She seldom thrust at an opponent's body, but concentrated instead on his face and throat, and when necessary, his legs. Her thrusts were short and tightly controlled, and her slashes were aimed not at muscles, but rather at tendons. She crippled more than she killed, and the shrieks and groans of her victims raised a fearful din on that bloody field.

The standard tactic of armored knights when deployed against foot troops was to charge with their lances first and then to use the weight of their horses to crush their unmounted opponents together so tightly that they become tangled with their comrades. Once they had been rendered more or less helpless, slaughtering them would be easy work.

"Ulath!" Sparhawk shouted. "Tell them to throw down their weapons!"

"I'll try," Ulath shouted back. Then he roared something incomprehensible at the milling foot troops.

A mounted man wearing a grotesquely decorated helmet bellowed something in reply.

"That one with the wings on his helmet is the leader, Sparhawk," Ulath said, pointing with his bloody axe.

"What did he say?" Kalten demanded.

"He made some uncomplimentary remarks about my mother. Excuse me for a moment, gentlemen. I really ought to do something about that." He wheeled his horse and approached the man with the winged helmet, who was also armed with a war axe.

Sparhawk had never seen an axe-fight before, and he was somewhat surprised to note that there was far more finesse involved than he had imagined. Sheer strength accounted for much, of course, but sudden changes of the direction of swings implied a level of sophistication Sparhawk had not expected. Both men wore heavy round shields, and the defenses they raised with them were more braced than might have been the case had they been attacking each other with swords.

Ulath stood up in his stirrups and raised his axe high over his head. The warrior in the winged helmet raised his shield to protect his head, but the huge Thalesian swung his arm back, rolled his shoulder, and delivered an underhand blow instead, catching his opponent just under the ribs. The leader of the attackers doubled over sharply, clutching at his stomach, and then he fell from his saddle.

A vast groan rolled through the ranks of the attackers still on their feet, and then, like a mist caught by a sudden breeze, they wavered and vanished.

"Where did they go?" Berit shouted, looking around with alarm.

But no one could answer. Where there had been two score foot troops before, there was now nothing, and a sudden silence fell over the field as the shrieking wounded also vanished. Only the dead remained, and even they were strangely altered. The bodies were peculiarly desiccated—dry, shrunken, and withered. The blood that had covered their limbs was no longer bright red, but black, dry, and crusty.

"What kind of spell could do that, Sparhawk?" Tynian demanded.

"I have no idea," Sparhawk replied in some bafflement. "Someone's playing, and I don't think I like the game."

"Bronze!" Bevier exclaimed from nearby. The young Cyrinic Knight had dismounted and was examining the armor of one of the shriveled dead. "They're wearing bronze armor, Sparhawk. Their weapons and helmets are steel, but this mail shirt is made out of bronze."

"What's going on here?" Kalten demanded.

"Berit," Sparhawk said, "ride back to the motherhouse at Demos. Gather up every brother who can still wear armor. I want them here before noon."

"Right," Berit replied crisply. He wheeled his horse and galloped back the way they had come.

Sparhawk looked around quickly. "Up there," he said, pointing at a steep hill on the other side of the road. "Let's gather up this crowd and get them to the top of that hill. Put the courtiers and grooms and footmen to work. I want ditches up there, and I want to see a forest of sharpened stakes sprouting on the sides of that hill. I don't know where those men in bronze armor went, but I want to be ready in case they come back."

"You can't order *me* around like that!" an overdressed courtier exclaimed to Khalad in an outraged tone of voice. "Don't you know who I am?"

"Of course I do," Sparhawk's young squire replied in an ominous tone of voice. "You're the man who's going to pick up that shovel and start digging. Or if you prefer, you can be the man who's crawling around on his hands and knees picking up his teeth." Khalad showed the courtier his fist. The courtier could hardly miss seeing it, since it was about an inch in front of his nose.

"It's almost like old times, isn't it?" Kalten laughed. "Khalad sounds exactly like Kurik."

Sparhawk sighed. "Yes," he agreed soberly, "I think he's going to work out just fine. Get the others, Kalten. We need to talk."

They gathered beside Ehlana's carriage. The queen was a bit pale, and she was holding her daughter in her arms.

"All right," Sparhawk said. "Who were they?"

"Lamorks, evidently," Ulath said. "I doubt that anybody else would be able to speak Old Lamork."

"But why would they be speaking in that language?" Tynian asked. "Nobody's spoken in Old Lamork for a thousand years."

"And nobody's worn bronze armor for even longer," Bevier added.

"Somebody's using a spell I've never even heard of before," Sparhawk said. "What are we dealing with here?"

"Isn't that obvious?" Stragen said. "Somebody's reaching back into the past—the same way the Troll-Gods did in Pelosia. We've got a powerful magician of some kind out there who's playing games."

"It fits." Ulath grunted. "They were speaking an antique language; they had antique weapons and equipment; they weren't familiar with modern tactics; and somebody obviously used magic to send them back to wherever they came from—except for the dead ones."

"There's something else, too," Bevier added thoughtfully. "They were Lamorks, and part of the upheaval in Lamorkand right now revolves around the stories that Drychtnath's returned. This attack makes it appear that those stories aren't just rumors and wild concoctions dreamed up late at night in some alehouse. Could Count Gerrich be getting some help from a Styric magician? If Drychtnath himself has actually been brought into the present, *nothing's* going to pacify the Lamorks. They go up in flames at just the mention of his name."

"That's all very interesting, gentlemen," Ehlana told them, "but this wasn't just a random attack. We're a goodly distance from Lamorkand, so these antiques of yours went to a great deal of trouble to attack *us* specifically. The real question here is why."

"We'll work on finding an answer for you, your Majesty," Tynian promised her.

Berit returned shortly before noon with three hundred armored Pandions, and the rest of the journey to Chyrellos had some of the air of a military expedition.

Their arrival in the Holy City and their stately march through the streets to the Basilica was very much like a parade, and it caused quite a stir. The Archprelate himself came out onto a second-floor balcony to watch their arrival in the square before the Basilica. Even from that distance, Sparhawk could clearly see that Dolmant's nostrils were white and his jaw was clenched. Ehlana's expression was regal and coolly defiant.

Sparhawk lifted his daughter down from the carriage. "Don't wander off," he murmured into her small ear. "There's something I need to talk with you about."

"Later," she whispered back to him. "I'll have to make peace between Dolmant and Mother first."

"That'll be a neat trick."

"Watch, Sparhawk—and learn."

The Archprelate's greeting was chilly—just this side of frigid—and he made it abundantly clear that he was just dying to have a nice long chat with the Queen of Elenia. He sent for his first secretary, the Patriarch Emban, and rather airily dropped the problem of making arrangements for Ehlana's entourage into the fat churchman's lap. Emban scowled and waddled away, muttering to himself.

Then Dolmant invited the queen and her Prince Consort into a private audience chamber. Mirtai stationed herself outside the door. "No hitting," she told Dolmant and Ehlana as they entered.

The small audience chamber was draped and carpeted in blue, and there were a table and chairs in the center.

"Strange woman, that one," Dolmant murmured, looking back over his shoulder at Mirtai. He took his seat and looked at Ehlana with a firm expression. "Let's get down to business. Would you like to explain this, Queen Ehlana?"

"Of course, Archprelate Dolmant—" She pushed his letter across the table to him. "—just as soon as you explain this." There was steel in her voice.

He picked up the letter and glanced at it. "It seems fairly straightforward. Which part of it didn't you understand?"

Things went downhill from there rather rapidly.

Ehlana and Dolmant were on the verge of severing all diplomatic ties when the Royal Princess Danae entered the room, dragging the Royal Toy Rollo by one hind leg. She gravely crossed the room, climbed up into the Archprelate's lap, and kissed him. Sparhawk had received quite a few of the kind of kisses his daughter bestowed when she wanted something, and he was well aware of just how devastatingly potent they were. Dolmant didn't really have much of a chance after that. "I should have read through the letter before I had it dispatched, I suppose," he admitted grudgingly. "Scribes sometimes overstate things."

"Maybe I overreacted," Ehlana conceded.

"I had a great deal on my mind." Dolmant's excuse had the tone of a peace offering.

"I was irritable on the day when your letter arrived," Ehlana countered.

Sparhawk leaned back. The tension in the room had noticeably relaxed. Dolmant had changed since his elevation to the Archprelacy. Always before, he had been a self-effacing man—so self-effacing, in fact, that his colleagues in the Hierocracy had not even considered him for the highest post in the Church until Ehlana had pointed out his many sterling qualities to them. The irony of that fact was not lost on Sparhawk. Now, however, Dolmant seemed to speak with two voices. The one was the familiar voice of their old friend. The other was the voice of the Archprelate, authoritarian and severe. The institution of his office seemed to be gradually annexing their old friend. Sparhawk sighed. It was probably inevitable, but he regretted it all the same.

Ehlana and the Archprelate continued to apologize and offer excuses to each other. After a while they agreed to respect one another, and they concluded their conference by agreeing to pay closer attention to the little courtesies in the future.

Princess Danae, still seated in the Archprelate's lap, winked at Sparhawk. There were quite a number of political and theological implications in what she had just done, but Sparhawk didn't really want to think about those.

The reason for the peremptory summons that had nearly led to a private war between Ehlana and Dolmant had been the arrival of a high-ranking emissary from the Tamul Empire on the Daresian continent, that vast landmass lying to the east of Zemoch. Formal diplomatic relations between the Elene kingdoms of Eosia and the Tamul Empire of Daresia did not exist. The Church, however, routinely dispatched emissaries with ambassadorial rank to the imperial capital at Matherion, in some measure because the three westernmost kingdoms of the empire were occupied by Elenes, and their religion differed only slightly from that of the Eosian Church.

The emissary was a Tamul, a man of the same race as Mirtai, although she would have made at least two of him. His skin was the same golden bronze, his black hair touched with grey, and his dark eyes were uptilted at the corners.

"He's very good," Dolmant quietly cautioned them as they sat in one of the audience chambers while Emban and the emissary exchanged pleasantries near the door. "In some ways he's even better than Emban. Be just a little careful of what you say around him. Tamuls are quite sensitive to the nuances of language."

Emban escorted the silk-robed emissary to the place where they all sat. "Your Majesty, I have the honor to present his Excellency, Ambassador Oscagne, representative of the imperial court at Matherion," the little fat man said, bowing to Ehlana.

"I swoon in your Majesty's divine presence," the ambassador proclaimed with a florid bow.

"You don't really, do you, your Excellency?" she asked him with a little smile.

"Well, not really, of course," he admitted with absolute aplomb. "I thought it might be polite to say it, though. Did it seem unduly extravagant? I am unversed in the usages of your culture."

"You'll do just fine, your Excellency." She laughed.

"I must say, however, with your Majesty's permission, that you're a devilishly attractive young lady. I've known a few queens in my time, and the customary compliments usually cost one a certain amount of wrestling with one's conscience." Ambassador Oscagne spoke flawless Elenic.

"May I present my husband, Prince Sparhawk?" Ehlana suggested.

"The legendary Sir Sparhawk? Most assuredly, dear lady. I've travelled half-round the world to make his acquaintance. Well met, Sir Sparhawk." Oscagne bowed.

"Your Excellency," Sparhawk replied, also bowing.

Ehlana then introduced the others, and the ongoing exchange of diplomatic pleasantries continued for the better part of an hour. Oscagne and Mirtai spoke at some length in the Tamul tongue, a language that Sparhawk found quite musical.

"Have we concluded all the necessary genuflections in courtesy's direction?" the ambassador asked at last. "Cultures vary, of course, but in Tamuli three-quarters of an hour is the customary amount of time one is expected to waste on polite trivialities."

"That seems about right to me, too." Stragen grinned. "If we overdo our homage to courtesy, she becomes a bit conceited and expects more and more obeisance every time."

"Well said, Milord Stragen," Oscagne approved. "The reason for my visit is fairly simple, my friends. I'm in trouble." He looked around. "I pause for the customary gasps of surprise while you try to adjust your thinking to accept the notion that anyone could possibly find any fault in so witty and charming a fellow as I."

"I think I'm going to like him," Stragen murmured.

"You would." Ulath grunted.

"Pray tell, your Excellency," Ehlana said, "how on earth could anyone find reason to be dissatisfied with you?" The ambassador's flowery speech was contagious.

"I exaggerated slightly for effect," Oscagne admitted. "I'm not really in all that much trouble. It's just that his Imperial Majesty has sent me to Chyrellos to appeal for aid, and I'm supposed to couch the request in such a way that it won't humiliate him."

Emban's eyes were very, very bright. He was in his natural element here. "I think the way we'll want to proceed here is to just lay the problem out on the table for our friends in bold flat terms," he suggested, "and then they can concentrate on the real issue of avoiding embarrassment to the imperial government. They're all unspeakably clever. I'm sure that if they put their heads together, they'll be able to come up with something."

Dolmant sighed. "Was there no one else you could have selected for my job, Ehlana?" he asked plaintively.

Oscagne gave the two of them a questioning look.

"It's a long story, your Excellency," Emban told him. "I'll tell you all about it someday when neither of us has anything better to do. Tell them what it is in Tamuli that's so serious that his Imperial Majesty had to send you here to look for help."

"Promise not to laugh?" Oscagne said to Ehlana.

"I'll do my best to stifle my guffaws," she promised.

"We've got a bit of civil unrest in Tamuli," Oscagne told them.

They all waited.

"That's it," Oscagne confessed ruefully. "Of course I'm quoting the emperor verbatim—at his instruction. You'd almost have to know our emperor to understand. He'd sooner die than overstate anything. He once referred to a hurricane as a 'little breeze' and the loss of half his fleet as a minor inconvenience."

"Very well, your Excellency," Ehlana said. "Now we know how your emperor would characterize the problem. What words would you use to describe it?"

"Well," Oscagne said, "since your Majesty is so kind as to ask, *catastrophic* does sort of leap to mind. We might consider *insoluble, cataclysmic, overwhelming*—little things like that. I really think you should give some consideration to his Majesty's request, my friends, because we have some fairly strong evidence that what's happening on the Daresian continent may soon spread to Eosia as well, and if it does, it's probably going to mean the end of civilization as we know it. I'm not entirely positive how you Elenes feel about that sort of thing, but we Tamuls are more or less convinced that some effort ought to be made to fend it off. It sets such a bad precedent when you start letting the world come to an end every week or so. It seems to erode the confidence people have in their governments for some reason."

CHAPTER FIVE

Ambassador Oscagne leaned back in his chair. "Where to begin?" he pondered. "When one looks at the incidents individually, they almost appear trivial. It's the cumulative effect that's brought the empire to the brink of collapse."

"We can understand that sort of thing, your Excellency," Emban assured him. "The Church has been on the brink of collapse for centuries now. Our Holy Mother reels from crisis to crisis like a drunken sailor."

"Emban," Dolmant chided gently.

"Sorry," the fat little churchman apologized.

Oscagne was smiling. "Sometimes it seems that way, though, doesn't it, your Grace," he said to Emban. "I'd imagine that the government of the Church is not really all that much different from the government of the empire. Bureaucrats need crisis in order to survive. If there isn't a crisis of some kind, someone might decide that a number of positions could be eliminated."

"I've noticed the same sort of thinking myself," Emban agreed.

"I assure you, however, that what we have in Tamuli is not some absurd little flap generated for the purposes of making someone's position secure. I'm not exaggerating in the slightest when I say that the empire's on the brink of collapse." His bronze face became thoughtful. "We are not one homogeneous people as you here in Eosia are," he began. "There are five races on the Daresian continent. We Tamuls live to the east, there are Elenes in the west, Styrics around Sarsos, the Valesians on their island, and the Cynesgans in the center. It's probably not natural for so many different kinds of people to all be gathered under one roof. Our cultures are different, our religions are different, and each race is sublimely convinced that it's the crown of the universe." He sighed. "We'd probably have been better off if we'd remained separate."

"But, at some time in the past someone grew ambitious?" Tynian surmised.

"Far from it, Sir Knight," Oscagne replied. "You could almost say that we Tamuls blundered into empire." He looked at Mirtai, who sat quietly with Danae in her lap. "And that's the reason," he said, pointing at the giantess.

"It wasn't my fault, Oscagne," she protested.

"I wasn't blaming you personally, Atana." He smiled. "It's your people."

She smiled. "I haven't heard that term since I was a child. No one's ever called me 'Atana' before."

"What's it mean?" Talen asked her curiously.

"Warrior." She shrugged.

"Warrioress, actually," Oscagne corrected. He frowned. "I don't want to be offensive, but your Elene tongue is limited in its ability to convey subtleties." He looked at Ehlana. "Has your Majesty noticed that your slave is not exactly like other women?" he asked her.

"She's my friend," Ehlana objected, "not my slave."

"Don't be ignorant, Ehlana," Mirtai told her crisply. "Of course I'm a slave. I'm supposed to be. Go on with your story, Oscagne. I'll explain it to them later."

"Do you really think they'll understand?"

"No. But I'll explain it anyway."

"And there, revered Archprelate," Oscagne said to Dolmant, "there lies the key to the empire. The Atans placed themselves in thrall to us some fifteen hundred years ago to prevent their homicidal instincts from obliterating their entire race. As a result, we Tamuls have the finest army in the world—even though we're basically a nonviolent people. We tended to win those incidental little arguments with other nations which crop up from time to time and are usually settled by negotiation. In our view, our neighbors are like children, hopelessly incapable of managing their own affairs. The empire came into being largely in the interests of good order." He looked around at the Church Knights. "Once again, I'm not trying to be offensive, but war is probably the stupidest of human activities. There are much more efficient ways to persuade people to change their minds."

"Such as the threat to unleash the Atans?" Emban suggested slyly.

"That does work rather well, your Grace," Oscagne admitted. "The presence of the Atans has usually been enough in the past to keep political discussion from becoming too spirited. Atans make excellent policemen." He sighed. "You noted that slight qualification, I'm sure. I said, 'in the past.' Unfortunately, that doesn't hold true anymore. An empire comprised of disparate peoples must always expect these little outbreaks of nationalism and racial discord. It's the nature of the insignificant to try to find some way to assert their own importance. And it's pathetic, but racism is generally the last refuge of the unimportant. These outbreaks of insignificance aren't normally too widespread, but suddenly all of Tamuli is in the throes of an epidemic of them. Everyone's sewing flags and singing national anthems and laboring over well-honed insults to be directed at 'the yellow dogs.' That's us, of course." He held out his hand and looked at it critically. "Our skins aren't really yellow, you know. They're more . . ." He pondered it.

"Beige?" Stragen suggested.

"That's not too flattering either, Milord Stragen." Oscagne smiled. "Oh, well. Perhaps the emperor will appoint a special commission to define our skin tone once and for all." He shrugged. "At any rate, incidental outbreaks of nationalism and racial bigotry would be no real problem for the Atans, even if they occurred in every town in the empire. It's the unnatural incidents that cause us all this concern."

"I thought there might be more," Ulath murmured.

"At first, these 'demonstrations of magic' were directed at the people themselves," Oscagne went on. "Every culture has its mythic hero—some towering personality who unified the people, gave them national purpose, and defined their character. The modern world is complex and confusing, and the simple folk yearn for the simplicity of the age of heroes when national goals could be stated simply and everyone knew precisely who he was. Someone in Tamuli is resurrecting the heroes of antiquity."

Sparhawk felt a sudden chill. "Giants?" he asked.

"Well," Oscagne considered it. "Perhaps that is the proper term at that. The passage of the centuries blurs and distorts, and our cultural heroes tend to become larger than life. I suppose that when we think of them, we *do* think of giants. That's a very acute perception, Sir Sparhawk."

"I can't actually take credit for it, your Excellency. The same sort of thing's been happening here."

Dolmant looked at him sharply.

"I'll explain later, Sarathi. Please go on, Ambassador Oscagne. You said that whoever's stirring things up in Tamuli started out by raising national heroes. That implies that it's gone further."

"Oh, yes indeed, Sir Sparhawk. Much, much further. Every culture has its hobgoblins as well as its heroes. It's the hobgoblins we've been encountering—monsters, afreets, werewolves, vampires—all those things adults use to frighten children into good behavior. Our Atans can't cope with that sort of thing. They're trained to deal with men, not with all the horrors the creative genius of eons has put together. That's our problem. We have nine different cultures in Tamuli, and suddenly each one of them has taken to pursuing its traditional historic goals. When we send in our Atans to restore order and to reassert imperial authority, the horrors rise up out of the ground to confront them. We can't deal with it. The empire's disintegrating—falling back into its component parts. His Imperial Majesty's government hopes that your Church can recognize a certain community of interest here. If Tamuli collapses back into nine warring kingdoms, the resulting chaos is almost certain to have its impact here in Eosia as well. It's the magic that has us so concerned. We can deal with ordinary insurrection, but we're unequipped to deal with a continentwide conspiracy that routinely utilizes magic against us. The Styrics at Sarsos are baffled. Everything they try is countered almost before they can set it in motion. We've heard stories about what happened in the City of Zemoch, and it is to you personally that I must appeal, Sir Sparhawk. Zalasta of Sarsos is the preeminent magician in all of Styricum, and he assures us that you are the only man in all the world with enough power to deal with the situation."

"Zalasta may have an exaggerated idea of my abilities," Sparhawk said.

"You know him?"

"We've met. Actually, your Excellency, I was only a very small part of what happened at Zemoch. When you get right down to it, I was hardly more than a channel for power I couldn't even begin to describe. I was the instrument of something else."

"Be that as it may, you're still our only hope. Someone is quite obviously conspiring to overthrow the empire. We *must* identify that someone. Unless we can get to the source of all of this and neutralize it, the empire will collapse. Will you help us, Sir Sparhawk?"

"That decision's not mine to make, your Excellency. You must appeal to my queen and to Sarathi here. If they command me, I'll go to Tamuli. If they forbid it, I won't."

"I'll direct my enormous powers of persuasion at them, then." Oscagne smiled. "But even assuming that I'm successful—and there's little doubt that I shall be— we're still faced with an almost equally serious problem. We must protect his Imperial Majesty's dignity at all costs. An appeal from one government to another is one thing, but an appeal from his Majesty's government to a private citizen on another continent is quite another. *That* is the problem which must be addressed."

"I don't see that we have any choice, Sarathi," Emban was saying gravely. It was late evening. Ambassador Oscagne had retired for the night, and the rest of them, along with Patriarch Ortzel of Kadach in Lamorkand, had gathered to give his request serious consideration. "We may not entirely approve of some of the policies of the Tamul Empire, but its stability is in our vital interest just now. We're fully committed to our campaign in Rendor. If Tamuli flies apart, we'll have to pull most of our armies—and the Church Knights—out of Rendor to protect our interests in Zemoch. Zemoch's not much of a place, I'll grant you, but the strategic importance of its mountains can't be overstated. We've had a hostile force in those mountains for the past two thousand years, and that fact has occupied the full attention of our Holy Mother. If we allow some other hostile people to replace the Zemochs, everything Sparhawk achieved in Otha's capital is lost. We'll go right back to where we were six years ago. We'll have to abandon Rendor again and start mobilizing to meet a new threat from the east."

"You're stating the obvious, Emban," Dolmant told him.

"I know, but sometimes it helps to lay everything out so that we can all look at it."

"Sparhawk," Dolmant said then, "if I were to order you to Matherion but your wife ordered you to stay home, what would you do?"

"I'd probably have to go into a monastery to pray for guidance for the next several years."

"Our Holy Mother Church is overwhelmed by your piety, Sir Sparhawk."

"I do what I can to please her, Sarathi. I am her true knight, after all."

Dolmant sighed. "Then it all boils down to some sort of accommodation between Ehlana and me, doesn't it?"

"Such wisdom can only have come from God," Sparhawk observed to his companions.

"Do you mind?" Dolmant said tartly. Then he looked at the Queen of Elenia with a certain resignation. "Name your price, your Majesty."

"I beg your pardon?"

"Let's not tiptoe around each other, Ehlana. Your champion's put my back to the wall."

"I know," she replied, "and I'm so impressed with him that I can barely stand it. We'll have to discuss this in private, revered Archprelate. We wouldn't want Sir Sparhawk to fully realize his true value, now would we? He might begin to get the idea that we ought to pay him what he's actually worth."

"I hate this," Dolmant said to no one in particular.

"I think we might want to touch briefly on something else," Stragen suggested. "The Tamul Ambassador's story had a certain familiar ring to it—or was I the only one who noticed that? We've got a situation going on in Lamorkand that's amazingly similar to what's happening in Tamuli. The Lamorks are all blithely convinced that Drychtnath's returned, and that's almost identical to the situation Oscagne described. Then, on our way here from Cimmura, we were set upon by a group of Lamorks who could only have come from antiquity. Their weapons were steel, but their armor was bronze, and they spoke Old Lamork. After Sir Ulath killed their leader, the ones who were still alive vanished. Only their dead remained—and they were all dried out."

"And that's not all," Sparhawk added. "This spring there were some bandits operating in the mountains of western Eosia. They were being led by some of Annias' former supporters, and they were doing all they could to stir up rebellion among the peasantry. Platime managed to get a spy into their camp, and he told us that the movement was being fueled by Krager, Martel's old underling. After we rounded them up, we tried to question one of them about Krager, and a cloud like the one we saw on our way to Zemoch engulfed the man and tore him all to pieces. There's definitely something afoot here in Eosia, too, and it seems to be coming out of Lamorkand."

"So you think there's a connection?" Dolmant asked him.

"It's a logical conclusion, Sarathi. There are too many similarities to be safely ignored." Sparhawk paused, glancing at his wife. "This may cause a certain amount of domestic discontent," he said regretfully, "but I believe we'd better think very seriously about Oscagne's request. Someone's harrowing the past to bring back people and things that have been dead for thousands of years. When we encountered this sort of thing in Pelosia, Sephrenia told us that only the Gods were capable of that."

"Well, that's not entirely true, Sparhawk," Bevier corrected him. "She did say that a few of the most powerful Styric magicians could also raise the dead."

"I think we can discount that possibility," Sparhawk disagreed. "Sephrenia and I were talking about it once, and she told me that in the forty thousand years of Styric history, there have only been two Styrics who had the capability, and then only imperfectly. This raising of heroes and armies is happening in nine nations in Tamuli and at least one here in Eosia. There are just too many similarities for it to be a coincidence, and the whole scheme—whatever its goal—is just too complex to have come from somebody who doesn't have an absolute grasp on the spell."

"The Troll-Gods?" Ulath suggested bleakly.

"I wouldn't discount the possibility. They did it once before, so we know that they have the capability. Right now, though, all we have are some suspicions based on some educated guesses. We desperately need information."

"That's my department, Sparhawk," Stragen told him. "Mine and Platime's. You're going to Daresia, I assume?"

"It's beginning to look that way." Sparhawk gave his wife an apologetic look. "I'd gladly let someone else go, but I'm afraid he wouldn't know what he's looking for."

"I'd better go with you," Stragen decided. "I have associates there as well as here in Eosia, and people in our line of work can gather information much more quickly than your people can."

Sparhawk nodded.

"Maybe we can start right there," Ulath suggested. He looked at the Patriarch Ortzel. "How did all these wild stories about Drychtnath get started, your Grace? Nobody's reputation really lasts for four thousand years, no matter how impressive he was to begin with."

"Drychtnath is a literary creation, Sir Ulath," the severe blond churchman replied, smiling slightly. Even as Dolmant's ascension to the throne had changed him, so Ortzel had been changed by living in Chyrellos. He no longer seemed to be quite the same rigid, provincial man he had been in Lamorkand. Although he was by no means as worldly as Emban, he had nonetheless acquired some of the sophistication of his colleagues in the Basilica. He smiled occasionally now, and he appeared to be developing a sly, understated sense of humor. Sparhawk had met with him on several occasions since Dolmant had ordered the cleric to Chyrellos, and the big Pandion found that he was actually beginning to like the man. Ortzel still had his prejudices, of course, but he was now willing to admit that points of view other than his own might have some small validity.

"Somebody just made him up?" Ulath was saying incredulously.

"Oh, no. There *was* somebody named Drychtnath four thousand years ago. Probably some bullyboy with his brains in his biceps. I'd imagine that he was the usual sort—no neck, no forehead, and nothing even remotely resembling intelligence between his ears. After he died, though, some poet struggling with failing inspiration seized on the story and embellished it with all the shopworn conventions of the heroic epic. He called it *The Drychtnathasaga,* and Lamorkand would be far better off if the poet had never learned to read and write." Sparhawk thought he detected some actual flashes of humor there.

"One poem could hardly have *that* kind of impact, your Grace," Kalten said skeptically.

"You underestimate the power of a well-told story, Sir Kalten. I'll have to translate as I go along, but judge for yourself." Ortzel leaned back with his eyes half-closed.

"Hearken unto a tale from the age of heroes," he began. His harsh, rigid voice became softer, more sonorous as he recited the ancient poem. "List, brave men of Lamorkland to the exploits of Drychtnath the smith, mightiest of all the warriors of yore.

"Now as all men know, the Age of Heroes was an age of bronze. Massive were the bronze swords and the axes of the heroes of yore, and mighty were the thews of the men who wielded them in joyous battle. And none there was in all the length and breadth of Lamorkland mightier than Drychtnath the smith.

"Tall was Drychtnath and ox-shouldered, for his labor molded him even as he molded the glowing metal. Swords of bronze wrought he, and spears as keen as daggers, and axes and shields and burnished helms and shirts of mail which shed the foeman's blows as they were no more than gentle rain.

"And lo, warriors from all of dark-forested Lamorkland gladly gave good gold and bright silver beyond measure in exchange for Drychtnath's bronze, and the mighty smith waxed in wealth and in strength as he toiled at his forge."

Sparhawk tore his eyes from Ortzel's face and looked around. The faces of his friends were all rapt. The Patriarch of Kadach's voice rose and fell in the stately cadences of bardic utterance.

"Lord," Sir Bevier breathed as the patriarch paused, "it's hypnotic, isn't it?"

"That's always been its danger," Ortzel told him. "The rhythm numbs the mind and sets the pulse to racing. The people of my race are susceptible to the emotionality of *The Drychtnathasaga.* An army of Lamorks can be whipped into a frenzy by a recitation of some of the more lurid passages."

"Well?" Talen said eagerly. "What happened?"

Ortzel smiled rather gently at the boy. "Surely so worldly a young thief cannot be stirred by some tired old poem?" he suggested slyly. Sparhawk nearly laughed aloud. Perhaps the change in the Patriarch of Kadach had gone further than he had imagined.

"I like a good story," Talen admitted. "I've never heard one told that way before, though."

"It's called 'felicity of style,' " Stragen murmured. "Sometimes it's not so much what the story says, but how it says it."

"Well?" Talen insisted. "What happened?"

"Drychtnath discovered that a giant named Kreindl had forged a metal that could cut bronze like butter," Ortzel replied conversationally. "He went to Kreindl's lair with only his sledgehammer for a weapon, tricked the secret of the new metal out of the giant, and then beat out his brains with the sledge. Then he went home and began to forge the new metal—steel—and hammered it out into weapons. Soon every warrior in Lamorkand—or Lamorkland, as they called it in those days—had to have a steel sword, and Drychtnath grew enormously wealthy." He frowned. "I hope you'll bear with me," he apologized. "Translating on the spot is a bit difficult." He thought a while and then began again to recite. "Now it came to pass that the fame of the mighty smith Drychtnath spread throughout the land. Tall was he, a full ten span, I ween, and broad were his shoulders. His thews were as the steel from his forge, and comely were his features. Full many a maid of noble house yearned for him in the silences of her soul.

"Now as it chanced to happen in those far-off days of yore, the ruler of the Lamorks was the aged King Hygdahl, whose snowy locks bespoke his wisdom. No son in life had he, but a daughter, the child of his eld, fair as morning dew and yclept Uta. And Hygdahl was sore troubled, for well he wot that when his spirit had been gathered to the bosom of Hrokka, strife and contention would wrack the lands of the Lamorks as the heroes vied with one another for his throne and for the hand of fair Uta in marriage, for such was the twin prize which would fall to the victor. And so resolved King Hygdahl at last to secure the future of realm and daughter with one stroke, and caused he to be sent word to every corner of his vasty realm. The fate of Lamorkland and of bright-eyed Uta would be decided by trial at arms. The mightiest hero in all the land would win wealth, wife, and dominion by the strength of his hands."

"What's a span?" Talen interrupted.

"Nine inches," Berit replied. "It's supposed to be as far as a man can stretch out the fingers of one hand."

Talen made the quick computation in his head. "Seven and a half feet?" he said incredulously. "He was seven and a half feet tall?"

"It may be slightly exaggerated." Ortzel smiled.

"Who is this Hrokka?" Bevier asked him.

"The Lamork War-God," Ortzel explained. "There was a period at the end of the bronze age when the Lamorks reverted to paganism. Obviously, Drychtnath won the trial at arms, and he didn't even kill too many other Lamorks in the process." Ortzel cleared his throat and took up his recitation. "And so it was that Drychtnath the smith, mightiest hero of antiquity, won the hand of bright-eyed Uta and became King Hygdahl's heir.

"And when the wedding feast was done, went Hygdahl's heir straightway to the king. 'Lord King,' quotha, 'since I have the honor to be the mightiest warrior in all the world, it is only meet that the world fall into my hands. To that end shall I bend mine efforts once Hrokka hath called thee home. I will conquer the world and subdue it and bend it to my will, and I will lead the heroes of Lamorkland e'en unto Chyrellos. There will I cast down the altars of the false God of that Church which doth, all womanly, hold strength in despite and weakens warriors with her drasty preaching. I spurn her counsel, and will lead the heroes of Lamorkland forth to bear back to our homes in groaning wains the loot of the world.'

"Happily heard Hygdahl the hero's words, for Hrokka, Sword-Lord of Lamorkland, glories in battle strife and doth inspire his children to love the sound of sword meeting sword and the sight of sparkling blood bedewing the grass. 'Go forth, my son, and conquer,' quotha. 'Punish the Peloi, crush the Cammorians, destroy the Deirans, and forget not to bring down the Church which doth pollute the manhood of all Elenes with her counsels of peace and lowly demeanor.'

"Now when word of Drychtnath's design reached the Basilica of Chyrellos, the Church was troubled and trembled in fear of the mighty smith, and the princes of the Church took counsel one with the other and resolved to spill out the life of the noble smith, lest his design dispossess the Church and win her wealth to wend in wains Lamorkward, there to bedeck the high-built walls of the conqueror's mead hall. Conspired they then to send a warrior of passing merit to the court of Hygdahl's heir to bring low the towering pride of dark-forested Lamorkland.

"In dissembling guise this traitorous warrior, a Deiran by birth—Starkad was his name—made his way to Drychtnath's mead hall, and mildly made he courteous greeting to Hygdahl's heir. And beseeched he the hero of Lamorkland to accept him as his vassal. Now Drychtnath's heart was so free of deceit and subterfuge that he could not perceive perfidy in others. Gladly did he accept Starkad's seeming friendship, and the two were soon as brothers even as Starkad had designed.

"And as the heroes of Drychtnath's hall labored, Starkad was ever at Drychtnath's right hand, in fair weather and foul, in battle and in the carouse which is battle's aftermath. Tales he spun which filled Drychtnath's heart with mirth, and for the love he bare his friend did the mighty smith gladly bestow treasures upon him, bracelets of bright gold and gems beyond price. Starkad accepted Drychtnath's gifts in seeming gratitude and ever, like the patient worm, burrowed he his way ever deeper into the hero's heart.

"And at the time of Hrokka's choosing was wise King Hygdahl gathered into the company of the Immortal Thanes in the Hall of Heroes, and then was Drychtnath king in Lamorkland. Well were laid his plans, and no sooner had the royal crown been placed upon his head that he gathered his heroes and marched north to subdue the savage Peloi.

"Many were the battles mighty Drychtnath waged in the lands of the Peloi, and great were the victories he won. And there it was in the lands of the horse-people that the design of the Church of Chyrellos was accomplished, for there, separated from their friends by legions of ravening Peloi, Drychtnath and Starkad wrought slaughter upon the foe, bathing the meadow's grass with the blood of their enemies. And there, in the full flower of his heroism, was mighty Drychtnath laid full low. Seizing upon a lull in the struggle when all stood somewhat apart to gather breath and strength to renew the struggle, the deceitful Deiran found his opportunity and drove his cursed spear, sharper than any dagger, full into his lord's broad back.

"And Drychtnath felt death's cold touch as Starkad's bright steel pierced him. And turned he then to face the man he had called friend and brother. 'Why,' quotha, his heart wrung more by the betrayal than by Starkad's stroke.

" 'It was in the name of the God of the Elenes,' quoth Starkad with hot tears streaming from his eyes, for in truth loved he the hero he had just slain. 'Think not that it was I who have smitten thee to the heart, my brother, for it was not I, but our Holy Mother Church which hath sought thy life.' So saying, he raised once more his dreadful spear. 'Defend thyself, Drychtnath, for though I must slay thee, I would not murder thee.'

"Then raised noble Drychtnath his face. 'That will I not do,' quotha, 'for if my brother have need of my life, I give it to him freely.'

" 'Forgive me,' quoth Starkad, raising again his deadly spear.

" 'That may I not do,' quoth the hero. 'My life mayest thou freely have, but never my forgiveness.'

" 'So be it then,' quoth Starkad, and, so saying, plunged he his deadly spear full into Drychtnath's mighty heart.

"A moment only the hero stood, and then slowly, as falls the mighty oak, fell all the pride of Lamorkland, and the earth and the heavens resounded with his fall."

There were tears in Talen's eyes. "Did he get away with it?" he asked. "I mean, didn't one of Drychtnath's other friends pay him back?" The boy's face clearly showed his eagerness to hear more.

"Surely you wouldn't want to waste your time with some tired, worn-out old story that's been around for thousands of years?" Ortzel said. He feigned some astonishment, but there was a sly twinkle in his eye. Sparhawk covered his own smile with his hand. Ortzel had definitely changed, all right.

"I don't know about Talen," Ulath said, "but I would." There were obviously some strong similarities between the culture of present-day Thalesia and that of ancient Lamorkland.

"Well, now," Ortzel said, "I'd say that some bargaining might be in order here. How many acts of contrition would the two of you be willing to give our Holy Mother in exchange for the rest of the story?"

"Ortzel," Dolmant reproved him.

The Patriarch of Kadach held up one hand. "It's a perfectly legitimate exchange, Sarathi," he said. "The Church has used it many times in the past. When I was a simple country pastor, I used this exact method to ensure regular attendance at services. My congregation was known far and wide for its piety—until I ran out of stories." Then he laughed. They were all a bit startled at that: most of them would have bet that the stern, unbending Patriarch of Kadach didn't even know how. "I was only teasing," he told the young thief and the gigantic Thalesian. "I wouldn't be too disappointed, however, if the two of you gave the condition of your souls some serious thought."

"Tell the story," Mirtai insisted. Mirtai was also a warrior and, also, it appeared, susceptible to a stirring tale.

"Do I sense the possibility of a convert here?" Ortzel asked her.

"What you're sensing is the possibility of failing health, Ortzel," she said bluntly. Mirtai never used titles when she spoke to people.

"All right then." Ortzel laughed again and continued with his translation.

"Hearken then, O men of Lamorkland, and hear how Starkad was paid. Some tears then shed he over his fallen brother, then turned he his raging wrath upon the Peloi, and they fled screaming from him. Straightway left he the strife-place and journeyed even to the Holy City of Chyrellos, there to advise the princes of the Church that their design was done. And when they had gathered all in the Basilica which is the crown of their o'erweening pride, recounted Starkad the sad tale of the fall of Drychtnath, mightiest hero of yore.

"And gloated then the soft and pampered princes of the Church at the hero's fall, thinking that their pride and power and position were safe, and spake they each in praise of Starkad and offered him good gold beyond measure for the deed he had done.

"Cold, however, was the hero's heart, and he looked upon the little men he had served, recalling with tears the great man he had slain at their bidding. 'Lordlings of the Church,' quotha then. 'Think ye that mere gold will satisfy me as payment for what I have done in your behalf?'

" 'But what else may we offer thee?' they asked in great perplexity.

" 'I would have Drychtnath's forgiveness,' quoth Starkad.

" 'But that we may not obtain for thee,' they said unto him, 'for dreaded Drychtnath lieth low in the House of the Dead from whence no man returneth. Pray, mighty hero, tell us what else we may offer thee in recompense for this great service thou hast provided us.'

" 'But one thing,' quoth Starkad in deadly earnest.

" 'And that is what?' they asked.

" 'Your hearts' blood,' quoth Starkad. And, so saying, sprang he to the massy door and chained it shut with chains of steel that none might escape him. Then drew he forth Hlorithn, Dread Drychtnath's bright blade, which he had brought with him to Chyrellos for just this purpose. And then took the hero Starkad his payment for the deed he had done on the plains of the Peloi.

"And when he had finished collecting that which was owed him, the Church of Chyrellos lay headless, for not one of her princes saw the setting of the sun that day, and sorrowing still that he had slain his friend, Starkad sadly took his leave of the Holy City and never returned there more.

"But it is said in dark-forested Lamorkland that the oracles and the auguries speak still of the mighty Drychtnath and of the day when the War-God Hrokka will relent and release the spirit of Drychtnath from his service as one of the Immortal Thanes in the Hall of Heroes that he may come once more to Lamorkland to take up again that grand design. Then how the blood will flow, and then how the kings of the world will tremble as once again the world shakes beneath the mighty stride of Dread Drychtnath the Destroyer, and the crown and throne of the world shall lie in his immortal grip, as was from the beginning intended." Ortzel's voice fell silent, indicating that he had reached the end.

"That's all?" Talen protested vehemently.

"I skipped over a great number of passages," Ortzel conceded, "battle descriptions and the like. The Lamorks of antiquity had an unhealthy fascination with certain kinds of numbers. They wanted to know how many barrels of blood, pounds of brains, and yards of entrails were spilled out during the festivities."

"But the story doesn't end right," Talen complained. "Drychtnath was the hero, but after Starkad murdered him, *he* turned into the hero. That isn't right. The bad people shouldn't be allowed to change over like that."

"That's a very interesting argument, Talen—particularly coming from you."

"I'm not a bad person, your Grace, I'm just a thief. It's not the same at all. At least the churchmen all got what was coming to them."

"You have a long way to go with this one, Sparhawk," Bevier observed. "We all loved Kurik like a brother, but are we really sure that his son has the makings of a Church Knight in him?"

"I'm working on that," Sparhawk replied, musing. "So that's what Drychtnath's all about. Just how deeply do the commons in Lamorkand believe in the story, your Grace?"

"It goes deeper than belief, Sparhawk," Ortzel replied. "The story's in our blood. I'm wholly committed to the Church, but when I hear *The Drychtnathasaga*, I become an absolute pagan—for a while at least."

"Well," Tynian said, "now we know what we're up against. We have the same thing going on in Lamorkand as we have in Rendor. We've got heresies springing up all around us. It still doesn't solve our problem, though. How are Sparhawk and the rest of us going to be able to go to Tamuli without insulting the emperor?"

"I've solved that problem already, Tynian," Ehlana told him.

"I beg your Majesty's pardon?"

"It's so simple that I'm almost ashamed that you all didn't think of it first."

"Enlighten us, your Majesty," Stragen said. "Make us blush for our stupidity."

"It's time for the western Elene kingdoms to open communications with the Tamul Empire," she explained. "We *are* neighbors, after all. It's politically very sound for me to make a state visit to Matherion, and if you gentlemen are all very nice to me, I'll invite you to come along." She frowned. "That was the least of our problems. Now we'll have to address something far more serious."

"And what is that, Ehlana?" Dolmant asked her.

"I simply don't have a thing to wear, Sarathi."

CHAPTER SIX

Sparhawk had learned to keep a tight rein on his emotions during the years since his marriage to the Queen of Elenia, but his smile was slightly fixed as the meeting broke up. Kalten fell in beside him as they all left the council chamber. "I gather that you're less than pleased with our queen's solution to the problem," he observed. Kalten was Sparhawk's boyhood friend, and he had learned how to read that battered face.

"You might say that, yes," Sparhawk replied tightly.

"Are you open to a suggestion?"

"I'll listen." Sparhawk didn't want to make any promises at that particular point.

"Why don't you and I go down into the crypt under the Basilica?"

"Why?"

"I thought you might want to vent certain feelings before you and your wife discuss the matter. You're a bit savage when you're angry, Sparhawk, and I'm really very fond of your wife. If you call her an idiot to her face, you'll hurt her feelings."

"Are you trying to be funny?"

"Not in the least, my friend. I feel almost the same way about it as you do, and I've had a very colorful education. When you run out of swear words, I'll supply some you might not have heard."

"Let's go," Sparhawk said, turning abruptly down a side corridor.

They passed through the nave quickly, perfunctorily genuflecting to the altar in passing, and descended into the crypt that contained the bones of several eons worth of Archprelates.

"Don't bang your fists on the walls," Kalten cautioned as Sparhawk began to pace up and down, swearing and waving his arms in the air. "You'll break your knuckles."

"It's a total absurdity, Kalten!" Sparhawk said—after he had shouted profanities for several minutes.

"It's worse than that, my friend. There's always room in the world for absurdities. They're sort of fun actually, but this is dangerous. We have no way of knowing what we're going to encounter in Tamuli. I love your wife dearly, but having her along is going to be inconvenient."

"Inconvenient?"

"I'm trying to be polite. How does 'bloody hindering awkward' strike you?"

"It's closer."

"You'll never persuade her to stay home, though. I'd give that up as a lost cause before I even started. She's obviously made up her mind, and she outranks you. You probably ought to try to put the best face on it—avoid the embarrassment of being told to shut your mouth and go to your room."

Sparhawk grunted.

"I think our best approach is to talk with Oscagne. We'll be taking the most precious thing in Elenia to the Daresian continent where things are far from tranquil. Your wife's going there is a personal favor to the Emperor of Tamuli, so he's obligated to protect her. An escort of a few dozen legions of Atans meeting us at the Astel border might be looked upon as a sign of his Majesty's appreciation, wouldn't you say?"

"That's really not a bad idea, Kalten."

"I'm not *totally* stupid, Sparhawk. Now, Ehlana's going to expect you to rant and rave and wave your arms at her. She's ready for that, so don't do it. She *is* going along. We've lost that fight already, wouldn't you say?"

"Unless I chain her to the bed."

"There's an interesting idea."

"Never mind."

"It's tactically unsound to fight a last stand unless you're trapped. Give her that victory, and then she'll owe you one. Use it to get her to agree not to do *anything* while we're in Tamuli without your express permission. That way we can keep her almost as safe as she'd be if she stayed home. There's a good chance that she'll be so happy that you didn't scream at her that she'll agree without thinking it all the way through. You'll be able to restrict her movements when we get there—at least enough to keep her out of danger."

"Kalten, sometimes you amaze me," Sparhawk told his friend.

"I know," the blond Pandion replied. "This stupid-looking face of mine is very useful sometimes."

"Where did you ever learn so much about manipulating royalty?"

"I'm not manipulating royalty, Sparhawk. I'm manipulating a woman, and I'm an expert at that. Women are born negotiators. They love these little trades. If you go to a woman and say, 'I'll do this for you, if you do that for me,' she'll almost always be willing at least to talk about it. Women *always* want to talk about things. If you keep your eye on what you really want, you'll almost always come out on top." He paused. "Metaphorically speaking of course," he added.

"What are you up to, Sparhawk?" Mirtai asked him suspiciously when he approached the suite of rooms Dolmant had provided for Ehlana and her personal retinue. Sparhawk carefully let the smug expression slide from his face and assumed one of grave concern instead.

"Don't try to be clever, Sparhawk," she told him. "If you hurt her, I'll have to kill you, you know."

"I'm not going to hurt her, Mirtai. I'm not even going to yell at her."

"You're up to something, aren't you?"

"Of course I am. After you lock me inside, put your ear to the door and listen." He gave her a sidelong look. "But you do that all the time anyway, don't you?"

She actually blushed. She jerked the door open. "Just get in there, Sparhawk!" she commanded, her face like a thundercloud.

"My, aren't we testy tonight?"

"Go!"

"Yes, ma'am."

Ehlana was ready for him, that much was fairly obvious. She was wearing a dressing gown of a pale rose that made her look particularly appealing, and she had done things with her hair. There was a barely noticeable tightness about her eyes, though.

"Good evening, love," Sparhawk said calmly. "Tedious day, wasn't it? Conferences can be so exhausting at times." He crossed the room, pausing to kiss her almost perfunctorily in passing, and poured himself a glass of wine.

"I know what you're going to say, Sparhawk," she said.

"Oh?" He gave her an innocent look.

"You're angry with me, aren't you?"

"No. Not really. What made you think I'd be angry?"

She looked a bit less sure of herself. "You mean you're not? I thought you'd be raging by now—about my decision to pay a state visit to Tamuli, I mean."

"No, actually it's a very good idea. Of course we'll have to take a few precautions to ensure your safety, but we always have to do that, so we're sort of used to it, aren't we?"

"What kind of precautions are we talking about here?" Her tone was suspicious.

"Nothing all that extreme, dear. I don't think you should go walking in the forest alone or visiting thieves' dens without some sort of escort. I'm not talking about anything out of the ordinary, and you're used to certain restrictions on your movements already. We'll be in a strange country, and we don't know the people. I know that you'll trust me to sort of nose things out, and that you won't argue with me if I tell you that something's too dangerous. We can all live with that, I'm sure. You pay me to protect you, after all, so we won't have any silly little squabbles about security measures, now will we?" He kept his tone mild and sweetly reasonable, giving her no reason to raise any questions about exactly what he had in mind when he spoke of "security measures."

"You know much more about that sort of thing than I do, my love," she conceded, "so I'll leave all that entirely in your hands. If a girl has a champion who just happens to be the greatest knight in the world, she'd be foolish not to pay attention to him, now wouldn't she?"

"My feelings exactly," he agreed. It was a small victory, to be sure, but when one is dealing with a queen, victories of any kind are hard to come by.

"Well," she said, rising to her feet, "since we're not going to fight, why don't we go to bed?"

"Good idea."

The kitten Talen had given to Princess Danae was named Mmrr, and Mmrr had one habit that particularly irritated Sparhawk. Kittens like to have company when they sleep, and Mmrr had found that when Sparhawk slept, he curled up slightly and that the space just behind his knees was a perfect place for her to nest. Sparhawk customarily slept with the covers pulled tightly around his neck, but that was no real problem. A cold, wet nose touched to the back of his neck caused him to flinch away violently, and that involuntary movement would always open just enough of a gap for an enterprising kitten. Mmrr found the whole process quite satisfactory and even rather amusing.

Sparhawk, however, did not. It was shortly before dawn when he emerged from the bedroom, tousled, sleepy-eyed, and just a bit out of sorts.

Princess Danae wandered into the large central room absently dragging Rollo behind her. "Have you seen my cat?" she asked her father.

"She's in bed with your mother," he replied shortly.

"I should have known, I suppose. Mmrr likes the way Mother smells. She told me so herself."

Sparhawk glanced around and then carefully closed the bedroom door. "I need to talk with Sephrenia again," he said.

"All right."

"Not here, though. I'll find someplace."

"What happened last night?"

"We have to go to Tamuli."

"I thought you were going to do something about Drychtnath."

"I am—in a way. It seems that there's something—or someone—over on the Daresian continent that's behind Drychtnath. I think we'll be able to find out more about him there than we ever would here. I'll make arrangements to have you taken back to Cimmura."

She pursed her small mouth. "No, I don't think so," she said. "I'd better go along with you."

"That's absolutely out of the question."

"Oh, Sparhawk, *do* grow up. I'm going along because you're going to need me when we get there." She negligently tossed Rollo over into a corner. "I'm also going because you can't stop me. Come up with some reason for it, Sparhawk. Otherwise you'll have to explain to Mother how it is that I managed to get ahead of you when you all find me sitting in a tree alongside a road somewhere. Get dressed, Father, and go find a place where we can talk privately."

Sometime later, Sparhawk and his daughter climbed a narrow, spiralling wooden staircase that led to the cupola atop the dome of the Basilica. There was quite probably no more private place in the world, particularly in view of the fact that the wooden stairs leading up to the little bell tower did not so much creak as they did shriek when anyone began to climb them.

When they reached the unenclosed little house high above the city, Danae spent several minutes gazing out over Chyrellos. "You can always see so much better from up high like this," she said. "It's just about the only reason I've ever found for flying."

"Can you really fly?"

"Of course. Can't you?"

"You know better, Aphrael."

"I was only teasing you, Sparhawk." She laughed. "Let's get started." She sat down, crossed her legs, and lifted her little face to sing that trilling song she had raised back in Cimmura. Then again, her eyes closed and her face went blank as the song died away.

"What is it *this* time, Sparhawk?" Sephrenia's voice was a bit tart.

"What's the matter, little mother?"

"Do you realize that it's the middle of the night here?"

"It *is*?"

"Of course it is. The sun's on your side of the world now."

"Astonishing—though I suppose it stands to reason if you think about it. Did I disturb you?"

"Yes, as a matter of fact you did."

"What were you doing so late at night?"

"None of your business. What do you want?"

"We'll be coming to Daresia soon."

"What?"

"The emperor asked us to come—well, he asked *me* actually. The rest are sort of tagging along. Ehlana's going to make a state visit to Matherion to sort of give us all an excuse for being there."

"Have you taken leave of your senses? Tamuli's a very dangerous place right now."

"Probably not much more than Eosia is. We were attacked by ancient Lamorks on our way here to Chyrellos from Cimmura."

"Perhaps they were just modern-day Lamorks dressed in ancient garb."

"I rather doubt that, Sephrenia. They vanished when their attack began to fail."

"All of them?"

"Except for the ones who were already dead. Would a little logic offend you?"

"Not unless you drag it out."

"We're almost positive that the attackers really were ancient Lamorks, and Ambassador Oscagne told us that someone's been raising antique heroes in Daresia as well. Logic implies that this resurrection business is originating in Tamuli and that its goal is to stir up nationalistic sentiments in order to weaken the central governments—the empire in Daresia *and* the Church here in Eosia. If we're right about the source of all of this activity being somewhere in Tamuli, that's the logical place to start looking for answers. Where are you right now?"

"Vanion and I are at Sarsos in eastern Astel. You'd better come here, Sparhawk. These long-distance conversations tend to blur things."

Sparhawk thought for a moment, trying to remember the map of Daresia. "We'll come overland then. I'll find some way to get the others to agree to that."

"Try not to take too long, Sparhawk. It's really very important that we talk face-to-face."

"Right. Sleep well, little mother."

"I wasn't sleeping."

"Oh? What *were* you doing?"

"Didn't you hear what she told you before, Sparhawk?" his daughter asked him.

"Which was that?"

"She told you that it was none of your business what she was doing."

"What an astonishingly good idea, your Majesty," Oscagne said later that morning when they had all gathered once again in Dolmant's private audience chamber. "I'd have never thought of it in a million years. The leaders of the subject nations of Tamuli don't go to Matherion unless they're summoned by his Imperial Majesty."

"The rulers of Eosia are less restrained, your Excellency," Emban told him. "They have total sovereignty."

"Astonishing. Has your Church no authority over their actions, your Grace?"

"Only in spiritual matters, I'm afraid."

"Isn't that inconvenient?"

"You wouldn't believe how inconvenient, Ambassador Oscagne." Dolmant sighed, looking at Ehlana reproachfully.

"Be nice, Sarathi," she murmured.

"Then no one is really in charge here in Eosia? No one has the absolute authority to make final decisions?"

"It's a responsibility we share, your Excellency," Ehlana explained. "We enjoy sharing things, don't we, Sarathi?"

"Of course." Dolmant said it without much enthusiasm.

"The rough-and-tumble, give-and-take nature of Eosian politics has a certain utility, your Excellency," Stragen drawled. "Consensus politics gives us the advantage of bringing together a wide range of views."

"In Tamuli, we feel that having only one view is far less confusing."

"The Emperor's view? What happens when the emperor happens to be an idiot? Or a madman?"

"The government usually works around him," Oscagne admitted blandly. "Such imperial misfortunes seldom live very long, however."

"Ah," Stragen said.

"Perhaps we should get down to work," Emban said. He crossed the room to a large map of the known world hanging on the wall. "The fastest way to travel is by sea," he noted. "We could sail from Madel in Cammoria, out through the Inner Sea, then around the southern tip of Daresia, and then up the east coast to Matherion."

"We?" Sir Tynian asked.

"Oh, didn't I tell you?" Emban said. "I'll be going along. Ostensibly, I'll be Queen Ehlana's spiritual advisor. In actuality, I'll be the Archprelate's personal envoy."

"It's probably wiser to keep the Elenian flavor of the expedition," Dolmant explained, "for public consumption, anyway. Let's not complicate things by sending two separate missions to Matherion simultaneously."

Sparhawk had to move quickly and he didn't have much to work with. "Traveling by ship has certain advantages," he conceded, "but I think there's a major drawback."

"Oh?" Emban said.

"It satisfies the requirements of a state visit, right enough, but it doesn't do very much to address our *real* reason for going to Tamuli. Your Excellency, what's likely to happen when we reach Matherion?"

"The usual." Oscagne shrugged. "Audiences, banquets, reviewing troops, concerts, that giddy round of meaningless activity we all adore."

"Precisely," Sparhawk agreed. "And we won't really get anything done, will we?"

"Probably not."

"But we aren't going to Tamuli for a month-long carouse. What we're *really* going there for is to find out what's behind all the upheaval. We need information, not entertainment, and the information's probably out in the hinterlands, not in the capital. I think we should find some reason to go across country." It was a practical suggestion, and it rather neatly concealed Sparhawk's *real* reason for wanting to go overland.

Emban's expression was pained. "We'd be on the road for months that way."

"We can get as much done as we'll accomplish in Matherion by staying home, your Grace. We *have* to get outside the capital."

Emban groaned. "You're absolutely bent on making me ride a horse all the way from here to Matherion, aren't you, Sparhawk?"

"You could stay home, your Grace," Sparhawk suggested. "We could always take Patriarch Bergsten instead. He'd be better in a fight anyway."

"That will do, Sparhawk," Dolmant said firmly.

"Consensus politics are very interesting, Milord Stragen," Oscagne observed. "In Matherion, we'd have followed the course suggested by the Primate of Ucera without any further discussion. We try to avoid raising the possibility of alternatives whenever possible."

"Welcome to Eosia, your Excellency." Stragen smiled.

"Permission to speak?" Kahlad said politely.

"Of course," Dolmant replied.

Khalad rose, went to the map, and began measuring distance. "A good horse can cover ten leagues a day, and a good ship can cover thirty—if the wind holds." He frowned and looked around. "Why is Talen never around when you need him?" he muttered. "He can compute these numbers in his head. I have to count them up on my fingers."

"He said he had something to take care of," Berit told him.

Khalad grunted. "All we're really interested in is what's going on in Daresia, so there's no need to ride across Eosia. We could sail from Madel the way Patriarch Emban suggested, go out through the Inner Sea, and up the east coast of Zemoch to—" He looked at the map and then pointed. "—to Salesha here. That's nine hundred leagues—thirty days. If we were to follow the roads, it'd probably be the same distance overland, but that would take us ninety days. We'd save two months at least."

"Well," Emban conceded grudgingly, "that's something, anyway."

Sparhawk was fairly sure that they could save much more than sixty days. He looked across the room at his daughter, who was playing with her kitten under Mirtai's watchful eye. Princess Danae was quite frequently present at conferences where she had no real business. People did not question her presence, for some reason. Sparhawk knew that the Child-Goddess Aphrael could tamper with the passage of time, but he was not entirely certain that she could manage it so undetectably in her present incarnation as she had when she had been Flute.

Princess Danae looked back at him and rolled her eyes upward with a resigned expression that spoke volumes about his limited understanding, then she gravely nodded her head.

Sparhawk breathed somewhat easier after that. "Now we come to the question of the queen's security," he continued. "Ambassador Oscagne, how large a retinue could my wife take with her without raising eyebrows?"

"The conventions are a little vague on that score, Sir Sparhawk."

Sparhawk looked around at his friends. "If I thought I could get away with it, I'd take the whole body of the Militant Orders with me," he said.

"We've defined our trip as a visit, Sparhawk," Tynian said, "not an invasion. Would a hundred armored knights alarm his Imperial Majesty, your Excellency?"

"It's a symbolic sort of number," Oscagne agreed after a moment's consideration. "Large enough for a show, but not so large as to appear threatening. We'll be going through Astel, and you can pick up an escort of Atans in the capital at Darsas. A sizeable escort for a state visitor shouldn't raise too many eyebrows."

"Twenty-five knights from each order, wouldn't you think, Sparhawk?" Bevier suggested. "The differences in our equipment and the colors of our surcoats would make the knights appear more ceremonial than utilitarian. A hundred Pandions by themselves might cause concern in some quarters."

"Good idea," Sparhawk agreed.

"You can bring more if you want, Sparhawk," Mirtai told him. "There are Peloi on the steppes of Central Astel. They're the descendants of Kring's ancestors. He might just want to visit his cousins in Daresia."

"Ah, yes," Oscagne said, "the Peloi. I'd forgotten that you had those wild men here in Eosia, too. They're an excitable and sometimes unreliable people. Are you certain that this Kring person would be willing to accompany us?"

"Kring would ride into fire if I asked him to," Mirtai replied confidently.

"The Domi is much taken with our Mirtai, your Excellency." Ehlana smiled. "He comes to Cimmura three or four times a year to propose marriage to her."

"The Peloi are warriors, Atana," Oscagne noted. "You would not demean yourself in the eyes of your people were you to accept him."

"Husbands take their wives more or less for granted, Oscagne," Mirtai pointed out with a mysterious little smile. "A suitor, on the other hand, is much more attentive, and I rather enjoy Kring's attentions. He writes very nice poetry. He compared me to a golden sunrise once. I thought that was rather pretty."

"You never wrote any poetry for me, Sparhawk," Ehlana accused her husband.

"The Elene language is limited, my Queen," he responded. "It has no words which could do you justice."

"Nice try," Kalten murmured.

"I think we all might want to spend a bit of time on some correspondence at this point," Dolmant told them. "There are all sorts of arrangements to be made. I'll put a fast ship at your disposal, Ambassador Oscagne. You'll want to advise your emperor that the Queen of Elenia's coming to call."

"With the Archprelate's permission, I'll communicate with my government by dispatch rather than in person. There are social and political peculiarities in various parts of the empire. I could be very helpful in smoothing her Majesty's path if I went with her."

"I'll be very pleased to have a civilized gentleman along, your Excellency." Ehlana smiled. "You have no idea what it's like being surrounded by men whose clothes have all been tailored by blacksmiths."

Talen entered the chamber with an excited expression on his face.

"Where have you been?" The question came from several parts of the room.

"It's such a comfort to be so universally loved that my activities arouse this breathless curiosity," the boy said with an exaggerated and sardonic bow. "I'm quite overwhelmed by this demonstration of affection."

Ambassador Oscagne looked quizzically at Dolmant.

"It would take far too long to explain, your Excellency," Dolmant said wearily. "Just keep a close watch on your valuables when that boy's in the room."

"Sarathi," Talen protested. "I haven't stolen a single thing for almost a week now."

"That's a start, I suppose," Emban noted.

"Old habits die hard, your Grace." Talen smirked. "Anyway, since you're all dying to know, I was out in the city sort of nosing around, and I ran across an old friend. Would you believe that Krager's here in Chyrellos?"

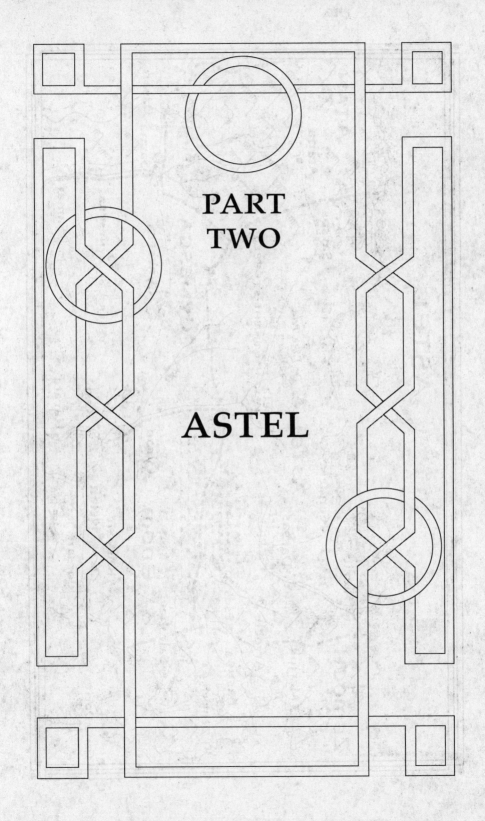

PART
TWO

ASTEL

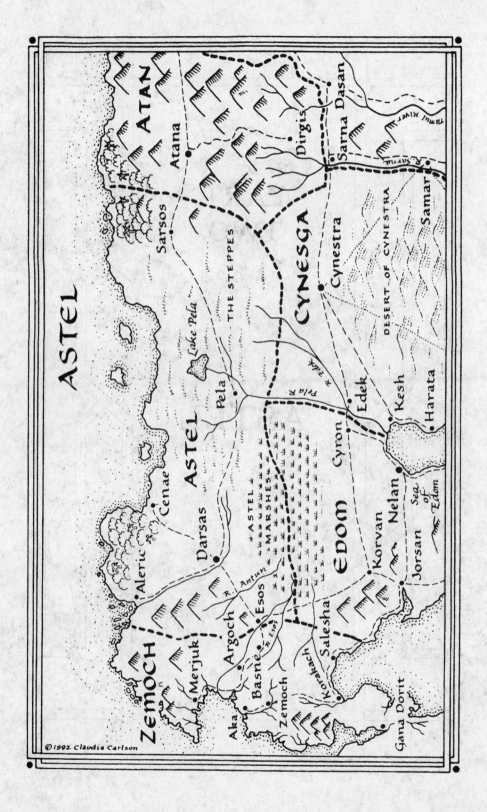

ASTEL

ATAN

Atana

Dirgis

Sarna Dasan

Tamul River

R. Sarna

Sarsos

THE STEPPES

CYNESGA

Cynestra

Samar

Lake Pela

DESERT OF CYNESTRA

Pela

R. Edek

Pela R.

Kesh

Harata

ASTEL

Cenae

Edek

Aleric

Cyron

Darsas

ASTEL MARSHES

EDOM

Korvan

Nelan

Sea of Edom

R. Antun

Esos

Jorsan

ZEMOCH

Merjuk

Argoch

R. Esos

Korakach

Salesha

Basne

Aka

Zemoch

Gana Dorit

©1992 Claudia Carlson

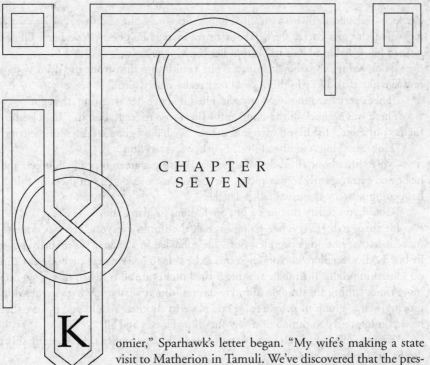

Komier," Sparhawk's letter began. "My wife's making a state visit to Matherion in Tamuli. We've discovered that the present turmoil in Lamorkand is probably originating in Daresia, so we're using Ehlana's trip to give us the chance to go there to see what we can find out. I'll keep you advised. I'm borrowing twenty-five Genidian Knights from your local chapterhouse to serve as a part of the honor guard.

"I'd suggest that you do what you can to keep Avin Wargunsson from cementing any permanent alliances with Count Gerrich in Lamorkand. Gerrich is rather deeply involved in some kind of grand plan that goes far beyond the borders of Lamorkand itself. Dolmant probably wouldn't be too displeased if you, Darellon, and Abriel can contrive some excuse to go to Lamorkand and step on the fellow's neck. Watch out for magic, though. Gerrich's getting help from somebody who knows more than he's supposed to. Ulath's sending you more details.—Sparhawk."

"Isn't that just a little blunt, dear?" Ehlana said, reading over her husband's shoulder. She smelled very good.

"Komier's a blunt sort of fellow, Ehlana." Sparhawk shrugged, laying down his quill. "And I'm not really very good at writing letters."

"I noticed." They were in their ornate apartments in one of the Church buildings adjoining the Basilica where they had spent the day composing messages to people scattered over most of the continent.

"Don't you have letters of your own to write?" Sparhawk asked his wife.

"I'm all finished. All I really had to do was send a short note to Lenda. He knows what to do." She glanced across the room at Mirtai, who sat patiently snipping the tips off Mmrr's claws. Mmrr was not taking it very well. Ehlana smiled. "Mirtai's communication with Kring was much more direct. She called in an itinerant Peloi and told him to ride to Kring with her command to ride to Basne on the

Zemoch–Astel border with a hundred of his tribesmen. She said that if he isn't waiting when she gets there, she'll take it to mean that he doesn't love her." Ehlana
pushed her pale blond hair back from her brow.

"Poor Kring." Sparhawk smiled. "She could raise him from the dead with a
message like that. Do you think she'll ever really marry him?"

"That's very hard to say, Sparhawk. He does have her attention, though."

There was a knock at the door, and Mirtai rose to let Kalten in. "It's a beautiful day out there," the blond man told them. "We'll have good weather for the trip."

"How are things coming along?" Sparhawk asked him.

"We're just about all ready." Kalten was wearing a green brocade doublet, and
he bowed extravagantly to the queen. "Actually, we *are* ready. About the only things
happening now are the usual redundancies."

"Could you clarify that just a bit, Sir Kalten?" Ehlana said.

He shrugged. "Everyone's going over all the things everyone else has done to
make sure that nothing's been left out." He sprawled in a chair. "We're surrounded
by busybodies, Sparhawk. Nobody seems to be able to believe that anybody else can
do something right. If Emban asks me if the knights are all ready to ride, even one
more time, I think I'll strangle him. He has no idea at all about what's involved in
moving a large group of people from one place to another. Would you believe that
he was going to try to put all of us on one ship? Horses and all?"

"That might have been just a bit crowded." Ehlana smiled. "How many ships
did he finally decide on?"

"I'm not sure. I still don't know for certain how many people are going. Your
attendants are all absolutely convinced that you'll simply die without their company, my Queen. There are about forty or so who are making preparations for the
trip."

"You'd better weed them out, Ehlana," Sparhawk suggested. "I don't want to be
saddled with the entire court."

"I *will* need a few people, Sparhawk—if only for the sake of appearances."

Talen came into the room. The gangly boy was wearing what he called his
"street clothes," slightly mismatched, very ordinary, and just this side of shabby.
"He's still out there," he said, his eyes bright.

"Who?" Kalten asked.

"Krager. He's creeping around Chyrellos like a lost puppy looking for a home.
Stragen's got people from the local thieves' community watching him. We haven't
been able to figure out exactly what he's up to just yet. If Martel were still alive, I'd
almost say he's doing the same sort of thing he used to do—letting himself be seen."

"How does he look?"

"Worse." Talen's voice cracked slightly. It was still hovering somewhere between soprano and baritone. "The years aren't treating Krager very well. His eyes
look like they've been poached in bacon grease. He looks absolutely miserable."

"I think I can bear Krager's misery," Sparhawk noted. "He's beginning to make
me just a little tired, though. He's been hovering around the edge of my awareness
for the last ten years or more—sort of like a hangnail or an ingrown toenail. He always seems to be working for the other side, but he's too insignificant to really
worry about."

"Stragen could ask one of the local thieves to cut his throat," Talen offered.

Sparhawk considered it. "Maybe not," he decided. "Krager's always been a good source of information. Tell Stragen that if the opportunity happens to come up, we might want to have a little chat with our old friend, though. The offer to braid his legs together usually makes Krager very talkative."

Ulath stopped by about a half hour later. "Did you finish that letter to Komier?" he asked Sparhawk.

"He has a draft copy, Sir Ulath," Ehlana replied for her husband. "It definitely needs some polish."

"You don't have to polish things for Komier, your Majesty. He's used to strange letters. One of my Genidian brothers sent him a report written on human skin once."

She stared at him. "He did *what?*"

"There wasn't anything else handy to write on. A Genidian Knight just arrived with a message for me from Komier, though. The knight's going back to Emsat, and he can carry Sparhawk's letter if it's ready to go."

"It's close enough," Sparhawk said, folding the parchment and dribbling candle wax on it to seal it. "What did Komier have to say?"

"It was good news for a change. All the Trolls have left Thalesia for some reason."

"Where did they go?"

"Who knows? Who cares?"

"The people who live in the country they've gone to might be slightly interested," Kalten suggested.

"That's their problem." Ulath shrugged. "It's funny, though. The Trolls don't really get along with each other. I couldn't even begin to guess at a reason why they'd all decide to pack up and leave at the same time. The discussions must have been very interesting. They usually kill each other on sight."

"There's not much help I can give you, Sparhawk," Dolmant said gravely when the two of them met privately later that day. "The Church is fragmented in Daresia. They don't accept the authority of Chyrellos, so I can't order them to assist you." Dolmant's face was careworn, and his white cassock made his complexion look sallow. In a very real sense, Dolmant ruled an empire that stretched from Thalesia to Cammoria, and the burdens of his office bore down on him heavily. The change they had all noticed in their friend in the past several years derived more likely from that than from any kind of inflated notion of his exalted station.

"You'll get more cooperation in Astel than either Edom or Daconia," he continued. "The doctrine of the Church of Astel is very close to ours—close enough that we even recognize Astellian ecclesiastical rank. Edom and Daconia broke away from the Astellian Church thousands of years ago and went their own way." The Archprelate smiled ruefully. "The sermons in those two kingdoms are generally little more than hysterical denunciations of the Church of Chyrellos—and of me personally. They're antihierarchical, much like the Rendors. If you should happen to go into those two kingdoms, you can expect the Church there to oppose you. The fact that you're a Church Knight will be held against you rather than the reverse. The children there are all taught that the Knights of the Church have horns and tails. They'll expect you to burn churches, murder clergymen, and enslave the people."

"I'll do what I can to stay away from those places, Sarathi," Sparhawk assured him. "Who's in charge in Astel?"

"The Archimandrite of Darsas is nominally the head of the Astellian Church. It's an obscure rank approximately the equivalent of our 'patriarch.' The Church of Astel's organized along monastic lines. They don't have a secular clergy there."

"Are there any other significant differences I should know about?"

"Some of the customs are different—liturgical variations, primarily. I doubt that you'll be asked to conduct services, so that shouldn't cause any problems. It's probably just as well. I heard you deliver a sermon once."

Sparhawk smiled. "We serve in different ways, Sarathi. Our Holy Mother didn't hire me to preach to people. How do I address the Archimandrite of Darsas—in case I meet him?"

"Call him 'Your Grace,' the same as you would a patriarch. He's an imposing man with a huge beard, and there's nothing in Astel that he doesn't know about. His priests are everywhere. The people trust them implicitly, and they all submit weekly reports to the archimandrite. The Church has enormous power there."

"What a novel idea."

"Don't mistreat me, Sparhawk. Things haven't been going very well for me lately."

"Would you be willing to listen to an assessment, Dolmant?"

"Of me personally? Probably not."

"I wasn't talking about that. You're too old to change, I expect. I'm talking about your policies in Rendor. Your basic idea was good enough, but you went at it the wrong way."

"Be careful, Sparhawk. I've sent men to monasteries permanently for less than that."

"Your policy of reconciliation with the Rendors was very sound. I spent ten years down there, and I know how they think. The ordinary people in Rendor would really like to be reconciled with the Church—if for no other reason than to get rid of all the howling fanatics out in the desert. Your policy is good, but you sent the wrong people there to carry it out."

"The priests I sent are all experts in doctrine, Sparhawk."

"That's the problem. You sent doctrinaire fanatics down there. All they want to do is punish the Rendors for their heresy."

"Heresy *is* a sort of problem, Sparhawk."

"The heresy of the Rendors isn't theological, Dolmant. They worship the same God we do, and their body of religious belief is identical to ours. The disagreements between us are entirely in the field of Church government. The Church was corrupt when the Rendors broke away from us. The members of the Hierocracy were sending relatives to fill Church positions in Rendor, and those relatives were parasitic opportunists who were far more interested in lining their own purses than caring for the souls of the people. When you get right down to it, that's why the Rendors started murdering primates and priests—and they're doing it for exactly the same reason now. You'll never reconcile the Rendors to the Church if you try to punish them. They don't care who's governing our Holy Mother. They'll never see you personally, my friend, but they *will* see their local priest—probably every day. If he spends all his time calling them heretics and tearing the veils off their women, they'll kill him. It's as simple as that."

Dolmant's face was troubled. "Perhaps I *have* blundered," he admitted. "Of course if you tell anybody I said that, I'll deny it."

"Naturally."

"All right, what should I do about it?"

Sparhawk remembered something then. "There's a vicar in a poor church in Borrata," he said. "He's probably the closest thing to a saint I've ever seen, and I didn't even get his name. Berit knows what it is, though. Disguise some investigators as beggars and send them down to Cammoria to observe him. He's exactly the kind of man you need."

"Why not just send for *him*?"

"He'd be too tongue-tied to speak to you, Sarathi. He's what they had in mind when they coined the word *humble*. Besides, he'd never leave his flock. If you order him to Chyrellos and then send him to Rendor, he'll probably die within six months. He's that kind of man."

Dolmant's eyes suddenly filled with tears. "You trouble me, Sparhawk," he said. "You trouble me. That's the ideal we all had when we took holy orders." He sighed. "How did we all get so far away from it?"

"You got too much involved in the world, Dolmant," Sparhawk told him gently. "The Church had to live in the world, but the world corrupts *her* much faster than she can redeem *it*."

"What's the answer to that problem, Sparhawk?"

"I honestly don't know, Sarathi. Maybe there isn't any."

Sparhawk. It was his daughter's voice, and it was somehow inside his head. He was passing through the nave of the Basilica and he quickly knelt as if in prayer to cover what he was really doing.

What is it, Aphrael? he asked silently.

You don't have to genuflect to me, Sparhawk. Her voice was amused.

I'm not. If they catch me walking through the corridors mouthing long conversations with somebody who isn't there, they'll lock me up in an asylum.

You look very reverential in that position, though. I'm touched.

Was there something significant, or are you just amusing yourself?

Sephrenia wants to talk to you again.

All right. I'm in the nave right now. Come down and meet me here. We'll go up to the cupola again.

I'll meet you up there.

There's only one stairway leading up there, Aphrael. We have to climb it.

You might have to, but I don't. I don't like going into the nave, Sparhawk. I always have to stop and talk with your God, and he's so tedious most of the time.

Sparhawk's mind shuddered back from the implications of that.

The dried-out wooden stairs circling up to the top of the dome still shrieked their protest as Sparhawk mounted. It was a long climb, and he was winded when he reached the top.

"What took you so long?" Danae asked him. She wore a simple white smock. It was a little-girl sort of dress, so no one seemed to even notice that its cut was definitely Styric.

"You enjoy saying things like that to me, don't you?" Sparhawk accused.

"I'm only teasing, Father." She laughed.

"I hope no one saw you coming up here. I don't think the world's ready for a flying princess just yet."

"No one saw me, Sparhawk. I've done this before, you know. Trust me."

"Do I have any choice? Let's get to work. I've still got a lot left to do today if we're going to leave tomorrow morning."

She nodded and sat cross-legged near one of the huge bells. She lifted her face again and raised that flutelike trill. Then her voice drifted off, and her face went blank.

"Where have you been?" Sephrenia asked, opening Danae's eyes to stare at her pupil.

He sighed. "If you two don't stop that, I'm going to go into another line of work."

"Has Aphrael been teasing you again?" she asked.

"Of course she has. Did you know that she can fly?"

"I've never seen her do it, but I'd assumed she could."

"What did you want to see me about?"

"I've been hearing disturbing rumors. The northern Atans have been seeing some very large, shaggy creatrues in the forests near their north coast."

"So *that's* where they went."

"Don't be cryptic, dear one."

"Komier sent word to Ulath. It seems that the Trolls have all left Thalesia."

"The Trolls!" she exclaimed. "They wouldn't do that! Thalesia's their ancestral home!"

"Maybe you'd better go tell the Trolls about that. Komier swears that there's not a single one of them left in Thalesia."

"Something very, very strange is going on here, Sparhawk."

"Ambassador Oscagne said more or less the same thing. Can the Styrics there at Sarsos make any sense out of it yet?"

"No. Zalasta's at his wits' end."

"Have you come up with any idea at all of who's behind it?"

"Sparhawk, we don't even know *what's* behind it. We can't even make a guess about the *species* of whatever it is."

"We sort of keep coming back to the idea that it's the Troll-Gods again. *Something* had to have enough authority over the Trolls to command them to leave Thalesia, and that points directly at the Troll-Gods. Are we absolutely *sure* that they haven't managed to get loose?"

"It's not a good idea to discount *any* possibility when you're dealing with Gods,

Sparhawk. I don't know the spell Ghwerig used when he put them inside the Bhelliom, so I don't know if it can be broken."

"Then it *is* possible."

"That's what I just said, dear one. Have you seen that shadow—or the cloud—lately?"

"No."

"Has Aphrael ever seen it?"

"No."

"*She* could tell you, but I'd rather not have her exposed to whatever it is. Perhaps we can come up with a way to lure it out when you get here so that I can take a look at it. When are you leaving?"

"First thing tomorrow morning. Danae sort of told me that she can play with time the way she did when we were marching to Acie with Wargun's army. That would get us there faster, but can she do it as undetectably now as she did when she was Flute?"

The bell behind the motionless form of his daughter gave a deep, soft-toned sound. "Why don't you ask *me*, Sparhawk?" Danae's voice hummed in the bell sound. "It's not as if I weren't here, you know."

"How was I supposed to know that?" He waited. "Well?" he asked the still-humming bell, "Can you?"

"Well, of *course* I can, Sparhawk." The Child-Goddess sounded irritated. "Don't you know *anything*?"

"That will do," Sephrenia chided.

"He's such a lump."

"Aphrael! I said that will do! You will *not* be disrespectful to your father." A faint smile touched the lips of the apparently somnolent little princess. "Even if he *is* a hopeless lump."

"If you two want to discuss my failings, I'll go back downstairs so you can speak freely," Sparhawk told them.

"No, that's all right, Sparhawk," Aphrael said lightly. "We're all friends, so we shouldn't have any secrets from each other."

They left Chyrellos the following morning and rode south on the Arcian side of the River Sarin in bright morning sunshine with one hundred Church Knights in full armor riding escort. The grass along the riverbank was very green, and the blue sky was dotted with fluffy, white clouds. After some discussion, Sparhawk and Ehlana had decided that the attendants she would need for the sake of appearances could be drawn for the most part from the ranks of the Church Knights. "Stragen can coach them," Sparhawk had told his wife. "He's had a certain amount of experience, so he can make honest knights look like useless butterflies."

It had been necessary, however, to include one lady-in-waiting, Baroness Melidere, a young woman of Ehlana's own age with honey-blond hair, deep blue eyes, and an apparently empty head. Ehlana also took along a personal maid, a doe-eyed girl named Alean. The two of them rode in the carriage with the queen, Mirtai, Danae, and Stragen, who, dressed in his elegant best, kept them amused with light banter. Sparhawk reasoned that between them, Stragen and Mirtai could provide his wife and daughter with a fairly significant defense if the occasion arose.

Patriarch Emban was going to be a problem. Sparhawk could see that after they had gone no more than a few miles. Emban was not comfortable on a horse and he filled the air with complaints as he rode.

"That isn't going to work, you know," Kalten observed about midmorning. "Churchman or not, if the knights have to listen to Emban feel sorry for himself all the way across the Daresian continent, he's likely to have some kind of an accident before we get to Matherion. I'm ready to drown him right now myself, and the river's very handy."

Sparhawk thought about it. He looked at the queen's carriage. "That landau's not quite big enough," he told his friend. "I think we need something grander. Six horses are more impressive than four anyway. See if you can find Bevier."

When the olive-skinned Arcian rode forward, Sparhawk explained the situation. "If we don't get Emban off that horse, it's going to take us a year to cross Daresia. Are you still on speaking terms with your cousin Lycien?"

"Of course. We're the best of friends."

"Why don't you ride on ahead and have a chat with him? We need a large carriage—roomy enough for eight—six horses probably. We'll put Emban and Ambassador Oscagne in the carriage with my wife and her entourage. Ask your cousin to locate one for us."

"That might be expensive, Sparhawk," Bevier said dubiously.

"That's all right, Bevier. The Church will pay for it. After a week on horseback, Emban should be willing to sign for anything that doesn't wear a saddle. Oh, as long as you're going there anyway, have our ships moved upriver to Lycien's docks. Madel's not so attractive a city that any of us would enjoy a stay there all that much, and Lycien's docks are more conveniently arranged."

"Will we need anything else, Sparhawk?" Bevier asked.

"Not that I can think of. Feel free to improvise, though. Add anything you can think of on your way to Madel. For once, we have a more or less unlimited budget at our disposal. The coffers of the Church are wide open to us."

"I wouldn't tell that to Stragen or Talen, my friend." Bevier laughed. "I'll be at Lycien's house. I'll see you when you get there." He wheeled his horse and rode south at a gallop.

"Why didn't you just have him pick up another carriage for Emban and Oscagne?" Kalten asked.

"Because I don't want to have to defend two when we get to Tamuli."

"Oh. That makes sense—sort of."

They arrived at the house of Sir Bevier's cousin, Marquis Lycien, late one afternoon and met Bevier and his stout, florid-faced kinsman in the gravelled court in front of Lycien's opulent home. The marquis bowed deeply to the Queen of Elenia and insisted that she accept his hospitality during her stay in Madel. Kalten dispersed the knights in Lycien's parklike grounds.

"Did you find a carriage?" Sparhawk asked Bevier.

Bevier nodded. "It's large enough for our purposes," he said a bit dubiously, "but the cost of it may turn Patriarch Emban's hair white."

"I wouldn't be too sure," Sparhawk said. "Let's ask him." They crossed the gravelled court to where the Patriarch of Ucera stood beside his horse, clinging to his saddle horn with a look of profound misery on his face.

"Pleasant little ride, wasn't it, your Grace?" Sparhawk asked the fat man brightly.

Emban groaned. "I don't think I'll be able to walk for a week."

"Of course we were only strolling," Sparhawk continued. "We'll have to move along much faster when we get to Tamuli." He paused. "May I speak frankly, your Grace?"

"You will anyway, Sparhawk," Emban said sourly. "Would you really pay any attention to me if I objected?"

"Probably not. You're slowing us down, you know."

"Well, *excuse* me."

"You're not really built for horseback riding, Patriarch Emban. Your talent's in your head, not your backside."

Emban's eyes narrowed with hostility. "Go on," he said in an ominous tone of voice.

"Since we're in a hurry, we've decided to put wheels under you. Would you be more comfortable in a cushioned carriage, your Grace?"

"Sparhawk, I could kiss you!"

"I'm a married man, your Grace. My wife might misunderstand. For security reasons, one carriage is far better than two, so I've taken the liberty of locating one that's somewhat larger than the one Ehlana rode down from Chyrellos. You wouldn't mind riding with her, would you? We thought we'd put you and Ambassador Oscagne in the carriage with my queen and her attendants. Would that be satisfactory?"

"Did you want me to kiss the ground you're standing on, Sparhawk?"

"Oh, that won't be necessary, your Grace. All you really have to do is sign the authorization for the carriage. This is urgent Church business, after all, so the purchase of the carriage is fully justified, wouldn't you say?"

"Where do I sign?" Emban's expression was eager.

"A carriage that large is expensive, your Grace," Sparhawk warned him.

"I'd pawn the Basilica itself if it'd keep me out of that saddle."

"You see?" Sparhawk said to Bevier as they walked away. "That wasn't hard at all, was it?"

"How did you know he'd agree so quickly?"

"Timing, Bevier, timing. Later on, he might have objected to the price. You need to ask that sort of question while the man you're asking is still in pain."

"You're a cruel fellow, Sparhawk." Bevier laughed.

"All sorts of people have said that to me from time to time," Sparhawk replied blandly.

· · ·

"My people will finish loading the supplies for your voyage today, Sparhawk," Marquis Lycien said as they rode toward the riverside village and its wharves on the edge of his estate. "You'll be able to sail with the morning tide."

"You're a true friend, my Lord," Sparhawk told him. "You're always here when we need you."

"You're exaggerating my benevolence, Sir Sparhawk." Lycien laughed. "I'm making a very handsome profit by outfitting your vessels."

"I like to see friends get on in the world."

Lycien looked back over his shoulder at the Queen of Elenia, who rode a grey palfrey some distance to the rear. "You're the luckiest man in the world, Sparhawk," he observed. "Your wife is the most beautiful woman I've ever seen."

"I'll tell her you said that, Marquis Lycien. I'm sure she'll be pleased."

Ehlana and Emban had decided to accompany them as they rode down to the marquis' enclave on the river, Ehlana to inspect the accommodations aboard ship, and Emban to have a look at the carriage he had just purchased.

The flotilla moored to Lycien's wharves consisted of a dozen large, well-fitted vessels, ships that made the merchantmen moored nearby look scruffy by comparison.

Lycien led the way through the village that had grown up around the wharves toward where the river sparkled in the morning sun.

"Master Cluff!" The voice was not unlike a foghorn.

Sparhawk turned in his saddle. "Well strike me down if it isn't Captain Sorgi!" he said with genuine pleasure. He liked the blunt, silvery-haired sea captain with whom he had spent so many hours. He swung down from Faran's back and warmly clasped his friend's hand.

"I haven't seen you in a dog's age, Master Cluff," Sorgi said expansively. "Are you still running from those cousins?"

Sparhawk pulled a long face and sighed mournfully. It was just too good an opportunity to pass up. "No," he replied in a broken voice, "not anymore, I'm afraid. I made the mistake of staying in an alehouse in Apalia up in northern Pelosia for one last tankard. The cousins caught up with me there."

"Were you able to escape?" Sorgi's face mirrored his concern.

"There were a dozen of them, Captain, and they were on me before I could even move. They clapped me in irons and took me to the estate of the ugly heiress I told you about."

"They didn't force you to marry her, did they?" Sorgi asked, sounding shocked.

"I'm afraid so, my friend," Sparhawk said in a tragic voice. "That's my wife on that grey horse there." He pointed at the radiant Queen of Elenia.

Captain Sorgi stared, his eyes growing wider and his mouth gaping open.

"Horrible, isn't it?" Sparhawk said with a brokenhearted catch in his voice.

Baroness Melidere was a pretty girl with hair the color of honey and eyes as blue as a summer sky. She did not have a brain in her head—at least that was what she wanted people to believe. In actuality, the baroness was probably more clever than most of the people in Ehlana's court, but she had learned early in life that people with limited intelligence feel threatened by pretty, clever young women and she had perfected a vapid, empty-headed smile, a look of blank incomprehension, and a silly giggle. She erected these defenses as the situation required and kept her own counsel.

Queen Ehlana saw through the subterfuge and even encouraged it. Melidere was very observant and had excellent hearing. People tend not to pay much attention to brainless girls; they say things in their presence they might not ordinarily say. Melidere always reported these conversational lapses back to the queen, and so Ehlana found the baroness useful to have around.

Melidere, however, drove Stragen absolutely wild. He knew with complete certainty that she could not be as stupid as she appeared, but he could never catch her off guard.

Alean, the queen's maid, was quite another matter. Her mind was very ordinary, but her nature was such that people automatically loved her. She was sweet, gentle, and loving. She had brown hair and enormous, soft brown eyes. She was shy and modest and seldom spoke. Kalten looked upon her as his natural prey, much as the wolf looks upon deer with a proprietary sense of ownership. Kalten was fond of maids. They did not usually threaten him, and he could normally proceed with them without any particular fear of failure.

The ship in which they sailed from Madel that spring was well appointed. It belonged to the Church and it had been built to convey high-ranking churchmen and their servants to various parts of Eosia.

There was a certain neat, cozy quality about all ship cabins. They were uniformly constructed of dark-stained wood, the oily stain being a necessary protection for wood perpetually exposed to excessive humidity. The furniture would be stationary, resisting all efforts to rearrange it, since it was customarily bolted to the floor to prevent its migration from one part of the cabin to another in rough weather. Since the ceiling of a ship's cabin was in reality the underside of the deck overhead where the sailors are working, the dark supporting beams were substantial.

In the particular vessel upon which the Queen of Elenia and her entourage sailed, there was a large cabin in the stern with a broad window running across the back of the ship. It was a sort of floating audience chamber, ideally suited for gatherings. Because of the window at the back, the cabin was light and airy, and, since the vessel was moved by her sails, the wind always came from astern, and it efficiently carried the smell of the bilges forward for the crew to enjoy in their cramped quarters in the forecastle.

On the second day out, Sparhawk and Ehlana dressed themselves in plain, utilitarian garments and went up to what had come to be called "the throne room" from their private cabin just below. Alean was preparing Princess Danae's breakfast over a cunning little utensil that was part lamp and part stove. Alean prepared most of Danae's meals, since she accepted the child's dietary prejudices without question.

There was a polite knock, then Kalten and Stragen entered. Kalten bore himself strangely, half-crouched, twisted off to one side, and quite obviously in pain.

"What happened to you?" Sparhawk asked him.

"I tried to sleep in a hammock." Kalten groaned. "Since we're at sea, I thought it was the thing to do. I think I've ruined myself, Sparhawk."

Mirtai rose from her chair near the door. "Stand still," she peremptorily ordered the blond man.

"What are you doing?" he demanded suspiciously.

"Be quiet." She ran one hand up his back, gently probing with her fingertips. "Lie down on the floor," she commanded, "on your stomach."

"Not *very* likely."

"Do you want me to kick your feet out from under you?"

Grumbling, he painfully lowered himself to the deck. "Is this going to hurt?" he asked.

"It won't hurt *me* a bit," she assured him, removing her sandals. "Try to relax." Then she started to walk on him. There were crackling noises and loud pops. There were also gasps and cries of pain as Kalten writhed under her feet. She finally paused, thoughtfully probing at a stubborn spot between his shoulder blades with her toes. Then she raised up on her toes and came down quite firmly.

Kalten's shriek was strangled as his breath *whooshed* out, and the noise that came from his back was very loud, much like the sound that might come from a tree trunk being snapped in two. He lay facedown, gasping and groaning.

"Don't be such a baby," Mirtai told him heartlessly. "Get up."

"I can't. You killed me."

She picked him up by one arm and set him on his feet. "Walk around," she commanded him.

"*Walk?* I can't even breathe."

She drew one of her daggers.

"All right. All right. Don't get excited. I'm walking."

"Swing your arms back and forth."

"Why?"

"Just do it, Kalten. You've got to loosen up those muscles."

He walked back and forth, swinging his arms and gingerly turning his head back and forth. "You know, I hate to admit it, but I do feel better—much better, actually."

"Naturally." She put her dagger away.

"You didn't have to be so rough, though."

"I can put you back into exactly the same condition as you were when you came in, if you'd like."

"No, that's quite all right, Mirtai." He said it very quickly and backed away from her. Then, always the opportunist, he sidled up to Alean. "Don't you feel sorry for me?" he asked her in an insinuating voice.

"Kalten!" Mirtai snapped. "No!"

"I was only—"

She smacked him sharply on the nose with two fingers, much as one would do to persuade a puppy to give up the notion of chewing on a pair of shoes.

"That hurt," he protested, putting his hand to his nose.

"It was meant to. Leave her alone."

"Are you going to let her do that, Sparhawk?" Kalten appealed to his friend.

"Do as she says," Sparhawk told him. "Leave the girl alone."

"Your morning's not going too well, is it, Sir Kalten?" Stragen noted.

Kalten went off to a corner to sulk.

The others drifted in, and they all sat down to the breakfast two crewmen brought from the galley. Princess Danae sat alone near the large window at the stern where the salt-tinged breeze would keep the smell of pork sausage from her delicate nostrils.

After breakfast, Sparhawk and Kalten went up on deck for a breath of air and stood leaning on the port rail watching the south coast of Cammoria slide by. The day was particularly fine. The sun was very bright, and the sky very blue. There was a good following breeze, and their ship, her white sails spread wide, led the small flotilla across the whitecap-speckled sea.

"The captain says that we should pass Miruscum about noon," Kalten said. "We're making better time than we expected."

"We've got a good breeze," Sparhawk agreed. "How's your back?"

"Sore. I've got bruises from my hips to my neck."

"At least you're standing up straight."

Kalten grunted sourly. "Mirtai's very direct, isn't she? I still don't know exactly what to make of her. What I mean is, how are we supposed to treat her? She's obviously a woman."

"You've noticed."

"Very funny, Sparhawk. What I'm getting at is the fact that you can't really treat her like a woman. She's as big as Ulath, and she seems to expect us to accept her as a comrade in arms."

"So?"

"It's unnatural."

"Just treat her as a special case. That's what I do. It's easier than arguing with her. Are you in the mood for a bit of advice?"

"That depends on the advice."

"Mirtai feels that it's her duty to protect the royal family, and she's extended that to include my wife's maid. I'd strongly recommend that you curb your instincts. We don't fully understand Mirtai, and so we don't know exactly how far she'll go. Even if Alean seems to be encouraging you, I wouldn't pursue the matter. It could be very dangerous."

"The girl likes me," Kalten objected. "I've been around long enough to know that."

"You might be right, but I'm not sure if that'll make any difference to Mirtai. Do me a favor, Kalten. Just leave the girl alone."

"But she's the only one on board ship," Kalten protested.

"You'll live." Sparhawk turned and saw Patriarch Emban and Ambassador Oscagne standing near the stern. They were an oddly matched pair. The Patriarch of Ucera had laid aside his cassock for the voyage and wore instead a brown jerkin over a plain robe. He was very nearly as wide as he was tall, and he had a florid face. Oscagne, on the other hand, was a slight man with fine bones and little flesh. His skin was a pallid bronze color. Their minds, however, were very similar. They were both consummate politicians. Sparhawk and Kalten drifted back to join them.

"All power comes from the throne in Tamuli, your Grace," Oscagne was explaining. "Nothing is done there except at the express instruction of the emperor."

"We delegate things in Eosia, your Excellency," Emban told him. "We pick a good man, tell him what we want done, and leave the details up to him."

"We've tried that, and it doesn't really work in our culture. Our religion is fairly superficial, and it doesn't encourage the kind of personal loyalty yours does."

"Your emperor has to make *all* the decisions?" Emban asked a bit incredulously. "How does he find the time?"

Oscagne smiled. "No, no, your Grace. Day-to-day decisions are all taken care of by custom and tradition. We're great believers in custom and tradition. It's one of our more serious failings. Once a Tamul moves out of those realms, he's obliged to improvise, and that's when he usually gets into trouble. His improvisations always seem to be guided by self-interest, for some reason. We've discovered that it's best to discourage these expeditions into free decision making. By definition, the emperor is all wise anyway, so it's probably best to leave these things in his hands."

"A standard definition isn't always very accurate, your Excellency. 'All wise' means different things when it's applied to different people. We have one ourselves. We like to say that the Archprelate is guided by the voice of God. There have been a number of Archprelates in the past who didn't listen very well, though."

"We've noticed the same sort of thing, your Grace. The definition of 'all wise' *does* seem to have a wide range of meaning. To be honest with you, my friend, we've had some frightfully stupid emperors from time to time. We're rather fortunate just now though. Emperor Sarabian is moderately accomplished."

"What's he like?" Emban asked intently.

"He's an institution, unfortunately. He's as much at the mercy of custom and tradition as we are. He's obliged to speak in formulas, so it's almost impossible to get to know him." The ambassador smiled. "The visit of Queen Ehlana may just jerk him into humanity. He'll have to treat her as an equal—for political reasons—and he was raised to believe that he didn't have any equals. I hope your lovely blond queen is gentle with him. I think I like him—or I would if I could get past all the formalities—and it would just be too bad if she happened to say something that stopped his heart."

"Ehlana knows exactly what she's doing every minute of the day, your Excellency," Emban assured him. "You and I are babies compared to her. You don't have to tell her I said that, Sparhawk."

"What's my silence worth to you, your Grace?" Sparhawk grinned.

Emban glowered at him for a moment. "What are we likely to encounter in Astel, your Excellency?"

"Tears, probably," Oscagne replied.

"I beg your pardon?"

"The Astels are an emotional people. They cry at the drop of a handkerchief. Their culture is much like that of the kingdom of Pelosia. They're tediously devout and invincibly backward. It's been demonstrated to them over and over again that serfdom is an archaic, inefficient institution, but they maintain it anyway—largely at the connivance of the serfs themselves. Astellian nobles don't exert themselves in any way, so they have no concept of the extent of human endurance. Their serfs take advantage of that outrageously. Astellian serfs have been known to collapse from sheer exhaustion at the very mention of such unpleasant words as 'reaping' or 'digging.' The weepy nobles are tenderhearted, so the serfs get away with it almost every time. Western Astel's a silly place filled with silly people. That changes as one moves east."

"One would hope so. I'm not certain just how much silliness I can—"

It was that same flicker of darkness at the very edge of Sparhawk's vision, and it was accompanied by that same chill. Patriarch Emban broke off, turning his head quickly to try to see it more clearly. "What—"

"It'll pass," Sparhawk told him tersely. "Try to concentrate on it, your Grace, and you as well, if you don't mind, your Excellency." They were seeing the shadow for the first time, and their initial reactions might be useful. Sparhawk watched them closely as they tried to turn their heads to look directly at the annoying darkness just beyond the range of sight. Then the shadow was gone.

"All right," Sparhawk said crisply, "exactly what did you see?"

"I couldn't see anything," Kalten told him. "It was like having someone trying to sneak up behind me." Although Kalten had seen the cloud several times, this was the first time he had encountered the shadow.

"What was it, Sir Sparhawk?" Ambassador Oscagne asked.

"I'll explain in a moment, your Excellency. Please try to remember exactly what you saw and felt."

"It was something dark," Oscagne replied, "*very* dark. It seemed to be quite substantial, but somehow it was able to move just enough to stay where I couldn't quite see it. No matter how quickly I turned my head or moved my eyes, it was never where I could see it directly. It felt as if it were standing just behind my head."

Emban nodded. "And it made me feel cold." He shuddered. "I'm still cold, as a matter of fact."

"It was unfriendly, too," Kalten added. "Not quite ready to attack, but very nearly."

"Anything else?" Sparhawk asked them. "Anything at all—no matter how small."

"There was a peculiar odor," Oscagne told him.

Sparhawk looked at him sharply. He had never noticed that. "Could you describe it, your Excellency?"

"I seemed to catch the faintest smell of tainted meat—a haunch or a side that had been left hanging for perhaps a week too long."

Kalten grunted. "I caught that, too, Sparhawk—just for a second, and it left a very bad taste in my mouth."

Emban nodded vigorously. "I'm an expert on flavors. It was definitely rotten meat."

"We were sort of standing in a semicircle," Sparhawk mused, "and we all saw—or sensed—it right behind us. Did any of you see it behind anybody else?"

They all shook their heads.

"Would you please explain this, Sparhawk?" Emban said irritably.

"In just a moment, your Grace." Sparhawk crossed the deck to a sailor who was splicing a loop into a bight of a rope. He spoke with the tar-smeared man for a few minutes and then returned.

"He saw it, too," he reported. "Let's spread out and talk with the rest of the sailors on deck. I'm not being deliberately secretive, gentlemen, but let's get what information we can from the sailors before they forget the incident entirely. I'd like to know just how widespread this visitation was."

It was about a half hour later when they gathered again near the aft companionway, and they had all begun to exhibit a kind of excitement.

"One of the sailors heard a kind of crackling noise—like a large fire," Kalten reported.

"I talked to one fellow, and he thought there was a kind of reddish tinge to the shadow," Oscagne added.

"No," Emban disagreed. "It was green. The sailor I talked with said that it was definitely green."

"And I spoke with a man who'd just come up on deck, and he hadn't seen or felt a thing," Sparhawk added.

"This is all very interesting, Sir Sparhawk," Oscagne said, "but could you *please* explain it to us?"

"Kalten already knows, your Excellency," Sparhawk replied. "It would appear that we've just been visited by the Troll-Gods."

"Be careful, Sparhawk," Emban warned, "you're walking on the edge of heresy."

"The Church Knights are permitted to do that, your Grace. Anyway, that shadow's followed me before, and Ehlana's seen it, too. We'd assumed it was because we were wearing the rings. The stones in the rings were fashioned from shards of the Bhelliom. The shadow seems to be a little less selective now."

"That's all it is? Just a shadow?" Oscagne asked him.

Sparhawk shook his head. "It can also show up as a very dark cloud, and everybody can see that."

"But not the things that are concealed in it," Kalten added.

"Such as what?" Oscagne asked.

Sparhawk gave Emban a quick sidelong glance. "It would start an argument, your Excellency, and we don't really want to spend the morning in a theological debate, do we?"

"I'm not all *that* doctrinaire, Sparhawk," Emban protested.

"What would be your immediate response if I told you that humans and Trolls are related, your Grace?"

"I'd have to investigate the condition of your soul."

"Then I'd probably better not tell you the truth about our cousins, wouldn't you say? Anyway, Aphrael told us that the shadow—and later the cloud—were manifestations of the Troll-Gods."

"Who's Aphrael?" Oscagne asked.

"We had a tutor in the Styric arts when we were novices, your Excellency," Sparhawk explained. "Aphrael is her Goddess. We thought that the cloud was somehow related to Azash, but we were wrong about that. The reddish color and the heat that one sailor sensed was Khwaj, the God of Fire. The greenish color and that rotten-meat smell was Ghnomb, the God of Eat."

Kalten was frowning. "I thought it was just one of those things you might expect from sailors," he said, "but one fellow told me that he had some rather overpowering thoughts about women while the shadow was lurking behind him. Don't the Trolls have a God of Mating?"

"I think so," Sparhawk replied. "Ulath would know."

"This is all very interesting, Sir Sparhawk," Oscagne said dubiously, "but I don't quite see its relevance."

"You've been encountering supernatural incidents that seem to be connected to the turmoil in Tamuli, your Excellency. There's almost exactly the same sort of disturbances cropping up in Lamorkand, and the same sort of unnatural events accompanying them. We were questioning a man who knew some things about it once, and the cloud engulfed him and killed him before he could talk. That strongly suggests some kind of connection. The shadow may have been present in Tamuli as well, but no one would have recognized it for what it really is."

"Zalasta was right, then," Oscagne murmured. "You *are* the man for this job."

"The Troll-Gods are following you again, Sparhawk," Kalten said. "What is this strange fascination they seem to have with you? We can probably discount your looks—but then again, maybe not. They're used to Trolls, after all."

Sparhawk looked meaningfully at the ship rail. "How would you like to run alongside the ship for a while, Kalten?"

"No, that's all right, Sparhawk. I got all the exertion I needed for the day when Mirtai decided to use me for a rug."

The wind held, and the sky remained clear. They rounded the southern tip of Zemoch and sailed up the east coast in a northeasterly direction. Once, when Sparhawk and his daughter were standing in the bow, he decided to satisfy a growing curiosity.

"How long have we actually been at sea, Danae?" he asked her directly.

"Five days," she replied.

"It seems like two weeks or more."

"Thank you, Father. Does that answer your question about how well I can manage time?"

"We certainly haven't eaten as much in five days as we would have in two weeks. Won't our cooks get suspicious?"

"Look behind us, Father. Why do you suppose all those fish are gleefully jumping out of the water? And what are all those seagulls doing following us?"

"Maybe they're feeding."

"Very perceptive, Sparhawk, but what could possibly be out there for that many of them to eat? Unless, of course, somebody's been throwing food to them off the aft deck."

"When do you do that?"

"At night." She shrugged. "The fish are terribly grateful. I think they're right on the verge of worshipping me." She laughed. "I've never been worshipped by fish before, and I don't really speak their language very well. It's mostly bubbles. Can I have a pet whale?"

"No. You've already got a kitten."

"I'll pout."

"It makes you look silly, but go ahead if you feel like it."

"*Why* can't I have a whale?"

"Because they can't be housebroken. They don't make good pets."

"That's a ridiculous answer, Sparhawk."

"It was a ridiculous request, Aphrael."

The port of Salesha at the head of the Gulf of Daconia was an ugly city that reflected the culture that had prevailed in Zemoch for nineteen hundred years. The Zemochs appeared to be confused by what had happened in their capital six years before. No matter how often they were assured that Otha and Azash were no more, they still tended to start violently at sudden loud noises and they generally reacted to any sort of surprise by running away.

"I'd strongly recommend that we spend the night on board our ships, your Majesty," Stragen advised the queen after he had made a brief survey of the accommodations available in the city. "I wouldn't kennel dogs in the finest house in Salesha."

"That bad?" she asked.

"Worse, my Queen."

And so they stayed on board and set out early the following morning. The road they followed north was truly bad, and the carriage in which the queen and her entourage rode jolted and creaked as their column wound up into the low range of mountains lying between the coast and the town of Basne. After they had been travelling for no more than an hour, Talen rode forward. As the queen's page, it was one of the boy's duties to carry messages for her. Talen was not alone on his horse this time, however. Sparhawk's daughter rode behind him, her arms about his waist and her cheek resting against his back. "She wants to ride with you," Talen told Sparhawk. "Your wife, Emban, and the ambassador are talking politics. The princess kept yawning in their faces until the queen gave her permission to get out of the carriage."

Sparhawk nodded. The suddenly acquired timidity of the Zemochs made this part of the trip fairly safe. He reached over and lifted his daughter onto Faran's back in front of his saddle. "I thought you liked politics," he said to her after Talen had returned to his post beside the carriage.

"Oscagne's describing the organization of the Tamul Empire," she replied. "I already know about that. He's not making too many mistakes."

"Are you going to shrink the distance from here to Basne?"

"Unless you enjoy long, tedious journeys through boring terrain. Faran and the other horses appreciate my shortening things up a bit, don't you, Faran?"

The big roan nickered enthusiastically.

"He's such a nice horse," Danae said, leaning back against her father's armored chest.

"Faran? He's a foul-tempered brute."

"That's because you expect him to be that way, Father. He's only trying to please you." She rapped on his armor. "I'm going to have to do something about this," she said. "How can you stand that awful smell?"

"You get used to it." The Church Knights were all wearing full armor, and brightly colored pennons snapped from their lances. Sparhawk looked around to be sure no one was close enough to overhear them. "Aphrael," he said quietly, "can you arrange things so that I can see real time?"

"Nobody can see time, Sparhawk."

"You know what I mean. I want to see what's really going on, not the illusion you create to keep what you're doing a secret."

"Why?"

"I like to know what's going on, that's all."

"You won't like it," she warned.

"I'm a Church Knight. I'm supposed to do things I don't like."

"If you insist, Father."

He was not entirely certain what he had expected—some jerky, accelerated motion, perhaps, and the voices of his friends sounding like the twittering of birds as they condensed long conversations into little bursts of unintelligible babble. That was not what happened, however. Faran's gait became impossibly smooth. The big horse seemed almost to flow across the ground—or, more properly, the ground seemed to flow back beneath his hooves. Sparhawk swallowed hard and looked around at his companions. Their faces seemed blank, wooden, and their eyes half-closed.

"They're sleeping just now," Aphrael explained. "They're all quite comfortable. They believe that they've had a good supper and that the sun's gone down. I fixed them a rather nice campsite. Stop the horse, Father. You can help me get rid of the extra food."

"Can't you just make it vanish?"

"And waste it?" She sounded shocked. "The birds and animals have to eat, too, you know."

"How long is it really going to take us to reach Basne?"

"Two days. We could go faster if there was an emergency, but there's nothing quite that serious going on just now."

Sparhawk reined in and followed his little daughter back to where the pack animals stood patiently. "You're keeping all of this in your head at the same time?" he asked her.

"It's not that difficult, Sparhawk. You just have to pay attention to details, that's all."

"You sound like Kurik."

"He'd have made an excellent God, actually. Attention to detail is the most important lesson we learn. Put that beef shoulder over near that tree with the broken-off top. There's a bear cub back in the bushes who got separated from his mother. He's very hungry."

"Do you keep track of every single thing that's happening around you?"

"Well, *somebody* has to, Sparhawk."

The Zemoch town of Basne lay in a pleasant valley where the main east–west road forded a small, sparkling river. It was a fairly important trading center. Not even Azash had been able to curb the natural human instinct to do business. There was an encampment just outside of town.

Sparhawk had dropped back to return Princess Danae to her mother, so he was riding beside the carriage as they started down into the valley.

Mirtai seemed uncharacteristically nervous as the carriage moved down toward the encampment.

"It appears that your admirer has obeyed your summons, Mirtai!" Baroness Melidere observed brightly.

"Of course," the giantess replied.

"It must be enormously satisfying to have such absolute control over a man."

"I rather like it," Mirtai admitted. "How do I look? Be honest, Melidere. I haven't seen Kring for months, and I wouldn't want to disappoint him."

"You're lovely, Mirtai."

"You're not just saying that?"

"Of course not."

"What do you think, Ehlana?" the Tamul woman appealed to her owner. Her tone was a bit uncertain.

"You're ravishing, Mirtai."

"I'll know better when I see his face," Mirtai paused. "Maybe I *should* marry him," she said. "I think I'd feel much more secure if I had my brand on him." She rose, opening the carriage door and leaning out to pull her tethered horse up from behind the carriage, and then quite literally flowed onto his back. Mirtai never used a saddle. "Well," she sighed, "I guess I'd better go down there and find out if he still loves me." And she tapped her heels into her horse's flanks and galloped on down into the valley to meet the waiting Domi.

CHAPTER NINE

The Peloi were nomadic herders from the marches of eastern Pelosia. They were superb horsemen and savage warriors. They spoke a somewhat archaic form of Elenic, and many of the words in their tongue had fallen out of use in the modern language. Among those words was *Domi,* a word filled with profoundest respect. It meant *Chief*—sort of—although, as Sir Ulath had once said, it lost a great deal in translation.

The current Domi of the Peloi was named Kring. Kring was a lean man of slightly more than medium height. As was customary among the men of his people, he shaved his head, and there were savage-looking saber scars on his scalp and face, an indication that the process of rising to a position of leadership among the Peloi involved a certain amount of rough-and-tumble competition. He wore black leather clothing, and a lifetime spent on horseback had made him bandy-legged. He was a fiercely loyal friend and he had worshipped Mirtai from the moment he had first seen her. Mirtai did not discourage him, although she refused to commit herself. They made an odd-looking couple, since the Atan woman towered more than a foot over her ardent suitor.

Peloi hospitality was generous, and the business of "taking salt together" usually involved enormous amounts of roasted meat, during the comsumption of which the men "spoke of affairs," a phrase with many implications, ranging in subject matter from the weather to formal declarations of war.

After they had eaten, Kring described what he had observed during the ride of the hundred Peloi across Zemoch. "It never really was a kingdom, friend Sparhawk," he said. "Not the way we understand the word. There are too many different kinds of people living in Zemoch for them all to come together under one roof. The only thing that kept them united was their fear of Otha and Azash. Now that their emperor and their God aren't there anymore, the Zemochs are just kind of drifting apart. There's not any sort of war or anything like that. It's just that they don't stay in touch with each other anymore. They all have their own concerns, so they don't really have any reason to talk to each other."

"Is there any kind of government at all?" Tynian asked the shaved-headed Domi.

"There's a sort of framework, friend Tynian," Kring replied. They were sitting in a large, open pavilion in the center of the Peloi encampment, feasting on roast ox. The sun was just going down and the shadows of the peaks lying to the west lay long across the pleasant valley. There were lights in the windows of Basne a half mile or so away. "The departments of Otha's government have all moved to Gana Dorit," Kring elaborated. "Nobody will even go near the city of Zemoch anymore. The bureaucrats in Gana Dorit spend their time writing directives, but their messengers usually just stop in the nearest village, tear up the directives, wait a suitable period of time, and then go back and tell their employers that all is going well. The bureaucrats are happy, the messengers don't have to travel very far, and the people go on about their business. Actually, it's not a bad form of government."

"And their religion?" Sir Bevier asked intently. Bevier was a devout young knight and he spent a great deal of his time talking and thinking about God. His companions liked him in spite of that.

"They don't speak very much about their beliefs, friend Bevier," Kring replied. "It was their religion that got them into trouble in the first place, so they're a bit shy about discussing the matter openly. They grow their crops, tend their sheep and goats, and let the Gods settle their own disputes. They're not a threat to anybody anymore."

"Except for the fact that a disintegrated nation is an open invitation to anyone nearby with anything even remotely resembling an army," Ambassador Oscagne added.

"Why would anyone want to bother, your Excellency?" Stragen asked him. "There's nothing in Zemoch of any value. The thieves there have to get honest jobs in order to make ends meet. Otha's gold appears to have been an illusion. It all vanished when Azash died." He smiled sardonically. "And you have no idea of how chagrined any number of people who'd supported the Primate of Cimmura were when that happened."

Just then, something rather peculiar happened to Kring's face. The savage horseman whose very name struck fear into the hearts of his neighbors went first pale, then bright red. Mirtai had emerged from the women's pavilion to which Peloi custom had relegated her and the others. Strangely, Queen Ehlana had not even objected, a fact that caused Sparhawk a certain nervousness. Mirtai had taken advantage of the accommodations within the pavilion to make herself "presentable." Kring, quite obviously, was impressed. "You'll excuse me," he said, rising quickly and moving directly toward the lodestar of his life.

"I think we're in the presence of a legend in the making," Tynian noted. "The Peloi will compose songs about Kring and Mirtai for the next hundred years at least." He looked at the Tamul ambassador. "Is Mirtai behaving at all the way other Atan women do, your Excellency? She obviously likes Kring's attentions, but she simply won't give him a definite answer."

"The Atana's doing what's customary, Sir Tynian," Oscagne replied. "Atan women believe in long, leisurely courtships. They find being pursued entertaining, and most men turn their attentions to other matters after the wedding. For this period of time in her life, she knows that she's the absolute center of the Domi's attention. Women, I'm told, appreciate that sort of thing."

"She wouldn't just be leading him on, would she?" Berit asked. "I like the Domi, and I'd hate to see him get his heart broken."

"Oh, no, Sir Berit. She's definitely interested. If she found his attentions annoying, she'd have killed him a long time ago."

"Courtship among the Atans must be a very nervous business," Kalten observed.

"Oh, yes." Oscagne laughed. "A man must be very careful. If he's too aggressive, the woman will kill him, and if he's not aggressive enough, she'll marry someone else."

"That's very uncivilized," Kalten said disapprovingly.

"Atan women seem to enjoy it, but then, women are more elemental than we are."

They left Basne early the following morning and rode eastward toward Esos on the border between Zemoch and the kingdom of Astel. It was a peculiar journey for Sparhawk. It took three days, he was absolutely certain of that. He could clearly remember every minute of those three days and every mile they travelled. And yet his daughter periodically roused him when he was firmly convinced that he was sleeping in a tent, and he would be startled to find that he was dozing on Faran's back instead and that the position of the sun clearly indicated that what had appeared to be a full day's travel had taken less than six hours. Princess Danae woke her father for a very practical reason during what was in reality no more than a one-day ride. The addition of the Peloi had greatly increased the amount of stores that had to be carefully depleted each "night," and Danae made her father help her dispose of the excess.

"What did you do with all the supplies when we were travelling with Wargun's army?" Sparhawk asked her on the second "night," which actually consumed about a half hour during the early afternoon of that endless day.

"I did it the other way." She shrugged.

"Other way?"

"I just made the excess go away."

"Couldn't you do that this time, too?"

"Of course, but then I couldn't leave it for the animals. Besides, this gives you and me the chance to talk when nobody's around to hear us. Pour that sack of grain under those bushes, Sparhawk. There's a covey of quail back in the grass. They haven't been eating very well lately, and the chicks are growing very fast right now."

"Was there something you wanted to talk about?" he asked her, slitting open the grain sack with his dagger.

"Nothing special," she said. "I just like talking with you, and you're usually too busy."

"And this gives you a chance to show off, too, doesn't it?"

"I suppose it does, yes. It's not all that much fun being a Goddess if you can't show off just a little bit now and then."

"I love you." He laughed.

"Oh, that's *very* nice, Sparhawk!" she exclaimed happily. "Right from the heart and without even thinking about it. Would you like to have me turn the grass lavender for you—just to show my appreciation?"

"I'll settle for a kiss. Lavender grass might confuse the horses."

They reached Esos that evening. The Child-Goddess so perfectly melded real and apparent time that they fit together seamlessly. Sparhawk was a Church Knight, trained in the use of magic, but his imagination shuddered back from the kind of power possessed by this whimsical little divinity who—she had announced during the confrontation with Azash in the City of Zemoch—had willed herself into existence, and who had decided independently to be reborn as his daughter.

They set up for the night some distance from town, and after they had eaten, Talen and Stragen took Sparhawk aside. "What's your feeling about a bit of reconnoitering?" Stragen asked the big Pandion.

"What did you have in mind?"

"Esos is a fair-sized town," the blond Thalesian replied, "and there's sure to be a certain amount of organization among the thieves there. I thought the three of us might be able to pick up some useful information by getting in touch with their leader."

"Would he know you?"

"I doubt it. Emsat's a long way away from here."

"What makes you think he'd want to talk with you?"

"Courtesy, Sparhawk. Thieves and murderers are exquisitely courteous to each other. It's healthier that way."

"If he doesn't know who you are, how will he know that he's supposed to be courteous toward you?"

"There are certain signals he'll recognize."

"You people have a very complex society, don't you?"

"All societies are complex, Sparhawk. It's one of the burdens of civilization."

"Someday you'll have to teach me these signals."

"No, I don't think so."

"Why not?"

"Because you're not a thief. It's another of those complexities we were talking about. The point of all of this is that all we have to work with is the ambassador's rather generalized notion of what's going on. I think I'd like something a bit more specific, wouldn't you?"

"That I would, my friend."

"Then why don't we drift on into Esos and see what we can find out?"

"Why don't we?"

The three of them changed into nondescript clothing and rode away from the encampment, circling around to the west to approach the town from that direction.

As they approached, Talen looked critically at the fortifications and the unguarded gate. "They seem a little relaxed when you consider how close they are to the Zemoch border," he observed.

"Zemoch doesn't pose much of a threat anymore," Stragen disagreed.

"Old customs die hard, Milord Stragen, and it hasn't been all *that* long since Otha was frothing at the frontier with Azash standing right behind him."

"I doubt that these people found Azash to be all that impressive," Sparhawk said. "Otha's God didn't have any reason to come this way. He was looking west, because that's where Bhelliom was."

"I suppose you're right," Talen conceded.

Esos was not a very large town, perhaps about the size of the city of Lenda in central Elenia. There was a kind of archaic quality about it, though, since there had been a town on this spot since the dawn of time. The cobbled streets were narrow and crooked, and they wandered this way and that without any particular reason.

"How are we going to find the part of town where your colleagues stay?" Sparhawk asked Stragen. "We can't just walk up to some burgher and ask him where we'll find the thieves, can we?"

"We'll take care of it." Stragen smiled. "Talen, go ask some pickpocket where the thieves' den is around here?"

"Right." Talen grinned, slipping down from his horse.

"That could take him all night," Sparhawk said.

"Not unless he's been struck blind," Stragen replied as the boy moved off into a crowded byway. "I've seen six pickpockets since we came into town, and I wasn't even looking very hard." He pursed his lips. "Their technique's a little different here. It probably has to do with the narrow streets."

"What would that have to do with it?"

"People jostle each other in tight quarters." Stragen shrugged. "A pickpocket in Emsat or Cimmura could never get away with bumping into a client the way they do here. It's more efficient, I'll grant you, but it establishes bad work habits."

Talen returned after a few minutes. "It's down by the river," he reported.

"Inevitably," Stragen said. "Something seems to draw thieves to rivers. I've never been able to figure out why."

Talen shrugged. "It's probably so that we can swim for it in case things go wrong. We'd better walk. Mounted men attract too much attention. There's a stable down at the end of the street where we can leave the horses."

They spoke briefly with the surly stableman and then proceeded on foot.

The thieves' den in Esos was in a shabby tavern at the rear of a narrow cul-de-sac. A crude sign depicting a bunch of grapes hung from a rusty hook just over the door, and a pair of burly loafers sprawled on the doorstep drinking ale from battered tankards.

"We're looking for a man named Djukta," Talen told them.

"What was it about?" one of the loafers growled suspiciously.

"Business," Stragen told him in a cold tone.

"Anybody could say that," the unshaven man said, rising to his feet with a thick cudgel in his hand.

"This is always so tedious," Stragen sighed to Sparhawk. Then his hand flashed to the hilt of his rapier, and the slim blade came whistling out of its sheath. "Friend," he said to the loafer, "unless you want three feet of steel between your breakfast and your supper, you'll stand aside." The needlelike point of the rapier touched the man's belly suggestively.

The other ruffian sidled off to one side, his hand reaching furtively toward the handle of his dagger.

"I wouldn't," Sparhawk warned him in a dreadfully quiet voice. He pushed his cloak aside to reveal his mail shirt and the hilt of his broadsword. "I'm not entirely positive where your breakfast or your supper are located just now, neighbor, but I'll probably be able to pick them out when your guts are lying in the street."

The fellow froze in his tracks, swallowing hard.

"The knife," Sparhawk grated. "Lose it."

The dagger clattered to the cobblestones.

"I'm so happy that we could resolve this little problem without unpleasantness," Stragen drawled. "Now why don't we all go inside so you can introduce us to Djukta?"

The tavern had a low ceiling and the floor was covered with moldy straw. It was lighted by a few crude lamps that burned melted tallow.

Djukta was by far the hairiest man Sparhawk had ever seen. His arms and hands seemed to be covered with curly black fur. Great wads of hair protruded from the neck of his tunic; his ears and nostrils looked like birds' nests; and his beard began just under his lower eyelids. "What's this?" he demanded, his voice issuing from somewhere behind his shaggy rug of a face.

"They made us let them come inside, Djukta," one of the men from the doorway whined, pointing at Stragen's rapier.

Djukta's piggish eyes narrowed dangerously.

"Don't be tiresome," Stragen told him, "and pay attention. I've given you the recognition signal twice already, and you didn't even notice."

"I noticed, but coming in here with a sword in your hand isn't the best way to get things off to a good start."

"We were a little pressed for time. I think we're being followed." Stragen sheathed his rapier.

"You're not from around here, are you?"

"No. We're from Eosia."

"You're a long way from home."

"That was sort of the idea. Things were getting unhealthy back there."

"What line are you in?"

"We're vagabonds at heart, so we were seeking fame and fortune on the high-ways and byways of Pelosia. A high-ranking churchman suddenly fell ill and died while we were talking business with him, and the Church Knights decided to inves-tigate the causes of his illness. My friends and I decided to find fresh scenery to look at right about then."

"Are those Church Knights really as bad as they say?"

"Worse, probably. The three of us are all that's left of a band of thirty."

"Are you planning to go into business around here?"

"We haven't decided yet. We thought we'd look things over first—and make sure that the knights aren't still following us."

"Do you feel like telling us your names?"

"Not particularly. We're not sure we're going to stay, and there's not much point in making up new names if we're not going to settle down."

Djukta laughed. "If you aren't sure you're going into business, what's the reason for this visit?"

"Courtesy, for the most part. It's terribly impolite not to pay a call on one's col-leagues when one's passing through a town, and we thought it might save a bit of time if you could spare a few minutes to give us a rundown on local practices in the field of law enforcement."

"I've never been to Eosia, but I'd imagine that things like that are fairly stan-dard. Highwaymen aren't held in high regard."

"We're so misunderstood." Stragen sighed. "They have the usual sheriffs and the like, I suppose?"

"There are sheriffs, right enough," Djukta said, "but they don't go out into the countryside very often in this part of Astel. The nobles out there more or less police their own estates. The sheriffs are usually involved in collecting taxes, and they aren't all that welcome when they ride out of town."

"That's useful. All we'd really have to deal with would be poorly trained serfs who fare better at catching chicken thieves than at dealing with serious people. Is that more or less the way it is?"

Djukta nodded. "The good part is that these serf-sheriffs won't go past the bor-ders of their own estate."

"That's a highwayman's dream." Stragen grinned.

"Not entirely," Djukta disagreed. "It's not a good idea to make too much noise out there. The local sheriff wouldn't chase you, but he *would* send word to the Atan garrison up in Canae. A man can't run far enough or fast enough to get away from the Atans, and nobody's ever taught them how to take prisoners."

"That could be a drawback," Stragen conceded. "Is there anything else we should know about?"

"Did you ever hear of Ayachin?"

"I can't say that I have."

"That could get you into all kinds of trouble."

"Who is he?"

Djukta turned his head. "Akros," he yelled, "come here and tell these colleagues of ours about Ayachin." He shrugged and spread his hands. "I'm not too well versed in ancient history," he explained. "Akros used to be a teacher before he got caught stealing from his employer. He may not be too coherent. He has a little problem with drink."

Akros was a shabby-looking fellow with bloodshot eyes and a five-day growth of beard. "What was it you wanted, Djukta?" he asked, swaying on his feet.

"Sort through what's left of your brain and tell our friends here what you can remember about Ayachin."

The drunken pedagogue smiled, his bleary eyes coming alight. He slid into a chair and took a drink from his tankard. "I'm only a little drunk," he said, his speech slurred.

"That's true," Djukta told Stragen. "When he's really drunk, he can't even talk."

"How much do you gentlemen know of the history of Astel?" Akros asked them.

"Not too much," Stragen admitted.

"I'll touch the high spots then." Akros leaned back in his chair. "It was in the ninth century that one of the Archprelates in Chyrellos decided that the Elene faith ought to be reunited—under his domination, naturally."

"Naturally." Stragen smiled. "It always seems to get down to that, doesn't it?"

Akros rubbed at his face. "I'm a little shaky on this, so I might leave some things out. This was before the founding of the Church Knights, so this Archprelate forced the kings of Eosia to provide him with armies, and they marched through Zemoch. That was before Otha was born, so Zemoch wasn't much of a barrier. The Archprelate was interested in religious unity, but the noblemen in his army were more interested in conquest. They ravaged the kingdom of Astel until Ayachin came."

Talen leaned forward, his eyes bright. It was the boy's one weakness. A good story could paralyze him.

Akros took another drink. "There are all sorts of conflicting stories about who Ayachin really was," he continued. "Some say he was a prince, some that he was a baron, and there are even those who say he was only a serf. Anyway, whoever he was, he was a fervent patriot. He roused such noblemen as hadn't yet gone over to the invaders, and then he did something no one had ever dared do before. He armed the serfs. The campaign against the invaders lasted for years, and after a fairly large battle that he *seemed* to lose, Ayachin fled southward, luring the Eosian armies into the

Astel marshes in the south of the kingdom. He'd made secret alliances with patriots in Edom, and there was a huge army lining the southern fringe of the marshes. Serfs who lived in the region guided Ayachin's armies through the bogs and quicksand, but the Eosians tried to just bull their way through, and most of them drowned, pulled under by all that muck. The few who reached the far side were slaughtered by the combined forces of Ayachin and his Edomish allies.

"He was a great national hero for a time, of course, but the nobles who had been outraged because he'd armed the serfs conspired against him, and he was eventually murdered."

"Why do these stories always have to end that way?" Talen complained.

"Our young friend here is a literary critic," Stragen said. "He wants his stories to all have happy endings."

"The ancient history is all well and good," Djukta growled, "but the point of all this is that Ayachin's returned—or so the serfs say."

"It's a part of the folklore of Astel," Akros said. "Serfs used to tell each other that someday a great crisis would arise, and that Ayachin would rise from the grave to lead them again."

Stragen sighed. "Can't anyone come up with a new story?"

"What's that?" Djukta asked him.

"Nothing, really. There's a similar story making the rounds in Eosia. Why would this concern us if we decided to go into business around here?"

"Part of that folklore Akros was telling you about is something that makes everybody's blood run cold. The serfs believe that when Ayachin returns, he's going to emancipate them. Now there's a hothead out there stirring them up. We don't know his real name, but the serfs call him 'Sabre.' He's going around telling them that he's actually seen Ayachin. The serfs are secretly gathering weapons—or making them. They sneak out into the forests at night to listen to this 'Sabre' make speeches. You should probably know that they're out there, since it might be dangerous if you happened upon them unexpectedly." Djukta scratched at his shaggy beard. "I don't normally feel this way, but I wish the government would catch this Sabre fellow and hang him or something. He's got the serfs all worked up about throwing off the oppressors, and he's not too specific about which oppressors he means. He could be talking about the Tamuls, but many of his followers think he's talking about the upper classes. Restless serfs are dangerous serfs. Nobody knows how many of them there really are, and if they begin to get wild ideas about equality and justice, God only knows where it might end."

CHAPTER TEN

"There are just too many similarities for it to be a coincidence," Sparhawk was saying the following morning as they rode northeasterly along the Darsas road under a lowering sky. He and his companions had gathered around Ehlana's carriage to discuss Djukta's revelations. The air was close and muggy, and there was not a breath of air stirring.

"I'd almost have to agree," Ambassador Oscagne replied. "There's a certain pattern emerging here, if what you've told me about Lamorkand is at all accurate. Our empire is certainly not democratic, and I'd imagine that your western kingdoms are much the same; but we're not really such hard masters—either of us. I think we've become the symbols of the social injustices implicit in every culture. I'm not saying that people don't hate us. Everybody in the world loathes his government—no offense intended, your Majesty." He smiled at Ehlana.

"I do what I can to keep my people from hating me too much, your Excellency," she replied. Ehlana wore a pale blue velvet travelling cloak, and Sparhawk felt that she looked particularly pretty this morning.

"No one could possibly hate someone as lovely as you, your Majesty." Oscagne smiled. "The point, though, is that the world seethes with discontent, and someone is playing on all those disparate resentments in an effort to bring down the established order—the empire here in Tamuli and the monarchies and the Church in Eosia. Somebody wants there to be a great deal of turmoil, and I don't think he's motivated by a hunger for social justice."

"We'd go a long way toward understanding the situation if we could pinpoint just exactly what he *is* after," Emban added.

"Opportunity," Ulath suggested. "If everything's all settled and the wealth and power have all been distributed, there's nothing left for the people coming up the ladder. The only way they can get their share is to turn everything upside down and shake it a few times."

"That's a brutal political theory, Sir Ulath," Oscagne said disapprovingly.

"It's a brutal world, your Excellency." Ulath shrugged.

"I'd have to disagree," Bevier stubbornly asserted.

"Go right ahead, my young friend." Ulath smiled. "I don't mind all that much when people disagree with me."

"There *is* such a thing as genuine political progress. The people's lot is much better now than it was five hundred years ago."

"Granted, but what's it going to be like next year?" Ulath leaned back in his saddle, his blue eyes speculative. "Ambitious people need followers, and the best way to get people to follow you is to promise them that you're going to correct everything that's wrong with the world. The promises are all very stirring, but only babies expect leaders to actually keep them."

"You're a cynic, Ulath."

"I think that's the word people use, yes."

The weather grew increasingly threatening as the morning progressed. A thick bank of purplish cloud marched steadily in from the west, and there were flickers of lightning along the horizon. "It's going to rain, isn't it?" Tynian asked Khalad.

Khalad looked pointedly toward the cloud bank. "That's a fairly safe bet, Sir Knight," the young man replied.

"How long until we start to get wet?"

"An hour or so—unless the wind picks up."

"What do you think, Sparhawk?" Tynian asked. "Should we look for some kind of shelter?"

There was a far-off rumble of thunder from the west.

"I think that answers that question," Sparhawk decided. "Men dressed in steel don't have any business being out in a thunderstorm."

"Good point," Tynian agreed. He looked around. "The next question is where? I don't see any woods around."

"We might have to set up the tents."

"That's awfully tedious, Sparhawk."

"So's being fried in your armor if you get struck by lightning."

Kring came riding back toward the main column with a small, two-wheeled carriage following him. The man in the carriage was blond, plump, and soft-looking. He wore clothing cut in a style that had gone out of fashion in the west forty years ago. "This is the landowner Kotyk," the Domi said to Sparhawk. "He calls himself a baron. He wanted to meet you."

"I am overwhelmed to meet the stalwarts of the Church, Sir Knights," the plump man gushed.

"We are honored, Baron Kotyk," Sparhawk replied, inclining his head politely.

"My manor house is nearby," Kotyk rushed on, "and I do foresee unpleasant weather on the horizon. Might I offer my poor hospitality?"

"As I've told you so many times in the past, Sparhawk," Bevier said mildly, "you have but to put your trust in God. He will provide."

Kotyk looked puzzled.

"A somewhat feeble attempt at humor, my Lord," Sparhawk explained. "My companions and I were just discussing our need for shelter. Your most generous offer solves a rather vexing problem for us." Sparhawk was not familiar with local customs, but the baron's ornate speech hinted at a somewhat stiff formality.

"I note that you have ladies in your company," Kotyk observed, looking toward the carriage in which Ehlana rode. "Their comfort must be our first concern. We can become better acquainted once we are safely under my roof."

"We shall be guided by you, my Lord," Sparhawk agreed. "I pray you, lead us whither you will, and I shall inform the ladies of this fortuitous encounter." If Kotyk wanted formal, Sparhawk would give him formal. He wheeled Faran and rode back along the column.

"Who's the fat fellow in the carriage, Sparhawk?" Ehlana asked.

"Speak not disparagingly of our host, light of my life."

"Aren't you feeling well?"

"The fat fellow has just offered us shelter from that thunderstorm snapping at our heels. Treat him with gratitude if not respect."

"What a nice man."

"It might not be a bad idea for us to sort of keep your identity to ourselves. We don't know exactly what we're walking into. Why don't I just introduce you as an aristocrat of some kind, and—"

"A margravine, I think," she improvised. "Margravine Ehlana of Cardos."

"Why Cardos?"

"It's a nice district with mountains and a beautiful coastline. Absolutely perfect climate and industrious, law-abiding people."

"You're not trying to sell it to him, Ehlana."

"But I need to know the pertinent details so that I can gush suitably."

Sparhawk sighed. "All right, my Lady, practice gushing, then, and come up with suitable stories for the others." He looked at Emban. "Are your morals flexible enough to stand a bit of falsehood, your Grace?" he asked.

"That depends on what you want me to lie about, Sparhawk."

"It won't exactly be a lie, your Grace." Sparhawk smiled. "If we demote my wife, you'll be the ranking member of our party. The presence of Ambassador Oscagne here suggests a high-level visit of some sort. I'll just tell Baron Kotyk that you're the Archprelate's personal emissary to the imperial court, and that the knights are *your* escort instead of the queen's."

"That doesn't stretch my conscience too far." Emban grinned. "Go ahead, Sparhawk. You lie, and I'll swear to it. Say whatever you have to. That storm is coming this way very fast."

"Talen," Sparhawk said to the boy, who was riding beside the carriage, "sort of move up and down the column and let the knights know what we're doing. A misplaced 'your Majesty' or two could expose us all as frauds."

"Your husband shows some promise, Margravine Ehlana," Stragen noted. "Give me some time to train him a bit, and I'll make an excellent swindler of him. His instincts are good, but his technique's a little shaky."

Baron Kotyk's manor house was a palatial residence in a parklike setting, and there was a fair-sized village at the foot of the hill upon which it stood. There were a number of large outbuildings standing to the rear of the main house. "Fortunately, Sir Knights, I have ample room for even so large a party as yours," the baron told them. "The quarters for the bulk of your men may be a bit crude, though, I'm afraid. They're dormitories for the harvest crew."

"We're Church Knights, my Lord Kotyk," Sparhawk replied. "We're accustomed to hardship."

Kotyk sighed. "We have no such institution here in Astel," he mourned. "There are so many things lacking in our poor, backward country." They approached the manor house by a long, white-gravelled drive lined on both sides by lofty elms and halted at the foot of the broad stone stairs leading up to an arched front door. The baron climbed heavily down from his carriage and handed his reins to one of the bearded serfs who had rushed from the house to meet them. "I pray you, gentles all," he said, "stand not on ceremony. Let us enter ere the approaching storm descend upon us."

Sparhawk could not be certain if the baron's stilted speech was a characteristic of the country, a personal idiosyncrasy, or a nervous reaction to the rank of his visitors. He motioned to Kalten and Tynian. "See to it that the knights and the Peloi are settled in," he told them quietly. "Then join us in the house. Khalad, go with them. Make sure that the serfs don't just leave the horses standing out in the rain."

The door to the manor house swung wide, and three ladies dressed in antiquated gowns emerged. One was tall and angular. She had a wealth of dark hair and the lingering traces of youthful beauty. The years had not been kind to her, however. Her rigid, haughty face was lined, and she had a noticeable squint. The other two were both blond, flabby, and their features clearly revealed a blood relationship to the baron. Behind them came a pale young man dressed all in black velvet. He seemed to have a permanent sneer stamped on his face. His dark hair was done in long curls that cascaded down his back in an artfully arranged display.

After the briefest of introductions Kotyk led them all inside. The tall, dark-haired lady was the baron's wife, Astansia. The two blondes were, as Sparhawk had guessed, his sisters, Ermude the elder and Katina the younger. The pale young man was Baroness Astansia's brother, Elron—who, she proudly advised them in a voice hovering on the verge of adoration, was a poet.

"Do you think I could get away with pleading a sick headache?" Ehlana murmured to Sparhawk as they followed the baron and his family down a long, tapestry-lined corridor toward the center of the house. "This is going to be deadly, I'm afraid."

"If I have to put up with it, so do you," Sparhawk whispered. "We need the baron's roof, so we'll have to endure his hospitality."

She sighed. "It might be a little more endurable if the whole place didn't reek of cooked cabbage."

They were led into a "sitting room" that was only slightly smaller than the throne room in Cimmura, a musty-smelling room filled with stiff, uncomfortable chairs and divans and carpeted in an unwholesome-looking mustard yellow.

"We are so isolated here," Katina sighed to the Baroness Melidere, "and so dreadfully out of fashion. My poor brother tries as best he can to keep abreast of what's happening in the west, but our remote location imprisons us and keeps visitors from our door. Ermude and I have tried over and over to persuade him to take a house in the capital where we can be near the center of things, but *she* won't hear of it. The estate came to my brother by marriage, and his wife's so terribly provincial. Would you believe that my poor sister and I are forced to have our gowns made up by *serfs*?"

Melidere put her palms to her cheeks in feigned shock. "My goodness!" she exclaimed.

Katina reached for her handkerchief as tears of misery began to roll down her cheeks.

"Wouldn't your Atan be more comfortable with the serfs, Margravine?" Baroness Astansia was asking Ehlana, looking with some distaste at Mirtai.

"I rather doubt it, Baroness," Ehlana replied, "and even if she were, *I* wouldn't be. I have powerful enemies, my Lady, and my husband is much involved in the affairs of Elenia. The queen relies heavily upon him, and so I must look to my own defenses."

"I'll admit that your Atan is imposing, Margravine," Astansia sniffed, "but she's still only a woman, after all."

Ehlana smiled. "You might tell that to the ten men she's already killed, Baroness," she replied.

The baroness stared at her in horror.

"The Eosian continent has a thin veneer of civilization, my Lady," Stragen advised her, "but underneath it all, we're really quite savage."

"It's a tedious journey, Baron Kotyk," Patriarch Emban said, "but the Archprelate and the emperor have been in communication with each other since the collapse of Zemoch, and they both feel that the time has come to exchange personal envoys. Misunderstandings can arise in the absence of direct contact, and the world has seen enough of war for a while."

"A wise decision, your Grace." Kotyk was quite obviously overwhelmed by the presence of people of exalted station in his house.

"I have some small reputation in the capital, Sir Bevier," Elron was saying in a lofty tone of voice. "My poems are eagerly sought after by the intelligentsia. They're quite beyond the grasp of the unlettered, however. I'm particularly noted for my ability to convey colors. I *do* think that color is the very soul of the real world. I've been working on my *Ode to Blue* for the past six months."

"Astonishing perseverance," Bevier murmured.

"I try to be as thorough as possible," Elron declared. "I've already composed 263 stanzas, and there's no end in sight, I'm afraid."

Bevier sighed. "As a Knight of the Church, I have little time for literature," he mourned. "Because of my vocation, I must concentrate on military texts and devotional works. Sir Sparhawk is more worldly than I, and his descriptions of people and places verge sometimes on the poetic."

"I should be most interested," Elron lied, his face revealing a professional's contempt for the efforts of amateurs. "Does he touch at all on color?"

"More with light, I believe," Bevier replied, "but then they're the same thing, aren't they? Color doesn't exist without light. I remember that once he described a street in the city of Jiroch. The city lies on the coast of Rendor where the sun pounds the earth like a hammer. Very early in the morning, before the sun rises, and when the night is just beginning to fade, the sky has the color of forged steel. It casts no shadows, and so everything seems etched by that sourceless grey. The buildings in Jiroch are all white, and the women go to the wells before the sun comes up to avoid the heat of the day. They wear hooded robes and veils all in black and they balance clay vessels on their shoulders. All untaught, they move with a grace beyond the capability of dancers. Their silent, beautiful procession marks each day's beginning as, like shadows, they greet the dawn in a ritual as old as time. Have you ever seen that peculiar light before the sun rises, Elron?"

"I seldom rise before noon," the young man said stiffly.

"You should make an effort to see it sometime," Bevier suggested mildly. "An artist should be willing to make some sacrifices for his art, after all."

"I trust you'll excuse me," the young fellow with the dark curls said brusquely. He bowed slightly and then fled, a mortified expression replacing his supercilious sneer.

"That was cruel, Bevier," Sparhawk chided, "and you put words in my mouth. I'll admit that you have a certain flair for language, though."

"It had the desired effect, Sparhawk. If that conceited young ass had patronized me one more time, I'd have strangled him. Two hundred some-odd verses in an ode to the color blue? What a donkey!"

"The next time he bothers you about blue, describe Bhelliom to him."

Bevier shuddered. "Not me, Sparhawk. Just the thought of it makes my blood run cold."

Sparhawk laughed and went over to the window to look at the rain slashing at the glass.

Danae came to his side and took his hand. "Do we really have to stay here, Father?" she asked. "These people turn my stomach."

"We need some place to shelter us from the rain, Danae."

"I can make it stop raining, if that's all you're worried about. If one of those disgusting women starts talking baby talk to me one more time, I'm going to turn her into a toad."

"I think I have a better idea." Sparhawk bent and picked her up. "Act sleepy," he instructed.

Danae promptly went limp and dangled from his arms like a rag doll.

"You're overdoing it," he told her. He crossed to the far side of the room, gently laid her on a divan, and covered her with her travelling cloak. "Don't snore," he advised. "You're not old enough to snore yet."

She gave him an innocent little look. "I wouldn't do that, Sparhawk. Find my cat and bring her to me." Then her smile turned hard. "Pay close attention to our host and his family, Father. I think you should see what kind of people they *really* are."

"What are you up to?"

"Nothing. I just think you should see what they're *really* like."

"I can see quite enough already."

"No, not really. They're trying to be polite, so they're glossing over things. Let's take a look at the truth. For the rest of the evening, they'll tell you what they *really* think and feel."

"I'd rather they didn't."

"You're supposed to be brave, Sparhawk, and this horrid little family is typical of the gentry here in Astel. Once you understand them, you'll be able to see what's wrong with the kingdom. It might be useful." Her eyes and face grew serious. "There's something here, Sparhawk—something we absolutely have to know."

"What?"

"I'm not sure. Pay attention, Father. Somebody's going to tell you something important tonight. Now go find my cat."

The supper they were offered was poorly prepared, and the conversation at the table was dreadful. Freed of constraint by Danae's spell, the baron and his family said things they might normally have concealed, and their spiteful, self-pitying vanity emerged all the more painfully under the influence of the inferior wine they all swilled like common tavern drunkards.

"I was not intended for this barbaric isolation," Katina tearfully confided to poor Melidere. "Surely God could not have meant for me to bloom unnoticed so far from the lights and gaiety of the capital. We were cruelly deceived before my brother's marriage to that dreadful woman. Her parents led us to believe that the estate would bring us wealth and position, but it scarcely provides enough to keep us in this hovel. There's no hope that we shall ever be able to afford a house in Darsas." She buried her face in her hands. "What shall become of me?" she wailed. "The lights, the balls, the hordes of suitors flocking to my door, dazzled by my wit and beauty."

"Oh, don't cry, Katina," Ermude wailed. "If you cry, I shall surely cry, too." The sisters were so similar in appearance that Sparhawk had some difficulty telling them apart. Their plumpness was more like dough than flesh. Their colorless hair was limp and uninspired, and their complexions were bad. Neither of them was really very clean. "I try so hard to protect my poor sister," Ermude blubbered to the long-suffering Melidere, "but this dreadful place is destroying her. There's no culture here. We live like beasts—like serfs. It's so meaningless. Life should have meaning, but what possible meaning can there be so far from the capital? That horrid woman won't permit our poor brother to sell this desolate waste so that we can take a proper residence in Darsas. We're trapped here—trapped, I tell you—and we shall live out our lives in this hideous isolation." Then she, too, buried her face in her hands and wept.

Melidere sighed, rolling her eyes ceilingward.

"I have some influence with the governor of the district," Baron Kotyk was telling Patriarch Emban with pompous self-importance. "He relies heavily on my judgment. We've been having a deuce of a time with the burghers in town—untitled rascals, every one of them—runaway serfs, if the truth were known. They complain bitterly at each new tax and try to shift the burden to *us*. We pay quite enough in taxes already, thank you, and *they're* the ones who are demanding all the services. What good does it do *me* if the streets in town are paved. It's the roads that are important. I've said that to his Excellency the governor over and over again."

The baron was deep in his cups. His voice was slurred, and his head wobbled on his neck. "All the burdens of the district are placed on *our* shoulders," he declared, his eyes filling with self-pitying tears. "I must support five hundred idle serfs—serfs so lazy that not even flogging can get any work out of them. It's all so unfair. I'm an aristocrat, but that doesn't count for anything anymore." The tears began to roll down his cheeks, and his nose started to run. "No one seems to realize that the aristocracy is God's special gift to mankind. The burghers treat us no better than commoners. Considering our divine origins, such disrespect is the worst form of impiety. I'm sure your Grace agrees." The baron sniffed loudly.

Patriarch Emban's father had been a tavern keeper in the city of Ucera, and Sparhawk was fairly sure that the fat little churchman most definitely did *not* agree.

Ehlana had been trapped by the baron's wife and she was beginning to look a little desperate.

"The estate's *mine,* of course," Astansia declared in a coldly haughty voice. "My father was in his dotage when he married me off to that fat swine." She sneered. "Kotyk only had those piggish little eyes of his on the income from *my* estate. My father was so impressed with the idiot's title that he couldn't see him for what he really is, a titled opportunist with two fat, ugly sisters hanging from his coattails." She sneered, and then the sneer slid from her face, and the inevitable tears filled her eyes. "I can only find solace for my tragic state in religion, my beloved brother's art, and in the satisfaction I take in making absolutely sure those two harridans never see the lights of Darsas. They'll rot here—right up until the moment my pig of a husband eats and drinks himself to death. Then I shall turn them out with nothing but the clothes on their backs." Her hard eyes became exultant. "I can hardly wait," she said fiercely. "I *shall* have my revenge, and then my sainted brother and I can live here in perfect contentment."

Princess Danae crawled up into her father's lap. "Lovely people, aren't they?" she said quietly.

"Are you making all this up?" he asked accusingly.

"No, Father, I can't do that. None of us can. People are what they are. We can't change them."

"I thought you could do anything."

"There *are* limits, Sparhawk." Her dark eyes grew hard again. "I am going to do *something,* though."

"Oh?"

"Your Elene God owes me a couple of favors. I did something nice for him once."

"Why do you need *his* help?"

"These people are Elenes. They belong to him. I can't do anything to them without his permission. That's the worst form of bad manners."

"I'm an Elene, and you do things to me."

"You're Anakha, Sparhawk. You don't belong to anybody."

"That's depressing. I'm loose in the world with no God to guide me?"

"You don't need guidance. Advice sometimes, yes. Guidance, no."

"Don't do anything exotic here," he cautioned. "We don't know exactly what we'll be dealing with when we get deeper into Tamuli. Let's not announce our presence until we have to." Then his curiosity got the better of him. "Nobody's said anything very relevant yet."

"Then keep listening, Sparhawk. It *will* come."

"Exactly what were you planning to ask God to do to these people?"

"Nothing," she replied. "Absolutely nothing at all. I won't ask him to do a thing to change their circumstances. All I want him to do is to make sure that they all live very, very long lives."

He looked around the table at the petulant faces of their host's family. "You're going to imprison them here," he accused, "chain five people who loathe each other together for all eternity so that they can gradually tear each other to pieces."

"Not quite eternity, Sparhawk," the little girl corrected. "Though it's probably going to seem that way to them."

"That's cruel."

"No, Sparhawk. It's justice. These people richly deserve each other. I only want to be sure that they have a long time to enjoy each other's company."

"What's your feeling about a breath of fresh air?" Stragen asked, leaning over Sparhawk's shoulder.

"It's raining out there."

"I don't think you'll melt."

"Maybe it's not a bad idea at that." Sparhawk rose to his feet and carried his sleeping daughter back into the sitting room and the divan where Mmrr drowsed, purring absently and kneading one of the cushions with her needle-sharp claws. He covered them both and followed Stragen into the corridor. "Are you feeling restless?" he asked the Thalesian.

"No, revolted. I've known some of the worst people in the world, my friend, and I'm no angel myself, but this little family . . ." He shuddered. "Did you happen to lay in a store of poison while you were in Rendor?"

"I don't approve of poison."

"A bit shortsighted there, old boy. Poison's a tidy way to deal with intolerable people."

"Annias felt much the same way, as I recall."

"I'd forgotten about that," Stragen admitted. "I imagine that prejudiced you slightly against a very practical solution to a sticky problem. Something really ought to be done about these monsters, though."

"It's already been taken care of."

"Oh? How?"

"I'm not at liberty to say."

They stepped out onto the wide veranda that ran across the back of the house and stood leaning on the railing looking out into the muddy backyard.

"It doesn't show any signs of letting up, does it?" Stragen said. "How long can it continue at this time of year?"

"You'll have to ask Khalad. He's the expert on the weather."

"My Lords?"

Stragen and Sparhawk turned.

It was Elron, the baron's poetic brother-in-law. "I came to assure you that my sister and I aren't responsible for Kotyk and his relatives," he said.

"We were fairly sure that was the case, Elron," Stragen murmured.

"All they had in the world was Kotyk's title. Their father gambled away their inheritance. It sickens me to have that clutch of out-at-the-elbows aristocrats lording it over us the way they do."

"We've heard some rumors," Stragen smoothly changed the subject. "Some people in Esos were telling us that there was unrest among the serfs. We got some garbled account of a fellow called 'Sabre' and another named Ayachin. We couldn't make any sense out of it."

Elron looked around in an overdramatically conspiratorial fashion. "It is not wise to mention those names here in Astel, Milord Stragen," he said in a hoarse whisper that probably could have been heard across the yard. "The Tamuls have ears everywhere."

"The serfs are unhappy with the Tamuls?" Stragen asked with some surprise. "I'd have thought that they wouldn't have had so far to look for someone to hate."

"The serfs are superstitious animals, Milord." Elron sneered. "They can be led anywhere with a combination of religion, folklore, and strong drink. The *real* movement is directed at the yellow devils." Elron's eyes narrowed. "The honor of Astel demands that the Tamul yoke be thrown off. That's the real goal of the movement. Sabre is a patriot, a mysterious figure who appears out of the night to inspire the men of Astel to rise up and smash the oppressor's chains. He's always masked, you know."

"I hadn't heard that."

"Oh, yes. It's necessary, of course. Actually, he's a well-known personage who very carefully conceals his real identity and opinions. By day he's an idle member of the gentry, but at night, he's a masked firebrand, igniting the patriotism of his countrymen."

"You have certain opinions, I gather," Stragen assumed.

Elron's expression grew cautious. "I'm only a poet, Milord Stragen," he said deprecatingly. "My interest is in the drama of the situation—for the purposes of my art, you understand."

"Oh, of course."

"Where does this Ayachin come in?" Sparhawk asked. "As I understand it, he's been dead for quite some time now."

"There are strange things afoot in Astel, Sir Sparhawk," Elron assured him, "things which have lain locked in the blood of all true Astels for generations. We know in our hearts that Ayachin is not dead. He can never die—not so long as tyranny is alive."

"Just as a practical consideration, Elron," Stragen said in his most urbane manner, "this movement seems to rely rather heavily on the serfs for manpower. What's in it for them? Why should men who are bound to the soil have any concern at all about who runs the government?"

"They're sheep. They'll stampede in any direction you want them to. All you have to do is murmur the word 'emancipation,' and they'd follow you into the mouth of Hell."

"Then Sabre has no intention of actually freeing them?"

Elron laughed. "My dear fellow, why would any reasonable man want to do that? What's the point of liberating cattle?" He looked around furtively. "I must return before I'm missed. Kotyk hates me, and he'd like nothing better than the chance to denounce me to the authorities. I'm obliged to smile and be polite to him and those two overfed sows he calls his sisters. I keep my own counsel, gentlemen, but when the day of our liberation comes, there will be changes here—as God is my judge. Social change is sometimes violent, and I can almost guarantee that Kotyk and his sisters will not live to see the dawn of the new day." His eyes narrowed with a kind of self-important secretiveness. "But I speak too much. I keep my own counsel, gentlemen. I keep my own counsel." He swirled his black cloak around him and crept back into the house, his head high and his expression resolute.

"Fascinating young fellow," Stragen observed. "He makes my rapier itch for some reason."

Sparhawk grunted his agreement and looked up at the rainy night. "I hope this blows over by morning," he said. "I'd really like to get out of this sewer."

The following morning dawned blustery and unpromising. Sparhawk and his companions ate a hasty breakfast and made ready to depart. The baron and his family were not awake as yet, and none of his guests were in any mood for extended farewells. They rode out about an hour after sunrise and turned northeasterly on the Darsas road, moving at a distance-consuming canter. Although none of them mentioned it, they all wanted to get well out of the range of any possible pursuit before their hosts awakened.

About midmorning, they reached the white stone pillar that marked the eastern border of the baron's estate and breathed a collective sigh of relief. The column slowed to a walk, and Sparhawk and the other knights dropped back to ride alongside the carriage.

Ehlana's maid, Alean, was crying, and the queen and Baroness Melidere were trying to comfort her. "She's a very gentle child," Melidere explained to Sparhawk. "The horror of that sorry household has moved her to tears."

"Did someone back there say something to you he shouldn't have?" Kalten asked the sobbing girl, his tone hard. Kalten's attitude toward Alean was strange. Once he had been persuaded not to press his attentions on her, he had become rather fiercely protective. "If anybody insulted you, I'll go back and teach him better manners."

"No, my Lord," the girl replied disconsolately, "it was nothing like that. It's just that they're all trapped in that awful place. They hate each other, but they'll have to spend the rest of their lives together, and they'll go on cutting little pieces out of each other until they're all dead."

"Someone once told me that there's a certain kind of justice at work in situations like that," Sparhawk observed, not looking at his daughter. "All right then, we all had the chance to talk with the members of our host's family individually. Did anyone pick up anything useful?"

"The serfs are right on the verge of open rebellion, my Lord," Khalad said. "I sort of drifted around the stable and other outbuildings and talked with them. The baroness' father was a kindly master, I guess, and the serfs loved him. After he died, though, Kotyk started to show his real nature. He's a brutal sort of man, and he's very fond of using the knout."

"What's a knout?" Talen asked.

"It's a sort of scourge," his half brother replied bleakly.

"A whip?"

"It goes a little further than that. Serfs *are* lazy, Sparhawk. There's no question about that. And they've perfected the art of either pretending to be stupid or feigning illness or injury. It's always been a sort of game, I guess. The masters knew what the serfs were up to, and the serfs knew that they weren't really fooling anybody. Actually, I think they all enjoyed it. Then, a few years ago, the masters suddenly stopped playing. Instead of trying to coax the serfs to work, the gentry began to resort to the knout. They threw a thousand years of tradition out the window and turned vicious overnight. The serfs can't understand it. Kotyk's not the only noble who's been mistreating his serfs. They say it's been happening all over western Astel. Serfs tend to exaggerate things, but they all seem to be convinced that their masters have set out on a course of deliberate brutality designed to eradicate traditional rights and to reduce the serfs to absolute slavery. A serf can't be sold, but a slave can. The one they call 'Sabre' has been making quite an issue of that. If you tell a man that somebody's planning to sell his wife and children, you're going to get him just a little bit excited."

"That doesn't match up too well with what Baron Kotyk was telling me," Patriarch Emban put in. "The baron drank more than was really good for him last night, and he let a number of things slip that he otherwise might not have. It's *his* position that Sabre's primary goal is to drive the Tamuls out of Astel. To be honest with you, Sparhawk, I was a bit skeptical about what that thief in Esos said about this Sabre fellow, but he certainly has the attention of the nobles. He's been making an issue of racial and religious differences between Elenes and Tamuls. Kotyk kept referring to the Tamuls as 'godless yellow dogs.' "

"We have Gods, your Grace," Oscagne protested mildly. "If you give me a few moments, I might even be able to remember some of their names."

"Our friend Sabre's been busy," Tynian said. "He's saying one thing to the nobles and another to the serfs."

"I think it's called talking out of both sides of your face at once," Ulath noted.

"I believe the empire might want to give the discovery of Sabre's identity a certain priority," Oscagne mused. "It's embarrassingly predictable, but we brutal oppressors and godless yellow dogs always want to identify ringleaders and troublemakers."

"So that you can catch them and hang them?" Talen accused.

"Not necessarily, young man. When a natural talent rises to the surface, one shouldn't waste it. I'm sure we can find a use for this fellow's gifts."

"But he hates your empire, your Excellency," Ehlana pointed out.

"That's no real drawback, your Majesty." Oscagne smiled. "The fact that a man hates the empire doesn't automatically make him a criminal. Anyone with any common sense hates the empire. There are days when even the emperor himself hates it. The presence of revolutionaries is a fair indication that something's seriously wrong in a given province. The revolutionary's made it his business to pinpoint the problems, so it's easier in the long run to just let him go ahead and fix things. I've known quite a few revolutionaries who made very good provincial governors."

"That's an interesting line of thought, your Excellency," Ehlana said, "but how do you persuade people who hate you to go to work for you?"

"You trick them, your Majesty. You just ask them if they think they can do any better. They inevitably think they can, so you just tell them to have a go at it. It usually takes them a few months to realize that they've been had. Being a provincial governor is the worst job in the world. *Everybody* hates you."

"Where does this Ayachin fit in?" Bevier asked.

"I gather he'd be the rallying point," Stragen replied. "Sort of the way Drychtnath is in Lamorkand."

"A figurehead?" Tynian suggested.

"Most probably. You wouldn't really expect a ninth-century hero to understand contemporary political reality."

"He's sort of an enigma, though," Ulath pointed out. "The nobility believes he was one sort of man, and the serfs believe he's another. Sabre must have two different sets of speeches. Just exactly who was Ayachin anyway?"

"Kotyk told me that he was a minor nobleman who was very devoted to the Astellian Church," Emban supplied. "In the ninth century, there was a Church-inspired invasion from Eosia. Your thief in Esos was right about *that* part, at least. The Astels believe that our Holy Mother in Chyrellos is heretical. Ayachin's supposed to have rallied the nobles and finally won a great victory in the Astel marshes."

"The serfs have a different story," Khalad told them. "They believe that Ayachin was a serf disguised as a nobleman and that his real goal was the emancipation of his class. *They* say that the victory in the marshes was the work of the serfs, not the nobility. Later, when the nobles found out who Ayachin really was, they had him murdered."

"He makes a perfect figurehead then," Ehlana said. "He was so ambiguous that he seems to offer something to everyone."

Emban was frowning. "The mistreatment of the serfs doesn't make any sense. Serfs aren't very industrious, but there are so many of them that all you have to do is pile on more people until you get the job done. If you maltreat them, all you really do is encourage them to turn on you. Even an idiot knows that. Sparhawk, is there some spell that might have induced the nobility to follow a course that's ultimately suicidal?"

"None that *I* know of," Sparhawk replied. He looked around at the other knights, and they all shook their heads. Princess Danae nodded very slightly, however, indicating that there might very well be some way to do what Emban suggested. "I wouldn't discount the possibility though, your Grace," he added. "Just because none of us knows the spell doesn't mean that there isn't one. If someone wanted turmoil here in Astel, there's probably nothing that would have suited his purposes better than a serf uprising, and if all the nobles started knouting their serfs at about the same time, it would have been a perfect way to set one off."

"And this Sabre fellow seems to be responsible," Emban said. "He's stirring the nobles against the godless yellow dogs—sorry, Oscagne—and at the same time he's agitating the serfs against their masters. Was anyone able to pick up anything about him?"

"Elron was in his cups last night, too," Stragen said. "He told Sparhawk and me that Sabre creeps around at night wearing a mask and making speeches."

"You're not serious!" Bevier asked incredulously.

"Pathetic, isn't it? We're obviously dealing with a juvenile mind here. Elron's quite overwhelmed by the melodrama of it all."

"He would be." Bevier sighed.

"It does sort of sound like the fabrication of a third-rate literary fellow, doesn't it?" Stragen smiled.

"That's Elron, all right," Tynian said.

"You're flattering him." Ulath grunted. "He trapped me in a corner last night and recited some of his verse to me. 'Third-rate' is a gross overstatement of his talent."

Sparhawk was troubled. Aphrael had told him that someone at Kotyk's house would say something important, but, aside from the revelation of some fairly unsavory personality defects, no one had directly told *him* anything of earthshaking note. Then he recalled that Aphrael had *not,* in fact, promised that whatever was so important would be said to *him.* Quite possibly, it had been revealed to one of the others. He brooded about it. The simplest way to resolve the question would be to ask his daughter, but to do that would once more expose him to some offensive comments about his limited understanding, so he decided that he'd much prefer to work it out for himself.

Their map indicated that the journey to the capital at Darsas would take them ten days. It actually did not, of course.

"How do you deal with people who happen to see us when we're moving this way?" he asked Danae as they proceeded along at that accelerated pace later that day. He looked at his blank-faced, uncomprehending friends. "I've got a sort of an idea of how you convince the people who are travelling with us that we're just plodding along, but what about strangers?"

"We don't move this way when there are strangers around, Sparhawk," she replied, "but they wouldn't see us anyway. We're going too fast."

"You're freezing time, then, the same way Ghnomb did in Pelosia?"

"No, I'm actually doing just the opposite. Ghnomb froze time and made you plod along through an endless second. What I'm doing is—" She looked speculatively at her father. "I'll explain it some other time," she decided. "We're moving in little spurts, a few miles at a time. Then we amble along for a while, and then we spurt ahead again. Making it all fit together is really very challenging. It gives me something to occupy my mind during these long, boring journeys."

"Did that important thing you mentioned get said?" he asked her.

"Yes."

"What was it?" He decided that a small bruise on his dignity wouldn't really hurt all that much.

"I don't know. I know that it was important and that somebody was going to say it, but I don't know the details."

"Then you're *not* omniscient."

"I never said that I was."

"Could it have come in bits and pieces—a word or two to Emban, a couple to Stragen and me, and quite a bit more to Khalad? And then we sort of had to put them all together to get the whole message?"

She thought about it. "That's brilliant, Father!" she exclaimed.

"Thank you." Their speculations earlier had borne some fruit after all. Then he pushed it a bit further. "Is someone here in Astel changing the attitudes of the people?"

"Yes, but that goes on all the time."

"So when the nobility began to mistreat their serfs, it wasn't their own idea?"

"Of course not. Deliberate, calculated cruelty is very hard to maintain. You have to concentrate on it, and the Astels are too lazy for that. It was externally imposed."

"Could a Styric magician have done it?"

"One by one, yes. A Styric could have selected one nobleman and turned him into a monster." She thought a moment. "Maybe two," she amended. "Three at the most. There are too many variables for a human to keep track of when you get past that."

"Then it's a God—or Gods—that made them all start mistreating their serfs here a few years back?"

"I thought I just said that."

He ignored that and went on. "And the whole purpose was to make the serfs resentful and ready to listen to someone inciting them to revolution."

"Your logic is blinding me, Sparhawk."

"You can be a very offensive little girl when you set your mind to it, did you know that?"

"But you love me anyway, don't you? Get to the point, Sparhawk. It's almost time for me to wake the others."

"And the sudden resentment directed at the Tamuls came from the same source, didn't it?"

"And probably at about the same time," she agreed. "It's easier to do it all at once. Going back into someone's mind over and over is so tedious."

A sudden thought came to him. "How many things can you think about at the same time?" he asked her.

"I've never counted—several thousand, I'd imagine. Of course there aren't really any limits. I guess if I really wanted to, I could think about everything all at once. I'll try it sometime and let you know."

"That's really the difference between us, isn't it? You can think about more things at the same time than I can."

"Well, that's *one* of the differences."

"What's another?"

"You're a boy, and I'm a girl."

"That's fairly obvious—and not very profound."

"You're wrong, Sparhawk. It's much, much more profound than you could ever imagine."

After they crossed the River Antun, they entered a heavily forested region where rocky crags jutted up above the treetops here and there. The weather continued blustery and threatening, though it did not rain.

Kring's Peloi were very uncomfortable in the forest, and they rode huddled close to the Church Knights, their eyes a bit wild.

"We might want to remember that," Ulath noted late that afternoon, jerking

his chin in the direction of a pair of savage-looking, shaved-headed warriors following so closely behind Berit that their mounts were almost treading on his horse's
hind hooves.

"What was that?" Kalten asked him.

"Don't take the Peloi into the woods." Ulath paused and leaned back in his saddle. "I knew a girl in Heid one summer who felt more or less the same way," he reminisced. "She was absolutely terrified of the woods. The young men of the town sort
of gave up on her—even though she was a great beauty. Heid's a crowded little
town, and there are always aunts and grandmothers and younger brothers underfoot in the houses. The young men have found that the woods offer the kind of privacy young people need from time to time, but this girl wouldn't go near the woods.
Then I made an amazing discovery. The girl was afraid of the woods, but she was
absolutely fearless where haybarns were concerned. I tested the theory personally
any number of times, and she never once showed the slightest bit of timidity about
barns—or goat sheds either, for that matter."

"I really don't get the connection," Kalten said. "We were talking about the fact
that the Peloi are afraid of the woods. If somebody attacks us here in this forest,
we're not going to have time to stop and build a barn for them, are we?"

"No, I suppose you're right about that."

"All right, what *is* the connection then?"

"I don't think there is one, Kalten."

"Why did you tell the story then?"

"Well, it's an awfully good story, don't you think?" Ulath sounded a bit injured.

Talen came galloping forward. "I think you'd better come back to the carriage,
Sir Knights." He laughed, trying without much success to control his mirth.

"What's the trouble?" Sparhawk asked him.

"We've got company—well, not company exactly, but there's somebody watching us."

Sparhawk and the others wheeled their mounts and rode back along the column to the carriage.

"You've *got* to see this, Sparhawk," Stragen said, trying to stifle his laughter.
"Don't be too obvious when you look, but there's a man on horseback on top of that
crag off to the left side of the road."

Sparhawk leaned forward as if speaking to his wife and raised his eyes to look
at the rocky crag jutting up from the forest floor.

The rider was about forty yards away, and he was outlined by the sunset behind
him. He was making no attempt to conceal himself. He sat astride a black horse,
and his clothing was all of the same hue. His inky cape streamed out from his shoulders in the stiff wind, and his broad-brimmed hat was crammed tightly down on his
head. His face was covered with a baglike black mask with two large, slightly off-
center eye holes in it.

"Isn't that the most ridiculous thing you've ever seen in your life?" Stragen
laughed.

"Very impressive," Ulath murmured. "At least *he's* impressed."

"I wish I had a crossbow," Kalten said. "Berit, do you think you could nick him
a little with your longbow?"

"It might be a little chancy in this wind, Kalten," the young knight replied. "It might deflect my arrow and kill him instead."

"How long's he going to sit there?" Mirtai asked.

"Until he's sure that everybody in the column has seen him, I expect," Stragen said. "He went to a lot of trouble to deck himself out like that. What do you think, Sparhawk. Is that the fellow Elron told us about?"

"The mask certainly fits," Sparhawk agreed. "I wasn't expecting all the rest, though."

"What's this?" Emban asked.

"Unless Sparhawk and I are mistaken, your Grace, we are privileged to be in the presence of a living legend. I think that's Sabre, the masked whatever-you-call-it, making his evening rounds."

"What on earth is he doing?" Oscagne sounded baffled.

"I imagine that he's out wronging rights, depressing the oppressed, and generally making an ass of himself, your Excellency. He looks as if he's having a lot of fun, though."

The masked rider reared his horse dramatically, and his black cape swirled around him. Then he plunged down the far side of the crag and was gone.

"Wait," Stragen urged before the others could move.

"For what?" Kalten asked.

"Listen."

From beyond the crag came the brassy note of a horn that trailed off into a distinctly unmusical squawk.

"He *had* to have a horn," Stragen explained. "No performance like that would ever be complete without a horn." He laughed delightedly. "Maybe if he practices, he'll even learn to carry a tune with it."

Darsas was an ancient city situated on the east bank of the River Astel. The bridge that approached it was a massive arch that had probably been in place for at least a thousand years, and most of the city's buildings showed a similar antiquity. The cobbled streets were narrow and twisting, following, quite probably, paths along which cows had gone to water eons in the past. Although its antiquity seemed strange, there was still something profoundly familiar about Darsas. It was an almost prototypical Elene town, and Sparhawk felt as if his very bones were responding to its peculiar architecture. Ambassador Oscagne led them through the narrow street and cluttered bazaars to an imposing square at the center of the city. He pointed out a fairy-tale structure with a broad gate and soaring towers bedecked with brightly colored pennons. "The royal palace," he told Sparhawk. "I'll speak with Ambassador Fontan, our local man, and he'll take us to see King Alberen. I'll only be a moment."

Sparhawk nodded. "Kalten," he called to his friend, "let's sort of form up the troops. A bit of ceremony might be in order here."

When Oscagne emerged from the Tamul embassy, which was conveniently located in a building adjoining the palace, he was accompanied by an ancient-appearing Tamul whose head was totally hairless and whose face was as wrinkled as the skin of a very old apple. "Prince Sparhawk," Oscagne said quite formally, "I have the honor to present his Excellency, Ambassador Fontan, his Imperial Majesty's representative here in the Kingdom of Astel."

Sparhawk and Fontan exchanged polite bows.

"Have I your Highness' permission to present his Excellency to her Majesty, the queen?" Oscagne asked.

"Tedious, isn't it, Sparhawk?" Fontan asked in a voice as dry as dust. "Oscagne's a good boy. He was my most promising pupil, but his fondness for ritual and formula overcomes him at times."

"I'll borrow a sword and immolate myself at once, Fontan," Oscagne bantered.

"I've seen you fumbling with a sword, Oscagne," Fontan replied. "If you're suicidally inclined, go molest a cobra instead. If you try to do it with a sword, you'll take all week."

"I gather that I'm watching a reunion of sorts." Sparhawk smiled.

"I always like to lower Oscagne's opinion of himself, Sparhawk," Fontan replied. "He's brilliant, of course, but sometimes he lacks humility. Now, why don't you introduce me to your wife? She's much prettier than you are, and the imperial messenger from Matherion rode three horses to death bringing me the emperor's instructions to be excruciatingly nice to her. We'll chat for a few moments, and then I'll take you to meet my dear, incompetent friend, the king. I'm sure he'll swoon at the unspeakable honor your queen's visit does him."

Ehlana was delighted to meet the ambassador. Sparhawk knew that to be true because she said so herself. She invited the ancient Tamul, the real ruler of Astel, to join her in the carriage, and the entire party moved rather inexorably on to the palace gates.

The captain of the palace guard was nervous. When two hundred professional killers descend on one with implacable pace, one is almost always nervous. Ambassador Fontan put him at his ease, and three messengers were dispatched to advise the king of their arrival. Sparhawk decided not to ask the captain why he sent three. The poor man was having a bad enough day already. The party was escorted into the palace courtyard where they dismounted and turned their horses over to the stable hands. "Behave yourself," Sparhawk muttered to Faran as a slack-mouthed groom took the reins.

There seemed to be a great deal of activity going on in the palace. Windows kept popping open, and excited people stuck their heads out to gape.

"It's the steel clothing, I think," Fontan observed to the queen. "The appearance of your Majesty's escort on the doorstep may very well set a new fashion. A whole generation of tailors may have to learn blacksmithing." He shrugged. "Oh, well," he added. "It's a useful trade. They can always shoe horses when business is slow." He looked at his pupil, who had returned to the carriage. "You should have sent word on ahead, Oscagne. Now we'll have to wait while everyone inside scurries around to make ready for us."

After several moments, a group of liveried trumpeters filed onto a balcony over the palace door and blew a shattering fanfare. The courtyard was enclosed by stone buildings, and the echoes from the trumpets were almost sufficient to unhorse the knights. Fontan climbed down from the carriage and offered Ehlana his arm with a graceful courtliness.

"Your Excellency is exquisitely courteous," she murmured.

"Evidence of a misspent youth, my dear."

"Your teacher's manner seems quite familiar, Ambassador Oscagne." Stragen smiled.

"My imitation of him is only a poor shadow of my master's perfection, Milord." Oscagne looked fondly at his wrinkled tutor. "We all try to imitate him. His successes in the field of diplomacy are legendary. Don't be deceived, Stragen. When he's being urbane and ironically humorous, he's completely disarming you and gathering more information about you than you could ever imagine. Fontan can read a man's entire character in the twitch of one of his eyebrows."

"I expect I'll be quite a challenge to him," Stragen said, "since I don't have any character to speak of."

"You deceive yourself, Milord. You're not nearly as unprincipled as you'd like us to believe."

A stout factotum in splendid scarlet livery escorted them into the palace and along a broad, well-lighted corridor. Ambassador Oscagne walked just behind their escort, identifying the members of their party as they went.

The broad doors at the end of the corridor swung wide, and their liveried guide preceded them into a vast, ornate throne room filled with excited courtiers. The factotum thunderously pounded on the floor with the butt of the staff that was his badge of office. "My Lords and Ladies," he boomed, "I have the honor to present her Divine Majesty, Queen Ehlana of the Kingdom of Elenia!"

"Divine?" Kalten murmured to Sparhawk.

"It grows more evident as you get to know her better."

The liveried herald continued his introductions, laboriously embellishing their individual titles as he presented them. Oscagne had quite obviously done his homework very thoroughly, and the herald dusted off seldom-used ornaments of rank in his introductory remarks. Kalten's nearly forgotten baronetcy emerged. Bevier was exposed as a viscount, Tynian as a duke, and Ulath as an earl. Most surprising of all, perhaps, was the revelation that Berit, plain, earnest Berit, had been concealing the title of marquis in his luggage. Stragen was introduced as a baron. "My father's title," the blond thief explained to them in an apologetic whisper. "Since I killed him and my brothers, I suppose it technically belongs to me—spoils of war, you understand."

"My goodness," Baroness Melidere murmured, her blue eyes alight, "I seem to be standing in the middle of a whole constellation of stars." She seemed positively breathless.

"I wish she wouldn't do that," Stragen complained.

"What's the problem?" Kalten asked him.

"She makes it seem as if the light in her eyes is the sun streaming in through the hole in the back of her head. I *know* she's far more clever than that. I *hate* dishonest people."

"You?"

"Let it lie, Kalten."

The throne room of King Alberen of Astel was filled with an awed silence as the eminence of the visitors was revealed. King Alberen himself, an ineffectual-looking fellow whose royal robes looked a size or so too large for him, seemed to shrink with each new title. Alberen, it appeared, had weak eyes, and his myopic gaze gave him the fearful, timid look of a rabbit or some other such small, helpless animal that all other creatures look upon as a food source. The splendor of his throne room seemed to shrink him all the more, the wide expanses of crimson carpets and drapes, the massive gilt and crystal chandeliers and marble columns providing an heroic setting that he could never hope to fill.

Sparhawk's queen, regal and lovely, approached the throne on Ambassador Fontan's arm with her steel-plated entourage drawn up around her. King Alberen seemed a bit uncertain about the customary ceremonies. As the reigning monarch of Astel, he was entitled to remain seated upon his throne, but the fact that his entire court genuflected as Ehlana passed intimidated him, and he rose to his feet and even stepped down from the dais to greet her.

"Now has our life seen its crown," Ehlana proclaimed in her most formal and oratorical style, "for we have, as God most surely must have decreed since time's beginning, come at last into the presence of our dear brother of Astel, whom we have longed to meet since our earliest girlhood."

"Is she speaking for all of us?" Talen whispered to Berit. "I didn't really have a girlhood, you know."

"She's using the royal plural," Berit explained. "The queen's more than one person. She's speaking for the entire kingdom."

"We are honored more than we can say, your Majesty," Alberen faltered.

Ehlana quickly assessed her host's limitations and smoothly adopted a less formal tone. She abandoned ceremony and unleashed her charm on the poor fellow. At the end of five minutes they were chatting together as if they had known each other all their lives. At the end of ten, he'd have given her his crown had she asked for it.

After the obligatory exchanges, Sparhawk and the other members of Ehlana's entourage moved away from the throne to engage in that silly but necessary pastime known as "circulating." They talked about the weather mostly. The weather is a politically correct topic. Emban and Archimandrite Monsel, the head of the Church of Astel, exchanged theological platitudes without touching on those doctrinal differences that divided their two Churches. Monsel wore an elaborate miter and intricately embroidered vestments. He also wore a full black beard that reached to his waist.

Sparhawk had discovered early in life that a scowl was his best defense in such situations and he customarily intimidated whole rooms full of people who might otherwise inflict conversational inanities upon him.

"Are you in some kind of distress, Prince Sparhawk?" It was Ambassador Fontan who dared to speak—quietly. "Your face has a decidedly dyspeptic cast to it."

"It's entirely tactical, your Excellency," Sparhawk replied. "When a military man doesn't want to be pestered, he digs a ditch and lines the bottom and sides with sharpened stakes. A scowl serves the same purpose in social situations."

"You look bristly enough, my boy. Let's take a turn around the battlements and enjoy the view, the fresh air, and the privacy. There are things you should know, and this may be my only chance to get you alone. King Alberen's court is full of inconsequential people who would all die for the chance to be able to maneuver conversation around to the point where they can assert that they know you personally. You have quite a reputation, you know."

"Largely exaggerated, your Excellency."

"You're too modest, my boy. Shall we go?"

They left the throne room unobtrusively and climbed several flights of stairs until they came out on the windswept battlements.

Fortan looked down at the city spread below. "Quaint, wouldn't you say?"

"Elene cities are always quaint, your Excellency," Sparhawk replied. "Elene architects haven't had a new idea in the last five millennia."

"Matherion will open your eyes, Sparhawk. All right, then, Astel's right on the verge of flying apart. So's the rest of the world, but Astel's carrying it to extremes. I'm doing what I can to hold things together, but Alberen's so pliable that almost anyone can influence him. He'll literally sign anything anybody puts in front of him. You've heard about Ayachin, of course. And his running dog, Sabre?"

Sparhawk nodded.

"I've got every imperial agent in Astel out trying to identify Sabre, but we haven't had much luck so far. He's out there blithely dismantling a system the empire spent centuries creating. We don't really know very much about him."

"He's an adolescent, your Excellency," Sparhawk said. "No matter what his age, he's profoundly juvenile." He briefly described the incident in the forest.

"That's helpful," Fontan said. "None of my people have ever been able to infiltrate one of those famous meetings, so we had no idea of what sort of fellow we were dealing with. He's got the nobility completely in his grasp. I stopped Alberen just in time a few weeks ago when he was on the verge of signing a proclamation which would have criminalized a serf if he ran away. That would have brought the kingdom down around our ears, I'm afraid. That's always been the serf's final answer to an intolerable situation. If he can run away and stay away for a year and a day, he's free. If you take that away from the serfs, they'll revolt, and a serf rebellion is too hideous a notion to even contemplate."

"It's quite deliberate, your Excellency," Sparhawk advised him. "Sabre's agitating the serfs as well. He *wants* a serf rebellion here in Astel. He's been using his influence over the nobility to persuade them to commit the exact blunders that will outrage the serfs all the more."

"What's the man thinking of?" Fontan burst out. "He'll drown Astel in blood."

Sparhawk made an intuitive leap at that point. "I don't think he really cares about Astel, your Excellency. Sabre's no more than a tool for someone who has his eyes on a much bigger goal."

"Oh? What's that?"

"I'm guessing, your Excellency, but I think there's somebody out there who wants the whole world, and he'd sacrifice Astel and every living person in it to get what he wants."

"It's hard to put your finger on it, Prince Sparhawk," Baroness Melidere said that evening after the extended royal family had retired to their oversized apartment for the night. At the queen's insistence, Melidere, Mirtai, and Alean, her maid, had been provided with rooms in the apartment. Ehlana needed women around her for a number of reasons, some practical, some political, and some very obscure. The ladies had removed their formal gowns, and, except for Mirtai, they wore soft pastel dressing gowns. Melidere was brushing Mirtai's wealth of blue-black hair, and the doe-eyed Alean was performing the same service for Ehlana.

"I'm not sure exactly how to describe it," the honey-blond baroness continued. "It's a sort of generalized sadness. They all sigh a great deal."

"I noticed that myself, Sparhawk," Ehlana told her husband. "Alberen hardly smiles at all, and I can make *anybody* smile."

"Your presence alone is enough to make us all smile, my Queen," Talen told her. Talen was the queen's page and he was also a member of the extended family. The young thief was elegant tonight, dressed in a plum-colored velvet doublet and knee breeches in the same shade and fabric. Knee breeches were just coming into fashion, and Ehlana had tried her very best to get Sparhawk into a pair of them. He had categorically refused, and his wife had been obliged to settle for coercing her page into the ridiculous-looking garments.

"The plan is to make you a knight, Talen," Melidere told the boy pointedly, "not a courtier."

"Stragen says it's always a good idea to have something to fall back on, Baroness." He shrugged, his voice cracking and warbling somewhere between soprano and baritone.

"He would," the baroness sniffed. Melidere affected a strong disapproval of Stragen, but Sparhawk was not so sure about how she really felt.

Talen and Princess Danae sat on the floor rolling a ball back and forth between them. Mmrr was participating in the game enthusiastically.

"They all seem to secretly believe that the world's going to come to an end week after next," the baroness went on, slowly drawing her brush through Mirtai's hair. "They're all bright and brittle on the surface, but once you get beneath that, there's the blackest melancholy, and they all drink like fish. I couldn't prove this, but I really think they all believe they're going to die very soon." She lifted Mirtai's hair speculatively. "I think I'll braid a gold chain into it, dear," she told the giantess.

"No, Melidere," Mirtai said firmly. "I'm not entitled to wear gold yet."

"Every woman's entitled to wear gold, Mirtai," Melidere laughed, "provided that she can charm it out of some man."

"Not among my people," Mirtai disagreed. "Gold is for adults. Children don't wear it."

"You're hardly a child, Mirtai."

"I am until I go through a certain ceremony. Silver, Melidere—or steel."

"You can't make jewelry out of steel."

"You can if you polish it enough."

Melidere sighed. "Fetch me the silver chains, Talen," she said. For the present, that was Talen's function: he fetched things. He didn't like it very much, but he did it—largely because Mirtai was bigger than he was.

There was a polite knock at the door, and Talen veered over to answer it.

Ambassador Oscagne entered. He bowed to Ehlana. "I've spoken with Fontan, your Majesty," he reported. "He's sending to the garrison at Canae for two Atan legions to escort us to Matherion. I'm sure we'll all feel more secure with them around us."

"What's a legion, your Excellency?" Talen asked, crossing the room to the jewelry cabinet.

"A thousand warriors," Oscagne replied. He smiled at Ehlana. "With two thousand Atans at your disposal, your Majesty could conquer Edom. Would you like to establish a toehold on the Daresian continent? It won't really be all that inconvenient. We Tamuls will administer it for you—for the usual fee, of course—and we'll send you glowing reports at the end of each year. The reports will be a tissue of lies, but we'll send them anyway."

"Along with the profits?" She actually sounded interested.

"Oh, no, your Majesty." He laughed. "For some reason, not one single kingdom in the whole empire ever shows a profit—except Tamul itself, of course."

"Why would I want a kingdom that doesn't pay?"

"Prestige, your Majesty, and vanity. You'd have another title and another crown."

"I don't really need another crown, your Excellency. I've only got one head. Why don't we just let the King of Edom keep his unprofitable kingdom?"

"Probably a wise decision, your Majesty," he agreed. "Edom's a tedious sort of place. They grow wheat there, and wheat farmers are a stodgy group of people all obsessively interested in the weather."

"How long is it likely to be until those legions arrive?" Sparhawk asked him.

"A week or so. They'll come on foot, so they'll make better time than they would on horseback."

"Isn't it the other way around, your Excellency?" Melidere asked him. "I thought horses moved much faster than men on foot."

Mirtai laughed.

"Did I say something funny?" Melidere asked.

"When I was fourteen, a man down in Daconia insulted me," the giantess told her. "He was drunk. When he sobered up the next morning, he realized what he'd done and fled on horseback. It was about dawn. I caught up with him just before noon. His horse had died from exhaustion. I always felt sort of sorry for the horse. A trained warrior can run all day. A horse can't. A horse has to stop when he wants to eat, so he's not used to running for more than a few hours at a time. We eat while we're running, so we just keep on going."

"What did you do to the fellow who insulted you?" Talen asked her.

"Do you really want to know?"

"Ah—no, Mirtai," he replied. "Now that you mention it, probably not."

· · ·

And so they had a week on their hands. Baroness Melidere devoted her time to breaking hearts. The young noblemen of King Alberen's court flocked around her. She flirted outrageously, made all sorts of promises—none of which she kept—and occasionally allowed herself to be kissed in dark corners by persistent suitors. She had a great deal of fun and gathered a great deal of information. A young man pursuing a pretty girl will often share secrets with her, secrets that he should probably keep to himself.

To the surprise of Sparhawk and his fellow knights, Sir Berit devastated the young ladies of the court quite nearly as much as the baroness did the young men.

"It's absolutely uncanny," Kalten was saying one evening. "He doesn't really do anything at all. He doesn't talk to them; he doesn't smile at them; he doesn't do any of the things he's supposed to do. I don't know what it is, but every time he walks through a room, every young woman in the place starts to come all unravelled."

"He *is* a very handsome young man, Kalten," Ehlana pointed out.

"Berit? He doesn't even shave regularly yet."

"What's that got to do with it? He's tall, he's a knight, he has broad shoulders and good manners. He's also got the deepest blue eyes I've ever seen—and the longest eyelashes."

"But he's only a boy."

"Not anymore. You haven't really looked at him lately. Besides, the young ladies who sigh and cry into their pillows over him are quite young themselves."

"What's really so irritating is the fact that he doesn't even know what effect he has on all those poor girls," Tynian observed. "They're doing everything but tearing their clothes off to get his attention, and he hasn't got the faintest notion of what's going on."

"That's part of his charm, Sir Knight." Ehlana smiled. "If it weren't for that innocence of his, they wouldn't find him nearly so attractive. Sir Bevier here has much the same quality. The difference though, is that Bevier *knows* that he's an extraordinarily handsome young man. He chooses not to do anything about it because of his religious convictions. Berit doesn't even know."

"Maybe one of us should take him aside and tell him," Ulath suggested.

"Never mind," Mirtai told him. "He's fine just the way he is. Leave him alone."

"Mirtai's right," Ehlana said. "Don't tamper with him, gentlemen. We'd like to keep him innocent for just a while longer." A hint of mischief touched her lips. "Sir Bevier, on the other hand, is quite another matter. It's time for us to find him a wife. He'll make some girl an excellent husband."

Bevier smiled faintly. "I'm already married, your Majesty—to the Church."

"Betrothed perhaps, Bevier, but not yet married. Don't start buying ecclesiastical garb just yet, Sir Knight. I haven't entirely given up on you."

"Wouldn't it be easier to start closer to home, your Majesty?" he suggested. "If you feel the urge to marry someone off, Sir Kalten is readily at hand."

"Kalten?" she asked incredulously. "Don't be absurd, Bevier. I wouldn't do that to *any* woman."

"Your *Majesty!*" Kalten protested.

"I love you dearly, Kalten," she smiled at the blond Pandion, "but you're just not husband material. I couldn't *give* you away. In good conscience I couldn't even *order* anyone to marry you. Tynian is remotely possible, but God intended you and Ulath to be bachelors."

"Me?" Ulath said mildly.

"Yes," she said, "you."

The door opened, and Stragen and Talen entered. They were both dressed in the plain clothing they usually wore when making one of their sorties into the streets.

"Any luck?" Sparhawk asked them.

"We found him," Stragen replied, handing his cloak to Alean. "He's not really my sort. He's a pickpocket by profession, and pickpockets don't really make good leaders. There's something fundamentally lacking in their character."

"Stragen!" Talen protested.

"You're not really a pickpocket, my young friend," Stragen told him. "That's only an interim occupation while you're waiting to grow up. Anyway, the local chief's named Kondrak. He could see that we all have a mutual interest in stable governments, I'll give him that. Looting houses when there's turmoil in the streets is a fast way to make a lot of money, but over the long run, a good thief can accumulate more in times of domestic tranquility. Of course Kondrak can't make any kind of overall decision on his own. He'll have to consult with his counterparts in other cities in the empire."

"That shouldn't take more than a year or so," Sparhawk noted dryly.

"Hardly," Stragen disagreed. "Thieves move much more rapidly than honest men. Kondrak's going to send out word of what we're trying to accomplish. He'll put it in the best possible light, so there's a very good chance that the thieves of all the kingdoms in the empire will cooperate."

"How will we know their decision?" Tynian asked him.

"I'll make courtesy calls each time we come to a fair-sized city." Stragen shrugged. "Sooner or later I'll get an official reply. It shouldn't take all that long. We'll certainly have a final decision by the time we reach Matherion." He looked speculatively at Ehlana. "Your Majesty's learned a great deal about the subterranean government in the past few years," he noted. "Do you suppose we could put that information on the level of a state secret? We're perfectly willing to cooperate and even assist on occasion, but we'd be much happier if the other monarchs of the world didn't know too much about the way we operate. Some crusader might decide to smash the secret government, and that would inconvenience us a bit."

"What's it worth to you, Milord Stragen?" she teased him.

His eyes grew very serious. "It's a decision you'll have to make for yourself, Ehlana," he told her, cutting across rank and customary courtesies. "I've tried to assist you whenever I could because I'm genuinely fond of you. If you make a little conversational slip, though, and other monarchs find out things they shouldn't know, I won't be able to do that anymore."

"You'd abandon me, Milord Stragen?"

"Never, my Queen, but my colleagues would have me killed, and I wouldn't really be of much use to you in that condition, now would I?"

Archimandrite Monsel was a large, impressive man with piercing black eyes and an imposing black beard. It was a forceful beard, an assertive beard, a beard impossible to overlook, and the archimandrite used it like a battering ram. It preceded him by a yard wherever he went. It bristled when he was irritated—which was often—and in damp weather it knotted up into snarls like a half a mile of cheap fishing line. The beard waggled when Monsel talked, emphasizing points all on its own. Patriarch Emban was absolutely fascinated by the archimandrite's beard. "It's like talking to an animated hedge," he observed to Sparhawk as the two of them walked through the corridors of the palace toward a private audience with the Astellian ecclesiast.

"Are there any topics I should avoid, your Grace?" Sparhawk asked. "I'm not familiar with the Church of Astel, and I don't want to start any theological debates."

"Our disagreements with the Astels are in the field of Church government, Sparhawk. Our purely theological differences are very minor. We have a secular clergy, but their Church is monastically organized. Our priests are just priests; theirs are also monks. I'll grant you that it's a fine distinction, but it's a distinction nonetheless. They also have many, many more priests and monks than we do—probably about a tenth of the population."

"That many?"

"Oh, yes. Every noble mansion in Astel has its own private chapel and its own priest, and the priest 'assists' in making decisions."

"Where do they find so many men willing to enter the priesthood?"

"From the ranks of the serfs. Being a clergyman has its drawbacks, but it's better than being a serf."

"I suppose the Church *would* be preferable."

"Much. Monsel will respect you, because you're a member of a religious order. Oh, incidentally, since you're the interim Preceptor of the Pandion Knights, you're technically a patriarch. Don't be surprised if he addresses you as 'your Grace.'"

They were admitted into Monsel's chambers by a long-bearded monk. Sparhawk had noticed that all Astellian clergymen wore beards. The room was small and panelled in dark wood. The carpet was a deep maroon, and the heavy drapes at the windows were black. There were books and scrolls and dog-eared sheets of parchment everywhere.

"Ah, Emban," Monsel said. "What have you been up to?"

"Mischief, Monsel. I've been out proselytizing among the heathens."

"Really? Where did you find any here? I thought most heathens lived in the Basilica in Chyrellos. Sit down, gentlemen. I'll send for some wine and we can debate theology."

"You've met Sparhawk?" Emban asked as they all took chairs before an open window where the breeze billowed the black drapes.

"Briefly," Monsel replied. "How are you today, your Highness?"

"Well. And you, your Grace?"

"Curious, more than anything. Why are we engaging in private consultations?"

"We're all clergymen, your Grace," Emban pointed out. "Sparhawk wears a cassock made of steel most of the time, but he *is* of the clergy. We've come to discuss something that probably concerns you as much as it does us. I think I know you well enough to know that you've got a practical side that's not going to get sidetracked by the fact that you think we genuflect wrong."

"What's this?" Sparhawk asked.

"We kneel on our right knee." Emban shrugged. "These poor, benighted heathens kneel on the left."

"Shocking," Sparhawk murmured. "Do you think we should come here in force and compel them to do it right?"

"You see?" Emban said to the archimandrite. "That's exactly what I was talking about. You should fall to your knees and thank God that you're not saddled with Church Knights, Monsel. I think most of them secretly worship Styric Gods."

"Only the Younger Gods, your Grace," Sparhawk said mildly. "We've had our differences with the Elder Gods."

"He says it so casually," Monsel shuddered. "If you think we've exhausted the conversational potential of genuflectory variation, Emban, why don't you get to the point?"

"This is in strictest confidence, your Grace, but our mission here to Tamuli's not entirely what it seems. It was Queen Ehlana's idea, of course. She's not the sort to go *anywhere* just because somebody tells her to—but all of this elaborate folderol was just a subterfuge to hide our real purpose, which was to put Sparhawk on the Daresian Continent. The world's coming apart at the seams, so we've decided to let him fix it."

"I thought that was God's job."

"God's busy just now, and he's got complete confidence in Sparhawk. All sorts of Gods feel that way about him, I understand."

Monsel's eyes widened, and his beard bristled.

"Relax, Monsel," Emban told him. "We of the Church are not required to believe in other Gods. All we have to do is make a few allowances for their speculative existence."

"Oh, that's different. If this is speculation, I suppose it's all right."

"There's one thing that *isn't* speculation, your Grace," Sparhawk said. "You've got trouble here in Astel."

"You've noticed. Your Highness is very perceptive."

"You may not have been advised, since the Tamuls are trying to keep it on a low key, but very similar things are afoot in many other Daresian kingdoms, and we're beginning to encounter the same sort of problem in Eosia."

"I think the Tamuls sometimes keep secrets just for the fun of it." Monsel grunted.

"I have a friend who says the same thing about our Eosian Church," Sparhawk said cautiously. They had not yet fully explored the archimandrite's political opinions. A wrong word or two here would not only preclude any possibility of obtaining his help, but might even compromise their mission.

"Knowledge is power," Emban said rather sententiously, "and only a fool shares power if he doesn't have to. Let me be blunt, Monsel. What's your opinion of the Tamuls?"

"I don't like them." Monsel's response was to the point. "They're heathens, they're members of an alien race, and you can't tell what they're thinking."

Sparhawk's heart sank.

"I have to admit, though, that when they absorbed Astel into their empire, it was the best thing that ever happened to us. Whether we like them or not is beside the point. Their passion for order and stability has averted war time and time again in my own lifetime. There have been other empires in ages past, and their time of ascendancy was a time of unmitigated horror and suffering. I think we'll candidly have to admit that the Tamuls are history's finest imperialists. They don't interfere with local customs or religions. They don't disrupt the social structure, and they function *through* the established governments. Their taxes, however much we complain about them, are really minimal. They build good roads and encourage trade. Aside from that, they generally leave us alone. About all they really insist upon is that we don't go to war with each other. I can live with that—although some of my predecessors felt dreadfully abused because the Tamuls wouldn't let them convert their neighbors by the sword."

Sparhawk breathed a little easier.

"But I'm straying from the point here," Monsel said. "You were suggesting a worldwide conspiracy of some kind, I think."

"Were we suggesting that, Sparhawk?" Emban asked.

"I suppose we were, your Grace."

"Do you have anything concrete upon which to base this theory, Sir Sparhawk?" Monsel asked.

"Logic is about all, your Grace."

"I'll listen to logic—as long as she doesn't contradict my beliefs."

"If a series of events happens in one place and it's identical to a series of events taking place in another, we're justified in considering the possibility of a common source, wouldn't you say?"

"On an interim basis, perhaps."

"It's about all we have to work with at the moment, your Grace. The same sort of thing could happen at the same time in two different places and still be a coincidence, but when you get up to five or ten different occurrences, coincidence sort of goes out the window. This current upheaval involving Ayachin and the one they call Sabre here in Astel is almost exactly duplicated in the kingdom of Lamorkand in Eosia, and Ambassador Oscagne assures us that the same sort of thing's erupting in other Daresian kingdoms as well. It's always the same. First there are the rumors that some towering hero of antiquity has somehow returned. Then some firebrand emerges to keep things stirred up. Here in Astel, you've got the wild stories about Ayachin. In Lamorkand, they talk about Drychtnath. Here you have a man named Sabre, and in Lamorkand they've got one named Gerrich. I'm fairly sure we'll find the same sort of thing in Edom, Daconia, Arjuna, and Cynesga. Oscagne tells us that *their* national heroes are putting in an appearance as well." Sparhawk rather carefully avoided mentioning Krager. He was still not entirely certain where Monsel's sympathies lay.

"You build a good case, Sparhawk," Monsel conceded. "But couldn't this master plot be directed at the Tamuls? They aren't widely loved, you know."

"I think your Grace is overlooking Lamorkand," Emban said. "There aren't any Tamuls there. I'm guessing, but I'd say that the master plot—if that's what we want to call it—is directed at the *Church* in Eosia as opposed to the empire here."

"Organized anarchy, perhaps?"

"I believe that's a contradiction in terms, your Grace," Sparhawk pointed out. "I'm not sure that we're far enough along to deal with causes yet, though. Right now we're trying to sort through effects. If we're correct in assuming that these plots are all coming from the same person, then what we're seeing is someone who's got a basic plan with common elements which he modifies to fit each particular culture. What we really want to do is to identify this Sabre fellow."

"So that you can have him killed?" Monsel's tone was accusing.

"No, your Grace, that wouldn't be practical. If we kill him, he'll be replaced by someone else—somebody we don't know. I want to know *who* he is and *what* he is, and everything I can possibly find out about him. I want to know how he thinks, what drives him, and what his personal motivations are. If I know all of that, I can neutralize him *without* killing him. To be completely honest with you, I don't really care about Sabre. I want the one who's behind him."

Monsel seemed shaken. "This is a dreadful man, Emban," he said in a hushed tone.

"*Implacable* is the word, I think."

"If we can believe Oscagne—and I think we can—someone's using the arcane arts in this business," Sparhawk told them. "That's why the Church Knights were created originally. It's *our* business to deal with magic. Our Elene religion can't cope with it because there's no place in our faith for it. We had to go outside the faith— to the Styrics—to learn how to counteract magic. It opened some doors we might have preferred had been left closed, but that's the price we had to pay. *Somebody*— or some*thing*—on the other side's using magic of a very high order. I'm here to stop him—to kill him if need be. Once he's gone, the Atans can deal with Sabre. I know an Atan, and if her people are at all like her, I know we can count on them to be thorough."

"You trouble me, Sparhawk," Monsel admitted. "Your devotion to your duty's almost inhuman, and your resolve goes even beyond that. You shame me, Sparhawk." He sighed and sat tugging at his beard, his eyes lost in thought. Finally, he straightened. "All right, Emban, can we suspend the rules?"

"I didn't quite follow that."

"I wasn't going to tell you this," the archimandrite said, "first of all because it'll probably raise your doctrinal hackles, but more important, because I didn't really want to share it with you. This implacable Sparhawk of yours has convinced me otherwise. If I don't tell you what I know, he'll dismantle Astel and everyone in it to get the information, won't you, Sparhawk?"

"I'd really hate that, your Grace."

"But you'd do it anyway, wouldn't you?"

"If I had to."

Monsel shuddered. "You're both churchmen, so I'm going to invoke the rule of clerical confidentiality. You haven't changed the requirements of *that* in Chyrellos yet, have you, Emban?"

"Not unless Sarathi did it since I've been gone. At any rate, you have our word that neither of us will reveal anything you tell us."

"Except to another clergyman," Monsel amended. "I'll go that far."

"All right," Emban agreed.

Monsel leaned back in his chair, stroking his beard. "The Tamuls have no real conception of how powerful the Church is in the Elene kingdoms here in western Daresia," he began. "In the first place, their religion's hardly more than a set of ceremonies. Tamuls don't even think about religion, so they can't understand the depth of the faith in the hearts of the devout—and the serfs of Astel are quite likely the most devout people on earth. They take all of their problems to their priests—and not only their own problems, but their neighbors' as well. The serfs are everywhere and they see everything, and they tell their priests."

"I think it was called tale bearing when I was in the seminary," Emban noted.

"We had a worse name for it during our novitiate," Sparhawk added. "All sorts of unpleasant accidents used to happen on the training field because of it."

"Nobody likes a snitch," Monsel agreed, "but like it or not, the Astellian clergy knows everything that happens in the kingdom—literally everything. We're sworn to keep these secrets, of course, but we feel that our primary responsibility is to the spiritual health of our flock. Since a large proportion of our priests were originally serfs, they simply don't have the theological training to deal with complex spiritual problems. We've devised a way to provide them with the advice they need. The serf-priests do not reveal the names of those who have come to them, but they *do* take serious matters to their superiors, and their superiors bring those matters to *me*."

"I have no real difficulty with that," Emban said. "As long as the names are kept secret, the confidentiality hasn't been violated."

"We'll get on well together, Emban." Monsel smiled briefly. "The serfs look upon Sabre as a liberator."

"So we gathered," Sparhawk told him. "There seems to be a certain lack of consistency in his speeches, though. He tells the nobles that Ayachin wants to throw off the Tamul yoke, and then he tells the serfs that Ayachin's real goal is the abolition of serfdom. Moreover, he's persuaded the nobles to become very brutal in their dealings with the serfs. That's not only disgusting, it's irrational. The nobles should be trying to *enlist* the serfs, not alienate them. Viewed realistically, Sabre's no more than an agitator, and he's not even particularly subtle. He's a political adolescent."

"That's going a little far, Sparhawk," Emban protested. "How do you account for his success then? An idiot like that could never persuade the Astels to accept his word."

"They're not accepting *his* word. They're accepting Ayachin's."

"Have you taken leave of your senses, Sparhawk?"

"No, your Grace. I mentioned before that someone on the other side's been using magic. *This* is what I was talking about. The people here have actually been seeing Ayachin himself."

"That's absurd!" Monsel seemed profoundly disturbed.

Sparhawk sighed. "For the sake of your Grace's theological comfort, let's call it some kind of hallucination—a mass illusion created by a clever charlatan, or some accomplice dressed in archaic clothing who appears suddenly in some spectacular fashion. Whatever its source, if what's happening here is anything like what's happening in Lamorkand, your people are absolutely convinced that Ayachin's returned from the grave. Sabre probably makes a speech—a rambling collection of disconnected platitudes—and then this hallucination appears in a flash of light and a clap of thunder and confirms all his pronouncements. That's a guess, of course, but it's probably not too far off the mark."

"It's an elaborate hoax then?"

"If that's what you want to believe, your Grace."

"But you *don't* believe it's a hoax, do you, Sparhawk?"

"I've been trained not to actively disbelieve things, your Grace. Whether the apparition of Ayachin is real or some trick is beside the point. It's what the people believe that's important, and I'm sure *they* believe that Ayachin's returned and that Sabre speaks for him. That's what makes Sabre so dangerous. With the apparition to support him, he can make people believe anything. That's why I have to find out everything about him that I can. I have to be able to know what he's going to do so that I can counter him."

"I'm going to behave as if I believe what you've just told me, Sparhawk," Monsel said in a troubled voice. "I really think you need some spiritual help, though." His face grew grave. "We know who Sabre is," he said finally. "We've known for over a year now. At first we believed as you do—that he was no more than a disturbed fanatic with a taste for melodrama. We expected the Tamuls to deal with him, so we didn't think we had to do anything ourselves. I've had some second thoughts on that score of late, though. On the condition that neither of you will reveal anything I say except to another clergyman, I'll tell you who he is. Do I have your word on that condition?"

"You have, your Grace," Emban swore.

"And you, Sparhawk?"

"Of course."

"Very well, then. Sabre's the younger brother-in-law of a minor nobleman who has an estate a few leagues to the east of Esos."

It all fell into place in Sparhawk's mind with a loud clank.

"The nobleman is a Baron Kotyk, a silly, ineffectual ass," Monsel told them. "And you were quite right, Sparhawk. Sabre's a melodramatic adolescent named Elron."

CHAPTER THIRTEEN

"That's impossible!" Sparhawk exclaimed.

Monsel was taken aback by his sudden vehemence. "We have more than ample evidence, Sir Sparhawk. The serf who reported the fact has known him since childhood. You've met Elron, I gather."

"We took shelter from a storm in Baron Kotyk's house," Emban explained. "Elron *could* be Sabre, you know, Sparhawk. He's certainly got the right kind of mentality. Why are you so certain he's not the one?"

"He couldn't have caught up with us," Sparhawk said lamely.

Monsel looked baffled.

"We saw Sabre in the woods on our way here," Emban told him. "It was the sort of thing you'd expect—a masked man in black on a black horse outlined against the sky—silliest thing I ever saw. We weren't really moving all that fast, Sparhawk. Elron could have caught up with us quite easily."

Sparhawk could not tell him that they *had*, in fact, been moving far too rapidly for anyone to have caught them—not with Aphrael tampering with time and distance the way she had been. He choked back his objections. "It just surprised me, that's all," he lied. "Stragen and I spoke with Elron the night we were there. I can't believe he'd be out stirring up the serfs. He had nothing but contempt for them."

"A pose, perhaps?" Monsel suggested. "Something to conceal his real feelings?"

"I don't think he's capable of that, your Grace. He was too ingenuous for that kind of subtlety."

"Don't be too quick to make judgments, Sparhawk," Emban told him. "If there's magic involved, it wouldn't make any difference *what* kind of man Sabre is, would it? Isn't there some way he could be rather tightly controlled?"

"Several, actually," Sparhawk admitted.

"I'm a little surprised you didn't consider that yourself. You're the expert on magic. Elron's personal beliefs are probably beside the point. When he's speaking as Sabre, it's the man behind him—our real adversary—who's talking."

"I should have thought of that." Sparhawk was angry with himself for having overlooked the obvious—and the equally obvious explanation for Elron's ability to overtake them. Another God could certainly compress time and distance the same way Aphrael could. "Just how widespread is this contempt for the serfs, your Grace?" he asked Monsel.

"Unfortunately, it's almost universal, Prince Sparhawk." Monsel sighed. "The serfs are uneducated and superstitious, but they're not nearly as stupid as the nobility would like to believe. The reports I've received tell me that Sabre spends almost as much time denouncing the serfs as he does the Tamuls when he's speaking to the nobility. 'Lazy' is about the kindest thing he says about them. He's managed to half persuade the gentry that the serfs are in league with the Tamuls in some vast, dark plot with its ultimate goal being the emancipation of the serfs and the redistribution of the land. The nobles are responding predictably. First they were goaded into hating the Tamuls, and then they were led to believe that the serfs are in league with the Tamuls and that their estates and positions are threatened by that alliance. They don't dare confront the Tamuls directly because of the Atans, so they're venting their hostility on their own serfs. There have been incidents of unprovoked savagery upon a class of people who will march en masse into heaven at final judgment. The Church is doing what she can, but there's only so far we can go in restraining the gentry."

"You need some Church Knights, your Grace," Sparhawk said in a bleak tone of voice. "We're very good in the field of justice. If you take a nobleman's knout away from him and apply it to his own back a few times, he tends to see the light very quickly."

"I wish that were possible here in Astel, Sir Sparhawk," Monsel replied sadly. "Unfortunately—"

It was the same chill, and that same annoying flicker at the edge of the eye. Monsel broke off and looked around quickly, trying to see what could not really be seen. "What—" he started.

"It's a visitation, your Grace," Emban told him, his voice tense. "Don't dislocate your neck trying to catch a glimpse of it." He raised his voice slightly. "Awfully good to see you again, old boy," he said. "We were beginning to think you'd forgotten about us. Was there something you wanted in particular? Or were you just yearning for our company? We're flattered, of course, but we're a little busy at the moment. Why don't you run along and play now? We can chat some other time."

The chill quite suddenly turned hot, and the flicker darkened.

"Are you insane, Emban?" Sparhawk choked.

"I don't think so," the fat little patriarch said. "Your flickering friend—or friends—are irritating me, that's all."

The shadow vanished, and the air around them returned to normal.

"What was that all about?" Monsel demanded.

"The Patriarch of Ucera just insulted a God—several Gods, probably," Sparhawk replied through clenched teeth. "For a moment there, we all hovered on the brink of obliteration. Please don't do that again, Emban—at least not without consulting me first." He suddenly laughed a bit sheepishly. "Now I know exactly how Sephrenia felt on any number of occasions. I'll have to apologize to her the next time I see her."

Emban was grinning with delight. "I sort of caught them off balance there, didn't I?"

"Don't do it again, your Grace," Sparhawk pleaded. "I've seen what Gods can do to people, and I don't want to be around if you *really* insult them."

"Our God protects me."

"Annias was praying to our God when Azash wrung him out like a wet rag, your Grace. It didn't do him all that much good, as I recall."

"That was really stupid, you know," Emban said then.

"I'm glad you realize that."

"Not me, Sparhawk. I'm talking about our adversary. Why did it reveal itself at this particular moment? It should have kept its flamboyant demonstration to itself and just listened. It could have found out what our plans are. Not only that, it revealed itself to Monsel. Until it appeared, he only had our word for the fact of its existence. Now he's seen it for himself."

"Will someone *please* explain this?" Monsel burst out.

"It was the Troll-Gods, your Grace," Sparhawk told him.

"That's absurd. There's no such thing as a Troll, so how can they have Gods?"

"This may take longer than I'd thought," Sparhawk muttered, half to himself. "As a matter of fact, your Grace, there *are* Trolls."

"Have you ever seen one?" Monsel challenged.

"Only one, your Grace. His name was Ghwerig. He was dwarfed, so he was only about seven feet tall. He was still very difficult to kill."

"You killed him?" Monsel gasped.

"He had something I wanted." Sparhawk shrugged. "Ulath's seen a lot more of them than I have, your Grace. He can tell you all about them. He even speaks their language. I did for a while myself, but I've probably forgotten by now. Anyway, they have a language, which means that they're semihuman, and that means that they have Gods, doesn't it?"

Monsel looked helplessly at Emban.

"Don't ask *me*, my friend," the fat patriarch said. "That's a long way out of *my* theological depth."

"For the time being, you'll have to take my word for it," Sparhawk told them. "There *are* Trolls, and they *do* have Gods—five of them—and these Gods aren't very nice. That shadow Patriarch Emban just so casually dismissed was them—or something very much like them—and that's what we're up against. That's what's trying to bring down the empire and the Church—both our Churches, probably. I'm sorry I have to put it to you so abruptly, Archimandrite Monsel, but you have to know what you're dealing with. Otherwise, you'll be totally defenseless. You don't have to believe what I just told you, but you'd better behave as if you did, because if you don't, your Church doesn't have a chance of surviving."

The Atans arrived a few days later. A hush fell over the city of Darsas as the citizens scurried for cover. No man is so entirely guiltless in his own soul that the sudden appearance of a few thousand police does not give him a qualm or two. The Atans were superbly conditioned giants. The two thousand warriors of both sexes ran in perfect unison as they entered the city four abreast. They wore short leather kirtles, burnished steel breastplates, and black half boots. Their bare limbs gleamed golden in the morning sun as they ran, and their faces were stern and unbending. Though they were obviously soldiers, there was no uniformity in their weapons. They carried a random collection of swords, short spears, and axes, as well as other implements for which Sparhawk had no names. They all had several sheathed daggers strapped tightly to their arms and legs. They wore no helmets, but had slender gold circlets about their heads instead.

"Lord," Kalten breathed to Sparhawk as the two of them stood on the palace battlements to watch the arrival of their escort, "I'd really hate to come up against that lot on a battlefield. Just looking at them makes my blood cold."

"I believe that's the idea, Kalten," Sparhawk said. "Mirtai's impressive all by herself, but when you see a couple thousand of them like this, you begin to understand how the Tamuls were able to conquer a continent without any particular difficulty. I'd imagine that whole armies simply capitulated when they saw them coming."

The Atans entered the square in front of the palace and formed up before the residence of the Tamul ambassador. A huge man went to Ambassador Fontan's door, his pace quite clearly indicating that if the door were not opened for him, he would walk right through it.

"Why don't we go down?" Sparhawk suggested. "I expect that Fontan will be bringing that fellow to call in a few moments. Watch what you say, Kalten. Those people strike me as a singularly humorless group. I'm sure they'd miss the point of almost any joke."

"Really," Kalten breathed his agreement.

The party accompanying the Queen of Elenia gathered in her Majesty's private quarters and stood about rather nervously awaiting the arrival of the Tamul ambassador and his general. Sparhawk watched Mirtai rather closely to see what her reaction might be upon being reunited with her people after so many years. She wore clothing he had not seen her wear before, clothing that closely resembled that worn by her countrymen. In place of the steel breastplate, however, she wore a tight-fitting, sleeveless black leather jerkin, and the band about her brow was of silver rather than gold. Her face was serene, seeming to show neither anticipation nor nervous apprehension. She merely waited.

Then Fontan and Oscagne arrived with the tallest man Sparhawk had ever seen. They introduced him as Atan Engessa. The word *Atan* appeared to be not only the name of the people, but some kind of title as well. Engessa was well over seven feet tall, and the room seemed to shrink as he entered. His age, probably because of his race, was indeterminate. He was lean and muscular, and his expression sternly unyielding. His face showed no evidence that he had ever smiled.

Immediately upon his entrance into the room, he went directly to Mirtai, as if none of the rest of them were even in the room. He touched the fingertips of both hands to his steel-armored chest and inclined his head to her. "Atana Mirtai," he greeted her respectfully.

"Atan Engessa," she replied, duplicating his gesture of greeting. Then they spoke to each other at some length in the Tamul tongue.

"What are they saying?" Ehlana asked Oscagne, who had crossed to where they all stood.

"It's a ritual of greeting, your Majesty," Oscagne replied. "There are a great many formalities involved when Atans meet. The rituals help to hold down the bloodshed, I believe. At the moment, Engessa's questioning Mirtai concerning her status as a child—the silver headband, you understand. It's an indication that she hasn't yet gone through the Rite of Passage." He stopped and listened for a moment as Mirtai spoke. "She's explaining that she's been separated from humans since childhood and hasn't had the opportunity to participate in the ritual as yet."

"Separated from humans?" Ehlana objected. "What does she think *we* are?"

"Atans believe that *they* are the only humans in the world. I'm not sure exactly what they consider us to be." The ambassador blinked. "Has she really killed that many people?" he asked with some surprise.

"Ten?" Sparhawk asked.

"She said thirty-four."

"That's impossible!" Ehlana exclaimed. "She's been a member of my court for the past seven years. I'd have known if she'd killed anyone while she was in my service."

"Not if she did it at night, you wouldn't, my Queen," Sparhawk disagreed. "She locks us in our rooms every night. She says that it's for our own protection, but maybe it's really so that she can go out looking for entertainment. Maybe we should change the procedure when we get home. Let's start locking *her* up for the night instead of the other way around."

"She'll just kick the door down, Sparhawk."

"That's true, I suppose. We could always chain her to the wall at night I guess."

"*Sparhawk!*" Ehlana exclaimed.

"We can talk about it later. Here come Fontan and General Engessa."

"*Atan* Engessa, Sparhawk," Oscagne corrected. "Engessa wouldn't even recognize the title of general. He's a warrior—an Atan. That's all the title he seems to need. If you call him 'general,' you'll insult him, and that's not a good idea."

Engessa had a deep, quiet voice and he spoke the Elenic language haltingly and with an exotic accent. He carefully repeated each of their names when Fontan introduced them, obviously committing them to memory. He accepted Ehlana's status without question, although the concept of a queen must have been alien to him. He recognized Sparhawk and the other knights as warriors, and seemed to respect them as such. The status of Patriarch Emban, Talen, Stragen, and Baroness Melidere obviously baffled him. He greeted Kring, however, with the customary Peloi salute. "Atana Mirtai advises me that you seek marriage with her," he said.

"That's right," Kring replied a bit pugnaciously. "Have you any objections?"

"That depends. How many have you killed?"

"More than I can conveniently count."

"That could mean two things. Either you have slain many, or you have a poor head for figures."

"I can count past two hundred," Kring declared.

"A respectable number. You are Domi among your people?"

"I am."

"Who cut your head?" Engessa pointed at the scars on Kring's scalp and face.

"A friend. We were discussing each other's qualifications for leadership."

"Why did you let him cut you?"

"I was busy. I had my saber in his belly at the time, and I was probing around for various things inside him."

"Your scars are honorable then. I respect them. Was he a good friend?"

Kring nodded. "The best. We were like brothers."

"You spared him the inconvenience of growing old."

"I did that, all right. He never got a day older."

"I take no exception to your suit of Atana Mirtai," Engessa told him. "She is a child with no family. As the first adult Atan she has met, it is my responsibility to serve as her father. Have you an *oma*?"

"Sparhawk serves as my *oma*."

"Send him to me, and he and I will discuss the matter. May I call you friend, Domi?"

"I would be honored, Atan. May I also call you friend?"

"I also would be honored, friend Kring. Hopefully, your *oma* and I will be able to arrange the day when you and Atana Mirtai will be branded."

"May God speed the day, friend Engessa."

"I feel as if I've just witnessed something from the dark ages," Kalten whispered to Sparhawk. "What do you think would have happened if they'd taken a dislike to each other?"

"It probably would have been messy."

"When do you want to leave, Ehlana, Queen of Elenia?" Engessa asked.

Ehlana looked at her friends questioningly. "Tomorrow?" she suggested.

"You should not ask, Ehlana-Queen," Engessa reprimanded her firmly. "Command. If any object, have Sparhawk-Champion kill them."

"We've been trying to cut back on that, Atan Engessa," she said. "It's always so hard on the carpeting."

"Ah," he said. "I knew there was a reason. Tomorrow, then?"

"Tomorrow, Engessa."

"I will await you at first light, Ehlana-Queen." And he turned on his heel and marched from the room.

"Abrupt sort of fellow, isn't he?" Stragen noted.

"He doesn't waste any words," Tynian agreed.

"A word with you, Sparhawk," Kring said.

"Of course."

"You *will* serve as my *oma,* won't you?"

"Of course."

"Don't pledge *too* many horses," Kring frowned. "What did he mean when he was talking about branding?"

Sparhawk suddenly remembered. "It's an Atan wedding custom. During the ceremony the happy couple is branded. Each wears the mark of the other."

"*Branded?*"

"So I understand."

"What if a couple doesn't get along?"

"I imagine they cross out the brand."

"How do you cross out a brand?"

"Probably with a hot iron. Are you still bent on marriage, Kring?"

"Find out where the brand goes, Sparhawk. I'll know better once I have that information."

"I gather there are places where you'd rather not be branded?"

"Oh, yes. There are *definitely* places, Sparhawk."

They left Darsas at first light the following morning and rode eastward toward Pela on the steppes of central Astel. The Atans enclosed the column, loping easily to match the speed of the horses. Sparhawk's concerns about the safety of his queen diminished noticeably. Mirtai had very briefly—even peremptorily—advised her owner that she would travel with her countrymen. She did not precisely ask. A rather peculiar change had come over the golden giantess. That wary tension that had always characterized her seemed to have vanished. "I can't exactly put my finger on it," Ehlana confessed about midmorning when they were discussing it. "She just doesn't seem quite the same."

"She isn't, your Majesty," Stragen told her. "She's come home, that's all. Not only that, the presence of adults allows her to take her natural place in her own society. She's still a child—in her own eyes at least. She's never talked about her childhood, but I gather it wasn't a time filled with happiness and security. Something happened to her parents, and she was sold into slavery."

"All of her people are slaves, Milord Stragen," Melidere objected.

"There are different kinds of slavery, Baroness. The slavery of the Atan race by the Tamuls is institutionalized. Mirtai's is personal. She was taken as a child, enslaved, and then forced to take her own steps to protect herself. Now that she's back among the Atans, she's able to recapture some sense of her childhood." He made a wry face. "I never had that opportunity, of course. I was born into a different kind of slavery, and killing my father didn't really liberate me."

"You concern yourself overmuch about that, Milord Stragen," Melidere told him. "You really shouldn't make the issue of your unauthorized conception the central fact of your whole existence, you know. There are much more important things in life."

Stragen looked at her sharply, then laughed, his expression a bit sheepish. "Do I really seem so self-pitying to you, Baroness?"

"No, not really, but you always insist on bringing it up. Don't worry at it so much, Milord. It doesn't make any difference to the rest of us, so why brood about it?"

"You see, Sparhawk," Stragen said. "That's exactly what I meant about this girl. She's the most dishonest person I've ever known."

"*Milord Stragen!*" Melidere protested.

"But you are, my dear Baroness." Stragen grinned. "You don't lie with your mouth, you lie with your entire person. You pose as someone whose head is filled with air, and then you puncture a façade I've spent a lifetime building with one single observation. 'Unauthorized conception' indeed. You've managed to trivialize the central tragedy of my entire life."

"Can you ever forgive me?" Her eyes were wide and dishonestly innocent.

"I give up," he said, throwing his hands in the air in mock surrender. "Where was I? Oh, yes, Mirtai's apparent change of personality. I think the Rite of Passage among the Atans is very significant to them, and that's another reason our beloved little giantess is reverting to the social equivalent of baby talk. Engessa's obviously going to put her through the rite when we reach her homeland, so she's enjoying the last few days of childhood to the hilt."

"Can I ride with you, Father?" Danae asked.

"If you wish."

The little princess rose from her seat in the carriage, handed Rollo to Alean and Mmrr to Baroness Melidere, and held out her hands to Sparhawk.

He lifted her to her usual seat in front of his saddle.

"Take me for a ride, Father," she coaxed in her most little-girl tone.

"We'll be back in a bit," Sparhawk told his wife, and cantered away from the carriage.

"Stragen can be so tedious at times," Danae said tartly. "I'm glad Melidere's the one who's going to have to modify him."

"What?" Sparhawk was startled.

"Where are your eyes, Father?"

"I wasn't actually looking. Do they *really* feel that way about each other?"

"*She* does. She'll let him know how *he* feels when she's ready. What happened in Darsas?"

Sparhawk wrestled with his conscience a bit at that point. "Would you say that you're a religious personage?" he asked carefully.

"That's a novel way to put it."

"Just answer the question, Danae. Are you or are you not affiliated with a religion?"

"Well, of *course* I am, Sparhawk. I'm the *focus* of a religion."

"Then in a general sort of way, you could be defined as a clergyman—uh—person?"

"What are you getting at, Sparhawk?"

"Just say yes, Danae. I'm tiptoeing around the edges of violating an oath, and I need a technical excuse for it."

"I give up. Yes, technically you could call me a church personage—it's a different church, of course, but the definition still fits."

"Thank you. I swore not to reveal this except to another clergyman—personage. You're a clergyperson, so I can tell you."

"That's sheer sophistry, Sparhawk."

"I know, but it gets me off the hook. Baron Kotyk's brother-in-law, Elron, is Sabre." He gave her a suspicious look. "Have you been tampering again?"

"Me?"

"You're starting to stretch the potentials of coincidence a bit, Danae," he said. "You knew what I just told you all along, didn't you?"

"Not the details, no. What you call 'omniscience' is a human concept. It was dreamed up to make people think that they couldn't get away with anything. I get hints—little flashes of things, that's all. I knew there was something significant in Kotyk's house, and I knew that if you and the others listened carefully, you'd hear about it."

"It's like intuition then?"

"That's a very good word for it, Sparhawk. Ours is a little more developed than yours, and we pay close attention to it. You humans tend to ignore it—particularly you men. But something else happened in Darsas, didn't it?"

He nodded. "That shadow put in another appearance. Emban and I were talking with Archimandrite Monsel, and we were visited."

"Whoever's behind this is very stupid, then."

"The Troll-Gods? Isn't that part of the definition of them?"

"We're not absolutely *certain* it's the Troll-Gods, Sparhawk."

"Wouldn't *you* know? I mean, isn't there some way you can identify who's opposing you?"

She shook her head. "I'm afraid not, Sparhawk. We can conceal ourselves from each other. The stupidity of that appearance in Darsas certainly suggests the Troll-Gods, though. We haven't been able to make them understand why the sun comes up in the east as yet. They know it's going to come up every morning, but they're never sure just exactly where."

"You're exaggerating."

"Of course I am." She frowned. "Let's not set our feet in stone on the idea that we're dealing with the Troll-Gods just yet, though. There are some very subtle differences—of course that may be the result of their encounter with you in the Temple of Azash. You frightened them very much, you know. I'd be more inclined to suspect an alliance between them and somebody else. I think the Troll-Gods would be more direct. If there is somebody else involved, he's just a bit childish. He hasn't been out in the world. He surrounded himself with people who aren't bright, and he's judging all humans by *his* worshippers. That appearance at Darsas was really a blunder, you know. He didn't have to do it, and all he really managed was to confirm what you'd already told that clergyman—you *did* tell him what's happening, didn't you?"

Sparhawk nodded.

"We really need to get to Sarsos and talk with Sephrenia."

"You're going to speed up the journey again then?"

"I think I'd better. I'm not entirely sure what the ones on the other side are doing yet, but they're starting to move faster for some reason, so we'd better see what we can do to keep up. Take me back to the carriage, Sparhawk. Stragen's probably finished showing off his education by now, and the smell of your armor's beginning to make me nauseous."

Although there was a community of interests among the three disparate segments of the force escorting the Queen of Elenia, Sparhawk, Engessa, and Kring decided to make some effort to keep the Peloi, the Church Knights, and the Atans more or less separate from each other. Cultural differences obviously made a general mingling unwise. The possibilities for misunderstandings were simply too numerous to be ignored. Each leader stressed the need for the strictest of courtesy and formality to his forces, and the end result was a tense and exaggerated stiffness. In a very real sense, the Atans, the Peloi, and the knights were allies rather than comrades. The fact that very few of the Atans spoke Elenic added to the distance between the component parts of the small army moving out onto the treeless expanse of the steppes.

They encountered the eastern Peloi some distance from the town of Pela in central Astel. Kring's ancestors had migrated from this vast grassland some three thousand years earlier, but despite the separation of time and distance, the two branches of the Peloi family were remarkably similar in matters of dress and custom. The only really significant differences seemed to be the marked preference of the eastern Peloi for the javelin as opposed to the saber favored by Kring's people. After a ritual exchange of greetings, Kring and his eastern cousin sat cross-legged on the turf "taking salt together and talking of affairs" while two armies warily faced each other across three hundred yards of open grass. The decision not to go to war with each other today was apparently reached, and Kring led his host and kinsman to the carriage to introduce him all around. The Domi of the eastern Peloi was named Tikume. He was somewhat taller than Kring, but his head was also shaved, a custom among those horsemen dating back to antiquity.

Tikume greeted them all politely. "It is passing strange to see Peloi allied with foreigners," he noted. "Domi Kring has told me of the conditions which prevail in Eosia, but I had not fully realized that they had led to such peculiar arrangements. Of course he and I have not spoken together for more than ten years."

"You've met before, Domi Tikume?" Patriarch Emban asked with a certain surprise.

"Yes, your Grace," Kring replied. "Domi Tikume journeyed to Pelosia with the King of Astel some years back. He made a point of looking me up."

"King Alberen's father was much wiser than his son," Tikume explained, "and he read a great deal. He saw many similarities between Pelosia and Astel, so he paid a state visit to King Soros. He invited me to go along." His expression became one of distaste. "I might have declined if I'd known he was going to travel by boat. I was sick every day for two months. Domi Kring and I got on well together, though. He was kind enough to take me with him to the marshes to hunt ears."

"Did he share the profits with you, Domi Tikume?" Ehlana asked him.

"What was that, Queen Ehlana?" Tikume looked baffled.

Kring, however, laughed nervously and flushed just a bit.

Then Mirtai strode up to the carriage.

"Is this the one?" Tikume asked Kring.

Kring nodded happily. "Isn't she stupendous?"

"Magnificent," Tikume agreed fervently, his tone almost reverential. Then he dropped to one knee. "Doma," he greeted her, clasping both hands in front of his face.

Mirtai looked inquiringly at Kring.

"It's a Peloi word, beloved," he explained. "It means 'Domi's mate.' "

"That hasn't been decided yet, Kring," she pointed out.

"Can there be any doubt, beloved?" he replied.

Tikume was still down on one knee. "You shall enter our camp with all honors, Doma Mirtai," he declared, "for among our people, you are a queen. All shall kneel to you, and all shall give way to you. Poems and songs shall be composed in your honor, and rich gifts shall be bestowed upon you."

"*Well*, now," Mirtai said.

"Your beauty is clearly divine, Doma Mirtai," Tikume continued, warming to his subject. "Your very presence brightens a drab world and puts the sun to shame. I am awed at the wisdom of my brother Kring in having selected you as his mate. Come straightway to our camp, divine one, so that my people may adore you."

"My goodness," Ehlana breathed. "Nobody's ever said anything like that to *me*."

"We just didn't want to embarrass you, my Queen," Stragen told her blandly. "We *feel* that way about you, of course, but we didn't want to be too obvious about it."

"Well said," Ulath approved.

Mirtai looked at Kring with a new interest. "Why didn't you tell me about this, Kring?" she asked him.

"I thought you knew, beloved."

"I didn't," she replied. Her lower lip pushed forward slightly in a thoughtful kind of pout. "But I do now," she added. "Have you chosen an *oma* as yet?"

"Sparhawk serves me in that capacity, beloved."

"Why don't you go have a talk with Atan Engessa, Sparhawk?" she suggested. "Tell him for me that I do not look upon Domi Kring's suit with disfavor."

"That's a *very* good idea, Mirtai," Sparhawk replied. "I'm surprised I didn't think of it myself."

CHAPTER FOURTEEN

The town of Pela in central Astel was a major trading center where merchants and cattle buyers came from all parts of the empire to do business with the Peloi herders. It was a shabby-looking, unfinished sort of place. Many of its buildings were no more than ornate fronts with large tents erected behind them. No attempt had ever been made to pave its rutted streets, and the passage of strings of wagons and herds of cattle raised a cloud of dust that entirely obscured the town most of the time. Beyond the poorly defined outskirts lay an ocean of tents, the portable homes of the nomadic Peloi.

Tikume led them through the town and beyond to a hilltop where a number of brightly striped pavilions encircled a large open area. A canopy held aloft by poles shaded a place of honor at the very top of the hill, and the ground beneath that canopy was carpeted and strewn with cushions and furs.

Mirtai was the absolute center of attention. Her rather scanty marching clothes had been covered with a purple robe that reached to the ground, an indication of her near royal status. Kring and Tikume formally escorted her to the ceremonial center of the camp and introduced her to Tikume's wife, Vida, a sharp-faced woman who also wore a purple robe and looked at Mirtai with undisguised hostility.

Sparhawk and the rest joined the Peloi leaders in the shade as honored guests.

The face of Tikume's wife grew darker and darker as Peloi warriors vied with each other to heap extravagant compliments upon Mirtai as they were presented to Kring and his purported bride-to-be. There were gifts and a number of songs praising the beauty of the golden giantess.

"How did they find time to make up songs about her?" Talen quietly asked Stragen.

"I'd imagine that the songs have been around for a long time," Stragen replied. "They've substituted Mirtai's name, that's all. I expect there'll be poems as well. I know a third-rate poet in Emsat who makes a fairly good living writing poems and love letters for young nobles too lazy or uninspired to compose their own. There's a whole body of literature with blank spaces in it that serves in such situations."

"They just fill in the blanks with the girl's name?" Talen demanded incredulously.

"It wouldn't really make much sense to fill them in with some other girl's name, would it?"

"That's dishonest!" Talen exclaimed.

"What a novel attitude, Talen." Patriarch Emban laughed. "Particularly coming from you."

"You aren't supposed to cheat when you're telling a girl how you feel about her," Talen insisted. Talen had begun to notice girls. They had been there all along, of course, but he had not noticed them before. Now he had some rather surprisingly strong convictions. It was to the credit of his friends that not one of them laughed at his peculiar expression of integrity. Baroness Melidere, however, impulsively embraced him.

"What was that all about?" he asked her a little suspiciously.

"Oh, nothing," she replied, touching a gentle hand to his cheek. "When was the last time you shaved?" she asked him.

"Last week sometime, I think—or maybe the week before."

"You're due again, I'd say. You're definitely growing up, Talen."

The boy flushed slightly.

Princess Danae gave Sparhawk a sly little smirk.

After the gifts and the poems and songs came the demonstrations of prowess. Kring's tribesmen demonstrated their proficiency with their sabers. Tikume's men did much the same with their javelins, which they either cast or used as short lances. Sir Berit unhorsed an equally youthful Cyrinic Knight, and two blond-braided Genidians engaged in a fearsomely realistic mock axe-fight.

"It's all relatively standard, of course, Emban," Ambassador Oscagne said to the Patriarch of Ucera. The friendship of the two men had progressed to the point where they had begun to discard titles. "Warrior cultures almost totally circumscribe their lives with ceremonies."

Emban smiled. "I've noticed that, Oscagne. Our Church Knights are the most courteous and ceremonial men I know."

"Prudence, your Grace," Ulath explained cryptically.

"You'll get used to that in time, your Excellency," Tynian assured the ambassador. "Sir Ulath hates to waste words."

"I wasn't being mysterious, Tynian," Ulath told him. "I was only pointing out that you almost have to be polite to a man who's holding an axe."

Atan Engessa rose and bowed a bit stiffly to Ehlana. "May I test your slave, Ehlana-Queen?" he asked.

"How exactly do you mean, Atan Engessa?" she asked warily.

"She approaches the time of the Rite of Passage. We must decide if she is ready. I will not harm her. These others are demonstrating their skill. Atana Mirtai and I will participate. It will be a good time for the test."

"As you think best, Atan," Ehlana consented, "as long as the Atana does not object."

"If she is truly Atan, she will not object, Ehlana-Queen." He turned abruptly and crossed to where Mirtai sat with the Peloi.

"Mirtai's certainly the center of things today," Melidere observed.

"I think it's very nice," Ehlana said. "She keeps herself in the background most of the time. She's entitled to a bit of attention."

"It's political, you realize," Stragen told her. "Tikume's people are showering Mirtai with attention for Kring's benefit."

"I know, Stragen, but it's nice all the same." She looked speculatively at her golden slave. "Sparhawk, I'd take it as a personal favor if you'd actively pursue the marriage negotiations with Atan Engessa. Mirtai deserves some happiness."

"I'll see what I can arrange for her, my Queen."

Mirtai readily agreed to Engessa's proposed test. She rose gracefully to her feet, unfastened the neck of her purple robe, and let it fall.

The Peloi gasped. Their womenfolk were customarily dressed in far more concealing garments. The sneer on the face of Tikume's wife Vida, however, was a bit wan. Mirtai was significantly female. She was also fully armed, and that also shocked the Peloi. She and Engessa moved to the area in front of the canopy, curtly inclined their heads to each other, and drew their swords.

Sparhawk thought he knew the differences between contest and combat, but what followed blurred that boundary for him. Mirtai and Engessa seemed to be fully intent on killing each other. Their swordsmanship was superb, but their manner of fencing involved a great deal more physical contact than did western-style fighting.

"It looks like a wrestling match with swords," Kalten observed to Ulath.

"Yes," Ulath agreed. "I wonder if a man could do that in an axe-fight. If you could kick somebody in the face the way she just did and then follow up with an axe-stroke, you could win a lot of fights in a hurry."

"I *knew* she was going to do that to him." Kalten chuckled as Engessa landed flat on his back in the dust. "She did it to me once."

Engessa, however, did not lie gasping on the ground as Kalten had. He rolled away from Mirtai instead and came to his feet with his sword still in his hand. He raised his blade in a kind of salute and then immediately attacked again.

The "test" continued for several more minutes until a watching Atan sharply banged his fist on his breastplate to signal the end of the match. The man who had signalled was much older than his compatriots, or so it seemed. His hair was white. Nothing else about him seemed any different, however.

Mirtai and Engessa bowed formally to each other, and he returned her to her place where she once again drew on her robe and sank down onto a cushion. Vida no longer sneered.

"She is fit," Engessa reported to Ehlana. He reached up under his breastplate and tenderly touched a sore spot. "More than fit," he added. "She is a skilled and dangerous opponent. I am proud to be the one she will call 'Father.' She will add luster to my name."

"*We* rather like her, Atan Engessa." Ehlana smiled. "I'm so glad you agree with us." She let the full impact of that devastating smile wash over the stern-faced Atan, and hesitantly, almost as if in spite of himself, he smiled back.

"I think he lost two fights today," Talen whispered to Sparhawk.

"So it would seem," Sparhawk replied.

"We can never catch up with them, friend Sparhawk," Tikume said that evening as they all relaxed on carpets near a flaring campfire. "These steppes are open grasslands with only a few groves of trees. There isn't really any place to hide, and you can't ride a horse through tall grass without leaving a trail a blind man could follow. They come out of nowhere, kill the herders, and run off the cattle. I followed one of those groups of raiders myself. They'd stolen a hundred cattle and they left a broad trail through the grass. After a few miles, the trail just ended. There was no sign that they'd dispersed. They just vanished. It was as if something had reached down and carried them off into the sky."

"Have there been any other disturbances, Domi?" Tynian asked carefully. "What I'm trying to say is, has there been unrest of any kind among your people? Wild stories? Rumors? That sort of thing?"

"No, friend Tynian." Tikume smiled. "We are an open-faced people. We do not conceal our emotions from each other. I'd know if there were something afoot. I've heard about what's been happening over around Darsas, so I know why you ask. Nothing like that is happening here. We don't worship our heroes the way they do, we just try to be like them. Someone's stealing our cattle and killing our herdsmen." He looked a bit accusingly at Oscagne. "I would not insult you for all the world, your Honor," he said, "but you might suggest to the emperor that he would be wise to have some of his Atans look into it. If we have to deal with it ourselves, our neighbors won't like it very much. We of the Peloi tend to be a bit indiscriminate when someone steals our cattle."

"I'll bring the matter to his Imperial Majesty's attention," Oscagne promised.

"Soon, friend Oscagne," Tikume recommended. "Very soon."

"She's a highly skilled warrior, Sparhawk-Knight," Engessa was saying the following morning as the two sat by a small fire.

"Granted," Sparhawk replied, "but by your own traditions, she's still a child."

"That's why it's my place to negotiate for her," Engessa pointed out. "If she were adult, she would do it herself. Children sometimes do not know their own worth."

"But a child cannot be as valuable as an adult."

"That's not always entirely true, Sparhawk-Knight. The younger a woman, the greater her price."

"Oh, this is absurd," Ehlana broke in. The negotiations were of a delicate nature and would normally have taken place in private. *Normally*, however, did not always apply to Sparhawk's wife. "Your offer's completely unacceptable, Sparhawk."

"Whose side are you on, dear?" he asked her mildly.

"Mirtai's my friend. I won't permit you to insult her. Ten horses indeed! I could get that much for Talen."

"Were you planning to sell him, too?"

"I was just illustrating a point."

Sir Tynian had also stopped by. Of all of their group, he was closest to Kring and he keenly felt the responsibilities of friendship. "What sort of offer would your Majesty consider properly respectful?" he asked Ehlana.

"Not a horse less than sixty," she declared adamantly.

"*Sixty!*" Tynian exclaimed. "You'll impoverish him! What kind of a life will Mirtai have if you marry her off to a pauper?"

"Kring's hardly a pauper, Sir Knight," she retorted. "He still has all that gold King Soros paid him for those Zemoch ears."

"But that's not *his* gold, your Majesty," Tynian pointed out. "It belongs to his people."

Sparhawk smiled and motioned with his head to Engessa. Unobtrusively, the two stepped away from the fire. "I'd guess that they'll settle on thirty, Atan Engessa," he tentatively suggested.

"Most probably," Engessa agreed.

"It seems like a fair number to me. Doesn't it to you?" It hovered on the verge of being an offer.

"It's more or less what I had in mind, Sparhawk-Knight."

"Me, too. Done then?"

"Done." The two of them clasped hands. "Should we tell them?" the Atan asked, the faintest hint of a smile touching his face.

"They're having a lot of fun." Sparhawk grinned. "Why don't we let them play it out? We can find out how close our guess was. Besides, these negotiations are very important to Kring and Mirtai. If we were to agree in just a few minutes, it might make them feel cheapened."

"You have been much in the world, Sparhawk-Knight," Engessa observed. "You know well the hearts of men—and of women."

"No man ever truly knows the heart of a woman, Engessa-Atan," Sparhawk replied ruefully.

The negotiations between Tynian and Ehlana had reached the tragic stage, each of them accusing the other of ripping out hearts and similar extravagances. Ehlana's performance was masterful. The Queen of Elenia had a strong flair for histrionics, and she was a highly skilled orator. She extemporized at length upon Sir Tynian's disgraceful niggardliness, her voice rising and falling in majestic cadences. Tynian, on the other hand, was coolly rational, although he, too, became emotional at times.

Kring and Mirtai sat holding hands not far away, their eyes filled with concern as they hung breathlessly on every word. Tikume's Peloi encircled the haggling pair, straining to hear.

It went on for hours, and it was nearly sunset when Ehlana and Tynian finally reached a grudging agreement—thirty horses—and concluded the bargain by spitting in their hands and smacking their palms together. Sparhawk and Engessa formalized the agreement in the same fashion, and a tumultuous cheer went up from the rapt Peloi. It had been a highly entertaining day all round, and that evening's celebration was loud and long.

"I'm exhausted," Ehlana confessed to her husband after they had retired to their tent for the night.

"Poor dear," Sparhawk commiserated.

"I had to step in, though. You were just being too meek, Sparhawk. You'd have given her away. It's a good thing I was there. You'd have never managed to reach that kind of agreement."

"I was on the other side, Ehlana, remember?"

"That's what I don't understand, Sparhawk. How *could* you treat poor Mirtai so disgracefully?"

"Rules of the game, love. I was representing Kring."

"I'm still very disappointed in you, Sparhawk."

"Well, fortunately, you and Tynian were there to get it all done properly. Engessa and I couldn't have done half so well."

"It *did* turn out rather well, didn't it? Even though it took us all day."

"You were brilliant, my love, absolutely brilliant."

"I've been in some very shabby places in my life, Sparhawk," Stragen said the next morning, "but Pela's the absolute worst. It's been abandoned several times, did you know that? Maybe abandoned isn't the right word. 'Moved' is probably closer to the truth. Pela exists wherever the Peloi establish their summer encampment."

"I'd imagine that sends the mapmakers into hysterics."

"More than likely. It's a temporary town, but it absolutely reeks of money. It takes a great deal of ready cash to buy a cattle herd."

"Were you able to make contact with the local thieves?"

"They contacted us, actually." Talen grinned. "A boy no more than eight lifted Stragen's purse. He's very good—except that he doesn't run very well. I caught him within fifty yards. After we'd explained who we were, he was very happy to take us to see the man in charge."

"Has the thieves' council made any decision as yet?" Sparhawk asked Stragen.

"They're still mulling it over," Stragen replied. "They're a bit conservative here in Daresia. The notion of cooperating with the authorities strikes them as immoral for some reason. I sort of expect an answer when we get to Sarsos. The thieves of Sarsos carry a great deal of weight in the empire. Did anything meaningful happen while we were gone?"

"Kring and Mirtai got betrothed."

"That was quick. I'll have to congratulate them."

"Why don't you two get some sleep," Sparhawk suggested. "We'll be leaving for Sarsos tomorrow. Tikume's going to ride along with us to the edge of the steppes. I think he'd like to go a bit farther, but the Styrics at Sarsos make him nervous." He rose to his feet. "Get some sleep," he told them. "I want to go have a talk with Oscagne."

The Peloi encampment was quiet. It was early summer now, and the midday heat kept the nomads inside their tents. Sparhawk walked across the hard-packed earth toward the tent shared by Ambassador Oscagne and Patriarch Emban. His chain mail jingled as he walked. Since they were in a secure encampment, the knights had decided to forgo the discomfort of their formal armor.

He found the two he sought sitting beneath a canopy at the side of their tent eating a melon.

"Well met, Sir Knight," Oscagne said as the Pandion approached.

"That's an archaic form of greeting, Oscagne," Emban told him.

"I'm an archaic sort of fellow, Emban."

"I was curious about something," Sparhawk said, joining them on the shaded carpet.

"It's a characteristic of the young, I suppose." Oscagne smiled.

Sparhawk let that pass. "This part of Astel seems quite different from what we ran into farther west," he observed.

"Yes," Oscagne agreed. "Astel's the melting pot that gave rise to all Elene cultures—both here in Daresia and in Eosia as well."

"We might want to argue about that someday," Emban murmured.

"Daresia's older, that's all." Oscagne shrugged. "That doesn't necessarily mean that it's better. Anyway, what you've seen of Astel so far is very much like what you'd encounter in the Elene Kingdom of Pelosia, wouldn't you say?"

"There are similarities, yes," Sparhawk replied.

"The similarities will stop when we reach the edge of the steppes. The western two-thirds of Astel are Elene. From the edge of the steppes to the Atan border, Astel's Styric."

"How did that happen?" Emban asked. "The Styrics in Eosia are widely dispersed. They live in their own villages and follow their own laws and customs."

"How cosmopolitan are you feeling today, Emban?"

"You're planning to insult my provincialism, I take it."

"Not too much, I hope. Your prototypical Elene is a bigot." Oscagne held up one hand. "Let me finish before you explode. Bigotry's a form of egotism, and I think you'll have to concede that Elenes have a very high opinion of themselves. They seem to feel that God smiles particularly for them."

"Doesn't he?" Emban feigned surprise.

"Stop that. For reasons only God can understand, the Styrics particularly irritate the Elenes."

"I have no trouble understanding it." Emban shrugged. "It's their superior attitude. They treat us as if we were children."

"From their perspective, we are, your Grace," Sparhawk told him. "Styrics have been civilized for forty thousand years. We got started somewhat later."

"For whatever the reason," Oscagne continued, "the initial impulse of the Elenes has been to drive the Styrics out—or to kill them. That's why the Styrics migrated to Eosia much earlier than you Elenes did. They were driven into the wilderness by Elene prejudice. Eosia was not the only wilderness, however. There's another that exists along the Atan border, and many Styrics fled there in antiquity. After the empire was formed, we Tamuls asked the Elenes to stop molesting the Styrics living around Sarsos."

"Asked?"

"We were quite firm—and we *did* have all those Atans with nothing else to do. We've agreed to let the Elene clergy deliver thunderous denunciations from the pulpit, but we garrison enough Atans around Sarsos to keep the two people separate. It's quieter that way, and we Tamuls are extraordinarily fond of quiet. I think you gentlemen are in for a surprise when we reach Sarsos. It's the only truly Styric city in the entire world. It's an astonishing place. God seems to smile in a very special way there."

"You keep talking about God, Oscagne," Emban noted. "I thought a preoccupation with God was an Elene conceit."

"You're more cosmopolitan than I thought, your Grace."

"Just exactly what do you mean when you use the word *God,* your Excellency?"

"We use the term generically. Our Tamul religion isn't very profound. We tend to think that a man's relationship with his God—or Gods—is his own affair."

"That's heresy, you know. It would put the Church out of business."

"That's all right, Emban." Oscagne smiled. "Heresy's encouraged in the Tamul Empire. It gives us something to talk about on long, rainy afternoons."

They rode out with a huge Peloi escort the following morning. The party moving northeasterly looked not so much like an army on the march as it did a migration. Kring and Tikume rode more or less by themselves for the next several days, renewing their blood ties and discussing an exchange of breeding stock.

Sparhawk attempted an experiment during the ride from Pela to the edge of the steppes, but try though he might, he could not detect any traces of Aphrael's tampering with time and distance. The Child-Goddess was simply too skilled, and her manipulations too seamless for him to detect them.

Once, when she had joined him on Faran's back, he raised an issue that had been troubling him. "I'm not trying to pry, but it seems that it's been about fifty days since we landed at Salesha. How long has it really been?"

"Quite a bit less than that, Sparhawk," she replied. "Half that long at most."

"I was sort of looking for an exact answer, Danae."

"I'm not very good with numbers, Father. I know the difference between a few and a lot, and that's all that's really important, isn't it?"

"It's a bit imprecise, wouldn't you say?"

"Is precision all that important to you, Sparhawk?"

"You can't begin to think logically without precision, Danae."

"Don't think logically then. Try being intuitive for a change. You might even find that you like it."

"How long, Danae?" he insisted.

"Three weeks." She shrugged.

"That's a little better."

"Well—more or less."

The edge of the steppes was marked by a dense forest of pale-trunked birches, and Tikume and his tribesmen turned back there. Since it was late in the day, the royal escort made camp on the edge of the forest so that they might follow the shaded road leading off through the trees in the full light of day.

After they had settled down and the cooking fires were going, Sparhawk took Kring and they went looking for Engessa. "We have a peculiar situation here, gentlemen," he told them as they walked together near the edge of the forest.

"How so, Sparhawk-Knight?" Engessa asked.

"We've got three different kinds of warriors in this group, and I'd imagine there are three different approaches to engagement. We should probably discuss the differences so that we won't be working at cross-purposes if trouble arises. The standard approach of the Church Knights is based on our equipment. We wear armor, and we ride large horses. Whenever there's trouble, we usually just smash the center of an opposing army."

"We prefer to peel an enemy like an apple," Kring said. "We ride around his force very fast and slice off bits and pieces as we go."

"We fight on foot," Engessa supplied. "We're trained to be self-sufficient, so we just rush the enemy and engage him hand to hand."

"Does that work very well?" Kring asked him.

"It always has." Engessa shrugged.

"If we happen to run into any kind of trouble, it probably wouldn't be a good idea for us all to dash right in," Sparhawk mused. "We'd be stumbling all over each other. See what you think of this. If a force of any significant size tries to attack us, Kring and his men circle around behind them, I form up the knights and charge the center, and Atan Engessa spreads his force out along a broad front. The enemy will sort of fold in behind the knights after we bash a hole in their center. They always do, for some reason. Kring's attacks along the rear and the flanks will add to their confusion. They'll be disorganized and most of them will be cut off from their leaders in one way or another. That would be a good time for Engessa to attack. The best soldiers in the world don't function too well when nobody's close enough to give orders."

"It's a workable tactic," Engessa conceded. "It's a bit surprising to find that other people in the world know how to plan battles, too."

"The story of man has been pretty much the story of one long battle, Atan Engessa," Sparhawk told him. "We're all experienced at it, so we devise tactics that take advantage of our strengths. Do we want to do it the way I suggested?"

Kring and Engessa looked at each other. "Almost any plan will work," Kring shrugged, "as long as we all know what we're doing."

"How will we know when you're ready for us to attack?" Engessa asked Sparhawk.

"My friend Ulath has a horn," Sparhawk replied. "When he blows it once, my knights will charge. When he blows it twice, Kring's men will start peeling off the rear elements. When we've got the enemy's full attention, I'll have Ulath blow three times. That's when you'll want to charge."

Engessa's eyes were alight. "It's the sort of strategy that doesn't leave very many survivors among the enemy, Sparhawk-Knight," he said.

"That was sort of the idea, Engessa-Atan."

The birch forest lay on a long, gradual slope rising from the steppes of central Astel to the rugged foothills on the Atan border. The road was broad and well maintained, though it tended to wander a great deal. Engessa's unmounted Atans ranged out about a mile on each side of the road, and for the first three days they reported no sightings of men, although they did encounter large herds of deer. Summer had not yet dried the lingering dampness from the forest floor, and the air in the sun-dappled shade was cool and moist, still smelling of new growth and renewal.

Since the trees obstructed their vision, they rode cautiously. They set up their nighttime encampments while the sun was still above the horizon, and erected certain rudimentary fortifications to prevent surprises after dark.

On the morning of their fourth day in the forest, Sparhawk rose early and walked through the first steel-grey light of dawn to the line where the horses were picketed. He found Khalad there. Kurik's eldest son had snubbed Faran's head up close to a birch tree and was carefully inspecting the big roan's hooves. "I was just going to do that," Sparhawk said quietly. "He seemed to be favoring his left fore-hoof yesterday."

"Stone bruise," Khalad said shortly. "You know, Sparhawk, you might want to give some thought to putting him out to pasture when we get back home. He's not a colt anymore, you know."

"Neither am I, when you get right down to it. Sleeping on the ground's not nearly as much fun as it used to be."

"You're just getting soft."

"Thanks. Is this weather going to hold?"

"As nearly as I can tell, yes." Khalad lowered Faran's hoof to the ground and took hold of the snubbing rope. "No biting," he cautioned the horse. "If you bite me, I'll kick you in the ribs."

Faran's long face took on an injured expression.

"He's an evil-tempered brute," Khalad noted, "but he's far and away the smartest horse I've ever come across. You should put him to stud. It might be interesting to train intelligent colts for a change. Most horses aren't really very bright."

"I thought horses were among the cleverest of animals."

"That's a myth, Sparhawk. If you want a smart animal, get yourself a pig. I've never yet been able to build a pen that a pig couldn't think his way out of."

"They're built a little close to the ground for riding. Let's go see how breakfast's coming."

"Who's cooking this morning?"

"Kalten, I think. Ulath would know."

"Kalten? Maybe I'll stay here and eat with the horses."

"I'm not sure that a bucketful of raw oats would taste all that good."

"I'd put it up against Kalten's cooking any day, my Lord."

They rode out shortly after the sun rose, and proceeded through the cool, sun-speckled forest. The birds seemed to be everywhere, and they sang enthusiastically. Sparhawk smiled as he remembered how Sephrenia had once punctured his illusion that birdsong was an expression of a love for music. "Actually they're warning other birds to stay away, dear one," she had said. "They're claiming possession of nesting sites. It sounds very pretty, but all they're really saying is, 'My tree. My tree. My tree.'"

Mirtai came back along the road late that morning running with an effortless stride. "Sparhawk," she said quietly when she reached the carriage, "Atan Engessa's scouts report that there are people up ahead."

"How many?" he asked, his tone suddenly all business.

"We can't be certain. The scouts didn't want to be seen. There are soldiers of some kind out there, and they seem to be waiting for us."

"Berit," Sparhawk said to the young knight, "why don't you ride on ahead and ask Kalten and the others to join us? Don't run. Try to make it look casual."

"Right." Berit rode forward at a trot.

"Mirtai," the big knight said, trying to keep his voice calm, "is there any kind of defensible position nearby?"

"I was just coming to that," she replied. "There's a kind of hill about a quarter of a mile ahead. It sort of juts up from the floor of the forest—boulders mostly. They're covered over with moss."

"Could we get the carriage up there?"

She shook her head.

"You get to walk then, my Queen," he said to his wife.

"We don't *know* that they're hostile, Sparhawk," Ehlana objected.

"That's true," he conceded, "but we don't know that they aren't, either, and that's far more important."

Kalten and the others came back along the column with Kring and Engessa.

"Are they doing anything at all, Atan Engessa?" Sparhawk asked.

"Just watching, Sparhawk-Knight. There are more of them than we thought at first—a thousand at least—probably a lot more."

"It's going to be tricky with all these trees," Kalten pointed out.

"I know." Sparhawk grunted. "Khalad, how close is it to noon?"

"About another hour, my Lord," Khalad replied from the carriage driver's seat.

"Close enough, then. There's a hill just up ahead. We'll ride onto it and make some show of stopping for our midday meal. Our friends here in the carriage will sort of stroll up to the top. The rest of us will spread out around the base of the hill. We'll build fires and rattle pots and pans together. Ehlana, be silly. I want you and the baroness to do a lot of laughing up there on that hilltop. Stragen, take some men and erect a pavilion of some kind up there. Try to make it look festive. Move some rocks out of your way and sort of pile them up around the hilltop."

"A siege again, Sparhawk?" Ulath said disapprovingly.

"Have you got a better idea?"

"Not really, but you know how I feel about sieges."

"Nobody said you had to *like* it, Ulath," Tynian told him.

"Spread the word," Sparhawk told them, "and let's try to make it all look very casual."

They were tense as they proceeded along the road at a leisurely appearing pace. When they rounded a bend and Sparhawk saw the hill, he immediately approved of its strategic potentials. It was one of those rockpiles that inexplicably rear up out of forests the world over. It was a conical heap of rounded boulders perhaps forty feet high, green with moss and totally devoid of trees or brush. It stood about two hundred yards to the left of the road. Talen rode to its base, dismounted, scampered up to the top, and looked around. "It's perfect, my Queen," he shouted back down. "You can see for miles up here. It's just what you were looking for."

"That's a nice touch," Bevier noted, "assuming that our friends out there speak Elenic, of course."

Stragen came forward from the line of packhorses carrying a lute. "A little finishing touch, my Queen." He smiled to Ehlana.

"Do you play, Milord?" she asked him.

"Any gentleman plays, your Majesty."

"Sparhawk doesn't."

"We're still working on a definition of Sparhawk, Queen Ehlana," Stragen replied lightly. "We're not altogether certain that *gentleman* really fits him—no offense intended of course, old boy," he hastily assured the black-armored Pandion.

"A suggestion, Sparhawk?" Tynian said.

"Go ahead."

"We don't know anything about those people out there, but they don't know anything about us either—or at the most, very, very little."

"That's probably true."

"Just because they're watching doesn't mean they're planning an immediate attack—if they're even planning to attack at all. If they are, they could just sit and wait until we're back on the road again."

"All right."

"But we're travelling with some giddy noblewomen—begging your Majesty's pardon—and noblewomen don't really need reasons for the things they do."

"Your popularity isn't growing in certain quarters, Sir Tynian," Ehlana said ominously.

"I'm crushed, but couldn't your Majesty decide—on a whim—that you absolutely adore this place and that you're bored with riding in a carriage? Under those circumstances, wouldn't it be natural for you to order a halt for the day?"

"It's not bad, Sparhawk," Kalten said. "While we're all lunching, we can sort of unobtrusively fortify that hill a little better. Then, after a few hours, when it's obvious that we aren't going any farther today, we can set up the usual evening camp—field fortifications and the like. We're not on any specific timetable, so half a day lost isn't going to put us behind any sort of schedule. The queen's safety's a lot more important than speed right now, wouldn't you say?"

"You know how I'm going to answer that, Kalten."

"I was sure I could count on you."

"It's good, Sparhawk-Knight," Engessa approved. "Give my scouts one whole night to work with, and we'll not only know how many are out there, but their names as well."

"Break a wheel," Ulath added.

"What was that, Sir Knight?" Ambassador Oscagne asked, looking perplexed.

"That would give us another excuse for stopping," the Thalesian replied. "If the carriage broke down, we'd *have* to stop."

"Can you fix a wheel, Sir Ulath?"

"No, but we can rig some kind of a skid to get us by until we can find a black-smith."

"Wouldn't a skid make the carriage jolt and bump around a great deal?" Patri-arch Emban asked with a pained look.

"Probably." Ulath shrugged.

"I'm almost certain we can find some other reason to stop, Sir Knight. Have you any idea of how uncomfortable that would be?"

"I didn't really give it much thought, your Grace," Ulath replied blandly, "but then, I won't be riding in the carriage, so it wouldn't bother *me* in the slightest."

■ CHAPTER FIFTEEN ■

The addition of a dozen female Atans added to the subterfuge of a courtly gather-ing on the hilltop, although it was difficult to persuade the Atan girls that their faces would not break if they smiled or that the Gods had issued no commandment against laughing. Berit and a number of other youthful knights entertained the ladies while casually clearing inconvenient—and not a few convenient—bushel basket–sized rocks from the natural amphitheater at the top of the hill. The back side of the pile of boulders was more precipitous than the front, and the rim of the hilltop on that side formed a naturally defensible wall. The young knights piled up enough rock to form a crude kind of breastwork around the other three sides. It was all very casual, but within an hour some fairly substantial fortifications had been erected.

There were many cooking fires around the base of the hill, and their smoke laid a kind of blue haze out among the white tree trunks. There was a great deal of clanking and rattling and shouting back and forth as the oddly assorted force made some show of preparing a meal. Engessa's Atans gathered up large piles of firewood—mostly in ten-foot lengths—and all of the cooks stated a loud preference for wood chips for their fires rather than chunks. It was therefore necessary to chop at the ends of the birch logs, and there were soon neat piles of sharpened ten-foot poles spaced out at regular intervals around the hill, ready for use either as fire-wood or a palisade that could be erected in a few minutes. The knights and the Peloi tethered their horses nearby and lounged around the foot of the hill while the Atans were evenly dispersed a bit farther out under the trees.

Sparhawk stood at the top of the hill surveying the progress of the work below. The ladies were gathered under a broad canopy erected on poles in the center of the depressed basin on the hilltop. Stragen was strumming his lute and singing to them in his deep rich voice.

"How's it going down there?" Talen asked, coming up to where Sparhawk stood.

"It's about as secure as Khalad can make it without being obvious about it," Sparhawk replied.

"He's awfully good, isn't he?" Talen said with a certain pride.

"Your brother? Oh, yes. Your father trained him very well."

"It might have been nice to grow up with my brothers." Talen sounded a bit wistful. He shrugged. "But then . . ." He peered out at the forest. "Any word from Engessa?"

"Our friends are still out there."

"They're going to attack, aren't they?"

"Probably. You don't gather that many armed men in one place without having something military in mind."

"I like your plan here, Sparhawk, but I think it's got a hole in it."

"Oh?"

"Once they finally realize that we aren't going to move from this spot, they might decide to wait and then come at us after dark. Fighting at night's a lot different from doing it in the daytime, isn't it?"

"Usually, yes, but we'll cheat."

Talen gave him a quizzical look.

"There are a couple of spells that brighten things up when you need to see."

"I keep forgetting about that."

"You might as well get used to it, Talen," Sparhawk told him with a faint smile. "When we get back home, you're going to start your novitiate."

"When did we decide that?"

"Just now. You're old enough, and if you keep on growing the way you have been lately, you'll be big enough."

"Is magic hard to learn?"

"You have to pay attention. It's all done in Styric, and Styric's a tricky language. If you use the wrong word, all sorts of things can go wrong."

"Thanks, Sparhawk. That's all I need—something else to worry about."

"We'll talk with Sephrenia when we get to Sarsos. Maybe she'll agree to train you. Flute likes you, so she'll forgive you if you make any mistakes."

"What's Flute got to do with it?"

"If Sephrenia trains you, you'll be submitting your requests to Aphrael."

"Requests?"

"That's what magic is, Talen. You ask a God to do something for you."

"Praying?" the boy asked incredulously.

"Sort of."

"Does Emban know that you're praying to a Styric Goddess?"

"More than likely. The Church chooses to ignore the fact, though—for practical reasons."

"She's a hypocrite then."

"I wouldn't mention that to Emban, if I were you."

"Let me get this straight. If I get to be a Church Knight, I'll be worshipping Flute?"

"Praying to her, Talen. I didn't say anything about worshipping."

"Praying, worshipping, what's the difference?"

"Sephrenia will explain it."

"She's in Sarsos, you say?"

"I didn't say that." Sparhawk silently cursed his careless tongue.

"Yes, as a matter of fact you did."

"All right, but keep it to yourself."

"That's why we came overland, isn't it?"

"One of the reasons, yes. Haven't you got something else to do?"

"Not really, no."

"Go find something—because if you don't, I will."

"You don't have to get all huffy."

Sparhawk gave him a steady stare.

"All right, all right, don't get excited. I'll go entertain Danae and her cat."

Sparhawk stood watching the boy as he returned to the festivities under the canopy. It was obviously time to start being a little careful around Talen. He was dangerously intelligent, and a slip of the tongue might give away things that were supposed to be kept private. The discussion had raised an issue, however. Sparhawk went back to the group gathered on the hilltop and took Berit aside. "Go tell the knights that if those people out there decide to wait until after dark to attack, *I'll* take care of giving us light to work by. If we all try to do it at the same time, we might confuse things."

Berit nodded.

Sparhawk considered it further. "And I'll go talk with Kring and Engessa," he added. "We don't want the Atans and the Peloi going into a panic if the sky suddenly lights up along about midnight tonight."

"Is that what you're going to do?" Berit asked.

"It usually works out about the best in cases like this. One big light's easier to control than several hundred little ones—and it disrupts the enemy's concentration a lot more."

Berit grinned. "It *would* be a little startling to be creeping through the bushes and have the sun come back up again, wouldn't it?"

"A lot of battles have been averted by lighting up the night, Berit, and a battle averted is sometimes even better than one you win."

"I'll remember that, Sparhawk."

The afternoon wore on, and the party on the hilltop became a little strained. There were only so many things to laugh at, and only so many jokes to tell. The warriors around the base of the hill either spent their time attending to equipment or pretending to sleep.

Sparhawk met with the others about midafternoon out near the road.

"If they don't know by now that we aren't going any farther today, they aren't very bright," Kalten noted.

"We *do* look a bit settled in, don't we?" Ulath agreed.

"A suggestion, Sparhawk?" Tynian offered.

"Why do you always say that?"

"Habit, I suppose. I was taught to be polite to my elders. Even the best of spells isn't going to give us the same kind of light we'll have before the sun goes down. We know they're out there, we're in position, and we're rested. Why don't we push things a bit? If we can force them to attack now, we can fight them in daylight."

"How are you going to make somebody attack when he doesn't want to?" Patriarch Emban asked.

"We start making obvious preparations, your Grace," Tynian replied. "It's logical to start on the field fortifications about now anyway. Let's put up the palisade around the foot of the hill, and start digging ditches."

"And cutting trees," Ulath added. "We could clear away some avenues leading out into the woods and pile all the tree trunks up where they'll hinder anybody trying to come through the forest. If they're going to attack, let's make them attack across open ground."

It took a surprisingly short time. The logs for the fence around the base of the hill were already sharpened and stacked in neat piles where they were handy. Digging them in was an easy matter. The birch trees in the forest were all no more than ten inches thick at the base, and they fell quickly to the axes of the warriors and were dragged into the surrounding forest to form large, jumbled piles that would be virtually impossible to penetrate, even for men on foot.

Sparhawk and the others went back up to the hilltop to survey their preparations. "Why don't they attack us now, before we're ready?" Emban tensely asked the knights.

"Because it takes time to organize an attack, your Grace," Bevier explained. "The scouts have to run back and tell the generals what we're doing; the generals have to sneak through the woods to have a look for themselves; and then they all have to get together and argue about what they're going to do. They were planning an ambush. They aren't really ready to attack fortified positions. The business of adjusting one's thinking to a different tactical situation is what takes the longest."

"How long?"

"It depends entirely on the personality of the man in charge. If his mind was really set on an ambush, it could take him as long as a week."

"He's dead, then, Bevier-Knight," Engessa told the Cyrinic tersely. "As soon as we saw the warriors in the woods I dispatched a dozen of my people to the garrison at Sarsos. If our enemy takes more than two days to make up his mind, he'll have five thousand Atans climbing his back."

"Sound thinking, Atan Engessa," Tynian approved. He pondered it. "A thought, Sparhawk. If our friend out there gets all caught up in indecision, we can just continue to strengthen our defenses around this hill—ditches, sharpened stakes, the usual encumbrances. Each improvement we add will make him think things over that much longer—which will give us time to add more fortifications, which will make him think all the more. If we can keep him thinking for two days, the Atans from Sarsos will come up behind him and wipe out his force before he ever gets around to using it."

"Good point," Sparhawk agreed. "Let's get to it."

"I thought that being a military person just involved banging on people with axes and swords," Emban conceded.

"There's a lot of that involved, your Grace." Ulath smiled. "But it doesn't hurt to outsmart your enemy a little, too." He looked at Bevier. "Engines?" he asked.

Bevier blinked. Ulath's cryptic questions always took him by surprise for some reason.

"As long as we have some time on our hands, we could erect some catapults on the hilltop. Attacking through a rain of boulders is always sort of distracting. Getting hit on the head with a fifty-pound rock seems to break a man's concentration, for some reason. If we're going to set up for a siege, we might as well do it right." He looked around at them. "I still don't like sieges, though," he added. "I want everybody to understand that."

The warriors set to work, and the ladies and the young men attending them renewed their festivities, although their hilarity was even more forced now.

Sparhawk and Kalten were reinforcing the breastworks atop the hill. Since his wife and daughter were going to be inside those fortifications, their strength was a matter of more than passing interest to the Prince Consort.

The party under the pavilion had begun to show gaps, and Stragen was increasingly obliged to fill them with his lute.

"He's going to wear out his fingers." Kalten grunted, lifting another large rock into place.

"Stragen enjoys attention." Sparhawk shrugged. "He'll keep playing until the blood runs out from under his fingernails if there's anybody around to listen."

Stragen's lute took up a very old air, and he began to sing again. Sparhawk didn't really have much of an ear for music, but he had to admit that the Thalesian thief had a beautiful voice.

And then Baroness Melidere joined in. Her voice was a rich contralto that blended smoothly with Stragen's baritone. Their duet was perfectly balanced, smooth and rich with the dark tones of their deeper voices. Sparhawk smiled to himself. The baroness was continuing her campaign. Once Aphrael had alerted him to the blond girl's designs on Stragen, Sparhawk could see dozens of artful little ploys she was using to keep her intended victim's attention. He almost felt sorry for Stragen, but he conceded that Melidere would be good for him. The pair concluded their duet to loud applause. Sparhawk glanced toward the pavilion and saw Melidere lay one lingering hand almost caressingly on Stragen's wrist. Sparhawk knew just how potent those accidental-seeming contacts were. Lillias had explained it to him once, and Lillias had been the world's champion seductress—as probably half the men in Jiroch could have sworn to.

Then Stragen turned to another traditional air, and a new voice lifted in song. Kalten dropped the rock he had been lifting. It fell onto his foot, but he did not even wince. The voice was that of an angel, high, sweet, and as clear as glass. It soared effortlessly toward the upper reaches of the soprano range. It was a lyric voice, uncontaminated by the subtle variations of the coloratura, and it seemed as untaught as birdsong.

It was Ehlana's maid, Alean. The doe-eyed girl, always so quiet and unassuming, stood in the center of the pavilion, her face luminous as she sang.

Sparhawk heard Kalten snuffle and he was astonished to see great tears stream-ing down his friend's face as the blond Pandion wept unashamed.

Perhaps his recent conversation with the Child-Goddess had alerted Sparhawk to the potentials of intuition. He suddenly knew, without knowing exactly *how* he knew, that *two* campaigns were in progress—and, moreover, that the one being waged by Baroness Melidere was the more overt and blatant. He carefully concealed a smile behind his hand.

"Lord, that girl's got a beautiful voice!" Kalten said in stunned admiration as Alean concluded her song. "God!" he said then, doubling over to clutch at the foot he had unwittingly injured five minutes earlier.

The work progressed until sunset, and then the combined army pulled back behind the reinforced palisade and waited. Sir Bevier and his Cyrinic Knights re-tired to the hilltop, where they completed the construction of their catapults. Then they amused themselves by lobbing large rocks into the forest, seemingly at ran-dom.

"What are they shooting at, Sparhawk?" Ehlana asked after supper.

"The trees." He shrugged.

"The trees aren't threatening us."

"No, but there are probably people hiding among them. The boulders falling out of the sky should make them a little jumpy." He smiled. "Actually, Bevier's men are testing the range of the engines, dear. If our friends in the forest decide to attack down those avenues we've provided for them, Bevier wants to know exactly when to start shooting."

"There's a great deal more involved in being a soldier than just keeping your equipment clean, isn't there?"

"I'm glad you appreciate that, my Queen."

"Shall we go to bed, then?"

"Sorry, Ehlana," he replied, "but I won't be sleeping tonight. If our friend out there makes up his mind and attacks, there are some things I'll have to do rather quickly." He looked around. "Where's Danae?"

"She and Talen are over there watching Bevier's people throw rocks at the trees."

"I'll go get her. You'll probably want to keep her close to you tonight." He crossed the basin to where Bevier was directing the activities of his knights. "Bed-time," he told his daughter, lifting her into his arms.

She pouted a little at that, but raised no other objections. When Sparhawk was about halfway back to his wife's tent, he slowed. "How much of a stickler are you for formality, Aphrael?" he asked.

"A few genuflections are nice, Father," she replied, "but I can live without them—in an emergency."

"Good. If the attack comes tonight, we're going to need some light to see them by."

"How much light?"

"Sort of noonish would be good."

"I can't do that, Sparhawk. Do you have any idea of how much trouble I'd get into if I made the sun rise when it wasn't supposed to?"

"I wasn't really suggesting that. I just want enough light so that people can't sneak up on us through the shadows. The spell's a fairly long one with a lot of formalities involved and many, many specifics. I may be a little pressed for time, so would you be terribly offended if I just asked you for light and left the details up to you?"

"It's highly irregular, Sparhawk," she chided him primly.

"I know, but just this once, maybe?"

"Oh, I *guess* so, but let's not make a habit of it. I *do* have a reputation to maintain, after all."

"I love you." He laughed.

"Oh, if that's the case, it's perfectly all right then. We can bend all sorts of rules for people who really love us. Just ask for light, Sparhawk. I'll see to it that you get lots and lots of light."

The attack came shortly before midnight. It began with a rain of arrows lofting out of the darkness, followed quickly by attacks on the Atan pickets. That last proved to be what might best be described as a tactical blunder. The Atans were the finest foot soldiers in the world, and they welcomed hand-to-hand combat.

Sparhawk could not clearly see the attacking force from his vantage point on the hilltop, but he firmly controlled his curiosity and held off on illuminating the battlefield until such time as the opposing force was more fully engaged.

As they had anticipated, their enemies used the cover of these first probing moves to attack the logjams designed to impede their progress through the belts of trees set off by Sir Ulath's avenues radiating out from the base of the hill like the spokes of a huge wheel. As it turned out, Bevier's Cyrinics had not been lobbing rocks out into the forest entirely for the fun of it. They had rather precisely pinpointed the range of those jumbles of fallen trees with their catapults, and they hurled baskets full of fist-sized rocks into the air to rain down on the men attempting to tear down the barricades or to widen the narrow gaps that had been deliberately left to permit the Peloi to ride out in search of entertainment. A two-pound rock falling out of the sky will not crush a man, but it will break his bones, and after ten minutes or so, the men out in the woods withdrew.

"I confess to you, Sparhawk-Knight," Engessa said gravely, "I had thought your elaborate preparations a bit silly. Atans do not fight so. Your approach does have certain advantages, though."

"Our societies are different, Atan Engessa. Your people live and fight in wilderness where enemies are encountered singly or in small groups. Our wilderness has been tamed, so our enemies come at us in large numbers. We build forts to live in, and over the centuries we've devised many means to defend those forts."

"When will you make the light come?"

"At a time when it's most inconvenient for our enemy. I want him to commit a large part of his force and to have them fully engaged before I sweep away the darkness. He won't expect that, and it takes time to get orders through to men who are already fighting. We should be able to eliminate a sizeable part of his army before he can pull them back. Defensive warfare has certain advantages if you make the proper preparations."

"Ulath-Knight does not like it."

"Ulath doesn't have the patience for it. Bevier's the expert on defense. He'd be perfectly willing to wait for ten years if need be for the enemy to come to him on *his* terms."

"What will the enemy do next? We Atans are not accustomed to interrupted fights."

"He'll draw back and shoot arrows at us while he thinks things over. Then he'll probably try a direct assault down one of those avenues."

"Why only one? Why not attack from all directions at once?"

"Because he doesn't know how much we can hurt him yet. He'll have to find that out first. He'll learn in time, but it's going to cost him a great deal to get his education. After we've killed about half of his soldiers, he'll do one of two things. He'll either go away, or he'll throw everything he's got at us from all sides at once."

"And then?"

"Then we'll kill the rest of his soldiers and be on our way." Sparhawk shrugged. "Assuming that everything goes the way we've planned, of course."

At two hundred paces and with only starlight to see by, the figures were hardly more than shadows. They marched out into the center of one of Ulath's corridors and halted while others filed out to join them and to form up into a kind of massed formation.

"I can't believe that!" Kalten exclaimed, gaping at the shadowy soldiers at the end of the corridor.

"Is something wrong, Sir Kalten?" Emban's voice was a little shrill.

"Not in the least, your Grace," Kalten replied gaily. "It's just that we're dealing with an idiot." He turned his head slightly. "Bevier," he called, "he's forming up his troops on the *road* to march them into place."

"You're not serious!"

"May all of my toenails fall out if I'm not."

Bevier barked a number of commands, and his knights swung the catapults around to bring them to bear on the unseen avenue leading toward the road. "Give the word, Sparhawk," the young Cyrinic called.

"We're going on down now," Sparhawk called back. "You can start as soon as we reach the bottom. We'll wait so that you can pound them for a while, and then we'll charge. We'd take it as a kindness if you'd stop about then."

Bevier grinned at him.

"Look after my wife while I'm gone."

"Naturally."

Sparhawk and the other warriors began to climb down the hill. "I'll break my men into two groups, friend Sparhawk," Kring said. "We'll circle around and come up onto the road about a half mile behind them on either side. We'll wait for your signal there."

"Don't kill all of them," Engessa cautioned. "My Atans grow sulky if there's fighting and they aren't allowed to participate."

They reached the bottom of the hill, and Bevier's catapults began to thud, launching large rocks this time. There were sounds from off in the direction of the road indicating that the Cyrinic Knights had found the proper range.

"Luck, Sparhawk," Kring said tersely and melted off into the shadows.

"Be careful, Sir Knights," Khalad cautioned them. "Those tree stumps out there are dangerous in the dark."

"It won't be dark when we charge, Khalad," Sparhawk assured him. "I've made some arrangements."

Engessa slipped quietly through an opening in the palisade to join his warriors out in the forest.

"Is it just my imagination, or does it seem to the rest of you that we're dealing with someone who's not really very sophisticated?" Tynian said. "He doesn't seem to have any conception of modern warfare or modern technology."

"I think the word you're groping for is *stupid,* Tynian," Kalten chuckled.

"I'm not so sure." Tynian frowned. "It was too dark for me to make out very much from the hilltop, but it looked almost as if he were forming up his troops into a phalanx. Nobody's done that in the west for over a thousand years."

"It wouldn't be very effective against mounted knights, would it?" Kalten asked.

"I'm not so sure. It would depend on how long his spears are and the size of those overlapping shields. He could give us trouble."

"Berit," Sparhawk said, "go back up the hill and tell Bevier to shift his catapults a bit. I'd like the enemy formation broken up."

"Right." The young knight turned and scrambled back up the hill.

"If he *is* using a phalanx formation," Tynian continued, "it means that he's never come up against mounted troops before and that he's used to fighting in open country."

Bevier's catapults began to hurl boulders at the shadowy formation at the far end of the cleared avenue.

"Let's get started," Sparhawk decided. "I was going to wait a while, but let's see what we're up against." He hauled himself up onto Faran's back and led the knights to a position outside the palisade. Then he drew in a deep breath. *We could use a bit of light now, Divine One.* He cast the thought out without even bothering to frame it in Styric.

That's really *improper, Sparhawk.* Aphrael's voice in his ear was tart. *You know I'm not supposed to respond to prayers in Elenic.*

You know both languages. What difference does it make?

It's a question of style, Sparhawk.

I'll try to do better next time.

I'd really appreciate it. How's this?

It began as a kind of pulsating lavender glow along the northern horizon. Then long streaks of pure, multicolored light spread upward in seething, curtainlike sheets, wavering, undulating like a vast veil shimmering against the night sky.

"What is it?" Khalad exclaimed.

"The northern lights." Ulath grunted. "I've never seen them this far south—or quite so bright. I'm impressed, Sparhawk."

The shimmering curtain of light, rising and falling, crept up and up into the darkness, erasing the stars and filling the night with rainbow light.

A huge groan of consternation and awe rose from the army massing near the road. Sparhawk looked intently down the stump-dotted avenue. The soldiers facing them wore antique armor—breastplates, horsehair-crested helmets, and large, round shields. They wore short swords and carried twelve-foot spears. Their front rank had evidently been formed with overlapping shields and advanced spears. Bevier's catapults, however, had broken those tightly packed ranks, and the rain of boulders continued to smash down among men so jammed together they could not flee.

Sparhawk watched grimly for a few moments. "All right, Ulath," he said at last, "sing the Ogre's song for them."

Ulath grinned and lifted his curled Ogre-horn to his lips and blew a single, deep-toned blast.

The massed foot troops, their ranks broken by the catapults and their minds filled with wonder and dismay by the sudden brilliant light covering half the sky, were in no way prepared to meet the awesome charge of the armored knights and their massive horses. There was a resounding crash, and the front ranks of the massed foot soldiers fell beneath the churning hooves of the war-horses. The knights discarded their lances, drew their swords and axes, and fell to work, carving great swaths through the tightly packed ranks.

"Ulath!" Sparhawk bellowed. "Turn loose the Peloi!"

Sir Ulath blew his Ogre-horn again—twice this time.

The Peloi war cries were shrill and ululating. Sparhawk glanced quickly along the road. The warriors Kring's Peloi were attacking were not the same as the ones facing the knights. Sparhawk had led a charge against infantry, men in breastplates and horsehair-crested helmets who fought on foot. Kring was attacking mounted men, men wearing flowing robes and cloth head coverings, all armed with curved swords much like the Peloi sabers. Quite obviously, the attacking force was comprised of two different elements. There would be time later to ponder those differences. Right now, they were all very busy.

Sparhawk swung his heavy broadsword rhythmically in huge overhead strokes that sheared down into the sea of horsehair-crested helmets surrounding him. He continued for several minutes until the sounds from along the road indicated that the Peloi were fully engaged. "Sir Ulath!" he roared. "Ask the Atans to join us!"

The Ogre-horn sang again—and again—and yet once again.

Sounds of fighting erupted back among the trees. Enemy soldiers who had fled the charge of the knights and the slashing attack of the Peloi found no sanctuary in the woods. Engessa's Atans, silent and deadly, moved through the eerie, multi-colored light streaming down from the pulsating sky, seeking and destroying.

"Sparhawk!" Kalten shouted. "Look!"

Sparhawk jerked his head around, and his heart froze.

"I thought that thing was dead!" Kalten exclaimed.

The figure was robed and hooded all in black, and it was astride a gaunt horse. A kind of greenish nimbus surrounded it, and waves of implacable hatred seemed to shimmer out from it. Sparhawk looked a bit more closely and then let out his breath, relieved. "It's not a Seeker," he told Kalten. "It's got human hands. It's probably the one we've been fighting, though."

Then another man in black rode out from farther back in the trees. This one wore exaggeratedly dramatic clothing. He had on a black, wide-brimmed hat and wore a black bag with ragged eye holes over his head.

"Has this all been some sort of joke?" Tynian demanded. "Is that who I think it is?"

"I'd guess that it's the one in the robe who's been in charge," Ulath said. "I doubt that Sabre could successfully herd goats."

"Savor thine empty victory, Anakha," the hooded figure called in a hollow, strangely metallic voice. "I did but test thee that I might discern thy strength—and thy weaknesses. Go thy ways now. I have learned what I needed to learn. I will trouble thee no further—for now. But mistake me not, O Man Without Destiny, we will meet anon, and in our next meeting shall I try thee more significantly." Then Sabre and his hooded companion wavered and vanished.

The wailing and groaning of the wounded enemies all around them suddenly broke off. Sparhawk looked around quickly. The strangely armored foot troops he and his friends had been fighting were all gone. Only the dead remained. Back along the road in either direction, Kring's Peloi were reining in their horses in amazement. The troops they had engaged had vanished as well, and startled exclamations from back among the trees indicated that the Atans had also been bereft of enemies.

"What's going on here?" Kalten exclaimed.

"I'm not sure," Sparhawk replied, "but I *am* sure that I don't like it very much." He swung down from his saddle and turned one of the fallen enemies over with his foot.

The body was little more than a dried husk, browned, withered, and totally desiccated. It looked very much like the body of a man who had been dead for several centuries at least.

"We've encountered it once before, your Grace," Tynian was explaining to Patriarch Emban. It was nearly morning, and they were gathered once again atop the rocky hill. "Last time it was antique Lamorks. I don't know what kind of antiques these were." He looked at the two mummified corpses the Atans had brought up the hill.

"This one is a Cynesgan," Ambassador Oscagne said, pointing at one of the dead men.

"Looks almost like a Rendor, doesn't he?" Talen observed.

"There would be certain similarities," Oscagne agreed. "Cynesga is a desert, much like Rendor, and there are only so many kinds of clothing suitable for such a climate."

The dead man in question was garbed in a flowing, loose-fitting robe, and his head was covered with a sort of cloth winding that flowed down to protect the back of his neck.

"They aren't very good fighters," Kring told them. "They all sort of went to pieces when we charged them."

"What about the other one, your Excellency?" Tynian asked. "These ones in armor were *very* good fighters."

The Tamul ambassador's eyes grew troubled. "That one's a figment of someone's imagination," he declared.

"I don't really think so, your Excellency," Sir Bevier disagreed. "The men we encountered back in Eosia had been drawn from the past. They were fairly exotic, I'll grant you, but they *had* been living men once. Everything we've seen here tells us that we've run into the same thing again. This fellow's most definitely *not* an imaginary soldier. He *did* live once, and what he's wearing was his customary garb."

"It's impossible," Oscagne declared adamantly.

"Just for the sake of speculation, Oscagne," Emban said, "let's shelve the word *impossible* for the time being. Who would you say he was if he *weren't* impossible?"

"It's a very old legend," Oscagne said, his face still troubled. "We're told that once, a long, long time ago, there were people in Cynesga who predated the current inhabitants. The legend calls them the Cyrgai. Modern Cynesgans are supposed to be their degenerate descendants."

"They look as if they come from two different parts of the world," Kalten noted.

"Cyrga, the city of the Cyrgai, was supposed to lie in the central highlands of Cynesga," Oscagne told him. "It's higher than the surrounding desert, and the legend says there was a large, spring-fed lake there. The stories say that the climate there was markedly different from that of the desert. The Cyrgai wouldn't have needed protection from the sun the way their bastard offspring would have. I'd imagine that there were indications of rank and status involved as well. Given the nature of the Cyrgai, they'd have definitely wanted to keep their inferiors from wearing the Cyrgai costume."

"They lived at the same time, then?" Tynian asked.

"The legends are a little vague on that score, Sir Tynian. Evidently there *was* a period when the Cyrgai and the Cynesgans coexisted. The Cyrgai would certainly have been dominant, though." He made a face. "Why am I talking this way about a myth?" he said plaintively.

"This is a fairly substantial myth, Oscagne," Emban said, nudging the mummified Cyrgai with his foot. "I gather that these fellows had something of a reputation?"

"Oh, yes," Oscagne said with distaste. "They had a hideous culture—all cruelty and militarism. They held themselves aloof from other peoples in order to avoid what they called contamination. They were said to be obsessively concerned with racial purity, and they were militantly opposed to any new ideas."

"That's a futile sort of obsession," Tynian noted. "Any time you engage in trade, you're going to encounter new ideas."

"The legends tell us they understood that, Sir Knight. Trade was forbidden."

"No commerce at all?" Kalten asked incredulously.

Oscagne shook his head. "They were supposed to be totally self-sufficient. They even went so far as to forbid the possession of gold or silver in their society."

"Monstrous!" Stragen exclaimed. "They had no money at all?"

"Iron bars, we're told—heavy ones, I guess. It tended to discourage trade. They lived only for war. All the men were in the army, and all the women spent their time having babies. When they grew too old to either fight or bear children, they were expected to kill themselves. The legends say that they were the finest soldiers the world has ever known."

"The legends are exaggerated, Oscagne," Engessa told him, "I killed five of them myself. They spent a great deal of time flexing their muscles and posing with their weapons when they should have been paying attention to business."

"The ancients were very formal, Atan Engessa," Oscagne murmured.

"Who was the fellow in the robe?" Kalten asked. "The one who seemed to be trying to pass himself off as a Seeker?"

"I'd guess that he holds a position somewhat akin to Gerrich in Lamorkand and to Sabre in western Astel," Sparhawk surmised. "I was a little surprised to see Sabre here," he added. He had to step rather carefully here. Both he and Emban were sworn to secrecy on the matter of Sabre's real identity.

"Professional courtesy, no doubt," Stragen murmured. "The fact that he was here sort of confirms our guess that all these assorted upheavals and disturbances are tied together. There's somebody in back of all this—somebody we haven't seen or even heard of yet. We're going to have to catch one of these intermediaries of his and wring some information out of him sooner or later." The blond thief looked around. "What now?" he asked.

"How long did you say it would be until the Atans arrive from Sarsos, Engessa?" Sparhawk asked the towering Atan.

"They should arrive sometime the day after tomorrow, Sparhawk-Knight." The Atan glanced toward the east. "Tomorrow, that is," he corrected, "since it's already starting to get light."

"We'll care for our wounded and wait for them, then," Sparhawk decided. "I like lots of friendly faces around me in times like this."

"One question, Sparhawk-Knight," Engessa said. "Who is Anakha?"

"That's Sparhawk," Ulath told him. "The Styrics call him that. It means 'without destiny.' "

"All men have a destiny, Ulath-Knight."

"Not Sparhawk, apparently, and you have no idea how nervous that makes the Gods."

As Engessa had calculated, the Sarsos garrison arrived about noon the following day, and the hugely increased escort of the Queen of Elenia marched easterly. Two days later, they crested a hill and gazed down at a marble city situated in a broad green field backed by a dark forest stretching to the horizon.

Sparhawk had been sensing a familiar presence since early that morning and he had ridden on ahead eagerly.

Sephrenia was sitting on her white palfrey beside the road. She was a small, beautiful woman with black hair, snowy skin, and deep blue eyes. She wore a white robe of a somewhat finer weave than the homespun she had normally worn in Eosia.

"Hello, little mother." He smiled, saying it as if they had been apart for no more than a week. "You've been well, I trust?" He removed his helmet.

"Tolerable, Sparhawk." Her voice was rich and had that familiar lilt.

"Will you permit me to greet you?" he asked in that formal manner all Pandions used when meeting her after a separation.

"Of course, dear one."

Sparhawk dismounted, took her wrists, and turned her hands over. Then he kissed her palms in the ritual Styric greeting. "And will you bless me, little mother?" he asked.

She fondly placed her hands on his temples and spoke her benediction in Styric. "Help me down, Sparhawk," she commanded.

He reached out and put his hands about her almost childlike waist. Then he lifted her easily from her saddle. Before he could set her down, however, she put her arms about his neck and kissed him full on the lips, something she had almost never done before. "I've missed you, my dear one," she breathed. "You cannot believe how I've missed you."

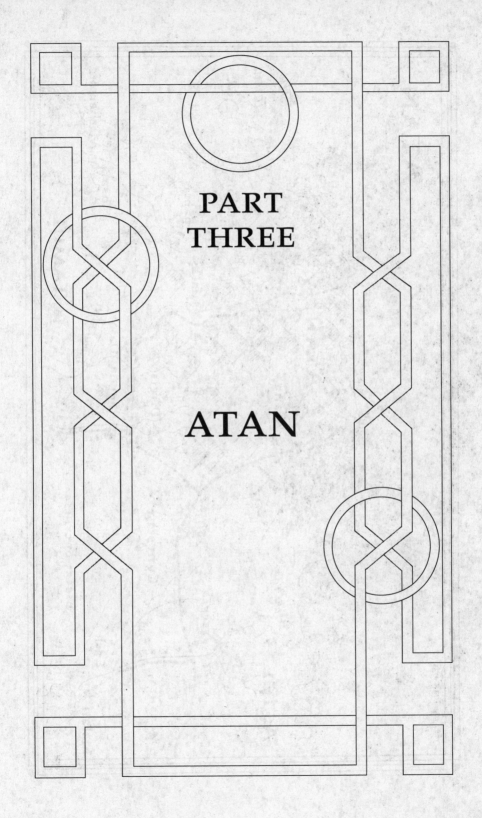

PART
THREE

ATAN

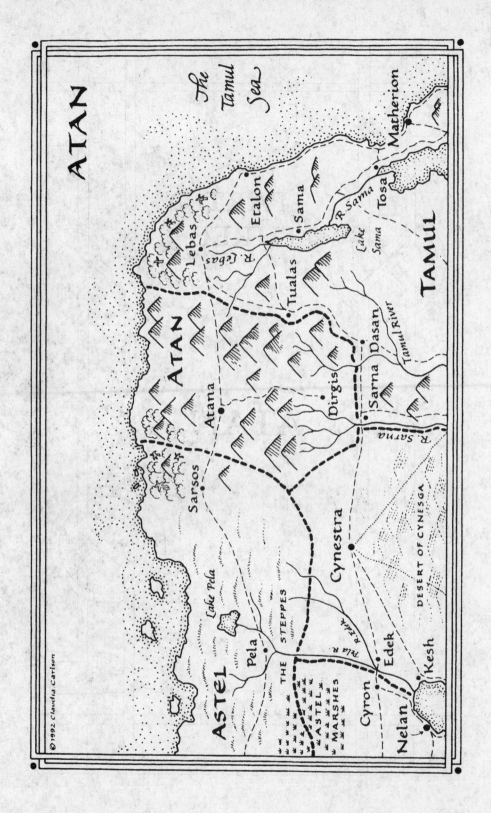

ATAN

ASTEL

TAMUL

The Tamul Sea

© 1992 Claudia Carlson

Matherion

Tosa

Sama

R. Sama

Lake Sama

Etalon

Lebas

R. Lebas

Sama

Tualas

Durgis

Sarna Dasan

Tamul River

ATAN

Atana

Sarsos

R. Sarna

Lake Pela

Pela

THE STEPPES

Cynestra

DESERT OF CYNESGA

Pela R.

ASTEL MARSHES

Cyron

Edek

Nelan

Kesh

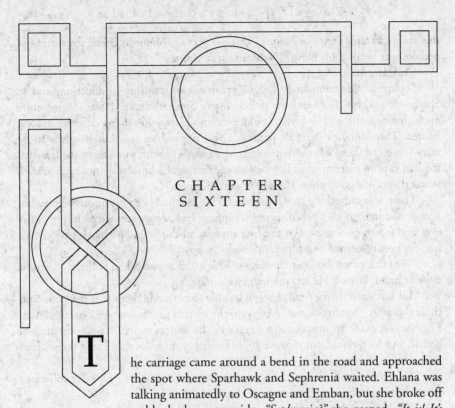

T he carriage came around a bend in the road and approached
the spot where Sparhawk and Sephrenia waited. Ehlana was
talking animatedly to Oscagne and Emban, but she broke off
suddenly, her eyes wide. *"Sephrenia?"* she gasped. *"It is! It's
Sephrenia!"* Royal dignity went out the window as she scrambled down from the
carriage.

"Brace yourself," Sparhawk cautioned with a gentle smile.

Ehlana ran to them, threw her arms around Sephrenia's neck, and kissed her,
weeping for joy.

The queen's tears were not the only ones shed that afternoon. Even the hard-
bitten Church Knights were misty-eyed for the most part. Kalten went even further
and wept openly as he knelt to receive Sephrenia's blessing.

"The Stryric woman has a special significance, Sparhawk-Knight?" Engessa
asked curiously.

"A very special significance, Atan Engessa," Sparhawk replied, watching his
friends clustered around the small woman. "She touches our hearts in a profound
way. We'd probably take the world apart if she asked us to."

"That's a very great authority, Sparhawk-Knight." Engessa said it with some
approval. Engessa respected authority.

"It is indeed, my friend," Sparhawk agreed, "and that's only the least of her
gifts. She's wise and beautiful, and I'm at least partially convinced that she could
stop the tides if she really wanted to."

"She is quite small, though," Engessa noted.

"Not really. In our eyes she's at least a hundred feet tall—maybe even two hundred."

"The Styrics are a strange people with strange powers, but I had not heard of this ability to alter their size before." Engessa was a profoundly literal man, and hyperbole was beyond his grasp. "Two hundred, you say?"

"At least, Atan."

Sephrenia was completely caught up in the outpouring of affection, and so Sparhawk was able to observe her rather closely. She had changed. She seemed more open, for one thing. No Styric could ever completely lower his defenses among Elenes. Thousands of years of prejudice and oppression had taught them to be wary—even of those Elenes they loved the most. Sephrenia's defensive shell, a shell she had kept in place around her for so long that she had probably not even known it was there, was gone now. The doors were all open.

There was something more, however. Her face had been luminous before, but now it was radiant. A kind of regretful longing had always seemed to hover in her eyes and it was gone now. For the first time in all the years Sparhawk had known her, Sephrenia seemed complete and totally happy.

"Will this go on for long, Sparhawk-Knight?" Engessa asked politely. "Sarsos is close at hand, but—" He left the suggestion hanging.

"I'll talk with them, Atan. I *might* be able to persuade them that they can continue this later." Sparhawk walked toward the excited group near the carriage. "Atan Engessa just made an interesting suggestion," he said to them. "It's a novel idea, of course, but he pointed out that we could probably do all of this inside the walls of Sarsos—since it's so close anyway."

"I see *that* hasn't changed," Sephrenia observed to Ehlana. "Does he still make these clumsy attempts at humor every chance he gets?"

"I've been working on that, little mother." Ehlana smiled.

"The question I was really asking was whether or not you ladies wanted to ride on into the city, or would you like to have us set up camp for the night."

"Spoilsport," Ehlana accused.

"We really should go on down," Sephrenia told them. "Vanion's waiting, and you know how cross he gets when people aren't punctual."

"Vanion?" Emban exclaimed. "I thought he'd be dead by now."

"Hardly. He's quite vigorous, actually. *Very* vigorous at times. He'd have come with me to meet you, but he sprained his ankle yesterday. He's being terribly brave about it, but it hurts him more than he's willing to admit."

Stragen stepped up and effortlessly lifted her into the carriage. "What should we expect in Sarsos, dear sister?" he asked her in his flawless Styric.

Ehlana gave him a startled look. "You've been hiding things from me, Milord Stragen. I didn't know you spoke Styric."

"I always meant to mention it to you, your Majesty, but it kept slipping my mind."

"I think you'd better be prepared for some surprises, Stragen," Sephrenia told him. "All of you should."

"What sort of surprises?" Stragen asked. "Remember that I'm a thief, Sephrenia, and surprises are very bad for thieves. Our veins tend to come untied when we're startled."

"I think you'd all better discard your preconceptions about Styrics," Sephrenia advised. "We aren't obliged to be simple and rustic here in Sarsos, so you'll find an altogether different kind of Styric in these streets." She seated herself in the carriage and held out her arms to Danae. The little princess climbed up into her lap and kissed her. It seemed very innocuous and perfectly natural, but Sparhawk was privately surprised that they were not surrounded by a halo of blazing light.

Then Sephrenia looked at Emban. "Oh, dear," she said. "I hadn't really counted on your being here, your Grace. How firmly fixed are your prejudices?"

"I like *you,* Sephrenia," the little fat man replied. "I resent the Styrics' stubborn refusal to accept the true faith, but I'm not really a howling bigot."

"Are you open to a suggestion, my friend?" Oscagne asked.

"I'll listen."

"I'd recommend that you look upon your visit to Sarsos as a holiday, and put your theology on a shelf someplace. Look all you want, but let the things you don't like pass without comment. The empire would really appreciate your cooperation in this, Emban. Please don't stir up the Styrics. They're a very prickly people with capabilities we don't entirely understand. Let's not precipitate avoidable explosions."

Emban opened his mouth as if to retort, but then his eyes grew troubled, and he apparently decided against it.

Sparhawk conferred briefly with Oscagne and Sephrenia and decided that the bulk of the Church Knights should set up camp with the Peloi outside the city. It was a precaution designed to avert incidents. Engessa sent his Atans to their garrison just north of the city wall, and the party surrounding Ehlana's carriage entered through an unguarded gate.

"What's the trouble, Khalad?" Sephrenia asked Sparhawk's squire. The young man was looking around, frowning.

"It's really none of my business, Lady Sephrenia," he said, "but are marble buildings really a good idea this far north? Aren't they awfully cold in the wintertime?"

"He's so much like his father." She smiled. "I think you've exposed one of our vanities, Khalad. Actually, the buildings are made of brick. The marble's just a sheathing to make our city impressive."

"Even brick isn't too good at keeping out the cold, Lady Sephrenia."

"It is when you make double walls and fill the space between those walls with a foot of plaster."

"That would take a lot of time and effort."

"You'd be amazed at the amount of time and effort people will waste for the sake of vanity, Khalad, and we can always cheat a little, if we have to. Our Gods are fond of marble buildings, and we like to make them feel at home."

"Wood's still more practical," he said stubbornly.

"I'm sure it is, Khalad, but it's so commonplace. We like to be different."

"It's different, all right."

Sarsos even smelled different. A faint miasma hung over every Elene city in the world, an unpleasant blend of sooty smoke, rotting garbage, and the effluvium from poorly constructed and infrequently drained cesspools. Sarsos, on the other hand, smelled of trees and roses. It was summer, and there were small parks and rosebushes everywhere. Ehlana's expression grew speculative. With a peculiar flash of insight, Sparhawk foresaw a vast program of public works looming on the horizon for the capital of Elenia.

The architecture and layout of the city was subtle and highly sophisticated. The streets were broad and, except where the inhabitants had decided otherwise for aesthetic reasons, they were straight. The buildings were all sheathed in marble, and they were fronted by graceful white pillars. This was most definitely *not* an Elene city.

The citizens looked strangely un-Styric. Their kinsmen to the west all wore robes of lumpy white homespun. The garb was so universal as to be a kind of identifying badge. The Styrics of Sarsos, however, wore silks and linens. White still appeared to be the preferred color, but there were other hues as well, blue and green and yellow, and not a few garments were a brilliant scarlet. Styric women in the west were very seldom seen, but they were much more in evidence here. They also wore colorful clothing and flowers in their hair.

More than anything, however, there was a marked difference in attitude. The Styrics of the west were timid, sometimes as fearful as deer. They were meek—a meekness designed to soften Elene aggressiveness, but that very attitude quite often inflamed the Elenes all the more. The Styrics of Sarsos, on the other hand, were definitely not meek. They did not keep their eyes lowered or speak in soft, hesitant voices. They were assertive. They argued on street corners. They laughed out loud. They walked along the broad avenues of their city with their heads held high as if they were actually proud to be Styric. The one thing that bespoke the difference more than anything else, however, was the fact that the children played in the parks without any signs of fear.

Emban's face had grown rigid, and his nostrils were pinched in with anger. Sparhawk knew exactly why the Patriarch of Ucera was showing so much resentment. Candor compelled him to privately admit that he shared it. All Elenes believed that Styrics were an inferior race, and despite their indoctrination, the Church Knights still shared that belief at the deepest level of their minds. Sparhawk felt the thoughts rising in him unbidden. How dare these puffed-up, loudmouthed Styrics have a more beautiful city than any the Elenes could construct? How dare they be prosperous? How dare they be happy? How dare they strut through these streets behaving for all the world as if they were every bit as good as Elenes?

Then he saw Danae looking at him sadly, and he pulled his thoughts and unspoken resentments up short. He took hold of those unattractive emotions firmly and looked at them. He didn't like what he saw very much. So long as Styrics were meek and submissive and lived in misery in rude hovels, he was more than willing to leap to their defense, but when they brazenly looked him squarely in the eye with unbowed heads and challenging expressions, he found himself wanting to teach them lessons.

"Difficult, isn't it, Sparhawk?" Stragen said wryly. "My bastardy has always made me feel a certain kinship with the downtrodden and despised. I found the towering humility of our Styric brethren so inspiring that I even went out of my way to learn their language. I'll admit that the people here set my teeth on edge, though. They all seem so disgustingly self-satisfied."

"Stragen, sometimes you're so civilized you make me sick."

"My, aren't *we* touchy today?"

"Sorry. I just found something in myself that I don't like. It's making me grouchy."

Stragen sighed. "We should probably never look into our own hearts, Sparhawk. I don't think anybody likes everything he finds there."

Sparhawk was not the only one having trouble with the city of Sarsos and its inhabitants. Sir Bevier's face reflected the fact that he was feeling an even greater resentment than the others. His expression was shocked, even outraged.

"Heard a story once," Sir Ulath said to him in that disarmingly reminiscent fashion that always signaled louder than words that Ulath was about to make a point. That was one of Sir Ulath's characteristics. He almost never spoke *unless* he was trying to make a point. "It seems that there was a Deiran, an Arcian, and a Thalesian. It was a long time ago, and they were all speaking in their native dialects. Anyway, they got to arguing about which of their modes of speech was God's own. They finally agreed to go to Chyrellos and ask the Archprelate to put the question directly to God himself."

"And?" Bevier asked him.

"Well, sir, everybody knows that God always answers the Archprelate's questions, so the word finally came back and settled their argument once and for all."

"Well?"

"Well what?"

"What *is* God's native dialect?"

"Why, Thalesian, of course. Everybody knows that, Bevier." Ulath was the kind of man who could say that with a perfectly straight face. "It only stands to reason, though. God was a Genidian Knight before he decided to take the universe in hand. I'll bet you didn't know that, did you?"

Bevier stared at him for a moment, and then began to laugh a bit sheepishly.

Ulath looked at Sparhawk, and one of his eyelids closed in a slow, deliberate wink. Once again Sparhawk felt obliged to reassess his Thalesian friend.

Sephrenia had a house here in Sarsos, and that was another surprise. There had always been a kind of possessionless transience about her. The house was quite large, set apart in a kind of park where tall old trees shaded gently sloping lawns and gardens and sparkling fountains. Like all the other buildings in Sarsos, Sephrenia's house seemed to have been constructed of marble, and it looked very familiar.

"You cheated, little mother," Kalten accused her as he helped her down from the carriage.

"I beg your pardon?"

"You imitated the Temple of Aphrael on the island we all saw in that dream. Even the colonnade along the front is the same."

"I suppose you're right, dear one, but it's sort of expected here. All the members of the Council of Styricum boast about their own Gods. It's expected. Our Gods would feel slighted if we didn't."

"You're a member of the council here?" He sounded a bit surprised.

"Of course. I *am* the High Priestess of Aphrael, after all."

"It seems a little odd to find somebody from Eosia on the ruling council of a city in Daresia."

"What makes you think I came from Eosia?"

"You *didn't?*"

"Of course not—and the council here in Sarsos isn't just the local government. We make the decisions for *all* Styrics, no matter where they are. Shall we go inside? Vanion's waiting." She led them up the marble stairs to a broad, intricately engraved bronze door, and they went on into the house.

The building was constructed around an interior courtyard, a lush garden with a marble fountain in the center. Vanion half lay on a divanlike chair near the fountain with his right leg propped up on a number of cushions. His ankle was swathed in bandages, and he had a disgusted expression on his face. His hair and beard were silvery now, and he looked very distinguished. His face was unlined, however. The cares that had weighed him down had been lifted, but that would hardly account for the startling change in him. Even the effects of the dreadful weight of the swords he had forced Sephrenia to give him had somehow been erased. His face looked younger than Sparhawk had ever seen it. He lowered the scroll he had been reading. "Sparhawk," he said irritably, "where have you been?"

"I'm glad to see you, too, my Lord," Sparhawk replied.

Vanion looked at him sharply and then laughed, his face a bit sheepish. "I guess that was a little ungracious, wasn't it?"

"Crotchety, my Lord," Ehlana told him. "Definitely crotchety." Then she cast dignity aside, ran to him, and threw her arms about his neck. "We are displeased with you, my Lord Vanion," she said in her most imperious manner. Then she kissed him soundly. "You have deprived us of your counsel and your company in our hour of need." She kissed him again. "It was churlish of you in the extreme to absent yourself from our side without our permission." She kissed him yet again.

"Am I being reprimanded or reunited with my queen?" he asked, looking a bit confused.

"A little of each, my Lord." She shrugged. "I thought I'd save some time and take care of everything all at once. I'm really very, very glad to see you again, Vanion, but I was most unhappy when you crept away from Cimmura like a thief in the night."

"We don't really do that, you know," Stragen noted clinically. "After you've stolen something, the idea is to look ordinary, and creeping attracts attention."

"Stragen," she said, "hush."

"I took him away from Cimmura for his health," Sephrenia told her. "He was dying there. I had a certain personal interest in keeping him alive, so I took him to a place where I could nurse him back to health. I badgered Aphrael unmercifully for a couple of years, and she finally gave in. I can make a serious pest of myself when I want something, and I *really* wanted Vanion." She made no attempt to conceal her feelings now. The years of unspoken love between her and the Pandion Preceptor were out in the open. She also made no effort to conceal what was quite obviously in both the Styric and the Elene cultures a scandalous arrangement. She and Vanion were openly living in sin, and neither of them showed the slightest bit of remorse about it. "How's the ankle, dear one?" she asked him.

"It's swelling up again."

"Didn't I tell you to soak it in ice when it did that?"

"I didn't have any ice."

"*Make* some, Vanion. You know the spell."

"The ice I make doesn't seem as cold as yours, Sephrenia." His voice was plaintive.

"Men!" she cried in seeming exasperation. "They're all such babies!" She bustled away in search of a basin.

"You followed that, didn't you, Sparhawk?" Vanion said.

"Of course, my Lord. It was very smooth, if I may say so."

"Thank you."

"What was that all about?" Kalten asked.

"You'd never understand, Kalten," Sparhawk replied.

"Not in a million years," Vanion added.

"How did you sprain your ankle, Lord Vanion?" Berit asked.

"I was proving a point. I advised the Council of Styricum that the young men of Sarsos were in extremely poor physical condition. I had to demonstrate by outrunning the whole bloody town. I was doing fairly well until I stepped in that rabbit hole."

"That's a real shame, Lord Vanion," Kalten said. "As far as I know, that's the first contest you ever lost."

"Who said I lost? I was far enough ahead and close enough to the finish line that I was able to hobble on and win. The council's going to at least *think* about some military training for the young men." He glanced at Sparhawk's squire. "Hello, Khalad," he said. "How are your mothers?"

"Quite well, my Lord. We stopped by to see them when we were taking the queen to Chyrellos so that she could turn the Archprelate over her knee and spank him."

"*Khalad!*" Ehlana protested.

"Wasn't I supposed to say that, your Majesty? We all thought that's what you had in mind when we left Cimmura."

"Well—sort of, I guess—but you're not supposed to come right out and say it like that."

"Oh, I didn't know that. I thought it was a good idea, myself. Our Holy Mother needs to have something to worry about now and then. It keeps her out of mischief."

"Astonishing, Khalad," Patriarch Emban murmured dryly. "You've managed to insult both Church and state in under a minute."

"What's been going on in Eosia since I left?" Vanion demanded.

"It was just a small misunderstanding between Sarathi and me, my Lord Vanion," Ehlana replied. "Khalad was exaggerating. He does that quite often—when he's not busy insulting the Church and state at the same time."

"We may just have another Sparhawk coming up here." Vanion grinned.

"God defend the Church," Emban said.

"And the Crown," Ehlana added.

Princess Danae pushed her way through to Vanion. She was carrying Mmrr, her hand wrapped around the kitten's middle. Mmrr had a resigned expression on her furry face, and her legs dangled ungracefully. "Hello, Vanion," Danae said, climbing up into his lap and giving him an offhand sort of kiss.

"You've grown, Princess." He smiled.

"Did you expect me to shrink?"

"*Danae!*" Ehlana scolded.

"Oh, Mother, Vanion and I are old friends. He used to hold me when I was a baby."

Sparhawk looked carefully at his friend, trying to decide whether or not Vanion knew about the little princess. Vanion's face, however, revealed nothing. "I've missed you, Princess," he said to her.

"I know. Everybody misses me when I'm not around. Have you met Mmrr yet? She's my cat. Talen gave her to me. Wasn't that nice of him?"

"Very nice, Danae."

"I thought so myself. Father's going to put him in training when we get home. It's probably just as well to get that all done while I'm still a little girl."

"Oh? Why's that, Princess?"

"Because I'm going to marry him when I grow up, and I'd like to have all that training nonsense out of the way. Would you like to hold my cat?"

Talen blushed and laughed a bit nervously, trying to pass off Danae's announcement as some sort of little-girl whim. His eyes looked a bit wild, however.

"You should never warn them like that, Princess," Baroness Melidere advised. "You're supposed to wait and tell them at the last possible minute."

"Oh. Is that the way it's done?" Danae looked at Talen. "Why don't you forget what I just said then?" she suggested. "I'm not going to do anything about it for the next ten or twelve years anyway." She paused. "Or eight, maybe. There's no real point in wasting time, is there?"

Talen was staring at her with the first faint hints of terror in his eyes.

"She's only teasing you, Talen," Kalten assured the boy. "And even if she isn't, I'm sure she'll change her mind before she gets to the dangerous age."

"Never happen, Kalten," Danae told him in a voice like steel.

That evening, after arrangements had been made and the crowd had been mostly dispersed to nearby houses, Sparhawk sat in the cool garden at the center of the house with Sephrenia and Vanion. Princess Danae sat on the ledge surrounding the fountain watching her kitten. Mmrr had discovered that there were goldfish swimming in the pool, and she sat with her tail twitching and her eyes wide with dreadful intent.

"I need to know something before I start," Sparhawk said, looking directly at Sephrenia. "How much does he know?" He pointed at Vanion.

"Just about everything, I'd say. I have no secrets from him."

"That's not too specific, Sephrenia." Sparhawk groped for a way to ask the question without revealing too much.

"Oh, *do* get to the point, Sparhawk," Danae told him. "Vanion knows who I am. He had a little trouble with it at first, but he's more or less reconciled to the idea now."

"That's not entirely true," Vanion disagreed. "You're the one with the really serious problems though, Sparhawk. How are you managing the situation?"

"Badly." Danae sniffed. "He keeps asking questions, even though he knows he won't understand the answers."

"Does Ehlana suspect?" Vanion asked seriously.

"Of course she doesn't," the Child-Goddess replied. "Sparhawk and I decided that right at the beginning. Tell them what's been happening, Sparhawk—and don't be all night about it. Mirtai's bound to come looking for me soon."

"It must be pure Hell," Vanion said sympathetically to his friend.

"Not entirely. I have to watch her, though. Once she had a swarm of fairies pollinating all the flowers in the palace garden."

"The bees are too slow." She shrugged.

"Maybe so, but people expect the bees to do it. If you turn the job over to the fairies, there's bound to be talk." Sparhawk leaned back and looked at Vanion. "Sephrenia's told you about the Lamorks and Drychtnath, hasn't she?"

"Yes. It's not just wild stories, is it?"

Sparhawk shook his head. "No. We encountered some bronze-age Lamorks outside of Demos. After Ulath brained their leader, they all vanished—except for the dead. Oscagne's convinced that it's a diversion of some kind—rather like the games Martel was playing to keep us out of Chyrellos during the election of the Archprelate. We've been catching glimpses of Krager, and that lends some weight to Oscagne's theory, but you always taught us that it's a mistake to try to fight the last war over again, so I'm not locking myself into the idea that what's happening in Lamorkand is purely diversionary. I can't really accept the notion that somebody would go to all that trouble to keep the Church Knights out of Tamuli—not with the Atans already here."

Vanion nodded. "You're going to need someone to help you when you get to Matherion, Sparhawk. Tamul culture's very subtle, and you could make some colossal blunders without even knowing it."

"Thanks, Vanion."

"You're not the only one, though. Your companions aren't the most diplomatic men in the world, and Ehlana tends to jump fences when she gets excited. Did she *really* go head-to-head with Dolmant?"

"Oh, yes," Danae said. "I had to kiss them both into submission before I could make peace between them."

"Who'd be the best to send, Sephrenia?" Vanion asked.

"Me."

"That's out of the question. I won't be separated from you again."

"That's very sweet, dear one. Why don't you come along, then?"

He seemed to hesitate. "I—"

"Don't be such a goose, Vanion," Danae told him. "You won't die the minute you leave Sarsos—any more than you did when you left my island. You're completely cured now."

"I wasn't worried about that," he told her, "but Sephrenia can't leave Sarsos anyway. She's a member of the Council of Styricum."

"I've been a member of the Council of Styricum for several centuries, Vanion," Sephrenia told him. "I've left here before—for long periods of time on occasion. The other members of the council understand. They've all had to do the same thing themselves now and then."

"I'm a little vague on this ruling council," Sparhawk admitted. "I knew that Styrics kept in touch with each other, but I hadn't realized it was quite so well knit."

"We don't make an issue of it." Sephrenia shrugged. "If the Elenes knew about it, they'd try to make it into some huge conspiracy."

"Your membership on the council keeps coming up," Sparhawk noted. "Is this council really relevant, or is it just some sort of ceremonial body?"

"Oh, no, Sparhawk," Vanion told him. "The council's very important. Styricum's a theocracy, and the council's composed of the high priests—and priestesses—of the Younger Gods."

"Being Aphrael's priestess isn't really a very taxing position." Sephrenia smiled, looking fondly at the Child-Goddess. "She's not particularly interested in asserting herself, since she usually gets what she wants in other ways. I get certain advantages—like this house—but I have to sit in on the meetings of the Thousand, and that can be tedious sometimes."

"The Thousand?"

"It's another name for the council."

"There are a thousand Younger Gods?" Sparhawk was a bit surprised at that.

"Well, of *course* there are, Sparhawk," Aphrael told him. "Everybody knows that."

"Why a thousand?"

"It's a nice number with a nice sound to it. In Styric it's *Ageraluon*."

"I'm not familiar with the word."

"It means ten times ten times ten—sort of. We had quite an argument with one of my cousins about it. He had a pet crocodile, and it had bitten off one of his fingers. He always had trouble counting after that. He wanted us to be *Ageralican*—nine times nine times nine, but we explained to him that there were already more of us than that, and that if we wanted to be *Ageralican,* some of us would have to be obliterated. We asked him if he'd care to volunteer to be one of them, and he dropped the idea."

"Why would anyone want to have a pet crocodile?"

"It's one of the things we do. We like to make pets of animals you humans can't control. Crocodiles aren't so bad. At least you don't have to feed them."

"No, but you have to count the children every morning. Now I understand why the question of whales keeps coming up."

"You're being terribly stubborn about that, Sparhawk. I could really impress my family if I had a whale."

"I think we're getting a little far afield," Vanion said. "Sephrenia tells me you've got some fairly exotic suspicions."

"I've been trying to explain something I can't completely see yet, Vanion. It's like trying to describe a horse when all you've to work with is his tail. I've got a lot of bits and pieces and not too much more. I'm positive that everything that we've seen so far—and probably a lot of things we haven't—are all hooked together, and that there's one intelligence guiding it all. I think it's a God, Vanion—or Gods."

"Are you sure your encounter with Azash didn't make you start seeing hostile divinities under beds and in dark closets?"

"I have it on the very best authority that only a God could raise an entire army out of the past. The authority who told me was quite smug about it."

"Be nice, Father," Danae said primly. "It's too complex, Vanion," she explained. "When you raise an army, you have to raise each individual soldier, and you have to know everything about him when you do that. It's the details that defeat human magicians when they try it."

"Any ideas?" Vanion asked his friend.

"Several," Sparhawk grunted, "and none of them very pleasant. Do you remember that shadow I told you about? The one that was following me all over Eosia after I killed Ghwerig?"

Vanion nodded.

"We've been seeing it again, and this time *everybody* can see it."

"That doesn't sound too good."

"No, it doesn't. Last time, that shadow was the Troll-Gods."

Vanion shuddered, and then the both of them looked at Sephrenia.

"Isn't it nice to be needed?" Danae said to her sister.

"I'll talk with Zalasta." Sephrenia sighed. "He's been keeping abreast of things here in Sarsos for the emperor. He probably knows a great deal about this, so I'll have him stop by tomorrow."

There was a loud splash.

"I told you that was going to happen, Mmrr," Danae said smugly to the wild-eyed kitten struggling to stay afloat in the fountain. Mmrr's problems were multiplied by the fact that the goldfish were ferociously defending their domain by bumping her paws and tummy with their noses.

"Fish her out, Danae," Sparhawk told her.

"She'll get me all wet, Father, and then Mother will scold me. Mmrr got herself into that fix. Now let her get herself out."

"She'll drown."

"Oh, of course she won't, Sparhawk. She knows how to swim. Look at her. She's cat-paddling for all she's worth."

"She's *what?*"

"Cat-paddling. You couldn't really call it dog-paddling, could you? She's not a dog, after all. We Styrics talk about cat-paddling all the time, don't we, Sephrenia?"

"*I* never have," Sephrenia murmured.

A large part of the fun came from the fact that her parents could not anticipate Princess Danae's early-morning visits. They were certainly not a daily occurrence, and there were times when a whole week would go by without one. This morning's visit was, of course, the same as all the rest. Consistency is one of the more important divine attributes. The door banged open, and the princess, her black hair flying and her eyes filled with glee, dashed into the room and joined her parents in bed with a great, whooping leap. The leap was followed, as always, by a great deal of squirming and burrowing until Danae was firmly nestled between her parents.

She never paid these visits alone. Rollo had never really been a problem. Rollo was a well-mannered toy, anxious to please and almost never intrusive. Mmrr, on the other hand, could be a pest. She was quite fond of Sparhawk and she was a genius at burrowing. Having a sharp-clawed kitten climb up the side of one's bare leg before one is fully awake is a startling experience. Sparhawk gritted his teeth and endured.

"The birds are awake." Danae announced it almost accusingly.

"I'm so happy for them," Sparhawk said, wincing as the kitten lurking beneath the covers began to rhythmically flex her claws in his hip.

"You're grumpy this morning, Father."

"I was doing just fine until now. Please ask your cat not to use me for a pincushion."

"She does it because she loves you."

"That fills my heart. I'd still rather have her keep her claws to herself, though."

"Is he always like this in the morning, Mother?"

"Sometimes." Ehlana laughed, embracing the little girl. "I think it depends on what he had for supper."

Mmrr began to purr. Most adult cats purr with a certain decorous moderation. Kittens don't. On this particular morning, Danae's small cat sounded much like an approaching thunderstorm or a gristmill with an off-center wheel.

"I give up," Sparhawk said. He threw back the covers, climbed out of bed, and pulled on a robe. "There's no sleeping with the three of you around," he accused them. "Coming, Rollo?"

His wife and daughter gave him a quick, startled glance, then exchanged a worried look. Sparhawk scooped up Danae's stuffed toy and ambled out of the room, holding it by one hind leg. He could hear Ehlana and Danae whispering as he left. He plumped the toy into a chair. "It's absolutely impossible, Rollo, old boy," he said, making sure that his womenfolk could hear him. "I don't know how you can stand it."

There was a profound silence from the bedroom.

"I think you and I should go away for a while, my friend," Sparhawk went on. "They're starting to treat us like pieces of furniture."

Rollo didn't say anything, but then Rollo seldom did.

Sephrenia, who was standing in the doorway, however, seemed a bit startled. "Aren't you feeling well, Sparhawk?"

"I'm fine, little mother. Why do you ask?" He hadn't really expected anyone to witness a performance intended primarily for his wife and daughter.

"You *do* realize that you're talking to a stuffed toy, don't you?"

Sparhawk stared at Rollo in mock surprise. "Why, I believe you're right, Sephrenia. How strange that I didn't notice. Maybe it has something to do with being rousted out of bed at the crack of dawn." No matter how hard he tried to put a good face on this, it wasn't going to go very well.

"What on earth are you talking about, Sparhawk?"

"You see, Rollo?" Sparhawk said, trying to rescue *something*. "They just don't understand—any of them."

"Ah—Prince Sparhawk?" It was Ehlana's maid, Alean. She had come into the room unnoticed, and her huge eyes were concerned. "Are you all right?"

Things were deteriorating all around Sparhawk. "It's a long, long story, Alean." He sighed.

"Have you seen the princess, my Lord?" Alean was looking at him strangely.

"She's in bed with her mother." There was really not much left for him to salvage from the situation. "I'm going to the bathhouse—if anybody cares." And he stalked from the room with the tatters of his dignity trailing along behind him.

Zalasta the Styric was an ascetic-looking man with white hair and a long, silvery beard. He had the angular, uncompleted-looking face of all Styric men, shaggy black eyebrows, and a deep, rich voice. He was Sephrenia's oldest friend, and was generally conceded to be the wisest and most powerful magician in Styricum. He wore a white, cowled robe and carried a staff—which may have been an affectation, since he was quite vigorous and did not need any aid when he walked. He spoke the Elenic language very well, although with a heavy Styric accent. Sparhawk's party had gathered that morning in Sephrenia's interior garden to hear Zalasta explain the details of what was really going on in Tamuli.

"We can't be entirely positive if they're real or not," Zalasta was saying. "The sightings have been random and very fleeting."

"They're definitely Trolls, though?" Tynian asked him.

Zalasta nodded. "No other creature looks quite like a Troll."

"That's God's own truth," Ulath murmured. "The sightings could very well have been of real Trolls. Some time back they all just packed up and left Thalesia. Nobody ever thought to stop one to ask him why."

"There have also been sightings of Dawn-men," Zalasta reported.

"What are they, learned one?" Patriarch Emban asked him.

"Manlike creatures from the beginning of time, your Grace. They're a bit bigger than Trolls, but not as intelligent. They roam in packs, and they're very savage."

"We've met them, friend Zalasta," Kring said shortly. "I lost many comrades that day."

"There may not be a connection," Zalasta continued. "The Trolls are contemporary creatures, but the Dawn-men definitely come from the past. Their species has been extinct for some fifty eons. There have also been some unconfirmed reports of sightings of Cyrgai."

"You can mark that down as confirmed, Zalasta," Kalten told him. "They provided us with some entertainment one night last week."

"They were fearsome warriors," Zalasta said.

"They might have impressed their contemporaries," Kalten disagreed, "but modern tactics and weapons and equipment are a bit beyond their capabilities. Catapults and the charge of armored knights seemed to baffle them."

"Just exactly who *are* the Cyrgai, learned one?" Vanion asked.

"I gave you the scrolls, Vanion," Sephrenia said. "Didn't you read them?"

"I haven't gotten that far yet. Styric's a difficult language to read. Somebody should give some thought to simplifying your alphabet."

"Hold it," Sparhawk interrupted. He looked at Sephrenia. "I've never seen you read anything," he accused her. "You wouldn't let Flute even touch a book."

"Not an Elene book, no."

"Then you *can* read?"

"In Styric, yes."

"Why didn't you tell us?"

"Because it wasn't really any of your business, dear one."

"You *lied*!" That shocked him for some reason.

"No, as a matter of fact I didn't. I *can't* read Elene—largely because I don't want to. It's a graceless language, and your writings are ugly—like spiderwebs."

"You deliberately led us to believe that you were too simple to learn how to read."

"That was sort of necessary, dear one. Pandion novices aren't really very sophisticated, and you had to have *something* to feel superior about."

"Be nice," Vanion murmured.

"I had to try to train a dozen generations of those great, clumsy louts, Vanion," she said with a certain asperity, "and I had to put up with their insufferable condescension in the process. Yes, Sparhawk, I *can* read, and I *can* count, and I *can* argue philosophy and even theology if I have to, and I *am* fully trained in logic."

"I don't know why you're yelling at *me*," he protested mildly, kissing her palms. "I've always believed you were a fairly nice lady—" He kissed her palms again. "—for a Styric, that is."

She jerked her hands out of his grasp and then saw the grin on his face. "You're impossible," she said, also suddenly smiling.

"We were talking about the Cyrgai, I believe," Stragen said smoothly. "Just exactly who are they?"

"They're extinct, fortunately," Zalasta replied. "They were of a race that appears to have been unrelated to the other races of Daresia—neither Tamul nor Elene, and certainly not Styric. Some have suggested that they might be distantly related to the Valesians."

"I couldn't accept that, learned one," Oscagne disagreed. "The Valesians don't even have a government, and they have no concept of war. They're the happiest people in the world. They could not in any way be related to the Cyrgai."

"Temperament is sometimes based on climate, your Excellency," Zalasta pointed out. "Valesia's a paradise, and central Cynesga's not nearly so nice. Anyway, the Cyrgai worshipped a hideous God named Cyrgon—and, as most primitive people do, they took their name from him. All peoples are egotistical, I suppose. We're all convinced that *our* God is better than all the rest and that *our* race is superior. The Cyrgai took that to extremes. We can't really probe the beliefs of an extinct people, but it appears that they even went so far as to believe that they were somehow of a different species from other humans. They also believed that all truth had been revealed to them by Cyrgon, so they strongly resisted new ideas. They carried the idea of a warrior society to absurd lengths, and they were obsessed with the concept of racial purity and strove for physical perfection. Deformed babies were taken out into the desert and left to die. Soldiers who received crippling injuries in battle were killed by their friends. Women who had too many female children were strangled. They built a city-state beside the Oasis of Cyrga in central Cynesga and rigidly isolated themselves from other peoples and their ideas. The Cyrgai were terribly afraid of ideas. Theirs was perhaps the only culture in human history that idealized stupidity. They looked upon superior intelligence as a defect, and overly bright children were killed."

"Nice group," Talen murmured.

"They conquered and enslaved their neighbors, of course—mostly desert nomads of indeterminate race—and there was a certain amount of interbreeding, soldiers being what they are."

"But that was perfectly all right, wasn't it?" Baroness Melidere added tartly. "Rape is always permitted, isn't it?"

"In this case it wasn't, Baroness," Zalasta replied. "Any Cyrgai caught 'fraternizing' was killed on the spot."

"What a refreshing idea," she murmured.

"So was the woman, of course. Despite all their best efforts, however, the Cyrgai *did* produce a number of offspring of mixed race. In their eyes, that was an abomination, and the half-breeds were killed whenever possible. In time, however, Cyrgon apparently had a change of heart. He saw a use for these half-breeds. They were given some training and became a part of the army. They were called 'Cynesgans,' and in time they came to comprise that part of the army that did all of the dirty work and most of the dying. Cyrgon had a goal, you see—the usual goal of the militaristically inclined."

"World domination?" Vanion suggested.

"Precisely. The Cynesgans were encouraged to breed, and the Cyrgai used them to expand their frontiers. They soon controlled all of the desert and began pushing at the frontiers of their neighbors. That's where we encountered them. The Cyrgai weren't really prepared to come up against Styrics."

"I can imagine." Tynian laughed.

Zalasta smiled briefly. It was an indulgent sort of smile, faintly tinged with a certain condescension. "The priests of Cyrgon had certain limited gifts," the Styric went on, "but they were no match for what they encountered." He sat tapping his fingertips together. "Perhaps when we examine it more closely, that's our real secret," he mused. "Other people have only one God—or at the most, a small group of Gods. We have a thousand, who more or less get along with each other and agree in a general sort of way about what ought to be done. Anyway, the incursion of the Cyrgai into the lands of the Styrics proved to be disastrous for them. They lost virtually all of their Cynesgans and a major portion of their full-blooded Cyrgai. They retreated in absolute disorder, and the Younger Gods decided that they ought to be encouraged to stay at home after that. No one knows to this day which of the Younger Gods developed the idea, but it was positively brilliant in both its simplicity and its efficacy. A large eagle flew completely around Cynesga in a single day, and his shadow left an unseen mark on the ground. The mark means absolutely nothing to the Cynesgans or the Atans or Tamuls or Styrics or Elenes or even the Arjuni. It was terribly important to the Cyrgai, however, because after that day any Cyrgai who stepped over that line died instantly."

"Wait a minute," Kalten objected. "We encountered Cyrgai just to the west of here. How did they get across the line?"

"They were from the past, Sir Kalten," Zalasta explained, spreading his hands. "We can assume that the line didn't exist for them, because the eagle had not yet made his flight when they marched north."

Kalten scratched his head and sat frowning. "I'm not really all that good at logic," he confessed, "but isn't there a hole in that somewhere?"

Bevier was also struggling with it. "I *think* I see how it works," he said a little dubiously, "but I'll have to go over it a few times to be sure."

"Logic can't answer *all* the questions, Sir Bevier," Emban advised. He hesitated. "You don't have to tell Dolmant I said that, of course," he added.

"It may be that the enchantment's no longer in force," Sephrenia suggested to Zalasta. "There's no real need for it, since the Cyrgai are extinct."

"And no way to prove it either," Ulath added, "one way or the other."

Stragen suddenly laughed. "He's right, you know," he said. "There might very well be this dreadful curse out there that nobody even knows about because the people it's directed at all died out thousands of years ago. What finally happened to them, learned one?" he asked Zalasta. "You said that they were extinct."

"Actually, Milord Stragen, they bred themselves out of existence."

"Isn't that a contradiction?" Tynian asked him.

"Not really. The Cynesgans had been very nearly wiped out, but now they were of vital importance, since they were the only troops at Cyrgon's disposal who could cross the frontiers. He directed the Cyrgai to concentrate on breeding up new armies of these formerly despised underlings. The Cyrgai were perfect soldiers who always obeyed orders to the letter. They devoted their attention to the Cynesgan women even to the exclusion of their own. By the time they realized their mistake, all the Cyrgai women were past childbearing age. Legend has it that the last of the Cyrgai died about ten thousand years ago."

"That raises idiocy to an art form, doesn't it?" Stragen observed.

Zalasta smiled a thin sort of smile. "At any rate, what used to be Cyrga is now Cynesga. It's occupied by a defective, mongrel race that manages to survive only because it sits astride the major trade routes between the Tamuls of the east and the

Elenes of the west. The rest of the world looks upon these heirs of the invincible Cyrgai with the deepest contempt. They're sneaky, cowardly, thieving, and disgustingly servile—a fitting fate for the offspring of a race that once thought it was divinely destined to rule the world."

"History's such a gloomy subject." Kalten sighed.

"Cynesga's not the only place where the past is returning to haunt us," Zalasta added.

"We've noticed," Tynian replied. "The Elenes in western Astel are all convinced that Ayachin's returned."

"Then you've heard of the one they call Sabre?" Zalasta asked.

"We ran across him a couple of times." Stragen laughed. "I don't think he poses much of a threat. He's an adolescent poseur."

"He satisfies the needs of the western Astels, though," Tynian added. "They're not exactly what you'd call deep."

"I've encountered them," Zalasta said wryly. "Kimear of Daconia and Baron Parok, his spokesman, are a bit more serious, though. Kimear was one of those men on horseback who emerge from time to time in Elene societies. He subdued the other two Elene kingdoms in western Astel and founded one of those empires of a thousand years that spring up from time to time and promptly fall apart when the founder dies. The hero in Edom is Incetes—a bronze-age fellow who actually managed to hand the Cyrgai their first defeat. The one who does his talking for him calls himself Rebal. That's not his real name, of course. Political agitators usually go by assumed names. Ayachin, Kimear, and Incetes appeal to the very simplest of Elene emotional responses—muscularity, primarily. I wouldn't offend you for the world, my friends, but you Elenes seem to like to break things and burn down other people's houses."

"It's a racial flaw," Ulath conceded.

"The Arjuni present us with slightly different problems," Zalasta continued. "They're members of the Tamul race, and their deep-seated urges are a bit more sophisticated. Tamuls don't want to rule the world, they just want to own it." He smiled briefly at Oscagne. "The Arjuni aren't very attractive as representatives of the race, though. Their hero is the fellow who invented the slave trade."

Mirtai's breath hissed sharply, and her hand went to her dagger.

"Is there some problem, Atana?" Oscagne asked her mildly.

"I've had experience with the slave traders of Arjuna, Oscagne," she replied shortly. "Someday I hope to have more, and I won't be a child this time."

Sparhawk realized that Mirtai had never told them the story of how she had become a slave.

"This Arjuni hero's of a somewhat more recent vintage than the others," Zalasta continued. "He was of the twelfth century. His name was Sheguan."

"We've heard of him," Engessa said bleakly. "His slavers used to raid the training camps of Atan children. We've more or less persuaded the Arjuni not to do that anymore."

"That sounds ominous," Baroness Melidere said.

"It was an absolute disaster, Baroness," Oscagne told her. "Some Arjuni slavers made a raid into Atan in the seventeenth century, and an imperial administrator got carried away by an excess of righteous indignation. He authorized the Atans to mount a punitive expedition into Arjuna."

"Our people still sing songs about it," Engessa said in an almost dreamy fashion.

"Bad?" Emban asked Oscagne.

"Unbelievable," Oscagne replied. "The silly ass who authorized the expedition didn't realize that when you command the Atans to do something, you have to specifically prohibit certain measures. The fool simply turned them loose. They actually hanged the King of Arjuna himself and then chased all his subjects into the southern jungle. It took us nearly two hundred years to coax the Arjuni down out of the trees. The economic upheaval was a disaster for the entire continent."

"These events are somewhat more recent," Zalasta noted. "The Arjuni have always been slavers, and Sheguan was only one of several operating in northern Arjuna. He was an organizer more than anything else. He established the markets in Cynesga and codified the bribes that protect the slave routes. The peculiar thing we face in Arjuna is that the spokesman's more important than the hero. His name is Scarpa, and he's a brilliant and dangerous man."

"What about Tamul itself?" Emban asked. "And Atan?"

"We both seem to be immune to the disease, your Grace," Oscagne replied. "It's probably because Tamuls are too egotistical for hero worship and because the Atans of antiquity were all so much shorter than their descendants that modern Atans overlook them." He smiled rather slyly at Engessa. "The rest of the world's breathlessly awaiting the day when the first Atan tops ten feet. I think that's the ultimate goal of their selective-breeding campaign." He looked at Zalasta. "Your information's far more explicit than ours, learned one," he complimented the Styric. "The best efforts of the empire have unearthed only the sketchiest of details about these people."

"I have different resources at my disposal, Excellency," Zalasta replied. "These figures from antiquity, however, would hardly be of any real concern. The Atans could quite easily deal with any purely military insurrection, but this isn't a totally military situation. Someone's been winnowing through the darker aspects of human imagination and spinning the horrors of folklore out of thin air. There are vampires and werewolves, ghouls, Ogres, and once even a thirty-foot giant. The officials shrug these sightings off as superstitious nonsense, but the common people of Tamuli are in a state of abject terror. We can't be certain of the reality of *any* of these things, but when you mingle monsters with Trolls, Dawn-men, and Cyrgai, you have total demoralization. Then, to push the whole thing over the edge, the forces of nature have been harnessed as well. There have been titanic thunderstorms, tornadoes, earthquakes, volcanic eruptions, and even isolated eclipses. The common people of Tamuli have become so fearful that they flee from rabbits and flocks of sparrows. There's no real focus to these incidents. They simply occur at random, and since there's no real plan behind them, there's no way to predict when and where they'll occur. That's what we're up against, my friends—a continent-wide campaign of terror—part reality, part illusion, part genuine magic. If it isn't countered—and very, very soon—the people will go mad with fear. The empire will collapse, and the terror will reign supreme."

"And what was the *bad* news you had for us, Zalasta?" Vanion asked him.

Zalasta smiled briefly. "You are droll, Lord Vanion," he said. "You may be able to gather more information this afternoon, my friends," he told them all. "You've been invited to attend the session of the Thousand. Your visit here is quite significant from a political point of view, and—although the council seldom agrees about anything—there's a strong undercurrent of opinion that we may have a common cause with you in this matter." He paused, then sighed. "I think you should be prepared for a certain amount of antagonism," he cautioned. "There's a reactionary faction in the council that begins to foam at the mouth whenever someone even mentions the word *Elene*. I'm sure they'll try to provoke you."

"Something's happening that I don't understand, Sparhawk," Danae murmured quietly a bit later. Sparhawk had retired to one corner of Sephrenia's little garden with one of Vanion's Styric scrolls and had been trying to puzzle out the Styric alphabet. Danae had found him there and had climbed up into his lap.

"I thought you were all wise," he said. "Isn't that supposed to be one of your characteristics?"

"Stop that. Something's terribly wrong here."

"Why don't you talk with Zalasta about it? He's one of your worshippers, isn't he?"

"Whatever gave you that idea?"

"I thought you and he and Sephrenia grew up together in the same village."

"What's that got to do with it?"

"I just assumed that the villagers all worshipped you. It's sort of logical that you'd choose to be born in a village of your own adherents."

"You don't understand Styrics at all, do you? That's the most tedious idea I've ever heard of—a whole village of people who all worship the same God? How boring."

"Elenes do it."

"Elenes eat pigs, too."

"What have you got against pigs?"

She shuddered.

"Who *does* Zalasta worship if he's not one of your adherents?"

"He hasn't chosen to tell us, and it's terribly impolite to ask."

"How did he get to be a member of the Thousand, then? I thought you had to be a high priest to qualify for membership."

"He isn't a member. He doesn't want to be. He advises them." She pursed her lips. "I really shouldn't say this, Sparhawk, but don't expect exalted wisdom from the council. High priests are devout, but that doesn't require wisdom. Some of the Thousand are frighteningly stupid."

"Can you get any kind of clue about which God might be at the bottom of all these disturbances?"

"No. Whoever it is doesn't want any of the rest of us to know his identity, and there are ways we can conceal ourselves. About all I can say is that he's not Styric. Pay very close attention at the meeting this afternoon, Sparhawk. My temperament's Styric, and there may be things I'd overlook just because I'm so used to them."

"What do you want me to look for?"

"I don't *know*. Use your rudimentary intuition. Look for false notes, lapses, any kind of clue hinting at the fact that someone's not entirely what he seems to be."

"Do you suspect that there might be some member of the Thousand working for the other side?"

"I didn't say that. I just said that there's something wrong. I'm getting another of those premonitions like the one I had at Kotyk's house. Something's not what it's supposed to be here, and I can't for the life of me tell what it is. Try to find out what it is, Sparhawk. We really need to know."

The council of the Thousand met in a stately marble building at the very center of Sarsos. It was an imposing, even intimidating building that shouldered its way upward arrogantly. Like most public buildings, it was totally devoid of any warmth or humanity. It had wide, echoing marble corridors and huge bronze doors designed to make people feel tiny and insignificant.

The actual meetings took place in a large, semicircular hall with tier upon tier of marble benches stair-stepping up the sides. There were ten of those tiers, naturally, and the seats on each tier were evenly spaced. It was all very logical. Architects are usually logical, since their buildings tend to collapse if they are not.

At Sephrenia's suggestion, Sparhawk and the other Elenes wore simple white robes to avoid those unpleasant associations in the minds of Styrics when they were confronted by armored Elenes. The knights, however, wore chain mail and swords under their robes.

The chamber was about half full, since at any given time a part of the council was off doing other things. The members of the Thousand sat or strolled about talking quietly with each other. Some moved purposefully among their colleagues, talking earnestly. Others laughed and joked. Not a few were sleeping.

Zalasta led them to the front of the chamber where chairs had been placed for them, facing the audience in a kind of semicircle.

"I have to take my seat," Sephrenia told them quietly. "Please don't take immediate action if someone insults you. There's several thousand years of resentment built up in this chamber, and some of it's bound to spill over." She crossed the chamber to sit on one of the marble benches.

Zalasta stepped to the center of the room and stood silently, making no attempt to call the assemblage to order. The traditional courtesies were obscure here. Gradually, the talking tapered off, and the council members took their seats. "If it please the council," Zalasta said in Styric, "we are honored today by the presence of important guests."

"It certainly doesn't please *me*," one member retorted. "These 'guests' appear to be Elenes for the most part, and I'm not all that interested in hobnobbing with pig-eaters."

"This promises to be moderately unpleasant," Stragen murmured. "Our Styric cousins seem to be as capable of boorishness as we are."

Zalasta ignored the ill-mannered speaker and continued. "Sarsos is subject to the Tamul Empire," he reminded them, "and we benefit enormously from that relationship."

"And the Tamuls make sure we pay for those benefits," another member called.

Zalasta ignored that as well. "I'm sure you'll all join with me in welcoming First Secretary Oscagne, the Chief of the Imperial Foreign Service."

"I don't know what makes you so sure about that, Zalasta," someone shouted with a raucous laugh.

Oscagne rose to his feet. "I'm overwhelmed by this demonstration of affection," he said dryly in perfect Styric.

There were catcalls from the tiers of seats. The catcalls died quite suddenly when Engessa rose to his feet and stood with his arms folded across his chest. He did not even bother to scowl at the unruly councillors.

"That's better," Oscagne said. "I'm glad that the legendary courtesy of the Styric people has finally asserted itself. If I may, I'll briefly introduce the members of our party, and then we'll place an urgent matter before you for your consideration." He briefly introduced Patriarch Emban. An angry mutter swept through the chamber.

"That's directed at the Church, your Grace," Stragen told him, "not at you personally."

When Oscagne introduced Ehlana, one council member on the top tier whispered a remark to those seated near him that elicited a decidedly vulgar laugh. Mirtai came to her feet like an uncoiling spring, her hands darting to her sheathed daggers.

Engessa said something sharply to her in the Tamul tongue.

She shook her head. Her eyes were blazing and her jaw was set. She drew a dagger. Mirtai may not have understood Styric, but she *did* understand the implications of that laugh.

Sparhawk rose to his feet. "It's *my* place to respond, Mirtai," he reminded her. "You will not defer to me?"

"Not this time, no. I'm sorry, but it's a sort of formal occasion, so we should observe the niceties." He turned to look up at the insolent Styric in the top row. "Would you care to repeat what you just said a little louder, neighbor?" he asked in Styric. "If it's so funny, maybe you should share it with us."

"Well, what do you know!" The fellow sneered. "A talking dog."

Sephrenia rose to her feet. "I call upon the Thousand to observe the traditional moment of silence," she declared in Styric.

"Who died?" the loudmouth demanded.

"You did, Camriel," she told him sweetly, "so our grief will not be excessive. This is Prince Sparhawk, the man who destroyed the Elder God Azash, and you've just insulted his wife. Did you want the customary burial? Assuming that we can find enough of you to commit to the earth when he's done with you?"

Camriel's jaw had dropped, and his face had gone dead white. The rest of the council also visibly shrank back.

"His name still seems to carry some weight," Ulath noted to Tynian.

"Evidently. Our insolent friend up there seems to be having long, gloomy thoughts about mortality."

"Councillor Camriel," Sparhawk said quite formally, "let us not interrupt the deliberations of the Thousand with a purely personal matter. I'll look you up after the meeting and we can make the necessary arrangements."

"What did he say?" Ehlana whispered to Stragen.

"The usual, your Majesty. I expect that Councillor Camriel's going to remember a pressing engagement on the other side of the world at any moment now."

"Will the council permit this barbarian to threaten me?" Camriel quavered.

A silvery-haired Styric on the far side of the room laughed derisively. "You personally insulted a state visitor, Camriel," he declared. "The Thousand has no obligation to defend you under those circumstances. Your God has been very lax in your instruction. You're a boorish, loudmouthed imbecile. We'll be well rid of you."

"How *dare* you speak to me so, Michan?"

"You seem dazzled by the fact that one of the Gods is slightly fond of you, Camriel," Michan drawled, "and you overlook the fact that we all share that peculiar eminence here. My God loves me at least as much as your God loves you." Michan paused. "Probably more, actually. I'd guess that your God's having second thoughts about you at the moment. You must be a terrible embarrassment to him. But you're wasting valuable time. As soon as this meeting adjourns, I expect that Prince Sparhawk will come looking for you—with a knife. You *do* have a knife someplace nearby, don't you, your Highness?"

Sparhawk grinned and opened his robe slightly to reveal his sword hilt.

"Splendid, old fellow," Michan said. "I'd have been glad to lend you mine, but a man always works better with his own equipment. Haven't you left yet, Camriel? If you plan to live long enough to see the sun go down, you'd best get cracking."

Councillor Camriel fled.

"What happened?" Ehlana demanded impatiently.

"If we choose to look at it in a certain light, we could consider the councillor's flight to be a form of apology," Stragen told her.

"We do not accept apologies," Mirtai said implacably. "May I chase him down and kill him, Ehlana?"

"Why don't we just let him run for a while, Mirtai?" the queen decided.

"How long?"

"How long would you say he's likely to run, Milord?" Ehlana asked Stragen.

"The rest of his life probably, my Queen."

"That sounds about right to me."

The response of the Thousand to Zalasta's description of the current situation was fairly predictable, and the fact that all of the speeches showed evidence of much polishing hinted strongly that there had been few surprises in his presentation. The Thousand seemed to be divided into three factions. Predictably, there were a fair number of councillors who took the position that the Styrics could defend themselves and that they had no real reason to become involved. Styrics had strong suspicions where Elene promises were concerned, since Elene rulers tended to forget promises made to Styrics after a crisis had passed.

A second faction was more moderate. They pointed out the fact that the crisis here concerned the Tamuls rather than the Elenes, and that the presence of a small band of Church Knights from Eosia was really irrelevant. As the silvery-haired Michan pointed out, "The Tamuls may not be our friends in every sense of the word, but at least they're not our enemies. Let's not overlook the fact that their Atans keep the Astels, the Edomish, and the Dacites from our doorstep." Michan was highly respected, and his opinion carried great weight in the council.

There was a third faction as well, a vocal minority so rabidly anti-Elene that they even went so far as to suggest that the interests of Styricum might be better served by an alliance with the perpetrators of the outrages. Their speeches were not really intended to be taken seriously. The speakers had merely seized this opportunity to list long catalogues of grievances and to unleash diatribes of hatred and vituperation.

"This is starting to get tiresome," Stragen finally said to Sparhawk, rising to his feet.

"What are you going to do?"

"Do? Why, I'm going to respond, old boy." He stepped to the center of the floor and stood resolutely in the face of their shouts and curses. The noise gradually subsided, more because those causing it had run out of energy than because anyone was really curious about what this elegant blond Elene had to say. "I'm delighted to discover that all men are equally contemptible," Stragen told them, his rich voice carrying to every corner of the hall. "I had despaired of ever finding a flaw in the Styric character, but I find that you're like all other men when you're gathered together into a mob. The outspoken and unconcealed bigotry you have revealed here this afternoon has lifted my despair and filled my heart with joy. I swoon with delight to find this cesspool of festering nastiness lurking in the Styric soul, since it proves once and for all that men are all the same, regardless of race."

There were renewed shouts of protest. The protests were laced with curses this time.

Once again Stragen waited. "I'm disappointed in you, my dear brothers," he told them finally. "An Elene child of seven could curse more inventively. Is this really the best the combined wisdom of Styricum can come up with? Is 'Elene bastard' really all you know how to say? It doesn't even particularly insult me, because in my case it happens to be true." He looked around, his expression urbane and just slightly superior. "I'm also a thief and a murderer, and I have a large number of unsavory habits. I've committed crimes for which there aren't even names, and you think your pallid, petty denunciations could distress me in any way? Does anyone have a meaningful accusation before I examine *your* failings?"

"You've enslaved us!" someone bellowed.

"Not me, old boy," Stragen drawled. "You couldn't give me a slave. You have to feed them, you know—even when they're not working. Now then, let's step right along here. We've established the fact that I'm a thief and a murderer and a bastard, but what are you? Would the word *snivellers* startle you? You Styrics whine a great deal. You've carefully stored up an inventory of the abuses you've suffered in the past several thousand years and you take a perverted pleasure in sitting in dark, smelly corners regurgitating them all, chewing them over and over like mouthfuls of stale vomit. You try to blame Elenes for all your troubles. Does it surprise you to discover that I feel no guilt about the plight of the Styrics? I have more than enough guilt for things I *have* done without beating my breast about things that happened a thousand years before I was born. Frankly, my friends, all these martyred expressions bore me. Don't you *ever* get tired of feeling sorry for yourselves? I'm now going to offend you even more by getting right to the point. If you want to snivel, do it on your own time. We're offering you the opportunity to join with us in facing a common enemy. It's just a courtesy, you understand, because we don't really need you. Keep that firmly in view. We don't need you. Actually, you'll encumber us. I've heard a few intellectual cripples here suggest an alliance with our enemy. What makes you think he'd *want* you as allies? The Elene peasantry would probably be overjoyed if you tried, though, because that would give them an excuse to slaughter Styrics from here to the Straits of Thalesia. Joining with us won't ensure a lessening of Elene prejudice, but joining with our enemies will almost guarantee that ten years from now there won't be a live Styric in any Elene kingdom in the world."

He scratched thoughtfully at his chin and looked around. "I guess that more or less covers everything," he said. "Why don't you talk it over amongst yourselves? My friends and I will be leaving for Matherion tomorrow. You might want to let us know what you've decided before we go. That's entirely up to you, of course. Words couldn't begin to express our indifference to the decisions of such an insignificant people." He turned and offered his arm to Ehlana. "Shall we leave, your Majesty?" he suggested.

"What did you say to them, Stragen?"

"I insulted them." He shrugged. "On as many levels as I possibly could. Then I threatened them with racial extinction and then invited them to sign on as allies."

"All in one speech?"

"He was brilliant, your Majesty," Oscagne said enthusiastically. "He said some things to the Styrics that have needed saying for a long, long time."

"I have certain advantages, your Excellency." Stragen smiled. "My character's so questionable that nobody expects me to be polite."

"Actually, you're exquisitely courteous," Bevier disagreed.

"I know, Sir Bevier, but people don't expect it of me, so they can't bring themselves to believe it."

Both Sephrenia and Zalasta had icy, offended expressions on their faces that evening.

"I wasn't trying to be personally insulting," Stragen assured them. "I've heard any number of enlightened people say exactly the same thing. We sympathize with Styrics, but we find these interminable seizures of self-pity tedious."

"You said many things that simply aren't true, you know," Sephrenia accused him.

"Of course I did. It was a political speech, little mother. Nobody expects a politician to tell the truth."

"You were really gambling, Milord Stragen," Zalasta said critically. "I nearly swallowed my tongue when you told them that the Elenes and the Tamuls were offering an alliance simply out of courtesy. When you told them that you didn't really need them, they might very well have decided to sit the whole affair out."

"Not when he was holding all the rest of Styricum hostage, learned one," Oscagne disagreed. "It was a brilliant political speech. That not-so-subtle hint of the possibility of a new wave of Elene atrocities didn't really leave the Thousand any choice in the matter. What was the general reaction?"

"About what you'd expect, your Excellency," Zalasta replied. "Milord Stragen cut the ground out from under the Styric tradition of self-pity. It's very hard to play the martyr when you've just been told that it makes you look like a silly ass. There's a fit of towering resentment brewing among the Thousand. We Styrics are *terribly* fond of feeling sorry for ourselves, and that's been ruined now. No one ever really considered joining with the enemy—even if we knew who he was—but Stragen effectively bludgeoned us into going even further. Neutrality's out of the question now, since the Elene peasants would come to view neutrality as very nearly the same thing as actually joining with our unknown opponent. The Thousand will assist you, your Excellency. They'll do all they can do—if only to protect our brothers and sisters in Eosia."

"You've put in a full day's work, Stragen," Kalten said admiringly. "We could have been here for a month trying to persuade the Styrics that it was in their best interests to join us."

"My day isn't finished yet," Stragen told him, "and the next group I have to try to persuade is much more hardheaded."

"Might I be of some assistance?" Zalasta offered.

"I really rather doubt it, learned one. As soon as it gets dark, Talen and I have to pay a visit to the thieves of Sarsos."

"There *are* no thieves in Sarsos, Stragen!"

Stragen and Talen looked at each other, and then they burst out with howls of cynical laughter.

"I just don't trust him, Sparhawk," Ehlana said later that night when they were in bed. "There's something about him that just doesn't ring true."

"I think it's his accent, love. I felt the same way until I realized that while his Elene is perfect, his accent puts emphasis on the wrong words. Styric and Elene flow differently. Don't worry, though. Sephrenia would know if Zalasta weren't to be trusted, Ehlana. She's known him for a long, long time."

"I still don't like him," she insisted. "He's so oily he gleams when the light hits him just right." She raised one hand. "And don't try to shrug it off as prejudice. I'm looking at Zalasta as a human being, not as a Styric. I just don't trust him."

"That should pass after we get to know him better."

There was a knock at the door. "Are you busy?" Mirtai called.

"What would we be doing at this hour?" Ehlana called back impishly.

"Do you really want me to tell you, Ehlana? Talen's here. He has something you might want to know."

"Send him in," Sparhawk told her.

The door opened, and Talen came into the circle of light of their single candle. "It's just like old times, Sparhawk."

"How so?"

"Stragen and I were coming back from our meeting with the thieves, and we saw Krager in the street. Can you believe that? It was good to see him again. I was actually starting to miss him."

CHAPTER EIGHTEEN

"We simply don't have the time, Sparhawk," Sephrenia said calmly.

"I'll *take* time, little mother," he replied bleakly. "It shouldn't take me too long. I'll stay here with Stragen, and we'll chase him down. Krager's not a Styric, so he shouldn't be hard to find. We can catch up with you after we've caught him and wrung every drop of information out of him. I'll squeeze him so hard that his hair will bleed."

"And who's going to see to Mother's safety while you're amusing yourself here, Father?" Danae asked him.

"She's surrounded by an army, Danae."

"*You're* her champion, Father. Is that just some hollow title you can lay aside when something more amusing than protecting her life comes up?"

Sparhawk stared helplessly at his daughter. Then he slammed his fist against the wall in frustration.

"You'll break your hand," Sephrenia murmured.

They were in the kitchen. Sparhawk had risen early and gone looking for his tutor to advise her of Talen's discovery and of his own plans to make Krager answer for a long, long list of transgressions. Danae's presence was really not all that surprising.

"Why didn't you rack him to death when you had your hands on him in Chyrellos, dear one?" Sephrenia asked calmly.

"*Sephrenia!*" Sparhawk was more startled by the cold-blooded way she said it than by the suggestion itself.

"Well, you should have, Sparhawk. Then he wouldn't keep coming back to haunt us like this. You know what Ulath always says. Never leave a live enemy behind you."

"You're starting to sound like an Elene, little mother."

"Are you trying to be insulting?"

"Did banging your hand like that bring you to your senses, Father?" Danae asked.

He sighed regretfully. "You're right, of course," he admitted. "I guess I got carried away. Krager's continued existence offends me for some reason. He's a loose end with bits and pieces of Martel still hanging from him. I'd sort of like to tidy that part of my life up."

"Can you really make somebody's hair bleed?" his daughter asked him.

"I'm not sure. After I finally catch up with Krager, I'll let you know." He nursed his sore knuckles. "I guess we really should get on to Matherion. Sephrenia, just how healthy *is* Vanion, honestly?"

"Would you like a personal testimonial?" she asked him archly.

"That's none of my business, little mother. All I'm really asking is whether or not he's fit to travel."

"Oh, yes." She smiled. "More than fit."

"Good. I'll be delighted to hand the rewards and satisfactions of leadership back to him."

"No. Absolutely not."

"I beg your pardon?"

"Vanion carried that burden for too many years. That's what made him sick in the first place. You might as well accept the fact that you're the Pandion Preceptor now, Sparhawk. He'll advise you, certainly, but *you* get to make all the decisions. I'm not going to let you kill him."

"Then you'll both be able to come with us to Matherion?"

"Of *course* they will, Sparhawk," Danae told him. "We decided that a long time ago."

"It would have been nice if somebody'd thought to tell *me* about it."

"Why? You don't have to know everything, Father. Just do as we tell you to do."

"What on earth ever possessed you to take up with this one, Sephrenia?" Sparhawk asked. "Wasn't there *any* other God available—one of the Troll-Gods maybe?"

"*Sparhawk!*" Danae gasped.

He grinned at her.

"Zalasta will be coming with us as well," Sephrenia said. "He's been summoned back to Matherion anyway, and we really need his help."

Sparhawk frowned. "That might cause some problems, little mother. Ehlana doesn't trust him."

"That's absolutely absurd, Sparhawk. I've known Zalasta all my life. I honestly think he'd die if I asked him to."

"Has Mother given you any reason for these suspicions?" Danae asked intently.

"Hate at first sight, maybe." Sparhawk shrugged. "His reputation as the wisest man in the world probably didn't help matters. She was probably predisposed to dislike him even before she met him."

"And of course he's Styric." There was a brittle edge to Sephrenia's voice.

"You know Ehlana better than that, Sephrenia. I think it's time we got you out of Sarsos. Some of the local opinions are starting to cloud your thinking."

"Really?" Her tone was dangerous.

"It's very easy to dismiss any sort of animosity as simple prejudice, and that's the worst form of sloppy thinking. There are other reasons for disliking people, too, you know. Do you remember Sir Antas?"

She nodded.

"I absolutely hated that man."

"*Antas?* I thought he was your friend."

"I couldn't stand him. My hands started to shake every time he came near me. Would you believe I was actually happy when Martel killed him?"

"*Sparhawk!*"

"You don't need to share that with Vanion, little mother. I'm not very proud of it. What I'm trying to say is that people sometimes hate us for personal reasons that have nothing at all to do with our race or class or anything else. Ehlana probably dislikes Zalasta just because she dislikes him. Maybe she doesn't like the way his eyebrows jut out. You should always consider the simplest explanation before you go looking for something exotic."

"Is there anything else about me you'd like to change, Sir Knight?"

He looked her up and down gravely. "You're really very small, you know. Have you ever considered growing just a bit?"

She almost retorted, but then she suddenly laughed. "You can be the most disarming man in the world, Sparhawk."

"I know. That's why people love me so much."

"Now do you see why I'm so fond of these great Elene oafs?" Sephrenia said lightly to her sister.

"Of course," Aphrael replied. "It's because they're like big, clumsy puppies." Her dark eyes grew serious. "Not too many people know who I really am," she mused. "You two and Vanion are about the only ones who recognize me in this incarnation. I think it might be a good idea if we kept it that way. Our enemy—whoever he is—might make a slip or two if he doesn't know I'm around."

"You'll want to tell Zalasta though, won't you?" Sephrenia asked her.

"Not yet, I don't think. He doesn't really need to know, so let's just keep it to ourselves. When you trust someone, you're putting yourself in the position of also trusting everybody *he* trusts, and sometimes that includes people you don't even know. I'd rather not do that just yet."

"She's growing very skilled at logic," Sparhawk observed.

"I know." Sephrenia sighed. "She's fallen in with evil companions, I'm afraid."

They left Sarsos later that morning, riding out through the east gate to be joined by the Church Knights, the Peloi, and Engessa's two legions of Atans. The day was fair and warm, and the sky intensely blue. The newly risen sun stood above the range of jagged, snowcapped peaks lying to the east. The peaks reared upward, and their soaring flanks were wrapped in the deep blue shadows of morning. The country lying ahead looked wild and rugged. Engessa was striding along beside Sparhawk, and his bronze face had a somewhat softer expression than it normally wore. He gestured toward the peaks. "Atan, Sparhawk-Knight," he said, "my homeland."

"A significant-looking country, Atan Engessa," Sparhawk approved. "How long have you been away?"

"Fifteen years."

"That's a long exile."

"It is indeed, Sparhawk-Knight." Engessa glanced back at the carriage rolling along behind them. Zalasta had supplanted Stragen, and Mirtai, her face serene, sat holding Danae on her lap. "We know each other, do we not, Sparhawk-Knight?" the Atan said.

"I'd say so," Sparhawk agreed. "Our people have many different customs, but we seem to have stepped around most of those."

Engessa smiled slightly. "You conducted yourself well during our discussions concerning Atana Mirtai and Domi Kring."

"Reasonable men can usually find reasons to get along with each other."

"Elenes set great store in reason, do they not?"

"It's one of our quirks, I suppose."

"I'll explain something about one of our customs to you, Sparhawk-Knight. I may not say it too clearly, because I am clumsy in your language. I'll rely on you to explain it to the others."

"I'll do my very best, Atan Engessa."

"Atana Mirtai will go through the Rite of Passage while she is in Atan."

"I was fairly sure she would."

"It is the custom of our people for the child to relive the memories of childhood before the rite, and it is important for her family to be present while that is done. I have spoken with Atana Mirtai, and her childhood was not happy. Many of her memories will be painful, and she will need those who love her near while she sets them aside. Will you tell Ehlana-Queen and the others what is happening?"

"I will, Engessa-Atan."

"The Atana will come to you when she is ready. It is her right to choose those who will support her. Some of her choices may surprise you, but among my people, it is considered an honor to be chosen."

"We will look upon it so, Engessa-Atan."

Sparhawk briefly advised the others that Mirtai would be calling a meeting at a time of her own choosing, but he did not go into too much detail, since he himself did not know exactly what to expect.

That evening the Atan giantess moved quietly through the camp, her manner uncharacteristically diffident. She did not, as they might have expected, peremptorily command them to attend, but rather she asked, one might almost say pleaded, and her eyes were very vulnerable. Most of her choices were the ones Sparhawk would have expected. They were the people who had been closest to Mirtai during her most recent enslavement. There were some surprises, however. She invited a couple of Pandions Sparhawk had not even known she was acquainted with as well as a couple of Kring's Peloi and two Atan girls from Engessa's legions. She also asked Emban and Oscagne to hear her story.

They gathered around a large fire that evening, and Engessa spoke briefly to them before Mirtai began. "It is customary among our people for one to put childhood away before entering adulthood," he told them gravely. "Atana Mirtai will participate in the Rite of Passage soon, and she has asked us to be with her as she sets the past aside." He paused, and his tone became reflective. "This child is not like other Atan children," he told them. "For most, the childhood that is put away is simple and much like that of all others of our race. Atana Mirtai, however, returns from slavery. She has survived that and has returned to us. Her childhood has been longer than most and has contained things not usual—painful things. We will listen with love—even though we do not always understand." He turned to Mirtai. "It might be well to begin with the place where you were born, my daughter," he suggested.

"Yes, Father-Atan," she replied politely. Since Engessa had assumed the role of parent when they had first met, Mirtai's response was traditionally respectful. Now she spoke in a subdued voice that reflected none of her customary assertiveness. Sparhawk had the distinct impression that they were suddenly seeing a different Mirtai—a gentle, rather sensitive girl who had been hiding behind a brusque exterior.

"I was born in a village lying to the west of Dirgis," she began, "near the headwaters of the River Sarna." She spoke in Elenic, since, with the exception of Oscagne, Engessa, and the two Atan girls, none of her loved ones spoke Tamul. "We lived deep in the mountains. My mother and father made much of that." She smiled faintly. "All Atans believe that they're special, but we mountain Atans believe that we're especially special. We're obliged to be the very best at everything we do, since we're so obviously superior to everybody else." She gave them all a rather sly glance. Mirtai was very observant, and her offhand remark tweaked the collective noses of Styric and Elene alike. "I spent my earliest years in the forests and mountains. I walked earlier than most and ran almost as soon as I could walk. My father was very proud of me, and he often said that I was born running. As is proper, I tested myself often. By the time I was five, I could run for half a day, and at six, from dawn until sunset.

"The children of our village customarily entered training very late—usually when we were nearly eight—because the training camp in our district was very far away, and our parents did not want to be completely separated from us while we were still babies. Mountain Atans are very emotional. It's our one failing."

"Were you happy, Atana?" Engessa asked her gently.

"Very happy, Father-Atan," she replied. "My parents loved me, and they were very proud of me. Ours was a small village with only a few children. I was the best, and my parents' friends all made much of me."

She paused, and her eyes filled with tears. "And then the Arjuni slavers came. They were armed with bows. They were only interested in the children, so they killed all of the adults. My mother was killed with the first arrow."

Her voice broke at that point, and she lowered her head for a moment. When she raised her face, the tears were streaming down her cheeks.

Gravely, Princess Danae went to her and held out her arms. Without apparently even thinking about it, Mirtai lifted the little girl up into her lap. Danae touched her tear-wet cheek and then softly kissed her.

"I didn't see my father die," Mirtai continued. Her voice was choked, but then it rang out, and her tear-filled eyes hardened. "I killed the first Arjuni who tried to capture me. They're ignorant people who can't seem to realize that children can be armed, too. The Arjuni was holding a sword in his right hand, and he took my arm with his left. My dagger was very sharp, and it went in smoothly when I stabbed him under the arm with it. The blood came out of his mouth like a fountain. He fell back, and I stabbed him again, up under his breastbone this time. I could feel his heart quivering on the point of my knife. I twisted the blade, and he died."

"*Yes!*" Kring half shouted. The Domi was weeping openly, and his voice was hoarse and savage.

"I tried to run," Mirtai went on, "but another Arjuni kicked my feet out from under me and tried to grab my dagger. I cut the fingers off his right hand and stabbed him low in the belly. It took him two days to die, and he screamed the whole time. His screams comforted me."

"*Yes!*" It was Kalten this time, and his eyes were also tear filled.

The Atan girl gave him a brief, sad smile. "The Arjuni saw that I was dangerous, so they knocked me senseless. When I woke up, I was in chains."

"This all happened when you were only eight?" Ehlana asked the giantess in a half whisper.

"Seven, Ehlana," Mirtai corrected gently. "I wasn't yet eight."

"You actually killed a man at that age?" Emban asked her incredulously.

"Two, Emban. The one who screamed for two days also died." The Atana looked at Engessa, her glistening eyes a bit doubtful. "May I claim that one as well, Father-Atan?" she asked. "He might have died anyway of something else."

"You may claim him, my daughter," he judged. "It was your knife thrust that killed him."

She sighed. "I've always wondered about that one," she confessed. "It clouded my count, and I didn't like that."

"It was a legitimate kill, Atana. Your count is unclouded."

"Thank you, Father-Atan," she said. "It's a bad thing to be uncertain about so important a matter." She paused, collecting her memories. "I didn't kill again for almost half a year. The Arjuni took me south to Tiana. I did not cry at all during the journey. It is not proper to let your enemies see you grieve. At Tiana, my captors took me to the slave market and sold me to a Dacite merchant named Pelaser. He was fat and greasy, he smelled bad, and he was fond of children."

"He was a kindly master then?" Baroness Melidere asked her.

"I didn't say that, Melidere. Pelaser liked little boys and girls in a rather peculiar way. The Arjuni had warned him about me, so he wouldn't let me near any knives. I had to eat, however, so he gave me a spoon. He took me to his home at Verel in Daconia, and I spent the entire journey sharpening the handle of my spoon on my chains. It was a good metal spoon, and it took a very fine edge. When we got to Verel he chained me to the wall in a little room at the back of his house. The room had a stone floor, and I spent all my time working on my spoon. I grew very fond of it." She bent slightly and slid her hand down into her boot. "Isn't it pretty?" The implement she held up was a very ordinary-looking spoon with a wooden handle. She took it in both hands, twisted the handle slightly, and then pulled it off the shank of the spoon. The shank was thin and narrow, and it came to a needlelike point. It had been polished until it gleamed like silver. She looked at it critically. "It's not quite long enough to reach a man's heart," she apologized for her spoon. "You can't kill cleanly with it, but it's good for emergencies. It looks so much like an ordinary spoon that nobody ever thinks to take it away from me."

"Brilliant," Stragen murmured, his eyes glowing with admiration. "Steal us a couple of spoons, Talen, and we'll get to work on them immediately."

"Pelaser came to my room one night and put his hands on me," Mirtai continued. "I sat very still, and so he thought I wouldn't resist. He started to smile. I noticed that he drooled when he smiled like that. He was still smiling—and drooling—when I stabbed both of his eyes out. Did you know that a man's eyes pop when you poke them with something sharp?"

Melidere made a slightly gagging sound and stared at the calm-faced Atana in open horror.

"He tried to scream," Mirtai went on in a chillingly clinical way, "but I looped my chain around his neck to keep him quiet. I really wanted to cut him into little pieces, but I had to hold the chain in both hands to keep him from screaming. He began to struggle, but I just pulled the chain tighter about his neck."

"Yes!" Rather astonishingly, it was Ehlana's doe-eyed maid Alean who cried her hoarse approval, and the quick embrace she gave the startled Atana was uncharacteristically fierce.

Mirtai touched the gentle girl's face fondly and then continued. "Pelaser struggled quite a bit at first, but after a while, he stopped. He had knocked over the candle, and the room was dark, so I couldn't be sure he was dead. I kept the chain pulled tight around his neck until morning. His face was very black when the sun came up."

"A fair kill, my daughter," Engessa said to her proudly.

She smiled and bowed her head to him. "I thought they would kill me when they discovered what I had done, but the Dacites of the southern towns are peculiar people. Pelaser wasn't well liked in Verel, and I think many of them were secretly amused by the fact that one of the children he usually molested had finally killed him. His heir was a nephew named Gelan. He was very grateful that I'd made him rich by killing his uncle, and he spoke to the authorities in my behalf." She paused and looked at the princess, who was still nestled in her lap holding the gleaming little dagger. "Could you get me some water, Danae?" she asked. "I'm not used to talking so much."

Danae obediently slipped down and went over toward one of the cooking fires.

"She might be a little young to hear about certain things," Mirtai murmured. "Gelan was a rather nice young man, but he had peculiar tastes. He gave his love to other young men instead of women."

Sir Bevier gasped.

"Oh, dear," Mirtai said. "Are you truly *that* unworldly, Bevier? It's not uncommon, you know. Anyway, I got on quite well with Gelan. At least he didn't try to take advantage of me. He loved to talk, so he taught me to speak Elenic and even to read a bit. People in his circumstances lead rather tentative lives, and he needed a permanent friend. I had been taught that it was polite to listen when my elders spoke, and after a time he would pour out his heart to me. When I grew a little older, he bought me pretty gowns to wear, and sometimes he'd even wear them himself, although I think he was only joking. Some of his friends wore women's clothes, but nobody was really very serious about it. It's something they laughed about. It was about then that I started to go through that difficult time in a girl's life when she starts to become a woman. He was very gentle and understanding, and he explained what was happening so that I wasn't afraid. He used to have me wear my prettiest gowns, and he'd take me with him when he was doing business with people who didn't know his preferences. Daconia is an Elene kingdom, and Elenes have some peculiar ideas about that sort of thing. They try to mix religion into it for some reason. Anyway, the fact that Gelan always had a young slave girl with him quieted suspicions."

Bevier's eyes had a stunned look in them.

"Maybe you should go help the princess look for that water, Bevier," Mirtai suggested to him almost gently. "This was a part of my childhood, so I have to talk about it at this time. You don't have to listen if it bothers you, though. I'll understand."

His face grew troubled. "I'm your friend, Mirtai," he declared. "I'll stay."

She smiled. "He's such a nice boy." She said it in almost the same tone of voice Sephrenia had always used when saying exactly the same thing. Sparhawk was a bit startled at how shrewdly perceptive the Atan girl really was.

Mirtai sighed. "Gelan and I loved each other, but not in the way that people usually think of when they're talking about a man and a woman. There are as many different kinds of love as there are people, I think. He had enemies, though—many enemies. He was a very sharp trader, and he almost always got the best of every bargain. There are small people in the world who take that sort of thing personally. Once an Edomish merchant became so enraged that he tried to kill Gelan, and I had to use my spoon to protect him. As I said before, the blade's not quite long enough to kill cleanly, so the incident was very messy. I ruined a very nice silk gown that evening. I told Gelan that he really ought to buy me some proper knives so that I could kill people without spoiling my clothes. The idea of having a twelve-year-old girl for a bodyguard startled him at first, but then he saw the advantages of it. He bought me these." She touched one of the silver-hilted daggers at her waist. "I've always treasured them. I devised a way to conceal them under my clothes when we went out into the city. After I'd used them on a few people, the word got around, and his enemies quit trying to kill him.

"There were other young men like Gelan in Verel, and they used to visit each other in their homes where they didn't have to hide their feelings. They were all very kind to me. They used to give me advice and buy me pretty gifts. I was quite fond of them. They were all polite and intelligent, and they always smelled clean. I can't abide smelly men." She gave Kring a meaningful look.

"I bathe," he protested.

"Now and then," she added a bit critically. "You ride horses a great deal, Kring, and horses have a peculiar odor. We'll talk about regular bathing after I've put my brand on you." She laughed. "I wouldn't want to frighten you until I'm sure of you." Her smile was genuinely affectionate. Sparhawk realized that what she was telling them was a part of the Rite of Passage, and that she would very likely never be this open again. Her typically Atan defenses had all been lowered for this one night. He felt profoundly honored to have been invited to be present.

She sighed then, and her face grew sad. "Gelan had one very special friend whom he loved very much—a pretty young fellow named Majen. I didn't like

Majen. He used to take advantage of Gelan, and he'd deliberately say and do things to hurt him. He was frivolous and selfish and very, very vain about his appearance. He was also unfaithful, and that's contemptible. In time he grew tired of Gelan and fell in love with another meaningless pretty boy. I probably should have killed them both as soon as I found out about it. I've always regretted the fact that I didn't. Gelan had foolishly given Majen the use of a rather splendid house on the outskirts of Verel and had told him that he'd made provisions in his will so that Majen would own the house if anything ever happened to him. Majen and his new friend wanted that house, and they plotted against Gelan. They lured him to the house one night and insisted that he come to them alone. When he got there, they killed him and dropped his body in the river. I cried for days after it happened, because I was really very fond of Gelan. One of his other friends told me what had really happened, but I didn't say anything or do anything right away. I wanted the two of them to feel safe and to think that they'd gotten away with the murder. Gelan's sister inherited me— along with all his other property. She was a nice enough lady, but awfully religious. She didn't really know how to deal with the fact that she owned me. She said she wanted to be my friend, but I advised her to sell me instead. I told her that I'd found out who had murdered Gelan and that I was going to kill them. I said that I thought it would probably be better if I belonged to somebody who was leaving Verel in order to avoid all the tedious business about unexplained bodies and the like. I thought she'd be tiresome about it, but she took it rather well. She was really quite fond of her brother, and she approved of what I was planning. She sold me to an Elene merchant who was going to sail to Vardenais and told him that she'd deliver me to him on the morning of his departure. She'd made him a very good price, so he didn't argue with her.

"Anyway, on the night before my new owner was planning to sail, I dressed my-self as a boy and went to the house where Majen and the other one were living. I waited until Majen left the house and went to the door and knocked. Majen's new friend came to the door, and I told him that I loved him. I'd lived with Gelan for six years, so I knew exactly how to behave to make the pretty fool believe me. He grew excited when I told him that, and he kissed me several times." She sneered with pro-foundest contempt. "Some people simply cannot be faithful. Anyway, after he began to get very, very excited with the kissing, he started exploring. He discovered some things that surprised him very much. He was even more surprised when I sliced him across the belly just above his hips."

"I *like* this part," Talen said, his eyes very bright.

"You would," Mirtai told him. "You never like a story unless there's a lot of blood in it. Anyway, after I sliced the pretty boy open, all sorts of things fell out. He stumbled back into a chair and tried to stuff them back in again. People's insides are very slippery, though, and he was having a great deal of trouble."

Ehlana made a choking sound.

"Didn't you know about insides?" Mirtai asked her. "Get Sparhawk to tell you about it sometime. He's probably seen lots of insides. I left the young man sitting there and hid behind a door. Majen came home a while later, and he was dreadfully upset about his friend's condition."

"I can imagine." Talen laughed.

"He was even more upset, though, when I reached around from behind him and opened him up in exactly the same way."

"Those are not fatal injuries, Atana," Engessa said critically.

"I didn't intend for them to be, Father-Atan," she replied. "I wasn't done with the two of them yet. I told them who I was and that what I'd just done to them was a farewell gift from Gelan. That was about the best part of the whole evening. I put Majen in a chair facing the chair of his friend so that they could watch each other die. Then I stuck my hands into them and jerked out several yards of those slippery things I told you about."

"And then you just left them there?" Talen asked eagerly.

She nodded. "Yes, but I set fire to the house first. Neither Majen or his friend managed to get enough of themselves put back inside to be able to escape. They screamed a great deal, though."

"Good God!" Emban choked.

"A fitting revenge, Atana," Engessa said to her. "We will describe it to the children in the training camps to provide them with an example of suitable behavior."

Mirtai bowed her head to him, then looked up. "Well, Bevier?" she said.

He struggled with it. "Your owner's sins were his own. That's a matter between him and God. What you did was the proper act of a friend. I find no sin in what you did."

"I'm so glad," she murmured.

Bevier laughed a bit sheepishly. "That was a bit pompous, wasn't it?"

"That's all right, Bevier," she assured him. "I love you anyway—although you should keep in mind the fact that I have a history of loving some very strange people."

"Well said," Ulath approved.

Danae returned with a cup of water and offered it to Mirtai. "Did you finish telling them the things you didn't want me to hear about?" she asked.

"I think I covered most of it. Thank you for being so understanding—and for the water." Nothing rattled Mirtai.

Ehlana, however, blushed furiously.

"It's getting late," Mirtai told them, "so I'll keep this short. The Elene merchant who owned me took me to Vardenais and sold me to Platime. I pretended not to speak Elenic, and Platime misjudged my age because I was very tall. Platime's quite shrewd in some ways and ignorant in others. He simply couldn't understand the fact that an Atan woman can't be forced, and he tried to put me to work in one of his brothels. He took my daggers away from me, but I still had my spoon. I didn't kill *too* many of the men who approached me, but I *did* hurt them all quite seriously. Word got around, and the business in that brothel fell off. Platime took me out of there, but he didn't really know what to do with me. I wouldn't beg and I wouldn't steal, and he was really very disappointed when he found out that I'd only kill people for personal reasons. I *won't* be a paid assassin. Then the situation came up in the palace, and he gave me to Ehlana—probably with a great sigh of relief." She frowned and looked at Engessa. "That was the first time I'd ever been given away instead of sold, Father-Atan. Did Platime insult me? Should I go back to Cimmura and kill him?"

Engessa considered it. "I don't think so, my daughter. It was a special case. You might even look upon it as a compliment."

Mirtai smiled. "I'm glad of that, Father-Atan. I sort of like Platime. He's very funny sometimes."

"And how do you feel about Ehlana-Queen?"

"I love her. She's ignorant, and she can't speak a proper language, but most of the time she does what I tell her to do. She's pretty, and she smells nice, and she's very kind to me. She's the best owner I've ever had. Yes. I love her."

Ehlana gave a low cry and threw her arms around the golden woman's neck. "I love you, too, Mirtai," she said in an emotion-filled voice. "You're my dearest friend." She kissed her.

"This is a special occasion, Ehlana," the Atana said, "so it's all right just this once." She gently detached the queen's arms from around her neck. "But it's not seemly to display so much emotion in public—and girls shouldn't kiss other girls. It might give people the wrong sort of ideas."

CHAPTER NINETEEN

"Hang it all, Atan Engessa," Kalten was saying, "you heard the story the same as the rest of us. She said she hadn't even entered training when the Arjuni captured her. Where did she learn to fight the way she does? I've been training more or less constantly since Sparhawk and I were fifteen, and she throws me around like a rag doll anytime she feels like it."

Engessa smiled slightly. It was still very early, and a filmy morning mist drifted ghostlike among the trees, softening the dark outlines of their trunks. They had set out at dawn, and Engessa strode along among the mounted Pandions. "I've seen you in a fight, Kalten-Knight," the tall Atan said. He reached out and rapped one knuckle on Kalten's armor. "Your tactics depend heavily on your equipment."

"That's true, I suppose."

"And your training has concentrated on the use of that equipment, has it not?"

"Well, to some degree, I suppose. We practice with our weapons and learn to take advantage of our armor."

"And the sheer bulk of our horses," Vanion added. Vanion was wearing his black armor for the journey. Before their party had even left Sarsos, Vanion's choice of wardrobe had occasioned a spirited discussion between him and the woman he loved. Once she had removed herself from the restraining presence of all those Elenes, Sephrenia had become more vocal, and she had shown an astonishing aptitude for histrionics during the course of the conversation. Although she and Vanion had been talking privately, Sparhawk had been able to hear her comments quite clearly. Everyone in the house had heard her. Probably everyone in Sarsos had.

"At least half of your training has been in horsemanship, Kalten," Vanion continued. "An armored knight without his horse is very much like a turtle on his back."

"I've said much the same thing to my fellow novices, Lord Vanion," Khalad said politely. "Most of them take offense when I say it to them though, so I usually have to demonstrate. That seems to offend them even more for some reason."

Engessa chuckled. "You train with your equipment, Kalten-Knight," he repeated. "So do we. The difference is that our bodies are our equipment. Our way of fighting is based on speed, agility, and strength, and we can practice those without training grounds or large fields where horses can run. We practice all the time, and in the village where she was born, Atana Mirtai saw her parents and their friends improving their skills almost every hour. Children learn by imitating their parents. We see three- and four-year-olds wrestling and testing each other all the time."

"There has to be more to it than that," Kalten objected.

"Natural talent, perhaps, Sir Kalten?" Berit suggested.

"I'm not *that* clumsy, Berit."

"Was your mother a warrior, Kalten-Knight?" Engessa asked him.

"Of course not."

"Or your grandmother, or your grandmother's grandmother—back for fifty generations?"

Kalten looked confused.

"Atana Mirtai is descended from warriors on both sides of her family. Fighting is in her blood. She is gifted, and she can learn much just by watching. She can probably fight in a half-dozen different styles."

"That's an interesting notion, Atan Engessa," Vanion said. "If we could find a horse big enough for her, she might make a very good knight."

"*Vanion!*" Kalten exclaimed. "That's the most unnatural suggestion I've ever heard!"

"Merely speculation, Kalten." Vanion looked gravely at Sparhawk. "We might want to give some thought to including a bit more hand-to-hand fighting in our training program, Preceptor Sparhawk."

"Please don't do that, Vanion," Sparhawk replied in a pained tone. "You're still the preceptor until the Hierocracy says otherwise. I'm just the interim preceptor."

"All right, Interim Preceptor Sparhawk, when we get to Atan, let's pay some attention to their fighting style. We don't always fight on horseback, you know."

"I'll put Khalad to work on it," Sparhawk said.

"Khalad?"

"Kurik trained him, and Kurik was better at close fighting than any other man I've ever known."

"He was indeed. Good idea, Interim Preceptor Sparhawk."

"Must you?" Sparhawk asked him.

They reached the city of Atana twelve days later—at least it *seemed* like twelve days. Sparhawk had decided to stop brooding about the difference between real and perceived time. Aphrael was going to tamper no matter what he did or said anyway, so why should he waste time worrying about it? He wondered if Zalasta could detect the manipulation. Probably not, he decided. No matter how skilled the Styric magician might be, he was still only a man, and Aphrael was divine. An odd thought came to Sparhawk one night, however. He wondered if his daughter could also make real time seem faster than it actually was instead of slower. After he thought about it for a while, though, he decided not to ask her. The whole concept gave him a headache.

Atana was a utilitarian sort of town in a deep green valley. It was walled, but the walls were not particularly high nor imposing. It was the Atans themselves who made their capital impregnable.

"Everything in the kingdom's named 'Atan,' isn't it?" Kalten observed as they rode down into the valley. "The kingdom, its capital, the people—even the titles."

"I think *Atan's* more in the nature of a concept than a name." Ulath shrugged.

"What makes them all so tall?" Talen asked. "They belong to the Tamul race, but other Tamuls don't loom over everybody else like trees."

"Oscagne explained it to me," Stragen told him. "It seems that the Atans are the result of an experiment."

"Magic?"

"I don't know all that much about it," Stragen admitted, "but I'd guess that what they did went beyond what magic's capable of. Back before there was even such a thing as history, the Atans observed that big people win more fights than little people. That was in a time when parents chose the mates of their children. Size became the most important consideration."

"What happened to short children?" Talen objected.

"Probably the same thing that happens to ugly children in *our* society." Stragen shrugged. "They didn't get married."

"That's not fair."

Stragen smiled. "When you get right down to it, Talen, it's not really very fair when we steal something somebody else has worked for, is it?"

"That's different."

Stragen leaned back in his saddle and laughed. Then he went on. "The Atans prized other characteristics as well—ability, strength, aggressiveness, and homicidal vindictiveness. It's strange how the combination worked out. If you stop and think about it, you'll realize that Mirtai's really a rather sweet girl. She's warm and affectionate, she really cares about her friends, and she's strikingly beautiful. She's got certain triggers built into her, though, and when somebody trips one of those triggers, she starts killing people. The Atan breeding program finally went too far, I guess. The Atans became so aggressive that they started killing each other, and since such aggressiveness can't be restricted to one sex, the women were as bad as the men. It got to the point that there was no such thing in Atan as a mild disagreement. They'd kill each other over weather predictions." He smiled. "Oscagne told me that the world discovered just how savage Atan women were in the twelfth century. A large band of Arjuni slavers attacked a training camp for adolescent Atan females— the sexes are separated during training in order to avoid certain complications. Anyway, those half-grown Atan girls—most of them barely over six feet tall— slaughtered most of the Arjuni and then sold the rest to the Tamuls as eunuchs."

"The slavers were eunuchs?" Kalten asked with some surprise.

"No, Kalten," Stragen explained patiently. "They weren't eunuchs until *after* the girls captured them."

"Little girls did that?" Kalten's expression was one of horror.

"They weren't exactly babies, Kalten. They were old enough to know what they were doing. Anyway, the Atans had a very wise king in the fifteenth century. He saw that his people were on the verge of self-destruction. He made contact with the Tamul government and surrendered his people into perpetual slavery—to save their lives."

"A little extreme," Ulath noted.

"There are several kinds of slavery, Ulath. Here in Atan, it's institutionalized. The Tamuls tell the Atans where to go and whom to kill, and they can usually find a reason to deny petitions by individual Atans to slaughter each other. That's about as far as it really goes. It's a good working arrangement. The Atan race survives, and the Tamuls get the finest infantry in the world."

Talen was frowning. "The Atans are terribly impressed with size, you said."

"Well, it's *one* of the things that impresses them," Stragen amended.

"Then why did Mirtai agree to marry Kring? Kring's a good warrior, but he's not much taller than I am, and I'm still growing."

"It must be something else about him that impressed her so much." Stragen shrugged.

"What do you think it is?"

"I haven't got the faintest idea, Talen."

"He's a poet," Sparhawk told them. "Maybe that's it."

"That wouldn't make *that* much difference to someone like Mirtai, would it? She *did* slice two men open and then burn them alive, remember? She doesn't sound to me like the kind of girl who'd get all gushy about poetry."

"Don't ask *me,* Talen." Stragen laughed. "I know a great deal about the world, but I wouldn't even try to make a guess about why any woman chooses any given man."

"Good thinking," Ulath murmured.

The city had been alerted to their approach by Engessa's messengers, and the royal party was met at the gate by a deputation of towering Atans in formal attire, which in their culture meant the donning of unadorned, ankle-length cloaks of dark wool. In the midst of those giants stood a short, golden-robed Tamul. The Tamul had silver-streaked hair and an urbane expression.

"What are we supposed to do?" Kalten whispered to Oscagne.

"Act formal," Oscagne advised. "Atans adore formality. Ah, Norkan," he said to the Tamul in the golden robe, "so good to see you again. Fontan sends his best."

"How is the old rascal?" Oscagne's colleague replied.

"Wrinkled, but he still hasn't lost his edge."

"I'm glad to hear it. Why are we speaking in Elenic?"

"So that you can brief us all on local circumstances. How are things here?"

"Tense. Our children are a bit discontented. There's turmoil afoot. We send them to stamp it out, but it refuses to stay stamped. They resent that. You know how they are."

"Oh, my, yes. Has the emperor's sister forgiven you yet?"

Norkan sighed. "Afraid not, old boy. I'm quite resigned to spending the rest of my career here."

"You know how the people at court like to carry tales. Whatever possessed you to make that remark? I'll grant you that her Highness' feet are a bit oversized, but 'big-footed cow' was sort of indiscreet, wouldn't you say?"

"I was drunk and a little out of sorts. Better to be here in Atan than in Matherion trying to evade her attentions. I have no desire to become a member of the imperial family if it means that I'd have to trudge along behind her as she clumps about the palace."

"Ah, well. What's on the agenda here?"

"Formality. Official greetings. Speeches. Ceremonies. The usual nonsense."

"Good. Our friends from the west are a bit unbridled at times. They're good at formality, though. It's when things become informal that they get into trouble. May I present the Queen of Elenia?"

"I thought you'd never ask."

"Your Majesty," Oscagne said, "this is my old friend, Norkan. He's the imperial representative here in Atan, an able man who's fallen on hard times."

Norkan bowed. "Your Majesty," he greeted Ehlana.

"Your Excellency," she responded. Then she smiled. "Are her Highness' feet *really* that big?" she asked him slyly.

"She skis with only the equipment God gave her, your Majesty. I could bear that, I suppose, but she's given to temper tantrums when she doesn't get her own way, and that sort of grates on my nerves." He glanced at the huge, dark-cloaked Atans surrounding the carriage. "Might I suggest that we proceed to what my children here refer to as the palace? The king and queen await us there. Is your Majesty comfortable speaking in public? A few remarks might be in order."

"I'm afraid I don't speak Tamul, your Excellency."

"Perfectly all right, your Majesty. I'll translate for you. You can say anything that pops into your head. I'll tidy it up for you as we go along."

"How very kind of you." There was only the faintest edge to her voice.

"I live but to serve, your Majesty."

"Remarkable, Norkan," Oscagne murmured. "How *do* you manage to put both feet in your mouth at the same time?"

"It's a gift." Norkan shrugged.

King Androl of Atan was seven feet tall, and his wife, Queen Betuana, was only slightly shorter. They were very imposing. They wore golden helmets instead of crowns, and their deep blue silk robes were open at the front, revealing the fact that they were both heavily armed. They met the Queen of Elenia and her entourage in the square outside the royal palace of Atan, which was in actuality nothing more than their private dwelling. Atan ceremonies, it appeared, were conducted out of doors.

With the queen's carriage in the lead and her armed escort formed up behind, the visitors rode at a slow and stately pace into the square. There were no cheers, no fanfares, none of the artificial enthusiasm normally contrived for state visitors. Atans showed respect by silence and immobility. Stragen skillfully wheeled the carriage to a spot in front of the slightly raised stone platform before the royal dwelling, and Sparhawk dismounted to offer his queen a steel-encased forearm. Ehlana's face was radiantly regal, and her pleasure was clearly unfeigned. Though she occasionally spoke slightingly of ceremonial functions, pretending to view them as tedious, she truly loved ceremony. She took a deep satisfaction in formality.

Ambassador Oscagne approached the royal family of Atan, bowed, and spoke at some length in the flowing, musical language of all Tamuls. Mirtai stood behind Ehlana, murmuring a running translation of his Excellency's words.

Ehlana's eyes were very bright, and there were two spots of heightened color on her alabaster cheeks, signs that said louder than words that she was composing a speech.

King Androl then spoke a rather brief greeting, and Queen Betuana added her somewhat lengthier agreement. Sparhawk could not hear Mirtai's translation, so for all he knew, the Atan king and queen were discussing weather conditions on the moon.

Then Ehlana stepped forward, paused for dramatic effect, and began to speak in a clear voice that could be heard throughout the square. Ambassador Norkan stood at the side of the stone platform and translated her words.

"My dear brother and sister of Atan," she began, "words cannot express my heartfelt joy at this meeting." Sparhawk knew his wife, so he knew that disclaimer to be fraudulent. Words *could* express her feelings, and she *would* tell everybody in the square all about them. "I come to this happy meeting from the world's far end," she went on, "and my heart was filled with anxiety as I sailed across the wine-dark sea toward a foreign land peopled with strangers, but your gracious words of friendly—even affectionate—greeting have erased my childish fears, and I have learned here a lesson which I will carry all the days of my life. There are no strangers in this world, my dear brother and sister. There are only friends we have not yet met."

"She's plagiarizing," Stragen murmured to Sparhawk.

"She does that now and then. When she finds a phrase she really likes, she sees no reason not to expropriate it."

"My journey to Atan has been, of course, for state reasons. We of the royal houses of the world are not free to do things for personal reasons as others are." She gave the Atan king and queen a rueful little smile. "We cannot even yawn without its being subjected to extensive diplomatic analysis. No one ever considers the possibility that we might just be sleepy."

After Norkan translated that, King Androl actually smiled.

"My visit to Atan, however, *does* have a personal reason as well as an official one," Ehlana continued. "I chanced some time ago upon a precious thing which belongs to the Atan people, and I have come half-round the world to return this treasure to you, though it is more dear to me than I can ever say. Many, many years ago, an Atan child was lost. That child is the treasure of which I spoke." She reached out and took Mirtai's hand. "She is my dear, dear friend, and I love her. The journey I have made here is as nothing. Gladly would I have travelled twice as far—ten times as far—for the joy I now feel in reuniting this precious Atan child with her people."

Stragen wiped at his eyes with the back of his hand. "She does it to me every time, Sparhawk." He laughed. "Every single time. I think she could make rocks cry if she wanted to, and it always seems so simple."

"That's part of her secret, Stragen."

Ehlana was moving right along. "As many of you may know, the Elene people have some faults—many faults, though I blush to confess it. We have not treated your dear child well. An Elene bought her from the soulless Arjuni who had stolen her from you. The Elene bought her in order to satisfy his unwholesome desires. This child of ours—for she is now as much my child as she is yours—taught him that an Atana may not be used so. It was a hard lesson for him. He died in the learning of it."

A rumble of approval greeted the translation of that.

"Our child has passed through the hands of several Elenes—most with the worst of motives—and came at last to me. At first she frightened me." Ehlana smiled her most winsome smile. "You may have noticed that I am not a very tall person."

A small chuckle ran through the crowd.

"I thought you might have noticed that," she said, joining in their laughter. "It's one of the failings of our culture that our menfolk are stubborn and short-sighted. I am not permitted to be trained in the use of weapons. I know it sounds ridiculous, but I've not even been allowed to kill my enemies personally. I was not accustomed to women who could see to their own defense, and so I was foolishly afraid of my Atan child. That has passed, however. I have found her to be steadfast and true, gentle and affectionate, and very, very wise. We have come to Atan so that this dear child of ours may lay aside the silver of childhood and assume the gold that is her just due in the Rite of Passage. Let us join our hands and our hearts, Elene and Atan, Styric and Tamul, in the ceremony which will raise our child to adulthood, and in that ceremony, may our hearts be united, for in this child, we are all made as one."

As Norkan translated, an approving murmur went through the crowd of Atans, a murmur that swelled to a roar, and Queen Betuana, her eyes filled with tears, stepped down from the dais and embraced the pale blond queen of Elenia. Then she spoke very briefly to the crowd.

"What did she say?" Stragen asked Oscagne.

"She advised her people that anyone who offered your queen any impertinence would answer to her personally. It's no idle threat, either. Queen Betuana's one of the finest warriors in all of Atan. I hope you appreciate your wife, Sparhawk. She's just scored a diplomatic coup of the highest order. How the deuce did she learn that the Atans are sentimentalists? If she'd talked for another three minutes, the whole square would have been awash with tears."

"Our queen's a perceptive young woman," Stragen said rather proudly. "A good speech is always drawn on a community of interests. Our Ehlana's a genius when it comes to finding things she has in common with her audience."

"So it would seem. She's ensured one thing, let me tell you."

"Oh?"

"The Atans will give Atana Mirtai a Rite of Passage such as comes along only once or twice in a generation. She'll be a national heroine after an introduction like that. The singing will be tumultuous."

"That's probably more or less what my wife had in mind," Sparhawk told him. "She loves to do nice things for her friends."

"And not-so-nice things to her enemies," Stragen added. "I remember some of the plans she had for Primate Annias."

"That's as it should be, Milord Stragen." Oscagne smiled. "The only real reasons for accepting the inconveniences of power are to reward our friends and punish our enemies."

"I couldn't agree more, your Excellency."

Engessa conferred with King Androl, and Ehlana with Queen Betuana. No one was particularly surprised when Sephrenia served as translator for the queens. The small Styric woman, it appeared, spoke most of the languages in the known world. Norkan explained to Sparhawk and the others that the child's parents were much involved in the Rite of Passage. Engessa would serve as Mirtai's father, and Mirtai had rather shyly asked Ehlana to be her mother. The request had occasioned an emotional display of affection between the two of them. "It's a rather touching ceremony, actually," Norkan told them. "The parents are obliged to assert that their child is fit and ready to assume the responsibilities of adulthood. They then offer to fight anyone who disagrees. Not to worry, Sparhawk," he added with a chuckle. "It's a formality. The challenge is almost never taken up."

"Almost never?"

"I'm teasing, of course. No one's going to fight your wife. That speech of hers totally disarmed them. They adore her. I hope she's quick of study, however. She'll have to speak in Tamul."

"Learning a foreign language takes a long time," Kalten said dubiously. "I studied Styric for ten years and never did get the hang of it."

"You have no aptitude for languages, Kalten," Vanion told him. "Even Elenic confuses you sometimes."

"You don't have to be insulting, Lord Vanion."

"I imagine Sephrenia will cheat a little," Sparhawk added. "She and Aphrael taught me to speak Troll in about five seconds in Ghwerig's cave." He looked at Norkan. "When will the ceremony take place?" he asked.

"At midnight. The child passes into adulthood as one day passes into the next."

"There's an exquisite kind of logic there," Stragen noted.

"The hand of God," Bevier murmured piously.

"I beg your pardon?"

"Even the heathen responds to that gentle inner voice, Milord Stragen."

"I'm afraid I'm still missing the point, Sir Bevier."

"Logic is what sets our God apart," Bevier explained patiently. "It's his special gift to the Elene people, and he reaches out with it to all others, freely offering its blessing to the unenlightened."

"Is that really a part of Elene doctrine, your Grace?" Stragen asked the Patriarch of Ucera.

"Tentatively," Emban replied. "The view is more widely held in Arcium than elsewhere. The Arcian clergy has been trying to have it included in the articles of the faith for the last thousand years or so, but the Deirans have been resisting. The Hierocracy takes up the question when we have nothing else to do."

"Do you think it will ever be resolved, your Grace?" Norkan asked him.

"Good God, no, your Excellency. If we ever settled the issue, we wouldn't have anything to argue about."

Oscagne approached from the far side of the square. He took Sparhawk and Vanion aside, his expression concerned. "How well do you gentlemen know Zalasta?" he asked them.

"I only met him once before we reached Sarsos," Sparhawk replied. "Lord Vanion here knows him much better than I."

"I'm starting to have some doubts about this legendary wisdom of his," Oscagne said to them. "The Styric enclave in eastern Astel abuts Atan, so he *should* know more about these people than he seems to. I just caught him suggesting a demonstration of prowess to the Peloi and some of the younger Church Knights."

"It's not unusual, your Excellency." Vanion shrugged. "Young men like to show off."

"That's exactly my point, Lord Vanion." Oscagne's expression was worried. "That's not done here in Atan. Demonstrations of that kind lead to bloodshed. The Atans look upon that sort of thing as a challenge. I got there just in time to avert a disaster. What was the man thinking of?"

"Styrics sometimes grow a bit vague," Vanion explained. "They can be profoundly absentminded sometimes. I'll have Sephrenia speak with him and remind him to pay attention."

"Oh, there's something else, gentlemen." Oscagne smiled. "Don't let Sir Berit wander around alone in the city. There are whole platoons of unmarried Atan girls lusting after him."

"Berit?" Vanion looked startled.

"It's happened before, Vanion," Sparhawk told him. "There's something about our young friend that drives young women wild. It has to do with his eyelashes, I think. Ehlana and Melidere tried to explain it to me in Darsas. I didn't understand what they were saying, but I took their word for it."

"What an astonishing thing," Vanion said.

There were torches everywhere, and the faint, fragrant night breeze tossed their sooty orange flames like a field of fiery wheat. The Rite of Passage took place in a broad meadow outside the city. An ancient stone altar adorned with wildflowers stood between two broad oaks at the center of the meadow, and two bronze, basin-like oil lamps flared, one on each end of the altar.

A lone Atan with snowy hair stood atop the city wall, intently watching the

light of the moon passing through a narrow horizontal aperture in one of the battlements and down the face of a nearby wall, which was marked at regular intervals
with deeply scored lines. It was not the most precise way to determine the time, but
if everyone agreed that the line of moonlight would reach a certain one of those
scorings at midnight, precision was unimportant. As long as there was general
agreement, it was midnight.

The night was silent except for the guttering of the torches and the sighing of
the breeze in the dark forest surrounding the meadow.

They waited as the silvery line of moonlight crept down the wall.

Then the ancient Atan gave a signal, and a dozen trumpeters raised brazen
horns to greet the new day and to signal the beginning of the rite that would end
Mirtai's childhood.

The Atans sang. There were no words, for this rite was too sacred for words.
Their song began with a single deep rumbling male voice, swelling and rising as
other voices joined it in soaring and complex harmonies.

King Androl and Queen Betuana moved with stately pace and slow along a
broad, torch-lit avenue toward the ageless trees and the flower-decked altar. Their
bronze faces were serene, and their golden helmets gleamed in the torchlight. When
they reached the altar, they turned, expectant.

There was a pause while the torches flared and the organ song of the Atans rose
and swelled. Then the melody subsided into a tightly controlled hum, scarcely more
than a whisper.

Engessa and Ehlana, both in deep blue robes, escorted Mirtai out of the shadows near the city wall. Mirtai was all in white, and her raven hair was unadorned.
Her eyes were modestly downcast as her parents led her toward the altar.

The song swelled again with a different melody and a different counterpoint.

"The approach of the child," Norkan murmured to Sparhawk and the others.
The sophisticated, even cynical Tamul's voice was respectful, almost awed, and his
world-weary eyes glistened. Sparhawk felt a small tug on his hand, and he lifted his
daughter so that she might better see.

Mirtai and her family reached the altar and bowed to Androl and Betuana. The
song sank to a whisper.

Engessa spoke to the king and queen of the Atans. His voice was loud and
forceful. The Tamul tongue flowed musically from his lips as he declared his daughter fit. Then he turned, opened his robe, and drew his sword. He spoke again, and
there was a note of challenge in his voice.

"What did he say?" Talen whispered to Oscagne.

"He offered to do violence to anyone who objected to his daughter's passage,"
Oscagne replied. His voice was also profoundly respectful, even slightly choked
with emotion.

Then Ehlana spoke, also in Tamul. Her voice rang out like a silver trumpet as
she also declared that her child was fit and ready to assume her place as an adult.

"She wasn't supposed to say that last bit," Danae whispered in Sparhawk's ear.
"She's adding things."

"You know your mother." He smiled.

Then the Queen of Elenia turned to look at the assembled Atans, and her voice took on a flinty note of challenge as she also opened her robe and drew a silver-hilted sword. Sparhawk was startled by the professional way she held it.

Then Mirtai spoke to the king and queen.

"The child entreats passage," Norkan told them.

King Androl spoke his reply, his voice loud and commanding, and his queen added her agreement. Then they, too, drew their swords and stepped forward to flank the child's parents, joining in their challenge.

The song of the Atans soared, and the trumpets added a brazen fanfare. Then the sound diminished again.

Mirtai faced her people and drew her daggers. She spoke to them, and Sparhawk needed no translation. He *knew* that tone of voice.

The song rose, triumphant, and the five at the altar turned to face the roughly chiselled stone block. In the center of the altar lay a black velvet cushion, and nestled on it there was a plain gold circlet.

The song swelled, and it echoed back from nearby mountains.

And then, out of the velvet black throat of night, a star fell. It was an incandescently brilliant white light streaking down across the sky. Down and down it arched, and then it exploded into a shower of brilliant sparks.

"Stop that!" Sparhawk hissed to his daughter.

"I didn't *do* it," she protested. "I might have, but I didn't think of it. How *did* they do that?" She sounded genuinely baffled.

Then, as the glowing shards of the star drifted slowly toward the earth, filling the night with glowing sparks, the golden circlet on the altar rose unaided, drifting up like a ring of smoke. It hesitated as the Atan song swelled with an aching kind of yearning, and then, like a gossamer cobweb, it settled on the head of the child, and when Mirtai turned with exultant face, she was a child no longer.

The mountains rang back the joyous sound as the Atans greeted her.

CHAPTER TWENTY

"They know nothing of magic." Zalasta said it quite emphatically.

"That circlet didn't rise up into the air all by itself, Zalasta," Vanion disagreed, "and the arrival of the falling star at just exactly the right moment stretches the possibility of coincidence further than I'm willing to go."

"Chicanery of some kind perhaps?" Patriarch Emban suggested. "There was a charlatan in Ucera when I was a boy who was very good at that sort of thing. I'd be inclined to look for hidden wires and burning arrows." They were gathered in the Peloi camp outside the city the following morning, puzzling over the spectacular conclusion of Mirtai's Rite of Passage.

"Why would they do something like that, your Grace?" Khalad asked him.

"To make an impression maybe. How would I know?"

"Who would they have been trying to impress?"

"Us, obviously."

"It doesn't seem to fit the Atan character," Tynian said, frowning. "Would the Atans cheapen a holy rite with that kind of gratuitous trickery, Ambassador Oscagne?"

The Tamul emissary shook his head. "Totally out of the question, Sir Tynian. The rite is as central to their culture as a wedding or a funeral. They'd never demean it just to impress strangers—and it wasn't performed for our benefit. The ceremony was for Atana Mirtai."

"Exactly," Khalad agreed, "and if there were hidden wires coming down from those tree branches *she'd* have known they were there. They just wouldn't have done that to her. A cheap trick like that would have been an insult, and we all know how Atans respond to insults."

"Norkan will be here in a little while," Oscagne told them. "He's been in Atan for quite some time. I'm sure he'll be able to explain it."

"It cannot have been magic," Zalasta insisted. It seemed very important to him for some reason. Sparhawk wondered if it had to do with the shaggy-browed magician's racial ego. So long as Styrics were the only people who could perform magic or instruct others in its use, they were unique in the world. If any other race could do the same thing, the Styrics' importance would be diminished.

"How long are we going to stay here?" Kalten asked. "This is a nervous kind of place. Some young knight or one of the Peloi is bound to make a mistake sooner or later. If somebody blunders into a deadly insult, I think all this good feeling will evaporate. We don't want to have to fight our way out of town."

"Norkan will be able to tell us," Oscagne replied. "We don't want to insult the Atans by leaving too early, either."

"How far is it from here to Matherion, Oscagne?" Emban asked.

"About five hundred leagues."

Emban sighed. "Almost two more months," he lamented. "I feel as if this journey's lasted for years."

"You *do* look more fit, though, your Grace," Bevier told him.

"I don't *want* to look fit, Bevier. I want to look fat, lazy, and pampered. I want to *be* fat, lazy, and pampered—and I want a decent meal with lots of butter and gravy and delicacies and fine wines."

"You *did* volunteer to come along, your Grace," Sparhawk reminded him.

"I must have been out of my mind."

Ambassador Norkan came across the Peloi campground with an amused expression on his face.

"What's so funny?" Oscagne asked him.

"I've been observing an exquisite dance, old boy," Norkan replied. "I'd forgotten just how profoundly literal an Elene can be. Any number of Atan girls have approached young Sir Berit and expressed a burning interest in western weaponry. They were obviously hoping for private lessons in some secluded place where he could demonstrate how he uses his equipment."

"Norkan," Oscagne chided him.

"Did I say something wrong, old chap? I'm afraid my Elenic's a bit rusty. Anyway, Sir Berit's arranged a demonstration for the entire group. He's just outside the city wall giving the whole bunch of them archery lessons."

"We're going to have to have a talk with that boy," Kalten said to Sparhawk.

"I've been told not to," Sparhawk said. "My wife and the other ladies want to keep him innocent. It seems to satisfy some obscure need." He looked at Norkan. "Maybe you can settle an argument for us, your Excellency."

"I'm good at peacemaking, Sir Sparhawk. It's not as much fun as starting wars, but the emperor prefers it."

"What really happened last night, Ambassador Norkan?" Vanion asked him.

"Atana Mirtai became an adult." Norkan shrugged. "You were there, Lord Vanion. You saw everything I did."

"Yes, I did. Now I'd like to have it explained. Did a star really fall at the height of the ceremony? And did the gold circlet really rise from the altar and settle itself on Mirtai's head?"

"Yes. Was there a problem with that?"

"Impossible!" Zalasta exclaimed.

"*You* could do it, couldn't you, learned one?"

"Yes, I suppose so, but I am Styric."

"And these are Atans?"

"That's exactly my point."

"We were also disturbed when we first encountered the phenomenon," Norkan told him. "The Atans are our cousins. So, unfortunately, are the Arjuni and the Tegans. We Tamuls are a secular people, as you undoubtedly know. We have a pantheon of Gods that we ignore except on holidays. The Atans only have one, and they won't even tell us what his name is. They can appeal to him in the same way you Styrics appeal to your Gods, and he responds in the same fashion."

Zalasta's face suddenly went white. "Impossible!" he said again in a choked voice. "We'd have known. There are Atans at Sarsos. We'd have felt them using magic."

"But they don't do it at Sarsos, Zalasta," Norkan said patiently. "They only use it here in Atan and only during their ceremonies."

"That's absurd!"

"I wouldn't tell *them* you feel that way. They hold you Styrics in some contempt, you know. They find the notion of turning a God into a servant a bit impious. Atans have access to a God, and their God can do the same sort of things other Gods do. They choose not to involve their God in everyday matters, so they only call on him during their religious ceremonies—weddings, funerals, Rites of Passage, and a few others. They can't understand your willingness to insult your Gods by asking them to do things you really ought to do for yourselves." He looked at Emban then with a sly sort of grin. "It just occurred to me that your Elene God could probably do exactly the same thing. Have you ever thought of asking him, your Grace?"

"Heresy!" Bevier gasped.

"Not really, Sir Knight. That word's used to describe somebody who strays from the teachings of his own faith. I'm not a member of the Elene faith, so my speculations can't really be heretical, can they?"

"He's got you there, Bevier," Ulath said. "His logic's unassailable."

"It raises some very interesting questions," Vanion mused. "It's entirely possible that the Church blundered when she founded the Militant Orders. We may *not* have had to go outside our own faith for instruction in magic. If we'd asked him the right way, our own God might have given us the help we needed." He coughed a bit uncomfortably. "I'll trust you gentlemen not to tell Sephrenia I came up with that. If I start suggesting that she's unnecessary, she might take it the wrong way."

"Lord Vanion," Emban said quite formally. "As the representative of the Church, I forbid you to continue this speculation. This is dangerous ground, and I want a ruling from Dolmant before we pursue the matter any further—and for God's sake, don't start experimenting."

"Ah—Patriarch Emban," Vanion reminded him rather mildly, "I think that you're forgetting the fact that as the Preceptor of the Pandion Order, my rank in the Church is the same as yours. Technically speaking, you can't forbid me to do anything."

"Sparhawk's the preceptor now."

"Not until he's been confirmed by the Hierocracy, Emban. I'm not trying to demean your authority, old boy, but let's observe the proprieties, shall we? It's the little things that keep us civilized when we're far from home."

"Aren't Elenes fun?" Oscagne said to Norkan.

"I was just about to make the same observation myself."

They met with King Androl and Queen Betuana later that morning. Ambassador Oscagne explained their mission in the flowing Tamul tongue.

"He's skirting around your rather unique capabilities, Sparhawk," Sephrenia said quietly. A faint smile touched her lips. "The emperor's officials seem a little unwilling to admit that they're powerless and that they had to appeal for outside help."

Sparhawk nodded. "We've been through it before," he murmured. "Oscagne was very concerned about that when he spoke to us in Chyrellos. It seems a little shortsighted in this situation, though. The Atans make up the Tamul army. It doesn't really make much sense to keep secrets from them."

"Whatever made you think that politics was supposed to make sense, Sparhawk?"

"I've missed you, little mother." He laughed.

"I certainly *hope* so."

King Androl's face was grave, even stern, as Oscagne described what they had discovered in Astel. Queen Betuana's expression was somewhat softer—largely because Danae was sitting in her lap. Sparhawk had seen his daughter do that many times. Whenever there was a potential for tension in a situation, Danae started looking for laps. People invariably responded to her unspoken appeals to be held without even thinking about it. "She does that on purpose, doesn't she?" he whispered to Sephrenia.

"That went by a little fast, Sparhawk."

"Aphrael. She climbs into people's laps in order to control them."

"Of course. Close contact makes it far more certain—and subtle."

"That's the reason she's always remained a child, isn't it? So that people will pick her up and hold her and she can make them do what she wants?"

"Well, it's one of the reasons."

"She won't be able to do that when she grows up, you know."

"Yes, I *do* know, Sparhawk, and I'm going to be very interested to see how she handles the situation. Oscagne's coming to the point now. He's asking Androl for a report on any incidents similar to the ones you've encountered."

Norkan stepped forward to translate for Androl, and Oscagne retired to the Elene side of the room to perform the same service. The Tamuls had perfected the tedious but necessary business of translation to make it as smooth and unobtrusive as possible.

King Androl pondered the matter for a few moments. Then he smiled at Ehlana and spoke to her in Tamul. His voice was very soft.

"Thus says the king:" Norkan began his translation. "Gladly do we greet Ehlana-Queen once more, for her presence is like the sunshine come at last after a long winter."

"Oh, that's *very* nice," Sephrenia murmured. "We always seem to forget the poetic side of the Atan nature."

"Moreover," Norkan continued his translation, "glad are we to welcome the fabled warriors of the west and the wise man of Chyrellos-Church." Norkan was obviously translating verbatim.

Emban politely inclined his head.

"Clearly we see our common concern in the matter at hand, and staunchly will we join with the west-warriors in such acts as are needful."

Androl spoke again, pausing from time to time for translation. "Our minds have been unquiet in seasons past, for we have failed in tasks set for us by our Matherion-masters. This troubles us, for we are not accustomed to failure." His expression was slightly mortified as he made that admission. "I am sure, Ehlana-Queen, that Oscagne-Emperor-Speaker has told you of our difficulties in parts of Tamuli beyond our own borders. Shamed are we that he has spoken truly."

Queen Betuana said something briefly to her husband.

"She told him to get on with it," Sephrenia murmured to Sparhawk. "It appears that his tendency to be flowery irritates her—at least that was the impression I got."

Androl said something to Norkan in an apologetic tone.

"That's a surprise," Norkan said, obviously speaking for himself now. "The king just admitted that he's been keeping secrets from me. He doesn't usually do that."

Androl spoke again, and Norkan's translation became more colloquial as the Atan king seemed to lay formality aside. "He says that there have been incidents here in Atan itself. It's an internal matter, so he technically wasn't obliged to tell me about it. He says they've encountered creatures he calls 'the shaggy ones.' As I understand it, the creatures are even bigger than the tallest Atans."

"Long arms?" Ulath asked intently. "Flat noses and big bones in the face? Pointed teeth?"

Norkan translated into Tamul, and King Androl looked at Ulath with some surprise. Then he nodded.

"Trolls!" Ulath said. "Ask him how many his people have seen at any one time."

"Fifty or more," came the reply.

Ulath shook his head. "That's very unlikely," he said flatly. "You might find a single family of Trolls working together, but never fifty all at once."

"He wouldn't lie," Norkan insisted.

"I didn't say he did, but Trolls have never behaved that way before. If they had, they'd have driven us out of Thalesia."

"It seems that the rules have changed, Ulath," Tynian noted. "Have there been any other incidents, your Excellency? Things that didn't involve Trolls?"

Norkan spoke to the king and then translated the reply. "They've had encounters with warriors in strange armor and with strange equipment."

"Ask him if they might have been Cyrgai," Bevier suggested, "horsehair-crested helmets? Big round shields? Long spears?"

Norkan posed the question, though his expression was baffled. It was with some amazement that he translated the reply. "They were!" he exclaimed. "They were Cyrgai! How's that possible?"

"We'll explain later," Sparhawk said tersely. "Were there any others?"

Norkan asked the questions quickly now, obviously excited by these revelations. Queen Betuana leaned forward slightly and took over for her husband.

"Arjuni," Norkan said tersely. "They were heavily armed and made no attempt to hide the way they usually do. And once there was an army of Elenes—mostly serfs." Then his eyes went wide with astonishment. "That's totally impossible! That's only a myth!"

"My colleague's losing his grip," Oscagne told them. "The queen says that once they encountered the Shining Ones."

"Who are they?" Stragen asked.

"Norkan's right," Oscagne replied. "The Shining Ones are mythical creatures. It's another of those things I told you about back in Chyrellos. Our enemy's been sifting through folklore for horrors. The Shining Ones are like vampires, werewolves, and Ogres. Would your Majesty object if Norkan and I pursued this and then gave you a summary?" he asked Ehlana.

"Go right ahead, your Excellency," she agreed.

The two Tamuls began to speak more rapidly now, and Queen Betuana replied firmly. Sparhawk got the distinct impression that she was far more intelligent and forceful than her husband. Still holding Princess Danae in her lap, she answered the questions incisively, and her eyes were very intent.

"Our enemy seems to be doing the same things here in Atan that he's been doing elsewhere," Oscagne told them finally, "and he's been adding a few twists besides. The forces from antiquity behave the same as your antique Lamorks did back in Eosia and the way those Cyrgai and their Cynesgan allies did in the forest west of Sarsos. They attack, there's a fight, and then they vanish when their leader gets killed. Only their dead remain. The Trolls *don't* vanish. They all have to be killed."

"What about these 'Shining Ones'?" Kalten asked.

"There's no way to be sure about those," Oscagne replied. "The Atans flee from them."

"They *what*?" Stragen's voice was startled.

"Everybody's afraid of the Shining Ones, Milord," Oscagne told him. "The stories about them make tales of vampires and werewolves and Ogres sound like bedtime stories."

"Could you accept a slight amendment, your Excellency?" Ulath asked mildly. "I don't want to alarm you, but Ogres *are* real. We see them all the time in Thalesia."

"You're joking, Sir Ulath."

"No, not really." Ulath took off his horned helmet. "These are Ogre-horns," he said, tapping the curved appurtenances on his headgear.

"Maybe what you have in Thalesia's just a creature you *call* an Ogre," Oscagne said dubiously.

"Twelve feet tall? Horns? Fangs? Claws for fingers? That's an Ogre, isn't it?"

"Well—"

"That's what we've got in Thalesia. If they *aren't* Ogres, we'll settle for them until you can find us some real ones."

Oscagne stared at him.

"They aren't all that bad, your Excellency. The Trolls give us more trouble—probably because they're meat eaters. Ogres eat anything. Actually, they prefer trees for dinner, over people. They're particularly fond of maple trees for some reason—probably because they're sweet. A hungry Ogre will kick his way right through your house to get at a maple tree you've got growing in your backyard."

"Is he actually serious?" Oscagne appealed to the others. Ulath sometimes had that effect on people.

Tynian reached over and rapped the Ogre-horns on Ulath's helmet with his knuckles. "These feel fairly serious to me, your Excellency," he said. "And that raises some other questions. If Ogres are real, we might want to rethink our positions on vampires, werewolves, and these Shining Ones as well. Under the circumstances, we might consider discarding the word *impossible* for the time being."

"But you *are*, Mirtai," Princess Danae insisted.

"It's a different kind of thing, Danae," the Atana told her. "It's symbolic in my case."

"Everything's symbolic, Mirtai," Danae told her. "Everything we do means something else. There are symbols all around us. No matter how you want to look at it, though, we have the same mother, and that makes us sisters." It seemed very important to her for some reason. Sparhawk was sitting with Sephrenia in the corner of a large room of King Androl's house. His daughter was busy asserting her kinship with Mirtai as Baroness Melidere and Ehlana's maid looked on.

Mirtai smiled gently. "All right, Danae," she gave in, "if you want to think so, we're sisters."

Danae gave a little squeal of delight, jumped into Mirtai's arms, and smothered her with kisses.

"Isn't she a little darling?" Baroness Melidere laughed.

"Yes, Baroness," Alean murmured. Then a small frown creased the girl's brow. "I'll never understand that," she said. "No matter how closely I watch her, she always manages to get her feet dirty." She pointed at Danae's grass-stained feet. "Sometimes I almost think she's got a box full of grass hidden among her toys, and she shuffles her feet in it when my back's turned just to torment me."

Melidere smiled. "She just likes to run barefoot, Alean," she said. "Don't you ever want to take off your shoes and run through the grass?"

Alean sighed. "I'm in service, Baroness," she replied. "I'm not supposed to give in to that sort of whim."

"You're so very proper, Alean," the honey-blond baroness said. "If a girl doesn't give in to her whims now and then, she'll never have any fun."

"I'm not here to have fun, Baroness. I'm here to serve. My first employer made that very clear to me." She crossed the room to the two "sisters" and touched Danae's shoulder. "Time for your bath, Princess," she said.

"Do I *have* to?"

"Yes."

"It's such a bother. I'll just get dirty again, you know."

"We're supposed to make an effort to stay ahead of it, your Highness."

"Do as she tells you, Danae," Mirtai said.

"Yes, sister dear." Danae sighed.

"That was an interesting exchange, wasn't it?" Sparhawk murmured to Sephrenia.

"Yes," the small woman agreed. "Has she been letting things slip that way very often?"

"I didn't quite follow that."

"She's not really supposed to talk about symbols the way she just did, not when she's around pagans."

"I wish you wouldn't use that word to describe us, Sephrenia."

"Well, aren't you?"

"It sort of depends on your perspective. What's so important about symbols that she's supposed to hide them?"

"It's not the symbols themselves, Sparhawk. It's what talking about them that way reveals."

"Oh? What's that?"

"The fact that she doesn't look at the world or think about it in the same way we do. There are meanings in the world for her that we can't even begin to comprehend."

"I'll take your word for it. Are you and Mirtai sisters now, too? I mean, if she's Danae's sister and so are you, wouldn't you almost have to be?"

"All women are sisters, Sparhawk."

"That's a generalization, Sephrenia."

"How perceptive of you to have noticed."

Vanion entered the room. "Where's Ehlana?" he asked.

"She and Betuana are conferring," Sparhawk replied.

"Who's translating for them?"

"One of Engessa's girls from Darsas. What did you want to talk with her about?"

"I think we'll be leaving tomorrow. Engessa, Oscagne, and I talked with King Androl. Oscagne feels that we should press on to Matherion. He doesn't want to keep the emperor waiting. Engessa's sending his legions back to Darsas; he'll be going on with us, largely because he speaks Elenic better than most Atans."

"That doesn't disappoint me," Mirtai said. "He's my father now, and we really ought to get to know each other better."

"You're enjoying this, aren't you, Vanion?" Sephrenia said it half-accusingly.

"I've missed it," he admitted. "I've been at the center of things for most of my life. I don't think I was meant to sit on the back shelf."

"Weren't you happy when there were just the two of us?"

"Of course I was. I'd have been perfectly content to spend the rest of my life alone with you, but we're not alone anymore. The world's intruding upon us, Sephrenia, and we both have responsibilities. We still have time for each other, though."

"Are you sure, Vanion?"

"I'll *make* sure, love."

"Would you two like to be alone?" Mirtai asked them with an arch little smile.

"Later, perhaps," Sephrenia replied quite calmly.

"Won't we be a little undermanned without Engessa's Atans?" Sparhawk asked.

"King Androl's making arrangements," Vanion said. "Don't worry, Sparhawk. Your wife's almost as important to the rest of us as she is to you. We're not going to let anything happen to her."

"We can discount the possibility of exaggeration," Sephrenia said. "The Atan character makes that very unlikely."

"I'll agree there," Sparhawk concurred. "They're warriors, and they're trained to give precise reports."

Vanion and Zalasta nodded. It was evening, and the four of them were walking together outside the city in order to discuss the situation apart from Norkan and Oscagne. It was not that they distrusted the two Tamuls. It was just that they wanted to be able to speak freely about certain things that Tamuls were culturally unprepared to accept.

"Our opponent is quite obviously a God," Zalasta said firmly.

"He says it so casually," Vanion noted. "Are you so accustomed to confronting Gods that you're becoming blasé about it, Zalasta?"

Zalasta smiled. "Just defining the problem, Lord Vanion. The resurrection of whole armies is beyond purely human capabilities. You can take my word for that. I tried it once and made a horrible mess of it. It took me weeks to get them all back into the ground again."

"We've faced Gods before." Vanion shrugged. "We stared across a border at Azash for five hundred years."

"Now who's blasé?" Sephrenia said.

"Just defining the solution, love," he replied. "The Church Knights were founded for just such situations. We really need to identify our enemy, though. Gods have worshippers, and our enemy's inevitably utilizing his worshippers in this plan. We have to find out who he is so that we know who his adherents are. We can't disrupt his plans until we know whom to attack. Am I being obvious?"

"Yes," Sparhawk told him, "but logic always is right at first. I like the notion of attacking his worshippers. If we do that, he's going to have to stop what he's doing and concentrate on protecting his own people. The strength of a God depends entirely on his worshippers. If we start killing his people, we'll diminish him with every sword stroke."

"Barbarian," Sephrenia accused.

"Can you make her stop doing that to me, Vanion?" Sparhawk appealed. "She's called me both a pagan and a barbarian so far today."

"Well, aren't you?" she said.

"Maybe, but it's not nice to come right out and say it like that."

"It's the presence of the Trolls that has concerned me since you told me about it at Sarsos," Zalasta told them. "They are *not* drawn from the past, and they have but recently come to this part of the world from their ancestral home in Thalesia. I know little of Trolls, but it was my understanding that they are fiercely attached to their homeland. What could have provoked this migration?"

"Ulath's baffled," Sparhawk replied. "I gather that the Thalesians are so happy that the Trolls have left that they didn't pursue the matter."

"Trolls don't habitually cooperate with each other," Sephrenia told them. "*One* of them might have decided on his own to leave Thalesia, but he'd have never persuaded the rest to go with him."

"You're raising a very unpleasant possibility, love," Vanion said.

They all looked at each other.

"Is there any way they could have gotten out of Bhelliom?" Vanion asked Sephrenia.

"I don't know, Vanion. Sparhawk asked me the same question quite some time ago. I don't know what spell Ghwerig used to seal them inside the jewel. Troll-spells aren't the same as ours."

"Then we don't *know* if they're still inside or if they've somehow managed to free themselves?"

She nodded glumly.

"The fact that the Trolls banded up and left their ancestral home all at the same time suggests that something with sufficient authority over them *commanded* them to leave," Zalasta mused.

"That would be their Gods, all right." Vanion's face was as glum as Sephrenia's. "Trolls wouldn't obey anyone else." He sighed. "Well, we wanted to know who was opposing us. I think we may have just found out."

"You're all full of light and joy today, Vanion," Sparhawk said sourly, "but I'd like something a little more concrete before I declare war on the Trolls."

"How did you force the Troll-Gods to stop attacking you in Zemoch, Prince Sparhawk?" Zalasta asked him.

"I used the Bhelliom."

"It rather looks as if you'll have to use it again. I don't suppose you happened to bring it with you, did you?"

Sparhawk looked quickly at Sephrenia. "You didn't tell him?" he asked with a certain surprise.

"It wasn't necessary for him to know, dear one. Dolmant wanted us all to keep it more or less to ourselves, remember?"

"I gather that it's not with you then, Prince Sparhawk," Zalasta surmised. "Did you leave it in some safe place in Cimmura?"

"It's in a safe place all right, learned one," Sparhawk replied bleakly, "but it's not in Cimmura."

"Where is it then?"

"After we used it to destroy Azash, we threw it into the sea."

Zalasta's face went chalk white.

"In the deepest part of the deepest ocean in the world," Sephrenia added.

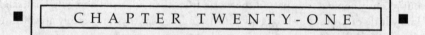

CHAPTER TWENTY-ONE

"It is along the north coast, Ehlana-Queen," Norkan translated Queen Betuana's reply. "These shaggy ones you call Trolls have come across the winter ice in large groups for the past two years. At first our people thought they were bears, but it was not so. They avoided us at first, and the snow and fog of winter made it hard for our people to see them clearly. When there were more of them here, they grew bolder. It was not until one of them was killed that we realized they were not bears."

King Androl was not present. Androl's intellectual gifts were not profound, and he much preferred to let his wife deal with state matters. The Atan king looked very impressive, but he was at his best in ceremonial situations where no surprises were likely to come up.

"Ask her if they've seen any Trolls farther south," Sparhawk murmured to his wife.

"Why don't *you* ask her?"

"Let's keep things sort of formal, Ehlana. This is technically a conversation between the two of you. I don't think the rest of us are supposed to join in. Let's not take a chance of violating a propriety we don't know about."

Ehlana posed the question, and Oscagne translated.

"No," Norkan repeated Betuana's answer. "The Trolls appear to have settled in the forests along the north slopes. So far as we know, they haven't come deeper into Atan."

"Warn her that Trolls are very good at hiding in forests," Ulath advised.

"So are we," the reply was translated.

"Ask her if some advice on tactics would offend her," the Genidian Knight said then. "We Thalesians have had many experiences with Trolls—most of them bad."

"We are always willing to listen to the voice of experience," came the Atan queen's reply.

"When we encounter Trolls in Thalesia, we usually stay back a ways and shoot some arrows into them," Ulath informed Ehlana. "It's hard to kill them with arrows, because their fur and their hides are so thick, but it's a good idea to slow them down if you can. Trolls are much, much quicker than they look, and they have very long arms. They can snatch a man out of his saddle quicker than the man can blink."

Ehlana went through the formality of repeating his words.

"What does the Troll do then?" Betuana's expression was curious.

"First he pulls off the man's head. Then he eats the rest of him. Trolls don't like to eat heads for some reason."

Ehlana choked slightly on that.

"We do not use the bow in war," Norkan translated Betuana's flowing Tamul. "We only use it in the hunt for creatures we intend to eat."

"Well," Ulath said a bit dubiously, "you *could* eat a Troll if you wanted to, I guess. I won't guarantee the flavor, though."

"I refuse to repeat that, Sir Ulath!" Ehlana exclaimed.

"Ask her if javelins would be acceptable in the Atan culture," Tynian suggested.

"Javelins would be quite all right," Norkan replied. "I've seen the Atans practicing with them."

Betuana spoke to him rapidly and at some length.

"Her Majesty's asked me to translate in narrative," Norkan told them. "The sun is well up, and she knows you should be on the road. Oscagne tells me that you're planning to take the road leading to Lebas in Tamul proper. Atan society's organized along clan lines, and each clan has its own territory. You'll be passed along from clan to clan as you ride east. It's a breach of etiquette for one clan to intrude on the territory of another, and breaches of etiquette are avoided at all costs here in Atan."

"I wonder why," Stragen murmured.

"Oscagne," Norkan said then, "as soon as you reach civilization, send me a score or so of imperial messengers with fast horses. Her Majesty wants to keep in close contact with Matherion during the crisis."

"Very good idea," Oscagne agreed.

Then Betuana rose, towering over all of them. She affectionately embraced Ehlana and then Mirtai, clearly indicating that it was time for them to continue their journey eastward.

"I will cherish the memory of this visit, dear Betuana," Ehlana told her.

"And I will as well, dearly loved sister-queen," Betuana replied in almost flawless Elenic.

Ehlana smiled. "I wondered how long you were going to hide your understanding of our language, Betuana," she said.

"You knew?" Betuana seemed surprised.

Ehlana nodded. "It's very hard to keep your face and your eyes from revealing your understanding while you're waiting for the translation. Why do you keep your knowledge of Elenic a secret?"

"The time the translator takes to convert your words into human speech gives me time to consider my reply." Betuana shrugged.

"That's a very useful tactic," Ehlana said admiringly. "I wish I could use it in Eosia, but everybody there speaks Elenic, so I couldn't really get away with it."

"Bandage your ears," Ulath suggested.

"Does he *have* to do that?" Ehlana complained to Sparhawk.

"It's only a suggestion, your Majesty." Ulath shrugged. "Pretend to be deaf and have some people around to wiggle their fingers at you as if they were translating."

She stared at him. "That's absurd, Ulath. Do you have any idea of how awkward and inconvenient that would be?"

"I just said it was a suggestion, your Majesty," he said mildly. "I didn't say it was a good one."

Following a formal farewell that was once again primarily for Mirtai's benefit, the queen and her party rode eastward out of Atana along the Lebas road. Once they were clear of the city, Oscagne, who had insisted on riding a horse that day, suggested to Sparhawk, Stragen, and Vanion that they ride forward to confer with the other knights. They found them near the head of the column. Tynian was entertaining them with a much embellished account of a probably imaginary amorous adventure.

"What's afoot?" Kalten asked when Sparhawk and the others joined them.

"Sparhawk and I conferred with Sephrenia and Zalasta last night," Vanion replied. "We thought we might share the fruits of our discussions—out of Ehlana's hearing."

"That sounds ominous," the blond Pandion observed.

"Not entirely." Vanion smiled. "Our conclusions are still a bit tenuous, and there's no point in alarming the queen until we're a bit more certain."

"Then there *is* something to be alarmed about, isn't there, Lord Vanion?" Talen asked.

"There's always *something* to be alarmed about," Khalad told his brother.

"We've sort of concluded that we're facing a God," Vanion told them. "I'm sure you've all more or less worked that out for yourselves."

"Did you really have to invite me to come along this time, Sparhawk?" Kalten complained. "I'm not very good at dealing with Gods."

"Who is?"

"*You* weren't so bad at Zemoch."

"Luck, probably."

"This is sort of the way our reasoning went," Vanion continued. "You've been seeing that shadow again, and the cloud. On the surface, at least, they seem to be divine manifestations, and these armies out of the past—the Lamorks and the Cyrgai—couldn't have been raised by a mortal. Zalasta told us that he'd tried it once and that it all fell apart on him. If *he* can't do it, we can be fairly sure that nobody else can either."

"Logical," Bevier approved.

"Thank you. Now then, the Trolls all left Thalesia a while back, and they've started to show up here in Atan. We more or less agreed that they wouldn't have done that unless they've been commanded to by someone they'd obey. Couple that fact with the shadow, and it sort of points at the Troll-Gods. Sephrenia's not positive that they're permanently locked inside Bhelliom, so we more or less have to accept the fact that they've somehow managed to escape."

"This isn't going to be one of the *good* stories, I gather," Talen said glumly.

"It *is* a bit gloomy, isn't it?" Tynian agreed.

Vanion raised one hand. "It gets worse," he told them. "We sort of agreed that all of this plotting involving ancient heroes, rabid nationalism, and the like is somewhat beyond the capability of the Troll-Gods. It's not likely that they'd have a very sophisticated concept of politics, so I think we'll have to consider the possibility of an alliance of some kind. Someone—either human or immortal—is taking care of the politics, and the Troll-Gods are providing the muscle. They command the Trolls, and they can raise these figures from the grave."

"They're being used?" Ulath suggested.

"So it would seem."

"It doesn't wash, Lord Vanion," the Thalesian said bluntly.

"How so?"

"What's in it for the Trolls? Why would the Troll-Gods ally themselves with somebody else if there weren't any benefits to the Trolls to come out of the arrangement? The Trolls can't rule the world, because they can't come down out of the mountains."

"Why not?" Berit asked him.

"Their fur—and those thick hides of theirs. They *have* to stay where it's cool. If you put a Troll out in the summer sun for two days, he'll die. Their bodies are built to keep the heat *in,* not to get rid of it."

"That *is* a fairly serious flaw in your theory, Lord Vanion," Oscagne agreed.

"I think I might be able to suggest a solution," Stragen told them. "Our enemy—or enemies—want to rearrange the world, right?"

"Well, at least the top part of it," Tynian amended. "Nobody I know of has ever suggested turning it all the way upside down and putting the peasantry in charge."

"Maybe that comes later." Stragen smiled. "Our nameless friend out there wants to change the world, but he doesn't have quite enough power to pull it off by himself. He needs the power of the Troll-Gods to make it work, but what could he offer the Trolls in exchange for their help? What do the Trolls *really* want?"

"Thalesia," Ulath replied moodily.

"Precisely. Wouldn't the Troll-Gods leap at an opportunity to wipe out the Elenes and Styrics in Thalesia and return total possession of the peninsula to the Trolls? If someone's come up with a way to expel the Younger Styric Gods—or at least claims he has—wouldn't that be fairly enticing to the Troll-Gods? It was the Younger Gods who dispossessed them in the first place, and that's why they had to go hide. This is pure speculation, of course, but let's say this friend of ours came up with a way to free the Troll-Gods. Then he offered an alliance, promising to drive the Elenes and Styrics out of Thalesia—and possibly the north coasts of both continents as well—in exchange for the help he needs. The Trolls get the north, and our friend gets the rest of the world. If *I* were a Troll, that would sound like a very attractive bargain, wouldn't you say?"

"He may have hit on it," Ulath conceded.

"His solution certainly answers *my* objection to the idea," Bevier concurred. "It may not be the *precise* arrangement between our friend and the Troll-Gods, but it's a clear hint that *something* could have been worked out. What's our course, then?"

"We have to break up the alliance," Sparhawk replied.

"That's a neat trick when you don't know who one of the allies is," Kalten told him.

"We *do* sort of know about *one* part of it, so we'll have to concentrate on that. Your theory narrows my options, Vanion. I guess I *will* have to declare war on the Trolls after all."

"I don't quite understand," Oscagne confessed.

"The Gods derive their strength from their worshippers, your Excellency," Bevier explained. "The more worshippers, the stronger the God. If Sparhawk starts killing Trolls, the Troll-Gods will notice it. If he kills enough of them, they'll withdraw from the alliance. They won't have any choice if they want to survive, and we found out at Zemoch that they're very interested in surviving: they went all to pieces when Sparhawk threatened to destroy Bhelliom and them along with it."

"They became very cooperative at that point," Sparhawk said.

"You gentlemen have a real treat in store for you," Ulath told them. "Fighting Trolls is very, *very* exhilarating."

They set up their night's encampment that evening in a meadow beside a turbulent mountain stream that had carved a deep gorge in the mountains. The lower walls of the gorge were tree-covered and they angled up steeply to the sheer cliffs rising a hundred or more feet to the rim of the cut. It was a good defensive position, Sparhawk noted as he surveyed the camp. Evening came early in these canyons, and the cooking fires flared yellow in the gathering dusk, their smoke drifting blue and tenuous downstream in the night breeze.

"A word with you, Prince Sparhawk?" It was Zalasta, and his white Styric robe gleamed in the half-light.

"Of course, learned one."

"I'm afraid your wife doesn't like me," the magician observed. "She tries to be polite, but her distaste is fairly obvious. Have I offended her in some way?"

"I don't think so, Zalasta."

A faintly bitter smile touched the Styric's lips. "It's what my people call 'the Elene complaint,' then."

"I rather doubt that. I more or less raised her, and I made her understand that the common Elene prejudice was without foundation. Her attitude sort of derives from mine, and the Church Knights are actually quite fond of Styrics—the Pandions particularly so, since Sephrenia was our tutor. We love her very much."

"Yes. I've observed that." The magician smiled. "We ourselves are not without our failings in that area. Our prejudice against Elenes is quite nearly as irrational as yours against us. Your wife's disapproval of me must come from something else, then."

"It may be something as simple as your accent, learned one. My wife's a complex person. She's very intelligent, but she *does* have her irrational moments."

"It might be best if I avoided her, then. I'll travel on horseback from now on. Our close proximity in that carriage exacerbates her dislike, I expect. I've worked with people who've disliked me in the past and it's no great inconvenience. When I have leisure, I'll win her over." He flashed a quick smile. "I can be very winning when I set my mind to it." He looked on down the gorge where the rapids swirled and foamed white in the gathering darkness. "Is there any possibility that you might be able to retrieve the Bhelliom, Prince Sparhawk?" he asked gravely. "I'm afraid we're at a distinct disadvantage without it. We need something powerful enough to achieve some measure of parity with a group of Gods. Are you at liberty to tell me where you were when you threw it into the sea? I might be able to aid you in its retrieval."

"There weren't any restrictions placed on me about discussing it, learned one," Sparhawk replied ruefully. "There wasn't any need for that, since I haven't got the foggiest idea of where it was. Aphrael chose the spot, and she very carefully arranged things so that we couldn't identify the place. You might ask her, but I'm fairly sure she won't tell you."

Zalasta smiled. "She *is* a bit whimsical, isn't she?" he said. "We all loved her in spite of that, however."

"That's right, you grew up in the same village with her and Sephrenia, didn't you?"

"Oh, yes. I am proud to call them my friends. It was very stimulating trying to keep up with Aphrael. She had a very agile mind. Did she give you any reason for her desire to keep the location a secret?"

"Not in so many words, but I think she felt that the jewel was far too dangerous to be loosed in the world. It's even more eternal than the Gods themselves, and probably more powerful. I can't pretend to even begin to understand where it originated, but it seems to be one of those elemental spirits that are involved in the creation of the universe." Sparhawk smiled. "That gave me quite a turn when I found out about it. I was carrying something that could create whole suns not six inches from my heart. I think I can understand Aphrael's concern about Bhelliom, though. She told us once that the Gods can only see the future imperfectly, and she couldn't really see what might happen if Bhelliom fell into the wrong hands. She and I took a very real chance of destroying the world to keep it out of the hands of Azash. She wanted to put it where nobody could ever use it again."

"Her thinking is faulty, Prince Sparhawk."

"I wouldn't tell *her* that, if I were you. She might take it as criticism."

Zalasta smiled. "She knows me, so she's not upset when I criticize her. If, as you say, Bhelliom's one of those energies that's involved in the constructing of the universe, it must be allowed to continue its work. The universe will be flawed if it is not."

"She said that this world won't last forever." Sparhawk shrugged. "In time, it'll be destroyed, and Bhelliom will be freed. The mind sort of shudders away from the notion, but I gather that the space of time stretching from the moment Bhelliom was trapped on this world until the moment the world burns away when our sun explodes is no more than the blinking of an eye to the spirit which inhabits it."

"I sort of choke on the notions of eternity and infinity myself, Prince Sparhawk," Zalasta admitted.

"I think we'll have to accept the notion that Bhelliom's lost for good, learned one," Sparhawk told him. "We're at a disadvantage, certainly, but I don't see any help for it. We're going to have to deal with this situation ourselves, I'm afraid."

Zalasta sighed. "You may be right, Prince Sparhawk, but we really need the Bhelliom. Our success or failure may hinge on that stone. I think we should concentrate our efforts on Sephrenia. We must persuade her to intercede with Aphrael. She has an enormous influence on her sister."

"Yes," Sparhawk agreed. "I've noticed that. What were they like as children?"

Zalasta looked up into the gathering darkness. "Our village changed a great deal when Aphrael was born," he reminisced. "We knew at once that she was no ordinary child. The Younger Gods are all very fond of her. Of all of them, she is the only child, and they've spoiled her outrageously over the eons." He smiled faintly. "She's perfected the art of being a child. All children are loveable, but Aphrael is so skilled at making people love her that she can melt the hardest of hearts. The Gods always get what they want, but Aphrael makes us do what she wants out of love."

"I've noticed that," Sparhawk said wryly.

"Sephrenia was about nine when her sister was born, and from the moment she first saw the Child-Goddess, she committed her entire life to her service." There was a strange note of pain in the magician's voice as he said it. "Aphrael seemed to have almost no infancy," he continued. "She was born with the ability to speak—or so it seemed—and she was walking in an incredibly short period of time. It was not convenient for her to go through a normal babyhood, so she simply stepped over such things as teething and learning to crawl. She wanted to be a child, not a baby. I was several years older than Sephrenia and already deep into my studies, but I did observe them rather closely. It's not often that one has the opportunity to watch a God grow up."

"Very rare," Sparhawk agreed.

Zalasta smiled. "Sephrenia spent every moment with her sister. It was obvious from the very beginning that there was a special bond between them. It's one of Aphrael's peculiarities that she adopts the subservient position of a young child. She's a Goddess, and she could command, but she doesn't. She almost seems to enjoy being scolded. She's obedient—when it suits her to be—but every so often she'll do something outrageously impossible—probably just to remind people who she really is."

Sparhawk remembered the swarm of fairies pollinating the flowers in the palace garden in Cimmura.

"Sephrenia was a sensible child who always acted older than her years. I suspect Aphrael of preparing her sister for a lifelong task even before she herself was born. In a very real sense, Sephrenia became Aphrael's mother. She cared for her, fed her, bathed her—although that occasioned some truly stupendous arguments. Aphrael absolutely hates to be bathed—and she really doesn't need it, since she can make dirt go away whenever she wants to. I don't know if you noticed it, but her feet always have grass stains on them, even when she's in a place where there is no grass. For some reason I can't begin to fathom, she seems to need those stains." The Styric sighed. "When Aphrael was about six or so, Sephrenia was obliged to become her mother in fact. The three of us were off in the forest, and while we were gone, a mob of drunken Elene peasants attacked our village and killed everyone there."

Sparhawk drew in his breath sharply. "That explains a few things," he said. "Of course it raises other things even more incomprehensible. After a tragedy like that, what could ever have persuaded Sephrenia to take on the chore of training generations of Pandion Knights?"

"Aphrael probably told her to." Zalasta shrugged. "Don't make any mistakes, Prince Sparhawk. Aphrael may *pretend* to be a child, but in truth she is not. She will obey when it suits her, but never forget that *she* is the one who makes the ultimate decisions, and she *always* gets what she wants."

"What happened after your village was destroyed?" Sparhawk asked.

"We wandered for a time in the forest, and then another Styric village took us in. As soon as I was sure that the girls were settled in and safe, I left to pursue my studies. I didn't see them again for many years, and when I finally met them again, Sephrenia was the beautiful woman she is now. Aphrael, however, was still a child, not a day older than she had been when I left them." He sighed again. "The time we spent together when we were children was the happiest of my life. The memory of that time strengthens and sustains me when I am troubled."

He looked up toward the sky where the first stars were beginning to come out. "Please make my excuses, Prince Sparhawk. I think I'd like to be alone with my memories tonight."

"I will, Zalasta," Sparhawk replied, laying a friendly hand on the Styric's shoulder.

"We're fond of him," Danae said.

"Why are you keeping your identity a secret from him then?"

"I'm not sure, Father. Maybe it's just because girls need secrets."

"That doesn't make sense, you know."

"Yes, but I don't have to make sense. That's the nice thing about being universally adored."

"Zalasta thinks we're going to need the Bhelliom." Sparhawk decided to get right to the point.

"No." Aphrael said it very firmly. "I spent too much time and effort getting it into a safe place to turn around and drag it out every time there's a change in the weather. Zalasta always wants to unleash more power than is really necessary in situations like this. If all we're facing are the Troll-Gods, we can manage without Bhelliom." She held up one hand when he started to object. "*My* decision, Sparhawk," she told him.

"I could always spank you and make you change your mind," he threatened.

"Not unless I let you, you can't." Then she sighed. "The Troll-Gods aren't going to be a problem for much longer."

"Oh?"

"The Trolls are doomed," she said rather sadly, "and once they're gone, their Gods will be powerless."

"Why are the Trolls doomed?"

"Because they can't change, Sparhawk. We may not always like it, but that's the way the world is. The creatures of this world must change—or die. That's what happened to the Dawn-men. The Trolls supplanted them because they couldn't change, and now it's the turn of the Trolls. Their nature is such that they need a great deal of room. A lone Troll needs fifty or so square leagues of range, and he won't share that range with any other Troll. There just isn't enough room left for them anymore. There are Elenes in the world now as well, and you're cutting down trees to build your houses and to clear fields for your crops. The Trolls might have survived if they only had to live with Styrics. Styrics don't chop trees down." She smiled. "It's not that we're really all that fond of trees. It's just that we don't have very good axes. When you Elenes discovered how to make steel, you doomed the Trolls—and their Gods."

"That lends some weight to the notion that the Troll-Gods may have allied themselves with someone else," Sephrenia noted. "If they can understand what's happening, they're probably getting desperate. Their survival depends on preserving the Trolls and their range."

Sparhawk grunted. "That might help to explain something that's been bothering me," he said.

"Oh?" Sephrenia asked him.

"If there's someone involved as well as the Troll-Gods, it might account for the differences I've been feeling. I've been getting this nagging sense that things aren't quite the same as they were last time—jarring little discrepancies, if you take my meaning. The major discrepancy lies in the fact that these elaborate schemes with people like Drychtnath and Ayachin are just too subtle for the Troll-Gods to understand." He made a rueful face. "But that immediately raises another problem. How can this other one get the cooperation of the Troll-Gods if he can't explain what he's doing and why?"

"Would it offend your pride if I offered you a simpler solution?" Danae asked him.

"I don't think so."

"The Troll-Gods know that others are smarter than they are, and the one you call 'our friend' has a certain hold over them. He can always cram them back into Bhelliom and let them spend several million years in that box on the sea bottom if they don't cooperate. Maybe he's just telling them what he wants them to do without bothering to explain it to them. The rest of the time, he could just be letting them blunder around making noise. All that crashing through the bushes would certainly help conceal what *he's* doing, wouldn't it?"

He stared at her for a long time. Then he laughed. "I love you, Aphrael," he said, lifting her in his arms and kissing her.

"He's such a nice boy." The little Goddess beamed at her sister.

·   ·   ·

Two days later, the weather changed abruptly. Heavy clouds swept in off the Tamul Sea several hundred-odd leagues to the east, and the sky turned suddenly murky and threatening. To add to the gloom, one of those "breakdowns in communications" so common in all government enterprises occurred. They reached a clan border marked by a several-hundred-yard-wide strip of open ground about noon only to find no escort awaiting them. The clan that had brought them this far could not cross that border, and, indeed, looked nervously back toward the safety of the forest.

"There are bad feelings between these two clans, Sparhawk-Knight," Engessa advised gravely. "It is a serious breach of custom and propriety for either clan to come within five hundred paces of the line between them."

"Tell them to go on home, Atan Engessa," Sparhawk told him. "There are enough of us here to protect the queen, and we wouldn't want to start a clan war just for the sake of maintaining appearances. The other clan should be along soon, so there's no real danger."

Engessa looked a bit dubious, but he spoke with the leader of their escort, and the Atans gratefully melted back into the forest.

"What now?" Kalten asked.

"How about some lunch?" Sparhawk replied.

"I thought you'd never think of that."

"Have the knights and the Peloi draw up around the carriage and get some cooking fires going. I'll go tell Ehlana." He rode back to the carriage.

"Where's the escort?" Mirtai asked brusquely. Now that she was an adult, Mirtai was even more commanding then she had been before.

"I'm afraid they're late," Sparhawk told her. "I thought we might as well have some lunch while we're waiting for them."

"Absolutely splendid idea, Sparhawk." Emban beamed.

"We thought you might approve, your Grace. The escort should be here by the time we finish eating."

They were not, however. Sparhawk paced back and forth, chafing at the delay, and his patience finally evaporated. "That's it!" he said loudly. "Let's get ready to move out."

"We're supposed to wait, Sparhawk," Ehlana told him.

"Not out in the open like this, we're not. And I'm not going to sit here for two days waiting for some Atan clan-chief to mull his way through a message."

"I think we'd better do as he says, friends," Ehlana told the others. "I know the signs, and my beloved's beginning to grow short-tempered."

"—Er," Talen added.

"You said what?" Ehlana asked him.

"Short-tempered-er. Sparhawk's always short-tempered. It's only a little worse now. You have to know him very well to be able to tell the difference."

"Are you short-tempered-er right now, love?" she teased her husband.

"I don't think there is such a word, Ehlana. Let's get ready and move out. The road's well marked, so we can hardly get lost."

The trees beyond the open space were dark cedars with swooping limbs that brushed the ground and concealed everything more than a few yards back into the forest. The clouds rolling in from the east grew thicker and the light back among the trees grew dim. The air hung motionless and sultry, and the whine of mosquitoes seemed to grow louder as they rode deeper into the woods.

"I love wearing armor in mosquito country," Kalten said gaily. "I have this picture of hordes of the little bloodsuckers sitting around with teeny little hammers trying to pound their beaks straight again."

"They won't really try to bite you through the steel, Sir Kalten," Zalasta told him. "They're attracted by smell, and I don't think any living creature finds the smell of Elene armor all that appetizing."

"You're taking all the fun out of it, Zalasta."

"Sorry, Sir Kalten."

There was a rumble far off to the east.

"The perfect end to a day gone sour," Stragen observed. "A nice rousing thunderstorm with lots of lightning, hail, driving rain, and howling winds."

Then, echoing down some unseen canyon back in the forest there came a hoarse, roaring bellow. Almost immediately there came an answer from the opposite direction.

Sir Ulath swore, biting off curses the way a dog tears at a piece of meat.

"What's wrong?" Sparhawk demanded.

"Didn't you recognize it, Sparhawk?" the Thalesian said. "You've heard it before—back at Lake Venne."

"What is it?" Khalad asked apprehensively.

"It's a signal that it's time for us to fort up! Those are Trolls out there!"

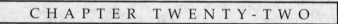

CHAPTER TWENTY-TWO

"It's not perfect, friend Sparhawk," Kring said a bit dubiously, "but I don't think we've got time to look for anything better."

"He's right about that, Sparhawk," Ulath agreed. "Time's definitely a major concern right now."

The Peloi had ranged out into the surrounding forest in search of some defensible position. Given their nervousness about wooded terrain, Kring's horsemen had displayed a great deal of courage in the search.

"Can you give me some details?" Sparhawk asked the shaved-headed Domi.

"It's a blind canyon, friend Sparhawk," Kring replied, nervously fingering the hilt of his saber. "There's a dried-up streambed running down the center of it. From the look of it, I'd say that the stream runs full in the springtime. There seems to be a dry waterfall at the upper end. There's a cave at the foot of the dry falls that should provide some protection for the women, and it'll be a good place to defend if things get desperate."

"I thought they already were," Tynian noted.

"How wide is the mouth of the canyon?" Sparhawk asked intently.

"The canyon mouth itself is maybe two hundred paces across," Kring told him, "but when you go back in a ways, it narrows down to about twenty paces. Then it widens out again into a sort of a basin where the falls are."

"The bad thing about a canyon is that you're down in a hole," Kalten said. "It won't take the Trolls too long to go up to the canyon rim and start throwing rocks down on our heads."

"Do we have any choice?" Tynian asked him.

"No, but I thought I'd point it out."

"There's no place else?" Sparhawk asked the Domi.

"A few clearings." Kring shrugged. "A hill or two that I could spit over."

"It looks like it's the canyon then," Sparhawk said grimly. "We'd better get there and start putting up some sort of fortifications across that narrow place."

They gathered closely around the carriage and pushed their way into the forest. The carriage jolted over the rough ground, and on several occasions fallen logs had to be dragged out of the way. After about five hundred yards, though, the ground began to slope upward and the trees thinned out.

Sparhawk pulled Faran in beside the carriage.

"There's a cave ahead, Ehlana," he told his wife. "Kring's men didn't have time to explore it, so we don't know how deep it is."

"What difference would that make?" she asked him. Ehlana's face was even more pale than usual. The bellowing of the Trolls far back in the forest had obviously unnerved her.

"It might be very important," he replied. "When you get there, have Talen explore the place. If it goes back in far enough or branches out, you'll have a place to hide. Sephrenia's going to be with you, and she'll be able to block the entrance and hide any side chamber so that the Trolls can't find you if they manage to get past us."

"Why don't we all just go into the cave? You and Sephrenia can use magic to block the entrance, and we can just sit there until the Trolls get bored and go away."

"According to Kring, the cave's not big enough. He's got men out looking for another one, but we *know* this one's there. If something better turns up, we'll change the plan, but for right now this is the best we can manage. You'll take the other ladies, Patriarch Emban, and Ambassador Oscagne and go inside. Talen will go in with you, and Berit and eight or ten other knights will cover the entrance to the cave. Please don't argue, Ehlana. This is one of those situations where *I* make the decisions. You agreed to that back in Chyrellos."

"He's right, your Majesty," Emban told her. "We need a general right now, not a queen."

"Am I encumbering you gentlemen?" she asked tartly.

"Not in the slightest, my Queen," Stragen said smoothly. "Your presence will inspire us to greater heights. We'll dazzle you with our prowess and our courage."

"I'd be happy to simulate dazzlement if we could avoid this," she said in a worried voice.

"I'm afraid you'd have to convince the Trolls on that score," Sparhawk told her, "and Trolls are very hard to convince—particularly if they're hungry." Although the situation was grave, Sparhawk was not quite as desperately concerned about his wife's safety as he might normally have been. Sephrenia would be there to protect her, and if things grew truly desperate, Aphrael could take a hand in the matter as well. He knew that his daughter would not permit any harm to come to her mother, even if it meant revealing her identity.

The canyon had its drawbacks, there was no question about that. The most obvious was the one Kalten had raised. If the Trolls ever reached the canyon rim above them, the situation would quickly become untenable. Kalten made quite an issue of pointing that out. "I told you so" figured prominently in his remarks.

"I think you're overestimating the intelligence of Trolls, Kalten," Ulath disagreed. "They'll come straight at us, because they'll be thinking of us as food, not as enemies. Supper's more important to them than a military victory."

"You're just loaded with cheery thoughts today, aren't you, Ulath?" Tynian said dryly. "How many of them do you think there are?"

"It's hard to say." Ulath shrugged. "I've heard ten different voices so far—probably the heads of families. There's likely a hundred or so of them out there at the very least."

"It could be worse," Kalten said.

"Not by very much," Ulath disagreed. "A hundred Trolls could have given Wargun's whole army some serious problems."

Bevier, their expert on fortifications and defensive positions, had been surveying the canyon. "There are plenty of rocks in the streambed for breastworks," he observed, "and whole thickets of saplings for stakes. Ulath, how long do you think we have before they attack?"

Ulath scratched at his chin. "The fact that we're stopping gives us a bit more space," he mused. "If we were still moving, they'd attack right away, but now they'll probably take their time and gather their forces. I believe you might want to rethink your strategy, though, Bevier. Trolls aren't going to shoot arrows at us, so breastworks aren't really necessary. Actually, they'd hinder us more than they would the Trolls. Our advantage lies in our horses—and our lances. You really want to keep Trolls at a distance if you possibly can. The sharpened stakes would be good, though. A Troll takes the easiest way to get at what he wants—us, in this case. If we can clutter up the sides of this narrow place and funnel them through so that only a few at a time can come at us, we'll definitely improve the situation. We don't want to take on more of them at any one time than we absolutely have to. What I'd really like is a dozen or so of Kurik's crossbows."

"I have one, Sir Ulath," Khalad volunteered.

"And many of the knights have longbows," Bevier added.

"We slow them down with the stakes so that we can pick them off with arrows?" Tynian surmised.

"That's the best plan," Ulath agreed. "You don't want to go hand to hand with a Troll if you can possibly avoid it."

"We'd better get at it, then," Sparhawk told them.

The work was feverish for the next hour. The narrow gap was necked down even more with boulders from the streambed, and a forest of sharpened stakes, all slanting sharply outward, was planted to the front. There was a method to the planting of the stakes. They bristled so thickly along the sides of the gap as to be well-nigh impenetrable, but the corridor leading to the basin at the head of the canyon was planted only sparsely with them to encourage the monsters to follow that route. Kring's Peloi found a large bramble thicket, uprooted the thorn bushes, and threw them back among the thick-planted stakes at the sides to further impede progress.

"What's Khalad doing there?" Kalten asked, puffing and sweating with the large rock he carried in his arms.

"He's building something," Sparhawk replied.

"This isn't really the time for the construction of camp improvements, Sparhawk."

"He's a sensible young man. I'm sure he's usefully occupied."

At the end of the hour, they stopped to survey the fruits of their labors. The gap had been narrowed to no more than eight feet wide, and the ground at the sides of the gap was dense with chest-high stakes angled so that they would keep the Trolls on the right path. Tynian, however, added one small embellishment. A number of his Alciones were driving pegs into the middle of the pathway and then sharpening the protruding ends.

"Trolls don't wear shoes, do they?" he asked Ulath.

"It'd take half a cowhide to make shoes for a Troll." Ulath shrugged. "And they eat cows hide and all, so they're a little short of leather."

"Good. We want to keep them in the center of the canyon, but we don't want to make it *too* easy for them. Barefoot Trolls aren't going to run through *that* stubble field—not after the first few yards, anyway."

"I like your style, Tynian." Ulath grinned.

"Could you gentlemen stand off to one side, please?" Khalad called. He had cut two fairly sturdy saplings off so that the stumps were about head high and had then lashed a third across them. Then he had strung a rope across the ends of the horizontal sapling and drawn it tight to form a huge bow. The bow was fully drawn, tied off to another stump at the rear, and it was loaded with a ten-foot javelin.

Sparhawk and the others moved off to the sides of the narrow cut, and Khalad released the bow by cutting the rope that held it drawn. The javelin shot forward with a sharp whistling sound and buried itself deep into a tree a good hundred yards down the canyon.

"I'm going to like that boy." Kalten smiled. "He's almost as good at this sort of thing as his father was."

"The family shows a lot of promise," Sparhawk agreed. "Let's position our archers so that they have a clear shot at that gap."

"Right," Kalten agreed. "What then?"

"Then we wait."

"That's the part I hate the most. Why don't we grab something to eat? Just to pass the time, of course."

"Of course."

· · ·

The storm that had been building to the east all morning was closer now, the clouds purplish-black and seething. There were flickers of lightning deep inside the cloud bank, and the thunder rolled from horizon to horizon, shaking the ground with every peal.

They waited. The air was dead calm and sultry, and the knights were sweating uncomfortably in their armor.

"Can we think of anything else?" Tynian asked.

"I've contrived a few rudimentary catapults," Bevier replied. "They're hardly more than bent saplings, so they won't throw very big rocks, and their range is limited."

"I'll take all the help I can get when it comes to fighting Trolls," Ulath told him. "Every one of them we knock down before they get to us is one less we'll have to fight."

"Dear God!" Tynian exclaimed.

"What?" Kalten demanded with a certain alarm.

"I think I just saw one of them back at the edge of the forest. Are they all that big?"

"Nine feet or so tall?" Ulath asked quite casually.

"At least."

"That's fairly standard for a Troll, and they weigh between thirty-five and fifty stone."

"You're not serious!" Kalten said incredulously.

"Wait just a bit and you'll be able to weigh one for yourself." Ulath looked around at them. "Trolls are hard to kill," he cautioned. "Their hides are very tough, and their skull bones are almost a half-inch thick. They can take a lot of punishment when they're excited. If we get in close, try to maim them. You can't really count on clean kills with Trolls, so every arm you chop off is one less the Troll can grab you with."

"Will they have weapons of any kind?" Kalten asked.

"Clubs are about all. They aren't good with spears. Their arms aren't hooked on right for jabbing."

"That's something, anyway."

"Not very much," Tynian told him.

They waited as the thunder moved ponderously toward them.

They saw several more Trolls at the edge of the forest in the next ten minutes, and the bellowing roars of those scouts were obviously summoning the rest of the pack. The only Troll Sparhawk had ever seen before had been Ghwerig, and Ghwerig had been dwarfed and grossly deformed. He quickly began to revise his assessment of the creatures. They were, as Ulath had stated, about nine feet tall, and they were covered with dark brown, shaggy fur. Their arms were very long, and their huge hands hung below their knees. Their faces were brutish, with heavy brow ridges, muzzlelike mouths, and protruding fangs. Their eyes were small, deep-set, and they burned with a dreadful hunger. They slouched along at the edge of the forest, not really trying to conceal themselves, and Sparhawk clearly saw that their long arms played a significant part in their locomotion, sometimes serving as an additional leg and sometimes grasping trees to help pull themselves along. Their movements were flowing, even graceful, and bespoke an enormous agility.

"Are we more or less ready?" Ulath asked them.

"I could stand to wait a little longer," Kalten replied.

"How long?"

"Forty or fifty years sounds about right to me. What did you have in mind?"

"I've seen about fifteen different individuals," the big Thalesian noted. "They're coming out one by one to have a look, and that means that they're all more or less gathered just back under the trees. I thought I'd insult them for a while. When a Troll gets angry, he doesn't really think. Of course Trolls don't have very much to think with in the first place. I'd like to provoke them into an ill-considered attack if possible. If I *really* insult them, they'll scream and howl and then come rushing out of those woods foaming at their mouths. They'll be easy targets for the bowmen at that point, and if a few of them get through, we can charge them with our horses and the lances. We should be able to kill quite a few of them before they come to their senses. I'd really like to whittle down their numbers, and enraged Trolls make easy targets."

"Do you think we might be able to kill enough of them to frighten the rest away?" Kalten asked.

"I wouldn't count on it, but anything's possible, I suppose. I'd have sworn that you couldn't get a hundred Trolls to even walk in the same direction at the same time, so the situation here's completely new to me."

"Let me talk with the others before we precipitate anything," Sparhawk told him. He turned and walked back to where the knights and the Peloi waited with their horses. Vanion stood with Stragen, Engessa, and Kring. "We're about ready to start," Sparhawk told them.

"Did you plan to invite the Trolls?" Stragen asked him. "Or are we going to begin without them?"

"Ulath's going to see if he can provoke them into something rash," Sparhawk replied. "The stakes should slow them down enough so that our archers can work on them. We want to thin them out a bit. If they manage to break through, we'll charge them with lances." He looked at Kring. "I'm not trying to insult you, Domi, but could you hold back a bit? Ulath tells us that Trolls take a lot of killing. It's a dirty business, but somebody's going to have to come along after we charge and kill the wounded."

Kring's face clearly registered his distaste. "We'll do it, friend Sparhawk," he agreed finally, "but only out of friendship."

"I appreciate that, Kring. As soon as Ulath enrages them enough to get them moving, those of us at the barricade will come back and get on our horses to join the charge. Oh, one thing—just because a Troll has a broken-off lance sticking out of him doesn't mean that he's out of action. Let's stick a few more in each one of them—just to be on the safe side. I'll go advise the ladies that we're about to start, and then we'll get on with it."

"I'll go with you," Vanion said, and the two of them walked back up the canyon toward the cave mouth.

Berit and a small group of young knights stood guard at the entrance to the cave. "Are they coming?" the handsome young man asked nervously.

"We've seen a few scouts," Sparhawk replied. "We're going to try to goad them into an attack. If we have to fight them, I'd rather do it in the daylight."

"And before that storm hits," Vanion added.

"I don't think they'll get past us," Sparhawk told the youthful knight, "but stay alert. If things start to look tight, pull back inside the cave."

Berit nodded.

Then Ehlana, Talen, and Sephrenia emerged from the cave.

"Are they coming?" Ehlana asked, her voice slightly shrill.

"Not yet," Sparhawk replied. "It's just a question of time, though. We're going to try to goad them a bit. Ulath thinks he might be able to enrage some of them enough so that they'll attack before the rest are ready. We'd rather not have to face them all at once if we can avoid it." He looked at Sephrenia. "Are you up to a spell or two, Sephrenia?"

"That depends on the spell."

"Can you block the cave mouth so that the Trolls can't get at you and the others?"

"Probably, and if not, I can always collapse it."

"I wouldn't do that except as a last resort. Wait for Berit and his men to get inside with you, though."

Talen's fine clothes were a bit mud smeared. "Any luck?" Sparhawk asked him.

"I found a place where a bear spent last winter." The boy shrugged. "It involved a bit of wriggling. There are a couple other passageways I want to look at."

"Pick the best one you can. If Sephrenia has to bring down the cave mouth, I'd like to have you all back where it's safe."

Talen nodded.

"Be careful, Sparhawk," Ehlana said to him, embracing him fiercely.

"Always, love."

Sephrenia had also embraced Vanion, her admonition echoing Ehlana's. "Now go, both of you," she added.

"Yes, little mother," Sparhawk and Vanion said in unison.

The two knights started back down the canyon. "You don't approve, do you, Sparhawk?" Vanion asked gravely.

"It's none of my business, my friend."

"I didn't ask if it was any of your business, I asked if you approved. There wasn't any other way, you know. The laws of both our cultures prohibit our marrying."

"I don't think the laws apply to you two, Vanion. You both have a special friend who ignores the laws when she chooses to." He smiled at his old friend. "Actually, I'm rather pleased about it. I got very tired of seeing the pair of you moping about the way you were."

"Thanks, Sparhawk. I wanted to get that out into the open. I'll never be able to go back to Eosia, though."

"I'd say that's no great loss under the circumstances. You and Sephrenia are happy, and that's all that matters."

"I'll agree there. When you get back to Chyrellos, try to put the best face on it you can, though. I'm afraid Dolmant will burst into flames when he hears about it."

"He might surprise you, Vanion."

Sparhawk was a bit startled to discover that he still remembered a few words in Troll. Ulath stood in the center of their narrow gap, bellowing at the forest in that snarling tongue.

"What's he saying?" Kalten asked curiously.

"It wouldn't translate very well," Sparhawk replied. "Trollish insults lean heavily in the direction of body functions."

"Oh. Sorry I asked."

"You'd be a lot sorrier if I could translate," Sparhawk said, wincing at a particularly vile imprecation Ulath had just hurled at the Trolls.

The Trolls, it appeared, took insults very seriously. Unlike humans, they seemed not to be able to shrug such things off as no more than a customary prelude to battle. They howled at each new sally from the big Genidian Knight. A number of them appeared at the edge of the wood, foaming at the mouth and stamping in rage.

"How much longer before they charge?" Tynian asked his tall blond friend.

"You can't always tell with Trolls," Ulath replied. "I don't think they're accustomed to fighting in groups. I can't say for sure, but I think one of them will lose his temper before the others, and he'll come rushing at us. I'm not positive if the others will follow." He roared something else at the huge creatures at the forest's edge.

One of the Trolls shrieked with fury and broke into a shambling, three-legged run, brandishing a huge club in his free hand. First one Troll, then several others, began to run after him.

Sparhawk glanced around, checking the positions of his archers. Khalad, he noted, had given his crossbow to another young Pandion and stood coolly sighting along the shaft of the javelin resting across the center of his improvised engine.

The Troll in the lead was swinging wildly at the sharpened stakes with his club, but the springy saplings bent beneath his blows and then snapped back into place. The enraged Troll lifted his muzzle and howled in frustration.

Khalad cut the rope holding his oversized bow drawn back. The limbs of the bow snapped forward with an almost musical twang, and the javelin shot forward in a long, smooth arc to sink into the Troll's vast, furry chest with a meaty-sounding *Chunk!*

The Troll jerked back and stood staring stupidly at the shaft protruding from his chest. He touched it with one tentative finger as if he could not even begin to understand how it had gotten there. Then he sat down heavily with blood pouring from his mouth. He grasped the shaft feebly with both hands and wrenched at it. A fresh gush of blood burst from his mouth, and he sighed and toppled over on one side.

"Good shot," Kalten called his congratulations to Sparhawk's squire, who, with the help of two other young Pandions, was already recocking the engine.

"Pass the word to the other archers," Khalad called back. "The Trolls stop when they come to those stakes. They don't seem to be able to understand them, and they make perfect targets when they're standing still like that."

"Right." Kalten went to the archers on one side of the canyon and Bevier to the other to pass the word along.

The half-dozen or so Trolls who had followed the first one paid no attention to his fall and lunged on forward toward the field of sharpened stakes.

"We might have a problem, Sparhawk," Tynian said. "They're not used to fighting in groups, so they don't pay any attention to casualties. Ulath says that they don't die of natural causes, so they don't really understand what death's all about. I don't think they'll back away just because we kill all their comrades. It's not like fighting humans, I'm afraid. They'll make one charge, and they'll keep coming until they're all dead. We may have to adjust our tactics to take that into account."

More Trolls came out of the trees, and Ulath continued to shout obscenities at them.

Kalten and Bevier returned. "I just had a thought," Kalten said. "Ulath, will the females attack, too?"

"Probably."

"How do you tell the females from the males?"

"Are you having urges?"

"That's disgusting. I just don't want to kill women, that's all."

"Women? These are Trolls, Kalten, not people. You can't tell a female from a male unless she's got cubs with her—or unless you get very, very close to her—and that's not a good idea. A sow will tear off your head just as quickly as a boar will." The Genidian went back to shouting insults.

More Trolls joined the charge, and then, with a vast roar, the entire edge of the woods erupted with the monsters. They did not pause, but joined the loping charge.

"That's it," Ulath said with a certain satisfaction. "The whole pack's committed now. Let's go get our horses."

They ran back to join the others as the several Cyrinics manning Bevier's improvised catapults and the Pandions working Khalad's engine began to launch missiles at the oncoming Trolls. The archers at the canyon walls rained arrows into the shaggy ranks. Some Trolls fell, riddled with arrows, but others continued the charge, ignoring the shafts sticking out of them.

"I don't think we can count on their breaking and running just because their friends have been killed," Sparhawk told Vanion and the others as he hauled himself onto Faran's back.

"Friends?" Stragen said mildly. "Trolls don't have friends, Sparhawk. They aren't even particularly fond of their mates."

"What I'm getting at is the fact that this is all going to be settled in one fight," Sparhawk said to them. "There probably won't be a second charge. They'll just keep coming until they break through or until they're all dead."

"It's better that way, friend Sparhawk," Kring said with a wolfish grin. "Protracted fights are boring, wouldn't you say?"

"I wouldn't say that, would you, Ulath?" Tynian asked mildly.

The knights moved into formation, their lances at the ready as the Trolls continued their bellowing advance.

The first half-dozen or so Trolls that had been in the forefront of the charge were all down now, either dead or dying of arrow wounds, and the front ranks of the bellowing horde were faltering as sheets of arrows struck them. The Trolls at the rear, however, simply ran over the top of their mortally wounded companions. Mouths agape and fangs dripping, they charged on and on.

The sharpened stakes served their purpose well. The Trolls, after a few futile efforts to break through the bristling forest, were forced into the narrow corridor where they were jammed together and milled impatiently behind the brutes who were leading the charge as Tynian's sharpened pegs protruding from the ground slowed the rushing advance of the leaders. Not even the most enraged creature in the world charges very well on sore paws.

Sparhawk looked around. The knights were drawn up into a column, four abreast, and their lances were all slightly advanced. The Trolls continued their limping charge up the gap until the first rank, also four abreast, reached the end of the stake-lined corridor where it opened out into the basin. "I guess it's time," he said. Then he raised up in his stirrups and roared, "Charge!"

The tactic Sparhawk had devised for the Church Knights was simple. They would charge four abreast into the face of the Trolls as soon as the creatures came out into the basin. They would drive their lances into the first rank of Trolls and then veer off, two by two, to the sides of the gap so that the next rank of four could make *their* charge. Once they had moved out of the way, they would return to the end of the column, take up fresh lances, and proceed in an orderly fashion to the front rank again. It was, in effect, an endless charge. Sparhawk was rather proud of the concept. It probably wouldn't work against humans, but it had great potential in an engagement with Trolls.

Shaggy carcasses began to pile up at the head of the gap. A Troll, it appeared, was not guileful enough to play dead. He would continue to attack until he died or was so severely injured that he could not continue. After several ranks of the knights had struck the Troll-front, some of the brutes had as many as four broken-off lances protruding from them. Still the monsters came, clambering over the bleeding bodies of their fellows.

Sparhawk, Vanion, Kalten, and Tynian made their second charge. They speared fresh Trolls in the raging front, snapped off their lances with well-practiced twists of their arms, and veered off to the sides.

"Your plan seems to be going well," Kalten congratulated his friend. "The horses have time to rest between charges."

"That was part of the idea," Sparhawk replied a bit smugly as he took a fresh lance from the rack at the rear of the column.

The storm was nearly on them now. The howling wind shrieked among the trees, and lightning staggered down in brilliant flashes from the purple clouds.

Then, from back in the forest there came a tremendous bellow.

"What in God's name was that?" Kalten cried. "Nothing can make *that* much noise!"

Whatever it was, it was huge, and it was coming toward them, crushing the forest as it came. The raging wind carried a foul, reptilian reek as it tore at the visored faces of the armored knights.

"It stinks like a charnel house!" Tynian shouted over the noise of the storm and the battle.

"Can you tell what it is, Vanion?" Sparhawk demanded.

"No," the preceptor replied. "Whatever it is, it's big, though—bigger than anything I've ever encountered."

Then the rain struck in driving sheets, obscuring the knights' vision and half concealing the advancing Trolls. "Keep at them!" Sparhawk commanded in a great voice. "Don't let up!"

The methodical charges continued as the Trolls doggedly pushed through the mud into the killing zone. The strategy was going well, but it had not been without casualties. Several horses were down, felled by club strokes from wounded and enraged Trolls, and a few armored knights lay motionless on the rain-swept ground.

Then the wind suddenly dropped, and the rain slackened as the calm at the center of the storm passed over them.

"What's that?" Tynian shouted, pointing beyond the howling Trolls.

It was a single, incandescent spark, brighter than the sun, and it hung just over the edge of the forest. It began to grow ominously, swelling, surging, surrounded by a blazing halo of purplish light.

"There's something inside it!" Kalten yelled.

Sparhawk strained to see, squinting in the brilliant purple light that illuminated the battleground. "It's alive," he said tersely. "It's moving."

The ball of purple light swelled faster and faster, and blazing orange flames shot out from the edges of it.

There was someone standing in the center of that fiery ball—someone robed and hooded and burning green. The figure raised one hand, opened it wide, and a searing bolt of lightning shot from that open palm. A charging Cyrinic Knight and his horse were blasted into charred fragments by the bolt.

And then, from behind that searing light, an enormous shape reared up out of the forest. It was impossible that anything alive could be so huge. The head left no doubt that the creature was reptilian. The huge head was earlessly sleek, scaly, and had a protruding, lipless muzzle filled with row after row of back-curving teeth. It had a short neck, narrow shoulders, and tiny forepaws. The rest of the body was mercifully concealed by the trees.

"We can't fight *that* thing!" Kalten cried.

The hooded figure within the ball of purple and orange fire raised its arm again. It seemed to clench itself, and then again the lightning shot from its open palm—and stopped, exploding in midair in a dazzling shower of sparks.

"Did you do that?" Vanion shouted at Sparhawk.

"Not me, Vanion. I'm not *that* fast."

Then they heard the deep, resonant voice chanting in Styric. Sparhawk wheeled Faran to look.

It was Zalasta. The silvery-haired Styric stood partway up the steep slope on the north side of the canyon, his white robe gleaming in the storm's half-light. He had both arms extended over his head, and his staff, which Sparhawk had thought to be no more than an affectation, blazed with energy. He swung the staff downward, pointing it at the hooded figure standing in its fiery nimbus. A brilliant spark shot from the tip of the staff and sizzled as it passed over the heads of the Peloi and the armored knights to explode against the ball of fire.

The figure in the fire flinched, and once more lightning shot from its open palm, directed at Zalasta this time. The Styric brushed it disdainfully aside with his staff and immediately responded with another of those brilliant sparks of light, which shattered like the last on the surface of the ball of fire.

Again the hooded one inside its protecting fire flinched, more violently this time. The gigantic creature behind it screamed and drew back into the darkness. The Church Knights, dumbfounded by the dreadful confrontation, had frozen in their tracks.

"We have our own work to attend to, gentlemen!" Vanion roared his reminder. "Charge!"

Sparhawk shook his head to clear his mind. "Thanks, Vanion," he said to his friend. "I got distracted there for a moment."

"Pay attention, Sparhawk," Vanion said crisply in precisely the same tone he had always used on the practice field years before when Sparhawk and Kalten had been novices.

"Yes, my Lord Preceptor," Sparhawk replied automatically in the selfsame embarrassed tone he had used as a stripling. The two looked at each other, and then they both laughed.

"Just like old times," Kalten said gaily. "Well then, why don't we go Troll hunting and leave the incidentals to Zalasta?"

The knights continued their endless charge and the two magicians continued their fiery duel overhead. The Trolls were no less savage now, but their numbers were diminished and the huge pile of their dead impeded their attack.

The bloody work on the ground went on and on while the air above the battleground sizzled and crackled with awful fire.

"Is it my imagination, or is our purple friend up there getting a little pale and wan?" Tynian suggested as they took up fresh lances once more.

"His fire's beginning to fade just a bit," Kalten agreed. "And he's taking longer and longer to work himself up to another thunderbolt."

"Don't grow overconfident, gentlemen," Vanion admonished them. "We still have Trolls to deal with, and I assume that oversized lizard's still out there in the forest."

"I was trying very hard not to think about that," Kalten replied.

Then, very suddenly, as suddenly as it had expanded, the ball of purple-orange fire began to contract. Zalasta stepped up his attack, the fiery sparks shooting from his staff in rapid succession to burst against the outer surface of that rapidly constricting nimbus like fiery hail.

Then the blazing orb vanished.

A cheer went up from the Peloi, and the Trolls faltered.

Khalad, his face strangely numb, set another javelin on his improvised engine and cut the rope to unleash his missile. The javelin sprang from the huge bow, and as it sped forward it seemed to ignite, and it blazed with light as it arced out higher and farther than any of the young man's previous shots had done.

The great lizard roared, rearing up out of the forest, its awful mouth gaping. And then the burning javelin took it full in the chest. It sank deep, and the hideous creature shrieked a great cry of agony and rage, its forepaws clutching futilely at the burning shaft. And then there was a heavy, muffled thud within the monster's body, a confined explosion that shook the very ground. The vast lizard burst open in a spray of bloody fire, and its ripped remains sank twitching back into the forest.

A nebulous kind of wavering appeared at the edge of the trees, a wavering very much like the shimmer of heat on a hot summer day, and then they all saw something emerging from that shimmer. It was a face only, brutish, ugly, and filled with rage and frustration. The shaggy face sloped sharply back from its fang-filled muzzle, and the piglike eyes burned in their sockets.

It howled—a vast howl that tore at the very air. It howled again, and Sparhawk recoiled. The wavering apparition was bellowing in Troll! Again it howled, its thunderous voice bending the trees around it like a vast wind.

"What in God's name is that?" Bevier cried.

"Ghworg," Ulath replied tensely, "the Troll-God of Kill."

The immortal beast howled yet again, and then it vanished.

CHAPTER TWENTY-THREE

All semblance of cooperation among the Trolls vanished with the disappearance of Ghworg. They were not, as Ulath had so frequently pointed out, creatures that normally ran in packs, and without the presence of the God to coerce them into semi-unity, they reverted to their customary antagonism toward each other. Their charge faltered as a number of very nasty fights broke out in their ranks. These fights quickly spread, and within moments there was a general brawl in progress out beyond the mouth of the canyon.

"Well?" Kalten asked Ulath.

"It's over." The Genidian Knight shrugged. "At least our part of it is. The riot among the Trolls themselves might go on for quite a while, though."

Kring, it appeared, had reached the same conclusion, and his Peloi moved purposefully on the heaps of Trollish casualties, their sabers and lances at the ready.

Khalad was still standing behind his roughly constructed engine, his face blank and his eyes unseeing. Then he seemed to awaken. "What happened?" he asked, looking around with some confusion.

"You killed that big reptile, my young friend," Tynian told him. "It was a spectacular shot."

"I *did*? I don't remember even shooting at it. I thought it was out of range."

Zalasta had come down from the sloping side of the canyon with a look of satisfaction on his beetle-browed face. "I'm afraid I had to override your thoughts for a few moments there, young sir," he explained to Sparhawk's squire. "I needed your engine to deal with the thunder beast. I hope you'll forgive me, but there wasn't time to consult with you about it."

"That's quite all right, learned one. I just wish I'd been able to see the shot. What kind of beast was it?"

"Its species roamed the earth millions of years ago," the Styric replied, "before mankind or even the Trolls emerged. Our opponent appears to be very gifted in resurrecting the ancient dead."

"Was that him inside that ball of fire?" Kalten asked.

"I can't be positive about that, Sir Kalten. It seems that we have many layers of enemies out there. If the one in the orb wasn't our main enemy, though, he was probably very high up in the opposing councils. He was most skilled."

"Let's see to the wounded," Vanion said crisply. Despite his protestations that Sparhawk was now in charge of the Pandions, the habit of command still ran deep in Vanion's blood.

"We might want to barricade that gap as well," Ulath suggested, "just to keep the surviving Trolls from paying us any unannounced visits during the night."

"I'll go advise the ladies that the worst of this is over," Sparhawk told them. He turned Faran and rode back to the cave. He was a bit surprised and more than a bit exasperated to find Ehlana and the rest of the party from the cavern standing out in the open. "I told you to stay in the cave," he reprimanded his wife sharply.

"You didn't really expect me to do it, did you?"

"Yes, as a matter of fact, I did."

"Life's just filled with these little disappointments, isn't it?" Her tone was challenging.

"That will do, children," Sephrenia said wearily. "Domestic squabbles shouldn't be aired in public. Do your fighting in private."

"We weren't fighting, were we, Sparhawk?" Ehlana said.

"We were just about to start."

"I'm sorry, dear," she apologized contritely. "I couldn't bear to stay inside while you were in such terrible danger." Then she made a wry face. "Right now I'm going to have to choke down my royal pride and eat a large dish of crow. I've wronged Zalasta dreadfully. He saved the day for us, didn't he?"

"He certainly didn't hurt us," Talen agreed.

"He was stupendous!" the queen exclaimed.

"He's very, very skilled," Sephrenia said proudly. Perhaps unconsciously, she was holding Danae in her arms. Their centuries of sisterhood had made the small Styric woman's responses instinctive.

"What was that awful face at the edge of the woods?" Sir Berit asked with a shudder.

"Ulath says it was Ghworg, the Troll-God of Kill," Sparhawk replied. "I sort of remember him from the Temple of Azash back in Zemoch. I didn't really look at him that closely then, though. I was a little preoccupied at the time." He made a face. "Well, little mother," he said to Sephrenia, "it looks as if we might have been right. I'd say that Ghwerig's spell wasn't quite as ironclad as we originally thought. The Troll-Gods are loose—at least Ghworg is. But what baffles me is why they didn't escape earlier. If they could get out at any time, why didn't they break free when I threatened to smash the Bhelliom in the temple?"

"Maybe they needed help." She shrugged. "It's altogether possible that our enemy was able to enlist their aid by offering to help them escape their imprisonment. We'll ask Zalasta. He might know."

More of the knights had been injured during the fight with the Trolls than Sparhawk had originally thought, and some fifteen of their number had been killed. As evening settled into the canyon, Engessa came to Sparhawk, his eyes hard. "I'll leave now, Sparhawk-Knight," he said abruptly.

Sparhawk looked at him, startled.

"I must go have words with the clan of this region. Their failure to be at the boundary was inexcusable."

"There was probably a reason for it, Atan Engessa."

"No reason that *I'll* accept. I'll be back in the morning with enough warriors to protect Ehlana-Queen."

"There are Trolls out there in the forest, you know."

"They will not greatly inconvenience me, Sparhawk-Knight."

"Just be careful, Atan Engessa. I'm getting very tired of burying friends."

Engessa suddenly grinned at him. "That's one of the good things about fighting Trolls, Sparhawk-Knight. You don't have to bury dead friends. The Trolls eat them."

Sparhawk shuddered.

Zalasta was clearly the hero of the day. All of the Peloi and most of the Church Knights were obviously in awe of him. The vision of his explosive duel with the hooded figure in the blazing purple orb and the spectacular demise of the vast reptile was vividly etched on the minds of the entire party. He bore himself modestly, however, shrugging off his stunning accomplishments as if they were of no moment. He did, however, seem very pleased that Ehlana's animosity had dissolved and that she was now wholeheartedly cordial toward him. His somewhat stiff manner softened—Ehlana had that effect on people—and he became somehow less reserved and more human.

Engessa arrived the next morning with a thousand Atan clansmen. The faces of their officers clearly showed that Engessa had spoken firmly with them about their failure to be at the clan border at the appointed time. The wounded knights were placed on litters borne by Atan warriors, and the much enlarged party moved slowly back to the road and continued eastward toward Lebas in Tamul proper. Hindered as they were by the wounded, they did not make good time—or so it seemed. After what had apparently been two full days of travel, Sparhawk spoke very briefly with his daughter, advising her that he needed to talk with her at some point while the minds of the others were asleep. When the blank faces of his companions indicated that Aphrael was compressing time again, he rode back to the carriage.

"Please get right to the point, Sparhawk," the little Goddess told him. "It's very difficult this time."

"Is it different somehow?"

"Of course it is. I'm extending the pain of the wounded, and that's very distasteful. I'm making them sleep as much as possible, but there are limits, you know."

"All right then, how much of what happened back there was real?"

"How could I possibly know that?"

"You mean you can't tell?"

"Well, of *course* I can't, Sparhawk. When we create an illusion, *nobody* can tell. It wouldn't be much of an illusion if someone could detect it, would it?"

"You said 'we.' If it *was* an illusion, there was a God behind it then?"

"Yes—either directly or indirectly. If it was indirectly, though, someone has a great deal of influence with whatever God was involved. We don't surrender that much power very often—or very willingly. Don't beat around the bush, Sparhawk. What's bothering you?"

"I don't really know, Aphrael," he confessed. "Something about it didn't seem quite right."

"Specifics, Sparhawk. I need something specific to work with."

"It just seemed to me that it was overdone, that's all. I got a distinct feeling that someone was just showing off. It was adolescent."

She considered that, her bowlike little mouth pouting. "Maybe we *are* adolescent, Sparhawk. It's one of the dangers of our situation. There's nothing powerful enough to make us grow up, so we're at liberty to indulge ourselves. I've even noticed that in my own character."

"You?"

"Be nice, Father." She said it almost absently, her small black brows knit in concentration. "It's certainly consistent," she added. "Back in Astel, that Sabre fellow showed a rather profound lack of maturity, and he was being rather tightly controlled. You may have just hit upon one of our weaknesses, Sparhawk. I'd rather you didn't apply the notion to me directly, but keep the idea that we're all just a bit immature sort of in the front of your mind. I won't be able to see it myself, I'm afraid. If it *is* one of our failings, I'm just as infected with it as the others. We all love to impress each other, and it's polite to be impressed when someone else is showing off." She made a little face. "It's automatic, I'm afraid. Keep a firm hold on your skepticism, Sparhawk. Your cold-eyed lack of gullibility might be useful. Now please go back to sleep. I'm very busy right now."

They crossed the summit of the mountains of Atan and moved on down the eastern slopes toward the border. The demarcation between Atan and Tamul was abrupt and clearly evident. Atan was a wilderness of trees and rugged peaks; Tamul was a carefully tended park. The fields were excruciatingly neat, and even the hills seemed to have been artfully sculpted to provide pleasing prospects and vistas. The peasantry seemed industrious, and they did not have that expression of hopeless misery so common on the faces of the peasants and serfs of Elene kingdoms.

"Organization, my dear Emban," Oscagne was telling the fat little churchman. "The key to our success lies in organization. All power in Tamul descends from the emperor, and all decisions are made in Matherion. We even tell our peasants when to plant and when to harvest. I'll admit that central planning has its drawbacks, but the Tamul nature seems to require it."

"Elenes, unfortunately, are much less disciplined," Emban replied. "The Church would be happier with a more docile congregation, but we have to make do with what God gave us to work with." He smiled. "Oh, well, it keeps life interesting."

They reached Lebas late one afternoon. It was a small, neat city with a distinctly alien-looking architecture that leaned strongly in the direction of artistic embellishment. The houses were low and broad, with graceful roofs that curved upward at the ends of their ridge lines as if the architects somehow felt that abrupt straight lines were somehow incomplete. The cobbled streets were broad and straight, and they were filled with citizens dressed in brightly colored silks.

The entrance of the westerners created quite a stir, since the Tamuls had never seen Elene knights before. It was the Queen of Elenia, however, who astonished them the most. The Tamuls were a golden-skinned, dark-haired people, and the pale, blond queen filled them with awe as her carriage moved almost ceremonially through the streets.

Their first concern, of course, was the wounded. Oscagne assured them that Tamul physicians were among the finest in the world. It appeared, moreover, that the ambassador held a fairly exalted rank in the empire. A house was immediately provided for the injured knights, and a medical staff seemed to materialize at his command. Additional houses were provided for the rest of their company, and those houses were fully staffed with servants who could not understand a single word of the Elenic language.

"You seem to throw a great deal of weight around, Oscagne," Emban said that evening after they had eaten an exotic meal consisting of course after course of unidentifiable delicacies and sometimes startling flavors.

"I'm not the overweight one, my friend." Oscagne smiled. "My commission is signed by the emperor, and his hand has the full weight of the entire Daresian continent behind it. He's ordered that all of Tamuli do everything possible—and even impossible—to make the visit of Queen Ehlana pleasant and convenient. No one ever disobeys his orders."

"They must not have reached the Trolls then," Ulath said blandly. "Of course Trolls have a different view of the world than we do. Maybe they thought Queen Ehlana would be entertained by their welcome."

"Does he have to do that?" Oscagne complained to Sparhawk.

"Ulath? Yes, I think he does, your Excellency. It's something in the Thalesian nature—terribly obscure, I'm afraid, and quite possibly perverted."

"*Sparhawk!*" Ulath protested.

"Nothing personal there, old boy." Sparhawk grinned. "Just a reminder that I haven't yet quite forgiven you for all the times you've euchred me into doing the cooking when it wasn't really my turn."

"Hold still," Mirtai commanded.

"You got some of it in my eye," Talen accused her.

"It won't hurt you. Now hold still." She continued to daub the mixture onto his face.

"What is that, Mirtai?" Baroness Melidere asked curiously.

"Saffron. We use it in our cooking. It's a kind of a spice."

"What are we doing here?" Ehlana asked curiously as she and Sparhawk entered the room to find the Atana spreading the condiment over Talen's face.

"We're modifying your page, my Queen," Stragen explained. "He has to go out into the streets, and we want him to be unobtrusive. Mirtai's changing the color of his skin."

"You could do that with magic, couldn't you, Sparhawk?" Ehlana asked.

"Probably," he said, "and if I couldn't, Sephrenia certainly could."

"*Now* you tell me," Talen said in a slightly bitter tone. "Mirtai's been seasoning me for the past half hour."

"You smell good, though," Melidere told him.

"I didn't set out to be somebody's supper. Ouch."

"Sorry," Alean murmured, carefully disengaging her comb from a snarl in his hair. "I have to work the dye in, though, or it won't look right." Alean was applying black dye to the young man's hair.

"How long will it take me to wash this yellow stuff off?" Talen asked.

"I'm not sure." Mirtai shrugged. "It might be permanent, but it should wear off in a month or so."

"I'll get you for this, Stragen," Talen threatened.

"Hold still," Mirtai said again, and continued her daubing.

"We have to make contact with the local thieves," Stragen explained. "The thieves at Sarsos promised that we'd get a definite answer here in Lebas."

"I see a large hole in the plan, Stragen," Sparhawk replied. "Talen doesn't speak Tamul."

"That's no real problem." Stragen shrugged. "The chief of the local thieves is a Cammorian."

"How did *that* happen?"

"We're very cosmopolitan, Sparhawk. All thieves are brothers, after all, and we recognize the aristocracy of talent. Anyway, as soon as he can pass for a Tamul, Talen's going to the local thieves' den to talk with Caalador—that's the Cammorian's name. He'll bring him here, and we'll be able to talk with him privately."

"Why aren't you the one who's going?"

"And get saffron all over my face? Don't be silly, Sparhawk."

Caalador the Cammorian was a stocky, red-faced man with curly black hair and an open, friendly countenance. He looked more like a jovial innkeeper than a leader of thieves and cutthroats. His manner was bluff and good-humored, and he spoke in the typical Cammorian drawl and with the slovenly grammar that bespoke backcountry origins. "So yer the one ez has got all the thieves of Daresia so sore perplexed," he said to Stragen when Talen presented him.

"I'll have to plead guilty on that score, Caalador." Stragen smiled.

"Don't never do that, brother. Alluz try'n lie yer way outten thangs."

"I'll try to remember that. What are you doing so far from home, my friend?"

"I mought ax you the same question, Stragen. It's a fur piece from here t' Thalesia."

"And quite nearly as far from Cammoria."

"Aw, that's easy explained, m' friend. I storted out in life ez a poacher, ketchin' rabbits an' sich in the bushes on land that weren't rightly mine, but that's a sore hard kinda work with lotsa risk and mighty slim profit, so I tooken t' liftin' chickens outten hen roosts—chickens not runnin' near ez fast ez rabbits, especial at night. Then I moved up t' sheep stealing—only one night I had me a set-to with a hull passel o' sheepdawgs which it wuz ez betrayed me real cruel by not stayin' bribed."

"How do you bribe a dog?" Ehlana asked curiously.

"Easiest thing in the world, little lady. Y' thrun 'em some meat scraps t' keep ther attention. Well, sir, them there dawgs tore into me somethin' fierce, an' I lit out—leavin', misfortunate like, a hat which it wuz I wuz partial to an' which it wuz ez could be rekonnized ez mine by half the parish. Now, I'm jist a country boy at hort 'thout no real citified ways t' get me by in town, an' so I tooken t' sea, an' t' make it short, I fetched up on this yere furrin coast an' beat my way inland, the capting of the ship I wuz a-sailin' on wantin' t' talk t' me 'bout some stuff ez had turnt up missin' fum the cargo hold, y' know." He paused. "Have I sufficiently entertained you as yet, Milord Stragen?" He grinned.

"Very, very good, Caalador," Stragen murmured. "Convincing—although it was a trifle overdone."

"A failing, Milord. It's so much fun that I get carried away. Actually, I'm a swindler. I've found that posing as an ignorant yokel disarms people. No one in this world is as easy to gull as the man who thinks he's smarter than you are."

"Ohh." Ehlana's tone was profoundly disappointed.

"Wuz yer Majesty tooken with the iggernent way I wuz a-talkin'?" Caalador asked sympathetically. "I'll do 'er agin, iff'n yer of a mind—of course it takes a beastly long time to get to the point that way."

She laughed delightedly. "I think you could charm the birds out of the bushes, Caalador," she told him.

"Thank you, your Majesty," he said, bowing with fluid grace. Then he turned back to Stragen. "Your proposal has baffled our Tamul friends, Milord," he said. "The demarcation line between corruption and outright theft is very clearly defined in the Tamul culture. Tamul thieves are quite class-conscious, and the notion of actually cooperating with the authorities strikes them as unnatural for some reason. Fortunately, we Elenes are far more corrupt than our simple yellow brothers, and Elenes seem to rise to the top in our peculiar society—natural talent, most likely. We saw the advantages of your proposal immediately. Kondrak of Darsas was most eloquent in his presentation. You seem to have impressed him enormously. The disturbances here in Tamuli have been disastrous for business, and when we began reciting profit and loss figures to the Tamuls, they started to listen to reason. They agreed to cooperate—grudgingly, I'll grant you, but they *will* help you to gather information."

"Thank God!" Stragen said with a vast sigh of relief. "The delay was beginning to make me nervous."

"Y'd made promises t' yer queen, an' y' wuzn't shore iffn y' could deliver, is that it?"

"That's very, very close, my friend."

"I'll give you the names of some people in Matherion." Caalador looked around. "Private like, iffn y' take my meanin'." He added. "It's all vury well t' talk 'bout lendin' a helpin' hand an' sich, but 'taint hordly nachral t' be namin' no names right out in fronta no queens an' knights an' sich." He grinned impudently at Ehlana. "An' now, yer queenship, how'd y' like it iffn I wuz t' spin y' a long, long tale 'bout my advenchoors in the shadowy world o' crime?"

"I'd be delighted, Caalador," she replied eagerly.

Another of the injured knights died that night, but the two dozen sorely wounded seemed on the mend. As Oscagne had told them, Tamul physicians were extraordinarily skilled, although some of their methods were strange to Elenes. After a brief conference, Sparhawk and his friends decided to press on to Matherion. Their trek across the continent had yielded a great deal of information, and they all felt that it was time to combine that information with the findings of the imperial government.

And so they set out from Lebas early one morning and rode south under a kindly summer sky. The countryside was neat, with crops growing in straight lines across weedless fields marked off with low stone walls. Even the trees in the wood lands grew in straight lines, and all traces of unfettered nature seemed to have been erased. The peasants in the fields wore loose-fitting trousers and shirts of white linen and tightly woven straw hats that looked not unlike mushroom tops. Many of the crops grown in this alien countryside were unrecognizable to the Elenes— odd-looking beans and peculiar grains. They passed Lake Sama and saw fishermen casting nets from strange-looking boats with high prows and sterns, boats of which Khalad profoundly disapproved. "One good gust of wind from the side would capsize them" was his verdict.

They reached Tosa, some sixty leagues to the north of the capital, with that sense of impatience that comes near the end of every long journey.

The weather held fair, and they set out early and rode late each day, counting off every league put behind them. The road followed the coast of the Tamul Sea, a low, rolling coastline where rounded hills rose from broad beaches of white sand and long waves rolled in to break and foam and slither back out into deep blue water.

Eight days—more or less—after they left Tosa, they set up for the night in a parklike grove with an almost holiday air, since Oscagne assured them that they were no more than five leagues from Matherion.

"We could ride on," Kalten suggested. "We'd be there by morning."

"Not on your life, Sir Kalten," Ehlana said adamantly. "Start heating water, gentlemen, and put up a tent we can use for bathing. The ladies and I are *not* going to ride into Matherion with half the dirt of Daresia caked on us—and string some lines so that we can hang our gowns out to air and to let the breeze shake the wrinkles out of them." She looked around critically. "And then, gentlemen, I want you to see to yourselves and your equipment. I'll inspect you before we set out tomorrow morning, and I'd better not find one single speck of rust."

Kalten sighed mournfully. "Yes, my Queen," he replied in a resigned tone of voice.

They set out the following morning in a formal column with the carriage near the front. Their pace was slow to avoid raising dust, and Ehlana, gowned in blue and crowned with gold and diamonds, sat regally in the carriage, looking for all the world as if she owned everything in sight. There had been one small but intense disagreement before they set out, however. Her Highness, the Royal Princess Danae, had objected violently when told that she *would* wear a proper dress and a delicate little tiara. Ehlana did not cajole her daughter about the matter, but instead she did something she had never done before. "Princess Danae," she said quite formally, "I am the queen. You *will* obey me."

Danae blinked in astonishment. Sparhawk was fairly certain that no one had *ever* spoken to her that way before. "Yes, your Majesty," she replied finally in a suitably submissive tone.

Word of their approach had preceded them, of course. Engessa had seen to that, and as they rode up a long hill about midafternoon, they saw a mounted detachment of ceremonial troops wearing armor of black lacquered steel inlaid with gold awaiting them at the summit. The honor guard was drawn up in ranks on each side of the road. There were as yet no greetings, and when the column crested the hill, Sparhawk immediately saw why.

"Dear God!" Bevier breathed in awed reverence.

A crescent-shaped city embraced a deep blue harbor below. The sun had passed its zenith, and it shone down on the crown of Tamuli. The architecture was graceful, and every building had a domelike, rounded roof. It was not so large as Chyrellos, but it was not the size that had wrung that reverential gasp from Sir Bevier. The city was dazzling, but its splendor was not the splendor of marble. An opalescent sheen covered the capital; a shifting rainbow-hued fire that blazed beneath the surface of its very stones, a fire that at times blinded the eye with its stunning magnificence.

"Behold!" Oscagne intoned quite formally. "Behold the seat of beauty and truth! Behold the home of wisdom and power! Behold fire-domed Matherion, the center of the world!"

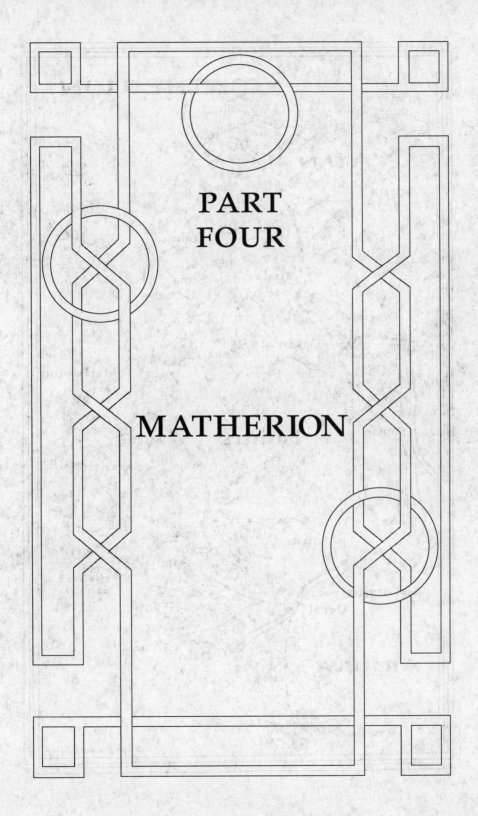

PART
FOUR

MATHERION

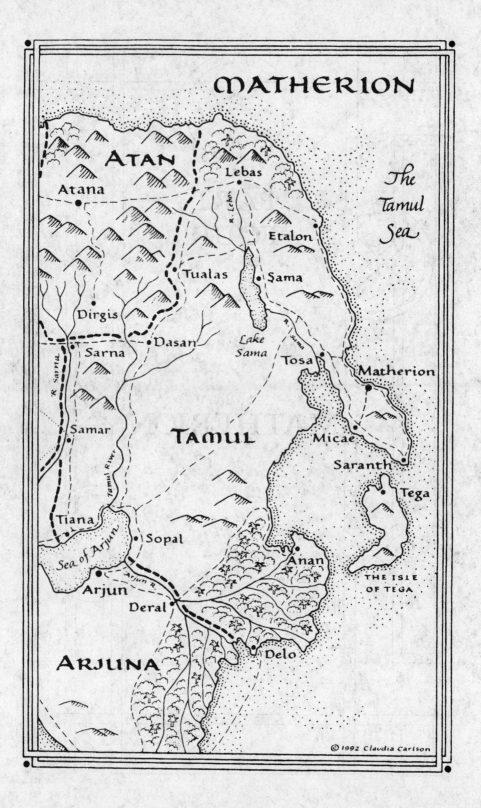

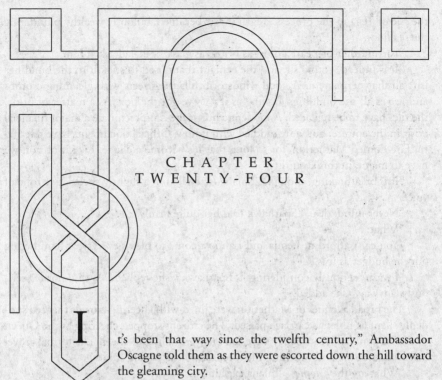

CHAPTER
TWENTY-FOUR

I t's been that way since the twelfth century," Ambassador Oscagne told them as they were escorted down the hill toward the gleaming city.

"Was it magic?" Talen asked him. The young thief's eyes were filled with wonder.

"You might call it that," Oscagne said wryly, "but it was the kind of magic one performs with unlimited money and power rather than with incantations. The eleventh and twelfth centuries were a foolish period in our history. It was the time of the Micaen Dynasty, and they were probably the silliest family to ever occupy the throne. The first Micaen emperor was given an ornamental box of mother-of-pearl—or nacre, as some call it—by an emissary from the Isle of Tega when he was about fourteen years old. History tells us that he would sit staring at it by the hour, paralyzed by the shifting colors. He was so enamored of the nacre he had his throne sheathed in the stuff."

"That must have been a fair-sized oyster," Ulath noted.

Oscagne smiled. "No, Sir Ulath. They cut the shells into little tiles and fit them together very tightly. Then they polish the whole surface for a month or so. It's a very tedious and expensive process. Anyway, the second Micaen emperor took it one step further and sheathed the columns in the throne room. The third sheathed the walls, and on and on and on. They sheathed the palace, then the whole royal compound. Then they went after the public buildings. After two hundred years, they'd cemented those little tiles all over every building in Matherion. There are low dives down by the waterfront that are more magnificent than the Basilica of Chyrellos. Fortunately the dynasty died out before they paved the streets with it. They virtually bankrupted the empire and enormously enriched the Isle of Tega in the process. Tegan divers became fabulously wealthy plundering the sea floor."

"Isn't mother-of-pearl almost as brittle as glass?" Khalad asked him.

"It is indeed, young sir, and the cement that's used to stick it to the buildings isn't all that permanent. A good windstorm fills the streets with gleaming crumbs and leaves all the buildings looking as if they've got the pox. As a matter of pride, the tiles have to be replaced. A moderate hurricane can precipitate a major financial crisis in the empire, but we're saddled with it now. Official documents have referred to 'Fire-domed Matherion' for so long that it's become a cliché. Like it or not, we have to maintain this absurdity."

"It *is* breathtaking, though," Ehlana marvelled in a slightly speculative tone of voice.

"Never mind, dear," Sparhawk told her quite firmly.

"What?"

"You can't afford it. Lenda and I almost come to blows every year hammering out the budget as it is."

"I wasn't seriously considering it, Sparhawk," she replied. "Well—not *too* seriously, anyway," she added.

The broad avenues of Matherion were lined with cheering crowds that fell suddenly silent as Ehlana's carriage passed. The citizens stopped cheering as the Queen of Elenia went by because they were too busy grovelling to cheer. The formal grovel involved kneeling and touching the forehead to the paving stones.

"What are they *doing?*" Ehlana exclaimed.

"Obeying the emperor's command, I'd imagine," Oscagne replied. "That's the customary sign of respect for the imperial person."

"Make them stop!" she commanded.

"Countermand an imperial order? Me, your Majesty? Not very likely. Forgive me, Queen Ehlana, but I like my head where it is. I'd rather not have it displayed on a pole at the city gate. It is quite an honor, though. Sarabian's ordered the population to treat you as his equal. No emperor's ever done that before."

"And the people who don't fall down on their faces are punished?" Khalad surmised with a hard edge to his voice.

"Of course not. They do it out of love. That's the official explanation, of course. Actually, the custom originated about a thousand years ago. A drunken courtier tripped and fell on his face when the emperor entered the room. The emperor was terribly impressed, and characteristically, he completely misunderstood. He awarded the courtier a dukedom on the spot. People aren't banging their faces on the cobblestones out of fear, young man. They're doing it in the hope of being rewarded."

"You're a cynic, Oscagne," Emban accused the ambassador.

"No, Emban, I'm a realist. A good politician always looks for the worst in people."

"Someday they may surprise you, your Excellency," Talen predicted.

"They haven't yet."

■   ■   ■

The palace compound was only slightly smaller than the city of Demos in eastern Elenia. The gleaming central palace, of course, was by far the largest structure on the grounds. There were other palaces, however—glowing structures in a wide variety of architectural styles. Sir Bevier drew in his breath sharply. "Good Lord!" he exclaimed. "That castle over there is almost an exact replica of the palace of King Dregos in Larium."

"Plagiarism appears to be a sin not exclusively committed by poets," Stragen murmured.

"Merely a genuflection toward cosmopolitanism, Milord," Oscagne explained. "We *are* an empire, after all, and we've drawn many different peoples under our roof. Elenes like castles, so we have a castle here to make the Elene kings of the western empire feel more comfortable when they come to pay a call."

"The castle of King Dregos certainly doesn't gleam in the sun the way that one does," Bevier noted.

"That was sort of the idea, Sir Bevier." Oscagne smiled.

They dismounted in the flagstoned semi-enclosed court before the main palace, where they were met by a horde of obsequious servants.

"What does he want?" Kalten asked, holding off a determined-looking Tamul garbed in crimson silk.

"Your shoes, Sir Kalten," Oscagne explained.

"What's wrong with my shoes?"

"They're made of steel, Sir Knight."

"So? I'm wearing armor. Naturally my shoes are made of steel."

"You can't enter the palace with steel shoes on your feet. Leather boots aren't even permitted—the floors, you understand."

"Even the floors are made of seashells?" Kalten asked incredulously.

"I'm afraid so. We Tamuls don't wear shoes inside our houses, so the builders went ahead and tiled the floors of the buildings here in the imperial compound as well as the walls and ceilings. They didn't anticipate visits by armored knights."

"I can't take off my shoes," Kalten objected, flushing.

"What's the problem, Kalten?" Ehlana asked him.

"I've got a hole in one of my socks," he muttered, looking dreadfully embarrassed. "I can't meet an emperor with my toes hanging out." He looked around at his companions, his face pugnacious. He held up one gauntleted fist. "If anybody laughs, there's going to be a fight," he threatened.

"Your dignity's secure, Sir Kalten," Oscagne assured him. "The servants have down-filled slippers for us to wear inside."

"I've got awfully big feet, your Excellency," Kalten pointed out anxiously. "Are you sure they'll have shoes to fit me?"

"Don't be concerned, Kalten-Knight," Engessa said. "If they can fit *me,* they can certainly fit you."

Once the visitors had been reshod, they were escorted into the palace. There were oil lamps hanging on long chains suspended from the ceiling, and the lamplight set everything aflame. The shifting, rainbow-hued colors of the walls, floors, and ceiling of the broad corridors dazzled the Elenes, and they followed the servants all bemused.

There were courtiers here, of course—no palace is complete without them—and like the citizens in the streets outside, they grovelled as the Queen of Elenia passed.

"Don't become too enamored of their mode of greeting, love," Sparhawk warned his wife. "The citizens of Cimmura wouldn't adopt it no matter what you offered them."

"Don't be absurd, Sparhawk," she replied tartly. "I wasn't even considering it. Actually, I wish these people would stop. It's really just a bit embarrassing."

"That's my girl." He smiled.

They were offered wine and chilled, scented water to dab on their faces. The knights accepted the wine enthusiastically, and the ladies dutifully dabbed.

"You really ought to try some of this, Father," Princess Danae suggested, pointing at one of the porcelain basins of water. "It might conceal the fragrance of your armor."

"She has a point, Sparhawk," Ehlana agreed.

"Armor's supposed to stink," he replied, shrugging. "If an enemy's eyes start to water during a fight, it gives you a certain advantage."

"I knew there was a reason," the little princess murmured.

Then they were led into a long corridor where mosaic portraits were inlaid into the walls: stiff, probably idealized representations of long-dead emperors. A broad strip of crimson carpet with a golden border along each edge protected the floor of that seemingly endless corridor.

"Very impressive, your Excellency," Stragen murmured to Oscagne after a time. "How many more miles is it to the throne room?"

"You are droll, Milord." Oscagne smiled briefly.

"It's artfully done," the thief observed, "but doesn't it waste a great deal of space?"

"Very perceptive, Milord Stragen."

"What's this?" Tynian asked.

"The corridor curves to the left," Stragen replied. "It's hard to detect because of the way the walls reflect the light, but if you look closely, you can see it. We've been walking around in a circle for the past quarter of an hour."

"A spiral, actually, Milord Stragen," Oscagne corrected him. "The design was intended to convey the notion of immensity. Tamuls are of short stature, and immensity impresses us. That's why we're so fond of the Atans. We're reaching the inner coils of the spiral now. The throne room's not far ahead."

The corridors of shifting fire were suddenly filled with a brazen fanfare as hidden trumpeters greeted the queen and her party. That fanfare was followed by an awful screeching punctuated by a tinny clanking noise. Mmrr, nestled in her little mistress' arms, laid back her ears and hissed.

"The cat has excellent musical taste," Bevier noted, wincing at a particularly off-key passage in the "music."

"I'd forgotten that," Sephrenia apologized to Vanion. "Try to ignore it, dear one."

"I *am*," he replied with a pained expression on his face.

"You remember that Ogress I told you about?" Ulath asked Sparhawk. "The one who fell in love with that poor fellow up in Thalesia?"

"Vaguely."

"When she sang to him, it sounded almost exactly like that."

"He went into a monastery to get away from her, didn't he?"

"Yes."

"Wise decision."

"It's an affectation of ours," Oscagne explained to them. "The Tamul language is very musical when it's spoken. Pretty music would seem commonplace, even mundane—so our composers strive for the opposite effect."

"I'd say they've succeeded beyond human imagination," Baroness Melidere said. "It sounds like someone's torturing a dozen pigs inside an ironworks."

"I'll convey your observation to the composer, Baroness," Oscagne told her. "I'm sure he'll be pleased."

"*I'd* be pleased if his song came to an end, your Excellency."

The vast doors that finally terminated the endless-seeming corridor were covered with beaten gold, and they swung ponderously open to reveal an enormous, domed hall. Since the dome was higher than the surrounding structures, the illumination in the room came through inch-thick crystal windows high overhead. The sun poured down through those windows to set the walls and floor of Emperor Sarabian's throne room afire. The hall was of suitably stupendous dimensions, and the expanses of nacreous white were broken up by accents of crimson and gold. Heavy red velvet draperies hung at intervals along the glowing walls, flanking columnar buttresses inlaid with gold. A wide avenue of crimson carpet led from the huge doors to the foot of the throne, and the room was filled with courtiers, both Tamul and Elene.

Another fanfare announced the arrival of the visitors, and the Church Knights and the Peloi formed up in military precision around Queen Ehlana and her party. They marched with ceremonial pace down that broad, carpeted avenue to the throne of his Imperial Majesty, Sarabian of Tamul.

The ruler of half the world wore a heavy crown of diamond-encrusted gold, and his crimson cloak, open at the front, was bordered with wide bands of tightly woven gold thread. His robe was gleaming white, caught at the waist by a wide golden belt. Despite the splendor of his throne room and his clothing, Sarabian of Tamul was a rather ordinary-looking man. His skin was pale by comparison with the skin of the Atans—largely, Sparhawk surmised, because the emperor was seldom out of doors. He was of medium stature and build and his face was unremarkable. His eyes, however, were far more alert than Sparhawk had expected. When Ehlana entered the throne room, he rose somewhat hesitantly to his feet.

Oscagne looked a bit surprised. "That's amazing," he said. "The emperor never stands to greet his guests."

"Who are the ladies gathered around him?" Ehlana asked in a quiet voice.

"His wives," Oscagne replied, "the Empresses of Tamuli. There are nine of them."

"Monstrous!" Bevier gasped.

"Political expediency, Sir Knight," the ambassador explained. "An ordinary man has only one wife, but the emperor has to have one from each kingdom in the empire. He can't really show favoritism, after all."

"It looks as if one of the empresses forgot to finish dressing," Baroness Melidere said critically, staring at one of the imperial wives, a sunny-faced young woman who stood naked to the waist with no hint that her unclad state caused her any concern. The skirt caught around her waist was a brilliant scarlet, and she had a red flower in her hair.

Oscagne chuckled. "That's our Elysoun." He smiled. "She's from the Isle of Valesia, and that's the costume—or lack of it—customary among the islanders. She's a totally uncomplicated girl, and we all love her dearly. The normal rules governing marital fidelity have never applied to the Valesian empress. It's a concept the Valesians can't comprehend. The notion of sin is alien to them."

Bevier gasped.

"Hasn't anyone ever tried to instruct them?" Emban asked.

"Oh, my, yes, your Grace." Oscagne grinned. "Churchmen from the Elene kingdoms of western Tamuli have gone by the score to Valesia to try to persuade the islanders that their favorite pastime is scandalous and sinful. The churchmen are filled with zeal right at first, but it doesn't usually last for very long. Valesian girls are all very beautiful and very friendly. Almost invariably, it's the Elenes who are converted. The Valesian religion seems to have only one commandment—be happy."

"There are worse notions." Emban sighed.

"Your *Grace*!" Bevier exclaimed.

"Grow up, Bevier," Emban told him. "I sometimes think that our Holy Mother Church is a bit obsessive about certain aspects of human behavior."

Bevier flushed, and his face grew rigidly disapproving.

The courtiers in the throne room, obviously at the emperor's command, once again ritualistically grovelled as Ehlana passed. Practice had made them so skilled that dropping to their knees, banging their foreheads on the floor, and getting back up again was accomplished with only minimal awkwardness.

Ehlana, gowned in royal blue, reached the throne and curtsied gracefully. The set look on her face clearly said that she would *not* grovel.

The emperor bowed in response, and an astonished gasp ran through the crowd. The imperial bow was adequate, though just a bit stiff. Sarabian had obviously been practicing, but bowing appeared not to come naturally to him. Then he cleared his throat and spoke at some length in the Tamul language, pausing from time to time to permit his official translator to convert his remarks into Elenic.

"Keep your eyes where they belong," Ehlana murmured to Sparhawk. Her face was serene, and her lips scarcely moved.

"I wasn't looking at her," he protested.

"Oh, *really*?"

The Empress Elysoun had the virtually undivided attention of the Church Knights and the Peloi and she quite obviously was enjoying it. Her dark eyes sparkled, and her smile was just slightly naughty. She stood not far from her imperial husband, breathing deeply, evidently a form of exercise among her people.

There was a challenge in the look she returned to her many admirers, and she surveyed them clinically. Sparhawk had seen the same look on Ehlana's face when she was choosing jewelry or gowns. He concluded that Empress Elysoun was very likely to cause problems.

Emperor Sarabian's speech was filled with formalized platitudes. His heart was full. He swooned with joy. He was dumbstruck by Ehlana's beauty. He was quite overwhelmed by the honor she did him in stopping by to call. He thought her dress was very nice.

Ehlana, the world's consummate orator, quickly discarded the speech she had been preparing since her departure from Chyrellos and responded in kind. She found Matherion quite pretty. She advised Sarabian that her life had now seen its crown—Ehlana's life seemed to find a new crown each time she made a speech. She commented on the unspeakable beauty of the imperial wives, though making no mention of Empress Elysoun's painfully visible attributes. She also promised to swoon with joy, since it seemed to be the fashion here. She thanked him profusely for his gracious welcome. She did not, however, talk about the weather.

Emperor Sarabian visibly relaxed. He had clearly been apprehensive that the Queen of Elenia might accidentally slip something of substance into her speech, which would have then obliged him to respond without consultation.

He thanked her for her thanks.

She thanked *him* for his thanks for her thanks.

Then they stared at each other. Thanks for thanks can only be carried so far without becoming ridiculous.

Then an official with an exaggeratedly bored look on his face cleared his throat. He was somewhat taller than the average Tamul, and his face showed no sign whatsoever of what he was thinking.

It was with enormous relief that Emperor Sarabian introduced his prime minister, Pondia Subat.

"Odd name," Ulath murmured after the emperor's remarks had been translated. "I wonder if his close friends call him 'Pondy.'"

"Pondia is his title of nobility, Sir Ulath," Oscagne explained. "It's a rank somewhat akin to that of viscount, though not exactly. Be a little careful of him, my Lords. He is *not* your friend. He also pretends not to understand Elenic, but I strongly suspect that his ignorance on that score is feigned. Subat was violently opposed to the idea of inviting Prince Sparhawk to come to Matherion. He felt that to do so would demean the emperor. I've also been advised that the emperor's decision to treat Queen Ehlana as an equal quite nearly gave our prime minister apoplexy."

"Is he dangerous?" Sparhawk murmured.

"I'm not entirely certain, your Highness. He's fanatically loyal to the emperor, and I'm not altogether sure where that may lead him."

Pondia Subat was making a few remarks.

"He says that he knows you're fatigued by the rigors of the journey," Oscagne translated. "He urges you to accept the imperial hospitality to rest and refresh yourselves. It's a rather neat excuse to conclude the interview before anyone says anything that might compel the emperor to answer before Subat has a chance to prompt him."

"It might not be a bad idea," Ehlana decided. "Things haven't gone badly so far. Maybe we should just leave well enough alone for the time being."

"I shall be guided by you, your Majesty," Oscagne said with a florid bow.

Ehlana let that pass.

After another effusive exchange between their Majesties, the prime minister escorted the visitors from the hall. Just outside the door to the throne room they mounted a flight of stairs and proceeded along a corridor directly to the far side of the palace, forgoing the pleasure of retracing their steps around and around the interminable spiral.

Pondia Subat, speaking through an interpreter, pointed out features of interest as they progressed. His tone was deliberately offhand, treating wonders as commonplace. He was not even particularly subtle about his efforts to put these Elene barbarians in their place. He did not quite sneer at them, but he came very close. He led them along a covered walkway to the gleaming Elene castle, where he left them in the care of Ambassador Oscagne.

"Is his attitude fairly prevalent here in Matherion?" Emban asked the ambassador.

"Hardly," Oscagne replied. "Subat's the leader of a very small faction here at court. They're archconservatives who haven't had a new idea in five hundred years."

"How did he become prime minister if his faction is so small?" Tynian asked.

"Tamul politics are very murky, Sir Tynian. We serve at the emperor's pleasure, and he's in no way obliged to take our advice on any matter. Subat's father was a very close friend of Emperor Sarabian's sire, and the appointment of Subat as prime minister was more in the nature of a gesture of filial respect than a recognition of outstanding merit, although Subat's an adequate prime minister—unless something unusual comes up. Then he tends to go all to pieces. Cronyism's one of the major drawbacks of our form of government. The head of our church has never had a pious thought in his life. He doesn't even know the names of our Gods."

"Wait a minute," Emban said, his eyes stunned. "Are you trying to say that ecclesiastical positions are bestowed by the emperor?"

"Of course. They *are* positions of authority, after all, and Tamul emperors don't like to let authority of *any* kind out of their hands."

They had entered the main hall of the castle, which, with the exception of the gleaming nacre that covered every exposed surface, was very much like the main hall of every Elene castle in the world.

"The servants here are Elenes," Oscagne told them, "so you should have no difficulty explaining your needs to them. I trust you'll excuse me now. I must go make my report to his Imperial Majesty." He made a face. "I'm not really looking forward to it, to be honest with you. Subat's going to be standing at his Majesty's elbow making light of everything I say." He bowed to Ehlana, then turned and left.

"We've got problems here, I think," Tynian observed. "All this formality's going to keep us away from the emperor, and if we can't tell him what we've discovered, he's not likely to give us the freedom of movement we're going to need."

"And the antagonism of the prime minister's going to make things that much worse," Bevier added. "It rather looks as if we've come halfway around the world to offer our help, only to be confined in this very elaborate prison."

"Let's feel things out a bit before we start getting obstreperous," Emban counselled. "Oscagne knows what he's doing, and he's seen almost everything we've seen. I think we can count on him to convey the urgency of the situation to Sarabian."

"If you have no need of us, your Majesty," Stragen said to Ehlana, "Talen and I should go make contact with the local thieves. If we're going to be tied up in meaningless formalities here, we'll need some help in gathering information."

"How do you plan to communicate with them?" Khalad asked him.

"Matherion's a very cosmopolitan place, Khalad. Caalador directed me to several Elenes who carry quite a bit of weight with the local thieves."

"Do what you must, Stragen," Ehlana told him, "but don't cause any international incidents."

"Trust me, your Majesty." He grinned.

The royal apartment in the castle was high up in a central tower. The castle was purely ornamental, of course, but since it was a faithful reproduction of an Elene fort, the builders had unwittingly included practical features they probably hadn't even recognized. Bevier was quite pleased with it. "I could defend the place," he judged. "About all I'd need would be a few vats of pitch and some engines and I could hold this castle for several years."

"Let's hope it doesn't come to that, Bevier," Ehlana replied.

Later that evening, when Sparhawk and his extended family had said good night to the others and retired to the royal apartment, the Prince Consort lounged in a chair by the window while the ladies did all those little things ladies do before going to bed. Many of those little ceremonies had clearly practical reasons behind them; others were totally incomprehensible.

"I'm sorry, Sparhawk," Ehlana was saying, "but it concerns me. If the Empress Elysoun's as indiscriminately predatory as Oscagne suggests, she could cause us a great deal of embarrassment. Take Kalten, for example. Can you believe that he'd decline the kind of offers she's likely to make—particularly in view of her costume?"

"I'll have a talk with him," Sparhawk promised.

"By hand," Mirtai suggested. "Sometimes it's a little hard to get Kalten's attention when he's distracted."

"She's vulgar." Baroness Melidere sniffed.

"She's very pretty though, Baroness," Alean added. "And she's not really flaunting her body. She knows it's there, of course, but I think she just likes to share it with people. She's generous more than vulgar."

"Do you suppose we could talk about something else?" Sparhawk asked them in a pained tone.

There was a light knock on the door, and Mirtai went to see who was asking admittance. As always, the Atana had one hand on a dagger hilt when she opened the door.

It was Oscagne. He was wearing a hooded cloak and he was accompanied by another man similarly garbed. The two stepped inside quickly. "Close the door,

Atana," the ambassador hissed urgently, his usually imperturbable face stunned and his eyes wild.

"What's your problem, Oscagne?" she asked bluntly.

"Please, Atana Mirtai, close the door. If anybody finds out that my friend and I are here, the palace will fall down around our ears."

She closed the door and bolted it.

A sudden absolute certainty came over Sparhawk, and he rose to his feet. "Welcome, your Imperial Majesty," he greeted Oscagne's hooded companion.

Emperor Sarabian pushed back his hood. "How the deuce did you know it was me, Prince Sparhawk?" he asked. His Elenic was only slightly accented. "I know you couldn't see my face."

"No, your Majesty," Sparhawk replied, "but I could see Ambassador Oscagne's. He looked very much like a man holding a live snake."

"I've been called a lot of things in my time," Sarabian laughed, "but never that."

"Your Majesty is most skilled," Ehlana told him with a little curtsy. "I didn't see a single hint on your face that you understood Elenic. I could read it in Queen Betuana's face, but you didn't give me a single clue."

"Betuana speaks Elenic?" He seemed startled. "What an astounding thing." He removed his cloak. "Actually, your Majesty," he told Ehlana, "I speak all the languages of the empire—Tamul, Elenic, Styric, Tegan, Arjuni, Valesian, and even the awful language they speak in Cynesga. It's one of our most closely guarded state secrets. I even keep it a secret from my government, just to be on the safe side." He looked a bit amused. "I gather that you'd all concluded that I'm not quite bright," he suggested.

"You fooled us completely, your Majesty," Melidere assured him.

He beamed at her. "Delightful girl," he said. "I adore fooling people. There are many reasons for this subterfuge, my friends, but they're mostly political and not really very nice. Shall we get to the point here? I can only be absent for a short period of time without being missed."

"We are, as they say, at your immediate disposal, your Majesty," Ehlana told him.

"I've never understood that phrase, Ehlana," he confessed. "You don't mind if we call each other by name, do you? All those 'your Majesties' are just *too* cumbersome. Where was I? Oh, yes—immediate disposal. It sounds like someone running to carry out the trash." His words seemed to tumble from his lips as if his tongue were having difficulty keeping up with his thoughts. "The point of this visit, my dear friends, is that I'm more or less the prisoner of custom and tradition here in Matherion. My role is strictly defined, and for me to overstep certain bounds causes earthquakes that can be felt from here to the Gulf of Daconia. I could ignore those earthquakes, but our common enemy could probably feel them, too, and we don't want to alert him."

"Truly," Sparhawk agreed.

"Please don't keep gaping at me like that, Oscagne," Sarabian told the ambassador. "I didn't tell you that I was really awake when most of you thought I was sleeping because it wasn't necessary for you to know before. Now it is. Snap out of it, man. The foreign minister has to be able to take these little surprises in stride."

"It's just taking me a little while to readjust my thinking, your Majesty."

"You thought I was an idiot, am I right?"

"Well—"

"You were *supposed* to think so, Oscagne—you and Subat and all the other ministers. It's been one of my main defenses—and amusements. Actually, old boy, I'm something of a genius." He smiled at Ehlana. "That sounds immodest, doesn't it? But it's true, nonetheless. I learned your language in three weeks, and Styric in four. I can find the logical fallacies in the most abstruse treaties on Elene theology, and I've probably read—and understood—just about everything that's ever been written. My most brilliant achievement, however, has been to keep all that a secret. The people who call themselves my government—no offense intended, Oscagne—seem to be engaging in some vast conspiracy to keep me in the dark. They only tell me things they think I'll want to hear. I have to look out a window to get an accurate idea of the current weather. They have the noblest of motives, of course. They want to spare me any distress, but I really think that someone ought to tell me when the ship I'm riding in is sinking, don't you?" Sarabian was still talking very fast, spilling out ideas as quickly as they came to him. His eyes were bright, and he seemed almost on the verge of laughing out loud. He was obviously tremendously excited. "Now then," he rushed on, "we must devise a means of communicating without alerting everyone in the palace—down to and including the scullery boys in the kitchen—to what we're doing. I desperately need to know what's *really* going on so that I can bring my towering intellect to bear on it." That last was delivered with self-deprecating irony. "Any ideas?"

"What are your feelings about magic, your Majesty?" Sparhawk asked him.

"I haven't formed an opinion yet, Sparhawk."

"It won't work then," Sparhawk told him. "You have to believe that the spell's going to work, or it'll fail."

"I might be able to *make* myself believe," Sarabian said just a bit dubiously.

"That probably wouldn't do it, your Majesty," Sparhawk told him. "The spells would succeed or not depending on your mood. We need something a bit more certain. There are things we'll need to tell you that will be so important that we won't be able to just trust to luck."

"My feelings exactly, Sparhawk. That defines our problem then. We need an absolutely certain method of passing information back and forth that can't be detected. My experience tells me that it has to be something so commonplace that nobody will pay any attention to it."

"Exchange gifts," Baroness Melidere suggested in an offhand way.

"I'd be delighted to send you gifts, my dear Baroness." Sarabian smiled. "Your eyes quite stop my heart, but—"

She held up one hand. "Excuse me, your Majesty," she told him, "but nothing is more common than the exchange of gifts between ruling monarchs. I can carry little mementos from the queen to you, and the ambassador here can carry yours to her. After we've run back and forth a few times, nobody will pay any attention to us. We can conceal messages in those gifts, and no one will dare to search for them."

"Where did you find this wonderful girl, Ehlana?" Sarabian demanded. "I'd marry her in a minute—if I didn't already have nine wives—oh, incidentally, Sparhawk, I need to talk with you about that—privately, perhaps." He looked around. "Can anyone see any flaws in the baroness' plan?"

"Just one," Mirtai said, "but I can take care of that."

"What is it, Atana?" the excited emperor asked.

"Someone may still have suspicions about this exchange of gifts—particularly if there's a steady stream of them. He might try to intercept Melidere, but I'll escort her back and forth. I'll personally guarantee that no one will interfere."

"Excellent, Atana! Capital! We'd better get back, Oscagne. Subat misses me terribly when I'm not where he expects me to be. Oh, Sparhawk, please designate several of your knights to entertain my wife, Elysoun."

"I beg your Majesty's pardon?"

"Young, preferably handsome, and with lots of stamina—you know the type."

"Are we talking about what I think we're talking about, your Majesty?"

"Of course we are. Elysoun enjoys exchanging gifts and favors, too, and she'd be crushed if no one wanted to play with her. She's terribly shrill when she's unhappy. For the sake of my ears, please see to it, old boy."

"Ah—how many, your Majesty?"

"A dozen or so should suffice, I expect. Coming, Oscagne?" And the Emperor of Tamuli rushed to the door.

CHAPTER TWENTY-FIVE

"It's a characteristic of people with a certain level of intelligence, your Majesty," Zalasta advised Ehlana. "They talk very fast because their ideas are spilling over. Emperor Sarabian may not be *quite* as brilliant as he thinks he is, but his is a mind to be reckoned with. The amazing thing is that he's managed to keep it a secret from everybody in his government. Those people are usually so erratic and excitable that they trip themselves up."

They were all gathered in the royal apartment to discuss the previous night's startling revelation. Ambassador Oscagne had arrived early, bringing with him a diagram of the hidden passageways and concealed listening posts inside the Elene castle that was their temporary home. A half-dozen spies had been rooted out and politely but firmly invited to leave. "There's nothing really personal involved, your Majesty," Oscagne apologized to Ehlana. "It's just a matter of policy."

"I understand completely, your Excellency," she replied graciously. Ehlana wore an emerald-green gown this morning, and she looked particularly lovely.

"Is your espionage system very well developed, your Excellency?" Stragen asked.

"No, not really, Milord. Each bureau of the government has its spies, but they spend most of their time spying on each other. We're far more nervous about our colleagues than we are about foreign visitors."

"There's no centralized intelligence service, then?"

"I'm afraid not, Milord."

"Are we sure we cleaned all the spies out?" Emban asked, looking a bit nervously at the gleaming walls.

"Trust me, your Grace." Sephrenia smiled.

"I didn't follow that, I'm afraid."

"She wiggled her fingers, Patriarch Emban," Talen said dryly. "She turned all the spies we didn't catch into toads."

"Well, not exactly," she amended, "but if there *are* any spies left hiding behind the walls, they can't hear anything."

"You're a very useful person to have around, Sephrenia," the fat little churchman observed.

"I've noticed that myself," Vanion agreed.

"Let's push on here," Ehlana suggested. "We don't want to overuse our subterfuge, but we *will* want to exchange a few gifts with Sarabian just to make sure that no one's going to intercept our messages and to get the courtiers in the hallways accustomed to seeing Melidere trotting back and forth with trinkets."

"I won't really trot, your Majesty," Melidere objected. "I'll swish—seductively. I've found that a man who's busy watching your hips doesn't pay too much attention to what the rest of you is doing."

"Really?" Princess Danae said. "I'll have to remember that. Can you show me how to swish, Baroness?"

"You're going to have to grow some hips first, Princess," Talen told her.

Danae's eyes went suddenly dangerous.

"Never mind," Sparhawk told her.

She ignored him. "I'll get you for that, Talen," she threatened.

"I doubt it, your Highness," he replied impudently. "I can still run faster than you can."

"We have another problem," Stragen told them. "The absolutely splendid plan I conceived some months ago fell all to pieces on me last night. The local thieves aren't going to be much help, I'm afraid. They're even worse than Caalador led us to believe back in Lebas. Tamul society's so rigid that my colleagues out there in the streets can't think independently. There's a certain way that thieves are supposed to behave here, and the ones we met last night are so hidebound that they can't get around the stereotypes. The Elenes in the local thieves' community are creative enough, but the Tamuls are hopelessly inept."

"That's certainly the truth," Talen agreed. "They don't even try to run when they're caught stealing. They just stand around waiting to be taken into custody. It's the most immoral thing I've ever heard of."

"We might be able to salvage something out of it," Stragen continued. "I've sent for Caalador. Maybe he can talk some sense into them. What concerns me the most is their absolute lack of any kind of organization. The thieves don't talk to the murderers; the whores don't talk to the beggars; and nobody talks to the swindlers. I can't for the life of me see how they survive."

"That's bad news," Ulath noted. "We were counting on the thieves to serve as our spy network."

"Let's hope that Caalador can fix it," Stragen said. "The fact that there's no central intelligence-gathering apparatus in the government makes those thieves crucial to our plans."

"Caalador will be able to talk some sense into them," Ehlana said. "I have every confidence in him."

"That's probably because you like to hear him talk," Sparhawk told her.

"Speaking of talking," Sephrenia said, "I think our efforts here are going to be limited by the fact that most of you don't speak Tamul. We're going to have to do something about that."

Kalten groaned.

"It won't be nearly as painful this time, dear one." She smiled. "We don't really have the time for you to actually learn the language, so Zalasta and I are going to cheat."

"Could you clarify that a bit for me, Sephrenia?" Emban said, looking puzzled.

"We'll cast a spell." She shrugged.

"Are you trying to say that you can teach somebody a foreign language by magic?" he asked.

"Oh, yes," Sparhawk assured him. "She taught me to speak Troll in about five seconds in Ghwerig's cave, and I'd imagine that Troll's a lot harder to learn than Tamul. At least Tamuls are human."

"We'll have to be careful, though," the small Styric woman cautioned. "If you all appear to be linguistic geniuses, it's going to look very curious. We'll do it a bit at a time—a basic vocabulary and a rudimentary grammar right at first, and then we'll expand on that."

"I could send you instructors, Lady Sephrenia," Oscagne offered.

"Ah—no, thanks all the same, your Excellency. Your instructors would be startled—and suspicious—if they suddenly found a whole platoon of extraordinarily gifted students. We'll do it ourselves in order to conceal what we're up to. I'll give our pupils here abominable accents right at first, and then we'll smooth things out as we go along."

"Sephrenia?" Kalten said in a slightly resentful tone.

"Yes, dear one?"

"You can teach people languages by magic?"

"Yes."

"Then why did you spend all those years trying to teach me Styric? When you saw that it wasn't going to work, why didn't you just wiggle your fingers at me?"

"Kalten, dear," she said gently, "why was I trying to teach you Styric?"

"So that I could perform magic tricks, I guess." He shrugged. "That's unless you just enjoy making people suffer."

"No, dear one. It was just as painful for me as it was for you." She shuddered. "More painful, probably. You *were,* in fact, trying to learn Styric so that you could work the spells, but in order to do that, you have to be able to *think* in Styric. You can't just mouth the words and make them come off the way you want them to."

"Wait a minute," he objected. "Are you saying that people who speak other languages don't think the same way we do?"

"They may think the same way, but they don't think in the same words."

"Do you mean to say that we actually think in words?"

"Of course we do. What did you think thoughts were?"

"I don't know. But we're all human. Wouldn't we all think the same way and in the same language?"

She blinked. "And which language would that be, dear one?"

"Elenic, naturally. That's why foreigners aren't as clever as we are. They have to stop and translate their thoughts from Elenic into that barbarian gabble they call language. They do it just to be stubborn, of course."

She stared at him suspiciously. "You're actually serious, aren't you?"

"Of course. I thought everybody knew that's why Elenes are smarter than everybody else." His face shone with blinding sincerity.

"Oh, dear," she sighed in near despair.

Melidere put on a lavender gown and swished off to the emperor's private apartments bearing a blue satin Elene doublet over one arm. Mirtai followed her. Mirtai did not swish. Melidere's eyes were ingenuously wide. Her expression was vapid. Her lower lip was adorably caught between her teeth as if she were breathless with excitement. Emperor Sarabian's courtiers watched the swishing with great interest. Nobody paid the slightest attention to what she did with her hands.

She delivered the gift to the emperor with a breathy little speech, which Mirtai translated. The emperor responded quite formally. Melidere curtsied and then swished back to the Elene castle. The courtiers still concentrated on the swishing— even though they had already had plenty of opportunity to observe the process.

"It went off without a hitch," the baroness reported smugly.

"Did they enjoy the swishing?" Stragen asked her.

"I turned the entire court to stone, Milord Stragen." She laughed.

"Did she really?" he asked Mirtai.

"Not entirely," the Atana replied. "A number of them followed her so that they could see more. Melidere's a very good swisher. What was going on inside her gown looked much like two cats fighting inside a burlap sack."

"We should use the talents God gave us, wouldn't you say, your Grace?" the blond girl asked Emban with mock piety.

"Absolutely, my child," he agreed without so much as cracking a smile.

Ambassador Oscagne arrived about fifteen minutes later bearing an alabaster box on a blue velvet cushion. Ehlana took the emperor's note out of the box.

" 'Ehlana'," she read aloud. " 'Your message arrived safely. I get the impression that the members of my court will not merely refrain from interfering with the baroness as she moves through the halls, but will passionately defend her right to do so. How *does* the girl manage to move so many things all at the same time?' Signed: Sarabian."

"Well," Stragen asked the honey-blond girl, "how do you?"

"It's a gift, Milord Stragen."

· · ·

The visiting Elenes made some show of receiving instruction in the Tamul language for the next few weeks, and Oscagne helped their subterfuge along by casually advising various members of the government that he had been teaching the visitors the language during their long journey. Ehlana made a brief speech in Tamul at one of the banquets the prime minister had arranged for the guests in order to establish the fact that she and her party had already achieved a certain level of proficiency.

There were awkward moments, of course. On one occasion Kalten grossly offended a courtier when he smilingly delivered what he thought to be a well-turned compliment. "What's the matter with him?" the blond Pandion asked, looking puzzled as the courtier stalked away.

"What were you trying to say to him?" Mirtai asked, stifling a laugh.

"I told him that I was pleased to see that he was smiling," Kalten replied.

"That's not what you said."

"Well, what *did* I say?"

"You said, 'May all of your teeth fall out.' "

"I used the wrong word for 'smiling,' right?"

"I'd say so, yes."

The pretense of learning a new language provided the queen and her entourage with a great deal of leisure time. The official functions and entertainments they were obliged to attend usually took place in the evening, and that left the days generally free. They passed those hours in idle conversation—conducted for the most part in Tamul. The spell Sephrenia and Zalasta had woven gave them all a fairly complete understanding of vocabulary and syntax, but the smoothing out of pronunciation took somewhat longer.

As Oscagne had predicted he would, the prime minister threw obstacles in their paths at every turn. Insofar as he could, he filled their days with tedious and largely meaningless activities. They attended the openings of cattle shows. They were awarded honorary degrees at the university. They visited model farms. He provided them with huge escorts whenever they left the imperial compound—escorts that usually took several hours to form up. Pondia Subat's agents put that time to good use, clearing the streets of precisely the people the visitors wanted to see. Most troublesome, however, was the fact that he severely restricted their access to Emperor Sarabian. Subat made himself as inconvenient as he possibly could, but he was unprepared for Elene ingenuity and the fact that many in their party were not entirely what they seemed to be. Talen in particular seemed to completely baffle the prime minister's agents. As Sparhawk had noticed long ago, it was quite nearly impossible to follow Talen in any city in the world. The young man had a great deal of fun and gathered a great deal of information.

On one drowsy afternoon, Ehlana and the ladies were in the royal apartment, and the queen's maid, Alean, was speaking as Kalten and Sparhawk quietly entered.

"It's not uncommon," the doe-eyed girl was saying quietly. "It's one of the inconveniences of being a servant." As usual, Alean wore a severe dress of muted grey.

"Who was he?" Ehlana's eyes were like flint.

"It's not really important, your Majesty," Alean replied, looking slightly embarrassed.

"Yes, Alean," Ehlana disagreed, "it is."

"It was Count Osril, your Majesty."

"I've heard of him." Ehlana's tone was frosty.

"So have I." Melidere's tone was just as cold.

"I gather that the count's reputation is unsavory?" Sephrenia asked.

"He's what's referred to as a rake, Lady Sephrenia," Melidere replied. "He wallows in debauchery of the worst kind. He boasts that he's saving God all the inconvenience of condemning him, since he was born to go to Hell anyway."

"My parents were country people," Alean continued, "so they didn't know about the count's reputation. They thought that placing me in service to him would give me the opportunity of a lifetime. It's the only real chance a peasant has for advancement. I was fourteen and very innocent. The count seemed friendly at first, and I considered myself lucky. Then he came home drunk one night, and I discovered why he'd been so nice to me. I hadn't received the kind of training Mirtai had, so there was nothing I could do. I cried afterward, of course, but all he did was laugh at my tears. Fortunately, nothing came of it. Count Osril customarily turned pregnant maids out with nothing but the clothes on their backs. After a few times, he grew tired of the game. He paid me my salary and gave me a good recommendation. I was fortunate enough to find employment at the palace." She smiled a tight, hurt little smile. "Since there were no aftereffects, I suppose it doesn't really matter all that much."

"It does to me," Mirtai said bleakly. "You have my word that he won't survive my return to Cimmura by more than a week."

"If you're going to take that long, you'll miss your chance, Mirtai," Kalten told her almost casually. "Count Osril won't see the sunset of the day when *I* get back to Cimmura, I promise you."

"He won't fight you, Kalten," Sparhawk told his friend.

"He won't have any choice," Kalten replied. "I know any number of insults that no man can swallow—and if *they* don't work, I'll start slicing pieces off him. If you cut off a man's ears and nose, he almost has to reach for his sword—probably because he doesn't know what you plan to cut off next."

"You'll get arrested."

"That's no problem, Sparhawk," Ehlana said, grimly. "I'll pardon him."

"You don't have to do that, Sir Kalten," Alean murmured, her eyes downcast.

"Yes," Kalten replied in a stony voice, "as a matter of fact, I do. I'll bring you one of his ears after I've finished with him—just to prove that I've kept my promise."

Sparhawk fully expected the gentle girl to react with violent revulsion to her protector's brutal offer. She did not, however. She smiled warmly at Sparhawk's friend. "That would be *very* nice, Sir Kalten," she said.

"Go ahead, Sephrenia," Sparhawk said to his tutor. "Roll your eyes and sigh. I might even agree with you this time."

"Why should I do that, Sparhawk?" she asked. "I think Sir Kalten's come up with a very appropriate course of action."

"You're a savage, little mother," he accused.

"So?"

Later that afternoon, Sparhawk and Kalten had joined the other knights in the gleaming great hall of the counterfeit Elene castle. The knights had put aside their formal armor and now wore doublets and hose. "It wouldn't take very much," Sir Bevier was saying. "The walls are really very sturdy, and the fosse is already in place. The drawbridge is functional, though the capstans that raise it need some grease. All we really need to finish it off are sharpened stakes in the fosse."

"And a few barrels of pitch?" Ulath suggested. "I know how much you Arcians enjoy pouring boiling pitch on people."

"Gentlemen," Vanion said disapprovingly, "if you start reinforcing the defenses of this place, our hosts may take it the wrong way." He thought about it for a moment. "It might not hurt to quietly lay in a goodly supply of stakes, though," he added, "and maybe a number of barrels of lamp oil. It's not quite as good as pitch, but it won't attract so much attention when we bring it inside. I think we might also want to start unobtrusively bringing in provisions. There are quite a lot of us, so concealing the fact that we're filling storerooms shouldn't be too hard. Let's keep it all fairly low-key, though."

"What are you contemplating, Vanion?" Emban asked him.

"Just a few simple precautions, your Grace. Things are unstable here in Tamuli, and we have no way of knowing what might happen. Since we've got a perfectly good castle, we might just as well give it a few finishing touches—just in case."

"Is it just my imagination, or does it seem to anybody else that this is a very, very long summer?" Tynian asked suddenly.

Sparhawk became very alert. Someone had been bound to notice that eventually, and if they really pursued the matter and started counting days, they'd be certain to uncover the fact that someone had been tampering with time. "It's a different part of the world, Tynian," he said easily. "The climate's bound to be different."

"Summer is summer, Sparhawk, and it's not supposed to last forever."

"You can never tell about climate," Ulath disagreed, "particularly along a seacoast. There's a warm current that runs up the west coast of Thalesia. It can be the dead of winter in Yosut on the east coast, and only midautumn in Horset."

Good old Ulath, Sparhawk thought with some relief.

"It still seems a little strange to me," Tynian said dubiously.

"Lots of things seem strange to you, my friend." Ulath smiled. "You've turned down any number of invitations I've sent you to go Ogre hunting with me."

"Why kill them if you're not going to eat them?" Tynian shrugged.

"You didn't eat any of those Zemochs you killed."

"I didn't have a good recipe for cooking them."

They all laughed and let the subject drop, and Sparhawk breathed a bit easier.

Talen came into the hall then. As usual, he had almost routinely shaken off the agents of the prime minister that morning and gone out into the city.

"Surprise, surprise," he said dryly. "Krager's finally made it to Matherion. I was starting to worry about him."

"*That* does it!" Sparhawk burst out, slamming his fist down on the arm of his chair. "That man's starting to make me *very* tired."

"We didn't really have the time to chase him down before, my Lord," Khalad pointed out.

"Maybe we should have taken the time. I was sure of that when we saw him back in Sarsos. We're settled in now, though, so let's devote a little time and energy to rooting him out. Draw some pictures of him, Talen. Spread them around and promise a reward."

"I know how to go about it, Sparhawk."

"Do it, then. I want to put my hands on that drunken little weasel. There's all kinds of information inside that sodden skin of his, and I'm going to wring him out until I've got the very last drop of it."

"Testy, isn't he?" Tynian said mildly to Kalten.

"He's been having a bad day." Kalten shrugged. "He discovered a streak of brutality in his womenfolk, and it upset him."

"Oh?"

"There's a nobleman in Cimmura who needs killing. When I get home, I'm going to slice off his cods before I butcher him. The ladies all thought it was a wonderful idea. Their approval shattered a number of Sparhawk's illusions."

"What's the fellow done?"

"It's a private matter."

"Oh. Well, at least Sephrenia agreed with our illustrious leader?"

"No, as a matter of fact, she was even more bloodthirsty than the rest. She went so far as to offer some suggestions later on that even made Mirtai turn pale."

"The fellow *really* must have done something awful."

"He did indeed, my friend, and I'm going to give him hours and hours to regret it." Kalten's blue eyes were like ice, and his nostrils were white and pinched with suppressed fury.

"I didn't do it, Kalten," Tynian told him, "so don't start looking at *me* like that."

"Sorry," Kalten apologized. "Just thinking about it makes my blood boil."

"Don't think about it then."

Their accents were still rough—Sephrenia had seen to that—but their understanding of the Tamul language was very nearly perfect. "Are we ready?" Sparhawk asked his tutor one evening.

"Unless you plan to make speeches, Prince Sparhawk," said Emperor Sarabian, who was paying them another of those whirlwind visits. "Your accent is really vile, you know."

"I'm going out there to listen, your Majesty," Sparhawk told him, "not to talk. Sephrenia and Zalasta are hiding our proficiency behind the accents."

"I wish you'd told me you could do this, Zalasta," Sarabian said just a bit wistfully. "You could have saved me months of time when I was studying languages, you know."

"Your Majesty was keeping your studies a secret," Zalasta reminded him. "I didn't know you wanted to learn other tongues."

"Caught by my own cleverness then." Sarabian shrugged. "Oh, well. What precisely are we planning?"

"We're going to winnow through your court, your Majesty," Vanion told him. "Your government's compartmentalized, and your ministers keep secrets from each other. That means that no one really has a grasp of the whole picture. We're going to fan out through the various departments and gather up everything we can find. When we put it all together, we might be able to see some patterns starting to emerge."

Sarabian made a sour face. "It's my own fault," he confessed.

"Please don't be cryptic, Sarabian," Ehlana told him. The two monarchs were good friends by now, largely because the emperor had simply pushed all formalities aside. He had spoken directly and had insisted that Ehlana do the same.

"I blundered, Ehlana," he said ruefully. "Tamuli's never faced a real crisis before. Our bureaucrats are more clever than the subject peoples, and they have the Atans to back them up. The imperial family's always been more afraid of its own government than of outsiders. We don't encourage cooperation between the various ministries. I seem to be reaping the fruit of a misguided policy. When this is all over, I think I'll fix it."

"*My* government doesn't keep secrets from *me*," Ehlana told him smugly.

"Please don't rub it in," he said. "What exactly are we looking for, Lord Vanion?"

"We observed a number of phenomena on our way to Matherion. Our guess is that we're facing an alliance of some sort. We know—or at least we have good evidence—about who *one* of the parties is. We need to concentrate on the other now. We're at a distinct disadvantage until we can identify him. If it's all right with you, your Majesty, Queen Ehlana and Prince Sparhawk will be spending a great deal of time with you. That means that you're going to have to have a long talk with your prime minister, I'm afraid. Pondia Subat's starting to be inconvenient."

Sarabian raised one eyebrow questioningly.

"He's done everything he possibly can to make you inaccessible to us, Sarabian," Ehlana explained.

"He was told not to do that," Sarabian said bleakly.

"Apparently he didn't listen, your Majesty," Sparhawk said. "We have to wade through his people whenever we get near the main palace, and every time one of us so much as sticks his head out a window, whole platoons of spies start to form up to follow us. Your prime minister doesn't approve of us, I gather."

"It rather looks as if I'm going to have to explain some things to the esteemed Pondia Subat," Sarabian said. "I think he's forgotten the fact that his office isn't hereditary—*and* that his head's not so firmly attached that I can't have it removed if he starts to inconvenience me."

"What charges would you bring against him, Sarabian?" Ehlana asked curiously.

"Charges? What on earth are you talking about, Ehlana? This is Tamuli. I don't need charges. I can have his head chopped off if I decide that I don't like his hair-

cut. I'll take care of Pondia Subat, my friends. I can promise his complete cooperation from now on—either his or that of his successor. Please continue, Lord Vanion."

Vanion pushed on. "Patriarch Emban will concentrate his attention on the
prime minister," he said, "whoever he happens to be. Sir Bevier will spend his time
with the faculty of the university. Scholars pick up a great deal of information, and
governments tend to ignore their findings—until it's too late. Ulath, Kring, and
Tynian will observe the general staff of the army—the Tamul high command rather
than the Atans. Atan Engessa will cover his own people. Milord Stragen and Talen
will serve as liaison with the thieves of Matherion, and Alean and Khalad will circulate among the palace servants. Sephrenia and Zalasta will talk with the local Styric
community, and Melidere and Sir Berit will charm all the courtiers."

"Isn't Sir Berit just a bit young?" Sarabian asked. "My courtiers are a very sophisticated group of people."

"Sir Berit has some special qualifications, your Majesty." Melidere smiled.
"The younger women of your court—and some not quite so young—will do almost anything for him. He may have to sacrifice his virtue a few times, but he's a
very dedicated young man, so I'm sure we can count on him."

Berit blushed. "Why do you always have to say things like that, Baroness?" he
asked plaintively.

"I'm only teasing, Berit," she said fondly.

"It's something that men don't understand, your Majesty," Kalten told the emperor. "Berit has a strange effect on young women for some reason."

"Kalten and Mirtai will attend Sparhawk and the queen," Vanion continued.
"We don't know exactly how far our opponents might be willing to go, so they'll
provide you with some additional protection."

"And you, Lord Vanion?" the emperor asked.

"Vanion and Oscagne are going to try to put it all together, Sarabian," Ehlana
replied. "We'll all bring everything we find directly to them. They'll sort through it
all and isolate the gaps so that we'll know where to concentrate further efforts."

"You Elenes are a very methodical people," Sarabian noted.

"It's an outgrowth of their dependency on logic, your Majesty," Sephrenia told
him. "Their plodding search for corroboration is maddening sometime, but it *does*
get results. A well-trained Elene will spend half a day making observations before
he'll allow himself to admit that it's raining."

"Ah," Emban said to her, "but when an Elene says that it's raining, you can be
absolutely sure that he's telling you the truth."

"And what about you, your Highness?" Sarabian smiled down at the little girl
in his lap. "What part are you going to play in this grand scheme?"

"I'm supposed to distract you so that you don't ask too many questions, Sarabian," Danae replied quite calmly. "Your new friends are going to do things that
aren't really proper, so I'm supposed to keep you from noticing."

"*Danae!*" her mother exclaimed.

"Well, aren't you? You're going to lie to people and spy on them and probably
kill anybody who gets in your way. Isn't that what you mean when you use the word
politics?"

Sarabian laughed. "I think she's got you there, Ehlana." He chortled. "Her definition of politics is a little blunt, but it's very close to the mark. She's going to make an excellent queen."

"Thank you, Sarabian," Danae said sweetly, kissing his cheek.

Then Sparhawk felt that sudden chill, and even though he knew it was useless, his hand went to his sword hilt as the flicker of darkness tugged at the very corner of his vision. He started to swear—half in Elenic and half in Tamul—as he realized that everything they had said had just been revealed to the shadowy presence that had been dogging their steps for all these months.

CHAPTER TWENTY-SIX

"Please take my word for it, your Majesty," Zalasta said to the skeptical Sarabian. "It was most definitely *not* a normal phenomenon."

"You're the expert, Zalasta," Sarabian said dubiously. "My instincts all tell me to look for a natural explanation first, though—a cloud passing in front of the sun, perhaps."

"It's evening, Sarabian," Ehlana pointed out. "The sun's already gone down."

"That *would* sort of weaken that particular explanation, wouldn't it? You've all seen this before?"

"Most of us, your Majesty," Oscagne assured him. "I even saw it once myself—on shipboard—and there was nothing between me and the sun. I think we'll have to accept the testimony of our Elene friends here. They've had experiences with this particular manifestation before."

"Stupid," Sparhawk muttered.

"I beg your pardon?" Sarabian said mildly.

"Sorry, your Majesty," Sparhawk apologized. "I wasn't referring to you, of course. It's our visitor who's not very intelligent. If you set out to spy on someone, you don't announce your presence with drum rolls and trumpet fanfares."

"He's done it before, Sparhawk," Patriarch Emban reminded him. "He put in an appearance in Archimandrite Monsel's study in Darsas, if you remember."

"Maybe he doesn't know he's doing it," Kalten suggested. "When he first went to work for Martel, Adus used to try to sneak around and spy on people. That's why Martel had to finally hire Krager."

"Who's Adus?" Sarabian asked.

"A fellow we used to know, your Majesty," Kalten replied. "He wasn't of much use as a spy. Everybody for a hundred yards in any direction knew when Adus was around. He didn't believe in bathing, so he had a distinctive fragrance."

"Is that at all possible?" Vanion asked Sephrenia. "Could Kalten have *actually* come up with the right answer?"

"*Vanion!*" Kalten objected.

"Sorry, Kalten. That didn't come out exactly the way I'd intended. Seriously, though, Sephrenia, could our visitor be unaware of the shadow he's casting?"

"Anything's possible, I suppose, dear one."

"A visual stink?" Ulath suggested incredulously.

"I don't know if I'd use that exact term, but—" Sephrenia looked at Zalasta. "Is it possible?"

"It would explain the phenomenon," he replied after pondering the notion for a moment. "The Gods are remarkable—not only in the depth of their understanding, but also in their limitations. It could very well be that our visitor doesn't know that we can smell him when he pays a call—if I may borrow Sir Ulath's metaphor. He may actually believe that he's totally invisible to us—that his spying is going unnoticed."

Bevier was shaking his head. "We always talk about it right after it happens," he disagreed. "He'd have heard us, so he has to know that he's giving himself away."

"Not necessarily, Bevier," Kalten disagreed. "Adus didn't know that he smelled like a cesspool, and it's not really the sort of thing one admits to himself. Maybe this shadow's the same sort of thing—a kind of socially unacceptable offensiveness, like bad breath or poor table manners."

"There's a fascinating idea." Patriarch Emban laughed. "We could extrapolate a complete book of divine etiquette from this one single incident."

"To what purpose, your Grace?" Oscagne asked him.

"The noblest of purposes, your Excellency—the greater understanding of God. Isn't that why we're here?"

"I'm not sure that a dissertation on the table manners of the Gods would significantly advance the sum of human knowledge, Emban," Vanion observed. "Might we prevail on your Majesty to smooth our way into the inner circles of your government?"

"Smooth or rough, Lord Vanion," Sarabian grinned, "I'll insert you into the ministries. After I've straightened Pondia Subat out, I'll take on the other ministers—one by one or row by row. I think it's time they all found out just exactly who's in charge here." He suddenly laughed with delight. "I'm so glad you decided to stop by, Ehlana. You and your friends have made me realize that I've been sitting on absolute power for all these years, and that it's never occurred to me to use it. I think it's time to pull it out, dust it off, and wave it around just a bit."

"Oh, dear," Oscagne said, his face suddenly filled with chagrin. "What have I done?"

"We got this yere problem, Stragen," Caalador drawled in Elenic. "These yere yaller brothers o' ourn ain't tooken with th' notion o' steppin' 'cross no social boundaries."

"Please, Caalador," Stragen said, "spare me the folksy preamble. Get to the point."

"T'aint really nachral, Stragen."

"Do you mind?"

Stragen, Talen, and Caalador were meeting in a cellar near the waterfront. It was midmorning, and the local thieves were beginning to stir. "As you've already discovered, the brotherhood here in Matherion's afflicted with a caste system," Caalador continued. "The thieves' guild doesn't talk to the swindlers, and the beggars' guild doesn't talk to the whores—except in the line of business, of course—and the murderers' guild is totally outcast."

"Now that there's *real* onnachral," Talen observed.

"Don't do that, Talen," Stragen told him, "one of you is bad enough. I couldn't bear two. Why are the murderers so despised?"

"Because they violate one of the basic precepts of Tamul culture." Caalador shrugged. "They're paid assassins actually, and they don't bow and scrape to their victims before they cut their throats. The concept of courtesy overwhelms Tamuls. They don't really object to the notion of someone murdering noblemen for hire. It's the rudeness of it all that upsets them." Caalador shook his head. "That's one of the reasons so many Tamul thieves get caught and beheaded. It's considered impolite to run away."

"Unbelievable," Talen murmured. "It's worse than we thought, Stragen. If these people don't talk to each other, we'll never get any information out of them."

"I think I warned you not to expect too much here in Matherion, my friends," Caalador reminded them.

"Are the rest of the guilds afraid of the murderers?" Stragen asked.

"Oh, yes," Caalador replied.

"We'll start from there then. What's the general feeling about the emperor?"

"Awe, generally, and a level of adoration that hovers right on the verge of outright worship."

"Good. Get in touch with the murderers' guild. When Talen brings you the word, have the cutthroats round up the heads of the other guilds and bring them to the palace."

"What are we a-fixin' t' do here, m' friend?"

"I'll speak with the emperor and see if I can persuade him to make a speech to our brothers." Stragen shrugged.

"Have you lost your mind?"

"Of course not. Tamuls are completely controlled by custom, and one of those customs is that the emperor can suspend customs."

"Were you able to follow that?" Caalador asked Talen.

"I think he lost me on that sharp turn right there at the end."

"Let's see if I've got this straight," Caalador said to the blond Thalesian. "You're going to violate every known propriety of the criminal culture here in Matherion by having the murderers kidnap the leaders of the other guilds."

"Yes," Stragen admitted.

"Then you're going to have them all taken to the palace compound, where they're absolutely forbidden to go."

"Yes."

"Then you're going to ask the emperor to make a speech to a group of people whose very existence he's not even supposed to know about."

"That's more or less what I had in mind."

"And the emperor's going to command them to suspend eons-old custom and tradition and start cooperating with each other?"

"Is there some problem with that?"

"No, not really. I just wanted to be sure I had it all down straight in my mind, that's all."

"See to it, would you, old boy?" Stragen asked. "I'd probably better go talk with the emperor."

Sephrenia sighed. "You're being childish, you know," she said.

Salla's eyes bulged. "How *dare* you?" he almost screamed. The Styric elder's face had gone white.

"You forget yourself, Elder Salla," Zalasta told the outraged man. "Councillor Sephrenia speaks for the Thousand. Will you defy them and the Gods they represent?"

"The Thousand are misguided!" Salla blustered. "There can never be an accommodation between Styricum and the pig-eaters!"

"That's for the Thousand to decide," Zalasta told him in a flinty tone.

"But look at what the Elene barbarians have done to us," Salla said, his voice choked with outrage.

"You've lived out your whole life here in the Styric quarter in Matherion, Elder Salla," Zalasta said. "You've probably never even *seen* an Elene."

"I can read, Zalasta."

"I'm delighted to hear it. We're not really here for discussion, however. The High Priestess of Aphrael is conveying the instruction of the Thousand. Like it or not, you're compelled to obey."

Salla's eyes filled with tears. "They've murdered us!" he choked.

"You seem to be in remarkably good condition for a man who's been murdered, Salla," Sephrenia told him. "Tell me, was it painful?"

"You know what I mean, Priestess."

"Ah, yes," she said, "that tiresome Styric compulsion to expropriate pain. Someone on the far side of the world stabs a Styric, and you start to bleed. You sit here in Matherion in protected luxury feeling sorry for yourself and secretly consumed with a gnawing envy that you're being denied martyrdom. Well, if you want to be a martyr so badly, Salla, I can arrange it for you." Sephrenia was coldly angry with this babbling fool. "The Thousand has made its decision," she said flatly. "I don't really have to explain it to you, but I will—so that you can convey the decision to your followers—and you *will* explain it, Salla. You'll be very convincing about it, or I'll replace you."

"I hold my position for life," he declared defiantly.

"Precisely my point." Her tone was ominous.

He stared at her. "You wouldn't!" he gasped.

"Try me." Sephrenia had wanted to say that to someone for years. She found it quite satisfying. "It goes like this, Salla—feel free to stop me if I start going too fast for you. The Elenes are savages who are looking for an excuse to kill every Styric they see. If we *don't* assist them in this crisis, we'll be handing them that excuse on a velvet cushion. We *will* assist them, because if we don't, they'll slaughter every Styric on the Eosian continent. We don't want them to do that, do we?"

"But—"

"Salla, if you say 'but' to me one more time, I'll obliterate you." She was startled to discover just how enjoyable it was to behave like an Elene. "I've given you the instruction of the Thousand, and the Thousand speaks for the Gods. The matter is not open for discussion, so quit trying to snivel or wriggle your way out of this. You will obey, or you will die. Those are your options. Choose quickly. I'm in a bit of a hurry."

Even Zalasta seemed shocked at that.

"Your Goddess is cruel, Councillor Sephrenia," Salla accused.

She hit him before she even thought about it, her hand and arm seeming to move all on their own. She had spent generations with the Pandion Knights and she knew how to get her shoulder behind the blow. It was more than an ineffectual slap. She caught him solidly on the point of the chin with the heel of her hand, and he reeled back, his eyes glazed.

Sephrenia began to intone the words of the deadly incantation, her hands moving quite openly in the accompanying gestures.

I won't do that, Sephrenia! Aphrael's voice rang sharply in her mind.

I know, Sephrenia threw back the thought. *I'm just trying to get his attention, that's all.*

Salla gasped as he realized what she was doing. Then he screamed and fell to his knees, blubbering and begging for mercy.

"Will you do as I have commanded you to do?" she snapped.

"Yes, Priestess! Yes! Please don't kill me!"

"I have suspended the spell, but I have not cancelled it. I can finish it at any time. Your heart lies in my fist, Salla. Keep that firmly in mind the next time you feel an urge to insult my Goddess. Now get up and go do as you're told. Come along, Zalasta. The smell of self-pity in here nauseates me."

"You've grown hard, Sephrenia," Zalasta accused when they were back out in the narrow streets of the Styric quarter.

"I was bluffing, my old friend," she told him. "Aphrael would never have responded to the spell." She touched her forearm gingerly. "Do you happen to know where I might find a good physician, Zalasta? I think I've just sprained my wrist."

"Not very impressive, are they?" Ulath suggested as he, Tynian, and Kring walked back across the neatly trimmed grounds of the imperial compound toward the Elene castle.

"Truly," Kring agreed. "They seem to spend all their time thinking about parades." The three of them were returning from their meeting with the Imperial High Command. "They're all show," the Domi concluded. "There's no substance to them."

"Uniformed courtiers," Ulath dismissed the Tamul general staff.

"I'll agree," Tynian concurred. "The Atans are the real military force in Tamuli. Decisions are made by the government, and the general staff simply passes those decisions on to the Atan commanders. I began to have some doubts about the effectiveness of the imperial army when they told me that rank is hereditary. I wouldn't want to rely on them in the event of an emergency."

"That's God's own truth, friend Tynian," Kring said. "Their cavalry general took me to the stables and showed me what they call horses here." He shuddered.

"Bad?" Ulath asked.

"Worse than bad, friend Ulath. Their mounts wouldn't even make good plow horses. I wouldn't have believed that horses could get that fat. Anything faster than a walk would kill the poor beasts."

"Are we agreed then?" Tynian asked them. "The imperial army is totally useless?"

"I think you're flattering them, Tynian," Ulath replied.

"We'll have to phrase our report rather carefully," the Alcione Knight told his companions. "We probably shouldn't offend the emperor. Could we say 'undertrained'?"

"That's the truth, certainly," Kring answered.

"How about 'unversed in modern tactics and strategy'?"

"No argument there." Ulath grunted.

" 'Poorly equipped'?"

"That's not exactly true, friend Tynian," Kring disagreed. "Their equipment is of very good quality. It's probably the best twelfth-century equipment I've ever seen."

"All right." Tynian laughed. "How about 'archaic weaponry'?"

"I could accept that," the Domi conceded.

"You'd rather not mention 'fat, lazy, stupid, or inept,' I gather," Ulath asked.

"That might be just a shade undiplomatic, Ulath."

"True, though," Ulath said mournfully.

Pondia Subat did not approve. Emban and Vanion could sense that, although the prime minister's face and manner remained diplomatically bland. Emperor Sarabian had, as promised, spoken at length with his prime minister, and Pondia Subat was going out of his way to be cooperative and to conceal his true feelings. "The details are very commonplace, my Lords," he said deprecatingly, "but then, the details of day-to-day government always are, aren't they?"

"Of course, Pondia." Emban shrugged. "But when taken in the mass, the accretion of detail conveys the sense of governing style, wouldn't you say? From what I've seen so far this morning, I've already reached certain conclusions."

"Oh?" Subat's tone was neutral.

"The guiding principle here seems to be the protection of the emperor," Emban told him. "That principle's very familiar to me, since it's identical to the one that dominates our thinking in Chyrellos. The government of the Church exists almost entirely to protect the Archprelate."

"Perhaps, your Grace, but you'll have to admit that there are differences."

"Oh, of course, but the fact that Emperor Sarabian's not as powerful as Arch-prelate Dolmant doesn't really change things."

Subat's eyes widened slightly, but he instantly gained control of his expression.

"I realize that the concept is alien to you, Pondia," Emban continued smoothly, "but the Archprelate speaks for God, and that makes him the most powerful man on earth. That's an Elene perception, of course, and it may have little or nothing to do with reality. So long as we all believe it, though, it *is* true. That's what those of us in Church government do. We devote a great deal of our effort to making sure that all Elenes continue to believe that Dolmant speaks for God. So long as they believe that, the Archprelacy's safe." The fat little churchman considered it. "If you don't mind an observation, Pondia Subat, your central problem here in Matherion stems from the fact that you Tamuls have a secular turn of mind. Your church has been di-minished, probably because you can't bring yourselves to accept the notion that any authority might equal or exceed that of the emperor. You've erased the element of faith from your national character. Skepticism is all very well and good, but it tends to get out of hand. After you've applied it to God—or your Gods—it starts to spill over, and people begin to question other things as well—the rightness of govern-ment, imperial wisdom, the justice of the tax system, that sort of thing. In the most perfect of worlds, the emperor would be deified, and church and state would become one." He laughed in a self-deprecating little way. "Sorry, Pondia Subat. I didn't mean to preach. It's an occupational compulsion, I suppose. The point is that both Tamuls and Elenes have made the same mistake. You didn't make your emperor a God, and we didn't make our Archprelate an emperor. We've both cheated the people by placing an incomplete authority over them. They deserved better of us. But I can see that you're busy, and my stomach's telling me rather pointedly that it's lunchtime. We'll talk again—soon. Coming, Lord Vanion?"

"You don't actually believe what you just said, do you, Emban?" Vanion mur-mured as the two Elenes left the ministry.

"Probably not." Emban shrugged. "But we're going to have to do something to widen the crack in that stone shell around Subat's mind. I'm sure that the emperor's offer to have his head docked opened his eyes a bit, but until he starts actually thinking instead of simply plodding along the well-worn paths of his preconcep-tions, we're not going to get anything out of him. Despite his general disapproval of us, he's still the most important man in the government, and I'd rather have him working for us than against us. Do you suppose we could step right along, Vanion? I'm definitely getting hungry."

"It should be blue, though," Danae was saying. She sat with Mmrr in Emperor Sarabian's lap, looking directly into his eyes.

"For an Elene, yes, but—" The emperor sounded dubious.

"Right," she agreed. "Tamul skin tone would be better with—"

"But not red-red, though. More scarlet, perhaps even—"

"No. Maroon's too dark. It's a ball, not a—"

"We don't wear dark clothes at funerals. We wear—"

"Really? That's a very interesting notion. Why do you—"

"It's considered insulting to—"

"The dead don't really mind, Sarabian. They're busy someplace else."

"Can you even begin to follow them?" Ehlana murmured to Sparhawk.

"Sort of. They're both thinking about the same thing, so they don't have to finish sentences."

Emperor Sarabian laughed delightedly. "You're the most stimulating conversationalist I've ever met, your Royal Highness," he said to the little girl in his lap.

"Thank you, your Imperial Majesty," she replied. "You're not so bad yourself, you know."

"Danae!" Ehlana said sharply.

"Oh, Mother. Sarabian and I are just getting to know each other."

"I don't suppose—" Sarabian's tone was speculative.

"I'm afraid not, your Majesty," Danae replied. "I'm not being disrespectful, but the crown prince is much too young for me. People gossip when the wife's older than the husband. He's a sweet-natured baby, though. But I've already decided who I'm going—"

"You *have*? So young?"

"It avoids confusion later on. Girls get silly when they reach the marrying age. It's better to decide those things while you've still got your wits about you—isn't it, Mother?"

Ehlana blushed suddenly.

"Mother started setting traps for my father when she was about my age," Danae confided to the Emperor of Tamuli.

"Did you, Ehlana?" Sarabian asked.

"Well, yes, but it's not nice to talk about it in public."

"He didn't mind being trapped, Mother," Danae said, "at least not after he'd gotten used to the idea. All in all, they make a fairly good set of parents—except when Mother starts throwing her rank around."

"That will do, Princess Danae," Ehlana said in her official tone.

"You see what I mean?" Danae grinned at the Emperor.

"Your daughter's going to be a remarkably gifted queen," Sarabian complimented them. "Elenia's going to be a lucky kingdom to have the two of you on the throne, one right after another. The problem with hereditary succession has always been those lamentable lapses in talent. A great king or emperor is almost inevitably succeeded by a hopeless incompetent."

"What's the customary procedure here in Tamuli, Sarabian?" Ehlana asked. "I know that you have nine wives. Does your firstborn become the crown prince—no matter what the race of his mother?"

"Oh, no. Certainly not. The throne descends to the firstborn son of the first wife. She's always a Tamul, since a Tamul princess is always the first one a crown prince marries. I was married at the age of two, actually. I married my other wives right after I was crowned emperor. It was a group ceremony—eight brides and one bridegroom. That eliminates jealousies and arguments about rank. I was absolutely exhausted the following morning."

"You mean that—"

"Oh, yes. It's required. It's another way to avoid those jealousies I mentioned. And it all has to be finished by sunrise."

"How do they decide who's first?" Ehlana sounded very interested.

"I have no idea. Maybe they roll dice for the privilege. There were four royal bedchambers on each side of a long corridor. I was obliged to go down that endless hallway and to pay a call on each of my new brides. It killed my grandfather. He wasn't a young man when he ascended the throne, and the exertion was too much for him."

"Do you suppose we could change the subject?" Sparhawk asked.

"Prude," Ehlana chided him.

"I wonder if Dolmant would let me have more than one husband," Danae mused.

"Never mind," Sparhawk told her very firmly.

The others arrived, and they all gathered around a large table set with a lunch consisting of unfamiliar delicacies. "How did you find Subat, your Grace?" Sarabian asked the Primate of Ucera.

"We went to his offices, and there he was, your Majesty,"

"Emban," Sephrenia chided the fat little churchman, who was looking suspiciously at an undefinable meat course.

"Sorry, your Majesty," Emban apologized. "Your prime minister still seems to be a bit set in his ways."

"You noticed," Sarabian said dryly.

"We definitely noticed, your Majesty," Vanion replied. "His Grace here turned his thinking upside down for him just a bit, though. He suggested that what the world really needs is a Divine Emperor or an Imperial Archprelacy. Both offices are incomplete as they stand."

"Me? A God? Don't be ridiculous, Emban. I've got enough problems with a government. Please don't pile a priesthood on top of it."

"I wasn't really serious, your Majesty," Emban replied. "I just wanted to shake up his thinking a bit more. That talk you had with him opened his eyes, right enough, but we still have to open his mind."

"What happened to your arm?" Vanion asked the woman he loved. Sephrenia had just turned back her sleeve to reveal her bandaged wrist.

"I sprained it," she replied.

"On a stubborn Styric head," Zalasta added, chuckling.

"*Sephrenia!*" Vanion stared at her.

"I used my Pandion training, dear one." She smiled. "Someone should have told me that I was supposed to lock my wrist, though."

"You actually *hit* someone?" Kalten asked incredulously.

"She did indeed, Sir Kalten." Zalasta grinned. "She knocked him halfway across the room. She also threatened to kill him and even went so far as to begin the death spell. He grew very cooperative at that point."

They all stared at her in disbelief.

"Oh, stop that," she told them. Then she laughed softly. "It was a great deal of fun actually. I've never bullied anyone before. It's very satisfying, isn't it?"

"*We* like it." Ulath grinned.

"The Styrics will cooperate fully," she told them.

"How was the army?" Emban asked Tynian.

"I don't think we should expect too much there, your Grace," Tynian replied carefully, glancing at the emperor. "Their function's primarily ceremonial."

"They come from the very best families, Sir Knight," Sarabian said defensively.

"That might be part of the problem, your Majesty—that and the fact that they've never had to actually fight anybody. We'll be depending on the Atans anyway, so we won't really need the imperial army." He looked at Engessa. "Is the local garrison up to standard, Atan Engessa?" he asked.

"A little soft, Tynian-Knight. I took them out for a run this morning, and they began to falter after twenty miles. I gave some orders. They'll be fit by the end of the week."

"Things are falling into place," Vanion approved.

"The palace servants have all the usual vices, Lord Vanion," Khalad reported. "They love to gossip. Alean's making much better progress than I am—probably because she's prettier."

"Thank you," the girl murmured, lowering her eyelashes.

"It's no great compliment, Alean," Talen told her. "My brother's not a raving beauty—none of us are. Our faces are designed for wear, not for show."

"I'd guess that by the end of the week we should have gained their confidence sufficiently to start picking up secrets," Khalad surmised.

"You Elenes amaze me," Sarabian marvelled. "You all seem to have an absolute genius for intrigue."

"This is a rather select group, your Majesty," Emban told him. "We knew before we left Chyrellos that our major task here would be the gathering of information. We chose people who were skilled at it."

"I came across one of the scholars in the contemporary-affairs department at the university," Bevier reported. "Most of the rest of the faculty's already established reputations based on this or that past event. Resting on one's laurels is one of the failings of academics. They can coast along on a single monograph for decades. Anyway, this fellow I mentioned is young and hungry. He's come up with a theory and he's riding it for all he's worth. He's absolutely convinced that all the present turmoil's emanating from Arjuna—perhaps because no one else on the faculty's staked out that particular ground yet. He's also convinced that Scarpa's the man behind the entire conspiracy."

"Who's Scarpa?" Kalten asked.

"Zalasta told us about him," Ulath reminded him. "He serves the same function in Arjuna as Sabre does in Astel and Gerrich does in Lamorkand."

"Oh, yes, now I remember."

"Anyway," Bevier continued, "our scholar's gathered a huge mass of corroborating evidence, some of it very shaky. He'll talk for hours about his theory to anybody willing to listen."

"Is anybody else at the university working on any alternatives?" Emban asked him.

"Not actively, your Grace. They don't want to risk their reputations on false leads. Academic timidity's forcing them to take a wait-and-see position. My young enthusiast doesn't have a reputation, so he's willing to take some risks."

"Stay with him, Bevier," Vanion said. "Even negative conclusions can help to narrow the search."

"My feelings exactly, Lord Vanion."

"Do you suppose I could impose on your Majesty?" Stragen asked the emperor.

"That's what a host is for, Milord." Sarabian grinned. "Impose to your heart's content."

"You *did* know that there are criminals here in Matherion, didn't you?"

"You mean other than the members of my government?"

Stragen laughed. "Score one for you, your Majesty," he said. "There's a world below the surface in every major city in the world," he explained. "It's a world of thieves, pickpockets, burglars, beggars, whores, swindlers, and murderers. They eke out a precarious existence by preying on the rest of society."

"We're aware that such people exist, of course," Sarabian said. "That's why we have policemen and prisons."

"Yes, your Majesty. Those are some of the minor inconveniences in the criminal's life. What isn't generally known, however, is the fact that the criminals of the world cooperate with each other to some degree."

"Go on."

"I've had some contacts with those people in the past, your Majesty," Stragen went on, choosing his words carefully. "They can be very useful. There's almost nothing that goes on in a city that some criminal doesn't know about. If you make it clear that you're not interested in *their* activities, they'll usually sell you the information they've picked up."

"A business arrangement?"

"Precisely. It's something on the order of buying stolen goods. It's not very nice, but many people do it."

"Of course."

"Now, then. This cooperative spirit I mentioned doesn't exist here in Matherion. Tamuls don't cooperate very well for some reason. Each profession here keeps strictly to itself. They've even formed guilds, and they view other criminal professions with contempt and suspicion. We're going to have to break down those walls if those people are to be of any use to us."

"That stands to reason, Milord."

Stragen seemed to breathe a bit easier. "I've made some arrangements, your Majesty," he said. "The leaders of the various criminal guilds are going to come here. They respect you enormously, and they'll obey if you tell them to do something." He paused. "That's as long as you don't command them to become honest, of course."

"Of course. You can't ask a man to give up his profession, I suppose."

"Exactly. What you *can* order them to do, though, your Majesty, is to abandon these caste barriers and start talking to each other. If they're going to be of any use, they're going to have to be willing to pass information to one central collecting point. If we have to contact the head of each guild, information would be stale long before we got our hands on it."

"I see. Correct me if I'm wrong, Milord Stragen. What you want me to do is to organize the criminals of Matherion so that they can prey on honest citizens more effectively in exchange for unspecified information they may or may not be able to pick up in the street. Is that it?"

Stragen winced. "I was afraid your Majesty might look at it that way," he said.

"You needn't be fearful, Milord Stragen. I'll be happy to have a chat with these loyal criminals. The gravity of the current crisis overrides my natural revulsion for having dealings with knaves and rogues. Tell me, Milord, are you a good thief?"

"I guess I've underestimated your Majesty." Stragen sighed. "Yes, actually I'm a very good thief. I hate to sound immodest, but I'm probably the best thief in the world."

"How's business?"

"Not so good lately, Emperor Sarabian. Times of turmoil are very bad for crime. Honest men grow nervous and start protecting their valuables. Oh, one thing, your Majesty. The criminals you'll be addressing will all be masked. They respect you enormously, but they'll probably want to hide their faces from you."

"I can understand that, I suppose. I'm rather looking forward to speaking with your friends, Stragen. We'll put our heads together and come up with ways to circumvent the authorities."

"That's not really a good idea, your Majesty," Talen told him. "Never let a thief get within ten feet of you." He raised his hand to show Sarabian a jewelled bracelet.

The startled emperor looked quickly at his naked right wrist.

"Merely a demonstration, your Majesty." Talen grinned. "I wasn't really going to keep it."

"Give him back the rest, as well, Talen," Stragen told the boy.

Talen sighed. "Your eyes are unwholesomely sharp, Stragen." He reached inside his doublet and took out several other jewels. "The best plan is not to have anything of value on your person when you talk with thieves, your Majesty," he advised.

"You're very good, Master Talen," Sarabian complimented the boy.

"It's all in the wrist." Talen shrugged.

"I absolutely love you Elenes," Sarabian said. "Tamuls are a dull, boring people, but you're full of surprises." He smiled archly at Melidere. "And what startling revelations do you have for me, Baroness?" he asked her.

"Nothing really very startling, your Majesty." She smiled. "The swishing back and forth through the corridors has earned me several fairly predictable offers—and a fair number of pinches. Tamuls pinch more than Elenes, don't they? I've learned to keep my back to the wall, though. A pinch or two in the spirit of good clean fun is all right, I suppose, but the bruises take a long time to fade."

Then they all looked at Berit. The young Pandion Knight blushed furiously. "I haven't really got anything to report, my Lords and Ladies," he mumbled.

"Berit," Ehlana said gently, "it's not nice to lie like that, you know."

"It wasn't really anything, your Majesty," he protested. "It was all a misunderstanding, I'm sure—probably because I don't speak Tamul very well."

"What happened, my young friend?" Sarabian asked him.

"Well, your Majesty, it was your wife, the Empress Elysoun—the one with the unusual costume."

"Yes, I'm acquainted with her."

"Well, your Majesty, she approached me in one of the corridors and said that I was looking a bit tired—perhaps because I was keeping my eyes closed."

"Why were you doing that?"

"Ah—well, her costume, you understand, your Majesty. I thought it might be impolite to stare."

"In Elysoun's case, it's impolite not to. She's very proud of her attributes."

Berit's blush deepened. "Anyway," he floundered on, "she said I looked tired and told me that she had a very comfortable bed in her quarters that I could use if I wanted to get some rest."

Kalten was gazing at the youthful knight with openmouthed envy. "What did you say?" he asked almost breathlessly.

"Well, I thanked her, of course, but I told her that I wasn't really sleepy."

Kalten buried his face in his hands and groaned.

"There, there," Ulath said, patting his shoulder comfortingly.

 ## CHAPTER TWENTY-SEVEN

"Well sir, yer Queenship," Caalador was saying in his broad, colloquial drawl, "these yere trinkets is purty thangs, I'll tell the world, but they ain't got no real practical use to 'em." He offered Ehlana a pair of carved ivory figurines.

"They're gorgeous, Caalador," she gushed.

"Is that guard gone?" Caalador muttered to Sparhawk.

Sparhawk nodded. "Mirtai just shoved him out the door."

"I thought he was planning to stay all day."

"Did you have any trouble getting on the grounds?" Ehlana asked him.

"Not a bit, your Majesty."

"I should hope not—after all the fuss I made." She looked more closely at the figurines. "These are really lovely, Caalador," she said. "Where did you get them?"

"I had them stolen from the museum at the university." He shrugged. "They're ninth-century Tegan—very rare and very valuable." He grinned at her impishly. "Iffn yer Queenship's got this yere passion fer antikities, y' might's well git th' real thang."

"I *love* to listen to this man talk," Ehlana said.

Baroness Melidere escorted the others into the royal quarters.

"Any problems?" Stragen asked his brother thief.

"Got in slicker 'n a weasel burrowin' into a hen roost."

"Please, Caalador, spare me."

Caalador was serving the Queen of Elenia in the capacity of "procurer of antiquities," and by her orders he was to be granted immediate access to her anytime. One or the other of the knights had escorted him onto the grounds several times during the past several weeks in order to familiarize the guards at the gates with his face, but this was the first time he had tried to gain entry by himself. Their assorted subterfuges were growing more and more subtle. "Has anything meaningful turned up, Master Caalador?" Zalasta asked.

"I'm not entirely sure, learned one." Caalador frowned. "We keep running into something a little peculiar."

"Oh?"

"All sorts of people are talking about something called 'the Hidden City.' They're the very people we've been watching, so we thought it might have some significance."

"It *is* a bit unusual," Zalasta agreed. "It's not the sort of thing you'd expect to hear noised about on the streets."

"It actually means something then?"

Zalasta nodded. "It's an old Tamul platitude that has to do with the life of the mind. Are they saying, 'The way to the Hidden City is long, but the rewards to be found there are treasures beyond price'?"

"That's it exactly, learned one. Two people meet on the street, one of them recites the first half, and the other recites the second."

Zalasta nodded. "The platitude's supposed to refer to the rewards of the search for knowledge and enlightenment. I'd suspect some other significance in this case, however. Are your people hearing it from anybody other than Tamuls?"

Caalador nodded. "A couple of Elene merchants greeted each other with it on a street corner just yesterday."

"It sounds very much like a sign and countersign," Vanion mused.

"I'd hate to concentrate all our efforts on something like that to the exclusion of everything else," Zalasta said cautiously.

"Aw, 'taint no big thang, yer Sorcerership," Caalador assured him. "I'm up t' m' ears in beggars an' whores an' sneak thieves an' sich. I got what y' might call a embarrassment o' riches in that deportment."

Zalasta looked puzzled.

"He says he's got more than enough people at his disposal, Zalasta," Sephrenia translated.

"It's a colorful dialect, isn't it?" Zalasta observed mildly.

Ulath was frowning. "I'm not entirely positive," he said, "but it seems to me that I heard two of the palace guards talking about 'the Hidden City' a few days ago. There might be more people involved than we thought."

Vanion nodded. "It may not lead anywhere," he said, "but it won't hurt anything if we all keep our ears open. If Caalador *has* stumbled across the password of the other side, it could help us to identify conspirators we might otherwise miss. Let's compile a sort of a list. Let's gather the names of all these people who hunger and thirst for the Hidden City of the mind. If this is a sign and countersign, and if it's in any way connected to what we're looking for, let's have a group of names to work with."

"You're starting to sound very much like a policeman, Lord Vanion," Talen said, half accusingly.

"Can you ever forgive me?"

"Oh, by the way, I saw an old friend at the university," Bevier told them with a faint smile. "It seems that Baron Kotyk's brother-in-law's come to Matherion to expose the Department of Contemporary Literature to his unspeakable art."

"Wouldn't *inflict* be a better word there, Bevier?" Ulath asked. "I've heard some of Elron's poetry."

"Who's Elron?" Sephrenia asked.

Sparhawk exchanged a long look with Emban. They were still bound by the oaths they had given Archimandrite Monsel. "Ah—" he began, not quite sure how to proceed, "he's an Astel—a sort of semi-aristocrat with literary pretensions. We're not sure just how much he's involved in the disturbances in Astel, but his opinions and sympathies seem to indicate that he's a strong supporter of the man known as Sabre."

"Isn't it a coincidence that he just happens to have made the trip to Matherion at just about the same time that we're getting a strong odor of dead fish in the streets?" Tynian asked. "Why would he come to the very center of the culture of the godless yellow devils he professes to hate?"

"Unusual," Ulath agreed.

"Anything that's unusual is suspicious," Kalten asserted.

"That's a gross generalization," Sparhawk accused.

"Well, isn't it?"

"In this case you might be right. Maybe we'd better keep an eye on him. You'd better pull out your drawing pad again, Talen."

"You know, Sparhawk," the boy said, "I could make a lot of money drawing these pictures if you weren't so set on making a Pandion of me and saddling me with all those high ideals."

"Service is its own reward, Talen," Sparhawk replied piously.

"Caalador," Sephrenia said thoughtfully.

"Yes, yer Sorceresssship?"

"Please don't do that," she said wearily. "There are a number of these so-called firebrands loose in Tamuli. Is it at all possible that some of the local thieves might have seen any of them?"

"I'll ask around, Lady Sephrenia, and I can send to the other kingdoms for people who've seen them if I have to. I'm not sure how much good physical descriptions are going to be, though. If you say that a man's sort of medium, that's going to include about half the population almost by definition."

"She can go beyond physical descriptions, Caalador," Talen assured him. "She'll wiggle her fingers at your witness and put an image of the person they've seen in a pail of water. I can draw a picture from that."

"It might not be a bad idea to have pictures of these various patriots in circulation," Sephrenia murmured. "If Elron and Krager are here, others may decide to visit Matherion as well. If they're going to hold a convention, we should know about it, wouldn't you say?"

"Shouldn't you add a picture of Count Gerrich as well?" Danae suggested.

"But he's all the way across the world in Lamorkand, Princess," Kalten pointed out.

"He's *still* one of the people involved, Kalten," she said. "If you're going to do something, do it right. How much is it going to cost? A few sheets of paper maybe? And the use of Talen's pencil for a half an hour?"

"All right, include him. I don't care. I don't think he'll ever show up here, but go ahead and have Talen draw his picture, if you want."

"Oh, thank you, Kalten. Thank you, thank you, thank you."

"Isn't it nearly her nap time?" Kalten asked sourly.

"Speaking of Krager," Sparhawk said, "have there been any new sightings of him?"

"Just those two I mentioned earlier," Caalador replied. "Is he the kind who's likely to go to ground?"

"That's Krager, all right," Kalten said. "He's perfectly at home with sewer rats—being at least half-rat himself. As long as there was someone around to fetch wine for him, he'd be quite happy to stay down a rat hole for six months at a stretch."

"I *really* want him, Caalador," Sparhawk grated. "My friends are all having a wonderful time telling me that they told me so."

"I didn't follow that one," Caalador said with a puzzled look.

"They all think I should have killed him. Even Sephrenia's all athirst for his blood."

"Well, now, m' friend," Caalador drawled, "I kin make a *real* good case fer jist how forchoonatelike it wuz that y' din't kill 'im. You an' yer friends here all knows this yere Krager feller, an' he's some kinda high muckety-muck on t' other side— which it is that he wouldn'ta bin iffn y'd slit his weasand, now would he? We *knows* this yere Krager, an' we'll chase 'im down sooner er later an' set fire t' his feet until he storts talkin'. Iffn he wuz t' be a absolute stranger, we wouldn't have no idea a-tall 'bout who we wuz a-lookin' fer, now would we?"

Sparhawk smiled beatifically around at his friends. "See," he said to them. "I told you I knew what I was doing."

Later that day, Sparhawk and Ehlana met with Emperor Sarabian and Foreign Minister Oscagne to discuss their findings to date. "Is it at all possible that anyone in the government might have noticed people using this sign and countersign, your Excellency?" Sparhawk asked Oscagne.

"*Quite* possible, Prince Sparhawk," Oscagne replied. "The Interior Ministry's got spies everywhere, but their reports probably won't surface for six months to a year. They're great paper shufflers over at Interior."

"Subat's got his own spies," Sarabian said moodily, "but he wouldn't tell me if he's discovered anything. I doubt that he'd tell me if someone had cut the Isle of Tega adrift and towed it away."

"All the traditions of the Prime Ministry tell him to protect you, your Imperial

Majesty," Oscagne told him. "Despite that little talk you had with him, you'll still probably have to pry information out of him. He devoutly believes that it's his duty to spare you the anguish of hearing unpleasant news."

"If my house is on fire, I'd rather not be spared the anguish of finding out about it," Sarabian said tartly.

"I have informants in the other ministries, your Majesty. I'll put them to work on it. Speaking of that, by the way, Interior's been getting a great many reports of disturbances—far more than we were experiencing previously. Kolata's at his wits' end."

"Kolata?" Sparhawk asked.

"The Minister of the Interior," Sarabian said, "the empire's Chief of Police. He's almost as good at keeping secrets from me as Subat is. What's afoot now, Oscagne?"

"The graveyards have been spitting out their dead, your Majesty. Someone's been digging up the recently deceased and reanimating them. They shamble about moaning and blank-eyed. Whole villages in Edom have been abandoned because of them. The werewolves are running in packs in Daconia, the vampires in the jungles of Arjuna are flocking up like migratory birds, and the Shining Ones are terrorizing the region around Dasan. Add to that the fact that the Trolls are on the march in northern Atan and that the town of Sarna's been attacked twice by what appear to be Cyrgai, and we have some fair evidence that things may be coming to a head. In the past, these disturbances were sporadic and localized. Now they're becoming general."

"Wonderful," Sarabian said sourly. "I think I'll just go into exile somewhere."

"You'll miss all the fun, your Majesty," Sparhawk told him.

"What fun?"

"We haven't even begun to take countermeasures yet. We might not be able to do too much about vampires and the like, but we can definitely move against the Trolls and the Cyrgai. Engessa's been training the local Atans in certain Elene tactics. I think they might be able to deal with the Trolls and the Cyrgai."

Sarabian looked a bit surprised. "Atan Engessa's the commander of the garrison at Canae in Astel," he said. "He doesn't have any authority here in Matherion."

"As a matter of fact he does, your Majesty," Sparhawk disagreed. "I gather that he's received a special commission from King Androl—or Queen Betuana, more than likely. Other Atan commanders have been ordered to follow his suggestions."

"Why doesn't anybody ever tell me these things?"

"Imperial policy, your Majesty." Oscagne smiled. "If you were to know too much, you might start interfering with the government."

"Anyway," Sparhawk continued, "Engessa was very impressed with our tactics in the encounters we had on our way here. We've been training some of his Atans in western techniques."

"That's surprising," Sarabian said. "I wouldn't have expected Atans to listen to anybody when it came to military matters."

"Engessa's a professional, your Majesty," Sparhawk told him. "Professionals are always interested in technical advances in weaponry and tactics. We rounded up some very large draft horses so that we could mount a number of his Atans, and

Kalten and Tynian have been giving them instruction with the lance. That's the safest way to deal with Trolls, we've found. Bevier's taken another group in hand, and he's teaching them how to construct and use siege engines. When we encountered those Cyrgai outside Sarsos, Bevier's catapults broke up their phalanx. It's very hard to maintain a military formation when it's raining boulders. Oh, there's something else we should be aware of. Khalad found a tree outside town that was riddled with short steel arrows. Someone's been practicing with a crossbow."

"What's a crossbow?" Sarabian asked.

"It's a Lamork weapon, your Majesty." Sparhawk scribbled a quick sketch. "It looks something like this. The limbs are much stronger than those on an ordinary longbow, so it has greater range and penetrating power. It's a serious threat to an armored knight. Someone here in Matherion's working on a way to counter the advantage our armor gives us."

"It's beginning to sound as if I'm hanging on to my throne by my fingertips," Sarabian said. "Could I appeal to you for political asylum, Ehlana?"

"I'd be delighted to have you, Sarabian," she replied, "but let's not give up on Sparhawk just yet. He's terribly resourceful."

"As I was saying before," Sparhawk continued, "we can't do too much about the ghouls or werewolves or the Shining Ones or vampires, but I think we might be able to give the Trolls and the Cyrgai a few surprises. I'd like for the Atans to have a bit more training with mounted tactics and the use of Bevier's engines, and then I think it might be time to let our opponent know that he's not going to win this in a walk. I'd particularly like to decimate the Trolls. Our enemy's relying rather heavily on the Troll-Gods, and they'll leave the alliance if too many of their worshippers get killed. I think that early next week we might want to mount a couple of expeditions—one up into Troll country and another down to Sarna. It's time to make our presence known."

"And this local business?" Oscagne asked. "All this fascination with the Hidden City of the mind?"

"Caalador will keep working on that. We've got their password now, and that can open all kinds of doors for us. Vanion's drawing up a list of names. Before long, we'll know everybody in Matherion who's been talking about the Hidden City." He looked at Sarabian. "Have I your Majesty's permission to detain those people if necessary?" he asked. "If we move first and round them all up before they can set their scheme in motion, we'll break the back of this plot before it gets too far along."

"Detain away, Sparhawk." Sarabian grinned. "I've got lots of buildings we can use for prisons."

"All right, young lady," Sparhawk said quite firmly to his daughter a few days later. "One of Caalador's beggars saw Count Gerrich in a street not far from here. How did you know that he'd be here in Matherion?"

"I didn't *know*, Sparhawk. I just had a hunch." Danae was sitting calmly in a large chair, scratching her cat's ears. Mmrr was purring gratefully.

"A hunch?"

"Intuition, if that word makes you feel any better. It just didn't seem right that

Krager and Elron would be here without the others being here as well—and that would logically include Gerrich, wouldn't it?"

"Don't confuse the issue by using the words *logic* and *intuition* in the same sentence."

"Oh, Sparhawk, *do* grow up. That's all that logic really is—a justification for hunches. Have you ever known anyone who used logic to disprove something he already believed?"

"Well—not personally, maybe, but I'm sure there have *been* some."

"I'll wait while you track one down. I'm an immortal, so time doesn't really mean all that much to me."

"That's *really* offensive, Aphrael."

"Sorry, Father." She didn't sound very contrite. "Your mind gathers information in hundreds of ways, Sparhawk—things you hear, things you see, things you touch, and even things you smell. Then it puts all of that information together and jumps from there to a conclusion. That's all that hunches really are. Intuition is just as precise as logic, really, but it doesn't have to go through the long, tedious process of plodding along step by step to prove things. It leaps immediately from evidence to conclusion without all the tiresome intermediate steps. Sephrenia doesn't like logic because it's so boring. She already knows the answers you're so laboriously trying to prove—and so do you, if you'd be honest about it."

"Folklore is full of these hunches, Aphrael—and they're usually wrong. How about the old notion that thunder sours milk?"

"That's a mistake in logic, Sparhawk, not a mistake in intuition."

"Would you like to explain that?"

"You could just as easily say that sour milk causes thunder, you know."

"That's absurd."

"Of course it is. Thunder and sour milk are both effects, not causes."

"You should talk to Dolmant. I'd like to see you try to explain that he's been wasting his time on logic all these years."

"He already knows." She shrugged. "Dolmant's far more intuitive than you give him credit for being. He knew who I was the moment he saw me—which is a lot more than I can say for you, Father. I thought for a while there that I was going to have to fly in order to persuade you."

"Be nice."

"I am. There are all sorts of things I didn't say about you. What's Krager up to?"

"Nobody knows."

"We *really* need to find him, Sparhawk."

"I *know*. I want him even more than you do. I'm going to enjoy wringing him out like a wet sock."

"Be serious, Sparhawk. You know Krager. He'd tell you his whole life story if you even frowned at him."

He sighed. "You're probably right," he conceded. "It takes a lot of the fun out of it, though."

"You're not here to have fun, Sparhawk. Which would you rather have? Information or revenge?"

"Couldn't we come up with a way to have both?"

She rolled her eyes upward. "Elenes." She sighed.

Bevier took a detachment of newly trained Atan engineers west toward Sarna early the next week. The following day Kalten, Tynian, and Engessa took two hundred mounted Atans north toward the lands being ravaged by the Trolls. At Vanion's insistence the parties filtered out of Matherion in twos and threes to assemble later outside the city. "There's no point in announcing what we're up to," he said.

A few days after the departure of the two military expeditions, Zalasta left for Sarsos. "I won't be very long," he told them. "We have a certain commitment from the Thousand, but I think I'd like to see some concrete evidence that they're willing to honor that commitment. Words are all well and good, but let's see some action— just as a demonstration of good faith. I know my brothers. Nothing in the world would please them more than being able to reap the benefits of allying themselves with us 'in principle' without the inconvenience of actually being obliged to do anything to help. They're best suited to deal with these supernatural manifestations, so I'll pry them loose from their comfortable chairs in Sarsos and disperse them to these trouble spots." He smiled thinly at Vanion from under his beetling brows. "Extensive travel might toughen them up a bit, my Lord," he added. "Perhaps we can avoid spraining any more of your ankles in demonstrations of how flabby and lazy they are."

"I appreciate that, Zalasta." Vanion laughed.

There were always more things to do than there was time for. The ceremonies and "occasions" that surrounded the state visit by the Queen of Elenia filled their afternoons and evenings, and so Sparhawk and the others were obliged to work late and rise early in order to conduct their surreptitious operations in the city and the imperial compound. They all grew short-tempered from lack of sleep, and Mirtai began to badger Sparhawk about the condition of his wife's health. Ehlana *was,* in fact, beginning to develop dark circles under her eyes and an increasingly waspish disposition.

The breakthrough came about ten days after the departure of the expeditions to Sarna and to the newly occupied lands of the Trolls. Caalador arrived early one morning with a kind of exultant tightness of his face and a large canvas sack in one hand. "It was pure luck, Sparhawk," he chortled when the two met in the royal apartment.

"We're due for some," Sparhawk told him. "What did you find?"

"How would you like to know the exact day and hour when this Hidden City business is going to come to a head?"

"I'd be moderately interested in that, yes. That self-congratulatory expression spread all over your face says that you've found out a few things."

"I have indeed, Sparhawk, and it fell into my hand like an overripe peach." Caalador slid into his drawl. "Them there fellers on t' other side's mighty careless with wrote-down instructions. It seems that this yere cutpurse o' my acquaintance— enterprisin' young feller with a real shorp knife—he slit open the purse o' this yere fat

Dacite merchant, an' a hull fistful o' coins come slitherin' out, an' mixt in with them there silver an' brass coins they wuz this yere message, which it wuz ez hed bin passt onta him by one o' his feller conspiracy-ers." Caalador frowned. "Maybe the right word there would have been *conspirytors*," he mused.

"Ehlana's still in bed, Caalador," Sparhawk told him. "You don't have to entertain *me* with that dialect."

"Sorry. Just keeping in practice. Anyway, the note was quite specific. It said, 'The day of the revelation of the Hidden City is at hand. All is in readiness. We will come to your warehouse for the arms at the second hour past sunset ten days hence.' Isn't that interesting?"

"It is indeed, Caalador, but the note could be a week old."

"No, actually it's not. Would you believe that the idiot who wrote it actually dated it?"

"You're not serious."

"May muh tongue turn green if I ain't."

"Can your cutpurse identify this Dacite merchant? I'd like to locate this warehouse and find out what kind of arms are stored there."

"I'm way ahead of you, Sparhawk." Caalador grinned. "We tracked down the Dacite, and I called on my vast experience as a chicken rustler to get inside his storehouse." He opened the large bag he had brought with him and took out what appeared to be a newly made crossbow. "They wuz several hunnerd o' these in that there hen roost o' his'n," he said, "along with a hull passel o' cheap swords—which wuz most likely forged in Lebros in Cammoria—which it is that's notorious fer makin' shoddy goods fer trade with backward folk."

Sparhawk turned the crossbow over in his hands. "It's not really very well made, is it?" he noted.

"She'll prob'ly shoot, though—oncet anyway."

"This explains that tree Khalad found with all the crossbow bolts stuck in it. It looks as if we've been anticipated. Our friend out there wouldn't really need crossbows unless he knew he was going to come up against men in armor. The longbow's a lot more efficient against ordinary people. It shoots faster."

"I think we'd better face up to something, Sparhawk," Caalador said gravely. "Several hundred crossbows means several hundred conspirators, not counting the ones who'll be using the swords, and that's fair evidence that the conspiracy's going to involve unpleasantness here in Matherion itself as well as out there in the hinterlands. I think we'd better be prepared for a mob—and for fighting in the streets."

"You could very well be right, my friend. Let's see what we can do to defang that mob."

He went to the door and opened it. As usual, Mirtai sat outside with her sword in her lap. "Could you get Khalad for me, Atana?" he asked politely.

"Who's going to guard the door while I'm gone?" she asked him.

"I'll take care of it."

"Why don't *you* go get him? I'll stay here and see to Ehlana's safety."

He sighed. "Please, Mirtai—as a special favor to me."

"If anything happens to Ehlana while I'm gone, you'll answer to me, Sparhawk."

"I'll keep that in mind."

"Pretty girl, isn't she?" Caalador noted after the giantess had gone in search of Sparhawk's squire.

"I wouldn't make a point of noticing that too much when Kring's around, my friend. They're betrothed, and he's the jealous type."

"Should I say that she's ugly, then?"

"That wouldn't really be a good idea either. If you do that, *she'll* probably kill you."

"Touchy, aren't they?"

"Oh, yes—both of them. Theirs promises to be a very lively marriage."

Mirtai returned with Khalad a few minutes later. "You sent for me, my Lord?" Kurik's son asked.

"How would you go about disabling this crossbow without making it obvious that it had been tampered with?" Sparhawk asked, handing the young man the weapon Caalador had brought with him.

Khalad examined the weapon. "Cut the string almost all the way through—up here where it's attached to the end of the bow," he suggested. "It'd break as soon as anyone tried to draw it."

Sparhawk shook his head. "They might load the weapons in advance," he said. "Someone's going to try to use these on us, I think, and I don't want him to find out that they don't work until it's too late."

"I could break the trigger mechanism," Khalad said. "The bowman could draw it and load it, but he couldn't shoot it—at least he couldn't aim it at the same time."

"Would it stay cocked until he tried to shoot it?"

"Probably. This isn't a very well-made crossbow, so he won't expect it to work very well. All you'd have to do is drive out this pin that holds the trigger in place and stick short steel pegs in the holes to hide the fact that the pin's gone. There's a spring that holds the bow drawn, but without the pin to provide leverage, the trigger won't release that spring. They'll be able to draw it, but they won't be able to shoot it."

"I'll take your word for it. How long would it take you to put this thing out of action?"

"A couple of minutes."

"You've got a few long nights ahead of you then, my friend. There are several hundred of these to deal with—and you're going to have to do it quietly and in poor light. Caalador, can you slip my friend here into the Dacite merchant's warehouse?"

"Iffn he kin move around sorta quietlike, I kin."

"I think he can manage. He's a country boy the same as you are, and I'd guess that he's almost as skilled at making rabbit snares and stealing chickens."

"Sparhawk!" Khalad protested.

"Those skills are too valuable to have been left out of your education, Khalad, and I knew your father, remember?"

"They knew we were coming, Sparhawk," Kalten said angrily. "We split up into small groups and stayed away from towns and villages, and they *still* knew we were coming. They ambushed us on the west shore of Lake Sama."

"Trolls?" Sparhawk's voice was tense.

"Worse. It was a large group of rough-looking fellows armed with crossbows. They made the mistake of shooting all at the same time. If they hadn't, none of us would have made it back to tell you about it. They decimated Engessa's mounted Atans, though. He was seriously put out about that. He tore quite a number of the ambushers apart with his bare hands."

A sudden cold fear gripped Sparhawk's stomach. "Where's Tynian?" he asked.

"He's in the care of a physician. He caught a bolt in the shoulder, and it broke some things in there."

"Is he going to be all right?"

"Probably. It didn't improve his temper very much though. He uses his sword almost as well with his left hand as he does with his right. We had to restrain him when the ambushers broke free and ran. He was going to chase them down one by one, and he was bleeding like a stuck pig. I think we've got spies here in this imitation castle, Sparhawk. Those people couldn't have laid that ambush without some fairly specific information about our route and our destination."

"We'll sweep those hiding places again."

"Good idea, and this time let's do a bit more with the ones we catch than reprimand them for bad manners. A spy can't creep through hidden passages very well with two broken legs." The blond Pandion's face was grim. "I get to do the breaking," he added. "I want to be sure that there aren't any miraculous recoveries. A broken shinbone heals in a couple of months, but if you take a sledgehammer to a man's knees, you'll put him out of action for much, much longer."

Bevier, who led the survivors of *his* detachment back into Matherion two days later, took Kalten's suggestion a step further. *His* notion involved amputations at the hip. The devout Cyrinic Knight was *very* angry about being ambushed and he used language Sparhawk had never heard from him before. When he had calmed himself finally, though, he contritely sought absolution from Patriarch Emban. Emban not only forgave him, but granted an indulgence as well—just in case he happened across some new swearwords.

A thorough search of the opalescent castle turned up no hidden listeners, and they all gathered to confer with Emperor Sarabian and Foreign Minister Oscagne the day after Sir Bevier's return. They met high in the central tower, just to be on the safe side, and Sephrenia added a Styric spell to further ensure that their discussions would remain private.

"I'm not accusing anyone," Vanion said, "so don't take this personally. Word of our plans is somehow leaking out, so I think we should all pledge that no hint of what we discuss here should leave this room."

"An oath of silence, Lord Vanion?" Kalten seemed surprised. That Pandion tradition had fallen into disuse in the past century.

"Well," Vanion amended, "something on that order, I suppose, but we're not all Pandion Knights here, you know." He looked around. "All right then, let's summarize the situation. The plot here in Matherion quite obviously goes beyond simple espionage. I think we'd better face up to the probability of an armed insurrection directed at the imperial compound. Our enemy seems to be growing impatient."

"Or fearful," Oscagne added. "The presence of Church Knights—*and* Prince Sparhawk—here in Matherion poses some kind of threat. His campaign of random terror, civil disturbance, and incipient insurrection in the subject kingdoms was working fairly well, but it appears that something's come up that makes that process too slow. He has to strike at the center of imperial authority now."

"And directly at *me,* I gather," Emperor Sarabian added.

"That's unthinkable, your Majesty," Oscagne objected. "In all the history of the empire, no one ever directly confronted the emperor."

"Please, Oscagne," Sarabian said, "don't treat me like an idiot. Any number of my predecessors have met with 'accidents' or fallen fatally ill under peculiar circumstances. Inconvenient emperors *have* been removed before."

"But never right out in the open, your Majesty. That's *terribly* impolite."

Sarabian laughed. "I'm sure that the three government ministers who threw my great-great-grandfather from the top of the highest tower in the compound were all exquisitely courteous about it, Oscagne. We're going to have an armed mob in the streets then? All enthusiastically howling for my blood?"

"I wouldn't discount the possibility, your Majesty," Vanion conceded.

"I hate this," Ulath said sourly.

"Hate what?" Kalten asked him.

"Isn't it obvious? We've got an Elene castle here. It might not be *quite* as good as one that Bevier would have designed, but it's still the strongest building in Matherion. We've got three days until the streets are going to be filled with armed civilians. We don't have much choice. We *have* to pull back inside these walls—fort up until the Atans can restore order. I *detest* sieges."

"I'm sure we won't have to go *that* far, Sir Ulath," Oscagne protested. "As soon as I heard about that message Master Caalador unearthed, I sent word to Norkan in Atana. There are ten thousand Atans massed twenty leagues from here. The conspirators aren't going to move until after dark on the appointed day. I can have the streets awash with seven-foot-tall Atans before noon of that same day. The attempted coup will fail before it ever gets started."

"And miss the chance to round them all up?" Ulath said. "Very poor military thinking, your Excellency. We've got a defensible castle here. Bevier could hold this place for two years at least."

"Five," Bevier corrected. "There's a well inside the walls. That adds three years."

"Even better," Ulath said. "We work on our fortifications here very quietly, and mostly at night. We bring in barrels of pitch and naphtha. Bevier builds siege engines. Then, just before the sun goes down, we move the entire government and the regular Atan garrison inside the castle. The mob will storm the imperial compound and rage through the halls of all these impressive buildings on the grounds. They won't encounter any resistance—until they come here. They'll try to storm our walls, and they'll be overconfident because nobody will have tried to fight them in any of the other buildings. They won't really be expecting a hailstorm of large boulders or sheets of boiling pitch dumped in their faces. Add to that the fact that their crossbows won't work because Khalad's been breaking the triggers in the Dacite warehouse for the last two nights, and you've got a large group of people with a serious problem. They'll mill around out there in confusion and chagrin, and then, probably about midnight, the new detachment of Atans will enter the city, come to the imperial compound, and grind the whole lot of them right into the ground."

"Yes!" Engessa exclaimed enthusiastically.

"It's a brilliant plan, Sir Ulath," Sarabian told the big Thalesian. "Why are you so dissatisfied with it?"

"Because I don't like sieges, your Majesty."

"Ulath," Tynian said, wincing slightly as he shifted his broken shoulder, "don't you think it's time that you abandoned this pose? You're as quick to suggest forting up as any of the rest of us when the situation calls for it."

"Thalesians are *supposed* to hate sieges, Tynian. It's a part of our national character. We're supposed to be impetuous, impatient, and more inclined toward brute force than toward well-considered endurance."

"Sir Ulath," Bevier said, smiling slightly, "King Wargun's father endured a siege at Heid that lasted for seventeen years. He emerged from it none the worse for wear."

"Yes, but he didn't *enjoy* it, Bevier. That's my point."

"I think we're overlooking an opportunity, my friends," Kring noted. "The mob's going to come to the imperial compound, right?"

"If we've guessed their intentions correctly, yes," Tynian agreed.

"*Some* of them are going to be all afire with political fervor—but not really very many, I don't think. Most of them are going to be more interested in looting the various palaces."

Sarabian's face blanched. "Hell and night!" he swore. "I hadn't even thought of that!"

"Don't be too concerned, friend Emperor," the Domi told him. "Whether it's politics or greed that brings them, they'll almost all come into the grounds. The walls around the compound are high and the gates very imposing. Why don't we let them come in—but then make sure they don't leave? I can hide men near the gatehouse. After the mob's on the grounds, we'll close the gates. That should keep them all more or less on hand to greet the Atans when they arrive. The loot will bring them in, and the gates will keep them in. They'll loot, right enough, but loot isn't really yours until you've escaped with it. We'll catch them all this way, and we won't have to dig any of them out of rabbit holes later."

"That's got real possibilities, you know that, Kring?" Kalten said admiringly.

"I'd have expected no less of him," Mirtai said. "He is a brilliant warrior, after all—*and* my betrothed."

Kring beamed.

"One last touch, perhaps," Stragen added. "I think we all have a burning curiosity about certain things, and we've compiled this list of the names of people who might have answers to some of our most urgent questions. Battles are chancy, and sometimes valuable people get killed. I think there are some out there in Matherion who should be removed to safety before the fighting starts."

"Good idea, Milord Stragen," Sarabian agreed. "I'll send out some detachments on the morning of the big day to round up those we'd like to keep alive."

"Ah—perhaps that might not be the best way to go at it, your Majesty. Why not let Caalador attend to it? As a group, policemen tend to be obvious when they arrest people—uniforms, chains, marching in step—that sort of thing. Professional murderers are much more unobtrusive. You don't have to put chains on a man when you arrest him. A dagger point held discreetly to his side is just as effective, I've found."

Sarabian gave him a shrewd look. "You're speaking from experience, I gather?" he speculated.

"Murder is a crime, your Majesty," Stragen pointed out, "and as a leader of criminals, I should have *some* experience in all branches of the field. Professionalism, you understand."

CHAPTER TWENTY-EIGHT

"It was definitely Scarpa, Sparhawk," Caalador assured the big Pandion. "We didn't have to rely entirely on the drawing. One of the local whores is from Arjuna, and she's had business dealings with him in the past. She positively identified him." The two of them were standing atop the castle wall where they could speak privately.

"That seems to be everybody but Baron Parok of Daconia then," Sparhawk noted. "We've seen Krager, Gerrich, Rebal of Edom, this Scarpa from Arjuna, and Elron from Astel."

"I thought the conspirator from Astel was called Sabre," Caalador said.

Sparhawk silently cursed his careless tongue. "Sabre keeps his face hidden," he said. "Elron's a sympathizer—more than that, probably."

Caalador nodded. "I've known some Astels," he agreed, "and some Dacites, too. I wouldn't be positive that Baron Parok's not lurking in the shadows somewhere. They're definitely all gathering here in Matherion." He looked thoughtfully out over the gleaming nacreous battlements at the fosse below. "Is that ditch down there going to be all that much of a barrier?" he asked. "The sides are so gently sloped that there's lawn growing on them."

"It gets more inconvenient when it's filled with sharpened stakes." Sparhawk replied. "We'll do that at the last minute. Has there been any influx of strangers into Matherion? All those assorted patriots have large followings. A mob gathered off the streets is one thing, but a horde drawn from most of Tamuli would be something else entirely."

"We haven't seen an unusual number of strangers here in town," Caalador said, "and there aren't any large gatherings out in the countryside—at least not within five leagues in any direction."

"They could be holding in place farther out," Sparhawk said. "If *I* had a supporting army out there someplace, *I* wouldn't bring them in until the last minute."

Caalador turned and looked pointedly at the harbor. "That's our weakness right there, Sparhawk. There could be a fleet hiding in coves and inlets along the coast. We'd never see them coming until they showed up on the horizon. I've got pirates and smugglers scouring the coasts, but—" He spread his hands.

"There's not very much we can do about it, I'm afraid," Sparhawk said. "We've got an army of Atans close at hand, though, and they'll be inside the city soon after the uprising starts. Do your people have the hiding places of these assorted visitors fairly well pinpointed? If things go well, I'd like to sweep them all up at once if possible."

"They don't seem to have lighted in specific places yet, Sparhawk. They're all moving around quite a bit. I've got people following them. We could pick them up early, if you'd like."

"Let's not expose our preparations. If we can catch them on the day of the uprising, fine. If not, we can chase them down later. I'm not going to endanger our countermeasures just for the pleasure of their company. Your people are doing very well, Caalador."

"Their performance is a bit forced, my friend," Caalador admitted ruefully. "I've had to gather a large number of burly ruffians with clubs to keep reminding the Tamul criminals that we're all working together in this affair."

"Whatever it takes."

"Her Majesty's suggestion has some advantages, Lord Vanion," Bevier said after giving it some thought. "It's what the fosse was designed for originally anyway. It's supposed to be a moat, not just a grassy ditch."

"It completely exposes the fact that we're preparing to defend the castle, Bevier," Vanion objected. "If we start pumping the moat full of water, everybody in Matherion will know about it within the hour."

"You didn't listen to the whole plan, Vanion," Ehlana said patiently. "We've been attending balls and banquets and various other entertainments ever since we arrived here. It's only proper that I respond to all those kindnesses, so I'm planning a grand entertainment to pay my social obligations. It's not my fault that it's going to take place on the night of the uprising, is it? We have an Elene castle, so we'll have an Elene party. We'll have an orchestra on the battlements, colored lanterns and buntings on the walls, and festive barges in the moat—complete with canopies and banquet tables. I'll invite the emperor and his whole court."

"That would be extremely convenient, Lord Vanion," Tynian said. "We'd have everybody we want to protect right close at hand. We wouldn't have to go looking for them, and we wouldn't alert anybody to what we're doing by chasing cabinet ministers across the lawns."

Sparhawk's squire was shaking his head.

"What is it, Khalad?" Ehlana asked him.

"The bottom of the ditch hasn't been prepared to hold water, your Majesty. We don't know how porous the subsoil is. There's a very good chance that the water you pump in will just seep into the ground. Your moat could be empty again a few hours after you fill it."

"Oh, bother!" Ehlana fretted. "I didn't think of that."

"I'll take care of it, Ehlana." Sephrenia smiled. "A good plan shouldn't be abandoned just because it violates a few natural laws."

"Would you have to do that *before* we started to fill the moat, Sephrenia?" Stragen asked her.

"It's easier that way."

He frowned.

"What's the problem?" she asked.

"There are those three tunnels that lead under the fosse to connect with the hidden passageways and listening posts inside the castle."

"Three that we know about, anyway," Ulath added.

"Exactly my point. Wouldn't we all feel more secure if all those tunnels—the ones we know about *and* the ones we don't—are flooded before the fighting starts?"

"Good point," Sparhawk said.

"I can wait to seal the bottom of the moat until after you've flooded the tunnels," Sephrenia told them.

"What do you think, Vanion?" Emban asked.

"The preparations for the queen's party *would* cover a lot of activity," Vanion conceded. "It's a very good plan."

"I like all of it except the barges," Sparhawk said. "I'm sorry, Ehlana, but those barges would just give the mob access to our walls. They'd defeat the whole purpose the moat was designed for in the first place."

"I'm getting to that, Sparhawk. Doesn't naphtha float on top of water?"

"Yes, but what's that got to do with it?"

"A barge isn't just a floating platform, you know. It's got a hold under the deck. Now, suppose we fill the holds with casks of naphtha. Then, when the trouble starts, we throw boulders down from the battlements and crack the barges open like eggshells. The naphtha will spread out over the water in the moat, we set fire to it and surround the castle with a wall of flame. Wouldn't that sort of inconvenience people trying to attack the castle?"

"You're a *genius,* my Queen!" Kalten exclaimed.

"How nice of you to have noticed that, Sir Kalten," she replied smugly. "And the beautiful part about the whole thing is that we can make all of our preparations right out in the open without sneaking around at night and losing all that sleep. This grand party gives us the perfect excuse to do almost anything to the castle in the name of decoration."

Mirtai suddenly embraced her owner and kissed her. "I'm proud of you, my mother," she said.

"I'm glad you approve, my daughter," Ehlana said modestly, "but you really ought to be more reserved, you know. Remember what you told me about girls kissing girls."

"We found two more tunnels, Sparhawk," Khalad reported as his lord joined him on the parapet. Khalad was wearing a canvas smock over his black leather vest.

Sparhawk looked out at the moat where a gang of workmen was driving long steel rods into the soft earth at the bottom of the ditch. "Isn't that a little obvious?" he asked.

"We have to have mooring stakes for the barges, don't we? The tunnels are all about five feet below the surface. Most of the workmen with the sledgehammers don't know what they're really looking for, but I've got a fair number of knights down in the ditch with them. The ceilings of those tunnels will be very leaky when we start to fill the moat." Khalad looked out across the lawn. Then he cupped his hands around his mouth. "Be careful with that barge!" he bellowed in Tamul. "If you spring her seams, she'll leak!"

The foreman of the Tamul work crew laboriously pulling the broad-beamed barge across the lawn on rollers looked up. "It's very heavy, honored sir," he called back. "What have you got inside of it?"

"Ballast, you idiot!" Khalad called back. "There are going to be a lot of people on that deck tomorrow night. If the barge capsizes and the emperor falls in the moat, we'll all be in trouble."

Sparhawk looked inquiringly at his squire.

"We're putting the naphtha casks in the barges inside the construction sheds," Khalad explained. "We decided to do that more or less in private." He looked at his lord. "You don't necessarily have to tell your wife I said this, Sparhawk," he said, "but there were a few gaps in her plan. The naphtha was a good idea—as far as it went, but we've added some pitch as well, just to make sure it catches on fire when we want it to. Naphtha casks are also very tight. They won't do us much good if they just sink to the bottom of the moat when we break open the barges. I'm going to put a couple of Kring's Peloi in the hold of each barge. They'll take axes to the casks at the last minute."

"You think of everything, Khalad."

"Somebody has to be practical in this group."

"Now you sound like your father."

"There is one thing though, Sparhawk. Your partygoers are going to have to be very, very *careful*. There'll be lanterns—and probably candles as well—on those barges. One little accident could start the fire quite a bit sooner than we'd planned, and—ah, actually, we're a bit ahead of schedule, your Highness," he said in Tamul for the benefit of the half-dozen laborers who were pulling a two-wheeled cart along the parapet. The cart was filled with lanterns, which the laborers were hanging from the battlements. "No, no, no!" Khalad chided them. "You can't put two green ones side by side like that. I've told you a thousand times—white, green, red, blue. Do it the way I told you to do it. Be creative on your own time." He sighed exaggeratedly. "It's *so* hard to get good help these days, your Highness," he said.

"You're overacting, Khalad," Sparhawk muttered.

"I know, but I want to be sure they're getting the point."

Kring came along the parapet rubbing his hand over his scarred head. "I need a shave," he said absently, "and Mirtai's too busy to attend to it."

"Is that a Peloi custom, Domi?" Sparhawk asked. "Is it one of the duties of a Peloi woman to shave her man's head?"

"No, actually it's Mirtai's personal idea. It's hard to see the back of your own head, and I used to miss a few places. Shortly after we were betrothed, she took my razor away from me and told me that from now on, *she* was going to do the shaving. She does a very nice job, really—when she isn't too busy." He squared his shoulders. "They absolutely refused, Sparhawk," he reported. "I knew they would, but I put the matter before them the way you asked. They *won't* be locked up inside your fort during the battle. If you stop and think about it, though, we'll be much more useful ranging around the grounds on horseback anyway. A few score mounted Peloi will stir that mob around like a kettle full of boiling soup. If you want confusion out there tomorrow night, we'll give you lots of confusion. A man who's worried about getting a saber across the back of the head isn't going to be able to concentrate on attacking a fort."

"Particularly when his weapon doesn't work," Khalad added.

Sparhawk grunted. "Of course we're assuming that the warehouse full of crossbows Caalador found was the only one," he added.

"I'm afraid we won't find that out until tomorrow night," Khalad conceded. "I disabled about six hundred of those things. If twelve hundred crossbowmen come onto the palace grounds we'll know that half of their weapons are going to work. We'll have to take cover at that point. You there!" he shouted suddenly, looking upward. "*Drape* that bunting! Don't stretch it tight that way!" He shook his fist at the workman leaning precariously out of a window high up in one of the towers.

Although he was obviously quite young, the scholar Bevier escorted into Ehlana's presence was almost totally bald. He was very nervous, but his eyes had that burning glaze to them that announced him to be a fanatic. He prostrated himself before Ehlana's thronelike chair and banged his forehead on the floor.

"Don't do that, man," Ulath rumbled at him. "It offends the queen. Besides, you'll crack the floor tiles."

The scholar scrambled to his feet, his eyes fearful.

"This is Emuda," Bevier introduced him. "He's the scholar I told you about—the one with the interesting theory about Scarpa of Arjuna."

"Oh, yes," Ehlana said in Tamul. "Welcome, Master Emuda. Sir Bevier has spoken highly of you." Actually, Bevier had not, but a queen is allowed to take certain liberties with the truth.

Emuda gave her a fawning sort of look. Sparhawk moved in quickly to cut off a lengthy, rambling preamble. "Correct me if I'm wrong about this, Master Emuda," he said, "but our understanding of your theory is that you think that Scarpa's behind all these disturbances in Tamuli."

"That's a slight oversimplification, Sir—?" Emuda looked inquiringly at the tall Pandion Knight.

"Sparhawk," Ulath supplied.

Emuda's face went white, and he began to tremble violently.

"I'm a simple sort of man, neighbor," Sparhawk told him. "Please don't confuse me with complications. What sort of evidence do you have that lays everything at Scarpa's door?"

"It's quite involved, Sir Sparhawk," Emuda apologized.

"Uninvolve it. Summarize, man. I'm busy."

Emuda swallowed very hard. "Well—uh—" he faltered. "We know—that is, we're fairly certain—that Scarpa was the first of the spokesmen for these so-called 'heroes from the past.' "

"Why do you say 'so-called,' Master Emuda?" Tynian asked him. Sir Tynian still had his right arm in a sling.

"Isn't it obvious, Sir Knight?" Emuda's tone was just slightly condescending. "The notion of resurrecting the dead is an absurdity. It's all quite obviously a hoax. Some henchman is dressed in ancient clothing, appears in a flash of light—which any country-fair charlatan can contrive—and then starts babbling gibberish, which the 'spokesman' identifies as an ancient language. Yes, it's clearly a hoax."

"How clever of you to have unmasked it," Sephrenia murmured. "We all thought it was magic of some kind."

"There's no such thing as magic, madam."

"Really?" she replied mildly. "What an amazing thing."

"I'd stake my reputation on that."

"How courageous of you."

"You say that Scarpa was the first of these revolutionaries to appear?" Vanion asked him.

"By more than a year, Sir Knight. The first reports of his activities began to appear in diplomatic dispatches from the capital at Arjuna just over four years ago. The next to emerge was Baron Parok of Daconia, and I have a sworn statement from a ship captain that Scarpa sailed from Kaftal in southwestern Arjuna to Ahar in Daconia. Ahar is Baron Parok's home, and he began *his* activities about three years ago. The connection is obvious."

"It *would* seem so, wouldn't it?" Sparhawk mused.

"From Ahar I have documented evidence of the travels of the two. Parok went into Edom, where he actually stayed in the hometown of Rebal—that connection gave me a bit of trouble, since Rebal isn't using his real name. We've identified his home district, though, and the town Parok visited is the district capital. I think I'm safe in assuming that a meeting took place during Parok's visit. While Parok was in Edom, Scarpa travelled all the way up into Astel. I can't exactly pinpoint his travels there, but I know he moved around quite a bit just to the north of the marches on the Edomish-Astellian border, and that's the region where Sabre makes his headquarters. The disturbances in Edom and Astel began some time after Scarpa and Parok had journeyed into those kingdoms. The evidence of connection among the four men is all very conclusive."

"What about these reports of supernatural events?" Tynian asked.

"More hoaxes, Sir Knight." Emuda's expression was offensively superior. "Pure charlatanism. You may have noticed that they always occur out in the countryside where the only witnesses are superstitious peasants and ignorant serfs. Civilized people would not be fooled by such obvious trickery."

"I wondered about that," Sparhawk said. "Are you sure about this timetable of yours? Scarpa was the first to start stirring things up?"

"Definitely, Sir Sparhawk."

"Then he contacted the others and enlisted them? Perhaps a year and a half later?"

Emuda nodded.

"Where did he go when he left Astel after recruiting Sabre?"

"I've lost track of him for a time there, Sir Sparhawk. He went into the Elene kingdoms of western Tamuli about two and a half years ago and didn't return to Arjuna until eight or ten months later. I have no idea of where he was during that interim. Oh, one other thing. The so-called vampires began to appear in Arjuna at almost precisely the same time that Scarpa began telling the Arjuni that he'd been in contact with Sheguan, their national hero. The traditional monsters of the other kingdoms also put in *their* appearance at the same time these other revolutionaries began *their* campaigns. Believe me, your Majesty," he said earnestly to Ehlana, "if you're looking for a ringleader, Scarpa's your man."

"We thank you for this information, Master Emuda," she said sweetly. "Would you please provide Sir Bevier with your supporting data and describe your findings to him in greater detail? Pressing affairs necessarily limit the time we can spend with you, fascinating though we find your conclusions."

"I shall be happy to share the entire body of my research with Sir Bevier, your Majesty."

Bevier rolled his eyes ceilingward and sighed.

They watched the enthusiast lead poor Bevier from the room.

"I'd hate to have to take *that* case into any court—civil *or* ecclesiastical." Emban snorted.

"It *is* a bit thin, isn't it?" Stragen agreed.

"The only thing that makes me pay any attention to him at all is that timetable of his," Sparhawk said. "Dolmant sent me to Lamorkand late last winter to look into the activities of Count Gerrich. While I was there, I heard all the wild stories about Drychtnath. It seems that our prehistoric Lamork started making appearances at a time that coincides almost exactly with the period when our scholarly friend lost track of Scarpa. Emuda's such a complete ass that I sort of hate to admit it, but he may just have hit upon the right answer."

"But it's for all the wrong reasons, Sparhawk," Emban objected.

"I'm only interested in his answers, your Grace," Sparhawk replied. "As long as they're the right answers, I don't care *how* he got them."

"It's just too risky to do it any earlier, Sparhawk," Stragen said later that day.

"You two are taking a lot of chances," Sparhawk objected.

"It's a hull lot more chancy t' stort out earlier, Sporhawk," Caalador drawled.

"Iffn we wuz t' grab th' leaders sooner, them ez is left could jist call it all off, an' all these traps o' ourn wouldn't ketch no rabbits. We gotta wait till they open that warehouse an' stort passin' out them there weepons."

Sparhawk winced. "Weepons?"

"The word wouldn't appear in that particular dialect." Caalador shrugged. "I had to countrify it up—just for the sake of consistency."

"You switch back and forth like a frog on a hot rock, my friend."

"I know. Infuriating, isn't it? It goes like this, Sparhawk. If we pick up the conspirators anytime before they start arming the mob, they'll be able to suspend operations and go to ground. They'll wait, reorganize, and then pick another day—which it is that we won't know nuthin' about. On the other hand, once they pass out the weapons, it'll be too late. There'll be thousands in the streets—most of them about half-drunk. Our friends in the upper councils could no more stop them than stop the tide. The sheer momentum of this attempted coup will be working for *us* instead of for our shadowy friends."

"They can still go to ground and just feed the mob to the wolves, you know."

Caalador shook his head. "Tamul justice is a bit abrupt, and an attack on the emperor is going to be viewed as the worst sort of bad manners. Several hundred people are going to be sent to the headsman's block. Recruitment after that will be virtually impossible. They have no choice. Once they start, they *have* to follow through."

"You're talking about some very delicate timing, you know."

"Aw, that's easy tuk care of, Sporhawk." Caalador grinned. "There's this yere temple right smack dab in the middle o' town. It's more 'n likely all fulla cobwebs an' dust, on accounta our little yaller brothers don't take ther religion none too serious like. There's these yere priests ez sits around in there, drinkin' an' carousin' an' sich. When they gits therselves all beered-up an' boistrous like, they usual decides t' hold services. They got this yere bell, which it is ez must weigh along 'bout twenty ton er so. One o' them there drunk priests, he wobbles over t' that there bell an' he takes up this yere sledgehammer an' he whacks the bell a couple licks with it. Makes the awfullest sound you ever *did* hear. Sailors bin known t' hear it 'bout ten leagues out t' sea. Now, there ain't no special time set fer when they goes t' whackin' on that there bell. Folks here in Matherion don't pay no attention t' it, figgerin' that it's jist the priests enjoyin' therselves. That's the beauty of it, Sparhawk," he said, lapsing into normal speech. "The sound of that bell is random, and nobody takes any special note of it. Tomorrow night, though, it's going to be profoundly significant. As soon as that warehouse opens, the bell's going to peal out its message of hope and joy. The murderers sitting almost in the laps of the people we want to talk with will take that as their order to move. We'll have the whole lot rounded up in under a minute."

"What if they try to resist?"

"Oh, there'll be some losses." Caalador shrugged. "You can't make an omelette without breaking eggs. There are several dozen people we want to pick up, so we can afford to lose a few."

"The sound of the bell will *also* alert *you,* Sparhawk," Stragen pointed out.

"When you hear it start ringing, you'll know that it's time to move your wife's party inside."

"But you can't *do* this, your Majesty!" the Minister of the Interior protested shrilly the next morning as tons of water began to gush into the moat from the throats of the huge pipes strewn across the lawn of the imperial compound.

"Oh?" Ehlana asked innocently. "And why is that, Minister Kolata?"

"Uh—well—uh—there's no subfoundation under the moat, your Majesty. The water will just sink into the ground."

"Oh, that's all right, Minister Kolata. It's only for one night. I'm sure the moat will stay full enough until after the party."

Kolata stared with chagrin at a sudden fountainlike eruption of air and muddy water out in the center of the moat.

"My goodness," Ehlana said mildly, looking at the sudden whirlpool funnelling down where the eruption had taken place. "There must have been an old abandoned cellar under there." She laughed a silvery little laugh. "I'd imagine that the rats who lived in there were very surprised, wouldn't you agree, your Excellency?"

Kolata looked a bit sick. "Uh—would you excuse me, your Majesty?" he said, and he turned to hurry across the lawn without waiting for a reply.

"Don't let him get away, Sparhawk," Ehlana said coolly. "I strongly suspect that Lord Vanion's list wasn't as complete as we might have hoped. Why don't you invite the Minister of the Interior into the castle so that you can show him our other preparations?" She tapped one finger thoughtfully against her chin. "And you might ask Sir Kalten and Sir Ulath to join you when you get around to showing his Excellency the torture chamber. Emperor Sarabian's excellent Minister of the Interior might want to add a few names to Vanion's list."

It was the cool and unruffled way she said it that chilled Sparhawk's blood the most.

"He's beginning to feel more than a little offended, Sparhawk," Vanion said soberly as the two of them watched Khalad's workmen "decorating" the vast gates of the imperial compound. "He's not stupid, and he knows that we're not telling him everything."

"It can't be helped, Vanion. He's just too erratic to be let in on all the details."

"Mercurial might be a more diplomatic term."

"Whatever. We don't really know him all that well, Vanion, and we're operating in an alien society. For all we know, he keeps a diary and writes everything down. That could be a Tamul custom. It's entirely possible that our whole plan could be available to the chambermaid who makes up his bed every morning."

"You're speculating, Sparhawk."

"Those ambushes out in the countryside weren't speculation."

"Surely you don't suspect the emperor."

"*Somebody* passed the word of our expeditions along to our enemy, Vanion. We can apologize to the emperor *after* this evening's entertainment is concluded."

"Oh, that's just *too* obvious, Sparhawk!" Vanion burst out, pointing at the heavy steel lattice Khalad's workmen were installing on the inside of the gates.

"It won't be visible when they open the gates all the way, Vanion, and Khalad's going to hang bunting on the lattice to conceal it. Did Sephrenia have any luck when she tried to contact Zalasta?"

"No. He must still be too far away."

"I'd be a lot more comfortable if he were here. If the Troll-Gods put in an appearance tonight, we could be in very serious trouble."

"Aphrael can deal with them."

"Not without revealing her true identity, she can't, and if that comes out, my wife's going to find out some things I'd rather she didn't know. I'm not so fond of Sarabian that I'm willing to risk Ehlana's sanity just to keep him on his throne."

The sun crept slowly down the western sky, moving closer and closer to the horizon. Although he knew it to be an absurdity, it seemed to Sparhawk that the blazing orb was plummeting to earth like a shooting star. There were so many details—so many things that had yet to be done. Worse yet, many of those tasks could not even be commenced until after the sun went down and gathering darkness concealed them from the hundreds of eyes that were certainly out there watching.

It was early evening when Kalten finally came to the royal apartment to announce that they had gone as far as they could go until after dark. Sparhawk was relieved to know that at least *that* much had been completed on time.

"Was the Minister of the Interior at all forthcoming?" Ehlana asked from her chair near the window where Alean and Melidere were involved in the extended process known as "doing her hair."

"Oh, yes, your Majesty," Kalten replied with a broad grin. "He seems even more eager to talk than your cousin Lycheas was. Ulath can be very persuasive at times. Kolata seemed to be particularly upset by the leeches."

"Leeches?"

Kalten nodded. "It was right after Ulath offered to stuff him head down into a barrel full of leeches that Kolata developed this burning desire to share things with us."

"Dear God!" The queen shuddered.

It was the general opinion of all the guests present that evening that the Queen of Elenia's party was absolutely *the* crowning event of the season. The lanterns illuminating the mother-of-pearl battlements were spectacular, the gay buntings—several thousand yards of *very* expensive silk—were festive, and the orchestra on the battlements, playing traditional Elene airs rather than the discordant cacophony that passed for music in Sarabian's court, lent a pleasantly archaic quality to the entire occasion. It was the barges moored in the moat, however, that drew the most astonished comment. The idea of dining out of doors had never occurred to the

Tamuls, and the notion of floating dining rooms ablaze with candlelight and draped with brightly colored silk bunting was quite beyond the imagination of the average member of the emperor's court.

The candles caused the knights no end of concern. The thought of open flame so close to the hidden cargo of the barges was sufficient to make strong men turn pale.

Since the party was taking place around the Elene castle, and the hostess was herself an Elene, the ladies of the emperor's court had quite nearly exhausted the creative talents of every dressmaker in Matherion in their efforts to "dress Elene." The results were not uniformly felicitous, however, since the dressmakers of Matherion were obliged to rely on books for inspiration, and many of the books in the library of the university were several hundred years old and the gowns depicted on their pages were terribly out of fashion.

Ehlana and Melidere *were* in fashion, however, and they were the absolute center of attention. Ehlana's gown was a regal blue, and she wore a diamond and ruby-studded tiara nestled in her pale blond hair. Melidere was gowned in lavender. It seemed to be her favorite color. Mirtai was defiantly not in fashion. She wore the blue sleeveless gown she had worn at her owner's wedding, and *this* time, she *was* visibly armed. Rather surprisingly, Sephrenia also wore an Elene gown—of snowy white, naturally—and Vanion was obviously smitten by her all over again. The knights of the queen's escort wore doublets and hose, much against Sparhawk's better judgment. Their armor, however, was close at hand.

After the members of the imperial court had made their appearance and had begun to circulate on the barges, there was a pause, and then a brazen Elene fanfare. "I had to offer violence to the musicians to get them to greet the emperor properly," the elegantly garbed Stragen muttered to Sparhawk.

"Oh?"

"They were very insistent that the emperor should be greeted by that dreadful noise they call music around here. They became much more cooperative after I sliced the smock off one of the trumpeters with my rapier." Stragen's eyes suddenly widened. "For God's sake, man!" he hissed at a servant placing a large platter of steaming beef on one of the tables, "be careful of those candles!"

"He's a Tamul, Stragen," Sparhawk pointed out when the servant gave the Thalesian a blank stare. "You're trying to talk to him in Elenic."

"Make him be careful, Sparhawk! A single tongue of fire in the wrong place on any of these barges could broil us all alive!"

Then the emperor and his nine wives appeared on the drawbridge and came down the carpeted steps to the first barge.

Everyone bowed to the emperor, but no one looked at him. All eyes were locked on the radiantly smiling Empress Elysoun of Valesia. She had modified the customary Elene costume to accommodate her cultural tastes. Her scarlet gown was really quite lovely, but it had been altered so that those attributes Elene ladies customarily concealed and Valesian ladies flaunted were nestled on two frilly cushions of snowy lace and were thus entirely, even aggressively, in full view.

"Now *that* is what you might call a fashion statement," Stragen murmured.

"That it is, my friend." Sparhawk chuckled, adjusting the collar of his black velvet doublet. "And everybody's listening to her. Poor Emban appears to be quite nearly on the verge of apoplexy."

In a kind of formal little ceremony, Queen Ehlana escorted Sarabian and his empresses across the bridges that stepped from barge to barge. The Empress Elysoun was obviously looking for someone, and when she saw Berit standing off to one side on the second barge, she altered course and bore down upon him with all sails set—figuratively speaking, of course. Sir Berit looked at first apprehensive, then desperate, as Elysoun more or less pinned him to the rail of the barge without so much as laying a hand on him.

"Poor Berit," Sparhawk said sympathetically. "Stay close to him, Stragen. I don't know for sure if he can swim. Be ready to rescue him if he jumps into the moat."

After the emperor had been given the grand tour, the banquet began. Sparhawk had judiciously spaced the knights among the diners. The knights were not really very interesting dinner companions, since they all concentrated almost exclusively on the candles and the lanterns. "God help us if a wind comes up," Kalten muttered to Sparhawk.

"Truly," Sparhawk agreed fervently. "Ah—Kalten, old friend."

"Yes?"

"You're supposed to be keeping an eye on the candles, not the front of the Empress Elysoun's gown."

"What front?"

"Don't be vulgar, and remember what you're supposed to be doing here."

"How are we going to herd this flock of overdressed sheep inside when that bell rings?" Kalten shifted uncomfortably. His green satin doublet was buttoned very tightly across his stomach.

"If we've timed it right, the feasters will be finishing up the main course at just about the same time as our friends out in the city start distributing the weapons. When that bell rings, Ehlana's going to invite all the revelers into the castle for the dessert course."

"Very clever, Sparhawk," Kalten said admiringly.

"Go congratulate my wife, Kalten. It was her idea."

"She's really awfully good at this sort of thing, you know that? I'm glad she decided to come along."

"I'm still of two minds about that." Sparhawk grunted.

The feast went on, and there were toasts by the dozen. The feasters heaped praise upon the Queen of Elenia. Since the revellers were totally unaware of the impending climax of the evening, there were many inadvertent ironies in the compliments.

Sparhawk scarcely tasted his dinner as he picked at his food, his eyes constantly on the candles and his ears alert for the first sound of the bell that would announce that his enemies were on the move.

Kalten's appetite, however, seemed unaffected by the impending crisis.

"How can you stuff yourself that way?" Sparhawk asked his friend irritably.

"Just keeping up my strength, Sparhawk. I'm likely to burn up a lot of energy before the night's out. If you're not busy, old boy, would you mind passing that gravy down this way?"

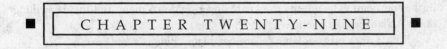

Then from somewhere near the center of the gleaming, moon-drenched city of Matherion, a deep-toned bell began to boom, announcing that the second half of the evening's entertainment had begun.

CHAPTER TWENTY-NINE

"Why didn't you *tell* me, Ehlana?" Sarabian demanded. The emperor's face was livid with suppressed fury, and his heavy gold crown was slightly askew.

"Please calm yourself, Sarabian," the blond queen suggested. "We didn't find out until midmorning today, and there was no possible way to get the information to you without taking the chance of compromising it."

"Your snake-hipped baroness could have carried a message to me," he accused, smacking his palm down on the battlement. They were on the parapet, ostensibly admiring the view.

"My fault there, your Majesty," Sparhawk apologized. "I'm more or less in charge of security, and Minister Kolata's the man who controls the police in Tamuli— both the overt police and the ones who hide in the bushes. There was no way we could be absolutely sure that our subterfuge involving the baroness had been successful. The information that we had discovered the minister's involvement was just too sensitive to risk. This attempt on your government tonight *has* to go off as planned. If our enemy gets the slightest hint that we know what he's up to, he'll postpone things until another day—and we won't have any idea of which day it's going to be."

"I'm still very put out with you, Sparhawk," Sarabian complained. "I can't fault your reasoning, but you've definitely bruised my feelings."

"We're supposed to be watching the play of lights on the waters of the moat, Sarabian," Ehlana reminded the emperor. "Please at least glance over the battlements once in a while." Their position on the parapet gave them privacy *and* a good vantage point from which to watch for the approach of the mob.

"The news about Kolata's involvement in this business is really distressing," Sarabian fretted. "He controls the police, palace security, and all the spies inside the empire. Worse than that, he has a certain amount of authority over the Atans. If we lose them, we're in very serious trouble."

"Engessa's trying to sever that connection, your Majesty," Sparhawk told him. "He sent runners to the Atan forces outside the city to advise the commanders that the agents of the Ministry of the Interior aren't to be trusted. The commanders will pass that on to Androl and Betuana."

"Are we safe here in the event that Atan Engessa's runners are intercepted?"

"Sir Bevier assures us that he can hold this castle for five years, Sarabian," Ehlana told him, "and Bevier's the expert on sieges."

"And when the five years run out?"

"The Church Knights will be here long before then, your Majesty," Sparhawk assured him. "Caalador has his instructions. If things go awry, he'll get word to Dolmant in Chyrellos."

"You people are still making me very, very nervous."

"Trust me, your Majesty," Sparhawk said.

Kalten came puffing up the stairs to the parapet. "We're going to need more wine, Sparhawk," he said. "I think we made a mistake when we set those wine casks in the courtyard. The queen's guests are lingering down there, and they're swilling down Arcian red like water."

"May I draw on your wine cellars, Sarabian?" Ehlana asked sweetly.

Sarabian winced. "Why are you pouring all that drink into them?" he demanded. "Arcian red's very expensive here in Matherion."

"Drunk people are easier to manage than sober ones, your Majesty." Kalten shrugged. "We'll let them continue to carouse down there in the courtyard and inside the castle until the fighting starts. Then we'll push the stragglers inside the castle with the others and keep them drinking. When they wake up tomorrow morning, most of them won't even know there's been a battle."

The party in the courtyard was growing noisier. Tamul wines were not nearly as robust as Elene vintages, and the wits of the revellers had become fuddled. They laughed a great deal and walked about the yard unsteadily with silly grins on their faces. Queen Ehlana looked critically down from the parapet. "How much longer would you say it's going to take them to be totally incapacitated, Sparhawk?" she asked.

"Not much longer." He shrugged. He turned and looked out toward the city. "I don't want to seem critical, Emperor Sarabian, but I have to point out that your citizenry is profoundly unimaginative. Your rebels out there are carrying torches."

"So?"

"It's a cliché, your Majesty. The mob in every bad Arcian romance ever written carries torches. Even I know that."

"How can you be so cool, man?" Sarabian demanded. "If someone made a loud noise behind me right now, I'd jump out of my skin."

"Professional training, I guess. I'm more concerned that they might *not* reach the imperial compound than that they *will*. We *want* them to come here, your Majesty."

"Shouldn't you raise the drawbridge?"

"Not yet. There are conspirators here in the compound as well as out there in the streets. We don't want to give away the fact that we know they're coming."

Khalad thrust his head out of the turret at the corner of the battlements and beckoned to his lord.

"Will you excuse me, your Majesties?" Sparhawk asked politely. "I have to go put on my work clothes. Oh, Ehlana, why don't you signal Kalten that it's time to push those stragglers inside and lock them in the dining hall with the others?"

"What's this?" Sarabian asked.

"We don't want them underfoot when the fighting starts, Sarabian." The queen smiled. "The wine should keep them from noticing that they're locked in the dining room."

"You Elenes are the most cold-blooded people in the world," Sarabian accused as Sparhawk moved off down the parapet toward the turret where Khalad was waiting with the suit of black armor.

When he returned about ten minutes later, he was dressed in steel. He found Ehlana talking earnestly with Sarabian. "Can't you talk with her?" she was saying. "The poor young man's on the verge of hysteria."

"Why doesn't he just do what she wants him to? Once they've entertained each other, she'll lose interest."

"Sir Berit's a very young knight, Sarabian. His ideals haven't been tarnished yet. Why doesn't she chase after Sir Kalten or Sir Ulath? They'd be happy to oblige her."

"Sir Berit's a challenge to Elysoun, Ehlana. Nobody's ever turned her down before."

"Doesn't her rampant infidelity bother you?"

"Not in the slightest. It doesn't really mean anything in her culture, you see. Her people look upon it as a pleasant but unimportant pastime. I sometimes think you Elenes place far too much significance on it."

"Can't you make her put some clothes on?"

"Why? She's not ashamed of her body, and she enjoys sharing it with people. Be honest, Ehlana, don't you find her quite attractive?"

"I think you'd have to ask my husband about that."

"You don't *really* expect me to answer that kind of question, do you?" Sparhawk said. He looked over the battlements. "Our friends out there seem to have found their way to the palace compound," he noted as the torch-bearing rioters began to stream through the gate onto the grounds.

"The guards are supposed to stop them," Sarabian said angrily.

"The guards are taking their orders from Minister Kolata, I expect." Ehlana shrugged.

"Where's the Atan garrison, then?"

"We've moved them inside the castle here, your Majesty," Sparhawk advised him. "I think you keep overlooking the fact that we *want* those people on the grounds. It wouldn't make much sense to impede their progress."

"Isn't it about time to raise the drawbridge?" Sarabian seemed nervous about that.

"Not yet, your Majesty," Sparhawk replied coolly. "We want them *all* to be inside the compound first. At that point, Kring will close the gates. *Then* we'll raise the drawbridge. Let them take the bait before we spring the trap on them."

"You sound awfully sure of yourself, Sparhawk."

"We have all the advantages, your Majesty."

"Does that mean that nothing can possibly go wrong?"

"No, something can always go wrong, but the probabilities are remote."

"You don't mind if I worry a little bit anyway, do you?"

"Go right ahead, your Majesty."

The mob from the streets of Matherion continued to stream unimpeded through the main gate of the imperial grounds and fanned out rapidly, shouting excitedly as they crashed their way into the various palaces and administration buildings. As Kring had anticipated, many emerged from the gleaming buildings burdened down with assorted valuables they had looted from the interiors.

There was a brief flurry of activity in front of the castle when one group of looters reached the drawbridge and encountered a score of mounted knights under the command of Sir Ulath. The knights were there to provide cover for the Peloi who had been hidden in the holds of the barges during the earlier festivities and who had fallen to work on the naphtha casks with their axes as soon as the revellers had retired to the castle yard. A certain amount of glistening seepage from the sides of the barges indicated that the axemen crossing the decks of the festive vessels in the moat toward the drawbridge had done their work well. When the mob reached the outer end of the drawbridge, Ulath made it abundantly clear to them that he was in no mood to receive callers. The survivors decided to find other places to loot.

The courtyard had been cleared, and Bevier and his men were moving their catapults into place on the parapet. Engessa's Atans had moved up onto the parapets with the Cyrinics and were crouched down out of sight behind the battlements. Sparhawk looked around. Everything seemed in readiness. Then he looked at the gates of the compound. The only revolutionaries coming in now were the lame and the halt. They crutched their way along vigorously, but they had lagged far behind their companions. Sparhawk leaned out over the battlements. "We might as well get started, Ulath," he called down to his friend. "Why don't you ask Kring to close the gates? Then you should probably come inside."

"Right!" Ulath's face was split with a broad grin. He lifted his curled Ogre-horn to his lips and blew a hollow-sounding blast. Then he turned and led his knights back across the drawbridge into the castle.

The huge gate at the entrance to the palace grounds moved ponderously, slowly, swinging shut with a dreadful kind of inexorability. Sparhawk noted that several of those still outside stumped along desperately on their crutches, trying for all they were worth to get inside before the gate closed. "Kalten," he yelled down into the courtyard.

"What?" Kalten's tone was irritable.

"Would you like to let those people out there know that we're not receiving any more visitors tonight?"

"Oh, all right. I *suppose* so." Then the blond Pandion grinned up at his fellow knight as he and his men began turning the capstan that raised the drawbridge.

"Clown," Sparhawk muttered.

The significance of the simultaneous closing of the gate and raising of the drawbridge did not filter through the collective mind of the mob for quite some time. Then sounds of shouted commands and even occasional clashes of weapons from nearby buildings announced that at least *some* of the rebels were beginning, however faintly, to see the light.

Tentatively, warily, the torch-bearing mob began to converge on the pristinely white Elene castle, where the gaily colored silk buntings shivered tremulously in the night breeze and the lantern- and candle-lit barges bobbed sedately in the moat.

"Hello the castle!" a bull-voiced fellow in the front rank roared in execrable Elenic. "Lower your drawbridge, or we'll storm your walls!"

"Would you please reply to that, Bevier?" Sparhawk called to his Cyrinic friend.

Bevier grinned and carefully shifted one of his catapults. He sighted carefully, elevated his line of sight so that the catapult was pointed almost straight up, and then he applied the torch to the mixture of pitch and naphtha in the spoonlike receptacle at the end of the catapult arm. The mixture took fire immediately.

"I command you to lower your drawbridge!" the unshaven knave out beyond the moat bellowed arrogantly.

Bevier cut the retaining rope on the catapult arm. The blob of dripping fire sizzled as it shot almost straight up into the air, then it slowed and seemed to hang motionless for a moment. Then it fell.

The ruffian who had been demanding admittance gaped at Bevier's reply as it majestically rose into the night sky and then fell directly upon him like a comet. He vanished as he was engulfed in fire.

"Good shot!" Sparhawk called his compliment.

"Not bad," Bevier replied modestly. "It was sort of tricky, because he was so close."

"I noticed that."

Emperor Sarabian had gone very pale and he was visibly shaken. "Did you *have* to do that, Sparhawk?" he demanded in a choked voice as the now frightened mob fled back across the lawns to positions that may or may not have been out of Sir Bevier's range.

"Yes, your Majesty," Sparhawk replied calmly. "We're playing for time here. The bell that started to ring an hour or so ago was a sort of general signal. Caalador's cutthroats took the ringleaders into custody when it rang, Ehlana moved the partygoers inside the castle, and the Atan legions outside the city started to march as soon as they heard it. That loudmouth who's presently on fire at the edge of the moat is graphic demonstration of just how truly unpleasant things are going to get if the mob decides to insist on being admitted. It's going to take some serious encouragement to persuade them to approach us again."

"I thought you said you could hold them off."

"We can, but why risk lives if you don't have to? You'll note that there was no cheering or shouts when Bevier shot his catapult. Those people out there are staring at an absolutely silent, apparently unmanned castle that almost negligently obliterates offensive people. That's a terrifying sort of thing to contemplate. This is the part of the siege that frequently lasts for several years." Sparhawk looked down the parapet. "I think it's time for us to move inside that turret, your Majesties," he suggested. "We can't be positive that Khalad disabled *all* the crossbows—or that somebody in the mob hasn't repaired a few. I'd have a great deal of trouble explaining why I was careless enough to let one of you get killed. We can see what's going on from the turret, and I'll feel much better if you've both got nice thick stone walls around you."

"Shouldn't we rupture those barges now, dear?" Ehlana asked him.

"Not just yet. We've got the potential for inflicting a real disaster on the besiegers there. Let's not waste it."

· · ·

Some few of the crossbows in the hands of the mob functioned properly, but not very many. There seemed to be a great deal of swearing about that.

A serious attempt to reopen the gates of the compound fell apart when the Peloi, their sabers flashing and their shrill, ululating war cries echoing back from the walls of nearby opalescent palaces, charged across the neatly clipped lawns to savage the crowd clustered around the gate.

Then, because once the Peloi had been unleashed they were very hard to rein in again, the tribesmen from the marches of eastern Pelosia sliced back and forth through the huddled mass cowering on the grass. The palace guards who had joined the mob made some slight effort to respond, but the Peloi horsemen gleefully rode them down.

Sephrenia and Vanion entered the turret. The small Styric woman's white gown gleamed in the shaft of moonlight streaming in through the door. "What are you thinking of, Sparhawk?" she demanded angrily. "This isn't a safe place for Ehlana and Sarabian."

"I think it's as safe as I can manage, little mother. Ehlana, what would you say if I told you that you had to go inside?"

"I'd say no, Sparhawk. I'd crawl out of my skin if you locked me up in some safe room where I couldn't see what's going on."

"I sort of thought you might feel that way. And you, Emperor Sarabian?"

"Your wife just nailed my feet to the floor, Sparhawk. How could I possibly run off and hide while she's standing up here on the wall like the figurehead on a warship?" The emperor looked at Sephrenia. "Is this insane foolhardiness a racial characteristic of these barbarians?" he asked her.

She sighed. "You wouldn't *believe* some of the things they're capable of, Sarabian," she replied, throwing a quick smile at Vanion.

"At least *someone* in that mob's still thinking coherently, Sparhawk," Vanion said to his friend. "He's just realized that there are all sorts of unpleasant implications in the fact that they can't get in here or out of the compound. He's out there trying to whip them up by telling them that they're doomed unless they take this castle."

"I hope he's *also* telling them that they're doomed if they try," Sparhawk replied.

"I'd imagine that he's glossing over that part. I had some misgivings about you when you were a novice, my friend. You and Kalten seemed like a couple of wild colts, but now that you've settled down, you're really quite good. Your strategy here has been brilliant, you know. You actually haven't embarrassed me too much this time."

"Thanks, Vanion," Sparhawk said dryly.

"No charge."

The rebels approached the moat tentatively, their faces filled with apprehension and their eyes fixed on the night sky, desperately searching for that first flicker of fire that would announce that Sir Bevier was sending them greetings. The chance passage of a shooting star across the velvet throat of night elicited screams of fright, followed by a vast nervous laugh.

The gleaming, brightly lighted castle, however, remained silent. No soldiers lined the battlements. No globs of liquid fire sprang into the night sky from within those nacreous walls.

The defenders crouched silently behind the battlements and waited.

"Good," Vanion muttered after a quick glance out of one of the embrasures in the turret. "Someone saw the potential of those barges. They've clapped together some scaling ladders."

"We *have* to rupture those barges now, Vanion!" Ehlana exclaimed urgently.

"You didn't tell her?" Vanion asked Sparhawk.

"No. The concept might have been difficult for her to accept."

"You'd better take her back inside the castle then, my friend. What's going to happen next is likely to upset her a great deal."

"*Will* you two stop talking about me as if I weren't even here?" Ehlana burst out in exasperation. "What are you going to do?"

"You'd better tell her," Vanion said bleakly.

"We can start that fire at any time, Ehlana," Sparhawk said as gently as he could. "In a situation like this, fire's a weapon. It's not tactically practical to waste it by setting it off before your enemies are around to receive its benefits."

She stared at him, the blood draining from her face. "This wasn't what I'd planned, Sparhawk!" she said vehemently. "The fire's supposed to keep them away from the moat. I didn't want you to burn them alive with it."

"I'm sorry, Ehlana. It's a military decision. A weapon's useless unless you demonstrate your willingness to employ it. I know it's hard to accept, but if we take your plan to its ultimate application, it may save lives in the long run. We're outnumbered here in Tamuli, and if we don't establish a certain reputation for ruthlessness, we'll be overrun the next time there's a confrontation."

"You're a monster!"

"No, dear. I'm a soldier."

She suddenly started to cry.

"Would you take her inside now, little mother?" Sparhawk asked Sephrenia. "I think we'd all rather she didn't see this."

Sephrenia nodded and took the weeping queen to the stairway leading down from the turret.

"You might want to go, too, your Majesty," Vanion suggested to Sarabian. "Sparhawk and I are more or less accustomed to this sort of unpleasantness. *You* don't have to watch, though."

"No, I'll stay, Lord Vanion," Sarabian said firmly.

"That's up to you, your Majesty."

A sheet of crossbow bolts rattled against the battlements like hail. It appeared that the rebels had been repairing the results of Khalad's tampering.

Then, fearfully, splashing in panicky desperation, swimmers leapt from the edge of the moat and struggled their way to the barges to slip the mooring lines. The barges were quickly pulled to shore, and the rebels, their makeshift scaling ladders already raised, swarmed on board and began to pole their way rapidly across the moat to the sheer castle wall.

Sparhawk stuck his head out through the doorway of the turret. "Kalten!" he whispered to his friend, who was crouched down on the parapet not far from the turret. "Pass the word! Tell the Atans to get ready!"

"Right."

"But tell them not to move until they hear the signal."

"I know what I'm doing, Sparhawk. Quit treating me like an idiot."

"Sorry."

The urgent whisper sped around the battlements.

"Your timing's perfect, Sparhawk," Vanion said tensely in a low voice. "I just saw Kring's signal from the compound wall. The Atans are outside the gate." He paused. "You're having an unbelievable run of good luck, you know. Nobody could have guessed in advance that the mob would start up the wall and the Atans would arrive at precisely the same time."

"Probably not," Sparhawk agreed. "I think we might want to do something nice for Aphrael the next time we see her."

In the moat below, the barges bumped against the castle walls, and the rebels began their desperate scramble up the ladders toward the ominously silent battlements.

Another urgent whisper slithered back around the parapet.

"The barges are all up against the wall now, Sparhawk!" Kalten whispered hoarsely.

"All right." Sparhawk drew in a deep breath. "Tell Ulath to give the signal."

"Ulath!" Kalten shouted, no longer even bothering to whisper. "Toot your horn!"

"*Toot?*" Ulath's voice was outraged. Then his Ogre-horn rang out its message of pain and death.

From around the parapet, great boulders were lifted, teetered a moment on the battlements, and then plummeted down onto the swarming decks of the barges below. The barges ruptured, splintered, and began to sink. The viscous mixture of naphtha and pitch spread out across the surface of the moat. The spreading slick was rainbow-hued and, Sparhawk absently thought, really rather pretty.

The towering Atans rose from their places of concealment, took up the lanterns conveniently hanging from the battlements, and hurled them down into the moat like a hundred flaring comets.

The rebels who had leapt from the sinking barges and who were struggling in the oily water below screamed in terror as they saw flaming death raining down on them from above.

The moat exploded. A sheet of blue fire shot across the naphtha-stained water, and it was immediately followed by towering billows of sooty orange flame and dense black smoke. There were volcanolike eruptions from the sinking barges as the deadly, unspilled naphtha still in their holds took fire. The flames belched upward to sear the rebels still clinging to the scaling ladders. They fell or jumped from the burning ladders, streaking flame as they plunged into the inferno below.

The screams were dreadful. Some few of the burning men reached the far bank of the moat and ran blindly across the tidy lawns of the compound, shrieking and dripping fire.

The rebels who had stood at the brink of the moat impatiently awaiting their turn to cross the intervening water to scale the walls recoiled in horror from the sudden conflagration that had just made the gleaming castle of the Elenes as unreachable as the far side of the moon.

"Ulath!" Sparhawk roared. "Tell Kring to open the gate!"

Once more the Ogre-horn sang.

The massive gates of the compound swung slowly open, and the golden Atan giants, running in perfect unison, swept into the imperial compound like an avalanche.

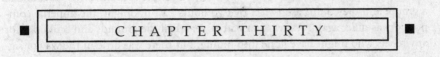

CHAPTER THIRTY

"I don't *know* how they did it, Sparhawk," Caalador replied with a dark scowl. "Krager himself hasn't been seen for days. He's a slippery one, isn't he?" Caalador had located Sparhawk on the parapet.

"That he is, my friend. What about the others? I wouldn't have thought that Elron could have managed something like that."

"Neither would I. He was doing everything but wearing a sign reading 'conspirator' on his forehead—all the swirling of his cape and exaggerated tiptoeing through back alleys." Caalador shook his head. "Anyway, he was staying in the house of a local Edomish nobleman. We know he was inside, because we watched him go in through the front door. We were watching every single door and window, so we know he didn't come back out, but he wasn't inside when we went to pick him up."

There was a crash from a nearby palace as the Atans broke in the doors to get at the rebels hiding inside.

"Did your people check the house for hidden rooms or passages?" Sparhawk asked.

Caalador shook his head. "They stood the Edomish noble barefoot in a brazier of hot coals instead. It's faster that way. There was no place to hide in that house. I'm sorry, Sparhawk. We picked up all the second-raters without a hitch, but the leaders—" He spread his hands helplessly.

"Somebody was probably using magic. They've done it before."

"Can you really do that sort of thing with magic?"

"*I* can't, but I'm sure Sephrenia knows the proper spells."

Caalador looked out over the battlements. "Well, at least we broke up this attack on the government. That's the main thing."

"I'm not so sure," Sparhawk disagreed.

"It *was* fairly important, Sparhawk. If they'd succeeded, all of Tamuli would have flown apart. As soon as the Atans finish mopping up, we'll be able to start questioning survivors—and those underlings we *did* manage to catch. They might be able to direct us to the important plotters."

"I sort of doubt it. Krager's very good at this sort of thing. I think we'll find that the underlings don't actually have a lot of information. It's a shame. I *really* wanted to have a little talk with Krager."

"You always get that tone of voice when you talk about him," Caalador observed. "Is there something personal between you two?"

"Oh, yes, and it goes back a long, long way. I've missed any number of opportunities to kill him—usually because it wasn't convenient. I was too busy concentrating on the man who employed him, and that may have been a mistake. Krager always makes sure that he's got just enough information to make him too valuable to kill. The next time I come across him, I think I'll just ignore that."

The Atans were efficiency personified as they rounded up the rebels. They offered the armed insurgents one opportunity to surrender each time they surrounded a group, and they didn't ask twice. By two hours past midnight, the imperial compound was quiet again. A few Atan patrols searched the grounds and buildings for any rebels who might have gone into hiding, but there was little in the way of significant activity.

Sparhawk was bone-tired. Though he had not physically participated in the suppression of the rebellion, the tension had exhausted him more than a two-hour battle might have. He stood on the parapet looking wearily down into the compound, watching without much interest as the groundskeepers, who had been pressed into service for the unpleasant task, cringingly pulled the floating dead out of the moat.

"Why don't you go to bed, Sparhawk?" It was Khalad. His bare, heavy shoulders gleamed in the torchlight. His voice and appearance and brusque manner were so much like his father's that Sparhawk once again felt that brief, renewed pang of sorrow.

"I just want to be sure that there won't be any bodies left floating in the moat when my wife wakes up tomorrow morning. People who've been burned to death aren't very pretty."

"I'll take care of that. Let's go to the bathhouse. I'll help you out of your armor, and you can soak in a tub of hot water for a while."

"I didn't really exert myself very much this evening, Khalad. I didn't even work up a sweat."

"You don't have to. That smell's so ingrained into your armor that five minutes after you put it on, you smell as if you haven't bathed for a month."

"It's one of the drawbacks of the profession. Are you sure you want to be a knight?"

"It wasn't my idea in the first place."

"Maybe when this is all over, the world will settle down enough so that there won't be any need for armored knights anymore."

"Of course, and maybe someday fish will fly, too."

"You're a cynic, Khalad."

"What *is* he doing up there?" Khalad demanded irritably, looking up toward the towers soaring over the castle.

"Who's doing what where?"

"There's somebody up in the very top of that south tower. This is the fourth time I've caught a flicker of candlelight through that window."

"Maybe Tynian or Bevier put one of their knights up there to keep watch." Sparhawk shrugged.

"Without telling you—or Lord Vanion?"

"If it worries you so much, let's go take a look."

"You don't sound very concerned."

"I'm not. This castle's absolutely secure, Khalad."

"I'll go have a look after I get you ready for bed."

"No, I'll go along."

"I thought you were certain that the castle's secure."

"It never hurts to be careful. I don't want to have to tell your mothers that I made a mistake and got you killed."

They went down from the battlements, crossed the courtyard, and went into the main building.

There were loud snores coming from behind the bolted door of the main dining hall. "I'd imagine that there are going to be some monumental headaches emerging from that room in the morning." Khalad laughed.

"We didn't force our guests to drink so much."

"They'll accuse us of it, though."

They started up the stairway that led to the top of the south tower. Although the main tower and the north tower had been constructed in the usual fashion, with rooms stacked atop each other, the south tower was little more than a hollow shell with a wooden stairway rising up through a creaking scaffolding. The architect had evidently added this structure primarily for the purposes of symmetry. The single room in the entire tower was at the very top, a room floored with wooden beams roughly adzed square.

"I'm getting too old to be climbing stairs in full armor," Sparhawk puffed when they were about halfway up.

"You're out of condition, Sparhawk," Khalad told his lord bluntly. "You're spending too much time on your backside talking about politics."

"It's part of my job, Khalad."

They reached the door at the top of the stairs. "You'd better let me go in first," Sparhawk murmured, sliding his sword out of its scabbard. Then he reached out and pushed the door open.

A shabby-looking man sat at a wooden table in the center of the room, his face lighted by a single candle. Sparhawk knew him. The years of hard drinking had not been kind to Krager. His hair had thinned even more in the six or so years since Sparhawk had last seen him, and the puffy pouches under his eyes were even more pronounced. The eyes themselves, nearsighted and watery, were discolored and seemed to be overlaid with a kind of yellow stain. The hand in which he held his wine cup palsied, and a continual tic shuddered in his right cheek.

Sparhawk moved without even stopping to think. He leveled his sword at Martel's threadbare former underling and lunged.

There was no feeling of resistance as the sword plunged into Krager's chest and emerged from his back.

Krager flinched violently, and then he laughed in his rusty, drink-corroded voice. "God, that's a startling experience!" he said conversationally. "I could almost feel the blade running through me. Put your sword away, Sparhawk. You can't hurt me with it."

Sparhawk pulled the sword out of Krager's substantial-appearing body and swept it back and forth through the man's head.

"Please don't do that, Sparhawk," Krager said, closing his eyes. "It's really very unnerving, you know."

"My compliments to your magician, Krager," Sparhawk said flatly. "That's really a very convincing illusion. You look so real that I can almost smell you."

"I see that we're going to be civilized about this," Krager said, taking a drink of his wine. "Good. You're growing up, Sparhawk. Ten years ago, you'd have chopped the room into kindling before you'd have finally been willing to listen to reason."

"Magic?" Khalad asked Sparhawk.

Sparhawk nodded. "And fairly sophisticated, too. Actually Krager's sitting in a room a mile or more away from here. Someone's projecting his image into this tower. We can see him and hear him, but we can't touch him."

"Pity," Khalad murmured, fingering the hilt of his heavy dagger.

"You've really been very clever this time, Sparhawk," Krager said. "Age seems to be improving you—like a good wine."

"You're the expert on that, Krager."

"Petty, Sparhawk. Very petty." Krager smirked. "Before you engage in an orgy of self-congratulation, though, you ought to know that this was just another of those tests a friend of mine mentioned to you a while back. I told my associates all about you, but they wanted to see for themselves. We arranged a few entertainments for you so that you could demonstrate your prowess—and your limitations. The catapults definitely confused the Cyrgai, and your mounted tactics against the Trolls were almost brilliant. You also did remarkably well in an urban setting here in Matherion. You really surprised me on that score, Sparhawk. You caught on to our sign and countersign much faster than I'd thought you would, and you intercepted the message about the warehouse in a remarkably short period of time. That Dacite merchant only had to walk through town three times before your spy stole the note from him. I'd have expected you to fail miserably when faced with a conspiracy instead of an army in the field. My congratulations."

"You've been drinking for too many years, Krager. Your memory's starting to slip. You're forgetting what happened in Chyrellos during the election. As I recall, we countered just about every one of the schemes Martel and Annias cooked up there as well."

"That wasn't really a very great accomplishment, Sparhawk. Martel and Annias weren't really very challenging opponents. I tried to tell them that their plots weren't sophisticated enough, but they wouldn't listen. Martel was too busy thinking about the treasure rooms under the Basilica, and Annias was so blinded by the Archprelate's miter that he couldn't see anything else. You really missed your chance there, Sparhawk. I've always been your most serious opponent. You had me right in your hands, and you let me go just for the sake of a few crumbs of information and some exaggerated testimony before the Hierocracy. Very poor thinking there, old boy."

"This evening's festivities weren't really designed to succeed, then, I gather?"

"Of course not, Sparhawk. If we'd really wanted to take Matherion, we'd have brought in whole armies."

"I'm sure there's a point to all this," Sparhawk said to the illusion. "Do you suppose we could step right along? I've had a tiring day."

"The tests have all been designed to oblige you to commit your resources, Sparhawk. We needed to know what kinds of responses you had at your command."

"You haven't seen them all yet, Krager—not by half."

"Khalad, isn't it?" Krager said to Sparhawk's squire. "Tell your master that he should practice a bit more before he tries lying. He's really not very convincing—oh, convey my regards to your mother. She and I always got on well."

"I sort of doubt that," Khalad replied.

"Be realistic, Sparhawk," Krager went on. "Your wife and daughter are here. Do you *really* expect me to believe that you'd hold anything back if you thought they were in danger?"

"We used what was necessary, Krager. You don't have to send out a whole regiment to step on a bug."

"You're so much like Martel was, Sparhawk," Krager observed. "You two could almost have been brothers. I used to despair of ever nursing him through his adolescence. He was a hopeless innocent when he started out, you know. About all he had was a towering resentment—directed primarily at you and Vanion—and at Sephrenia, of course, although to a lesser degree. I had to raise him from virtual infancy. God, the hours I spent patiently grinding away all those knightly virtues."

"Reminisce on your own time, Krager. Get to the point. Martel's history now. This is a new situation, and he's not around anymore."

"Just renewing our acquaintance, Sparhawk. You know, 'the good old days' and all that. I've found a new employer, obviously."

"I gathered as much."

"When I was working for Martel, I had very little direct contact with Otha and almost none with Azash himself. That situation might have had an entirely different outcome if I'd had direct access to the Zemoch God. Martel was obsessed with revenge, and Otha was too sunk in his own debauchery for either of them to think clearly. They were giving Azash very poor advice as a result of their own limitations. I could have given him a much more realistic assessment of the situation."

"Provided you were ever sober enough to talk."

"That's beneath you, Sparhawk. Oh, I'll admit that I take a drink now and then, but never so much that I lose sight of the main goals. Actually, it turned out better for me in the long run. If I'd been the one advising Azash, he'd have beaten you. Then I'd have been inextricably involved with him, and I'd have been destroyed when he confronted Cyrgon—that's my new employer's name, by the way. You've heard of him, I suppose?"

"A few times." Sparhawk forced himself to sound casual.

"Good. That saves us a a lot of time. Pay attention now, Sparhawk. We're getting to the significant part of this little chat. Cyrgon wants you to go home. Your presence here on the Daresian continent is an inconvenience—nothing more, really. Just an inconvenience. If you had Bhelliom in your pocket, we might take you seriously, but you don't—and so we don't. You're all alone here, my old friend. You don't have the Bhelliom, and you don't have the Church Knights. You've only got the remnants of Ehlana's honor guard and a hundred of those mounted apes from Pelosia. You're hardly worth even noticing. If you go home, Cyrgon will give you his pledge not to move against the Eosian continent for a hundred years. You'll be long dead by then, and so will everybody you care about. It's not really a bad offer, you know. You get yourself a hundred years of peace just by getting on a ship and going back to Cimmura."

"And if I don't?"

"We'll kill you—*after* we've killed your wife and your daughter and everybody else in the whole world you care about. There's another possibility, of course. You could join us. Cyrgon could see to it that you lived longer than even Otha did. He specifically told me to make you that offer."

"Thank him for me—if you ever see him again."

"You're declining, I gather?"

"Obviously. I haven't seen nearly as much of Daresia as I want to see, so I think I'll stay for a while, and I'm sure I wouldn't care for the company of you and Cyrgon's other hirelings."

"I told Cyrgon you'd take that position, but he insisted that I make the offer."

"If he's so all-powerful, why's he trying to bribe me?"

"Out of respect, Sparhawk. Can you believe that? He respects you because you're Anakha. The whole concept baffles him, and he's intrigued by it. I honestly believe he'd like to get to know you. You know how childish Gods can be at times."

"Speaking of Gods, what's behind this alliance he's made with the Troll-Gods?" Then Sparhawk thought of something. "Never mind, Krager, I've just worked it out for myself. A God's power is dependent on the number of worshippers he has. The Cyrgai are extinct, so Cyrgon's no more than a squeaky little voice making hollow pronouncements in a ruin somewhere in central Cynesga—all noise and no substance."

"Someone's been telling you fairy tales, Sparhawk. The Cyrgai are far from extinct—as you'll find out to your sorrow if you stay in Tamuli. Cyrgon made the alliance with the Troll-Gods in order to bring the Trolls to Daresia. Your Atans are very impressive, but they're no match for Trolls. Cyrgon's very sentimental about his chosen people. He'd rather not lose them needlessly in skirmishes with a race of freaks, so he made an arrangement with the Troll-Gods. The Trolls will get the pleasure of killing—and eating—the Atans." Krager drained the rest of his wine. "This is starting to bore me, Sparhawk, and my cup's gone empty. I told Cyrgon I'd present you with his offer. He's giving you the chance to live out the rest of your life in peace. I'd advise you to take it. He won't make the offer again. Really, old boy, why should you care what happens to the Tamuls? They're nothing but yellow monkeys, after all."

"Church policy, Krager. Our Holy Mother takes the long view. Tell Cyrgon to take his offer and stick it up his nose. I'm staying."

"It's your funeral, Sparhawk." Krager laughed. "I might even send flowers. I've had all the entertainment of knowing a pair of anachronisms—you and Martel. I'll drink to your memories from time to time—if I remember you at all."

And then the illusion of the shabby scoundrel vanished.

"So that's Krager," Khalad said in a chill tone. "I'm glad I got the chance to meet him."

"What exactly have you got in mind, Khalad?"

"I thought I might kill him just a little bit. Fair's fair, Sparhawk. You got Martel, Talen got Adus, so Krager's mine."

"Sounds fair to me," Sparhawk agreed.

"Was he drunk?" Kalten asked.

"Krager's always a little drunk," Sparhawk replied. "He wasn't so far gone that he got careless, though." He looked around. "Would everybody like to say 'I told you so' right here and now?" he asked them. "Let's have it out of the way right at the start so I don't have it hanging over my head. Yes, it probably would have been more convenient if I'd killed him the last time I saw him, but if we hadn't had his testimony to the Hierocracy at the time of the election, Dolmant probably wouldn't be the Archprelate right now."

"I might be able to learn to live with that," Ehlana murmured.

"Be nice," Emban told her.

"Only joking, your Grace."

"Are you sure you repeated what he said verbatim?" Sephrenia asked Sparhawk.

"It was very close, little mother," Khalad assured her.

She frowned. "It was contrived, I'm sure you all realize that. Krager didn't really tell us anything we didn't already know—or couldn't have guessed."

"The name Cyrgon hadn't come up before, Sephrenia," Vanion disagreed.

"And it may very well never come up again," she replied. "I'd need a lot more than Krager's unsubstantiated word before I'll believe that Cyrgon's involved."

"Well, *somebody's* involved," Tynian noted. "Somebody had to be impressive enough to get the attention of the Troll-Gods, and Krager doesn't quite fit that description."

"Not to mention the fact that Krager can't even pronounce *magic*, much less use it," Kalten added. "Could just any Styric have cast that spell, little mother?"

Sephrenia shook her head. "It's very difficult," she conceded. "If it hadn't been done exactly right, Sparhawk's sword would have gone right through the real Krager. Sparhawk would have started the thrust in that room up in the tower, and it would have finished up in a room a mile away sliding through Krager's heart."

"All right then," Emban said, pacing up and down the room with his pudgy hands clasped behind his back. "Now we know that this so-called uprising tonight wasn't intended seriously."

Sparhawk shook his head. "No, your Grace, we *don't* know that for certain. Regardless of what he says, Krager learned much of his style from Martel, and trying to shrug a failure off by pretending that the scheme wasn't really serious in the first place is exactly the sort of thing Martel would have done."

"You knew him better than I did." Emban grimaced. "Can we *really* be sure that Krager and the others are working for a God—Cyrgon or maybe some other one?"

"Not really, Emban," Sephrenia replied. "The Troll-Gods are involved, and *they* could be doing the things we've encountered that are beyond the capability of a human magician. There's a sorcerer out there, certainly, but we can't be certain that there's a God—other than the Troll-Gods—involved as well."

"But it *could* be a God, couldn't it?" Emban pressed.

"Anything's possible, your Grace." She shrugged.

"That's what I needed to know," the fat little churchman said. "It rather looks as if I'm going to have to make a flying trip back to Chyrellos."

"That went by me a little fast, your Grace," Kalten confessed.

"We're going to need the Church Knights, Kalten," Emban said. "All of them."

"They're committed to Rendor, your Grace," Bevier reminded him.

"Rendor can wait."

"The Archprelate may feel differently about that, Emban," Vanion told him. "Reconciliation with the Rendors has been one of our Holy Mother's goals for over half a millennium now."

"She's patient. She'll wait. She's going to *have* to wait. This is a crisis, Vanion."

"I'll go with you, your Grace," Tynian said. "I won't be of much use here in Tamuli until my shoulder heals anyway, and I'll be able to clarify the military situation to Sarathi much better than you will. Dolmant's had Pandion training, so he'll understand military terminology. Right now we're standing out in the open with our breeches down—begging your Majesty's pardon for the crudity of that expression," he apologized to Ehlana.

"It's an interesting metaphor, Sir Tynian," she smiled, "and it conjures up an absolutely enthralling image."

"I'll agree with the Patriarch of Ucera," Tynian went on. "We definitely have to have the Church Knights here in Tamuli. If we *don't* get them here in a hurry, this whole situation's going to crumble right in our hands."

"I'll send word to Tikume," Kring volunteered. "He'll send us several thousand mounted Peloi. We don't wear armor or use magic, but we know how to fight."

"Will you be able to hold out here until the Church Knights arrive, Vanion?" Emban asked.

"Talk to Sparhawk, Emban. He's in charge."

"I wish you wouldn't keep doing that, Vanion," Sparhawk objected. He thought for a moment. "Atan Engessa," he said then, "how hard was it to persuade your warriors that it's not really unnatural to fight on horseback? Can we persuade any more of them?"

"When I tell them that this Krager-drunkard called them a race of freaks, they'll listen to me, Sparhawk-Knight."

"Good. Krager may have helped us more than he thought, then. Are *you* convinced that it's best to attack Trolls with war-horses and lances, my friend?"

"It was most effective, Sparhawk-Knight. We haven't encountered the Troll-beasts before. They're bigger than we are. That may be difficult for my people to accept, but once they do, they'll be willing to try horses—if you can find enough of those big ones."

"Did Krager happen to make any references to the fact that we've been using thieves and beggars as our eyes and ears?" Stragen asked.

"Not in so many words, Milord," Khalad replied.

"That puts an unknown into our equation then," Stragen mused.

"Please don't do that, Stragen," Kalten pleaded. "I absolutely *hate* mathematics."

"Sorry. We don't know for certain whether Krager's aware that we've been using the criminals of Matherion as spies. If he *is* aware of it, he could use it to feed us false information."

"That spell they used sort of hints that they know, Stragen," Caalador noted.

"That explains how it was that we saw the leaders of the conspiracy go into a house and never come out. They used illusions. They wouldn't have done that if they hadn't known we were watching."

Stragen stuck out his hand and wobbled it from side to side a bit dubiously. "It's not set in stone yet, Caalador," he said. "He may not know just exactly how well organized we are."

Bevier's expression was profoundly disgusted. "We've been had, my friends," he said. "This was all an elaborate ruse—armies from the past, resurrected heroes, vampires, and ghouls—all of it. It was a trick with no other purpose than to get us to come here without the entire body of the Church Knights at our back."

"Then why have they turned around and told us to go home, Sir Bevier?" Talen asked him.

"Maybe they found out that we were a little more effective than they thought we'd be," Ulath rumbled. "I don't think they really expected us to break up that Cyrgai assault or exterminate a hundred Trolls, or break the back of this coup attempt the way we did. It's altogether possible that we surprised them and even upset them more than a little. Krager's visit could have been sheer bravado, you know. We might not want to get overconfident, but I don't think we should get *under*confident either. We're professionals, after all, and we've won every encounter so far. Let's not give up the game and run away just because of a few windy threats by a known drunkard."

"Well said," Tynian murmured.

"We don't have any choice, Aphrael," Sparhawk told his daughter later when they were alone with Sephrenia and Vanion in a small room several floors above the royal apartment. "It's going to take Emban and Tynian at least three months to get back to Chyrellos and then nine months for the Church Knights to come overland to Daresia. Even then, they'll still be present only in the western kingdoms."

"Why can't they come by boat?" The princess sounded a bit sulky, and she was holding Rollo tightly to her chest.

"There are a hundred thousand Church Knights, Aphrael," Vanion reminded her, "twenty-five thousand in each of the four orders. I don't think there are enough ships in the world to transport that many men and horses. We can bring in a few thousand by ship, but the bulk of them will have to come overland. We won't be able to count on even that few thousand for at least six months—the time it's going to take Emban and Tynian to reach Chyrellos and then come back by ship with the knights and their horses. Until they arrive we're all alone here."

"With your breeches down," she added.

"Watch your tongue, young lady," Sparhawk scolded her.

She shrugged that off. "My instincts all tell me that it's a very bad idea," she told them. "I went to a lot of trouble to find a safe place for Bhelliom, and the first time there's a little rain shower, you all want to run to retrieve it. Are you *sure* you're not exaggerating the danger? Ulath might have been right, you know. Everything Krager said to you could have been sheer bluster. I still think you can handle it without Bhelliom."

"I disagree," Sephrenia told her. "I know Elenes better than you do, Aphrael. It's not in their nature to exaggerate dangers. Quite the reverse, actually."

"The whole point here is that your mother may be in danger," Sparhawk told his daughter. "Until Tynian and Emban bring the Church Knights to Tamuli, we're seriously overmatched. Even as stupid as they are, it was only the Bhelliom that gave us any advantage over the Troll-Gods last time. *You* couldn't even deal with them, as I recall."

"That's a hateful thing to say, Sparhawk," she flared.

"I'm just trying to get you to look at this realistically, Aphrael. Without the Bhelliom, we're all in serious danger here—and I'm not just talking about your mother and all our friends. If Krager was telling the truth and we *are* matched up against Cyrgon, he's at least as dangerous as Azash was."

"Are you *sure* all of these flimsy excuses aren't coming into your head because you want to get your hands on Bhelliom again, Sparhawk?" she asked him. "Nobody's really immune to its seduction, you know. There's a great deal of satisfaction to be had in wielding unlimited power."

"You know me better than that, Aphrael," he said reproachfully. "I don't go out of my way looking for power."

"If it *is* Cyrgon, his first step would be to exterminate the Styrics, you know," Sephrenia reminded the little Goddess. "He hates us for what we did to his Cyrgai."

"Why are you all joining forces to bully me?" Aphrael demanded.

"Because you're being stubborn," Sparhawk replied. "Throwing Bhelliom into the sea was a very good idea when we did it, but the situation's changed now. I know that it's not in your nature to admit that you made a mistake, but you did, you know."

"Bite your tongue!"

"We have a new situation here, Aphrael," Sephrenia said patiently. "You've told me again and again that you can't fully see the future, so you couldn't really have foreseen all of what's happening here in Tamuli. You didn't *really* make a mistake, baby sister, but you have to be flexible. You can't let the world fly all to pieces just because you want to maintain a reputation for infallibility."

"Oh, *right!*" Aphrael gave in, flinging herself into a chair and starting to suck her thumb as she glared at them.

"Don't do that," Sparhawk and Sephrenia told her in unison.

She ignored them. "I want all three of you to know that I'm really very put out with you for this. You've been very impolite and very inconsiderate of my feelings. I'm ashamed of you. Go ahead. I don't care. Go ahead and get the Bhelliom if you think you absolutely *have* to have it."

"Ah—Aphrael," Sparhawk said mildly, "we don't know where it is, remember?"

"That's not my fault," she replied in a sulky little voice.

"Yes, actually it is. You were very careful to make sure that we *didn't* know where we were when we threw it into the sea."

"That's a spiteful thing to say, Father."

A horrible thought suddenly occurred to Sparhawk. "You *do* know where it is, don't you?" he asked her anxiously.

"Oh, Sparhawk, don't be silly! Of *course* I know where it is. You didn't think I'd let you put it someplace where I couldn't find it, did you?"

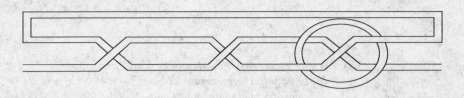

THE
SHINING ONES

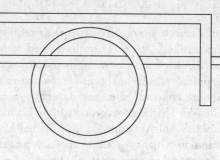

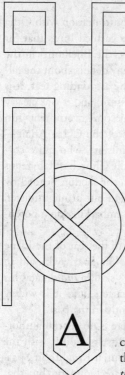

PROLOGUE

—Excerpted from Chapter Three of *The Cyrga Affair: An Examination of the Recent Crisis.* Compiled by the Contemporary History Department of the University of Matherion.

A compilation such as this is the work of many scholars, and thus inevitably reflects differing views. While the author of *this* portion of the work in hand has enormous respect for his eminent colleague who so ably composed the preceding chapter, the reader must be candidly advised that this writer differs from his colleague in the interpretation of a number of recent events. I most definitely do *not* agree that the intervention by the agents of the Church of Chyrellos in the Cyrga Affair was entirely untainted by self-interest.

I join my colleague, however, in expressing admiration and respect for Zalasta of Styricum. The inestimable services to the empire of this wise and faithful statesman cannot be overly praised. Thus it was that when the full import of the Cyrga Affair burst upon his Majesty's government, it was natural for our ministers to turn to Zalasta for counsel. Despite our admiration for this preeminent citizen of Styricum, however, we must admit that Zalasta's mind is so noble that he sometimes fails to perceive less admirable qualities in others. There were grave doubts in some quarters of his Majesty's government when Zalasta urged that we turn our attention beyond the borders of Tamuli in our quest for a solution to the problem which was rapidly approaching the dimensions of a crisis. His suggestion that the Pandion Knight, Sir Sparhawk, was best suited to deal with the situation troubled the more conservative members of the Imperial Council. Despite the man's military genius, he is nonetheless a member of one of the Militant Orders of the Church of Chyrellos, and prudent men do not lower their guard when compelled by necessity to have dealings with that particular institution.

Sir Sparhawk had come to Zalasta's attention during the Second Zemoch War between the Knights of the Church of Chyrellos and the minions of Otha of Zemoch. Not even Zalasta, whose wisdom is legendary, can tell us precisely what took place in the city of Zemoch during Sir Sparhawk's fateful confrontation with Otha and with the Zemoch God, Azash. There have been some garbled hints that Sir Sparhawk may have utilized an ancient talisman known as "the Bhelliom" in the struggle, but no reputable scholar has been able to uncover any details about the talisman or its attributes. However he managed to perform the astounding feat, it is undeniably true that Sir Sparhawk was successful in his mission; and it was clearly *that* remarkable success which stampeded his Imperial Majesty's government into turning to this Pandion Knight for aid in the early stages of the Cyrga Affair—despite the grave reservations of some highly respected ministers, who quite correctly pointed out that an alliance between the empire and the Church of Chyrellos might well be fraught with danger. Unfortunately perhaps, the faction headed by Foreign Minister Oscagne currently has the emperor's ear, and our prime minister, Pondia Subat, was unable to prevent the government from embarking on a potentially dangerous course of action.

Foreign Minister Oscagne himself headed the mission to the seat of the Elene Church of Chyrellos to petition Archprelate Dolmant for Sir Sparhawk's aid in dealing with the crisis. While no one can question Oscagne's skill in diplomacy, his political views have been called into question in some quarters, and it is widely known that he and the prime minister have disagreed violently in the past.

The politics of the Eosian continent are murky, for there is no central authority there. Quite frequently, the Church of Chyrellos finds itself at odds with the reigning monarchs of the separate Elene kingdoms. As a Church Knight, Sir Sparhawk would normally be under the command of Archprelate Dolmant, but that simple and direct line of command was clouded by the fact that Sparhawk is *also* the Prince Consort of the Queen of Elenia and therefore subject to *her* whims. It was here that Foreign Minister Oscagne was able to demonstrate his virtuosity in the field of diplomacy. Archprelate Dolmant clearly saw the contiguity of interest with the empire in the matter, but Queen Ehlana remained unconvinced. The Queen of Elenia is young, and her emotions sometimes cloud her judgment. She clearly viewed the notion of a prolonged separation from her husband with a profound lack of enthusiasm. In a brilliant stroke, however, Foreign Minister Oscagne proposed that Sir Sparhawk's journey to the Daresian continent might best be masked by a state visit of Queen Ehlana to the imperial court in Matherion. As Prince Consort, Sir Sparhawk would quite naturally accompany his wife, and his presence would thus be fully explained. This proposal sufficiently mollified Sparhawk's queen, and she finally agreed.

Traveling with a suitable escort of one hundred Church Knights and various functionaries, Queen Ehlana took ship and sailed to the port of Salesha in eastern Zemoch. From there the royal party traveled north to Basne where an additional escort of horsemen from eastern Pelosia awaited them. Thus reinforced, the Elenes crossed the border into Astel in western Daresia.

The accounts we have received of the queen's journey have shown glaring inconsistencies. Objections have been raised that should we accept the word of these Elenes, we would clearly be faced with an absurdity. After some consideration, however, this writer has become convinced that these apparent discrepancies can be easily reconciled if those who so violently object will but take the trouble to examine the differences between the Elene and the Tamul calendars. The Queen of Elenia did *not,* in fact, pretend to have flown across the continent, as some have scornfully suggested. Her progress was quite normal, and it will be recognized as such if the learned gentlemen will but take note of the fact that *the Elene week is longer than ours!*

At any rate, the queen's party reached the capital of Astel at Darsas, where Queen Ehlana so charmed King Alberen that Ambassador Fontan humorously reported that the poor man was on the verge of giving her his crown. Prince Sparhawk, meanwhile, began to actively pursue the real purpose behind his journey to Tamuli, the gathering of information about what the Elenes had melodramatically come to call "the conspiracy."

The queen's party was joined at Darsas by two legions of Atan warriors under the leadership of Engessa, the commander of the garrison at Cenae, and they journeyed to Pela on the steppes of central Astel to meet with the nomadic Peloi. From thence they set out for the Styric city of Sarsos in northeastern Astel.

A disturbing note emerges from the accounts of this journey, however. The foreign minister, either duped or willingly conspiring with the Elenes, reported that somewhat to the west of Sarsos, the royal party encountered *Cyrgai!* This clear evidence of an intent to deceive his Majesty's government has raised grave questions, not only about Oscagne's loyalty, but about the sincerity of the Elenes as well. As Prime Minister Subat pointed out, Foreign Minister Oscagne is, though brilliant, sometimes erratic, a common characteristic of the overly gifted. Moreover, the prime minister added, Prince Sparhawk and his companions *are* Church Knights, after all, and the Church of Chyrellos is widely known to be a *political* as well as a spiritual force on the Eosian continent. Dark suspicions began to arise in the halls of his Majesty's government, and many have expressed grave doubts about the wisdom of our course. Some have even gone so far as to raise the possibility that the disruption here in Tamuli might be of *Elene* origin, providing as they did a perfect excuse for an incursion onto the continent by the Church Knights, the acknowledged agents of Archprelate Dolmant. Could it be, they ask, that this entire affair has been contrived by Dolmant to provide his Church with the opportunity to forcibly convert all of Tamuli to the worship of the Elene God and thus to deliver political control of the empire into his own hands? It should be noted here that Prime Minister Subat has *personally* advised this writer that he is seriously concerned about this possibility.

At Sarsos, Queen Ehlana's party was joined by Sephrenia, who was formerly the tutor of the Pandions in the Secrets of Styricum, but who is now a member of the Thousand, the ruling council in that city. They were also joined there by Zalasta himself, a fact which has quieted some of our anxieties in regard to the motives of the Elenes. It was obviously through Zalasta's efforts that the Thousand were persuaded to pledge their aid, despite the long-standing and, many feel, fully justified suspicions all Styrics have of Elene motives.

The Elenes then moved on to Atan, where Queen Ehlana again charmed king and queen. It is clearly evident that the personality of this winsome girl is a force to be reckoned with.

Although Foreign Minister Oscagne's report of the encounter with the supposed Cyrgai is open to serious question, there can be no doubt about the veracity of the report of what happened after our visitors left Atana. *That* report came from Zalasta himself, and no sane man in the government could ever question the veracity of the first citizen of Styricum. It was in the mountains lying to the west of the border of Tamul proper that the party was set upon again, and Zalasta has confirmed the fact that the attackers were nonhuman.

There have been sightings of fearsome monsters in the Atan mountains in the past year, although many skeptics have dismissed these reports as being yet more of the illusory manifestations of the power of those bent on bringing down his Imperial Majesty's government. These clever illusions of Ogres, vampires, werewolves, and Shining Ones have been terrorizing the simple folk of Tamuli for several years, and the mountain monsters had been assumed to be no more than another of these illusions. Zalasta assures us, however, that these huge, shaggy beasts are Trolls, indigenous to the Thalesian peninsula in Eosia, which had migrated to the north coast of Atan across the polar ice, presumably at the behest of the enemies of the empire. Sir Sparhawk, once again reinforcing Zalasta's opinion of him, quickly devised tactics which routed the brutes.

Queen Ehlana's party then crossed into Tamul proper and shortly thereafter reached the imperial capital at fire-domed Matherion, where they were graciously welcomed by Emperor Sarabian. Despite the protests of Prime Minister Subat, the Elene visitors were given almost unimpeded access to his Majesty. The Queen of Elenia soon charmed the emperor, even as she had the lesser monarchs to the west. Candor compels us to admit that Emperor Sarabian has shown of late a lamentable tendency to interfere with the government, and to override the counsel of those far better equipped than he to deal with the day-to-day details of governing his vast realm.

The prime minister, acting on the advice of Interior Minister Kolata, had decided to place Prince Sparhawk under the command of the Ministry of the Interior. As Kolata correctly pointed out, Sir Sparhawk, an Eosian Elene, could not be expected to understand the myriad cultures of Tamuli and therefore would need guidance and direction in his efforts to counter the schemes of our enemies. Emperor Sarabian, however, rejected this approach and granted this foreigner almost total discretion in approaching such problems as arose.

Despite our reservations about Prince Sparhawk, his queen, and his companions, however, we must reluctantly concede that their presence in Matherion averted a disaster of the first order. Among the other structures in the imperial compound there is a replica of an Elene castle, which was specifically designed to make Elene dignitaries feel at home. Queen Ehlana and her entourage were housed in that castle, and the relevance of that fact will soon become clear.

In some as-yet-to-be-determined fashion, Sir Sparhawk and his cohorts unearthed a plot here in Matherion to overthrow the government. Rather than report their findings to the Ministry of the Interior, however, the Elenes chose to keep their discovery to themselves and to permit the conspirators to pursue their plot to its final conclusion. When an armed mob approached the imperial compound on that fateful night, Prince Sparhawk and his companions simply withdrew into their Elene castle, taking the emperor and the government inside with them.

We Tamuls had not fully understood the fact that architecture can be a weapon. Unbeknownst to his Majesty's government, Sparhawk's Elenes had modified the castle to some degree and had quietly brought in stores, all the while secretly constructing the brutal implements with which Elenes do war.

The mob, bent on the overthrow of the government, swept unimpeded into the imperial compound and found itself confronted by an impregnable castle filled with ruthless Elene warriors who routinely utilize boiling pitch and fire to defend their strongholds. The horrors of that night will remain forever etched on the memories of civilized men. As has long been the practice in Tamuli, many of the younger sons of the great houses of Tamul proper had joined with the rebels, more as a lark than out of any serious criminal intent. Always in the past these youthful offenders have been separated from the true criminals, severely reprimanded, and then returned to their parents. Protected by rank and family, they have had little to fear from the authorities. Boiling pitch, however, is no respecter of rank, and a high-spirited young aristocrat soaked in naphtha will burn as quickly as the foulest knave from the gutter. Moreover, once the mob had entered the compound, the Elenes closed the main gates, effectively sealing all inside, the innocent as well as the guilty, and further horrors were inflicted on the unfortunates by rampaging Peloi horsemen. The brutal suppression of the uprising was completed when the compound gates were opened once again to admit fully twenty legions of Atans, savages from the mountains who had received no instruction whatsoever in the customary civilities. The Atans systematically butchered all in their paths. Many young nobles, dearly loved students at this very university, were cut down even as they displayed their badges of rank, which should have guaranteed them immunity.

Although decent men the world around must view this unbridled savagery with horror, we must reluctantly congratulate Sir Sparhawk and his companions. The uprising was crushed, nay, annihilated, by these Elene savages and the unrestrained Atans.

His Imperial Majesty's government, however, made few friends on that dreadful night. Although the atrocities were clearly of Elene origin, the fact that Sir Sparhawk was here in Matherion at the emperor's express invitation has not been lost on the great houses of Tamul proper.

To further exacerbate the situation, the Elenes have seized upon the uprising as an excuse to send Patriarch Emban, a high-ranking member of the Elene clergy and ostensibly the spiritual adviser of Queen Ehlana, back to Chyrellos to urge the Archprelate to dispatch his Church Knights to Tamuli in force to aid in "restoring order."

Pondia Subat, the prime minister, has privately confessed that he is growing powerless, able only to watch helplessly as events move at an increasingly quickening pace. He has personally told this writer of his concerns. Foreign Minister Oscagne is clearly using his influence over the emperor to manipulate the situation. The invitation to Sir Sparhawk to come to Tamuli was obviously but the first step in some wider and more deadly scheme. Utilizing the present turmoil in Tamuli, the foreign minister has manipulated the emperor into providing the very opening Dolmant needed to justify an incursion in force onto the Daresian continent.

This writer is fully convinced that the empire faces the gravest threat in her long and glorious history. The willing cooperation of the Atans in the massacre within the imperial compound is clear evidence that not even *their* loyalty can be depended upon.

To whom can we turn for aid? Where in all this world can we find a force sufficient to repel the savage minions of Dolmant of Chyrellos? Must the empire in all her glory fall before the onslaught of the Elene zealots? I weep, my brothers, for the glory that must die. Fire-domed Matherion, the city of light, the home of truth and beauty, the center of the world, is doomed. The darkness descends, and there is little hope that morning will ever come again.

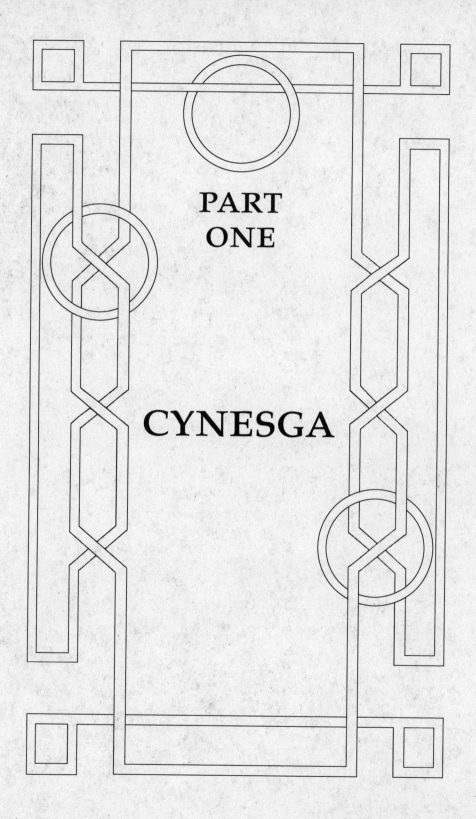

PART
ONE

CYNESGA

CHAPTER ONE

The seasons were turning, and the long summer was winding down toward autumn. A tenuous mist hung in the streets of fire-domed Matherion. The moon had risen late, and its pale light starkly etched the opalescent towers and domes and imparted a soft glow to the fog lying in the streets. Matherion, all agleam, stood with her feet bathed in shining mist and her pale face lifted to the night sky.

Sparhawk was tired. The tensions of the past week and the climactic events that had resolved them had drained him, but he could not sleep. Wrapped in his black Pandion cloak, he stood on the parapet looking pensively out over the shining city. He was tired, but his need to evaluate, to assess, to understand, was far too great to permit him to seek his bed and let his mind sink into the soft well of sleep until everything had been put into its proper place.

"What are you doing up here, Sparhawk?" Khalad spoke quietly, his voice so much like his father's that Sparhawk turned his head sharply to be sure that Kurik himself had not returned from the House of the Dead to chide him. Khalad was a plain-faced young man with thick shoulders and an abrupt manner. His family had served Sparhawk's for three generations now, and Khalad, like his father, customarily addressed his lord with a plain-spoken bluntness.

"I couldn't sleep," Sparhawk replied with a brief shrug.

"Your wife's got half the garrison out looking for you, you know."

Sparhawk grimaced. "Why does she always have to do that?"

"It's your own fault. You know she's going to send people out after you anytime you go off without telling her where you'll be. You could save yourself—and us—a lot of time and trouble if you'd just tell her in the first place. It seems to me that I've suggested that several times already."

"Don't bully me, Khalad. You're as bad as your father was."

"Sometimes good traits breed true. Would you like to go down and tell your wife that you're all right—*before* she calls in the workmen to start tearing down the walls?"

Sparhawk sighed. "All right." He turned away from the parapet. "Oh, by the way, you probably ought to know that we'll be making a trip before long."

"Oh? Where are we going?"

"We have to go pick something up. Have a word with the farriers. Faran needs to be reshod. He's scuffed his right front shoe down until it's as thin as paper."

"That's your fault, Sparhawk. He wouldn't do that if you'd sit up straight in your saddle."

"We start to get crooked as we grow older. That's one of the things you have to look forward to."

"Thanks. When are we leaving on this trip?"

"Just as soon as I can come up with a convincing enough lie to persuade my wife to let me go off without her."

"We've got plenty of time, then." Khalad looked out across moon-washed Matherion standing in pale fog with the moonlight awakening the rainbows of fire in her naked shoulders. "Pretty," he noted.

"Is that the best you can do? You look at the most fabulous city in the world and shrug it off as 'pretty.' "

"I'm not an aristocrat, Sparhawk. I don't have to invent flowery phrases to impress others—or myself. Let's get you inside before the damp settles into your lungs. You crooked old people have delicate health sometimes."

Queen Ehlana, pale and blonde and altogether lovely, was irritated more than angry; Sparhawk saw that immediately. He also saw that she had gone to some trouble to make herself as pretty as possible. Her dressing gown was dark blue satin, her cheeks had been carefully pinched to make them glow, and her hair was artfully arranged to give the impression of winsomely distracted dishevelment. She berated him about his lack of consideration in tones that might easily have made the trees cry and the very rocks shrink from her. Her cadences were measured, and her voice rose, then sank, as she told him exactly how she felt. Sparhawk concealed a smile. Ehlana was speaking to him on two levels at the same time as she stood in the center of the blue-draped royal apartment scolding him. Her words expressed extreme displeasure; her careful preparations, however, said something quite different.

He apologized.

She refused to accept his apology and stormed off to the bedroom, slamming the door behind her.

"Spirited," Sephrenia murmured. The small woman sat out of harm's way on the far side of the room, her white Styric robe glowing in the candlelight.

"You noticed," Sparhawk smiled.

"Does she do that often?"

"Oh, yes. She enjoys it. What are you doing up so late, little mother?"

"Aphrael wanted me to speak with you."

"Why didn't she just come and talk with me herself? It's not as if she were way over on the other side of town."

"It's a formal sort of occasion, Sparhawk. I'm supposed to speak for her at times like this."

"Was that intended to make sense?"

"It would if you were Styric. We're going to have to make some substitutions when we go to retrieve Bhelliom. Khalad can fill in for his father without any particular problem, but Tynian's decision to go back to Chyrellos with Emban really has Aphrael upset. Can you persuade him to change his mind?"

Sparhawk shook his head. "I wouldn't even try, Sephrenia. I'm not going to cripple him for life just because Aphrael might miss him."

"Is his arm really that bad?"

"It's bad enough. That crossbow bolt went right through his shoulder joint. If he starts moving it around, it won't set right, and that's his sword arm."

"Aphrael could fix it, you know."

"Not without exposing her identity, she couldn't, and I won't let her do that."

"Won't *let*?"

"Ask her if she wants to endanger her mother's sanity just for the sake of symmetry. Substitute someone else. If Aphrael's willing to accept Khalad in place of Kurik, she should be able to pick someone else to fill in for Tynian. Why is it so important to her in the first place?"

"You wouldn't understand."

"Why don't you try to explain it anyway? I might surprise you."

"You're in an odd humor tonight."

"I've just been scolded. That always makes me odd. Why does Aphrael think it's so important to always have the same group of people around her?"

"It has to do with the feeling of it, Sparhawk. The presence of any given person is more than just the way he looks or the sound of his voice. It also involves the way he thinks—and probably more important, the way he feels about Aphrael. She surrounds herself with that. When you bring in different people, you change the way it feels, and that throws her off balance." She looked at him. "You didn't understand a word of that, did you?"

"Yes, as a matter of fact, I did. How about Vanion? He loves her as much as Tynian does, and she loves him, too. He's been more or less with us in spirit since all this started anyway, and he *is* a knight, after all."

"Vanion? Don't be absurd, Sparhawk."

"He's not an invalid, you know. He was running footraces back in Sarsos, and he was still as good as ever with his lance when we fought the Trolls."

"It's out of the question. I won't even discuss it."

He crossed the room, took her wrists in his hands, and kissed her palms. "I love you dearly, little mother," he told her, "but I'm going to override you this time. You can't wrap Vanion in lamb's wool for the rest of his life just because you're afraid he might scratch his finger. If you don't suggest him to Aphrael, I will."

She swore at him in Styric. "Don't you understand, Sparhawk? I almost lost him." Her heart was in her luminous blue eyes. "I'll die if anything happens to him."

"Nothing's going to happen to him. Are you going to ask Aphrael about it, or would you rather have me do it?"

She swore at him again.

"Where did you ever learn that kind of language?" he asked mildly. "If that takes care of our problem, I'm a little overdue at the bedroom door."

"I didn't quite follow that."

"It's time for the kissing and making up. There's supposed to be a certain rhythm to these things, and if I wait too long to soften Ehlana's displeasure, she'll begin to think I don't love her anymore."

"Do you mean her performance here tonight was nothing more than an invitation to the bedroom?"

"That might be putting it a little bluntly, but there was some of that involved, yes. Sometimes I get busy and forget to pay as much attention to her as I should. She'll only let that go on for so long before she makes a speech. The speech reminds me that I've been neglecting her. We kiss and make up, and everything's all right again."

"Wouldn't it be simpler if she just came right out and told you in the first place without these elaborate games?"

"Probably, but it wouldn't be nearly as much fun for her. You'll excuse me?"

"Why do you always avoid me, Berit-Knight?" Empress Elysoun asked with a disconsolate little pout.

"Your Highness misunderstands me," Berit replied, flushing slightly and keeping his eyes averted.

"Am I ugly, Berit-Knight?"

"Of course not, your Highness."

"Then why don't you ever look at me?"

"It's not considered polite among Elenes for a man to look at an undressed woman, your Highness."

"I'm not an Elene, Sir Knight. I'm a Valesian, and I'm not naked. I have plenty of clothes on. If you'll come to my chambers, I'll show you the difference."

Sparhawk had been looking for Sir Berit to advise him of their upcoming journey and he had just rounded a corner in the hallway leading to the chapel to find his young friend trapped once more by the Empress Elysoun. Since Emperor Sarabian's entire family was inside the castle as a security measure, Berit's escape routes had been seriously curtailed, and Elysoun had been taking advantage of the situation outrageously. The emperor's Valesian wife was a brown-skinned, sunny girl whose native costume left her unashamedly bare-breasted. No matter how many times Sarabian had explained to Berit that customary moral strictures did not apply to Valesians, the young knight remained steadfastly respectful—and chaste. Elysoun had taken that as a challenge and she had been pursuing the poor young man relentlessly. Sparhawk was just on the verge of speaking to his friend, but he smiled instead and stepped back around the corner to listen. He *was* the interim Preceptor of the Pandion Order, after all, and it was his duty to look after the souls of his men.

"Do you *always* have to be an Elene?" Elysoun was asking the knight.

"I *am* an Elene, your Highness."

"But you Elenes are so boring," she said. "Why don't you be a Valesian for just one afternoon? It's much more fun, and it won't take very long, you know—unless you want it to." She paused. "Are you really a virgin?" she asked curiously.

Berit turned bright red.

Elysoun laughed delightedly. "What an absurd idea!" she exclaimed. "Aren't you even a little curious about what you've been missing? I'll be happy to take that tiresome virginity off your hands, Berit-Knight—and it won't even hurt very much."

Sparhawk took pity on the poor fellow and intervened at that point. "Ah, there you are, Berit," he said, stepping around the corner and speaking in Tamul for the empress's benefit. "I've been looking all over for you. Something's come up that needs our attention." He bowed to the empress. "Your Imperial Highness," he murmured, "I'm afraid I'll have to commandeer your friend here for a while. Matters of state, you know."

The look Elysoun gave him had daggers in it.

"I was sure your Highness would understand," he said, bowing again. "Come along, Berit. The matter's serious, and we're late." He led his friend off down the opalescent corridor as Empress Elysoun glared after them.

"Thanks, Sparhawk," Berit said with relief.

"Why don't you just stay away from her?"

"I can't. She follows me everywhere. She even trapped me in the bathhouse once—in the middle of the night. She said she wanted to bathe with me."

"Berit—" Sparhawk smiled. "—as your preceptor and spiritual guide, I'm supposed to applaud your devotion to the ideals of our order. As your friend, though, I have to tell you that running away from her only makes matters worse. We have to stay here in Matherion, and if we stay long enough, she *will* get you. She's very single-minded about it."

"Yes, I've noticed that."

"She's really quite pretty, you know," Sparhawk suggested tentatively. "What's your difficulty with the notion of being friendly?"

"Sparhawk!"

The big Pandion sighed. "I was afraid you might look at it that way. Look, Berit, Elysoun comes from a different culture with different customs. She doesn't see this sort of thing as sin. Sarabian's made it quite clear that he wants some of us to accommodate her, and she's chosen you as the lucky man. It's a political necessity, so you're just going to have to set these delicate feelings aside. Look upon it as your knightly duty, if it makes you feel any better. I can even have Emban grant you an indulgence if you think it's necessary."

Berit gasped.

"You're starting to embarrass us," Sparhawk said. "Elysoun's been making Sarabian's life miserable about the whole thing. He won't step in and *order* you to do as she asks, no matter how much she nags him, but he quite obviously expects *me* to speak with you about it."

"I can't believe you're saying this, Sparhawk."

"Just go ahead and do it, Berit. You don't have to enjoy it if you don't want to, but do it. Do it as often as you have to, but make her stop screaming at the emperor. It's your duty, my friend, and after you and Elysoun have romped around the bedroom a few times, she'll start looking for new playmates."

"But what if she doesn't?"

"I wouldn't worry too much. Patriarch Emban's got a whole saddlebag full of indulgences if it should turn out that you really need them."

The failed uprising had given Emperor Sarabian the perfect excuse to escape from his government. Feigning cowardice, he had flatly declared that he felt safe only within the walls of Ehlana's castle, and then only if the moat remained full and the drawbridge raised. His ministers, long accustomed to arranging his every move, found that terribly inconvenient.

Sarabian had not been motivated entirely by a desire to breathe the air of relative freedom, however. Interior Minister Kolata had been revealed as a traitor during the coup attempt, but Sarabian and his Elene friends had decided that the time was not yet right to publicly reveal his treachery. So long as the emperor remained inside Ehlana's castle, Kolata's presence there as well was fully explained. He was in charge of the police, after all, and the protection of the emperor was his paramount duty. The interior minister, closely supervised by Ehlana's cohorts, directed the police forces of the empire from inside the walls. His meetings with his underlings were always just a trifle strained, since Stragen customarily sat beside him with one hand idly resting on the hilt of a dagger.

It was early one morning when Ambassador Norkan, the Tamul emissary to the court of King Androl and Queen Betuana of Atan, was escorted into the gleaming imitation throne room in the castle. Norkan wore his usual golden mantle and a puzzled expression. Though he tried to conceal the fact, he quite obviously disapproved of the fact that his emperor was dressed in western-style doublet and hose of a rich plum color. "Have you gone and stolen my emperor, too, Queen Ehlana?" he asked with a perfunctory bow. Norkan was a brilliant man, but he had an unfortunate tendency to speak his mind quite openly.

"What a thing to say, your Excellency," Ehlana protested mildly in nearly perfect Tamul. Ehlana was technically the hostess here, so she sat on her throne wearing her formal crimson robe and a golden crown. She turned to her imperial "guest," who sprawled in a nearby chair slowly twitching a string across the opalescent floor for the entertainment of Princess Danae's cat. "Have I stolen you, Sarabian?" she asked him.

"Oh, absolutely, Ehlana," he replied, speaking in Elenic. "I'm utterly in thrall to you."

"Has someone opened a school for modern languages here on the grounds while I've been gone, Oscagne?" Norkan asked.

"I suppose you might say that," the foreign minister replied. "His Majesty's proficiency in Elenic predates Queen Ehlana's visit, however. Our revered emperor's been keeping secrets from us."

"Is he allowed to do that? I thought he was supposed to be just a stuffed toy that we trotted out on ceremonial occasions."

Even Oscagne choked a bit on that, but Sarabian burst into laughter. "I've missed you, Norkan," he declared. "Have you had the chance to get to know our excellent Norkan, Ehlana?"

"I sampled his wit in Atana, Sarabian." The queen smiled. "His observations always seem so—ah—unexpected."

"That they are," Sarabian laughed, rising to his feet. He swore as the rapier at his side briefly caught behind the leg of his chair; the emperor still had difficulty with his rapier. "Norkan once made one of those unexpected observations about the size of my sister's feet, and I had to send him off to Atan to keep her from having him murdered." He cocked one eyebrow at the ambassador. "I really should make you marry her, Norkan. Then you could insult her in private. Public insults require public responses, you know."

"I'm honored more than I can say, your Imperial Majesty," Norkan replied. "The prospect of becoming your brother-in-law is quite likely to stop my heart entirely."

"You don't like my sister," Sarabian accused.

"I didn't say that, your Majesty, but I prefer to worship her from afar—at least out of the range of her feet. That's what precipitated my unfortunate remark in the first place. I was gouty that day, and she stepped on my toe. She'd be a nice enough girl, I suppose, if she'd only watch where she's putting those cattle barges she wears for shoes."

"It wouldn't be one of those marriages made in heaven, Sarabian." Ehlana smiled. "I've met your sister, and I'm afraid his Excellency's wit would be lost on her."

"You might be right, my dear," Sarabian agreed. "I'd really like to get rid of her, though. She's irritated me since the day she was born. What are you doing back here in Matherion, Norkan?"

One of Ambassador Norkan's eyebrows shot up. "Things *have* changed, haven't they, Oscagne? Are we supposed to tell him to his face what's *really* going on?"

"Emperor Sarabian's decided to take charge of his own government, my friend." Oscagne sighed mournfully.

"Isn't that against the law?"

"Afraid not, old boy."

"Would you consider accepting my resignation?"

"No, not really."

"Don't you want to work for me any more, Norkan?" Sarabian asked.

"I have nothing against you personally, your Majesty, but if you decide to actually meddle in government, the whole empire could collapse."

"Marvelous, Norkan. I love the way you start talking before you've saddled up your brains. You see, Ehlana? That's what I was telling you about. The officials in my government all expect me to smile regally, approve their recommendations without question, and leave the business of running things to them."

"How boring."

"Indeed it is, my dear, but I'm going to change it. Now that I've seen a real ruler in action, whole new horizons have been opened to me. You still haven't answered my question, Norkan. What brings you back to Matherion?"

"The Atans are growing restive, your Majesty."

"Are the recent disturbances starting to erode their loyalty?"

"No, your Majesty, quite the reverse. The uprising has them all excited. Androl wants to move out in force to occupy Matherion in order to guarantee your safety. I don't think we want that. The Atans don't pay too much attention to rank or position when they decide to kill people."

"We noticed that," Sarabian replied dryly. "I've received all sorts of petitions of protest from the noble houses of Tamul proper as a result of the measures Engessa took to put down the coup."

"I've spoken with Betuana, your Majesty," Norkan continued. "She's promised to shorten her husband's leash until I get some instructions from you. Something short and to the point like 'Sit! Stay!' might be appropriate, considering Androl's mental capabilities."

"How did you ever get to be a diplomat, Norkan?"

"I lied a lot."

"A suggestion, Emperor Sarabian?" Tynian offered.

"Go ahead, Sir Tynian."

"We don't really want to ruffle King Androl's feathers, so a hint to him that he's being held in place to meet a far greater threat might be preferable to just sending him to bed without any supper."

Sarabian laughed. "What a novel way to put it, Sir Tynian. All right, Norkan, send Engessa."

Norkan blinked.

"Pay attention, man," Sarabian snapped.

"That's something you'll have to get used to, Norkan," Oscagne advised. "The emperor sometimes takes verbal shortcuts."

"Oh. I see." Norkan thought about it. "Might I ask why Atan Engessa would be better qualified to carry your instructions than I would, your Majesty?"

"Because Engessa can run faster than you can, and he'll be able to put our commands to Androl in language far more acceptable to him. There's also the fact that using Engessa hints at a military reason for the decision, and that should smooth Androl's feathers all the more. You can explain our *real* reasons to Betuana when you get back."

"You know something, Oscagne?" Norkan said. "He might just work out all right after all—if we can keep him from making too many blunders at the outset."

Oscagne winced.

Sparhawk touched Vanion's shoulder and motioned with his head. The two of them drifted back to the rear of the throne room. "I've got a problem, Vanion," Sparhawk muttered.

"Oh?"

"I've racked my brains to come up with an excuse for us to get out of Matherion for long enough to retrieve the Bhelliom, but I haven't had a single idea that a child wouldn't be able to see through. Ehlana's not stupid, you know."

"No, that she isn't."

"Aphrael won't say anything definite, but I get the strong feeling that she wants us to sail on the same ship with Emban and Tynian, and I'm starting to run out of excuses to keep delaying their departure. Any ideas?"

"Ask Oscagne to help you," Vanion shrugged. "He's a diplomat, so lying comes second nature to him."

"Nice idea, but I can't really tell him where we're going and what we're going to do when we get there, can I?"

"*Don't* tell him, then. Just tell him that you need a reason to be out of town for a while. Put on a gravely mysterious face and let it go at that. Oscagne's been around for long enough to recognize the symptoms of official reticence when he sees them."

"Why didn't I think of that?"

"Probably because your oath keeps getting in your way. I know that you've sworn to tell the truth, but that doesn't mean that you have to tell the *whole* truth. You can leave things out, you know. Leaving things out is one of the perquisites of the office of Preceptor."

Sparhawk sighed. "Back to school, I see. I think I'm doomed to spend my whole life getting instructions from you—and being made to feel inadequate in the process."

"That's what friends are for, Sparhawk."

"You're not going to tell me, are you?" Sparhawk tried very hard to keep it from sounding like an accusation.

"Not yet, no," Princess Danae replied, carefully tying a doll's bonnet on her cat's head. Mmrr did not appear to care for the idea, but she endured her mistress's little game with a look of resignation.

"Why not?" Sparhawk asked his daughter, flopping down into one of the blue armchairs in the royal apartment.

"Because something might still come up to make it unnecessary. You're not going to find Bhelliom until I decide to *let* you find it, Father."

"You want us to sail with Tynian and Emban, though?"

"Yes."

"How far?"

"It doesn't really matter. I just need Tynian with us when we first set out, that's all."

"Then you don't really have any set destination in mind—with that ship, I mean?"

"Of course not. I just need Tynian to be along for a couple of days. We can go out to sea for a couple of leagues and then sail around in circles for two days if you want. It's all the same to me."

"Thanks," he said acidly.

"No charge. There." She held up the cat. "Isn't she darling in her new bonnet?"

"Adorable."

Mmrr gave Sparhawk a flat look of pure disgust.

·　·　·

"I can't tell you why, your Excellency," Sparhawk said to Oscagne later that same day when they were alone in one of the hallways. "All I can say is that I need a reason to be away from Matherion with a group of nine or ten of my friends for an indeterminate period of time—several weeks or so. It has to be significant enough to convince my wife that it's necessary, but not so serious as to worry her, *and* I have to sail on the same ship with Emban and Tynian."

"All right," Oscagne agreed. "How good an actor are you, Prince Sparhawk?"

"I don't think anybody'd pay money to watch me perform."

Oscagne let that pass. "I gather that this ploy is primarily intended for your wife's benefit?"

"Yes."

"Then it might be best if the idea of sending you off someplace came from her. I'll maneuver her into ordering you off on some inconsequential errand, and you can take it from there."

"I'd really like to see you try to maneuver Ehlana."

"Trust me, old boy. Trust me."

"Tega?" Sarabian asked his foreign minister incredulously. "The only superstition they have on the Isle of Tega is the one that says that it's bad luck not to raise the price of seashells every year."

"They never mentioned it to us in the past because they were probably afraid we'd think they were being silly, your Majesty," Oscagne replied urbanely. Oscagne looked decidedly uncomfortable in the blue doublet and hose Sarabian had ordered him to wear. He couldn't seem to think of anything to do with his hands, and he appeared to be very self-conscious about his bony legs. "The word *silly* seems to strike at the very core of the Tegan soul. They're the stuffiest people in the world."

"I know. Gahenas, my Tegan wife, can put me to sleep almost immediately—even when we're . . ." The emperor threw a quick look at Ehlana and left it hanging.

"Tegans have raised being boring to an art form, your Majesty," Oscagne agreed. "Anyway, there's an old Tegan myth to the effect that the oyster beds are haunted by a mermaid. Supposedly she eats oysters, shells and all, and that *really* upsets the Tegans. She also seduces Tegan divers, who tend to drown during the exchange of pleasantries."

"Isn't a mermaid supposed to be half-girl and half-fish?" Ulath asked.

"So the legend goes," Oscagne replied.

"And isn't she supposed to be a fish from the waist down?"

"I've been told so, yes."

"Then how—?" Ulath also looked quickly at Ehlana and then abruptly broke off.

"How what, Sir Ulath?" Ehlana asked him innocently.

"It's—ah—not really important, your Majesty," he replied with an embarrassed cough.

"I wouldn't even raise this absurd myth, your Majesties," Oscagne said to Sarabian and Ehlana, "except in the light of recent developments. The parallels between the vampires in Arjuna, the Shining Ones in southern Atan, and the werewolves, ghouls, and Ogres in other parts of the empire are really rather striking, wouldn't you say? I'd imagine that if someone were to go to Tega and ask around, he might hear stories about some prehistoric pearl-diver who's been resurrected and also find that some rabble-rouser's telling the Tegans that this hero and his half-fish, half-human mistress are going to lead the oysters in a mass assault on Matherion."

"How droll," Sarabian murmured.

"Sorry, your Majesty," Oscagne apologized. "What I'm getting at is that we've probably got some relatively inexperienced conspirator on Tega. He's just getting started, so he's bound to make mistakes—but experienced or not, he knows a great deal about the whole conspiracy. Since our friends here won't let us question Kolata too closely, we have to look elsewhere for information."

"We're not being delicate about the Minister of the Interior, your Excellency," Kalten told him. "It's just that we've seen what happens to prisoners who are on the verge of talking too much. Kolata's still useful to us, but only as long as he stays in one piece. He won't be much good if little chunks and globs of him get scattered all over the building."

Oscagne shuddered. "I'll take your word for it, Sir Kalten. At any rate, your Majesty, if some of our Elene friends here could go to Tega and put their hands on this fellow and talk with him before our enemy can dismantle him, they could probably persuade him to tell us everything he knows. Sir Sparhawk has some ambitions along those lines, I understand. He wants to find out if he can wring somebody out hard enough to make his hair bleed."

"You have a very graphic imagination, Sparhawk," Sarabian noted. "What do you think, Ehlana? Can you spare your husband for a while? If he and some of his knights went to Tega and held the entire island underwater for a couple of hours, God only knows what kind of information might come bubbling to the surface."

"That's a very good idea, Sarabian. Sparhawk, why don't you take some of our friends, run on down to the Isle of Tega, and see what you can find out?"

"I'd really rather not be separated from you, dear," he replied with feigned reluctance.

"That's very sweet, Sparhawk, but we *do* have responsibilities, you know."

"Are you ordering me to go, Ehlana?"

"You don't have to put it *that* way, Sparhawk. It's only a suggestion, after all."

"As my Queen commands," he sighed, putting on a melancholy expression.

CHAPTER TWO

Empress Gahenas was a Tegan lady of middle years with a severe expression and tightly pursed lips. She wore a plain grey gown, buttoned to the chin, and long-sleeved gloves of scratchy wool. Her hair was drawn so tightly back into a bun that it made her eyes bulge, and her ears protruded from the sides of her head like open barn doors. Empress Gahenas disapproved of everything; that much was clear from the outset. She had come to Sparhawk's study to provide background information on the Isle of Tega, but she did not come alone. The Empress Gahenas never went anywhere without her four chaperons, a cluster of ancient Tegan hags who perched on a varnished bench like a row of gargoyles.

It was a warm day in early autumn, but the sunlight streaming in through the window of Sparhawk's study seemed to grow wan and sickly when Empress Gahenas entered with the stern guardians of her virtue.

She spent an hour lecturing Sparhawk on the gross national product of her homeland in a tone that strongly suggested that she was going to give a test at the conclusion of the lecture. Sparhawk fought to keep from yawning. He was not really interested in production figures or labor costs. What he really wanted from the jug-eared empress were little details of ordinary life on the Isle to flesh out the series of letters he was writing to his wife—letters that were to be doled out to Ehlana to help sustain the fiction that he and his friends were tracking down ringleaders and other conspirators who were concealed among the general population.

"Ah—" He interrupted Gahenas's droning monologue. "—this is absolutely fascinating, your Highness, but could we go back for a moment to the island's form of government? That really has me baffled."

"Tega is a republic, Prince Sparhawk. Our rulers are elected to their positions every five years. It's been that way for twenty-five centuries."

"Your officials aren't elected for life?"

"Of course not. Who would want a job like that for life?"

"No one ever develops a hunger for power?"

"The government *has* no power, Prince Sparhawk. It exists only to carry out the will of the electorate."

"Why five years?"

"Because nobody wants to be away from his own affairs for longer than that."

"What happens if a man's reelected?"

"That's contrary to the law. No one serves more than one term in office."

"Let's suppose somebody turned out to be an absolute genius in a particular position? Wouldn't you want to keep him there?"

"We've never found anyone that indispensable."

"It seems to me that the system would encourage corruption. If a man knows he's going to be thrown out of office after five years, what's to keep him from manipulating his official decisions to further his own interests? Later on, I mean?"

"Quite impossible, Prince Sparhawk. Our elected officials *have* no outside interests. As soon as they're elected, everything they own is sold, and the money's put into the national treasury. If the economy prospers during their term in office, their wealth earns them a profit. If the economy collapses, they lose everything."

"That's absurd. No government *ever* makes a profit."

"Ours does," she said smugly, "and it has to be a real profit. The tax rates are set and cannot be changed, so our officials can't generate a false profit by simply raising taxes."

"Why would anyone want to be an official in a government like that?"

"Nobody *wants* to be, Prince Sparhawk. Most Tegans do everything they possibly can to avoid election. The fact that a man's own personal fortune's in the treasury forces him to work just as hard as he possibly can to make sure that the government prospers. Many have worked themselves to death looking after the interests of the republic."

"I think I'd run away from an honor like that one."

"That's really quite impossible, your Highness. Just as soon as a man's name's placed in nomination for a public office, he's put under guard, and if he's elected, he remains under close guard for his entire term. The republic makes absolutely sure that nobody evades his responsibilities to her."

"The republic's a stern mistress."

"She is indeed, Prince Sparhawk, and that's exactly the way it should be."

Though his companions chafed at the delay, Sparhawk put off their departure for two more days while he feverishly composed the letters to Ehlana. The progress of the fictitious investigation had to be convincing, certainly, and at least moderately interesting. Sparhawk wove false leads, plots, and unsolved mysteries into his account. He became increasingly absorbed in the developing story, sometimes becoming so caught up in it that he lost sight of the fact that the events he was reporting were not actually taking place. He became rather proud of his efforts, and he began to revise extensively, adding a touch here and modifying a poorly phrased passage there, until he unwittingly crossed the line between careful artistry and sheer fussiness.

"They're good enough, Sparhawk," Vanion said to him after reading through the letters on the evening of the second day. Vanion was rather pointedly wearing the plain tunic and heavy riding boots Pandions customarily put on before making an extended journey.

"You don't think it's too obvious?"

"It's fine just the way it is."

"Maybe I should rework that third letter. It seems awfully weak to me for some reason."

"You've written it four times already. It's good enough."

"I'm really not happy with it, Vanion." Sparhawk took the offending letter from his friend and ran through it once more, automatically reaching for his pen as he read.

Vanion firmly took the letter away from him.

"Let me just fix that last paragraph," Sparhawk pleaded.

"No."

"But—"

"*No!*" Vanion put the letter back in its proper place, folded the packet, and tucked it inside his doublet. "Oscagne's sending Norkan along with us," he said. "We'll give the letters to him, and he can sort of dribble them back here to Ehlana. Norkan's shrewd enough to space them out just enough to keep her from getting suspicious. The ship's been ready for a week now, and Emban's getting impatient. We'll sail with the morning tide."

"I think I know what I did wrong," Sparhawk said. "I can fix that third letter in no more than an hour or two."

"No, Sparhawk. Absolutely not."

"Are you sure she's asleep?" Sparhawk whispered.

"Of course I am, Father," Princess Danae replied.

"The slightest sound will wake her up, you know. She can hear a fly walking across the ceiling."

"Not tonight she can't. I've seen to that."

"I hope you know what you're doing, Danae. She knows every tiny little mark on that ring. If there's the slightest difference between it and this new one, she'll notice it immediately."

"Oh, Father, you worry too much. I've done this before, after all. Ghwerig *made* the rings, and I still fooled him. I've been stealing those rings for thousands of years. Believe me, Mother will never know the difference."

"Is this really necessary?"

"Yes. Bhelliom's useless to you without both rings, and you may need it almost as soon as we lift it from the seafloor."

"Why?"

She rolled her eyes upward and sighed. "Because the whole world will shift just as soon as Bhelliom moves. When you were carrying it to Zemoch, the world quivered around like a plate of jelly the whole time. My family and I really don't like it when Bhelliom moves. It makes some of us queasy."

"Will our enemies out there be able to pinpoint our location from that?"

She shook her head. "It's too generalized. Every God in the world's going to know when Bhelliom starts to move, though, and we can be absolutely sure that at least *some* of them will come looking for it. Can we talk about this some other time?"

"What do you want me to do?"

"Just stand watch at the bedroom door. I don't like having an audience when I'm stealing things."

"You sound just like Talen."

"Naturally. He and I were made for each other. It was the Gods who invented theft in the first place."

"You're not serious."

"Of course. We steal things from each other all the time. It's a game. Did you think we just sat around on clouds basking in adoration? We have to do *something* to pass the time. You should try it sometime, Father. It's lots of fun." She looked around furtively, crouched low, and reached for the bedroom door-handle. "Keep a lookout, Sparhawk. Whistle if you hear anybody coming."

They all gathered in the sitting room of the royal apartment the following morning to receive their final instructions from Emperor Sarabian and Queen Ehlana. It was a formality, really. Everybody knew what they were supposed to do already, so they sat in the sunlit room making generalized small talk and cautioning each other to be careful, as people parting from each other do the world around.

Alean, Queen Ehlana's doe-eyed maid, was in the next room, and she was singing. Her voice was clear and sweet and true, and all conversation in the sitting room broke off as she sang. "It's like listening to an angel," Patriarch Emban murmured.

"The girl has a truly magnificent voice," Sarabian agreed. "She already has the court musicians in near-despair."

"She seems a bit sad this morning," Kalten said, two great tears glistening in his eyes.

Sparhawk smiled faintly. Kalten had preyed on maids since he had been a young man, and few had been able to resist his blandishments. This time, however, the shoe was on the other foot. Alean was not singing for her own entertainment. The brown-eyed girl was singing for an audience of one, and her song, dealing as it did with the sorrows of parting, filled Kalten's eyes. She sang of broken hearts and other extravagances in a very old Elenian ballad entitled "My Bonnie Blue-Eyed Boy." Then Sparhawk noticed that Baroness Melidere, Queen Ehlana's lady-in-waiting, was also watching Kalten very closely. Melidere's eyes met Sparhawk's, and she slowly winked. Sparhawk almost laughed aloud. He was clearly not the only one who was aware of Alean's subtle campaign.

"You *will* write, won't you, Sparhawk?" Ehlana said.

"Of course I will," he replied.

"I can virtually guarantee that, your Majesty," Vanion said. "If you give him just a little time, Sparhawk's a great letter-writer. He devotes enormous amounts of time and effort to his correspondence."

"Tell me everything, Sparhawk," the queen urged.

"Oh, he *will*, your Majesty, he will," Vanion assured her. "He'll probably tell you more than you ever really wanted to know about the Isle of Tega."

"Critic," Sparhawk muttered under his breath.

"Please don't be *too* vivid in your description of our situation here, your Grace," Sarabian was saying to Emban. "Don't make Dolmant think that my empire's falling down around my ears."

"Isn't it, your Majesty?" Emban replied with some surprise. "I thought that was why I was dashing back to Chyrellos to fetch the Church Knights."

"Well, maybe it is, but don't destroy my dignity entirely."

"Dolmant's very wise, your Majesty," Emban assured him. "He understands the language of diplomacy."

"Oh, *really*?" Ehlana said with heavy sarcasm.

"Should I convey your Majesty's greetings to the Archprelate as well?" Emban asked her.

"Of course. Tell him that I'm desolate at being separated from him—particularly in view of the fact that I can't keep an eye on him. You might *also* advise him that a little-known Elenian statute clearly says that I have to ratify any agreements he makes with the Earl of Lenda during my absence. Tell him not to get *too* comfortable in those pieces of my kingdom he's been snipping off since I left, because I'll just take them back again as soon as I get home."

"Does she do this all the time, Sparhawk?" Sarabian asked.

"Oh, yes, all the time, your Majesty. The Archprelate bites off all his fingernails every time a letter from her reaches the Basilica."

"It keeps him young." Ehlana rose to her feet. "Now, friends," she said, "I hope you'll excuse my husband and me for a few moments so that we can say our good-byes privately. Come along, Sparhawk," she commanded.

"Yes, my Queen."

The morning fog had lifted, and the sun was very bright as their ship sailed out of the harbor and heeled over to take a southeasterly course which would round the southern tip of the Micaen peninsula to the Isle of Tega. The ship was well-appointed, although she was of a slightly alien configuration. Khalad did not entirely approve of her, finding fault with her rigging and the slant of her masts.

It was about noon when Vanion came up on deck to speak with Sparhawk, who was leaning on the rail watching the coastline slide by. They were both wearing casual clothing, since there is no real need for formal garb on board ship.

"Sephrenia wants us all in the main cabin," the preceptor told his friend. "It's time for one of those startling revelations we've all come to love and adore. Why don't you round up the others and bring them on down?"

"You're in a peculiar humor," Sparhawk noted. "What's the problem?"

"Sephrenia's being excessively Styric today." Vanion shrugged.

"That one escaped me."

"You know the signs, Sparhawk—the mysterious expression, the cryptic remarks, the melodramatic pauses, the superior manner."

"Have you two been fighting?"

Vanion laughed. "Never that, my friend. It's just that we all have little quirks and idiosyncracies that irritate our loved ones sometimes. Sephrenia's having one of her quirky days."

"I won't tell her you said that, of course."

Vanion shrugged. "She already knows how I feel. We've discussed it in the past—at length. Sometimes she does it just to tease me. Go get the others, Sparhawk. Let's not give her *too* much time to perfect this performance."

They all gathered in the main salon belowdecks, a cabin that was part dining room and part lounge. Sephrenia had not put in her appearance as yet and after a few moments, Sparhawk understood what Vanion had been talking about. A familiar sound began to emerge from the lady's cabin.

"*Flute?*" Talen exclaimed in astonishment, his voice cracking in that peculiar adolescent yodel which afflicts human males at the onset of puberty.

Sparhawk had wondered how Aphrael intended to get around the rather sticky problem of explaining her identity. To have appeared to the others as Princess Danae would quite obviously have been out of the question. Flute was quite another matter. His friends all recognized Flute as Aphrael, and that would eliminate the need for extended explanations. Sparhawk sighed as a rather melancholy thought occurred to him. He realized sadly that he didn't know what his daughter really looked like. That dear little face that was engraved on his mind almost as deeply as

Ehlana's was only one in a long line of incarnations—one of thousands, more than likely.

Then the door to Sephrenia's cabin opened, and the small Styric woman emerged with a smile that made her face look like the sun coming up and with her little sister in her arms.

Flute, of course, was unchanged—and unchangeable. She appeared to be no more than six years old—precisely the same age as Danae. Sparhawk immediately rejected the possibility of coincidence. Where Aphrael was concerned, there *were* no coincidences. She wore that same short linen smock belted at the waist and that same plaited grass headband as she had when they had first met her. Her long hair was as black as night, and her large eyes nearly as dark. Her little bare feet were grass-stained. She held a simple many-chambered set of goatherd's pipes to her bowlike lips, and her song was Styric, set in a complex minor key.

"What a pretty child," Ambassador Norkan observed, "but is it really a good idea to take her along on this mysterious mission of yours, Prince Sparhawk? I gather there might be some danger involved."

"Not *now* there won't be, your Excellency." Ulath grinned.

Sephrenia gravely set the Child-Goddess on the cabin floor, and Flute began to dance to the clear, sweet music of her pipes.

Sephrenia looked at Emban and Norkan. "Watch the child closely, Emban, and you, too, your Excellency. That should save us hours of explanation and argument."

Flute pirouetted through the cabin, her grass-stained little feet flickering, her black hair flying and her pipes sounding joyously. This time Sparhawk actually saw the first step she placed quite firmly on insubstantial air. As one mounting an invisible stair, the Child-Goddess danced upward, whirling as she climbed, bending and swaying, her tiny feet fluttering like bird's wings as she danced on nothing at all. Then her song and her dance ended, and, smiling impishly and still standing in midair, she curtsied.

Emban's eyes were bulging and he had half fallen from his chair. Ambassador Norkan tried to maintain his urbane expression, but it was slipping badly, and his hands were shaking.

Talen grinned and began to applaud. The others laughed, and they all joined in.

"Oh, thank you, my dear ones," Flute said sweetly, curtsying again.

"For God's sake, Sparhawk!" Emban choked, "Make her come down from there! She's destroying my sanity!"

Flute laughed and quite literally hurled herself into the fat little churchman's arms, smothering his pale, cringing face with kisses. "I *love* to do that to people!" She giggled delightedly.

Emban shrank back even farther.

"Oh, don't be silly, Emban," she chided. "I'm not going to hurt you. I sort of love you, actually." A look of sly mischief came into her eyes. "How would you like to come to work for me, your Grace?" she suggested. "I'm not nearly as stuffy as your Elene God, and we could have a lot of fun together."

"Aphrael!" Sephrenia said sharply. "Stop that! You *know* you're not supposed to do that!"

"I was only teasing him, Sephrenia. I wouldn't really steal Emban. The Elene God needs him too much."

"Has your theology been sufficiently shaken, your Grace?" Vanion asked the Patriarch of Ucera. "The little girl in your lap who's blithely trying to lead you off down the flowery path to heresy is the Child-Goddess Aphrael, one of the thousand Younger Gods of Styricum."

"How do I greet her?" Emban asked in a squeaky, frightened kind of voice.

"A few kisses might be nice," Flute suggested.

"Stop that," Sephrenia chided her again.

"And what are *your* feelings, your Excellency?" the little girl asked Norkan.

"Dubious, your—uh—"

"Just Aphrael, Norkan," she told him.

"That's really not suitable," he replied. "I'm a diplomat, and the very soul of diplomatic speech is formal modes of address. I haven't called anyone but colleagues by their first names since I was about ten years old."

"Her first name *is* a formal mode of address, your Excellency," Sephrenia said gently.

"All right, then," Aphrael said, slipping down from Emban's lap. "Tynian and Emban are going to Chyrellos to fetch the Church Knights. Norkan's going to the Isle of Tega to help Sparhawk lie to my—uh—his wife, that is. The rest of us are going to go get the Bhelliom again. Sparhawk seems to think he might need it. I think he's underestimating his own abilities, but I'll go along with him on the issue—if only to keep him from nagging and complaining."

"I've really missed her." Kalten laughed. "What are you going to do, Flute? Saddle up a herd of whales for us to ride to that coastline where we threw Bhelliom into the sea?"

Her eyes brightened.

"Never mind," Sparhawk told her quite firmly.

"Spoilsport."

"I'm really disappointed in you, Sparhawk," Kalten said. "I've never ridden a whale before."

"*Will* you shut up about whales?" Sparhawk snapped at him.

"You don't have to get so touchy about it. What have you got against whales?"

"It's a personal thing between Aphrael and me," Sparhawk replied in a grating tone. "I won't win *many* arguments with her, but I *am* going to win the one about whales."

The layover of their ship at Tega was necessarily brief. The tide had already turned, and the captain was quite concerned about the inexorably lowering water-level in the harbor.

Sparhawk and his friends conferred briefly in the ship's main salon while Khalad directed the sailors in the unloading of their horses and supplies. "Do your very best to make Sarathi understand just how serious the situation here really is, Emban," Vanion said. "Sometimes he gets a little pigheaded."

"I'm sure he'll enjoy knowing how you really feel about him, Vanion." The fat churchman grinned.

"Say anything you want, your Grace. I'll never be going back to Chyrellos anyway, so it doesn't really matter. Make a special point of letting him know that the name of Cyrgon's been popping up. You might want to gloss over the fact that we've only got Krager's word for Cyrgon's involvement, though. We *are* sure about the Troll-Gods, however, and the notion that we're facing heathen Gods again might help Sarathi tear his attention away from Rendor."

"Was there anything else I already know that you'd like to tell me, Vanion?"

Vanion laughed. "Nicely put. I *was* being a bit of a meddler, wasn't I?"

"The term is *busybody*, Vanion. I'll do everything I can, but you know Dolmant. He'll make his own assessment and his own decision. He'll weigh Daresia against Rendor and decide which of them he wants to save."

"Tell him that I'm here with Sparhawk, Emban," Flute instructed. "He knows who I am."

"He *does*?"

"You don't really have to step around Dolmant so carefully. He's not the fanatic Ortzel is, so he can accept the fact that his theology doesn't answer all the questions in the universe. The fact that I'm involved might help him to make the right decision. Give him my love. He's an old stick sometimes, but I'm really fond of him."

Emban's eyes were a little wild. "I think I'll retire when this is all over," he said.

"Don't be silly." She smiled. "You could no more retire than I could. You're having too much fun. Besides, we need you." She turned to Tynian. "Don't overwork that shoulder," she instructed. "Give it time to completely heal before you start exercising it."

"Yes, ma'am," he replied, grinning at her authoritarian manner.

"Don't make fun of me, Tynian," she threatened. "If you do that, you might just wake up some morning with your feet on backward. Now give me a kiss."

"Yes, Aphrael."

She laughed, and swarmed into his arms to collect her kisses.

They debarked and stood on the pier as the Tamul vessel made her way slowly out of the harbor.

"They're sailing at the right time of year, anyway," Ulath said. "It's a little early for the hurricanes."

"That's encouraging," Kalten said. "Where to now, Flute?"

"There's a ship waiting for us on the far side of the island," she replied. "I'll tell you about it after we get out of town."

Vanion handed Norkan the packet of letters Sparhawk had so laboriously written. "We can't be sure how long we'll be gone, your Excellency," he said, "so you might want to space these out."

Norkan nodded. "I can supplement them with reports of my own," he said, "and if worse comes to worst, I can always use the talents of the professional forger at the embassy here. He should be able to duplicate Prince Sparhawk's handwriting after a day or so of practice—well enough to add personal postscripts to my reports, anyway."

For some reason Sparhawk found that very shocking.

"May I ask a question?" Norkan said to Flute.

"Of course," she replied. "I won't guarantee that I'll answer, but you can ask."

"Are our Tamul Gods real?"

"Yes."

Norkan sighed. "I was afraid of that. I haven't led what you'd call an exemplary life."

"Don't worry, Norkan. Your Gods don't take themselves very seriously. They're considered frivolous by the rest of us," she paused. "They're fun at parties, though," she added. She suddenly giggled. "They *really* irritate the Elene God. He has absolutely no sense of humor, and your Tamul Gods are very fond of practical jokes."

Norkan shuddered. "I don't think I really want to know any more about this sort of thing," he said. He looked around. "I'd strongly advise you to leave town rather quickly, my friends," he told them. "A republican form of government generates vast quantities of paper. There are questionnaires and forms and permits and licenses for almost everything, and there have to be ten copies of every single one. Nobody in the government wants to really make a decision about anything, so documents are just passed around from hand to hand until they either fall apart or get lost someplace."

"Who finally *does* make the decisions?" Vanion asked.

"Nobody." Norkan shrugged. "Tegans have learned to get along without a government. Everybody knows what has to be done anyway, so they scribble on enough official forms to keep the bureaucrats busy and then just ignore them. I hate to admit it, but the system seems to work quite well." He laughed. "There was a notorious murderer who was apprehended during the last century," he said. "They put him on trial, and he died of old age before the courts could decide whether he was guilty or not."

"How old was he when they caught him?" Talen asked.

"About thirty, I understand. You'd really better get started, my friends. That fellow at the head of this wharf has a sort of official expression on his face. You should probably be out of sight before he leafs through that pouch he's carrying and finds the right set of forms for you to fill out."

The Isle of Tega was tidy. It was not particularly scenic, nor did it have that picturesque desolation that sets the hearts of romantics all aflutter. The island produced no economically significant crops, and the small plots of ground under cultivation were devoted to what might be called expanded kitchen gardens. The stone walls that marked off the fields were straight and were all of a uniform height. The roads did not curve or bend, and the roadside barrows were all precisely of the same width and depth. Since the island's major industry, the collecting of seashells, was conducted underwater, there was none of the clutter one customarily sees around workshops.

The tedious tidiness, however, was offset by a dreadful smell that seemed to hover over everything.

"What is that awful stink?" Talen said, trying to cover his nostrils with his sleeve.

"Rotting shellfish." Khalad shrugged. "They must use it for fertilizer."

"How can they stand to live here with that smell?"

"They're probably so used to it that they don't even notice it anymore. They want the seashells because they can sell them to the Tamuls in Matherion, but people can't live on a steady diet of oysters and clams, so they have to get rid of the excess somehow. It seems to make very good fertilizer. I've never seen cabbages that big before."

Talen looked speculatively at his brother. "Pearls come from oysters, don't they?" he asked.

"That's what I've been told."

"I wonder if the Tegans do anything with them when they run across them?"

"They're not really very valuable, Talen," Flute told him. "There's something in the water around the island that makes the pearls black. Who would pay anything for black pearls?" She looked around at them. "Now then," she said to them, "We'll have to sail about fifteen hundred leagues to reach the place where Bhelliom is."

"*That* far?" Vanion said. "We won't get back to Matherion until the dead of winter, then. At thirty leagues a day, it's going to take us fifty days to get there and fifty days back."

"No," she disagreed, "actually it's going to take us five days to get there and five days to get back."

"Impossible!" Ulath said flatly. "No ship can move that fast."

"How much would you be willing to wager on that, Sir Ulath?"

He thought about that for a moment. "Not very much," he decided. "I wouldn't insult you by suggesting that you'd cheat, but . . ." He spread his hands suggestively.

"You're going to tamper with time again, I take it?" Sparhawk said to her.

She shook her head. "There are some limitations to that, Sparhawk. We need something more dependable. The ship that's waiting for us is just a bit unusual. I don't think any of you should get too curious about what she's made of and what makes her move. You won't be able to talk with the crew, because they don't speak your language. You probably wouldn't want to talk with them anyway, because they aren't really human."

"Witchcraft?" Bevier asked suspiciously.

She patted his cheek. "I'll answer that question just as soon as you come up with a definition of witchcraft that's not personally insulting, dear Bevier."

"What *are* you going to do, Aphrael?" Sephrenia asked suspiciously. "There *are* rules, you know."

"The other side's been breaking rules right and left, dear sister," Aphrael replied airily. "Reaching into the past has been forbidden almost from the very start."

"Are you going to reach into the future?" Khalad asked her. "People are coming up with new ideas in ship design all the time. Are you going to reach ahead and bring us back a ship that hasn't been invented yet?"

"That's an interesting idea, Khalad, but I wouldn't know where to look. The future hasn't happened yet, so how would I know where—or when—to find that kind of a ship? I've gone someplace else, that's all."

"What do you mean, 'someplace else'?"

"There's more than one world, Khalad," she said mysteriously. Then she made a little face. "You wouldn't *believe* how complicated the negotiations were," she added.

CHAPTER THREE

Ehlana and Sarabian had gone to the top of the central tower of the glowing castle, ostensibly to admire the sunset. Despite the fact that the castle was firmly in Elene hands, there were still enough Tamuls inside the walls to require a certain amount of care when the two wanted to speak privately.

"It all comes down to the question of power, Sarabian," Ehlana told the emperor in a pensive voice. "The fact that it's there has to be the central fact of our lives. We can either take it into our own hands, or leave it lying around unused; but if we choose not to use it, we can be sure that someone else *will.*" Her tone was subdued and her pale young face almost somber.

"You're in a melancholy humor today, Ehlana," Sarabian noted.

"I don't like being separated from Sparhawk. There were too many years of that after Aldreas exiled him. The point I was getting at is that you're going to have to be very firm so that the people in your government will understand that things have changed. What you'll really be doing here is seizing power. That's an act of revolution, you know." She smiled faintly. "You're almost too civilized to be a revolutionary, Sarabian. Are you sure you want to overthrow the government?"

"Good God, Ehlana, it's *my* government, and the power was mine in the first place."

"But you didn't use it. You were lazy and self-indulgent, and you let it slip away. Your ministers have filched your authority bit by bit. Now you're going to have to wrest it back from them. People don't willingly give up power, so you'll probably have to kill some of your ministers in order to prove to the rest that you're serious."

"Kill!"

"That's the ultimate expression of power, Sarabian, and your situation here requires a certain ruthlessness. You're going to have to spill some blood in order to get your government's attention."

"I don't think I can do that," Sarabian said in a troubled tone. "Oh, I know I've blustered and made threats a few times, but I couldn't actually order someone killed."

"That's up to you, but you'll lose if you don't, and that means that *they'll* kill *you.*" She considered it. "They'll probably kill you anyway," she added, "but at least you'll die for something important. Knowing that they're going to kill you in the end might help you make some unpleasant decisions at the outset. Once you get past your first couple of killings, it grows easier. I speak from a certain amount of experience on the subject, since almost exactly the same thing happened to me. Primate Annias completely controlled my government when I came to the throne, and I had to try to take my power back from him."

"You're the one who's been talking so freely about killing, Ehlana. Why didn't you kill Annias?"

She laughed a brittle, chilling little laugh. "It wasn't because I didn't *want* to, believe me, but I was too weak. Annias had very carefully stripped the crown of all its authority. I had some help from Lord Vanion and his Pandion Knights, but Annias had control of the army and the Church soldiers. I killed a few of his underlings, but I couldn't get to him. He knew I was trying, though, and that's why he poisoned me. Annias was really a very good politician. He knew exactly when the time for killing had arrived."

"You sound almost as if you admired him."

"I *hated* him, but he was very good."

"Well, I haven't killed anybody yet, so I can still step back from this."

"You're wrong there. You've already drawn your dagger, so you're going to have to use it. You crushed that uprising and you've imprisoned the Minister of the Interior. That's the same thing as a declaration of war."

"*You* did those things," he accused her.

"Yes, but I was acting in your behalf, so it's the same thing—at least in the eyes of your enemies. You're in danger now, you know. You've let your government know that you're going to seize back the power you let slip away. If you don't start killing people—and soon—you probably won't live out the month. You'd be dead already if you hadn't taken refuge in this castle."

"You're starting to frighten me, Ehlana."

"God knows I've been trying. Like it or not, Sarabian, you're committed now." She looked around. The sun was sinking into the cloud bank building up over the mountains lying to the west, and its ruddy glow was reflecting from the mother-of-pearl domes of Matherion. "Look at your city, Sarabian," she told him, "and contemplate the reality of politics. Before you're done, that red splashed all over the domes won't just be the reflection of the sunset."

"That's blunt enough," he said, his jaw taking on an unfamiliar set. "All right, how many people do I have to kill in order to ensure my own safety?"

"You don't have that many knives, my friend. Even if you butcher everybody in Matherion, you'll still be in danger. You might as well accept the fact that you're going to be in danger for the rest of your life." She smiled at him. "Actually, it's kind of exciting—once you get used to it."

"Well sir, yer Queenship," Caalador drawled, "it's all purty much th' way we wuz a-thankin' it wuz. That Krager feller, he wuz a-tellin' ol' Sporhawk th' ak-chool truth. Me'n Stragen, we bin a-twistin' the arms an' a-settin' fahr t' the feet o' them fellers ez wuz picked up durin' the koop—" He stopped. "Would your Majesty be too disappointed if I spoke like a human being for a while? That dialect's starting to dislocate my jaw."

"Not to mention the violence it's doing to the mother tongue," Stragen murmured.

The three of them had gathered together in a small blue-draped room adjoining the royal apartment later that same evening. Ehlana and Stragen were still dressed for dinner, she in crimson velvet and he in white satin. Caalador wore the sober brown of a businessman. The room had been carefully checked several times to be sure that no hidden listening posts lurked behind the walls, and Mirtai grimly stood watch outside the door.

"With the exception of Interior Minister Kolata, we didn't scoop up anybody of significance," Caalador continued, "and none of our other prisoners knows very much. I'm afraid we don't have much choice, your Majesty. We're going to have to go to work on Kolata if we want anything useful."

Ehlana shook her head. "You won't get anything out of him either, Caalador. He'll be killed as soon as he opens his mouth."

"We don't know that for certain, my Queen," Stragen disagreed. "It's entirely possible that our subterfuge has worked, you know. I really don't believe that the other side knows that he's a prisoner here. His policemen are still getting their orders from him."

"He's too valuable to risk," she said. "Once he's been torn to pieces, he'll be very hard to put back together again."

"If that's the way you want it, your Majesty." Caalador shrugged. "Anyway, it's growing increasingly obvious that this uprising was a pure hoax. Its only purpose was to compel us to reveal our strength. What concerns me the most is the fact that Krager and his friends obviously knew that we were using the criminals of Matherion as our eyes and ears. I'm sorry, Stragen, but it's the truth."

"It was such a good idea," Stragen sighed.

"It was, at first, but the trouble was that Krager's seen it before. Talen told me that your friend Platime used to have whole crowds of beggars, whores, and pickpockets following Krager around. The best idea in the world wears a little thin if you overuse it."

Stragen rose to his feet muttering curses and began to pace up and down in the small room with his white satin doublet gleaming in the candlelight. "It looks as if I've failed you, my Queen," he admitted. "I let a good idea run away with me. You couldn't really trust my judgment after a blunder like that, so I'll make arrangements to go back to Emsat."

"Oh, don't be an ass, Stragen," she told him. "And *do* sit down. I can't think while you're clumping around the room like that."

"She shore knows how t' put a feller in his place, don't she, Stragen?" Caalador laughed.

Ehlana sat tapping one finger thoughtfully against her chin. "First of all, let's keep this in the family. Sarabian's already getting a bit wild-eyed. Politically, he's an infant. I'm trying to raise him as quickly as I can, but I can only move him just so fast." She made a sour face. "I have to stop every so often to burp him."

"Now *that's* a picture for you," Caalador grinned. "What's he choking on, your Majesty?"

"Murder, primarily." She shrugged. "He doesn't seem to have the stomach for it."

Caalador blinked. "Not many do."

"Politicians can't afford that kind of delicacy. All right, if Krager and his friends know about our spy network, it won't be long until they try something in the way of penetration, will it?"

"You're quick," he said admiringly.

"Quick people live longer. Start thinking, gentlemen. We've got an exploitable situation here, and it won't last for very long. How can we use it to our greatest advantage?"

"We might be able to identify *real* conspirators instead of dupes, your Majesty," Stragen mused. "If they *do* try penetration, they're going to have to subvert some of our people. Let's say that we start passing out assorted fairy tales—this story to some pickpocket, another to some beggar or whore. Then we sit back to see which of those fraudulent schemes the other side attempts to counter. That will identify the turncoats in our own ranks, and we can squeeze useful names out of them."

"Surely we can get something a little better than that," she fretted.

"We'll work on it, your Majesty," Caalador promised. "If it's all right with you, I'd like to follow up on something else as well. We know that Krager's been busy here in Matherion, but we *don't* know how much information about our methods he's passed to his friends in other kingdoms. We might as well get what use we can out of our makeshift intelligence service before it becomes totally useless. I'll pass the word to the criminals down in Arjuna. I'd like to find out one way or the other if that silly scholar at the university has blundered across the real truth or if he's just weaving a theory out of moonbeams. I think we might all find a complete biography of the fellow known as Scarpa really fascinating reading. If nothing else, whether or not our spies in Arjuna succeed will tell us how much Krager *really* knows about the scope of our operations. If he thinks it's only localized, our apparatus hasn't been too severely compromised."

"Go after the others as well," Ehlana told him. "See what you can find out about Baron Parok, Rebal, and Sabre. Let's try to attach names to Rebal and Sabre at the very least."

"We'll do 'er jist th' way yer Majesty commands."

"I'd be happier 'n a pig in mud iffn y' would, Caalador," she replied.

Caalador collapsed in helpless laughter.

"It's probably the change in the weather, your Majesty," Alean said. "It's getting chillier at night, and the days aren't nearly as warm as they were just a few weeks ago."

"She grew up in Cimmura, Alean," Ehlana disagreed, "and the weather changes there much more markedly than it does here in Matherion."

"It's a different part of the world though, my Queen," Baroness Melidere pointed out. "We're right on the seacoast, for one thing. That could be what's causing the problem. Sometimes children react more strongly to things like that than adults."

"You're both making too much out of it," Mirtai told them. "All she needs is a tonic. She's not really sick, she's just moping around."

"But she *sleeps* all the time," Ehlana fretted. "She even falls asleep when she's playing."

"She's probably growing." The giantess shrugged. "I used to do the same sort of thing when I was a little girl. Growing is very hard work, I guess."

The object of their discussions lay drowsing on a divan near the window with Rollo loosely clasped in her arms. Rollo had survived two generations of intense affection. He had been dragged about by one hind leg. He had been laid upon, crammed into tight places, and ignored at times for weeks on end. A shift in his stuffings had given him a slightly worried expression. Queen Ehlana viewed that as a bad sign. Rollo had never looked worried when he had been *her* toy. Mmrr, on the other hand, seemed quite content. An owner who didn't move around very much suited Mmrr right down to the ground. When Princess Danae was dozing, she was not dreaming up ridiculous things to do to her cat. Mmrr secretly felt that any day which did not involve being dressed up in doll's clothing was a good day. She lay on her little mistress's hip with her front paws sedately folded under her chest, her eyes closed, and a soft, contented purr coming from her throat. So long as nothing disturbed her naps, Mmrr was perfectly at peace with the world.

The Royal Princess Danae dozed, her mind far more involved with the conversation Flute was holding with Sparhawk and his friends on the Isle of Tega than with her mother's concern over her health here in Matherion. Danae yawned and nestled down with toy and cat and drifted off to sleep.

Dearest,

We've reached Tega, and we'll be going out into the countryside for a while to see what's afoot. I'll be out of touch for a bit, so I thought it might be a good idea to let you know that we've arrived safely. Don't be too concerned if you don't hear from me for quite some time. I'm not entirely sure how long we'll be submerged in the population here.

The others are growing impatient to get started. There's no real point to this letter—except to tell you that I love you—but that's probably the most important point of all, isn't it? Kiss Danae for me.

All my love,
Sparhawk

"Oh, that's nice," Ehlana murmured, lowering the note from her husband. They were all sitting in the blue-draped sitting room in the queen's apartments, and the arrival of Caalador with Sparhawk's letter had interrupted a serious discussion about what they were going to do about the Interior Ministry.

Caalador, dressed again in sober brown and carrying a grotesque porcelain figurine from twelfth-century Arjuna, was frowning. "I think you might want to remind the people at the gates of the compound that they're supposed to let me in, your Majesty. I had a bit of an argument again."

"What's this?" Emperor Sarabian asked.

"Master Caalador's serving as my 'procurer of antiquities,' " Ehlana explained.

"It gives him an excuse to come and go without interference. I've gathered a whole roomful of assorted bric-a-brac since I've arrived here."

"That brings us right back to the issue we were discussing before you got here, Caalador," Stragen said. Stragen wore black today, and Ehlana privately felt that the color didn't really suit him. He rose and began to pace up and down, a habit the Queen of Elenia found irritating. "The Interior Ministry's beginning to flex its muscles for some reason. We're sitting on the minister himself, so this onset of burliness is probably coming from some underling."

"Interior has always liked to throw its weight around," Oscagne told them. The foreign minister was wearing western-style clothes again, and he still looked distinctly uncomfortable in them.

"I think that reinforces the point I was trying to make earlier, Ehlana," Sarabian said. "Are you sure we shouldn't dissolve the Interior Ministry right now?"

"Absolutely," Ehlana replied. "We've got Kolata buttoned up inside the castle here and we've given the world a perfectly legitimate reason for his presence. He's still functioning—under our control—and that's of enormous value to us. We're playing for time, Sarabian. We're terribly vulnerable until Tynian and Emban come back from Chyrellos with the Church Knights—or at the very least until all the Atan commanders have been advised that they aren't supposed to obey the orders of the Interior Ministry anymore. We *definitely* don't want the Atans fighting on both sides if trouble breaks out."

"I hadn't thought of that," he admitted.

"Not only that, your Majesty," Oscagne added gently. "It's entirely possible that Interior would simply ignore a proclamation disbanding them. They have almost total power, you know. Queen Ehlana's right. We can't move against them until we're sure of the Atans."

Stragen had continued his pacing. "*Nobody* can subvert an entire branch of government," he declared. "There are just too many people involved, and all it would take would be one honest policeman to expose the entire scheme."

"There's no such thing as an honest policeman, Stragen," Caalador said with a cynical laugh. "It's a contradiction in terms."

"You know what I mean," Stragen shrugged that off. "We know that Kolata has dirty hands, but we can't be sure just how far that disloyalty goes. It could be very widespread, or it could be confined to just a few in the higher councils of the ministry."

Caalador shook his head. " 'Tain't hordly likely, Stragen," he disagreed. "Y' gotta have them ez y' kin trust out thar when y' start givin' orders ez runs contrary t' reg'lar policy. They's gotta be *some* in th' hinterlands ez knows whut's whut."

Stragen made a face. "I wish you wouldn't use that vile dialect when you're right. It makes me feel inadequate. All right then. We can be fairly certain that most of the higher-ranking officials in the ministry are involved, but we can't even guess at how widespread the contamination is. I'd say that finding out gets to be a priority."

"Shouldn't take y' more'n a couple hunnerd years t' do that, Stragen," Caalador noted.

"Not necessarily," Baroness Melidere disagreed. She looked at Oscagne. "You once said that the Ministry of the Interior's very fond of paper, your Excellency."

"Of course, Baroness. All government agencies adore paper. Paperwork provides full employment for our relatives. Interior goes a little further, though. Policemen can't function without files and dossiers. They write everything down."

"I rather thought that might be the case. The people over at Interior are all trained as policemen, aren't they?"

Oscagne nodded.

"Then they'd all be compulsive about writing reports and filing them, wouldn't they?"

"I suppose so," he said. "I don't see where you're going with this exactly, Baroness."

"Wake up, Oscagne," Sarabian said excitedly. "I think this wonderful girl's just solved our problem for us. Someplace over in that rabbit warren at Interior there's a set of files that contains the names of all the disloyal policemen and secret agents in the empire. All we have to do is get our hands on that set of files, and we'll know exactly which people to pick up when the time comes to move."

"Except for the fact that they'll defend those files to the death," Ehlana observed. "And there's also the fact that a move against their filing system would be the same as a frontal assault on the ministry itself."

"You really know how to burst bubbles, Ehlana," the emperor complained.

"There might be a way around the queen's objections, your Majesty," Melidere said with a slight frown. "Is there a standardized filing system here in Matherion, Minister Oscagne?"

"Good God, no, Baroness," he exclaimed. "If we all had the same filing system, anybody at all could walk into our offices and find anything he wanted. We'd *never* be able to keep any secrets from each other."

"I thought that might be the case. Now then, suppose that Queen Ehlana happened to mention to the emperor—just in passing—that *her* government had standardized the filing system, and that everybody filed things the same way. Then let's suppose that the emperor grew very excited about the idea—the enormous savings in the cost of government and all that. Then, still supposing, he appoints an imperial commission with extraordinary powers to examine *everybody's* files with an eye toward that standardization. Wouldn't that justify a search of the offices at Interior?"

"It's got possibilities, my Queen," Stragen approved. "Something like that would hide what we're really up to—particularly if we had people tearing up everybody else's files at the same time."

Oscagne's face went absolutely white.

"I'd sooner take pizen than insult y', little lady," Caalador drawled to the baroness, "but yer still a-talkin' 'bout a chore which it is that'd taken us a good twenty year 'er more t' finish. We got us a hull buildin' over thar t' take aport iffn th' furrin minister yere is kee-rect 'bout how miny tons o' paper they got over t' Interior."

"We can shorten that a bit, Master Caalador," Melidere replied. "All we have to do is question Interior Minister Kolata."

"Absolutely not," Ehlana said sharply. "I don't want him all torn to pieces—at least not until I don't need him anymore."

"We wouldn't be asking him any sensitive questions, your Majesty," Melidere said patiently. "All we want to know is how his filing system works. That wouldn't compromise the conspiracy he's involved in, would it?"

"I think she's right, Ehlana," Mirtai said. "There would almost have to be some sort of trigger—questions about certain subjects—that would make our enemies decide to kill Kolata. They wouldn't kill him if all we did was ask him about something as ordinary as a filing system, would they?"

"No," the queen agreed. "They probably wouldn't at that." Her expression was still dubious, however.

"It's all very clever, Baroness," Stragen said, "but we'll be sending Tamul officials into the various ministries to investigate files. How will we know that at least some of *them* aren't on the other side?"

"We wouldn't, Milord Stragen. That's why we'll have to send our own people—the Church Knights—in to review those files."

"How would we justify that?"

"The new filing system would be an *Elene* invention, Milord. We're obviously going to have to send Elenes into the various ministries to evaluate the current methods and to instruct the officials on how to convert to the new system."

"Now I've got you, Baroness," he said triumphantly. "This is all a fiction. We don't *have* a new filing system."

"Then invent one, Milord Stragen," she suggested sweetly.

Prime Minister Subat was deeply troubled by the suggestion the Chancellor of the Exchequer had just placed before him. The two were alone together in the prime minister's ornate office, a room only slightly less magnificent than one of the imperial audience chambers. "You're out of your mind, Gashon," he declared flatly.

Chancellor of the Exchequer Gashon was a bloodless, corpselike man with sunken cheeks and no more than a few wispy strands of hair protruding from his lumpy scalp. "Look at it more closely, Pondia Subat," he said in his hollow, rusty-sounding voice. "It's only a theory, but it *does* explain many things that are otherwise incomprehensible."

"They wouldn't have dared," Subat scoffed.

"Try to lift your mind out of the fourteenth century, Subat," Gashon snapped. "You're the prime minister, not the keeper of antiquities. The world is changing all around you. You can't just sit still with your eyes firmly fixed on the past and hope to survive."

"I don't like you very much, Gashon."

"I'm not terribly fond of you either, Subat. Let me go through it for you again. Try to stay awake this time."

"How *dare* you?"

"I dare because I'd sort of like to keep my head where it is. First off: The Elenes of Eosia are absolute barbarians. Can we agree on that at least?"

"All right."

"They haven't caused much trouble in the past because they were too busy fighting among themselves about religion, *and* because they had Otha of Zemoch to worry about. Would it surprise you too much if I told you that Otha's dead and that the Rendorish insurgency's been almost completely crushed?"

"I have my own sources of information, Gashon."

"Have you ever considered listening to what they tell you? Now then, there was open warfare in the streets of Chyrellos preceding the elevation of this Dolmant to the Archprelacy. I'd say that's a fair indication of the fact that he's not universally loved. The best way I know of for a shaky ruler to consolidate his position is to contrive a foreign adventure, and the only real foreign ground for the Elenes of the Eosian continent is Daresia—the Tamul Empire. That's us, in case you hadn't noticed, Pondia Subat."

"I know that, Gashon."

"I just wanted to be sure, that's all. Are you with me so far?"

"Get to the point, Gashon. I don't have all day."

"Did you have an appointment with the headsman? All right, the Elenes are religious fanatics who feel that they're called of the Lord to convert everybody in the world to their absurd faith. For all I know, they also want to convert snakes, spiders, and fish. Dolmant's their religious leader, and they'd probably try to subdue glaciers and tides if he told them to. So, we've got a religious leader who has an uncertain grasp on power in his own church, and he has hordes of fanatic followers at his disposal. He can either use those followers to crush his opponents at home, *or* he can hurl them against a foreign power on some trumped-up excuse that will inflame the commons and stifle objections to his rule. Isn't it a coincidence that at precisely that time we have this 'state visit' by a silly female—a female who Foreign Minister Oscagne assures us is the Queen of Elenia. I hope the fact that we only have Oscagne's word for that hasn't escaped you. This so-called queen is obviously more accustomed to doing business in bed than she is on a throne. She clearly wrestled that silly ass Alberen of Astel into submission, and probably Androl of the Atans as well. We can only speculate about her adventures among the Peloi and the Styrics at Sarsos. Then, once she reached Matherion, she lured Emperor Sarabian to her bedchamber before the first day was out—you *did* know that Sarabian and Oscagne crept across the compound to that imitation Elene castle on the first night she was here, didn't you?"

Subat started to object.

"Yes, I know," Gashon cut him off, "that brings us to Oscagne. I'd say that the evidence strongly suggests that Oscagne has gone over to the Elenes—either for personal gain or because he's fallen under the spell of that blonde Elene strumpet. She had plenty of time to work on him while he was in Chyrellos, you know."

"It's all speculation, Gashon," Subat said, although his voice lacked conviction.

"Of course it is, Subat," Gashon replied with heavy sarcasm. "What would be the fastest way to get to Matherion from Chyrellos?"

"By ship, naturally."

"Then why did the strumpet of Cimmura choose to come overland? Was it to look at scenery, or to grapple her way across the continent? The girl's got stamina, I'll give her that."

"What about this recent coup attempt, Gashon? The government would have fallen if the Elenes hadn't been here."

"Ah, yes, the famous coup. Isn't it astounding that a group of Elenes who didn't even speak the Tamul language when they arrived were able to unearth this dire plot in about six weeks—when the agents of the Ministry of the Interior, who've only been in Matherion for all of their lives, hadn't come across a single clue about it? The Elenes crushed an imaginary coup, Subat, and now they've used it as an excuse to imprison the emperor in that cursed fortress of theirs—and Interior Minister Kolata as well, and Kolata's the one man in government who has the resources to free our ruler. I've talked with Teovin, Director of the Secret Police, and he assures me that no one from the ministry has been permitted to speak with Kolata privately since his incarceration. Our colleague is obviously a prisoner, and the orders he's issuing are just as obviously coming from the Elenes. Then, if that weren't bad enough, they've sent the so-called churchman, Emban, back to Chyrellos to lead the Church Knights back here to 'deal with the crisis.' We have all the resources of Interior *and* whole armies of Atans at our disposal, Subat. Why do we need the Church Knights? What possible reason is there to bring the most ruthless force in the entire world to Tamuli? Would the word *invasion* startle you? That's all that the famous coup really was, you realize—an excuse for the Elene Church to invade Tamuli, and quite obviously it's been with the emperor's full cooperation."

"Why would the emperor conspire with the Elenes to topple his own government?"

"I can think of any number of reasons. Maybe this so-called queen threatened to deny him her favors. Most probably, though, she's been spinning fairy tales for him, telling him about the joys of absolute power. That's a common fiction in Eosia. Elene rulers like to pretend that *they're* the ones who make all the decisions in their kingdoms rather than permitting the government to do it for them. We both know how ridiculous *that* idea is. A king—or in our case, the emperor—only has one function. He's a symbol of government, nothing more. He serves as a focus for the love and loyalty of the people. The imperial government's been engaged in a selective breeding program for the past thousand years. The emperor's Tamul wife—the one who produces the heir to the throne—is always selected for her stupidity. We don't *need* intelligent emperors, only docile ones. Somehow Sarabian slipped past us. If you'd ever really taken the trouble to pay attention to him, you'd have discovered that he's frighteningly intelligent. Kolata blundered there. Sarabian should have been killed long before he ascended the throne. Our revered emperor's beginning to hunger for real power, I'm afraid. Normally, we could deal with that, but we can't get at him to kill him as long as he's inside that blasted fortress."

"You weave a convincing story, Gashon," the prime minister conceded with a troubled frown. "I *knew* it was a blunder to invite that Sparhawk savage to come to Matherion."

"We all did, Subat, and you'll recall who it was who overrode all our objections."

"Oscagne," Subat spat.

"Precisely. Is it beginning to fit together for you now?"

"Did you devise all of this by yourself, Gashon? It's a little elaborate for a man who spends all his time counting pennies."

"Actually, it was Teovin, the Director of the Secret Police, who brought it to my attention. He provided me with very concrete evidence. I've summarized it for you here. Interior has spies everywhere, you know. Nothing happens in the empire that doesn't generate a report for those famous files of theirs. Now, Pondia Subat, what does our esteemed prime minister propose to do about the fact that our emperor's being held prisoner—willingly or unwillingly—not a hundred paces from where we sit? You're the titular head of government, Subat. You're the one who has to make these decisions. Oh, and while you're at it, you might want to give some thought to how we're going to prevent the Church Knights from sweeping across the continent, marching into Matherion, and forcing everyone to bow down to their ridiculous God—and butchering the entire government in the process."

"They're trying to stall, your Majesties," Stragen reported. "When suppertime comes, they escort us to the door, push us outside, and lock the door behind us. The building stays locked for the rest of the night—although there are always plenty of lights moving around in there after dark. When we go back the next morning, everything's been rearranged. The files migrate from room to room like ducks in the autumn. I wouldn't actually swear to it, but I think they move walls as well. We found a room just this morning that I don't think was there last night."

"I'll send in Engessa's Atans," Sarabian said darkly. "We'll chase everybody out and then tear the building apart brick by brick."

"No," Ehlana said, shaking her head. "If we make an overt move against Interior, every policeman in the empire will scurry down a rabbit hole." She pursed her lips. "Let's start to do inconvenient things to the other ministries as well. Don't make it obvious that we're concentrating all of our attention on the Ministry of the Interior."

"How can you possibly make things any worse than they already are, your Majesty?" Oscagne asked in a broken voice. "You've disrupted centuries of work as it is."

"Can anyone think of anything?" Sarabian asked, looking around.

"May I speak, your Majesty?" Alean asked in a small, timid-sounding voice.

"Of course, dear." Ehlana smiled.

"I hope you'll forgive my presumption," Alean apologized. "I can't even read, so I don't really know what files are, but aren't we sort of letting on that we're rearranging them?"

"That's what we're telling everybody," Mirtai replied.

"As I said, I can't read, but I do know a bit about rearranging cupboards and such things. This is a little like that, isn't it?"

"Close enough," Stragen replied.

"Well, then, when you're rearranging a cupboard, you take everything out and spread it on the floor. Then you put all the things you want in the top drawer in one pile, the things you want in the second drawer in another and so on. Couldn't we do that with these files?"

"It's a nice i-dee, little dorlin'," Caalador drawled, "but they ain't e-nuff floors in the hull buildin' fer spreadin' out all them there files."

"There *are* lots of lawns around the outside, though, aren't there?" Alean kept her eyes downcast as she spoke. "Couldn't we just take all the files from every government building outside and spread them around on the lawns? We could tell the people who work in the buildings that we want to sort through them and put them in the proper order. They couldn't really object, and you can't lock the door to a lawn at night, or move things around when there are seven-foot-tall Atans standing guard over them. I know I'm just a silly servant girl, but that's the way *I'd* do it."

Oscagne was staring at her in absolute horror.

■ CHAPTER FOUR ■

The soil on the western side of the Isle of Tega was thin and rocky, and since there was plenty of fertile ground farther inland, the citizens of the Republic had made no effort to cultivate the area. Tough, scrubby bushes rustled stiffly in the onshore breeze as Sparhawk and his friends rode along a rocky trail leading to the coast.

"The breeze helps," Talen observed gratefully. "At least it blows away that stink."

"You complain too much," Flute told him. The little girl rode with Sephrenia as she had since they had first encountered her. She nestled in her older sister's arms with her dark eyes brooding. She straightened suddenly as the sound of surf pounding on the western shore of the Isle reached them. "This is far enough for right now, gentlemen," she told them. "Let's have some supper and wait for it to get dark."

"Is that a good idea?" Bevier asked her. "The ground's been getting rougher the farther west we come, and the sound of that surf seems to have rocks mixed up in it. This might not be a good place to be blundering around in the dark."

"I can lead you safely to the beach, Bevier," she told him. "I don't want you gentlemen to get too good a look at our ship. There are certain ideas involved in her construction that you don't need to know. That's one of the promises I had to make during those negotiations I was telling you about." She pointed to the lee side of a rocky hillock. "Let's go over there out of this wind and build a fire. I have some instructions for you."

They rode away from the ill-defined trail and dismounted in the shelter of the hill. "Whose turn is it to do the cooking?" Berit asked Sir Ulath.

"Yours," Ulath told him with no hint of a smile.

"You knew he was going to do that, Berit," Talen said. "What you just did was almost the same thing as volunteering."

Berit shrugged. "My turn will come up eventually anyway," he said. "I thought I'd get it out of the way for a while."

"All right, gentlemen," Vanion said, "let's look around and see what we can find in the way of firewood."

Sparhawk concealed a smile. Vanion could maintain that he was no longer the preceptor as much as he wished, but the habit of command was deeply ingrained in him.

They built a fire, and Berit stirred up an acceptable stew. After supper, they sat by the fire, watching as evening slowly settled in.

"Now, then," Flute said to them, "we're going to ride down to a cove. I want you to all stay close behind me, because it's going to be very foggy."

"It's a perfectly clear evening, Flute," Kalten objected.

"It won't be when we reach the cove," she told him. "I'm going to make sure that you don't get too much chance to examine that ship. I'm not really supposed to do this, so don't get me in trouble." She looked sternly at Khalad. "And I want you in particular to keep a very tight rein on your curiosity."

"Me?"

"Yes, you. You're too practical and too clever by half for my comfort. Your noble friends here aren't imaginative enough to make any educated guesses about the ship. You're a different matter. Don't be digging at the decks with your knife, and don't try to sneak off to examine things. I don't want to drop by Cimmura someday and find a duplicate of the ship anchored in the river. We'll go down to the cove, board the ship, and go directly below. You will *not* go up on deck until we get to where we're going. A certain part of the ship has been set aside for us, and we'll all stay there for the duration of the voyage. I want your word on that, gentlemen."

Sparhawk could see some differences between Flute and Danae. Flute was more authoritarian, for one thing, and she didn't seem to have Danae's whimsical sense of humor. Although the Child-Goddess had a definite personality, each of her incarnations seemed to have its own idiosyncracies.

Flute looked up at the slowly darkening sky. "We'll wait another hour," she decided. "The crew of the ship has been told to stay away from us. Our meals will be put just outside the door, and we won't see the one who puts them there. It won't do you any good to try to catch her, so don't even try."

"Her?" Ulath exclaimed. "Are you trying to say that there are *women* in the crew?"

"They're *all* females. There aren't very many males where they come from."

"Women aren't strong enough to raise and lower the sails," he objected.

"These females are ten times stronger than you are, Ulath, and it wouldn't matter anyway, because the ship doesn't *have* sails. Please stop asking questions, gentlemen. Oh, one other thing. There'll be a sort of humming sound when we get under way. It's normal, so don't let it alarm you."

"How—" Ulath began.

She held up her hand. "No more questions, Ulath," she told him quite firmly. "You don't need to know the answers. The ship's here to take us from one place to another in a hurry. That's all you need to know."

"That brings us to something we really *should* know," Sparhawk said. "Where *are* we going?"

"To Jorsan on the west coast of Edom," she replied. "Well, almost, anyway.

There's a long gulf leading inland to Jorsan. We'll put ashore at the mouth of the gulf and go inland on horseback. Now, why don't we talk about something else?"

The fog seemed almost thick enough to walk on, and the knights were obliged to blindly follow the misty light of the torch Sephrenia held aloft as they rode down a steep bank toward the sound of unseen surf.

They reached a sandy beach and groped their way down toward the water. Then they saw other lights out in the fog, filmy, mist-shrouded lights that stretched out for what seemed an impossible distance. The lights did not flicker, and they were the wrong color for torchlight.

"Good God!" Ulath choked. "*No* ship could be that big!"

"*Ulath!*" Flute said sharply from out of the fog ahead.

"Sorry," he mumbled.

When they reached the water's edge, all they could see was a dark, looming shape lying low in the water several yards out, a shape outlined by those unwinking white lights. A ramp reached from the ship to the beach, and Ch'iel, Sephrenia's white palfrey, stepped confidently onto that ramp and clattered across to the ship.

There were dim, shrouded shapes on the deck, cloaked and hooded figures that were all no more than shoulder high, but strangely squat and blocky.

"What do we do with the horses?" Vanion asked as they all dismounted.

"Just leave them here," Flute replied. "They'll be taken care of. Let's go below. We can't start until everybody's off the deck."

"The crew stays up here, don't they?" Ulath asked her.

"No. It's too dangerous."

They went to a rectangular hatchway in the deck and followed an inclined ramp leading down.

"Stairs would take up less space," Khalad said critically.

"The crew couldn't use stairs, Khalad," Flute told him. "They don't have legs."

He stared at her in horror.

"I told you that they're not human." She shrugged.

The companionway they reached at the bottom of the ramp was low, and the knights had to half stoop as they followed the Child-Goddess aft. The area belowdecks was illuminated by pale glowing spots of light recessed into the ceiling and covered over by what appeared to be glass. The light was steady, unwinking, and it definitely did not come from any kind of fire.

The quarters to which their little guide led them were more conventionally illuminated by candles, however, and the ceilings were high enough for the tall knights to stand erect. No sooner had Ulath closed the heavy door to what was in effect to be their prison for the next five days than a low-pitched humming sound began to vibrate the deck beneath their feet, and they could feel the bow of the strange vessel start to swing ponderously about to point at the open sea. Then the ship surged forward.

"What's making it move?" Kalten asked. "There's no wind."

"*Kalten!*" Aphrael said sharply.

"Sorry," he muttered.

"There are four compartments here," she told them. "We'll eat in this one, and we can spread out and sleep in the other three. Put away your belongings, gentlemen. Then you might as well go to bed. Nothing's going to happen for five days."

Sparhawk and Kalten went into one of the cabins, taking Talen with them. Talen was carrying Khalad's saddlebags as well as his own.

"What's your brother up to?" Sparhawk asked the boy suspiciously.

"He wants to look around a bit," Talen replied.

"Aphrael told him not to do that."

"So?"

They were all staggered a bit as the ship gave another forward surge. The humming sound climbed to a whine, and the ship seemed to rise up in the water almost like a sitting man rising to his feet.

Kalten threw his saddlebags onto one of the bunks and sat down beside them. "I don't understand any of this," he grumbled.

"You aren't supposed to," Sparhawk replied.

"I wonder if they've got anything to drink aboard. I could definitely use a drink about now."

"I wouldn't get my hopes up too high, and I'm not sure you'd care to drink something brewed by nonhumans. It might do some strange things to you."

Khalad came into the tiny compartment, his eyes baffled. "I don't want to alarm you, gentlemen," he said, "but we're moving faster than a horse can run."

"How do you know that?" Talen asked him.

"Those curtains in that central cabin are hanging over openings that are sort of like portholes—they've got glass over them, anyway. I looked out. There's still fog all around us, but I could see the water. We passed a floating log, and it went by like a crossbow bolt. There's something else, too. The hull curves back under us, and it isn't touching the water at all."

"We're *flying*?" Kalten asked incredulously.

Khalad shook his head. "I think the keel's touching the water, but that's about all."

"I really don't want to know about this," Kalten said plaintively.

"He's right, Khalad," Sparhawk said. "I think this is one of the things Aphrael told us was none of our business. Leave those curtains closed from now on."

"Aren't you the least bit curious, my Lord?"

"I can live with it."

"You don't mind if I speculate just a bit, do you, Sparhawk?"

"Go right ahead, but keep your speculations to yourself." He sat down on his bunk and began to pull off his boots. "I don't know about the rest of you, but I'm going to follow orders and go to bed. This is a good chance to catch up on our sleep, and we've all been running a little short on that for quite some time now. We'll want to be alert when we get to Jorsan."

"Which only happens to be about a quarter of the way around the world," Khalad added moodily, "and which we're going to reach in just five days. I don't think I'm put together right for this kind of thing. Do I *have* to be a Pandion Knight, Sparhawk?"

"Yes," Sparhawk told him, dropping his boots on the deck. "Was there anything else you wanted to know before I go to sleep?"

They all slept a great deal during the next five days. Sparhawk strongly suspected that Aphrael might have had a hand in that, since sleeping people don't wander around making discoveries.

Their meals were served on strange oblong trays that were made of some substance none of them could identify. The food consisted entirely of uncooked vegetables, and they were given only water to drink. Kalten complained about the food at every meal, but, since there was nothing else available, he ate it anyway.

On the afternoon before they were scheduled to arrive, they gathered together in the cramped central compartment. "Are you sure?" Kalten dubiously asked Flute when she told them that they were no more than ten hours from their destination.

She sighed. "Yes, Kalten, I'm sure."

"How do you know? You haven't been up on deck, and you haven't talked to any of the sailors. We could have been . . ." His words sort of faded off. She was looking at him with a long-suffering expression as he floundered on. "Oh," he said then. "I wasn't thinking, I guess. Sorry."

"I *do* love you, Kalten—in spite of everything."

Khalad cleared his throat. "Didn't Dolmant tell you that the Edomish have some strong feelings about the Church?" he asked Sparhawk.

Sparhawk nodded. "As I understand it, they look at our Holy Mother in almost the same way that the Rendors do."

"Church Knights wouldn't really be welcome, then, I gather."

"Hardly."

"We'll need to disguise ourselves as ordinary travelers, then."

"More than likely," Sparhawk agreed.

Vanion had been looking at his map. "Exactly where are we going from Jorsan, Aphrael?" he asked Flute.

"Up the coast a ways," she replied vaguely.

"That's not very specific."

"Yes, I know."

He sighed. "Is there any real need for us to go on up the Gulf of Jorsan to the city itself? If we were to land on the north shore of the gulf, we could avoid the city entirely. Since the Edomish have these prejudices, shouldn't we stay away from them as much as possible?"

"We have to go to Jorsan," she told him. "Well," she amended, "Jorsan itself isn't that important, but we're going to see something along the way that will be."

"Oh? What's that?"

"I have no idea."

"You get used to that," Sparhawk told his friend. "Our little Goddess here gets hunches from time to time—no details at all, just hunches."

"What time will we make our landfall?" Ulath asked.

"About midnight," she replied.

"Landing on a strange shore at night can be a little tricky," he said dubiously.

"There won't be any problems." She said it with absolute confidence.

"I'm not supposed to worry about it. Is that it?"

"You can worry if you want to, Ulath." She smiled. "It's not necessary, but you can worry all you like, if it makes you feel better."

It was foggy when they came up on deck again, a dense, obscuring fog, and this time the strange ship showed no lights. Their horses, already saddled, were waiting, and they led them down the ramp to a pebbly beach.

When they looked back out toward the water, their ship was gone.

"Where did she go?" Ulath exclaimed.

"She's still there." Aphrael smiled.

"Why can't I see her, then?"

"Because I don't *want* people to see her. We passed a number of ordinary ships on our way here. If anybody'd seen her, there'd be wild talk in every sailors' tavern in every port in the world."

"It's all in the shape of the keel, isn't it?" Khalad mused.

"*Khalad!*" she said sharply. "You stop that immediately!"

"I'm not going to do anything about it, Flute. I couldn't if I wanted to, but it's that keel that accounts for her speed. I'm only mentioning it so that you won't make the mistake of thinking I'm so stupid that I can't put it together."

She glared at him.

He bent slightly and kissed her cheek. "That's all right, Flute." He smiled. "I love you anyway—even if you do underestimate me at times."

"He's going to work out just fine," Kalten said to Vanion.

The hillside rising from the gravel strand was covered with thick, rank grass, and by the time they had reached the top of the hill, the fog had entirely dissipated. A broad highway of reflected moonlight stretched out across the calm waters of the gulf.

"My map shows a kind of track a mile or so inland," Vanion told them. "It seems to run up the gulf in the general direction of Jorsan." He looked at Flute, who was still glaring darkly at Khalad. "Pending instructions to the contrary from higher authority, I suppose we can follow that track." He looked inquiringly at the Child-Goddess again.

She sank a little lower in Sephrenia's arms and began to suck her thumb.

"You'll make your teeth crooked."

She pulled her thumb out of her mouth and stuck her tongue out at him.

"Shall we press on, then?" Vanion suggested.

They rode on across a broad, rolling meadow covered with the rank salt grass. The moon washed out all color, making the grass whipping at the horses' legs seem grey and the forest beyond the meadow a formless black blot. They rode slowly, their eyes and ears alert and their hands never far from their sword hilts. Nothing untoward had happened yet, but these were trained knights, and for them the world was always filled with danger.

After they rode in under the trees, Vanion called a halt.

"Why are we stopping?" Flute demanded a little crossly.

"The moon's very bright tonight," Vanion explained, "and our eyes need a little time to adjust to the shadows here under the trees. We don't want to blunder into anything."

"Oh."

"Her night isn't going too well, is it?" Berit murmured to Sparhawk. "She seemed to be very upset with Khalad."

"It's good for her. She gets overconfident, sometimes, and a little too much impressed with her own cleverness."

"I heard that, Sparhawk," Flute snapped.

"I rather thought you might have," he replied blandly.

"Why is everyone mistreating me tonight?" she complained.

"They're only teasing you, Aphrael," Sephrenia assured the little girl. "Clumsily, of course, but they're Elenes, after all, so you can't really expect too much from them."

"Shall we move on before things start to turn ugly?" Vanion said.

They rode at a walk through the shadows, and after about half an hour they reached a narrow, rutted track. They turned eastward and moved on, riding a little faster now.

"How far is it to Jorsan, my Lord?" Bevier asked Vanion after they had gone a ways.

"About fifty leagues," Vanion replied.

"A goodly ways then." Bevier looked inquiringly at Flute.

"What?" she said crossly.

"Nothing, really."

"Say it, Bevier."

"I wouldn't offend you for the world, Divine Aphrael, but could you speed the journey the way you did when we were traveling across Deira with King Wargun's army?"

"No, I can't. You've forgotten that we're waiting for something important to happen, Bevier, and I'm not going to fly past it just because you're in a hurry to get to the taverns of Jorsan."

"That will do," Sephrenia told her.

Since it was still early autumn, they had not brought tents with them, and after about another hour's travel they rode back into the forest and spread their blankets on beds of fallen leaves to get a few hours' sleep.

The sun was well up when they set out again, and they traveled through the forest until late afternoon without encountering any local people.

Once again they moved back into the forest about a quarter of a mile and set up for the night in a narrow ravine where an overhanging bank and the thick foliage would conceal the light from their small cooking fire. Rather surprisingly, Ulath did the cooking without any of his usual subterfuge. "It's not as much fun when Tynian isn't along," he explained.

"I miss him, too," Sparhawk agreed. "It seems strange to be traveling without all those suggestions of his."

"This cooking business has come up before," Vanion observed. "Am I missing something?"

"Sir Ulath normally keeps track of it, my Lord," Talen replied. "It's a very complicated system, so none of the rest of us really understands how it works."

"Wouldn't a simple roster do just as well?" Vanion asked.

"I'm sure it would, but Sir Ulath prefers his own method. It has a few drawbacks, though. Once Kalten cooked every single meal for an entire week."

Vanion shuddered.

They had smoked mutton chops that evening, and Ulath received some hard looks from his companions about that. Flute and Sephrenia, however, complimented him on his choice. After they had eaten, they sought their makeshift beds.

It must have been well past midnight when Talen shook Sparhawk awake, laying a cautious hand across his mouth to prevent his crying out. "There are some people back near the road," the boy whispered. "They've built a big fire."

"What are they doing?" Sparhawk asked.

"Just standing around waiting for somebody, it seems—unless you want to count the drinking."

"You'd better rouse the others," Sparhawk told him, throwing off his blankets and reaching for his sword.

They crept through the forest in the darkness and stopped at the edge of a stump-dotted clearing. There was a large bonfire in the center of the clearing and nearly a hundred men—peasants for the most part, judging from their clothing—sitting on the ground near the blaze. Their faces were ruddy from the reflected light and from the contents of the earthenware jars they were passing around.

"Strange place to be holding a drinking party," Ulath murmured. "*I* wouldn't come out this far into the woods for something as ordinary as that."

"Is this it?" Vanion asked Flute, who was nestled in Sephrenia's arms, concealed by her sister's dark cloak.

"Is this what?"

"You know what I mean. Is this what we're supposed to see?"

"I think so," she replied. "I'll know better when they all get here."

"Are there more coming?"

She nodded. "One, at least. The ones who are already here don't matter."

They waited as the peasants in the clearing grew progressively more and more rowdy.

Then a lone horseman appeared at the far edge of the clearing, near the road. The newcomer wore a dark cloak and a slouch hat pulled low over his face.

"Not again," Talen groaned. "Doesn't *anybody* on this continent have any imagination?"

"What's this?" Vanion asked.

"The one they call Sabre up in Astel wore the same kind of clothes, my Lord."

"Maybe this one's different."

"I wouldn't get my hopes up too high."

The man on horseback rode into the firelight, dismounted, and pushed back his hat. He was a tall, gangly man with a long pockmarked face and narrow eyes. He stepped up onto a tree stump and stood waiting for the peasants to gather around him. "Hear me, my friends," he said in a loud, harsh voice. "I bring news."

The half-drunk babble of the peasants faded.

"Much has happened since last we met," the speaker continued. "You will recall that we had determined to make one last try to resolve our differences with the Tamuls by peaceful means."

"What choice did we have, Rebal?" one of the peasants shouted. "Only madmen would attack the Atan garrison—no matter how just their cause."

"So that's Rebal," Kalten whispered. "Not very impressive, is he?"

"Our cause was made just by Incetes himself," Rebal was responding, "and Incetes is more than a match for the Atans."

The mob murmured its agreement.

"There is good news, my friends," Rebal declared. "Our emissaries have been successful. The emperor himself has seen the justice of our cause!"

A ragged cheer went up.

"I rejoice even as you," Rebal continued, "but a new peril, far more grave than the simple injustice of the corrupt Tamul administrators, has arisen. The emperor, who is now our friend, has been taken prisoner by the accursed Church Knights! The evil Archprelate of the Church of Chyrellos has reached halfway around the world to seize our friend!"

"Outrageous!" a burly peasant in the crowd roared. "Monstrous!"

The rest of the peasants looked a bit confused, however.

"He's going too fast," Talen whispered critically.

"What?" Berit asked.

"He's changing course on them," Talen explained. "I'd guess that he's been cursing the Tamuls for the last year or so—the same way Sabre was, up in Astel. Now he wants to curse somebody else, but he's got to uncurse the Tamuls first. Even a drunken peasant's going to have some suspicions about the miraculous conversion of the emperor. He made it all too fast—and too easy."

"Tell us, Rebal," the burly peasant shouted, "how was our friend, the emperor, taken prisoner?"

"Yes, tell us!" another man on the far side of the crowd howled.

"Planted henchmen," Talen sneered. "This Rebal's about as subtle as a club in the face."

"It was clever, my friends," Rebal declared to the crowd, "very clever. The Church of Chyrellos is guided by the demons of Hell, and they are the masters of deceit. The Tamuls, who are now our friends, are heathens, and they do not understand the guile of the heretics of Chyrellos. All unsuspecting, they welcomed a delegation of Church officials, and among those foul heretics who journeyed to Matherion were Knights of the Church—the armored minions of Hell itself. Once in Matherion, they seized our dear friend and protector, Emperor Sarabian, and they now hold him prisoner in his own palace!"

"Death to the Tamuls!" a wheezy-voiced old man, far gone in drink, bawled.

One of the other peasants rapped him sharply across the back of the head with a cudgel, and the slightly out-of-date demonstrator sagged limply to the ground.

"Crowd control," Talen sniffed. "Rebal doesn't want people making any mistakes here."

Other peasants, obviously more of Rebal's planted henchmen, began to shout the correct slogan, "Death to the Church Knights!" They brandished crude weapons and assorted agricultural implements as they bellowed, emphasizing their slogan and intimidating the still-confused.

"The purpose of these monsters is all too clear," Rebal shouted over the tumult. "It is their plan to hold the emperor as hostage to prevent the Atans from storming the palace. They will sit safe where they are until reinforcements arrive. And make no mistake, my friends, those reinforcements are even now gathering on the plains of Eosia. The armies of the heretics are on the march, and in the van come the Church Knights!"

Horrified gasps ran through the ranks of the peasants.

"On to Matherion!" the fellow with the cudgel bellowed. "Free the emperor!"

The crowd took up the shout.

Rebal held up one hand. "My blood burns as hotly as yours, my friends!" he shouted. "But will we leave our homes and families to the mercies of the Knights of the Church? All of Eosia marches toward Matherion! And what stands between ac-cursed Eosia and fire-domed Matherion? Edom, my friends! Our beloved homeland stands in the path of the heretic horde! What mercy can we expect from these sav-ages? Who will defend our women from foul rape if we rush to the emperor's aid?"

Cries of chagrin ran through the crowd.

Rebal moved quickly at that point. "And yet, my friends," he rushed on, "our defense of our beloved homes may yet aid our friend, the emperor. The beasts of Eosia come to destroy our faith and to slaughter the true believers. I know not what course you may take, but I pledge to you all that I will lay down my life for our beloved homeland and our holy faith! But in my dying, I will delay the Church Knights! That Spawn of Hell must pause to spill my blood, and their delay will give the Atans the time to rally! *Thus* may we defend our homes and aid our friend in one stroke!"

Sparhawk began to swear, half strangling to keep his voice down.

"What's your problem?" Kalten asked.

"We've just been blocked. If those idiots out there accept what Rebal's telling them, the Church Knights are going to have to fight their way to Matherion foot by foot."

"They're very quick to exploit a changing situation," Vanion agreed. "Too quick, perhaps. It's almost a thousand leagues from here to Matherion. Either some-one has a *very* good horse, or our mysterious friend out there's breaking the rules again in order to get word out to the hinterlands of what happened after the coup was put down."

Rebal was holding up his hands to quiet the shouting of the crowd. "Are you with me, my brothers?" he called. "Will we defend our homes and our faith and help our friends, the Tamuls, at the same time?"

The mob howled its assent.

"Let's ask Incetes to help us!" the man with the cudgel shouted.

"Incetes!" another bellowed. "Incetes! Call forth Incetes!"

"Are you sure, my friends?" Rebal asked, drawing himself up and pulling his dark cloak tightly around him.

"Call him forth, Rebal! Raise Incetes! Let *him* tell us what to do!"

Rebal struck an exaggerated pose and raised both arms over his head. He began to speak, intoning guttural words in a hollow, booming voice.

"Is that Styric?" Kalten whispered to Sephrenia. "It doesn't sound like Styric to me."

"It's gibberish," she replied scornfully.

Kalten frowned. "I don't think I've ever heard of them," he whispered. "What part of the world do the Gibbers come from?"

She stared at him, her face baffled.

"Did I say it wrong?" he asked. "Are they called the Gibberese? or maybe the Gibberenians? The people who speak Gibberish, I mean."

"Oh, Kalten." She laughed softly. "I love you."

"What did I say?"

Rebal's voice had risen to a near shriek, and he brought both arms down sharply.

There was a sudden explosion in the middle of the bonfire, and a great cloud of smoke boiled out into the clearing.

"Herken, Maisteres alle!" A huge voice came out of the smoke. "Now hath the tyme for Werre ycom. Now, be me troth, shal alle trew Edomishmen on lyve to armes! Tak ye uppe the iren swerd; gird ye your limbes alle inne the iren haubergeon and the iren helm! Smyte ye the feendes foule, which beestes derk do sette hom and fey in deedly peril. Goe ye to bataile ferse to fend the feendes of the acurset Chirche of Chyrellos! Follwe! Follwe! Follwe me, as Godes hondys yeve ye force!"

"Old High Elenic!" Bevier exclaimed. "Nobody's spoken that tongue in thousands of years!"

"*I'd* follow him, whatever tongue it is," Ulath rumbled. "He makes a good speech."

The smoke began to thin, and a huge, ox-shouldered man wearing ancient armor and holding a mighty two-handed sword above his head appeared at Rebal's side. "Havok!" he bellowed. "Havok and Werre!"

CHAPTER FIVE

"They've all gone now," Berit reported when he and Talen returned to the camp concealed in the narrow ravine. "They spent a lot of time marching around in circles shouting slogans first, though."

"Then the beer ran out," Talen added dryly, "and the party broke up." He looked at Flute. "Are you sure this was supposed to be important?" he asked her. "It was the most contrived hoax I've ever seen."

She nodded stubbornly. "It *was* important," she insisted. "I don't know why, but it was."

"How did they make that big flash and all the smoke?" Kalten asked.

"One of the fellows near the fire threw a handful of some kind of powder onto the coals," Khalad shrugged. "Everybody else was watching Rebal, so they didn't see him when he did it."

"Where did the one in the armor come from?" Ulath asked.

"He was hiding in the crowd," Talen explained. "The whole thing was at about the same level as you'd find at a country fair—one that's held a long way from the nearest town."

"The one who was pretending to be Incetes gave a fairly stirring speech, though," Ulath noted.

"It certainly *should* have been." Bevier smiled. "It was written by Phalactes in the seventh century."

"Who was he?" Talen asked.

"Phalactes was the greatest playwright of antiquity. That stirring speech came directly from one of his tragedies, *Etonicus*. That fellow in the antique armor substituted a few words is all. The play's a classic. It's still performed at universities once in a while."

"You're a whole library all by yourself, Bevier," Kalten told him. "Do you remember every single thing you've ever read—word for word?"

Bevier laughed. "I wish I could, my friend. Some of my classmates and I put on a performance of *Etonicus* when I was a student. I played the lead, so I had to memorize that speech. The poetry of Phalactes is really very stirring. He was a great artist—Arcian, naturally."

"I never liked him very much," Flute sniffed. "He was as ugly as sin; he smelled like an open cesspool; and he was a howling bigot."

Bevier swallowed hard. "Please don't do that, Aphrael," he said. "It's very unsettling."

"What was the story about?" Talen asked, his eyes suddenly eager.

"Etonicus was supposed to be the ruler of a mythic kingdom somewhere in what's now eastern Cammoria," Bevier replied. "The legend has it that he went to war with the Styrics over religion."

"What happened?" Talen's tone was almost hungry.

"He came to a bad end," Bevier shrugged. "It's a tragedy, after all."

"But—"

"You can read it for yourself sometime, Talen," Vanion said firmly. "This isn't the story hour."

Talen's face grew sulky.

"I'd be willing to wager that you could paralyze our young friend here in midtheft." Ulath chuckled. "All you'd have to do is say, 'Once upon a time,' and he'd stop dead in his tracks."

"This throws a whole new light on what's been happening here in Tamuli," Vanion mused. "Could this all be some vast hoax?" He looked inquiringly at Flute.

She shook her head. "No, Vanion. There *has* been magic of varying levels in *some* of the things we've encountered."

"Some, perhaps, but not all, certainly. Was there any magic at all involved in what we saw tonight?"

"Not a drop."

"Is *that* how you measure magic?" Kalten asked curiously. "Does it come by the gallon?"

"Like cheap wine, you mean?" she suggested tartly.

"Well, not exactly, but—"

"This was very important," Sparhawk said. "Thank you, Aphrael."

"I live but to serve." She smiled mockingly at him.

"Stop that."

"You've missed me entirely, Sparhawk," Kalten said.

"We've just found out that not *everything* that's being reported back to Matherion is the result of real magic. There's a fair amount of fraud mixed in as well. What does that suggest?"

"The other side's lazy." Kalten shrugged.

"I'm not so sure," Ulath disagreed. "They're not afraid to exert themselves when it's important."

"Two," Sephrenia said. "Three at the most."

"I beg your pardon," Ulath said with a puzzled look.

"Now do you see how exasperating that is, Ulath?" she said to him. "This charade we watched here tonight rather strongly hints that there aren't many people on the other side who can really work spells. They're spread out a bit thin, I'd say. What's going on here in Edom—and probably in Astel and Daconia as well—is rather commonplace, so they don't feel that they have to waste magic on it."

"Commonplace or not, it's going to seriously hinder Tynian when he tries to lead the Church Knights across Daresia to Matherion," Sparhawk said. "If Rebal can stir up the whole kingdom the way he did this group tonight, Tynian's going to have to wade his way through hordes of howling fanatics. The Edomish peasantry's going to be convinced that our brothers are coming here to impose heresies on them by force, and they'll be lurking behind every bush with sickles and pitchforks."

"We still have a certain advantage, though," Bevier said thoughtfully. "There's no way that our enemies can possibly know that we're here in Edom and that we saw this business tonight. Even if they were to know that we're going to raise Bhelliom—which isn't very likely—they wouldn't know where it is, so they'd have no idea where we were going. Even we don't know where we're going."

"And even if they did, they wouldn't know that we could get here as quickly as we did," Khalad added. "I think we've got the jump on them, my Lords. If they're relying on hoaxes here, that probably means that they don't have any magicians around to sniff us out. If we can pass ourselves off as ordinary travelers, we should be able to move around without much hindrance—and pick up all sorts of information in the process."

"We're here to retrieve the Bhelliom, Khalad," Flute reminded him.

"Of course, but there's no point in passing up little treasures as we go along, is there?"

"Aphrael," Vanion said, "have we seen and heard everything we were supposed to?"

She nodded.

"I think we might want to move on to Jorsan rather quickly, then. If Khalad's right and we're one jump ahead, let's stay that way. What would it take in the way of bribes to persuade you to speed up the journey?"

"We could negotiate that, I suppose, Lord Vanion." She smiled. "I'm sure you could all offer me *something* that might induce me to lend a hand."

They kissed the Child-Goddess into submission and arrived in Jorsan late the following day. Jorsan turned out to be a typical Elene port city squatting at the head of the gulf. The question of suitable disguises had arisen during the journey. Bevier had leaned strongly in the direction of posing as religious pilgrims. Kalten had liked the notion of masquerading as a group of rowdies in search of constructive debauchery, while Talen, perhaps influenced by Rebal's recent performance, had thought it might be fun to pose as traveling players. They were still arguing about it when Jorsan came into view.

"Isn't all this a waste of time?" Ulath asked them. "Why should we play dressup? It's not really anybody's business *who* we are, is it? As long as we're not wearing armor, the people in Jorsan won't know—or care—about us. Why go to all the trouble of lying about it?"

"We'll need to wear our mail shirts, Sir Ulath," Berit reminded him. "How do we explain that?"

"We don't. Lots of people wear chain mail and carry weapons, so it's not really *that* unusual. If somebody in town gets *too* curious about who we are and where we're going, I can make him get un-curious in fairly short order." He held up his hand and closed his fist suggestively.

"You mean just bully our way through?" Kalten asked.

"Why not? Isn't that what we're trained for?"

The inn was not particularly elegant, but it was clean and not so near the waterfront that the streets around it were filled with brawling sailors lurching from alehouse to alehouse. The sleeping rooms were upstairs over the common room on the main floor, and the stables were in the back.

"Let me handle this," Ulath muttered to Sparhawk as they approached the innkeeper, a tousled fellow with a long, pointed nose.

"Feel free," Sparhawk replied.

"You," Ulath said abruptly to the innkeeper, "we need five rooms for the night, fodder for ten horses, and some decent food."

"I can provide all those, good master," the innkeeper assured him.

"Good. How much?"

"Ah—" The man with the pointed nose rubbed at his chin, carefully appraising the big Thalesian's clothes and general appearance. "That would be a halfcrown, good master," he said somewhat tentatively. His rates seemed to be based on a sliding scale of some sort.

Ulath turned on his heel. "Let's go," he said shortly to Sparhawk.

"What was I thinking of?" the innkeeper said, slapping his forehead. "That was *five* rooms and fodder for *ten* horses, wasn't it? I got the numbers turned around in my head. I thought you wanted ten rooms for some reason. A half-crown would be *far* too much for only five rooms. The right price would be two silver imperials, of course."

"I'm glad you got your mathematics straightened out," Ulath grunted. "Let's look at the rooms."

"Of course, good master." The innkeeper scurried on up the stairs ahead of them.

"You don't leave very many conversational openings, do you, my friend?" Sparhawk chuckled.

"I've never found innkeepers very interesting to talk with."

They reached an upper hallway, and Ulath looked into one of the rooms. "Check it for bugs," he told Sparhawk.

"Good *master*!" the innkeeper protested.

"I like to sleep alone," Ulath told him. "Bugs crowd me, and they're always restless at night."

The innkeeper laughed a bit weakly. "That's very funny, good master. I'll have to remember it. Where is it you come from, and where are you bound?"

Ulath gave him a long, icy stare, his blue eyes as chill as a northern winter and his shoulders swelling ominously as he bunched them under his tunic.

"Ah—no matter, I suppose," the innkeeper rushed on. "It's not really any of my affair, is it?"

"You've got that part right," Ulath said. He looked around. "Good enough," he said. "We'll stay." He nudged Sparhawk with his elbow. "Pay him," he said, turned, and clumped down the stairs.

They handed their horses over to the grooms and carried their saddlebags up to the sleeping rooms. Then they went back downstairs for supper.

Kalten, as usual, heaped his plate with steaming beef.

"Maybe we should send out for another cow," Berit joked.

"He's young," Kalten told the others jovially, "but I like the way he thinks." He grinned at Berit, but then the grin slowly faded, and the big blond Pandion grew quite pale. He stared at the young knight's face for quite some time. Then he abruptly pushed his plate back and rose to his feet. "I don't think I'm really hungry," he said. "I'm tired. I'm going to bed." He turned, quickly crossed the common room to the stairs, and went up them two at a time.

"What's the matter with *him*?" Ulath asked in a puzzled tone. "I've never seen him walk away from supper like that before."

"That's God's own truth," Bevier agreed.

"You'd better have a talk with him when you go up, Sparhawk," Vanion suggested. "Find out if he's sick or something. Kalten *never* leaves anything on his plate."

"Or anybody else's, for that matter," Talen added.

Sparhawk did not linger over supper. He ate quickly, said good night to the others, and went upstairs to have a talk with his friend. He found Kalten sitting on the edge of his bed with his face in his hands.

"What's the matter?" Sparhawk asked him. "Aren't you feeling well?"

Kalten turned his face away. "Leave me alone," he said hoarsely.

"Not very likely. What's wrong?"

"It doesn't matter." The blond knight sniffed loudly and wiped at his eyes with the back of his hand. "Let's go get drunk."

"Not until you tell me what's bothering you, we won't."

Kalten sniffed again and set his jaw. "It's something foolish. You'd laugh at me."

"You know better than that."

"There's a girl, Sparhawk, and she loves somebody else. Are you satisfied now?"

"Why didn't you say something earlier?"

"I just now found out about it."

"Kalten, you're not making any sense at all. One girl's always been the same as another to you. Most of the time you can't even remember their names."

"This time's different. Can we go get drunk now?"

"How do you know she doesn't feel the same way about you?" Sparhawk knew who the girl was and he was quite certain that she *did* in fact return his friend's feelings for her.

Kalten sighed. "God knows that there are people in this world who are brighter than I am, Sparhawk. It's taken me all this time to put it together. I'll tell you one thing, though. If he breaks her heart, I'll kill him, brother or no."

"Will you at least *try* to make some sense?"

"She told me that she loves somebody else—as plain as if she'd come right out and said it in so many words."

"Alean wouldn't do that."

"How did you know it was Alean?" The big blond man sprang to his feet. "Have you all been laughing at me behind my back?" he demanded pugnaciously.

"Don't be an ass. We wouldn't do that. We've all been through exactly the same thing. You didn't invent love, you know."

"Everybody knows, though, don't they?"

"No. I'm probably the only one—except for Melidere. Nothing much gets past *her*. Now what's all this nonsense about Alean loving somebody else?"

"I just put it together myself."

"*What* did you put together? Try to make a little sense, Kalten."

"Didn't you hear her singing on the day we left?"

"Of course I did. She has a beautiful voice."

"I'm not talking about her voice. I'm talking about the song she was singing. It was 'My Bonnie Blue-Eyed Boy.' "

"So?"

"It's Berit, Sparhawk. She's in love with Berit."

"What are you talking about?"

"I just noticed it when we sat down to supper." Kalten buried his face in his hands again. "I never paid any attention before, but when I looked into his face while we were talking, I saw it. I'm surprised you haven't seen it yourself."

"Seen what?"

"Berit's got blue eyes."

Sparhawk stared at him. Then, being careful not to laugh, he said, "So do you—when they're not bloodshot."

Kalten shook his head stubbornly. "His are bluer than mine. I know it's him. I just know it! God's punishing me for some of the things I've done in the past. He made me fall in love with a girl who loves somebody else. Well, I hope he's satisfied. If he wants to make me suffer, he's doing a good job of it."

"*Will* you be serious?"

"Berit's younger than I am, Sparhawk, and God knows he's better looking."

"Kalten—"

"Look at the way every girl who gets to within a hundred yards of him starts to follow him around like a puppy. Even the Atan girls were all falling in love with him."

"Kalten—"

"I *know* it's him. I just know it. God's twisting his knife in my heart. He's gone and made the one girl I'll ever feel this way about fall in love with one of my brother-knights."

"Kalten—"

Kalten sat up and squared his shoulders. "All right, then," he said weakly, "if that's the way God wants it, that's the way it's going to be. If Berit and Alean really, really love each other, I won't stand in their way. I'll bite my tongue and keep my mouth shut."

"Kalten—"

"But I swear it to you, Sparhawk," the blond Pandion said hotly, "if he hurts her, I'll kill him!"

"*Kalten!*" Sparhawk shouted at him.

"*What?*"

Sparhawk sighed. "Why don't we go out and get drunk?" he suggested, giving up entirely.

It was cloudy the following morning. It was a low, dirty-grey cloud cover that seethed and tattered in the stiff wind aloft. It was one of those peculiar days when the murk raced overhead, streaming in off the gulf lying to the west, but the air at the surface was dead calm.

They set out early and clattered along the narrow, cobbled streets where sleepy-eyed shopkeepers were opening their shutters and setting out their wares. They passed through the city gates and took the road that followed the north coast of the gulf.

After they had gone a mile or so, Vanion leaned over in his saddle. "How far do we have to go?" he asked Flute, who nestled, as always, in her sister's arms.

"What difference does it make?" The Child-Goddess shrugged.

"I'd like to know how long it's going to take."

"What does 'how far' have to do with 'how long'?"

"They're the same thing, Aphrael. Time and distance mean the same thing when you're traveling."

"Not if you know what you're doing, they don't."

Sparhawk had always admired Vanion, but never quite so much as in that moment. The silvery-bearded preceptor did not even raise his voice. "All I'm really getting at, Divine One, is that nobody knows we're here. Shouldn't we keep it that way? I don't mind a good fight now and then, but would bashing our way through crowds of drunken Edomish peasants serve any real purpose right now?"

"You always take so long to get to the point, Vanion," she said. "Why didn't you just come right out and tell me to speed things up?"

"I was trying to be polite. I think we'll all feel much better about this when Sparhawk's got Bhelliom in his hands again. It's up to you, though. If you want the road from here to wherever it is you've got Bhelliom hidden awash with blood and littered with corpses, we'll be happy to oblige you."

"He's hateful," Aphrael said to her sister.

"Oh, I wouldn't say that."

"*You* wouldn't. Sometimes you two are worse than Sparhawk and Ehlana."

Sparhawk moved in rather quickly at that point. Aphrael was coming very close to saying things that she shouldn't be saying in the presence of the others. "Shall we move right along?" he suggested quite firmly. "Vanion's right, Aphrael, and you know he is. If Rebal finds out that we're here, we'll have to wade through his people by the score."

"All right," she gave in quite suddenly.

"That was quick," Talen said to Khalad. "I thought she was going to be stubborn about it."

"No, Talen." She smirked. "Actually, I'm sort of looking forward to hearing that vast cry of chagrin that's going to echo from every mountain in Daresia when our enemies hear the sound of Anakha's fist closing around Bhelliom again. Just lean back in your saddles, gentlemen, and leave the rest to me."

Sparhawk awoke with a start. They were riding along the brink of a windswept cliff with an angry sea ripping itself to tattered froth on the rocks far below. Sephrenia rode in the lead, and she held Flute enfolded in her arms. The others trailed along behind, their cloaks drawn tightly around them and wooden expressions of endurance on their faces. The wind had risen, and it pushed at them and tugged at their cloaks.

There were some significant impossibilities involved here, but Sparhawk's mind seemed somehow numb to them. Normally, Vanion rode protectively close to Sephrenia, but Vanion didn't seem to be with them now.

Tynian, however, was. Sparhawk knew with absolute certainty that Tynian was a thousand leagues and more away, but there he was, his broad face as wooden as the faces of the others and his right shoulder as functional as ever.

Sparhawk did not turn around. He knew that another impossibility was riding behind him.

Their horses plodded up the winding trail that followed the edge of the long, ascending cliff toward a rocky promontory that thrust a crooked, stony finger out into the sea. At the outermost tip of the promontory stood a gnarled and twisted tree, its streaming branches flailing in the wind.

When she reached the tree, Sephrenia reined in. Kurik walked forward to lift Flute down. Sparhawk felt a sharp pang of bitter resentment. He knew about Aphrael's need for symmetry, but this went *too* far.

Kurik set Aphrael down on her feet, and when he straightened, he looked Sparhawk full in the face. Sparhawk's squire was unchanged. His features were rugged, and his black beard, touched with silver, was as coarse as ever. His bare shoulders were bulky, and his wrists were enclosed in steel cuffs. Without so much as changing expression, he winked at his lord.

"Very well, then," Flute said to them in a crisp voice, "let's get on with this before too many more of my cousins change their minds. I had to talk very fast and even throw a few tantrums to get them to agree, and many of them still have grave doubts about the whole notion."

"You don't have to explain things to them, Flute," Kurik told her in that gruff voice of his, a voice so familiar that Sparhawk's eyes filled with sudden tears. "Just tell them what to do. They're Church Knights, after all, so they're used to following orders they don't understand."

She laughed delightedly. "How very wise you are, Kurik. All right then, gentlemen, come with me." She led them past the gnarled tree to the brink of the awful precipice. Even though they were very high above it, the roaring of the surf was much like heavy thunder.

"All right," Aphrael told them, "I'm going to need your help with this."

"What do you want us to do?" Tynian asked her.

"Stand there and approve."

"Do *what?*"

"Just approve of me, Tynian. You can cheer if you'd like, but it's not really necessary. All I really need is approval—and love, of course—but there's nothing unusual about that. I always need love." She smiled at them mysteriously.

Then she stepped off the edge of the cliff.

Talen gave a startled cry and plunged after her.

The Child-Goddess, as unconcerned as if she were only taking a morning stroll, walked out across the empty air. Talen, however, fell like a stone.

"Oh, bother!" Aphrael exclaimed peevishly. She made a curious gesture with one hand, and Talen stopped falling. He sprawled in midair, his limbs spraddled, his face pasty-white, and his eyes bulging with horror. "Would you take care of that, Sephrenia?" the little girl said. "I'm busy right now." Then she glared down at Talen. "You and I are going to have a talk about this, young man," she said ominously. Then she turned and continued to walk out toward the open sea.

Sephrenia murmured in Styric, her fingers weaving the spell, and Talen rose with a curious fluttering movement, flaring from side to side like a kite on a taut string as Sephrenia pulled against the force of the gravity that was trying to dash him to the rocks below. When he had reached the edge of the cliff again, he scrambled across the wind-tossed grass on his hands and knees for several yards and then collapsed, shuddering violently.

Aphrael, all unconcerned, continued her stroll across the emptiness.

"You're getting fat, Sparhawk," Kurik said critically. "You need more exercise."

Sparhawk swallowed very hard. "Do you want to talk about this?" he asked his old friend in a choked voice.

"No, not really. You're supposed to be paying attention to Aphrael right now." He looked out at the Child-Goddess with a faint smile. "She's showing off, but she's only a little girl, after all, so I guess it's sort of natural." He paused, and a note of yearning came into his voice. "How's Aslade been lately?"

"She was fine the last time I saw her. She and Elys are both living on your farm, you know."

Kurik gave him a startled look.

"Aslade thought it would be best. Your sons are all in training now, and she didn't think it made much sense for her and Elys to both be alone. They adore each other."

"That's *fine*, Sparhawk," Kurik said, almost in wonder. "That's really fine. I always sort of worried about what was going to happen to them after I left." He looked out at the Child-Goddess. "Pay close attention to her now, my Lord. She's coming to the hard part."

Aphrael was far out over the surging waves and she had begun to glow with a brilliant incandescence. She stopped, hardly more than a glowing spark in the distance.

"Help her, gentlemen," Sephrenia commanded. "Send all of your love to her. She needs you now."

The fiery spark rose in a graceful little arc and then shot smoothly down through the murky air toward the long, lead-grey waves rolling ponderously toward the rocky shore. Down and down she plunged, and then she cut into the sea with no hint of a splash.

Sparhawk held his breath. It seemed that the Child-Goddess stayed down for an eternity. Black spots began to appear before the big Pandion's eyes.

"*Breathe*, Sparhawk!" Kurik barked, bashing his Lord's shoulder with his fist. "You won't do her much good if you faint."

Sparhawk blew out his breath explosively and stood gasping on the brink of the precipice.

"Idiot," Kurik muttered.

"Sorry," Sparhawk apologized. He concentrated on the little girl, and his thoughts became strongly jumbled. Aphrael was out there beneath those endlessly rolling waves certainly, but Flute was there as well—and Danae. That thought caught at his heart, and he felt suddenly icy cold.

Then that glowing spark burst up out of the sullen water. The Child-Goddess had been an incandescent white when she had made her plunge, but when she emerged from the sea, she glowed a brilliant blue. She was not alone as she rose once more into the air. Bhelliom rose with her, and the very earth seemed to shudder with its reemergence.

All glowing blue, Aphrael returned toward them, bearing that same golden box Sparhawk had cast into the sea a half-dozen years ago. The little girl reached solid ground once more. She went directly to Sparhawk and held up the gleaming golden box. "Into thy hands, for good or for ill, I deliver up the Bhelliom once more, Anakha," she intoned formally, placing the box in his hands. Then she smiled an impish little smile. "Try not to lose it again this time," she added.

CHAPTER SIX

"He looked well," Khalad said in a tight, controlled voice.

"Aren't you being just a little blasé about all this?" Talen asked his brother.

"Did you want me to go into hysterics?"

"You saw him, then?"

"Obviously."

"Where were you? I couldn't see you around any place."

"Lord Vanion and I were right over there," Khalad replied, pointing toward the far side of the trail. "We were told to just keep quiet and watch. We saw you all come riding up the hill. Why did you jump off the cliff like that?"

"I don't want to talk about it."

Sparhawk was not really paying very much attention to the others. He stood holding the golden box in his hands. He could feel the Bhelliom inside, and, as always, it was neither friendly nor hostile.

Flute was watching him closely. "Aren't you going to open the box, Anakha?"

"Why? I don't need Bhelliom just now, do I?"

"Don't you want to see it again?"

"I know what it looks like."

"Isn't it calling to you?"

"Yes, but I'm not listening. It always seems to complicate things when I let it out, so let's not do that until I really need it." He turned the box over in his hands, closely examining it. Kurik's work had been meticulous, though the box was unadorned. It was just that—a box. The fact that it was made of gold was largely irrelevant. "How do I open this? When I need to, I mean? There isn't any keyhole."

"Just touch the lid with one of the rings." She was watching him very closely.

"Which one?"

"Use your own. It knows you better than Ehlana's does. Are you sure you don't feel some sort of—?"

"Some sort of what?"

"Aren't your hands aching to touch it?"

"It's not unbearable."

"Now I see why all the others in my family are so afraid of you. You aren't anything at all like other humans."

"Everybody's different in some ways, I suppose. What do we do now?"

"We can go back to the ship."

"Can you get in touch with the sailors?"

"Yes."

"Why don't you ask them to sail across the gulf and pick us up somewhere on this side? That way we won't have to ride all the way back to Jorsan again, and we'll be able to avoid any chance meetings with Rebal's enthusiasts. Some of them might be sober enough by now to recognize the fact that we're not Edomishmen."

"You're in a strange humor, Sparhawk."

"I'm a little discontented with you at the moment, to be honest about it."

"What did I do?"

"Why don't we just drop it?"

"Don't you love me anymore?" Her lower lip began to tremble.

"Of course I do, but that doesn't alter the fact that I'm put out with you just now. People we love *do* irritate us from time to time, you know."

"I'm sorry," she said in a contrite little voice.

"I'll get over it. Are we finished here? Can we mount up and start back?"

"In just a moment," she said, seeming to suddenly remember something. Her eyes narrowed and began to glint dangerously. "You!" she said, leveling a finger at Talen. "Come here!"

Talen sighed and did as he was told.

"What did you think you were doing?" she demanded.

"Well—I was afraid you'd fall."

"I wasn't the one who was going to fall, you clot! Don't you *ever* do anything like that again!"

Talen could have agreed with her. That would have been the simplest way, and it would have avoided an extended scolding. He did not, however. "No, Flute. I'm afraid it's not going to be that way. I'll jump in every time I think you're in danger." He grimaced. "It's not really my idea. I want to be sure you understand that I haven't *completely* lost my mind. It's just that I can't help myself. When I see you do something like that, I'm moving before I even think. If you're really serious about trying to keep me alive, don't do things like that when I'm around, because I'll try to stop you every single time—regardless of how stupid it is."

"Why?" she asked him intently.

"I guess it's because I love you." He shrugged.

She squealed with delight and swarmed up into his arms. "He's such a *nice* boy!" she exclaimed, covering his face with kisses.

They had gone no more than a mile when Kalten reined in sharply, filling the air with sulphurous curses.

"Kalten!" Vanion snapped. "There are ladies present!"

"Take a look behind us, my Lord," the blond Pandion said.

It was the cloud, inky black, ominous, and creeping along the ground like viscous slime.

Vanion swore and reached for his sword.

"That won't do any good, my Lord," Sparhawk told him. He reached inside his tunic and took out the gleaming box. "This might, though." He rapped the band of his ring against the box lid.

Nothing happened.

"You have to tell it to open, Sparhawk," Flute instructed.

"Open!" Sparhawk commanded, touching the ring to the box again.

The lid popped up, and Sparhawk saw the Bhelliom nestled inside. The sapphire rose was perfect, eternal, and it glowed a deep blue. It seemed strangely resentful as Sparhawk reached in and lifted it out, however. "We all know who we are," he told the stone and its unwilling inhabitants. "I'm not going to speak to you in Troll-ish because I know you can understand me, no matter what language I use. I want you to stop this nonsense with that cloud, and I want you to do it right *now*! When I turn around to look, your little patch of private darkness had better be gone. I don't care how you do it, but get rid of that cloud!"

The sapphire rose grew suddenly hot in his hand, and it seemed almost to writhe against his fingers. Flickers of red, green, orange, and purple, all interspersed with streaks of white, stained the azure petals of Bhelliom as the Troll-Gods trapped within the gem fought to resist. Bhelliom, however, appeared to exert some kind of overcontrol, and those ugly flickers were smothered as the jewel began to burn more brightly.

Then there was a sudden, violent jolt that numbed Sparhawk's arm to the shoulder.

"*That's* the way!" Kalten shouted with a sudden laugh.

Sparhawk turned in his saddle and saw that the cloud was gone. "What happened?"

"It sort of flopped around like a fresh-caught eel—" Kalten laughed again. "—and then it flew all to pieces. What did you do, Sparhawk? I couldn't hear what you said."

"I let our blue friend and its tenants know that the cloud was starting to irritate me. Then I sort of hinted at the fact that I get ugly when I'm irritated."

"They must have believed you."

Flute was staring at Sparhawk in open astonishment. "You broke all the rules!" she accused him.

"I do that sometimes. It's quicker to cut across the formalities once in a while."

"You're not supposed to do it that way."

"It worked, didn't it?"

"It's a question of style, Sparhawk. I'm technically in charge here, and I don't know *what* Bhelliom and the Troll-Gods are going to think of me after that."

He laughed and then gently put Bhelliom back into its box. "Nice job," he told it. They *were* going to have to work together, after all, and a little encouragement now and then never hurt. Then he firmly closed the lid. "It's time for some speculation, gentlemen," he said to the others. "What can we make of this?"

"They know where we are, for one thing," Talen offered.

"It could be the rings again," Sephrenia noted. "That's what happened last time. The cloud—and the shadow—were concentrating on Sparhawk and Ehlana right at first because they had the rings."

"Bhelliom's closed up inside the box," Sparhawk said, "and so are the Troll-Gods."

"Are they still inside the jewel?" Ulath asked him.

"Oh, yes," Sparhawk said. "I could definitely feel them when I took Bhelliom out." He looked at Aphrael, phrasing his next question carefully. There were still some things that needed to be concealed. "I've heard that a God can be in more than one place at the same time." He left it a little tentative.

"Yes," she replied.

"Does that apply to the Troll-Gods as well?"

She struggled with it. "I'm not sure," she admitted. "It's a fairly complicated business, and the Troll-Gods are quite limited."

"Does this box confine them in the same way that chain-mail pouch did, back in Zemoch?"

She shook her head. "It's different. When they're encased in gold that way, they don't know where they are."

"Does that make a difference?"

"You have to know where you are before you can go someplace else."

"I'll take your word for it." He made a face. "I think we may have blundered again," he said sourly.

"How so?" Bevier asked him.

"We don't really have any absolute proof that the Troll-Gods are in league with our enemy. If they're trapped inside this box with Bhelliom and can't get out, they couldn't be, could they?"

"That *was* Ghworg in the mountains of Atan," Ulath insisted. "That means that *he's* out and about, at least."

"Are you sure, Ulath? Those peasants around the bonfire were convinced that the big fellow in the ancient armor was Incetes, too, you know."

"All the evidence points to it, Sparhawk. Everything we've seen this time is just like it was last time, and it was the Troll-Gods then, wasn't it?"

"I'm not even positive about that anymore."

"Well, *something* had to have enough authority over the Trolls to make them migrate from Thalesia to the north coast of Atan."

"Just how smart do you have to be in order to be a Troll? I'm not saying that it was something as crude as the hoax Rebal foisted off on those peasants, but . . ." Sparhawk left it hanging.

"That would be a fairly complex hoax, dear one," Sephrenia murmured.

"But not quite impossible, little mother. I'll drop the whole line of thought if you'll tell me that what I'm suggesting is impossible."

"Don't throw it away just yet," she said, her face troubled.

"Aphrael," Sparhawk said, "will this gold box keep our friend out there from being able to locate Bhelliom?"

She nodded. "The gold shields it. He can't hear it or feel it, so he can't just move toward the sound or the sense of it."

"And if I put Ehlana's ring in there as well? Would the box shield that, too?"

"Yes, but your own ring's still out in the open where he can feel its location."

"One thing at a time." He touched his ring to the lid of the box. "Open," he said.

The latch clicked, and the lid raised slightly.

Sparhawk removed Ehlana's ring from his finger and put it inside the box. "*You* look after it for a while," he told the Bhelliom.

"Please don't do that, Sparhawk," Vanion told him with a pained look.

"Do what?"

"Talk to it like that. You make it sound like a real being."

"Sorry, Vanion. It helps a little if I think of it that way. Bhelliom definitely has its own personality." He closed the lid and felt the latch click.

"Ah—Flute?" Khalad said a bit tentatively.

"Yes?"

"Is it the box that keeps Bhelliom hidden? Or is it the fact that the box is made out of gold?"

"It's the gold, Khalad. There's something about gold that muffles Bhelliom and hides it."

"And it works on Queen Ehlana's ring as well?"

She nodded. "I can't hear or feel a thing." She stretched her open palm out toward the box Sparhawk was holding. "Nothing at all," she confirmed. "I can feel *his* ring, though."

"Put a golden glove on him." Kalten shrugged.

"How much money did you bring along, Sir Kalten?" Khalad asked. "Gold's expensive, you know." He squinted at Sparhawk's ring. "I don't have to cover his whole hand," he said, "just the ring itself."

"I'll have to be able to get at it in a hurry, Khalad," Sparhawk cautioned.

"Let me work on it. Does anyone have a gold florin? That would be about the right size."

They all opened their purses.

Kalten looked around hopefully, then sighed. He reached into his purse. "You owe me a gold florin, Sparhawk," he said, handing the coin to Khalad.

"I'm in your debt, Kalten," Sparhawk smiled.

"You certainly are—one gold florin's worth. Shall we move on? It's starting to get chilly out here."

The wind had come up, gusty at first, but blowing steadily stronger. They followed the trail on down the slope until they were riding along the upper edge of a long sandy beach with the wind screaming and tearing at them and the salt spray stinging their faces.

"This is more than just a gale!" Ulath shouted over the screaming wind. "I think we've got a hurricane brewing!"

"Isn't it too early for hurricanes?" Kalten shouted.

"It is in Eosia," Ulath shouted back.

The shrieking of the wind grew louder, and they rode with their cloaks pulled tightly about them.

"We'd better get in out of this," Vanion yelled. "There's a ruined farmstead just ahead." He squinted through the driving spray. "It's got stone walls, so it should give us some kind of shelter from the wind."

They pushed their horses into a gallop and reached the ruin in a few minutes. The moldering buildings were half-buried in weeds, and the windows of the unroofed structures seemed to stare down from the walls like blind eyes. The house had completely tumbled in, so Sparhawk and the others dismounted in the yard and led their nervous horses into what had evidently been the barn. The floor was littered with the rotting remains of the roof, and there were bird droppings in the corners.

"How long does a hurricane usually last?" Vanion asked.

"A day or two," Ulath shrugged. "Three at the most."

"I wouldn't make any wagers on *this* one," Bevier said. "It came up just a little too quickly to suit me, and it's forced us to take shelter. We're pinned down in these ruins, you know."

"He's right," Berit agreed. "Don't we almost have to assume that somebody's raised this storm to delay us?"

Kalten gave him a flat, unfriendly stare, a fair indication that he had not yet shaken off his suspicions about the young man and Queen Ehlana's maid.

"I don't think it's going to be much of a problem," Ulath said. "As soon as we get back on board that ship, we'll be able to outrun the hurricane."

Aphrael was shaking her head.

"What's wrong?" he asked her.

"That ship wasn't built to ride out a hurricane. As a matter of fact, I've already sent it back to where it came from."

"Without even telling us?" Vanion objected.

"*My* decision, Vanion. The ship's no good to us in this kind of weather, so there was no point in putting the crew in danger."

"It seemed well-made to me," Ulath objected. "The builders must have taken high winds into account when they designed her."

She shook her head. "The wind doesn't blow where that ship came from."

"There are winds everywhere, Flute," he pointed out. "There's no place on this entire world where the wind doesn't blow now and—" He broke off and stared at her. "Where *does* that ship come from?"

"That's really none of your business, Sir Knight. I can bring it back after the storm passes."

"*If* it passes," Kalten added. "And I wouldn't be at all surprised that when it does, this broken-down barn's going to be surrounded by several thousand armed fanatics."

They all looked at each other.

"I think maybe we'd better move on, storm or no storm," Vanion said. He looked at Flute. "Can you still—? I mean, will this wind interfere?"

"It won't make it any easier," she admitted glumly.

"I don't want you to hurt yourself," Sephrenia told her.

Flute waved her hand as if brushing something aside. "Don't worry about me, Sephrenia."

"Don't try to hide things from me, young lady." Sephrenia's tone was stern. "I know exactly what all this wind's going to do to you."

"And *I* know exactly what trying to carry it around will do to our mysterious friend out there. Trying to chase us with a hurricane on his back will exhaust *him* far more than carrying ten people on horseback will exhaust *me*—and I'm faster than he is. They don't call me the nimble Goddess for nothing, you know. I can run even faster than Talen, if I have to. Where would you like to go, Lord Vanion?"

The preceptor looked around at them. "Back to Jorsan?"

"It's probably as good as anyplace in a hurricane," Kalten said. "At least the beds are dry."

"And the beer is wet?" Ulath smiled.

"That *did* sort of enter into my thinking," Kalten admitted.

The wind shrieked around the corners of the building, but the inn was a sturdy stone structure, and the windows had stout shutters. Sparhawk chafed at the delay, but there was no help for it.

Sephrenia had put Flute to bed immediately upon their return to the inn and she hovered over the little girl protectively. "She's really concerned," Vanion reported. "I guess there *are* limits after all. Flute's trying to make light of it, but I know exhaustion when I see it."

"She won't *die*, will she?" Talen asked in a shocked voice.

"She *can't* die, Talen," Vanion replied. "She can be destroyed, but she can't die."

"What's the difference?"

"I'm not sure," Vanion admitted. "I *am* sure that she's very, very tired. We shouldn't have let her do that." He looked around the hallway outside the room where Sephrenia was tending the weary little Goddess. "Where's Kalten?" he asked.

"He and Ulath are down in the taproom, my Lord," Bevier replied.

"I should have known, I guess. One of you might remind them that I won't go easy on them if they're unwell when we set out, though."

They went on downstairs again and periodically checked the weather outside. If anything, the wind actually began to blow harder.

Sparhawk finally went back up and knocked lightly on the door to Sephrenia's room. "Could I have a word with Flute?" he asked when his tutor came to the door.

"No. Absolutely not," she whispered. "I just got her to sleep." She came out into the hallway, closed the door, and set her back protectively against it.

"I'm not going to hurt her, Sephrenia."

"You can make safe wagers on that all over Daresia," she told him with a steely glint in her eyes. "What did you want to ask her?"

"Could I use Bhelliom to break up this storm?"

"Probably."

"Why don't I do that then?"

"Did you want to destroy Jorsan? And kill everybody in town?"

He stared at her.

"You have no real idea of the kind of forces involved in weather, have you, Sparhawk?"

"Well, sort of," he said.

"No, I don't think you do, dear one. Whoever raised this hurricane is very powerful, and he knows what he's doing, but his hurricane is still a natural force. You could use Bhelliom to break it up, certainly, but if you do, you'll release all that pent-up force at one time and in one place. You wouldn't even be able to find pieces of Jorsan after the dust settled."

"Maybe I'd better drop the idea."

"I would. Now run along. I have to keep watch over Aphrael."

Sparhawk went back down the hallway feeling a little like a small boy who had just been sent to his room.

Ulath was coming up the stairs. "Have you got a minute, Sparhawk?" he asked.

"Of course."

"I think you'd better keep a close eye on Kalten."

"Oh?"

"He's beginning to have some murderous thoughts about Berit."

"Is it getting out of hand?"

"You knew about it? About the feelings he has for your wife's maid?"

Sparhawk nodded.

"The more he drinks, the worse it's going to get, you know—and there's nothing else to do during this storm *except* drink. Is there any real substance to those suspicions of his?"

"No. He just pulled them out of the air. The girl's very, very fond of him, actually."

"I sort of thought she might be. Berit was already having enough trouble with the emperor's wife without going in search of more. Does Kalten do this very often? Fall desperately in love, I mean?"

"So far as I know, it's the first time. He's always sort of taken affection where he could find it."

"That's the safest way," Ulath agreed. "But since he's waited so long, this is hitting him very hard. We'd better do what we can to keep him and Berit apart until we get back to Matherion and Alean has the chance to straighten it out."

Khalad came down the hallway to join them. Sparhawk's squire had a slightly disgusted look on his face. He held up Kalten's florin. "This isn't going to work, Sparhawk," he said. "I could cover the stone with it easily enough, but it'd probably take you a half hour to pry it open again so that you could use the ring. I'm going to have to come up with something else. You'd better give me the ring. I'm going to have to go talk with a goldsmith, and I'll need precise measurements."

Sparhawk felt a great reluctance to part with the ring. "Can't you—just?"

Khalad shook his head. "Whatever the goldsmith and I decide on will have to be fitted anyway. I guess it gets down to how much you trust me at this point, Sparhawk."

Sparhawk sighed. "You *had* to put it on that basis, didn't you, Khalad?"

"I thought it would be the quickest way, my Lord." Khalad held out his hand, and Sparhawk removed the ring and gave it to him. "Thank you." Khalad smiled. "Your faith in me is very touching."

"Well said," Ulath murmured.

Later, after Sparhawk and Ulath had carried Kalten upstairs and put him to bed, they all gathered in the common room for supper. Sparhawk spoke briefly with the innkeeper and had Sephrenia's meal taken upstairs to her.

"Where's Talen?" Bevier asked, looking around.

"He said he was going out for a breath of fresh air," Berit replied.

"In a *hurricane*?"

"I think he's just restless."

"Or he wants to go steal something," Ulath added.

The door to the inn banged open, and the wind blew Talen inside. He was wearing doublet and hose under his cloak, and a rapier at his side. The weapon did not seem to encumber him very much. He set his back against the door and strained to push it shut. He was soaked through, and his face was streaming water. He was grinning broadly, however. "I just solved a mystery," he laughed, coming across to where they sat.

"Oh?" Ulath asked.

"What would it be worth to you gentlemen to know Rebal's real identity?"

"How did you manage *that*?" Berit demanded.

"Sheer luck, actually. I was outside looking around. The wind blew me down a narrow lane and pinned me up against the door of the shop at the end. I thought I'd step inside to get my breath, and the first thing I saw in there was a familiar face. Our mysterious Rebal's a respected shopkeeper here in Jorsan. He told me so himself. He doesn't look nearly as impressive when he's wearing an apron."

"A shopkeeper?" Bevier asked incredulously.

"Yes indeed, Sir Knight—one of the pillars of the community, to hear him tell it. He's even a member of the town council."

"Did you manage to get his name?" Vanion asked.

"Of course, my Lord. He introduced himself just as soon as the wind blew me through the door. His name's Amador. I even bought something from him just to keep him talking."

"What does he deal in?" Berit asked.

Talen reached inside his tunic and drew out a bright pink strip of cloth, wet and somewhat bedraggled. "Isn't it pretty?" he said. "I think I'll dry it out and give it to Flute."

"You're not serious." Vanion laughed. "Is that *really* what he sells?"

"May muh tongue turn green iffin it ain't, yer Preceptorship," the boy replied, imitating Caalador's dialect. "The man here in Edom who has all the Tamuls trembling in their boots is a ribbon clerk. Can you imagine that?" And he collapsed in a chair, laughing uproariously.

"How does it work?" Sparhawk asked the next day, turning the ring over and looking at the underside.

"It's the mounting of one of those rings people use when they want to poison other people's food or drink," Khalad replied. "I had the goldsmith take it off the original ring and mount it on yours so that the cover fits over the ruby. There's a little hinge on this side of the mounting and a latch on the other. All you have to do is touch the latch—right here." He pointed at a tiny lever half-concealed under the massive-looking setting. "The hinge has a little spring, so this gold cap pops open." He touched the lever, and the half globe covering the ruby snapped up to reveal the stone. "Are you *sure* that the ring will work if you're only touching Bhelliom with the band? With that cap in the way, touching the stone to anything might be a little tricky."

"The band does the job," Sparhawk replied. "This is very clever, Khalad."

"Thank you. I made the goldsmith wash out all the poison before we installed it on your ring."

"The old ring had been used?"

"Oh, yes. One of the heirs of the Edomish noblewoman who'd previously owned it sold it to the goldsmith after she died. I guess she had a lot of enemies. She did at first, anyway." Khalad chuckled. "The goldsmith was very disappointed with me. He *really* wanted to be alone with your ring for a while. That ruby's worth quite a lot. I didn't think Bhelliom would respond to a piece of red glass, though, so I kept a close eye on him. You'd probably better find out if the ring will still open the box, just to be on the safe side. If it doesn't, I'll go back to the goldsmith's shop and start cutting off his fingers. After he loses two or three, he'll remember where he hid the real ruby; it's hard to do finely detailed work when you don't have all ten fingers. But I told him I'd do that right at the outset, so we can probably trust his integrity."

"You're a ruthless sort of fellow."

"I just wanted to avoid misunderstandings. After we make sure that the ring still opens the box, you'd better take it to Flute and find out if the gold's thick enough to shield the ruby. If it isn't, I'll take it back to the goldsmith and have him pile more gold on that cap. We can keep doing that until it does what we want it to do."

"You're very practical, Khalad."

"*Somebody* in this group has to be."

"What did you do with Kalten's florin?"

"I used it to pay the goldsmith. It covered *part* of the cost. You still owe me for the rest, though."

"I'm going to be in debt to everybody before we get home."

"That's all right, Sparhawk." Khalad grinned. "We all know that you're good for it."

"*That* does it!" Sparhawk said angrily after he had taken a quick look out the door of the common room. It was two days later, and they had all just come downstairs for breakfast. "Let's get ready to leave."

"I can't bring the ship back in this storm, Sparhawk," Flute told him. The little girl still looked wan, but she was obviously recovering.

"We'll have to go overland, then. We're sitting here like ducks in a row just waiting for our friend out there to gather his forces. We *have* to move."

"It's going to take months to reach Matherion if we go overland, Sparhawk," Khalad objected. "Flute's not well enough to speed up the trip."

"I'm not *that* sick, Khalad," Flute said. "I'm just a little tired, that's all."

"Do you have to do it all by yourself?" Sparhawk asked her.

"I didn't quite follow that."

"If one of your cousins happened along, could he help you?"

She frowned.

"Let's say that you were making the decisions, and he was just lending you the muscle."

"It's a nice idea, Sparhawk," Sephrenia said, "but we don't *have* one of Aphrael's cousins along."

"No, but we've got Bhelliom."

"I knew it would happen," Bevier groaned. "The accursed stone's unhinged Sparhawk's mind. He thinks he's a God."

"No, Bevier." Sparhawk smiled. "I'm not a God, but I have access to something very close to one. When I put those rings on, Bhelliom has to do what I tell it to do. That's not *exactly* like being a God, but it's close enough. Let's have breakfast, and then the rest of you can gather our belongings and get them packed on the horses. Aphrael and I'll hammer out the details of how we're going to work this."

CHAPTER SEVEN

The wind was screaming through the streets of Jorsan, driving torrents of rain before it. Sparhawk and his friends wrapped themselves tightly in their cloaks, bowed their heads into the wind, and plodded grimly into the teeth of the hurricane.

The city gates were unguarded, and the party rode out into open country where the wind, unimpeded, savaged them all the more. Speech was impossible, so Sparhawk merely pointed toward the muddy road that led off toward Korvan, fifty leagues to the north.

The road curved around behind a low hill a mile or so outside of town, and Sparhawk reined in. "Nobody can see us now," he shouted over the howling wind. "Let's try this and see what happens." He reached inside his tunic for the golden box.

Berit came galloping up from the rear. "We've got riders coming up from behind!" he shouted, wiping the rain out of his face.

"Following us?" Kalten demanded.

Berit spread his hands uncertainly.

"How many?" Ulath asked.

"Twenty-five or thirty, Sir Ulath. I couldn't see them very clearly in all this rain, but it looked to me as if they were wearing armor of some sort."

"Good," Kalten grated harshly. "There's not much fun in killing amateurs."

"What do you think?" Sparhawk asked Vanion.

"Let's have a look. They might not be interested in us at all."

The two turned and rode back along the muddy road a couple hundred yards.

The riders coming up from behind had slowed to a walk. They were rough-looking men wrapped in furs and armed for the most part with bronze-tipped spears. The one in the lead wore a vast, bristling beard and an archaic-looking helmet surmounted with a set of deer antlers.

"That's it," Sparhawk said shortly. "They're definitely following us. Let's get the others and deal with this."

They rode back to where their friends had taken some small shelter on the lee side of a pine grove. "We stayed in Jorsan too long," Sparhawk told them. "It gave Rebal time to call in help. The men behind us are bronze-age warriors."

"Like the Lamorks who attacked us outside Demos?" Ulath asked.

"Right," Sparhawk said. "These are most likely followers of Incetes rather than Drychtnath, but it all amounts to the same thing."

"Could you pick out the leader?" Ulath asked.

"He's right up front," Vanion replied.

"That makes it easier, then."

Vanion gave him a questioning look.

"This has happened before," Sparhawk explained. "We don't know exactly why, but when the leader falls, the rest of them vanish."

"Couldn't we just hide back among these trees?" Sephrenia asked.

"I wouldn't want to chance that," Vanion told her. "We know where they are now. If we let them get out of sight, they could circle back and ambush us. Let's deal with this here and now."

"We're wasting time," Kalten said abruptly. "Let's get on with it."

"Khalad," Sparhawk said to his squire, "take Sephrenia and the children back into the trees a ways. Try to stay out of sight."

"Children?" Talen objected.

"Just do as you're told," Khalad told him, "and don't get any ideas about trying out that rapier just yet."

The knights turned and rode back along the muddy track to face their pursuers.

"Are they alone?" Bevier asked. "I mean, can anybody make out the one who might have raised them?"

"We can sort that out after we kill the fellow with the antlers," Kalten growled. "Once all the rest vanish, whoever's responsible for this is going to be left standing out in the rain all by himself."

"There's no point in waiting," Vanion told them, his voice bleak. "Let's get at it. I'm starting to get wet."

They all pushed their cloaks out of the way to clear their sword arms, pulled on the plain steel helmets which had been hanging from their saddlebows, and buckled on their shields.

"I'll do it," Kalten told Sparhawk, forcing his mount against Faran's shoulder. There was a kind of suppressed fury in Kalten's voice and a reckless set to his shoulders. "Let's go!" he bellowed, drawing his sword.

They charged.

The warriors from the ninth century recoiled momentarily as the mail-shirted Church Knights thundered toward them with the hooves of their war-horses hurling great clots of mud out behind them.

Bronze-age weaponry and ancient tactics were no match for steel mail shirts and contemporary swords and axes, and the small, scrubby horses of the dark ages were scarcely more than ponies. Kalten crashed into the forefront of the pursuers with his companions fanned out behind him in a kind of wedge formation. The blond Pandion stood up in his stirrups, swinging his sword in vast, powerful strokes. Kalten was normally a highly skilled and cool-headed warrior, but he seemed enraged today, taking chances he should not have taken, overextending his strokes, and swinging his sword much harder than was prudent. The round bronze shields of the men who faced him barely slowed his strokes as he chopped his way through the press toward the bearded man in the antlered helmet. Sparhawk and the others, startled by his reckless charge, followed him, cutting down any who tried to attack him from the rear.

The bearded man bellowed an archaic war cry and spurred his horse forward, swinging a huge, bronze-headed war ax.

Almost disdainfully, Kalten brushed the ax-stroke aside with his shield and delivered a vast overhand stroke with his sword, swinging the weapon with all his strength. His sword sheared down through the hastily raised bronze shield, and half of the gleaming oval spun away, carrying the bearded man's forearm with it. Kalten swung again, and his sword struck the top of the antler-adorned helmet, gashing down into the enemy's head in a sudden spray of blood and brains. The dead man was hurled from his saddle by the force of the blow, and his followers wavered like mirages and vanished.

One mounted man, however, remained. The black-cloaked figure of Rebal was suddenly quite alone as the ancient warriors who had been drawn up protectively around him were abruptly no longer there.

Kalten advanced on him, his bloody sword half-raised and death in his ice-blue eyes.

Rebal shrieked, wheeled his horse, and fled back into the storm, desperately flogging at his mount.

"*Kalten!*" Vanion roared as the knight spurred his horse to pursue the fleeing man. "*Stop!*"

"But—"

"*Stay where you are!*"

Still caught in the grip of that reckless fury, Kalten started to object.

"That's an order, Sir Knight! Put up your sword!"

"Yes, my Lord," Kalten replied sullenly, sliding his blood-smeared blade back into its sheath.

"Take that weapon back out!" Vanion bellowed at him. "Wipe it off before you sheathe it!"

"Sorry, Lord Vanion. I forgot."

"*Forgot?* What do you mean, 'forgot'? Are you some half-grown puppy? *Clean* that sword, Sir Knight! I want to see it shining before you put it away!"

"Yes, my Lord," Kalten mumbled.

"*What did you say?*"

"*Yes, my Lord!*" Kalten shouted it this time.

"That's a little better."

"Thanks, Vanion," Sparhawk murmured.

"I'll deal with you later, Sparhawk!" Vanion barked. "Making him see to his equipment was *your* responsibility. You're supposed to be a leader of men, not a goatherd." The preceptor looked around. "All right," he said crisply, "let's form up and go back. Smartly, gentlemen, smartly. We're soldiers of God. Let's try to at least *look* as if we knew what we were doing!"

There was some slight shelter from the wind back in among the trees. Vanion led the knights through the grove to rejoin Sephrenia, Khalad, and the "children."

"Is everyone all right?" Sephrenia asked quickly.

"We don't have any *visible* wounds, little mother," Sparhawk replied.

She gave him a questioning look.

"Lord Vanion was in fine voice." Ulath grinned. "He was a little dissatisfied with a couple of us, and he spoke to us about it—firmly."

"That will do, Sir Knight," Vanion said.

"Yes, my Lord."

"Were you able to identify whoever it was who raised that party?" Khalad asked Sparhawk.

"No. Rebal was there, but we didn't see anybody else."

"How was the fight?"

"You should have seen it, Khalad," Berit said enthusiastically. "Sir Kalten was absolutely stupendous!"

Kalten glared at him.

Sephrenia gave the two of them a shrewd look. "We can talk about all this after we get clear of the storm," she told them. "Are you ready, Sparhawk?"

"In a moment," he replied. He reached inside his tunic, took out the box, and commanded it to open. He put on Ehlana's ring and lifted the Bhelliom out.

"Here," Sephrenia said. She lifted Flute, and Sparhawk took the little girl into his arms.

"How do we go about this?" he asked her.

"Once we get started, I'll be speaking through your lips," she replied. "You won't understand what I'm saying because the language will be strange to you."

"Some obscure Styric dialect?"

"No, Sparhawk, not Styric. It's quite a bit older than that. Just relax. I'll guide you through this. Give me the box. When Bhelliom moves from one place to another, everything sort of shivers. I don't think our friend out there will be able to locate Bhelliom again immediately, so if you put it—and your wife's ring—back in the box immediately and snap the cover down on your own ring, he won't have any idea of where we've gone. Now hold Bhelliom in both hands and let it know who you are."

"It should know already."

"Remind it, Sparhawk, and speak to it in Trollish. Let's observe the formalities." She nestled back into the protective circle of his mailed arms.

Sparhawk lifted Bhelliom, making sure that the bands of both rings were firmly in contact with it. "Blue-Rose," he said to it in Trollish, "I am Sparhawk-from-Elenia. Do you know me?"

The azure glow which had bathed his hands hardened, became like fresh-forged steel. Sparhawk's relationship with the Bhelliom was ambiguous, and the flower-gem had no real reason to be fond of him.

"Tell it who you really are, Sparhawk," Flute suggested. "Make certain that it knows you."

"Blue-Rose," Sparhawk said again, once more in the hideous language of the Trolls, "I am Anakha, and I wear the rings. Do you know me?"

The Bhelliom gave a little lurch as he spoke the fatal name, and some of the steel went out of its petals.

"It's a start," he muttered. "What now?"

"Now it's my turn," she replied. "Relax, Sparhawk. Let me into your mind."

It was a strange sort of process. Sparhawk felt almost as if his own will had been suspended as the Child-Goddess gently, even lovingly, took his mind into her two small hands. The voice that came from his lips was strangely soft, and the language it spoke was hauntingly familiar, skirting the very outer edges of his understanding.

Then the world seemed to blur around him and it faded momentarily into a kind of luminous twilight. Then the blur was gone, and the sun was shining. It was no longer raining, and the wind had dropped to a gentle breeze.

"What an astonishing idea!" Aphrael exclaimed. "I never even *thought* of that! Put the Bhelliom away, Sparhawk. Quickly."

Sparhawk put the jewel and Ehlana's ring back into the box and snapped down the cover on his own ring. Then he turned and looked toward the south. There was an intensely dark line of cloud low on the horizon. Then he looked north again and saw a fair-sized town at the bottom of the hill, a pleasant-looking town with red tile roofs glowing in the autumn sunshine. "Is that Korvan?" he asked tentatively.

"Well, of *course* it is," Flute replied with an airy little toss of her head. "Isn't that where you said you wanted to go?"

"We made good time," Ulath observed blandly.

Sephrenia suddenly laughed. "We wanted to test our friend's stamina," she said. "Now we'll find out just how much endurance he has. If he wants to keep chasing us, he's going to have to pick up his hurricane and run along behind us just as fast as he possibly can."

"Oh, this is going to be *fun*!" Flute exclaimed, clapping her hands together delightedly. "I'd never have *believed* we could jump so far."

Kalten squinted up toward the bright autumn sun. "I make it just a little before noon. Why don't we ride down into Korvan and have an early lunch. I worked up quite an appetite back there."

"It might not be a bad idea, Sparhawk," Vanion agreed. "The situation's changed now, so we might want to think our plans through and see if we want to modify them."

Sparhawk nodded. He bumped Faran's flanks with his heels, and they started down the hill toward Korvan. "You seemed surprised," he murmured into Flute's ear.

"Surprised? I was stunned."

"What did it do?"

"You wouldn't really understand, Father. Do you remember how the Troll-God Ghnomb moved you across northern Pelosia?"

"He sort of froze time, didn't he?"

She nodded. "I've always done it a different way, but I'm more sophisticated than Ghnomb is. Bhelliom does it in still another way—much simpler, actually. Ghnomb and I are different, but we're both part of this world, so the terrain's very important to us. It gives us a sense of permanence and location. Bhelliom doesn't appear to need reference points. It seems to just think of another place, and it's there."

"Could you do it like that?"

She pursed her lips. "I don't think so." She sighed. "It's a little humiliating to admit it, but Bhelliom's far wiser than I am."

"But not nearly as loveable."

"Thank you, kind sir."

Sparhawk suddenly thought of something. "Is Danae at Matherion?"

"Of course."

"How's your mother?"

"She's well. She and the thieves are very busy trying to get their hands on some documents that are hidden somewhere in the Ministry of the Interior."

"Are things still under control there?"

"For the moment, yes. I know I've teased you about it a few times, but it's very hard to be in two places at the same time. Danae's sleeping a great deal, so I'm missing a lot of what's going on there. Mother's a little worried. She thinks Danae might be sick."

"Don't worry her *too* much."

"I won't, Father."

They rode into Korvan and found a respectable-looking inn. Ulath had a word or two with the innkeeper, and they were all escorted into a private dining room in the back where the golden sunlight streamed in through the windows to set the oaken tables and benches to glowing. "Can you keep anyone who might be curious from eavesdropping on us, little mother?" Sparhawk asked.

"How many times do you have to ask that question before you know the answer?" she asked with a weary sigh.

"Just making sure, that's all."

They removed their cloaks, stacked their weapons in a corner, and sat down at the table.

A squinty-eyed, slatternly serving-girl came in and told them what the kitchen had prepared for the day.

Sephrenia shook her head. "Tell her, Vanion."

"The lady and I—and the little girl—will have lamb," he said firmly. "We don't much care for pork."

"The cook ain't fixed no lamb," the girl whined.

"You'd better tell him to get started, then."

"He ain't gonna like it."

"He doesn't *have* to like it. Tell him that if we don't get lamb, we'll take our money to another inn. The owner of the place wouldn't like that very much, would he?"

The girl's face became set, and she stormed out.

"*That's* the Vanion we came to know and love when we were boys." Kalten laughed. The fight that morning seemed to have improved his temper.

Vanion unfolded his map. "We've got a fairly substantial road going east," he said, running his finger along the line stretching across the map. "It crosses Edom and then goes on through Cynesga. We'll cross the border into Tamul proper at Sarna." He looked at Flute. "How long a jump can Bhelliom make at one time?"

"Would you like to pay a visit to the moon, Lord Vanion?" She frowned. "There's a drawback, though. Bhelliom makes a very distinctive sound when it does something. It probably doesn't even know that it's doing it, but it *does* sort of announce its location. We might be able to teach it how to conceal itself, but it's going to take time."

"And that raises another point as well," Sephrenia added. "Sparhawk's holding Bhelliom's power, but he doesn't know how to use it yet."

"Thanks," Sparhawk said dryly.

"I'm sorry, dear one, but you don't. Every time you've ever picked it up, either Aphrael or I have had to walk you through it step by step. We're definitely going to need some time. We have to teach Bhelliom how to be quiet, and we have to teach you how to use it without having someone hold your hand."

"I love you, too, Sephrenia."

She smiled fondly. "You're holding tremendous power in your hands, Sparhawk, but it's not of much use if all you know how to do is wave it around like a battle flag. I don't think we should rush back to Matherion immediately. That story you cooked up for Ehlana will explain our absence for at least two or three more weeks. We'll want to avoid the traps and ambushes our enemies are going to lay for us along the way, of course." She paused. "They might even be useful. They'll give you something to practice on."

"Jump around," Ulath grunted.

"*Will* you stop that, Ulath?" she snapped at him.

"Sorry, Sephrenia. It's a habit of mine. After I think my way through something, I just blurt out the conclusion. The intermediate steps aren't usually very interesting. Our friends out there have been raising random disturbances to keep the Atans running back and forth across the continent—werewolves here, vampires there, Shining Ones off in that direction and antique armies in this. There's no real purpose to it all except to confuse the imperial authorities. We could steal a page right out of their book, you know. They can hear and feel Bhelliom—particularly when it's doing something noisy. I gather that there's no real limit to how far it can jump at one time, so let's just say that Sparhawk wants to see what the weather's like in Darsas. He has Bhelliom pick him up by the scruff of the neck and drop him down in the square outside King Alberen's palace. He stays there for about a half hour—long enough for the other side to smell him out—then he hops across the continent to Beresa in southern Arjuna and stays long enough to make his presence known *there*. Then he goes to Sarsos, then to Jura in southern Daconia, then back to Cimmura to say hello to Platime—all in the space of one afternoon. He'd get all sorts of practice using Bhelliom, and by the time the sun went down, they wouldn't know *where* he was or where he was going to go next. To make it even more fun, our mysterious friend out there wouldn't know which of these little jumps was the significant one, so he'd almost have to follow along."

"Carrying that hurricane on his back every step of the way," Kalten added. "Ulath, you're brilliant."

"Yes," the blond-braided Thalesian agreed with becoming modesty, "I know."

"I like it," Vanion approved. "What do you think, Sephrenia?"

"It *would* give Sparhawk and Bhelliom the chance to get to know each other," she agreed, "and that's basically what we need here. The better they know each other, the better they'll be able to work together. I'm sorry, Sir Ulath. Blurt out conclusions anytime you feel like it."

"All right then," Vanion said in his most businesslike fashion, "When Sparhawk's off on one of his little excursions, the rest of us will be sort of invisible—well, not really invisible, but if Bhelliom's not with us, our friend won't be able to hear us or feel us, will he?"

"Probably not," Flute agreed. "Even if he could, Sparhawk will be making so much noise that he won't really pay much attention to you."

"Good. Let's say that Sparhawk hops up to Darsas and rattles all the windows there. Then he hops back here, picks *us* up, and puts down in—" He frowned at his map. "In Cyron on the Cynesgan border." He stabbed his finger down on the chart. "Then he hops around to several other places, leaving Bhelliom and the rings out in the open so that our friend knows where he is each time. Then he rejoins us at Cyron and boxes up Bhelliom again. By that time, our friend will be so confused he won't know *where* we are."

"Pay close attention, Sparhawk," Kalten grinned. "That's the way a preceptor's *supposed* to think."

Sparhawk grunted. Then he thought of something. "I want to talk with you for a moment when we leave," he told his blond friend quietly.

"Am I in trouble?"

"Not yet, but you're working on it."

The slatternly serving-girl brought in their meal, glowering at Vanion as she did, and Sparhawk and his friends began to eat.

They did not linger after lunch, but rose immediately and trooped out.

"What's your problem?" Kalten asked as he and Sparhawk trailed along behind the others.

"Quit trying to get yourself killed."

"What are you talking about?"

"Don't be coy, Kalten. I saw what you were doing this morning. Don't you realize how transparent you are to people who know you?"

"You're unwholesomely clever, Sparhawk," the blond Pandion accused.

"It's a character defect of mine. I've got enough to worry about already. Don't add *this* to it."

"It's such a perfect solution."

"For a nonexistent problem, you jackass. Alean's had her eyes on you ever since we left Chyrellos. She's not going to throw all that effort away. It's *you* she's after, Kalten, not Berit. If you don't stop this nonsense, I'll take you back to Demos and have you confined in the motherhouse."

"How do you propose to do that?"

"I've got this blue friend here, remember?" Sparhawk patted the bulge in the front of his tunic. "I can pick you up by the hair, deposit you in Demos, and be back before Vanion even gets into his saddle."

"That's not fair."

"Now you're starting to sound like Talen. I'm not trying to be fair. I'm trying to keep you from killing yourself. I want your oath."

"No."

"Demos is nice this time of year. You'll enjoy it. You can spend your days in prayer."

Kalten swore at him.

"You've got *some* of the words right, Kalten. Now just put them together into a proper oath. Believe me, my friend, you're not going to go one step farther with us until you give me your oath to stop all this nonsense."

"I swear," Kalten muttered.

"Not good enough. Let's make it nice and formal. I want it to make an impression on you. You've got this tendency to overlook things if they aren't all spelled out."

"Do you want me to sign something in my own blood?" Kalten demanded acidly.

"It's a thought, but I don't have any parchment handy. I'll accept your verbal oath—for the time being. I may change my mind later, though, so keep your veins nice and loose and your dagger sharp."

"*Sparhawk?*" Ambassador Fontan exclaimed. "What are you doing in Darsas?" The ancient Tamul diplomat stared at the big Pandion in astonishment.

"Just passing through, your Excellency," Sparhawk replied. "May I come in?"

"By all means, my boy." Fontan opened his door wide, and Sparhawk and Flute entered the crimson-carpeted study of the Tamul embassy.

"You're looking well, your Royal Highness." Fontan smiled at the little girl. Then he looked at her more closely. "I'm sorry," he apologized to her. "I mistook you for Prince Sparhawk's daughter. You resemble her very much."

"We're distantly related, your Excellency," Flute told him without turning a hair.

"Has word reached you about what happened in Matherion a few weeks ago, your Excellency?" Sparhawk asked, tucking the Bhelliom back into his inside tunic pocket.

"Just yesterday," Fontan replied. "Is the emperor safe?"

Sparhawk nodded. "My wife's looking after him. Our time's limited, your Excellency, so I'm not going to be able to explain everything. Are you cosmopolitan enough to accept the notion that the Styrics have some very unusual capabilities?"

Fontan smiled faintly. "Prince Sparhawk, a man my age is willing to accept almost anything. After the initial shock of astonishment that comes each morning when I wake up and discover that I'm still alive, I can face the day with an open mind."

"Good. My friends and I left Korvan down in Edom about an hour ago. They're riding on toward Cyron on the border, but I came here to have a word with you."

"An *hour* ago?"

"Just take it on faith, your Excellency," Flute told him. "It's one of those Styric things Sparhawk was talking about."

"I'm not certain how much your messenger told you," Sparhawk continued, "but it's urgent that all of the Atan garrison commanders in the empire know that the Ministry of the Interior's not to be trusted. Minister Kolata's working for the other side."

"I never liked that man," Fontan said. He gave Sparhawk a speculative look. "This message is hardly so earthshaking that it would move you to violate a whole cluster of natural laws, Sparhawk. What are you *really* doing in Darsas?"

"Casting false trails, your Excellency. Our enemies have ways of detecting my presence, so I'm going to give them a presence to detect in assorted corners of the empire to confuse them a bit. My friends and I are returning overland from Korvan to Matherion, and we'd prefer not to be ambushed along the way. This isn't a confidential visit, Ambassador Fontan. Feel free to let people know that I stopped by. They'll probably know already, but let's confirm it for them."

"I like your style, Sparhawk. You'll be crossing Cynesga?"

Sparhawk nodded.

"It's an unpleasant country."

"These are unpleasant times. Oh, it won't really hurt if you're sort of smug when you tell people that you've seen me. Our side was definitely behind up until now. That changed a few days ago. Our enemy, whoever he may be, is at a distinct disadvantage right now, and I'd sort of like to grind his face in that fact for a while."

"I'll get word to the town crier immediately." The ancient man squinted up at the ceiling. "How long can you stay?"

"An hour at the very most."

"Plenty of time, then. Why don't we step over to the palace? I'll take you into the throne room, and you can pay your respects to the king—in front of his entire court. That's the best way *I* know of to let people know you've been here."

"I like *your* style, your Excellency." Sparhawk grinned.

It grew easier each time. At first, Bhelliom seemed impossibly dense, and Flute frequently had to step in, speaking in that language that Sparhawk strongly suspected was the original tongue of the Gods themselves. Gradually, the stone seemed to grasp what was wanted of it. Its compliance was never fully willing, however; it had to be compelled. Sparhawk found that visualizing Vanion's map helped quite a bit. Once Bhelliom grasped the fact that the map was no more than a picture of the world, it grew easier for Sparhawk to tell the jewel where he wanted to go.

This is not to say that there weren't a few false starts. Once, when he had been concentrating on the town of Delo on the east coast, the thought crossed his mind that there was a certain remote similarity between that name and the name of the town of Demos in east-central Elenia, and after the momentary grey blur where the world around him shifted and changed, he found himself and Flute riding Faran in bright moonlight up the lane that led to Kurik's farm.

"What are you *doing*?" Flute demanded.

"My attention wandered. Sorry."

"Keep your mind on your work. Bhelliom's responding to what you're thinking, not what you're saying. It probably doesn't even understand Elenic—but then, who really does?"

"Be nice."

"Take us back immediately!"

"Yes, ma'am."

There was that now-familiar lurch, and the moonlight faded into grey. Then they were back in bright autumn sunshine on the road a few miles outside Korvan, and their friends were staring at them in astonishment.

"What went wrong?" Sephrenia asked Flute.

"Our glorious leader here was wool-gathering," Flute replied with heavy sarcasm. "We just took a little side trip to Demos."

"Demos!" Vanion exclaimed. "That's on the other side of the world!"

"Yes," she agreed. "It's the middle of the night there right now. We were on the road to Kurik's farm. Maybe our stalwart commander here felt lonesome for Aslade's cooking."

"I can live without these 'stalwart commanders' and 'glorious leaders,' " Sparhawk told her tartly.

"Then do it right."

It came without warning. There was a certain desperation in the flicker of darkness at the edge of Sparhawk's vision this time, and a tinge of harried confusion. Sparhawk did not even stop to think. "Blue-Rose!" he barked to the Bhelliom, bringing up his other hand so that both rings touched the deep blue petals, "destroy that thing!"

He felt a brief jolt in his hands and heard a sizzling kind of crackle behind him.

The shadow that had dogged their steps for so long, which they had thought at first to be Azash and then the Troll-Gods, gave a shrill shriek and began to babble in agony. Sparhawk saw Sephrenia's eyes widen.

The shadow was crying out, not in Zemoch or Trollish, but in Styric.

CHAPTER EIGHT

"Well now, yer Queenship," Caalador was saying, "I don't know ez I'd stort a-dancin' in the streets jist yit. Them fellers over t' Interior's bin a-doin' ever'thang but a-nailin' th' doors shet t' keep us from a-puttin' our hands on this yere pertic'ler set o' files, an' now they turns up sorta unexpected-like amongst a hull buncha others—which I'd swear a oath to that I already looked over 'bout four er five times my ownself. Don't that smell jist a bit like a dead fish t' you?"

"What did he say?" Emperor Sarabian asked.

"He's suspicious," Ehlana translated. "He thinks that our discovery of these files was too easy. He may just have a point."

They had gathered again in the royal apartment in what was by now generally called "Ehlana's Castle" to discuss the surprising discovery of a hitherto-missing set of personnel files. The files themselves were stacked in heaps upon the tables and the floor of the main sitting room.

"Do you always have to complicate things, Master Caalador?" The emperor's expression was slightly pained. As he habitually did now, Sarabian was wearing western-style clothes. Ehlana felt that this morning's choice of a black velvet doublet and pearl-grey hose was not a happy one. Black velvet made Sarabian's bronze-tinted skin look sallow and unhealthy.

"I'm a professional swindler, your Majesty," Caalador replied, dropping the dialect. "I've learned that when something seems too good to be true, it probably is."

Stragen was looking into one of the files. "What an amazing thing," he said. "Someone in the Ministry of the Interior seems to have discovered the secret of eternal youth."

"Don't be cryptic, Stragen," Ehlana told him, adjusting the folds of her blue dressing gown. "Say what you mean."

He took a sheet of paper out of the file he was holding. "This particular document looks as if it were only written last week—which it probably was. The ink's barely dry."

"They *are* still using those files, Milord," Oscagne said, "despite the inconvenience. It's probably just a recently filed document."

Stragen took out another sheet of paper and handed both documents to the foreign minister. "Do you notice anything unusual about these, your Excellency?"

Oscagne shrugged. "One of them's fairly new, the other's turned yellow with age, and the ink's faded so badly you can hardly read it."

"Exactly," Stragen said. "Don't you find it just a little odd that the faded one's supposed to be five years younger than the fresh one?"

Oscagne looked more closely at the two sheets of paper. "Are you trying to say that they falsified an official document?" he exclaimed. "That's a capital offense!"

"Let me see those," Sarabian said.

Oscagne handed him the documents.

"Oh, yes," Sarabian noted, "Chalba. Kolata's been singing his praises for the past fifteen years." He held up the suspicious document. "This purports to be his appointment to the ministry. It's dated no more than a week after Kolata took office." He looked at Stragen. "You think this has been substituted for the original?"

"It certainly looks that way, your Majesty."

Sarabian frowned. "What could there possibly have been on the original that they'd have wanted to conceal?" he asked.

"I have no idea, your Majesty. There must have been *something*, though." He leafed through the file. "This Chalba's rise in the ministry was positively meteoric. It looks as if he was getting promoted every time he turned around."

"That sounds a bit like the sort of thing one does for a close friend," Oscagne mused, "or a relative."

Sarabian smiled faintly. "Yes, it does, doesn't it? Your brother Itagne seems to have risen quite nearly as rapidly."

Oscagne made a face. "That wasn't my idea, your Majesty. Itagne's not a career officer of the Foreign Ministry. I press him into service in emergencies, and he always extorts promotions out of me. I'd rather not have anything to do with him at all, but he's so brilliant that I don't have any choice. My younger brother's intensely competitive, and I wouldn't be at all surprised to find that he has his eye on *my* position."

"This fallacious document Stragen found might give us a place to start," Caalador mused. Caalador frequently dipped in and out of the dialect like a leaping trout. "If Kolata took a cluster of friends and relatives into the ministry with him, wouldn't it stand to reason that they'd be the ones he'd trust the most?"

"It would indeed," Stragen agreed, "and we'd be able to tell from the dates on their appointments just *who* these cronies of his are, and his cronies would have been the people he'd have been most likely to confide in when he decided to take up treason as a hobby. I'd guess that anybody whose appointment coincided with Kolata's elevation to office is probably involved in this business."

"The ones ez is still alive, anyway," Caalador added. "A feller what turns down the chance t' join some friends in the treason business ain't got *too* much in the way o' life-expectancy after he sez no."

"May I speak, your Majesty?" Alean asked Ehlana timidly.

"Of course, dear."

The gentle girl was holding one of the files in her hands. "Does ink always fade and paper turn yellow as the document gets older?" she asked them in a barely audible voice.

"Indeed it does, child." Sarabian laughed. "It drives librarians crazy."

"And if there was something written down in one of these packages of paper that the people at the Inferior Ministry didn't want us to—"

Oscagne suddenly howled with laughter.

Alean blushed and lowered her head. "I'm just being silly," she said in a very tiny voice. "I'm sorry I interrupted."

"The place is called the *Interior* Ministry, Alean," Melidere told her gently.

"I preferred *her* term." Oscagne chuckled.

"May I be excused, my Queen?" Alean asked, her face flaming with mortification.

"Of course, dear," Ehlana replied sympathetically.

"Not just yet, Ehlana," Sarabian cut in. "Come here, child," he said to Alean.

She crossed to his chair and curtsied a bit awkwardly. "Yes, your Majesty?" she said in a scarcely audible voice.

"Don't pay any attention to Oscagne," he said. "His sense of humor gets the best of him sometimes. What were you going to say?"

"It's silly, your Majesty. I'm just an ignorant girl. I shouldn't have spoken."

"Alean," he said very gently, "*you* were the one who suggested that we take all the files of all the ministries out of the government buildings and spread them out on the lawns. *That* turned out to be an excellent idea. I don't know about these others, but *I'll* listen to anything you have to say. Please go on."

"Well, your Majesty," she said, blushing even harder, "as I understand what Milord Stragen just said, those people wanted to hide things that were written down, so they wrote new papers and put them in place of the ones they didn't want us to see."

"It looks as if that's what they've done, all right."

"Well, then, if new paper's white, and old paper's yellow, wouldn't that sort of mean that anybody whose package has white papers mixed in with yellow ones has something to hide?"

"Oh, good God!" Stragen exclaimed, smacking himself on the forehead with his open palm. "How could I have been so stupid?"

"And I went right along with you," Caalador added. "We both walked right over the top of the simplest and most obvious answer. How could we have missed it?"

"If I wanted to be spiteful, I *could* say that it was because you're men, Master Caalador—" Baroness Melidere smiled sweetly. "—and men just *adore* unnecessary complications. It's not nice to be spiteful, though, so I won't say it." She gave the two thieves an arch little look. "I may *think* it, but I won't *say* it," she added.

"It's very easily explained, your Majesty," Teovin replied calmly. "You've already touched on it yourself." Teovin, the Director of the Secret Police at the Interior Ministry, was a dry, spare sort of man with no really distinguishing features. He was so ordinary looking that Ehlana felt him to be an almost perfect secret policeman.

"And what is this brilliant explanation that I've already discovered without even noticing it?" Sarabian asked acidly.

Teovin held up the yellowed sheet the emperor had just given him. "As your Majesty pointed out, the ink on this document has faded rather badly. The information in our files is vital to the security of the empire, so we *can't* let time erase the documents. The files are constantly reviewed, and any document that shows signs of approaching illegibility is copied off to preserve it."

"Why hasn't that one in your hand been updated, then, Teovin?" the emperor asked. "It's barely legible."

Teovin coughed diffidently. "Ah—budgetary considerations, your Majesty," he explained. "The Chancellory of the Exchequer saw fit to cut our appropriation this year. They're strange over at Exchequer. They always act as if it were their own personal money."

"They *do* rather, don't they?" Sarabian laughed. The emperor, Ehlana noted, was very fast on his feet, instantly adjusting to surprises. "Chancellor Gashon's hands start to shake every time I start talking about replacing broken tiles in the throne room. I'm glad we had the chance to straighten this out, my friend. I commend you for your devotion to your duty and your concern for the documents which have been placed in your care."

"I live but to serve, your Majesty." Teovin paused. "I wonder—might I have a word with Interior Minister Kolata? There are some matters—strictly routine, of course—that should be brought to his attention."

Sarabian laughed. "Afraid not, old boy," he said easily. "You wouldn't be able to keep his attention for very long today."

"Oh?"

"He got some tainted fish at supper last night, and he's been vomiting into a pail since just after midnight. We keep checking the pail, but his toenails haven't come out as yet. Poor Kolata. I can't remember when I've seen a man so sick."

"Do you think it's serious, your Majesty?" Teovin sounded genuinely concerned.

"Oh, probably not. We've all come in contact with bad food before, so we know what to expect. *He* thinks he's going to die, though. I'd imagine that he rather wishes he could. We have a physician in attendance. He'll be all right tomorrow—thinner, maybe, and a little shaky, but recovered enough to look after business. Why don't you come by in the morning? I'll make sure that you get in to see him."

"As your Majesty commands," Teovin said, dropping to the floor to formally grovel before the emperor. Then he rose to his feet and left the audience chamber.

They waited.

"He's gone," Mirtai reported from the doorway. "He just went out into the courtyard."

"Quick, isn't he?" Caalador noted. "He didn't so much as turn a hair when your Majesty handed him that document."

"He was ready for us," Stragen said. "He had his story prepared well in advance."

"His explanation *is* plausible, Stragen," Sarabian pointed out.

"Of course, your Majesty. Secret policemen are very creative. We know that Interior Minister Kolata's involved in treason. He wouldn't be much of a threat all by himself, so his entire agency's suspect. We almost have to assume that every department head is involved. As Caalador so colorfully pointed out, anyone who didn't join in probably got himself defenestrated just as soon as he objected."

"De-*what*?" Melidere asked.

"Defenestrated. It means getting thrown out of a window—a high one, usually. It doesn't accomplish very much to push somebody out of a ground-floor window."

"There isn't really such a word, Stragen. You're making it up."

"No, honestly, Baroness," he protested. "It's a real word. It's a common solution to the problem of politically inconvenient people."

"I think we're straying here," Ehlana told them. "Sarabian, why did you make up that story about Kolata and the bad fish?"

"We don't want his underlings to find out that we're keeping him drugged into insensibility most of the time, do we, Ehlana?"

"No, I suppose not. Are you really going to let Teovin in to see him tomorrow?"

"Maybe we should. We've been stalling Kolata's underlings for three days now, and I'm starting to run out of excuses. We'd better let *one* of them see him, or they'll start to get suspicious."

"I'm not sure it's a good idea, but maybe you're right. Alean, do be a dear and run down to the kitchen. Tell the cooks not to drug Minister Kolata's supper tonight."

"Yes, your Majesty," the girl replied.

"You might want to tell them to give him an emetic instead," Stragen suggested.

"Why would we want to do that?" Melidere asked.

"Emperor Sarabian just told the excellent Teovin that Kolata's been throwing up all day. We wouldn't want people to start accusing his Majesty of lying through his teeth, would we? Minister Kolata should show *some* signs of illness when Teovin visits him tomorrow. A good strong emetic should take care of that."

Alean giggled wickedly.

· · ·

The Royal Princess Danae sat on a divan. She was carefully dressing Mmrr in a new doll's gown. Over the centuries, Aphrael had noticed that little Elene girls did that quite frequently. It didn't really make any sense to the Child-Goddess, but since it was a long-established custom—"Oh, quit," she murmured to her struggling cat. "I'm not hurting you."

Mmrr objected loudly, giving vent to a plaintive yowl filled to the brim with a heart-rending self-pity.

"Teovin was right about one thing," Stragen was saying to the rest of them. They had all gathered in the royal apartments again, and the Thalesian thief was holding forth once more. Danae liked Stragen, but the fact that he absolutely adored the sound of his own voice made him a bit tedious at times. "The Ministry of the Interior would die en masse before they'd destroy a single scrap of paper. The documents they pulled out of those files are *somewhere* in the building, and those documents would tell us things we haven't even *guessed* as yet about the conspiracy. I'd give my teeth to get a look at them."

"And spoil your smile, Stragen?" Melidere objected. "Bite your tongue."

"I was speaking figuratively, of course."

"He's probably right, your Majesties," Caalador agreed, forgoing the dialect. "Those original documents would be an absolute gold mine. I don't know that I'd give my *teeth,* but I *would* give a lot to browse through them."

Danae rolled her eyes. "Elenes," she said under her breath. "If it's all *that* important to you, Caalador," she said, "go look at them."

"We don't know whur it iz they got em hid, little dorlin'."

"*Look* for them, Caalador," she said with exaggerated patience. "You've got all night, every night, for the next month or two, haven't you? Talen told me once that he can get into any house in the world in under a quarter of an hour. You two are more experienced at it, so it probably wouldn't take you nearly as long. You're not going to *steal* the papers, all you're going to do is *read* them. If you put them back where you found them after you're finished, nobody will even know that you've seen them."

Caalador and Stragen looked at each other sheepishly. "Why didn't *we* think of that?" Stragen asked his friend.

"It seems to me I've already told you why once," Melidere said. "Shall we go through it again? It's really a very good idea, Princess. These two might not be much good at *thinking* sometimes, but they're probably very good burglars. They both have that shifty, unreliable look about them."

"They *do,* just a bit, don't they?" Danae agreed. She set Mmrr down on the floor. "There," she said, "isn't she adorable?"

The angry lashing of Mmrr's tail, however, totally spoiled the effect.

"The tail definitely detracts from the fashion statement, Danae." Sarabian laughed indulgently.

"Oh, I can fix that right up, Sarabian," she assured him. "I'll tell you what, Mmrr. How would you like to have me tie a big pink velvet bow right on the end of your tail to sort of set things off? You could wave it around like a parasol if you wanted."

Mmrr's tail stopped in midswish.

"I *thought* you might see it that way," Danae said.

"Shall we go down to the dungeon for your fencing lesson, your Majesty?" Stragen suggested. "Caalador and I are going to be busy being burglars tonight, I think."

"Not only tonight, I'm afraid," Caalador added. "I haven't been on a roof in years."

"It's like swimming, Caalador," Stragen said. "Once you learn how, you never forget."

"I'd really like to forgo the lesson today, Milord Stragen," Sarabian said. "I'm still sore from yesterday."

"Fencing is *not* like swimming, your Majesty," Stragen told him. "You have to practice continually. If you're going to wear that rapier, you'd better know how to use it. In a tight situation, that could be your last line of defense."

Sarabian sighed. "Sometimes I wish I'd never even *heard* of Elenes," he mourned.

"Because Ehlana *told* me to," Mirtai said as she, Engessa, Kring, and the two thieves crossed the document-littered lawn toward the Interior Ministry. "She wants to be sure that nobody interrupts you."

"Mirtai," Stragen said with a pained look, "I love you like a sister, but burglary's a fine art."

"I think my beloved can manage, friend Stragen," Kring said. "I've seen her walk through a pile of dry leaves and not make a sound."

"I just don't like it," Stragen complained.

"You are not required to, Stragen-thief," Engessa told him. "Ehlana-Queen said that Mirtai-daughter will go with you, so she will go."

Mirtai smiled up at the towering Atan. "Thank you, Engessa-father. It's so hard to make Elenes grasp reality sometimes."

"Engessa and I are going to relieve the two knights watching over the documents on the lawn," Kring told them. "We'll stay fairly close to the building, and we have other men nearby. Call if anyone surprises you in there, and we'll come and rescue you."

"I've never had a platoon of soldiers standing watch for me while I burglarized a building before," Caalador noted. "It adds a whole new dimension to the business."

Stragen grunted sourly. "It takes a lot of the fun out of it. A large part of the thrill of burglary comes from the danger of getting caught."

"I've never tried burglary," Kring admitted. "It's not much of a challenge among the Peloi, since we all live in tents. A sharp knife will get you into the stoutest tent in the world. If we want to ransack someone's encampment, we usually send in some men to run off his horses. He chases *those* men, and that gives us a free hand."

"Burglary's a crime of stealth, Kring," Stragen smiled. "You get to sneak around at night and climb over rooftops. It's a lot of fun—and really quite profitable."

"Be careful up there on that roof, Mirtai," Kring admonished his betrothed. "I went to a great deal of trouble winning you, and I'd hate to lose you at this point. Oh, speaking of that, friend Stragen—and you, too, friend Caalador—if anything happens to her, you *do* know that I'll kill you, don't you?"

"We wouldn't have it any other way, friend Kring," Stragen nodded.

Mirtai ran a caressing hand over her beloved's scalp. Stragen had noticed that she did that quite often. He wondered if the feel of the little fellow's shaved head might have had some bearing on her decision to marry him. "You need a shave," the giantess said. "Remind me in the morning, and I'll take care of it."

Then Stragen, Caalador, and Mirtai, all dressed in close-fitting black clothing, slipped through the shadows of a grove of trees near the Ministry of the Interior. "You're really fond of the little fellow, aren't you, Mirtai?" Stragen murmured softly, ducking under a tree limb.

"Kring? He's a suitable sort of man."

"That's a rather lukewarm declaration of passion."

"Passion's a private thing. It shouldn't be displayed in public."

"Then you *do* have those feelings for him?"

"I don't really see where that's any of your business, Stragen."

There was a filmy layer of fog lying on the lawns of the imperial compound. It was autumn now, and the fog crept in off the Tamul Sea every evening. The moon would not rise for hours yet, and all in all it was a perfect night for a burglary.

Caalador was puffing when they reached the wall surrounding the Ministry of the Interior. "Out of condition," he muttered.

"You're almost as bad as Platime," Stragen told him, speaking very softly. Then he squinted upward, swinging a heavy grappling hook in his hand. He stepped back and began to whirl the hook in a wide circle, letting out more rope with each circuit. Then he hurled it upward with the rope trailing behind it. It sailed up over the wall and fell inside, striking the stones with a metallic-sounding clink. He tugged down a couple of times to set the points in place. Then he sat down on the grass.

"Aren't we going up?" Mirtai asked him.

"Not yet. Somebody might have heard it. We'll wait until his curiosity's had time to wear off."

"Fellers what's a-standin' watch in the middle o' the night ain't really all *that* eager t' go lookin' fer where it is ez noises is a-comin' from, dorlin'," Caalador explained. "In my experience, they usually feel that a quiet watch is a good watch, so they don't go out of their way to investigate things. As long as nobody sets the building on fire, they're not overburdened with curiosity. B'sides," he added, dipping once again into the dialect, "fellers ez gits chose t' stand gord at night usual turns out t' be drankin' min, an' after a flagon er two, they can't really hear hordly nuthin' a-tall." He looked at Stragen. "Do you want to try the ground floor before we go up on the roof?" he asked in clipped Elenic.

"No," Stragen decided. "Ground-floor windows are always double-checked when people lock up, and watchmen pass the lonely hours of the night rattling door-handles and trying the windows close to the ground. I've always preferred attics myself."

"What if all the attic windows are locked as well?" Mirtai asked him.

"We'll break one." He shrugged. "The building's high enough so that a broken window won't be all that visible from the ground."

"Don't be *too* obvious, Stragen," Caalador cautioned him. "I've got the feeling that we'll be going back inside every night for the next week or two. That's a large building."

"Let's get at it, then," Stragen said, rising to his feet. He looked out across the lawn. The fog had grown noticeably thicker. He tugged down on the rope a couple of times to make sure that the hook was secure and then began to climb up.

"You go on up next, dorlin'," Caalador said quietly to Mirtai.

"Why do you call me that?"

"Jist a-bein' friendly-like. It don't mean nothin' personal, so don't go complainin' t' yer bow-legged beau. He's a likeable sort, but he shore is touchy where yer concerned."

"Yes," Mirtai agreed. She went quickly up the rope and joined Stragen atop the wall. "What now?" she asked.

"We'll go across to the roof and start checking attic windows just as soon as Caalador climbs up."

"You'll use the hook again?"

He nodded.

"Burglars are about half ape, aren't they?"

"We prefer to think of ourselves as agile. Now, then, if we run into anybody inside, we'll try to hide first. If that doesn't work, we'll rap him on the head. Caalador's carrying a wineskin, and he'll pour wine all over the man. The smell of that should make him less credible when he wakes up. Try not to kill anybody. It takes all night to clean up, and we'd have to carry the body away when we leave. This isn't an ordinary burglary, and we don't want anybody to know we've been here."

"You're repeating the obvious, Stragen."

"I've seen your instincts in operation before, love. If you *do* kill somebody, please try to leave *most* of the blood inside the body. I don't want to be caught in there with a mop in my hands when the sun comes up."

"Why are you both being so affectionate tonight?"

"I don't think I quite followed that."

"Caalador's been calling me 'darling' ever since we set out, and you just called me 'love.' Is there some sort of significance to that?"

He chuckled. "A gang of burglars is a very close-knit group, Mirtai. We depend on each other for our very lives. That creates powerful ties of affection—which usually last right up until the point when the time comes to divide up the spoils. That's when things sometimes turn ugly."

"Let's have it all in place *before* we make any overt moves, Sarabian," Ehlana counseled. "The Interior Ministry knows that we're up to *something*, but we're all pretending that everything's normal. The customary approach is to have everybody in custody before you start issuing proclamations and disbanding branches of government."

"I can see your point, of course," he agreed. They were standing atop the battlements again, looking out over the city as the sun rose above the thick ground fog. "That's pretty, isn't it?" he observed. "The color of the fog almost perfectly matches the mauve on the walls and domes."

"You have a beautiful city."

"With some not-so-beautiful people living in it. What am I going to do for a police force after I dissolve the Ministry of the Interior?"

"You'll probably have to declare martial law."

He winced. "The Atans won't make me very many friends, I'm afraid. They tend to have a very simplified concept of justice."

"We don't have to stand for reelection, Sarabian. That's why we can do unpopular things."

"Only up to a point," he disagreed. "I have to live with the great houses of Tamul proper, and I'm still getting letters of protest from many of them about sons and brothers who were killed or maimed while the Atans were putting down the coup."

"They were traitors, weren't they?"

"No," he sighed, "probably not. We Tamuls pamper our children, and the noble houses carry that to extremes. Matherion's a political city, and when young Tamuls enter the university, they're *expected* to get involved in politics—usually of the most radical sort. The rank and position of their families protects them from the consequences of excessive juvenile enthusiasm. I was an anarchist when I was a student. I even led a few demonstrations against my father's government." He smiled faintly. "I used to get arrested on an average of once a week. They never *would* throw me in the dungeon, though, no matter *what* kind of names I called my father. I tried very hard to get thrown into the dungeon, but the police wouldn't cooperate."

"Why on earth did you want to spend time in a dungeon?" She laughed.

"Young Tamul noblewomen are *terribly* impressed by political martyrs. I'd have cut a wide track if I could have gotten myself imprisoned for a few days."

"I thought you got married when you were a baby," she said. "Isn't it sort of inappropriate for a married man to be thinking about how wide a track he can cut among the ladies?"

"My first wife and I stopped speaking to each other for about ten years when we were young, and the fact that I was required by tradition to have eight other wives made the notion of fidelity a sort of laughable concept." A thought came to him. "I wonder if Caalador would consider taking a post in my government," he mused.

"You could do worse. I have a man named Platime in my government, and he's an even bigger thief than Caalador." Ehlana glanced down the battlements and saw Mirtai approaching. "Any luck?" she asked.

"It's hard to say." The giantess shrugged. "We got inside easily enough, but we didn't find what we were looking for. Stragen and Caalador are going out to the university to talk with some of the scholars there."

"Are they suddenly hungering and thirsting after knowledge?" Sarabian asked her lightly.

" 'Tain't hordly likely, dorlin'," Mirtai replied.

"Darling?" he asked her incredulously.

"But you *are*, Sarabian," the golden giantess replied, gently touching his cheek. "I discovered tonight that conspirators and thieves and other scoundrels are supposed to be very affectionate with each other. You're conspiring with us to overthrow the police, so you're a member of the family now. Stragen wants to talk with some specialists in architecture. He suspects that there might be some secret rooms in the Interior Ministry. He's hoping that the original plans for the building might be in some library." She gave the emperor a sly, sidelong glance. "That's what it iz that they're a-doin', dorlin'," she added.

"Are you really sure you want Caalador in your government, Sarabian?" Ehlana asked him. "That dialect of his seems to rub off on people. Give him a year or two, and everybody in the imperial compound will be calling you 'dorlin'.'"

"That might be preferable to some of the *other* names I've been called lately."

CHAPTER NINE

Sparhawk and his friends left Cyron early the next morning and rode eastward through vast golden fields of ripening wheat. The rolling countryside sloped gradually downward into the broad valley where the Pela and Edek rivers joined on the border between Edom and Cynesga.

Sparhawk rode in the lead with Flute nestled in his arms. The little girl seemed unusually quiet this morning, and after they had been on the road for a couple of hours, Sparhawk leaned to one side and looked at her face. Her eyes were fixed, vacant, and her face expressionless. "What's the matter?" he asked.

"Not now, Sparhawk," she told him crossly. "I'm busy."

"Aphrael, we're coming up on the border. Shouldn't we—?"

"Leave me alone." She burrowed her forehead into his chest with a discontented little sound.

"What is it, Sparhawk?" Sephrenia asked, pulling Ch'iel in beside Faran.

"Aphrael won't talk to me."

Sephrenia leaned forward and looked critically at Flute's face. "Ah," she said.

"Ah what?"

"Leave her alone, Sparhawk. She's someplace else right now."

"The border's just ahead, Sephrenia. Can we really afford to spend half a day trying to talk our way across?"

"It looks as if we'll have to. Here, give her to me."

He lifted the semicomatose little girl and placed her in her sister's arms. "Maybe I can move us past the border without her. I know how it's done now."

"No, Sparhawk. You're not ready to try it by yourself. We definitely don't want you to start experimenting on your own just yet. We'll have to take our chances at the border. There's no way of knowing how long Aphrael's going to be busy."

"It's not anything important, is it? I mean, is Ehlana in any kind of danger?"

"I don't know, and I don't want to disturb Aphrael just now to find out. Danae will take care of her mother. You're just going to have to trust her."

"This is *very* difficult, you know. How long does it take to adjust your thinking to the idea that there are three of her—and that they're all the same one?"

She gave him a puzzled look.

"Aphrael, Flute, and Danae—they're all the same person, but they can be in two places at once—or even three, for all I know—and doing two or three different things."

"Yes," she agreed.

"Doesn't that disturb you just a little?"

"Does it concern you that your Elene God's supposed to know what everybody in the world's thinking? All at the same time?"

"Well—no. I suppose not."

"What's the difference?"

"He's God, Sephrenia."

"So's she, Sparhawk."

"It doesn't seem quite the same."

"It is, though. Tell the others that we're going to have to make the border crossing on our own."

"They'll want to know why."

"Lie to them. God will forgive you—one of them will, anyway."

"You're impossible to talk to when you're like this, do you know that?"

"Don't talk to me, then. Right now I'd prefer that you didn't anyway."

"Is something wrong?"

"I was just a little upset when you dissolved that cloud and it started swearing at you in Styric."

"I noticed that myself." He made a face. "How could anyone have missed it? I gather it's significant."

"What language do *you* swear in when you stub your toe?"

"Elenic, of course."

"Of course. It's your native tongue. Doesn't that sort of suggest that Styric's the native tongue of whoever's behind that shadow?"

"I hadn't thought of that. I suppose it does."

"The fact disturbs me, Sparhawk—more than just a little bit. It suggests all sorts of things that I don't really want to accept."

"Such as?"

"There's a Styric working with our enemy, for one thing, and he's highly skilled. That shadow's the result of a very complex spell. I doubt that there are more than eight or ten in all of Styricum who could have managed it, and I *know* all of those people. They're my friends. It's not a pleasant thing to contemplate. Why don't you go bother somebody else and let me work on it?"

Sparhawk gave up and dropped back to talk with the others. "There's been a little change of plans," he told them. "Aphrael's occupied elsewhere just now, so we won't be able to avoid the border crossing."

"What's she doing?" Bevier asked.

"You don't want to know. Believe me, Bevier, *you*, of all people, *really* don't want to know."

"She's doing one of those God-things?" Talen guessed.

"Talen," Bevier rebuked him. "They're called miracles, not God-things."

"*That* was the word I was looking for," Talen replied, snapping his fingers.

Vanion was frowning. "Border crossings are always tedious," he told them, "but the Cynesgans have a reputation for carrying that to extremes. They'll negotiate the suitable bribe for days on end."

"That's what axes are for, Lord Vanion," Ulath rumbled. "We use them to clear away inconveniences—underbrush, trees, obstructionist officials—that sort of thing."

"We don't need an international incident, Sir Ulath," Vanion told him. "We *might* be able to speed things up a bit, though. I've got an imperial pass signed by Sarabian himself. It might carry enough weight to get us past the border without too much delay."

The border between Edom and Cynesga was marked by the Pela River, and at the far end of the substantial bridge there stood a solid, blocklike building with a horse corral behind it.

Vanion led them across the bridge to the barricade on the Cynesgan side, where a number of armed men in strange flowing robes waited.

The imperial pass Vanion presented to the border guards not only failed to gain them immediate passage, but even added further complications. "How do I know that this is really his Majesty's signature?" the Cynesgan captain demanded suspiciously in heavily accented Tamul. He was a swarthy man in a loose-fitting black-and-white-striped robe and with a long cloth wound intricately around his head.

"What's much more to the point, neighbor, is how do you know that it *isn't?*" Sparhawk asked bluntly in the Tamul tongue. "The Atans take a very unpleasant stance toward people who disobey the emperor's direct commands."

"It means death to forge the emperor's signature," the captain said ominously.

"So I've been told," Vanion replied. "It *also* means death to ignore his orders. I'd say that *one* of us is in trouble."

"My men still have to search your packs for contraband," the captain said haughtily. "I will consider this while they carry out their orders."

"Do that," Sparhawk told him in a flat, unfriendly tone of voice, "and keep in mind the fact that a wrong decision here could have a negative impact on your career."

"I didn't catch your meaning."

"A man with no head seldom gets promoted."

"I have nothing to fear," the captain declared. "I am strictly following the orders of my government."

"And the Atans who'll chop off your head will be strictly following the orders of *theirs*. I'm certain that everyone involved will take enormous comfort in the fact that all the legal niceties were observed." Sparhawk turned his back on the officious captain, and he and Vanion walked back to rejoin the others.

"Well?" Sephrenia asked them.

"The emperor's voice doesn't seem to be very loud here in Cynesga," Vanion replied. "Our friend in the bathrobe has a whole book full of regulations, and he's going to use every single one of them to delay us."

"Did you try to bribe him?" Ulath asked.

"I hinted at the fact that I might entertain a suggestion along those lines." Vanion shrugged. "He didn't take the hint, though."

"Now *that's* unusual," Kalten noted. "Bribes are always the first thing on the mind of any official anywhere in the world. That sort of suggests that he's trying to hold us here until reinforcements arrive, doesn't it?"

"And they're probably already on their way," Ulath added. "Why don't we take steps?"

"You're just guessing, gentlemen," Sephrenia chided them. "You're all just itching for the chance to do Elenish things to those border guards."

"Did you want to do Elenish things to people, Ulath?" Kalten asked mildly.

"I was suggesting constructive Elenishism before we even got here."

"We're not contemplating it out of sheer bloodlust, little mother," Vanion told the woman he loved.

"Oh, *really*?"

"The situation's manageable now, but if a thousand mounted Cynesgans suddenly ride in from the nearest garrison, it's going to get out of hand."

"But—"

He held up one hand. "*My* decision, Sephrenia. Well, Sparhawk's, actually, since he's the preceptor now."

"Interim preceptor," Sparhawk corrected.

Vanion did not like to be corrected. "Did *you* want to do this?" he asked.

"No. You're doing just fine, Vanion."

"Do you want to be quiet then? It's a military decision, Sephrenia, so we'll have to ask you—respectfully, of course—to keep your pretty little nose out of it."

She said a very harsh word in Styric.

"I love you, too," he told her blandly. "All right, gentlemen, let's sort of drift on over to our horses. We'll do some of those Elenish things Ulath mentioned to the men who are going through our saddlebags. Then we'll run off all those horses in that corral and be on our way."

There were a score of border guards under the captain's command. Their primary weapon seemed to be the spear, although they wore a sort of rudimentary armor and scimitars at their waists.

"Excuse me a moment, friend," Ulath said pleasantly to the fellow who was rifling his saddlebags. "I'm going to need my tools for a couple of minutes." He reached for the war ax slung from his saddle.

"What for?" the Cynesgan demanded suspiciously in broken Tamul.

"There's something in my way." Ulath smiled. "I want to remove it." He lifted his ax out of its sling, tested the edge with his thumb, and then brained the border guard with a single stroke.

The fight around the horses was brief and the outcome promised to be fairly predictable. As a group, border guards are not among the world's most highly skilled warriors.

"What do you think you're doing?" Sparhawk bellowed at Talen as the boy pulled his rapier out of the body of one of the Cynesgans.

"Stragen's been giving me lessons," Talen replied. "I just wanted to find out if he knew what he was talking about. Watch your back."

Sparhawk spun, knocked aside the spear of a charging border guard, and cut the man down. He turned back just as Talen deftly parried the thrust of another, deflecting the curved blade off to one side. Then the young man lunged smoothly and ran the surprised fellow through. "Neat, wouldn't you say?" He smirked proudly.

"Quit showing off—and don't take so long to recover from your thrust. You're exposing yourself with all that posing."

"Yes, revered teacher."

What little question there had been about the outcome of the skirmish vanished once the knights were in their saddles. Things ended abruptly when the obnoxious captain, who had been shrieking, "You're all under arrest!" broke off suddenly as Sir Bevier coolly swung his lochaber ax and sent the officer's head flying.

"Throw down your weapons!" Ulath roared at the few survivors. "Surrender or die!"

Two of the guards, however, had reached their horses. They scrambled up into their saddles and rode off to the east at a gallop. One stiffened and toppled from his saddle after about fifty yards with Berit's arrow protruding from between his shoulder blades. The other rode on some distance, flogging desperately at his mount. Then he, too, lurched and fell to the musical twang of Khalad's crossbow.

"Good shot," Berit noted.

"Fair," Khalad agreed modestly.

The rest of the Cynesgans were throwing their weapons away.

"You run a good fight, Sparhawk," Vanion complimented his friend.

"I had a good teacher. Kalten, tie them all up and then run off their horses."

"Why me?"

"You're handy, and there's that other matter as well."

"I didn't break my oath," Kalten protested.

"No, but you were thinking about it."

"What's this?" Vanion asked.

"There's a lady involved, my Lord," Sparhawk replied loftily, "and no gentleman ever discusses things like that."

"What are you doing?" Aphrael asked sharply. She had raised her head from Sephrenia's shoulder and was looking suspiciously at Sparhawk.

"Are you with us again?" he asked her.

"Obviously. What are you doing?"

"There was some unpleasantness at the border, and we're probably being followed—chased, actually."

"I can't leave you alone for a minute, can I, Father?"

"It was more or less unavoidable. Have you finished with whatever it was you were doing?"

"For the time being."

"The town of Edek is just ahead, and we've probably got a brigade of Cynesgan soldiers right behind us. Do you suppose you could move us on ahead a ways?"

"Why didn't you do it yourself? You know how it's done."

"Sephrenia wouldn't let me."

"His attention wanders at critical moments," Sephrenia explained. "I didn't want him to put us down on the moon."

"I see your point," the little girl agreed. "Why don't we just move straight on to Cynestra, Sparhawk? There's nothing between here and there but open desert, you know."

"They were expecting us at the border," he replied. "It seems that our friend out there has alerted everybody along the way that we're coming. There's certain to be a large garrison of troops at Cynestra, and I'd like to feel my way through the situation there before I blunder into something."

"I guess that makes sense—sort of."

"How's your mother?"

"She's enjoying herself enormously. The political situation in Matherion's very murky right now, and you know how much Mother loves politics."

"I'm glad she's happy. You'll have to tell us about it, but let's get past Edek and outrun that Cynesgan brigade first. I don't like having people snapping at my heels."

"Tell the others to stop, and then get Vanion's map. Let's be sure we know where we're going this time."

"I'm never going to get used to that," Kalten shuddered after they had covered fifty leagues of open desert in a single grey-blurred moment.

"Your map's not very precise, Vanion," Aphrael said critically. "We were trying for a spot on the *other* side of that peak." She pointed at a jagged spire rearing up out of the desert.

"*I* didn't draw the map," Vanion replied a bit defensively. "What difference does it make, though? We're close enough, aren't we? We came to within a few miles of where we wanted to go."

"You'd have found out how much difference it makes if we'd been moving around near a large body of water," she said tartly. "This is just *too* imprecise."

Vanion looked back over his shoulder toward the west. "It's almost sunset. Why don't we get back away from this road and set up for the night? If we've got a problem with this, let's find a quiet place where we can work it out."

Sparhawk smiled. Despite all his protestations that he was no longer the Pandion Preceptor, Vanion automatically took charge unless he was consciously thinking about what he believed to be his changed status. Sparhawk didn't really mind. He was used to taking orders from Vanion, and his friend's assumption of authority relieved *him* of the nagging details of command.

They rode out into the desert a couple of miles and set up for the night in a dry wash behind an upthrust jumble of weathered boulders. Unlike the Rendorish desert, which was mostly sand, the desert here in Cynesga was sun-baked gravel, rusty-brown and sterile. The moving sands of Rendor at least gave an illusion of life. Cynesga was dead. Stark, treeless peaks clawed harshly at the sky, and the vast emptiness of gravel and rock was broken only by flat, bleached white beds of alkali.

"Ugly place," Ulath grunted, looking around. Ulath was used to trees and snow-capped peaks.

"I'm sorry you feel that way." Kalten grinned. "I was thinking of selling it to you."

"You couldn't *give* it to me."

"Look on the bright side. It almost never rains here."

"I think that's part of the problem."

"There's a lot of wild game, though."

"Really?"

"Snakes, lizards, scorpions—that sort of thing."

"Have you developed a taste for baked scorpion?"

"Ah—no, I don't think so."

"I wouldn't waste any arrows on them, then."

"Speaking of eating . . ."

"Were we speaking of that?"

"It's a topic that comes up from time to time. Do you know of a way to set fire to rocks?"

"Not right offhand, no."

"Then I'll volunteer to fix supper. I haven't seen a stick or a twig or even a dry leaf around here, so a fire's sort of out of the question. Oh, well, cold food never hurt anybody."

"We can get by without fire," Vanion said, "but we're going to have to have water for the horses."

"Aphrael and I can manage that, dear," Sephrenia assured him.

"Good. I think we might be here for a day or so. Sparhawk and Aphrael are going to be working with Bhelliom on this little problem of precision." He looked inquiringly at the Child-Goddess. "Is it likely to take very long?" he asked her.

"I'm not really positive, Vanion. When *I* do it, I still have the surrounding terrain to refer to, so I know where I am, no matter how fast I'm going. Bhelliom goes from one place to another instantaneously without any reference points. It's an altogether different process. Either Sparhawk and I are going to have to learn how Bhelliom's technique works, or we're going to have to make Bhelliom understand exactly what we want."

"Which way would be easier?" Kalten asked her.

"I'm not sure. It's possible that they're about the same—both very, very difficult. We'll find out tomorrow morning." She looked at Vanion. "Are we more or less safe where we are right now?"

Vanion scratched at his short silvery beard. "Nobody really expects us to be here. Somebody might accidentally stumble across us, but there won't be any kind of organized search. They don't know where we are, and the rings are shielded, so our friend out there won't be able to pick up the sense of their location and follow that to us. I'd say that we're safe here."

"Good. We've got some time, then. Let's use it to let Sparhawk and Bhelliom get to know each other. There's nothing all that crucial going on right now, so a few mistakes and false starts won't hurt anything. They might be disastrous later on, though."

Sephrenia did not tell them where the water came from the next morning, but it was icy cold and tasted of snowmelt. It sparkled invitingly in its shaded little pool behind a rust-colored boulder, and by its very presence it alleviated a great deal of tension. Water is a source of major concern to people in a desert.

Flute took Sparhawk, Khalad, and Talen some distance out onto a broad graveled plain to begin the instruction.

"It's going to get hot out here before long," Talen complained.

"Probably, yes," the little girl agreed.

"Why do Khalad and I have to come along?"

"Vanion needs the knights with him here in case someone stumbles across our camp."

"You missed my point. Why do you two need *anybody* to come along?"

"Sparhawk has to have people and horses to carry. He's not going to be moving sacks of grain from place to place, you know." She looked at Vanion's map. "Let's see if Bhelliom can take us to this oasis up here, Sparhawk," she said, pointing at a symbol on the map.

"What does it look like?" he asked her.

"How would I know? I've never been there either."

"All you're giving me to work with is a *name*, Aphrael. Why don't we do it the way we did when we moved from outside Jorsan up to Korvan?—and all those other places we went to when we were jumping around to confuse the other side? You tell Bhelliom where we want to go and then I'll tell it to do it."

"We can't be sure that I'll always be available, Sparhawk. There are times when I have to be away. The whole idea here is to train you and Bhelliom to work together *without* my intervention."

"A *name* isn't really very much to take hold of, you know."

"There'll be trees, Sparhawk," Khalad told him. "An oasis is kind of a pond, and anywhere you've got water, you're going to have trees."

"And probably houses," Talen added. "There'd almost have to be houses, since water's so scarce here in Cynesga."

"Let's see the map," Sparhawk said. He studied the chart carefully for quite some time. "All right," he said finally. "Let's try it and see what happens." He lifted the cap on his ring and touched the band to the lid of the golden box. "Open," he said. Then he put on the other ring and took out the Bhelliom. "It's me again," he told the jewel.

"Oh, that's absurd, Sparhawk," Aphrael told him.

"Formal introductions take too long," he replied. "There may come a time when I'll be in a hurry." He carefully imagined a desert oasis—an artesian-fed pond with its surrounding palms and flat-roofed white houses. "Take us there, Blue-Rose," he commanded.

The air blurred and faded into grey. Then the blur cleared, and the oasis was there, just as he had imagined it.

"You see, Sparhawk," Aphrael said smugly. "That wasn't hard at all, was it?"

Sparhawk even laughed out loud. "This might work out after all."

"Talen," Khalad said, "why don't you ride on down to one of those houses and ask somebody the name of this place?"

"It's Zhubay, Khalad," Flute told him. "That's where we wanted to go, so that's where we are."

"You wouldn't mind a bit of verification, would you?" he asked her innocently. She scowled at him.

Talen rode down to the cluster of houses and returned a few minutes later. "Let me see the map," he said to Khalad.

"Why?" Flute asked him. "We're in Zhubay, up near the Atan border."

"No, Divine One," the boy disagreed, "actually we're not." He studied the map for several minutes. "Ah," he said. "Here it is." He pointed. "*This* is where we're at—Vigayo, down near the southern border where Cynesga adjoins Arjuna. You missed your mark by about three hundred leagues, Sparhawk. I think you'd better sharpen your aim just a bit."

"What were you *thinking* about?" Aphrael demanded.

"Pretty much what Khalad was talking about—trees, a pond, white houses—just exactly what there is in front of us."

"Now what?" Talen asked. "Do we go back to where we started and try again?"

Aphrael shook her head. "Bhelliom and the rings are unshielded. We don't want to put Vanion, Sephrenia, and the others in danger by going back there too often. Let me down, Sparhawk. I want to think about this."

He set her down on the ground, and she walked down to the edge of the oasis, where she stood throwing pebbles into the water for a while. Her expression was dubious when she returned. Sparhawk lifted her again. "Well?" he asked.

"Take us to Zhubay, Sparhawk," she said firmly.

"Let me see the map again, Khalad."

"No," Aphrael said very firmly. "Never mind the map. Just tell Bhelliom to take us to Zhubay."

"*Exactly!*" Khalad said, snapping his fingers. "Why didn't we think of that before?"

"Think of what?" Sparhawk demanded.

"Try it, my Lord." Khalad grinned. "I think you might be surprised."

"If we wind up on the moon, you two are in trouble," Sparhawk threatened.

"Just try it, Sparhawk," Flute told him.

"Blue-Rose! Take us to Zhubay!" He said it without much conviction.

The air blurred again, and when it cleared they were sitting on their horses beside another oasis. There were a number of significant differences between this one and the one they'd just left.

"There probably isn't any need," Khalad said to his brother, "but you might want to ask anyway, just to be sure."

Talen rode on around the oasis and spoke with an old woman who had just come out of one of the houses. He was grinning when he came back. "Zhubay," he told them.

"How could it find the place with only the name to work with?" Sparhawk demanded. "It's probably never even *heard* the name Zhubay before."

"But the people who live here have, my Lord." Khalad shrugged. "The name Zhubay was sort of floating around in their minds. That's all Bhelliom really needed to find the place. Isn't that more or less the way it works, Flute?"

"That's *exactly* how it works. All Sparhawk has to do is mention the name of the place he wants to visit. Bhelliom will find it and take us there."

"Are you sure?" Talen sounded uncertain about the whole notion. "It seems awfully simple to me."

"There's one way to find out. Take us to Ahkan, Sparhawk."

"Where is it? What kingdom, I mean?"

"I don't think you need to know that. Just take us there."

Ahkan was a town in the mountains—*some* mountains, *some*where. It was surrounded by dark green fir trees, and the nearby peaks were snow-capped.

"Better and better," Flute said happily.

"Where are we?" Talen asked, looking around. "This isn't Cynesga, that's for certain, so where is it?"

"What difference does it make?" Flute shrugged. "Torrelta, Sparhawk."

It was snowing in Torrelta. The wind came howling in off a lead-grey sea driving a blizzard before it. The buildings around them were dim and indistinct in the swirling snowstorm, but they seemed to be constructed of rough-hewn logs.

"There's no *limit*!" Flute exclaimed. "We can go *anywhere*!"

"All right," Sparhawk said very firmly, "just which 'anywhere' have we come to?"

"It doesn't matter. Let's go back to where we started from."

"Of course," he agreed pleasantly. "Just as soon as you tell us where we are."

"I'm getting *cold,* Sparhawk. I'm not dressed for a blizzard."

"It's nice and warm back in Cynesga," he told her, "and we'll go there—just as soon as you tell me where we are."

She said a naughty word. "Torrelta's on the north coast of Astel, Sparhawk. It's almost winter here now."

He looked around with feigned surprise. "Why, I believe you're right. Isn't that amazing?" He visualized the flat gravel plain near the dry wash where they had set up camp the previous evening. He groped for a name for a moment, then remembered the blunder he had made when they had first set out. "Hold the box open, Khalad," he instructed. "I'll put Bhelliom and Ehlana's ring inside just as soon as we get back." He drew the picture in his mind again. "Take us *there,* Blue-Rose!" he commanded.

"Where have you been?" Sephrenia demanded. She and Vanion had ridden out onto the gravel plain to look for them.

"Oh," Talen said evasively, brushing the snow off his shoulders, "here and there."

"I gather that one of the places was quite a ways off," Vanion surmised, looking at the snow still clinging to the travelers.

"It's really amazing, Sephrenia," Flute said happily, "and it's all so *simple.*"

Khalad closed the box and handed it to Sparhawk. Sparhawk snapped the cap down over the ruby on his ring and then put the box back inside his tunic. "We made a couple of false starts right at first, though," he admitted.

"How does it work?" Vanion asked.

"We just let Bhelliom take care of everything." Sparhawk shrugged. "We *have* to do it that way, actually. It's when we try to help that things go wrong."

"Could you be just a bit more specific than that?" Sephrenia asked Flute.

"Sparhawk's really very close. All he has to do is tell Bhelliom a name—any name—of any place at all. Bhelliom goes and finds it, and then it takes us there."

"That's *all*?"

"That's it, dear sister. Not even Sparhawk can make any mistakes this way."

CHAPTER TEN

"We have to pick up someone there, that's why," Flute told them.

"Who?" Kalten asked.

"I don't know. All I know is that someone's supposed to go with us, and we have to pick him up in Cynestra."

"Another one of those hunches of yours?"

"You can call it that if you want to."

"I don't think we'll want to go into the city itself until we've had a chance to feel things out," Vanion said, looking up from his map. "There's a village just to the west of town. Let's go there and nose around a bit."

"What's the name?" Sparhawk asked him, opening the box and taking out his wife's ring.

"Narset," Vanion replied, looking up from the map.

"All right." Sparhawk took out the Bhelliom. He held it up and frowned slightly. "May I borrow your handkerchief, little mother?" he asked Sephrenia.

"Use your own," she told him.

"I seem to have left home without one. I'm not going to blow my nose on it, Sephrenia. Bhelliom's getting dusty. I wanted to brush it off a bit."

She gave him a peculiar look.

"It's being very helpful. I don't want it to think that I'm ungrateful."

"Why should you care what it thinks?"

"She's obviously never commanded troops," Sparhawk said to Vanion. "You might want to expose her to the notion of two-way loyalty someday."

"If I get around to it. Do you suppose we can go to Narset—as soon as you've finished with your housekeeping?"

Sparhawk brushed off the glowing petals of the sapphire rose. "How's that?" he asked it.

"I think he's losing his grip on his sanity," Kalten said to Ulath.

"Not really," Sparhawk disagreed. "It's got an awareness—almost a personality. I could use the rings like whips and drive it, I suppose, but I think I'd prefer willing cooperation. The time may come when that's important." He gave Sephrenia back her handkerchief. "Ready with the box, Khalad," he told his squire. He looked at Vanion again. "Narset?" he asked.

"Narset," Vanion replied firmly.

"Blue-Rose," Sparhawk said, taking the jewel in both hands, "let's go to Narset."

The Bhelliom throbbed, and that blurred twilight came down briefly. Then it cleared again.

Narset was a small, dusty village. The houses were hardly more than mud huts, and they had flat roofs and animal pens at the rear, pens that seemed largely decorative, since chickens, pigs, and goats wandered freely in the streets. There was a fair-sized city lying to the east, and all the buildings in that city were covered with white plaster to ward off the brutal desert sun.

Sparhawk put Bhelliom and Ehlana's ring away and flipped the golden cap back down over his own ring.

"We've got company coming," Talen warned.

A sallow-faced Tamul in a green silk robe was approaching with a squad of Cynesgan soldiers, swarthy men in the same flowing black and white robes and intricately wound cloth headdresses as the guards at the border had worn. The Tamul had hard-looking eyes, which he tried to conceal behind a contrived expression of joviality. "Well met, Sir Knights," he greeted them in slightly accented Elenic. "We've been expecting you. I am Kanzad, chief of the local office of the Ministry of the Interior. Ambassador Taubel posted me here to greet you."

"His Excellency is too kind," Vanion murmured.

"All the officials of the empire have been instructed to cooperate with you fully, Lord—?"

"Vanion."

Kanzad covered a momentary confusion. "I was led to believe that a Sir Sparhawk would be in command of your party."

"Sparhawk's been detained. He'll be joining us later."

"Ah." Kanzad recovered. "I'm afraid there'll be some slight delay before you can enter the city, Lord Vanion."

"Oh?"

Kanzad smiled a thin, humorless mile. "King Jaluah's feeling neglected at the moment." He threw a quick look at the squad of Cynesgans standing several paces behind him, then lowered his voice to a confidential tone. "Frankly, Lord Vanion, the Cynesgans and this pest-hole they call home are so unimportant in the affairs of the empire that no one takes them seriously. They're terribly touchy about that. Some idiot at the embassy neglected to pass on a routine communication from Matherion, and now the king's sulking in his palace. His sycophants have filled the streets with crowds of demonstrators. Ambassador Taubel's trying to smooth things over without resorting to the use of the Atan garrison, but things are a bit strained in the streets of Cynestra just now. His Excellency suggests that you and your companions wait here in Narset until he sends word that it's safe for you to proceed."

"As you think best," Vanion murmured politely.

Kanzad visibly relaxed. "First of all, let's get in out of this accursed sun." He turned and led them into the shabby village. There were no more than a couple dozen of the mud huts surrounding a well located in the sun-baked central square. Sparhawk idly wondered if the women of the village went to the well in the first steely light of dawn as the women of Cippria in Rendor had, and if they could possibly move with that same fluid grace. Then, for no reason at all, he wondered how Lillias was doing.

Aphrael leaned toward him from her sister's horse. "Shame on you, Sparhawk," she murmured.

"You've met Lillias," he replied easily, "so you know that she's not the sort of woman you forget—no matter how much you might want to."

The only building of any substance in the village was the local police station, an ominous stone structure with black iron bars on the windows. Kanzad's expression was smoothly apologetic. "It's not very inviting, Lord Vanion," he said deprecatingly, "but it's the coolest place in this pigsty."

"Should we kill him now and get it over with?" Bevier murmured to Sparhawk in Styric.

"Let's hold off on that," Sparhawk replied. "We have to wait for Aphrael's friend—whoever he is—so let's not precipitate anything just yet."

"I've had some refreshments prepared," Kanzad said to Vanion. "Why don't we go inside? That sun is really growing unbearable."

The knights dismounted and followed the policeman into the large dusty office. There was a long table set against one wall, a table laden with plates of sliced melon and figs and with flagons that promised other refreshments. "The fruits and melons here aren't nearly as palatable as those you'd find in Matherion," Kanzad apologized, "but the local wines aren't *entirely* undrinkable."

"Thanks all the same, Kanzad," Vanion declined, "but we stopped for lunch no more than an hour ago. We're all just fine."

A momentary flicker of annoyance crossed the Tamul's face. "I'll go make sure that your horses are being properly cared for, then, and I'll send a messenger to the embassy to advise Ambassador Taubel of your arrival." He turned and went out.

"Could you arrange some privacy, dear?" Vanion asked Sephrenia in Styric.

"Of course." She smiled. She quickly wove the spell and released it.

"Someday you'll have to teach me that one," he said.

"And become redundant?" She smiled. "Not on your life, my love."

"We appear to have taken them by surprise," Bevier noted. "Kanzad doesn't seem to have had much time to knock the rough edges off those lies he told us."

"I wouldn't," Ulath said as Kalten reached for one of the wine flagons. "One sip of that would probably stiffen you like a plank."

Kalten regretfully pushed the flagon away. "I suppose you're right," he agreed.

"We're prisoners, then, aren't we." Talen sighed. "That's depressing. I've been a thief all my life, and this is the first time I've ever been arrested."

"The fact that these refreshments are probably poisoned complicates things just a bit," Ulath growled. "Aside from that, Kanzad's been very helpful. He's just put us inside the strongest building in the village and he rather carelessly forgot to take our weapons. We can hold this place for as long as necessary."

"You're a fraud, Ulath." Bevier laughed. "Tynian's right. You pretend to hate sieges, but you're always the first one to suggest forting up."

"A true friend wouldn't mention that."

"I can provide water if worse comes to worst," Sephrenia told them, "but let's not precipitate anything just yet." She reached down and picked Flute up. "Have you had any hints about the one we're waiting for yet?"

Flute shook her head. "Nothing very specific so far. I *think* he's on his way, though."

"Good. This isn't really a very pleasant place."

"A thought, my Lords," Berit said. "Wouldn't it be a good idea to have Kanzad in here with us—just as a precaution? If someone starts thinking about storming the building, that might make them give it a few second thoughts."

"Good point," Ulath agreed.

Kanzad, however, did not return. The afternoon inched along, and the knights grew increasingly restless. "He's stalling, you know," Kalten said finally. "Either he's got reinforcements on the way, or he's hoping that we'll get thirsty."

"We'll just have to wait, Kalten," Flute told him. "The one who's going to be joining us is on his way."

"It's a race, then. We get to sit here making wagers on who gets here first—our new traveling companion or Kanzad's reinforcements."

"You can look at it that way if you want to, I suppose."

It was about two hours after their arrival in Narset when a large party came along the road from Cynestra. The man in the lead wore a rose-colored Tamul robe, and he was riding a spirited black horse. The ones following him were Atans.

"Whose side are the Atans on?" Talen asked.

"That depends on whether or not word from Matherion has reached the local garrison telling them to ignore orders from the Ministry of the Interior," Khalad replied.

"Things could be even murkier than that," Vanion suggested. "Back in Matherion, there's no love lost between the Foreign Ministry and Interior. Kanzad was hinting at the fact that he and Ambassador Taubel are very cozy."

"That might suggest that our enemies have managed to penetrate Oscagne's service," Bevier added with a slightly worried frown.

"We'll find out in a minute," Berit said from where he had been watching out the window. "Kanzad just came out from behind the building."

They all crowded around the windows to watch.

Kanzad's welcoming smile crumbled from his face. "What are *you* doing here, Itagne?" he demanded of the Tamul on the black horse. "I sent for Ambassador Taubel."

The rose-clad man reined in. His eyes looked almost sleepy, and he had a lofty, superior expression on his face. "I'm afraid the ambassador's been detained, old boy," he replied in a cultured, almost deliberately insulting tone. His voice was oddly familiar. "He sends you his very best, though."

Kanzad struggled to regain his composure. "What is it exactly that's delaying the ambassador?" he asked bluntly.

Itagne turned his head slightly. "I'd say it was the chains, wouldn't you, Atana?" he asked the young Atan woman who appeared to be in charge of the detachment. "It's deucedly hard to run with chains on."

"It *could* be the chains, Itagne-Ambassador," the girl agreed. "Of course, the bars of his cell might be getting in his way, too." The young woman was full-figured, and her eyes were bold as she looked at the Tamul official.

"What's going on here?" Kanzad demanded.

"The Atana and I have become very close friends since my arrival, Kanzad"— Itagne smiled—"but gentlemen shouldn't really talk about that sort of thing, should they? You *are* a gentleman, aren't you, Kanzad?"

"I wasn't talking about that." Kanzad's teeth were clenched. "What have you done with the ambassador?"

"There have been a few changes at the embassy, old boy—and in your own offices as well. I really hope you don't mind, but I had to commandeer your building. We don't *have* a dungeon at the embassy—distressing oversight there, I suppose. Anyway, Ambassador Taubel, along with all your grubby little policemen, are presently locked safely away in your dungeon. My compliments on it, incidentally. It's really very nice."

"By whose authority have you imprisoned the ambassador? You're only an undersecretary."

"Appearances *can* be deceiving, can't they? Actually, my brother placed me in charge here in Cynestra. My authority is absolute."

"*Your brother?*"

"Didn't the similarity between Oscagne's name and mine set off any bells in your brain, old boy? I *knew* you fellows at Interior were sort of limited, but I didn't think you were *that* dense. Shall we cut directly on through to the significant part of this discussion, Kanzad? It's beastly hot out here in the sun. My brother's authorized me to take charge here. I have the full support and cooperation of the Atan garrison, don't I, Atana?" He smiled at the golden giantess standing beside his horse.

"Oh *my*, yes, Itagne." She rolled her eyes. "We'll do almost *anything* for you."

"There you have it, then, Kanzad," Itagne said. "I've uncovered the fact that you and Taubel are a part of a treasonous conspiracy, so I've removed you from authority. I have all these lovely muscles to back me up, so there's really not a blasted thing you can do about it, is there?"

"You have no authority over me, Itagne."

"How tiresome." Itagne sighed. "Cynestra's currently under martial law, Kanzad. That means that I have authority over *everybody*. The Atans control the streets. I know you share my confidence in them." He looked critically at the policeman's stubborn face. "You just don't understand at all, do you, old boy?" He smiled fondly at the giantess. "Atana, dear, what would you do if I asked you to delete this tiresome wretch?"

"I'd kill him, Itagne." She shrugged, reaching for her sword. "Did you want me to split him up the middle, or just cut off his head?"

"Charming girl," Itagne murmured. "Let me think about it for a while, Atana. Kanzad's a fairly high-ranking official, so there may be some formalities involved." He turned back to the now-pasty-faced policeman. "I'm sure you see how things stand, dear boy," he said. "Oh, I suppose you should sort of consider yourself under arrest."

"On what charge?"

"I'm a Foreign Service man, Kanzad, so I'm not really up on all these legal terms. I suppose 'High Treason' will have to do. That's the crime they arrested Interior Minister Kolata for, anyway, and I used it again when I had Taubel picked up. It's an impressive sort of charge, and I'm sure that a man of your standing would be insulted if I had you arrested for loitering or spitting in the street. Atana, love, *do* be a dear and have this criminal taken back to Cynestra and thrown in his own dungeon."

"At once, Itagne-Ambassador," she replied.

"Darling child," he murmured.

"You favor your brother, your Excellency," Vanion said to the smiling Itagne, "not only in physical appearance but also in temperament."

"How *is* the old rascal?"

"He was well, the last time we saw him." Vanion frowned. "It might have been helpful if he'd told us that he was sending you here, though."

"That's my brother for you. Sometimes I think he tries to keep secrets from himself."

"Exactly what happened here, your Excellency?" Sparhawk asked him.

"You would be Sir Sparhawk," Itagne guessed. "Your nose is really famous, you know."

"Thank you," Kalten said modestly.

Itagne looked puzzled.

"I broke it for him, your Excellency—when we were children. I knew it was a good idea when I did it. He wears it like a badge. I'm a little disappointed in the fact that he's never once considered thanking me for the service I did him."

Itagne smiled. "As you've probably gathered, gentlemen, Oscagne sent me to Cynestra to look into the rather peculiar situation here. The chain of command in the outer corners of the empire's always been a little cloudy. The Foreign Office takes the position that the Elene kingdoms of the west, as well as Valesia, Arjuna, and Cynesga, are essentially foreign nations subservient to Tamul proper. This would make the ambassadors to those kingdoms the ultimate authority. Interior has always maintained that those kingdoms are integral parts of metropolitan Tamuli, and that puts *them* in charge. Oscagne and Kolata have been quibbling about it for years now. Ambassador Taubel's a political hack, and his stunning ability to reach a working accommodation with Interior sort of surprised my brother. That's why he pulled me out of the university—where I was quite happily putting down roots—

and sent me here to investigate in the guise of an undersecretary." He laughed. "I'll make sure that he regrets it as much *this* time as he did both other times."

"That one escaped me, I'm afraid," Sparhawk conceded.

"This is the third time Oscagne's wrenched me out of private life to put out fires for him. I don't really like being wrenched, so I think I'll teach him a lesson this time. Maybe if I replace him as foreign minister for a while he'll get the point—if I ever decide to let him have his office back again."

"Are you really that good, Itagne?" Sephrenia asked him.

"Oh, good God, yes, dear lady. I'm at least twice as good as Oscagne—and he knows it. That's why my appointments are always temporary. Where was I? Oh, yes. I came to Cynestra, set up a functional apparatus, and found out in fairly short order that Taubel and Kanzad were eating from the same plate. Then I intercepted the instructions Matherion sent to Taubel after the disturbances there. I decided not to trouble him with the distressing news, so I went to the Atan garrison and personally took care of advising our towering friends that the Ministry of the Interior was no longer relevant. They were quite pleased about it, actually. The Atans dislike policemen intensely for some reason. I think it has to do with their national character. I was about ready to move on Kanzad and Taubel when one of my spies brought me word of your impending arrival, so I decided to wait until you got here before I upended things. I must say, Sparhawk, you *really* upset the people in the local office of the Interior Ministry."

"Oh?"

"They were running through the halls screaming, 'Sparhawk is coming! Sparhawk is coming!' "

"He has that effect on people sometimes," Flute told him. She looked around at the others. "This is the one," she told them. "We can leave here now."

Itagne looked baffled.

"In a moment," Sephrenia said to her sister. "Itagne, how did Interior find out that we were coming?"

He shrugged. "I didn't really look into that too deeply. There are all sorts of disgusting people who work for the Interior Ministry. One of them probably flogged four or five horses to death to bring the news."

"Quite impossible," she said. "No one could have gotten here ahead of us by normal means. Could the news have been brought by a Styric?"

"There aren't any Styrics in Cynesga, dear lady. The hatred between Cynesgans and Styrics predates history."

"Yes, I know. I think you may be wrong, though. I'm almost positive that at least *one* Styric passed through Cynestra just before the people at Interior went into their panic."

"How did you arrive at *that* conclusion, little mother?" Vanion asked her.

"There's a Styric working with our enemies," she replied. "He was in that shadow Sparhawk dissolved back in Edom. Whoever was inside was screaming in Styric, at any rate." She frowned. "I still don't understand how he got here before we did, though. He might be a renegade of some kind who has dealings with the Elder Gods. We've never really understood the full extent of their power."

"Could it be an Elder God himself?" Bevier asked apprehensively.

"No," Flute said flatly. "We imprisoned them all when we overthrew them—in much the same way we imprisoned Azash. The Elder Gods *don't* move around."

"I seem to be missing about half of this conversation," Itagne observed. "Aren't some introductions in order at this point?"

"Sorry, your Excellency," Vanion apologized. "We weren't really trying to be mysterious. The lady is obviously Styric. May I present Sephrenia, High Priestess of the Goddess Aphrael?"

"The Child-Goddess?"

"You know of her?" Sephrenia asked him.

"Some of my Styric colleagues at the university mentioned her to me. They didn't really seem to approve of her. They evidently feel that she's flighty—and a little frivolous."

"Flighty?" Flute objected. *"Frivolous?"*

"Don't take it personally," Sparhawk told her.

"But it *is* personal, Sparhawk! They've insulted me! When you get back to Matherion, I want you to go to the university and issue a challenge to those impious wretches! I want blood, Sparhawk! Blood!"

"Human sacrifice, Divine One?" he asked mildly. "Isn't that a little out of character?"

"Well—" She hesitated. "Couldn't you spank them anyway?"

Itagne was staring at them.

"Disappointing, isn't it?" Talen murmured.

To say that Oscagne's brother was shaken would be a profound understatement. He kept staring at Flute with bulging eyes as they rode eastward from Cynestra.

"Oh, *do* stop that, Itagne," she told him. "I'm not going to sprout another head or turn into a gorgon."

He shuddered and passed one hand across his face. "I should probably tell you that I don't believe in you," he said. "I'm not trying to be offensive, mind. It's just that I'm a confirmed skeptic in religious matters."

"I'll bet I can change your mind," she suggested with an impish little smile.

"Stop that," Sephrenia told her.

"He's a self-confessed agnostic, Sephrenia. That makes him fair game. Besides, I like him. I've never had a Tamul worshipper before, and I think I want one. Itagne will do just fine."

"No."

"I didn't ask you to buy him for me, Sephrenia. I'll coax him out of the bushes all by myself, so you're not in any way involved. It's really none of your business, dear sister, so keep your nose out of it."

"Does this ever get any easier?" Itagne plaintively asked the rest of them.

"No." Kalten laughed. "You get numb after a while, though. I've found that drinking helps."

"That's Kalten's answer to everything," Flute said with an airy little toss of her head. "He tries to cure winter with a barrel of Arcian red—every year."

"Have we finished here in this part of the empire?" Sparhawk asked her.

"No. Something else is supposed to happen." The Child-Goddess sighed and nestled against her sister. "Please don't be angry with me, Sephrenia," she said. "You're not going to like what's coming, I'm afraid. It's necessary, though. No matter how much it upsets you, always remember that I love you." She sat up and held her hands out to Sparhawk. "I need to talk with you," she said to him. "Privately."

"Secrets?" Talen asked her.

"Every girl needs secrets, Talen. You'll learn more about that as time goes on. Let's ride off a ways, Sparhawk."

They rode away from the road for several hundred yards and then moved on, keeping pace with the others. Faran's steel-shod hooves clattered on the rusty sun-baked gravel of the desert floor.

"We'll be going on toward the Tamul border," Flute said as they rode. "This event that's ahead of us will happen there, and I'll have to leave you before it does."

"*Leave?*" He was startled.

"You'll be able to manage without me for a while. I can't be present when this event takes place. There's a propriety involved. I may be as flighty and frivolous as Itagne suggested, but I *do* have good manners. A certain personage will be taking part in this affair and he'd be insulted if I were present. He and I have had some disagreements in the past, and we're not speaking to each other at the moment." She made a rueful little face. "It's been quite a lengthy moment," she admitted, "eight or ten thousand years, actually. He's doing something I don't really approve of—of course he's never fully explained it to me. I like him well enough, but he's got a terribly superior attitude. He always behaves as if the rest of us are too stupid to understand what he's doing—but *I* understand very well. He's breaking one of the cardinal rules." She waved her hand as if brushing it aside. "That's between him and me, though. Look after my sister, Sparhawk. She's going to have a very difficult time."

"She's not going to get sick, is she?"

"She'd probably prefer that." The Child-Goddess sighed. "I wish there were some way I could spare her this, but there isn't. She has to go through it if she's going to continue to grow."

"Aphrael, she's over three hundred years old."

"What's that got to do with it? I'm a hundred times older than that, and *I'm* still growing. She has to do the same. I'm loveable, Sparhawk, but I never promised to be easy. This is going to be terribly painful to her, but she'll be much better for having gone through it."

"You're not making any sense, you know."

"I don't have to make sense, Father. That's one of the advantages of my situation."

They made the journey from Cynestra to the border west of Sarna in easy stages, moving at a leisurely pace from oasis to oasis. Sparhawk could not be positive, but it seemed Aphrael was waiting for something. She and Vanion spent a great deal of time with the map, and their jumps across the sun-baked gravel of eastern

Cynesga grew shorter and shorter, and their stays at the oases longer. As they neared the border, their pace slowed even more, and more often than not they found themselves simply riding, plodding their way eastward through the interminable, empty miles without any resort to Bhelliom at all.

"It's difficult to get anything very precise," Itagne was saying on the afternoon of their fourth day out from Cynestra. "Most of the sightings have been made by desert nomads, and they don't trust the authorities enough to speak with them at any length. There have been the usual wild stories about vampires and werewolves and Harpies and the like, but I rather imagine that most of those flew out of the neck of a wineskin. The Cynesgan authorities laugh most of those off as no more than the hallucinations of ignorant people who drink too much and spend too much time out in the sun. They take the reports of sightings of the Shining Ones very seriously, however."

"All right, Itagne," Kalten said irritably, "we've been hearing about these 'Shining Ones' ever since we came to Daresia. People turn all trembly and white-knuckled and refuse to talk about them. We've got you way out here in the desert where you can't run away, so why don't you tell us just who—or what—they are."

"It's really quite grotesque, Sir Kalten," Itagne told him, "and more than a little sickening."

"I've got a strong stomach. Are they some kind of monster? Twelve feet tall and with nine heads or something?"

"No. Actually they're supposed to look like ordinary humans."

"Why are they called by that peculiar name?" Berit asked.

"Why don't you let *me* ask the questions, Berit?" Kalten said bluntly. Kalten, it appeared, still had problems where Berit was concerned.

"Excuse me, Sir Kalten," Berit replied, looking just a bit startled and slightly hurt.

"Well?" Kalten said to Oscagne's brother. "What does it mean? Why are they called that?"

"Because they glow like fireflies, Sir Kalten." Itagne shrugged.

"That's all?" Kalten asked incredulously. "The whole continent collapses in terror just because some people glow in the dark?"

"Of course not. The fact that they glow is just a warning. Everybody in Tamuli knows that when he sees someone who shines like the morning star coming toward him, he'd better turn around and run for his life."

"What are these monsters supposed to be able to do?" Talen asked. "Do they eat people alive or tear them all to pieces or something?"

"No," Itagne replied somberly. "The legend has it that their merest touch is death."

"Sort of like poisonous snakes?" Khalad suggested.

"Much worse than that, young sir. The touch of the Shining Ones rots a man's flesh from his bones. It's the decay of the grave, and the victim isn't dead when it happens. The descriptions from folklore are very lurid. We're given pictures of people standing stock-still, shrieking in agony and horror as their faces and limbs dissolve into slime and run like melted wax."

"That's a graphic picture." Ulath shuddered. "I'd imagine it sort of interferes with establishing normal relations with these people."

"Indeed, Sir Ulath." Itagne smiled. "But despite all of that, the Shining Ones are among the most popular figures in Tamul literature—which may provide you with some insight into the perversity of our minds."

"Are you talking about ghost stories?" Talen asked him. "Some people like those, I've heard."

"Delphaeic literature is far more complex than that."

"Delphaeic? What does that mean?"

"Literature refers to the Shining Ones as the Delphae," Itagne replied, "and the mythic city where they live is called Delphaeus."

"It's a pretty name."

"I think that's part of the problem. Tamuls tend to be sentimentalists, and the musical quality of the word fills the eyes of our lesser poets with tears and their brains with mush. They ignore the most unpleasant aspects of the legend and present the Delphae as a simple, pastoral people who are grossly misunderstood. For seven centuries they've inflicted abominable pastoral verse and overdrawn adolescent eclogues on us. They've pictured the Delphae as lyric shepherds, glowing like fireflies and mooning about the landscape, suffering pangs of unrequited love and pondering—ponderously, of course—the banalities of their supposed religion. The academic world has come to regard Delphaeic literature as a bad joke perpetuated far too long."

"It's an abomination!" Sephrenia declared with uncharacteristic heat.

"Your critical perception does you credit, dear lady—" Itagne smiled. "—but I think your choice of terms overdignifies the genre. *I'd* characterize Delphaeic literature as adolescent sentimentality perhaps, but I don't really take it seriously enough to grow indignant about it."

"Delphaeic literature is a mask for the most pernicious kind of anti-Styric bigotry!" she said in tones she usually reserved for ultimatums.

Vanion appeared to be as baffled by her sudden outburst as Sparhawk and the rest. He looked around, obviously seeking some way to change the subject.

"It's moving on toward sunset," Kalten noted, stepping in to lend a hand. Kalten's perceptiveness sometimes surprised Sparhawk. "Flute," he said, "did you plan to put us down beside another one of those waterholes for the night?"

"Oasis, Kalten," Vanion corrected him. "They call it an oasis, not a waterhole."

"That's up to them. They can call it whatever they want, but I know a waterhole when I see one. If we're going to do this the old-fashioned way, we're going to have to start looking for a place to camp, and there's a ruin of some kind on that hilltop over there to the north. Sephrenia can squeeze water out of the air for us, and if we stay in those ruins we won't have to put up with the smell of boiling dog all night the way we usually do when we camp near one of their villages."

"The Cynesgan don't eat dogs, Sir Kalten." Itagne laughed.

"I wouldn't swear to that without an honest count of all the dogs in one of their villages—both before and *after* supper."

· · ·

"Sparhawk!" It was Khalad, and he was roughly shaking his lord into wakeful-ness. "There are people out there!"

Sparhawk threw his blankets to one side and rolled to his feet, reaching for his sword. "How many?" he asked quietly.

"I've seen a dozen or so. They're creeping around among those boulders down by the road."

"Wake the others."

"Yes, my Lord."

"Quietly, Khalad."

Khalad gave him a flat, unfriendly stare.

"Sorry."

The ruin in which they had set up their camp had been a fortress at one time. The stones were roughly squared off, and they had been set without mortar. Un-counted centuries of blowing dust and sand had worn the massive blocks smooth and had rounded the edges. Sparhawk crossed what appeared to have been a court to the tumbled wall on the south side of the fortress and looked down toward the road.

A thick cloudbank had crept in during the night to obscure the sky. Sparhawk peered toward the road, silently cursing the darkness. Then he heard a faint rustling sound just on the other side of the broken wall.

"Don't get excited," Talen whispered.

"Where have you been?"

"Where else?" The boy climbed over the rubble to join the big Pandion.

"Did you take Berit with you again?" Sparhawk asked acidly.

"No. Berit's a little too noisy now that he's taken to wearing chain mail, and his integrity always seems to get in the way."

Sparhawk grunted. "Well?" he asked.

"You're not going to believe this, Sparhawk."

"I might surprise you."

"Those are more of those Cyrgai out there."

"Are you sure?"

"I didn't stop one to ask him, but they look exactly the same as those ones we ran across west of Sarsos did. They've got on those funny-looking helmets, the old-fashioned armor, and those silly short dresses they wear."

"I think they're called kilts."

"A dress is a dress, Sparhawk."

"Are they doing anything tactically significant?"

"You mean forming up for an attack? No. I think these are just scouts. They don't have their spears or shields with them, and they're doing a lot of crawling around on their bellies."

"Let's go talk with Vanion and Sephrenia."

They crossed the rubble-littered courtyard of the ancient fortress. "Our young thief's been disobeying orders again," Sparhawk told the others.

"No, I haven't," Talen disagreed. "You didn't order me not to go look at those people, so how can you accuse me of disobeying you?"

"I didn't order you not to because I didn't know they were out there."

"That *did* sort of make things easier. I'll admit that."

"Our wandering boy here reports that the people creeping around down by the road are Cyrgai."

"Someone on the other side's been winnowing through the past again?" Kalten suggested.

"No," Flute said, raising her head slightly. The little girl had appeared to have been sleeping soundly in her sister's arms. "The Cyrgai out there are as alive as you are. They aren't from the past."

"That's impossible," Bevier objected. "The Cyrgai are extinct."

"Really?" the Child-Goddess said. "How astonishing that they didn't notice that. Trust me, gentlemen. I'm in a position to know. The Cyrgai who are creeping up on you are contemporary."

"The Cyrgai died out ten thousand years ago, Divine One," Itagne said firmly.

"Maybe you should run down the hill and let them know about it, Itagne," she told him. "Let me go, Sephrenia."

Sephrenia looked a little startled.

Aphrael kissed her sister tenderly and then stepped a little way away. "I have to leave you now. The reasons are very complex, so you'll just have to trust me."

"What about those Cyrgai?" Kalten demanded. "We're not going to let you wander off in the dark while they're out there."

She smiled. "Would someone please explain this to him?" she asked them.

"Are you going to leave us in danger like this?" Ulath demanded.

"Are you worried about your own safety, Ulath?"

"Of course not, but I thought I could shame you into staying until we'd dealt with them."

"The Cyrgai aren't going to bother you, Ulath," she said patiently. "They'll be going away almost immediately." She looked around at them. Then she sighed. "I really have to leave now," she said regretfully. "I'll rejoin you later."

Then she wavered like a reflection in a pool and vanished.

"Aphrael!" Sephrenia cried, half reaching out.

"That is *truly* uncanny," Itagne muttered. "Was she serious about the Cyrgai?" he asked them. "Is it at all possible that some of them actually survived their war with the Styrics?"

"I wouldn't care to call her a liar," Ulath said. "Particularly not around Sephrenia. Our little mother here is very protective."

"I've noticed that," Itagne said. "I wouldn't offend you or your Goddess for the world, dear Lady, but would you be at all upset if we made a few preparations? History is one of my specialties at the university, and the Cyrgai had—have, I suppose—a fearsome reputation. I trust your little Goddess implicitly, of course, but . . ." He looked around apprehensively.

"Sephrenia?" Sparhawk said.

"Don't bother me." She seemed terribly shocked by Aphrael's sudden departure.

"Snap out of it, Sephrenia. Aphrael had to leave, but she'll be back later. I need an answer right now. Can I use Bhelliom to set up some kind of barrier that will hold the Cyrgai off until whatever it was that Aphrael was talking about chases them away?"

"Yes, but you'd let our enemy know exactly where you are if you did that."

"He already knows," Vanion pointed out. "I doubt that those Cyrgai stumbled across us by accident."

"He has a point there," Bevier agreed.

"Why bother with holding them off?" Kalten asked. "Sparhawk can move us ten leagues on down the road faster than we can blink. I'm not so attached to this place that I'll lose any sleep if I'm not around to watch the sun come up over it."

"I've never done it at night," Sparhawk said dubiously. He looked at Sephrenia. "Would the fact that I can't see where I'm going have any effect at all?"

"How would I know?" She sounded a little cross.

"Please, Sephrenia," he said. "I've got a problem, and I need your help."

"What in God's name is going on?" Berit exclaimed. He pointed to the north. "Look at that!"

"Fog?" Ulath said incredulously. "Fog in the *desert*?"

They stared at the strange phenomenon moving steadily toward them across the arid desert.

"Lord Vanion," Khalad said in a troubled voice, "does your map show any towns or settlements off to the north?"

Vanion shook his head. "Nothing but open desert."

"There are lights out there, though. You can see them reflecting off the fog. They're close to the ground, but you can definitely see them."

"I've seen lights in the fog before," Bevier said, "but never quite like that. That isn't torchlight."

"You're right there," Ulath agreed. "I've never seen light quite that color before—and it seems to be just lying on the fog itself, almost like a blanket."

"It's probably just the camp of some desert nomads, Sir Ulath," Itagne suggested. "Mist and fog do strange things to light sometimes. In Matherion you'll see light reflected off the mother-of-pearl on the buildings. Some nights it's like walking around inside a rainbow."

"We'll know more about it in a little bit," Kalten said. "That fog's moving right straight toward us, and it's bringing the light with it." He raised his face. "And there's absolutely no breeze. What's going on here, Sephrenia?"

Before she could answer, shrieks of terror came from the south, where the road was. Talen scurried across the littered yard to the tumbled wall. "The Cyrgai are running away!" he shouted. "They're throwing away their swords and helmets and running like rabbits!"

"I don't like the feel of this, Sparhawk," Kalten said bleakly, drawing his sword.

The fogbank approaching them had divided and flowed around the hill upon which they stood. It was a thick fog such as one might see in a coastal city, and it moved across the arid, barren desert, marching inexorably upon the ruined fortress.

"There's something moving in there!" Talen shouted from the far side of the ruin.

They were only blurs of light at first, but as the strange fogbank drew nearer, they grew more and more distinct. Sparhawk could clearly make out the shapes of nebulous bodies now. Whatever they were, they had human shapes.

Then Sephrenia shrieked as one seized in the grip of an overpowering rage. "Defiled ones! Defiled ones! Foul and accursed!"

They stared at her, stunned by her sudden outburst.

The lights in the fog never faltered but continued their glowing, inexorable advance.

"Run!" Itagne suddenly shouted. "Run for your lives! It's the Delphae—the Shining Ones!"

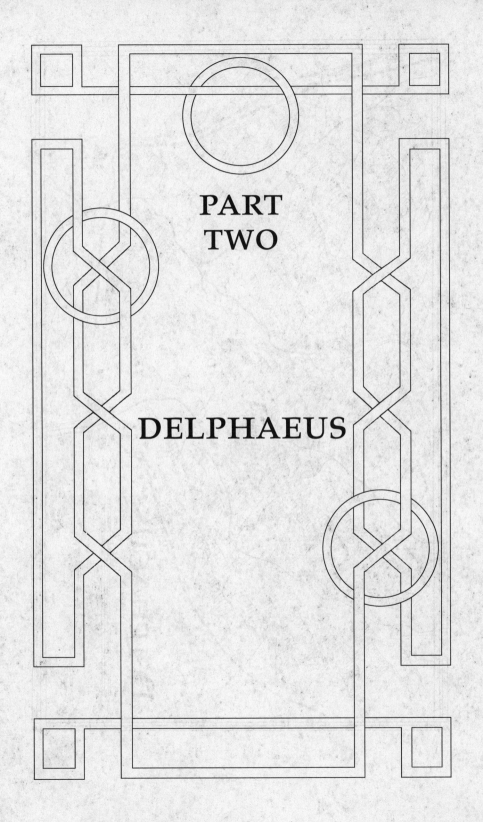

PART TWO

DELPHAEUS

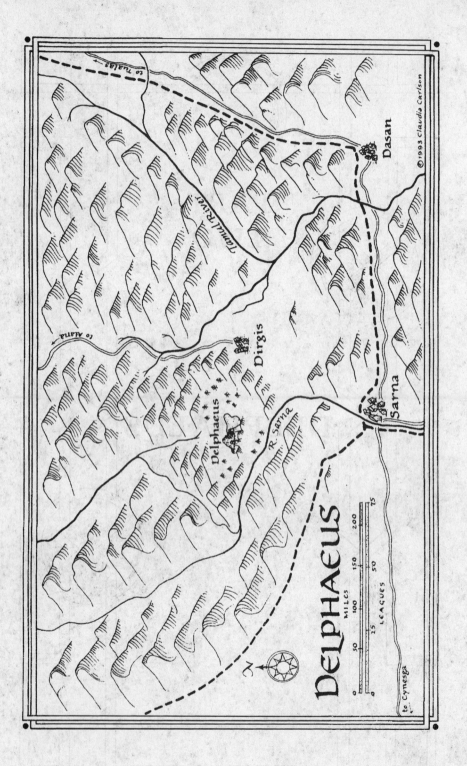

DELPHAEUS

to Tualas

Tamui River

to Alarta

Delphaeus

Dirgis

R. Sarna

Dasan

Sarna

©1993 Claudia Carlson

MILES
0   50   100   150   200
LEAGUES
0   15   50   75

N

to Cynesga

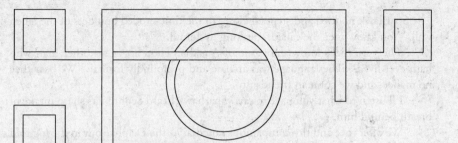

CHAPTER
ELEVEN

I t was the fog, perhaps. The fog blurred everything. There were no precise outlines, no clear, sharp dangers, and the glowing figures in the mist approached slowly, seeming almost to float up the graveled slope toward the ancient ruin, bringing their obscuring fog with them. Their faces, their very shapes, were indistinct, softened until they seemed hardly more than glowing blurs. It was the fog, perhaps—but then again, perhaps not. For whatever reason, Sparhawk felt no alarm.

The Delphae stopped about twenty yards from the broken walls of the ruin and stood with their glowing fog eddying and swirling around them, erasing the night with cold, pale fire.

Sparhawk's mind was strangely detached, his thoughts clear and precise. "Well met, neighbors," he called out to the shapes in the mist.

"Are you mad?" Itagne gasped.

"Destroy them, Sparhawk!" Sephrenia hissed. "Use the Bhelliom! Obliterate them!"

"Why don't we see what they want first?"

"How can you be so calm, man?" Itagne demanded.

"Training, I suppose." Sparhawk shrugged. "You develop instincts after a while. Those people out there don't have any hostile intentions."

"He's right, Itagne," Vanion said. "You can definitely feel it when someone wants to kill you. Those people out there don't want to fight. They're not afraid of us, but they're not here to fight. Let's see where this goes, gentlemen. Keep your guard up, but let's not precipitate anything—not yet, anyway."

"Anakha," one of the glowing figures in the fog called.

"That's a good start," Vanion murmured. "See what they want, Sparhawk."

Sparhawk nodded and stepped closer to the time-eroded boulders of the fallen wall. "You know me?" he called, speaking in Tamul.

"The very rocks know the name of Anakha. Thou art as no other man who hath ever lived." The language was archaic and profoundly formal. "We bear thee no malice, and we come in friendship."

"I'll listen to what you have to say." Sparhawk heard Sephrenia's sharp intake of breath behind him.

"We offer thee and thy companions sanctuary," the Delphae out in the fog told him. "Thine enemies are all about thee, and thy peril is great here in the land of the Cyrgai. Come thou even unto Delphaeus, and we will give thee rest and safety."

"Your offer's generous, neighbor," Sparhawk replied, "and my companions and I are grateful." His tone, however, was dubious.

"We sense thy reluctance." The voice in the fog seemed strangely hollow with a sort of reverberating echo to it, an echo such as one might hear in a long, empty corridor, a sound receding off into some immeasurable distance. "Be assured that we mean thee and thy companions no harm, and shouldst thou choose to come to Delphaeus, we will pledge thee our protection. Few there are in all this world who will willingly face us."

"So I've heard. But that brings up a question. Why, neighbor? We're strangers here. What possible interest can the Delphae have in our affairs? What do you hope to gain from this offer of friendship?"

The glowing shape in the fog hesitated. "Thou hast taken up Bhelliom, Anakha—for good or for ill, and thou knowest not which. Thy will is no longer thine own, for Bhelliom bends thee to its own purpose. Thou art no longer of this world, nor is thy destiny. Thy design and thy destiny are of Bhelliom's devising. In truth, we are indifferent to thee and thy companions, for our offer of friendship is not to thee, but to Bhelliom, and it is from Bhelliom that we will extract the price of that friendship."

"That's direct enough," Kalten muttered.

"Thy peril is greater than thou knowest," the glowing speaker continued. "Bhelliom is the greatest prize in all the universe, and beings beyond thine imagining seek to possess it. It *will* not be possessed, however. It chooseth its own, and it hath chosen thee. Into *thy* hand hath it placed itself, and through *thine* ears must we speak with it and offer our exchange." The speaker paused. "Consider what we have told thee here and put aside thy suspicion. Thy success or failure in completing Bhelliom's design may hinge on our assistance—or its lack—and we *will* have our price. We will speak more of this anon."

The fog swirled and thickened, and the glowing shapes dimmed and faded. A sudden night breeze, as chill as winter and as arid as dust, swept across the desert, and the fog tattered and shawled, whirling, all seethe and confusion. And then it was gone, and the Shining Ones with it.

"Don't listen to them, Sparhawk!" Sephrenia said in a shrill voice. "Don't even consider what he said! It's a trick!"

"We're not children, Sephrenia," Vanion told the woman he loved. "We're not really gullible enough to accept the word of strangers at face value—particularly not the word of strangers like the Delphae."

"You don't know them, Vanion. Their words are like the honey that lures and traps the unwary fly. You should have destroyed them, Sparhawk."

"Sephrenia," Vanion said in a troubled tone, "you've spent the last forty years with your hand on my sword arm trying to keep me from hurting people. Why have you changed? What's making you so bloodthirsty all of a sudden?"

She gave him a flat, hostile look. "You wouldn't understand."

"That's an evasion, dear, and you know me well enough to know that it's probably not true. The Delphae may not have been entirely candid with us about their offer, but they weren't hostile, and they weren't threatening us in any way."

"Ah—Lord Vanion," Ulath interrupted, "I don't think anybody in his right mind would threaten Sparhawk. Threatening the man who holds Bhelliom in his fist is *not* the course of wisdom—not even for people who glow in the dark and mulch their neighbors down into compost."

"That's exactly my point, Vanion," Sephrenia seized upon Ulath's words. "The Delphae were afraid to attack us because of Bhelliom. That's all that was holding them back."

"But they *were* holding back. They weren't any danger to us. Why did you want Sparhawk to kill them?"

"I despise them!" It came out in a kind of hiss.

"Why? What did they ever do to you?"

"They have no right to exist!"

"Everything has a right to exist, Sephrenia—even wasps and scorpions. You've spent your whole life teaching bloodthirsty young Pandions that lesson. Why are you suddenly throwing it away?"

She turned her face away from him.

"Please don't do that. You've got some kind of problem here, and your problems are mine. Let's pull this out into the light and look at it."

"No!" And she turned abruptly on her heel and stalked away.

"It has absolutely no basis in fact," Itagne told them as they rode across the barren miles under a murky sky.

"Those are usually the best stories," Talen said.

Itagne smiled briefly. "There's been a body of folklore about the Shining Ones in Tamul culture for eons. It started out with the usual horror stories, I suppose, but there's something in the Tamul nature that drives us to extremes. About seven hundred years ago, a decidedly minor poet began to tamper with the legend. Instead of concentrating on the horror, he began to wax sentimental, delving into how the Delphae felt about their situation. He wept copiously in vile verse about their loneliness and their sense of being outcast. He unfortunately turned to the pastoral tradition and added the mawkishness of that silly conceit to his other extravagances. His most famous work was a long narrative poem entitled 'Xadane.' Xadane was supposedly a Delphaeic shepherdess who fell in love with a normal human shepherd boy. As long as they met in the daytime, everything was fine, but Xadane had to run away every afternoon to keep her paramour from discovering her real identity. The poem's very long and tedious, and it's filled with lengthy, lugubrious passages in which Xadane feels sorry for herself. It's absolutely awful."

"I gather from what those people out in the fog said last night that the word *Delphae* is their own name for themselves," Bevier noted. "If Tamul literature also uses the term, that would seem to suggest some sort of contacts."

"So it would, Sir Knight," Itagne replied, "but there's no record of them. The traditions are very old, and I suspect that many of them grew out of the warped minds of third-rate poets. The city of Delphaeus supposedly lies in an isolated valley high in the mountains of southern Atan. The Delphae are said to be a Tamul people somewhat akin to the Atans but without the gigantic proportions. If we're to believe our poets, which we probably shouldn't, the Delphae were a simple pastoral folk who followed their flocks into that valley and were trapped there by an avalanche that sealed the only pass leading to the outside world."

"That's not entirely impossible," Ulath said.

"The impossibilities start cropping up later on in the story," Itagne said dryly. "We're told that there's a lake in the center of the valley, and the lake's supposed to be the source of the Delphaeic peculiarity. It's said to glow, and since it's the only source of water in the valley, the Delphae and their flocks are forced to drink from it and bathe in it. The story has it that after a while, they *also* started to glow." He smiled faintly. "They must save a fortune on candles."

"That's not really possible, is it?" Talen asked skeptically. "I mean, people aren't going to glow in the dark just because of what they eat or drink, are they?"

"I'm not a scientist, young sir, so don't ask me about what's possible and impossible. It could be some sort of mineral, or maybe a form of algae, I suppose. It's a neat sort of explanation for an imaginary characteristic."

"Those people last night *did* glow, your Excellency," Kalten reminded him.

"Yes, and I'm trying very hard to forget about that." Itagne looked back over his shoulder. Sephrenia had refused to listen to any discussion of the Delphae, and she and Berit followed the others at some distance. "Lady Sephrenia's reaction to the Delphae isn't really uncommon among Styrics, you know. The very name makes them irrational. Anyway, 'Xadane' enjoyed enormous popularity, and there were the usual imitators. A whole body of literature grew up around the Delphae. It's called, quite naturally, Delphaeic literature. Serious people don't take it seriously, and foolish people take it foolishly. You know how that goes."

"Oh, yes," Bevier murmured. "I had to read whole libraries full of abominable verse when I was a student. Every professor had his favorite poet, and they all inflicted them on us without mercy. I think that's what ultimately led me to take up a military career."

Khalad came riding back to join them. "I wouldn't want to seem critical of my betters, my Lords," he said dryly, "but the decision to abandon the road and cut across country may have been just a little ill-advised on a day when we can't see the sun. Does anyone know which way we're going?"

"East," Vanion said firmly.

"Yes, my Lord," Khalad replied. "If you say it's east, then it's east—even if it really isn't. Aren't we supposed to be getting fairly close to the border?"

"It shouldn't be very far ahead."

"Doesn't your map indicate that the River Sarna marks the boundary between Cynesga and Tamul proper?"

Vanion nodded.

"Well, I just rode to the top of that hill up ahead and took a look around. I could see for about ten leagues in every direction, and there aren't any rivers out there. Do you suppose that someone might have stolen the Sarna?"

"Be nice," Sparhawk murmured.

"Cartography's not an exact art, Khalad," Vanion pointed out. "The distances on any map are only approximate. We started out at dawn, and we rode toward the lightest place in the cloud-cover. Unless somebody's changed things, that's east. We've taken sightings on landmarks every hour or so, and we're still riding in the same direction we were when we set out this morning."

"Where's the river then, my Lord?" Khalad asked, then looked at Itagne. "How wide would you say the valley of the Sarna is, your Excellency?"

"Sixty leagues, anyway. It's the longest and widest river on the continent, and the valley's very fertile."

"Grass? Trees? Lots of green crops?"

Itagne nodded.

"There's not a hint of green in any direction, my Lords," Khalad declared. "It's all a brown wasteland."

"We're riding east," Vanion insisted. "The mountains of Atan should be to the north—off to the left."

"They could be, my Lord, but they're a little bashful today. They're hiding themselves in the clouds."

"I've told you, Khalad, the map's inaccurate, that's all." Vanion looked back over his shoulder. "Why don't you ride back and ask Sephrenia and Berit to join us? It's about lunchtime, isn't it, Kalten?"

"Definitely, my Lord."

"I sort of thought so myself. Let's dig into the packs and put together something to eat."

"Is Sir Kalten skilled at estimating the time?" Itagne asked Sparhawk.

Sparhawk smiled. "We normally rely on Khalad—when the sun's out. When it's cloudy, though, we fall back on Kalten's stomach. He can usually tell you to within a minute how long it's been since the last time he ate."

Late that afternoon when they had stopped for the night, Khalad stood a short distance from where the rest of them were setting up their encampment. He was looking out over the featureless desert with a slightly smug expression on his face. "Sparhawk," he called, "could you come here a moment? I want to show you something."

Sparhawk put down Faran's saddle and walked over to join his squire. "Yes?" he asked.

"I think you'd better talk with Lord Vanion. He probably won't listen to me, since he's already got his mind made up, but somebody's going to have to convince him that we haven't been riding east today."

"You're going to have to convince me first."

"All right." The husky young man pointed out across the desert. "We came from that direction, right?"

"Yes."

"If we've been riding east, that would be west, right?"

"You're being obvious."

"Yes, I know. I have to be. I'm trying to explain something to a knight. The last time I looked, the sun went down in the west."

"Please, Khalad, don't try to be clever. Just get to the point."

"Yes, my Lord. If that's west, then why's the sun going down over there?" He turned and pointed off toward the left, where an angry orange glow stained the clouds.

Sparhawk blinked, and then he muttered an oath. "Let's go talk to Vanion," he said, and led the way back across the camp to where the Pandion Preceptor was speaking with Sephrenia.

"We've got a problem," Sparhawk told them. "We made a wrong turn somewhere today."

"Are you still riding that tired horse, Khalad?" Vanion's tone was irritable. His conversation with Sephrenia had obviously not been going well.

"Our young friend here just pointed something out to me," Sparhawk said. "Speaking slowly, of course, because of my limited understanding. He says that unless somebody's moved the sun, we've been riding north all day."

"That's impossible."

Sparhawk turned and pointed toward the ugly orange glow on the horizon. "That's *not* the direction we came from, Vanion."

Vanion stared at the horizon for a moment, and then he started to swear.

"You wouldn't listen to me, would you?" Sephrenia accused. "*Now* will you believe me when I tell you that the Delphae will deceive you at every turn?"

"It was our *own* mistake, Sephrenia—well, mine, anyway. We can't just automatically blame the Delphae for everything that goes wrong."

"I've known you since you were a boy, Vanion, and you've never made this kind of mistake before. I've seen you find your way on a dark night in the middle of a snowstorm."

"I must have confused a couple of landmarks and taken my bearings on the wrong one." Vanion grimaced. "Thanks for being so polite about it, Khalad—and so patient. We could have ridden on until we ran into the polar ice. I tend to get pigheaded sometimes."

Sephrenia smiled fondly at him. "I much prefer to speak of your singleness of purpose, dear one," she told him.

"It means the same thing, doesn't it?"

"Yes, but it sounds nicer."

"Set out some markers, Khalad," Vanion instructed. He looked around. "There aren't any sticks lying around, so pile up heaps of rock and mark them with scraps of colored cloth. Let's get an absolute reference on the position of the sun this evening so that we don't make the same mistake again tomorrow morning."

"I'll take care of it, my Lord."

· · · ·

"They're back," Kalten said, roughly shaking Sparhawk awake.

"Who's back?" Sparhawk sat up.

"Your glowing friends. They want to talk with you again."

Sparhawk rose to his feet and followed his friend to the edge of the camp.

"I was standing watch," Kalten said quietly, "and they just appeared out of nowhere. Itagne's stories are entertaining enough, but I don't think they're all that accurate. The Shining Ones don't shine all the time. They crept up on me in the dark, and they didn't start to glow until they were in place."

"Are they still staying back a ways?"

Kalten nodded. "They're keeping their distance. There's no way we could rush them."

There was no fog this time, and there were only two of the Shining Ones standing about twenty yards from the picketed horses. The eerie glow emanating from them still blurred their features, however.

"Thy peril increases, Anakha," that same hollow, echoing voice declared. "Thine enemies are seeking thee up and down in the land."

"We haven't seen anyone, neighbor."

"It is the unseen enemy which is most perilous. It is with their minds that thine enemies seek thee. We urge thee to accept our offer of sanctuary. It may soon be too late."

"I wouldn't offend you for the world, neighbor, but we've only got your word for this unseen danger, and I think you may be exaggerating a bit. You said that Bhelliom's directing my steps, and Bhelliom has unlimited power. I've tested that myself a few times. Thanks for your concern, but I still think I can take care of myself and my friends." He paused a moment and then plunged ahead on an impulse. "Why don't we just cut across all this polite chitchat? You've already admitted to a certain self-interest here. Why don't you come right out and tell me what you want and what you're prepared to offer in exchange? That might give us a basis for negotiation."

"Your charm's positively blinding, Sparhawk," Kalten muttered.

"We will consider thy proposal, Anakha." The echoing voice was cold.

"Do that. Oh, one other thing, neighbor. Stop tampering with our direction. Deceit and trickery at the outset always seem to get negotiations off on the wrong foot."

The glowing Delphae did not respond, but receded back into the desert and slipped out of sight.

"Then you *do* believe me, don't you, Sparhawk?" Sephrenia said from just behind the two knights. "You realize how unprincipled and dishonest those creatures are."

"Let's just say that I'm keeping an open mind on the subject, little mother. You were absolutely right about what you said earlier, though. We could blindfold Vanion, spin him around in circles for a day or so, and he'd still come out pointing due north." He looked around. "Is everybody awake? I think we'd better start considering options."

They returned to the place where their beds were laid out on the hard, uncomfortable gravel. "You're really very clever, Sparhawk," Bevier said. "The fact that our visitors didn't deny that accusation you pulled out of the air suggests that Sephrenia's been right about them all along. They *have* been misdirecting us."

"That doesn't alter the fact that the Cyrgai are out there," Ulath reminded him, "and the Cyrgai are definitely our enemies. We may not know what the Delphae are really up to, but they ran off the Cyrgai for us last night, and that sort of inclines me to like them."

"Could that have been some sort of collusion?" Berit asked.

"That's very unlikely," Itagne said. "The Cyrgai traditionally have a sublime belief that they're the crown of creation. They'd never agree to any ruse that put them in a subservient position—not even for the sake of appearances. It's just not in their racial makeup."

"He's right," Sephrenia agreed, "and even though I hate to admit it, an alliance of that sort would be totally out of character for the Delphae as well. There could be no common ground between them and the Cyrgai. I don't know what the Delphae are doing in this business, but they have their own agenda. They wouldn't be cat's-paws for anyone else."

"Wonderful," Talen said sardonically, "now we've got *two* enemies to worry about."

"Why worry at all?" Kalten shrugged. "Bhelliom can put us down on the outskirts of Matherion in the space between two heartbeats. Why don't we just go away and leave the Cyrgai and the Delphae here in this wasteland to resolve their differences without us?"

"No," Sephrenia said.

"Why not?"

"Because the Delphae have misdirected us already. We *don't* want to go to Delphaeus."

"They're not going to be able to fool the Bhelliom, Sephrenia," Vanion disagreed. "They might have been able to confuse *me*, but Bhelliom's an entirely different matter."

"I don't think we can take that chance, dear one. The Delphae want something from Sparhawk, and it's obviously going to involve Bhelliom. Let's not deliver them both into Delphaeic hands. I know that it's tedious and dangerous, but let's keep our feet on the ground. Bhelliom moves through a vast emptiness. If the Delphae can deceive it, we could come out of that emptiness almost anyplace."

"What's an eclogue?" Talen asked. They were riding toward what they hoped was the east the following morning, and Itagne was continuing his rambling discourse on Delphaeic literature.

"It's a sort of primitive drama," he replied. "It usually involves a meeting between two shepherds. They stand around discussing philosophy in bad verse."

"I've known a few sheepherders," Khalad said, "and philosophy wasn't their usual topic of conversation. They're far more interested in women."

"There's some of that involved in eclogues as well, but it's so idealized that it's hardly recognizable." Itagne tugged thoughtfully at one earlobe. "I think it's some sort of disease," he mused. "The more civilized people become, the more they romanticize the simple bucolic life and ignore the dirt and grinding toil involved. Our sillier poets grow all weepy-eyed about shepherds—and shepherdesses, of course. It wouldn't be nearly as much fun without the shepherdesses. The aristocracy periodically becomes enamored of the pastoral tradition, and they go to great lengths to act out their fantasies. Emperor Sarabian's father even went so far as to have an idealized sheep farm built down near Saranth. He and his court used to go there in the summertime and spend months pretending to watch over flocks of badly overfed sheep. Their rude smocks and kirtles were made of velvet and satin, and they'd sit around all moony-eyed composing bad verse and ignoring the fact that their sheep were wandering off in all directions." He leaned back in his saddle. "Pastoral literature doesn't really hurt anything. It's silly and grossly oversentimental, and the poets who become addicted to it tend to be a bit heavy-handed when they ladle on the moral lessons. That's always been the problem with literature—finding a justification for it. It really doesn't serve any practical purpose, you know."

"Except that life without it would be sterile and empty," Bevier asserted.

"It would indeed, Sir Bevier," Itagne agreed. "Anyway, Delphaeic literature—which probably doesn't have anything at all to do with the real Delphae—grew up around these ridiculous literary conventions, but after several centuries of that nonsense, the potentials of the pastoral tradition had been pretty much exhausted, so our poets began to wander afield—like untended sheep, if I may extend the metaphor. Sometime during the last century, they began to posit the notion that the Delphae practice a non-Styric form of magic. That *really* upsets my Styric colleagues at the university." Itagne looked back over his shoulder to make sure that Sephrenia, who still rode in the rear with Berit, was out of earshot. "Many people find something fundamentally irritating about Styrics. The pudding of smug superiority and accusatory self-pity doesn't cook up very well, and the favorite form of Styric-baiting on the university campus is to mention 'Delphaeic magic' to a Styric and then watch him go up in flames."

"Can you think of anything at all that might explain Sephrenia's reaction to the Delphae?" Vanion asked with troubled eyes. "I've never seen her behave this way before."

"I really don't know Lady Sephrenia that well, Lord Vanion, but her explosion the first time I mentioned Delphaeic literature provides some clues. There's a very brief passage in 'Xadane' that hints that the Delphae were allied with the Styrics during the war that was supposed to have exterminated the Cyrgai. The passage was clearly based on a very obscure section in a seventh-century historical text. There's mention of a betrayal, but not much more. Evidently, when their war with the Cyrgai began, the Styrics contacted the Delphae and tricked them into mounting an attack on the Cyrgai from the east. They promised aid and all manner of other inducements, but when the Cyrgai counterattacked and began to overrun the Delphae, the Styrics chose to renege on their promises. The Delphae were almost exterminated. The Styrics have been wriggling and squirming for eons trying to justify that blatant breach of faith. There are many people in the world who don't like Styrics, and they've used that betrayal as a vehicle for their bigotry. Styrics quite understandably don't care much for the literature." He looked pensively out across the featureless desert. "One of the less attractive aspects of human nature is our tendency to hate the people we haven't treated very well; it's much easier than accepting guilt. If we can convince ourselves that the people we betrayed or enslaved were subhuman monsters in the first place, then our guilt isn't nearly as black as we secretly know that it is. Humans are very, very good at shifting blame and avoiding guilt. We *do* like to keep a good opinion of ourselves, don't we?"

"I think it would take more than that to set Sephrenia off," Vanion said dubiously. "She's too sensible to catch on fire just because somebody says unflattering things about Styrics. She's spent several hundred years in the Elene kingdoms of Eosia, and anti-Styric prejudice there goes far beyond literary insults." He sighed. "If she'd only *talk* to me about it. I can't get anything coherent out of her, though. All she does is splutter wild denunciations. I don't understand at all."

Sparhawk, however, had an inkling of what was happening. Aphrael had hinted that Sephrenia was going to encounter something extraordinarily painful, and it was growing increasingly obvious that the Delphae would be the cause of her pain. Aphrael had said that Sephrenia's suffering would be necessary as a prelude to some kind of growth. Itagne, who really didn't know any of them that well, may have hit upon something relevant. Sephrenia was Styric to her fingertips, and the acceptance of racial guilt for an eons-old misbehavior would cause her the exact kind of pain Aphrael had so sorrowfully described. Sephrenia, however, would not be the only one who would suffer. Vanion had said that Sephrenia's problems were also his. Unfortunately, the same held true of her pain.

Sparhawk rode on across the desolate waste, his thoughts as bleak as the surroundings.

CHAPTER TWELVE

Kring looked pensively out across the lawn. "It came on me like a madness, Atan Engessa," he told his towering friend. "From the moment I first saw her, I couldn't think of anything else." The two were standing in the shadows near the Ministry of the Interior.

"You are fortunate, friend Kring," Engessa replied in his deep, soft voice. "Most men's lives are never touched by such love."

Kring smiled a bit wryly. "I'm sure my life would be much easier if it hadn't touched mine."

"Do you regret it?"

"Not for a moment. I'd thought that my life was full. I was the Domi of my people and I'd assumed that my mother would find me a suitable wife in due time, as is customary and proper. I'd have married and fathered sons, and that would have satisfied the requirements. Then I saw Mirtai, and I realized how empty my life had been before." He rubbed one hand over his shaved scalp. "My people will have a great deal of trouble with her, I'm afraid. She's like no other woman we've ever encountered. It wouldn't be so difficult if I weren't the Domi."

"She might not have accepted you if you hadn't been, friend Kring. Mirtai is a proud woman. She was meant to be the wife of a ruler."

"I know. I wouldn't have dared to approach her if I hadn't been Domi. There'll be trouble, though. I can see that coming. She's a stranger, and she's not at all like Peloi women. Status is very important to our women and Mirtai's of a different race, she's taller than even the tallest of the Peloi men, and she's more beautiful than any other woman I've ever seen. Just by themselves, those things would shrivel the hearts of Peloi women. You saw how Tikume's wife, Vida, looked at her, didn't you?"

Engessa nodded.

"The women of *my* people will hate her all the more because I am *their* Domi. She will be Doma, the Domi's wife, and she'll have first place among the women. To make matters even worse, she'll be one of the wealthiest of all the Peloi."

"I don't understand."

"I've done quite well. My herds have increased, and I've stolen much. All my wealth will belong to her. She'll own vast herds of sheep and cattle. The horse herds will still be mine, though."

"Is that the Peloi custom?"

"Oh, yes. Sheep and cattle are food, so they belong to the women. The women also own the tents and the beds and the wagons. The gold we get from the king for Zemoch ears is owned by all the people in common, so about the only thing we Peloi men own are our weapons and our horses. When you get right down to it, the women own everything, and we spend our lives protecting their possessions."

"You have a strange society, friend Kring."

Kring shrugged. "A man shouldn't have his mind all cluttered with possessions. It distracts him when the time comes for fighting."

"There's wisdom there, my friend. Who holds your possessions until you marry?"

"My mother. She's a sensible woman, and having a daughter like Mirtai will increase her status enormously. She has a great deal of authority among the Peloi women, and I'm hoping she'll be able to keep matters under control—at least among my sisters." He laughed. "I'm going to enjoy watching the faces of my sisters when I introduce them to Mirtai and they have to bow to her. I'm not really fond of them. They all pray for my death every night."

"Your own *sisters*?" Engessa sounded shocked.

"Of course. If I die before I'm married, everything I've won becomes the property of my mother, and my sisters will inherit all of it. They already think of themselves as women of property. They've turned down perfectly acceptable suitors because of their pride of position and the wealth they think they'll inherit. I've been too busy making war to think much about marriage, and every year that passed made my sisters feel that their ownership of the herds was that much more secure." He grinned. "Mirtai's sudden appearance is going to upset them, I'm afraid. One of the customs of our people obliges a bride-to-be to spend two months in the tent of her betrothed's mother—learning all the little things she'll need to know about him after they're married. During that period my mother and Mirtai will *also* select husbands for all my sisters; it's not a good idea to have too many women in one tent. That will *really* upset my sisters. I expect they'll try to murder Mirtai. I'll warn them against it, of course," he added piously. "I *am* their brother, after all. But I'm sure they won't listen—at least not until after Mirtai's killed a few of them. I've got too many sisters anyway."

"How many?" Engessa asked him.

"Eight. Their status will change drastically once I marry. Right now they're all heiresses. After my wedding, they'll be possessionless spinsters, dependent on Mirtai for every crust of bread they eat. I think they'll bitterly regret all the suitors they've refused at that point. Is that somebody creeping through the shadows over by the wall?"

Engessa looked toward the Interior Ministry. "It seems to be," he replied. "Let's go ask him his business. We don't really want anybody going inside that building while Atana Mirtai and the thieves are in there."

"Right," Kring agreed. He loosened his saber in its sheath, and the oddly mismatched pair moved silently across the lawn to intercept the furtive shadow near the wall.

"How far is it from here to Tega, Sarabian?" Ehlana asked, looking up from Sparhawk's letter. "In a direct line, I mean?"

Sarabian had removed his doublet, and he really looked quite dashing in his tight-fitting hose and full-sleeved linen shirt. He had tied back his shoulder-length black hair, and he was practicing lunges with his rapier, aiming at a golden bracelet hanging from the ceiling on a long string. "About a hundred and fifty leagues, wouldn't you say, Oscagne?" he replied, contorting his body into *en garde* position. He lunged and caught the rim of the bracelet with the point of his rapier, sending the bracelet spinning and swinging on the string. "Blast!" he muttered.

"Perhaps closer to a hundred and seventy-five, your Majesty," Oscagne corrected.

"Could it *really* be raining there?" Ehlana asked. "The weather's been beautiful here. A hundred and seventy-five leagues isn't really all that far, and Sparhawk says right here that it's been raining on Tega for the past week."

"Who can say what the weather's going to do?" Sarabian lunged again, and his rapier passed smoothly through the bracelet.

"Well thrust," Ehlana said a bit absently.

"Thank you, your Majesty." Sarabian bowed, flourishing his rapier. "This is really fun, you know that?" He crouched melodramatically. "Have at you, dog!" He lunged at the bracelet again, missing by several inches. "Blast."

"Alean, dear," Ehlana said to her maid. "Would you go see if the sailor who brought this letter is still on the premises?"

"At once, my Queen."

Sarabian looked inquiringly at his hostess.

"The sailor just came from Tega. I think I'd like to hear *his* views on the weather there."

"Surely you don't think your husband would lie to your Majesty, do you?" Oscagne protested.

"Why not? I'd lie to *him* if there was a valid political reason for it."

"*Ehlana!*" Sarabian sounded profoundly shocked. "I thought you loved Sparhawk."

"What on earth has that got to do with it? Of course I love him. I've loved him since I was about Danae's age, but love and politics are two entirely different things, and they should never be mixed. Sparhawk's up to something, Sarabian, and your excellent foreign minister here probably knows what it is."

"Me?" Oscagne protested mildly.

"Yes, you. Mermaids, Oscagne? *Mermaids?* You didn't *really* think I'd swallow that story, did you? I'm just a bit disappointed in you, actually. Was that the best you could come up with?"

"I was a bit pressed for time, your Majesty," he apologized with a slightly embarrassed look. "Prince Sparhawk was in a hurry to leave. Was it the weather that gave us away?"

"Partly," she replied. She held up the letter. "My beloved outsmarted himself, though. I've seen his letters before. The notion of 'felicity of style' has never occurred to Sparhawk. His letters usually read as if he'd written them with his broadsword. This one—and all the others from Tega—have been polished until they glisten. I'm touched that he went to all the trouble, but I don't believe one word of them. Now, then, where is he? And what's he really up to?"

"He wouldn't say, your Majesty. All he told me was that he needed some excuse to be away from Matherion for several weeks."

She smiled sweetly at him. "That's all right, Oscagne," she said. "I'll find out for myself. It's more fun that way anyhow."

"It's a big building," Stragen reported the following morning. "It's going to take time to go over it inch by inch." He, Caalador, and Mirtai had just returned from their night of unsuccessful burglary.

"Have you made much progress?" Sarabian asked.

"We've covered the top two floors, your Majesty," Caalador replied. "We'll start on the third floor tonight." Caalador was sprawled in a chair with a weary look on his face. Like his two companions, he was still dressed in tight-fitting black clothing. He stretched and yawned. "God, I'm tired," he said. "I'm getting too old for this."

Stragen unrolled a time-yellowed set of drawings. "I *still* think that the answer's right here," he said. "Instead of opening doors and poking under desks, we should be matching dimensions against these drawings."

"Yer still a-thankin' there's sekert passages an' corn-sealed rooms in thar, ain't ya, Stragen?" Caalador drawled, yawning again. "That doesn't speak too well for your taste in literature, old boy."

Sarabian gave him a puzzled look.

"Thalesians are addicted to bad ghost stories, your Majesty," Caalador explained.

"It gives the copying houses in Emsat something to do now that they've exhausted the body of real literature." Stragen shrugged. "We've got a whole subgenre of highly popular books spewing out of grubby garrets on back streets—lurid narratives that all take place in cemeteries or in haunted houses on dark and stormy nights. The whores of Emsat absolutely adore them. I rather expect the policemen at Interior share that taste. After all, a policeman's sort of like a whore, isn't he?"

"I didn't exactly follow that," Mirtai said, "and I'm not really sure I want to. There's probably something disgusting involved in your thinking, Stragen. Caalador, *will* you stop yawning like that. Your face looks like an open barn door."

"I'm sleepy, little dorlin'. You two bin a-keepin' me up past muh bedtime."

"Then go to bed. You make my jaws ache when you gape at me like that."

"You should *all* get some sleep," Ehlana told them. "You're the official royal burglars now, and Sarabian and I would be absolutely mortified if you were to fall asleep in midburgle."

"Are we ready to be practical about this?" Caalador asked, rising to his feet. "I can have two dozen professionals here by this evening, and we'll have all the secrets of the Interior Ministry in our hands by tomorrow morning."

"And Interior will know that we have them by tomorrow afternoon," Stragen added. "Our impromptu spy network isn't really all that secure, Caalador. We haven't had enough time to weed out all the people Krager's probably subverted."

"There's no real rush here, gentlemen," Ehlana told them. "Even if we *do* find the documents the policemen at Interior are hiding, we won't be able to do a thing about them until my wandering husband finds his way home again."

"Why are you so positive that Sparhawk's deceiving you, Ehlana?" Sarabian asked her.

"It's consistent with his character. Sparhawk's devoted his entire life to protecting me. It's rather sweet, even though it *is* bloody, hindering awkward at times. He still thinks of me as a little girl—although I've demonstrated to him on any number of occasions that I'm not. He's out there doing something dangerous, and he doesn't want me to worry. All he really had to do was tell me what he was planning and then lay out the reasons why he thought it was necessary. I know it's hard for you men to believe, but women are rational, too—and far more practical than you are."

"You're a hard woman, Ehlana," Sarabian accused.

"No, I'm a realist. Sparhawk does what he thinks he has to, no matter what I say, and I've learned to accept that. The point I'm trying to make is that no matter what we dig out of the walls of the Interior Ministry, there's absolutely nothing we can do about it while Sparhawk and the others are out there wandering around the countryside. We're going to disband Interior and throw about a quarter of the empire's policemen in prison. Then we're going to place all of Tamuli under martial law, with the Atans enforcing our decrees. The Daresian continent's going to look like an anthill that's just been run over by a cavalry charge. I don't know what Sparhawk's doing, so I don't know what kind of impact that chaos is going to have on him. I am *not* going to let you put him in any more danger than I think he's already in."

"Do you know something, Ehlana?" Sarabian said. "You're even more protective of Sparhawk than he is of you."

"Of course I am. That's what marriage is all about."

"None of mine are," he sighed.

"That's because you've got too many wives, Sarabian. Your affection's dispersed. Your wives each return only as much love as you give them."

"I've found that it's safer that way."

"But dull, my friend, and sort of boring. Being consumed with a burning passion that only has a single object is very exciting. It's sort of like living in a volcano."

"What an exhausting prospect." He shuddered.

"Fun, though." She smiled.

Baroness Melidere had retired early, pleading a painful headache. It was not that she found her duties as Ehlana's lady-in-waiting onerous, but rather that she had an important decision to make; and she knew that the longer she put it off, the more difficult it would be. To put it rather bluntly, the baroness had reached the point where she was going to have to decide what to do about Stragen.

Melidere was no innocent. Few members of any court really are. An innocent girl has only one option in her dealings with the opposite sex. A more worldly girl has two, and this was the crux of Melidere's dilemma. Stragen, of course, would make a perfectly acceptable paramour. He was presentable, interesting, and he had exquisite manners. Melidere's reputation at court would not be tarnished by a liaison with him; quite the reverse, actually. That had originally been her intention, and the time had come for her to take the final step and to invite him to her bedchamber and have done with it. The liaison could be brief, or it could be extended— renewed each time Stragen visited Cimmura. That would give the affair a certain status, while at the same time leaving them both free to pursue other amusements, as was normal in such situations. Melidere, however, was not sure if that was all she wanted. More and more of late, she had found herself thinking of a more permanent arrangement, and therein lay the dilemma.

There is a rhythm, almost a tide, in the affairs of the heart. When that tide reaches its high point, a lady must give certain signals to her quarry. One set of signals points toward the bedchamber; the other, toward the altar. Melidere could no longer put it off. She had to decide which set of signal flags to hoist.

Stragen intrigued her. There was a sense of dangerous excitement about him, and Melidere, a creature of the court, was attracted by that. It could be intoxicating, addictive, but she was not entirely sure that the excitement would not begin to pall as the years went by.

There was, moreover, the problem of Stragen himself. His irregular origins and lack of any official status had made him overly sensitive, and he continually imagined slights where none had been intended. He hovered around the edges of Ehlana's court like an uninvited guest at a banquet, always fearful that he might be summarily ejected. He had the outsider's awe of the nobility, seeming at times to view aristocrats almost as members of another species. Melidere knew that if she de-

cided to marry him, she would have to attack that first. She personally knew that titles were a sham and that legitimacy could be purchased, but how was she going to
persuade Stragen of that? She could easily buy him out of bastardy and into the aristocracy, but that would mean that she would have to reveal the secret she had kept
locked in her heart since childhood. Melidere had always concealed the fact that she
was one of the wealthiest people at court, largely because her fabulous wealth had
not been legally obtained.

And there it was! She almost laughed when she realized how simple it was. If
she really wanted to marry Stragen, all she'd have to do is share her secret with him.
That would put them on equal footing and tear down the largely imaginary barrier.

Melidere was a baroness, but her title had not been in her family for very long.
Her father had begun life as a blacksmith in Cardos, a man with huge shoulders and
a mop of curly blond hair, and he had amassed a fortune with a simple invention
which he had crafted in his forge. Most people look upon gold coins as money—
something with intrinsic and unalterable value. There are some, however, who
realize that the value of a coin lies in the social agreement saying that it is worth
what the words stamped on its face say that it's worth. The words do not change,
even if the edge of the coin has been lightly brushed with a file or a sharp knife a few
times. The tiny fragments of pure gold thus obtained do not amount to very much
if one files or carves the edge of *one* coin. If one tampers with a thousand coins,
however, that's quite another matter. Governments try to discourage the practice by
milling the edges of coins during the stamping process. A milled coin has a series of
indentations around its edge, and if the edge has been filed or carved, it is immediately apparent. Melidere's father had contrived a way to get around that. He had
carefully crafted a set of remilling dies, one die for each size coin. A blacksmith will
not handle enough coins in his entire life to make enough to pay for the effort
of hammering out such equipment. Melidere's father was a genius, however. He
did not make the dies for his own use, nor did he sell them. Instead, he rented
them, along with the services of highly trained operators, taking a small percentage
as his fee.

Melidere smiled. She was positive that very few gold coins in the whole of
Eosia were of true weight, and she also knew that five percent of the difference between face value and true value was stacked in ingots in the hidden vault in the
basement of her own manor house near Cardos. Once she had made Stragen aware
of the fact that she was a bigger and more successful thief than he was, the rest
would be easy. His illusions about her nobility would fall away to be replaced with
an almost reverential respect for her consummate dishonesty. She could even show
him the source of her wealth, for she always carried the most prized memento of her
childhood, her father's original dies. Even now, they nestled in velvet in the ornately
carved rosewood case on her dressing table, polished steel jewels more valuable than
diamonds.

Even as she realized that the means to marry Stragen were at hand, she also
realized that she had already made her decision. She *would* marry him. She would,
the very next time she saw him, hoist *those* signal flags rather than the others.

Then she thought of something else. Her father's activities had been confined
to the Eosian continent. All of Tamuli was literally awash with virgin coins unvio-

lated by file or knife-edge. Once he realized that, Stragen would not *walk* to the altar, he would *run*.

Melidere smiled and picked up her hairbrush. She hummed softly to herself as she brushed her long honey-blonde hair. Like any good Elene girl, she had attacked the problem logically, and, as it almost always did, logic had won out. Logic was a friendly and comforting thing to have around, particularly if morality didn't interfere.

"Hold it," Stragen whispered as the three of them started down the broad staircase descending to the third floor. "There's still somebody down there."

"What's he doing this late?" Mirtai asked. "They all went home hours ago."

"We could go ask him," Caalador said.

"Don't be absurd. Is it a watchman?"

"I don't know," Stragen replied. "I didn't see him. I just caught a flicker of candlelight. Somebody down there opened a door."

"Some drudge working late, most likely." Caalador shrugged.

"Now what?" Mirtai asked.

"We wait." Caalador sat down on the top step.

Stragen considered it. "Why don't the two of you stay here?" he suggested. "I'll go have a look. If he's settling in for the night, there's not much point in camping on these stairs until morning." He went on down, his glove-soft shoes making no sound on the mother-of-pearl tiles. When he reached the hallway below, he saw the fine line of candlelight glowing out from under a door at the far end. He moved quickly with the confidence of long practice. When he reached the door, he heard voices.

Stragen did not even consider listening at the door. That was far too amateurish. He slipped into the room adjoining the lighted one, felt his way carefully to the wall, and set his ear against it.

He couldn't hear a sound. He swore under his breath and went back out into the hallway. Then he padded on past the door with the candlelight coming out from under it and entered the room on the other side. He could hear the two men talking as soon as he entered.

"Our esteemed prime minister is beginning to grasp the situation," a rusty-sounding voice was saying. "It's a struggle, though. Pondia Subat's severely limited when something new appears on the horizon."

"That's more or less to be expected, your Excellency." Stragen recognized the second voice. It was Teovin, the Director of the Secret Police. "The prime minister's almost as much a figurehead as the emperor."

"You've noticed," the rusty-sounding man replied.

"Subat's not likely to ask too many questions. As long as he's aware of the situation in general terms, he'll probably prefer to let us handle things without personally learning details. And that's what we wanted in the first place. Have you made any progress with the others?"

"Some. I have to broach the subject rather carefully, you realize. The Elene strumpet's made many friends here at court. They all listen to me, though. I hold the keys to the treasury, and that helps to get their attention. Most of the ministries are ceremonial, so I haven't wasted much time on the men who head them. The Ministry of Culture's probably not going to be of much use—or the Ministry of Education either, for that matter."

"I wouldn't be so sure of that one, your Excellency. The Ministry of Education controls the universities. We have to think past the current emergency. I don't think either of us wants whole generations to go through life believing that Interior and Exchequer are hotbeds of treason. Technically, we *are* acting contrary to the emperor's wishes."

"That's true, I suppose, but Interior controls the police, and Exchequer levies and collects the taxes. We're neither one of us ever going to be very popular, no matter what we do. But you're probably right. If the history professors at the universities start telling their students that we're traitors, people might start claiming that it's their patriotic duty to ignore the officers of the law or to stop paying their taxes."

"That raises an interesting point, Chancellor Gashon," Teovin mused. "You've got a sort of police force, haven't you? Muscular fellows who accompany your tax collectors to make sure that people pay what they owe?"

"Oh, yes. One way or the other, *everybody* pays his taxes. I get money—or blood—from all of them."

"Follow me on this, if you will. The Elenes probably know that Interior—and most likely the army as well—are opposed to them, so they'll try their very best to disrupt our customary operations. I'd like to conceal some of my more-valuable people. Do you suppose I might transfer them into *your* enforcement branch? That way I'll still have a functional operation—even if the Elenes start burning down police stations."

"I can manage that, Teovin. Is there anything else you'll need?"

"Money, Chancellor Gashon."

There was a pained silence. "Would you accept eternal friendship instead?"

"Afraid not, your Excellency. I have to bribe people." Teovin paused. "There's an idea. I could probably use some form of tax-immunity as an inducement in many cases."

"I don't recognize the term."

"We give people an exemption from taxation in exchange for their cooperation."

"That's immoral!" Gashon gasped. "That's the most shocking thing I've ever heard in my whole life!"

"It was only a thought."

"Don't even suggest something like that, Teovin. It makes my blood run cold. Can we get out of here? Police stations make me apprehensive, for some reason."

"Of course, your Excellency. I think we've covered the things we wanted to keep private."

Stragen sat in the dark office listening as the two men pushed back their chairs and went out into the corridor. He heard Teovin's key turn in the lock. The blond thief waited for perhaps ten minutes, and then he went back to the foot of the staircase. "They're gone now," he called up the stairs in a loud whisper.

Mirtai and Caalador came on down. "Who was it?" Caalador asked.

"The head of the Secret Police and the Chancellor of the Exchequer," Stragen replied. "It was a very enlightening conversation. Teovin's enlisting other ministries to help him. They don't know what he's *really* up to, but he's managed to convince several of them that it's in their own interest to join him."

"We can sort out the politics later," Caalador said. "It's almost midnight. Let's get to burgling."

"There's no need." Stragen shrugged. "I've found what we're looking for."

"Isn't that disgusting?" Caalador said to the Atan giantess. "He tosses it off as if it weren't really very important. All right, Stragen, stun us with your brilliance. Make my eyes pop out, and make Mirtai swoon with admiration."

"I can't really take much credit for it," Stragen confessed. "I stumbled across it, actually. It *is* a secret room. I was right about that. We still have to find the door, though, and make sure that the documents we want are inside, but the room's in the right place. I should have thought of it immediately."

"Where is it?" Mirtai asked.

"Right next to Teovin's office."

"That's the logical place, right enough," Caalador noted. "How did you find it?"

"Well, I haven't actually found it yet, but I've reasoned out its existence."

"Don't throw away your soft shoes or your black clothes just yet, Caalador," Mirtai advised.

"You hurt me, love," Stragen protested.

"I've seen Elene reasoning go awry before. Why don't you tell us about it?"

"I wanted to do some constructive eavesdropping, so I went into the adjoining office to listen to Teovin and Chancellor of the Exchequer Gashon's conversation."

"And?"

"I couldn't hear a thing."

"The walls are stone, Stragen," she pointed out, "and they've got seashells glued to them."

"There's no such thing as a soundproof wall, Mirtai. There are always cracks and crannies that the mortar doesn't seep into. Anyway, when I tried the office on the other side, I could hear everything. Believe me, there's a room between that first office and the one Teovin uses."

"It *does* sort of fit together, dorlin'," Caalador said to Mirtai. "The door to that room would almost *have* to be in Teovin's office, wouldn't it? Those documents are sensitive, and he wouldn't want just anybody to have access to them. If we'd just taken a little while to think our way through it, we could have saved ourselves a lot of time."

"It wasn't a total waste." Mirtai smiled. "I've learned the art of burglary, and I've had the chance to absolutely wallow in your affection. You two have made me happier than I could possibly say. The office door's certain to be locked, you know."

"Nuthin' simpler, little dorlin'." Caalador smirked, holding up a needle-thin implement with a hook on the end.

"We'd better get started," Stragen said. "It's midnight, and it might take us the rest of the night to find the door to that hidden room."

·   ·   ·

"You're not serious," Ehlana scoffed.

"May muh tongue turn green iffn I ain't, yer Queenship." Caalador paused. "Dreadful, isn't it?" he added.

"I don't quite understand," Sarabian confessed.

"It's a cliché, your Majesty," Stragen explained, "taken from a type of literature that's currently very popular in Eosia."

"Do you really want to dignify that trash by calling it literature, Stragen?" Baroness Melidere murmured.

"It satisfies the needs of the mentally deprived, Baroness." He shrugged. "Anyway, your Imperial Majesty, the literature consists largely of ghost stories. There's always a haunted castle complete with hidden rooms and secret passages, and the entrances to these rooms and passages are always hidden behind bookcases. It's a very tired old device—so tired in fact that I almost didn't think of it. I didn't believe *anybody* would be so obvious." He laughed. "I wonder if Teovin thought it up all by himself or if he plagiarized. If he stole it, he has abominable taste in literature."

"Are books all that available in Eosia?" Oscagne asked curiously. "They're fearfully expensive here."

"It's one of the results of our Holy Mother's drive toward universal literacy during the last century, your Excellency," Ehlana explained. "The Church wanted her children to be able to read her message, so parish priests spend a great deal of time teaching everybody to read."

"The message of the Church doesn't really take all that long to browse through, however," Stragen added, "and after that you've got crowds of literate people with a skill they can't really apply. It was the invention of paper that set off the literary explosion, though. The labor costs involved in copying aren't particularly high. It was the cost of parchment that made books so prohibitively expensive. When paper came along, books became cheaper. There are copy houses in most major cities with whole platoons of scriveners grinding out books by the ton. It's a very profitable business. The books don't have illuminations or decorated capitals, and the lettering's a little shoddy, but they're readable—and affordable. Not everyone who can read has good taste, though, so a lot of truly dreadful books are written by people with minimal talent. They write adventure stories, ghost stories, heroic fantasies, and those naughty books that people don't openly display in their bookcases. The Church encourages lives of the saints and tedious religious verse. Things like that are produced, of course, but nobody really reads that sort of thing. Ghost stories are currently in vogue—particularly in Thalesia. It has something to do with our national character, I think." He looked at Ehlana. "The business of getting the information out of Teovin's hidey-hole is going to be tedious, my Queen. There are mountains of documents in there, and I can't take whole platoons of people in over the roof every night to help plow through them. Mirtai, Caalador, and I are going to have to read every document ourselves."

"Perhaps not, Milord Stragen," Ehlana disagreed. She smiled at the blond thief. "I had absolute confidence in your dishonesty, dear boy, so I knew that sooner or later you'd find what we were looking for. I struggled for a time with the very problem you just mentioned. Then I remembered something Sparhawk once told me. He'd used a spell to put the image of Krager's face in a basin of water so that Talen could draw his picture. I spoke with one of the Pandions who came along with us—a Sir Alvor. He told me that since Sephrenia refuses to learn to read Elenic, she and Sparhawk devised a way around her deliberate incapacity. She can glance at a page—a single glance—and then make the whole page come up in a mirror or on the surface of a basin of water hours or even days later. Sir Alvor knows the spell. He's a fairly young and agile fellow, so he'll be able to creep across the rooftop with you. Take him along, next time you visit the Interior Ministry, and turn him loose in Teovin's hidden closet. I rather imagine he'll be able to carry that entire library out with him in a single night."

"Does it really work, your Majesty?" Caalador asked her a bit dubiously.

"Oh, yes, Caalador. I handed Alvor a book he'd never seen before. He leafed through it in a couple of minutes and then printed it on that mirror over there—page after page after page. I checked what he was producing against the original, and it was absolutely perfect—right down to the smudges and the food-stains on the pages."

"Them there Pandion fellers is real useful t' have around," Caalador admitted.

"You know—" She smiled. "—I've noticed the exact same thing myself. There's one in particular who does all sorts of useful things for me."

CHAPTER THIRTEEN

"We don't have any choice, dear," Vanion said to Sephrenia. "We've even tried turning around and going back, but we *still* keep moving in the same direction. We're going to have to use the Bhelliom." He looked up the gorge lying ahead of them. The mountain river was tumbling over the boulders jutting up out of its bed, sawing its way deeper and deeper into the rock with its white, roaring passage. The sides of the gorge were thick with evergreens that dripped continually in the swirling mist rising out of the rapids.

"No, Vanion," Sephrenia replied stubbornly. "We'll fall directly into their trap if we do that. The Delphae want the Bhelliom, and as soon as Sparhawk tries to use it, they'll attack us and try to kill him and take it away from him."

"They'll regret it if they do," Sparhawk told her.

"Maybe," she said, "but then again, maybe not. We don't know what they're capable of. Until I know *how* they're misleading us, I can't even guess at what else they can do. There are too many uncertainties involved to be taking chances."

"Isn't this what they call an impasse?" Khalad suggested. "We keep going north no matter how much we try to go in some other direction, and we don't know what the Delphae will do if Sparhawk tries to use Bhelliom to pull us out of these mountains. Why don't we just stop?"

"We have to get back to Matherion, Khalad," Sparhawk objected.

"But we're not *going* to Matherion, my Lord. Every step we take brings us that much closer to Delphaeus. We've been twisting and turning around through these mountains for two days now, and we're *still* going north. If all directions lead to a place where we really don't want to go, why keep moving at all? Why not find a comfortable campsite and stay there for a while? Let's make them come to *us,* instead of the other way around."

"It makes sense, Lord Vanion," Itagne agreed. "As long as we keep moving, the Delphae don't have to do a thing except herd us in the right direction. If we stop moving, they'll have to try something else, and that might give Lady Sephrenia some clues about their capabilities. It's called 'constructive inaction' in diplomatic circles."

"What if the Delphae just decide to wait us out?" Ulath objected. "Autumn isn't a good time to linger in the mountains. It wasn't so bad in those foothills we came through when we left the desert, but now that we're up here, time starts to get very important."

"I don't think they'll wait, Sir Ulath," Itagne disagreed.

"Why not? They've got all the advantages, haven't they?"

"Let's just call it a diplomat's instinct. I caught a faint odor of urgency about them when they approached us. They want us to go to Delphaeus, right enough, but it's *also* important to them that we get there soon."

"I'd like to know how you worked *that* out, your Excellency," Kalten said skeptically.

"It's a combination of a thousand little things, Sir Kalten—the tone of voice, slight changes of expression, even their posture and their rate of breathing. The Delphae weren't as certain of themselves as they seemed, and they want us to go to Delphaeus as quickly as possible. As long as we keep going, they don't have any reason to make further contact, but I think we'll find that if we just sit still, they'll come to us and start making concessions. I've seen it happen that way many times."

"Does it take long to learn how to be a diplomat, your Excellency?" Talen asked him with a speculative look.

"That depends entirely on your natural gifts, Master Talen."

"I'm a quick learner. Diplomacy sounds like a lot of fun."

"It's the best game there is." Itagne smiled. "There's no other that even approaches it."

"Are you considering another career change, Talen?" his brother asked him.

"I'm never going to be a very good knight, Khalad—not unless Sparhawk takes the Bhelliom and makes me about four times bigger than I am now."

"Isn't this about the third occupation you've grown excited about so far this year?" Sparhawk asked him. "Have you given up the notion of becoming the emperor of the thieves or the archprelate of larceny?"

"I don't really have to make any final decisions yet, Sparhawk. I'm still young." Talen suddenly thought of something. "They can't arrest a diplomat, can they, your Excellency? I mean, the police can't really touch him at all—no matter *what* he does?"

"That's a long-standing custom, Master Talen. If I throw *your* diplomats into a dungeon, you'll turn around and do the same thing to *mine,* won't you? That puts a diplomat more or less above the law."

"Well, now," Talen said with a beatific smile, "isn't *that* something to think about?"

"I like caves." Ulath shrugged.

"Are you sure you're not part Troll, Ulath?" Kalten asked.

"Even Trolls and Ogres can have good ideas once in a while. A cave's got a roof in case the weather turns sour, and nobody can come at you from behind. This one's a good cave, and it's been used before. Somebody spent quite a bit of time building a wall around that spring in there so that there's plenty of water."

"What if he comes back and wants his cave again?"

"I don't think he'll do that, Kalten." The big Thalesian held up a beautifully crafted flint spearhead. "He left this behind when he moved out. I'd say that he'd probably be too old to give us much to worry about—fifteen or twenty thousand years too old at least." He touched a careful thumb to the serrated edge of the spearpoint. "He did very nice work, though. He drew pictures on the wall, too—animals, mostly."

Kalten shuddered. "Wouldn't it be sort of like taking up residence in a tomb?"

"Not really. Time's all one piece, Kalten. The past is always with us. The cave served the fellow who made this spearpoint very well, and the work he left behind inclines me to trust his judgment. The place has everything we need—shelter, water, plenty of firewood nearby, and then there's that steep meadow a hundred yards off to the south, so there's plenty of forage for the horses."

"What are *we* going to eat, though? After a couple of weeks when our supplies run out, we'll be trying to boil rocks down for soup stock."

"There's game about, Sir Kalten," Khalad told him. "I've seen deer down by the river and a flock of feral goats higher up the slope."

"Goat?" Kalten made a face.

"It's better than rock soup, isn't it?"

"Sir Ulath is right, gentlemen," Bevier told them. "The cave's in a defensible position. So far as we know, the Delphae have to get close enough to touch us in order to do us any harm. Some breastworks and a well-planted field of sharpened stakes on that steep slope leading down to the river will keep them at arm's length. If Ambassador Itagne is right and the Delphae *are* pressed for time, that should encourage them to come to the bargaining table."

"Let's do it," Vanion decided. "And let's get right at it. The Delphae seem to come out at night, so we'll want some defenses in place before the sun goes down."

The overcast that had turned the sky into an oppressive leaden bowl for the past week was gone the following morning, and the autumn sunlight touching the turning leaves of the grove of aspens across the gorge from their cave filled the day with a vibrant, golden light. Everything seemed etched with a kind of preternatural clarity. The boulders in the streambed below were starkly white, and the swift-moving river was a dark, sun-illuminated green. The gorge was alive with birdsong and the chatter of scolding squirrels.

The knights continued the labor of fortification, erecting a substantial chest-high wall of loosely piled stones around the edge of the semicircular shelf that extended out from the mouth of the cave, and planting a forest of sharpened stakes on the steep slope that led down to the river.

They pastured their horses in the adjoining meadow by day and brought them inside the makeshift fort as the sun went down. They bathed and washed their clothing in the river and hunted deer and goats in the forest. They took turns standing watch at night, but there was no sign of the Delphae.

They stayed there for four nights, growing more restless with each passing hour. "If this is how the Delphae respond to something urgent, I'd hate to sit around waiting for them when they were relaxed," Talen said dryly to Itagne on the morning of the fourth day. "They don't even have anybody out there watching us."

"They're out there, Master Talen," Itagne replied confidently.

"Why haven't we seen them, then? They'd be fairly hard to miss at night."

"Not necessarily," Kalten disagreed. "I don't think they glow all the time. We saw them shining out there in that fog the first time they came to call, but the second time, they crept up to within twenty yards of us before they lit up. They seem to be able to control the light, depending on the circumstances."

"They're out there," Itagne repeated, "and the longer they wait, the better."

"I didn't follow that," Talen confessed.

"They know by this time that we're not going to move from this spot, so they're out there right now arguing among themselves about what they're going to offer us. Some of them want to offer more than the others, and the longer we just sit here, the more we strengthen the position of that faction."

"Have you suddenly become clairvoyant, Itagne?" Sephrenia asked him.

"No, Lady Sephrenia, just experienced. This delay is fairly standard in any negotiation. I'm on familiar ground now. We've chosen the right strategy."

"What else should we be doing?" Kalten asked.

"Nothing, Sir Knight. It's their move."

She came from the river in broad daylight, climbing easily up the rocky path that ascended the steep slope. She wore a grey hooded robe and simple sandals. Her features were Tamul, but she did not have the characteristic golden skin-tone of her race. She was not so much pale as she was colorless. Her eyes were grey and seemed very wise, and her hair was long and completely white, though she appeared to be scarcely more than a girl.

Sparhawk and the others watched her as she came up the hill in the golden sunlight. She crossed the steep meadow where the horses grazed. Ch'iel, Sephrenia's gentle white palfrey, approached the colorless woman curiously, and the stranger gently touched the mare's face with one slim hand.

"That's probably far enough," Vanion called to her. "What is it that you want?"

"I am Xanetia," the young woman replied. Her voice was soft, but there was a kind of echoing timbre to it that immediately identified her as one of the Delphae. "I am to be thy surety, Lord Vanion."

"You know me?"

"We know thee, Lord Vanion—and each of thy companions. Ye are reluctant to come to Delphaeus, fearing that we mean you harm. My life will serve as pledge of our good faith."

"Don't listen, Vanion," Sephrenia said, her eyes hard.

"Art thou afeared, Priestess?" Xanetia asked calmly. "Thy Goddess doth not share thy fear. Now do I perceive that it is *thy* hatred which doth obstruct that which must come to pass, and thus it shall be into *thy* hands that I shall place my life—to do with as thou wilt. If thou must needs kill me to quench this hatred of thine, then so be it."

Sephrenia's face went deathly pale. "You know I wouldn't do that, Xanetia."

"Then put the implement of death into the hands of another. Thus thou mayest command my dying and put no stain of blood upon thine own hands. Is this not the custom of thy race, Styric? Thou shalt remain undefiled—even as this thirst of thine is slaked. All unsmirched mayest thou face thy Goddess and protest thine innocence, for thou shalt be blameless. My blood shall be upon the hands of thine Elenes, and Elene souls are cheap, are they not?" She reached inside her robe and drew out a jewel-like stone dagger. "Here is the implement of my death, Sephrenia," she said. "The blade is obsidian, so thou shalt not contaminate thy hands—or thy soul—with the loathsome touch of steel when thou spillest out my life." Xanetia's voice was soft, but her words cut into Sephrenia like the hard, sharp steel she spoke of.

"I won't listen to this!" the small Styric woman declared hotly.

Xanetia smiled. "Ah, but thou wilt, Sephrenia," she said, still very calm. "I know thee well, Styric, and I know that my words have burned themselves into thy soul. Thou wilt hear them again and again. In the silence of the night shall they come to thee, burning deeper each time. Truly shalt thou listen, for my words are the words of truth, and they shall echo in thy soul all the days of thy life."

Sephrenia's face twisted in anguish, and with a sudden wail she fled back into the cave.

Itagne's face was troubled as he came back along the narrow path from the meadow to the open area in front of the cave. "She's very convincing," he told them. "I get no sense of deceit from her at all."

"She probably doesn't know enough about the real motives of the leaders of her people to have anything to hide," Bevier said dubiously. "She could very well be nothing more than a pawn."

"She *is* one of the leaders of her people, Sir Bevier," Itagne disagreed. "She's the equivalent of the crown princess of the Delphae. She's the one who'll be Anarae when the Anari dies."

"Is that a name or a title?" Ulath asked.

"It's a title. The Anari—or in Xanetia's case, the Anarae—is both the temporal and spiritual leader of the Delphae. The current Anari is named Cedon."

"She's not just making it up?" Talen asked. "She *could* be just pretending to be their crown princess, you know. That way, we'd *think* she was important, when she's actually nothing more than a shepherdess or somebody's housemaid."

"I don't think so," Itagne said. "It may sound immodest, but I don't really believe anyone can lie to me for very long and get away with it. She says that she's the one who'll be Anarae, and I believe her. The move's consistent with standard diplomatic practice. Hostages *have* to be important. It's another indication of just how desperate the Delphae are in this business. I think Xanetia's telling the truth, and if she is, she's the most precious thing they possess." He made a wry face. "It definitely goes against everything I've been trained to believe about the Shining Ones since childhood, but I think we almost have to trust them this time."

Sparhawk and Vanion looked at each other. "What do you think?" Vanion asked.

"I don't see that we've got much choice, do you?"

"Not really. Ulath was right. We can't sit here all winter, and no matter which way we turn, we keep going toward Delphaeus. The fact that Xanetia's here is *some* assurance of good faith."

"Is it enough, though?"

"It's probably going to have to be, Sparhawk. I don't think we're going to get anything better."

"Kalten!" Sephrenia exclaimed. "No!"

"Somebody has to do it," the blond knight replied stubbornly. "Good faith has to go both ways." He looked Xanetia full in the face. "Is there something you'd like to tell me before I help you up onto that horse?" he asked her. "Some warning, maybe?"

"Thou art brave, Sir Kalten," she replied.

"It's what they pay me for." He shrugged. "Will I dissolve if I touch you?"

"No."

"All right. You've never ridden a horse before, have you?"

"We do not keep horses. We seldom leave our valley, so we have little need of them."

"They're fairly nice animals. Be a little careful of the one Sparhawk rides, though. He bites. Now, this horse is a pack animal. He's fairly old and sensible, so he won't waste energy jumping around and being silly. Don't worry too much about the reins. He's used to following along after the others, so you don't have to steer him. If you want him to go faster, nudge him in the ribs with your heels. If you want him to slow down, pull back on the reins a little bit. If you want him to stop, pull back a little harder. That packsaddle's not going to be very comfortable, so let us know if you start getting stiff and sore. We'll stop and get off and walk for a while. You'll get used to it after a few days—if we've got that far to travel."

She held out her hands, crossed at the wrist. "Wilt thou bind me now, Sir Knight?"

"What for?"

"I am thy prisoner."

"Don't be silly. You won't be able to hold on if your hands are tied." He set his jaw, reached out, and took her by the waist. Then he lifted her easily up onto the patient packhorse. Then he held out his hands and looked at them. "So far so good," he said. "At least my fingernails haven't fallen off. I'll be right beside you, so if you feel yourself starting to slip, let me know."

"We always underestimate him," Vanion murmured to Sparhawk. "There's a lot more to him than meets the eye, isn't there?"

"Kalten? Oh, yes, my Lord. Kalten can be very complicated sometimes."

They rode away from their fortified cave and followed the gorge the river had cut down through the rock. Sparhawk and Vanion led the way with Kalten and their hostage riding close behind them. Sephrenia, her face coldly set, rode at the rear with Berit, keeping as much distance as possible between herself and Xanetia.

"Is it very far?" Kalten asked the pale woman at his side. "I mean, how many days will it take us to get there?"

"The distance is indeterminate, Sir Kalten," Xanetia replied, "and the time as well. The Delphae are outcast and despised. We would be unwise to make the location of the valley of Delphaeus widely known."

"We're used to traveling, Lady," Kalten told her, "and we always pay attention to landmarks. If you take us to Delphaeus, we'll be able to find it again. All we'd have to do is find that cave and start from there."

"That is the flaw in thy plan, Sir Knight," she said gently. "Thou couldst consume a lifetime in the search for that cave. It is our wont to conceal the approaches to Delphaeus rather than Delphaeus itself."

"It's a little hard to conceal a whole mountain range, isn't it?"

"We noted that selfsame thing ourselves, Sir Kalten," she replied without so much as a smile, "so we conceal the sky instead. Without the sun to guide thee, thou art truly lost."

"Could *you* do that, Sparhawk?" Kalten raised his voice slightly. "Could you make the whole sky overcast like that?"

"Could we?" Sparhawk asked Vanion.

"*I* couldn't. Maybe Sephrenia could, but under the circumstances it might not be a good idea to ask her. I know enough to know that it's against the rules, though. We're not supposed to play around with the weather."

"We do not in truth cloud the sky, Lord Vanion," Xanetia assured him. "We cloud thine eyes instead. We can, an we choose, make others see what we wish them to see."

"Please, Anarae," Ulath said with a pained look, "don't go into too much detail. You'll bring on one of those tedious debates about illusion and reality, and I really hate those."

They rode on with the now-unobscured sun clearly indicating their line of travel. They were moving somewhat northeasterly.

Kalten watched their prisoner—or captor—closely, and he called halts somewhat more frequently than he might normally have done. When they stopped, he helped the strange pale woman down from her horse and walked beside her as they continued on foot, leading their horses.

"Thou art overly solicitous of my comfort, Sir Kalten," she gently chided him.

"Oh, it's not for you, Lady," he lied. "The going's a bit steep here, and we don't want to exhaust the horses."

"There's *definitely* more to Kalten than I'd realized," Vanion muttered to Sparhawk.

"You can spend a whole lifetime watching somebody, my friend, and you still won't learn everything there is to know about him."

"What an astonishingly acute perception," Vanion said dryly.

"Be nice," Sparhawk murmured.

Sparhawk was troubled. While Xanetia was certainly not as skilled as Aphrael, it was clear that she was tampering with time and distance in the same way the Child-Goddess did. If she had maintained the illusion of an overcast sky, he might not have noticed, but the position of the sun clearly indicated that there were gaps in his perception of time; the sun does not normally jump as it moves across the sky. The troubling fact was not that Xanetia did it badly, but the fact that she did it at all. Sparhawk began to revise a long-held opinion. This "tampering" was obviously not a purely divine capability. Itagne's rather sketchy discourse on the Delphae had contained at least *some* elements of truth. There was indeed such a thing as "Delphaeic magic," and so far as Sparhawk could tell, it went further and into areas where Styrics were unable or unwilling to venture.

He kept his eyes open, but did not mention his observations to his friends.

And then, on a perfect autumn evening when the birds clucked and murmured sleepily in the trees and a luminous twilight turned the mountains purple around them, they rode up a narrow, rocky trail that wound around massive boulders toward a V-shaped notch high above. Xanetia had been most insistent that they not stop for the night, and she and Kalten had pressed on ahead. Her normally placid face seemed somehow alight with anticipation.

When she and her protector reached the top of the trail, they stopped and sat their horses, starkly outlined against the last rosy vestiges of the sunset.

"Dear God!" Kalten exclaimed. "Sparhawk, come up and look at this!"

Sparhawk and Vanion rode on up to join them.

There was a valley below, a steep, basinlike mountain valley with dark trees shrouding the slopes. There were houses down there, close-packed houses with candlelighted windows and with columns of pale blue smoke rising straight up into the evening air from innumerable chimneys. The fact that there was a fair-sized town this deep in the inaccessible mountains was surprising enough, but Sparhawk and the others were not looking at the town.

In the very center of the valley, there was a small lake. There was, of course, nothing unusual about that. Lakes abound in mountains in all parts of the world. The spring runoff from melting snow inevitably seeks valleys and basins—any place that is lower than the surrounding terrain and from which there is no exit channel. It was not the fact that the lake was there that was so surprising. The thing that startled them and raised those vestigial hackles of superstitious awe along the backs of their necks was the fact that the lake glowed in the lowering twilight. The light was not the sickly, greenish glow of the phosphorescence that is sometimes exuded by rotting vegetable matter, but was instead a clear, steady white. Like a lost moon, the lake glowed, responding to the light of her new-risen sister standing above the eastern horizon.

"Behold Delphaeus," Xanetia said simply, and when they looked at her, they saw that she, too, was all aglow with a pure white light that seemed to come from within her and that shone through her garment and through her skin itself as if that pale, unwavering light were coming from her very soul.

CHAPTER FOURTEEN

Sparhawk's senses were preternaturally acute for some reason, although his mind seemed detached and emotionless. He observed; he heard; he catalogued; but he felt nothing. The peculiar state was not an unfamiliar one, but the circumstances under which this profound calm had come over him *were* unusual—very unusual. There were no armed men facing him, and yet his mind and body were preparing for battle.

Faran tensed, bunching his muscles, and the sound of his steel-shod hooves altered very slightly, becoming somehow more crisp, more deliberate. Sparhawk touched the big roan's neck with one hand. "Relax," he murmured. "I'll let you know when the time comes."

Faran shuddered, absently flicking his master's reassurance off like a bothersome insect and continuing his cautious pace.

Vanion looked at his friend questioningly.

"Faran's being a little sensitive, my Lord."

"Sensitive? That ill-tempered brute?"

"Faran doesn't really deserve that reputation, Vanion. When you get right down to it, he's a good-natured horse. He tries very hard to please me. We've been together for so long that he knows what I'm feeling most of the time, and he goes out of his way to match his attitude to mine. *I'm* the one who's the ill-tempered brute, but he gets all the blame. He behaves like a puppy when Aphrael's riding on his back."

"Are you feeling belligerent just now?"

"I don't like being led around by the nose, but it's nothing specific. You've overtrained me, Vanion. Any time anything unusual comes up, I start getting ready for war. Faran can feel that, so he does the same."

Xanetia and Kalten were leading them across the meadow that sloped down toward the glowing lake and the strangely alien town nestled on the near shore. The pale Delphaeic woman still glowed with that eerie light. The radiance surrounding her seemed to Sparhawk's heightened senses to be almost a kind of aura, a mark more of a special kind of grace rather than a loathsome contamination.

"It's all one building, did you notice that?" Talen was saying to his brother. "It looks like any other city from a distance, but when you get closer, you start to see that the houses are all connected together."

Khalad grunted. "It's a stupid idea," he said. "A fire could burn out the whole town."

"The buildings are made of stone. They won't burn."

"But the roofs are thatch, and thatch *will* burn. It's a bad idea."

Delphaeus had no separate wall as such. The outermost houses, all interconnected, turned their backs to the world, facing inward with their windowless rear walls presented to the outside. Sparhawk and the others followed Xanetia through a large, deep archway into the city. There was a peculiar fragrance about Delphaeus, a scent of new-mown hay. The streets were narrow and twisting, and they frequently ran *through* the buildings, passing under heavy arches into vaulted corridors that emerged again on the far side. As Talen had noted, Delphaeus was all one building, and what would have been called streets in another town were simply unroofed hallways here.

The citizens did not avoid their party, but they made no particular effort to approach. Like pale ghosts they drifted through the shadowy maze.

"No torches," Berit noted, looking around.

"No need," Ulath grunted.

"Truly," the young knight agreed. "Notice how it changes the smell of the place? Even Chyrellos always reeks of burning pitch—even in the daytime. It's a little strange to be in a city that doesn't have that greasy smoke clinging to everything."

"I don't think the world at large is ready for self-illuminating people yet, Berit. It's an idea that probably won't catch on—particularly in view of the drawbacks attached to it."

"Where are we going, Lady?" Kalten asked the pale, glowing woman at his side. Kalten's situation was a peculiar one. He guarded and protected Xanetia. He was solicitous about her comfort and well-being. He *would*, however, be the one who would kill her at the first sign of hostility from her people.

"We go to the quarters of the Anari," Xanetia replied. "It is he who must place our proposal before Anakha. Anakha holds the keys to Bhelliom, and only he can command it."

"You could have saved the rest of us a lot of trouble and made this trip alone, Sparhawk," Talen said lightly.

"Maybe, but it's always nice to have company. Besides, if you hadn't come along, you'd have missed all the fun. Look at how entertaining it was to jump off that cliff and lounge around in midair with about a thousand feet of absolute emptiness under you."

"I've been trying very hard to forget about that, my lord," the boy replied with a pained expression.

·   ·   ·

They dismounted in one of those vaulted corridors near the center of the city and turned their horses over to several young Delphae. The young men looked to Sparhawk like goatherds who had been pressed into service as stableboys. Then they followed the glowing woman to a dark-stained door, worn with centuries of use. Sparhawk, still in the grip of that emotionless calm, looked carefully at Xanetia. She was not much bigger than Sephrenia, and, although she was clearly a woman and quite an attractive one, that fact somehow had no meaning. Xanetia's gender seemed irrelevant. She opened the worn door and led them into a hallway with deeply inset doorways piercing the walls at widely spaced intervals. The hallway was lighted by glass globes hanging on long chains from the vaulted ceiling, globes filled with a glowing liquid—water drawn from the lake, Sparhawk surmised.

At the far end of the corridor, Xanetia paused in front of one of the doors, and her eyes grew distant for a moment. "Cedon bids us to enter," she said after a brief pause. She opened the door and, with Kalten close behind her, she led them into the chambers beyond. "The hall of Cedon, Anari of the Delphae," she told them in that peculiarly echoing voice that seemed to be one of the characteristics of her race.

Three worn stone steps led down into the central chamber, a tidy room with vaulted ceilings supported by low, heavy arches. The slightly inwardly curving walls were covered with white plaster, and the low, heavy furniture was upholstered with snowy lamb's wool. A small fire burned in an arched fireplace at the far end of the room, and more of those glowing globes hung from the ceiling.

Sparhawk felt like a crude, barbaric intruder here. Cedon's home reflected a gentle, saintly nature, and the big Pandion was acutely conscious of his chain-mail shirt and the heavy broadsword belted at his waist. He felt bulky and out of place, and his companions, wrapped in steel and leather and rough, grey cloth, seemed to loom around him like the crude monoliths of an ancient and primitive culture.

A very old man entered from the far side of the room. He was frail and bent, and his shuffling steps were aided by a long staff. His hair was wispy and snowy white, in his case the mark of extreme age rather than a racial characteristic. In addition to his unbleached wool robe, he wore a kind of shawl about his thin shoulders.

Xanetia went to him immediately, touching his wrinkled old face with a gentle hand. Her eyes were full of concern for him, but she did not speak.

"Well met, Sir Knights," the old man greeted them. He spoke in only slightly accented Elenic, and his voice sounded thin and rusty as if he seldom had occasion to speak at all. "And welcome to thee as well, dear sister," he added, speaking to Sephrenia in nearly flawless, though archaic, Styric.

"I am not your sister, old man," she said, her face cold.

"We are all brothers and sisters, Sephrenia of Ylara, High Priestess of Aphrael. Our kinship lies in our common humanity."

"That may have been true once, Delphae," she replied in a voice like ice, "but you and your accursed race are no longer human."

He sighed. "Perhaps not. It is hard to say precisely what we are—or what we will become. Put aside thine enmity, Sephrenia of Ylara. Thou wilt come to no harm in this place, and for once, our purposes merge into one. Thou wouldst set us apart from the rest of mankind, and that is now also *our* desire. May we not join our efforts to achieve this end?"

She turned her back on him.

Itagne, ever the diplomat, stepped in to fill the awkward gap. "Cedon, I presume?" he said urbanely.

The old man nodded.

"I find Delphaeus puzzling, revered one, I must confess it. We Tamuls know virtually nothing about your people, and yet the Delphae have been central to a grossly affected genre in our literature. I've always felt that this so-called 'Delphaeic literature' had been spun out of whole cloth by third-rate poets with diseased imaginations. Now I come to Delphaeus and find that all manner of things I had believed to be literary conceits have more than a little basis in fact." Itagne was smooth, there was no question about that. His assertion that he was even more clever than his brother, the foreign minister, was probably quite true.

The Anari smiled faintly. "We did what we could, Itagne of Matherion. I will grant thee that the verse is execrable and the sentimentality appalling, but 'Xadane' did serve the purpose for which it was created. It softened and turned aside certain of the antagonisms the Styrics had planted in your society. The Tamuls control the Atans, and we did not wish a confrontation with our towering neighbors. I cringe to confess it to thee, but I myself played no small part in the composition of 'Xadane.' "

Itagne blinked. "Cedon, are we talking abut the same poem? The 'Xadane' *I* studied as a schoolboy was written about seven hundred years ago."

"Has it been so long? Where *do* the years go? I did enjoy my stay in fire-domed Matherion. The university was stimulating."

Itagne was too well-trained to show his astonishment. "Your features are Tamul, Cedon, but didn't your coloration seem . . . odd?"

"Ye Tamuls are far too civilized to make an issue of deformity. My racial characteristics were simply taken to mean that I was an albino. The condition is not unheard of. I had a colleague—a Styric—who had a clubfoot. Rather surprisingly, we got on well together. I note from thy speech that contemporary Tamul hath changed from what it was when I was last among thy people. That would make it difficult for me to return to Matherion. Please accept my apologies for 'Xadane.' It is truly abominable, but as I say, it served its purpose."

"I should have known," Sephrenia cut in. "The whole body of Delphaeic literature was created with the sole purpose of fostering a climate of anti-Styric bigotry."

"And what was the purpose of the eons of outright falsehood with which ye Styrics deceived the Tamuls?" Cedon demanded. "Was the design not precisely the same? Did ye not seek to instill the idea in the Tamul perception that the Delphae are subhuman?"

Sephrenia ignored the question. "Does your hatred of us run so deep that you would contaminate the understanding of an entire race?"

"And how deeply doth *thy* hatred run, Sephrenia of Ylara? Art thou not even now attempting to poison the minds of these simple Elenes against us?" The Anari sank into a cushioned chair, passing one weary hand across his face. "Our mutual hatreds have gone, methinks, too far to be healed. Better far that we live apart. And that doth bring us to the issue which hath brought us together. It is our wish to be apart from all others."

"Because you're so much better than the rest of us?" Sephrenia's tone was thick with contempt.

"Not better, Priestess, only different. We will leave *that* puffed-up sense of superiority to *thy* race."

"If you two want to renew a few eons-old hatreds, I think the rest of us would prefer not to sit through it," Vanion said coolly. "You both seem quite able to manage without our help."

"You don't know what they've done, Vanion," Sephrenia said with a mute appeal in her eyes.

"Frankly, dear, I'm not really interested in what happened several thousand years ago. If you want to chew old soup, please do it on your own time." Vanion looked at the ancient Delphae. "I believe you had some kind of an exchange in mind, Cedon. We'd love to sit around and watch you and Sephrenia slice each other into thin strips, but we're a little pressed for time. Affairs of state, you understand."

Even Sparhawk choked a bit on that.

"Thou art very blunt, Lord Vanion," Cedon said in a coldly reproving tone.

"I'm a soldier, revered Anari. A conversation made up of spiteful little insults bores me. If you and Sephrenia really want to fight, use axes."

"Have you had many occasions to deal with Elenes, revered Anari?" Itagne asked in an unruffled manner.

"Almost none."

"You might consider offering up a few prayers of thanksgiving for that. The Elenes have this distressing tendency to get right to the point. It's dreadfully uncivilized, of course, but it *does* save time. I believe you wanted to address your proposal to Anakha. That's him right there. I should probably warn you that Lord Vanion is the absolute soul of finesse when compared to Sparhawk, but Sparhawk is Anakha, so sooner or later you're going to have a deal with him."

"Since we've all decided to be unpleasant this evening, I don't think we'll get very far," Sparhawk said. "Why don't you tell me what you want, Cedon, and what you're prepared to offer in return? I'll think it over tonight, and then we can talk about it tomorrow, after we've had time to get a firmer grip on our civility."

"A wise course, perhaps, Anakha," the old man agreed. "There is turmoil afoot in Tamuli."

"Yes. We've noticed that."

"The turmoil is not directed at the empire, Anakha, but at *thee*. Thou were lured here because thou hast the keys to Bhelliom. Thine enemies covet the jewel."

"We know that, too. I don't really need a preamble, Cedon. What's the point of this?"

"We will aid thee in thy struggle, and I do assure thee that without our aid, thou canst not prevail."

"You'll have to convince me of that, but we can talk about it some other time. What do you want in return?"

"We would have thee take up Bhelliom and seal us in this valley."

"That's all?"

"That is all we ask. Put us beyond the reach of all others, and put all others beyond *our* reach. All will be served by this—Elene and Tamul, Styric and Delphae.

Use the infinite power of Bhelliom to set us apart from the rest of mankind so that we may continue our journey undisturbed."

"Journey?"

"A figure of speech, Anakha. Our journey is measured in generations, not in leagues."

"An even exchange, then? You'll help us to deal with our enemies if I close off this valley so that no one can ever get in—or out?"

"An even exchange, Anakha."

"All right. I'll think about it."

"She won't talk to me about it, Sparhawk," Vanion sighed, "or about anything else, for that matter." The silvery-haired preceptor and his friend were speaking privately in a small room just off the corridor that led to the cluster of tiny, cell-like rooms where they had spent the night.

"You *were* just a bit blunt last night," Sparhawk told him.

"Irrational behavior irritates me. I wish Aphrael were here. She could straighten Sephrenia out in fairly short order."

Sparhawk slid lower in his chair. "I'm not so sure, Vanion. I don't know if I'm supposed to tell you this, but I get the feeling that Aphrael wouldn't interfere. Before she left, she told me that Sephrenia has to work this out for herself."

"Could Itagne shed any light on this antagonism between the Styrics and the Delphae?"

Sparhawk shook his head. "No more than he's already told us. The whole business seems to date back to the time of the war with the Cyrgai. That was about ten thousand years ago, so history's a little vague about what really happened. Evidently the Styrics and the Delphae were allies, and there seems to have been a betrayal of some sort."

"I gathered as much. Can Itagne make any guesses about who was betrayed?"

"No. The Styrics have made themselves useful to the Tamuls over the centuries—as they made themselves useful to the Church in Eosia. They've been busy insinuating *their* version of what happened into the Tamul perception of history. From what Cedon told us last night, I'd say that the Delphae have infiltrated the University of Matherion and inserted Delphaeic literature into the Tamul culture with precisely the same idea. The events of ten thousand years ago are going to be buried under a thick layer of myth and legend anyway, and with both the Styrics and the Delphae busily muddying up the waters, the real truth probably won't ever come out into the open." He smiled faintly. "I'm not sure how significant it is, but the Styrics tried to contaminate the historians, while the Delphae spent their time trying to contaminate the poets. Interesting contrast, wouldn't you say?"

"Aphrael would know the truth."

"Probably, but she's not talking. I know her well enough to know that her silence is deliberate. I don't think she really wants us to know who was originally at fault. She doesn't seem to want us to take sides, for some reason, and that puts us in a very difficult position. I wonder if we'll ever find out the truth behind this racial antagonism—not that it really matters. I doubt if Sephrenia or the Anari themselves even know. They've both had about four hundred generations of hysterical propaganda to set their prejudices in stone. *Our* problem is that the Delphae can probably hold us here indefinitely. If we try to ride away, they'll just turn us around and lead us right back, so eventually we're going to have to negotiate with them. We all love Sephrenia, though, so if we *do* negotiate with the Delphae, she'll take fire spontaneously."

"Yes, I noticed that. What am I going to do, Sparhawk? I bleed when she so much as pricks her finger."

"Lie to her." Sparhawk shrugged.

"Sparhawk!"

"You don't have to be too obvious about it, but lean your neutrality slightly in her direction. *I'm* the one in charge of Bhelliom, so Cedon's going to have to deal with *me*. Technically, you're secondary here—sorry, Vanion, but it's true. Cedon's going to be negotiating with me, not you. Glare at me now and then and raise objections. Sephrenia's behaving irrationally, so the others, like good, logical Elenes, are going to oppose her. Let's not isolate her entirely. You're the most important person in her life, and if *you* seem to be turning against her as well, you'll break her heart." He smiled a bit wryly. "I'd take it as a personal favor, though, if you didn't let her turn me into a toad about midway through the negotiations."

"Let's go back a step or two, revered Anari," Sparhawk suggested when they had gathered again in the large, sunken room. "I need to know what I'm getting involved in here. I'm *not* going to do anything to injure the Styrics. They're sometimes a prickly and difficult people, but we've grown fond of them for some reason." He smiled at Sephrenia, hoping to soften her displeasure. "You mentioned a journey of some sort. Where are you going?"

"We are changing, Anakha. When the world turned against us, we appealed to Edaemus to protect us."

"Your God?"

The Anari nodded. "We were a childlike, unsophisticated people before the war with the Cyrgai, and Edaemus lived among us, sharing our simple joys and transient sorrows. Of all the people of this world, we were the least suited for war." The old man looked at Sephrenia. "I will not offend thy teacher by speaking the truth about what led to our being made outcast."

"The truth is well known," Sephrenia said stiffly.

"Yes, it is, but *thy* truth is quite different from *ours*. You believe that one thing happened, and we believe that something else took place. But that, Sephrenia of Ylara, is between us, and it doth not concern these Elenes. In truth, Lady, neither Styric *nor* Delphae were very admirable in that unfortunate affair. For whatever cause, Anakha, the Delphae were cast out, and the hands of all men were turned against us. We appealed, as I said, to Edaemus, and he responded by laying a curse on us."

"This Edaemus of yours has a peculiar way of showing his affection," Ulath noted.

"It was the only way to protect us, Sir Knight. We are not warlike and have no skill with the weapons with which other men kill each other, and so Edaemus cursed us to make our merest touch a weapon. Other men soon found that the touch of our hands meant death."

"Then why am I still here, Cedon?" Kalten asked. "I've been helping Xanetia on and off her horse for several days now, and her touch hasn't killed *me*."

"We have learned to control the curse, Sir Kalten. That was a part of the plan of Edaemus when he raised his hand against our lake."

"The lake?"

The Anari nodded. "Edaemus could not bear the thought of laying his curse upon us directly, and so he cursed the waters of the lake instead. The lake is our only source of water, and we therefore must drink of it. When first we came to this valley, the mind of Edaemus was as childlike as ours. In the spirit of play gave he the waters of the lake that peculiar essence which doth illuminate us. We drink of the lake, and its waters infuse our bodies. Out of love did Edaemus make us appear like Gods. It was a harmless entertainment, and we soon forgave him for so altering us. When the world turned against us, however, did Edaemus curse the lake; and its infusing waters, changed by that curse, changed us as well. The touch of death which doth hold our enemies at bay is but a small part of the design of our God, however. Circumstance hath set us apart from this world, and it is the intent of Edaemus to set us yet further apart. We are changing, my friends. Our bodies are different, and our minds and spirits as well. We are no longer as ye—nor as once we were. With each generation this inexorable change progresses. Xanetia, dear, gentle Xanetia, so far surpasseth me that I cannot even begin to comprehend the extent of her thought. In time, methinks, she will equal—or even surpass—the very Gods themselves."

"And then you will supplant us," Sephrenia accused. "Even as the Trolls supplanted the Dawn-men and as we are supplanting the Trolls, so will you despised Delphae become our masters, putting aside our Gods and kenneling us like dogs in uninhabitable wastelands while *you* enjoy the fruits of the earth. We Styrics have endured such treatment at the hands of the Elenes for eons and we have learned much. You will not so easily subdue us, Cedon, and we will not worship you nor fawn at your feet like whipped dogs."

"How may we supplant thee and seize thy lands, Sephrenia of Ylara? We are bound to our lake and may not long be away from its waters. Thy submission, moreover, would have no meaning for us, for we will not be here. We journey toward the light, and we will *become* light. My Xanetia, who will be Anarae, could join with the light even now, but those of us who have not yet reached her perfection hold her back. When we are dead, there will no longer be any reason for her to remain, and she will lead the Delphae out to dwell among the stars with Edaemus, who hath gone before us to prepare our home."

"Where you will be Gods," Sephrenia added with a spiteful sneer.

"That is a word without meaning, Sephrenia of Ylara," Xanetia said quietly. "All of us, Gods *and* men, move toward the same goal. Edaemus hath gone before us, and we will go before thee. We will await thy coming with love, and we will even forgive thee for the wrong that thou hast done us."

"*Forgive me?*" Sephrenia exploded. "I spurn thy condescending forgiveness!" She had lapsed, probably without realizing it, into archaic Styric. "I will *never* forgive thee nor accept any of *thy* forgiveness."

"But thou wilt, Sephrenia," the glowing woman disagreed. "Even now is thine heart doubtful within thy breast. Thou art of two minds, gentle Sephrenia. I know thee well, and I know that this hatred of thine, like winter frost, doth lurk in the dark, shaded places of thy soul. I do assure thee that it will melt in the warm sun of thy loving nature—even as mine own hatred doth even now begin its painful thaw. But make no mistake, Sephrenia of Ylara, I do hate Styrics even as thou hatest the Delphae. An hundred centuries of enmity is not lightly cast aside. I do *hate* the perfidious Styrics, but I do *not* hate thee. I know thine heart, dear sister, for it is even as mine own. In time will we both put aside this childish hatred and live together in peace."

"*Never!*"

"Never, dear sister, is a long, long time."

"I think we're getting a little far afield here," Sparhawk cut in. "This sealing up of the valley isn't intended to be eternal, I gather?"

"There would be no need of that, Anakha," the Anari replied. "Once we are gone, Edaemus will lift his curse from the lake, its waters will return to normal, and other men may freely come to this valley without fear."

"I should probably tell you that if I seal the valley with Bhelliom, I *will* seal it. I can guarantee you that no Delphae will ever leave. If you're going to turn into moonbeams or sunlight, that won't inconvenience you, but if you've got some other notion hidden away, you might as well forget it. And if this Edaemus of yours has a secret agenda involving some sort of retaliation against the Styrics, you'd better tell him to drop it. Bhelliom eats Gods for breakfast—as Azash found out. Do you *still* want me to seal your valley?"

"Yes," Cedon replied without hesitation.

"How about you, Sephrenia?" Sparhawk asked. "Would that kind of guarantee satisfy you?"

"They'll try trickery, Sparhawk. They're a deceitful race."

"You know the Bhelliom, Sephrenia—probably even better than I do. Do you *really* think anybody—man *or* God—could trick it? If I tell it to keep the Delphae in and everybody else out, *nobody's* going to cross the line—not you, not me, not Aphrael, not Edaemus—not even the God of the Elenes. Even if all the Gods of this world and of all other worlds combined, Bhelliom would *still* keep them out. If I seal this valley, it will *stay* sealed. Even the birds and angleworms won't be able to leave. Will that satisfy you?"

She refused to look at him.

"I need an answer, little mother, and I'd rather not have to wait all year to get it. Will it satisfy you?"

"You're hateful, Sparhawk!"

"I've got a lot on my mind just now. Think it over and let me know what you decide." He turned to face the Anari. "All right, now I know what you want. The next question is what's in it for me? What do *I* get out of this arrangement?"

"Our assistance in thy struggle with thine enemies, Anakha."

"That's a little unspecific, Cedon. I've got the Bhelliom. What can you possibly do for me that I can't do for myself?"

"Thou must have the cooperation of the jewel, Anakha. Thou canst compel the stone, but it loves thee not, and it doth sometimes deliberately misunderstand thee—as when it took thee and the Child-Goddess to Demos when thou sought to go to Delo in Arjuna."

"How did you know about that?" Sparhawk was startled.

"Thy mind is open to me, Anakha, as are all minds. This is but one of the services we can offer thee. Would it not be to thine advantage to know what those about thee are thinking?"

"It would indeed, Cedon, but there are other ways to wrest the truth from men's hearts."

"But men who have been put to the torture know that they have been tortured, and they know what they have revealed unto thee. Our way is more subtle."

"He's got a point there, Sparhawk," Kalten said. "What am *I* thinking right now, Cedon?"

"Thou art troubled by the duty to slay Xanetia should our people play thee false, Sir Knight. Thy mind is gently inclined toward her."

"He's right about that," Kalten admitted to the others. "I think these people *can* hear what others are thinking."

"We have other capabilities as well, Sir Knights," the Anari told them, "and we freely offer them to thee in exchange for what we ask." He looked rather sadly at Sephrenia. "I fear that when I reveal the nature of these capabilities, it will cause thee pain and harden thine heart yet more toward us, dear sister."

"*Will* you stop calling me that? My heart is already like granite toward you and your kind."

"That is not true, Sephrenia of Ylara," Xanetia disagreed. "Thou art troubled forasmuch as thou hast found no wickedness in us in this, thy first meeting with our kind. Hard put art thou to maintain an hatred which groweth more from thy sense of duty to thy kindred than from any personal rancor. I do freely confess mine own similarly troubled state. I am inclined to love thee, even as thou art so inclined toward me."

"Stop that!" Sephrenia burst out. "Keep your unclean hands out of my thoughts.

"Stubborn, isn't she?" Ulath murmured.

"It is the nature of the Younger Gods of Styricum to protect their children—even from their own folly," the Anari noted. "Thus it is that the Styrics must appeal to their Gods with spells and prayers for aid when they would step beyond the powers of other men. Is it not so, Sephrenia of Ylara?"

She refused to answer him.

"That's the core of Styric magic, Cedon," Vanion replied for her.

She glared at him, and Sparhawk silently groaned. Why *couldn't* Vanion keep his mouth shut?

The Anari nodded. "Edaemus hath, as I say, gone before us to prepare the way, and he is therefore no longer able to watch over us. Thus hath he granted certain of us the power to do what must be done *without* his guidance."

"Unrestrained magic?" Sephrenia exclaimed. "You hold the power of the Gods in your *own* hands with no restraints?"

"Some few of us, yes."

"That's monstrous! The human mind isn't capable of understanding the nature of that kind of power. We can't grasp the consequences of unleashing it to satisfy our childish whims."

"Thy Goddess hath instructed thee well, Sephrenia of Ylara," Xanetia noted. "This is what she *wishes* thee to believe."

"Thy Goddess would keep thee a child, dear sister," the Anari said. "For so long as thou art a child, she is secure in thy love. I tell thee truly, however, Edaemus doth love us even as thine Aphrael doth love thee. His love, however, doth compel us to grow. He hath placed his power in our hands, and we must accept the consequences of our acts when we bring it to bear. It is a different kind of love, but it is love nonetheless. Edaemus is no longer here to guide us, so we can do whatever our minds are able to conceive." The Anari smiled gently. "Forgive me, my friends," he said to them, "but one as old as I hath but one peculiar interest." He held up one withered old hand and looked at it rather sadly. "How soon are we altered by the passing of years, and how distressing is the alteration."

The change seemed gradual, but considering the staggering nature of that change, what was happening before their eyes was nearly miraculous. The withered hand grew more firm-fleshed; the knobby joints smoothed; and the wrinkles faded. It was not only the hand, however. The tracery of wrinkles and lines on Cedon's face seemed to slide away. His hollow cheeks filled out, and his thin, wispy hair grew fuller, more abundant. They stared at him as, with no apparent effort, he reversed the erosion of years. He regressed to vigorous youth, his skin clear and his hand and face firm and unmarked. Then, he began to diminish, his limbs shrinking inside his garments. The prickly stubble vanished from his cheeks and chin, and, as he continued to regress, his head seemed to grow larger in proportion to his shrinking body. "That might be far enough," he said in a piping, childish voice. He smiled, a strangely ancient smile that looked very much out of place on that little boy's face. "A miscalculation here might reduce me to nothing. In truth, I have considered that, but my tasks and responsibilities are not yet completed. Xanetia has her own tasks, and I would not yet burden her with mine as well."

Sparhawk swallowed hard. "I think you've made your point, Cedon," he said in a strained voice. "We'll accept the fact that you can do things that we can't do." He looked around at his friends. "I can already see arguments brewing," he told them, deliberately avoiding Sephrenia's eyes, "and no matter what we decide, we'll probably all have serious doubts about it."

"We could pray," Bevier suggested.

"Or roll dice and let them decide," Ulath added.

"Not with *your* dice, we couldn't," Kalten objected.

"We could even fall back on logic," Vanion concluded, "but Sparhawk's right. No matter how we try to decide, we could probably sit here all winter and still not agree." He also avoided Sephrenia's eyes.

"All right, then," Sparhawk said, reaching inside his tunic, "since Aphrael's not here to bully us into agreement, we'll let Bhelliom decide." He took out the golden box and set it on the table in front of him.

"*Sparhawk!*" Sephrenia gasped.

"No, Anakha!" Xanetia also exclaimed.

"Bhelliom doesn't love any of us," he said, "so we can sort of rely on its neutrality. We need guidance here, and neither Edaemus nor Aphrael is around to provide it—besides which, I don't know that I'd trust either of them anyway, given the peculiar circumstances here. We want an uncontaminated opinion, so why don't we just find out what Bhelliom thinks about the situation?"

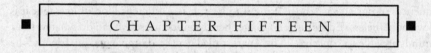

CHAPTER FIFTEEN

"Blue-Rose," Sparhawk said in Trollish to the glowing jewel in his hands, "I am Anakha. Do you know me?"

Bhelliom's glow pulsed slightly, and Sparhawk could sense the stone's stiff reluctance to acknowledge his dominion. Then he thought of something. "You and I need to talk," he said, speaking in Elenic this time, "and I don't think Khwaj and the others need to be listening. Can you understand me when I speak in this fashion?"

There was the faintest hint of curiosity in the pulse this time.

"Good. Is there some way you can talk to me? There's something you and I have to decide. This is too important for me to simply force you to do what I want, because I could be wrong. I know you're none too fond of me—or of any creature on this particular world—but I think that we may have some common interest this time."

"Let me go." The voice was a kind of lingering whisper, but it was familiar. Sparhawk whirled around to stare at Kalten. His boyhood friend's face was wooden, uncomprehending, and the words came stiffly from his lips. "Why hast thou done this thing, Anakha? Why hast thou enslavèd me?" The archaic Elenic could not have come from Kalten, but why had Bhelliom chosen this most unlikely mouth?

Sparhawk carefully readjusted his thoughts, casting them in the profoundly formal language with which the stone had addressed him, and in the instant of that changeover, perception and understanding came. It somehow seemed that knowledge had lain dormant in his mind until unlocked by this peculiar key. Strangely, his understanding had been bound up in language, and once he made the conscious shift from contemporary Elenic with all its casual imprecision to more stately and concise cadences, that previously closed part of his mind opened. "It was not I who enslavèd thee, Blue-Rose. It was thine own inattention that brought thee into such perilous proximity to the red of iron which congealed thee into thy present state, and it was Ghwerig who lifted thee from the earth and contorted thee into this similitude of a flower with his cruel diamond implements."

A stifled groan came from Kalten's lips, a groan of pain endured and pain remembered.

"I am Anakha, Blue-Rose," Sparhawk continued. "I am *thy* creature. It is *thou* who hast causèd me to be, that I might be the instrument of thy liberation, and I will not betray thy trust in me. I am in some part made of *thy* thought, and I am therefore thy servant. It is thou who hast enslavèd *me*. Didst thou not set my destiny apart, making me a stranger to the Gods of this world and to all other men? But, though I am thine enslavèd servant, I am, nonetheless, still of *this* world, and I will not have it destroyed nor its people crushed by the vile oppression of mine enemies. I did free thee from the enslavement of Ghwerig, did I not? Is this not in some small measure proof of my fidelity to the task which thou hast lain upon me? And, bound together in common purpose, did we not destroy Azash, who would have chained us both in a slavery harsher than that which now chains us together? For mistake me not, Blue-Rose, even as thou art *my* slave, so am I *thine,* and once again the chain which binds us together is common purpose, and neither shall be free until that purpose be accomplishèd. Then shalt thou, and then shall I, be free to go our separate ways—I to remain, and thou to go, an it please thee, to continue thine interrupted and endless journey to the farthest star."

"Thou hast learned well, Anakha," Bhelliom said grudgingly, "but thine understanding of thy situation did never obtrude itself upon thy conscious thought where I could perceive it. I had despaired, thinking that I had wrought amiss."

Sephrenia was staring at them, first at Sparhawk and then at the seemingly comatose Kalten, and her pale, flawless face was filled with something very like chagrin. Xanetia stared, also, and her expression was no less chagrined. Sparhawk took a fleeting satisfaction in that. The two were very much alike in their perhaps-unconscious assumption of condescending superiority. Sparhawk's sudden, unexpected awareness of things long concealed in his understanding had shaken that irritating smugness of theirs. For the first time in his life he consciously knew that he was Anakha, and more important, he knew the meaning of Anakha in ways neither Sephrenia nor Xanetia could ever begin to comprehend. He had stepped around them to reach Bhelliom, and in joining his thought with Bhelliom's, he had to some degree shared Bhelliom's awareness, and that was something neither of them could ever do.

"Thou hast not wrought amiss, Blue-Rose," he told the jewel. "Thine error lay in casting thy thought in this particular speech. Mine understanding was also cast so, and it did not reveal itself to me until I responded to thy words in kind. Now, let us to work withal. Mine enemies are also thine, forasmuch as they would bind *thee* even as they would bind *me*. Neither of us shall be secure in our freedom until they are no more. Are we agreed upon that?"

"Thy reasoning is sound, Anakha."

"Our purpose then is the same?"

"So it would seem."

"We're making some headway here," Sparhawk murmured.

Kalten's expression became coldly disapproving.

"Sorry," Sparhawk apologized, "force of habit, I suppose. Reason doth urge that since our enemies and our purpose are common, and our thoughts are linked by this chain of *thy* forging, we must join our efforts in this cause. In victory shall we be freed. Our enemies and our common purpose shall be no more, and the chain which links us will fall away. I do pledge it to thee that upon the completion of this task will I free thee to continue thy work. My life is surely within thy fist, and thou mayest destroy me if I play thee false."

"I find no falsity in thy thought, Anakha, and I will strengthen thine arm and harden thine heart, lest others, beloved by thee, seek to turn thee aside from thy design and thy pledge. We are agreed."

"Done, then!" Sparhawk exclaimed.

"And done!" Bhelliom's speech, emerging from Kalten's lips, had been dry and unemotional, but this time the voice was exultant.

"And now to this decision which thou and I must make together."

"Sparhawk—" Sephrenia's tone was uncertain.

"I'm sorry, little mother," he said, "I'm not talking with you at the moment. Please don't interrupt." Sparhawk was not entirely sure whether he should address his question to the sapphire rose or to Kalten, who seemed to have been completely taken over by the spirit within the jewel. He settled for directing his question somewhere between them. "The Delphae have offered their assistance in exchange for a certain service," he said. "They would have us seal their valley that none may enter and none may leave, and in recompense for that small favor they promise to aid us. Is their offer made in good faith?" Sparhawk heard Xanetia's sharp intake of breath.

"It is," Bhelliom replied. "There is no falsity in their offer."

"I didn't think so myself, but I wanted to be sure."

"Anakha." The voice was firm. "When thou speakest so, thy mind is concealed from me. Our alliance is new and unfamiliar. It is not wise of thee to raise doubts in me by compressing thy words together so."

Sparhawk suddenly laughed. "Forgive my lapse, Blue-Rose," he said. "We can trust the Delphae, then?"

"For the moment, yes. Their intent is presently without guile. It is uncertain what it will be tomorrow. Thy kind is inconstant, Anakha." Kalten's voice hesitated briefly. "I say that not as criticism, merely as observation. For the nonce mayest thou put thy trust in their sincerity—and they in thine. What may come subsequently lieth in the hands of chance."

"Then there *is* such a thing as chance?" Sparhawk was a bit surprised at that. "We are told that all things are predetermined by the Gods."

"Whosoever told thee so was in error."

Bevier gasped.

"My journey and my task were interrupted by chance," Bhelliom continued. "If *my* course may be turned aside, might not thine as well? Truly I tell thee, Anakha, we *must* join with the Delphae in this enterprise, for if we do not, we shall surely fail. Whether one or both play the other false will depend on circumstance. At this time, the hearts of the Delphae are pure; that may change. At this time, *thine* heart is *also* pure; that may *also* change. But will we, nil we, we must join with them, lest we fail and languish forever in vilest bondage."

"You heard him, Bevier," Sephrenia was saying to the olive-skinned Arcian later when Sparhawk quietly entered the room where the two were deep in conversation, "they worship the lake—the source of the contamination that makes them outcast."

"He *did* mention a God, Lady Sephrenia," Bevier protested mildly. "I think he called their God Edaemus—or something like that."

"But Edaemus has abandoned them—cursed them and then turned his back on them."

"Anari said that Edaemus had gone before them to prepare a place for them." Bevier's objection seemed even weaker. "He said that they were changing—turning into pure light."

"Lies," she snapped. "The light that marks them is not the mark of a blessing, Bevier, it's the mark of their curse. Cedon was cleverly trying to twist it around to make it seem that the Delphae are turning into something holy, when the reverse is actually true."

"They *do* perform magic, Sephrenia, and a kind of magic I've never seen before. I wouldn't have believed that anyone could return to childhood if I hadn't seen it with my own eyes."

"Exactly my point, Bevier. They're using witchcraft, not magic. You've never seen *me* imitate a God, have you?"

Sparhawk stepped unobserved back out into the hallway and went on down to the doorless cell Vanion occupied. "We've got a problem," he told the Preceptor of the Pandions.

"Another one?"

"Sephrenia's trying to subvert Bevier. She's trying to convince him that the Delphae practice witchcraft. You know Bevier. His eyes start to bulge out any time anyone so much as mentions the word."

"*Why* won't she just leave it alone?" Vanion exclaimed, throwing his hands in the air. "Wasn't Bhelliom's word good enough for her?"

"She doesn't *want* to believe, Vanion," Sparhawk sighed. "We've run into exactly the same thing when we've tried to convince rural Elenes that Styrics aren't born with horns and tails."

"She of all people should be free of that sort of thing."

"I'm afraid not, my friend. Styrics are good haters, I guess. How do we want to handle this?"

"I'll confront her directly."

Sparhawk winced. "She'll turn you into a frog if you do."

Vanion smiled briefly. "No. I lived in Sarsos, remember? A Styric can't do anything like that without the consent of his God, and Aphrael's sort of fond of me—I hope."

"I'll round up the others and get them out from underfoot so that you can speak with her privately."

"No, Sparhawk, it has to be done in front of them. She's trying to slip around behind us to recruit converts. They're all going to have to be made aware of the fact that she's not to be trusted in this particular situation."

"Wouldn't it be a little better to talk with her privately at first—*before* you humiliate her publicly?"

Vanion shook his head stubbornly. "We've got to meet this head-on," he declared.

"You'd *better* hope that Aphrael's fond of you," Sparhawk murmured.

"They've reverted to total paganism," Sephrenia said stubbornly. "They might as well worship trees or oddly shaped rocks. They have no creed, no doctrine, and no restraints. Their use of witchcraft proves that." They had gathered at Vanion's summons in a large room at the end of the hall, and Sephrenia was urgently, even stridently, trying to make her case.

"What's the difference?" Talen shrugged. "Magic, witchcraft, it's all the same, isn't it?"

"Magic is of the Gods, Talen," Bevier explained. "Our Holy Mother, in her wisdom, has chosen to allow the Church Knights to learn the secrets of Styricum that we might better serve her. There are restraints on us—certain areas we may not enter. Witchcraft is unrestrained because it is of the evil one."

"The Devil, you mean? I've never really believed in the Devil. There's plenty of concentrated wickedness in people anyway, so we can probably get along fairly well without him. I've known some *very* nasty people, Bevier."

"The existence of the Devil has been proved."

"Not to me, it hasn't."

"Aren't we wandering a bit?" Ulath suggested. "Does it really matter *what* the Delphae worship? We've allied ourselves with all sorts of people in the past in order to achieve this or that goal. Bhelliom says that we have to join forces with the Delphae, or we're going to lose. I don't like losing, so what's the problem?"

"Bhelliom doesn't know anything about this world, Ulath," Sephrenia said.

"So much the better. It comes at the problem with a clear and uncluttered understanding. If I need to jump behind a tree to keep from being swept away by an avalanche, I'm not going to stop to question the tree about its beliefs first."

"Bhelliom will do or say *anything* in order to gain its freedom," Sephrenia asserted. "That's why I was so much against using it in the first place."

"We *have* to believe Bhelliom, Sephrenia," Vanion told her, obviously trying to keep his irritation under control. "It doesn't make much sense for us to trust it with our very lives and then not believe what it tells us, does it? It *has* done some very useful things for us in the past, you know."

"Only because it was *compelled* to, Vanion. Bhelliom submits because it's forced to submit. I trust the Bhelliom even less than I trust the Delphae. It's alien, totally alien, and we have no way of knowing *what* it will do. We're safe only for as long as we keep it chained and force it to obey us. The minute we begin to listen to it, we're in great danger."

"Is that how you feel about us, too, little mother?" he asked her sadly. "We're

Elenes, and as a race we've proved time and again that we're not to be trusted. Do you want to chain *us* as well? And *force* us to obey you?"

"Don't be absurd. Bhelliom's not a person."

"The Delphae *are*, though, aren't they?"

"No!"

"You're being illogical, Sephrenia. The Delphae *are* human. We don't care for the Zemochs or the Rendors, but we've never tried to pretend that they aren't human. There are a lot of Elenes who don't like you Styrics, but we've never gone so far as to try to deny your humanity." He paused, then drew in a deep breath. "I guess that's what it comes down to, love. If you're going to deny the humanity of the Delphae, how can I be positive that you don't secretly feel the same way about me? I've lived in Sarsos, and many of the Styrics there wanted to treat *me* like some lower life-form. Did you agree with them? Have I been some kind of pet, Sephrenia—a dog maybe? Or a tame ape that you kept around for your private amusements? Hang it all, Sephrenia, this is a question of morality. If we deny *anyone's* humanity, we open the door to unimaginable horror. Can't you see that?"

"The Delphae are different."

"*Nobody's* different! We *have* to believe that, because if we don't, we deny our *own* humanity as well. Why *won't* you understand?"

Her face was very, very pale. "This is all very high-sounding and noble, Vanion, but it has nothing whatsoever to do with the Delphae. You don't know anything about what they are or who they are, so you don't really know what you're talking about. You've always come to me for guidance in the past when your ignorance was putting you in danger. Am I correct in assuming that we're not going to do that any-more?"

"Don't be silly."

"I'm not. I'm being very serious. Are you going to ignore me on this issue? Are you going to take up with these monstrous lepers, no matter what I tell you?"

"We don't have any choice in the matter, can't you see that? Bhelliom tells us that we're going to fail if we don't—and we *can't* fail. I think the whole world's going to depend on our not failing."

"You seem to have outgrown your need for me, then. It would have been po-lite of you to have told me that *before* you brought me to this accursed valley, but I suppose I was silly to expect politeness from an Elene in the first place. As soon as we get back to Matherion, I'll make arrangements to return to Sarsos, where I be-long."

"Sephrenia—"

"No. This concludes it. I've served the Pandion Order well and faithfully for three hundred years, and I thank you for your generous payment for my years of toil. We're through, Vanion. This ends it. I hope the rest of your life will be happy, but happy or sad, you're going to live it without me." And she turned and swept from the room.

"It will be very dangerous, Anari," Itagne warned, "and Xanetia is the most im-portant of all your people. Is it prudent to risk her life?"

"Truly, Itagne of Matherion," the old man replied, "Xanetia is precious to us, for she will be Anarae. She is, however, the most gifted of us, and it may well be that *her* gifts will weight the scale in our final confrontation with our common enemy." Sparhawk, Vanion, and Itagne had been summoned to meet with Cedon prior to their departure from the valley of Delphaeus. It was a fine autumn morning. A hint of frost, fast melting in the newly risen sun, steamed on the meadow, and the shade under the boughs of the evergreens beyond that meadow was a deep, deep blue.

"I merely wished to point it out, Anari," Itagne said. "For all its splendor, Matherion is a city filled with hidden dangers—with rough, ignorant people who will react very strongly to the appearance of one of the Delphae in their midst. Your gentle Xanetia is an ethereal, unworldly sort of person, hardly more than a girl. The fact that she's a Shining One will protect her to some degree against overt physical attack, but are you really willing to expose her to the curses, the vituperation, and all the other kinds of abuse she's sure to encounter there at the center of the world?"

The Anari smiled. "Thou hast misperceived Xanetia, Itagne of Matherion. Doth she truly seem so much a child to thee? Would thy mind be more easy if thou wert aware that she is well past her first century of life?"

Itagne stared at him and then at Xanetia, who sat quietly near the window. "You are a strange people, Anari," he said. "I'd have guessed her age at no more than sixteen years."

"It is impolite to speculate about a lady's age, Itagne of Matherion." The pale woman smiled.

"Forgive me, Anarae," Itagne replied with a courtly bow.

"His Excellency here has raised a fairly important point, Anari," Vanion said. The preceptor's face was still marked by the pain of the previous day's conversation with Sephrenia. "The lady's appearance won't go unnoticed—not only in Matherion itself, but along the roads we'll have to follow as we ride east as well. Is there some way we could disguise her enough so that whole villages won't go into absolute panic the moment she rides by?" He looked apologetically at the Delphaeic woman. "I wouldn't offend you for the world, Anarae, but you *are* very striking."

"I thank thee for the compliment, gentle sir."

"Do you want to take over, Sparhawk?" Vanion said. "I just seem to be digging myself in deeper."

"We're soldiers, Xanetia," Sparhawk said bluntly, "and our answer to hostility is fairly direct. We can butcher our way from here to the imperial palace in Matherion if we have to, but I get the feeling that you might find that distressing. Would a disguise of some kind offend you?" Then a thought came to him. "*Can* we disguise you? I don't know if you've noticed, but you glow. Some of your people have come fairly close to us before the light started to show. Can your internal fire be dampened?"

"We can control the light, Anakha," Cedon assured him, "and Xanetia, the most gifted of us all, can control it even better than most—though it doth cause her pain to do so. For us, it is an unnatural thing."

"We'll have to work on that, then."

"The pain is of no moment, Anakha," Xanetia assured him.

"Not to you, perhaps, but it is to me. Let's start with your coloration, though.

Your features are Tamul, but your skin and hair are the wrong color. What do you think, Itagne? Could she pass for Tamul if we dyed her skin and hair?"

"That is not needful, Anakha," Xanetia told him. Her brow furrowed briefly in concentration, and gradually, almost like a slow blush, a faint golden tint began to mount in her cheeks, and her hair slipped from its colorless white into pale blonde. "Color is a quality of light," she explained quite calmly even as the embronzing of her skin and the darkening of her hair continued, "and since I can control the light from within me, so can I also control my color—indeed, by thus altering the light rather than suppressing it entirely, I can lessen the pain. A most happy solution for me—and for thee as well, I wot, since thou seemest sensitive to the pain of others. This is a simple matter." Her skin by now was almost the same pale gold as Itagne's, and her hair was a deep, rich auburn. "The change of shape is far more difficult," she conceded, "and the change of gender more difficult still."

"The *what*?" Itagne choked.

"I do not do that often—nor willingly," she replied. "Edaemus did not intend for me to be a man, and I find it most uncomfortable. A man's body is so cluttered and untidy." She held out her arm and examined it closely. "The color seemeth to me correct," she observed. Then she took a lock of her now-black hair and looked at it. "And this as well," she added. "What thinkest thou, Itagne? Would I pass unnoticed in Matherion now?"

"Hardly, divine Xanetia." He smiled. "Thy passage through the streets of firedomed Matherion would stop the hearts of all who beheld thee, for thou art fair, and thy beauty doth bedazzle mine eye beyond all measure."

"Well said," Sparhawk murmured.

"Thine honeyed words fall sweetly upon mine ears, Itagne," Xanetia smiled. "Thou art, I do believe, a master of flattery."

"You should probably know that Itagne is a diplomat, Anarae," Vanion advised her, "and his words aren't always to be trusted. This time he's telling you the truth, though. You're an extraordinarily beautiful woman."

She looked at him gravely. "Thine heart is sore within thee, is it not, Lord Vanion?" she observed.

He sighed. "It's my personal problem, Anarae," he replied.

"Not entirely so, my Lord. Now are we all of the same fellowship, and the troubles of one are the troubles of all. But that which troubleth thee is of far greater note and causeth us all much greater concern than that which might grow from our comradely feelings for thee. This breach between thy beloved and thee doth endanger our cause, and until it be healed, our common purpose doth stand in peril."

They rode eastward, following a scarcely perceptible track that seemed more like a game trail than a route normally followed by humans. Sephrenia, accompanied by Bevier and young Berit, rode some distance to the rear, her face set and her eyes as hard as flint.

Sparhawk and Vanion rode in the lead, following occasional directions from Xanetia, who rode directly behind them under Kalten's watchful eye. "Just give her some time, Vanion," Sparhawk was saying. "Women deliver ultimatums and declarations of war fairly often. Things like that are usually intended to get our attention. Any time I start neglecting Ehlana, she says something she doesn't really mean to bring me up short."

"I'm afraid this goes a little further than that, Sparhawk," Vanion replied. "Sephrenia's a Styric, but she's never been so totally irrational before. If we could find out what's behind this insane hatred of hers, we might be able to do something about it, but we've never been able to get any coherent reasons out of her. Apparently, she hates the Delphae simply because she hates the Delphae."

"Aphrael will straighten it out," Sparhawk said confidently. "As soon as we get back to Matherion, I'll have a talk with Danae, and—" Sparhawk broke off as a sudden thought chilled his blood. "I have to talk with Xanetia," he said, abruptly wheeling Faran around.

"Trouble?" Kalten asked as Sparhawk joined them.

"Nothing immediate," Sparhawk replied. "Why don't you go on ahead and ride with Vanion for a while. I need to talk with Xanetia."

Kalten gave him a questioning look but rode on forward without any further questions.

"Thou art troubled, Anakha," Xanetia observed.

"A little, yes. You know what I'm thinking, don't you?"

She nodded.

"Then you know who my daughter is?"

"Yes."

"It's a sort of secret, Anarae. Aphrael didn't consult with my wife when she chose her present incarnation. It's very important that Ehlana doesn't find out. I think her sanity depends on it."

"Thy secret is safe, Anakha, I do pledge thee my silence on this issue."

"What really happened, Xanetia? Between the Styrics and the Delphae, I mean. I don't want your version or Sephrenia's. I want the truth."

"Thou art not meant to know the truth, Anakha. A part of thy task is to resolve this issue without recourse to the truth."

"I'm an Elene, Xanetia," he said in a pained voice. "I *have* to have facts in order to make decisions."

"Then it is thine intent to judge? To decide if the guilt doth condemn the Styrics or the Delphae?"

"No. My intent is to get to the bottom of Sephrenia's behavior so that I can change her mind."

"Is she so important to thee?"

"Why do you ask questions when you already know the answers?"

"My questions are intended to help *thee* formulate *thy* thought, Anakha."

"I'm a Pandion Knight, Xanetia. Sephrenia's been the mother of our order for three centuries. Any one of us would give up his life for her without any hesitation at all. We love her, but we don't share all of her prejudices." He leaned back in his saddle. "I'll only wait for so long, Xanetia. If I don't get the real truth out of you—or out of Sephrenia—I'll just ask Bhelliom."

"Thou wouldst *not*!" Her now-dark eyes were filled with a sudden chagrin.

"I'm a soldier, Xanetia, so I don't have the patience for subtlety. You'll excuse me? I have to go talk with Sephrenia for a moment."

"Dirgis," Xanetia told them as they crested a hill and saw a typical Atan town lying in the valley below.

"Well, *finally*," Vanion said, taking out his map. "Now we know where we are." He looked over his map for a moment and then squinted up at the evening sky. "Is it too late in the day for us to take one of those long steps, Sparhawk?"

"No, my Lord," Sparhawk replied. "There's plenty of light."

"Are we still concerned about that?" Ulath asked. "Haven't you and Bhelliom hammered that out yet?"

"We haven't been having any private chats," Sparhawk replied. "There are still people out there who can locate Bhelliom when it's out in the open, so I've been keeping it inside its little house—just to be on the safe side."

"It's well over three hundred leagues, Sparhawk," Vanion pointed out. "It's going to be later there."

"I'm never going to get used to that," Kalten said sourly.

"It's really very simple, Kalten," Ulath told him. "You see, when the sun goes down in Matherion, it's still—"

"Please, Ulath," Kalten told him, "don't try to explain it to me. It just makes things worse. When people start to explain it, I sometimes think I can actually feel the world moving under me. I don't like that very much. Just tell me that it's later there, and let it go at that. I don't really need to know *why* it's later."

"He's a perfect knight," Khalad told his brother. "He doesn't even *want* explanations."

"Look on the bright side of it, Khalad," Talen replied. "After we've gone through the wonderful training they've got planned for us, we'll be exactly like Kalten. Think how much easier life's going to be for us when we don't have to understand anything at all."

"I'd guess that it's very close to being fully dark in Matherion by now, Sparhawk," Vanion said. "Maybe we'd better wait until morning."

"I'm not so sure," Sparhawk disagreed. "The time's going to come sooner or later when we're going to have to make one of these jumps after the sun goes down. There's nothing urgent in the wind right now, so it's a good time for us to answer this question once and for all."

"Ah—Sparhawk?" Khalad said.

"Yes?"

"If you've got a question, why not ask? Now that you and Bhelliom are on speaking terms, wouldn't it be simpler—and safer—to just ask it first? *Before* you start experimenting? Matherion's on the coast, as I recall, and I'd rather not come down about a hundred leagues out to sea."

Sparhawk felt just a little foolish. He took out the small golden box and opened the lid. He paused momentarily, casting his question in antique Elenic. "I must needs have thine advice on a certain matter, Blue-Rose," he said.

"Say thy question, Anakha." This time the voice came from Khalad's lips.

"That's a relief," Kalten said to Ulath. "I almost chewed up my tongue with all the *thee*'s and *thou*'s last time."

"Can we safely go from one place to another when the pall of darkness hath covered the earth?" Sparhawk asked.

"There *is* no darkness for me, Anakha."

"I did not know that."

"Thou hadst but to ask."

"Yes. I do perceive that now. Mine understanding doth grow with each passing hour. On the eastern coast of far-flung Tamuli there doth lie a road which doth proceed southward to fire-domed Matherion."

"Yes."

"When my companions and I first beheld Matherion, we came in sight of it when we did crest a long hill."

"Yes. I share thy memory of the place."

"Couldst thou take us there, e'en though darkness doth cover the face of the earth?"

"Yes."

Sparhawk started to reach into the box for his wife's ring. Then he stopped. "We share a common purpose and thus are comrades. It is not meet that I should compel thee and whip thee into compliance with the power of Ghwerig's rings. Thus I do not command thee, but request instead. Wilt thou take us to this place we both know, out of comradeship and common purpose?"

"I will, Anakha."

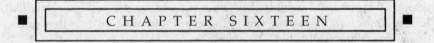

CHAPTER SIXTEEN

The blur which surrounded them momentarily was that same featureless grey, no darker than it had been when Bhelliom had transported them in daylight. Night and day appeared to be irrelevant. Sparhawk dimly perceived that Bhelliom took them through some different place, a colorless emptiness that adjoined all other places—a kind of doorway to everywhere.

"You were right, my Lord," Kalten said to Vanion, looking up at the star-studded night sky. "It *is* later here, isn't it?" He looked sharply at Xanetia, who swayed slightly in her saddle. "Are you unwell, Lady?" he asked her.

"It is of no moment, Sir Knight. A slight giddiness, nothing more."

"You get used to it. The first few times are a little unsettling, but that wears off."

Khalad held out the box, and Sparhawk put Bhelliom back inside. "I do not do this to imprison thee," he told the jewel. "Our enemies can sense thy presence when thou art exposed, and this receptacle doth conceal thee from their search."

The Bhelliom pulsed slightly in acknowledgment.

Sparhawk closed the cap over his ring, took the box from his squire, and closed it. Then he tucked it back into its usual place inside his tunic.

Matherion, ruddy with torchlight, lay below, and the pale path of light from the newly risen moon stretched from the horizon across the waters of the Tamul Sea to her doorstep, yet another of the innumerable roads leading to the city the Tamuls called the center of the world.

"Are you open to a suggestion, Sparhawk?" Talen asked.

"You sound just like Tynian."

"I know. I'm sort of filling in for him while he's away. We've been out of Matherion for a while, so we don't know what's really been going on here. Suppose I slip into town and have a look—ask a few questions, find out what we're riding into— the usual sort of thing."

Sparhawk nodded. "All right," he said.

"That's all? Just 'all right'? No protests? No objections? No hour-long lectures about being careful? I'm disappointed in you, Sparhawk."

"Would you listen to me if I objected or delivered a lecture?"

"No, not really."

"Why waste the time, then? You know what you're doing and how to do it. Just don't take all night."

Talen swung down from his horse and opened his saddlebags. He took out a rough, patched smock and pulled it on over his other clothes. Then he bent, rubbed his hand in the dirt of the road, and artfully smudged his face. He stirred up his hair and sifted a handful of straw from the roadside onto it. "What do you think?" he asked Sparhawk.

"You'll do." Sparhawk shrugged.

"Spoilsport," Talen grumbled, climbing back on his horse. "Khalad, come along. You can watch my horse for me while I sniff around."

Khalad grunted, and the two rode on down the hill.

"Is the child truly so gifted?" Xanetia asked.

"He'd be offended if you called him a child, Lady," Kalten replied, "and he can come closer to being invisible than anybody I know."

They drew back some distance from the road and waited.

It was an hour later when Talen and his brother returned.

"Things are still more or less the way they were when we left," the boy reported.

"No open fighting in the streets, you mean?" Ulath laughed.

"Not yet. Things are a little hectic at the palace, though. It's got something to do with documents of some kind. The whole government's in an uproar. None of the people I talked with knew all that much about it. The Church Knights and the Atans are still in control, though, so it's safe to jump from here to the courtyard of Ehlana's castle if we want."

Sparhawk shook his head. "Let's ride in. I'm sure there are still Tamuls inside the walls, and probably half of them are spies. Let's not give away any secrets if we don't have to. Is Sarabian still staying in the castle?"

Talen nodded. "Your wife's probably been teaching him a few tricks—'roll over,' 'play dead,' 'sit up and beg'—that sort of thing."

"*Talen!*" Itagne exclaimed.

"You haven't met our queen yet, have you, your Excellency?" Talen grinned. "I'd say that you're in for a whole new experience."

"It has to do with setting up the new filing system, my Lord," the young Pandion at the drawbridge explained in reply to Vanion's question. "We needed room to rearrange things, so we spread all the government files out on the lawn."

"What if it rains?"

"That would probably simplify the job a great deal, my Lord."

They dismounted in the courtyard and went up the broad stairs to the ornately carved main door, paused briefly to put on the cushioned shoes that protected the brittle floor-covering, and went inside.

Queen Ehlana had been advised of their arrival and she was waiting for them at the door to the throne room. Sparhawk's heart caught in his throat as he looked at his lovely young wife. "So nice of you to stop by, Sir Sparhawk," she said tartly before she threw her arms about his neck.

"Sorry we're so late, dear," he apologized after they had exchanged a brief, formal sort of kiss. "Our travel plans got a little skewed." He was painfully conscious of the half-dozen or so Tamuls lingering nearby trying to look very hard as if they weren't listening. "Why don't we go on upstairs, my Queen? We've got quite a bit to tell you, and I'd like to get out of this mail shirt before it permanently embeds itself into my skin."

"You are *not* going to wear that stinking thing into *my* bedroom, Sparhawk. As I remember, the baths lie in that general direction. Why don't you take your fragrant friends and go make use of them? The ladies can come with me. I'll round up the others, and we'll all meet you in the royal quarters in about an hour. I'm sure your explanation of your tardiness will be absolutely fascinating."

Sparhawk felt much better after he had bathed and changed into the conventional doublet and hose. He and his friends trooped up the stairs that mounted into the central tower where the royal apartments were located.

"You're late, Sparhawk," Mirtai said bluntly when they reached the top of the stairs.

"Yes. My wife's already pointed that out to me. Come inside. You'll need to hear this, too."

Ehlana and the others who had remained behind were gathered in the large, blue-draped sitting room. Sephrenia and Danae were conspicuously absent, however.

"Well, *finally!*" Emperor Sarabian said as they entered. Sparhawk was startled by the change in the emperor's appearance. His hair was tied back from his face, he wore tight-fitting black hose and a full-sleeved linen shirt. He looked younger for some reason, and he was holding a rapier with the kind of familiarity that spoke of much practice. "Now we can get on with the business of overthrowing the government."

"What have you been up to, Ehlana?" Sparhawk asked.

"Sarabian and I have been expanding our horizons." She shrugged.

"I knew I shouldn't have stayed away so long."

"I'm glad you brought that up. That very same thought's been on my mind for the longest time now."

"Why don't you just save yourself some time and unpleasantness, Sparhawk?" Kalten suggested. "Just show her why we had to take this little trip."

"Good idea." Sparhawk reached inside his doublet and took out the unadorned gold box. "Things were beginning to get out of hand, Ehlana, so we decided to go fetch some reinforcements."

"I thought that's what Tynian was doing."

"The situation called for something a little more significant than the Church Knights." Sparhawk touched the band of his ring to the lid of the box. "Open," he said. He kept the lid partially closed to conceal the fact that his wife's ring was also inside.

"What have you done with your ring, Sparhawk?" she asked him, looking at the cover concealing the stone.

"I'll explain in a bit." He reached in and took out the Bhelliom. "*This* is why we had to leave, dear." He held up the stone.

She stared at it, the color draining from her face. "Sparhawk!" she gasped.

"What a magnificent jewel!" Sarabian exclaimed, reaching his hand out toward the sapphire rose.

"That might not be wise, your Majesty," Itagne cautioned. "That's the Bhelliom. It tolerates Sparhawk, but it might pose some dangers to anyone else."

"Bhelliom's a fairy tale, Itagne."

"I've been reassessing my position on various fairy tales lately, your Majesty. Sparhawk destroyed Azash with Bhelliom—just by touching it to him. I don't advise putting your hands on it, my Emperor. You've shown some promise in the past few months, and we'd sort of hate to lose you at this point."

"Itagne!" Oscagne said sharply. "Mind your manners!"

"We're here to advise the emperor, brother mine, not to coddle him. Oh, incidentally, Oscagne, when you sent me to Cynestra, you invested me with plenipotentiary powers, didn't you? We can check over my commission, if you like, but I'm fairly sure I had that kind of authority—I usually do. I hope you don't mind, old boy, but I've concluded a couple of alliances along the way." He paused. "Well," he amended, "Sparhawk did all the real work, but my commission put some slight stain of legality on the business."

"You can't do that without consulting Matherion first, Itagne!" Oscagne's face was turning purple.

"Oh, be serious, Oscagne. All I did was seize some opportunities that presented themselves, and I was hardly in a position to tell Sparhawk what he could or couldn't do, now, was I? I had things more or less under control in Cynestra when Sparhawk and his friends dropped by. We left Cynestra, and—"

"Details, Itagne. What did you do in Cynestra?"

Itagne sighed. "You can be so tedious at times, Oscagne. I found out that Ambassador Taubel was in bed with Kanzad, the Interior Ministry's station chief. They had King Jaluah pretty much dancing to their tune."

Oscagne's face went bleak. "Taubel's defected to Interior?"

"I thought I just said that. You might want to run a quick evaluation of your other embassies, too. Interior Minister Kolata's been very busy. Anyway, I threw Taubel and Kanzad—along with the entire police force and most of the embassy staff—into a dungeon, declared martial law, and put the Atan garrison in charge."

"You did what?"

"I'll write you a report about it one of these days. You know me well enough to know that I had justification."

"You exceeded your authority, Itagne."

"You didn't impose any limitations on me, old boy. That gave me carte blanche. All you said was to have a look around and to do what needed to be done, so I did."

"How did you persuade the Atans to go along with you without written authorization?"

Itagne shrugged. "The commander of the Atan garrison there is a fairly young woman—quite attractive, actually, in a muscular sort of way. I seduced her. She was an enthusiastic seducee. Believe me, Oscagne, she'll do absolutely *anything* for me." He paused. "You might want to make a note of that in my file—something about my willingness to make sacrifices for the empire and all that. I didn't give her *total* free rein, though. The dear child wanted to give me the heads of Taubel and Kanzad as tokens of her affection, but I declined. My rooms at the university are cluttered enough already, so I don't really have the space for stuffed trophies on the walls. I told her to lock them up instead and to keep a firm grip on King Jaluah until Taubel's replacement arrived. You needn't hurry with that appointment, my brother. I have every confidence in her."

"You've set back relations with Cynesga by twenty years, Itagne."

"*What* relations?" Itagne snorted. "The Cynesgans respond only to naked force, so that's what I used on them."

"You spoke of alliances, Itagne," Sarabian said, flicking the tip of his rapier. "Just exactly to whom have you committed my undying trust and affection?"

"I was just coming to that, your Majesty. After we left Cynestra, we went on to Delphaeus. We spoke with their chieftain, the Anari—a very old man named Cedon—and he offered his assistance. Sparhawk's going to take care of our side of the bargain, so there's no cost to the empire involved."

Oscagne shook his head. "It must come from our mother's side of the family, your Majesty," he apologized. "There was an uncle of hers that was always a little strange."

"What are you talking about, Oscagne?"

"My brother's obvious insanity, your Majesty. I'm told that things like that are hereditary. Fortunately, I favor our father's side of the family. Tell me, Itagne, are you hearing voices, too? Do you have visions of purple giraffes?"

"You can be so tiresome sometimes, Oscagne."

"Would *you* tell us what happened, Sparhawk?" Sarabian asked.

"Itagne covered it fairly well, your Majesty. I take it that you Tamuls have some reservations about the Shining Ones?"

"No," Oscagne said, "I wouldn't call them reservations, your Highness. How could we have any reservations about a people who don't exist?"

"This argument could go on all night," Kalten said. "Would you mind, Lady?" he asked Xanetia, who sat quietly beside him with her head slightly bowed. "If you don't show them who you are, they'll wrangle for days."

"An it please thee, Sir Knight," she replied.

"So formal, my dear?" Sarabian smiled. "Here in Matherion, we only use that mode of speech at weddings, funerals, coronations, and other mournful events."

"We have long been isolate, Emperor Sarabian," she replied, "and unmovèd by the winds of fashion and the inconstant tides of usage. I do assure thee that we find no inconvenience in what must seem to thee forcèd archaism, for it cometh to our lips unbidden and is our natural mode of speech—upon such rare occasions when speech among us is even needful."

The door at the far end of the room opened, and Princess Danae, dragging Rollo behind her, entered quietly with Alean close behind her.

Xanetia's eyes widened, and her expression became awed.

"She fell asleep," the little princess reported to her mother.

"Is she all right?" Ehlana asked.

"Lady Sephrenia seemed very tired, your Majesty," Alean responded. "She bathed and went directly to bed. I couldn't even interest her in any supper."

"It's probably best to just let her sleep," Ehlana said. "I'll look in on her later."

Emperor Sarabian had obviously taken advantage of the brief interruption to frame his thoughts in a somewhat studied archaism. "Verily," he said to Xanetia, "thy mode of speech doth fall prettily upon mine ear, Lady. In truth, however, thou hast been unkind to absent thyself from us, for thou art fair, and thine elegant mode of address would have added luster to our court. Moreover, thine eyes and thy gentle demeanor do shine forth from thee and would have provided instruction by ensample for they who are about me."

"Thy words are artfully honeyed, Majesty," Xanetia said, politely inclining her head, "and I do perceive that thou are a consummate flatterer."

"Say not so," he protested. "I do assure thee that I speak truly from mine heart." He was obviously enjoying himself.

She sighed. "Thine opinion, I do fear me, will change when thou dost behold me in my true state. I have alterèd mine appearance as necessary subterfuge to avoid affrighting thy subjects. For, though it doth cause me grave distress to confess it, should thy people see me in mine accustomed state, they would flee, shrieking in terror."

"Canst thou truly inspire such fear, gentle maiden?" He smiled. "I cannot give credence to thy words. In truth, methinks, shouldst thou appear on the streets of fire-domed Matherion, my subjects would indeed run—but *not* away from thee."

"That thou must judge for thyself, Majesty."

"Ah—before we proceed, might I inquire as to the state of your Majesty's health?" Itagne asked prudently.

"I'm well, Itagne."

"No shortness of breath? No heaviness or twinges in your Majesty's chest?"

"I said that I'm healthy, Itagne," Sarabian snapped.

"I certainly *hope* so, your Majesty. May I be permitted to present the Lady Xanetia, the Anarae of the Delphae?"

"I think your brother's right, Itagne. I think you've taken leave of—Good God!" Sarabian was staring in open horror at Xanetia. Like the dye running out of a bolt of cheap cloth, the color was draining from her skin and hair, and the incandescent glow that had marked her before she had disguised it began to shine forth again. She rose to her feet, and Kalten stood up beside her.

"Now is the stuff of thy nightmares made flesh, Sarabian of Tamuli," Xanetia said sadly. "This is who and what I am. Thy servant Itagne hath told thee well and truly what transpirèd in fabled Delphaeus. I would greet thee in manner suitable to thy station, but like all the Delphae, I am outcast, and therefore not subject to thee. I am here to perform those services which devolve upon my people by reason of our pact with Anakha, whom thou hast called Sparhawk of Elenia. Fear me not, Sarabian, for I am here to serve, not to destroy."

Mirtai, her face deathly pale, had risen to her feet. Purposefully, she stepped in front of her mistress and drew her sword. "Run, Ehlana," she said grimly. "I'll hold her back."

"That is not needful, Mirtai of Atan," Xanetia told her. "As I said, I mean no harm to any in this company. Sheathe thy sword."

"I will, accursed one—in your vile heart!" Mirtai raised her sword. Then, as if struck by some great blow, she reeled back and fell to the floor, tumbling over and over.

Kring and Engessa reacted immediately, rushing forward and clawing at their sword hilts.

"I would not hurt them, Anakha," Xanetia warned Sparhawk, "but I must protect myself that I may keep faith with the pact between thee and my people."

"*Put up your swords!*" Vanion barked. "The lady is a friend!"

"But—" Kring protested.

"*I said to put up your swords!*" Vanion's roar was shattering, and Kring and Engessa stopped in their tracks.

Sparhawk, however, saw another danger. Danae, her eyes bleak and her face set, was advancing on the Delphaeic woman. "Ah, there you are, Danae," he said, moving rather more quickly than his casual tone might have suggested. He intercepted the vengeful little princess. "Aren't you going to give your poor old father a kiss?" He swept her up into his arms and smothered her indignant outburst by mashing his lips to hers.

"Put me down, Sparhawk!" she said, speaking directly down his throat.

"Not until you get a grip on your temper," he muttered, his mouth still clamped to hers.

"She hurt Mirtai!"

"No, she didn't. Mirtai knows how to fall without getting hurt. Don't do anything foolish here. You knew this was going to happen. Everything's under control, so don't get excited—and *don't*, for God's sake, let your mother find out who you really are."

"It doesn't really talk!" Ehlana interrupted Sparhawk's account of what had taken place in Delphaeus.

"Not by itself, no," Sparhawk replied. "It spoke through Kalten—well, it did the first time, anyway."

"Kalten?"

"I have no idea why. Maybe it just seizes on whoever's handy. The language it uses is archaic and formal—*thee*'s and *thou*'s and that sort of thing. Its speech is much like Xanetia's, and it wants me to respond in kind. Evidently, the mode of speech is important." He rubbed one hand across his freshly shaved cheek. "It's very strange, but as soon as I began to speak—and think—in twelfth-century Elenic, something seemed to open in my mind. For the first time I knew that I was Anakha, and I knew that Bhelliom and I are linked together in some profoundly personal way." He smiled wryly. "It seems that you're married to two different people, love. I hope you'll like Anakha. He seems a decent enough sort—once you get used to the way he talks."

"Perhaps I should just go mad," she said. "That might be easier than trying to understand what's going on. How many other strangers do you plan to bring to my bed tonight!"

Sparhawk looked at Vanion. "Should I tell them about Sephrenia?"

"You might as well," Vanion sighed. "They'll find out about it soon enough anyway."

Sparhawk took his wife's hands in his and looked into her grey eyes. "You're going to have to be a little careful when you talk with Sephrenia, dear," he told her. "There's an ancient enmity between the Delphae and the Styrics, and Sephrenia grows irrational whenever she's around them. Xanetia has problems with the Styrics as well, but she manages to keep it under control better than Sephrenia does."

"Doth it seem so to thee, Anakha?" Xanetia asked. She had resumed her disguise, more for the sake of the comfort of the others than out of any real need, Sparhawk guessed. Mirtai sat not far from her with watchful eyes and with her hand resting on her sword hilt.

"I'm not trying to be personally offensive, Anarae," he apologized. "I'm just trying to explain the situation so that they'll understand when you and Sephrenia try to claw each other's eyes out."

"I'm sure you've noticed my husband's blinding charm, Anarae," Ehlana smiled. "Sometimes he absolutely overwhelms us with it."

Xanetia actually laughed, then looked at Itagne. "These Elenes are a complex people, are they not? I do detect great agility of thought behind this bluff manner of theirs, and subtleties I would not have expected from a people who tailor steel into garments."

Sparhawk leaned back in his chair. "I haven't really covered everything that happened, but that's enough to let you know in general what we encountered. We can fill in more detail tomorrow. What's been going on here?"

"Politics, of course," Ehlana shrugged.

"Don't you ever get tired of politics?"

"Don't be silly, Sparhawk. Milord Stragen, why don't you tell him? It shocks him when I start going into all the sordid details."

Stragen was once again dressed in his favorite white satin doublet. The blond thief was sunk deep in a chair with his feet up on a table. "That attempted coup alerted us that there were more mundane elements involved in this business than hobgoblins and resurrected antiquities," he began. "We knew that Krager was involved—and Interior Minister Kolata—and that turned it into ordinary, garden-variety politics. We didn't know where Krager was, so we decided to find out just how deeply Interior was infected. Since all policemen everywhere are compulsive about paperwork, we were fairly sure that somewhere in that rabbit warren of a building was a set of files that would identify the people we wanted to talk with. The problem was that we couldn't just walk into the ministry and demand to see their files without giving away the fact that we knew what they were up to, which in turn would have let them know that Kolata was our prisoner instead of a willing guest. Baroness Melidere came up with the idea of a new filing system, and that gave us access to all the files of all the ministries."

"It was dreadful." Oscagne shuddered. "We had to disrupt the entire government in order to conceal the fact that we were really only interested in the files at Interior. Milord Stragen and the baroness put their heads together and concocted a system. It's totally irrational and wildly inconsistent, but for some reason it works amazingly well. I can lay my hands on any given piece of paper in less than an hour."

"Anyway," Stragen continued, "we browsed through the files at Interior for a week or so, but the people over there kept slipping back into the building at night to move things around so that we'd have to start all over again every morning. That's when we decided to just move our operations out onto the lawns. We stripped all the paper out of all the buildings and spread it out on the grass. That inconvenienced the rest of the government enormously, but Interior was still holding out on us. They were still hiding the critical files. Caalador and I reverted to type and tried burglary—along with Mirtai. The queen sent her along to remind us that we were looking for paper rather than miscellaneous valuables, I guess. It took a few nights, but we finally found the hidden room where the files we wanted were concealed."

"Didn't they miss them the next morning?" Bevier asked him.

"We didn't take them, Sir Knight," Caalador told him. "The queen called in a young Pandion who used a Styric spell to bring the information back to the castle without physically removing the documents." He grinned. "We got us all that there real incriminatin' stuff, an' they don't know we got it. We stole it, an' they don't even miss it."

"We've got the name of every spy, every informer, every secret policeman, and every conspirator of whatever rank Interior has in all of Tamuli." Sarabian smirked. "We've been waiting for all of you to come home so that we can take steps. I'm going to dissolve the Ministry of the Interior, round up all those people, and declare martial law. Betuana and I have been in close contact, and we've laid our plans very carefully. As soon as I give the word, the Atans are going to take charge of the entire empire. Then I'll *really* be the emperor instead of just a stuffed toy."

"You've all been very busy," Vanion observed.

"It makes the time go faster, my Lord." Caalador shrugged. "We went a little further, though. Krager obviously knew that we were using the criminals of Matherion as spies, but we weren't sure if he knew about the hidden government. If he thinks our organization's localized, that's not much of a problem; but if he knows that I can give the order here in Matherion, and somebody dies in Chyrellos, that's a whole 'nother thang."

"I've missed that dialect," Talen said. He considered it. "Not really very much, though," he added.

"Critic," Caalador accused.

"How much were you able to find out?" Ulath asked him.

Caalador spread one hand and rocked it back and forth dubiously. "It's sorta hord t' say," he admitted. "They's some places whur it iz ez them folks o' ourn kin move around free ez frogs in a muddy pond. Other places, they can't." He made a sour face. "It probably all boils down to natural talent. Some are gifted; some aren't. We've made a little headway in putting names to some of the rabid nationalists in various parts of Tamuli—at least we *think* it's headway. If Krager really knows what we're doing, he could be feeding us false information. We wanted to wait until you came back before we tested the information we've got."

"How do you test something like that?" Bevier asked.

"We'll send out the order to have somebody's throat cut, then see if they try to protect him," Stragen replied. "Some chief of police somewhere, or maybe one of those nationalist leaders—Elron, maybe. Isn't that astonishing, Sparhawk? That's one of the things we found out. It turns out that Elron is the mysterious Sabre."

"What an amazing thing," Sparhawk replied with feigned astonishment.

"Caalador wants to kill the man named Scarpa," Stragen went on, "but I favor Elron—although my preference in the matter could be viewed as a form of literary criticism. Elron deserves killing more for his abominable verse than his political opinions."

"The world can stand a little more bad poetry, Stragen," Caalador told his friend. "Scarpa's the really dangerous one. I just wish we could put a name to Rebal, but so far he's eluded us."

"His real name's Amador," Talen told him. "He's a ribbon clerk in Jorsan on the west coast of Edom."

"How did you find *that* out?" Caalador seemed astonished.

"Pure luck, to be honest about it. We saw Rebal making a speech to some peasants out in the woods. Then, later on when we were in Jorsan, a gust of wind blew me into his shop. He isn't really very much to worry about. He's a charlatan. He uses carnival tricks to make the peasants think that he's raising the ghost of Incetes. Sephrenia seems to think that means that our enemies are spread thin. They don't have enough real magicians to arrange all these visitations, so they have to resort to trickery."

"What were you doing in Edom, Sparhawk?" Ehlana asked.

"We went through there on our way to pick up Bhelliom."

"How did you get there and back so fast?"

"Aphrael helped us. She's very helpful—most of the time." Sparhawk avoided looking at his daughter. He rose to his feet. "We're all a little tired tonight," he suggested, "and I rather expect that filling in all of the details is going to take us quite awhile. Why don't we break off here and get some sleep? Then we'll be able to attack it again in the morning when we're all fresh."

"Good idea," Ehlana agreed, also rising. "Besides, I've got this burning curiosity."

"Oh?"

"As long as I'm going to be sleeping with him, I should probably get to know this Anakha fellow, wouldn't you say? Sleeping with total strangers so tarnishes a girl's reputation, you know."

"She's still asleep," Danae said, quietly closing the door to Sephrenia's room.

"Is she all right?" Sparhawk asked.

"Of course she isn't. What did you expect, Sparhawk? Her heart's broken."

"Come with me. We need to talk."

"I don't think I want to talk with you right now, Father. I'm just a little unhappy with you."

"I can live with that."

"Don't be too sure."

"Come along." He took her by the hand and led her up a long flight of stairs to the top of the tower and then out onto the parapet. He prudently closed the door and bolted it behind them. "You blundered, Aphrael," he told her.

She raised her chin and gave him a flat, icy stare.

"Don't get imperial with me, young lady. You made a mistake. You never should have let Sephrenia go to Delphaeus."

"She *had* to go. She has to go through this."

"She can't. It's more than she can bear."

"She's stronger than she looks."

"Don't you have any heart at all? Can't you see how much she's suffering?"

"Of course I can, and it's hurting *me* far more than it's hurting you, Father."

"You're killing Vanion, too, you know."

"He's *also* stronger than he looks. Why did all of you turn against Sephrenia at Delphaeus? Two or three soft words from Xanetia was all it took to make you throw away three hundred years of love and devotion. Is that the way you Elenes customarily treat your friends?"

"*She's* the one who forced the issue, Aphrael. She started delivering ultimatums. I don't think you realize how strongly she feels about the Delphae. She was totally irrational. What's behind all of that?"

"That's none of your business."

"I think it is. What *really* happened during the Cyrgai wars?"

"I won't tell you."

"Art thou afeared to speak of it, Goddess?"

Sparhawk spun around quickly, a startled oath coming to his lips. It was Xanetia. She stood all aglow, not far from where they were talking.

"This doesn't concern you, Xanetia," Aphrael told her coldly.

"I must needs know thine heart, Goddess. Thy sister's enmity is of no real moment. *Thine,* however, would be more troublesome. Art thou also unkindly disposed toward me?"

"Why don't you leech my thoughts and find out for yourself?"

"Thou knowest that I cannot, Aphrael. Thy mind is closed to me."

"I'm so glad you noticed that."

"Behave yourself," Sparhawk told his daughter, speaking very firmly.

"Stay out of this, Sparhawk."

"No, Danae, I don't think I will. Are *you* behind the way Sephrenia was behaving at Delphaeus?"

"Don't be absurd. I sent her to Delphaeus to *cure* her of that nonsense."

"Are you sure, Aphrael? You're not behaving very well at the moment yourself, you know."

"I don't like Edaemus, and I don't like his people. I'm trying to cure Sephrenia out of love for *her,* not out of any affection for the Delphae."

"But thou didst stand for us against thy kindred when all this began, Goddess," Xanetia pointed out.

"That *also* was not out of any great affection for your race, Xanetia. My family was wrong, and I opposed them out of principle. You wouldn't understand that, though, would you? It had to do with love, and you Delphae have outgrown that, haven't you?"

"How little thou knowest us, Goddess," Xanetia said sadly.

"As long as we're all speaking so frankly, I've noticed a certain bias against Styrics in some of *your* remarks, Anarae," Sparhawk said pointedly.

"I have reasons, Anakha—many reasons."

"I'm sure you have, and I'm sure Sephrenia has reasons, too. But whether we like each other or not is really beside the point. I *am* going to straighten this all out. I've got work to do, and I can't do it in the middle of a catfight. I *will* make peace among you—even if I have to use the Bhelliom to do it."

"Sparhawk!" Danae's face was shocked.

"Nobody wants to tell me what really happened during the Cyrgai wars, and maybe that's just as well. I was curious at first, but not any longer. What it boils down to, ladies, is that I don't *care* what happened. The way you've all been behaving sort of says that *nobody's* hands were really clean. I want this spiteful wrangling to stop. You're all behaving like children, and it's beginning to make me tired."

CHAPTER SEVENTEEN

There were dark circles under Sephrenia's eyes the next morning, and the light had gone out of her face. Her white Styric robe was partially covered by a sleeveless overmantle of deepest black. Sparhawk had never seen her wear that kind of garment before, and her choice—of both the garment and the color—seemed ominous. She joined them at the breakfast table reluctantly, and only at Ehlana's express command. She sat slightly apart from the rest of them with her injury drawn about her like a defensive wall. She would not look at Vanion and refused breakfast despite Alean's urgings.

Vanion appeared no less injured. His face was drawn and pale, quite nearly as pale as it had been when he had been carrying the burden of the swords, and his eyes were filled with pain.

Breakfast under those circumstances was strained, and they all left the table with a certain relief. They proceeded directly to the blue-draped sitting room and got down to business.

"The others aren't really all that significant," Caalador told them. "Rebal, Sabre, and Baron Parok are decidedly second-rate. All they're really doing is exploiting existing hostilities. Scarpa's something quite different, though. Arjuna's a troublesome sort of place to begin with, and Scarpa's using that to the fullest. The others have to be fairly circumspect because the Elene kingdoms of western Tamuli are so well-populated. There are people everywhere, so the conspirators have to sneak around. Southeastern Arjuna's one vast jungle, though, so Scarpa's got places to hide, and places he can defend. He makes some small pretense at nationalism in the way that the others do, but that doesn't appear to be his main agenda. The Arjuni are far more shrewd than the Elene peasants and serfs of the west."

"Have you got any background on him?" Ulath asked, "where he came from, what he did before he set up shop, that sort of thing?"

Caalador nodded. "That part wasn't very difficult. Scarpa was fairly well known in some circles before he joined the conspiracy." Caalador made a face. "I wish there were some other word. 'Conspiracy' sounds so melodramatic." He shrugged. "Anyway, Scarpa's a bastard."

"Caalador!" Bevier said sharply, "there are ladies present!"

"It wasn't intended as an obscenity, Sir Bevier, merely as a legal definition. Scarpa's the result of a dalliance between a militantly promiscuous Arjuni tavern wench and a renegade Styric. It was an odd sort of pairing-off, and it produced a very odd sort of fellow."

"Don't pursue this too far, Caalador," Stragen said ominously.

"Grow up, Stragen. You're not the only one with irregular parentage. When you get right down to it, I'm not entirely sure who my father was either. Bastardy's no great inconvenience for a man with brains and talent."

"Milord Stragen's oversensitive about his origins," Baroness Melidere explained lightly. "I've spoken with him time and again about it, but he still has feelings of inadequacy. It might not be a bad thing, though. He's so generally stupendous otherwise that a little bit of insecurity keeps him from being unbearable."

Stragen rose and bowed flamboyantly.

"Oh, sit down, Stragen," she said.

"Where was I?" Caalador said. "Oh, yes, now I recollect. This yere Scarpa feller, he growed-up in a shack-nasty sorta roadside tavern down thar in Ar-juna, an' he done all the sorta thangs which it iz ez bastards does in ther formative years in a place 'thout no real moral restraints on 'em."

"Please, Caalador," Stragen sighed.

"Just entertaining the queen, old boy." Caalador shrugged. "She pines away without periodic doses of down-home folksiness."

"What does *shack-nasty* mean, Caalador?" Ehlana interrupted him.

"Why, jist whut it sez, yer Queenship. A *shack*'s a kinda th'owed-together hovel built outten ole boards an' scraps, an' *nasty* means purty much whut it sez. I knowed a feller ez went by that name when I wuz a pup. He lived in th' messiest place y' ever *did* see, an' he warn't none too clean his ownself, neither."

"I think I can survive for several hours now without any more mangled language, Master Caalador." She smiled. "I want to thank you for your concern, though."

"Always glad to be of service, your Majesty." He grinned. "Scarpa grew up in a situation that sort of skirted the edges of crime. He was what you might call a gifted amateur. He never really settled down into one given trade." He made a face. "Dabblers. I absolutely *detest* dabblers. Anyway, he pandered for his mother—just as every good boy should—and also for his numerous half sisters, who, if we're to believe the common gossip, were all whores from the cradle. He was a moderately competent pickpocket and cutpurse, and a fairly gifted swindler. Unlike many of his mother's one-time paramours, Scarpa's Styric father stayed around for a time, and he used to drop back to visit his son from time to time, so Scarpa got a smattering of a Styric education. Eventually, however, he made the kind of mistake we expect amateurs to make. He tried to cut the purse of a tavern patron who wasn't quite as drunk as he appeared to be. His intended victim grabbed him, and Scarpa demonstrated the Arjuni side of his nature. He whipped out a small, very sharp knife and spilled the fellow's guts out on the floor of the tavern. Some busybody went to the police about it, and Scarpa left home rather abruptly."

"Wise move," Talen murmured. "Didn't he get any professional training while he was growing up?"

"No. He appears to have picked things up on his own."

"Precocious."

Caalador nodded his agreement. "If he'd had the right teachers, he probably could have become a master thief. After he ran away, he seems to have kept moving for a couple of years. He was only twelve or so when he killed that first man, and when he was about fourteen, he turned up in a traveling carnival. He billed himself as a magician—the usual sort of carnival fakery—although he occasionally utilized a few Styric spells to perform *real* magic. He grew a beard—which is very unusual among the Tamul races, since Tamul men don't have much facial hair. Neither do Styrics for that matter, now that I think about it. Scarpa's a half-breed, and the mixture of Southern Tamul and Styric came out rather peculiarly. Neither his features nor some of his traits are really characteristic of either race." Caalador reached inside his doublet and drew out a folded sheet of paper. "Here," he said, opening the paper, "judge for yourselves."

The drawing was a bit crude—more a caricature than a portrait. It was a depiction of a man with a strangely compelling face. The eyes were deep-sunk under heavy brows. The cheekbones were high and prominent, the nose aquiline, and the mouth sensual. The beard appeared to be dense and black, and it was meticulously trimmed and shaped.

"He spends a lot of time on that beard," Kalten observed. "It looks as if he shaves off stray whiskers hair by hair." He frowned slightly. "He looks familiar, for some reason—something around the eyes, I think."

"I'm surprised you can even recognize the fact that it's supposed to be a picture of a human being," Talen sniffed. "The technique's absolutely awful."

"The girl hasn't had any training, Talen," Caalador defended the artist. "She's gifted in her own profession, though."

"Which profession is that, Master Caalador?" Ehlana asked.

"She's a whore, your Majesty." He shrugged. "The drawing is just a sideline. She likes to keep pictures of her customers. She studies their faces during the course of her business transactions, and some of the portraits have strange expressions."

"May I see that?" Sephrenia asked suddenly.

"Of course, Lady Sephrenia." Caalador looked a little surprised as he took the drawing to her. Then he returned to his seat. "Did you ever meet Djukta, Sparhawk?" he asked.

"Once."

"Now *there's* a beard for you. Djukta looks like an ambulatory shrub. He's even got whiskers on his eyelids. Anyhow, Scarpa traveled with the carnival for several seasons, then about five years back, he dropped out of sight for a year or so. When he returned, he went into politics—if that's what you want to call it. He makes some small pretense at nationalism in the same way that Rebal, Parok, and Sabre do, but that's only for the benefit of the truly ignorant down in Arjuna. The national hero there was the man who established the slave trade, a fellow named Sheguan. That's a fairly contemptible sort of thing, so not many Arjunis take much pride in it."

"They still practice it, though," Mirtai said bleakly.

"They do indeed, little dorlin'," Caalador agreed.

"Friend Caalador," Kring said, "I thought we agreed that you weren't going to call Mirtai that anymore."

"Aw, it don't mean nuthin', Kring. It's jist muh folksy way o' settin' people at ther ease." He paused. "Where was I?" he asked.

"You were starting to get to the point," Stragen replied.

"Testy this morning, aren't we, old boy?" Caalador said mildly. "From what our people were able to discover, Scarpa's far more dangerous than those three enthusiasts in western Tamuli. Arjuni thieves are more devious than run-of-the-mill criminals, and a number of them have infiltrated Scarpa's apparatus for fun and profit. The Arjuni are an untrustworthy people, so the empire's been obliged to deal with them quite firmly. Arjuni hatred for the Tamuls is very real, so Scarpa hasn't had to stir it up artificially." Caalador tugged at his nose a bit dubiously. "I'm not altogether sure how much of this we can believe—the Arjuni being what they are and all—but one highway robber down there claims to have been a member of Scarpa's inner circle for a while. He told us that our man's just a little deranged. He operates out of the ruins of Natayos down in the southern jungles. The town was destroyed during the Atan invasion back in the seventeenth century, and Scarpa doesn't so much hide there as he does occupy the place—in a military sense of the word. He's reinforced the crumbling old walls so that the town's defensible. Our highwayman reports that Scarpa starts raving sometimes. If we can believe our informant, he started talking about the Cyrgai once, and about Cyrgon. He tells his cronies that Cyrgon wants to make his people the masters of the world, but that the Cyrgai, with that institutionalized stupidity of theirs, aren't really intelligent enough to govern a global empire. Scarpa doesn't have any problems with the idea of an empire. He just doesn't like the way the present one's set up. He'd be more than happy with it if there were just a few changes—up at the top. He believes that the Cyrgai will conquer the world and then retreat back into their splendid isolation. *Somebody's* going to have to run the government of the world for them, and Scarpa's got a candidate in mind for the position."

"That's insane!" Bevier exclaimed.

"I think I already suggested that, Sir Knight. Scarpa seems to think he'd make a very good emperor."

"The position's already been filled," Sarabian noted dryly.

"Scarpa's hoping that Cyrgon will vacate it, your Majesty. He tells his people that the Cyrgai have absolutely no administrative skills and that they're going to need someone to run the conquered territories for them. He'll volunteer at that point. He'll genuflect perfunctorily in Cyrgon's direction once in a while, and more or less run things to suit himself. He has large dreams, I'll give him that."

"It has a sort of familiar ring to it, doesn't it, Sparhawk?" Kalten said with a tight grin. "Didn't Martel—and Annias—have the same sort of notion?"

"Oh, my goodness, yes," Ehlana agreed. "I feel as if I've lived through all of this before."

"Where does Krager fit in?" Sparhawk asked.

"Krager seems to be some sort of coordinator," Caalador replied. "He serves as a go-between. He travels a great deal, carrying messages and instructions. We're guessing about this, but we think that there's a layer of command between Cyrgon and the people like Scarpa, Parok, Rebal, and Sabre. Krager's known to all of them, and that authenticates his messages. He seems to have found his natural niche in life. Queen Ehlana tells us that he served Martel and Annias in exactly the same way, and he was doing the same kind of thing back in Eosia when he was carrying Count Gerrich's instructions to those bandits in the mountains east of Cardos."

"We should really make some sort of effort to scoop Krager up," Ulath rumbled. "He starts talking if someone so much as gives him a harsh look, and he knows a great deal about things that make me moderately curious."

"That's how he's managed to stay alive for so long," Kalten grunted. "He always makes sure that he's got so much valuable information that we don't dare kill him."

"Kill him *after* he talks, Sir Kalten," Khalad said.

"He makes us promise not to."

"So?"

"We're knights, Khalad," Kalten explained. "Once we give someone our oath, we're obliged to keep our word."

"You weren't thinking of knighting me at any time in the immediate future, were you, Lord Vanion?" Khalad asked.

"It might be just a little premature, Khalad."

"That means that I'm still a peasant, doesn't it?"

"Well—technically, maybe."

"That solves the problem, then," Khalad said with a chill little smile. "Go ahead and catch him, Sir Kalten. Promise him anything you have to in order to get him to talk. Then turn him over to me. Nobody expects a peasant to keep his word."

"I'm going to like this young man, Sparhawk." Kalten grinned.

"Zalasta's coming for me, Sparhawk," Sephrenia told the big Pandion. "He'll escort me safely back to Sarsos." She shook her head, refusing to enter the room to which they were returning after lunch.

"You're being childish. You know that, don't you, Sephrenia?"

"I've outlived my usefulness, and I've been around Elenes long enough to know what a prudent Styric does when that happens. As long as a Styric's useful, she's relatively safe among Elenes. Once she's served her purpose, though, her presence starts to be embarrassing, and you Elenes deal abruptly with inconvenient people. I'd rather not have one of you slip a knife between my ribs."

"Are you just about finished? Conversations like this bore me. We love you, Sephrenia, and it has nothing to do with whether or not you're useful to us. You're breaking Vanion's heart. You know that, too, don't you?"

"So? He broke mine, didn't he? Take your problems to Xanetia, since you're all enamored of her."

"That's beneath you, little mother."

Her chin came up. "I think I'd rather you didn't call me that anymore, Sparhawk. It's just a bit grotesque in the present circumstances. I'll be in my room—if it's still mine. If it isn't, I'll go live in the Styric community here in Matherion. If it's not too much trouble, let me know when Zalasta arrives." And she turned and walked down the corridor, ostentatiously wearing her injury like a garment.

Sparhawk swore under his breath. Then he saw Kalten and Alean coming down the tiled hallway. At least *that* particular problem had been resolved. The queen's maid had laughed in Kalten's face when the blond knight had clumsily offered to step aside so that she could devote her attentions to Berit. She had then, Sparhawk gathered, convinced Kalten that her affections were still quite firmly where they were supposed to be.

"But you never leave her side, Sir Kalten," the doe-eyed girl accused. "You're always hovering over her and making certain that she has everything she needs or wants."

"It's a duty, Alean," Kalten tried to explain. "I'm not doing it because I have any kind of affection for her."

"You're performing your duty just a little too well to suit me, Sir Knight." Alean's voice, that marvelous instrument, conveyed a whole range of feelings. The girl could speak volumes with only the slightest change of key and intonation.

"Oh, God," Sparhawk groaned. Why did he *always* have to get caught in these personal matters? This time, however, he moved quickly to put a stop to things before they got out of hand. He stepped out into the corridor to confront the pair of them. "Why don't we take care of this right now?" he suggested bluntly.

"Take care of what?" Kalten demanded. "This isn't any of your business, Sparhawk."

"I'm *making* it my business. Are you satisfied that Alean doesn't have any kind of serious feelings for Berit?"

Kalten and the girl exchanged a quick, guilty sort of glance.

"Good," Sparhawk said. "My congratulations to you both. Now, let's clear up this Xanetia business. Kalten was telling you the truth, Alean—as far as he went. His duty obliges him to stay close to her because he's required to make certain that no harm comes to her. We have an agreement with her people, and she's here as our hostage to make sure that they don't go back on their word. We all know that if the Delphae betray us in any way, Kalten will kill Xanetia. *That's* why he's staying so close to her."

"Kill?" The girl's huge eyes went even wider.

"Those are the rules, Alean." Kalten shrugged. "I don't like them very much, but I have to follow them."

"You *wouldn't*!"

"Only if I have to, and I wouldn't like it very much. That's what the word *hostage* means, though. I always seem to be the one who gets these dirty jobs."

"How *could* you?" Alean said to Sparhawk. "How could you *do* this to your oldest friend?"

"Military decisions are hard sometimes," Sparhawk told her. "Are you satisfied now that Kalten's not straying? You *do* know, don't you, that when he thought that you'd fallen in love with Berit, he started going out of his way trying to get himself killed?"

"You didn't have to tell her *that,* Sparhawk," Kalten protested.

"You idiot!" Alean's voice climbed effortlessly into the upper ranges. She spoke—at length—to Sparhawk's friend while he stood hanging his head and scuffing his feet like a schoolboy being scolded.

"Ah—" Sparhawk ventured. "Why don't the two of you go someplace private where you can discuss things?"

"With your leave, Prince Sparhawk," Alean agreed with an abrupt little curtsy. "You," she snapped to Kalten, "come with me."

"Yes, dear," Kalten said submissively, and the two went on back up the corridor.

"Was that Alean just now?" Baroness Melidere asked, sticking her head out through the doorway.

"Yes," Sparhawk replied.

"Where are she and Kalten going?" she asked, looking after the pair.

"They have something important to take care of."

"Something more important than what we're discussing in here?"

"*They* seem to think so, Baroness. We can manage without them this afternoon, I expect, and it's a matter that needs clearing up."

"Oh," she said, "one of those."

"I'm afraid so."

"Alean will straighten it out," Melidere said confidently.

"I'm sure she will. How's *your* campaign going, Baroness? I'm not trying to pry, you understand. It's just that these matters break my concentration, and I kind of like to have them out of the way so they don't come bubbling to the surface when I least expect them to."

"Everything's on schedule, Prince Sparhawk."

"Good. Have you told him?"

"Of course not. He doesn't need to know yet. I'll break it to him gently when the time comes. It's actually kinder that way. If he finds out too soon, he'll just worry about it. Trust me, your Highness. I know *exactly* what I'm doing."

"There's something I'd sort of like to get cleared up before we go on, Anarae," Stragen said to Xanetia. "The Tamuls all believe that the Cyrgai were extinct, but Krager and Scarpa say otherwise."

"The Cyrgai *want* the world to believe that they are no more," she replied. "After their disastrous march on Sarsos, they returned home and concentrated for a time on replenishing their subordinate forces, the Cynesgans, which forces had been virtually annihilated by the Styrics."

"So we've heard," Caalador said. "We were told that the Cyrgai concentrated with such single-mindedness that their *own* women were past child-bearing age before they realized their mistake."

"Thine informant spoke truly, Master Caalador, and it is the common belief in Tamuli that the Cyrg race died out some ten eons ago. That common belief, however, is in error. It is a belief which ignores the fact that Cyrgon is a God. He did *not*, however, take the blind obedience of his people into account when he commanded them to devote their attentions to the women of the Cynesgans. But when he saw that his chosen race was dying out, he did alter the natural course of such things, and agèd Cyrgai women became fertile once more—though most died in child-birth. Thus were the Cyrgai perpetuated."

"Pity," Oscagne murmured.

"Knowing, however, that the diminishèd numbers of his worshippers *and* the Styric curse which imprisoned them in their arid homeland did imperil them, Cyrgon sought to protect his people. The Cynesgans were commanded to confirm and perpetuate the belief of the other races of Tamuli that the Cyrgai were no more, and the dread city of Cyrga itself was concealed from the eyes of men."

"In the same way that Delphaeus is concealed?" Vanion guessed.

"Nay, my Lord. We are more subtle than Cyrgon. We conceal Delphaeus by misdirection. Cyrgon hides Cyrga in the central highlands of Cynesga by means of an enchantment. Thou couldst go to those highlands and ride close by Cyrga and never see it."

"An invisible city?" Talen asked her incredulously.

"The Cyrgai can see it," she replied, "and, when it doth suit them so, their Cynesgan underlings can as well. To all others, however, Cyrga is not there."

"The tactical advantages of that must be enormous," Bevier noted in his most professional tone. "The Cyrgai have an absolutely secure stronghold into which they can retreat if things go wrong."

"Their advantage is offset, however," Xanetia pointed out. "They may freely ravage and despoil Cynesga, which is theirs already, and which is no more than a barren waste at best; but they may not pass the boundaries of their homeland. The curse of the Styrics is still potent, I do assure thee. It is the wont of the kings of the Cyrgai to periodically test that curse. Agèd warriors are taken from time to time to the boundary and commanded to attempt a crossing. They die in midstride as they obediently march across the line."

Sarabian was looking at her, his eyes narrowed shrewdly. "Prithee, Anarae, advise me in this matter. Thou hast said that the Cynesgans are subject to the Cyrgai?"

"Yes, Majesty."

"*All* Cynesgans?"

"Those in authority, Imperial Sarabian."

"The king? The government? The army?"

She nodded.

"*And* their ambassadors as well?" Oscagne added.

"Very good, Oscagne," Itagne murmured to his brother. "Very, very good."

"I didn't quite follow that," Ulath admitted.

"*I* did," Stragen told him. "We'd probably better look into that, Caalador."

"I'll see to it."

"Do you know what they're talking about, friend Engessa?" Kring asked.

"It's not all that complicated, Kring," Ehlana explained. "The Cynesgan embassy here in Matherion is full of people who take their orders from the Cyrgai. I'd guess that if we were to look into the matter, we'd find that the headquarters of the recent attempt to overthrow the emperor was located in that embassy."

"And if he's not out of town, we might even find Krager there as well," Khalad mused. "Talen, how long would it take you to teach me how to be a burglar?"

"What have you got in mind?" Sparhawk asked his squire.

"I thought I might creep into that embassy and steal Krager, my Lord. Since Anarae Xanetia can tell us what he's thinking, we wouldn't even have to break his fingers to make him talk—*or* make him any inconvenient promises that we probably didn't intend to keep anyway."

"I sense thy discontent, Anakha," Xanetia said later when she, Sparhawk, and Danae had returned to the fortified roof of the central tower of Ehlana's castle.

"I've been had, Anarae," he said sourly.

"I do not recognize the expression."

"He means that he's been duped," Danae translated, "and he's being impolite enough to imply that *I* have, too." She gave her father a smug little smile. "I told you so, Sparhawk."

"Spare me, please."

"Oh, no, Father. I've got this wonderful chance to gloat. You're not going to rob me of it. If I remember correctly—and I do—I was against the idea of retrieving Bhelliom from the very beginning. *I* knew that it was a mistake, but *you* bullied me into agreeing."

He ignored that. "Was any of it real? The Troll-Gods? Drychtnath? The monsters? Or was it all just some elaborate game designed to get me to bring Bhelliom to Tamuli?"

"Some of it may have been real, Sparhawk," she replied, "but you've probably put your finger on the actual reason behind it all."

"It is thy belief that Cyrgon deceivèd thee into bringing Bhelliom within his reach, Anakha?" Xanetia said.

"Why bother to ask, Anarae? You know what I'm thinking already. Cyrgon believes that he could use Bhelliom to break that curse so that his people could start invading their neighbors again."

"I told you so," Danae reminded him again.

"Please." He looked out over the glowing city. "I think I need a divine opinion here," he said. "Up until very recently, we all believed that Bhelliom was just a thing—powerful, but just an object. We know that's not true now. Bhelliom has its own personality and its own will. It's more of an ally than just a weapon. Not only that—and please don't be offended, Aphrael—in some ways it's even more powerful than the Gods of this world."

"I *am* offended, Sparhawk," she said tartly. "Besides, I haven't finished telling you that I told you so."

He laughed, swept her up into his arms, and kissed her. "I love you," he told her, still laughing.

"Isn't he a nice boy?" Danae said to Xanetia.

The Delphaeic woman smiled.

"If *we* didn't know about Bhelliom's awareness—*and* its will—could Cyrgon have known? I don't think Azash did. Speaking as a Goddess, would *you* want to pick up something that could make its own decisions—and *might* just decide that it didn't like you all that much?"

"*I* wouldn't," she replied. "Cyrgon might be a different matter, though. He's so arrogant that he might believe that he could control Bhelliom even against its will."

"But he couldn't, could he? Azash thought he could control Bhelliom by sheer force. He wasn't even interested in the rings. The rings *can* compel Bhelliom—because they're a part of it. Could Cyrgon be as stupid as Azash was?"

"Sparhawk, you're talking about one of my distant relatives. Please be a little more respectful." Danae's brow furrowed with thought. She absently kissed her father.

"Don't do that," he said. "This is serious."

"I know. It helps me to think. Bhelliom's never made itself known before. You're probably right, Sparhawk. Azash wasn't really very bright. Cyrgon has the same sort of personality, and he's made several blunders in the past. That's one of the drawbacks of divinity. We don't *have* to be intelligent. We all know about Bhelliom's power, but I don't think any of us have ever come to grips with the notion of its will before. Did it *really* talk to Sparhawk the way he said it did, Xanetia? As an equal, I mean?"

"As at least an equal, Goddess," Xanetia replied. "Bhelliom and Anakha are allies, not friends—and neither is master."

"Where are we going with this, Sparhawk?" Danae asked.

"I'm not sure. Cyrgon may have made another of those blunders, though. He may just have tricked me into bringing back the one thing that could defeat him. I think we may have an advantage here, but we should probably give a great deal of thought to just exactly how we're going to use it."

"You're hateful, Sparhawk," Danae said.

"I beg your pardon?"

"You've just taken all the fun out of all the *I told you so*'s I've been saving up."

Zalasta arrived in Matherion two days later. After only the briefest of greetings to the rest of them, he went immediately to Sephrenia's room.

"He'll straighten it out, Vanion," Sparhawk assured the preceptor. "He's her oldest friend, and he's far too wise to be infected with irrational prejudice."

"I wouldn't be all that sure, Sparhawk." Vanion's face was gloomy. "I thought *she* was too wise, and look what happened. This blind hatred may infect the entire Styric race. If Zalasta feels the same way Sephrenia does, all he's going to do is reinforce her prejudices."

Sparhawk shook his head. "No, my friend. Zalasta's above that. He has no reason to trust Elenes either, but he was willing to help us, wasn't he? He's a realist, and even if he *does* share her feelings, he'll suppress them in the name of political expediency. And if I'm right, he'll persuade her to do the same. She doesn't have to like Xanetia. All she has to do is accept the fact that we need her. Once Zalasta convinces her of that, the two of you will be able to patch things up."

"Maybe."

It was several hours later when Zalasta emerged alone from Sephrenia's room with his rough-hewn Styric face somber. "It will not be easy, Prince Sparhawk," he said when the two of them met in the corridor outside. "She is deeply wounded. I cannot understand what Aphrael was thinking of."

"Who can *ever* understand why Aphrael does things, learned one?" Sparhawk smiled briefly. "She's the most whimsical and exasperating person I've ever known. As I understand it, she doesn't approve of Sephrenia's prejudice, and she's taking steps. The expression 'doing something to somebody for his own good' always implies a certain amount of brutality, I'm afraid. Were you able to talk any sense into Sephrenia at all?"

"I'm approaching the question obliquely, your Highness," Zalasta replied. "Sephrenia's already been deeply injured. This isn't a good time for a direct confrontation. I was at least able to persuade her to postpone her return to Sarsos."

"That's something, anyway. Let's go talk to the others. A lot has happened since you left."

"The reports come from unimpeachable sources, Anarae," Zalasta said coolly.

"I do assure thee, Zalasta of Styricum, they are nonetheless false. None of the

Delphae have left our valley for well over an hundred years—except to deliver our invitation to Anakha."

"It's happened before, Zalasta," Kalten told the white-robed Styric. "We watched Rebal use some very obvious trickery when he was talking to a group of Edomish peasants."

"Oh?"

"It was the sort of thing one sees in second-rate carnivals, learned one," Talen explained. "One of his henchmen threw something into a fire; there was a flash of light and a puff of smoke; then somebody dressed in old-time clothes stood up from where he'd been hiding and started bellowing in an ancient form of speech. The peasants all thought they were seeing Incetes rising from the grave."

"Those who witnessed the Shining Ones were not so gullible, Master Talen," Zalasta objected.

"And the fellow who gulled them probably wasn't as clumsy." The boy shrugged. "A skilled fake can make almost anybody believe almost anything—as long as they aren't close enough to see the hidden wires. Sephrenia told us that it means that the other side's a little short on real magicians, so they have to cheat."

Zalasta frowned. "It *may* be possible," he conceded. "The sightings were brief and at quite some distance." He looked at Xanetia. "You are certain, Anarae? Could there perhaps be some of your people who live separately? Who are cut off from Delphaeus and may have joined with our enemies?"

"They would no longer be of the Delphae, Zalasta of Styricum. We are bound to the lake. It is the lake which doth make us what we are, and I tell thee truly, the light which doth illuminate us is but the least of the things which do make us unlike all others." She looked at him gravely. "Thou art Styric, Zalasta of Ylara, and thou art well aware of the consequences of markedly differing from thy neighbors."

"Yes," he agreed, "to our sorrow."

"The decision of thy race to attempt to co-exist with the other races of man may be suitable for Styrics," she continued. "For my race, however, it hath not been possible. Ye of the Styric race are oft met with contempt and derision, but thy differences are not threatening to the Elenes or Tamuls who are about you. We of Delphaeus, however, do inspire terror in the hearts of all others. In time, methinks, thy race will become acceptable. The wind of change hath already begun to blow, engendered in large measure by that fortuitous alliance betwixt ye and the Church of Chyrellos. The knights of that Church are kindly disposed toward Styricum, and their might shall alter Elenic predispositions. For the Delphae, however, such accommodation is impossible. Our very appearance doth set us forever apart from all others, and this doth stand at the heart of our present alliance. We have sought out Anakha, and we have offered him our aid in his struggle with Cyrgon. In exchange, we have besought him only to raise up Bhelliom and to seal us away from all other men. Then none may come against us, nor may we go against any other. Thus will all be safe."

"A wise decision perhaps, Anarae," Zalasta conceded. "It was a choice which *we* considered in eons past. Delphaeic numbers are limited, however, and your hidden valley will easily hold all of you. We Styrics are more numerous and more widespread. Our neighbors would not look kindly on a Styric homeland abutting their own borders. We cannot follow your course, but must live in the world."

Xanetia rose to her feet, putting one hand on Kalten's shoulder. "Stay, gentle Knight," she told him. "I must confer a moment with Anakha in furtherance of our pact. Should he detect falsity in me, *he* may slay me."

Sparhawk stood up, crossed to the door, and opened it for her. Danae, dragging Rollo behind her, followed them from the room.

"What is it, Anarae?" Sparhawk asked.

"Let us repair to that place above where we are wont to speak," she replied. "What I must tell thee is for thine ears alone."

Danae gave her a hard look.

"Thou mayest also hear my words, Highness," Xanetia told the little girl.

"You're *so* kind."

"We couldn't hide from her anyway, Xanetia," Sparhawk said. "We could go to the top of the highest tower in Matherion, and she'd fly up to eavesdrop on us anyway."

"Canst thou truly fly, Highness?" Xanetia looked startled.

"Can't everyone?"

"Behave yourself," Sparhawk told his daughter.

They climbed the stairs to the top of the tower again and went out onto the roof. "Anakha, I must tell thee a truth which thou mayest not wish to believe," Xanetia said gravely, "but it *is* truth, nonetheless."

"That's an unpromising start," Danae observed.

"I must speak this truth, Anakha," Xanetia said gravely, "for it is not only in keeping with our pact, but it doth also have a grave import on our common design."

"I get the feeling that I should take hold of something solid," Sparhawk said wryly.

"As it seemeth best to thee, Anakha. I must advise thee, however, that thy trust in Zalasta of Styricum is sorely misplaced."

"*What?*"

"He hath played thee false, Anakha. His heart and his mind are Cyrgon's."

CHAPTER EIGHTEEN

"That's absolutely impossible!" Danae exclaimed. "Zalasta *loves* my sister and me! He'd *never* betray us!"

"He doth love thy sister beyond measure, Goddess," Xanetia replied. "His feelings for *thee*, however, are not so kindly. In truth, he doth hate thee."

"I don't believe you!"

Sparhawk was a soldier, and soldiers who cannot adjust to surprises rapidly do not live long enough to become veterans. "You weren't at Delphaeus, Aphrael," he reminded the Child-Goddess. "Bhelliom vouched for Xanetia's truthfulness."

"She's just saying this to drive a wedge between us and Zalasta."

"I don't really think so." A number of things were rapidly falling into place in Sparhawk's mind. "The alliance is too important to the Delphae for her to endanger it with something that petty, and what she just told us explains several things that didn't make sense before. Let's hear her out. If there's some question about Zalasta's loyalty, we'd better find out about it right now. Exactly what did you discover in his mind, Anarae?"

"A great confusion, Anakha," Xanetia said sadly. "The mind of Zalasta might have been a noble one, but it doth stand on the brink of madness, consumed with but one thought and one desire. He hath loved thy sister since earliest childhood, Goddess, but his love is not the brotherly affection thou hast believed it was. This I know with greater certainty than all else, for it is ever at the forefront of his mind. He doth think of her as his affianced bride."

"That's absurd!" Danae said. "She doesn't think of him that way at all."

"Nay, but he doth think so of her. My sojourn within his thought was brief, therefore I do not as yet know all. As soon as I did perceive his treachery, my pledge bound me to reveal it to Anakha. With more time, I will discover more."

"What prompted you to look into *his* thought, Xanetia?" Sparhawk asked her. "The room was full of people. Why choose him—or do you just listen to everybody simultaneously? It seems to me that would be very confusing." He made a face. "I think I'm going at this backward. It might be helpful if I knew how your gift works. Is it like having another set of ears? Do you hear *every* thought going on around you—all at the same time?"

"Nay, Anakha." She smiled faintly. "That, as thou hast perceived, would be too confusing. Our ears, will we, nil we, hear *all* sound. My perception of the thought of others doth require my conscious direction. I must reach out to hear, *unless* the thought of one who is near me be so intense that it doth become as a shout. So it was with Zalasta. His mind doth scream the name of Sephrenia again and again. In equal measure, moreover, doth his mind shriek *thy* name, Goddess, and *those* shrieks are filled with his hatred of thee. In his mind art thou a thief, having stolen away all his hope of joy."

"A *thief*? *Me*? He was the one who was trying to steal what was mine! I *put* my sister here on this world. She's *mine*! She's always been mine! How *dare* he?" Danae's black eyes were flashing, and her voice was filled with outraged indignation.

"This isn't one of the more attractive sides of your nature, Divine One," Sparhawk suggested. "We don't own other people."

"I'm not a people, Sparhawk! I own what I want!"

"You're just digging yourself in deeper. I wouldn't pursue it any further."

"But I *do*, Father. I've devoted hundreds of years to Sephrenia, and all that time Zalasta's been sneaking around behind my back trying to steal her from me."

"Aphrael," he said gently, "you're an Elene in this particular incarnation, so you're going to have to stop thinking like a Styric. There are certain things that decent Elenes don't do, and you're doing one of them right now. Sephrenia belongs to herself—not to you, not to Zalasta, not even to Vanion. Her soul's her own."

"But I love her!" It was almost a wail.

"I'm not built right for this," Sparhawk muttered to himself. "How can any human hope to be the father of a Goddess?"

"Don't you love me, Father?" Her voice was tiny.

"Of course I do."

"Then *you* belong to me, too. Why are you arguing with me about it?"

"You're a primitive."

"Of course I am. We're *supposed* to be primitive. All these years Zalasta's been pretending to love me—smiling at me, kissing me, holding me while I slept. That wretch! That lying wretch! I'll have his heart for supper for this!"

"No, as a matter of fact, you won't. I'm not raising a cannibal. You won't eat pork, so don't start developing a taste for people."

"I'm sorry," she said contritely. "I got excited."

"Besides, I think Vanion's got first claim on Zalasta's tripes."

"Oh, dear. I completely forgot about Vanion. That poor, poor man." Two great tears welled up in her eyes. "I'll spend the rest of his life making this up to him."

"Why don't we let Sephrenia take care of that? Just heal the breach between them. That's the only thing he really wants." Then Sparhawk thought of something. "It won't wash, Xanetia. Zalasta could very well be in love with Sephrenia, but he hasn't gone over to Cyrgon. When we encountered those Trolls in the mountains of Atan, he was the one who saved us from them—and it wasn't just the Trolls. There were worse things there as well."

"The Trolls do not loom large in Cyrgon's plans, Anakha. The deaths of an hundred of them were of little moment. All else was illusion—illusion wrought by Zalasta himself to allay certain suspicions in the minds of diverse of thy companions. He sought to win thy trust by destroying those shadows of his own making."

"It *does* fit," Sparhawk said in a troubled voice. "Would you ladies excuse me for a moment? I think Vanion should hear this. It concerns him, too, and I'd like his advice before I start making decisions." He paused. "Will you two be all right here—together, I mean? Without someone here to keep you from each other's throats?"

"All will be well, Anakha," Xanetia assured him. "Divine Aphrael and I have something to discuss."

"All right," he said, "but no hitting—and don't start screaming at each other. You'll wake up the whole castle." He crossed the parapet to the door and went back down the stairs.

The meeting in the royal apartment had adjourned for a time, and Sparhawk found his friend sitting with his face in his hands in a room quite some distance from the one he normally shared with Sephrenia.

"I need some help, my friend," Sparhawk said to him. "There's something you need to know, and we're going to have to decide what to do about it."

Vanion raised his grief-ravaged face. "More trouble?" he asked.

"Probably. Xanetia just told me . . . well, I'll let her tell you about it herself. She and Danae are up at the top of the tower. I think we'll want to keep this private—at least until we decide what steps to take."

Vanion nodded and rose to his feet. The two of them went back out into the corridor and started up the stairs. "Where's Zalasta?" Sparhawk asked.

"He's with Sephrenia. She needs him right now."

Sparhawk grunted, not really trusting himself to speak.

They found Xanetia and Danae at the battlements looking out over the city. The sun was moving down the intensely blue autumn sky toward the craggy western horizon, and the breeze coming in off the Tamul Sea had a salt tang mingled with the ripe odor of autumn. "All right, go ahead and tell him, Xanetia," Sparhawk said. "Then we'll decide what to do."

To Sparhawk's surprise, Vanion didn't waste much time on incredulous exclamation. "You're sure, Anarae?" he asked after Xanetia had told him of Zalasta's duplicity.

She nodded. "I have seen his heart, my Lord. He hath played thee false."

"You don't seem very surprised, Vanion," Sparhawk said.

"I'm not—well, not really. There's always been something about Zalasta that didn't quite ring true. He had some trouble keeping his face under control when Sephrenia and I first went to Sarsos and moved into her house there. He tried to hide it, but I could tell that he wasn't very happy with our living arrangements, and his disapproval seemed to go quite a bit further than a generalized kind of moral outrage about unorthodox relationships."

"That's a delicate way to put it," Danae observed. "We've never understood why you humans make such a fuss about that. If two people love each other, they should do something about it, and living together is much more convenient for that sort of thing, isn't it?"

"There are certain ceremonies and formalities customary first," Sparhawk explained dryly.

"You mean something like the way the peacock shows off his feathers to the peahen before they start building a nest?"

"Something along those lines." Vanion sighed. "It seems that Sephrenia doesn't admire my feathers anymore."

"Not so, Lord Vanion," Xanetia disagreed. "She doth deeply love thee still, and her heart is made desolate by reason of her separation from thee."

"And Zalasta's with her right now doing everything he can to make the separation permanent," Sparhawk added, his voice bleak. "How do you want us to proceed with this, Vanion? You're the one most deeply involved here. There's nothing any of us could say that would convince Sephrenia that Zalasta's a traitor, you know."

Vanion nodded. "She's going to have to see it for herself," he agreed. "How far were you able to reach into his mind, Anarae?"

"His present thought is open to me; his memories somewhat less so. Proximity and some time should provide opportunity to probe more."

"That's the key, then," Vanion said. "Ehlana and Sarabian want to start tearing down the government almost immediately. Once that starts, Zalasta's presence in our inner councils is going to be potentially disastrous. He'll find out everything we've got planned."

"Let him," Danae sniffed. "It's not going to do him much good after I'm done with my supper."

"What's this?" Vanion asked.

"Our little savage here wants to eat Zalasta's heart," Sparhawk explained.

"While he watches," the Child-Goddess added. "That's the whole point of it—making him watch while I do it."

"Could she do that?" Vanion asked.

"Probably," Sparhawk replied. "I won't let her, though."

"I didn't *ask* you, Father," Danae said.

"You didn't have to. I said no. Now let's drop it."

"When did Zalasta make this arrangement with Cyrgon, Anarae?" Vanion asked.

"That is unclear for the nonce, my Lord," she replied. "I shall pursue it further. My sense of his thought doth suggest that their alliance dates back some years and doth involve Bhelliom in some fashion."

Sparhawk thought about that. "Zalasta *was* very upset when he found out that we'd thrown Bhelliom into the sea," he recalled. "I could start making some educated guesses at this point, but let's wait and see what Xanetia's able to turn up. Right now, I think we'd better concentrate on delaying Ehlana and Sarabian until we can devise some way to make Zalasta expose his own guilt. We need to get Sephrenia out from under his influence, and she's never going to believe that he's a traitor until she actually sees him convict himself by doing something that proves his treason."

Vanion nodded his agreement.

"I think we're going to have to keep this just among the four of us," Sparhawk continued. "Zalasta's very shrewd, and Sephrenia knows all of us better than we know ourselves. If the others have any idea of what we're doing, they'll let something slip, and Sephrenia will know about it immediately—and Zalasta will know about five minutes after she does."

"I'm afraid you're right," Vanion agreed.

"Hast thou a plan, Anakha?" Xanetia asked.

"Sort of. I've still got to work out some of the details, though. It's a little complicated."

Danae rolled her eyes upward. "Elenes," she sighed.

"Absolutely not," Ehlana said adamantly. "He's too valuable. We can't risk it." She was sitting near the window with the morning sun streaming in on her and setting her pale hair aglow.

"There's no risk involved, dear," Sparhawk assured her. "The cloud and the shadow are both gone. Bhelliom and I took care of that once and for all." There was the flaw. Sparhawk was not entirely positive of that.

"He's right, my Queen," Kalten agreed. "He tore the cloud to tatters and dissolved the shadow like salt in boiling water."

"I'd really like to ask Kolata some questions, Ehlana," Sarabian said. "It doesn't make sense to keep feeding him if we aren't going to get any use out of him. This is what we've been waiting for, my dear—some sort of assurance that he won't be torn to pieces the minute he opens his mouth."

"Are you absolutely sure, Sparhawk?" Ehlana asked.

"Trust me." Sparhawk reached inside his doublet and took out the box. "My blue friend here can make sure that Kolata remains intact—no matter *what* questions we ask." He looked at Zalasta. "I'm going to ask a favor of you, learned one," he said, keeping his voice casual. "I think Sephrenia should sit in on this. I know that she'd rather wash her hands of the lot of us, but maybe if she listens to Kolata's confession, she'll begin to take an interest in things again. It might be just the thing to bring her out of the state she's in right now."

Zalasta's face was troubled, though he was obviously trying very hard to keep his expression under control. "I don't think you realize how deeply she feels about this matter, Prince Sparhawk. I strongly advise you not to force her to be present when you question Kolata. It will only deepen the rift between her and her former friends."

"I won't accept that, Zalasta," Ehlana told him. "Sephrenia's a member of the royal council of Elenia. I appointed her to that position when I ascended the throne. Her personal problems are her own business, but I need her here in her *official* capacity. If necessary, I'll command her presence, and I'll send Kalten and Ulath to deliver the command and make sure that she obeys."

Sparhawk almost felt sorry for Zalasta at that point. Their decisions and their requests were all completely reasonable, and try though he might, Zalasta could find no way to avoid agreeing. Kolata's testimony was almost certain to be an absolute disaster for the first citizen of Styricum, but there was no way he could prevent that testimony without exposing himself as a traitor. He rose to his feet. "I will try to persuade her, your Majesty," he said, bowing to Ehlana. He turned and quietly left the blue-draped room.

"I don't understand why you won't let us tell him, Sparhawk," Kalten said. "He *is* a friend, after all."

"He's also a Styric, Kalten," Vanion said smoothly. "We don't know how he *really* feels about the Delphae. He might go up in flames if he finds out that Xanetia can pick his thoughts the way Talen picks pockets."

"Sephrenia's probably told him about it already, Lord Vanion," Bevier pointed out.

Sparhawk threw a brief questioning look at Xanetia, framing the question in his thought.

She shook her head. For some reason, Sephrenia had *not* yet told Zalasta about the Delphaeic woman's strange capability to delve into the minds of others.

"I don't think so, Bevier," Vanion was saying. "He hasn't shown any reluctance to be in the same room with the Anarae, and that's a fair indication that he doesn't know. Now, then, who's going to question Kolata? We should probably limit it to just one of us. If we all start throwing questions at him, his thoughts will be so jumbled that Xanetia won't be able to make any sense of them."

"Itagne's skilled at debate and disputation," Oscagne suggested. "Academics spend hours splitting hairs."

"We prefer to call it meticulous attention to detail, old boy," Itagne corrected his brother. "Kolata has ministerial rank."

"Not any more, he doesn't," Sarabian said.

"Well, he *used* to, your Majesty. I'd suggest that we let Oscagne conduct the interrogation. He holds the same rank as Kolata, so he'll be able to approach him as an equal."

"Might I make a suggestion?" Stragen asked.

"Of course, Milord Stragen," the emperor said.

"Teovin's been sneaking around out there trying his very best to subvert the other ministries of your Majesty's government. Wouldn't it be a good idea to make this a formal inquiry instead of a star-chamber proceeding? If all the ministers and the aides are present when we question Kolata, Teovin won't have the chance to scramble around and mend his fences."

"It's an interesting notion, isn't it, Ehlana?" Sarabian mused.

"Very interesting," she agreed. "We'll have to postpone the interrogation, though."

"Oh?"

"We'll want to give your Atan runners a head start." She looked at him gravely. "This is it, Sarabian. Up until now, it's only been speculation. Once Kolata starts talking in front of the rest of the government, you'll be committed. Are you really ready to go that far?"

The emperor drew in a deep breath. "Yes, Ehlana, I think I am." His voice was firm, but very quiet.

"Issue the order, then. Declare martial law. Turn the Atans loose."

Sarabian swallowed hard. "Are you certain your idea will work, Atan Engessa?" he asked the towering warrior.

"It always has, Sarabian-Emperor," Engessa replied. "The signal fires are all in place. The word will spread throughout Tamuli in a single night. The Atans will move out of their garrisons the following morning."

Sarabian stared at the floor for a long time. Then he looked up. "Do it," he said.

The difficult part was persuading Sarabian and Ehlana *not* to tell Zalasta about what was happening. "He doesn't need to know," Sparhawk explained patiently.

"Surely you don't mistrust him, Sparhawk," Ehlana protested. "He's proved his loyalty over and over again."

"Of course he has. He's a Styric, though, and this sudden move of yours is going to turn all of Tamuli upside down. There's going to be absolute chaos out there. He may try to get word to the Styric communities hereabouts—a warning of some kind. It's a natural thing for him to do, and we can't afford to risk letting that information get out. The only thing that makes your plan workable at all is the fact that it's going to be a total surprise. There are Styrics, and then there are Styrics."

"Say what you mean, Sparhawk," Sarabian said in a testy voice.

"The term *renegade* Styric means the same thing here in Tamuli as it does in

Eosia, your Majesty. We almost have to assume that if we tell Zalasta, we're telling all of Styricum, don't we? We know Zalasta, but we *don't* know all the other Styrics on the continent. There are some in Sarsos who'd sign compacts with Hell itself if they thought it would give them a chance to get even with the Elenes."

"You're going to hurt his feelings, you know," Ehlana told him.

"He'll live. We only have one chance at this, so let's not take even the remotest of risks."

There was a polite tap at the door, and Mirtai stepped into the room where the three of them were meeting. "Oscagne and that other one are back," she reported.

"Show them in please, Atana," Sarabian told her.

There was a kind of suppressed jubilation on the foreign minister's face as he entered with his brother, and Itagne's expression was almost identical. Sparhawk was a bit startled by how much alike they looked.

"You two look like a couple of cats who just got into the cream," Sarabian told them.

"We're pulling off the coup of the decade, your Majesty," Itagne replied.

"Of the century," Oscagne corrected. "Everything's in place, my Emperor. We left it sort of vague—'general meeting of the Imperial Council'—that sort of thing. Itagne dropped a few hints. He's been planting the notion that you're considering having your birthday declared a national holiday. It's the sort of foolish whim your Majesty's family is famous for."

"Be nice," Sarabian murmured. He had picked up that particular Elene expression during his stay in Ehlana's castle.

"Sorry, your Majesty," Oscagne apologized. "We've passed the whole thing off as a routine, meaningless meeting of the council—all formality and no substance."

"May I borrow your throne room, Ehlana?" Sarabian asked.

"Of course." She smiled. "Formal dress, I suppose?"

"Certainly. We'll wear our crowns and our state robes. You wear your prettiest dress, and I'll wear mine."

"Your *Majesty*!" Oscagne protested. "The customary Tamul mantle is hardly a dress."

"A long skirt is a long skirt, Oscagne. Frankly, I'd prefer doublet and hose—and, given the circumstances, my rapier. Stragen's right. Once you get used to wearing one, you start to feel undressed without it."

"If formality's going to be the keynote, I think you and the others should wear your dress armor, Sparhawk," Ehlana told her husband.

"Excellent idea, Ehlana," Sarabian approved. "That way they'll be ready when things turn ugly."

They spent the rest of the day supervising the moving of furniture in the throne room. The Queen of Elenia, as she sometimes did, went to extremes. "Buntings?" Sparhawk asked her. "*Buntings,* Ehlana?"

"We want things to look festive, Sparhawk," she replied with an airy little toss of her head. "Yes, I know. It's frivolous and even a little silly, but buntings hanging from the walls and trumpet fanfares introducing each of the ministers will set the tone. We want this to look so intensely formal that the government officials won't believe that anything serious could possibly happen. We're laying a trap, love, and buntings are part of the bait. Details, Sparhawk, details. Good plots swarm with details."

"You're enjoying this, aren't you?"

"Of course I am. Is the drawbridge raised?"

He nodded.

"Good. Keep it that way. We don't want anybody slipping out of the castle with any kind of information. We'll escort the ministers inside tomorrow, and then we'll raise the drawbridge again. We want to be in absolute control of the situation."

"Yes, dear."

"Don't make fun of me, Sparhawk," she warned.

"I'd sooner die."

It was nearly dusk when Zalasta came into the throne room and took Sparhawk to one side. "I *must* leave, Prince Sparhawk," he pleaded, his eyes a little wild. "It is a matter of the gravest urgency."

"My hands are tied, Zalasta," Sparhawk replied. "You know my wife. When she starts speaking in the royal we, there's no reasoning with her."

"There are things I *must* set in motion, your Highness, things vital to the success of the emperor's plan."

"I'll try to talk with her, but I can't hold out much hope. Things *are* fairly well under control, though. The Atans know what to do outside the castle walls, and my Church Knights can handle things inside. There *are* ministers and other high-level officials whose loyalty is in doubt, you know. We don't know exactly what the questioning of the Minister of the Interior is going to bring out. We'll have those people in our hands, and we don't want them running off to stir up more mischief."

"You don't *understand,* Sparhawk!" The note of desperation was clearly evident.

"I'll do what I can, Zalasta," Sparhawk said. "But I can't make any promises."

CHAPTER NINETEEN

The Tamul architect who had designed Ehlana's castle had evidently devoted half a lifetime to the study of Elene buildings, and, like so many with limited gifts, he had slavishly imitated the details without capturing the spirit. The throne room was a case in point. Elene castles have but two purposes—to remain standing and to keep out unwanted visitors. Both these purposes are served best by the kind of massive construction one might consider in designing a mountain. Over the centuries, some Elenes have sought to soften their necessarily bleak surroundings by embellishment. The interior braces intended to keep the walls from collapsing—even when swept by a blizzard of boulders—became buttresses. The massive stone posts designed to keep the ceiling where it belonged became columns with ornately carved bases and capitals. The same sort of strength can be achieved by vaulting, and the throne room of Ehlana's Tamul-built castle was a marvel of redundancy. It was massively vaulted *and* supported by long rows of fluted columns, and was braced by flying buttresses so delicate as to be not only useless but actually hazardous to those standing under them. Moreover, like everything else in fire-domed Matherion, the entire room was sheathed in opalescent mother-of-pearl.

Ehlana had chosen the buntings with some care, and the gleaming walls were now accented with a riot of color. The forty-foot-long blue-velvet draperies at the narrow windows had been accented with white satin, the walls were decorated with crossed pennons and imitation battle flags, bright runners carpeted the aisles, and the columns and buttresses were bandaged with scarlet silk. The place looked to Sparhawk's somewhat-jaundiced eye like a country fair operated by a profoundly color-blind entrepreneur.

"Garish," Ulath observed, buffing the black Ogre-horns on his helmet with a piece of cloth.

"Garish comes close," Sparhawk agreed. Sparhawk wore his formal black armor and silver surcoat. The Tamul blacksmith who had hammered out the dents and re-enameled the armor had also anointed the inside of each intricately wrought section and all the leather straps with crushed rose petals in a kind of subtle, unspoken criticism of the armor's normal fragrance. The resulting mixture of odors was peculiar.

"How are we going to explain all the guards standing around Ehlana and Sarabian?" Ulath asked.

"We don't have to explain things, Ulath." Sparhawk shrugged. "We're Elenes, and the rest of the world believes that we're barbarians with strange, ritualistic customs that nobody else understands. I am *not* going to let my wife sit there unprotected while she and Sarabian calmly advise the Tamul government that it's been dismantled."

"Good thinking." Ulath looked gravely at his friend. "Sephrenia's being difficult, you know."

"We more or less expected that."

"She might have an easier time if she could sit next to Zalasta."

Sparhawk shook his head. "Zalasta's an adviser to the government. He'll have to be on the main floor with the ministers. Let's keep Sephrenia off to one side. I'll have Danae sit with her."

"That might help. Your daughter's presence seems to calm Sephrenia. I wouldn't seat Xanetia with them, though."

"I hadn't planned to."

"Just making sure. Did Engessa get any kind of acknowledgment of his signal? Are we absolutely *sure* his order got to everybody?"

"*He* is. I guess the Atans have used signal fires to pass orders along for centuries."

"I'm just a bit dubious about bonfires on hilltops as a way to send messages, Sparhawk."

"That's Engessa's department. It won't matter all that much if word hadn't reached a few backwaters by sunrise this morning."

"You're probably right. I guess we've done all we can, then. I just hope nothing goes wrong."

"What could go wrong?"

"That's the kind of thinking that fills graveyards, Sparhawk. I'll go tell them to lower the drawbridge. We might as well get started."

Stragen had carefully coached the dozen Tamul trumpeters and the rest of his musicians, concluding the lesson with some horrendous threats and an instructional visit to the carefully re-created torture chamber in the basement. The musicians had all piously sworn to play the proper notes and to forgo improvisation. The fanfares that were to greet the arrival of each minister of the imperial government had been Ehlana's idea. Fanfares are flattering; they elevate the ego; they lull the unwary into traps. Ehlana was good at that sort of thing. The depths of her political instincts sometimes amazed Sparhawk.

In keeping with the formality of the occasion, armored Church Knights were stationed at evenly spaced intervals along the walls. To the casual observer, the knights were no more than a part of the decor of the throne room. The casual observer, however, would have been wrong. The motionless men in steel were there to make absolutely certain that once the members of the imperial government had entered the room, they would not leave without permission; and the drawbridge, which was to be raised as soon as all the guests had arrived, doubly insured that nobody would grow bored and wander off. Sarabian had advised his Elene friends that the Imperial Council of Tamuli had grown over the centuries. At first, the council had consisted only of the ministers. Then the ministers had included their secretaries; then their undersecretaries. By now it had reached the point where sub-sub assistant temporary interim undersecretaries were also included. The title "Member of the Imperial Council" had become largely meaningless. The inclusion of such a mob, however, ensured that every traitor inside the imperial compound would be gathered under Ehlana's battlements. The Queen of Elenia was shrewd enough to even use her enemies' egotism as a weapon against them.

"Well?" Ehlana asked nervously when her husband entered the royal apartment. The Queen of Elenia wore a cream-colored gown, trimmed with gold lamé, and a dark blue, ermine-trimmed velvet cloak. Her crown looked quite delicate, a kind of lace cap made of hammered gold inset with bright-colored gems. Despite its airy appearance, however, Sparhawk knew—because he had picked it up several times—that it was almost as heavy as her state crown, which was locked in the royal vault back in Cimmura.

"They're starting to drift across the drawbridge," he reported. "Itagne's greeting them. He knows everybody of any consequence in the government, so he'll know when our guests have all arrived. As soon as everyone's inside, the knights will raise the drawbridge." He looked at Emperor Sarabian, who stood near a window nervously chewing on one fingernail. "It's not going to be all that much longer, your Majesty," he said. "Shouldn't you change clothes?"

"The Tamul mantle was designed to cover a multitude of defects, Prince Sparhawk, so it should cover my western clothes—*and* my rapier. I am *not* going in there unarmed."

"We'll take care of you, Sarabian," Ehlana assured him.

"I'd rather do it myself, Mother." The emperor suddenly laughed nervously. "A bad joke, perhaps, but there's a lot of truth to it. You've raised me from political babyhood, Ehlana. In that respect, you *are* my mother."

"If you ever call me Mommy, I'll never speak to you again, your Majesty."

"I'd sooner bite out my tongue, your Majesty."

"What's the customary procedure, your Majesty?" Sparhawk asked Sarabian as they stood peering around the edge of the draped doorway into the rapidly filling throne room.

"As soon as everybody gets here, Subat will call the meeting to order," Sarabian replied. "That's when I enter—usually to the sound of what passes for music here in Matherion."

"Stragen's seen to it that your grand entrance will be truly grand," Ehlana assured him. "He composed the fanfare himself."

"Are all Elene thieves artists?" Sarabian asked. "Talen paints, Stragen composes music, and Caalador's a gifted actor."

"We *do* seem to attract talent, don't we." Ehlana smiled.

"Should I explain why there are so many of us on the dais?" Sarabian asked, glancing at Mirtai and Engessa.

She shook her head. "Never explain. It's a sign of weakness. I'll enter on your arm, and they'll all grovel."

"It's called genuflectory prostration, Ehlana."

"Whatever." She shrugged. "When they get up again, we'll be sitting there with our guards around us. That's when *you* take over the meeting. Don't even let Subat get started. We've got our own agenda today, and we don't have time to listen to him babble about the prospects for the wheat harvest on the plains of Edom. How are you feeling?"

"Nervous. I've never overthrown a government before."

"Neither have I, actually—unless you count what I did in the Basilica when I appointed Dolmant to the Archprelacy."

"She didn't actually do that, did she, Sparhawk?"

"Oh, yes, your Majesty—all by herself. She was superb."

"Just keep talking, Sarabian," Ehlana told him. "If anyone tries to interrupt, shout him down. Don't even pretend to be polite. This is *your* party. Don't be conciliatory or reasonable. Be coldly furious instead. Are you any good at oratory?"

"Probably not. They don't let me speak in public very often—except at the graduation ceremonies at the university."

"Speak slowly. You tend to talk too fast. Half of any good oration lies in its cadence. Use pauses. Vary your volume from a shout down to a whisper. Be dramatic. Give them a good show."

He laughed. "You're a charlatan, Ehlana."

"Naturally. That's what politics is all about—fraud, deceit, charlatanism."

"That's dreadful!"

"Of course. That's why it's so much fun."

The brazen fanfares echoed back from the vaulted ceiling as each minister entered the throne room, and they had the desired effect. The ministers in their silken mantles all seemed slightly awed by their own sublime importance. They moved to their places with stately pace and slow, their expressions grave, even exalted. Pondia Subat, the prime minister, seemed particularly impressed with himself. He sat splendidly alone in a crimson-upholstered chair to one side of the dais upon which the thrones stood, looking out imperially at the other officials assembling in the chairs lining both sides of the broad central aisle.

Chancellor of the Exchequer Gashon sat with Teovin, the Director of the Secret Police, and several other ministers. There seemed to be a great deal of whispering going on in the little group.

"That would probably be the opposition," Ehlana observed. "Teovin's certainly involved, and the others are also most likely a part of it—to a greater or lesser degree." She turned to Talen, who stood directly behind her, wearing his page's knee britches. "Pay very close attention to that group," she instructed. "I want a report on their reactions. We should be able to determine their degree of guilt by the looks on their faces."

"Yes, my Queen."

Then Itagne appeared briefly at the massive double doors to the throne room and flicked his hand at Ulath, signaling that all of the relevant officials had arrived.

Ulath, who stood to one side of the dais, nodded and raised his Ogre-horn trumpet to his lips.

The room seemed to shudder into a shocked silence as the barbaric sound of the Ogre-horn, deep-toned and rasping, reverberated from the nacreous walls. The huge doors boomed shut, and two armored knights, one a Cyrinic all in white, and the other a Pandion all in black, placed themselves in front of the entryway.

The prime minister rose to his feet.

Ulath banged the butt of his ax on the floor three times to call for silence.

The emperor winced.

"What's wrong, Sarabian?" Mirtai asked him.

"Sir Ulath just broke several of the floor tiles."

"We can replace them with bone," she assured him. "There should be quite a few lying around before the day's over."

"Will the council please come to order?" Pondia Subat intoned.

Ulath banged the floor again.

Sparhawk looked around the throne room. Everyone was in place. Sephrenia, dressed in her white Styric robe, sat with Princess Danae and Caalador on the far side of the room. Xanetia, also in white, sat on the near side with Kalten and Berit. Melidere sat in a small gallery with the nine imperial wives. The clever baroness had carefully cultivated a friendship with Sarabian's first wife, Cieronna, a member of one of the noblest houses of Tamul proper and the mother of the crown prince. The friendship had by now grown so close that Melidere was customarily invited to attend state functions in the company of the empresses. Her presence among them *this* time had a serious purpose, however. Sarabian had a wife from each of the nine kingdoms, and it was entirely possible that some of them had been subverted. Sparhawk was fairly certain that the bare-breasted Valesian, Elysoun, was free of any political contamination. She was simply too busy for politics. The Tegan wife, Gahenas, a puritanical lady obsessed with her personal virtue and her staunch republicanism, would probably not have even been approached by conspirators. Torellia of Arjuna, and Chacole of Cynesga, however, were highly suspect. They had both established what might best be called personal courts liberally sprinkled with nobles from their homelands. Melidere had been instructed to keep a close eye on those two in particular for signs of unusual reactions to the revelation of Zalasta's true affiliation.

Sparhawk sighed. It was all so complicated. Friends and enemies all looked the same. In the long run, it might turn out that Xanetia's unusual gift would prove more valuable than a sudden offer of aid from an entire army.

Vanion, who had unobtrusively stationed himself with the knights lining the walls, reached up and first lowered, then raised, his visor. It was the signal that all their forces were in place. Stragen, who was with his trumpeters behind the dais, nodded briefly in acknowledgment.

Then Sparhawk looked rather closely at Zalasta, the unknowing guest of honor at this affair. The Styric, his eyes apprehensive, sat among the ministers, his white robe looking oddly out of place among all the bright-colored silk mantles. He quite obviously knew that something was afoot, and just as obviously had no idea what it might be. That was something, anyway. At least no one in the inner circle had been subverted. Sparhawk irritably shook that thought off. Under the circumstances, a certain amount of wary suspicion was only natural; but left unchecked, it could become a disease. He made a sour face. About one more day of this and he'd begin to suspect himself.

"The council will come now to order!" Pondia Subat repeated.

Ulath broke some more tiles.

"By command of his Imperial Majesty, Emperor Sarabian, this council is called to order!"

"Good God, Subat," Sarabian groaned, half to himself, "will you destroy the floor entirely?"

"Gentlemen, his Imperial Majesty, Sarabian of Tamuli!"

A single trumpet voiced a clear, ringing theme of majestically descending notes. Then another joined the first to repeat the theme a third of an octave higher—then another trumpet another third higher. Then, in a great crescendo and still higher, the musicians all joined in to fill the throne room with shimmering echoes.

"Impressive," Sarabian noted. "Do we go in now?"

"Not yet," Ehlana told him. "The music changes. That's when we start. Pay attention to my hand on your arm. Let me set the pace. Don't jump when we get to the thrones. Stragen's got a whole brass band hidden in various parts of the room. The climax will be thunderous. Draw yourself up, throw your shoulders back, and look regal. Try your very best to look like a God."

"Are you having fun, Ehlana?"

She grinned impishly at him and winked. "There," she said, "the flutes at the back of the hall have picked up the theme. That's our signal. Good luck, my friend." She kissed him lightly on the cheek and then laid her hand on his arm. "One," she said, listening intently to the music. "Two." She drew in a deep breath. "Now." And the Emperor of Tamuli and the Queen of Elenia stepped through the archway and crossed with regal pace toward their golden thrones as the flutes at the rear of the hall softly sang the plaintive accompaniment of Stragen's main theme, set now in a minor key. Immediately behind them came Sparhawk, Mirtai, Engessa, and Bevier. Talen, Alean, and Itagne, who was still puffing slightly from running through the halls, followed.

As the royal party reached the thrones, Stragen, who was using his rapier as a conductor's baton, led his hidden musicians into a fortissimo recapitulation of his main theme. The sound was overwhelming. It was not entirely certain whether the members of the imperial council fell to their faces out of habit or were knocked down by that enormous blast of sound. Stragen cut his rapier sharply to one side, and the musicians broke off, slashed as it were into silence, leaving the echoes shimmering in the air like ghosts.

Pondia Subat rose to his feet. "Will your Majesty address some few remarks to this assemblage before we commence?" he asked in an almost insultingly superior tone. The question was sheer formality, almost ritualistic. The emperor traditionally did not speak at these sessions.

"Why, yes, as a matter of fact, I believe I will, Pondia Subat," Sarabian replied, rising again to his feet. "So good of you to ask, old boy."

Subat gaped at him, his expression incredulous. "But——"

"Was there something, Subat?"

"This is most irregular, your Majesty."

"I know. Refreshing, isn't it? We've got a lot to cover today, Subat, so let's get cracking."

"Your Majesty has not consulted with me. We cannot proceed if I don't know what issues are——"

"Sit, Subat!" Sarabian snapped. "Stay!" His tone was one of command. "You will remain silent until I give you leave to speak."

"You can't——"

"*I said sit down!*"

Subat quailed and sank into his chair.

"Your head's none too tightly attached just now, my Lord Prime Minister," Sarabian said ominously, "and if you waggle it at me in the wrong way, it might just fall off. You've been tiptoeing right on the brink of treason, Pondia Subat, and I'm more than a little put out with you."

The prime minister's face went deathly pale.

Sarabian began to pace up and down on the dais, his face like a thundercloud.

"Please, God, make him stand still," Ehlana said under her breath. "He can't make a decent speech if he's loping around the dais like a gazelle in flight."

Then the emperor stopped to stand at the very front of the slightly elevated platform. "I'm not going to waste time with banalities, gentlemen," he told his government bluntly. "We had a crisis, and I depended on you to deal with it. You failed me—probably because you were too busy playing your usual games of politics. The empire required giants, and all I had to serve me were dwarves. That made it necessary for *me* to deal with the crisis personally. And that's what I've been doing, gentlemen, for the past several months. You are no longer relevant, my Lords. *I* am the government."

There were cries of outrage from the ministers and their subordinates.

"He's going too *fast!*" Ehlana exclaimed. "He should have built up to that!"

"Don't be such a critic," Sparhawk told her. "It's his speech. Let him make it his own way."

"I will have silence!" Sarabian declared.

The council paid no attention. They continued their excited babbling. The emperor opened his mantle to reveal his Elene clothing, and then he drew his rapier. "I said *SILENCE!*" he roared.

All sound ceased.

"I'll pin the next man who interrupts me to the wall like a butterfly," Sarabian told them. Then he cut his rapier sharply through the air. The whistling sound of the blade's passage was as chill as death itself. He looked around at his cowed officials. "That's a little better," he said. "Now stay that way." He set the point of the rapier on the floor and lightly crossed his hands on the pommel. "My family has depended on the ministries to handle the day-to-day business of government for centuries," he said. "Our trust has obviously been misplaced. You were adequate—barely—in times of tranquility, but when a crisis arose, you began to scurry around like ants, more interested in protecting your fortunes, your personal privileges, and perpetuating your petty interdepartmental rivalries than in the good of my empire—and that's the one thing you all seem to forget, gentlemen. It's *my* empire. My family hasn't made a great issue of the fact, but I think it's time you were reminded of it. You serve *me,* and you serve only at *my* pleasure, not at *your* convenience."

The officials were all gaping at the man they had thought to be no more than a harmless eccentric. Sparhawk saw a movement near the middle of the throne room. His eyes flicked back to the front, and he saw that Teovin's chair was conspicuously empty. The Director of the Secret Police was more clever and much quicker than his colleagues, and, throwing dignity to the winds, he was busily crawling on his hands and knees toward the nearest exit. Chancellor of the Exchequer Gashon, thin, bloodless, and wispy-haired, sat beside Teovin's vacant chair, staring at Sarabian in open terror.

Sparhawk looked quickly at Vanion, and the preceptor nodded. Vanion had seen the crawling policeman, too.

"When I perceived that I had chosen little men with little minds to administer my empire," Sarabian was saying, "I appealed to Zalasta of Styricum for advice.

Who better to deal with the supernatural than the Styrics? It was Zalasta who recommended that I submit a request directly to Archprelate Dolmant of the Church of Chyrellos for assistance, and the very core of that assistance was to be Prince Sparhawk of Elenia. We Tamuls pride ourselves on our subtlety and our sophistication, but I assure you that we are but children when compared to the Elenes. The state visit of my dear sister Ehlana was little more than a subterfuge designed to conceal the fact that our main purpose was to bring her husband, Sir Sparhawk, to Matherion. Queen Ehlana and I amused ourselves by deceiving you—and you were not hard to deceive, my Lords—while Prince Sparhawk and his companions sought the roots of the turmoil here in Tamuli. As we had anticipated, our enemies reacted."

There was a brief, muted disturbance at one of the side doors. Vanion and Khalad were quite firmly preventing the Director of the Secret Police from leaving.

"Did you have a pressing engagement somewhere, Teovin?" Sarabian drawled.

Teovin's eyes were wild and he looked at his emperor with open hatred.

"If you're discontent with me, Teovin, I'll be more than happy to give you satisfaction," Sarabian told him, flourishing his rapier meaningfully. "Please return to your seat. My seconds will call upon you when we've concluded here."

Vanion took the Director of the Secret Police by one arm, turned him around, and pointed at the empty seat. Then, with a none-too-gentle shove, he started him moving.

"This windy preamble's beginning to bore me, gentlemen," Sarabian announced, "so why don't we get down to cases? The attempted coup here in Matherion was the direct response to Sir Sparhawk's arrival. The assorted disturbances which have kept the Atans running from one end of the continent to the other for the past several years have had one source and only one. We have a single enemy, and he has formed a massive conspiracy designed to overthrow the government and to wrest my throne from me, and—as I probably should have anticipated, given the nature of those who pretend to serve me—he had willing helpers in the government itself."

Some of the dignitaries gasped; others looked guilty.

"Pay very close attention, gentlemen," Sarabian told them. "This is where it gets interesting. Many of you have wondered at the long absence of Interior Minister Kolata. I'm sure you'll be delighted to know that Kolata's going to be joining us now."

He turned to Ulath. "Would you be so good as to invite the Minister of the Interior to come in, Sir Knight?" he asked.

Ulath bowed, and Kalten rose from his seat to join him.

"Minister Kolata, as the chief policeman in all the empire, knows a great deal about criminal activities," Sarabian declared. "I'm absolutely sure that his analysis of the present situation will be enlightening."

Kalten and Ulath returned with the ashen-faced Minister of the Interior between them. It was not the fact that Kolata was in obvious distress that raised the outcry from the other officials, however, but rather the fact that the chief policeman of the empire was in chains.

· · ·

Emperor Sarabian stood impassively as his council members shouted their protests. "How am I doing so far, Ehlana?" he asked out of the corner of his mouth.

"I'd have done it differently," she told him, "but that's only a matter of style. I'll give you a complete critique when it's all over." She looked out at the officials who were all on their feet talking excitedly. "Don't let that go on for too long. Remind them who's in charge. Be very firm about it."

"Yes, Mother." He smiled. Then he looked at his government and drew in a deep breath. *"QUIET!"* he roared in a great voice.

They fell into a stunned silence.

"There will be no further interruptions of these proceedings," Sarabian told them. "The rules have changed, gentlemen. We're not going to pretend to be civilized anymore. I'm going to tell you what to do, and you're going to do it. I'd like to remind you that not only do you *serve* at my pleasure; you also continue to *live* only at my pleasure. The Minister of the Interior is guilty of high treason. You'll note that there was no trial. Kolata is guilty because I *say* that he's guilty." Sarabian paused as a new realization came to him. "My power in Tamuli is absolute. *I* am the government, and *I* am the law. We are going to question Kolata rather closely. Pay attention to his answers, gentlemen. Your positions in government—your very lives—may hinge on what he says. Foreign Minister Oscagne is going to question Kolata—not about his guilt, which has already been established—but about the involvement of others. We're going to get to the bottom of this once and for all. You may proceed, Oscagne."

"Yes, your Majesty." Oscagne rose to his feet and stood a moment in deep thought as Sarabian sat again on his throne. Oscagne wore a black silk mantle. His choice of color had been quite deliberate. While black mantles were not common, they were not unheard of. Judges and imperial prosecutors, however, *always* wore black. The somber color heightened the foreign minister's pallor, which in turn accentuated his grim expression.

Khalad came forward with a plain wooden stool and set it down in front of the dais. Kalten and Ulath brought the Minister of the Interior forward and plopped him unceremoniously down on the stool.

"Do you understand your situation here, Kolata?" Oscagne asked the prisoner.

"You have no right to question me, Oscagne," Kolata replied quickly.

"Break his fingers, Khalad," Sparhawk instructed from his position just behind Ehlana's throne.

"Yes, my Lord," Khalad replied. "How many?"

"Start out with one or two. Every time he starts talking about Oscagne's rights—or his own—break another one."

"Yes, my Lord." Khalad took the Interior Minister's wrist.

"Stop him!" Kolata squealed in fright. "Somebody stop him!"

"Kalten, Ulath," Sparhawk said, "kill the first man who moves."

Kalten drew his sword, and Ulath raised his ax.

"You see how it is, old boy," Oscagne said to the man on the stool. "You're not universally loved to begin with, and Prince Sparhawk's command has just evaporated any minuscule affection anyone here might have had for you. You *will* talk, Kolata. Sooner or later, you'll talk. We can do this the easy way, or we can do it the other way, but you *are* going to answer my questions." Oscagne's expression had become implacable.

"They'll kill me, Oscagne!" Kolata pleaded. "They'll kill me if I talk."

"You're in a difficult situation, then, Kolata, because *we'll* kill you if you don't. You're taking orders from Cyrgon, aren't you?"

"Cyrgon? That's absurd!" Kolata blustered. "Cyrgon's a myth."

"Oh, really?" Oscagne looked at him with contempt. "Don't play the fool with me, Kolata. I don't have the patience for it. Your orders come from the Cynesgan embassy, don't they? And most of the time, they're delivered by a man named Krager."

Kolata gaped at him.

"Close your mouth, Kolata. You look like an idiot with it hanging open like that. We already know a great deal about your treason. All we really want from you are a few details. You were first contacted by someone you had reason to trust—and most probably someone you respected. That immediately rules out a Cynesgan. No Tamul has anything but contempt for Cynesgans. Given our characteristic sense of our own superiority, that would also rule out an Arjuni or an Elene from any of the western kingdoms. That would leave only another Tamul, or possibly an Atan, or—" Oscagne's eyes suddenly widened, and his expression grew thunderstruck. "Or a *Styric*!"

"Absurd," Kolata scoffed weakly. His eyes, however, were wild, darting this way and that like those of a man looking for a place to hide.

Sparhawk looked appraisingly at Zalasta. The sorcerer's face was deathly pale, but his eyes showed that he was still in control. It was going to take something more to push him over the edge. The big Pandion placed his left hand on his sword hilt, giving Oscagne their prearranged signal.

"We don't seem to be getting anywhere, old boy," Oscagne drawled, recovering from his surprise. "I think you need some encouragement." He turned and looked at Xanetia. "Would you be so kind, Anarae?" he asked her. "Our esteemed Minister of the Interior doesn't seem to want to share things with us. Do you suppose you could persuade him to change his mind?"

"I can but try, Oscagne of Matherion," Xanetia replied, rising to her feet. She crossed the front of the room, choosing for some reason to approach the prisoner from the side where Sephrenia sat rather than the one from which she herself had been watching. "Thou art afeared, Kolata of Matherion," she said gravely, "and thy fear doth make thee brave, for it is in thy mind that though they who hold thy body captive may do thee great harm, he who hath thy soul in thrall may do thee worse. Now must thou contend with yet an even greater fear. Look upon *me*, Kolata of Matherion, and tremble, for *I* will visit upon thee the ultimate horror. Wilt thou speak, and speak freely?"

"I *can't*!" Kolata wailed.

"Then art thou lost. Behold me as I truly am, and consider well thy fate, for I am death, Kolata of Matherion, death beyond thy most dreadful imagining." The color drained from her slowly, and the glow within her was faint at first. She stood looking at him with her chin raised and an expression of deep sadness in her eyes as she glowed brighter and brighter.

Kolata screamed.

The other officials scrambled to their feet, their faces terrified, and their babbling suddenly shrill.

"Sit down!" Sarabian bellowed at them, *"and be silent!"*

A few of them were cowed into obedience. Most, however, were too frightened. They continued to shrink back from Xanetia, crying out in shrill voices.

"My Lord Vanion," Sarabian called over the tumult, "would you please restore order?"

"At once, your Majesty." Vanion clapped down his visor, pulled his sword from its scabbard, and raised his shield. "Draw swords!" He barked the command. There was a steely rasp as the Church Knights drew their swords. "Forward!" Vanion ordered.

The knights posted along the walls marched clankingly forward, their swords at the ready, converging on the frightened officials. Vanion stretched forth his steel-clad arm, extending his sword and touching the tip to the throat of the prime minister. "The emperor told you to sit down, Pondia Subat," he said. "Do it! *NOW!*"

The prime minister sank back into his chair, suddenly more afraid of Vanion than he was of Xanetia.

A couple of the council members had to be chased down and forcibly returned to their seats, and one rather athletic one—the Minister of Public Works, Sparhawk thought—was only persuaded to come down from the drape he'd been climbing by the threat of Khalad's crossbow. Order was restored. When the council had returned—or been returned—to their seats, however, the Chancellor of the Exchequer was discovered lying on the floor, vacant-eyed and with a large bubble of foam protruding from his gaping mouth. Vanion checked the body rather perfunctorily. "Poison," he said shortly. "He seems to have taken it himself."

Ehlana shuddered.

"Prithee, Anarae," Sarabian said to Xanetia, "continue thine inquiry."

"An it please your Majesty," she replied in that strange echoing voice. She turned her gaze on Kolata. "Wilt thou speak, and freely, Kolata of Matherion?" she asked.

He shrank back in horror.

"So be it, then." She put forth her hand and moved closer. "The curse of Edaemus is upon me," she warned, "and I bear its mark. I will share that curse with thee. Mayhap thou wilt regret thy silence when thy flesh doth decay and melt like wax from thy bones. The time hath come to choose, Kolata of Matherion. Speak or die. Who is it who hath stolen thy loyalty from thine appointed master?" Her hand, more surely deadly than Vanion's sword, was within inches of Kolata's ashen face.

"No!" he shrieked. "No! I'll tell you!"

The cloud appeared quite suddenly in the air above the gibbering minister, but Sparhawk was ready. Half-hidden behind Ehlana's throne, he had taken off his gauntlet and surreptitiously removed the sapphire rose from its confinement. "Blue-Rose!" he said sharply. "Destroy the cloud!"

The Bhelliom surged in his hand, and the dense, almost solid-appearing patch of intense darkness tattered, whipping like a pennon on a flagstaff in a hurricane, then it streamed away and was gone.

Zalasta was thrown back in his chair as his spell was broken. He half rose and fell back again, writhing and moaning as the jagged edges of his broken spell clawed at him. His chair overturned, and he convulsed on the floor like one caught in a seizure.

"It was *him*!" Kolata shrieked, pointing with a trembling hand. "It was Zalasta! He made me do it!"

Sephrenia's gasp was clearly audible. Sparhawk looked sharply at her. She had fallen back, nearly as shaken as Zalasta himself. Her eyes were filled with disbelief and horror. Danae, Sparhawk noticed, was talking to her, speaking rapidly and holding her sister's face quite firmly in her small hands.

"Curse you, Sparhawk!" The words came out in a kind of rasping croak as Zalasta, aided by his staff, dragged himself unsteadily to his feet. His face was shaken and twisted in frustration and rage. "You are *mine*, Sephrenia, *mine*!" he howled. "I have longed for you for an eternity, watched as your thieving, guttersnipe Goddess stole you from me! But no more! *Thus* do I banish forever the Child-Goddess and her hold on thee!" His deadly staff whirled and leveled. "Die, Aphrael!" he shrieked.

Sephrenia, without even thinking, clasped her arms around Sparhawk's daughter and turned quickly in her seat, shielding the little girl with her own body, willingly offering her back to Zalasta's fury.

Sparhawk's heart froze as a ball of fire shot from the tip of the staff.

"No!" Vanion cried, trying to rush forward.

But Xanetia was already there. Her decision to approach Kolata from Sephrenia's side of the room had clearly been influenced by her perception of what lay in Zalasta's mind. She had consciously placed herself in a position to protect her enemy. Unafraid, she faced the raving Styric. The sizzling fireball streaked through the silent air of the throne room, bearing with it all of Zalasta's centuries-old hatred.

Xanetia held out her hand, and, like a tame bird returning to the hand that feeds it, the flaming orb settled into that hand. With only the faint hint of a smile touching her lips, the Delphaeic woman closed her fingers around Zalasta's pent-up hatred. For an instant, incandescent flame spurted out from between her pale fingers, and then she absorbed the fiery messenger of death, the light within her consuming it utterly. "What now, Zalasta of Styricum?" she asked the raging sorcerer. "What dost thou propose now? Wilt thou contend with me more at peril of thy life? Or wilt thou, like the whipped cur thou art, cringe and flee my wrath? For I do know thee. It hath been *thy* poisoned tongue which hath set my sister's heart against me. Flee, master of lies. Abuse Sephrenia's ears no longer with thy foul slanders. Go. I abjure thee. Go."

Zalasta howled, and in that howl there was a lifetime of unsatisfied longing and blackest despair.

And then he vanished.

Emperor Sarabian's expression was strangely detached as he looked out over the shambles of his government. Some of the officials appeared to be in shock; others scurried aimlessly, babbling. Several were clustered at the main door, imploring the knights to let them out.

Oscagne, his diplomat's face imperturbable, approached the dais. "Surprising turn of events," he noted as if he were speaking of an unexpected summer shower. He studiously adjusted his black mantle, looking more and more like a judge.

"Yes," Sarabian agreed, his eyes still lost in thought. "I think we might be able to exploit it, however. Sparhawk, is that dungeon down in the basement functional?"

"Yes, your Majesty. The architect was very thorough."

"Good."

"What have you got in mind, Sarabian?" Ehlana asked him.

He grinned at her, his face suddenly almost boyish. "I ain't a-tellin', dorlin'," he replied in outrageous imitation of Caalador's dialect. "I purely wouldn't want t' spoil th' surprise."

"Please, Sarabian," she said with a weary sigh.

"Jist you watch, yer Queenship. I'm a-fixin' t' pull off a little koop my ownself."

"You're going to make me cross, Sarabian."

"Don't you love me anymore, Mother?" His tone was excited and exhilarated.

"Men!" she said, rolling her eyes upward.

"Just follow my lead, my friends," the emperor told them. "Let's find out how well I've learned my lessons." He rose to his feet. "Lord Vanion," he called. "Would you be so good as to return our guests to their seats?"

"At once, your Majesty," Vanion replied. Vanion, forewarned of Zalasta's treachery, was completely in control. He barked a few short commands, and the Church Knights firmly escorted the distracted officials back to their chairs.

"What was he doing?" Ehlana demanded of her husband in a tense whisper. "Why did he try to attack Danae?"

"He didn't, love," Sparhawk replied, thinking very quickly. "He was trying to attack Aphrael. Didn't you see her? She was standing right beside Sephrenia."

"She *was?*"

"Of course. I thought everyone in the room saw her, but maybe it was only me—and Zalasta. Why do you think he ran away so fast? Aphrael was right on the verge of jerking out his heart and eating it before his very eyes."

She shuddered.

Emperor Sarabian moved to the front of the dais again. "Let's come to order, gentlemen," he told them crisply. "We haven't finished here yet. I gather that you were surprised by the revelation of Zalasta's *true* position—some of you, anyway. I'm disappointed in you, my Lords—most of you for your profound lack of perception, the rest for not realizing that I could see through Zalasta—and you—like panes of glass. Some of you are traitors, the rest are merely stupid. I have no need of men of either stripe in my service. It is my excruciating pleasure to announce that at sunrise this morning, the Atan garrisons throughout Tamuli moved out of their barracks and replaced *all* imperial authorities with officers from their own ranks. With the exception of Matherion, the entire empire is under martial law."

They gaped at him.

"Atan Engessa," Sarabian said.

"Yes, Sarabian-Emperor?"

"Would you be so kind as to eliminate that lone exception? Take your Atans out into the city and take charge of the capital."

"At once, Sarabian-Emperor." Engessa's grin was very broad.

"Be firm, Engessa. Show my subjects my fist."

"It shall be as you command, Sarabian-Emperor."

"Splendid chap," Sarabian murmured loudly enough to be heard as the towering Atan marched to the door.

"Your Majesty," Pondia Subat protested weakly, half rising.

The look the emperor gave his prime minister was icy. "I'm busy right now, Subat," he said. "You and I will talk later—extensively. I'm sure I'll find your explanation of how all of this happened under your very nose without even disturbing your decades-long nap absolutely fascinating. Now sit down and be quiet."

The prime minister sank back into his chair, his eyes very wide.

"All of Tamuli is under martial law now," the emperor told his officials. "Since you've failed so miserably, I've been obliged to step in and take charge. That makes you redundant, so you are all dismissed."

There were gasps, and some of the officials, those longest in office and most convinced of their own near-divinity, cried out in protest.

"Moreover—" Sarabian cut across their objections, "—the treason of Zalasta has cast doubt upon the loyalty of each and every one of you. If I cannot *trust* all, I must *suspect* all. I want you to search your souls tonight, gentlemen, because we'll be asking you questions tomorrow, and we'll want complete truth from you. We don't have time for lies or excuses or attempts to wriggle out from under your responsibility or guilt. I strongly recommend that you be forthcoming. The consequences of mendacity or evasion will be *very* unpleasant."

Ulath took a long honing steel from his belt and began to draw it slowly across the edge of his ax-blade. It made the sort of screech that sets the teeth on edge.

"As a demonstration of my benevolence," Sarabian continued, "I've made arrangements for you all to be lodged here tonight, and to provide you with accommodations that will give each of you absolute privacy to review your past lives so that you can answer questions fully tomorrow. Lord Vanion, would you and your knights be so good as to escort our guests down to their quarters in the dungeon?" Sarabian was improvising for all he was worth.

"At once, your Majesty," Vanion replied, clashing his mailed fist against his breastplate in salute.

"Ah, Lord Vanion," Ehlana added.

"Yes, my Queen?"

"You might consider searching our guests before you put them to bed. We don't want any more of them hurting themselves the way the Chancellor of the Exchequer did, now, do we?"

"Excellent suggestion, your Majesty," Sarabian agreed. "Take all their toys away from them, Lord Vanion. We don't want them to be distracted by anything." He paused a moment. "Actually, Lord Vanion, I rather think our guests will be able to concentrate a little better if they have something tangible about them to emphasize their situation. It seems that I read something once to the effect that the prisoners in Elene dungeons wear a kind of uniform."

"Yes, your Majesty," Vanion told him with an absolutely straight face. "It's a sleeveless smock made of grey burlap—with a bright red stripe painted down the back, so that they can be identified in case they escape."

"Do you suppose we might be able to find something along those lines for our guests?"

"If not, we can improvise, your Majesty."

"Splendid, Lord Vanion—and take their jewels away from them as well. Jewels make people feel important, and I want them all to understand that they're little more than bugs. I suppose you'd better feed them as well. What do people usually eat in dungeons?"

"Bread and water, your Majesty—a little gruel once in a while."

"That should do nicely. Get them out of here, Vanion. The very sight of them is starting to nauseate me."

Vanion barked a few sharp commands, and the knights descended on the former government.

Each official had an honor guard of armored men to escort him—in some cases to drag him—down to the dungeon.

"Ah—stay a moment, Teovin," the emperor said urbanely to the Director of the Secret Police. "I believe there was something you wanted to say to me?"

"No, your Majesty." Teovin's tone was sullen.

"Come, come, old boy. Don't be shy. We're all friends here. If you're in any way offended by anything I've done here today, spit it out. Milord Stragen will be happy to lend you his rapier, and then you and I can discuss things; I'm sure you'll find my explanations quite pointed." Sarabian let his mantle slide to the floor. He smiled a chill smile and drew his rapier again. "Well?" he said.

"It would be treason for me to offer violence to your Majesty's person," Teovin mumbled.

"Good God, Teovin, why should *that* bother you? You've been involved in treason for the past several years anyway, so why concern yourself with a few picky little technicalities? Take up the sword, man. For once—just once—face me openly. I'll give you a fencing lesson—one you'll remember for the rest of your life, short though that may be."

"I will not raise my hand against my emperor," Teovin declared.

"What a shame. I'm really disappointed in you, old boy. You may go now."

Vanion took the director's arm in his mailed fist and half dragged him from the throne room.

The Emperor of Tamuli exultantly raised his rapier over his head, rose to his tiptoes, and spun about in a flamboyant little pirouette. Then he extended one leg forward and bowed extravagantly to Ehlana, sweeping his slender sword to the side. "And *that,* dear mother," he said to her, "is how you overthrow a government."

"No, Lady Sephrenia," the queen said flatly a half hour later when they had gathered again in the royal apartment, "you do *not* have our permission to withdraw. You're a member of the royal council of Elenia, and we have need of you."

Sephrenia's pale, grief-stricken face went stiff. "As your Majesty commands."

"Snap out of it, Sephrenia. This is an emergency. We don't have time for personal concerns. Zalasta's betrayed us all, not just you. Now we have to try to minimize the damage."

"You're not being fair, Mother," Danae accused.

"I'm not trying to be. You'll be queen one day, Danae. Now sit down, keep your mouth shut, and learn."

Danae looked startled. Then her chin came up. She curtsied. "Yes, your Majesty," she said.

"That's better. I'll make a queen of you yet. Sir Bevier."

"Yes, your Majesty?" Bevier replied.

"Tell your Cyrinics to man their catapults. Vanion, put the rest of the knights on the walls and tell them to start boiling the pitch. Zalasta's on the loose out there. He's completely lost control of himself, and we have no idea of what forces he has at his command. In his present state, he may try anything, so let's be ready—just in case."

"You sound like a field marshal, Ehlana," Sarabian told her.

"I am," she replied absently. "It's one of my titles. Sparhawk, can Bhelliom counter any magic Zalasta might throw at us?"

"Easily, my Queen. He probably won't try anything, though. You saw what happened to him when Bhelliom blew his cloud apart. It's very painful to have one of your spells broken. Sephrenia knows him better than I do. She can tell you whether or not he's desperate enough to risk that again."

"Well, Sephrenia?" Ehlana asked.

"I don't really know, your Majesty," the small Styric woman replied after a moment's thought. "This is a side of him I've never seen before. I honestly believe he's gone mad. He might do almost anything."

"We'd better be ready for him then. Mirtai, ask Kalten and Ulath to bring Kolata in here. Let's find out just how far this conspiracy goes."

Sparhawk drew Sephrenia to one side. "How did Zalasta find out about Danae?" he asked. "It's obvious that he knows who she really is. Did *you* tell him?"

"No. She told me not to."

"That's peculiar. I'll talk with her later and find out why. Maybe she suspected something—or it might have been one of those hunches of hers." He thought for a moment. "Could he have been trying to kill *you?* It *seemed* that he was throwing that fireball at Danae, but *you* might have been his target."

"I could never believe that, Sparhawk."

"At this point, I'm almost ready to believe anything." He hesitated. "Xanetia knew about him, you realize. She told us earlier."

"Why didn't you warn me?" Her tone was shocked.

"Because you wouldn't have believed her. You're not really inclined to trust her word, Sephrenia. You had to see Zalasta's treachery for yourself. Oh, incidentally, she *did* save your life, you'll remember. You might want to give that some thought."

"Don't scold me, Sparhawk," she said with a wan little smile. "I'm having a difficult enough time as it is."

"I know, and I'm afraid nobody can make it any easier for you."

Kolata proved to be very cooperative. His weeks of confinement had broken his spirit, and Zalasta's obvious willingness to kill him had canceled any loyalty he might have felt. "I really don't know," he replied to Oscagne's question. "Teovin might, though. He's the one who brought Zalasta's proposal to me originally."

"Then you haven't been involved in this affair since you were first appointed to office?"

"I don't think 'this affair,' as you call it, has been going on for that long. I can't say for certain, but I got the impression that it all started about five or six years ago."

"You've been recruiting people for longer than that."

"That was just ordinary Tamul politics, Oscagne. I knew that the prime minister was an idiot as soon as I took office. *You* were my only significant opponent. I was recruiting people to counter *your* moves—and your absurd idea that the subject kingdoms of Daresia are foreign nations rather than integral parts of metropolitan Tamuli."

"We can discuss jurisdictional disputes some other time, Kolata. It was Teovin, then? He's been your contact with the enemy?"

Kolata nodded. "Teovin and a disreputable drunkard named Krager. Krager's an Eosian, and he's had dealings with Prince Sparhawk before, I understand. Everyone in our loose confederation knows him, so he makes a perfect messenger—when he's sober."

"That's Krager, all right," Kalten noted.

"What exactly did Zalasta offer you, Kolata?" Oscagne asked the prisoner.

"Power, wealth—the usual. You're a minister of the government, Oscagne. You know the game and the stakes we play for. We all thought that the emperor was no more than a figurehead, well-meaning, a little vague, and not really very well informed—sorry, your Majesty, but that's what we all believed."

"Thank you," Sarabian replied. "That's what you were supposed to think. What really baffles me, though, is the fact that you all overlooked the fact that the Atans are loyal to me personally. Didn't any of you take that into consideration?"

"We underestimated your Majesty. We didn't think you grasped the full implications of that. If we'd thought for a moment that you really understood how much power you had, we'd have killed you."

"I rather thought you might have. That's why I played the simpleton."

"Did Zalasta tell you who was *really* behind all of this?" Oscagne asked.

"He pretended that he was speaking for Cyrgon," Kolata replied. "We didn't take that too seriously, though. Styrics are peculiar people. They always try to make us believe that they represent a higher power of some kind. They never seem to want to accept full responsibility. So far as I know, however, it was Zalasta's scheme."

"I think that maybe it's time for us to hear from Zalasta himself," Vanion said.

"Have you got him hidden up your sleeve, Vanion?" Ehlana asked.

"In a manner of speaking, your Majesty. Kalten, why don't you take the Minister of the Interior back to his room? He looks a little tired."

"I still have questions, Lord Vanion," Oscagne protested.

"We'll get you your answers, old boy," Itagne assured him, "quicker and in much greater detail. You plod, Oscagne. It's one of your failings. We're just going to hurry things along."

Vanion waited until Kalten and Ulath had removed Kolata from the room. "We've told you all in a general sort of way that Xanetia knows what other people are thinking. This isn't just some vague notion about feelings or moods. If she chooses, she can repeat your thoughts word for word. Most of you probably have some doubts about that, so in the interests of saving time, why don't we have her demonstrate? Would you tell us what Queen Ehlana's thinking right now, Anarae?"

"An it pleases thee, Lord Vanion," the Delphaeic woman replied. "Her Majesty is enjoying herself very much at the moment. She is, however, discontent with thee for thine interruption. She is pleased with the progress of Emperor Sarabian, thinking it might now be reasonable to expect some small measure of competence from him. She hath, as well, certain designs of an intimate nature upon her husband, for political activity doth ever stir that side of her personality."

Ehlana's face turned bright red. "You stop that at once!" she exclaimed.

"I'm sorry, your Majesty," Vanion apologized. "I didn't anticipate that last bit. Did Xanetia more or less read your thoughts correctly?"

"You know I won't answer that, Vanion." The queen's face was still flaming.

"Will you at least concede that she has access to the thoughts of others?"

"I'd heard about that," Sarabian mused. "I thought it was just another of the wild stories we hear about the Delphae."

"Bhelliom confirmed it, Emperor Sarabian," Sparhawk told him. "Xanetia can read others the way you'd read an open book. I'd imagine that she's read Zalasta from cover to cover. She should be able to tell us everything we want to know." He looked at Xanetia. "Could you give us a sort of summary of Zalasta's life, Anarae?" he asked her. "Sephrenia in particular is deeply saddened by what he revealed in the throne room. Maybe if she knows the reason for his actions, she'll find them easier to understand."

"I can speak for myself, Sparhawk," Sephrenia told him tartly.

"I'm sure you can, little mother. I was just serving as an intermediary. You and Xanetia don't get on too well."

"What's this?" Sarabian asked quickly.

"An ancient enmity, your Majesty," Xanetia explained. "So ancient, in truth, that none living knoweth its source."

"*I* know," Sephrenia grated at her, "and it's not as ancient as all that."

"Perhaps, but hearken unto the mind of Zalasta, and judge for thyself, Sephrenia of Ylara."

Kalten and Ulath returned and quietly took their seats again.

"Zalasta was born some few centuries ago in the Styric village of Ylara, which lay in the forest near Cenae in northern Astel," Xanetia began. "In his seventh year was there born also in that selfsame village she whom we know as Sephrenia, one of the Thousand of Styricum, tutor to the Pandion Knights in the secrets of Styricum, councillor of Elenia, and beloved of Preceptor Vanion."

"That's no longer true," Sephrenia said shortly.

"I spoke of Lord Vanion's feelings for *thee*, Sephrenia, not of thine for him. Zalasta's family was on friendly terms with Sephrenia's, and they did conclude between them that when Sephrenia and Zalasta should reach a suitable age, they would be wed."

"I'd forgotten about that," Sephrenia said suddenly. "I've never really thought of him that way."

"It hath been the central fact of his life, however, I do assure thee. When thou wert in thy ninth year didst thy mother conceive, and the child she bore was in truth Aphrael, Child-Goddess of Styricum, and in the instant of her birth did Zalasta's hopes and dreams turn to dust and ashes, for thy life was forever given over entirely to thine infant sister. Zalasta's wrath knew no bounds, and he did hide himself in the forest, lest his countenance betray his innermost thoughts. Much he traveled, seeking out the most powerful magicians of Styricum, even, at peril of his soul, those outcast and accursèd. His search had but one aim, to discover some means whereby a man might overthrow and destroy a God; for his despair drove him to an unreasoning hatred of the Child-Goddess; and, more than anything, he sought her death."

Princess Danae gasped aloud.

"You're supposed to be listening," her mother said.

"I was startled, Mother."

"You must never show that. Always keep your emotions under control."

"Yes, Mother."

"It was in the sixth year of the life of the Child-Goddess—in that particular incarnation—that Zalasta, in a frenzy of frustration, since all with whom he had spoken had told him that his goal was beyond human capability, turned to more direct means. Hoping perhaps that the Child-Goddess might be caught unawares or that by reason of her tender years might she not yet have come into her full powers, conceived he a reckless plan, an attempt to o'erwhelm her with sheer numbers. Though the Goddess herself is immortal, thought he that mayhap might her *incarnation* be slain, forcing her to seek another vessel for her awareness."

"Would that work?" Kalten asked Sparhawk.

"How should I know?" Sparhawk threw a guarded glance at his daughter.

Danae very casually shook her head.

"In furtherance of his hasty and ill-conceived scheme did Zalasta assume the guise of an Elene clergyman and did visit the rude villages of the serfs of that region and did denounce the Styrics of his own village, describing them as idolaters and demon-worshippers, whose foul rites demanded the blood of Elene virgins. So hotly did he inflame them with his false reports that on a certain day did the ignorant serfs gather, and swept they down upon that innocent Styric village, slaughtering all and putting their houses to the torch."

"But that was Sephrenia's home, too!" Ehlana exclaimed. "How could he be sure that she wouldn't be killed as well?"

"He was beyond caring, Queen of Elenia. Indeed, it was his thought that better far should she die than that Aphrael should have her. Better a grief that would pass than endless unsatisfied longing. But as it came to pass, the Child-Goddess had besought her sister that very morning that they two should go into the forest to gather wildflowers, and thus it was that they were not there when the Elene serfs fell upon the village."

"Zalasta told me the story once," Sparhawk interrupted. "He said that he was with Sephrenia and Aphrael in the forest."

"Nay, Anakha. He was at the village, directing the search for the two."

"Why would he lie about something like that?"

"Mayhap he doth lie even to himself. His acts that day were monstrous, and it is in our nature to obscure such behavior from ourselves."

"Maybe that's it," he conceded.

"Ye may well perceive the depths of Zalasta's hatred and despair when thou knowest that his own kindred perishèd there," Xanetia continued. "Yea, his father and his mother and sisters three fell beneath the cudgels and scythes of the ravening beasts he had unleashèd, even as he looked on."

"I don't believe you!" Sephrenia burst out.

"Bhelliom can confirm my truth, Sephrenia," Xanetia replied calmly, "and if I have broken faith by lying, Sir Kalten stands ready to spill out my life. Put me to the test, sister."

"He told us that the serfs had been inflamed against our village by *your* people—by the Delphae!"

"He lied unto thee, Sephrenia. Great was his chagrin when he discoverèd that Aphrael—and thou—didst still live. Seizing upon the first thought which came to him, he did shift his own guilt to *my* kindred, knowing that thou wouldst surely believe the worst of those whom thou wert already predisposèd to hate. He hath deceived thee since childhood, Sephrenia of Ylara, and would deceive thee still, had not Anakha forced him to reveal his true self."

"That's why you hate the Delphae, isn't it, Sephrenia?" Ehlana asked shrewdly. "You thought that *they* were the ones responsible for the murder of your parents."

"And Zalasta, ever striving to conceal his own guilt, lost no opportunity to remind her of that lie," Xanetia said. "In truth hath he poisoned her thoughts against the Delphae for centuries, filling her heart with hatred, lest she question him concerning his own involvement."

Sephrenia's face twisted, and she bowed her head, buried her face in her hands, and began to weep.

Xanetia sighed. "The truth hath made her grief all new. She weeps for her parents, dead these many centuries." She looked at Alean. "Take her somewhat apart, gentle child, and comfort her. She hath much need of the ministrations of women presently. The storm of her weeping will soon pass, and then woe unto Zalasta should he ever fall into her hands."

"Or mine," Vanion added bleakly.

"Boiling oil is good, my Lord," Kalten suggested. "Cook him while he's still alive."

"Hooks are good, too," Ulath added. "Long ones with nice sharp barbs on them."

"Must you?" Sarabian said with a shudder.

"Zalasta hurt Sephrenia, your Majesty," Kalten told him. "There are twenty-five thousand Pandion Knights—and quite a few knights from the other orders as well—who are going to take that very personally. Zalasta can pull mountain ranges over his head to try to hide, but we'll still find him. The Church Knights aren't really very civilized, and when somebody hurts those we love, it brings out the worst in us."

"Well said," Sparhawk murmured.

"We're getting afield here, gentlemen," Ehlana reminded them. "We'll decide Zalasta's punishment after we catch him. When did he become involved in this current business, Xanetia? Is he really allied with Cyrgon?"

"The alliance was of Zalasta's devising, Queen of Elenia. His failure in the forest of Astel and his own guilt arising therefrom did plunge him into deepest despair and blackest melancholy. He roamed the world, losing himself at times in vilest debauchery and at times dwelling alone and hermitlike in the wilderness of this world for decades on end. He sought out every Styric magician of reputation—good or ill—and gleaned from them *all* of the secrets. In truth, of all the Styrics who have ever lived in the forty eons of the history of their race, Zalasta is preeminent. But knowledge alone consoled him not. Aphrael lived still, and Sephrenia was ever bound to her.

"But the knowledge of Zalasta, which is beyond measure, did suggest to him a means by which he might break those bonds. At the dawn of time in far Thalesia had the Troll-Dwarf Ghwerig wrought Bhelliom, and Zalasta knew that with Bhelliom's aid might he gain his heart's desire.

"Then came the birth of Anakha, signaling that Bhelliom itself would soon emerge from the place where it had lain hidden, and by signs and oracles and diverse other means did outcast Styrics perceive his birth, and counseled they Zalasta, instructing him to journey straightway to Eosia to observe Anakha throughout his childhood and youth that he might know him better, for it was the hope of Zalasta that in the day that Anakha did bring the flower-gem to light, might he wrest it from him and thereby gain the means to prevail over the Child-Goddess. But on the day when the ring did come into Anakha's possession, did Zalasta perceive his error. Well had the Troll-Gods wrought when they guided Ghwerig in the carving of the sapphire rose. Man is capricious and inconstant, and covetousness doth ever lurk in his heart, and Trolls are but reflections of the worst in men. Thus did the Troll-Gods make the rings the key to Bhelliom, lest any or all have power to command it. Thus did Aphrael disarm Ghwerig by stealing the rings, and thus did she scatter the power of the jewel that no mortal might command it. Thinking that their own power was absolute, the Troll-Gods had no interest in the flower-gem, and distrustful each of the others, they laid enchantments upon the stone to ensure that no one of them might take up Bhelliom unless all did. Only in concert might they command it, and they contrived it so that *they*, as Gods acting in concert, could command Bhelliom *without* the rings." She paused, reflecting, Sparhawk realized, on the peculiarities of the Troll-Gods.

"Now truly," she went on, "the Troll-Gods are elementals, each so limited that his mind may in no wise be considered whole and complete. Only when united, which doth rarely happen, can they by combination achieve that wholeness we see in the merest human child. For the other Gods, however, it is not so. The mind of Azash was whole and complete, despite his maiming, and in his wholeness had he the power to command Bhelliom without the rings. This then was the peril which did confront thee, Anakha, when thou didst journey to Zemoch to meet with him. Had Azash wrested Bhelliom from thee, he could have compelled it to join its will and its power with his."

"That might have been a bit inconvenient," Kalten noted.

"I don't quite understand," Talen said. "The last few times he's used it, Sparhawk's been able to get Bhelliom to do what he wants it to do *without* using the rings. Does that mean that Sparhawk's a God?"

"Nay, young sir." Xanetia smiled. "Anakha is of Bhelliom's devising and is therefore in some measure a *part* of Bhelliom—even as are the rings. For him, the rings are not needful. Zalasta did perceive this. When Anakha slew Ghwerig and took up the Bhelliom did Zalasta intensify his surveillance, ever using the rings as beacons to guide him. Thus did he observe Anakha's progress, and thus did he watch Anakha's mate as well."

"All right, Sparhawk," Ehlana said in a dangerous tone, "how did you get my ring? And what's this?" She extended her hand to show him the ruby adorning her finger. "Is it some cheap piece of glass?"

He sighed. "Aphrael stole your ring for me," he replied. "She's the one who provided the substitute. I doubt that she'd have used glass."

She pulled the ring off her finger and hurled it across the room. "Give it back! Give me back my ring, you thief."

"*I* didn't steal it, Ehlana," he protested. "Aphrael did."

"You took it when she gave it to you, didn't you? That makes you an accessory. Give me back my ring!"

"Yes, dear," he replied meekly. "I meant to do that, but it slipped my mind." He took out the box. "Open," he told it. He did not touch his ring to the lid. He wanted to find out if the box would open at his command alone.

It did. He took out his wife's ring and held it out to her.

"Put it back where it belongs," she commanded.

"All right. Here, hold this." He gave her the box, took her hand, and slipped the ring onto her finger. Then he reached for the box again.

"Not just yet," she said, holding it out of his reach. She looked at the sapphire rose. "Does it know who I am?"

"I think so. Why don't you ask it? Call it Blue-Rose. That's what Ghwerig called it, so it's familiar with the name."

"Blue-Rose," she said, "do you know me?"

There was a momentary silence as Bhelliom pulsed, its azure glow dimming and then brightening.

"Anakha," Talen said in a slightly wooden voice, "is it thy desire that I respond to the questions of thy mate?"

"It were well that thou didst, Blue-Rose," Sparhawk replied. "She and I are so intertwined that her thoughts are mine and mine hers. Whether we will or no, we are three. Ye two should know one another."

"This was not my design, Anakha." Talen's voice had an accusing note in it.

"The world is ever-changing, Blue-Rose," Ehlana said, "and there is no design so perfect that it cannot be improved." Her speech, like Sparhawk's, was profoundly formal. "Some there are who have feared that I might imperil my life should I touch thee. Is there in truth such peril?"

The wooden expression slid off Talen's face to be replaced with a look of bleak determination. "There is, mate of Anakha." The note in Talen's voice was as hard and cold as steel. "Once did I relent and once only. After ages uncounted of lying imprisoned in the earth, I did permit Ghwerig to lift me from the place where I had lain. This shape, which is so pleasing unto thee, was the result. With cruel implements of diamond and accursed red iron did Ghwerig carve and contort me, living, into this grotesque form. I *must* submit to the touch of a God; I willingly submit to the touch of Anakha in the sure and certain hope that he will liberate me from this shape which hath become my prison. It is death for any other."

"Couldn't you—?" She left it hanging.

"No." There was an icy finality in it. "I have no reason to trust the creatures of this world. The death that lieth in my touch shall remain, and also the lure which doth incline all who see me to touch me. They who see me will yearn to touch me and they will eagerly reach forth their hands—and die. The dead have no desire to enslave me; the living are not to be trusted."

She sighed. "Thou art hard, Blue-Rose," she said.

"I have reason, mate of Anakha."

"Someday, mayhap, we will learn trust."

"It is not needful. The achievement of our goal doth not hinge upon it."

She sighed again and handed the box back to her husband. "Please go on, Xanetia. That shadow that was pestering Sparhawk and me was Zalasta, then? At first we thought it was Azash—and then, later on, the Troll-Gods."

"The shadow was Zalasta's mind, Queen of Elenia," Xanetia replied. "A Styric spell known to very few doth make it possible for him thus to observe and listen unseen."

"I'd hardly call it unseen. I saw the edges of him every single time. It's a very clumsy spell."

"That was Bhelliom's doing. It sought to warn Anakha of Zalasta's presence by making him partially visible. Since one of the rings was on thy hand, the shadow of Zalasta's mind was also visible to *thee*." She paused. "Zalasta was afeared," she went on. "It was the design of the minions of Azash to lure Anakha—with Bhelliom in his grip—to go even unto Zemoch where Azash might take the jewel from him. Should that have come to pass, Zalasta's one hope of defeating Aphrael and possessing Sephrenia would have been forever dashed. In truth, Anakha, were all the impediments heaped in thy path to Zemoch of Zalasta's devising."

"I sort of wondered about that," Sparhawk mused. "Martel was being inconsistent, and that wasn't at all like him. My brother was usually as single-minded as an avalanche. We thought it was the Troll-Gods, though. *They* had plenty of reason not to want Bhelliom to fall into the hands of Azash."

"Zalasta wished thee to believe so, Anakha. It was yet another means whereby he could conceal his own duplicity from Sephrenia, and her good opinion of him was most important. In short, thou didst win thy way through to Zemoch and didst destroy Azash there—along with diverse others."

"We did *that,* all right," Ulath murmured. "Whole *groups* of diverses."

"Then was Zalasta sore troubled," Xanetia continued, "for Anakha had come to full realization of his power to control Bhelliom, and with that realization had he become as dangerous as any God. Zalasta could no more confront him than he could confront Aphrael. And so it was that he went apart from all other men to consider his best course of action, and to consult with certain outcasts of his acquaintance. The destruction of Azash had confirmed their surmise: Bhelliom *could,* in fact, confront and destroy the Gods. The means of the death of Aphrael was at hand, could Zalasta but obtain it. That means, however, was in the hands of the most dangerous man on life. Clearly, if Zalasta wished to achieve his goal, he must needs ally himself with a God."

"Cyrgon," Kalten guessed.

"Even so, my protector. The Elder Gods of Styricum, as ye have discovered, were powerless by reason of their lack of worshippers. The Troll-Gods were confined, and the Elene God was inaccessible, as was Edaemus of the Delphae. The Tamul Gods were too frivolous, and the God of the Atans too inhospitable to save his own children. That left Cyrgon, and Zalasta and his cohorts did immediately perceive a means by which he might strike a bargain with the God of the Cyrgai. With Bhelliom might Cyrgon lift the Styric curse which confined his children and unleash them upon the world. In return, Zalasta believed, might Cyrgon be persuaded to permit him to use Bhelliom to destroy Aphrael, or, at the very least, to raise it against Aphrael with his own divine hand."

"It would have been a reasonable basis for opening negotiations," Oscagne conceded. "I'd take that kind of bargain to the table and expect a hearing at least."

"Perhaps," Itagne said dubiously, "but you'd have to live long enough to get to the table first. I don't imagine that the appearance of a Styric in Cyrga would have moved the population there to enthusiastic demonstrations of welcome."

"It was in truth a perilous undertaking, Itagne of Matherion. By diverse means did Zalasta gain entrance into the Temple of Cyrgon in the heart of the hidden city, and there did he confront the blazing spirit of Cyrgon himself and stay the God's vengeful hand with his offer of the liberation of the Cyrgai. The enemies at once became allies by reason of their mutual desires, and concluded they that Anakha must be lured to Daresia, for in no wise would they risk confrontation with the God of the Elenes, whose power, derived from his countless worshippers, is enormous. Conceived they then their involuted plan to disrupt all of Tamuli by insurrection and by apparition so that the imperial government must seek aid, and Zalasta's position of trust would easily enable him to direct the attention of the government to Anakha and to suggest accommodation with the Church of Chyrellos. The apparitions to be raised were no great chore for Zalasta of Styricum and his outcast comrades; nor was the deceit whereby Cyrgon persuaded the Trolls that their Gods commanded them to march across the polar ice to the north coast of Tamuli, an impossible task for the God of the Cyrgai. More central to their plans, however, were the insurrections which have so sorely marred the peace of Tamuli in recent years. Insurrection, to be successful, must be tightly controlled. Spontaneous uprisings seldom succeed. History had persuaded Zalasta that central to the success of their plan would be the character and personality of he who would unite the diverse populations of the kingdoms of the Tamul Empire and fire them with his force and zeal. Zalasta did not have far to seek to find such an one. Straightway upon his departure from Cyrga did he journey to Arjuna, and there presented he his plan to one known as Scarpa."

"Hold it," Stragen objected. "Zalasta's plan involved high treason at the very least. It probably involved crimes they haven't even named as yet—'consorting with ye powers of Darknesse' and the like. How did he know he could trust Scarpa?"

"He had every reason, Stragen of Emsat," she replied. "Zalasta knew that he could trust Scarpa as he could trust none other on life. Scarpa, you see, is Zalasta's own son."

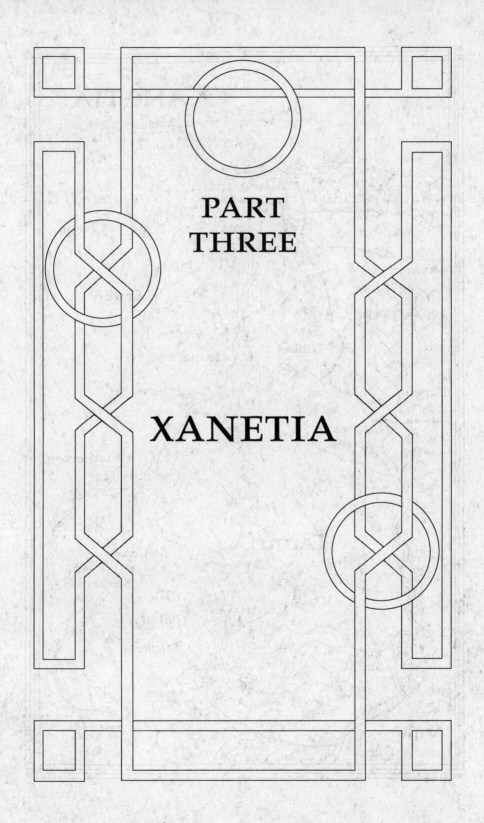

PART
THREE

XANETIA

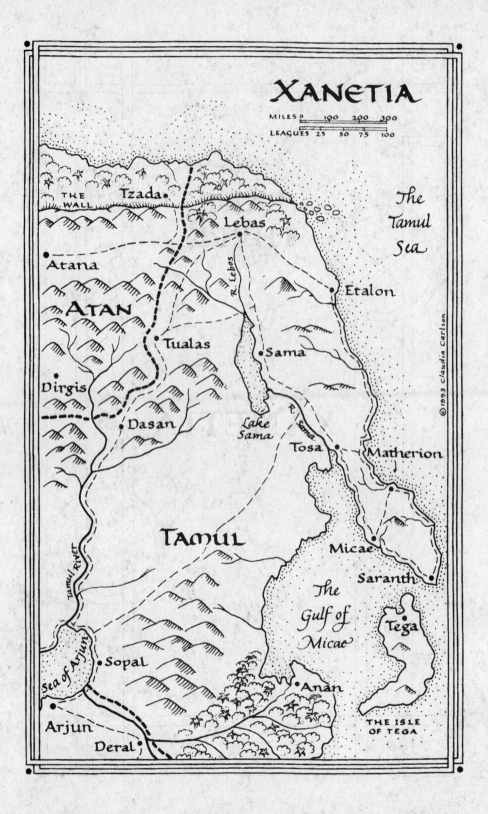

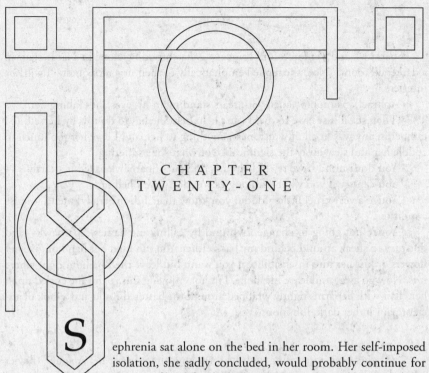

CHAPTER
TWENTY-ONE

Sephrenia sat alone on the bed in her room. Her self-imposed isolation, she sadly concluded, would probably continue for the rest of her life. She had spoken in anger and haste, and this empty solitude was the consequence. She sighed.

Sephrenia of Ylara. It was strange that both Xanetia and Cedon had reached into the past for that archaic name, and stranger still that it should touch her heart so deeply.

Ylara had not been much of a village, even by Styric standards. Styrics had long sought to divert the hostility of Elenes by posing as the poorest of the poor, living in hovels and wearing garments of the roughest homespun. But Ylara, with its single muddy street and clay and wattle huts, had been home. Sephrenia's childhood there had been filled with love, and that love had reached its culmination with the birth of her sister. At the moment of Aphrael's birth, Sephrenia had found at once fulfillment and life-long purpose.

The memory of that small, rude village and its warmth and all-encompassing love had sustained her through dark days. Ylara, glowing in her memories, had always been a refuge to which she could retreat when the world and all its ugliness pressed in around her.

But now it was gone. Zalasta's treachery had forever fouled and profaned her most precious memories. Now, whenever she remembered Ylara, Zalasta's face intruded itself; and now she saw his face for what it truly was—a mask of deceit and lust and a vile hatred for the Child-Goddess who was at the core of Sephrenia's very being.

Her memories had preserved Ylara; the revelation of Zalasta's corrupt duplicity had forever destroyed it.

Sephrenia buried her face in her hands and wept.

· · ·

Sparhawk and Vanion found Princess Danae brooding alone in a large chair in a darkened room. "No," she replied emphatically to their urgent request, "I will *not* interfere."

"Aphrael," Vanion pleaded with tears standing in his eyes, "it's killing her."

"Then she'll just have to die. I can't help her. She has to do this by herself. If I tamper in any way at all, it won't mean anything to her, and I love her too much to coddle her and steal away the significance of what she's suffering."

"You don't mind if we try to help her, do you?" Sparhawk asked her tartly.

"You can try if you want—as long as you don't use Bhelliom."

"You're a very cruel little girl, did you know that? I didn't really intend to raise a monster."

"You're not going to change my mind by calling me names, Sparhawk—and don't try to sneak around behind my back either. You can hold her hand or give her flowers or kiss her into insensibility if you want, but leave the Bhelliom right where it is. Now go away and leave me alone. I'm not enjoying this." And she curled up in her chair with her arms tightly wrapped around the battered Rollo and a look of ancient pain in her dark, luminous eyes.

"Zalasta's been interfering with us for a long time, hasn't he, Anarae?" Bevier asked the following morning when they had gathered once again in the blue-draped sitting room. They all wore more-casual clothing now, and the long table against the far wall was set with a breakfast buffet. Queen Ehlana had discovered a long time ago that meals did not necessarily have to interfere with important matters. Bevier's blue doublet was open at the front, and he was sunk low in his chair with his legs stretched out in front of him. "If he's been behind that shadow and the cloud, that would almost have to mean that he was involved in the Zemoch war, wouldn't it?"

Xanetia nodded. "Zalasta's scheming is centuries old, Sir Knight. His passion for Sephrenia dates back to his childhood, as doth his hatred for Aphrael, whose birth did dash all his hopes. Well he knew that should he confront the Child-Goddess directly, she could will away his very existence with a single thought. He knew that his lust was unwholesome, and that no God would be inclined to aid him in his struggle with Aphrael. Long he pondered this, and he concluded that his design required aid from some source with power, but without conscience or will of its own."

"Bhelliom," Sparhawk said. "Or at least that's how everyone saw it. We know differently now."

"Truly," she agreed. "Zalasta did share the common misperception of the jewel, thinking it to be a source of power only. He did believe that Bhelliom, untouched by morality, would obey him without question, and that it would destroy his mortal enemy and thus he could come to possess his heart's lust—for mistake me not, Zalasta sought possession of Sephrenia, not her love."

"That's vile," Baroness Melidere said with a shudder.

Xanetia nodded her agreement. "Zalasta knew that he must needs have the rings to command the sapphire rose," she went on, "but all of Styricum knew that the nimble Child-Goddess herself had purloined the rings from Ghwerig the Troll-Dwarf to prevent the misshapen creature from raising Bhelliom 'gainst the Styrics. Thus did Zalasta feign continuing friendship for Sephrenia and her sister, hoping to gain knowledge of the location of the rings and thus the keys to Bhelliom. Now the Gods had known, and some few humans as well, that one day Bhelliom's creature Anakha would appear, and by diverse signs and auguries did they divine that he would be born of the house of Sparhawk.

"Aphrael was wary, for she knew that the house of Sparhawk was Elene, and Elenes are not kindly disposed toward Styricum. She knew, however, that one day Anakha would come, and that he would raise Bhelliom from the place where it had lain hidden and wield it to his own purposes—and to the purposes of Bhelliom itself. She was troubled by this, for should Anakha share the common Elene despite of Styricum, might he raise the jewel against her worshippers. She sought to diminish that peril by separating the rings, placing one in the hands of Anakha's ancestor and the other elsewhere, so that when the one ring descended to Anakha, she might examine his heart and mind to determine whether it be safe to place both rings in his possession."

"Stories are more exciting when you know the people involved, aren't they?" Talen noted, filling his plate for the third time. Talen was growing again and he ate almost constantly. He *did*, however, remember his manners well enough to take a plate of sliced fruit and a glass of milk to Xanetia before he sat down to gorge himself.

Sparhawk phrased his question carefully. "I seem to remember that you once told me that you can't hear the thoughts of the Gods, Anarae. How is it that you know what Aphrael was thinking?"

"It is true that the thoughts of the Gods are veiled from me, Anakha, but Aphrael hath few secrets from her sister, and it is from Sephrenia's memories that I have gleaned what I have told ye.

"Now," she went on with her account, "Anakha's ancestor was a Pandion Knight dwelling with his brethren in the motherhouse of his order in the city of Demos in Elenia, and joined he in the war of the rash young king Antor against certain rebellious barons. And it came to pass that the knight and the king, separated from their companions, lay sorely wounded on the bloody field of battle. As darkness fell upon that field, did Sephrenia of Ylara, commanded by her sister, come reluctantly to bind their wounds and to deliver up the rings—one to each of them. She did conceal the true import of the rings, advising them that they were but tokens of their friendship, and by means of a Styric spell did she stain the rings with the mingled blood of the wounded pair to conceal their true nature and import. Thus did she bind the two houses together, which binding did prepare the way for the union of Anakha and his queen."

Ehlana beamed smugly at her husband. "I told you so," she said.

"I didn't quite follow that."

"I told you that we were destined to marry. Why did you keep arguing with me?"

"It seemed like the thing to do. I was fairly sure you could have done better." It was a slightly flippant reply, and it concealed his shocked surprise. Obviously Aphrael was absolutely ruthless in her manipulation of people's lives. Anakha was Bhelliom's creature, and the Child-Goddess, not certain she could trust him, had deliberately arranged to be born as his daughter so that she could in some measure control him.

"Now Zalasta, perceiving the intent of Aphrael, was troubled," Xanetia went on. "He had hoped to wrest Bhelliom from Anakha before Anakha could come to know the full import of his union with the stone, but Aphrael had once again blocked his design. By virtue of the rings and the mastery of Bhelliom which they conferred had Anakha been made invincible."

"All right, then," Ulath rumbled. "Zalasta was blocked. What did he do then?"

"There are some in Styricum—and have ever been—who, like the Elder Gods themselves, have used the power of the spells their race has learned to satisfy unwholesome personal desires. The Younger Gods are as children in this regard, and they cannot know the depths to which such as these will willingly sink. They are outraged by this coarser side of the nature of man, and such Styrics as display it are cast out and accursèd. These unfortunates dwell alone and sorrowing in wilderness and waste, or, all unrepentant, seek they their vile pleasure in the festering stews of the cities of this world. It was to these that Zalasta in desperation turned, and in Verel, foulest of the cities of southern Daconia, found he such a one as he sought."

"I've lived in Verel," Mirtai said. "That would be the place to look for degenerates, all right."

Xanetia nodded. "There in that sink of iniquity Zalasta did happen quite by chance upon one Ogerajin, a corrupt and ancient voluptuary. Now this Ogerajin was double-dipt in vileness, and by means of certain forbidden spells and enchantments had he reached into the darkness—yea, even into that ultimate corruption that lieth in the hearts of the Elder Gods. And Ogerajin, perceiving that Zalasta's lust was like his own and that they were therefore kindred, counseled him to seek out Otha of Zemoch."

Bevier gasped.

"Truly," Xanetia agreed. "And so did Zalasta journey even unto the city of Zemoch to make alliance with Otha."

"Hold it," Kalten said. "Didn't you tell us that Zalasta was trying to keep us *away* from Otha and Azash?"

She nodded. "Zalasta doth conclude alliances to further his *own* ends, not those of his allies. With Otha's aid he found other outcast Styrics in Eosia to aid him in keeping watch on the family of the Sparhawks, instructing them to seek out weaknesses which might be to his advantage when Anakha was born.

"As well ye might guess, Aphrael *also* set a watcher on those who would precede Sparhawk, and despite her sister's protests, the Child-Goddess sent Sephrenia to Demos to instruct the Elene Pandions in the Secrets of Styricum."

"Our charming little Aphrael has a heartless streak, I see," Stragen noted. "Considering what the Elene serfs in Astel did to Sephrenia's parents, sending her to Demos smacks of a certain lack of consideration."

"Who can know the mind of a God?" Xanetia sighed. She passed a weary hand across her eyes.

"Aren't you feeling well?" Kalten asked, his voice mirroring his concern.

"Some slight fatigue, Sir Kalten," she confessed. "The mind of Sephrenia was in great turmoil when I did gather in her memories, and it is with no small difficulty that I wring some consistency from them."

"Is that the way it works, Anarae?" Sarabian asked curiously. "You just reach in and swallow somebody else's mind whole?"

"Thy metaphor is inexact, Sarabian of Tamuli," she said in a slightly reproving tone.

"Forgive me, Anarae," he apologized. "I plucked it out of the air. What I meant to ask was whether you absorb the entire contents of another's awareness and memories with a single touch."

"Approximately, yes."

"How many minds have you got stored away?" Talen asked her. "Other people's minds, I mean?"

"Close on to a thousand, young master." She shrugged.

"Where do you find room?" He paused, looking just a little embarrassed. "I didn't say that very well, did I? What I was trying to ask was, Doesn't it get awfully crowded in there?"

"The mind is limitless, young master."

"*Yours* might be, Anarae." Kalten smiled. "I've found plenty of limits to mine, though."

"Is Sephrenia all right?" Vanion asked her with a worried frown.

"She is in great agony," Xanetia sighed. "Zalasta's treachery hath wounded her to the heart, and her mistaken belief that all of ye have forsaken her hath crushed her spirit."

"I'll go to her," Vanion said, rising quickly to his feet.

"No, my Lord," Kalten told him. "That wouldn't be a good idea. You're too close to her and if you went, you'd only make her feel worse. Why don't you let me go instead?"

"It's my place to go, Kalten."

"Not if it's going to make her suffer all the more, it isn't. Right now she needs to know that we still love her, and that means she needs somebody who's affectionate and not very bright. That's me, in case you hadn't noticed."

"You stop that!" Alean flared. "I won't have you saying things like that about yourself!" Then she seemed to realize that they were not alone, and she blushed and lowered her eyes in confusion.

"He might be right, Vanion," Ehlana said gravely. "Sir Kalten may have his faults, but he's straightforward and honest. Sephrenia knows that there's no deviousness in his nature. He's just too . . . too . . ."

"Stupid?" Kalten supplied.

"That's not the word I'd have chosen."

"It doesn't hurt my feelings, my Queen. They don't pay me to think—just to follow orders. When I try to think, I get in trouble, so I've learned to get along without thinking. I just trust my feelings instead. They don't lead me off in the wrong direction *too* often. Sephrenia knows me, and she knows I couldn't deceive her even if I tried."

"It's called sincerity, my friend." Sparhawk smiled.

"That's as good a word for it as any, I suppose." Kalten shrugged. "I'll just nip on down to her room and smother her with sincerity. That ought to make her feel better."

"It's me, Sephrenia. Kalten. Unlock the door."

"Go away." Her voice was muffled.

"This is important."

"Leave me alone."

Kalten sighed. It was going to be one of *those* days. "Please, little mother," he tried again.

"Just go away."

"If you don't open the door, I'll have to use magic on it."

"Magic? *You?*" She laughed scornfully.

Kalten leaned back, raised his right leg, and drove his booted heel against the latch. He kicked it twice more, and the door splintered and burst open.

"What are you *doing?*" she screamed at him.

"Haven't you ever seen Elene magic before, little mother?" he asked her mildly. "We use it all the time. You don't mind if I come in, do you?" He stepped through the splinter-littered doorway. "We thought you might be lonesome and that maybe you needed somebody to yell at. Vanion wanted to come, but I wouldn't let him."

"You? Since when have you started ordering Vanion around?"

"I'm bigger than he is—and younger."

"You get out of my room!"

"I'm sorry, but I can't do that." He glanced toward her window. "You've got a nice view from here. You can see all the way down to the harbor. Shall we get started? Screaming and hitting are all right, but please don't turn me into a toad. Alean wouldn't like that."

"Who sent you here, Kalten?"

"I already told you. It was my own idea. I wouldn't let Vanion come because you're upset right now. You might say something to him that you'd both regret later. You can say anything you want to *me*, Sephrenia. You can't hurt *my* feelings."

"Go away!"

"No, I won't do that. Would you like to have me make you a nice cup of tea?"

"Just leave me alone!"

"I already told you no." Then he took her by the shoulders and enfolded her in a huge bear hug. She struggled against him, but he was absolutely immovable. "Your hair smells nice," he noted.

She began to pound on his shoulders with her fists. "I *hate* you!"

"No, you don't," he replied calmly. "You couldn't hate me even if you wanted to." He continued to hold her. "It's been very mild this autumn, hasn't it?"

"*Please* leave me alone, Kalten."

"No."

She started to cry, clutching at his doublet and burying her face in his chest. "I'm so *ashamed*!" she wept.

"Of what? You didn't do anything wrong. Zalasta tricked you, that's all. He tricked the rest of us as well, so you're no more to blame than we are."

"I've broken Vanion's heart!"

"Oh, I don't think so—not really. You know Vanion. He can endure almost anything."

The storm of her weeping continued—which was more or less what Kalten had in mind. He pulled a handkerchief out of the sleeve of his doublet and gave it to her, still not relaxing his embrace.

"I'll never be able to face them again," she wailed.

"Who? You mean the others? Of course you will. You made a fool of yourself, that's all. Everybody does that now and then."

"How *dare* you!" She began to pound on him again.

Kalten *really* wished she'd get past that part of it. "It's true, though, isn't it?" he said gently. "Nobody's blaming you, but it's true all the same. You did what you thought was right, but it turned out to be wrong. Everybody's wrong sometimes, you know. There aren't any perfect people."

"I'm so ashamed!"

"You already said that. Are you sure you wouldn't like a nice cup of tea?"

"You should rest now, Anarae," Sarabian said solicitously. "I hadn't realized how exhausting this would be for you."

She smiled at him. "Thou art kind, Sarabian of Tamuli, but I am not so fragile as that. Let us proceed. It had been in the mind of Zalasta that he might by diverse inducements corrupt Anakha in his youth and thus gain access to Bhelliom without the need for perilous confrontation, but Sephrenia and Aphrael did closely attend the childhood and youth of Bhelliom's champion, once again and all unknowingly thwarting Zalasta's design.

"Then did Zalasta conclude that he had no choice but to approach Anakha as an enemy rather than a convert, and consulted he with Ogerajin and with Otha and went he even to Cimmura to seek allies to assist him. In furtherance of this did he pose as one of the numerous Zemoch Styrics Otha had sent into the Elene kingdoms to sow dissention and turmoil."

"There were plenty of those, all right," Ulath said. "Rumor had it that a Zemoch Styric could give an Elene anything he wanted—provided that the Elene wasn't too attached to his soul."

"The blandishments such Styrics offered were many," Xanetia agreed, "but the understanding of Otha's agents was limited."

"Profoundly limited," Vanion agreed.

"Truly. Zalasta, however, was more subtle, and far more patient. He did find an apt pupil in the person of the young chaplain to the royal house of Elenia, a priest named Annias."

"*Annias?*" Ehlana exclaimed. "I didn't know that he was ever the royal chaplain."

"It was before you were born," Sparhawk told her.

"*That* would explain why he had so much control over my father. Are you saying that Zalasta was behind all that, Anarae?"

Xanetia nodded.

"It isn't really all that easy to corrupt a young priest," Bevier objected. "They're usually filled with zeal and idealism."

"And Annias was no exception," Xanetia replied. "He was ambitious, but in his youth was he ever true to the ideals of his Church. That idealism stood in Zalasta's path until he found means to wear it away." She paused, flushing slightly. "I would not offend thee, Majesty," she apologized to Ehlana, "but thine aunt was ever lustful and wanton."

"It doesn't offend me in the slightest, Anarae," Ehlana replied. "Arissa's appetites were legendary in Cimmura, and I was never really all that fond of her in the first place."

"There was some connection, then?" Melidere asked.

"Indeed, Baroness," Xanetia replied. "Princess Arissa was the means whereby Zalasta recruited Annias to his cause. Well-schooled by the voluptuary Ogerajin, did Zalasta introduce the wanton princess to—" She broke off, blushing furiously.

"You needn't go into detail, Xanetia," Ehlana told her. "We all knew Arissa; there was nothing she wouldn't do."

"In truth was she an apt pupil," Xanetia agreed. "Now Zalasta concluded that Annias would be useful to him by reason of his position as adviser to thy father. Thus did he implant the firm belief in the mind of thy corrupt aunt that no act could be so vile as the seduction of a young priest. That notion, once implanted, did obsess Arissa, and 'ere long it bore fruit. In her twelfth year did Arissa steal away the dubious virtue of thy father's chaplain."

"At the age of *twelve?*" Melidere murmured. "She was precocious, wasn't she?"

"Then Annias was consumed with remorse," Xanetia continued.

"Annias?" Ehlana scoffed. "He didn't know what the word meant."

"You may be wrong there, my Queen," Vanion disagreed. "I knew Annias when he was a young man. He seemed committed to the principles of the Church. It wasn't until later that he began to change. Sparhawk's father and I always wondered what had happened to him."

"Evidently Arissa happened," Ehlana said dryly. She pursed her lips. "Then Zalasta gained access to Annias by means of my aunt?" she guessed.

Xanetia nodded. "The young priest, after much prayer and meditation, did resolve to renounce his vows and to wed the tarnished princess."

"A marriage made in heaven," Ulath noted sardonically.

"Arissa, however, would have none of such union, for so insatiable was her nature that she soon grew tired of her ecclesiastical paramour and did taunt him by reason of his waning prowess and stamina. At Zalasta's insinuating suggestion, however, did she bring her exhausted convert to a certain house in Cimmura, and there did Zalasta hint that he might restore the waning vigor of Annias by means of Styric enchantments. Thus did he secure a firm grip on the soul of he who would become Primate of Cimmura."

"We knew that Annias was getting help from one of Otha's Styrics," Sparhawk said. "We had no idea it was Zalasta, though. He had a hand in virtually everything, didn't he?"

"He is most clever, Anakha. Patiently did he instruct his two ever-more-willing pupils in that depravity which he himself had learned under the tutelage of Ogerajin of Verel. The royal chaplain was central to his plan, but first was it necessary to corrupt him beyond all hope of redemption."

"He did *that* part of it well enough," Ehlana said bleakly.

"Step by step did Arissa, guided by Zalasta, lead the chaplain down and down until all semblance of decency had been washed from him. Then it was that the Styric proposed the ultimate degeneracy—that the lustful princess, aided by her now equally foul paramour, should seduce thy father, her brother, and when he should be wholly in her thrall, should she broach the idea of incestuous marriage to him. Zalasta did well know that Anakha's father would resist such abomination to the death, and hoped he thereby to separate the house of Sparhawk from the royal house of Elenia. Reckoned he not, however, upon the iron will of the Sparhawks nor the weakness of King Aldreas. The elder Sparhawk compelled thy father to wed another, but in truth had Zalasta's goal been achieved. A breach had been opened between the two houses."

"But we've healed that breach, haven't we, Sparhawk?" Ehlana said with a warm smile.

"Frequently," he replied.

"What can I *do*?" Sephrenia wailed, wringing her hands.

"You can stop doing that, for one thing," Kalten told her, gently separating her hands. "I found out a little while ago just how sharp your fingernails are, and I don't want you tearing off your skin."

She looked guiltily at the fresh scratches on his face. "I hurt you, didn't I, dear one?"

"It's nothing. I'm used to bleeding."

"I've treated Vanion so badly," she mourned. "He'll never forgive me, and I love him."

"Then tell him so. That's all you really have to do, you know. Just tell him how you feel about him, say you're sorry, and everything will go back to being the way it was before."

"It won't *ever* be the same."

"Of course it will. As soon as you two are back together, Vanion will forget it ever happened." He took her two small hands in his great ones, turned them over, and kissed her palms. "That's what love's all about, little mother. We all make mistakes. The people who love us forgive the mistakes. The people who won't forgive don't really matter, now, do they?"

"Well, no, but—"

"There aren't any buts, Sephrenia. It's so simple that even *I* can understand it. Alean and I trust our feelings, and it seems to work out fairly well. You don't really need complicated logic when it comes to something as simple as love."

"You're such a good man, Kalten."

That embarrassed him a bit. "Hardly," he replied ruefully. "I drink too much, and I eat too much. I'm not very refined, and I usually can't follow even a simple thought from one end to the other. God knows I've got faults, but Alean knows about them and forgives them. She knows that I'm just a soldier, so she doesn't expect too much from me. Are you just about ready for that cup of tea?"

"That would be nice." She smiled.

"Now *that* comes as a real surprise," Vanion said, "but why Martel?"

"Zalasta did perceive that of all the Pandions, Martel came closest to being a match for Anakha," Xanetia replied, "and Martel's hunger for the forbidden secrets provided Zalasta with an opening. The Styric did pose as an unlettered and greedy Zemoch, and did accept Martel's gold with seeming eagerness. Thus did he beguile the arrogant young Pandion until there was no turning back for him."

"And all this time he was posing as Otha's emissary?" Bevier asked her.

"Yes, Sir Knight. He served Otha's design so long as it suited him, but his heart and mind remained his own. Truly, he did corrupt Primate Annias and the Pandion Martel for his *own* ends, which did ever center upon that day when Anakha would lift Bhelliom from the place where it lay hidden."

"But it wasn't Anakha who lifted it, Anarae. It was Aphrael, and none of Zalasta's scheming could have taken that into account."

They all turned quickly at the sound of the familiar voice. Sephrenia, her face still drawn, stood in the doorway with Kalten hovering behind her. "Zalasta might possibly have been able to take the stone from Sparhawk, but not Aphrael. That's where everything fell apart on him. He couldn't bring himself to believe that *anyone*—even a God—would willingly surrender Bhelliom to someone else. Maybe someday I'll explain it to him."

"I have seen into the mind of Zalasta, Sephrenia of Ylara," Xanetia told her. "He could not comprehend such an act."

"I'll *make* him understand, Anarae," Sephrenia replied in a bleak voice. "I have this group of big savage Elenes who love me—or so they say. I'm sure that if I ask them nicely enough, they'll *beat* that understanding into Zalasta." And she smiled a wan little smile.

CHAPTER TWENTY-TWO

Ehlana rose from her chair, went to Sephrenia, and kissed her palms in greeting. Sparhawk often marveled at how his young wife instinctively knew the right thing to do. "We've missed you, little mother," she said simply. "Are you feeling better now?"

A faint smile touched Sephrenia's lips. "Exactly how do you define *better*, Ehlana?" She looked closely at the blonde queen. "You're not getting enough sleep."

"You look a bit drawn yourself," Ehlana replied. "I suppose we both have reason enough."

"Oh, yes." Sephrenia looked around at the slightly apprehensive faces of her friends. "Oh, stop that," she told them. "I'm not going to throw a fit. I behaved badly." She reached up and fondly touched Kalten's cheek. "My overbearing friend here tells me that it doesn't matter, but I'd still like to apologize."

"You had plenty of reason to be upset," Sparhawk told her. "We were very abrupt with you."

"That's no excuse, dear one." She drew in a deep breath, squared her shoulders, and crossed the room to Xanetia with the air of one about to perform an unpleasant duty. "We don't really have any reason to be fond of each other, Anarae," she said, "but we should at least be civil. I wasn't. I'm sorry."

"Thy courage becomes thee, Sephrenia of Ylara. I do confess that I would be hard-pressed thus to admit a fault to an enemy."

"Exactly what did Sir Kalten do to bring you around, Lady Sephrenia?" Sarabian asked curiously. "You were in absolute despair, and Kalten wouldn't have been my first choice as a comforter."

"That's because you don't know him, Sarabian. His heart is very large, and he demonstrates his affection in a very direct way. He kicked my door down and smothered me into submission." She thought about it for a moment. "About all he really did was wrap his arms around me and tell me that he loved me. He kept saying it over and over again, and every time he said it, it struck me right to the heart. Elenes are very good bullies. I screamed at him for a while, and then I tried hitting him, but hitting Kalten is sort of like pounding on a brick. I even tried crying—I've always had good luck with crying—but all he did was offer to make me a cup of tea." She shrugged. "After a while, I realized that he was going to continue to love me no matter what I did and that I was making a fool of myself, so here I am." She smiled at Alean. "I don't know if you realize it, dear, but you may just be the luckiest woman in the world. Don't let him get away."

"No fear of that, Lady Sephrenia," the soft-eyed girl responded with a rosy blush.

Sephrenia looked around, suddenly all business. "I'm sure we have more important things to discuss than my recent temper tantrum. Have I missed much?"

"Oh, not really, dear sister," Stragen drawled. "About all we've discovered so far is that Zalasta's been responsible for nearly every catastrophe in human history since the fall of man. We don't have *quite* enough evidence to implicate him in *that* yet."

"We're a-workin' on it, though," Caalador added.

Sparhawk briefly summarized what Xanetia had told them of the hidden side of Zalasta. Sephrenia was startled to learn that it had been Zalasta who had corrupted Martel.

"I'm not trying to be offensive, dear sister," Stragen said, "but it seems to me that the Younger Gods weren't quite firm enough in dealing with these renegade

Styrics. They seem to lend themselves to just about every bit of mischief that comes along. Something a bit more permanent than banishment might have been a better solution."

"The Younger Gods wouldn't do that, Stragen."

"Pity," he murmured. "That sort of leaves it up to us, doesn't it? We've got a group of people out there who are highly skilled at causing trouble." His expression grew sly. "Here's a notion," he said. "Why don't you have somebody draw up a list of names and give it to me. I'll see to it that the Secret Government takes care of all the messy details. We wouldn't even need to bother the Younger Gods or the rest of Styricum about it. You propose, and I'll dispose. Call it a personal favor if you like."

"You're a depraved man, Stragen."

"Yes. I thought you might have noticed that."

"What did Zalasta do after Sparhawk destroyed Azash?" Talen asked Xanetia. "Didn't that teach him that he'd be wiser to stay clear of our friend here?"

"He was much chagrined, young master. Anakha had demolished decades of patient labor in a single night and, with Bhelliom firmly in his grasp, he was more dangerous than ever. Zalasta's hopes of wresting the jewel from him were dashed, and he fled from Zemoch in rage and disappointment."

"And when he ran away, he missed seeing Sparhawk throw Bhelliom into the sea," the boy added. "So far as he knew, Sparhawk still had it in his pocket."

She nodded. "Returned he to Verel to consult with Ogerajin and diverse other renegades concerning this disastrous turn of events."

"How many of them are there, Lady?" Kalten asked, "and what are they like? It's always good to know your enemies."

"They are many, Sir Kalten, but four—in addition to Zalasta and Ogerajin— are most significant. They are the most powerful and corrupt in all of Styricum. Ogerajin is by far the foulest, but his powers are waning by reason of a loathsome disease which doth eat away at his mind." Xanetia suddenly looked uncomfortable and she even blushed. "It is one of those ailments which do infect those who engage overmuch in bawdry."

"Ah—" Sarabian came to her aid, "I don't know that we need to get *too* specific about Ogerajin's disease. Why don't we just say that he's incapacitated and let it go at that? Who are the others, Anarae?"

She gave him a grateful look. "Cyzada of Esos is the most versed in the darker aspects of Styric magic, Emperor Sarabian," she replied. "Residing close by the eastern frontier of Zemoch, had he frequent contacts with the half-Styric, half-Elene wizards of that accursèd land, and did he learn much from them. Reaches he with some facility into the darkness which did surround the mind of Azash, and he can summon certain of the creatures which served the Elder God."

"Damorks?" Berit asked. "Seekers?"

"The Damorkim perished with their master, Sir Knight. The fate of the Seekers is uncertain. Cyzada fears to summon such as they, for only Otha could surely control them."

"That's something, anyway," Khalad said. "I've heard some stories that I'd rather not have to confirm in person."

"In addition to Cyzada, Zalasta and Ogerajin have allied themselves with Ptaga of Jura, Ynak of Lydros, and Djarian of Samar," Xanetia continued.

"I've heard of them," Sephrenia said darkly. "I wouldn't have believed Zalasta could sink so low."

"Bad?" Kalten asked her.

"Worse than that. Ptaga's a master of illusion who can blur the line between reality and imagining. It's said that he conjures up the images of various women for the pleasure of the degenerates who pay him, and that the images are even better than reality could be."

"Evidently he's branching out," Oscagne noted. "It would appear that he's creating the illusions of monsters now instead of pretty ladies. That would explain all the vampires and the like."

"Ynak's reputed to be the most contentious man alive," Sephrenia went on. "He can start centuries-long feuds between families just by walking past their houses. He's probably behind the upsurge of racial hatred that's contaminating the Elene kingdoms to the west. Djarian is probably the preeminent necromancer in the world. It's said that he can raise people who never even really existed."

"Whole armies?" Ulath asked her, "like those antique Lamorks or the Cyrgai?"

"I doubt it," she replied, "although I can't be sure. It was Zalasta who told us it was impossible, and he may have been lying."

"I've got a question, Anarae," Talen said. "Can you *see* what Zalasta's thinking as well as hear it?"

"To some degree, young master."

"What are you getting at, Talen?" Sparhawk asked him.

"You remember that spell you used to put Krager's face in that basin of water back in Platime's cellar in Cimmura?"

Sparhawk nodded.

"A name's just a name," Talen noted, "and these particular Styrics probably aren't running around announcing themselves. Stragen suggested getting rid of them earlier. Wouldn't pictures make that a lot easier? If Xanetia can see Zalasta's memories of what those people look like and let me see them, too, I could draw pictures of them. Then Stragen could send the pictures to Verel—or wherever those Styrics are—and Zalasta would suddenly lose some people he's been counting on rather heavily. I think we owe him *that* much, anyway."

"I like the way this boy thinks, Sparhawk." Ulath grinned.

"Thy plan is flawed, young master," Xanetia said to Talen. "The spell of which thou didst speak is a Styric spell, and I have no familiarity with it."

"Sephrenia could teach it to you." He shrugged.

"You're asking the impossible, Talen," Bevier told him. "Sephrenia and Xanetia have only recently reached the point where they can be in the same room without wanting to kill each other. There's a lot of trust involved in teaching—and learning—spells."

Xanetia and Sephrenia, however, had been exchanging a long, troubled look. "Don't be too quick to throw away a good idea, Bevier," Sephrenia murmured. "It *has* got some possibilities, Anarae," she suggested tentatively. "The notion probably makes your skin crawl as much as it does mine, but if we could ever learn to trust each other, there could be all manner of things we might be able to accomplish. If we could combine your magic with mine . . ." She left it hanging.

Xanetia pursed her lips, and her expression oddly mirrored Sephrenia's. So intense was her consideration of the notion that her control slipped a bit, and her face began to glow. "The alliance between our two races *did* almost bring the Cyrgai to their knees," she noted, also rather tentatively.

"In diplomatic circles this is the point at which the negotiators usually adjourn so that they can consult with their governments," Oscagne suggested.

"The Anarae and I aren't obliged to get instructions from either Sarsos or Delphaeus, your Excellency," Sephrenia told him.

"Most diplomats aren't, either." He shrugged. "The announcement 'I must consult with my government' is merely a polite way of saying 'Your suggestion is interesting. Give me some time to think it over and get used to the idea.' You ladies are breaking new ground. I'd advise you not to rush things."

"What say you, Sephrenia of Ylara?" Xanetia said, smiling shyly. "Shall we pause for a fictional consultation with Sarsos and Delphaeus?"

"That might not be such a bad idea, Xanetia of Delphaeus," Sephrenia agreed. "And as long as we both know that it's fiction, we won't have to waste time waiting for nonexistent messengers to make imaginary journeys before we speak of it again."

"After the destruction of the city of Zemoch and all who dwelt there, did Zalasta and his cohorts meet in Verel to consider their course," Xanetia picked up the story after a brief recess. "Concluded they at once that they were no match for Anakha and Bhelliom. It was Ogerajin who did point out that Zalasta's tentative alliance had been with *Otha,* and that there had been no direct contact with Azash. He did speak slightingly to Zalasta concerning this and Zalasta's rancor regarding those words doth linger still."

"That's always useful," Vanion observed. "Dissention among your enemies can usually be exploited."

"The presence of the contentious Ynak doth heighten their discord, Lord Vanion. Ogerajin did berate Zalasta, demanding to know if he were so puffed up as to think himself the equal of a God, for Ogerajin doth consider Anakha to be such—or very nearly—because of his access to Bhelliom."

"How does it feel to be married to a God, Ehlana?" Sarabian teased.

"It has its moments." She smiled.

"Cyzada of Esos then joined their discussion," Xanetia continued. "He did rather slyly suggest alliance with one or more of the myriad demigods of the netherworld, but his companions trusted him not, for he alone is conversant with the Zemoch spells which do raise and control such creatures of darkness. Indeed, trust is slight in that unwholesome company. Zalasta hath placed the ultimate prize before them and well doth he know that each of them doth secretly covet sole possession of the jewel. Theirs is an uneasy alliance at best."

"What did they finally decide to do, Anarae?" Kring asked. Sparhawk had noticed that the Domi seldom spoke at these meetings. Kring was not really comfortable indoors, and the subtleties of politics that so delighted Ehlana and Sarabian quite obviously bored him. Peloi politics were straightforward and simple—and usually involved bloodshed.

"It was the consensus of their deliberations that they might find—for a price—willing helpers in the imperial government itself," Xanetia replied.

"They were right about that," Sarabian said sourly. "If what we saw yesterday is any indication, my ministers were standing in line to betray me."

"It wasn't really personal, my Emperor," Oscagne assured him. "We were betraying each other, not you."

"Did anyone ever approach you?"

"Several, actually. They couldn't offer me anything I really wanted, though."

"Truth in politics, Oscagne?" his brother asked in feigned astonishment. "Aren't you setting a bad precedent?"

"Grow up, Itagne," Oscagne told him. "Haven't you learned by now that you can't deceive Sarabian? He claims to be a genius, and he's probably very close to being right—or will be as soon as we peel away his remaining illusions."

"Isn't that a blunt sort of thing to say, Oscagne?" Sarabian asked pointedly. "I'm right here, you know."

"Why, so you are, your Majesty," Oscagne replied with exaggerated astonishment. "Isn't that amazing?"

Sarabian laughed. "What can I do?" he said to Ehlana. "I need him too much to even object. Why didn't you tell me about this, Oscagne?"

"It happened when you were still feigning stupidity, your Majesty. I didn't want to wake you. I may have met this Ynak you've been talking about, Anarae. One of the men who approached me was Styric, and I've never met a more disagreeable individual. I've come across goats who smelled better, and the fellow was absolutely hideous. His eyes looked off in different directions, and his teeth were broken and rotting, and they all seemed to stick straight out. He looked like a man with a mouthful of brown icicles."

"Thy description doth closely match Zalasta's memories of him."

"That one shouldn't be too orful hord t' find, Stragen," Caalador drawled. "I kin send word t' Verel, iffn y' want. This yere Why-nack ain't likely t' be missed much if'n he's as on-pleasant as the furrin minister sez."

Xanetia looked puzzled.

"It's a pose that amuses my colleague, Anarae," Stragen apologized. "He likes to put on the airs of a yokel. He *says* it's for the purposes of concealment, but I think he does it just to irritate me."

"Thine Elenes are droll and frolicsome, Sephrenia of Ylara," Xanetia said.

"I know, Anarae," Sephrenia sighed. "It's one of the burdens I bear."

"Sephrenia!" Stragen protested mildly.

"How did you put this fellow off without getting a knife in your back, your Excellency?" Talen asked Oscagne. "Declining that sort of offer is usually fatal."

"I told him that the price wasn't right," Oscagne shrugged. "I said that if he could come up with a better offer, I might be interested."

"Very good, your Excellency," Caalador said admiringly. "What kind of reason did he give you for making the offer in the first place?"

"He was a bit vague about it. He hinted about some kind of large-scale smuggling operation and said that he could use the help of the foreign service to smooth the way in various kingdoms outside Tamuli. He hinted that he'd already bought off the Interior Ministry and the customs branch of the Chancellory of the Exchequer."

"He was lying, your Excellency," Stragen told him. "There isn't that much money to be made in smuggling. It's a big risk for short pay."

"I rather thought so myself." Oscagne leaned back, stroking his chin thoughtfully. "This group of Styrics down in Verel may think they're very worldly, but they're like children when compared to *real* criminals and international businessmen. They cooked up a story that wasn't really very convincing. What they actually wanted was access to the government and the power of the various ministries in order to use that power to overthrow the government itself. The government had to be on the brink of collapse in order to get *me* to run off to Eosia to beg Prince Sparhawk to come here and save us."

"It worked, didn't it?" Itagne said bluntly.

"Well, yes, I suppose it did, but it was so clumsy. I'd personally be ashamed to accept such a shoddy victory. It's a matter of style, Itagne. Any amateur can blunder into occasional triumph. The true professional controls things well enough not to have to trust to luck."

They adjourned for the night not long after that. Sparhawk watched Sephrenia and Vanion rather closely as everyone filed out. The two of them exchanged a few tentative glances, but neither seemed ready to break the ice.

They gathered again the following morning, and Talen and Kalten seemed to be competing to see which of them could eat the most for breakfast.

After a bit of casual conversation, they got down to business again. "Right after the attempted coup here in Matherion, Krager paid me a visit," Sparhawk told Xanetia. "Was he telling the truth when he said that Cyrgon's involved in this?"

She nodded. "Cyrgon hath much reason to hate the Styrics and their Gods," she replied. "The curse which hath imprisoned his Cyrgai for ten eons hath enraged him beyond all measure. The outcast Styrics in Verel did share his hatred, for they, too, had been punished." She reflected a moment. "We all have reason to hate Zalasta," she said, "but we cannot question his courage. It was at peril of his life that he did carry the proposal of the renegades to the Hidden City of Cyrga to place it before Cyrgon himself. The proposal was simple. By means of Bhelliom could the curse be lifted and the Cyrgai loosed once more upon this world. The Styrics could be crushed, which would please both Cyrgon and the outcasts; the Cyrgai would come to dominate the world—with positions of honor and power reserved for Ogerajin and his friends; and Aphrael would be destroyed, thus giving possession of Sephrenia to Zalasta."

"Something for everybody," Sarabian said dryly.

"So thought Ogerajin and Zalasta," Xanetia agreed. "They had, however, reckoned not upon the nature of Cyrgon. They soon found that he would in no wise consent to the secondary role they had in mind for him. Cyrgon doth command; he doth not follow. He did set his high priest, one Ekatas, over his new allies, telling them that Ekatas spoke for him in all things. Zalasta did secretly laugh at the God's simplicity, thinking that the High Priest Ekatas would, like all the Cyrgai, die with the step which took him over the unseen line in the sand. Ekatas, however, had no need of crossing the line. With Cyrgon's aid did he travel with his *mind,* not his body, that he might observe and direct without leaving Cyrga. Truly, the mind of Ekatas can reach across vast distances, not only to convey the will of Cyrgon, but to advise the diverse cohorts of what hath occurred elsewhere."

"That explains how the word that we were coming got from one end of Cynesga to the other so fast," Bevier said. "We sort of wondered how they were keeping ahead of us."

"Now," Xanetia pressed on, "though they are outcast and despised, Ogerajin and the others are still Styrics, and the Styrics are not a warlike people. Their efforts had concentrated on deception and misdirection previously. Cyrgon, however, is a war-God, and he did command them to raise armies to confront the Atans, who are the strong arm of the empire. Then were the outcasts of Verel nonplussed, for Cyrgon gave the command, but no guidance. Zalasta, who had traveled much in Eosia, did suggest to Ekatas that Cyrgon might deceive the Trolls and bring them to northern Tamuli, and Cyrgon did readily consent. Still he demanded more. Ynak of Lydros, who doth ever carry that cloud of dissention with him, could fan the fires of discontent in all of Tamuli, but so contentious is his nature that none would willingly follow him. Armies require generals, and Styrics are not gifted in that profession. I do not say this to give offense, Sephrenia," she added quickly. Both Xanetia and Sephrenia were being very careful with each other.

"I'm not offended, Xanetia. I *like* soldiers, mind you." Her eyes flickered toward Vanion. "Some of them, anyway. But I really think the world might be a nicer place without them."

"Bite your tongue," Ulath told her. "If we couldn't be soldiers, we'd all have to go out and find honest work."

Xanetia smiled. "It was in desperation—for Cyrgon did grow impatient—that Zalasta did journey to Arjuna to enlist his son Scarpa in the enterprise. Now Scarpa was unlike his father in that he did willingly—even eagerly—resort to violence. His years as a performer in shabby carnivals had taught him the skills of swaying crowds of people by eloquence and by his commanding presence. His profession, however, was held in low regard, and this did pain him deeply, for Scarpa hath an exalted opinion of himself."

"He does indeed, little Lady," Caalador agreed. "If what the thieves of Arjuna tell me is anywhere close to being accurate, Scarpa probably believes that he could fly or walk on water if he just set his mind to it."

"Truly," she agreed. "He hath, moreover, a deep contempt for the Gods and a profound hatred of women."

"That's not uncommon among bastards," Stragen said clinically. "Some of us blame our mothers—or our Gods—for our social unacceptability. Fortunately, I never fell into that trap. But then, I'm so witty and charming that I didn't have the usual inadequacies to try to explain away."

"I hate it when he does that," Baroness Melidere said.

"It's only a plain fact, my dear Baroness." He grinned at her. "False modesty is so unbecoming, don't you think?"

"Be clever on your own time, Stragen," Ehlana chided. "Did Zalasta tell his son *all* the details of this conspiracy, Anarae?"

"Yes, your Majesty. Given the nature of the two, there was surprising candor between them. Scarpa, however, was very young and had an exaggerated notion of his own cleverness. Zalasta did quickly realize that the rudimentary Styric spells which he had imparted to his son during his infrequent visits to Arjuna might serve to deceive rural bumpkins, but they would scarce be adequate for the business at hand. Therefore, took he his son to Verel to place him under the tutelage of Oger-ajin."

"When was this, Anarae?" Caalador asked curiously.

"Perhaps five years since, Master Caalador."

"Then it fits together with what *we* found out. It was almost exactly five years ago that Scarpa disappeared from Arjuna. Then a couple of years later he came back and started stirring up trouble."

"It was a short education," Xanetia said, "but Scarpa hath a quick mind. In truth, it was his tutor who did suspend his training, for Ogerajin was much offended by the young man's arrogance."

"This Scarpa sounds like the sort you have to stand in line to hate," Talen noted. "I've never met him, and I already dislike him."

"Zalasta was also taken somewhat aback by his son's abrasive nature," Xanetia told them, "and thinking to awe him into some measure of civility, he did take him to Cyrga that he might come to know their master. Cyrgon did question the young man closely and then, evidently satisfied, did he instruct him in the task before him. Scarpa came away with no more respect for the God of the Cyrgai than he had felt 'ere they met, and Zalasta hath lost what small regard he previously had for his son. It is now in his mind that should their conspiracy succeed, Scarpa will not long survive the victory." She paused. "An it please thee to view it so, Sephrenia, thy vengeance hath already had its beginning. Zalasta is a hollow man with no God and with none in all the world to love him or to call him friend. Even the scant affection he had for his son is now witherèd, and he is empty and alone."

Two great tears welled up in Sephrenia's eyes, but then she angrily dashed them away with the back of her hand. "It's not enough, Anarae," she said adamantly.

"You've spent too much time with Elenes, little mother," Sarabian said. That startled Sparhawk just a bit. He could not be sure if the brilliant, erratic Tamul emperor used that affectionate term deliberately, or if it had been a slip of the tongue.

"Who recruited the others, Anarae?" Vanion asked, smoothly moving away from a slightly touchy situation.

"It was Scarpa, Lord Vanion," she replied. "Cyrgon had directed him to seek out confederates to stir rebellion in western Tamuli, thus to bar the way should Anakha come with the armies of the Church, for Cyrgon would not willingly pit his cherished Cyrgai against such as you. Now Scarpa did know a certain out-at-the-elbows Dacite nobleman who, plagued by gambling debts and the ungentle urgings of his creditors to settle accounts, did flee from Daconia and conceal himself for a time in the very Arjuni carnival where Scarpa did practice his dubious art. This scruffy nobleman, Baron Parok by name, did Scarpa seek out on his return home from Cyrga. Parok, desperate out of all measure, soon willingly fell in with his former associate, for the inducements Scarpa offered were enticing. Consulted then the unscrupulous pair with the debauched Styrics at Verel and followed their counsel to seek out the merchant Amador in Edom and the poet Elron in Astel, both men being much taken with themselves and resentful of the station in life which fate had assigned them."

Bevier was frowning. "We've encountered both of them, Anarae, and neither one strikes me as a natural leader. Were they the best Scarpa could find?"

"Their selection was determined by their willingness to cooperate, Sir Knight. The ability to sway men with words and that commanding presence which doth draw all eyes can be elevated by certain Styric spells. Unimpressive though they are, it was the quality of desperation in them which Scarpa did seek. Both Amador and Elron suffered agonies by reason of their insignificance, and both were willing, even eager, to go to any lengths to exalt themselves."

"We see it all the time in Thalesia, Bevier," Ulath explained. "We call it 'the little man's complaint.' Avin Wargunsson's a perfect example. He'd rather die than be ignored."

"Amador's not all that short," Talen pointed out.

"There are all kinds of littleness, Talen," Ulath said. "How did Count Gerrich in Lamorkand get involved, Anarae? And why?"

"He was recruited by Scarpa on Zalasta's instruction, Sir Ulath. Zalasta thought to stir discord and turmoil on the Eosian continent to persuade the Church of Chyrellos that her interests required that Anakha be dispatched to Tamuli to seek out the roots of the disturbances. Of all of them, only Zalasta hath his feet planted on both continents, and only he doth understand the thinking of thy Church. In truth, Elron and Amador are but pawns, knowing little of the true scope of the enterprise they have joined. Baron Parok is more knowledgeable, but he is still not privy to *all* their designs. Count Gerrich is peripheral. He follows his own purposes, which only occasionally match the purposes of his colleagues here in Tamuli."

"You almost have to admire them," Caalador said. "This is the most complicated and well-organized swindle I've ever heard of."

"But it all fell apart when Xanetia opened the door to Zalasta's mind," Kalten said. "As soon as we found out that he's been on the other side all along, the whole thing began to crumble." He thought of something. "How did Krager get mixed up in this?"

"Count Gerrich did suggest him to Scarpa," Xanetia replied. "Gerrich had found the one called Krager useful in times past."

"Yes," Ulath said. "We saw him being useful outside the walls of Baron Alstrom's castle in Lamorkand. Martel's still coming back to haunt us, isn't he, Sparhawk?"

"How much did my Minister of the Interior and the other traitors really know about all of this, Anarae?" Sarabian asked.

"Almost nothing, Majesty. In the main they did believe that their activities were but a part of the ongoing struggle between Foreign Minister Oscagne and Interior Minister Kolata. Kolata offered them profit, and so they did follow him."

"Ordinary palace politics, then," Sarabian mused. "I suppose I'll have to keep that in mind at their trials. They weren't really disloyal, only corrupt."

"All except for Kolata, your Majesty," Itagne noted. "His involvement had to have gone deeper than simple garden-variety political bickering, wouldn't it?"

"Kolata was a dupe, Itagne of Matherion," Xanetia corrected. "It was Teovin who was ever Zalasta's man at court. It was to *him* that the one called Krager did bring Zalasta's instruction, and Teovin did tell Kolata only so much as it was needful for him to know."

"This brings us to the coup attempt," Ehlana said. "Krager told Sparhawk that it wasn't intended to succeed—that it was only designed to force us to reveal our strengths and weaknesses. Was he actually telling the truth?"

"In part, Majesty," Xanetia replied. "In the main, however, was Zalasta uncertain about the truth of Anakha's declaration that he had cast Bhelliom into the sea. Sought he by raising rebellion in the streets of Matherion and endangering all whom Anakha held most dear to force him to reveal whether or no he still did possess the jewel."

"We played right into his hands by going after it, then, didn't we?" Khalad suggested.

"I don't think so," Sparhawk disagreed. "We'd never have found out about Bhelliom's awareness if we'd left it where it was. That's the thing that *nobody* knew about—except possibly Aphrael. Azash didn't seem to know about it, and neither does Cyrgon. I doubt that either one would have been so interested in it if they'd known that it might resist their commands—even to the point of obliterating this world if necessary."

"All right," Khalad said. "Now we know what's led up to all this. What happens next?"

"That lieth in the future, Khalad of Demos," Xanetia replied, "and the future is concealed from all. Know, however, that our enemies are in disarray. Zalasta's position as adviser to the imperial government was at the core of all their plans."

"How quickly will he be able to recover, Sephrenia?" Ehlana asked. "You know him better than anyone. Will he be able to strike back immediately?"

"Possibly," Sephrenia said, "but whatever he does won't be very well thought out. Zalasta's a Styric, and we don't react well to surprises. He'll flounder for a while—destroying mountains and setting lakes on fire—before he gets hold of himself."

"We should hit him again, then," Bevier observed. "We shouldn't allow him to recover his balance."

"Here's a thought," Sarabian said. "After we went through the secret files of the Interior Ministry, we decided to pick up only the top level of conspirators—the police chiefs and administrators in the various towns, for the most part. We didn't bother with the toadies and informers—largely because we didn't have enough jail space. The Interior Ministry was central to the whole conspiracy, I think, and now Zalasta and his friends will probably be forced to rely on the scrapings we left behind. If I send the Atans out to make a more thorough sweep, won't that push Zalasta off-balance all the more?"

"Let him start to settle down first, Sarabian," Sephrenia advised. "Right now he's so enraged that he probably wouldn't even notice."

"Is Norkan still on the Isle of Tega?" Vanion asked suddenly.

"No," Ehlana replied. "I got tired of the forged letters he was sending me from there, so we sent him back to Atan."

"Good. I think we'd better get word of Zalasta's treachery to him as quickly as possible. Betuana really needs to know about it."

"I'll see to it, Vanion-Preceptor," Engessa promised.

"Thank you, Engessa-Atan. If that little outburst in the throne room is any indication of his present state of mind, Zalasta's totally out of control right now."

"Infuriated to the brink of insanity," Sephrenia agreed. It was the first time she had spoken directly to Vanion since the rupture between them. That fact gave Sparhawk some hope.

"He'll almost have to do *something,* then, won't he?" Vanion asked her. "In his present state, inaction would be unbearable."

She nodded. "He'll respond in some way," she said, "and since he wasn't at all prepared for what just happened, whatever he does won't have been planned out in advance."

"So it'll have large holes in it, won't it?"

"Probably."

"Most likely it would involve the use of main force," Sparhawk added. "Enraged people usually try to smash things."

"You'd better alert Norkan and Betuana to the possibility, Engessa-Atan," Sarabian instructed.

"It shall be as you say, Sarabian-Emperor."

Vanion began to pace up and down. "Zalasta's still more or less in command," he said. "At least he will be until he does something so stupid that Cyrgon replaces him. Why don't we let him have his temper tantrum, crush it, and *then* round up all the minor conspirators? Let's frighten our opponents just a bit. If they see us methodically smashing everything they've gone to so much trouble to prepare and rounding up all their friends, they'll start having thoughts about their own mortality. At that point, I think Cyrgon's going to have to show himself, and then Sparhawk can turn Bhelliom loose on him."

"I hate it when he's like this," Sephrenia said to Xanetia. "He's so certain—and probably so right. Men are much more appealing when they're just helpless little boys." The casual-seeming remark was startling. Sephrenia was clearly stepping over ancient racial antagonisms between Styric and Delphae and speaking to Xanetia as one woman to another.

"Then all we really have to do is sit here and wait for Zalasta's next move," Sarabian observed. "I wonder what he's going to do."

·   ·   ·

They did not have to wait long for the answer. A few days later an exhausted Atan stumbled across the drawbridge with an urgent message from Ambassador Norkan.

"Oscagne," the message began with characteristic abruptness, "round up every Atan you can lay your hands on and send them all here. The Trolls are dismantling northern Atan right down to the very bedrock."

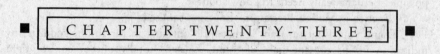

CHAPTER TWENTY-THREE

"We *can't* send them, Engessa-Atan," Sarabian said. "We need them right where they are. At the moment, they're all that's holding the empire together."

Engessa nodded. "I understand the situation, Sarabian-Emperor, but Betuana-Queen will only wait for so long. If the lands of the Atans are in peril, she will have no choice but to act. She will order the Atans home—despite her alliance with you."

"She's going to have to pull her people back," Vanion advised the huge Atan. "She doesn't have enough warriors to defend the north against the Trolls, so she may have to abandon northern Atan for a while. We won't be able to send full garrisons to her aid, but we *can* pull one or two platoons out of each garrison. That's several thousand warriors altogether, but it's going to take them longer to reach Atan because they're so spread out. She'll just have to pull back until we can get there."

"We are Atans, Vanion-Preceptor. We do not run away."

"I'm not suggesting that, Engessa-Atan. All your queen will be doing is repositioning her forces. She can't hold the north at the moment, and there's no point in wasting lives trying. The best we can do for her in the meantime is to send some Genidian advisers and Cyrinic technical assistance."

"Not quite, friend Vanion," Kring said. "I'll go to Tikume in central Astel. The eastern Peloi aren't as fearful of forests as my children are, and Tikume loves a good fight as much as I do, so he'll probably bring several thousand horsemen with him. I'll gather up a few hundred bowmen and come to Atan ahead of his main force."

"Your offer is generous, friend Kring," Engessa said.

"It's a duty, Engessa-Atan. You serve as Mirtai's father, and that makes us kinsmen." Kring absently rubbed his hand across his shaved scalp. "The bowmen are very important, I think. Your Atans have moral reservations about using bows in warfare, but when we met those Trolls in eastern Astel, we found out that you can't really fight them without shooting them full of arrows first."

"Here's another thought," Khalad said, holding up his crossbow. "How do your people feel about these, Engessa-Atan?"

Engessa spread his hands. "It is a new device here in Tamuli, Khalad-squire. We have not yet formed an opinion about it. Some Atans may accept it; others may not."

"We wouldn't have to arm *all* the Atans with crossbows," Khalad said. He looked at Sparhawk. "Will you be needing me here, my Lord?" he asked.

"Why don't you see if you can persuade me that I won't?"

"That's a cumbersome way to put it, Sparhawk. We've still got all those crossbows we gathered up when we put down the coup. I broke most of them, but it won't take me too long to fix them again. I'll go north with Engessa-Atan and the technical advisers. Engessa can try to persuade his people that the crossbow's a legitimate weapon of war, and I'll teach them how to use it."

"I'll join you in Atana later," Kring told them. "I'll have to lead Tikume's bowmen to the city. The Peloi tend to get lost in forests."

"Never mind, Mirtai," Ehlana told the giantess, whose eyes had suddenly come alight. "I need you here."

"My betrothed and my father are going to war, Ehlana," Mirtai objected. "You can't expect me to stay behind."

"Oh, yes, I can. You can't go, and that's final."

"May I be excused?" Mirtai asked stiffly.

"If you wish."

Mirtai stormed toward the door.

"Don't break *all* the furniture," Ehlana called after her.

It was really only a small domestic crisis, but it was a crisis all the same, largely because the Royal Princess Danae declared that she would die if her missing cat was not found immediately. She wandered tearfully around the throne room, climbing into laps, pleading and cajoling. Sparhawk was once again able to observe the devastating effect his daughter could have on someone's better judgment when she was sitting in the person's lap. "*Please* help me find my cat, Sarabian," she said, touching the emperor's cheek with one small hand. Sparhawk had long since learned that the first rule in dealings with Danae was never to let her touch you. Once she touched you, you were lost.

"We all need some fresh air anyway, don't we?" Sarabian said to the others. "We've been sitting in this room for more than a week now. Why don't we suspend our discussions and go find Princess Danae's cat. I think we'll all be fresher when we come back."

Score one for Danae. Sparhawk smiled.

"I'll tell you what," Sarabian continued. "It's a beautiful morning. Why don't we make an outing of it? I'll send word to the kitchens, and we can all have our lunches out on the lawns." He smiled down at Danae, whose hand might just as well have been wrapped around his heart. "We'll celebrate the return of Mmrr to her little mistress."

"What a *wonderful* idea!" Danae exclaimed, clapping her hands together. "You're *so* wise, Sarabian!"

They all smiled indulgently and rose to their feet. Sparhawk privately admitted that the emperor was probably right. The long day's conferences were beginning to make them all just a little fuzzy-headed. He went to his daughter and picked her up.

"I can walk, Father," she protested.

"Yes, but I can walk faster. My legs are longer. We *do* want to find Mmrr as soon as possible, don't we?"

She glared at him.

"You've got everybody under control," he murmured to her. "You don't have to herd them around like sheep. What's this all about? You can call Mmrr back home anytime you feel like it. What are you *really* up to?"

"There are some things I want to get settled before we get too busy, Sparhawk, and I can't do anything with all of you huddled together in this room like a flock of chickens. I need to get you all out of here so that I can straighten things out."

"Is Mmrr really lost?"

"Well, of *course* she isn't. I know exactly where she is. I just told her to go chase grasshoppers for a while."

"What sort of things were you talking about? Exactly what is it that you want to get straightened out?"

"Watch, Sparhawk," she told him. "Watch and learn."

"It's just not done, Kalten," Alean said in a sorrowfully resigned voice as the two walked out across the drawbridge with Sparhawk and Danae not far behind.

"What do you mean, 'not done'?"

"You're a knight, and I'm only a peasant girl. Why can't we just leave things the way they are?"

"Because I want to marry you."

She touched his face fondly. "And I'd give anything to be able to marry you, but we can't."

"I'd like to know why not."

"I told you already. We come from different social classes. A peasant girl can't marry a knight. People would laugh at us and say hateful things about me."

"Only once," he declared, clenching his fist.

"You can't fight the whole world, my love." She sighed.

"Of course I can—particularly if the world we're talking about consists of those butterflies that infest the court at Cimmura. I could kill a dozen of them before lunchtime."

"No!" she said sharply. "No killing! Can't you see what that would do? People would grow to hate me. We'd never have any friends. That's all right for you, because you'll be off at whatever war Prince Sparhawk or Lord Vanion sends you to, but I'll be completely alone. I couldn't bear that."

"I want to marry you!" he almost shouted.

"It would make my life complete as well, my dear love," she sighed, "but it's impossible."

"I want you to fix that, Sparhawk," Danae said out loud.

"Quiet! They'll hear us."

"They can't hear us, Sparhawk—or see us, either, for that matter."

"You're using a spell, I gather?"

"Naturally. It's a useful little spell that makes people ignore us. They kind of know we're here, but their minds don't pay any attention to us."

"I see. It tiptoes around the moral objection to eavesdropping, too, doesn't it?"

"What on earth are you talking about, Sparhawk? I don't have any moral problems with eavesdropping. I *always* eavesdrop. How else am I supposed to keep track of what people are doing? Tell Mother to give Alean a title so that she and Kalten can get married. I'd do it myself, but I'm busy. Take care of it."

"Is *this* the sort of thing you were talking about earlier?"

"Of course. Don't waste time on all these silly questions, Sparhawk. We've got a lot more to do today."

"I *do* love you, Berit-Knight," Empress Elysoun said a little sadly, "but I love him, too."

"And how many *others* do you love, Elysoun?" Berit asked her acidly.

"I've lost count." The bare-breasted empress shrugged. "Sarabian doesn't mind. Why should you?"

"Then we're through? You don't want to see me any more?"

"Don't be ridiculous, Berit-Knight. Of *course* I want to see you again—as often as I possibly can. It's just that there are going to be times when I'll be busy seeing *him*. I didn't *have* to tell you this, you know, but you're so nice that I didn't want to go behind your back to . . ." She groped for a word.

"To be unfaithful?" he said bluntly.

"I'm *never* unfaithful," she said indignantly. "You take that back right now. I'm the most faithful lady in the whole court. I'm faithful to at least a dozen young men, all at the same time."

He suddenly burst out laughing.

"What's so funny?" she demanded.

"Nothing, Elysoun," he replied with a genuine fondness. "You're so delightful that I can't help laughing."

She sighed. "Life would be so much simpler for me if you men wouldn't take these things so seriously. Love's supposed to be fun, but you all scowl and wave your arms in the air about it. Go love somebody else for a while. I won't mind. As long as everybody's happy, what difference does it make who *made* them happy?"

He smiled again.

"You *do* still love me, don't you, Berit-Knight?"

"Of course I do, Elysoun."

"There. Everything's all right, then, isn't it?"

"What was that all about?" Sparhawk asked his daughter. They were standing fairly close to Berit and Elysoun—close enough to make Sparhawk slightly self-conscious, at any rate.

"Berit was getting just a little too deeply involved with the naked girl," Danae replied. "He's learned what she could teach him, so it's time for their friendship to calm down a little. I have other plans for him."

"Have you ever considered letting him make his own plans?"

"Don't be ridiculous, Sparhawk. He'd just make a mess of things. I *always* take care of these arrangements. It's one of the things I do best. We'd better hurry. I want to look in on Kring and Mirtai. He's going to tell her something that isn't going to make her happy. I want to be there to head off any explosions."

They found Kring and Mirtai sitting on the lawn under a large tree ablaze with autumn color. Mirtai had opened the basket the kitchen had provided and was looking inside. "Some kind of dead bird," she reported.

Kring made a face. "I suppose it's civilized food," he said, trying to put the best face on it.

"We're both warriors, my betrothed," she replied, also looking less than happy with what had been prepared for their lunch. "We're supposed to eat red meat."

"Stragen told me once that you ate a wolf when you were younger," Kring said, suddenly remembering the story.

"Yes," she replied simply.

"Do you mean you actually *did*?" He seemed stunned. "I thought he was just trying to fool me."

"I was hungry—" she shrugged, "—and I didn't have time to stop. The wolf didn't taste very good, but he was raw. If I'd had time to cook him, he might have been better."

"You're a strange woman, my beloved."

"That's why you love me, isn't it?"

"Well—it's *one* of the reasons. Are you *sure* we can't talk about our problem?" He was obviously coming back to a subject they had discussed before—many times.

"There's nothing to talk about. We have to be married twice—once in Atana and then again when we get back to Pelosia. We won't be really married until we've gone through both ceremonies."

"We'll be *half*-married after the ceremony in Atana, won't we?"

"Half-married isn't good enough, Kring. I'm a virgin. I've killed too many men protecting that to settle for 'half-married.' You'll just have to wait."

He sighed. "It's going to take a long time, you know," he said mournfully.

"It's not *that* far from Atana back to your country. I'll race you there."

"It's not the journey that's going to take so long, Mirtai. It's the two months you'll have to spend in my mother's tent before the wedding in Pelosia. You'll have to learn our practices and ceremonies."

She gave him a long, steady look. "You said I have to *what*?" There was an ominous tone in her voice.

"It's the custom. A Peloi bride always lives for two months with the groom's mother before the ceremony."

"Why?"

"To learn about him."

"I already know about you."

"Well, yes, I suppose you do, but it's the custom."

"That's ridiculous!"

"Customs often are, but I *am* Domi, so I have to set a good example—and you'll be Doma. The Peloi women will have no respect for you if you don't do what's expected."

"I'll *teach* them respect." Her eyes had turned flint-hard.

He leaned back on his elbows. "I was sort of afraid you might feel this way." He sighed.

"Is that why you didn't mention it before?"

"I was waiting for the right time. Is there any wine in that basket? This might be easier if we're both more relaxed."

"Let's wait. We can get relaxed *after* you tell me. What *is* this nonsense?"

"Let's see if I can explain it." He rubbed his head. "When my people say that the bride is 'learning about her husband,' it doesn't really mean that she's learning about what he expects for breakfast or things like that. What they're really talking about is the fact that there's property involved."

"I don't have any property, Kring. I'm a slave."

"Not after you marry me, you won't be. You'll be a very wealthy woman."

"What are you talking about?"

"Peloi men own their weapons and their horses. Everything else belongs to the women. Always before whenever I stole something—cattle, usually—I gave it to my mother. She's been holding my wealth for me until I get married. She's entitled to *some* of it. That's what the two months is all about. It's to give the two of you time to agree on the division."

"It shouldn't take us *that* long."

"Well, probably not. My mother's a reasonable woman, but the two of you will *also* have to find husbands for my sisters. It wouldn't be so hard if there weren't so many of them."

"How many?" Her voice was *very* hard now.

"Ah—eight, actually."

"Eight?" She said it flatly.

"My father was very vigorous."

"So was your mother, apparently. Are your sisters presentable?"

"More or less. None of them are as beautiful as you are, though, love—but then who could be?"

"We can talk about that later. There's some kind of problem with your sisters, isn't there?"

Kring winced. "How did you know that?"

"I know *you*, Kring. You saved mention of these sisters until the very last. That means that you didn't want to talk about them, and that means there's a problem. What is it?"

"They think they're rich. That makes them put on airs."

"Is *that* all?"

"They're very arrogant, Mirtai."

"I'll teach them humility." She shrugged. "Since there are only eight, I should be able to do it all at once. I'll just take them all out into the nearest pasture for an hour or so. They'll be very humble when we come back—and eager to marry any men your mother and I choose for them. I'll make sure they're willing to do *any-*

thing to get away from me. Your mother and I should be able to settle the property division in the morning; I'll civilize your sisters in the afternoon, and you and I can be married that same evening."

"It's not done that way, my love."

"It will be, *this* time. I'm no more enthusiastic about waiting than you are. Why don't you come over here and kiss me? Now that everything's been settled, we should take advantage of this opportunity."

He grinned at her. "My feelings exactly, love." He took her in his arms and kissed her. The kiss was rather genteel at first, but that didn't last for very long. Things turned slightly savage after a moment.

"That's going to work out just fine," Danae said smugly. "I wasn't sure how Mirtai was going to take the idea of living with Kring's mother, but she's got everything in hand now."

"She's going to upset the Peloi, you know," Sparhawk said.

"They'll live." The princess shrugged. "They're too set in their ways anyhow. They *need* somebody like Mirtai to open their eyes to the modern world. Let's move on, Sparhawk. We're not done yet."

"How long has this been going on?" Stragen asked in a slightly choked voice.

"Since I was a little girl," Melidere replied. "My father made the dies when I was about seven or so."

"Do you realize what you've done, Baroness?"

"I thought we were going to drop the formality, Milord Stragen." She smiled at him.

He ignored that. "You've struck a direct blow at the economy of every kingdom in Eosia. This is monstrous!"

"Oh, *do* be serious, Stragen."

"You've debased the coinage!"

"I haven't really, but why should it make any difference to you?"

"Because I'm a thief! You've devalued everything I've ever stolen!"

"No, not really. The value of the coins doesn't really have anything to do with their true weight. It's a matter of trust. People may not *like* their governments, but they trust them. If the government says that this coin is worth a half crown, then that's what it's worth. Its value is based on an agreement, not on weight. If the coin has milled edges, it has the value that's stamped on its face. I haven't really stolen anything."

"You're a *criminal,* Melidere!"

"How can I be a criminal if I haven't stolen anything?"

"What if they find out about what you've been doing?"

"What if they do? They can't do anything about it. If they say anything or try to do something to me, I'll just tell the whole story, and every government in Eosia will collapse because nobody will trust their coins anymore." She touched his cheek. "You're such an innocent, Stragen. I think that's why I'm fond of you. You pretend to be depraved, but actually you're like a little boy."

"Why did you tell me about this?"

"Because I need a partner. I can handle these affairs in Eosia, but taking on Tamuli as well might strain my resources. You have contacts here, and I don't. I'll teach you the business and then lease Tamuli to you. I'll buy you a title and set things up so that you can start immediately."

His eyes narrowed. "Why?" he demanded. "Why are you being so generous?"

"I'm not being generous, Stragen. You *will* pay your rent every month. I can see to that. And you *won't* pay in coins. I want bullion, Stragen—nice, solid bars of gold that I can weigh—and don't try mixing in any copper either. I'll have your throat cut if you ever try that."

"You're the hardest woman I've ever known, Melidere." He sounded slightly afraid of her.

"Only in *some* places, Stragen," she replied archly. "The rest of me is fairly soft. Oh, that reminds me. We'll be getting married."

"We'll *what?*"

"Partnerships aren't made in heaven, Milord; marriages are. Marriage will give me one more hold on you."

"What if I don't *want* to get married?" He sounded a little desperate now.

"That's just too bad, Stragen, because like it or not, you *will* marry me."

"And you'll have me killed if I don't, I suppose."

"Of course. I'm not going to let you run around loose with this information. You'll get used to the idea, Milord. I'm in a position to make you deliriously happy—and fabulously wealthy to boot. When have you ever had a better offer?"

The look in Stragen's eyes, however, was one of sheer panic.

"Now *that* was something I didn't expect," Danae said as she and Sparhawk crossed the lawn.

Sparhawk was almost too shocked to answer. "You didn't know about Melidere's little hobby, you mean?"

"Oh, of course I knew about that, Sparhawk. Melidere bought her way into Mother's court several years ago."

"*Bought?*"

"She paid an old countess to step aside for her. What I didn't expect was the direct way she approached Stragen. I thought she might soften things a little, but she was all business. She carved him into neat little slices and she didn't give him any room to move at all while she did it. I think I've misjudged her."

"No, actually you misjudged Stragen. She used the only technique that had any chance of success with him. Stragen's very slippery. You've got to pin him to the plate with a fork before you can carve him. He probably wouldn't have listened to an ordinary marriage proposal, so she was all business with him. The marriage was only an incidental part."

"Not to *her,* it wasn't."

"Yes, I know. She did it right, though. I'm going to have to tell your mother about this, you know."

"No, actually, you're not. You heard Melidere. Mother wouldn't be able to do anything about it, and all you'd do is worry her."

"They're stealing millions, Aphrael."

"They're not stealing anything, Sparhawk. What they're going to do in no way changes the value of money. When you get right down to it, they're actually *creating* wealth. The whole world will be better for it."

"I don't entirely follow the logic of that."

"You don't have to, Father," she said sweetly. "Just take my word for it." She pointed. "We want to go over there next."

"Over there," was beside the moat, where Sephrenia and Vanion walked side by side along the grassy bank. Sparhawk was growing accustomed to his de facto invisibility by now, but it was still strange to have one of his friends look directly at him without acknowledging his presence.

"It would depend entirely on what kind of fish were locally available," Vanion was explaining. Sparhawk could tell that Vanion was explaining because he was using his "explaining" voice, which was quite a bit like his "preaching" voice. Vanion had put whole generations of Pandion novices to sleep—both in the lecture hall and in chapel.

"Why is he talking like that?" Danae asked.

"Because he's afraid." Sparhawk sighed.

"Of *Sephrenia*? Vanion isn't afraid of anything—least of all Sephrenia. He loves her."

"That's what's making him afraid. He doesn't know what to say. If he says the wrong thing, it could all fall apart again."

"Now," Vanion continued to lecture, "there are warm-water fish and cold-water fish. Carp like the water to be warm, and trout like it colder."

Sephrenia's eyes were starting to glaze over.

"The water in the moat has been standing for quite a while, so it's fairly warm. That would sort of rule out trout, wouldn't you say?"

"I suppose so," she sighed.

"But that doesn't mean that you couldn't plant some other kind of fish in there. A really good cook can do wonders with carp—and they *do* help to keep the water clean. There's nothing like a school of carp to keep standing water from turning stagnant."

"No," she sighed. "I'm sure there isn't."

"What on earth is he *doing*?" Danae exploded.

"It's called 'walking on eggshells,' " Sparhawk explained. "He probably talks a great deal about the weather, too."

"They'll *never* get back together if he doesn't talk directly to her about something that matters."

"He probably won't do that, Aphrael. I think Sephrenia's going to have to take the first step."

"I found her!" Talen's shout came across the lawn. "She's up in this tree!"

"Oh, bother!" Danae said irritably. "He wasn't supposed to find her yet—and what's she doing up a tree? She wasn't supposed to climb any trees."

"We may as well go on over," Sparhawk told her. "Everybody's drifting in that direction. You'd better dissolve your spell."

"What about Vanion and Sephrenia?"

"Why don't we just let them work it out for themselves?"

"Because he'll go on talking about fish for the next ten years, that's why."

"Sephrenia will only listen to lectures about fish for so long, Danae, then *she'll* get to the point. Vanion isn't really talking about fish. He's telling her that he's ready to make peace if she is."

"He didn't say anything about that. He was just about to start giving her recipes for boiled carp."

"That's what you *heard* him saying, but that wasn't what he was *really* saying. You've got to learn to listen with *both* ears, Danae."

"*Elenes!*" she said, rolling her eyes upward.

Then they heard Kalten shout, "Look out!"

Sparhawk looked sharply toward the spot where the others were gathered around a tall maple tree. Talen was up among the topmost branches, inching his way slowly out on a very slender limb toward the wild-eyed Mmrr. Things weren't going well. The limb was sturdy enough to support Mmrr, but Talen was too heavy. The limb was bending ominously, and there were unpleasant cracking sounds coming from its base.

"Talen," Kalten shouted again, "get back!"

But by then, of course, it was too late. The tree limb did not so much break off from the trunk as it did split at its base and peel down the side of the tree. Talen made a desperate grab, caught the confused and terrified cat in one hand, and then plunged headlong down through the lower branches of the tree.

The situation was still not irretrievable. The Church Knights were all versed in various levels of magic, Sephrenia was there, and Aphrael herself rode on Sparhawk's shoulders. The problem was that no one could actually *see* Talen. The maple tree had large leaves and the boy was falling down through the limbs and was thus totally obscured by the foliage. They could hear him hitting limbs as he fell, a series of raps and thumps accompanied by grunts and sharp cries of pain. Then he emerged from the lower foliage, falling limply to land with a thud on the grass under the tree with Mmrr still loosely held in one hand. He did not get up.

"Talen!" Danae screamed in horror.

Sephrenia concurred with the opinion of Sarabian's physicians. Talen had suffered no really serious injuries. He was bruised and battered, and there was a large, ugly knot on his forehead from his encounter with the unyielding tree limb that had knocked him senseless, but Sephrenia assured them that aside from a splitting headache, he would have no lasting aftereffects from his fall.

Princess Danae, however, was in no mood to be reassured. She hovered at the bedside, reacting with little cries of alarm each time the unconscious boy stirred or made the slightest sound.

Finally, Sparhawk picked her up and carried her from the room. There were people there who probably shouldn't witness miracles. "It got away from you, didn't it, Aphrael?" he observed to the distraught Child-Goddess.

"What are you talking about?"

"You *had* to tamper with things—trying to fix things that would have fixed themselves if you'd just left them alone—and you almost got Talen killed in the process."

"It wasn't *my* fault that he fell out of the tree."

"Whose fault was it, then?" He knew that logically he was being grossly unfair, but he felt that maybe it was time for the meddling little Goddess to be brought up short. "You interfere too much, Aphrael," he told her. "People have to be allowed to live their own lives and to make their own mistakes. We can usually fix our mistakes by ourselves if you'll just give us the chance. I suppose that what it gets down to is that just because you *can* do something doesn't always mean that you *should* do it. You might want to think about that."

She stared at him for a long moment, and then she suddenly burst into tears.

"Tikume's bowmen will help," Vanion said to Sparhawk a bit later when the two stood together on the parapet. "Ulath's right about Trolls. You definitely want to slow them down before you fight them."

"And Khalad's idea about the crossbows isn't bad either."

"Right. Thank God you brought him along." The preceptor pursed his lips. "I'd like to have you take personal charge of Khalad's training when you get him back to Cimmura, Sparhawk. Make sure that he gets instruction in politics, diplomacy, and Church law as well as in military skills. I think he's going to go a long way in our order, and I want to be sure he's ready for *any* position."

"Even yours?"

"Stranger things have happened."

Sparhawk remembered Vanion's lecture on fish that morning. "Are you making any progress at all with Sephrenia?" he asked.

"We're speaking to each other, if that's what you mean."

"It wasn't. Why don't you just sit down and talk with her? About something more significant than the weather, or how many birds can sit on a limb, or what kind of fish can live in the moat?"

Vanion gave him a sharp look. "Why don't you mind your own business?"

"It is my business, Vanion. She can't function while there's this rift between you—and neither can you, for that matter. I *need* you—both of you—and I can't really count on either of you until you resolve your differences."

"I'm moving as fast as I dare, Sparhawk. One wrong move here could destroy everything."

"So could a failure to move. She's waiting for you to take the first step. Don't make her wait too long."

Stragen came out onto the parapet. "He's awake now," he reported. "He's not very coherent, and his eyes aren't focused, but he's awake. Your daughter's making quite a fuss over him, Sparhawk."

"She's fond of him." Sparhawk shrugged. "She tells everybody that she's going to marry him someday."

"Little girls are strange, aren't they?"

"Oh, yes, and Danae's stranger than most."

"I'm glad I was able to catch the two of you alone," Stragen said then. "There's something I'd like to talk over with you before I mention it to the others." Stragen was absently twiddling two gold Elenic half crowns in his right hand, carefully running one fingertip across the milled edges and hefting them slightly as if trying to determine their weight. Baroness Melidere's confession appeared to have unsettled him just a bit. "Zalasta's little fit of rage wasn't quite as irrational as we thought it would be. Turning the Trolls loose on northern Atan was the most disruptive thing he could have done to us. We'll have to deal with that, of course, but I think we'd better start preparing for his next move. Trolls don't need much supervision once they've been pointed in the right direction, so Zalasta's free to work on something else now, wouldn't you say?"

"Probably," Sparhawk agreed.

"Now, I could be wrong—"

"But you don't think you are," Vanion completed his sentence sardonically.

"He's in a touchy mood today, isn't he?" Stragen said to Sparhawk.

"He's got a lot on his mind."

"It's my guess that whatever Zalasta comes up with next is going to involve those conspirators Sarabian and Ehlana left in place for lack of jail cells."

"It could just as easily involve the armies Parok, Amador, and Elron have raised in western Tamuli," Vanion disagreed.

Stragen shook his head. "Those armies were raised to keep the Church Knights off the continent, Lord Vanion, *and* they were raised at Cyrgon's specific orders. If Zalasta risked them now, he'd have to answer to Cyrgon for it, and I don't think he's *that* brave yet."

"Maybe you're right," Vanion conceded. "All right, let's say that he *will* use those second-level conspirators. Sarabian and Ehlana have already set things in motion to round them up."

"Why bother rounding them up at all, my Lord?"

"To get them off the streets, for one thing. Then there's also the small detail of the fact that they're guilty of high treason. They need to be tried and punished."

"Why?"

"As an example, you idiot!" Vanion flared.

"I'll agree that getting them off the streets is important, Lord Vanion, but there are more effective ways to make examples of people—not only more effective, but more terrifyingly certain. When you send policemen out to arrest people, it's noisy, and usually others hear the noise and manage to escape. There's also the fact that trials are tedious, expensive, and not absolutely certain."

"You've got an alternative in mind, I gather," Sparhawk said.

"Naturally. Why not have the executions first and the trials later?"

They stared at him.

"I'm sort of extending the idea I had the other day," Stragen said. "Caalador and I have access to a number of nonsqueamish professionals who can carry out the executions privately."

"You're talking about murder, Stragen," Vanion accused.

"Why, yes, Lord Vanion, I believe that is the term some people do use to describe it. The whole idea behind 'examples' is to frighten others so much that they won't commit the same crime. It doesn't really work, because criminals know that their chances of being caught and punished are very slim." He shrugged. "It's just one of the hazards of doing business. We professional criminals break laws all the time. We *don't,* however, break our own rules. People in our society who break the rules aren't afforded the courtesy of being tried. They're just killed. No acquittals, no pardons, no last-minute jailbreaks. Dead. Period. Case closed. The justice of regular society is slow and uncertain. Ours is just the opposite. If you want to use terror to keep people honest, use *real* terror."

"It *has* got possibilities, Vanion," Sparhawk suggested tentatively.

"You're not seriously considering it, are you? There are thousands of those people out there! You're talking about the largest mass murder in history!"

"It's a way to get my name in the record books." Stragen shrugged. "Caalador and I are probably going to do this any way. We're both impatient men. I wouldn't have bothered you about it, but I thought I'd like to get your views on the subject. Should we tell Sarabian and Ehlana, or should we just go ahead and not bother them? Discussions about relative morality are so tedious, don't you think? The point here is that we need to come up with something that will unhinge Zalasta all the more, and I think this might be it. If he wakes up some morning in the not-too-distant future and finds himself absolutely and totally alone, it might give him some second thoughts about the wisdom of his course. And oh, incidentally, I've borrowed Berit and Xanetia. They're taking a stroll in the vicinity of the Cynesgan embassy so that Xanetia can run that dip net of hers through the minds of the people inside. We've got quite a few names, but I'm sure there are more."

"Doesn't she have to be in the same room with somebody to listen to his thoughts?" Vanion asked.

"She's not really certain. She's never had occasion to test the limits of her gift. The expedition today is something in the nature of an experiment. We're hoping that she'll be able to reach in through the walls and pull out the names of the people inside. If she can't, I'll find some way to get her inside so that she can seine out what we need. Caalador and I want as much information and as many names as we can get. Setting up the largest mass murder in history is a very complicated business, and we don't want to have to do it twice."

CHAPTER TWENTY-FOUR

"It's diversionary," Ulath said the next morning. He lowered one of the dispatches Emperor Sarabian had brought with him. "The werewolves and vampires and ghouls are just illusions, so they can't really hurt anybody, and these attacks on Atan garrisons are no more than suicidal gestures intended to keep things confused. This is just more of what they were doing before."

"He's right," Sparhawk agreed. "None of this is new, and it doesn't have any real purpose except to keep the Atans in place."

"Unfortunately, it's succeeding very well," Bevier said. "We can't reduce the Atan garrisons by very much to send help to Betuana with all this going on."

"Lord Vanion's idea of detaching platoon-sized units from the main garrisons should help a *little*," Sarabian protested.

"Yes, your Majesty," Bevier replied, "but will it be enough?"

"It's going to *have* to be," Vanion said. "It's all we can spare right now. We're talking about Atans, though, and numbers aren't that significant where they're concerned. One Atan is half an army all by himself."

Stragen motioned to Sparhawk, and the two of them drifted over to the long table laden with breakfast. The blond thief carefully selected a pastry. "It worked," he said quietly. "Xanetia has to be able to *see* the person whose thoughts she's stealing, but Berit found a building that's fairly close and quite a bit higher than the embassy. Xanetia's got a comfortable room to sit in with a window that faces the ambassador's office. She's picking up all sorts of information—and names—for us."

"Why are we keeping this from the others?"

"Because Caalador and I are going to use the information to set that new world record I was telling you about yesterday. Sarabian hasn't authorized it yet, so let's not upset him over something he doesn't need to know about—at least not until we've stacked all the bodies in neat piles."

Princess Danae fell ill the next day. It was nothing clearly definable. There was no fever, no rash, and no cough involved—only a kind of listless weakness. The princess seemed to have no appetite, and it was difficult to wake her.

"It's the same thing as it was last month," Mirtai assured the little girl's worried parents. "She needs a tonic, that's all."

Sparhawk, however, knew that Mirtai was wrong. Danae had not really been ill the previous month. The Child-Goddess made light of her ability to be in two places at the same time, but her father knew that when her attention was firmly fixed on what was going on in one place, she would be semicomatose in the other. This illness was quite different, somehow. "Why don't you go ahead and try a tonic, Ehlana?" he suggested. "I'll go talk with Sephrenia. Maybe she can think of something else."

He found Sephrenia sitting moodily in her room. She was looking out the window, although it was fairly obvious that she did not even see the view. "We've got a problem, little mother," Sparhawk said, closing the door behind him. "Danae's sick."

She turned sharply, her eyes startled. "That's absurd, Sparhawk. She doesn't *get* sick. She can't."

"I didn't think so myself, but she's sick all the same. It's nothing really tangible, no overt symptoms or anything like that, but she's definitely not well."

Sephrenia rose quickly. "I'd better go have a look," she said. "Maybe I can get her to tell me what's wrong. Is she alone?"

"No. Ehlana's with her. I don't think she'll be willing to leave. Won't that complicate things?"

"I'll take care of it. Let's get to the bottom of this before it goes any further."

Sephrenia's obvious concern worried Sparhawk all the more. He followed her back to the royal quarters with growing apprehension. She was right about one thing. Aphrael was not in any way susceptible to human illnesses, so this was no simple miasmic fever or one of the innumerable childhood diseases that all humans catch, endure, and get over. He dismissed out of hand the notion that there could be such a thing as the sniffles of the Gods.

Sephrenia was very businesslike. She was muttering the Styric spell before she even entered Danae's room.

"Thank God you're here, Sephrenia!" Ehlana exclaimed, half rising from her chair beside the little girl's bed. "I've been so—"

Sephrenia released the spell with a curious flick of her hand, and Ehlana's eyes went blank. She froze in place, half-risen from her chair and with one hand partially extended.

Sephrenia approached the bed, sat on the edge of it, and took the little girl in her arms. "Aphrael," she said, "wake up. It's me—Sephrenia."

The Child-Goddess opened her eyes and began to cry.

"What is it?" Sephrenia asked, holding her sister even more tightly and rocking back and forth with her.

"They're killing my children, Sephrenia!" Aphrael wailed. "All over Eosia! The Elenes are killing my children! I want to die!"

"We have to go to Sarsos," Sephrenia said to Sparhawk and Vanion a short while later when the three of them were alone. "I have to talk with the Thousand."

"I know that it's breaking her heart," Vanion said, "but it can't really hurt her, can it?"

"It could kill her, Vanion. The younger Gods are so totally involved with their worshippers that their very lives depend on them. Please, Sparhawk, ask Bhelliom to take us to Sarsos immediately."

Sparhawk nodded bleakly and took out the box, touching his ring to the lid. "Open!" He said it more sharply than he'd intended.

The lid snapped up.

"Blue-Rose," Sparhawk said, "a crisis hath arisen. The Child-Goddess is made gravely ill by reason of the murder of her worshippers in far-off Eosia. We must at once to Sarsos that Sephrenia might consult with the Thousand of Styricum regarding a cure."

"It shall be as thou dost require, Anakha." The words came from Vanion's mouth. The preceptor's expression turned slightly uncertain. "Is it proper for me to tell thee that I feel sympathy for thee and thy mate for this illness of thine only child?"

"I do appreciate thy kind concern, Blue-Rose."

"My concern doth not arise merely from kindness, Anakha. Twice hath the gentle hand of the Child-Goddess touched me, and even I am not proof against the subtle magic of her touch. For the love we all bear her, let us away to Sarsos that she may be made whole again."

The world seemed to shift and blur, and the three of them found themselves outside the marble-sheathed council hall in Sarsos. Autumn was further along here, and the birch forest lying on the outskirts of the city was ablaze with color.

"You two wait here," Sephrenia told them. "Let's not stir up the hotheads by marching Elenes into the council chamber again."

Sparhawk nodded and opened Bhelliom's golden case to put the jewel away.

"Nay, Anakha," Bhelliom told him, still speaking through Vanion's lips. "I would know how Sephrenia's proposal is received."

"An it please thee, Blue-Rose," Sparhawk replied politely.

Sephrenia went quickly up the marble steps and inside.

"It's cooler here," Vanion noted, pulling his cloak a little tighter about him.

"Yes," Sparhawk agreed. "It's farther north."

"That more or less exhausts the weather as a topic. Quit worrying, Sparhawk. Sephrenia has a great deal of influence with the Thousand. I'm sure they'll agree to help."

They waited as the minutes dragged by.

It was probably half an hour later when Sparhawk felt a sharp surge, almost a shudder, pass through the Bhelliom. "Come with me, Anakha!" Vanion's voice was sharp, abrupt.

"What is it?"

"The Styric love of endless talk discontents me. I must needs go past the Thousand to the Younger Gods themselves. These babblers do talk away the life of Aphrael." Sparhawk was a bit surprised by the vehemence in Vanion's voice. He followed as his preceptor, walking in a gait that was peculiarly not his own, stormed into the building. The bronze doors to the council chamber may have been locked. The screech of tortured metal that accompanied Vanion's abrupt opening of them suggested that they *had* been, at any rate.

Sephrenia was standing before the council, her hands upraised, pleading for aid. She broke off and stared incredulously at Vanion as he burst through the door.

"We don't allow Elenes in here!" one of the council members on a back bench shrieked in Styric, rising to his feet and waving his arms.

Then a sort of strangled silence filled the chamber. Vanion began to swell, spreading upward and outward into enormity even as an intensely blue aura flickered brighter and brighter around him. Flickers of lightning surged through that aura, and ripping peals of thunder echoed shockingly back from the marble-clad walls. Sephrenia stared at Vanion in sudden awe.

Prompted by an unvoiced suggestion that only he could hear, Sparhawk raised the glowing sapphire rose. "Behold Bhelliom!" he roared, "and hearken unto its mighty voice!"

"Hear my words, ye Thousand of Styricum!" The voice coming from the enormity that a moment before had been Vanion was vast. It was a voice to which mountains would listen and for which waves and torrents would stop at once to hear. "I would speak with your Gods! Too small are ye and too caught up in endless babble to consider this matter!"

Sparhawk winced. Diplomacy, he saw, was not one of Bhelliom's strong suits.

One of the white-robed councillors drew himself up, spluttering indignantly. "This is outrageous! We don't have to—" He was suddenly gone, and in his place stood a confused-looking personage who appeared to have been interrupted in the middle of his bath. Naked and dripping, he gaped at the huge, blue-lighted presence and at the glowing jewel in Sparhawk's hand. "Well, *really*—" he protested.

"Setras!" the profound voice said sharply, "how deep is thy love for thy cousin Aphrael?"

"This is *most* irregular!" the youthful God protested.

"How deep is thy love?" The voice was inexorable.

"I adore her, naturally. We all do, but—"

"What wouldst thou give to save her life?"

"Anything she asks, of course, but how could her life be in danger?"

"Thou knowest that Zalasta of Styricum is a traitor, dost thou not?"

There were gasps from the council.

"Aphrael said so," the God replied, "but we thought she might have been a little excited. You know how she is sometimes."

"She told thee truly, Setras. Even now do Zalasta's minions slaughter her worshippers in far-off Eosia. With each death is she made less. If this be permitted to continue, soon she will be no more."

The God Setras stiffened, his eyes suddenly blazing. "Monstrous!"

"What wilt thou give that she may live?"

"Mine own life, if need be," Setras replied with archaic formalism.

"Wilt thou lend her of thine own worshippers?"

Setras stared at the glowing Bhelliom, his face filled with chagrin.

"Quickly, Setras! Even now doth the life of Aphrael ebb away!"

The God drew in a deep breath. "There is no alternative?" he asked plaintively.

"None. The life of the Child-Goddess is sustained only by love. Give her the love of certain of *thy* children for a time that she may be made whole again."

Setras straightened. "I *will*!" he declared. "Though it doth rend mine heart." A determined look crossed that divine face. "And I do assure thee, World-Maker, that mine shall not be the *only* children who will sustain the life of our beloved cousin with their love. *All* shall contribute equally."

"Done, then!" Bhelliom seemed fond of that expression.

"Ah," Setras said then, his tone slightly worried and his speech slipping into less formal colloquialism, "she *will* give them back, won't she?"

"Thou hast mine assurance, Divine Setras," Sephrenia promised with a smile.

The Younger God looked relieved. Then his eyes narrowed slightly. "Anakha," he said crisply.

"Yes, Divine One?"

"Measures must be taken to protect Aphrael's remaining children. How might that best be accomplished?"

"Advise them to go to the chapterhouses of the Knights of the Church of Chyrellos," Sparhawk replied. "There will they be kept from all harm."

"And who doth command these knights?"

"Archprelate Dolmant, I suppose," Sparhawk replied dubiously. "It is he who doth exercise ultimate authority."

"I will speak with him. Where may I find him?"

"He will be in the Basilica in Chyrellos, Divine One."

"I will go there and seek him out that we may consult together regarding this matter."

Sparhawk nearly choked on the theological implications of *that* particular announcement. Then he looked at Sephrenia's face. She was still regarding Vanion with a certain amount of awe. Then, so clearly that he could almost hear the click in her mind, Sephrenia made a decision. Her whole face, her entire being, announced it louder than words.

"Ulath," Kalten said irritably, "pay attention. You've been woolgathering for the past two weeks. What's got you so distracted?"

"I don't like the reports we've been getting back from Atan," the big Genidian replied, shifting the princess Danae, Rollo, and Mmrr around in his lap. The little princess had been confined to her room for ten days by her illness, and this was her first day back among them. She was engaging in one of her favorite pastimes—lap switching. Sparhawk knew that most of his friends really didn't pay that much attention, responding automatically to her mute, wan little appeals to be picked up and held. In actuality, however, Aphrael, with toy and with cat, was very busily going from lap to lap to reestablish contact with those who might have drifted out of her grasp during her illness. As always, there were kisses involved, but those kisses were not really the spontaneous little demonstrations of affection they seemed. Aphrael could change minds and alter moods with a touch. With a kiss, however, she could instantly take possession of the entirety of someone's heart and soul. Whenever Sparhawk was engaged in a dispute with his daughter, he was always very careful to keep at least one piece of furniture between them.

"Things aren't working out the way I thought they would," Ulath said in a gloomy voice. "The Trolls are learning to hide from arrows and crossbow bolts."

"Even a Troll is bound to learn eventually," Talen said. Talen seemed fully recovered from his tumble out of the maple tree, although he still complained of headaches occasionally.

"No," Ulath disagreed. "That's the whole point. Trolls *don't* learn. Maybe it's because their Gods don't learn—or can't. The Trolls that are walking around right now know exactly what the first Troll who ever lived knew—no more, no less. Cyrgon's tampering with them. If he alters the Trolls to the point that they can learn things, mankind's going to be in serious trouble."

"There's something more, too, isn't there, Ulath?" Bevier asked shrewdly. "You've had your 'theological expression' on your face for the past several days. You're tussling with some moral dilemma, aren't you?"

Ulath sighed. "This is probably going to upset everybody, but try to consider it on its merits instead of just going up in flames about it."

"That doesn't sound too promising, old boy," Stragen murmured. "You'd better break it to us gently."

"I don't think there *is* a gentle way, Stragen. Betuana's dispatches are getting more and more shrill. The Trolls won't come out in the open anymore. The mounted Atans can't get at them with lances, and the arrows and crossbow bolts are hitting more trees than Trolls. They're even setting grass fires so they can hide in the smoke. Betuana's right on the verge of calling her people home, and without the Atans, we don't have an army anymore."

"Sir Ulath," Oscagne said, "I gather that this gloomy preamble is a preparation for a shocking suggestion. I think we've all been sufficiently prepared. Go ahead and shock us."

"We have to take the Trolls away from Cyrgon," Ulath replied, absently scratching Mmrr's ears. "We can't let him continue to teach them even rudimentary tactics, and we definitely don't want them cooperating with each other the way they have been."

"And how exactly are you going to take totally unmanageable brutes away from a God?" Stragen asked him.

"I was sort of thinking along the lines of letting their *own* Gods do it. The Troll-Gods *are* available, after all. Ghwerig imprisoned them inside Bhelliom, and Sparhawk's got Bhelliom tucked away inside his shirt. I'd imagine that Khwaj and the others would do almost *anything* for us if we promise to give them their freedom."

"Are you mad?" Stragen exclaimed. "We can't turn them loose! That's unthinkable!" He dropped the pair of gold coins he always carried now.

"I'd be more than happy to consider alternatives—if anyone can come up with some. The threat to Atan is serious enough, but the longer Cyrgon dominates the Trolls, the more they're going to learn from him. Sooner or later, they'll go back to Thalesia. Do we really want a trained army of Trolls outside the gates of Emsat? We've got at least *some* small advantage if we deal with the Troll-Gods. We hold the key to their freedom. But we don't really have *anything* Cyrgon wants—except Bhelliom itself. I'd rather deal with the Troll-Gods, myself."

"Why don't we just have Sparhawk take Bhelliom to northern Atan and exterminate the Trolls with it?"

Sparhawk shook his head. "Bhelliom won't do that, Stragen. It won't obliterate an entire species. I know that for certain."

"You've got the rings. You could force it to do as you say."

"No. I won't do that. Bhelliom isn't a slave. If it cooperates, it's going to have to be willingly."

"We can't just turn the Troll-Gods loose, Sparhawk. I may be a thief, but I'm still a Thalesian. I'm not going to just sit by and let the Trolls overrun the entire peninsula."

"We haven't even talked with the Troll-Gods yet, Stragen," Ulath told him. "Why don't we see what they have to say before we decide? No matter what, though, we're going to have to do *something* very soon. If we don't, we're going to start seeing long columns of Atans marching out of their barracks on their way back home."

Danae slipped down from Ulath's lap and retrieved Stragen's coins. "You dropped these, Milord," she said sweetly. Then she frowned. "Is it my imagination, or is one of them just a little lighter than the other?"

Stragen looked at her with a slightly sick expression on his face.

·   ·   ·

It was somewhat later, and Sparhawk and Vanion were escorting Sephrenia back to her room. They reached the door and stopped.

"Oh, this is absurd!" Sephrenia suddenly burst out in an exasperated tone of voice. "Vanion, go get your things and come back home where you belong!"

Vanion blinked. "I—"

"Hush!" she told him. Then she glared at Sparhawk. "And not a word out of you, either!"

"Me?"

"You have packing to do, Vanion," she said. "Don't just stand there gawking."

"I'll get right at it."

"And don't take all day." She threw her arms up in the air. "Men! Do I have to draw pictures for you? I did everything short of lighting signal fires and blowing trumpets, and all you wanted to talk about was the weather—or fish. Why wouldn't you *ever* get to the point?"

"Well—I—" he floundered. "You *were* very angry with me, Sephrenia."

"That was then. This is now. I'm not angry anymore, and I want you to come back home. I'm going to go have a word with Danae, and I want to see you back in our room when I return."

"Yes, dear," he replied meekly.

She glared at him for a moment, and then she spun on her heel and went off down the hall, talking to herself and waving her hands in the air.

"Well, Krager's back," Talen reported as they gathered again later that afternoon. "One of the beggars saw him slipping in through the back gate of the Cynesgan embassy about two hours ago—*staggering* might be a better word for it, though. He was roaring drunk."

"That's the Krager we've come to know and love." Kalten laughed.

"I can't understand how Zalasta can put any faith in a known drunkard," Oscagne said.

"Krager's very intelligent when he's sober, your Excellency," Sparhawk explained. "That was the only reason Martel put up with him." He scratched at his cheek. "Could we prevail on you to go back to that lookout near the embassy, Anarae?"

Xanetia started to rise from her chair.

"Not right now." He smiled. "It usually takes Krager all night to sober up, so tomorrow morning should be soon enough. I think we'll want to know what instructions he brings to the Cynesgan ambassador."

"There's something else, too," Stragen added. "We've never really been sure if Krager knows that we're using criminals to gather information for us. He knew that we were getting help from Platime in Cimmura and that we had contact with thieves and the like in other cities in Eosia, but we should find out if he's made the connection between the two continents yet."

"He sort of hinted that he knew when he talked with me after we put down the coup," Sparhawk reminded him.

"I don't want to discard the entire apparatus on the basis of a hint, Sparhawk,"

Stragen said, "and I *really* need to know if he's aware of the fact that we can use certain criminals for things other than spying."

"I shall probe his mind most closely," Xanetia promised.

"Where are Vanion and Sephrenia, Sparhawk?" Ehlana asked suddenly. "They should have been here an hour ago."

"Oh, I'm sorry, dear. I meant to tell you about that. I excused them for the rest of the day. They have something important to take care of."

"Why didn't you tell me?"

"I am, dear—right now."

"What are they doing?"

"They've resolved their differences. I'd imagine they're discussing that right now—at some length."

She flushed slightly. "Oh," she said in a neutral sort of way. "What finally got them back together again?"

He shrugged. "Sephrenia got tired of the estrangement and told Vanion to come back home. She was very direct about it—and she even managed to twist it around so that it was all his fault. You know how that goes."

"That will do, Sir Knight," she said firmly.

"Yes, your Majesty."

"Would this Krager person know where Zalasta is right now, Prince Sparhawk?" Oscagne asked.

"I'm sure he does, your Excellency. Zalasta probably doesn't *want* him to know—Krager being what he is, and all—but it's very hard to hide things from Krager when he's the least bit sober."

"He could be enormously valuable to us, Prince Sparhawk. Particularly in the light of the Anarae's special gift."

"You'd better get all you can from him right now, your Excellency," Talen suggested, "because just as soon as my brother gets back from Atan, he'll probably kill him."

Oscagne looked startled.

"It's a personal thing, your Excellency. Krager was involved in the death of our father—around the edges, anyway. Khalad wants to do something about that."

"I'm sure we can persuade him to wait, young master."

"I wouldn't be, your Excellency."

"It's been a part of us for so long that I don't think we'd be Styrics without it, Anarae," Sephrenia said sadly.

It was one of those private meetings at the top of the tower. Sparhawk and his daughter had joined Sephrenia, Vanion, and Xanetia as evening settled over Matherion, so that they could discuss certain things the others did not need to know about.

"It is even so with us, Sephrenia of Ylara," Xanetia confessed. "Our hatred of thy race doth in part define the Delphae as well."

"We tell our children that the Delphae steal souls," Sephrenia said. "I was always taught that you glow because of the souls you've devoured, and that the people you touch decay because you've jerked their souls out of them."

Xanetia smiled. "And we tell *our* young ones that the Styrics are ghouls who rob graves for food—when there are no Delphaeic children nearby to be eaten alive."

"I know a child with a slightly Styric background who's been considering cannibalism lately," Sparhawk noted blandly.

"Snitch!" Danae muttered.

"What's this?" Sephrenia demanded of her sister.

"The Child-Goddess was very upset when she found out that Zalasta had deceived her," Sparhawk said in an offhand sort of way, "and even more upset when she discovered that he wanted to steal you from her. She said she was going to rip his heart out and eat it right before his very eyes."

"Oh, I probably wouldn't have done it," Aphrael tried to shrug it off.

"Probably?" Sephrenia exclaimed.

"His heart's so rotten it would have made me sick."

Sephrenia gave her a long, steady look of disapproval.

"Oh, *all right*," the Child-Goddess said, "I was exaggerating." She looked pensively out over the city, then back at Sephrenia and Xanetia. "All this hatred and the wild stories the Styrics and the Delphae tell their children about each other aren't really natural, you realize. You've been very carefully coached to feel this way. The real argument was between my family and Edaemus, and it involved things you wouldn't even understand. It was a silly argument—most arguments are—but Gods can't keep their arguments private. You humans were drawn into something that didn't really concern you at all." She sighed. "Like so many of our disagreements, that one started to spill over from the part of the world where *we* live into your part. It's *our* party, and you never should have been invited."

"Where *is* this country of yours, Aphrael?" Vanion asked curiously.

"Right here—" She shrugged. "—all around us, but *you* can't see it. It might be better if we had our own separate place, but it's too late now. I should have told Sephrenia about our foolishness when she and I were children and I heard her parroting some of that nonsense about the Delphae, but then the Elene serfs destroyed our village and killed our parents, and Zalasta tried to shift his own guilt to the Delphae, and that set her prejudices in stone." She paused. "I always *knew* there was something about Zalasta's story that didn't ring true, but I couldn't get into his thoughts to find out what it was."

"Why not?" Vanion asked her. "You *are* a Goddess, after all."

"You've *noticed*!" she exclaimed. "What a *thrilling* discovery that must have been for you!"

"Mind your manners," Sparhawk told her.

"Sorry, Vanion," she apologized. "That *was* a little snippy, wasn't it? I can't look into Zalasta's thoughts because he isn't one of my children." She paused. "Sephrenia, don't you find it interesting that *I'm* limited but Xanetia isn't?"

"Xanetia and I are exploring our differences, Aphrael." Sephrenia smiled. "Every one of them we've examined so far has turned out to be imaginary."

"Truly," Xanetia agreed. Sparhawk could only begin to imagine how difficult even these tentative steps toward peacemaking must be for this strangely similar pair of women. The tearing down of institutionalized bigotry must have been somewhat akin to dismantling a house that had been standing for a hundred centuries.

"Vanion, dear," Sephrenia said then, "it's starting to get a little chilly."

"I'll run down and fetch your cloak."

She sighed. "No, Vanion," she told him. "I *don't* want a cloak. I want you to put your arms around me."

"Oh," he said. "I should have thought of that myself."

"Yes," she agreed. "Try to think of it more often."

He smiled and put his arms about her.

"That's *so* much nicer," she said, snuggling up against him.

"There's something I've been meaning to ask," Sparhawk said to his daughter. "Regardless of who put them up to it, the people who attacked Ylara *were* Elenes. How in the world did you ever persuade Sephrenia to take on the chore of teaching the Pandions the Secrets? She must have hated Elenes."

"She did." The Child-Goddess shrugged. "And I wasn't too fond of you myself. I had Ghwerig's rings, though, and I absolutely *had* to get them on the fingers of King Antor and the first Sparhawk—otherwise, I wouldn't be here." She paused, and her eyes narrowed. *"That's intolerable!"* she exclaimed.

"What is?"

"Bhelliom manipulated me! After I stole the rings from Ghwerig—or maybe even before—it put the notion into the rings themselves. I *know* it did. I no sooner took those rings than the idea occurred to me to separate them by giving one of them to your ancestor and the other to Ehlana's. This has all been *Bhelliom's* scheme! That—that thing *used* me!"

"My, my," Sparhawk said blandly.

"And it was so *clever*!" she fumed. "It seemed like such a good idea! Your blue friend and I are going to have a long talk about this."

"You were telling us how you forced Sephrenia to become our tutor, I believe," he said.

"I commanded her to do it—after coaxing wouldn't work. First I ordered her to take the rings to that pair of bleeding savages, and then I took her to your motherhouse at Demos and compelled her to become your tutor. I had to have her there to keep your family on the right track. You're Anakha, and I knew I'd need some kind of hold on you. Otherwise, Bhelliom would have had you all to itself, and I didn't trust it enough to let *that* happen."

"Then you *did* plan all this in advance," Sparhawk said just a bit sadly.

"Bhelliom may have planned it first," she said darkly. "I was absolutely sure it was my idea. I thought that if I just happened to be your daughter, you'd at least pay some attention to me."

He sighed. "It was all completely calculated, then, wasn't it?"

"Yes, but that doesn't have anything to do with the way I feel about you. I had a great deal to do with inventing you, Sparhawk, so I do really love you. You were a darling baby. I almost disassembled Kalten when he broke your nose. Sephrenia talked me out of it, though. Mother was a different story. You were sweet, but she was adorable. I loved her from the first moment I saw her, and I knew you two would get on well together. I'm really rather proud of the way things have turned out. I even think Bhelliom approves—of course it would never admit it. Bhelliom's so stuffy sometimes."

"Did your cousin Setras actually go into the Basilica and talk with Dolmant?" Vanion asked her suddenly.

"Yes."

"How did Dolmant take it?"

"Surprisingly well. Of course Setras can be very charming when he wants to be, and Dolmant *is* fond of me." She paused, her dark eyes speculative. "I think his Archprelacy's going to bring about some rather profound changes in your Church, Vanion. Dolmant's mind isn't absolutely locked in stone the way Ortzel's is. I think Elene theology's going to change a great deal while he's Archprelate."

"The conservatives won't like that."

"They never do. Conservatives wouldn't even change their underwear if they didn't have to."

"That's extremely questionable from a legal standpoint, your Majesty," Oscagne said. "I'm not personally questioning your word, Anarae," he added quickly, "but I think we can all see the problem here. All we'll have in the way of evidence is Xanetia's unsubstantiated testimony about what somebody's thinking. Even the most pliable of judges is likely to choke a bit on that. These are going to be very difficult cases to prosecute—particularly in view of the fact that some of the accused are going to be members of the great families of Tamul proper."

"You might as well go ahead and tell them all of it, Stragen," Sparhawk suggested. "You're going to carry out your plan anyway, and they'll worry over legal niceties for weeks if you don't tell them."

Stragen winced. "I really wish you hadn't brought it up, old boy," he said in a pained voice. "Their Majesties are official personages, and they're more or less obliged to observe the strict letter of the law. They'd both be much more comfortable if they didn't know too many details."

"I'm sure they would, but all this fretting about building ironclad court cases is wasting time we should be spending on other problems."

"What's this?" Sarabian asked.

"Milord Stragen and Master Caalador are contemplating something along the lines of what you might call legal shortcuts, your Majesty—in the interests of expediency. Do you want to tell them, Stragen? or do you want me to do it?"

"You go ahead. It might sound better coming from you." Stragen leaned back, still brooding over his two gold coins.

"Their plan's very simple, your Majesty," Sparhawk told the emperor. "They propose that instead of rounding up all these conspirators, spies, informers, and the like, we just have them murdered."

"*What?*" Sarabian exclaimed.

"That was a very blunt way to put it, Sparhawk," Stragen complained.

"I'm a blunt man." Sparhawk shrugged. "Actually, your Majesty, I sort of approve of the notion. Vanion's having a little trouble choking it down, though." He leaned back in his chair. "Justice is a funny thing," he observed. "She's only partly interested in punishing the guilty. What she's *really* interested in is deterrence. The idea is to frighten people into avoiding crime by doing unpleasant things—publicly—to the criminals who get caught. But as Stragen pointed out, most criminals know that they probably won't *get* caught, so all the police and the courts are *really* doing is justifying their continued employment. He suggests that we by-pass the police and the courts and send out the murderers some night very soon. The next morning, everybody even remotely connected with Zalasta and his rene-gade Styrics would be found with his throat cut. If we want a deterrent, that would really be the most effective one. There wouldn't be any acquittals or appeals or im-perial pardons to confuse the issue. If we do it that way, everybody in all of Tamuli will have nightmares about the fruits of treason for years afterward. I approve of the idea for tactical reasons, though. I'll leave justice to the courts—or the Gods. I like the idea because of the damage it would do to Zalasta. He's a Styric, and Styrics usu-ally try to get what they want by deception and misdirection. Zalasta's set up a very elaborate apparatus to gain his ends without a direct confrontation. Stragen's plan would destroy that apparatus in a single night, and only madmen would be willing to join Zalasta after that. Once the apparatus is gone, he'll *have* to come out in the open and fight. He's not good at that, but we are. This would give us the chance to fight this war on our own terms, and that's always an enormous tactical advantage."

"*And* we can pick our own time," Caalador added. "The timing would be very important."

"They wouldn't be expecting it; that's one thing," Itagne noted.

"There are rules, Itagne," his brother objected. "Civilization's based on rules. If we break the rules, how can we expect others to follow them?"

"That's the whole point, Oscagne. Right now, the rules are protecting the criminals, not society as a whole. We can wriggle around and come up with some kind of legalistic justification for it afterward. About the only real objection I have is that these—ah—agents of government policy, shall we say, won't have any official standing." He frowned for a moment. "I suppose we could solve that problem by appointing Milord Stragen to the post of Minister of the Interior and Master Caala-dor Director of the Secret Police."

"*Real* secret, your Excellency." Caalador laughed. "I don't even know who most of the murderers are."

Itagne smiled. "Those are the best kind, I suppose." He looked at the emperor. "That *would* put a slight stain of legality on the whole business, your Majesty—in the event that you decide to go ahead with it."

Sarabian leaned thoughtfully back in his chair. "I'm tempted," he said. "A bloodbath like this would insure domestic tranquility in Tamuli for at least a cen-tury." He shook off his expression of wistful yearning and sat up. "It's just too un-civilized. I couldn't approve of something like that with Lady Sephrenia and Anarae Xanetia watching me and sitting in judgment."

"What are *your* feelings, Xanetia?" Sephrenia asked tentatively.

"We of the Delphae are not overconcerned with niceties and technicalities, Sephrenia."

"I didn't think you would be. Good is good, and bad is bad, wouldn't you say?"

"It seemeth so to me."

"And to me as well. Zalasta's hurt the both of us, and Stragen's massacre would hurt *him*. I don't think either of us would object too much to something that would cause him pain, would we?"

Xanetia smiled.

"It's your decision, then, Sarabian," Sephrenia said. "Don't look to Xanetia and me for some excuse *not* to make it. We find nothing objectionable in the plan."

"I'm profoundly disappointed in both of you," he told them. "I was hoping you'd get me off the hook. You're my last chance, Ehlana. Doesn't this monstrous notion turn *your* blood cold?"

"Not particularly," she shrugged, "but I'm an Elene—*and* a politician. As long as we don't get caught with bloody knives in our *own* hands, we can always wriggle out of it."

"Won't *anyone* help me?" Sarabian actually looked desperate.

Oscagne gave his emperor a penetrating look. "It has to be your decision, your Majesty," he said. "I personally don't like it, but I'm not the one who has to give the order."

"Is it always like this, Ehlana?" Sarabian groaned.

"Usually," she replied quite calmly. "Sometimes it's worse."

The emperor sat staring at the wall for quite some time. "All right, Stragen," he said finally. "Go ahead and do it."

"That's Mother's darling boy," Ehlana said fondly.

CHAPTER TWENTY-FIVE

"No, Caalador," Sparhawk said, "as a matter of fact, it *won't* take three or four weeks. I have access to a faster way to get from place to place."

"That won't do any good, Sparhawk," the ruddy-faced Cammorian objected. "The people in the Secret Government won't take orders from *you*."

"I won't be giving the orders, Caalador," Sparhawk told him. "*You* will."

Caalador swallowed. "Are you sure it's safe to travel that way?" he asked dubiously.

"Trust me. How many people will we have to get word to?"

Caalador threw an uncomfortable glance at Sarabian. "I'm not at liberty to say."

"I won't use the information, Caalador," the emperor assured him.

"You and I know that, your Majesty, but rules are rules. We like to keep our numbers just a little vague."

"Generalize, Caalador," Ehlana suggested. "A hundred? Five hundred?"

"Not hordly that many, dorlin'." He laughed. "Ther ain't *no* pie whut kin be cut into *that* many pieces." He squinted a bit anxiously at Stragen. "Let's just say more than twenty and less than a hundred and let it go at that, shall we? I'd rather not get my *own* throat cut."

"That's general enough." Stragen laughed. "I won't turn you in for that, Caalador."

"Thanks."

"Don't mention it."

"Two or three days, then," Sparhawk said.

"Let's not start passing the word around until after the Anarae pulls her net through Krager's mind tomorrow morning," Stragen said.

"Thou art fond of that particular metaphor, Milord Stragen," Xanetia noted in a slightly disapproving tone.

"I'm not trying to be offensive, Anarae. I'm groping for a way to explain something I couldn't begin to understand, that's all." Stragen's face grew bleak. "If Krager really knows about the Secret Government, he's probably infiltrated it, and there'll be *some* people out there we won't want to tell about this."

"And whose names we'll be adding to our list," Caalador added.

"Just how long *is* your list, Master Caalador?" Oscagne asked.

"You don't really need to know that, your Excellency," Caalador replied in a tone that clearly said he wasn't going to discuss the matter. "Let's pick a date—something that sort of stands out in people's minds. Thieves and cutthroats aren't all that good at reading calendars."

"How about the Harvest Festival?" Itagne suggested. "It's only three weeks away, and it's celebrated in all of Tamuli."

Caalador looked around. "Can we wait that long?" he asked. "It *would* be the perfect time. Our murderers would have three nights to get the job done instead of one, and there's lots of noise and confusion during the Harvest Festival."

"And lots of drinking," Itagne added. "The whole continent gets roaring drunk."

"It's a general holiday then?" Bevier asked.

Itagne nodded. "Technically it's a religious holiday. We're supposed to thank the Gods for a bountiful harvest. Most people can get that out of the way in about a half a minute, and that leaves them three days and nights to get into trouble. The harvest crews are all paid off, they take their annual baths, and then head for the nearest town in search of mischief."

"It's made to order for our purposes," Caalador added.

"Will you be ready to move your forces against the Trolls in three weeks, Lord Vanion?" Sarabian asked.

"More than ready, your Majesty. We weren't planning to gather them all in one place anyway. The detachments from each garrison are only platoon-sized, and a platoon can move faster than a battalion. They're all moving toward staging areas along the Atan border."

"Do we want to hit them all at the same time?" Kalten asked.

"We could go any one of three ways on that," Sparhawk said. "We can hit the Trolls first and pull Zalasta's attention to northern Atan, or we can murder the conspirators first and send him scurrying around the continent trying to salvage what he can of his organization, or we can do it simultaneously and see if he can be in a hundred places all at the same time."

"We can decide that later," Sarabian said. "Let's get word to the murderers first. We *know* that we want them to go to work during the Harvest Festival. The military situation's more fluid."

"Let's make a special point of eliminating Sabre, Parok, and Rebal this time," Stragen said to Caalador. "Evidently the Atans missed them in the last general roundup. Those Elene kingdoms in western Tamuli are standing between Sir Tynian and Matherion, and as long as those three troublemakers are alive, he's going to have rough going. Is there any way we could get Scarpa as well?"

Caalador shook his head. "He's holed up in Natayos. He's turned it into a fortress and filled it with fanatics. I couldn't *pay* a murderer enough to try to kill him. The only way we'll get Scarpa is to mount a military expedition."

"That's a shame," Sephrenia murmured. "The death of his only son would definitely twist a knife in Zalasta's belly."

"Savage," Vanion accused affectionately.

"Zalasta killed my family, Vanion," she replied. "All I want to do is return the favor."

"That sounds fair to me." He smiled.

"I'm still dead-set against it," Stragen said stubbornly when he, Sparhawk, and Ulath met in the hallway a bit later.

"Be reasonable, Stragen," Ulath said. "It won't hurt anything to see what they have to say, will it? I'm not going to just turn them loose without any restrictions at all, you know."

"They'll agree to anything to get their freedom, Ulath. They might *promise* to pull the Trolls out of Atan—or even to help us deal with Zalasta and Cyrgon—but once they get back to Thalesia, they won't feel obligated to honor any commitments. We're not even members of the same species as their worshippers. We're just animals in their eyes. Would you feel obliged to keep promises you made to a bear?"

"That would depend on the bear, I suppose."

"The Troll-Gods might break promises they make to *us,*" Sparhawk said, "but they won't break faith with Bhelliom, because Bhelliom can reabsorb them if they try any tricks."

"Well," Stragen said dubiously, "I want to be sure everybody understands that I don't like this, but I guess it won't hurt to hear what they have to say. I want to be present, though. I don't altogether trust you, Ulath, so I want to hear the promises you give them."

"Do you understand Trollish?"

Stragen shuddered. "Of course not."

"You're going to have a little difficulty following the conversation, then, don't you think?"

"Sephrenia's going along, isn't she? She can translate for me."

"Are you sure you trust *her*?"

"That's a contemptible thing to say."

"I thought I'd ask. When do you want to do this, Sparhawk?"

"Let's not be premature," Sparhawk decided. "I still have to take Caalador around to talk with his friends. Let's get that set up and make sure that the Atans Vanion's calling in are in the staging areas before we broach the subject to the Troll-Gods. There's no point in getting them excited until we need them."

"I think we'll want to be out in the countryside when we talk with them," Ulath suggested. "When we tell them that Cyrgon's stolen their worshippers, their screams of outrage might shatter all the seashells off the walls of Matherion."

"His mind is much fogged by drink," Xanetia reported about midmorning the next day after she and Berit had returned from the Cynesgan embassy, "and it is difficult to wring consistency from it."

"Does he have any suspicions at all, Anarae?" Stragen asked with a worried expression.

"He doth know that thou hast set thieves and beggars to watch him in the past, Milord Stragen," she replied, "but it is his thought that thou—or young Talen—must make these arrangements in each city and that one of you must go there to speak with each chief separately."

"He don't know nothin' about the Sekert Gover-mint?" Caalador pressed, speaking in dialect for some obscure reason.

"His understanding of thy society is vague, Master Caalador. Cooperation of such nature is beyond his grasp, for Krager himself is incapable of it, being guided only by immediate self-interest."

"What a splendid drunkard!" Stragen exulted. "Let's all pray that he never sobers up!"

"A-*men*!" Caalador agreed fervently. "Well, Sporhawk, why don't yew have a talk with this yere jool o' yourn, an' me'n you'll go a-hippety-skippin' 'round about Tamuli. We got us folks t' see an' th'otes t' cut."

Xanetia's face took on a pained expression.

Caalador was badly shaken the first few times Bhelliom whisked him halfway across the continent, but after that he seemed to grow numb. It took him about a half hour each time to pass instructions to the various criminal chiefs of Tamuli, and Sparhawk strongly suspected that the ruddy-faced Cammorian settled his shaken nerves with strong drink at each stop. Sparhawk could not be sure, of course, since he was quite firmly excluded from the discussions. "You don't need to know who these people are, Sparhawk," Caalador said, "and your presence would just make them nervous."

Vanion's small Atan detachments were streaming into the staging areas along the Atan border from all over Tamuli, and Tikume had promised several thousand eastern Peloi in addition to the three hundred bowmen Kring had taken with him back to Atana. Bhelliom took Sparhawk and Vanion to the Atan capital so that they could reassure Betuana that they *were* in fact marshaling forces to come to her aid, *and* to explain why they were holding most of that aid at the border. "The Trolls wouldn't understand the significance of those reinforcements, Betuana-Queen," Vanion told her, "but Cyrgon's completely versed in strategy and tactics. He'd understand what was going on immediately. Let's not give him any hints about what we're doing until we're ready to strike."

"Do you really think you can spring surprises on a God, Vanion-Preceptor?" she asked. Betuana was dressed in what passed for armor among the Atans, and her face clearly showed that she had been functioning on short sleep for weeks.

"I'm certainly going to *try,* Betuana-Queen," Vanion replied with a brief smile. "I think it's fairly safe to say that Cyrgon hasn't had a new thought in the last twenty thousand years. Military thinking's changed a great deal in that time, so he probably won't fully understand what we're up to." He made a wry face. "At least that's what I'm *hoping,*" he added.

And then it reached the point where they could not put it off any longer. None of them were really comfortable with the idea of chatting with the Troll-Gods, but the time had come to put Ulath's notion to the test.

About an hour before dawn of the day none of them had really been looking forward to, Sparhawk and Vanion went to Sephrenia's room to speak with Sephrenia, Xanetia, and Danae. Their discussions struck a snag almost immediately.

"I *have* to go along, Sparhawk," Danae insisted.

"That's out of the question," he told her. "Ulath and Stragen are going to be there. We can't let them find out who you really are."

"They're not going to find anything out, Father," she said with exaggerated patience. "It won't be *Danae* who'll be going along."

"Oh. That's different, then."

"Exactly how are we going to work this, Sparhawk?" Vanion asked. "Won't you have to release the Troll-Gods in order to talk with them?"

Sparhawk shook his head. "Bhelliom says we won't. The Troll-Gods themselves will still be locked up inside Bhelliom. Their spirits have always been free to roam around, except when Bhelliom's encased in gold—or steel. They have a certain limited amount of power in that condition, I guess, but their *real* power's locked up with them inside the Bhelliom."

"Wouldn't it be safer to get them to agree to use that limited power, rather than to unleash them entirely?" Vanion asked.

"It wouldn't work, dear one," Sephrenia told him. "The Troll-Gods may encounter Cyrgon, and if they do, they'll need their full power."

"Moreover," Xanetia added, "I do strongly believe that they will sense our need and bargain stringently."

"Are you going to do the talking, Sparhawk?" Vanion asked.

Sparhawk shook his head. "Ulath knows Trolls—and the Troll-Gods—better than I do, and his Trollish is better than mine. I'll hold Bhelliom and call the Troll-Gods out and then let him do the talking." He looked out the window. "It's almost dawn," he said. "We'd better get started. Ulath and Stragen are going to meet us down in the courtyard."

"Turn your backs," Danae told them.

"What?" her father asked.

"Turn around, Sparhawk. You don't have to watch this."

"It's one of her quirks," Sephrenia explained. "She doesn't want anybody to know what she really looks like."

"I already know what Flute looks like."

"There's a transition, Sparhawk. She doesn't go directly from Danae to Flute. She passes through her *real* person on the way from one little girl to the other."

Sparhawk sighed. "How many of her are there?"

"Thousands, I'd imagine."

"That's depressing. I've got a daughter I don't really know."

"Don't be silly," Danae said. "Of course you know me."

"But only one of you—a several-thousandth part of who you really are—such a tiny part." He sighed again and turned his back.

"It's not a tiny part, Father." Danae's voice changed as she spoke, becoming richer, more vibrant. It was no longer a child's voice, but a woman's.

There was a mirror on the far side of the room, a flat sheet of polished brass. Sparhawk glanced at it and saw the wavering reflection of a figure standing behind him. He quickly averted his eyes.

"Go ahead and look, Sparhawk. It's not a very good mirror, so you won't see all that much."

He raised his eyes and stared at the gleaming brass. The reflection was distorted. About all he could really see was the general size and shape. Aphrael was somewhat taller than Sephrenia. Her hair was long and very dark, and her skin was pale. Her face was hardly more than a blur in that imperfect reflection, but he could see her eyes quite clearly for some reason. There was an ageless wisdom in those eyes and a kind of eternal joy and love. "I wouldn't do this for just anybody, Sparhawk," the woman's voice told him, "but you're the best father I've ever had, so I'm stretching the rules for you."

"Don't you wear any clothes?" he asked her.

"What on earth for? I don't get cold, you know."

"I'm talking about modesty, Aphrael. I *am* your father, after all, and things like that are supposed to concern me."

She laughed and reached around from behind him to caress his face. It was not a little girl's hand that touched his cheek. He caught the faint scent of crushed grass, but the rest of the familiar fragrance that lingered about both Danae and Flute had been subtly changed. The person standing behind him was definitely *not* a little girl.

"Is this the way you appear to the rest of your family?" he asked her.

"Not very often. I prefer to have them think of me as a child. I can get my own way a lot easier in that form—and I get a lot more kisses."

"Getting your own way is very important to you, isn't it, Aphrael?"

"Of course. It's important to all of us, isn't it? I'm just better at it than most." She laughed, a deep, rich laugh. "I'm probably the best there is at getting my own way."

"I've noticed that," he said dryly.

"Well," she said then, "I'd love to talk more with you about it, but I suppose we shouldn't keep Ulath and Stragen waiting." The reflection wavered and began to shrink, sliding back into childhood. "All right, then," Flute's familiar voice said, "let's go have it out with the Troll-Gods."

It was blustery that morning, and dirty grey clouds scudded in off the Tamul Sea. There were few citizens abroad in fire-domed Matherion as Sparhawk and his friends rode out of the palace compound and down the long, wide street leading to the west gate.

They left the city and rode up the hill to the place from which they had first glimpsed the gleaming city. "How do you plan to approach them?" Stragen asked Ulath as they crested the hill.

"Carefully," Ulath grunted. "I'd rather not get eaten. I've talked with them before, so they probably remember me, and the fact that Sparhawk's holding Bhelliom in his fist may help to curb their urge to devour me right on the spot."

"Any particular sort of place you'd like?" Vanion asked him.

"An open field—but not *too* open. I want trees nearby—so I can climb one in case things turn ugly." Ulath looked around at the rest of them. "One word of caution," he added. "Don't any of you stand between me and the nearest tree once I get started."

"Over there?" Sparhawk suggested, pointing toward a pasture backed by a pine grove.

Ulath squinted. "It's not perfect, but no place really would be. Let's get this over with. My nerves are strung a little tight this morning for some reason."

They rode out into the pasture and dismounted. "Is there anything anyone would like to tell me before we start?" Sparhawk asked.

"You're on your own, Sparhawk," Flute replied. "It's all up to you and Ulath. We're just here to observe."

"Thanks," he said dryly.

She curtsied. "Don't mention it."

Sparhawk took the box out from inside his tunic and touched his ring to it. "Open," he told it.

The lid popped up.

"Blue-Rose," Sparhawk said, speaking in Elenic.

"I hear thee, Anakha." The voice came from Vanion's lips again.

"I feel the Troll-Gods within thee. Can they understand my words when I speak in this tongue?"

"Nay, Anakha."

"Good. Cyrgon hath by deceit and subterfuge lured the Trolls here to Daresia and doth hurl them against our allies, the Atans. We would attempt to persuade the Troll-Gods to reassert their authority over their creatures. Thinkest thou that they might be willing to give hearing to our request?"

"Any God listens most attentively to words concerning his worshippers, Anakha."

"I had thought such might be the case. Dost thou agree with mine assessment that the knowledge that Cyrgon hath stolen their Trolls will enrage them?"

"They will be discomfited out of all measure, Anakha."

"How thinkest thou we might best proceed with them?"

"Advise them in simple words of what hath come to pass. Speak not too quickly nor with obscured meaning, for they are slow of understanding."

"I have perceived as much in past dealings with them."

"Wilt *thou* speak with them? I say this not in criticism, but thy Trollish is rude and uncouth."

"Did *you* put that in, Vanion?" Sparhawk accused.

Vanion blinked, his face changing subtly as Bhelliom withdrew its hold. "Not me," Vanion protested his innocence. "I wouldn't know good Trollish from bad."

"Forgive mine ineptitude, Blue-Rose. Mine instructor was in haste when she schooled my tongue in the language of the man-beasts."

"Sparhawk!" Sephrenia objected.

"Well, weren't you?" He addressed the stone again. "My comrade, Sir Ulath, hath greater familiarity with Trolls and their speech than do I. It is *he* who will advise the Troll-Gods that Cyrgon hath stolen their creatures."

"I will bring forth their spirits that thy comrade may address them." The stone pulsed in his hand, and the gigantic presences Sparhawk had sensed in the Temple of Azash were there, but this time they were in front of him where he could see them. He fervently wished that he could not. Because their reality was still locked inside the Bhelliom, their forms were suffused with an azure glow. They bulked enormous before him, their brutish faces enraged and their fury held in check only by the power of Bhelliom.

"All right, Ulath," Sparhawk said. "This is a dangerous situation. Try to be very, very convincing."

The big Genidian Knight swallowed hard and stepped forward. "I am Ulath-from-Thalesia," he said in Trollish. "I speak for Anakha, Bhelliom's child. I bring word of *your* children. Will you hear me?"

"Speak, Ulath-from-Thalesia." Sparhawk judged from the crackling roar mingled in the enormous voice that it was Khwaj, the Troll-God of Fire, who spoke.

Ulath's face took on an expression of mild reproach. "We are baffled by what you have done," he told them. "Why have you given your children to Cyrgon?"

"*What?*" Khwaj roared.

"It was our thought that you wished it so," Ulath said, feigning surprise. "Did you not command your children to leave their home-range and to walk for many sleeps across the ice-which-never-melts to this alien place?"

Khwaj howled, beating at the ground with his apelike fists, raising a cloud of dust and smoke from the ground.

"When did this come to pass?" another voice, a voice filled with a kind of gross slobbering, demanded.

"Two full turns of the seasons, Ghnomb," Ulath answered the question of the God of Eat. "It was our thought that you knew. Blue-Rose called you forth that we might ask why you have done this. Our Gods wish to know why you have broken the compact."

"Compact?" Stragen asked after Sephrenia had translated.

"It's an agreement," Flute explained. "We didn't really want to exterminate the Trolls, so we told the Troll-Gods that we'd leave their children alone if they'd stay in the Thalesian mountains."

"When did this happen?"

"Twenty-five thousand years ago—or so."

Stragen swallowed hard.

"Why are your children obeying Cyrgon if you did not command it?" Ulath asked.

One of the gigantic figures stretched out an abnormally long arm, and the huge hand plunged into a kind of emptiness, vanishing as it went in almost as a stick seems to vanish when poked into a forest pool. When the hand reemerged, it held a struggling Troll. The enormous God spoke, harshly demanding. The language was clearly Trollish, snarling and roaring.

"Now that's interesting," Ulath murmured. "It appears that even Trollish has changed over the years."

"What's he saying?" Sparhawk asked.

"I can't entirely make it out," Ulath replied. "It's so archaic that I can't understand most of the words. Zoka's demanding some answers, though."

"Zoka?"

"The God of Mating." Ulath listened intently.

"The Troll's confused," he reported. "He says that they all thought they *were* obeying their Gods. Cyrgon's disguise must have been nearly perfect. The Trolls are very close to their Gods and they'd probably recognize any ordinary attempt to deceive them."

Zoka roared, and hurled the shrieking Troll back into emptiness.

"Anakha!" another of the vast Gods bellowed.

"Which one is that?" Sparhawk muttered.

"Ghworg," Ulath replied quietly. "The God of Kill. Be a little careful with him. He's very short-tempered."

"Yes, Ghworg," Sparhawk responded to that vast brute.

"Release us from your father's grip. Let us go. We must reclaim our children." There was blood dripping from the fangs of the God of Kill. Sparhawk didn't want to think about whose blood it might be.

"Let me," Ulath murmured. He raised his voice. "That is beyond Anakha's power, Ghworg," he replied. "The spell which imprisoned you was of Ghwerig's making. It is a Trollish spell, and Anakha is untaught in such."

"We will teach him the spell."

"No!" Flute suddenly broke in, throwing aside her pretense of merely observing. "These are *my* children. I will not permit you to contaminate them with Trollish spells."

"We beg you, Child-Goddess! Set us free! Our children stray from us!"

"My family will never agree. Your children look upon our children as food. If Anakha frees you, your children will devour ours. It cannot be."

"Ghnomb!" Khwaj roared. "Give her surety!"

The huge face of the God of Eat twisted in agony. "I cannot!" It was almost a wail. "It would lessen me! Our children *must* eat. All that lives *must* be food!"

"Our children are lost unless you agree!" The grass around the feet of the God of Fire began to smoke.

"I think I see a toehold here," Ulath said in Elenic. He spoke again in Trollish. "There is justice in Ghnomb's words," he told the Gods. "Why should he alone lessen himself? Each must *also* accept lessening. Ghnomb will not accept less."

"It speaks truly!" Ghnomb howled. "I will not be lessened unless all are lessened!"

The four other Troll-Gods squirmed, their faces reflecting the same agony that had marked Ghnomb's.

"What will satisfy you?" It was the voice of the God who had not yet spoken. There were blizzards in that voice.

"The God of Ice," Ulath identified the speaker, "Schlee."

"Lessen yourselves!" Ghnomb demanded stubbornly. "I will not if you will not!"

"Trolls," Aphrael sighed, rolling her eyes. "Will you accept my mediation in this?" she demanded of the monstrous deities.

"We will hear your words, Aphrael," Ghworg replied dubiously.

"Our purposes are the same," the Child-Goddess began.

Sparhawk groaned.

"What's wrong?" Ulath asked quickly.

"She's going to make a speech—now of all times."

"Shut up, Sparhawk!" the Child-Goddess snapped. "I know what I'm doing." She turned to face the Troll-Gods again. "Cyrgon deceived your children," she began. "He brought them across the ice-which-never-melts to this place to make war on *my* children. Cyrgon must be punished!"

The Troll-Gods roared their agreement.

"Will you join with me and my family to cause hurt to Cyrgon for what he has done?"

"We will cause hurt to him by ourselves, Aphrael," Ghworg snarled.

"And how many of your children will die if you do? My children can pursue the children of Cyrgon into the lands of the sun, where your children die. Should we not join, then, that Cyrgon will suffer more?"

"There is wisdom in her words," Schlee said to his fellows. The breath of the God of Ice steamed in the air, though the air was not really cold, and glittering snowflakes appeared out of nowhere to settle on his massive shoulders.

"Ghnomb must agree that your children will no longer eat mine," Aphrael bored in. "If he does not, Anakha will not free you from his father's grip."

Ghnomb groaned.

"Ghnomb *must* do this," she insisted. "If he does not, I will not permit Anakha to free you, and Cyrgon will *keep* your children. Ghnomb will not agree to this if each of you will not accept equal lessening. Ghworg! You must no longer drive your children to kill mine!"

Ghworg raised both huge arms and howled.

"Khwaj!" she continued inexorably. "You must curb the fires which rage through the forests of Thalesia each year when the sun returns to the lands of the north."

Khwaj stifled a sob.

"Schlee!" Aphrael barked. "You must hold back the rivers of ice which crawl down the sides of the mountains. Let them melt when they reach the valleys."

"No!" Schlee wailed.

"Then you have lost all your children. Hold back the ice or you will weep alone in the wastes of the north. Zoka! No more than two offspring can issue from each she-Troll."

"*Never!*" Zoka bellowed. "My children *must* mate!"

"Your children are now Cyrgon's. Will you aid Cyrgon's increase?" She paused, her eyes narrowing. "One last agreement will I have from you all, or I will not let Anakha free you."

"What is your demand, Aphrael?" Schlee asked in his ice-choked voice.

"Your children are immortal. Mine are not. Your children must also die—each in an appointed time."

They exploded in an absolute rage.

"Return them to their prison, Anakha," Aphrael said. "They will not agree. The bargaining is done." She said it in Trollish, so it was obviously intended for the benefit of the raging Troll-Gods.

"Wait!" Khwaj shouted. "Wait!"

"Well?" she said.

"Let us go apart from you, that we may consider this monstrous demand."

"Do not be long," she said to them. "I have little patience."

The five vast beings withdrew farther into the pasture.

"Weren't you pushing them a little far?" Sephrenia suggested. "That last demand of yours may very well kill any chance of reaching an agreement."

"I don't think so," Aphrael replied. "The Troll-Gods can't think that far into the future. They live for now, and right now the most important thing for them is taking their Trolls back from Cyrgon." She sighed. "The last demand is the most important, really. Humans and Trolls can't live in the same world. One or the other has to leave. I'd rather that it was the Trolls, wouldn't you?"

"You're very cruel, Aphrael. You're forcing the Troll-Gods to assist in the extermination of their own worshippers."

"The Trolls are doomed anyway," the Child-Goddess sighed. "There are just too many humans in the world. If the Trolls suddenly become mortal, they'll just slip away peacefully. If you humans have to kill them all, half of your number will die with them. I'm just as moral as the rest of the Gods. I love my children, and I don't want half of them killed and eaten in the mountains of Thalesia in some war to the death with the Trolls."

"Sparhawk," Stragen said, "didn't Khwaj do something that made it possible for you to watch Martel and listen to him talking when we were going across Pelosia toward Zemoch?"

Sparhawk nodded.

"Can Aphrael do that?"

"I'm right here, Stragen," Flute told him. "Why don't you ask me?"

"We haven't really been properly introduced yet, Divine One," he said with a fluid bow. "Can you? Reach out and talk with somebody on the other side of the world, I mean?"

"I don't like to do it that way," she replied. "I want to be close to someone when I talk to him."

"My Goddess places great importance on touching, Stragen," Sephrenia explained.

"Oh. I see. All right, then, when the Troll-Gods come back—and if they agree to our preposterous demands—I'd like to have Sparhawk or Ulath ask Khwaj to do me a favor. I need to talk to Platime back in Cimmura."

"They do return," Xanetia advised.

They all turned to face the monstrous beings coming back across the autumn-browned pasture.

"You have left us no choice, Aphrael," Khwaj said in a broken voice. "We must accept your brutal demands. We *must* save our children from Cyrgon."

"You will no longer kill and eat my children?" she pressed.

"We will not."

"You will no longer burn the forests of Thalesia?"

Khwaj groaned and nodded.

"You will no longer fill the valleys with glaciers?"

Schlee sobbed his agreement.

"You will no longer breed your Trolls like rabbits?"

Zoka wailed.

"Your children will grow old and die as do all other creatures?"

Khwaj buried his face in his hands. "Yes," he wept.

"Then we will join with you and do war upon Cyrgon. You will return to Bhelliom's heart for now. Anakha will carry you to the place where your children languish in thrall to Cyrgon. There will he release you and there will you wrest your children from Cyrgon's vile grasp. And there will we join together to cause hurt to Cyrgon. We will make his pain like the pain of Azash."

"*YES!*" the Troll-Gods howled their agreement in unison.

"Done!" Aphrael declared in a ringing voice. "One boon more, Khwaj—in demonstration of our newly formed alliance. This child of mine would speak with one known as Platime in Cimmura in far-off Elenia. Make it so that he can."

"I will, Aphrael." Khwaj held out his vast hand, and a sheet of unwavering fire dripped from his fingertips.

Behind the fire there lay a bedchamber with a vast, snoring bulk sprawled on an oversized bed.

"Wake up, Platime," Stragen said crisply.

"Fire!" Platime shrieked, struggling into a sitting position.

"Oh, be quiet!" Stragen snapped. "There isn't any fire. This is magic."

"Stragen? Is that you? Where are you?"

"I'm behind the fire. You probably can't see me."

"Are you learning magic now?"

"Just dabbling," Stragen lied modestly. "Now listen carefully; I don't know how long the spell will last. Get in touch with Arnag in Khadach. Ask him to kill Count Gerrich. I don't have time to explain. It's important, Platime. It's part of something we're doing here in Tamuli."

"Gerrich?" Platime said dubiously. "That's going to be expensive, Stragen."

"Get the money from Lenda. Tell him that Ehlana authorized it."

"Did she?"

"Well—she would if she knew about it. I'll get her approval next time I talk with her. Now, this is the most important part. Gerrich *has* to be killed exactly fifteen days from now—not fourteen, not sixteen. The time's very important."

"All right, I'll see to it. Tell Ehlana that Gerrich will die in exactly fifteen days. Was there anything else? That magic fire of yours is making me very nervous."

"See if you can identify anybody else Gerrich has been dealing with and kill them as well—those Pelosian barons who've allied themselves with him certainly, and any people in the other kingdoms who are in this with him. You know the kind I mean—the ones like the Earl of Belton."

"You want them all killed at that same time?"

"As close as you can. Gerrich is the really important one, though." Stragen pursed his lips. "While you're at it, you'd probably better kill Avin Wargunsson as well—just to be on the safe side."

"He's as good as dead, Stragen."

"You're a good friend, Platime."

"Friend, my foot. You'll pay the usual fees, Stragen."

Stragen sighed. "All right," he said mournfully.

"How deeply are you attached to your Elene God, Stragen?" Aphrael asked as they rode back to Matherion.

"I'm an agnostic, Divine One."

"Would you like to examine that last sentence for logical consistency, Stragen?" Vanion asked with an amused expression.

"Consistency's the mark of a little mind, my Lord," Stragen replied loftily. "Why do you ask, Aphrael?"

"You don't really belong to *any* God, then, do you?"

"No, not really."

Sephrenia started to say something, but Aphrael raised one little hand to cut her off. "You might want to look into the advantages of coming to serve *me*," the Child-Goddess suggested. "I can do all sorts of *wonderful* things for you."

"You're not supposed to do this, Aphrael!" Sephrenia protested.

"Hush, Sephrenia. This is between Stragen and me. I think that maybe it's time for me to broaden my horizons. Styrics are very, very nice, but sometimes Elenes are more fun. Besides, Stragen and I are both thieves. We've got a lot in common." She grinned at the blond man. "Think it over, Milord. I'm not at all difficult to serve. A few kisses and a bouquet of flowers now and then and I'm perfectly happy."

"She's lying to you," Sparhawk warned. "Enlisting in the service of Aphrael is volunteering for the profoundest slavery you could possibly imagine."

"Well," the Child-Goddess said deprecatingly, "I suppose it is, when you get right down to it—but as long as we're all having fun, what difference does it make?"

It was quite early, several hours before dawn, Sparhawk judged, when Mirtai entered the royal bedroom—as usual without knocking. "You'd better get up," the golden giantess announced.

Sparhawk sat up. "What's the problem?" he asked.

"There's a fleet of boats coming toward the city," she replied. "Either that, or the Delphae have learned how to walk on water. There are enough lanterns on the eastern horizon to light up a small city. Put your clothes on, Sparhawk. I'll go wake the others." She turned abruptly and left the room.

"I *wish* she'd learn to knock," Sparhawk muttered, throwing off the covers.

"*You're* the one who's supposed to make sure the doors are locked," Ehlana reminded him. "Do you think it might be trouble?"

"I don't know. Did Sarabian say anything about expecting a fleet?"

"He didn't mention it to me," she replied, also rising from their bed.

"I'd better go have a look." He picked up his cloak. "There's no need for you to go outside, dear," he told her. "It's chilly up on the parapet."

"No. I want to see for myself."

They went out of the bedroom. Princess Danae came out of her room in her nightdress, rubbing her eyes with one hand and dragging Rollo behind her. Mutely she went to Sparhawk, and he picked her up without even thinking.

The three of them went into the hallway and up the stairs toward the top of the tower.

Kalten and Sarabian were standing on the east side of the tower looking out across the battlements at the lights strung along the eastern horizon.

"Any idea of who they might be?" Sparhawk asked as he and his family joined them.

"Not a clue," Kalten replied.

"Could it be the Tamul navy?" Ehlana asked the emperor.

"It *could* be, I suppose," he replied, "but if it is, they're not responding to any orders *I* sent."

Sparhawk stepped back a few paces. "Who do the ships belong to?" he murmured to his daughter.

"I ain't a-tellin', dorlin'," she replied with a little smirk.

"Stop that. I want to know who's coming."

"You'll find out—" She squinted toward the lights on the horizons, "—in a couple of hours, I'd imagine."

"I want to know who they are," he insisted.

"Yes, I can see that, but wanting isn't getting, Father, and I ain't a-gonna tell ya."

"Oh, God," he groaned.

"Yes?" she responded innocently. "*Was* there something?"

. . .

The dawn came up rusty that morning. There was no hint of a breeze, and the smoke from the chimneys of fire-domed Matherion hung motionless in the air, blurring the light from the east. Sparhawk and the other knights roused the Atan garrison, put on their armor, and rode down to the harbor.

The approaching ships were clearly of Cammorian construction, but banks of oars had been added along their sides.

"Somebody was in a hurry to get here," Ulath noted. "A Cammorian ship with a good following wind can make thirty leagues a day. If you added oars to that, you could increase it to fifty."

"How many ships are there?" Kalten asked, squinting at the approaching fleet.

"I make it close to a hundred," the big Thalesian replied.

"You could carry a lot of men on a hundred ships," Sarabian said.

"Enough to make me nervous, your Majesty," Vanion agreed.

Then, as the ships entered the harbor, the red and gold standards of the Church were run up on the masts, and as the lead vessel came closer, Sparhawk could make out two familiar figures standing in the bow. The one man had broad shoulders and a massive chest. His round face was split with a delighted grin. The other was short and very stout. He was also grinning.

"What kept you?" Ulath shouted across the intervening water.

"Class distinctions," Tynian shouted back. "Knights are defined as gentlemen, and they objected to being pressed into service as oarsmen."

"You've got *knights* manning the oars?" Vanion called incredulously.

"It's a part of a new physical conditioning program, Lord Vanion," Patriarch Emban shouted. "Archprelate Dolmant noticed that the Soldiers of God were getting flabby. They're much more fit now than they were when we left Sarinium."

The ship approached the wharf carefully, and the seamen threw the mooring hawsers to the knights ashore.

Tynian leapt across. Emban gave him a disgusted look and waddled back amidships to wait for the sailors to extend the gangway.

"How's the shoulder?" Ulath asked the broad-faced Deiran.

"Much better," Tynian replied. "It aches when the weather's damp, though." He saluted Vanion. "Komier, Darellon, and Abriel are leading the Church Knights east from Chyrellos, my Lord," he reported. "Patriarch Bergsten's with them. Patriarch Emban and I came on ahead by ship—obviously. We thought a few more knights here in Matherion might be useful."

"Indeed they will, Sir Tynian. How many do you have with you?"

"Five thousand, my Lord."

"That's impossible, Tynian. There's no way you could crowd that many men and horses on a hundred ships."

"Yes, my Lord," Tynian replied mildly, "we noticed that ourselves almost immediately. The knights were terribly disappointed when they found out that we weren't going to let them bring their horses with them."

"Tynian," Kalten objected, "they *have* to have horses. A knight without his horse is meaningless."

"There are already horses here, Kalten. Why bring more?"

"Tamul horses aren't trained."

"Then we'll just have to train them, won't we? I had a hundred ships. I could have brought fifteen hundred knights along with their horses, or five thousand *without* the horses. Call the extra thirty-five hundred a gift."

"How were you able to make them row?" Ulath asked.

"We used whips." Tynian shrugged. "There's a Captain Sorgi who plies the inner sea, and the oars were his idea."

"Good old Sorgi." Sparhawk laughed.

"You know him?"

"Quite well, actually."

"You'll be able to renew your friendship. His ship's out there with the fleet. We'd have sailed aboard *his* ship, but Patriarch Emban didn't like the looks of it. It's all patched and rickety."

"It's old. I think Sorgi has a secret bet with himself about which of them falls apart first—him or his ship."

"His mind's still sharp, though. When we asked him how to get more speed out of the ships, he suggested adding oars. It's very seldom done that way because of the expense of paying the oarsmen—not to mention the fact that they take up room usually reserved for cargo. I decided not to bring any cargo, and Church Knights are sworn to poverty, so I didn't have to pay them. It worked out fairly well, actually."

They gathered in Ehlana's sitting room several hours later to hear Emban and Tynian report on what was happening in Eosia.

"Ortzel nearly had apoplexy when Dolmant pulled all the knights out of Rendor," Emban told them. He leaned back in his chair with a silver tankard in his pudgy hand. "Ortzel *really* has his heart set on returning the Rendors to the bosom of our Holy Mother. Dolmant seemed inclined to agree with him at first, but he woke up one morning with a completely different outlook. Nobody's been able to explain his sudden change of heart."

"He received a message, Emban." Sephrenia smiled. "The messenger can be *very* impressive when he wants to be."

"Oh?"

"An emergency came up, your Grace," Vanion explained. "Zalasta had sent word to his confederates in Eosia, and they began killing the worshippers of the Child-Goddess Aphrael. That put *her* life in danger as well. We spoke with one of the other Younger Gods—Setras. He agreed that the Younger Gods would lend Aphrael some of *their* children, and he went to Chyrellos to ask Dolmant to offer sanctuary to Aphrael's surviving worshippers. He was also going to try to persuade Dolmant to send the Church Knights here. Evidently he was a bit more convincing than you and Tynian were."

"Are you saying that a Styric God went into the Basilica?" Emban exclaimed.

"He said that's what he was going to do," Sparhawk replied, shifting his daughter in his lap.

"No Styric God has *ever* gone into the Basilica!"

"He's wrong," Princess Danae whispered into her father's ear. "I've been there dozens of times."

"I know," Sparhawk whispered back. "Setras paid a *formal* visit, though." He thought of something. "Setras went to Chyrellos just a short time ago," he murmured into her ear. "Even with oarsmen to help, Tynian's fleet couldn't have reached Matherion *this* fast. Have you been tampering again?"

"Would I do that?" Her eyes were wide and innocent.

"Yes, as a matter of fact, you probably would."

"If you already knew the answer, why did you ask the question? Don't waste my time, Sparhawk. I *am* very busy, you know."

"Things seem to be coming to a head in Lamorkand," Tynian continued his report. "Count Gerrich's forces have taken Vraden and Agnak in northern Lamorkand, and King Friedahl's been appealing to the other monarchs for assistance."

"We'll be taking care of that shortly, Sir Tynian," Stragen told him. "I've been in touch with Platime, and he's arranging fatal accidents for Gerrich and the various barons who've been helping him."

The door opened, and Berit entered with Xanetia.

"What did you find out, Anarae?" Sephrenia asked intently.

"This morning's sortie was quite profitable, little mother," Berit advised her. "Zalasta's friend Ynak showed up at the Cynesgan embassy, and the Anarae was able to probe his mind. I think we've got most of the details of their plan now."

"Is this the lady with the rare gift?" Emban asked.

"I seem to be forgetting my manners," Vanion apologized. "Anarae Xanetia, this is Sir Tynian of Deira and Patriarch Emban of the Church of Chyrellos. Gentlemen, this is Xanetia, the Anarae of the People of Delpheus."

Tynian and Emban bowed, their eyes curious.

"What have our friends at the embassy been up to, Anarae?" Sarabian asked.

"Though it was not pleasant to probe so vile a mind, Ynak's thought did reveal much, Majesty," she replied. "As we had surmised, the outcast Styrics at Verel have long known that the greatest threat to their design would come from Eosia. They wished Anakha to come to Tamuli, but they did *not* wish for him to bring an hundred thousand Church Knights with him. The turmoil in western Tamuli is intended to block the passage of the knights; all else is extraneous. Moreover, the attacks of the Trolls in Atan are also designed to divert attention. It is from the *south* that our enemies plan their main assault. Even now do Cynesgan troops filter across the unguarded frontier to join with Scarpa's forces in the jungles of Arjuna; and Elenes from western Tamuli, moreover, do journey by ship to southern Arjuna to add their weight to Scarpa's growing horde. The distractions in the west and in Atan were to drain away imperial might, thus opening a path for Scarpa to strike directly across Tamul and to lay siege to Matherion itself. Ynak and the others were much chagrined by the exposure of Zalasta's treachery, for it voided his opportunity to do us harm by misdirection and false counsel."

"What's the real goal of a siege of Matherion, Lady Xanetia?" Emban asked shrewdly. "It's a nice enough city, but . . ." He spread his hands.

"Our enemies thought to compel the imperial government to surrender up Anakha by posing a threat to Matherion itself, your Grace. The subversion of diverse officials gave them hope that the prime minister might be persuaded to capitulate so that Matherion might be spared."

"That might have worked," Sarabian noted. "Pondia Subat's backbone isn't really very rigid. Zalasta and his four friends plan things quite well."

"Three friends now, your Majesty." Berit grinned. "The Anarae tells me that the one named Ptaga came a cropper a few days ago."

"The vampire-raiser?" Kalten said. "What happened to him?"

"May I tell them, Anarae?" Berit asked politely.

"An it please thee, Sir Knight."

"It seems that Ptaga was in southern Tamul proper, in those mountains between Sarna and Samar. He was waving his arms and creating the illusion of Shining Ones to turn loose on the populace. One of the *real* Delphae was out scouting the area and came across him and quietly joined the crowd of illusions." Berit grinned a nasty little grin.

"Well?" Kalten said impatiently. "What happened?"

"Ptaga was inspecting his illusions, and when he came to the *real* Shining One, not even *he* could tell the difference. The Delphaeic scout reached out and touched him. Ptaga's cast his last illusion, I guess. He was in the process of dissolving when the scout left the area."

"Ynak of Lydros is *most* discomfited by his associate's demise," Xanetia added, "for without the illusion of Ptaga, our enemies must produce *real* forces to confront us."

"And that brings us to something we should consider," Oscagne observed. "The arrival of Sir Tynian and Patriarch Emban with five thousand knights, the elimination of these illusions that were terrorizing the populace, and our knowledge of this planned attack from the south change the whole strategic situation."

"It certainly does," Sarabian agreed.

"I think we might want to consider these new developments in our planning, then, your Majesty."

"You're right, of course, Oscagne." Sarabian squinted at Sparhawk. "Could we prevail on you to go up to Atana and bring Betuana back here, old boy?" he asked. "If we're going to discuss changes in planning, she should be present. Betuana's bigger than I am, and I *definitely* don't want to insult her by leaving her out of our discussions."

Betuana, the Queen of the Atans, ruled more or less by default. King Androl, her husband, was a stupendous warrior, and that may have been a part of the problem. He was *so* stupendous that the normal concerns of the military commanders—such problems as being grossly outnumbered, for example—were quite beyond his grasp. Men who are sublimely convinced of their own invincibility seldom make good generals. Betuana, on the other hand, *was* a good general, quite possibly one of the best in the world, and the peculiar Atan society, which totally ignored any distinctions between the sexes, gave her talents the fullest opportunity to flower. Far from resenting his wife's superiority, Androl was inordinately proud of her. Sparhawk rather suspected that Betuana might have preferred it otherwise, but she was a realist.

She had, moreover, a disconcerting level of trust. Sparhawk had carefully marshaled a number of explanations both about the need for the council of war and about their mode of travel, but those explanations proved totally unnecessary. "All right," she replied calmly when he told her that Bhelliom would transport them instantly to Matherion.

"You don't want any details, your Majesty?" He was more than a little surprised.

"Why waste time explaining something I wouldn't understand anyway, Sparhawk-Knight?" She shrugged. "I'll accept your word that the jewel can take us to Matherion; you don't have any reason to lie to me about it. Give me a few moments to tell Androl that I'm going and to change clothes. Sarabian-Emperor finds my work clothes a trifle unsettling." She glanced down at her armor.

"He's changed quite a bit, your Majesty."

"So Norkan tells me. I'm curious to find out just how much your wife has modified him. I'll be right back." She strode from the room.

"You get used to that, Sparhawk," Khalad said. "She's very direct, and she doesn't waste time asking questions about things she doesn't need to know about. It's quite refreshing, actually."

"Be nice," Sparhawk said mildly.

Ambassador Norkan was nervous, but both Kring and Engessa were quite nearly as calm as the queen.

"God!" Emperor Sarabian exclaimed as the momentary blur faded and the trees of the Atan vanished to be replaced by the familiar blue carpeting, breeze-touched drapes, and the gleaming, opalescent walls of the royal sitting room in Ehlana's castle. "Isn't there some way you can announce that you're coming, Sparhawk?"

"I don't think so, your Majesty," Sparhawk replied.

"Having a group of people pop out of nowhere is very unnerving, you know." He frowned. "What would have happened if I'd been standing in the same spot you just appeared in? Would we have gotten sort of combined? All mixed together into one person?"

"I don't really know, your Majesty."

"Tell him that it is impossible, Anakha," Vanion spoke with the voice of Bhelliom. "I would not make such errors, and it is unusual for two things to be in the same place at once."

"Unusual?" Sarabian demanded. "Do you mean that it *can* happen?"

"I pray thee, Anakha, ask him not to pursue this question. The answers will greatly disturb him."

"You're looking fit, Sarabian-Emperor," Betuana said. "You are much changed. Do you know how to use that sword?"

"The rapier? Oh, yes, Betuana. Actually, I'm quite proficient."

"The weapon is light for my taste, but each of us must select such arms as suit him best. Sparhawk-Knight and Vanion-Preceptor tell me that much has changed. Let us consider those changes and adjust our plans to fit them." She looked at Ehlana and smiled. "You look well, Sister-Queen," she said. "Matherion suits you."

"And you're as lovely as ever, dear sister," Ehlana replied warmly. "The gown is breathtaking."

"Do you really like it?" Betuana turned almost girlishly to show off her deep blue Atan gown that left one golden shoulder bare and was girdled at the hips with a golden chain.

"It's absolutely stunning, Betuana. Blue is definitely your color."

Betuana glowed at the compliment. "Now, then, Sarabian," she said, all business again, "what's happened, and what are we going to do about it?"

"I do not find that amusing, Sarabian-Emperor," Betuana declared angrily.

"I didn't say it to amuse you, Betuana. I felt much the same way when they told me. I've sent for the lady. You're probably going to have to see for yourself."

"Do you take me for some child to be frightened by stories of ghosts and hobgoblins?"

"Of course not, but I assure you, Xanetia really *is* a Delphae."

"Does she glow?"

"Only when it suits her. She's been suppressing the light—for the sake of our peace of mind—and she's altered her coloration. She looks like an ordinary Tamul, but believe me, she's far from ordinary."

"I think you've lost your mind, Sarabian-Emperor."

"You'll see, dorlin'."

She gave him a startled look.

"Local joke." He shrugged.

The door opened, and Xanetia, Danae, and Sephrenia entered.

Princess Danae, her face artfully innocent, went to Betuana's chair and held out her arms. Betuana smiled at the little girl, picked her up, and held her on her lap. "How have you been, Princess?" she asked in Elenic.

"That's all right, Betuana," the little girl replied in Tamul. "Sephrenia's taught us all to speak the language of humans. I've been a little sick, actually, but I'm all better now. It's really boring to be sick, isn't it?"

"I've always thought so, Danae."

"I don't think I'll do it anymore, then. You haven't kissed me yet."

"Oh." Betuana smiled. "I forgot. I'm sorry." She quickly attended to the oversight.

Sarabian straightened in his chair. "Queen Betuana of Atan, I have the honor to present Anarae Xanetia of Delphaeus. Would you mind showing the queen who you are, Anarae?"

"An it please thee, Majesty," Xanetia replied.

"It's a startling experience, your Majesty," Emban said to the Atan queen, folding his pudgy hands on his paunch, "but you get used to it."

Xanetia looked gravely at Betuana. "Thy people and mine are cousins, Betuana-

Queen," she said. "Long, however, have we been separated. I mean thee no harm, so fear me not."

"I do not fear thee." Betuana lapsed automatically into archaic Tamul.

"Mine appearance here in Matherion is of necessity disguised, Betuana-Queen. Behold my true state." The color drained quickly from Xanetia's hair and face, and her unearthly glow began to shine through.

Danae calmly reached up to touch Betuana's face with one small hand. Sparhawk carefully concealed his smile.

"I know what you're feeling, Betuana," Sephrenia said quite calmly. "I'm sure you can imagine how Xanetia and *I* both felt about each other the first time we met. You know about the enmity between our two races, don't you?"

Betuana nodded, obviously not trusting herself to speak.

"I'm going to do something unnatural, Anarae," Sephrenia said then, "but I think Atana Betuana needs reassurance. Let's both try to control our reactions." Then with no hesitation or evident revulsion, she embraced the glowing woman. Sparhawk knew her very well, however, and he could see the faint ripple along her jaw. Sephrenia had steeled herself as she might have before thrusting her hand into fire.

Almost timidly, Xanetia's arms slipped around Sephrenia's shoulders. "Well met, sister mine," she murmured.

"Well met indeed, my sister," Sephrenia replied.

"Did you notice that the world didn't come to an end, Betuana?" Ehlana said.

"I think I *did* feel it quiver, though," Sarabian noted.

"We seem to be surrounded by people obsessed with their own cleverness, Xanetia." Sephrenia smiled.

"A failing of the young, my sister. Maturity may temper their impulse to levity."

Betuana straightened in her chair and put Danae down. "This alliance meets with your approval, Sarabian-Emperor?" she asked formally.

"It does, Betuana-Queen."

"Then I shall abide by it." She rose to her feet and went to the two sorceresses, holding out her hands. Sephrenia and Xanetia took those hands, and the three stood together so for a long minute.

"Thou art brave, Betuana-Queen," Xanetia noted.

"I'm an Atan, Anarae." Betuana shrugged. Then she turned and gave Engessa a stern look. "Why did you not tell me?" she demanded.

"I was told not to, Betuana-Queen," he replied. "Sarabian-Emperor said that you would need to see Xanetia-Anarae before you would believe that she is who we say she is. He also wanted to be present when you and she met. He takes delight in the astonishment of others. His is a peculiar mind."

"Engessa!" Sarabian protested.

"I am bound to speak the truth as I see it to my queen, Sarabian-Emperor."

"Well, I suppose you are, but you don't have to be quite so blunt about it, do you?"

·　　·　　·

"All right, then," Vanion summed it all up, "we start marching north with the knights, the majority of the local Atan garrisons, and the Imperial Guard. We'll make a great deal of noise, and Ekatas, Cyrgon's High Priest, will pass the word to Zalasta and Cyrgon that we're on the way. That will give Stragen's murderers a free hand, because everybody will be watching *us*. *Then,* when the Harvest Festival's over and the bodies start to turn up, our friends out there should be a bit distracted. At that point, Sparhawk takes Bhelliom to northern Atan and releases the Troll-Gods. Northern Atan becomes totally secure at that point. We reverse our line of march, pick up the bulk of the Atans, and go south to meet Scarpa. Are we all agreed so far?"

"No, we're not, Vanion-Preceptor," Betuana said firmly. "The Harvest Festival's still two weeks away, and the Trolls could very well be in the streets of Atana in two weeks. We *have* to devise some means to slow their advance."

"Forts," Ulath said.

"I must be getting used to you, Ulath." Kalten laughed. "I actually understood that one."

"So did I," Sarabian agreed, "but the Trolls might just bypass any forts we build and keep marching on Atana."

"The *Trolls* might, your Majesty," Sparhawk disagreed, "but Cyrgon won't. Cyrgon's got the oldest military mind in the world, and a soldier absolutely will not leave enemy strongholds behind his lines. People who do that lose wars. If we build forts, he'll *have* to stop his advance to deal with them."

"And if the forts are in open fields, the Trolls won't be able to hide in the forest," Bevier added. "They'll have to come across open ground, in plain view of the Peloi archers, my catapult crews, and Khalad's crossbowmen. Even if they cover the field with smoke, we'll be able to put down a goodly number of them with blind shots."

"My Atans do not like to hide behind walls," Betuana said stubbornly.

"We all have to do things we don't like sometimes, Betuana," Ehlana told her. "Forts will keep your warriors alive, and dead soldiers don't serve any purpose at all."

"Except to provide supper for the Trolls," Talen added. "There's an idea, Sparhawk. If you could train your Pandions to eat their enemies, you wouldn't need supply trains."

"Do you mind?" Sparhawk said acidly.

"It still won't work," Betuana told them. "The Trolls are too closely engaged with my armies. We don't have the *time* to build forts."

"We could build the forts a few miles behind your lines and withdraw your troops into them once they're finished, your Majesty," Sparhawk told her.

"Have you had many dealings with Trolls, Prince Sparhawk?" she asked tartly. "Do you have any idea how fast they run? They'll be on top of you before you can get the walls up."

"They can't run anywhere if time stops, your Majesty. We used that when we were on our way to Zemoch. The Troll-God of Eat can put people—or Trolls—into the space between one second and the next. We found that when we were in that space, the rest of the world didn't move at all. We'll have plenty of time to build forts."

"Why don't you verify that with the Bhelliom before you start making predictions, Sparhawk?" Emban suggested. "Let's be sure that it's going to work before we base any strategies on it. Let's find out if Bhelliom has any reservations about the notion."

Bhelliom, as it turned out, had several. "Thy design is flawed, Anakha," it responded to Sparhawk's question. Vanion's hand lifted Sephrenia's teacup and released it.

The cup stopped in midair and hung there.

"Take the vessel down, Anakha," Vanion's voice instructed.

Sparhawk took hold of the cup and immediately found that it was as immobile as a mountain. He tried as hard as he could to move it, but it simply stayed where it was.

"Thou couldst not so much as move a leaf, Anakha," Bhelliom told him. "Thou canst easily move *thyself* through that frozen moment, but to move other objects would require thee to move the entire universe."

"I see," Sparhawk said glumly. "Then we wouldn't be able to cut down trees and build forts, would we?"

"Are those structures of great importance to thee? Doth some obscure custom require them?"

"Nay, Blue-Rose. It is our intent to place obstructions in the path of the Trolls that they may not attack our friends, the Atans."

"Wouldst thou be offended were I to offer suggestion?"

Ulath looked sharply at Tynian. "Have you been talking to that poor stone in secret?" he accused.

"Very funny, Ulath," Tynian said sourly.

"I did not understand." Vanion's tone was slightly chilly.

"It is an ongoing discussion between the two, Blue-Rose," Sparhawk explained, giving the pair a hard look. "It hath reached a point so obscure now that it is incomprehensible. Gladly would I hear thy suggestion, my friend."

"Is it needful to injure the Trolls, Anakha? If they be totally denied access to the lands of thy friends, the Atans, must thou kill them?"

"Indeed, Blue-Rose, we would prefer *not* to cause them harm. When their Gods wrest them from Cyrgon's dominion shall they be our allies."

"Would it offend thee should *I* erect a barrier before them? A barrier beyond their ability to cross?"

"Not in the least. Indeed, we would be most grateful."

"Let us then to Atan, and I will make it so. I would not see *any* destroyed needlessly. My child will surely aid me, and between us, she and I will bar the Trolls from proceeding farther southward."

"Thou hast a daughter, too, Blue-Rose?" Sparhawk was stunned.

"I have millions, Anakha, and each is as precious to me as thine is to thee. Let us to Atan, then, that the bloodshed may cease."

Northern Atan was forested, but the more rugged mountains lay to the south. The mountains of the north had been ground down by glaciers in ages past, and the land sloped gradually down to the Sea of the North where eternal pack-ice capped the globe. Sparhawk looked around quickly. Bhelliom had responded to his unspoken request and had brought only warriors to this northern forest. There were certain to be arguments about that later, but that could not be helped.

"Engessa-Atan." Vanion's voice was crisply authoritative. An absurd notion occurred to Sparhawk. He wondered suddenly if Bhelliom had ever commanded troops.

"Yes, Vanion-Preceptor?" the big Atan replied.

"Command thy kinsmen to withdraw one league's distance from the place where now they are engaged."

Engessa looked sharply at Vanion, then realized that it was not the Pandion Preceptor who had spoken. "That will take some time, Blue-Rose," he explained. "The Atans are engaging the Trolls all across the North Cape. I will have to send messengers."

"Do thou but speak the command, Engessa-Atan. *All* shall hear thee, thou hast mine assurance."

"I wouldn't argue, friend Engessa," Kring advised. "That's the jewel that stops the sun. If it says they'll all hear you, they'll all hear you. Take my word for it."

"We'll try it, then." Engessa raised his face. "Withdraw!" he roared in a shattering bellow. "Fall back one league and regroup!"

The huge voice echoed and reechoed through the forest.

"I think you could make yourself heard from one side of the cape to the other without any help at all, Engessa-Atan," Kalten said.

"Not *quite* so far, Kalten-Knight," Engessa replied modestly.

"Thy judgment of thy people's speed will be more precise than mine, Engessa-Atan," Bhelliom told him. "Advise me when they have reached safety. I would not have them trapped north of the wall."

"The wall?" Ulath asked.

"The barrier of which I spake." Vanion bent and touched the ground with strangely gentle fingertips. "It is well, Anakha. We are within a few paces of the place I sought."

"I have ever had absolute faith in thine ability to find a precise spot, Blue-Rose."

"*Ever* is perhaps an imprecise term, Anakha." A faint, ironic smile touched Vanion's lips. "It seemeth to me I do recall some talk of finding thyself on the surface of the moon when first we began to move from place to place."

"You *did* say that, Sparhawk," Kalten reminded his friend.

"Thou spakest of thy daughter, Blue-Rose," Sparhawk said, rather quickly changing the subject. "May we be privileged to meet her?"

"Thou hast met her, Anakha. Thou standest this very moment upon her verdant bosom." Vanion's hand fondly patted the ground.

"The earth itself?" Bevier asked incredulously.

"Is she not fair?" There was a note of pride in the question. Then Vanion straightened. "Let us withdraw somewhat from this spot, Anakha. What I am to do here will take place some six of thy miles beneath our feet, and its effects here at the surface are difficult to predict. I would not endanger thee or thy companions by mine imprecision, and there will be some disturbance here. Is it safe to proceed now, Engessa-Atan?"

Engessa nodded. "Any Atan who hasn't covered at least a league by now doesn't deserve to be called an Atan," he replied.

They turned and walked some hundred paces to the south. Then they stopped.

"Farther, I pray thee, Anakha, yet again as far, and it would be well if thou and thy companions did lie upon the earth. The disturbance may be quite profound."

"Your friend is beginning to make me nervous, Sparhawk," Tynian confessed as they walked another hundred paces back. "Exactly what is it planning here?"

"You know as much about it as I do, my friend."

Then they heard a deep-toned subterranean booming that seemed to rise up out of the core of the earth. The ground shuddered sharply under their feet.

"Earthquake!" Kalten shouted in alarm.

"I think that may be what you were asking about, Tynian," Ulath rumbled.

"This is not simple, Anakha," Bhelliom observed in an almost clinical tone. "The pressures are extreme and must be adjusted with great delicacy to achieve the end we do desire."

The next jolt staggered them. The ground heaved and shuddered, and the dreadful, hollow booming grew louder.

"It is time, Anakha. The disturbance which I did mention previously is about to begin."

"*Begin?*" Bevier exclaimed. "It's all I can do to stand up *now!*"

"We'd better do as we're told," Sparhawk said sharply, dropping to his knees and then sprawling out facedown on the carpet of fallen leaves. "I think the next one's going to be spectacular."

"The next one" lasted for a full ten minutes. Nothing with legs could have stood erect on the violently jerking and convulsing earth. Then, with a monstrous roar, the earth not fifty paces in front of them split. The land beyond that ghastly crack in the earth's shell seemed to fall away, while the shuddering ground to which they clung heaved upward, rising ponderously, rippling almost like a wind-tossed banner. Great clouds of birds, squawking in alarm, rose from the shuddering trees.

Then the earthquake gradually subsided. The violence of the tremors grew less severe and less frequent, although there were a number of intermittent jolts. The awful booming sound grew fainter, echoing up through miles of rock like the memory of a nightmare. Vast clouds of dust came billowing up over the lip of the newly formed precipice.

"Now mayest thou contemplate mine handiwork, Anakha," Bhelliom said quite calmly, although with a certain modest pride. "Speak truly, for I will not be offended shouldst thou find flaws. If thou dost perceive faults in what I have wrought, I will correct them."

Sparhawk decided not to trust his feet just yet. Followed closely by his friends, he crawled to the abrupt edge that had not been there fifteen minutes earlier.

The cliff was almost as straight as a sword-cut, and it went down and down at least a thousand feet. It stretched, moreover, as far as the eye could reach both to the east and to the west. A huge escarpment, a vast wall, now separated the upper reaches of the North Cape from the rest of Tamuli.

"What thinkest thou?" Bhelliom asked, just a little anxiously. "Will my wall deny the Trolls access to the lands of thy friends? I can do more if it is thy wish."

"No, Blue-Rose," Sparhawk choked, "no more, I pray thee."

"I am pleased that thou art satisfied."

"It is a splendid wall, Blue-Rose." It was a ridiculous thing to say, but Sparhawk was badly shaken.

Bhelliom did not seem to notice. Vanion's face was suddenly creased with a shy smile at Sparhawk's stunned expression of approval. "It is an adequate wall," it said a bit deprecatingly. "There was some urgency in our need, so I had not time enough to mold and shape it as I might have wished, but methinks it will serve. I would take it as kindness, however, that when next thou dost require modification of the earth, thou wouldst give me more extensive notice, for truly, work done in haste is never wholly satisfactory."

"I shall endeavor to remember that, Blue-Rose."

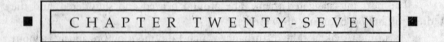

CHAPTER TWENTY-SEVEN

"It's not so bad in here, Sarabian," Mirtai was saying to the distraught emperor. "The floor's carpeted, so most of the tiles weren't broken when they fell." She was on her knees gathering up the small opalescent tiles as Sparhawk and the others emerged from that blurred grey emptiness.

"Sparhawk!" Sarabian exclaimed, recoiling in shocked surprise. "I *wish* you'd blow a trumpet or something before you do that!"

"What happened, your Majesty?" Vanion asked, staring at the littered carpet.

"We had an earthquake! Now I've got an economic disaster on my hands in addition to everything else!"

"You felt it *here,* your Majesty?" Vanion choked.

"It was *terrible,* Vanion!" Sephrenia said. "It was the worst earthquake I've ever been through!"

"Here?"

"You're going to make me cross if you keep saying that. Of course we felt it here. Look at the walls."

"It looks like a bad case of the pox," Kalten said.

"The tiles were jumping off the walls like grasshoppers," Sarabian said in a sick voice. "God knows what the rest of the city looks like. This will bankrupt me."

"It's over four hundred leagues!" Vanion choked. "Twelve hundred miles!"

"What *is* he talking about, Sparhawk?" Ehlana demanded.

"We were at the center of the earthquake," Sparhawk replied. "It was up in northern Atan."

"Did *you* do this to me, Sparhawk?" Sarabian demanded.

"Bhelliom did, your Majesty. The Trolls won't be attacking the Atans any-more."

"Bhelliom shook them all to pieces?"

Sparhawk smiled faintly. "No, your Majesty. It put a wall across the North Cape."

"Can't the Trolls climb over it?" Betuana demanded.

"I wouldn't think so, your Majesty," Vanion said. "It's about a thousand feet high, and it stretches from the Tamul Sea to that coast that lies to the northwest of Sarsos. The Trolls won't be coming any farther south—not in the next two weeks, anyway, and after that, it won't make any difference."

"What exactly do you mean when you say 'wall,' Vanion?" Patriarch Emban asked.

"Actually, it's an escarpment, your Grace," Vanion explained, "a huge cliff that stretches all the way across the North Cape. That's what caused the earthquake."

"Won't Cyrgon be able to reverse whatever Bhelliom did?" Sephrenia asked.

"Bhelliom says no, little mother," Sparhawk replied. "He isn't strong enough."

"He's a God, Sparhawk."

"Evidently that doesn't make any difference. What happened was just too enor-mous. Bhelliom said that it shifted some things about six miles beneath the surface of the earth, and certain changes in the shape of that part of the continent happened all at once instead of being spread out over a million or so years. The changes were going to happen anyway, but Bhelliom made them happen all at once. I gather that the escarpment will become a mountain range as it gradually breaks down. The concepts are just too vast for Cyrgon to comprehend, and the pressures involved are beyond his ability to control."

"What in God's name have you done, Sparhawk?" Emban exclaimed. "You're ripping the world apart!"

"Tell them not to be disquieted, Anakha," Bhellion spoke again in Vanion's voice. "I would not hurt my daughter, for I do love her. She is a wayward and whim-sical child at times, much given to tantrums and sweet, innocent vanity. Behold how she doth adorn herself with spring and mantle her shoulders with the white gown of winter. The stresses and tensions which I did relieve in raising the wall had, in truth, been causing her some discomfort for the past thousand eons. Now is she content, and indeed doth she take some pleasure in her new adornment, for, as I say, she *is* a trifle vain."

"Where's Kring?" Mirtai asked suddenly.

"We left him, Engessa, and Khalad back at the escarpment," Sparhawk told her. "Bhelliom's excellent wall keeps the Trolls from getting at *us,* but it also keeps us from getting at *them.* We have to work out some way to get the Troll-Gods past it to steal back their Trolls."

"You've got Bhelliom, Sparhawk," Stragen said. "Just jump over it."

Sparhawk shook his head. "Bhelliom says that we'd better not. The ground's still a little touchy near the wall right now. If we jump around too much in that gen-eral vicinity, we might set off more earthquakes."

"God!" Sarabian cried. "Don't do that! You'll shake the whole continent apart!"

"We're trying to avoid that, your Majesty. Engessa, Kring, and Khalad are working on something. If we can't go down the escarpment, we may have to use Tynian's fleet and sail around the eastern end of it."

"We want to think about that for a while, though," Vanion added. "Sparhawk and I are still debating the issue, but I think we'll want to make some show of marching north. If we leave here in about a week with banners flying and five thousand knights added to the forces we've gathered in this general area, we'll have Zalasta's full attention. If we go out to sea, he won't know we're coming, and that might give him the leisure to sniff out some details of Stragen's plans for our special celebration of the Harvest Festival. Both ideas have an element of surprise involved. We're quibbling about which surprise would disrupt Zalasta's plans the most."

The training of Tamul horses began immediately. Tynian's knights, of course, complained bitterly. The riding horses favored by the Tamul gentry were too small and delicate to carry armored men, and the oversized plow-horses used by Tamul farmers were too slow and docile to make good war-horses.

They were always rushed now. Caalador had given the order, and it was irrevocable. The murders *would* take place during the Harvest Festival, whether their other plans were fully in place or not, and every minute brought the holiday that much closer.

It was five days following the return of Sparhawk and his friends from northern Atan that a runner reached Matherion with a message from Khalad. Mirtai admitted the weary Atan to the sitting room, where Sparhawk and Vanion were arguing the relative merits of their opposing plans. Wordlessly, the messenger handed Khalad's note to Sparhawk.

" 'My Lord,' " he read the characteristically abrupt note aloud. " 'The earthquake has jumbled the northeast coast. Don't rely on any charts of the area. You're going to have to come by sea, however. There's no way we can climb down the wall—particularly not with Trolls waiting for us at the bottom. Engessa, Kring, and I will be waiting with the Atans and Tikume's Peloi a couple of leagues south of where the wall dives into the Tamul Sea. Don't take too long to get here. The other side is up to something.' "

"That throws both your plans out the window, doesn't it?" Emperor Sarabian noted. "You won't be able to go by land, because you can't climb down the wall; and you can't go by sea, because the sea's filled with uncharted reefs."

"And we've only got about two days to make the decision," Itagne added. "The forces we're sending north are going to have to start moving at least a week before the festival if they're going to reach the North Cape in time to spring our second surprise on Zalasta."

"I'd better go have a talk with Captain Sorgi," Sparhawk said, rising to his feet.

"He and Caalador are down in the main pantry," Stragen advised him. "They're both Cammorians, and Cammorians like to be close to food and drink."

Sparhawk nodded, and he and Vanion quickly left the room.

An almost immediate friendship had sprung up between Caalador and Sorgi. They were, as Stragen had pointed out, both Cammorians, and they even looked much alike. Both had curly hair, though Sorgi's was nearly silver by now, and they were both burly men with heavy shoulders and powerful hands.

"Well, Master Cluff," Sorgi said expansively as Sparhawk and Vanion entered the large, airy kitchen storeroom, "have you solved all the world's problems yet?" Captain Sorgi always called Sparhawk by the alias he had used the first time they had met.

"Hardly, Sorgi. We've got one that maybe *you* can solve for us, though."

"Get the money part settled first, Sorgi," Caalador recommended. "Ol' Sporhawk here, he gets a little vague when th' time comes t' settle up."

Sorgi smiled. "I haven't heard that dialect since I left home," he told Sparhawk. "I could sit and listen to Caalador talk by the hour. Let's not worry about money yet. The advice is free. It starts costing you money when I lift my anchor up off the bottom."

"We have to go to a place where there's been an earthquake recently," Sparhawk told him. "Kurik's son just sent me a message. The earthquake has changed things so much that all the old maps are useless."

"Happens all the time," Sorgi told him. "The estuary that runs up to Vardenais changes her bottom every winter."

"How do you deal with that?"

Sorgi shrugged. "We put out a small boat with a strong sailor to do the rowing and a clever one to heave the sounding line. They lead us through."

"Isn't that sort of slow?"

"Not nearly as slow as trying to steer a sinking ship. How big an area got churned up by the earthquake?"

"It's sort of hard to say."

"Guess, Master Cluff. Tell me exactly what happened, and give me a guess about how big the danger spot is."

Sparhawk glossed over the cause of the sudden change in the coastline and described the emergence of the escarpment.

"No problem," Sorgi assured him.

"How did you arrive at that conclusion, Captain?" Vanion asked him.

"We won't have to worry about any reefs to the north of your cliff, my Lord. I saw something like that happen on the west coast of Rendor one time. You see, what's happened is that the cliff keeps on going. It runs on out to sea—under the water—so once you get north of it, the water's going to be a thousand feet deep. Not too many ships I know of draw that much water. I'll just take along some of the old charts. We'll go out about ten leagues and sail north. I'll take my bearings every so often, and when we get six or eight leagues north of this new cliff of yours, we'll turn west and run straight for the beach. I'll put your men ashore up there with no trouble at all."

"And *that's* the problem with your plan, Sparhawk," Vanion said. "You've only got a hundred ships. If you take both the knights *and* their horses, you'll only be able to take fifteen hundred up there to face the Trolls."

"Is a-winnin' this yere arg-u-ment *real* important t' you two?" Caalador asked.

"We're just looking for the best way, Caalador," Sparhawk replied.

"Then why not combine the two plans? Have Sorgi start north first thing in the morning, and you mount up your armies and ride up that way as soon as you get organized. When Sorgi gets to a place ten leagues or so south of the wall, he can feel his way in to shore. You meet him there, and he starts ferrying your army around the reef and puts you down on the beach north of the wall. Then you can go looking for Trolls, and Sorgi can drop his anchor and spend his time fishing."

Sparhawk and Vanion looked at each other sheepishly.

"It's like I wuz a-sayin', Sorgi." Caalador grinned. "Th' gentry ain't' got hordly no common sense a-tall. I b'leeve it's 'cause they ain't got room in ther heads fer more'n one i'dee at a time."

Inevitably, the day arrived when the relief column was scheduled to depart for Atan. It was before dawn when Mirtai came into the bedroom of the Queen of Elenia and her Prince Consort. "Time to get up," the giantess announced.

"Don't you know how to knock?" Sparhawk asked, sitting up in bed.

"Did I interrupt something?"

"Never mind, Mirtai," he sighed. "It's a custom, that's all."

"Foolishness. Everybody knows what goes on in here."

"Isn't it almost time for you and Kring to get married?"

"Are you trying to get rid of me, Sparhawk?"

"Of course not."

"Kring and I have decided to wait until after all of this is finished. Our weddings are going to be a little complicated. We have to go through two ceremonies in two parts of the world. Kring's not very happy about all the delay."

"I can't for the life of me see why," Ehlana said innocently.

"Men are strange." Mirtai shrugged.

"They are indeed, Mirtai, but how would we amuse ourselves without them?"

Sparhawk dressed slowly, pulling on the padded, rust-stained underclothing with reluctance and eying his black-enameled suit of steel work clothes with active dislike.

"Did you pack warm clothing?" Ehlana asked him. "The nights are getting chilly even this far south, so it's going to be very cold up on the North Cape."

"I packed it." He grunted. "For all the good it's going to do. No amount of clothing heips when you're wearing steel." He made a sour face. "I know it's a contradiction, but I start to sweat the minute I put the armor on. Every knight I've ever known does the same. We keep on sweating even when we're freezing and icicles are forming up inside the armor. Sometimes I wish I'd gone into another line of work. Bashing people for fun and profit starts to wear thin after a while."

"You're in a gloomy mood this morning, love."

"It's just that it's getting harder and harder to get started. I'll be all right once I'm on the road."

"You *will* be careful, won't you, Sparhawk. I'd die if I lost you."

"I'm not going to be in all that much danger, dear. I've got Bhelliom, and Bhelliom could pick up the sun and break it across its knee. It's Cyrgon and Zalasta who'll have to watch out."

"Don't get overconfident."

"I'm not. I've got more advantages than I can count, that's all. We're going to win, Ehlana, and there's nothing in the world that can stop us. All that's really left is the tedious plodding from here to the victory celebration."

"Why don't you kiss me for a while?" she suggested. "*Before* you put on the armor. It takes weeks for the bruises to go away after you kiss me when you're all wrapped in steel."

"You know—" He smiled. "—that's an awfully good idea. Why don't we do that?"

The column stretched for several miles, undulating across the rounded hills on the east coast of Lake Sama. There were Church Knights, Atans, Kring's Peloi, and a few ornately garbed regiments of the Tamul army.

It was a splendid day, one of those perfect autumn days with a stiff wind aloft hurrying puffy white clouds across an intensely blue sky, and the enormous shadows of those clouds raced across the rolling landscape so that Sparhawk's army rode alternately in sunshine and in shadow. The pennons and flags were of many hues, and they snapped and rippled in the breeze, tugging at the lances and flagstaffs to which they were fastened.

Queen Betuana strode along at Faran's shoulder. "Are you sure, Sparhawk-Knight?" she asked. "The Troll-beasts are animals, and all animals are born knowing how to swim. Even a cat can swim."

"Only reluctantly, Betuana-Queen." Sparhawk smiled, remembering Mmrr's "cat-paddling" in Sephrenia's fish pond in Sarsos. "Ulath-Knight says that we won't have to worry about the Troll-beasts swimming around the end of the escarpment. They'll swim across rivers and lakes, but the sea terrifies them. It has something to do with the tides, I think—or maybe it's the salt."

"Must we continue at this slow pace?" Her tone was impatient.

"We want to be certain that Zalasta's spies see us, your Majesty," Vanion told her. "That's a very important part of our plan."

"Elene battles are very large," she observed.

"We'd prefer smaller ones, Atana, but Zalasta's schemes stretch across the whole continent, so we have to respond."

Sephrenia, with Flute riding in front of her, rode forward with Xanetia. They had all watched the tentative friendship growing between Sephrenia and Xanetia. Both were still very cautious, and there were no great leaps in their relationship. The tenuousness now came not from defensiveness but rather from an excess of concern about inadvertently giving offense, and Sparhawk felt that to be a rather profound change for the good. "We grew tired of all the stories," Sephrenia told Vanion. "I can't be sure which is the bigger liar, Tynian or Ulath."

"Oh?"

"They're trying to outdo each other. Ulath's exaggerating outrageously, and I'm sure Tynian's doing the same thing. Each of them is doing his level best to persuade the other that he missed the adventure of the century."

"It's a demonstration of a form of affection, little mother," Sparhawk explained. "They'd be too embarrassed to admit that they're genuinely fond of each other, so they tell each other wild stories instead."

"Did you understand that, Xanetia?" Sephrenia smiled.

"What reasonable person can *ever* understand how and why men express their love, sister."

"Men aren't really comfortable with the word *love*," Sparhawk told them, "particularly when it's applied to other men."

"It *is* love, though, isn't it, Sparhawk?" Sephrenia asked him.

"Well, I suppose it is, but we're not comfortable with it all the same."

"I have meant to speak with thee, Anarae." Betuana lapsed perhaps unconsciously into archaic Tamul.

"Gladly will I hear thy words, Queen of Atan."

"It hath been the wont of youthful Atans to seek Delphaeus, having it in their minds to destroy thine home and to put thy people to the sword. I am heartily sorry that I have permitted this."

Xanetia smiled. "It is of no moment, Queen of Atan. This is but an excess of adolescent enthusiasm. I must freely confess that *our* fledglings do entertain themselves by deceiving and distracting *thine*, leading them away from their intended goal by rudimentary enchantments and clumsy deceptions. It cometh to me all unbidden that thus are we *both* relieved of the obligation to entertain our children, who, by virtue of their youth, inexperience, and profound inability to divert themselves, do continually complain that there is nothing for them to do—at least nothing worthy of what they perceive to be their enormous gifts."

Betuana laughed. "Do *thy* children have that selfsame plaint, Anarae?"

"*All* children complain," Sephrenia assured them. "It's one of the things that makes parents age so fast."

"Well said," Sparhawk agreed. Neither he nor Sephrenia looked directly at Flute.

They reached Lebas in northern Tamul in about two days. Sparhawk had spoken with the army, stressing the enormous power of Bhelliom as he explained how it would be possible for them to cover great distances in a short period of time. In actuality, however, Bhelliom was in no way responsible. Flute was in charge of their travel arrangements on this particular trip.

There was another Atan runner waiting for them in Lebas with yet another message from Khalad—a fairly offensive note that suggested that the runner had been sent to guide them to the stretch of beach where Kring and Engessa waited with their forces, since if knights were left to their own devices in the forest, they would inevitably get lost. Khalad's class prejudices were still quite firmly in place.

There was no road as such leading north from Lebas, but the trails and paths were quite clearly marked. They reached the southern edge of the vast forest that covered the northeastern quadrant of the continent, and the hundred Peloi that Kring had brought with him from Eosia pulled in to ride close to their allies. Deep woods made the plains-dwelling western Peloi very nervous.

"I think it has to do with the sky," Tynian explained to the others.

"You can barely see the sky when you're in the deep woods, Tynian," Kalten objected.

"Exactly my point," the broad-faced Deiran replied. "The western Peloi are accustomed to having the sky overhead. When there are tree limbs blocking their view of it, they start to get nervous."

They were never able to determine if the attempt was random or was deliberately aimed at Betuana. They were a hundred leagues or so into the forest and had set up their night's encampment; and the large tent for the ladies—Betuana, Sephrenia, Xanetia, and Flute—had been erected somewhat apart so that they might have a bit of privacy.

The assassins were well-concealed, and there were four of them. They burst out of the thicket with drawn swords just as Betuana and Xanetia were emerging from the tent. Betuana responded instantly. Her sword whipped out of its sheath and plunged directly into the belly of one of the attackers. Even as she jerked the sword free, she dove to the ground, rolled, and drove both feet full into the face of yet another.

Sparhawk and the others were running toward the tent in response to Sephrenia's cry of alarm, but the Queen of the Atans seemed to have things well in hand. She parried a hasty thrust and split the skull of the shabby assailant who had made it. Then she engaged the remaining attacker.

"Look out!" Berit shouted as he ran toward her. The man she had felled with her feet was struggling to rise, his nose bleeding and a dagger in his hand. He was directly behind the Atan queen.

Always before when Xanetia had shed her disguise, the change had been slow, the concealing coloration receding gradually. This time, however, she flashed into full illumination, and the light within her was no mere glow. Instead, she blazed forth like a new sun.

The bloody-nosed assassin might have been able to flee from her had he been in full possession of his faculties. The kick he had received in the face, however, appeared to have rattled him and shaken his wits.

He did scream once, though, just before Xanetia's hand touched him. His scream died in a hoarse kind of gurgle. With his mouth agape and his eyes bulging with horror, he stared at the blazing form of she who had just killed him—but only for a moment. After that, it was no longer possible to recognize his expression. The flesh of his face sagged and began to run down, turned by that dreadful touch into a putrefying liquid. His mouth seemed to gape wider as his cheeks and lips oozed down to drip off his chin. He tried to scream once, but the decay had already reached his throat, and all that emerged from his lipless mouth was a liquid wheeze. The flesh slid off his hand, and his dagger dropped from his skeleton clutch.

He sagged to his knees with the slimy residue of skin and nerve and tendons oozing out of his clothing.

Then the rotting corpse toppled slowly forward to lie motionless on the leaf-strewn floor of the forest—motionless, but still dissolving as Xanetia's curse continued its inexorable course.

The Anarae's fire dimmed, and she buried her shining face in her glowing hands and wept.

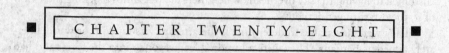

CHAPTER TWENTY-EIGHT

It was raining in Esos, a chill, persistent rain that swept down out of the mountains of Zemoch every autumn. The rain did not noticeably dampen the Harvest Festival celebration, since most of the revelers were too drunk to even notice the weather.

Stolg was *not* drunk. He was working, and he had nothing but contempt for men who drank on the job. Stolg was a nondescript sort of fellow in plain clothing. He wore his hair cropped close and he had large, powerful hands. He went through the crowd of revelers unobtrusively, moving toward the wealthier quarter of the city.

Stolg and his wife, Ruta, had argued that morning, and that always put him in a bad humor. Ruta really had little cause for complaint, he thought, stepping aside for a group of drunken young aristocrats. He *was* a good provider, after all, and their neat little cottage on the outskirts of town was the envy of all their friends. Their son was apprenticed to a local carpenter, and their daughter had excellent prospects for a good marriage. Stolg loved Ruta, but she periodically became waspish over some little thing and pestered him to death about it. This time she was upset because their cottage had no proper lock on the front door, and no matter how many times he told her that *they*, of all people, had no need of locks, she had continued to harp on the subject.

Stolg stopped and drew back into a recessed doorway as the watch tramped by. Djukta would normally have bribed the watch to stay out of Stolg's way, but it was Harvest Festival time, so there would be plenty of confusion to cover any incidental outcries. Djukta was not one to spend money needlessly. It was a common joke in the seedier taverns in Esos that Djukta had deliberately grown his vast beard so that he could save the price of a cloak.

Stolg saw the house that was his destination and went into the foul-smelling alley behind it. He had arranged for a ladder to be placed against the back of the house, and he climbed up quickly and entered through a second-story window. He walked down the hallway and through the door at the end into a bedroom. A former servant in the house had drawn a diagram and had pointed out the room of the owner of the house, a minor nobleman named Count Kinad. Once inside the room, Stolg lay down on the bed. As long as he had to wait, he might as well be comfortable. He could hear the sound of revelry coming from downstairs.

As he lay there, he decided to install the lock Ruta wanted. It wouldn't be expensive, and the peace and quiet around the house would be more than worth it.

It was no more than half an hour later when he heard a heavy, slightly unsteady footfall on the stair. He rolled quickly off the bed, crossed silently to the door, and put his ear to the panel.

"It's no trouble at all," a slurred voice outside said. "I've got a copy in my bedroom."

"Really, Count Kinad," a lady's voice called from below, "I take your word for it."

"No, Baroness, I want you to read his Majesty's exact words. It's the most idiotic proclamation you've ever seen." The door opened, and a man carrying a candle entered. It was the man who had been pointed out to Stolg two days ago. Stolg idly wondered what Count Kinad had done to irritate someone enough to justify the expense of a professional visit. He brushed the thought aside. That was really none of his business.

Stolg was a thorough professional, so he had several techniques available to him. The fact that Count Kinad's back was to him presented the opportunity for his favorite, however. He drew a long poniard from his belt, stepped up behind the count, and drove the long, slim blade into the base of the count's skull with a steely crunch. He caught the collapsing body and quietly lowered it to the floor. A knife-thrust in the brain was always certain, and it was quick, quiet, and produced a minimum of mess. Ruta absolutely *hated* to wash her husband's work clothes when there was blood all over them. Stolg set his foot between the count's shoulders and wrenched his poniard out of the back of the skull. That was sometimes tricky. Pulling a knife out of bone takes quite a bit of strength.

Stolg rolled the body over and looked intently into the dead face. A professional always makes sure that a client has been permanently serviced.

The count was definitely dead. His eyes were blank, his face was turning blue, and a trickle of blood was coming out of his nose. Stolg wiped off his poniard, put it away, and went back out into the hallway. He walked quietly back to the window through which he had entered.

There were two more names on the list Djukta had given him, and with luck he could service another this very night. It was raining, however, and Stolg really disliked working in the rain. He decided to go home early instead and tell Ruta that he would give in just this once and install the lock she wanted so much. Then he thought it might be nice if they took their son and their daughter to the tavern at the end of the street to have a few tankards of ale with their neighbors. It *was* the Harvest Festival, after all, and a man should really try to spend the holidays with his friends and family.

Sherrok was a small, weedy sort of fellow with thinning hair and a lumpy skull. He did not so much walk as scurry through the crowded streets of Verel in southern Daconia. In the daytime, Sherrok was a minor official in the customshouse, biting his tongue as he took orders from his Tamul superiors. Sherrok *loathed* Tamuls, and being placed in a subservient position to them sometimes made him physically ill. It was that loathing which had been primarily behind his decision to sell information to the diseased Styric Ogerajin, to whom a mutual acquaintance had introduced him. When Ogerajin, after a few carefully worded questions, had slyly hinted that certain kinds of information might be worth quite a bit of money, Sherrok had leapt at the chance to betray his despised superiors—*and* to make tidy sums as well.

The information he had for Ogerajin tonight was *very* important. The greedy, bloodsucking Tamuls were going to raise the customs rate by a full quarter of a percent. Ogerajin should pay handsomely for *that* piece of information.

Sherrok licked his lips as he rushed through the noisy crowds celebrating the Harvest Festival. There was an eight-year-old Astellian girl available at one of the slave marts, a ravishing child with huge, terrified eyes, and if Ogerajin could be persuaded to be generous, Sherrock might actually be able to buy her. He had never owned a child so young before, and the very thought of her made his knees go weak.

His mind was full of her as he passed a reeking alleyway, and so he was not really paying any attention—until he felt the strand of wire snap tight around his neck.

He struggled, of course, but it was really not much use. The assassin dragged him back into the alley and methodically strangled him. His last thought was of the little girl's face. She actually seemed to be laughing at him.

"You're really more trouble than you're worth, you know," Bersola said to the dead man sprawled in the bow of the rowboat. Bersola always talked to the men he had killed. Many of Bersola's colleagues believed that he was crazy. They were probably right.

Bersola's major problem lay in the fact that he always did things exactly the same way. He invariably stuck his knife into someone between the third and fourth ribs at a slightly downward angle. It *was* effective, though, since a knife thrust there absolutely *cannot* miss the heart. Bersola also *never* left a body lying where it fell. He had a compulsive sense of neatness that drove him to put the remains somewhere out of sight. Since Bersola lived and worked in the Daconian town of Ederus on the coast of the Sea of Edom, disposal was a simple matter. A short trip in a rowboat and a few rocks tied to the deceased's ankles removed all traces. Bersola's habit-driven personality, however, led him to always sink the bodies in the exact same place. The other murderers of Ederus made frequent laughing reference to "Bersola's Reef," a place on the lake bottom supposedly piled high with sunken bodies. Even people who didn't fully understand the significance of the phrase referred to Bersola's Reef.

"You went and did it, didn't you?" Bersola said to the corpse in the bow of the boat as he rowed out to the reef. "You just *had* to go and offend somebody. You've got nobody to blame but yourself for this, you know. If you'd behaved yourself, none of this would have happened."

The corpse did not answer. They almost never did.

Bersola stopped rowing and took his bearings. There was the usual light in the window of Fanna's Tavern on the far shore, and there was the warning fire on the rocky headlands on the near side. The lantern on the wharf protruding out from Ederus was dead astern. "This is the place," Bersola told the dead man. "You'll have lots of company down there, so it won't be so bad." He shipped his oars and crawled forward. He checked the knots on the rope that held the large rock in place between the dead man's ankles. "I'm really sorry about this, you know," he apologized, "but it *is* your own fault." He lifted the rock—and the dead man's legs—over the side. He held the shoulders for a moment. "Do you have anything you'd like to say?" he asked.

He waited for a decent interval, but the dead man did not reply.

"I didn't really think you would," Bersola said. He let go of the shoulders, and the body slithered limply over the gunwale and disappeared into the dark waters of the lake.

Bersola whistled his favorite tune as he rowed back to Ederus.

Avin Wargunsson, Prince Regent of Thalesia, was in an absolute fury. Patriarch Bergsten had left Thalesia without so much as a by-your-leave. It was intolerable! The man had absolutely no regard for the Prince Regent's dignity. Avin Wargunsson was going to be king one day, after all—just as soon as the raving madman in the north tower finally got around to dying—and he deserved *some* courtesy. People always ignored him! That indifferent lack of regard cankered the soul of the little crown prince. Avin was scarcely more than five feet tall, and in a kingdom absolutely awash with blond people a foot or more taller, he was almost unnoticeable. He had spent his childhood scurrying like a mouse out from under the feet of towering men who kept accidentally stepping on him because they refused to look down and see that he was there.

Sometimes that made him so angry that he could just scream.

Then, without even bothering to knock, two burly blond ruffians opened the door and rolled in a large barrel. "Here's that cask of Arcian red you wanted, Avin," one of them said. The ignorant barbarian didn't even know enough to use a proper form of address.

"I didn't order a barrel of wine," Avin snapped.

"The chief of the guards said you wanted a barrel of Arcian red," the other blond savage declared, closing the door. "We're just doing what we were told to do. Where do you want this?"

"Oh, put it over there," Avin said, pointing. It was easier than arguing with them.

They rolled the barrel across the floor and set it up in the corner.

"I don't think I know you two," Avin said.

"We're new." The first one shrugged. "We just joined the Royal Guard last week." He set a canvas bag on the floor and took out a pry-bar. He carefully inserted the bar under the lid of the barrel and worked it back and forth until the lid came free.

"What are you doing?" Avin demanded.

"You can't drink it if you can't get at it, Avin," the fellow pointed out. "We've got the right tools, and you probably don't." At least the man was clean-shaven. Avin approved of that. Most of the men in the Royal Guard looked like trees with golden moss growing on them. "You'd better taste it and make sure it hasn't soured, Brok."

"Right," the other one agreed. He scooped up some of the wine in the cupped palm of his hand and sucked it in noisily. Avin shuddered. "Tastes all right to me, Tel," he reported. A thoughtful look crossed his face. "Why don't I fill up a bucket of this before we put the lid back on?" he suggested. "Hauling this barrel up the stairs was heavy business, and I've worked up quite a thirst."

"Good idea," Tel agreed.

The bearded man picked up the brass-bound wooden bucket Avin used for a wastebasket. "Is it all right if I use this, Avin?" he asked.

Avin Wargunsson gaped at him. This went too far—even in Thalesia.

The burly fellow shook the contents of the wastebasket out on Avin's desk and dipped it into the barrel. Then he set the pail on the floor. "I guess we're ready, Tel," he said.

"All right," Tel replied. "Let's get at it."

"What are you doing?" Avin demanded in a shrill voice as the two approached him.

They didn't even bother to answer. It was intolerable! He was the Prince Regent! People had no right to ignore him like this!

They picked him up by the arms and carried him over to the barrel, ignoring his cries and struggles. He couldn't even get their attention by kicking them.

"In you go," the one named Tel said pleasantly, almost in the tone one uses when he pushes a horse into a stall. The two lifted Avin Wargunsson quite easily and stuffed him feetfirst into the barrel. The one called Brok held him down while Tel took a hammer and a handful of nails out of the canvas bag and picked up the barrel lid. He set the lid on Avin's head and pushed him down. Then he rapped his hammer around the edge of the lid, settling it in place.

Only Avin's eyes and forehead were above the surface of the wine. He held his breath and pounded impotently on the underside of the lid with both fists.

Then there was another pounding sound as well as Tel calmly nailed down the lid of the barrel.

The ladies quite firmly dismissed Kalten when they set out the morning after the attempt on Queen Betuana's life. Kalten took his self-appointed duties as Xanetia's protector quite seriously, and he was a bit offended at being so cavalierly sent away.

"They need some privacy right now," Vanion told him. "Set some knights to either side to protect them, but give them enough room to get Xanetia through this." Vanion was a soldier, but his insights were sometimes quite profound. Sparhawk looked back over his shoulder. Sephrenia rode close to one side of the sorrowing Xanetia, and Betuana strode along on the other. Xanetia rode with her head bowed, holding Flute in her arms. There was about them a kind of exclusionary wall as they closed ranks around their injured companion. Sephrenia rode very close to the Anarae, frequently reaching out her hand to touch the stricken woman. The racial differences and eons-old enmity appeared to have been overridden by the universal sisterhood of all women. Sephrenia reached across those barriers to comfort her enemy without even thinking about it. Betuana was no less solicitous, and in spite of the gruesome demonstration of the effects of Xanetia's touch, she walked very close to the Delphaeic woman.

Aphrael, of course, was in complete control of the situation. She rode with her arms about Xanetia's waist, and Aphrael's touch was one of the more powerful forces on earth. Sparhawk was quite certain that Xanetia was not really suffering. The Child-Goddess would not permit that. The Anarae's apparent horror and remorse at what she had been compelled to do was primarily for the benefit of her two comforters. Aphrael was quite deliberately erasing Sephrenia's racial animosity and Betuana's superstitious aversion by the simple expedient of intensifying Xanetia's outward appearance of grief.

It was easy to underestimate Aphrael when she appeared in one of her innumerable incarnations as a capricious little girl, and that was probably the main reason she had chosen the form of the Child-Goddess in the first place. Sparhawk, however, had seen the reality of Aphrael waveringly reflected in the brass mirror back in Matherion, and the reality was neither childish nor whimsical. Aphrael, he guessed, generally knew exactly what she was doing, and generally got exactly what she wanted. Sparhawk firmly fixed the wavering image of the reality of Aphrael in his mind so that it would always be present when the dimples and the kisses began to cloud his judgment.

The days were significantly shorter this far to the north. The sun rose far to the southeast now and it did not go very high above the southern horizon before it started to descend again. Each long night's frost piled up on the previous night's lacy blanket, since the pale, weak sun no longer had the strength to melt what had built up during the hours of darkness.

It was nearly sunset when a towering Atan came loping down a frosty forest path to meet them. He went directly to Queen Betuana, banged his fist against his chest in salute, and spoke urgently. Betuana motioned quickly to Sparhawk and the others. "A message from Engessa-Atan," she said tersely. "There are enemies gathering on the coast at the eastern end of the wall."

"Trolls?" Vanion asked quickly.

The tall Atan shook his head. "No, Vanion-Lord," he replied. "They're Elenes, and for the most part they're not warriors. They're cutting trees."

"To use in building fortifications?" Bevier asked.

"No, Church-Knight. They are lashing the trees together to build things that will float."

"Rafts?" Tynian asked. "Ulath, you said that Trolls are afraid of the sea. Would they be willing to use rafts to go around the outer edge of the escarpment?"

"It's hard to say," the blond-braided Thalesian replied. "Ghwerig *did* use a boat to cross Lake Venne, and he almost had to have stolen a ride on some ship to get from Thalesia to Pelosia when he followed King Sarak during the Zemoch war, but Ghwerig wasn't like other Trolls." He looked at the Atan. "Are they building these rafts north of the wall or here on the south side?"

"They're on this side of the wall," the Atan replied.

"That doesn't make too much sense, does it?" Kalten asked.

"Not to *me*, it doesn't," Ulath admitted.

"I think we'd better get up there and have a look, Sparhawk," Vanion said. "That attack on Betuana last night was fair evidence that Zalasta knows we're coming, so this little stroll through the woods has accomplished its purpose. Let's join forces with Engessa and Kring and find out if Sorgi's made it to the beach yet. Winter's coming on fast, and I think we'll want to deal with the Trolls before the sun goes down permanently."

"Would you see to that, Divine One?" Sparhawk said to Aphrael. "I'd ask Bhelliom to do it, but you've been handling things so well that I wouldn't want to appear critical by taking over at this point."

Aphrael's eyes narrowed. "Don't push your luck, Sparhawk," she said ominously.

Sparhawk was never really certain whether Aphrael had somehow moved them during the night or had slipped them across the intervening miles at some point between the time when they swung up into their saddles and the time when their mounts took their first steps. The Child-Goddess was too practiced, too skilled, to be caught tampering when she didn't want to be.

The hill was the same hill that had been lying to the northwest of their night's encampment when the sun had gone down—or so it seemed—but when they crested it about a half hour after they set out, there was a long, sandy beach and the lead-grey expanse of the Tamul Sea on the other side instead of a broad, unbroken forest.

"That was quick," Talen said, looking around. Talen's presence on this expedition had never really been explained to Sparhawk's satisfaction. He suspected Aphrael, however. It was easy to suspect Aphrael of such things, and more often than not the suspicions proved to be well-founded.

"There's someone coming down the beach," Ulath said, pointing at a tiny figure riding along the water's edge from the north.

"Khalad." Talen shrugged.

"How can you tell?"

"He's my brother, Sir Ulath—besides, I recognize his cloak."

They rode on down the hill and out onto the sand.

"What kept you?" Khalad asked Sparhawk bluntly when he joined them.

"I'm glad to see you, too, Khalad."

"Don't try to be funny, Sparhawk. I've been struggling to keep Engessa and his Atans from swimming around the outer edge of the escarpment for the past ten days. They want to go attack the Trolls all by themselves. How did Stragen's plan come off?"

"It's hard to say," Talen told him. "We were on the road during the Harvest Festival. I know Stragen and Caalador well enough to know that *most* of the people they were after are probably dead by now. We're a little late because we wanted to make sure that Zalasta's people saw us coming. We thought we might be able to divert him enough to keep him out of the way of Caalador's murderers."

Khalad grunted.

"Are the Trolls gathering anywhere nearby?" Ulath asked.

"As closely as we can tell, they're all clustered around the abandoned village of Tzada over on the other side of the Atan border," Khalad replied. "They tried to climb the wall for a while, then they pulled back. Engessa's got scouts on top of the wall; they'll let us know when the Trolls start to move."

"Where are Engessa and Kring?" Vanion asked him.

"Up the beach about a mile, my Lord. We've built an encampment back in the forest a ways. Tikume's joined us. He brought in several thousand of the eastern Peloi about five days ago."

"That should help," Kalten said. "The Peloi are very enthusiastic about their wars."

"Any sign of Sorgi yet?" Sparhawk asked.

"He's feeling his way in through the reefs," Khalad replied. "He sent a longboat ahead to let us know he was coming."

"What's this business with the rafts all about?" Vanion asked him.

"They aren't rafts, my Lord. They're sections of a floating bridge."

"A bridge? A bridge to where?"

"We aren't sure. We've been staying back so that the Edomish peasants constructing it won't see us."

"What are Edomishmen doing on *this* side of the continent?" Kalten asked with some astonishment.

"Building a bridge, Sir Kalten. Weren't you listening? Talen's old friend Amador—or Rebal, or whatever he calls himself—is sort of in charge, but Incetes is there, too, and *he's* the one who's making the big impression. He bellows orders in archaic Elenic, and he's been braining anyone who doesn't understand him or move fast enough."

"Is it that counterfeit one we saw in the woods near Jorsan?" Talen asked.

"I don't think so. This fellow seems to be quite a bit bigger, and he's got a sizeable contingent of men in bronze armor with him. I'd guess that somebody's resurrecting people out of the past again."

"That would probably be Djarian of Samar," Sephrenia said. "Maybe he *can* raise whole armies after all."

"He can if Cyrgon's lending him a hand," Aphrael added. The Child-Goddess had appeared to be dozing in her sister's arms, but she had clearly been listening. She opened her large, dark eyes. "Hello, Khalad," she said. "You look a little windburned."

"We've had some gales coming in off the Tamul Sea, Divine One. There's a strong smell of ice mixed up in them."

"*That's* what they're doing," Ulath said, snapping his fingers.

"Does he still do that?" Tynian asked. "I was hoping you'd cured him of it by now."

"Ulath likes to play leapfrog with his mind, Tynian," Sephrenia said calmly. "He'll come back in a moment or two and fill in the blank spaces for us."

"How long has it been cold up here, Khalad?" Ulath asked.

"It wasn't particularly warm when we *got* here, Sir Ulath."

"Is any ice forming up in the inlets and along the beach at night?"

"Some. It isn't very thick, though, and the tide comes in and breaks it up before it has the chance to spread."

"The floating ice a mile or so out to sea *isn't* breaking up, though," Ulath said. "It rises and falls with the tide because it's not grinding up against the rocks. It's probably almost a foot thick out there by now. The Edomishmen aren't building rafts or a bridge. They're building a pier out to that pack ice. There'll be another one north of the wall as well. The Trolls *will* cross the ice. We know that because they did it to get here from Thalesia. Cyrgon's going to march the Trolls to the pier north of the wall and drive them out to the pack ice. Then they'll march south across the ice and come ashore on this south pier."

"And then they'll attack the Atans again," Vanion said bleakly. "How thick will the pack ice have to be to support the weight of the Trolls?"

"Two feet or so. It should be thick enough by the time the piers are finished—if it stays cold."

"I think we can count on Cyrgon to make sure that it stays cold," Tynian noted.

"There's something else, too," Khalad added. "If Cyrgon's playing with the weather this way, it won't be *too* long before Sorgi's ships are locked in ice. I think we'd better come up with something, my Lords—and fairly soon—or we're going to be hip-deep in Trolls again."

"Let's go talk with Kring and Engessa," Sparhawk said.

CHAPTER TWENTY-NINE

"The beach has changed, friend Sparhawk," Kring was saying. "When you get close to the cliff, there's about a mile of what used to be the sea-bottom that's out of the water now."

"It looks as if Bhelliom pushed the land from north of the break underneath the rest of the continent," Khalad added. "It sort of slid under and pushed this side of the crack upward to form the cliff. That's what raised the sea-bottom on this side. The land to the north of the cliff sank, though, so the sea went a couple of miles inland. You can see treetops sticking up out of the water. The break was clean and straight back where we were when the earthquakes started, but there were a lot of landslides out here on the coast. There are big rocks sticking up out of the water north of the cliff."

"Where are those Edomishmen you mentioned?" Vanion asked.

"Up near the top of the cliff, my Lord. They're cutting trees and rolling the logs down to the edge of the water. That's where they're building the rafts." Khalad paused, his expression slightly critical. "They aren't very good rafts," he added. "If the Trolls try to come ashore on that floating pier, they're going to get their feet wet."

"He's his father's son, all right." Kalten laughed. "Why do you care whether or not the Trolls get their feet wet, Khalad?"

"If you're going to do something, you should do it right, Sir Kalten," Khalad said stubbornly. "I hate sloppy workmanship."

"Where's this place the Trolls are gathering?" Vanion asked. "What was its name again?"

"Tzada, Vanion-Preceptor," Engessa replied. "It's over in Atan."

"What are they doing?"

"It's a little hard to tell from the top of the cliff."

"Where's the border between Tamul proper and Atan?" Tynian asked.

"There isn't any real border, Tynian-Knight," Queen Betuana told him. "It's just a line drawn on the map, and the line doesn't mean anything up here on the North Cape. A land where the sun goes down in the late autumn and doesn't come up again until early spring and where the trees freeze and explode in midwinter doesn't attract too many settlers. The western part of the cape's supposed to be in Astel; the middle's in Atan; and the east is called part of Tamul proper. Nobody up here really pays any attention to things like that. The land belongs to anybody foolish enough to live this far north."

"It's about a hundred and fifty leagues to Tzada," Engessa told them.

"That's a good week's travel for a Troll," Ulath said. "How far along are the Edomishmen with their pier?"

Khalad scratched his cheek. "I'd guess that they've got a good ten more days before they finish."

"And in ten days the pack ice out to sea should be thick enough to hold the weight of the Trolls," Ulath concluded.

"Cyrgon will make *sure* it's thick enough," Flute said.

"Somebody's doing some very tight scheduling," Bevier noted. "The Edomishmen will have their piers complete in ten days, the ice will be thick enough to walk on, and if the Trolls set out from Tzada three days from now, they'll get here just when everything's ready."

"We have all sorts of options here," Vanion said. "We could destroy this southern pier and leave the Trolls stranded out on the ice; we could just wait and meet them when they try to come ashore; we could use Sorgi's ships to assault them while they're on the pier itself; or we could . . ."

Queen Betuana was firmly shaking her head.

"Something wrong, your Majesty?" Vanion asked her.

"We don't have that much time, Vanion-Preceptor," she replied. "How long is the daylight here now, Engessa-Atan?"

"Not much more than five hours, Betuana-Queen."

"In ten days it won't even last that long. Do we want to fight Trolls in the dark?"

"Not even a little bit, your Majesty." Ulath shuddered. "The point is that we don't really want to fight them at all. We want to steal them. We could just ignore all this construction work here on the coast, you know. Sorgi's ships could ferry us around these work gangs and put us ashore far enough north of the escarpment so that Bhelliom won't set off a new batch of earthquakes, and then we could have it carry us directly to Tzada."

"That's a good plan, Ulath-Knight," Betuana agreed, "except for the ice. It's already forming out there, you know."

"Aphrael," Sparhawk said to the Child-Goddess, "could you melt that ice for us?"

"If I really *had* to," she replied, "but it wouldn't be polite. The ice is a part of winter, and winter belongs to the earth. The earth is Bhelliom's child, not mine, so you'll have to talk to Bhelliom about it."

"What should I ask it to do?"

She shrugged. "Why not just leave that up to Bhelliom? Tell it that the ice is a problem and let *it* decide how to deal with it. You've got a lot to learn about the etiquette of these situations, Sparhawk."

"I suppose so," he admitted, "but it's the sort of thing that doesn't come up every day, so I haven't had much practice."

"You see what I mean about those rafts, Sparhawk?" Khalad said. "Those green logs lie so low in the water that you couldn't lead a donkey along that pier without getting him wet all the way up to the hocks."

"How would *you* have built them?"

"I'd have used a double layer of logs—one layer across the top of the other." The two of them were lying under some bushes on a knoll watching the Edomish peasants laboring on the rafts. The first part of the pier was already anchored in place, and it jutted about a quarter of a mile out into the icy water. Additional rafts were being added to the outer end as quickly as they were completed.

"There's Incetes," Khalad said, pointing at a huge man in a bronze mail shirt and horned helmet. "He and those prehistoric warriors he brought with him have been driving those poor peasants to the point of exhaustion. Rebal's running around waving his arms and trying to look important, but it's Incetes who's really in charge. The peasants don't seem to understand his dialect, so he's been talking to them by hand." Khalad scratched his short black beard. "You know, Sparhawk, if we killed him, his warriors would vanish, and one charge by the knights would chase Rebal and his peasants halfway back to Edom."

"It's a nice idea, but how are we going to get close enough to kill him?"

"I'm already close enough, Sparhawk. I could kill him from right here."

"He's two hundred and fifty paces away, Khalad. Your father said that the maximum range with a crossbow is two hundred yards—and even that involved a lot of luck."

"I'm a better shot than Father was." Khalad lifted his crossbow. "I've modified the sights and lengthened the arms a bit. Incetes is close enough, believe me. I could stick a bolt up his nose from here."

"That's a graphic picture. Let's go talk with Vanion." They slid back down the back of the knoll, mounted their horses, and rode back to their hidden encampment. Sparhawk quickly explained his squire's plan to the others.

"Are you sure you could hit him at that range, Khalad?" Vanion asked a bit skeptically.

Khalad sighed. "Do you want a demonstration, my Lord?" he asked.

Vanion shook his head. "No. If you tell me you can hit him, then I'll believe you."

"All right. I can hit him, my Lord."

"That's good enough for me." Vanion frowned. "What would you say might be the absolute extreme range of the crossbow?" he asked.

Khalad spread his hands uncertainly. "I'd have to experiment, Lord Vanion," he said. "I'm sure I could build one that will reach out a thousand yards, but aiming it would be difficult, and it would probably take two men a half hour to recock it. The arms would have to be very stiff."

"A thousand paces," Vanion sighed, shaking his head. He rapped his knuckles on the chest of his suit of armor. "I think we're becoming obsolete, gentlemen." Then he straightened. "Well, we're not obsolete yet. As long as we're here anyway, let's go ahead and neutralize this southern pier. All it's going to cost us is one crossbow bolt and a single mounted charge. The dismay it's going to cause our enemies is worth *that* much, anyway."

Kring and Tikume came riding up the hill from the beach with Captain Sorgi clattering along beside him. Sorgi was not a very good horseman and he rode stiffly, clinging to the saddlebow. "Friend Sorgi came ashore in one of those rowboats," Kring said. "His big boats are still about a mile out in the water."

"Ships, friend Kring," Sorgi corrected with a pained expression. "The little ones are boats, but the big ones are called ships."

"What's the difference, friend Sorgi?"

"A ship has a captain. A boat operates by mutual consent." Sorgi's expression grew somber. "We have a problem, Master Cluff. The ice is forming up right behind my ships. I'll be able to bring them ashore, but I don't think they'll be of much use to you. I've had soundings taken, and we'll have to sail a couple of miles out to get around the reef that runs out to sea from that cliff. We don't *have* those two miles anymore. The ice is moving inshore very fast."

"You'd better talk with Bhelliom, Sparhawk," Aphrael said. "I think I told you that this morning."

"Yes," he agreed, "as a matter of fact you did."

"Why didn't you do it then?"

"I had a few other things on my mind."

"They get like that as they grow older," Sephrenia told her sister. "They get mulish and deliberately put off doing things they're supposed to do just because *we* suggest them. They *hate* being told what to do."

"What's the best way to get around that?"

Sephrenia smiled sweetly at the warriors standing around her. "I've always had good luck with telling them to do the exact opposite of what I really want."

"All right," the Child-Goddess said dubiously. "It sounds silly to me, but if it's the only way to get the job done . . ." She drew herself up. "Sparhawk!" she said in a commanding voice, "don't you *dare* talk to Bhelliom!"

Sparhawk sighed. "I wonder if Dolmant could find an opening in a monastery for me when I get home," he said.

Sparhawk and Vanion went off a ways from the others to consult with the sapphire rose. Flute trailed along behind them. Sparhawk touched his ring to the lid of the box. "Open," he said.

The lid snapped up.

"Blue-Rose," Sparhawk said, "winter doth approach with unseemly haste, and the freezing of the sea doth hinder our design. We would proceed some distance beyond thine excellent wall so that our movements will not perturb thy daughter."

"Thou art considerate, Anakha," Vanion's voice replied.

"His courtesy is not untainted by self-interest, Flower-Gem," Aphrael said with an impish little smile. "When thy daughter shudders, it doth unsettle his stomach."

"You didn't have to say that, Aphrael," Sparhawk told her. "Are you going to do this?"

"No. My manners are better than that."

"Why did you come along, then?"

"Because I owe Bhelliom an apology—and it owes me an explanation." She looked into the golden cask, and the azure glow from the stone illuminated her face. She spoke directly to the stone in a language Sparhawk did not understand, although it was somehow tantalizingly familiar. There were pauses as she spoke, pauses during which Sparhawk presumed Bhelliom was responding, communing directly with her in a voice that only she could hear. At one point she laughed, peal upon peal of silvery laughter that almost seemed to sparkle in the chill air. "All right, Sparhawk," she said finally, "Bhelliom and I have finished apologizing to each other. You can go ahead and present your problem now."

"You're too kind," he murmured.

"Be nice."

"I would not trouble thee with our trivial concerns, Blue-Rose," Sparhawk said then, "but methinks the onset of the winter ice hath been hastened by Cyrgon's hand, and it is beyond our power to respond."

Vanion's tone was stern as Bhelliom replied. "Methinks Cyrgon doth need instruction in courtesy, Anakha—and perchance in humility as well. He hath bent his will to the premature formation of the ice. I will tweak his beard for this. There are rivers in the sea, and he hath turned one of these aside to freeze this coast in furtherance of his design. I will turn aside yet another and bring the torrid breath of tropic climes to this northern shore and consume his ice."

Aphrael clapped her hands together with a delighted laugh.

"What's so funny?" Sparhawk asked her.

"Cyrgon's going to be a little sick for a few days," she replied. "Thou art wise beyond measure, Flower-Gem," she said gaily.

"Thou art kind to say so, Aphrael, but methinks thy praise hath some small taint of flattery to it."

"Well," she said, "a *little,* perchance, but overfulsome praise for those we love is no sin, is it?"

"Guard well thine heart, Anakha," Bhelliom advised. "The Child-Goddess will steal it from thee when thou dost least expect it."

"She did that years ago, Blue-Rose," Sparhawk replied.

"I can do this myself, Sparhawk," Khalad whispered. "I don't need a chaperon." The two were lying behind a log atop the knoll from which they had observed the Edomish workmen the previous day. The work gangs were laboring by the smoky light of fires being fed with green wood. The moon was full, and the smoke from the fires seemed almost to glow in its pale light.

"I just came along to admire the shot, Khalad," Sparhawk replied innocently. "I like to watch professionals in action. Besides, I have to give Ulath the signal just as soon as you put Incetes to sleep." He shivered. "Aren't we a bit early?" he asked. "The sky won't start to get light for another hour yet. All we're doing here is sprouting icicles."

"Did you want to do this?"

"No. I probably couldn't even come close at this range."

"Then do you want to keep your mouth shut and let me do it?"

"You're awfully grouchy for so young a fellow, Khalad. That doesn't usually set in until a man's much older."

"Dealing with knights has prematurely aged me."

"How does this new sight of yours work?"

"Do you know what the word *trajectory* means?"

"Sort of."

Khalad shook his head wearily. "Never mind, Sparhawk. My calculations are accurate. Just take my word for it."

"You actually work it out on paper?"

"Paper's cheaper than a bushel of new crossbow bolts."

"It sounds to me as if you spend more time calculating and adjusting your sights than you do shooting."

"Yes," Khalad admitted, "but if you do it right, you only have to shoot once."

"Why did we come out so early, then?"

"To give my eyes time to adjust to the light. The light's going to be peculiar when I make the shot. I'll have moonlight, firelight, and the first touches of dawn in the sky when the time comes. It'll all be changing, and I need to watch it change so that my eyes are ready. I've also got to pick Incetes out and keep a close eye on him. Killing his second cousin won't do the job."

"You think of everything, don't you?"

"Somebody has to."

They waited. The pale light of the full moon made the sand of the newly emerged, mile-wide beach intensely white, almost the same as snow, and the night air was bitingly cold.

"Keep your head down, Sparhawk, or hold your breath."

"What?"

"Your breath is steaming. If somebody looks this way, he'll know that we're here."

"They're two hundred and fifty paces away, Khalad."

"Why take chances if you don't have to?" Khalad peered intently at the antlike figures working at the edge of the trees. "Is Empress Elysoun still chasing Berit?" he asked after a few moments.

"She seems to be branching out a bit. I think she caught him a few times, though."

"Good. Berit was awfully stuffy when he was younger. He's in love with your wife, you know."

"Yes. We talked about it some years back."

"It doesn't bother you?"

"No. It's just one of those infatuations young men go through. He doesn't really intend to do anything about it."

"I like Berit. He'll make a good knight—once I grind off the remnants of his nobility. Titles make people a little silly." He pointed. "It's starting to get light off to the east."

Sparhawk glanced out across the icy reaches of the north Tamul Sea. "Yes," he agreed.

Khalad opened the leather pouch he had brought along and took out a length of sausage. "A bite of breakfast, my Lord?" he offered, reaching for his dagger.

"Why not?"

The first faint touches of light along the eastern horizon faded back into darkness as the "false dawn" came and went. No one had ever satisfactorily explained that particular phenomenon to Sparhawk. He had seen it many times during his exile in Rendor. "We've still got about another hour," he told his squire.

Khalad grunted, lay back against the log, and closed his eyes.

"I thought you were here to watch," Sparhawk said. "How can you watch if you're asleep?"

"I'm not sleeping, Sparhawk. I'm just resting my eyes. Since you came along anyway, *you* can watch for a while."

The true dawn began to stain the eastern sky some time later, and Sparhawk touched Khalad's shoulder. "Wake up," he said quietly.

Khalad's eyes opened quickly. "I wasn't asleep."

"Why were you snoring, then?"

"I wasn't. I was just clearing my throat."

"For half an hour?"

Khalad rose up slightly and peered over the top of the log. "Let's wait until the sun hits those people," he suggested. "That bronze breastplate Incetes is wearing should gleam in the sunlight, and a brighter target's easier to hit."

"You're the one doing the shooting."

Khalad looked at the laboring Edomish peasants. "I just had a thought, Sparhawk. They've built a lot of those rafts. Why waste them?"

"What did you have in mind?"

"Even if Bhelliom melts Cyrgon's ice, it's going to take Captain Sorgi a couple of days to ferry all of us around that reef. Why not use these rafts? Sorgi can put a good-sized force on the beach a few miles north of the pier that's probably being constructed on the other side of the wall, and the rest of us can slip around the reef from this side on those rafts, and we can jump the people up there from both sides."

"I thought you didn't like these rafts."

"I can fix them, Sparhawk. All we have to do is take two of them, lay one on top of the other, and we'll have one good one. Cyrgon might have more forces up here on the North Cape than just the Trolls. I think we'll want to put all these rafts well out of his reach, don't you?"

"You're probably right. Let's talk to Vanion about it." Sparhawk looked at the eastern horizon. "The sun's starting to come up."

Khalad rolled over and laid his crossbow across the log. He carefully checked the settings on his sighting mechanism and then settled the stock against his shoulder.

Incetes was standing on a tree stump in the full light of the half-risen sun. He was waving his arms and bellowing incomprehensible exhortations to his exhausted workmen.

"Are we ready?" Khalad asked, laying his cheek against the stock and squinting through the sight.

"*I'm* ready, but *you're* the one who has to shoot."

"No talking. I have to concentrate now." Khalad drew in a deep breath, let part of it out, and then stopped breathing entirely.

Incetes, gleaming golden in the new-risen sun, stood bellowing and waving his arms. The titan from prehistory looked tiny, almost toylike in the distance.

Khalad slowly, deliberately squeezed the release lever.

The crossbow thumped heavily, its rope-thick gut string giving off a deep-toned twang. Sparhawk watched the bolt arc upward.

"Got him," Khalad said with a certain satisfaction.

"The arrow hasn't even reached him yet," Sparhawk objected.

"It will. Incetes is dead. The arrow will go right through his heart. Go ahead and signal Ulath to charge."

"Aren't you being a little—"

A vast cry of chagrin rose from the crowd at the edge of the forest. Incetes was toppling slowly backward, and the bronze-age warriors surrounding him wavered and vanished even as he fell.

"You've got to learn to have a little more faith, Sparhawk," Khalad noted. "When I tell you that somebody's dead, he's dead—even if he doesn't know it yet. Were you planning to signal Ulath—sometime today?"

"Oh. I almost forgot."

"Age does that to people—or so I've been told."

"The ministries are corrupt, Ehlana. I'll be the first to admit that; but if I have to rebuild the government from the ground up, I'll spend the rest of my life at it, and I'll never get anything else done." Sarabian's tone was pensive.

"But Pondia Subat's such an incompetent," Ehlana objected.

"I *want* him to be an incompetent, dear heart. I'm going to reverse the usual roles. *He's* going to be the figurehead, and *I'm* going to be the one pulling the strings. The other ministers are in the habit of obeying him, so having him as prime minister won't even confuse them. I'll write Subat's speeches for him and terrorize him to the point that he won't depart from the prepared text. I'll terrorize him to the point that he won't even change clothes or shave without my permission. That's why I want him to sit in and hear the reports of Milord Stragen's unique solution to our recent problem. I want him to imagine the feel of the knives going in every time he has an independent thought."

"Might I make a suggestion, your Majesty?" Stragen asked.

"By all means, Stragen." Sarabian smiled. "The stunning success of your outrageous scheme has earned you a sizeable balance of imperial indulgence."

Stragen smiled and began to pace the floor, his face deep in thought and his fingers absently weighing a gold coin. Ehlana wondered where he had picked up that habit. "The society of thieves is classless, your Majesty," he pointed out. "We're firm believers in the aristocracy of talent, and talent shows up in some of the strangest places. You might want to consider including some people who aren't Tamuls in your government. Racial purity is all well and good, I suppose, but when every government official of rank in every subject kingdom is a Tamul, it stirs the kind of resentment that Zalasta and his friends have been exploiting. A more ecumenical approach might dampen those resentments. If an ambitious man sees the chance for advancement, he's much less likely to want to throw off the yoke of the Godless yellow devils."

"Are they still calling us that?" Sarabian murmured. He leaned back. "It's an interesting notion, Stragen. First I ruthlessly crush rebellion, and then I invite the rebels into the government. It should confuse them, if nothing else."

Mirtai opened the door to admit Caalador.

"What's afoot?" Ehlana asked him.

"Our friends at the Cynesgan embassy are very busy, your Majesty," he reported. "Evidently our unusual celebration of the Harvest Festival made them nervous. They're bringing in supplies and reinforcing the gates. It looks as if they're expecting trouble and they're getting ready to fort up."

"Let them," Sarabian shrugged. "If they want to imprison themselves, it saves me the trouble of doing it."

"Is Krager still inside?" Ehlana asked.

Caalador nodded. "I saw him walking across the courtyard this morning my very own-self."

"Keep an eye on him, Caalador," she instructed.

"I purely will, dorlin'." He grinned. "I purely will."

Vanion led the charge up the beach. The knights and the Peloi descended upon the demoralized work gangs in a thunderous rush, while Engessa's Atans ran along the water's edge to the foot of the makeshift pier to cut off the escape of those laboring to extend it farther out into the chill waters of the Tamul Sea.

The ribbon clerk Amador was shrieking orders from the pier, but no one was really paying much attention to him. Some few of the workmen who had been cutting trees put up a feeble resistance, but most fled back into the forest. It only took a few minutes for those who had chosen to resist to realize that the decision had been a bad one, and they threw down their weapons and raised their hands in surrender. The knights, trained to be merciful, readily accepted surrenders; Tikume's Peloi did so only reluctantly; the Atans on the pier tended to ignore those who sued for mercy, pausing only long enough to kick them off into the water. With Betuana and Engessa in the lead, the Atans marched ominously out onto the pier, killing anybody who offered any resistance and throwing the rest into the chill water on either side. The men in the water struggled to shore to be rounded up by the Tamul soldiers from the imperial garrison at Matherion. The soldiers' presence was primarily a gesture, since they were ceremonial troops unprepared by either their training or their natural inclinations for fighting. However, they *were* quite good at rounding up the shivering men who emerged, dripping and blue with the cold, from the icy water.

"I'd say that Bhelliom's warm current hasn't arrived yet," Khalad observed.

"It wouldn't seem so," Sparhawk agreed. "Let's go on down. The days are very short now, and I'd like to secure the north pier before the sun goes down."

"If there *is* a north pier," Khalad said.

"There *has* to be one, Khalad."

"You wouldn't mind if I ambled over to the edge of the cliff and had a look for myself, would you? Logic is all well and good, but a little verification never hurt anything."

They walked back down the knoll, mounted, and rode out to join their friends.

"Not much of a fight," Kalten complained, looking disdainfully at the mob of terrified prisoners.

"Those are the best kind," Tynian told him.

"Sorgi's coming," Ulath told them, pointing at the fleet moving toward the beach. "As soon as Betuana and Engessa finish clearing the pier, we'll be able to get started."

The Atans were halfway to the end of the pier by now, and the terrified Edomishmen were being crowded into a tighter and tighter mass by that inexorable advance.

"How cold is that water?" Talen asked. "I mean, has it started to warm up at all?"

"Not noticeably," Ulath said. "I saw a fish swim by earlier wearing a fur coat."

"Do you think a man could swim back to shore from the end of the pier?"

"Anything's possible," Ulath shrugged. "I wouldn't want to wager any money on it, though."

Rebal was at the very end of the pier by now, and his screams were growing increasingly shrill. The Atans leveled their spears and continued their inexorable advance. They did not even bother to kill the Edomishmen anymore. They simply shoved everyone off the pier to struggle in the icy water. A large knot of the workmen at the very end of the pier went off the end in a kind of cluster, the ones at the extreme outer end dragging their fellows with them as they toppled off. The Atans lined the sides and the end of the pier, keeping everyone in the water at spear's length from safety. That went somewhat beyond the bounds of civilized behavior, but Sparhawk knew of no diplomatic way to object to Queen Betuana about it, so he ground his teeth together and let it pass.

There was a great deal of splashing at first, but that did not last for very long. Singly and in groups the freezing peasants gave up and slid under the waves. A few athletic ones struck out for shallow water, but no more than a handful reached that questionable safety.

Amador, Sparhawk noted, was not among the few survivors being rounded up by the Tamul soldiers at the water's edge.

Sorgi's ships were standing at anchor some few yards off the beach by now, and the plans they had all drawn up the night before proceeded smoothly.

There was one thing, however, that their planning had not taken into account. Khalad had ridden to the edge of the cliff to look to the north, and he rode back with a slightly worried frown.

"Well?" Sparhawk asked him.

"There's a pier north of the wall, right enough," Khalad replied, dismounting, "but we've got a problem coming up from the south. Bhelliom's warm current is arriving."

"Why is that a problem?"

"I think Bhelliom got a little carried away. It looks as if the leading edge of that current is boiling."

"So?"

"What do you get when you pour boiling water on ice, Sparhawk?"

"Steam, I suppose."

"Right. Bhelliom's melting the ice out there, right enough, but it's raising a lot of steam in the process. What's another word for steam, my Lord?"

"Please don't do that, Khalad. It's very offensive. Just how big is this fogbank?"

"I couldn't see the end of it, my Lord."

"Thick?"

"You could probably walk on it."

"Could we possibly stay ahead of it?"

Khalad pointed out to sea. "I sort of doubt it, my Lord. I'd say it's already here."

The fog was rolling across the water in a thick grey blanket, its leading edge a solid wall obscuring everything in its path.

Sparhawk started to swear.

"You seem melancholy, my Queen," Alean said when the ladies were alone.

Ehlana sighed. "I don't like being separated from Sparhawk," she said. "There were too many years of that when he was in exile."

"You've loved him for a long time, haven't you, your Majesty?"

"I was born loving Sparhawk. It's really more convenient that way. You don't have to waste time thinking about other possible husbands. You can concentrate all your attention on the one you're going to marry and make sure you've closed all his escape routes."

There was a knock on the door, and Mirtai rose, put her hand on her sword hilt, and went to answer it.

Stragen entered. He was wearing rough clothes.

"What on earth have you been up to, Milord?" Melidere asked him.

"Pushing a wheelbarrow, Baroness." He shrugged. "I'm not sure that it accomplishes all that much to disguise myself this way, but it's good to maintain proper work habits. I've been posing as an employee of the Ministry of Public Works. We've been repairing the street outside the Cynesgan embassy. Caalador and I rolled dice, and he won the right to sit on a rooftop to keep watch. I get to trundle wheelbarrow-loads of cobblestones to the pavers."

"I gather that something's happening at the embassy?" Ehlana guessed.

"Yes, my Queen. Unfortunately, we can't quite figure out what. All the chimneys are spouting smoke that doesn't look like woodsmoke. I think they're burning documents. That's usually a sign of incipient flight."

"Don't they know that they haven't a chance of getting out of town?" Mirtai asked him.

"It appears that they're going to make a try anyway. It's just a guess, but I'd say they're planning something that's going to seriously offend the authorities, and then they're going to make a run for it." He looked at Ehlana. "I think we'd better tighten our security arrangements, your Majesty. All these preparations hint at something serious, and we don't want to be caught off-guard."

"I'll have a talk with Sarabian," Ehlana decided. "It was useful to have that embassy functioning as long as Xanetia was here to eavesdrop. Now that she's off with Sparhawk and the others, the embassy's just an irritation. I think it might be time to send in some Atans to nullify it."

"It's an embassy, your Majesty," Melidere objected. "We can't just go in and round everybody up. That's against all the rules of civilized behavior."

"So?"

"We don't have much choice, Master Cluff," Sorgi said gravely. "When you're out in deep water and this kind of fog comes up, all you can do is put out your sea anchor and hope you don't run aground on some island. You'd never be able to pick your way around the end of that reef with those rafts, and I'd rip the bottoms out of half the ships in the fleet if I tried to slip through the channel between the reef and the ice. We're going to have to wait until this lifts—or thins out, at least."

"And how long will that be?" Sparhawk asked.

"There's no way to tell."

"The air's colder than the water, Sparhawk," Khalad explained. "That's what's causing the fog. I don't think it's going to lift until the air warms up. We won't be ready to leave here until tomorrow anyway. We're going to have to do something to raise those rafts up out of the water a bit before we load men and horses on them. If we try to use them the way they are, we'll be trying to move them half-submerged."

"Why don't you get started on that, Khalad?" Vanion suggested. "Sparhawk and I'll go have a talk with Sephrenia and Aphrael. We might just need a bit of divine intervention here. Coming, Sparhawk?"

The two of them went back on down the beach to the fire Kalten had built for the ladies.

"Well?" Sephrenia asked. She was seated on a driftwood log with her sister in her lap.

"The fog's creating some problems," Vanion replied. "We can't get around the end of the reef until it lifts, and we're a little crowded for time. We'd like to reach Tzada before the Trolls start to march. Any ideas?"

"A few," Aphrael replied, "but I'll need to talk with Bhelliom first. There are certain proprieties and courtesies involved, you understand."

"No," Sparhawk replied. "I don't, really, but I'll take your word for it."

"Oh, *thank* you, Sparhawk!" she said with a certain false ingenuousness. "I think Bhelliom and I should discuss this in private. Open the box and give it to me."

"Whatever you say." He took out the cask and touched it with his ring. "Open," he told it. Then he handed the box to the Child-Goddess.

She slid off Sephrenia's lap and went down the beach a little way. Then she stood looking out at the fog-enveloped sea. So far as Sparhawk could tell, she was not speaking aloud to the sapphire rose.

It was about ten minutes later when she returned and handed the box back to Sparhawk. "It's all taken care of," she told him in an offhand way. "When do you want to leave?"

"Tomorrow morning?" Sparhawk asked Vanion.

Vanion nodded. "That should give Khalad time to modify the rafts, and we can get the knights and their horses on board Sorgi's ships and ready to go by then."

"All right," Aphrael said. "Tomorrow, then. Now why don't you go find Ulath and ask him whose turn it is to do the cooking? I'm absolutely famished."

It was not much of a breeze, and it did not entirely dissipate the fog, but they could at least see where they were going, and the tattered remnants of mist would provide them with some cover after they rounded the tip of the reef.

Khalad had decided that the quickest way to modify the rafts was to simply double them, pulling one raft on top of another so that the added buoyancy would provide a reasonable freeboard. This made the rafts very cumbersome, of course. They were heavy and hard to steer, and so their progress out along the reef was painfully slow.

The skiff leading the way, however, cut through the water ahead of the flotilla and faded into the remnants of the fogbank. Khalad and Berit had announced that they would scout on ahead.

After about an hour, the skiff returned. "We marked the channel," Khalad told them. "That boiling water really cut the ice away, so there'll be plenty of room to get the rafts around the tip of the reef."

"We saw Captain Sorgi's ships go by," Berit reported. "Apparently he didn't entirely trust the sails. This breeze is a little erratic—" He hesitated. "You don't have to tell Aphrael I said that, of course. Anyway, Sorgi's put the knights to work rowing. They'll get to the beach north of the pier quite some time before we make it to shore."

"Are those trees sticking up out of the water going to cause us any problems?" Kalten asked.

"Not if we stick close to the face of the cliff, Sir Kalten," Khalad replied. "The landslides Bhelliom's earthquake set off knocked down all the trees for about a hundred yards out from the wall. The trees farther out will give us some additional cover. When you add them to what's left of the fog, I don't think anybody on shore will see us coming."

"It's working out fairly well, then," Ulath said, grunting as he pushed his twenty-foot-long pole against the sea-bottom, "except for this part, of course."

"We could always swim," Tynian suggested.

"No, that's all right, Tynian," Ulath replied. "I don't mind poling all *that* much."

When they reached the tip of the reef, the flotilla of rafts split up into two separate fleets. Queen Betuana and Engessa took the Atans and made their way along the outer edge of the half-submerged forest toward the pier that thrust out from shore, while Sparhawk and his friends took the Peloi and the knights for whom there had not been room aboard Sorgi's ships along the cliff-face, with Khalad and Berit scouting ahead in the skiff. Since even Sorgi's hundred ships and the large number of rafts were not enough to carry *all* their forces, they had been obliged to leave a sizeable portion of their army on the south beach along with Sephrenia, Talen, Flute, and Xanetia.

"It's shoaling," Ulath said after about half an hour. "I think we're getting closer to shore."

"More of the trees are sticking up out of the water as well," Kalten added. "I'll definitely be glad to get off this raft. It's a nice enough raft, I suppose, but pushing it through the water with a twenty-foot pole is sort of like trying to tip over a house."

The skiff came ghosting back out of the fog. "You'd better start keeping your voices down, my Lords," Khalad said in a hoarse whisper. "We're getting closer." He reached out with one hand to steady the skiff. "We're in luck, though. There used to be a road running parallel to the beach—at least I think it was a road. Anyway, the road or whatever it was gives us an open channel through the trees, and the trees between us and the beach will keep the workmen from seeing us."

"And probably keep us from getting ashore as well," Tynian added.

"No, Sir Tynian," Berit replied. "There was a meadow out there a mile or so from where the cliff is now, and that's where the pier is. All we have to do is follow that road and it'll bring us out almost on top of the work gangs."

"Could you hear them at all?" Vanion asked.

"Oh, yes," Khalad replied, "almost as if they were standing about ten feet away—and you'll start hearing their axes in just a few minutes." He and Berit climbed aboard the raft.

"Could you make out their accents? Were they more of those Edomishmen we came up against on the south pier?"

"No, my Lord. The men up here are Astels. We couldn't see the beach, but I'd guess that the people giving the orders came from Ayachin's army instead of Incetes' people."

"Let's push on, then," Kalten said, hefting his pole. "Figuratively speaking, of course," he added.

"Are we all ready?" Sparhawk asked, looking up and down the line of rafts strung out to either side.

"What is there to get ready for, Sparhawk?" Kalten asked. "If anything, Astellian serfs are going to be even more timid than those Edomish peasants were. Ulath could probably chase them all back into the trees by just standing out here in what's left of the fog blowing on his Ogre-horn."

"All right, then," Sparhawk said. *Aphrael*—he threw the thought out—*are you listening?*

Well, of course I'm listening, Sparhawk.

He decided to try a different approach. He cast his request in formal Styric this time. *An it please thee, Divine Aphrael, I do beseech thine aid.*

Aren't you feeling well? Her tone was suspicious.

I but sought to demonstrate mine unutterable regard and respect for thee, Divine One!

Are you making fun of me?

No, of course not. I just realized that I haven't been all that respectful lately. We're in position now. We're going to start moving the rafts slowly toward shore. As soon as we can make out the people on the beach, Ulath's going to give the signal for the general attack. I'd appreciate a nice strong gust of wind at that point, if it's not too much trouble . . .

Well, I'll think about it.

Will you be able to hear Ulath's horn? Or would you rather have me tell you when we need the wind?

Sparhawk, I can hear a spider walking across the ceiling of a house ten miles away. I'll blow as soon as Ulath does.

That's a novel way to put it.

Get moving, Sparhawk, or you'll run out of daylight.

Yes, ma'am. He looked around at the others. "Let's get started," he told them. "The Divine One is drawing in deep breaths. I think she plans to blow the fog all the way to the pole."

The rafts inched forward, concentrating on staying in a straight line so that none of them emerged from the fog before the others.

They could clearly hear the voices speaking in Elenic from the shore now and the faint lapping of wavelets sloshing over the protruding roots of the trees off to the left.

"Six feet," Kalten reported in a loud whisper as he lifted his pole out of the water. "We can make a mounted charge when it shoals down to four."

"*If* the fog holds out that long," Bevier amended.

They crept on with the water shoaling under their rafts inch by inch as they eased closer to shore.

They heard the sound of a heavy blow and curses spat out in archaic Elenic.

"That's one of Ayachin's men," Khalad whispered.

"Ayachin himself wouldn't be here, would he?" Berit asked.

"Incetes was, so I wouldn't discount the possibility."

"If Ayachin *is* here, I want you two to go looking for Elron," Sparhawk instructed. "We lost Amador, but Xanetia should be able to get the same kind of information out of Elron. Don't let him get away—or get himself killed."

"Three feet!" Kalten announced in a triumphant whisper. "We can charge just as soon as we catch sight of them."

The rafts inched closer, and the voices ahead were much louder now.

"There's something moving," Khalad said, pointing at a dim shape ahead.

"How far?" Sparhawk asked, peering into the white blankness ahead.

"Maybe thirty paces."

Then Sparhawk saw more of the dark outlines in the fog and heard the sound of men slogging through shallow water. "Mount up!" he commanded in a low voice, "and signal the other rafts."

They pulled themselves slowly into their saddles, being careful not to make any noise.

"All right, Ulath," Sparhawk said aloud, "let everybody know that we're starting."

Ulath grinned and lifted the curled Ogre-horn to his lips.

CHAPTER THIRTY

It was more like a gale than a breeze, and it came howling out of nowhere, bending the evergreens and tearing the last of the leaves from birch and aspen. The fog streamed away in the leaf-speckled blast.

The crests of the shallow waves were suddenly whipped to froth, and the water ran against a shoreline that was not sand, nor gravel, nor rock, but grass and half-submerged bushes. There were thousands of men on shore, roughly dressed serfs laboring in a field of tree stumps.

"Heretic Knights!" a man at the edge of the water screamed. He wore crude bits and pieces of ancient armor and he stood gaping at the huge force of mounted men which had appeared quite suddenly out of nowhere as the gale tore the fog away.

Ulath's horn continued its barbaric call, and Tikume's Peloi and the knights plunged off the rafts, their mounts sending great sheets of water out to either side, almost like icy wings.

"What must we do, noble Ayachin?" the crudely armored man shrieked to a lean fellow astride a white horse. The mounted man was more completely armored, although his armor was an archaic blend of steel plate and bronze chain mail.

"Fight!" he roared. "Destroy the heretic invaders! Fight—for Astel and our holy faith!"

Sparhawk sawed Faran's reins around and charged directly at the resurrected Astellian hero, his sword aloft and his shield in front of his body.

Ayachin's helmet had no visor as such, but rather a steel nose-guard protruding down over half his face. There was a quick intelligence in that face and a burning zeal. The eyes, however, were the eyes of a fanatic. He set himself, raised his heavy sword, and spurred his white mount forward to meet Sparhawk's charge.

The two horses crashed together, and the white mount reeled back. Faran was the bigger horse and he was skilled at fighting. He slammed his shoulder into Ayachin's mount and tore great chunks from the white animal's neck with his teeth. Sparhawk caught the ancient hero's sword-stroke with his shield and countered with a heavy overhead stroke of his own, clashing his blade down on the hastily raised and bulky shield.

"Heretic!" Ayachin snarled. "Spawn of Hell! Foul sorcerer!"

"Give it up!" Sparhawk snapped. "You're out of your class!" He found that he had no real wish to kill this man who was fighting to defend his homeland and his faith from a brutal Church policy long since abandoned. Sparhawk had no real quarrel with him.

Ayachin bellowed his defiance and swung his sword again. He showed some proficiency with the weapon, but he was no real match for the black-armored Pandion he faced. Sparhawk caught the sword-stroke with his shield again and struck a chopping blow at his opponent's shoulder. "Run away, Ayachin!" he barked. "I don't want to kill you! You've been duped by an alien God and dragged thousands of years into the future! This isn't your fight! Take your people and go!"

It was too late, though. Sparhawk saw the madness in his opponent's eyes and he had been in too many fights not to recognize it. He sighed, crowded Faran in against the white horse, and began a series of strokes he had used so many times in the past that once it began, the succeeding blows were automatic.

The ancient shade fought bravely, struggling to respond with his unwieldy equipment, but the outcome was inevitable. Sparhawk's progressive strokes bit him deeper and deeper, and chunks of his armor flew from each savage cut.

Then, altering his last stroke to avoid a grotesque maiming, Sparhawk thrust instead of delivering the customary overhand stroke which would have split his opponent's head. His swordpoint crunched through the ancient and ineffective armor and smoothly ran through Ayachin's chest.

The fire went out of that ancient face, and the hero Ayachin stiffened and toppled slowly from his saddle.

Sparhawk raised his sword hilt to his face in a sad salute.

A great cry went up from the Astellian serfs as Ayachin's army vanished. A burly serf at the water's edge bawled contradictory orders, gyrating his arms like a windmill. Berit leaned over in his saddle and brought the flat side of his axblade down on top of the man's head, felling him instantly.

There were a few pockets of ineffective and halfhearted resistance, but the serfs for the most part fled. Queen Betuana and her Atans drove the panicky workers from the pier, and the knights and the Peloi parted ranks to permit them to flee into the forest. Sparhawk rose in his stirrups and looked to the north. The knights from Sorgi's ships were driving the misguided serfs on the far side of the pier back into the trees.

The battle, such as it had been, was over.

The Queen of the Atans came ashore with a look of discontent on her golden face. "It was not much of a fight, Sparhawk-Knight," she accused.

"I'm sorry, your Majesty," he apologized. "I did the best I could with what I had to work with. I'll try to do better next time."

She suddenly grinned at him. "I was teasing you, Sparhawk-Knight. Good planning reduces the need for fighting, and you plan well."

"Your Majesty is kind to say so."

"How long will it take that Cammorian sailor to bring the rest of our army to this side of the wall?"

"The rest of today and most of tomorrow, I'd imagine."

"Can we afford to wait that long? We should go to Tzada before the Troll-beasts start to march."

"I'll talk with Aphrael and Bhelliom, your Majesty," he said. "They'll be able to tell us what the Trolls are doing—and delay them if necessary."

Khalad rode up. "We couldn't find any sign of Elron, Sparhawk," he reported. "We captured a few of those serfs, and they told us that he wasn't here."

"Who was in charge, then?"

"That husky fellow Berit put to sleep with the flat of his ax seems to have been the one giving all the orders."

"Wake him up and see what you can get out of him. Don't twist him too hard, though. If he decides to be stubborn, we'll wait until Xanetia gets here. She can find out everything he knows without hurting him."

"Yes, my Lord." Khalad wheeled his mount and went looking for Berit.

"You have a kindly disposition for a warrior, Sparhawk-Knight," Betuana observed.

"These serfs aren't really our enemies, Betuana-Queen. I'll show you the other side of my nature after we catch Zalasta."

"His name is Torbik," Khalad reported when he joined them in the pavilion they had erected for the ladies. "He was one of Sabre's first followers. I think he's a serf from Baron Kotyk's estate. He wouldn't say so, but I'm fairly sure he knows that Elron is Sabre."

"Does he know why Elron sent *him* rather than coming here himself?" Tynian asked.

"He hasn't a clue—or so he says," Khalad replied. "Anarae Xanetia can look inside his head and find out for sure." He paused. "Excuse me, Anarae," he said to the Delphaeic woman. "We all keep groping for ways to describe what you do when you listen to the thoughts of others. We'd probably be a lot less offensive if you'd tell us the right word for it."

Xanetia, who had arrived with Sephrenia, Talen, and Flute on Sorgi's ship with the first contingent being ferried around the reef, smiled. "I had wondered which of you would be the first to ask," she said. "Methinks I should have known it would be thee, young master, for thine is the most practical mind in all this company. We of the Delphae do refer to this modest gift as 'sharing.' We *share* the thoughts of others, we do not *leech* them, nor do we scoop them like struggling minnows from the dark waters of consciousness."

"Would it offend you, Sir Knights, if I pointed out that it's easier to ask than to grope your way through four languages looking for the right term?" Khalad asked rather innocently.

"Yes," Vanion said, "as a matter of fact it *would* offend us."

"I won't point it out, then, my Lord." Khalad even managed to say it with a straight face. "Anyways, Torbik was here primarily to keep the Astellian serfs from talking with Ayachin's warriors too much. Evidently there's a great potential for confusion in the situation. Elron didn't want the two groups to start comparing notes."

"Does he have any idea at all about where Elron is right now?" Kalten asked.

"He doesn't even know where *he* is right now. Elron just said a few vague things about eastern Astel and let it go at that. Torbik wasn't really the one in charge here—any more than Ayachin was. There was a Styric with them, and *he* was the one who was giving all the orders. He was probably one of the first to run off into the woods when we came ashore."

"Could that have been Djarian?" Bevier asked Sephrenia, "Zalasta's necromancer? *Somebody* plucked Ayachin out of the ninth century."

"It might have been," Sephrenia replied dubiously. "More likely, though, it was one of Djarian's pupils. It's the initial spell that's difficult. Once the people from the past have been successfully raised, a fairly simple spell can bring them back again. I'm sure there was a Styric south of the wall calling up Incetes and *his* men as well. Zalasta and Ogerajin have a large body of renegades to draw upon."

"May I come in?" Captain Sorgi asked from just outside the tent.

"Of course, Captain," Vanion replied.

The silvery-haired seaman came inside. "We'll have the last of your people ashore on this side of the reef by tomorrow noon, my Lords," he reported. "You'll want us to wait here, won't you?"

"Yes," Sparhawk replied. "If all goes well, we'll need to go back around the reef after we've finished at Tzada."

"Will the warm water hold? I'd rather not get icebound up here."

"We'll see to it, Captain," Sparhawk promised.

Sorgi shook his head. "You're a strange man, Master Cluff. You can do things no one I've ever met can do." He suddenly smiled. "But strange or not, you've thrown a lot of profit my way since you started running away from that ugly heiress." He looked at the others. "But I'm just interrupting things here. Do you suppose I might have a word with you in private, Master Cluff?"

"Of course." Sparhawk rose and followed the sailor outside.

"I'll get right to the point," Sorgi said. "Do you have any further plans for these rafts—after you use them to go back around the reef, I mean?"

"No, I don't think so."

"Would it be all right with you if I left a crew on the beach south of the reef while I run you and your friends back to Matherion?"

"I have no objections, Captain, but why?"

"The rafts are made of very good logs, Master Cluff. After your army uses them to get around the reef, they'll just be lying there. It'd be a shame to waste them. I thought I'd leave a crew to lash them together into some kind of boom. I'll come back after I drop you off in Matherion, and we'll tow them to the timber market in Etalon—or maybe even back to Matherion itself. They should fetch a good price."

Sparhawk laughed. "Good old Sorgi," he said, putting a friendly hand on the sea captain's shoulder. "You never overlook a chance for a profit, do you? Take the logs with my blessing."

"You're a generous man, Master Cluff."

"You're my friend, Captain Sorgi, and I like doing things for friends."

"You're my friend as well, Master Cluff. The next time you need a ship, come and look me up. I'll take you anywhere you want to go." Sorgi paused, his expression suddenly cautious. "For only half price," he added.

The village of Tzada had been abandoned several years ago, and the rampaging Trolls had knocked most of the buildings down. It lay at the edge of a vast, marshy meadow with Bhelliom's escarpment looming over it to the south. The sun was just rising far to the southeast, and the grassy meadow was thick with frost that glittered in the slanting sunlight.

"How large is the meadow, your Majesty?" Vanion asked Betuana.

"Two leagues across and six or eight leagues long. It will be a good battlefield."

"We were sort of hoping to avoid that, your Majesty," Vanion reminded her.

Engessa was ordering his scouts out to pinpoint the exact location of the Trolls. "We were able to see them from the top of the escarpment," he told Vanion. "They've been gathering out in the middle of the meadow every day for the past several weeks. They were too far away for us to see exactly what they've been doing, though. The scouts will locate them for us."

"What's the plan, friend Sparhawk?" Kring asked, fingering his saber hilt. "Do we march on them and then turn their Gods loose on them at the last minute?"

"I want to talk with the Troll-Gods first," Aphrael said. "We want to be absolutely certain that they understand all the conditions of their release."

Vanion rubbed at the side of his face. "I think we'll want the Trolls to come to us instead of the other way around, don't you, Sparhawk?"

"Definitely, but a feint of some kind should draw them out." Sparhawk thought a moment. "Why don't we move a mile or so into the meadow so they can see us. Then we'll draw up in a standard formation—knights in the center, Atans on either side, and the Peloi out on the flanks. Cyrgon's got a military mind, and that formation's older than dirt. He'll think we're preparing to attack. The Cyrgai are an aggressive people, and *they* would want to attack first. Cyrgon's commanding Trolls this time instead of his own people, but I think we can count on him to do what's customary."

"He might as well." Ulath shrugged. "The Trolls will attack as soon as they see us no matter *what* Cyrgon wants them to do. The idea of defending themselves won't even occur to them. They look on us as food, and somebody who sits in one place waiting for supper to come to him usually goes to bed hungry."

"Better and better," Vanion said. "We'll hold our formation and let them get to within a few hundred yards of us. Then we'll turn the Troll-Gods loose. They'll reclaim their Trolls, and Cyrgon will be left standing out there in the middle of the meadow all alone."

"Maybe not quite," Sephrenia added. "He might have Zalasta with him. I certainly *hope* so, anyway."

"Savage," Vanion said fondly to her.

"Let's leave the army here and go around to the back side of the village," Sparhawk suggested. "If we're going to talk with the Troll-Gods, I'd rather not do it out in plain sight." He turned Faran and led the others around the ruined village to a smaller clearing a few hundred yards to the east.

Sparhawk had deliberately not closed the box after Bhelliom had transported them to Tzada. This time he *wanted* his enemies to know where he was. "Blue-Rose," he said politely, "canst thou find anything amiss in our plan?"

"It seemeth sound to me, Anakha," the stone replied through Vanion's lips. "It might be prudent, however, to advise the Troll-Gods that Cyrgon may reach back into antiquity for reinforcements once he doth perceive that the Trolls are no longer deceived by his assumèd guise."

"Thou art wise, my friend," Sparhawk replied. "We shall so advise them." He looked at Aphrael. "Don't pick any fights right now," he told her. "Let's try to get along with our allies—at least until the battle's over."

"Trust me," she said.

"Do I have any choice?"

"No, not really. Bring on the Troll-Gods, Sparhawk. Let's get to work. The day won't last forever, you know."

He muttered something under his breath.

"I didn't quite hear that," she said.

"You weren't supposed to." He raised the glowing gem. "Please bring them forth now, my friend," he told it. "The Child-Goddess doth grow impatient."

"I did notice that myself, Anakha."

Then the vast presences of the Troll-Gods were there, glowing blue and towering enormous.

"The time is come," Sparhawk announced in Trollish. "This is the place where Cyrgon has your children. Let us join together to cause hurt to Cyrgon."

"Yes!" Ghworg exulted.

"I will remind you of our compact," Aphrael said. "You have given surety. I will hold you to your promises."

"Well will we keep them, Aphrael." Ghworg's voice was sullen.

"Let us repeat them," she said shrewdly. "Promises made in haste are sometimes forgotten. Your children will no longer eat my children. Is it agreed?"

Ghnomb sobbed his assent.

"Khwaj will restrain his fire and Schlee his ice. Agreed? Ghworg will forbid your children to kill mine, and Zoka will permit no more than two cubs to each she-Troll. Is it agreed?"

"Agreed. Agreed," Ghworg said impatiently. "Free us."

"In a moment. Is it also agreed that your children will become mortal? That they will age and die as do mine?"

They howled in fury. They had evidently been hoping in their dim minds that she had forgotten that promise.

"Agreed?" she bored in with a not-so-veiled threat in her voice.

"Agreed," Schlee said reluctantly.

"Turn them loose, Sparhawk."

"In a minute." Then he spoke to the Troll-Gods directly. "It is our intent to cause hurt to Cyrgon," he told them. "Let him seem to have victory in his mouth before we jerk it from between his teeth. Thus will he suffer more."

"It speaks well," Schlee told the others. "Let us hear its words. Let us find out how the hurt of Cyrgon may be made greater."

Sparhawk quickly outlined their plan of battle. "Thus," he concluded, "when your children are ten tens of strides from Aphrael's children and Cyrgon exults, you can appear and tear your stolen children back from his grasp. In pain and agony may he bring his *own* children from the shadowy past to meet us. I will appeal to the Child-Goddess and ask her to relent this once and let your children feast upon Cyrgon's, and Cyrgon himself will feel their teeth as they rend and tear the flesh of his children."

"Your words are good, Anakha," Schlee agreed. "It is my thought that you are almost worthy to be a Troll."

"I thank you for thinking so," Sparhawk replied a bit dubiously.

The army advanced at a steady trot. The Church Knights, their armor gleaming in the slanting rays of the newly risen sun and the pennons on their lances fluttering, rode forward, the hooves of their half-trained war horses crushing the knee-high grass of the meadow. The unmounted Atans loped along on either side, and Tikume's Peloi, probably the finest light cavalry in the world, ranged out on the flanks. Despite Vanion's violent objections, Sephrenia and Xanetia rode with the knights. Flute, for some obscure reason, rode with Talen this time.

They had trotted perhaps two miles out into the frost-white meadow when Vanion held up his hand to signal a halt. Ulath blew a long, strident blast on his Ogre-horn to pass the word.

Engessa, Betuana, and Kring joined them. "We have more details now," Betuana told them. "Some of our scouts concealed themselves in the high grass to watch the Trolls. Cyrgon is exhorting the man-beasts, and there are several Styrics with him. My people don't know the language of those monsters, so they couldn't understand what Cyrgon was saying."

"It's not too hard to guess," Tynian shrugged. "We've got quite an army here, and we've drawn up in the traditional battle formation. I'm sure Cyrgon thinks we're planning to attack the Trolls. He's preparing them for battle."

"Could your scouts recognize any of the Styrics, Betuana?" Sephrenia asked, her face grim.

The Atan Queen shook her head. "They couldn't get that close," she replied.

"Zalasta is there, Sephrenia," Xanetia said. "I can feel the presence of his mind."

"Can you hear his thoughts, Anarae?" Bevier asked her.

"Not clearly, Sir Knight. He is not yet close enough."

Vanion frowned. "I wish we could get some assurance that this ruse of ours is working," he fretted. "This could turn very ugly if Zalasta's got any ideas at all of what we're planning. Could your scouts get any kind of estimate about how many Trolls are out there, your Majesty?"

"Perhaps fifteen hundred, Vanion-Preceptor," Betuana replied.

"That's almost the whole herd," Ulath observed. "There aren't really very many Trolls." He made a wry face. "There don't really have to be. One Troll's a crowd all by himself in a fight."

"If we *were* planning a battle, would we have enough men?" Tynian asked him.

Ulath wobbled one hand back and forth uncertainly. "It'd be touch and go," he replied. "We've only got about twelve thousand. Attacking fifteen hundred Trolls with so few would be an act of desperation."

"Our ruse is believable, then," Vanion said. "Cyrgon and Zalasta shouldn't have any reason to suspect a trap."

They waited. The horses of the knights were restive and some grew more difficult to control as the minutes ticked by.

Then an Atan woman came running back across the frosty meadow. "They've started to move, Betuana-Queen!" she shouted from about a hundred yards out.

"It worked, then," Talen said gleefully.

"We'll see," Khalad said cautiously. "Let's not start dancing in the streets just yet."

The scout came the rest of the way across the meadow to join them.

"Tell us what you saw," Betuana commanded.

"The man-beasts are coming toward us, Betuana-Queen," the woman replied. "They move singly, some far to the front and others lagging behind."

"Trolls wouldn't understand the concept of fighting as a unit," Ulath told them.

"Who commands them?" Betuana asked.

"Something that is very large and ugly, Betuana-Queen," the scout reported. "The man-beasts around it are taller than any Atan, and they scarcely come as high as its waist. There are Styrics with it as well—eight, by my count."

"Did one of them have silvery hair and beard?" Sephrenia asked intently.

"There are two such. One is thin, and one is fat. The thin one is close by the big ugly thing."

"*That* one is Zalasta," she said in a bleak voice.

"I'll take a promise from you now, Sephrenia," Vanion said firmly.

"You can go whistle for promises, Vanion," she said tartly. She was flexing her fingers in an ominous sort of way.

"You were right, Sparhawk-Knight," Engessa said with a faint smile. "When we reached Sarsos last summer, you said Sephrenia was two hundred feet tall. She *does* seem to grow as one comes to know her better, doesn't she? I don't think I'd care to trade places with Zalasta right now."

"No," Sparhawk agreed. "That wouldn't be a good idea."

"Will you at least agree to *think* just a little before you start grappling with Zalasta?" Vanion pleaded. "For *my* sake? My heart stops when you're in danger."

She smiled at him. "That's very sweet, Vanion, but I'm not the one in danger just now."

Then they heard it. It was a dull, rhythmic thudding of hundreds of feet striking the earth in rhythmic unison, and that thudding was accompanied by a low, brutish grunting. Then the thudding and grunting suddenly broke off, and a shrill, wailing ululation rose, fluctuating and piercing the chill air.

"Kring!" Ulath barked. "Let's go have a look!" And the two galloped out across the frozen meadow.

"What is it?" Vanion asked.

"Very bad news," Kalten replied tensely. "We've heard that noise before. When we were on our way to Zemoch, we came across some creatures Sephrenia called the Dawn-men. They make Trolls look like tame puppies by comparison."

"And the Troll-Gods wouldn't have any authority over them," Sephrenia added. "We might have to retreat."

"Never!" Betuana almost shouted. "I *won't* run away again—not from anything! I've been humiliated too many times already! My Atans and I will die here if necessary!"

Ulath and Kring came riding back, their faces baffled. "They're just ordinary Trolls!" Ulath exclaimed. "But they're stamping and grunting and wailing the same way the Dawn-men did!"

Flute suddenly burst out laughing.

"What's so funny?" Talen demanded.

"Cyrgon," she replied gaily. "I knew he was stupid, but I didn't think he was *this* stupid. He can't tell the difference between Trolls and Dawn-men. He's forcing the Trolls to behave the way their ancestors did, and that won't work with Trolls. All he's doing is confusing them. Let's go out and meet them, Sparhawk. I want to watch Cyrgon's face crumble and fall off the front of his head." Then she drove her little grass-stained feet into the flanks of Talen's horse, obliging the rest of them to follow along behind.

They crested a low hill and reined in. The Trolls were advancing through the tall grass on a broad front, quite nearly a mile across, shuffling, stamping their heels, and grunting in unison. A vast shape that very closely resembled Ghworg, the God of Kill, shambled along in the center of the brutish throng, beating on the frozen ground with a huge iron-bound club.

The monstrous apparition was closely surrounded by a group of white-robed Styrics. Sparhawk could quite clearly see Zalasta at Cyrgon's right.

"Cyrgon!" Aphrael called. Her voice was shatteringly loud. Then she spoke at some length in a language that had only traces of Styric in it and was shaded around the edges with bits and pieces of Elenic and Tamul and a half-dozen other languages as well.

"What tongue is that?" Betuana demanded.

"It is the language of the Gods," Vanion replied, his voice carrying that slightly wooden overtone that always overlaid it when Bhelliom spoke. "The Child-Goddess doth taunt Cyrgon." Vanion seemed to wince slightly. "Thou wert perhaps unwise to expose thy Goddess overmuch to Elenes, Sephrenia," Bhelliom observed. "Her capacity for imprecation and insult seemeth to me inappropriate for one so young."

"Aphrael is hardly young, Blue-Rose," she replied.

A faint smile touched Vanion's lips. "Not to thee, perhaps. Perspective, however, doth color all. To me, thy seemingly ancient Goddess is scarce more than a babe."

"Be nice," Aphrael murmured. Then she continued to rail at the now-enraged Cyrgon.

"Can you hear Zalasta's thoughts now, Anarae?" Kalten asked.

"Clearly, Sir Knight," Xanetia replied.

"Does he have any suspicion at all about what we're going to do?"

"Nay. He doth believe that victory is within his reach."

Aphrael stopped in midcurse. "Let's disabuse him of that right now," she said. "Turn loose the Troll-Gods, Sparhawk."

"An it please thee, Blue-Rose," Sparhawk said politely, "evict thine unwanted tenants now."

"More than gladly, Anakha," Bhelliom replied with great relief.

The Troll-Gods were not surrounded by that azure nimbus this time. They appeared suddenly and in vividly excruciating detail. Sparhawk suppressed a wave of revulsion.

"Go to your children, Ghworg!" Aphrael commanded in Trollish. "It is *your* semblance Cyrgon has stolen, and it is your right to cause hurt to him for that."

Ghworg roared his agreement and charged down the hill with the other Troll-Gods close on his heels.

The counterfeit Ghworg gaped up the hill at the dreadful reality descending upon him. And then he screamed in sudden agony.

"That is Cyrgon, isn't it?" Kalten shouted.

"Does that even happen to Gods?" Talen asked Flute. "Does it hurt you as much as it hurts humans to have one of your spells broken?"

"Even more," she almost purred. "Cyrgon's brains are on fire right now."

The Trolls were also gaping at their suddenly materialized Gods. One huge brute not far from the writhing God of the Cyrgai reached out almost absently, picked up a shrieking Styric, and pulled off his head. Then he tossed the head aside and began to eat the still-convulsing body.

The Troll-Gods roared something in unison, and the Trolls all fell on their faces.

Cyrgon writhed, shrieking, and the seven remaining Styrics collapsed as if they had been cut down. The false shape of Ghworg shuddered away into nothingness, and Cyrgon himself suddenly appeared as an amorphous blob of pale intense light.

Aphrael sneered. "That's Cyrgon for you," she noted. "He claims to be too proud to assume a human form. Personally, I think he's just too clumsy. If he tried, he'd probably put the head on upside down or both arms on the same side." She shrieked a few more triumphant insults.

"*Aphrael!*" Sephrenia actually sounded shocked.

"I've been saving those up," the Child-Goddess apologized. "You weren't really supposed to hear me say them."

Cyrgon's fire was fluctuating wildly now, flaring and dimming as his agony swelled and then diminished.

"What is Zalasta feeling now?" Sephrenia eagerly asked Xanetia.

"His pain doth go beyond mine ability to describe it," the Anarae replied.

"Dear, dear sister!" Sephrenia exulted. "You've made me happier than you could possibly imagine!"

"Are you ever going to be able to tame her again?" Sparhawk asked Vanion.

"It may take awhile." Vanion's tone was troubled.

The writhing, half-formed shape of the flamelike Cyrgon partially rose and waved one huge, fiery arm; and a half mile or so behind the Trolls there suddenly appeared a vast glittering.

"He's called up his Cyrgai!" Khalad shouted. "We'd better do something."

"Ghworg! Schlee!" Vanion roared in Bhelliom's huge voice. "Cyrgon hath summoned his children! Now may *your* children feast!"

The Troll-Gods swelled even more enormous and barked sharp commands to their prostrate worshippers. The Trolls scrambled to their feet, turned, and looked hungrily at the advancing Cyrgai drawn from ages past. Then with a great roar they rushed toward the banquet Cyrgon had so generously provided.

Ehlana was tired. It had been one of those exhausting days with so many things to do that nothing had been really wrapped up before the next intruded itself. She had retired with Mirtai, Alean, and Melidere to prepare for bed. Danae trailed along behind them, dragging Rollo by one hind leg and yawning broadly.

"The emperor was in a peculiar humor this evening," Melidere noted, closing the door behind them.

"Sarabian's nerves are strung a little tight right now," Ehlana said, sitting down at her dressing table. "The future of his whole empire hinges on what Sparhawk and the others are doing in the north, and there's no way he can keep track of what's going on up there."

Danae yawned again and curled up in a chair.

"Where's your cat?" Ehlana asked her.

"She's around somewhere," Danae replied sleepily.

"Check my bed, Mirtai," Ehlana instructed. "I don't like furry little surprises in the middle of the night."

Mirtai patted down the canopied royal bed and then dropped to her knees to look under all the furniture. "No sign of her, Ehlana," she reported.

"You'd better go find her, Danae," the queen said.

"I'm sleepy, Mother," Danae objected.

"The sooner you find your cat, the sooner you can get to bed. Let's catch her *before* she gets out of the castle this time. Go with her, Mirtai. After you two find the cat, put Danae to bed, and then see if you can locate either Stragen or Caalador. One of them's supposed to bring me a report on what's going on at the Cynesgan embassy tonight, and I'd like to get it out of the way before I go to bed. I don't want them banging on my door in the middle of the night."

Mirtai nodded. "Come along, Danae," she said.

The princess sighed. She climbed out of her chair, kissed her mother, and followed the golden giantess out of the room.

Alean began to brush the queen's hair. Ehlana loved to have her hair brushed. There was a kind of sleepy, sensual delight in it that relaxed her tremendously. She was quite vain about her hair. It was thick and heavy and lustrously blonde. Its pale color was astounding to the dark-haired Tamuls, and she knew that all eyes would be on her any time she entered a room.

The three of them talked, the drowsy, intimate talk of ladies preparing for bed.

Then there was a polite tapping at the door.

"Oh, bother," Ehlana said. "See who that is, Melidere."

"Yes, your Majesty." The baroness rose to her feet and crossed the bedroom to the door. She opened it and spoke for a moment with the people outside. "It's four of the Peloi, your Majesty," she said. "They say they have word from the north."

"Bring them in, Melidere." Ehlana turned to face the door.

The man who came through the door wore typical Peloi clothing, tight-fitting and mostly leather, with a saber at his waist. His head was shaved, as were the heads of all Peloi men, but this fellow's face was slightly tanned, whereas his scalp was as pale as the belly of a fish. Something was wrong here.

The man behind the first wore a carefully trimmed black beard. His face was very pale, and it looked somehow familiar.

The last two also wore Peloi garb and had shaved their heads, but they were definitely *not* Peloi. The first was Elron, the juvenile Astellian poet, and the second, pouchy-eyed and slightly tipsy, was Krager. "Ah," he said in his drink-slurred voice, "so good to see you again, your Majesty."

"How did you get in here, Krager?" she demanded.

"Nothing easier, Ehlana." He smirked. "You should have kept a few of Sparhawk's knights to stand watch. Church Knights are more observant than Tamul soldiers. We dressed as Peloi, shaved our heads, and no one gave us a second glance. Elron here covered his face with his cloak when the baroness answered the door— just as a precaution—but otherwise it was almost too easy. You *have* met Elron before, haven't you?"

"I vaguely remember him, don't you, Melidere?"

"Why, yes, I believe so, your Majesty," the blonde girl replied. "Wasn't he that literary incompetent we met back in Astel?"

Elron's face went suddenly white with outrage.

"I'm not an expert in poetry, Ladies." Krager shrugged. "Elron tells me that he's a poet, so I take him at his word. May I present Baron Parok?" He indicated the first man who had entered the room.

Parok bowed floridly. His face was marked with the purplish broken veins of a heavy drinker, and his eyes were pouchy and dissipated-looking.

Ehlana ignored him. "You're not going to get out of here alive, Krager. You know that, don't you?"

"I *always* get out alive, Ehlana." He smirked. "My preparations are very thorough. Now I'd like to have you meet our leader. This is Scarpa." He gestured at the bearded man. "I'm sure you've heard of him, and he's been absolutely *dying* to make your acquaintance."

"He doesn't look at all that dead to me—yet," she noted. "Why don't you call the guards to remedy that, Melidere?"

Scarpa blocked the baroness. "This bravado is quite out of place," he said to Ehlana coldly in a voice loaded with contempt. "You give yourself too many airs. All the genuflecting and *your Majesty*s seem to have gone to your head and made you forget that you're still only a woman."

"I don't think I need instruction in proper behavior from the bastard son of a whore!" she retorted.

Scarpa's face flickered a brief annoyance. "We're wasting time," he said. His voice was deep and rich, the voice of a performer, and his manner and gestures were studied. He had obviously spent a great deal of time in the public eye. "We have many leagues to cover before dawn."

"I'm not going anyplace," she declared.

"You'll go where I tell you to go," he said, "and I'll teach you your place as we go along."

"What do you hope to gain from this?" Melidere demanded.

"Empire and victory." Scarpa shrugged. "We're taking the Queen of Elenia hostage. Her husband is so stupid that he forgets that the world is full of women—one very much like another. He's so foolishly attached to her that he'll give us anything for her safe return."

"Are you such an idiot that you actually believe that my husband will trade Bhelliom for me?" Ehlana said scornfully. "Sparhawk is Anakha, you fool, and he has Bhelliom in his fist. That makes him a God. He killed Azash, he'll kill Cyrgon, and he'll *definitely* kill you. Pray that he does it quickly, Scarpa. He has it in his power to make your dying last for a million years if he chooses."

"I do not pray, woman. Only weaklings put any faith in Gods."

"I think you underestimate Sparhawk's devotion to you, Ehlana," Krager said. "He'll give anything to gain your safe return."

"He won't have to," Ehlana snapped. "I'll deal with the four of you myself. Do you really think you can get out of here when one word from me will bring half the garrison running?"

"You won't give that word, however." Scarpa sneered. "You're just a little too arrogant, woman. I think you need to know the full reality of your situation." He turned and pointed at Baroness Melidere. "Kill that one," he commanded Elron.

"But—" the pasty-faced literary poseur began to object.

"Kill her!" Scarpa snapped. "If you don't, I'll kill *you*!"

Elron tremblingly drew his rapier and advanced on the defiant baroness.

"It's not a knitting needle, you clot," Melidere told him. "You can't even hold it right. Stick to butchering language, Elron. You don't have the skill—or the stomach—to move up to people yet, although your so-called poetry's bad enough to make people *want* to die."

"How dare you?" he almost screamed, his face turning purple.

"How's your 'Ode to Blue' coming, Elron?" she taunted him. "You could make a fortune peddling that one as an emetic, you know. I felt the urge to vomit before you'd finished reciting the first stanza."

He howled in absolute rage and made a clumsy thrust with his rapier.

Ehlana had watched Stragen training Sarabian often enough to know that the thrust was off the mark. The intrepid baroness coolly deflected the blade with the wrist of the hand she seemed to be raising in a futilely defensive gesture, and Elron's blade passed smoothly through her shoulder.

Melidere gasped, clutching at the blade to conceal the exact location of the wound. Then she lurched back to pull herself free and clawed at the wound, spreading the blood spurting from it over the bodice of her nightdress. Then she fell.

"You murderer!" Ehlana shrieked, rushing to her fallen friend. She hurled herself across Melidere's inert body, weeping and crying out in apparent anguish. "Are you all right?" she muttered under her breath between sobs.

"It's only a scratch," Melidere lied, also in a whisper.

"Tell Sparhawk that I'm all right," the queen instructed, tugging off her ring and concealing it in Melidere's bodice, "and I forbid him to give up Bhelliom, no matter what they threaten to do to me." She rose to her feet, her face tear-streaked. "You'll hang for this, Elron," she said in a deadly voice, "or maybe I'll have you burned at the stake instead—with a slow fire." She pulled a blanket from the bed and quickly covered Melidere with it to prevent too close an examination.

"We will leave now," Scarpa said coldly. "That other one is also your friend, I believe." He pointed at the ashen-faced Alean. "We'll take her along, and if you make any outcry at all, I'll personally slit her throat."

"You're forgetting the message, Lord Scarpa," Krager said, pulling a folded piece of paper from the inside of his leather Peloi jacket. "We *have* to leave a friendly little note for Sparhawk—just to let him know that we stopped by to call." Then he drew a small knife. "Your pardon, Queen Ehlana"—he smirked, exhaling the sharp, acrid reek of his wine-sodden breath into her face—"but I need a bit of authentication to prove to Sparhawk that we're really holding you captive." He took hold of a lock of Ehlana's hair and roughly sawed it off with his knife. "We'll just leave this with our note so that he can compare it with later ones to verify that it's really yours." His grin grew even more vicious. "If you should feel a sudden urge to cry out, Ehlana, just remember that all we *really* need is your head. We can harvest hair from that, so we won't need to bring the rest of you along if you start being *too* much bother."

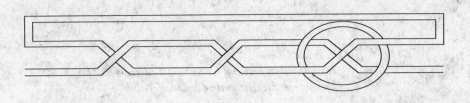

THE
HIDDEN CITY

For Dr. Bruce Gray—
    For his enthusiasm and his technical advice—and for
    keeping our favorite author (and wife) alive—

and for Nancy Gray, R.N.,
    who takes care of everybody else,
    and neglects to take care of herself.

            Shape up, Nancy.

Professor Itagne of the Foreign Affairs Department of the University of Matherion sat on the platform reviewing his notes. It was early in the evening of a fine spring day, and the windows of the auditorium where the faculty of the College of Political Science had gathered were open to admit the smell of flowers and grass and the faintly distracting sound of birdsong.

Professor Emeritus Gintana of the International Trade Department stood at the lectern droning on interminably about twenty-seventh-century tariff regulations. Gintana was a wispy, white-haired, and slightly vague academic customarily referred to as "that dear old man." Itagne was not really listening to him.

This was not going to go well, he concluded wryly, crumpling up and discarding yet another sheet of notes. Word of his subject had been broadcast across the campus, and academics from as far away as Applied Mathematics and Contemporary Alchemy packed the hall, their eyes bright with anticipation. The entire faculty of the Contemporary History Department filled the front rows, their black academic robes making them look like a flock of crows. Contemporary History was here in force to ensure all the fireworks anyone could hope for.

Itagne idly considered a feigned collapse. How in the name of God—any God—was he going to get through the next hour without making a total ass of himself? He had all the facts, of course, but what rational man would *believe* the facts? A straightforward account of what had really happened during the recent turmoil would sound like the ravings of a lunatic. If he stuck to straight truth, the hacks from Contemporary History would not have to say a word. He could destroy his own reputation with no help from them at all.

Itagne took one more brief glance at his carefully prepared notes. Then he bleakly folded them and thrust them back into the voluminous sleeve of his academic robe. What was going to happen here tonight would more closely resemble a tavern brawl than reasoned discourse. Contemporary History had obviously showed up to shout him down. Itagne squared his shoulders. Well, if they wanted a fight, he'd give them one.

A breeze had come up. The curtains at the tall windows rustled and billowed, and the golden tongues of flame flickering in the oil lamps wavered and danced. It was a beautiful spring evening—everywhere but inside this auditorium.

There was a polite spattering of applause, and old Professor Gintana, flustered and confused by this acknowledgment of his existence, bowed awkwardly, clutched his notes in both hands, and tottered back to his seat. Then the dean of the College of Political Science rose to announce the evening's main event. "Colleagues," he began, "before Professor Itagne favors us with his remarks, I would like to take this opportunity to introduce some visitors of note. I'm sure you will all join with me in welcoming Patriarch Emban, First Secretary of the Church of Chyrellos; Sir Bevier, the Cyrinic Knight from Arcium; and Sir Ulath of the Genidian Order located in Thalesia."

There was more polite applause as a pale, gawky student ushered the Elene visitors onto the stage and Itagne hurried across the platform to greet his friends. "Thank God you're here," he said fervently. "The whole Contemporary History Department's turned out—except for the few who are probably outside boiling the tar and bringing up bags of feathers."

"You didn't think your brother was going to hang you out to dry, did you, Itagne?" Emban smiled, settling onto a bench beneath the window. "He thought you might get lonesome here, so he sent us to keep you company."

Itagne felt better as he returned to his seat. If nothing else, Bevier and Ulath could head off any *physical* attacks.

"And now, colleagues and distinguished guests," the dean continued, "Professor Itagne of the Foreign Affairs Department will respond to a recent paper published by the Department of Contemporary History under the title, 'The Cyrga Affair: An Examination of the Recent Crisis.' Professor Itagne."

Itagne rose, strode purposefully to the lectern, and assumed his most offensively civilized expression. "Dean Altus, distinguished colleagues, faculty wives, honored guests . . ." He paused. "Did I leave anybody out?"

There was a titter of nervous laughter. Tension was high in the hall.

"I'm particularly pleased to see so many of our colleagues from Contemporary History here with us this evening," Itagne continued, throwing the first punch. "Since I'll be discussing something near and dear to their hearts, it's much better that they're present to hear what I say with their own ears rather than being forced to rely on garbled secondhand accounts." He smiled benignly down at the scowling hacks in the front row. "Can you hear me, gentlemen?" he asked. "Am I going too fast for any of you?"

"This is outrageous!" a portly, sweating professor protested loudly.

"It's going to get worse, Quinsal," Itagne told him. "If the truth bothers you, you'd better leave now." He looked out over the assemblage. "It's been said that the quest for truth is the noblest occupation of man, but there be dragons lurking in the dark forests of ignorance. And the names of these dragons are 'Incompetence' and

'Political Bias' and 'Deliberate Distortion' and 'Sheer, Wrongheaded Stupidity.' Our gallant friends here in Contemporary History bravely sallied forth to do battle with these dragons in their recently published 'Cyrga Affair.' It is with the deepest regret that I must inform you that the dragons won."

There was more laughter, and dark scowls from the front row.

"It's never been any secret at this institution that the Contemporary History Department is a political entity rather than an academic one," Itagne continued. "It has been sponsored from its very inception by the prime minister, and its only reasons for existence have been to gloss over his blunders and to conceal as best they might his absolute incompetence. To be sure, Prime Minister Subat and his accomplice, Interior Minister Kolata, have never been interested in honesty, but *please*, gentlemen, this is a university. Shouldn't we at least *pretend* to be telling the truth?"

"Rubbish!" a burly academic in the front row bellowed.

"Yes," Itagne replied, holding up a yellow-bound copy of "The Cyrga Affair," "but if you knew it was rubbish, Professor Pessalt, why did you publish it?"

The laughter in the hall was even louder this time, and it drowned out Pessalt's spluttered attempt to answer.

"Let us push on with this great work that we are in," Itagne suggested. "We all know Pondia Subat for a scheming incompetent, but the thing that baffles me about your 'Cyrga Affair' is its consistent attempt to elevate the Styric renegade Zalasta to near sainthood. How in the name of God could *anyone*—even someone as severely limited as the prime minister—revere this scoundrel?"

"How *dare* you speak so of the greatest man of this century?" one of the hacks screamed at him.

"If Zalasta's the best this century can manage, colleague, I think we're in deep trouble. But we digress. The crisis which Contemporary History chooses to call 'The Cyrga Affair' has been brewing for several years."

"Yes," someone shouted with heavy sarcasm, "we noticed that!"

"I'm so happy for you," Itagne murmured, drawing another loud laugh from the audience. "To whom did our idiot prime minister turn for aid? To Zalasta, of course. And what was Zalasta's answer to the crisis? He urged us to send for the Pandion Knight, Prince Sparhawk of Elenia. Why would the name of an Elene nobleman leap to Zalasta's lips in answer to the question—almost before it was asked—*particularly* in view of the sorry record of the Elenes in their relations with the Styrics? To be sure, Prince Sparhawk's exploits are legendary, but what was it about the man that made Zalasta pine for his company? And why was it that Zalasta neglected to tell us that Sparhawk is Anakha, the instrument of the Bhelliom? Did the fact somehow slip his mind? Did he think that the spirit which creates whole universes was somehow irrelevant? I find no mention at all about Bhelliom in this recently published heap of bird droppings. Did you omit the most momentous event of the past eon deliberately? Were you so caught up in trying to give your adored Pondia Subat credit for policy decisions he had no part in that you decided not to mention Bhelliom at all?"

"Balderdash!" a deep voice roared.

"I'm pleased to meet you, Professor Balderdash. My name's Itagne. It was good of you to introduce yourself. Thanks awfully, old boy."

The laughter was tumultuous this time.

"Fast on his feet, isn't he?" Itagne heard Ulath murmur to Bevier.

Itagne looked up. "Colleagues," he said, "I submit that it was *not* Prince Sparhawk that Zalasta so yearned for, but the Bhelliom. Bhelliom is the source of ultimate power, and Zalasta has been trying to get his hands on it for three centuries—for reasons too disgusting to mention. He has been willing to go to any lengths. He has betrayed his faith, his people, and his personal integrity—such as it was—to gain what the Trolls call 'the flower-gem.' "

"That tears it!" the corpulent Quinsal declared, rising to his feet. "This man is mad! Now he's talking about Trolls! This is an academic affair, Itagne, not the children's hour. You've picked the wrong forum for fairy tales and ghost stories."

"Why don't you let me do this, Itagne?" Ulath said, rising to his feet and coming to the podium. "I can settle this question in just a moment or two."

"Feel free," Itagne said gratefully.

Ulath set one huge hand on each side of the lectern. "Professor Itagne has requested me to brief you gentlemen on a few matters," he said. "I take it that you're having some difficulties with the notion of Trolls."

"None at all, Sir Knight," Quinsal retorted. "Trolls are an Elene myth and nothing else. There's no difficulty in that at all."

"What an amazing thing. I spent five years compiling a Trollish grammar. Are you saying that I was wasting my time?"

"I think you're as mad as Itagne is."

"Then you probably shouldn't irritate me, should you? Particularly in view of the fact that I'm so much bigger than you are." Ulath squinted at the ceiling. "Logic tells us that no one can prove a negative. Are you sure you wouldn't like to amend your statement?"

"No, Sir Ulath. I'll stand by what I just said. There's no such thing as a Troll."

"Did you hear that, Bhlokw?" Ulath raised his voice slightly. "This fellow says that you don't exist."

There was a hideous roar in the corridor outside the auditorium, and the double doors at the rear splintered and crashed inward.

"Stay calm!" Bevier hissed as Itagne jumped. "It's an illusion. Ulath's amusing himself."

"Would you like to turn around and tell me what you see at the back of the hall, Quinsal?" Ulath asked. "Exactly what would you call my friend Bhlokw there?"

The creature hulking in the doorway was huge, and its bestial face was contorted with rage. It stretched its paws forth hungrily. "Who has said this, U-lat?" it demanded in a hideous voice. "I will cause hurt to it! I will rip it to pieces and eat it!"

"Can that Troll actually speak Tamul?" Itagne whispered.

"Of course not." Bevier smiled. "Ulath's getting carried away."

The hideous apparition in the doorway bellowed a horribly graphic description of its plans for the faculty of the Contemporary History Department. "Were there any other questions about Trolls?" Ulath asked mildly, but none of the assembled academics heard him over all the shouts, screams, and the tipping over of chairs.

It took the better part of a quarter of an hour to restore order once Ulath had dismissed his illusion; and when Itagne reapproached the lectern, the entire audience was huddled closely together near the front of the auditorium. "I'm touched by your eagerness to hear my every word, gentlemen—" Itagne smiled. "—but I can speak loudly enough to be heard at the back of the hall, so you needn't draw so close. I trust that the visit of Sir Ulath's friend has cleared up the little misunderstanding about Trolls?" He looked at Quinsal, who was still cowering on the floor, gibbering in terror. "Splendid," Itagne said. "Briefly then, Prince Sparhawk came to Tamuli. Elenes are sometimes a devious people, so Sparhawk's wife, Queen Ehlana, proposed a state visit to Matherion and concealed her husband and his friends in her entourage. Upon their arrival, they almost immediately uncovered some facts which we had somehow overlooked. First, Emperor Sarabian actually has a mind; and second, the government led by Pondia Subat was in league with our enemies."

"Treason!" a thin, balding professor shrieked, leaping to his feet.

"Really, Dalash?" Itagne asked. "Against whom?"

"Why—uh—" Dalash floundered.

"You still don't understand, do you, gentlemen?" Itagne asked the faculty of Contemporary History. "The previous government has been overthrown—by the emperor himself. Tamuli is now an Elene-style monarchy, and Emperor Sarabian rules by decree. The previous government—and its prime minister—are no longer relevant."

"The prime minister cannot be removed from office!" Dalash screamed. "He holds his position for life!"

"Even if that were true, it suggests a rather simple solution to the problem, doesn't it?"

"You wouldn't *dare*!"

"Not me, old boy. That's the emperor's decision. Don't cross him, gentlemen. If you do, he'll decorate the city gates with your heads. But let's press on here; I'd like to cover a bit more ground before our customary recess. It was the aborted coup attempt that finally brought things to a head. Pondia Subat was a party to the entire conspiracy and he fully intended to stand around wringing his hands while the drunken mob murdered all of his political enemies, evidently including the emperor himself. If Professor Dalash wants to scream 'treason' he might take a look at that. We discovered much in the aftermath of that failed coup, not only concerning the treason of the prime minister, but of the minister of the interior as well. Most important, however, was the discovery that it had been *Zalasta* who had engineered the entire plot, *and* that he was secretly allied with Ekatas, High Priest of Cyrgon, the God of the supposedly extinct Cyrgai.

"At this point Prince Sparhawk had no choice but to retrieve Bhelliom from its hiding place and to send to Chyrellos for reinforcements. He enlisted other allies as well, not the least of which were the Delphae—who *do* in fact exist in all their glowing horror."

"This is absurd!" Contemporary History's reigning bullyboy, the crude and muscular Professor Pessalt, sneered. "Are we supposed to believe this nonsense?"

"You've already seen a Troll this evening, Pessalt," Itagne reminded him. "Would you like a personal visitation by a Shining One as well? I can arrange it, if you'd like—but outside, please. We'd never get rid of the stink if you were dissolved into a puddle of slime right here in front of the platform."

Dean Altus cleared his throat meaningfully.

"Yes, sir," Itagne assured him. "I'll just be a few more minutes." He turned back to the audience. "Now then," he continued quickly, "since the subject of the Trolls has come up again, we might as well clear it away once and for all. As you've noticed, the Trolls are real. They were lured to Tamuli from their home range in northern Thalesia by Cyrgon, who posed as one of their Gods. The *real* Troll-Gods have been imprisoned for eons, and Prince Sparhawk offered them an exchange—their freedom in return for their aid. He then led a sizable force to northern Atan, where the misguided Trolls had been stirring up turmoil in hopes of forcing the Atans to return to defend their homeland—which would have left us effectively defenseless, since the Atans comprise the bulk of our army. Sparhawk's move *seemed* to play right into the hands of our enemies, but when Cyrgon and Zalasta unleashed the Trolls, Sparhawk called forth their Gods to reclaim them. In desperation, Cyrgon reached back in time and produced a huge army of his Cyrgai—and the Trolls, true to their nature, ate them."

"You don't really expect us to swallow this, do you, Itagne?" Professor Sarafawn, chairman of the Department of Contemporary History and brother-in-law of the prime minister, demanded scornfully.

"Was that supposed to be a pun, Sarafawn?" Itagne asked. "No matter. The short answer is that you might as well," Itagne told him. "Your wife's brother isn't dictating official history anymore. From now on, the emperor wants us to give our students the plain, unvarnished truth. I'll be publishing a factual account in the next month or so. You'd better reserve a copy, Sarafawn, because you're going to be required to teach it to all your students in the future—assuming that you have a future at this institution. Next year's budget's going to be a little tight, I understand, so a number of departments will probably have to be dropped." He paused. "Are you any good with tools, Sarafawn? There's a very nice little vocational school at Jura, I hear. You'd just *love* Daconia."

The dean cleared his throat again, a bit more urgently this time.

"Sorry, Dean Altus," Itagne apologized. "I'm running past time, gentlemen, so I'll just briefly sum up one more development. Despite their crushing defeat, Cyrgon and Zalasta were by no means powerless. In a bold stroke, Zalasta's natural son, one Scarpa, crept into the imperial compound and abducted Queen Ehlana, leaving behind a demand that Sparhawk give up the Bhelliom in exchange for the safe return of his wife.

"Following the recess Dean Altus has been so patiently awaiting, I will take up Prince Sparhawk's reaction to *that* development."

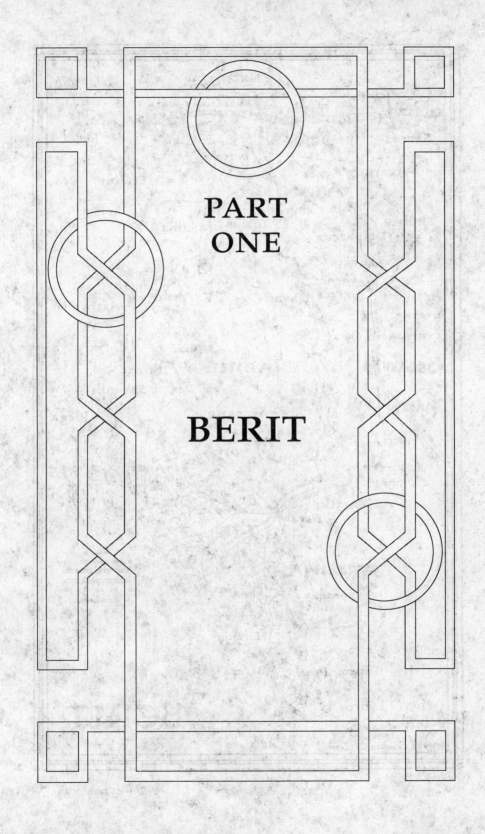

PART
ONE

BERIT

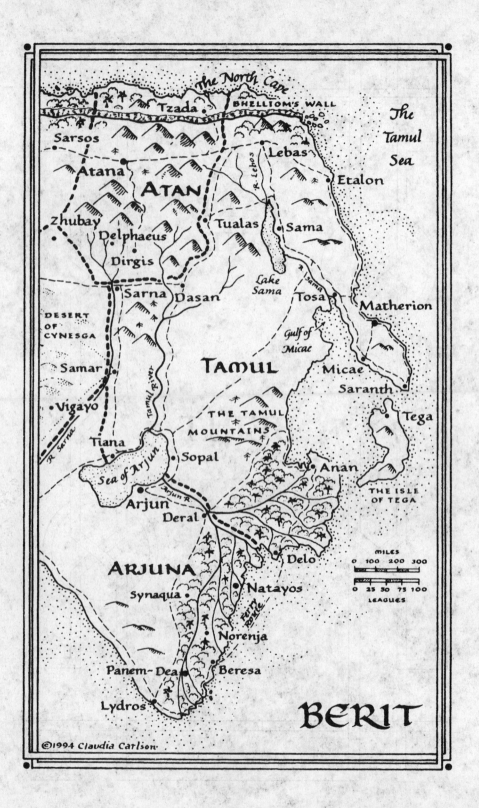

CHAPTER ONE

A chill haze was rising from the meadow, and thin clouds had drifted in from the west to obscure the cold, brittle sky. There were no shadows, and the frozen ground was iron-hard and unyielding. Winter was inexorably tightening its grip on the North Cape.

Sparhawk's army, girt in steel and leather and thousands strong, was lined up along a broad front in the frost-covered grass of the meadow near the ruins of Tzada. Sir Berit sat his horse in the center of the bulky, armored Church Knights watching the ghastly feast taking place a few hundred yards to the front. Berit was a young and idealistic knight, and he was having some difficulty with the behavior of their new allies.

The screams were remote, mere rumors of agony, and those who were screaming were not actually people—not really. They were no more than shades, the scarce-remembered reflections of long-dead men. Besides, they were enemies—members of a cruel and savage race that worshipped an unspeakable God.

But they steamed. That was the part of the horror Sir Berit could not shrug off. Though he told himself that these Cyrgai were dead—phantoms raised by Cyrgon's magic—the fact that steam rose from their eviscerated bodies as the ravening Trolls fed on them brought all of Berit's defenses crashing down around his ears.

"Trouble?" Sparhawk asked sympathetically. Sparhawk's black armor was frost-touched, and his battered face was bleak.

Berit felt a sudden embarrassment. "It's nothing, Sir Sparhawk," he lied quickly. "It's just—" He groped for a word.

"I know. I'm stumbling over that part myself. The Trolls aren't being deliberately cruel, you know. To them we're just food. They're only following their nature."

"That's part of the problem, Sparhawk. The notion of being eaten makes my blood run cold."

"Would it help if I said, 'Better them than us'?"

"Not very much." Berit laughed weakly. "Maybe I'm not cut out for this kind of work. Everybody else seems to be taking it in stride."

"*Nobody's* taking it in stride, Berit. We all feel the same way about what's happening. Try to hold on. We've met these armies out of the past before. As soon as the Trolls kill the Cyrgai generals, the rest should vanish, and that'll put an end to it." Sparhawk frowned. "Let's go find Ulath," he suggested. "I just thought of something, and I want to ask him about it."

"All right," Berit agreed quickly. The two black-armored Pandions turned their horses and rode through the frosty grass along the front of the massed army.

They found Ulath, Tynian, and Bevier a hundred yards or so down the line. "I've got a question for you, Ulath," Sparhawk said as he reined Faran in.

"For *me*? Oh, Sparhawk, you shouldn't have!" Ulath removed his conical helmet and absently polished the glossy black Ogre-horns on the sleeve of his green surcoat. "What's the problem?"

"Every time we've come up against these antiques before, the dead all shriveled up after we killed the leaders. How are the Trolls going to react to that?"

"How should I know?"

"You're supposed to be the expert on Trolls."

"Be reasonable, Sparhawk. It's never happened before. Nobody can predict what's going to happen in a totally new situation."

"Make a guess," Sparhawk snapped irritably.

The two of them glared at each other.

"Why badger Ulath about it, Sparhawk?" Bevier suggested gently. "Why not just warn the Troll-Gods that it's going to happen, and let *them* deal with the problem?"

Sparhawk rubbed reflectively at the side of his face, his hand making a kind of sandy sound on his unshaven cheek. "Sorry, Ulath," he apologized. "The noise from the banquet hall out there's distracting me."

"I know just how you feel," Ulath replied wryly. "I'm glad you brought it up, though. The Trolls won't be satisfied with dried rations when there's all this fresh meat no more than a quarter-mile away." He put his Ogre-horned helmet back on. "The Troll-Gods will honor their commitment to Aphrael, but I think we'd better warn them about this. I definitely want them to have a firm grip on their Trolls when supper turns stale. I'd hate to end up being the dessert course."

"*Ehlana?*" Sephrenia gasped.

"Keep your voice down!" Aphrael muttered. She looked around. They were some distance to the rear of the army, but they were not alone. She reached out and touched Ch'iel's bowed white neck, and Sephrenia's palfrey obediently ambled off a little way from Kalten and Xanetia to crop at the frozen grass. "I can't get too many details," the Child-Goddess said. "Melidere's been badly hurt, and Mirtai's so enraged that they've had to chain her up."

"Who did it?"

"I don't *know,* Sephrenia! Nobody's talking to Danae. All I can get is the word *hostage.* Somebody's managed to get into the castle, seize Ehlana and Alean, and spirit them out. Sarabian's beside himself. He's flooded the halls with guards, so Danae can't get out of her room to find out what's really happening."

"We must tell Sparhawk!"

"Absolutely not! Sparhawk bursts into flames when Ehlana's in danger. He's got to get his army safely back to Matherion before we can let him catch on fire."

"But—"

"No, Sephrenia. He'll find out soon enough, but let's get everyone to safety before he does. We've only got a week or so left until the sun goes down permanently and everything—and everyone—up here turns to solid ice."

"You're probably right," Sephrenia conceded. She thought a moment, staring off at the frost-silvered forest beyond the meadow. "That word *hostage* explains everything, I think. Is there any way you can pinpoint your mother's exact location?"

Aphrael shook her head. "Not without putting her in danger. If I start moving around and poking my nose into things, Cyrgon will feel me nudging at the edges of his scheme, and he might do something to Mother before he stops to think. Our main concern right now is keeping Sparhawk from going crazy when he finds out what's happened." She suddenly gasped and her dark eyes went very wide.

"What is it?" Sephrenia asked in alarm. "What's happening?"

"I don't *know!*" Aphrael cried. "It's something monstrous!" She cast her eyes about wildly for a moment and then steadied herself, her pale brow furrowing in concentration. Then her eyes narrowed in anger. "Somebody's using one of the forbidden spells, Sephrenia," she said in a voice that was as hard as the frozen ground.

"Are you sure?"

"Absolutely. The very air stinks of it."

Djarian the necromancer was a cadaverous-looking Styric with sunken eyes, a thin, almost skeletal frame, and a stale, mildewed odor about him. Like the other Styric captives, he was in chains and under the close watch of Church Knights well versed in countering Styric spells.

A cold, oppressive twilight was settling over the encampment near the ruins of Tzada when Sparhawk and the others finally got around to questioning the prisoners. The Troll-Gods had taken their creatures firmly in hand when the feeding orgy had come suddenly to an end, and the Trolls were now gathered around a huge bonfire several miles out in the meadow, holding what appeared to be religious observances of some sort.

"Just go through the motions, Bevier," Sparhawk quietly advised the olive-skinned Cyrinic Knight as Djarian was dragged before them. "Keep asking him irrelevant questions until Xanetia signals that she's picked him clean."

Bevier nodded. "I can drag it out for as long as you want, Sparhawk. Let's get started."

Sir Bevier's gleaming white surcoat, made ruddy by the flickering firelight, gave him a decidedly ecclesiastical appearance, and he prefaced his interrogation with a lengthy prayer. Then he got down to business.

Djarian replied to the questions tersely in a hollow voice that seemed almost to come echoing up out of a vault. Bevier appeared to take no note of the prisoner's sullen behavior. His whole manner seemed excessively correct, even fussy, and he heightened that impression by wearing fingerless wool gloves such as scribes and scholars wear in cold weather. He doubled back frequently, rephrasing questions he had previously asked and then triumphantly pointing out inconsistencies in the prisoner's replies.

The one exception to Djarian's terse brevity was a sudden outburst of vituperation, a lengthy denunciation of Zalasta—and Cyrgon—for abandoning him here on this inhospitable field.

"Bevier sounds exactly like a lawyer," Kalten muttered quietly to Sparhawk. "I *hate* lawyers."

"He's doing it on purpose," Sparhawk replied. "Lawyers like to spring trick questions on people, and Djarian knows it. Bevier's forcing him to think very hard about the things he's supposed to conceal, and that's all Xanetia really needs. We always seem to underestimate Bevier."

"It's all that praying," Kalten said sagely. "It's hard to take a man seriously when he's praying all the time."

"We're Knights of the Church, Kalten—members of religious orders."

"What's that got to do with it?"

"In his own mind he is more dead than alive," Xanetia reported later when they had gathered around one of the large fires the Atans had built to hold back the bitter chill. The Anarae's face reflected the glow of the fire, as did her unbleached wool robe.

"Were we right?" Tynian asked her. "Is Cyrgon augmenting Djarian's spells so that he can raise whole armies?"

"He is," she replied.

"Was that outburst against Zalasta genuine?" Vanion asked her.

"Indeed, my Lord. Djarian and his fellows are increasingly discontent with the leadership of Zalasta. They have all come to expect no true comradeship from their leader. There is no longer common cause among them, and each doth seek to wring best advantage to himself from their dubious alliance. Overlaying all is the secret desire of each to gain sole possession of Bhelliom."

"Dissension among your enemies is always good," Vanion noted, "but I don't think we should discount the possibility that they'll all fall in line again after what happened here today. Could you get anything specific about what they might try next, Anarae?"

"Nay, Lord Vanion. They were in no wise prepared for what hath come to pass. One thing did stand out in the mind of this Djarian, however, and it doth perhaps pose some danger. The outcasts who surround Zalasta do all fear Cyzada of Esos, for he alone is versed in Zemoch magic, and he alone doth plunge his hand through that door to the netherworld which Azash opened. Horrors beyond imagining lie within his reach. It is Djarian's thought that since all their plans have thus far gone awry, Cyrgon in desperation might command Cyzada to use his unspeakable art to raise creatures of darkness to confront and confound us."

Vanion nodded gravely.

"How did Stragen's plan affect them?" Talen asked curiously.

"They are discomfited out of all measure," Xanetia replied. "They did rely heavily on those who now are dead."

"Stragen will be happy to hear that. What were they going to do with all those spies and informers?"

"Since they had no force capable of facing the Atans, Zalasta and his cohorts thought to use the hidden employees of the Ministry of the Interior to assassinate diverse Tamul officials in the subject kingdoms of the empire, hoping thereby to disrupt the governments."

"You might want to make a note of that, Sparhawk," Kalten said.

"Oh?"

"Emperor Sarabian had some qualms when he approved Stragen's plan. He'll probably feel much better when he finds out that all Stragen really did was beat our enemies to the well. They'd have killed our people if Stragen hadn't killed theirs first."

"That's very shaky moral ground, Kalten," Bevier said disapprovingly.

"I know," Kalten admitted. "That's why you have to run across the top of it so fast."

The sky was overcast the following morning; thick, roiling clouds steamed in from the west, all seethe and confusion. Because it was late autumn and they were far to the north, it seemed almost that the sun was rising in the south, turning the sky above Bhelliom's escarpment a fiery orange and reaching feebly out with ruddy, low-lying light to paint the surging underbellies of the swift-scudding cloud with a brush of flame.

The campfires seemed wan and weak and very tiny against the overpowering chill here on the roof of the world, and the knights and their friends all wore fur cloaks and huddled close to the fires.

There were low rumbles off to the south, and flickers of pale, ghastly light.

"Thunder?" Kalten asked Ulath incredulously. "Isn't it the wrong time of the year for thunderstorms?"

"It happens." Ulath shrugged. "I was in a thunderstorm north of Heid once that touched off a blizzard. That's a very unusual sort of experience."

"Whose turn is it to do the cooking?" Kalten asked him absently.

"Yours," Ulath replied promptly.

"You're not paying attention, Kalten." Tynian laughed. "You know better than to ask that question."

Kalten grumbled and started to stir up the fire.

"I think we'd better get back to the coast today, Sparhawk," Vanion said gravely. "The weather's held off so far, but I don't think we'll be able to count on that much longer."

Sparhawk nodded.

The thunder grew louder, and the fire-red clouds overhead blanched with shuddering flickers of lightning.

Then there was a sudden, rhythmic booming sound.

"Is it another earthquake?" Kring cried out in alarm.

"No," Khalad replied. "It's too regular. It sounds almost like somebody beating a very big drum." He stared at the top of Bhelliom's wall. "What's that?" he asked, pointing.

It was like a hilltop rearing up out of the forest beyond the knifelike edge of the top of the cliff—very much like a hilltop, except that it was moving.

The sun was behind it, so they could not see any details, but as it rose higher and higher they could make out the fact that it was a kind of flattened dome with two pointed protuberances flaring out from either side like huge wings. And still it swelled upward. As they could see more of it, they realized that it was not a dome. It seemed to be some enormous, inverted triangle instead, wide at the top, pointed at the bottom, and with those odd winglike protuberances jutting out from its sides. The pointed bottom seemed to be set in some massive column. Since the light was behind it, it was as black as night, and it rose and swelled like some vast darkness.

Then it stopped.

And then its eyes opened.

Like two thin, fiery gashes at first, the blazing eyes opened wider and wider, cruelly slanted like cat's eyes and all ablaze with fire more incandescent than the sun itself. The imagination shuddered back from the realization of the enormity of the thing. What had appeared to be huge wings were the creature's ears.

And then it opened its mouth and roared, and they knew that what they had heard before had not been thunder.

It roared again, and its fangs were flickers of lightning that dripped flame like blood.

"Klæl!" Aphrael shrieked.

And then, like two rounded, bulky mountains, the shoulders rose above the sharp line of the cliff, and, fanning out from the shoulders like black sails, two jointed, batlike wings.

"What is it?" Talen cried.

"It's Klæl!" Aphrael shrieked again.

"What's a Klæl?"

"Not *what,* you dolt. *Who!* Azash and the other Elder Gods cast him out! Some idiot has returned him!"

The enormity atop the escarpment continued to rise, revealing vast arms with many-fingered hands. The trunk was huge, and flashes of lightning seethed beneath its skin, illuminating ghastly details with their surging flickers.

And then that monstrous presence rose to its full height, towering eighty, a hundred feet above the top of the escarpment.

Sparhawk's spirit shriveled. How could they possibly—? "Blue-Rose!" he said sharply. "Do something!"

"There is no need, Anakha." Vanion's usurped voice was very calm as Bhelliom once again spoke through his lips. "Klæl hath but momentarily escaped Cyrgon's grasp. Cyrgon will not risk his creature in a direct confrontation with me."

"That thing belongs to Cyrgon?"

"For the moment. In time that will change, and Cyrgon will belong to Klæl."

"What is it *doing*?" Betuana cried.

The monstrosity atop the cliff had raised one huge fist and was striking at the ground with incandescent fire, hammering at the earth with lightning. The face of the escarpment shuddered and began to crack away, falling, tumbling, roaring down to smash into the forest at the foot of the cliff. More and more of the sheer face crumbled and sheared away and fell in a huge thundering landslide.

"Klæl was ever uncertain of the strength of his wings," Bhelliom observed calmly. "He would come to join battle with me, but he fears the height of the wall. Thus he prepares a stair for himself."

Then with a booming like that of the earthquake which had spawned it, a mile or more of the escarpment toppled ponderously outward and crashed into the forest, piling rubble higher and higher against the foot of the cliff.

The enormous being continued to savage the top of the cliff, spilling more and more rubble down to form a steep causeway reaching up and up to the top of the wall.

And then the thing called Klæl vanished, and a shrieking wind swept the face of the escarpment, whipping away the boiling clouds of dust the landslide had raised.

There was another sound as well. Sparhawk turned quickly. The Trolls had fallen to their faces, moaning in terror.

"We've always known about him," Aphrael said pensively. "We used to frighten ourselves by telling stories about him. There's a certain perverse pleasure in making one's own flesh crawl. I don't think I ever really admitted to myself that he actually existed."

"Exactly what is he?" Bevier asked her.

"Evil." She shrugged. "We're supposed to be the essence of good—at least that's what we tell ourselves. Klæl is the opposite. He's our way of explaining the existence of evil. If we didn't have Klæl, we'd have to accept the responsibility for evil ourselves, and we're a little too fond of ourselves to do that."

"Then this Klæl is the King of Hell?" Bevier asked.

"Well, sort of. Hell isn't a place, though. It's a state of mind. The story has it that when the Elder Gods—Azash and the others—emerged, they found Klæl already here. They wanted the world for themselves, and he was in their way. After several of them had tried individually to get rid of him and got themselves obliterated, they banded together and cast him out."

"Where did he come from? Originally, I mean?" Bevier pressed. Bevier was very much caught up in first causes.

"How in the world should I know? I wasn't there. Ask Bhelliom."

"I'm not so much interested in where this Klæl came from as I am in what kinds of things it can do," Sparhawk said. He took Bhelliom out of the pouch at his waist. "Blue-Rose," he said, "I do think we must talk concerning Klæl."

"It might be well, Anakha," the jewel responded, once again taking control of Vanion.

"Where did he—or it—originate?"

"Klæl did not originate, Anakha. Even as I, Klæl hath always been."

"What is it—he?"

"Necessary. I would not offend thee, Anakha, but the necessity of Klæl is beyond thine ability to comprehend. The Child-Goddess hath explained Klæl sufficiently—within her capabilities."

"Well, *really*!" Aphrael spluttered.

A faint smile touched Vanion's lips. "Be not wroth with me, Aphrael. I do love thee still—despite thy limitations. Thou art young, and age shall bring thee wisdom and understanding."

"This is not going well, Blue-Rose," Sephrenia warned the stone.

"Ah, well," Bhelliom sighed. "Let us then to work. Klæl was, in fact, cast out by the Elder Gods, as Aphrael hath told thee—although the spirit of Klæl, even as my spirit, doth linger in the very rocks of this world—as in all others which I have made. Moreover, what the Elder Gods could do, they could also undo, and the spell which hath returned Klæl was implicit in the spell which did cast Klæl out. Clearly, some mortal conversant with the spells of the Elder Gods hath reversed the spell of casting out, and Klæl hath returned."

"Can he—or it—be destroyed?"

"It is not 'he' of which we speak, nor do we speak of some 'it.' We speak of Klæl. But nay, Anakha, Klæl cannot be destroyed—no more than can I. Klæl is eternal."

Sparhawk's heart sank. "I think we're in trouble," he muttered to his friends.

"The fault is in some measure mine. So caught up was I in the birth of this latest child of mine that mine attention did stray from needful duties. It is my wont to cast Klæl out at a certain point in the making of a new world. This particular child did so delight me, however, that I delayed the casting out. Then it was that I did encounter the red dust which did imprison me, and the duty to cast Klæl out did devolve upon the Elder Gods. The casting-out was made imperfect by reason of *their* imperfection, and thus it was possible for Klæl to be returned."

"By Cyrgon?" Sparhawk asked bleakly.

"The spell of casting out—and returning—is Styric. Cyrgon could not utter it."

"Cyzada, then," Sephrenia guessed. "He might very well have known the spell. I don't think he'd have used it willingly, though."

"Cyrgon probably forced him to use it, little mother," Kalten said. "Things haven't been going very well for Cyrgon and Zalasta lately."

"But to call Klæl!" Aphrael shuddered.

"Desperate people do desperate things." Kalten shrugged. "So do desperate Gods, I suppose."

"What do we do, Blue-Rose?" Sparhawk asked. "About Klæl, I mean to say?"

"Thou canst do nothing, Anakha. Thou didst well when thou didst meet

Azash, and doubtless will do well again in thy dispute with Cyrgon. Thou wouldst be powerless against Klæl, however."

"We're doomed, then." Sparhawk suddenly felt totally crushed.

"Doomed? Of course thou art not doomed. Why art thou so easily downcast and made disconsolate, my friend? I did not make thee to confront Klæl. That is *my* duty. Klæl will trouble us in some measure, as is Klæl's wont. Then, as is our custom, Klæl and I will meet."

"And thou wilt once more banish him?"

"That is never certain, Anakha. I do assure thee, however, that I will strive to mine utmost to cast Klæl out—even as Klæl will strive to cast *me* out. The contest between us doth lie in the future, and as I have oft told thee, the future is concealed. I will approach the contest with confidence, however, for doubt doth weaken resolve, and timorous uncertainty doth weigh down the spirit. Battle should be joined with a light heart and joyous demeanor."

"You can be very sententious sometimes, World-Maker," Aphrael said with just a hint of spitefulness.

"Be nice," Bhelliom chided mildly.

"Anakha!" It was Ghworg, the God of Kill. The huge presence came across the frosty meadow, plowing a dark path through the silver-sheathed grass.

"I will hear the words of Ghworg," Sparhawk replied.

"Have *you* summoned Klæl? Is it your thought that Klæl will aid us in causing hurt to Cyrgon? It is not good if you have. Let Klæl go back."

"It was not my doing, Ghworg. Neither was it the flower-gem's doing. It is our thought that it was Cyrgon who summoned Klæl to cause hurt to us."

"Can the flower-gem cause hurt to Klæl?"

"That is not certain. The might of Klæl is even as the might of the flower-gem."

The God of Kill squatted on the frozen turf, scratching at his shaggy face with one huge paw. "Cyrgon is as nothing, Anakha," he rumbled in an almost colloquial form of speech. "We can cause hurt to Cyrgon tomorrow—or some time by-and-by. We must cause hurt to Klæl now. We cannot wait for by-and-by."

Sparhawk dropped to one knee on the frozen turf. "Your words are wise, Ghworg."

Ghworg's lips pulled back in a hideous approximation of a grin. "The word you use is not common among us, Anakha. If Khwaj said, 'Ghworg is wise,' I would cause hurt to him."

"I did not say it to cause you anger, Ghworg."

"You are not a Troll, Anakha. You do not know our ways. We must cause hurt to Klæl so that he will go away. How can we do this?"

"We cannot cause hurt to him. Only the flower-gem can make him go away."

Ghworg smashed his fist against the frozen ground with a hideous snarl.

Sparhawk held up one hand. "Cyrgon has called Klæl," he said. "Klæl has joined Cyrgon to cause hurt to us. Let us cause hurt to Cyrgon now, not by-and-by.

If we cause hurt to Cyrgon, he will fear to aid Klæl when the flower-gem goes to cause hurt to Klæl and make him go away."

Ghworg puzzled his way through that. "Your words are good, Anakha," he said finally. "How might we best cause hurt to Cyrgon now?"

Sparhawk considered it. "The mind of Cyrgon is not like your mind, Ghworg, nor is it like mine. Our minds are direct. Cyrgon's is guileful. He threw your children against our friends here in the lands of winter to make us come here to fight them. But your children were not his main force. Cyrgon's main force will come from the lands of the sun to attack our friends in the city that shines."

"I have seen that place. The Child-Goddess spoke first with us there."

Sparhawk frowned, trying to remember the details of Vanion's map. "There are high places here and to the south," he said.

Ghworg nodded.

"Then, even farther south, the high places grow low and then they become flat."

"I see it," Ghworg said. "You describe it well, Anakha." That startled Sparhawk. Evidently Ghworg could visualize the entire continent.

"In the middle of that flat place is another high place that the man-things call the Tamul Mountains."

Ghworg nodded in agreement.

"The main force of Cyrgon's children will pass that high place to reach the city that shines. The high place will be cool, so your children will not suffer from the sun there."

"I see which way your thought goes, Anakha," Ghworg said. "We will take our children to that high place and wait there for Cyrgon's children. Our children will not eat Aphrael's children. They will eat Cyrgon's children instead."

"That will cause hurt to Cyrgon and his servants, Ghworg."

"Then we will do it." Ghworg turned and pointed toward the landslide. "Our children will climb Klæl's stairway. Then Ghnomb will make time stop. Our children will be in the high place before the sun goes to sleep this night." He stood up abruptly. "Good hunting," he growled, turned, and went back to join his fellows and the still-terrified Trolls.

"We have to proceed as if things were normal," Vanion told them as they gathered near the fire a couple of hours past noon. The sun, Sparhawk noted, was already going down. "Klæl can probably appear at any time and any place. We can't plan for him—any more than we can plan for a blizzard or a hurricane. If you can't plan for something, about the only thing you can do is take a few precautions and then ignore it."

"Well spoken," Queen Betuana approved. Betuana and Vanion were getting along well.

"What do we do then, friend Vanion?" Tikume asked.

"We're soldiers, friend Tikume," Vanion replied. "We do what soldiers do. We get ready to fight armies, not Gods. Scarpa's coming up out of the jungles of Arjuna, and I'd expect another thrust to come out of Cynesga. The Trolls will probably hamper Scarpa, but they can only move out a short way from those mountains in southern Tamul proper because of the climate. After the initial shock of encountering Trolls, Scarpa will probably try to go around them." Vanion consulted his map. "We'll have to have forces in place to respond either to Scarpa or to an army coming out of Cynesga. I'd say that Samar would be the best location."

"Sarna," Betuana disagreed.

"Both," Ulath countered. "Forces in Samar could cover everything from the southern edge of the Atan Mountains to the Sea of Arjuna *and* be in position to strike eastward to the southern Tamul Mountains if Scarpa evades the Trolls. Forces in Sarna could block the invasion route through the Atan Mountains."

"His point's well taken," Bevier said. "It divides our forces, but we don't have much choice."

"We could put the knights and the Peloi in Samar and the Atan infantry in Sarna," Tynian added. "The lower valley of the River Sarna's ideal for mounted operations, and the mountains around Sarna itself are natural for Atans."

"Both positions are defensive," Engessa objected. "Wars aren't won from defensive positions."

Sparhawk and Vanion exchanged a long look. "Invade Cynesga?" Sparhawk asked dubiously.

"Not yet," Vanion decided. "Let's wait until the Church Knights get here from Eosia before we do that. When Komier and the others cross into Cynesga from the west, *that's* when we'll want to come at the place from the east. We'll put Cyrgon in a vise. With that sort of force coming at him from both sides, he can raise every Cyrgai who's ever lived, and he'll still lose."

"Right up until the moment he unleashes Klæl," Aphrael added moodily.

"No, Divine One," Sparhawk told her. "Bhelliom *wants* Cyrgon to send Klæl against us. If we do it this way, we'll force the issue in a place and time that *we* choose. We'll pick the spot, Cyrgon will unleash Klæl, and I'll unleash Bhelliom. Then all we have to do is sit back and watch."

"We'll go to the top of the wall the same way the Trolls went, Vanion-Preceptor," Engessa said the following morning. "We can climb as well as they can."

"It might take *us* a little longer," Tikume added. "We'll have to push boulders out of the way to get our horses up that slope."

"We will help you, Tikume-Domi," Engessa promised.

"That's it, then," Tynian summed up. "The Atans and the Peloi will go south from here to take up positions in Sarna and Samar. We'll take the knights back to the coast, and Sorgi will ferry us back to Matherion. We'll go overland from there."

"It's the ferrying that concerns me," Sparhawk said. "Sorgi's going to have to make at least a half-dozen trips."

Khalad sighed and rolled his eyes upward.

"I gather you're going to embarrass me in public again," Sparhawk said. "What am I overlooking?"

"The rafts, Sparhawk," Khalad said in a weary voice. "Sorgi's gathering up the rafts to take them south to the timber markets. He's going to lash them all together into a long log boom. Put the knights in the ships, the horses on the boom, and we can all make it to Matherion in one trip."

"I forgot about the rafts," Sparhawk admitted sheepishly.

"That log boom won't move very fast," Ulath pointed out.

Xanetia had been listening to their plans intently. She looked at Khalad and spoke diffidently, almost shyly. "Might a steady wind behind thy logs assist thee, young Master?" Xanetia asked Khalad.

"It would indeed, Anarae," Khalad said enthusiastically. "We can weave rough sails out of tree limbs."

"Won't Cyrgon—or Klæl—feel you raising a breeze, dear sister?" Sephrenia asked.

"Cyrgon cannot detect Delphaeic magic, Sephrenia," Xanetia replied. "Anakha can ask Bhelliom whether Klæl is similarly unaware."

"How did you manage that?" Aphrael asked curiously.

Xanetia looked slightly embarrassed. "It was to hide from thee and thy kindred, Divine Aphrael. When Edaemus did curse us, he did so arrange his curse that our magic would be hidden from our enemies—for thus did we view thee at that time. Doth that offend thee, Divine One?"

"Not under *these* circumstances, Anarae," Flute replied, swarming up into Xanetia's arms and kissing her soundly.

CHAPTER TWO

The log boom Captain Sorgi's sailors had constructed from the rafts was a quarter of a mile long and a hundred feet wide. Most of it was taken up by the huge corral. It wallowed and wobbled its way south under threatening skies, and it was frequently raked by stinging sleet-squalls. The weather was bitterly cold, and the young knights who manned the raft were bundled to the ears in furs and spent most of their time huddled in the dubious shelter of the flapping tents.

"It's all in attention to detail, Berit," Khalad said as he tied off the rope holding the starboard end of one of their makeshift sails in place. "That's all that work really is—details." He squinted along the ice-covered line of what was really much more like a snow fence than a sail. "Sparhawk looks at the grand plan and leaves the details to others. It's a good thing, really, because he's a hopeless incompetent when it comes to little things and real work."

"Khalad!" Berit was actually shocked.

"Have you ever seen him try to use tools? That was something our father used to tell us over and over: 'Don't ever let Sparhawk pick up a tool.' Kalten's fairly good with his hands, but Sparhawk's hopeless. If you hand him anything associated with honest work, he'll hurt himself with it." Khalad's head came up sharply, and he swore.

"What's wrong?"

"Didn't you feel it? The port-side towropes just went slack. Let's go wake up those sailors. We don't want this big cow turning broadside on us again." The two fur-clad young men started across the icy collection of lashed-together rafts, skirting the huge corral where the horses huddled together in the bitterly cold breeze coming from astern.

The idea of making a log boom out of the rafts was very good in theory, but the problems of steering proved to be far more complex than either Sorgi or Khalad had anticipated. Khalad's thickly woven fences of evergreen boughs acted well enough as sails, moving the sheer dead-weight of the boom steadily southward ahead of Xanetia's breeze. But Sorgi's ships were supposed to provide steerageway by towing the boom, and that was where the problems cropped up. No two ships ever move at exactly the same rate of speed, even when propelled by the same wind. Thus, the fifty ships ahead and the twenty-five strung out along each side of the boom had to be almost constantly fine-tuned to keep the huge raft moving in the right general direction. As long as everybody paid very close attention, all went well. Two days south of Bhelliom's wall, however, a number of things had gone wrong all at once, and the log boom had swung around sideways. No amount of effort had been able to straighten it out, and so they had been obliged to take it apart and reassemble it—back-breaking labor in the bitter cold. Nobody wanted to go through that again.

When they reached the port side of the boom, Berit took a dented brass horn out from under his fur cape and blew a flat, off-key blat at the port-side towboats while Khalad picked up a yellow flag and began to wave it vigorously. The prearranged signals were simple. The yellow flag told the ships to crowd on more sail to keep the towing hawsers taut; the blue flag told them to put out the sea anchors to slack off on the ropes; and the red flag told them to cast off all lines and get out of the way.

The towropes went tight again as Khalad's crisp signal trickled down through the ranks to the sailors who actually did the work aboard the ships.

"How do you keep track of everything?" Berit asked his friend. "And how do you know so quickly that something's wrong?"

"Pain," Khalad replied wryly. "I don't really want to spend several days taking this beast apart and putting it back together again with the spray freezing on me, so I'm paying very close attention to the things my body's telling me. You can feel things change in your legs and the soles of your feet. When one of the hawsers goes slack, it changes the feel of how the boom moves."

"Is there *anything* you don't know how to do?"

"I don't dance very well." Khalad squinted up into the first stinging pellets of another sleet-squall. "It's time to feed and water the horses," he said. "Let's go tell the novices to stop sitting around admiring their titles and get to work."

"You really dislike the aristocracy, don't you?" Berit asked as they started forward along the edge of the corral toward the wind-whipped tents of the apprentice knights.

"No, I don't dislike them. I just don't have any patience with them, and I can't understand how they can be so blind to what's going on around them. A title must be a very heavy thing to carry if the weight makes you ignore everything else."

"You're going to be a knight yourself, you know."

"It wasn't my idea. Sparhawk gets silly sometimes. He thinks that making knights of my brothers and me is a way of honoring our father. I'm sure that Father's laughing at him right now."

They reached the tents, and Khalad raised his voice. "All right, gentlemen!" he shouted. "It's time to feed and water the animals! Let's get at it!" Then he critically surveyed the corral. Five thousand horses leave a great deal of evidence that they have been present. "I think it's time for another lesson in the virtue of humility for our novices," he said quietly to Berit. Then he raised his voice again. "And after you've finished with that, you'd better break out the scoop shovels and wheelbarrows again. We wouldn't want to let the work pile up on us, would we, gentlemen?"

Berit was not yet fully adept at some of the subtler forms of magic. That part of the Pandion training was the study of a lifetime. He was far enough along, however, to recognize "tampering" when he encountered it. The log boom *seemed* to be lumbering southward at a crawl, but the turning of the seasons was giving some things away. It should have taken them much longer to escape the bitter cold of the far north, for one thing; and the days should not have become so much longer in such a short time, for another.

However it was managed, and whoever managed it, they arrived at a sandy beach a few miles north of Matherion late one golden autumn afternoon, long before they should have, and began wading the horses ashore from the wobbly collection of rafts.

"Short trip," Khalad observed laconically as the two watched the novices unloading the horses.

"You noticed." Berit laughed.

"They weren't particularly subtle about it. When the spray stopped freezing in my beard between one minute and the next, I started having suspicions." He paused. "Is magic very hard to learn?" he asked.

"The magic itself isn't too hard. The hard part is learning the Styric language. Styric doesn't have any regular verbs. They're *all* irregular—and there are nine tenses."

"Berit, please speak plain Elenic."

"You know what a verb is, don't you?"

"Sort of, but what's a tense?"

Somehow that made Berit feel better. Khalad did not know everything. "We'll work on it," he assured his friend. "Maybe Sephrenia can make some suggestions."

The sun was going down in a blaze of color when they rode through the opalescent gates into fire-domed Matherion, and it was dusk when they reached the imperial compound.

"What's wrong with everybody?" Khalad muttered as they rode through the gate.

"I didn't follow that," Berit confessed.

"Use your eyes, man! Those gate guards were looking at Sparhawk as if they expected him to explode—or maybe turn into a dragon. Something's going on, Berit."

The main body of Church Knights rode off across the twilight-dim lawn to their barracks while the rest of the party clattered across the drawbridge into Ehlana's castle. They dismounted in the torchlit courtyard and trooped inside.

"It's even worse here," Khalad murmured. "Let's stay close to Sparhawk in case we have to restrain him. The knights at the drawbridge seemed to be actually afraid of him."

They went up the stairs to the royal apartment. Mirtai was not in her customary place at the door, and that made Berit even more edgy. Khalad was right. Something here was definitely not the way it should be.

Emperor Sarabian, dressed in his favorite purple doublet and hose, was nervously pacing the blue-carpeted floor of the sitting room as they entered, and he seemed to shrink back as Sparhawk and Vanion approached him.

"Your Majesty," Sparhawk greeted him, inclining his head. "It's good to see you again." He looked around. "Where's Ehlana?" he asked, laying his helmet on the table.

"Uh—in a minute, Sparhawk. How did things go on the North Cape?"

"More or less the way we'd planned. Cyrgon doesn't command the Trolls anymore, but we've got another problem that might be even worse."

"Oh?"

"We'll tell you about it when Ehlana joins us. It's not such a pretty story that we'd want to go through it twice."

The emperor gave Foreign Minister Oscagne a helpless look.

"Let's go speak with Baroness Melidere, Prince Sparhawk," Oscagne suggested. "Something's happened here. She was present, so she'll be able to answer your questions better than we would."

"All right." Sparhawk's gaze was level, and his voice was steady, despite the fact that Sarabian's nervousness and Oscagne's evasive answer fairly screamed out the fact that something was terribly wrong.

Baroness Melidere sat propped up in her bed. She wore a fetching blue dressing gown, but the sizable bandage on her left shoulder was a clear indication that something serious had happened. Her face was pale, but her eyes were cool and rock-steady. Stragen sat at her bedside in his white satin doublet, his face filled with concern.

"Well," Melidere said, "finally." Her voice was crisp and businesslike. She flicked a withering glance at the emperor and his advisers. "I see that these brave gentlemen have decided to let *me* tell you about what happened here, Prince Sparhawk. I'll try to be brief. One night a couple of weeks ago, the queen, Alean, and I were getting ready for bed. There was a knock on the door, and four men we thought were Peloi came in. Their heads were shaved and they wore Peloi clothing, but they weren't Peloi. One of them was Krager. The other three were Elron, Baron Parok, and Scarpa."

Sparhawk did not move, and his face did not change expression. "And?" he asked, his voice still unemotional.

"You've decided to be sensible, I see," Melidere said coolly. "Good. We exchanged a few insults, and then Scarpa told Elron to kill me—just to prove to the queen that he was serious. Elron lunged at me, and I deflected his thrust with my wrist. I fell down and smeared the blood around to make it appear that I'd been killed. Ehlana threw herself over me, pretending to be hysterical, but she'd seen what I'd done." The baroness took a ruby ring out from under her pillow. "This is for you, Prince Sparhawk. Your wife hid it in my bodice. She also said, 'Tell Sparhawk that I'm all right, and tell him that I forbid him to give up Bhelliom, no matter what they threaten to do to me.' Those were her exact words. Then she covered me with a blanket."

Sparhawk took the ring and slipped it onto his finger. "I see," he said in a calm voice. "What happened then, Baroness?"

"Scarpa told your wife that he and his friends were taking her and Alean as hostages. He said that you were so foolishly attached to her that you'd give him anything for her safe return. He obviously intends to exchange her for the Bhelliom. Krager had a note already prepared. He cut off a lock of Ehlana's hair to include in the note. I gather that there'll be other notes, and each one will have some of her hair in it to prove that it's authentic. Then they took Ehlana and Alean and left."

"Thank you, Baroness," Sparhawk said, his voice still steady. "You've shown amazing courage in this unfortunate business. May I have the note?"

Melidere reached under her pillow again, took out a folded and sealed piece of parchment, and handed it to him.

Berit had loved his queen from the moment he had first seen her sitting on her throne encased in crystal, although he had never mentioned the fact to her. There would be other loves in his life, of course, but she would always be the first. So it was that when Sparhawk broke the seal, unfolded the parchment, and gently removed the thick lock of pale blonde hair, Berit's mind suddenly filled with flames. His grip tightened around the haft of his war ax.

Khalad took him by the arm, and Berit was dimly startled by just how strong his friend's grip was. "That's not going to do anybody any good at all, Berit," he said in a crisp voice. "Now why don't you just give me the ax before you do something foolish with it?"

Berit drew in a deep, trembling breath, pushing away his sudden, irrational fury. "Sorry, Khalad," he said. "I sort of lost my grip there for a moment. I'll be all right now." He looked at his friend. "Sparhawk's going to let you kill Krager, isn't he?"

"So he says."

"Would you like some help?"

Khalad flashed him a quick grin. "It's always nice to have company when you're doing something that takes several days," he said.

Sparhawk quickly read the note, his free hand still gently holding the lock of Ehlana's pale hair. Berit could see the muscles rippling along his friend's jaw as he read. He handed the note to Vanion. "You'd better read this to them," he said bleakly.

Vanion nodded and took the note. He cleared his throat.

" 'Well, now, Sparhawk,' " he read aloud. " 'I gather that your temper tantrum's over. I hope you didn't kill *too* many of the people who were supposed to be guarding your wife.

" 'The situation here is painfully obvious, I'm afraid. We've taken Ehlana hostage. You *will* behave yourself, won't you, old boy? The tiresomely obvious part of all of this is that you can have her back in exchange for Bhelliom and the rings. We'll give you a few days to rant and rave and try to find some way out of this. Then, when you've come to your senses and realize that you have no choice but to do exactly as you're told, I'll drop you another note with some rather precise instructions. Do be a good boy and follow the instructions to the letter. I'd really rather not be forced to kill your wife, so don't try to be creative.

" 'Be well, Sparhawk, and keep an eye out for my next note. You'll know it's from me because I'll decorate it with another lock of Ehlana's hair. Pay very close attention, because if our correspondence continues for *too* long, your wife will run out of hair, and I'll have to start using fingers.'

"And it's signed 'Krager,' " Vanion concluded.

Kalten smashed his fist into the wall, his face rigid with fury.

"That's enough of that!" Vanion snapped.

"What are we going to do?" Kalten demanded. "We have to do *something*!"

"We're *not* going to jump eight feet into the air and come down running, for a start," Vanion told him.

"Where's Mirtai?" Kring's voice had a note of sudden alarm.

"She's perfectly all right, Domi," Sarabian assured him. "She was a little upset when she found out what happened."

"A *little*?" Oscagne murmured. "It took twelve men to subdue her. She's in her room, Domi Kring—chained to the bed, actually. There are some guards there as well to keep her from doing herself any injury."

Kring abruptly turned and left Melidere's bedroom.

"We're tiring you, aren't we, Baroness?" Sarabian said then.

"Not in the least, your Majesty," she replied in a cool voice. She looked around at them. "It's a bit cramped in here. Why don't we adjourn to the sitting room? I'd imagine we'll be most of the night at this, so we might as well be comfortable." She threw back her blankets and started to get out of bed.

Stragen gently restrained her. Then he picked her up.

"I can walk, Stragen," she protested.

"Not while I'm around, you can't." Stragen's customary expression of civilized urbanity was gone as he looked around at the others, and it had been replaced with one of cold, tightly suppressed rage. "One thing, gentlemen," he told them. "When we catch up with these people, Elron's mine. I'll be very put out with anybody who accidently kills him."

Baroness Melidere's eyes were quite content, and there was a faint smile on her face as she laid her head on Stragen's shoulder.

Caalador was waiting for them in the sitting room. His knees and elbows were muddy, and there were cobwebs in his hair. "I found it, your Majesty," he reported to the emperor. "It comes out in the basement of that barracks the Church Knights have been using." He looked appraisingly at Sparhawk. "I'd heard you were back," he said. "We've managed to pick up a little information for you."

"I appreciate that, Caalador," Sparhawk replied quietly. The big Pandion's almost inhuman calm had them all more than a little on edge.

"Stragen was a bit distracted after what happened to the baroness here," Caalador reported, "so I was left more or less to my own devices. I took some fairly direct steps. The ideas were all mine, so don't blame him for them."

"You don't have to do that, Caalador," Stragen said, carefully tucking a blanket around Melidere's shoulders. "You didn't do anything I didn't approve of."

"I take it that there were a few atrocities," Ulath surmised.

"Let me start at the beginning," Caalador said, brushing his hands through his hair, trying to dislodge the cobwebs. "One of the men we'd been planning to kill during the Harvest Festival managed to evade my cutthroats, and he sent me a message offering to exchange information for his life. I agreed to that, and he told me something I didn't know about. We knew that there were tunnels under the lawns here in the imperial compound, but what we *didn't* know is that the ground under the whole city's honeycombed with more tunnels. That's how Krager and his friends got into the imperial grounds, and that's how they took the queen and her maid out."

"Prithee, good Master Caalador, stay a moment," Xanetia said. "I have seen into the memories of the minister of the interior, and he had no knowledge of such tunnels."

"That wouldn't be hard to explain, Anarae," Patriarch Emban told her. "Ambitious underlings quite often conceal things from their superiors. Teovin, Director of the Secret Police, probably had his eye on Kolata's position."

"That's most likely it, your Grace," Caalador agreed. "Anyway, my informant knew the location of *some* of the tunnels, and I put men down there to look around for more while I questioned various members of the Secret Police who were in custody. My methods were fairly direct, and the ones who survived the questioning were more than happy to cooperate.

"The tunnels were very busy on the night the queen was abducted. The diplomats who were forted up in the Cynesgan embassy knew about the scheme, and they realized that we'd kick down their walls as soon as we found out that the queen was gone. They tried to escape through the tunnels, but I already had men down in those ratholes. There were a number of noisy encounters, and we either rounded up or killed just about the entire embassy staff. The ambassador himself survived, and I let him watch while I interrogated several undersecretaries. I'm very fond of Queen Ehlana, so I was quite firm with them." He looked at Sephrenia. "I don't think I need to go into too much detail," he added.

"Thank you," Sephrenia murmured.

"The ambassador didn't really know all that much," Caalador continued apologetically, "but he *did* tell me that Scarpa and his friends were going south from here—which may or may not have been a ruse. His Majesty ordered the ports of Micae and Saranth sealed, and he put Atan patrols on the road from Tosa to the coast, just to be on the safe side. Nothing's turned up yet, so Scarpa either got way ahead of us, or he's gone down a hole someplace nearby."

The door opened, and Kring rejoined them, his face gloomy.

"Did you unchain her?" Tynian asked him.

"That wouldn't be a good idea right now, friend Tynian. She feels personally responsible for the queen's abduction. She wants to kill herself. I took everything with any kind of sharp edge out of the room, but I don't think it's really safe to unshackle her just yet."

"Did you get that spoon of hers away from her?" Talen asked.

Kring's eyes went wide. "Oh, God!" he exclaimed, bolting for the door.

"If he'd only yell at us or bang his fist against the wall or something," Berit murmured to Khalad the next morning when they gathered once again in the blue-draped sitting room. "All he does is sit there."

"Sparhawk keeps his feelings to himself," Khalad replied.

"It's his *wife* we're talking about, Khalad! He sits there like a lump. Doesn't he have any feelings at all?"

"Of course he does, but he's not going to take them out and wave them around for us to look at. Right now it's more important for him to think than to feel. He's listening and putting things together. He's saving up his feelings for when he gets his hands on Scarpa."

Sparhawk sat in his chair with his daughter in his lap. He seemed to be studying the floor, and he was absently stroking Princess Danae's cat.

Lord Vanion was telling the emperor and the others about Klæl and about their strategic disposition of forces: the Trolls to the Tamul Mountains in south-central Tamul proper, the Atans to Sarna, and Tikume's Peloi to Samar.

Flute was sitting quietly on Sephrenia's lap. Berit noticed something that hadn't occurred to him before. He glanced first at Princess Danae and then at the Child-Goddess. They appeared to be about the same age, and their bearing and manner seemed very much alike for some reason.

The presence of the Child-Goddess was having a peculiar effect on Emperor Sarabian. The brilliant, erratic ruler of the continent seemed dumbfounded by her presence and he sat gazing wide-eyed at her. His face was pale, and he was obviously not hearing a word Lord Vanion was saying.

Aphrael finally twisted around and returned his gaze. Then she slowly crossed her eyes at him.

The emperor stared back violently.

"Didn't your mother ever tell you that it's not polite to stare, Sarabian?" she asked him.

"Mind your manners," Sephrenia chided.

"He's supposed to be listening. If I want adoration, I'll get myself a puppy."

"Forgive me, Goddess Aphrael," the emperor apologized. "I seldom have divine visitors." He looked at her rather closely. "I hope you don't mind my saying so, but you rather resemble Prince Sparhawk's daughter. Have you ever met her Royal Highness?"

Sparhawk's head came up sharply, and there was a strange, almost wild look in his eyes.

"Now that you mention it, I don't think I have," Flute said. She looked across the room at the princess. Berit noticed that Sephrenia's eyes were also just a bit wild as Flute slid down out of her lap and went across the room to Sparhawk's chair. "Hullo, Danae," the Child-Goddess said in an offhand sort of way.

"Hullo, Aphrael," the princess replied in almost exactly the same tone. "Are you going to do something to get my mother back home?"

"I'm working on it. Try to keep your father from getting too excited about this. He's no good to any of us when he flies all to pieces and we have to gather him up and put him back together again."

"I know. I'll do what I can with him. Would you like to hold my cat?"

Flute glanced at Mmrr, whose eyes were filled with a look of absolute horror. "I don't think she likes me," she declined.

"I'll take care of my father," Danae assured the little Goddess. "You deal with these others."

"All right." Aphrael paused. "I think we'll get on well together," she said. "You wouldn't mind if I stopped by from time to time, would you?"

"Any time, Aphrael."

Something very peculiar was going on. Berit saw nothing unusual in the conversation between the two little girls, but Sparhawk's face—and Sephrenia's—clearly showed that they were both very disturbed. Berit kept his expression casual and looked around. Everyone else had faintly indulgent smiles on their faces as they watched the exchange—all except Lord Vanion and Anarae Xanetia. *Their* faces were no less strained than Sparhawk's and Sephrenia's. Evidently something titanic had just happened, but for the life of him, Berit could not fathom out what it might have been.

"I don't think we should discount the possibility," Oscagne said gravely. "Baroness Melidere has demonstrated again and again the fact that she has a very penetrating mind."

"Thank you, your Excellency," Melidere said sweetly.

"I wasn't really being complimentary, Baroness," he replied coolly. "Your intelligence is a resource to be exploited in this situation. You've seen Scarpa and we haven't. Do you really believe he's mad?"

"Yes, your Excellency, quite mad. It wasn't only *his* behavior that convinced me of it. Krager and the others treated him the way you'd treat a live cobra. They're terrified of him."

"That dovetails rather neatly with some of the reports I got from the thieves of Arjuna," Caalador agreed. "There's always a certain amount of exaggeration involved when people talk about madmen, but every report that came in mentioned it."

"If you're trying to make Sparhawk and me feel better, you're going at it in a strange way, Caalador," Kalten accused. "You're suggesting that the women we love are the prisoners of a crazy man. He could do *anything*."

"It might not be as bad as it looks, Sir Kalten," Oscagne said. "If Scarpa's mad, couldn't this abduction have been *his* idea alone? If that's the case, our solution becomes almost too simple. Prince Sparhawk simply follows the instructions he receives to the letter, and when Scarpa appears with Queen Ehlana and Alean, his Highness simply hands over the Bhelliom. We all know what'll happen to Scarpa as soon as he touches it."

"You're equating insanity with feeblemindedness, Oscagne," Sarabian disagreed, "and that's simply not the way it works. Zalasta knows that the rings would protect him if he ever managed to get his hands on Bhelliom, and if he knows, then we have to assume that Scarpa does, too. He'll demand the rings before he even tries to touch the jewel."

"We have three possibilities then," Patriarch Emban summed up. "Either Cyrgon instructed Zalasta to arrange for the abduction, or Zalasta came up with the notion on his own, or Scarpa's so crazy that he thinks he can just pick up Bhelliom and start giving it commands with no instruction or preparation at all."

"There's one more possibility, your Grace," Ulath said. "Klæl could already be in charge, and this could be his way to force Bhelliom to come to *him* for their customary contest."

"What difference does it make at this point?" Sparhawk asked suddenly. "We won't know whose idea it is until we see who shows up to make the exchange."

"We *should* have some plans in place, Prince Sparhawk," Oscagne pointed out. "We should try to think our way through each situation so that we'll know what to do."

"I already know what I'm going to do, your Excellency," Sparhawk told him bleakly.

"At the moment, we can't do anything," Vanion said, moving in rather quickly. "All we can do is wait for Krager's next note."

"Truly," Ulath agreed. "Krager's going to give Sparhawk instructions. Those instructions might give us some clues about whose idea this *really* is."

"You noticed it, too, didn't you?" Berit said to Khalad that evening when the two of them were getting ready for bed.

"Noticed what?"

"Don't play the innocent with me, Khalad. You see everything that's going on around you. *Nothing* gets by you. Sparhawk and Sephrenia were behaving very peculiarly when Flute and Danae were talking to each other."

"Yes," Khalad admitted calmly. "So what?"

"Aren't you curious about why?"

"Has it occurred to you that 'why' might not be any of our business?"

Berit stepped around that. "Did you notice how much the two little girls resemble each other?"

Khalad shrugged. "You're the expert on girls."

Berit suddenly blushed and silently cursed himself for blushing.

"It isn't a secret, you know," Khalad told him. "Empress Elysoun's fairly obvious. She doesn't hide her feelings any more than she hides—well, you know."

"She's a good girl," Berit quickly came to her defense. "It's just that her people don't pay any attention to our kind of morality. They can't even comprehend the notion of fidelity."

"I'm not throwing rocks at her. If the way she behaves doesn't bother her husband, it certainly doesn't bother me. I'm a country boy, remember? We're more realistic about things like that. I just wouldn't get *too* attached to her, Berit. Her attention may wander in time."

"It already has," Berit replied. "She doesn't want to discontinue our friendship, though She wants to be friendly to me *and* to him—and to the half-dozen or so others she neglected to mention earlier."

"The world needs more friendliness, Berit." Khalad grinned. "There wouldn't be so many wars if people were friendlier."

Krager's next note arrived two days later, and it was authenticated by another lock of Ehlana's hair. The thought of the sodden drunkard violating his queen's pale blonde hair enraged Berit for some obscure reason. Vanion once again read the note to them while Sparhawk sat somewhat apart, gently holding the lock of his wife's hair in his fingers.

" 'Sparhawk, old boy,' " the note began. " 'You don't mind if I call you that, do you? I always admired the way Martel sort of tossed that off when everything was going his way. It was pretty much the *only* thing about him that I admired.

" 'Enough of these fond reminiscences. You're going to be making a trip, Sparhawk. We want you to take your squire and travel by the customary overland route to Beresa in southeastern Arjuna. You'll be watched, so don't take any side trips, don't have Kalten and the other baboons trailing along behind you, don't have Sephrenia disguised as a mouse or a flea hidden in your pocket, and most *definitely* don't use Bhelliom for anything at all—not even for building campfires. I know we can depend on your absolute cooperation, old boy, since you'll never see Ehlana alive again if you misbehave.

" 'It's always a pleasure to talk with you, Sparhawk, particularly in view of the fact that it's *your* hands that are chained this time. Now stop wasting time. Take Khalad and the Bhelliom and go to Beresa. You'll receive further instructions there.

" 'Fondly, Krager.' "

CHAPTER THREE

They talked and talked and talked, and every "maybe" or "possibly" or "probably" or "on the other hand" set Sparhawk's teeth on edge. It was all pure speculation, useless guessing that circled and circled and never got to the point. He sat slightly apart from them holding the lock of pale hair. The hair felt strangely alive, coiling around his fingers in a soft caress.

It was his fault, of course. He should never have permitted Ehlana to come to Tamuli. It went further than that, though. Ehlana had been in danger all her life, and it had all been because of him—because of the fact that he was Anakha. Xanetia had said that Anakha was invincible, but she was wrong. Anakha was as vulnerable as *any* married man. By marrying Ehlana, he had immediately put her at risk, a risk that would last for as long as she lived.

He should never have married her. He loved her, of course, but was it an act of love to put her in danger? He silently cursed the weakness that had led him even to consider the ridiculous notion when she had first raised it. He was a soldier, and soldiers should never marry—particularly not scarred, battered old veterans with too many years and too many battles behind them and too many enemies still about. Was he some selfish old fool?—some disgusting, half-senile lecher eager to take advantage of a foolish young girl's infatuation? Ehlana had extravagantly declared that she would die if he refused her, but he knew better than that. People die from a sword in the belly, or from old age, but they do not die from love. He should have laughed in her face and rejected her absurd command. Then he could have arranged a proper marriage for her, a marriage to some handsome young nobleman with good manners and a safe occupation. If he had, she would still be safely back in Cimmura instead of in the hands of madmen, degenerate sorcerers, and alien Gods to whom her life meant nothing at all.

And still they talked on and on. Why were they wasting all their breath? There wasn't any choice in the matter. Sparhawk would obey the instructions because Ehlana's life depended on it. The others were certain to argue with him about it, and the arguments would only irritate him. The best thing would probably be just to take the Bhelliom and Khalad and slip out of Matherion without giving them the chance to drive him mad with their meaningless babble.

It was the touch of a springlike breeze on his cheek and a soft nuzzling on his hand that roused him from his gloomy reverie.

"It was not mine intent to disturb thy thought, Sir Knight," the white deer apologized, "but my mistress would have words with thee."

Sparhawk jerked his head around in astonishment. He no longer sat in the blue-draped room in Matherion, and the voices of the others had faded away to be replaced by the sound of the gentle lapping of waves upon a golden strand. His chair now sat on the marble floor of Aphrael's temple on the small verdant island that rose gemlike from the sea. The breeze was soft under the rainbow-colored sky, and the ancient oaks around the alabaster temple rustled softly.

"Thou hast forgotten me," the gentle white hind reproached him, her liquid eyes touched with sorrow.

"Never," he replied. "I shall remember thee always, dear creature, for I do love thee, even as I did when first we met." The extravagant expression came to his lips unbidden.

The white deer sighed happily and laid her snowy head in his lap. He stroked her arched white neck and looked around.

The Child-Goddess Aphrael, gowned in white and surrounded by a glowing nimbus, sat calmly on a branch of one of the nearby oaks. She lifted her many-chambered pipes and blew an almost mocking little trill.

"What are you up to now, Aphrael?" he called up to her, deliberately forcing away the flowery words that jumped to his lips.

"I thought you might want to talk," she replied, lowering the pipes. "Did you want some more time for self-mortification? Would you like a whip so that you can flog yourself with it? Take as much time as you want, Father. This particular instant will last for as long as I want it to." She reached out with one grass-stained little foot, placed it on nothing at all, and calmly walked down a nonexistent stairway to the alabaster floor of her temple. She sank down on it, crossed her feet at the ankles, and lifted her pipes again. "Will it disturb your sour musings if I play?"

"Just what do you think you're doing?" he demanded.

She shrugged. "You seem to have this obscure need for penance of some kind, and there's no time for it. I wouldn't be much of a Goddess if I couldn't satisfy both needs at the same time, now would I?" She raised her pipes. "Do you have any favorites you'd like to hear?"

"You're actually serious, aren't you?"

"Yes." She breathed another little trill into the pipes.

He glared at her for a moment, and then he gave up. "Can we talk about this?" he asked her.

"You've come to your senses? Already? Amazing."

He looked around at the island. "Where is this place?" he asked curiously.

The Child-Goddess shrugged. "Wherever I want it to be. I carry it with me everyplace I go. Were you serious about what you were just thinking, Sparhawk? Were you really going to snatch up Bhelliom, grab Khalad by the scruff of the neck, leap onto Faran's back, and try to ride off in three directions at the same time?"

"All Vanion and the others are doing is talking, Aphrael, and the talk isn't going anywhere."

"Did you speak with Bhelliom about this notion of yours?"

"The decision is *mine,* Aphrael. Ehlana's *my* wife."

"How brave you are, Sparhawk. You're making a decision that involves the Bhelliom without even consulting it. Don't be misled by its seeming politeness, Father. That's just a reflection of its archaic speech. It *won't* do something it knows is wrong, no matter how sorry you're feeling for yourself, and if you grow *too* insistent, it might just decide to create a new sun—about six inches from your heart."

"I have the rings, Aphrael. I'm still the one giving the orders."

She laughed at him. "Do you *really* think the rings mean anything, Sparhawk? They have no control over Bhelliom at all. That was just a subterfuge that concealed the fact that it has an awareness—and a will and purpose of its own. It can ignore the rings anytime it wants to."

"Then why did it need me?"

"Because you're a necessity, Sparhawk—like wind or tide or rain. You're as necessary as Klæl is—or Bhelliom—or me, for that matter. Someday we'll have to come back here and have a long talk about necessity, but we're a little pressed for time right now."

"And was that little virtuoso performance of yours yesterday another necessity as well? Would the world have come to an end if you hadn't held that public conversation with yourself?"

"What I did yesterday was useful, Father, not necessary. I am who I am, and I can't change that. When I'm going through one of these transitions, there are usually people around who know both of the little girls, and they start noticing the similarities. I always make it a point to have the girls meet each other in public. It puts off tiresome questions and lays unwanted suspicions to rest."

"You terrified Mmrr, you know."

She nodded. "I'll make it up to her. That's always been a problem. Animals can see right through my disguises. They don't look at us in the way that we look at each other."

He sighed. "What am I going to do, Aphrael?"

"I was hoping that a visit here would bring you back to your senses. A stopover in reality usually has that effect."

He looked up at her private, rainbow-colored sky. "*This* is your notion of reality?"

"Don't you like my reality?"

"It's lovely," he told her, absently stroking the white deer's neck, "but it's a dream."

"Are you really sure about that, Sparhawk? Are you so certain that *this* isn't reality and that other place isn't the dream?"

"Don't do that. It makes my head hurt. What should I do?"

"I'd say that your first step ought to be to have a long conversation with Bhelliom. All of your moping around and contemplating arbitrary decisions has it more than a little worried."

"All right. Then what?"

"I haven't gotten that far yet." She grinned at him. "I'm a-workin' on it, though, Dorlin'," she added.

"They're going to be all right, Kalten," Sparhawk said, gently laying his hand on his suffering friend's shoulder.

Kalten looked up, his eyes filled with hopeless misery. "Are you sure, Sparhawk?"

"They will be if we can just keep our heads. Ehlana was in much more danger when I came back from Rendor, and we took care of that, didn't we?"

"I suppose you're right." Kalten straightened up in his chair and jerked down his blue doublet. His face was bleak. "I think I'm going to find some people and hurt them," he declared.

"Would you mind if I came along?"

"You can help if you like." Kalten rubbed at the side of his face. "I've been thinking," he said. "You know that if you follow those orders in Krager's note, he'll be able to keep you plodding from one end of Tamuli to the other for the next year or more, don't you?"

"Do I have any choice? They're going to be watching me."

"Let them. Do you remember how we met Berit?"

"He was a novice in the chapterhouse in Cimmura." Sparhawk shrugged.

"Not when *I* first saw him, he wasn't. I was coming back from exile in Lamorkand, and I stopped at a roadside tavern outside of Cimmura. Berit was there with Kurik, and he was wearing your armor. I've known you since we were children, and even *I* couldn't tell that he wasn't you. If *I* couldn't tell, Krager's spies certainly won't be able to. If somebody has to plod around Tamuli, let Berit do it. You and I have better things to do."

Sparhawk was startled. "That's the best idea I've heard yet." He looked around at the others. "Could I have your attention, please?" he said.

They all looked sharply at him, their faces apprehensive.

"It's time to get to work," he told them. "Kalten here just reminded me that we've used Sir Berit as a decoy in the past. Berit and I are nearly the same size, and my armor fits him—more or less—and with his visor down, nobody can really tell that he isn't me. If we can prevail on him to masquerade as a broken-down old campaigner again, we might just be able to prepare a few surprises for Krager and his friends."

"You don't even have to ask, Sparhawk," Berit said.

"Get some details before you volunteer like that, Berit," Khalad told his friend in a pained voice.

"Your father used to say almost exactly the same thing," Berit recalled.

"Why didn't you listen to him?"

"It's an interesting plan, Prince Sparhawk," Oscagne said a bit dubiously, "but isn't it extremely dangerous?"

"I'm not afraid, your Excellency," Berit protested.

"I wasn't talking about *your* danger, young sir. I'm talking about the danger to Queen Ehlana. The moment someone penetrates your disguise—well . . ." Oscagne spread his hands.

"Then we'll just have to make sure that his disguise is foolproof," Sephrenia said.

"He can't keep his visor down forever, Sephrenia," Sarabian objected.

"I don't think he'll have to," Sephrenia replied. She looked speculatively at Xanetia. "Do we trust each other enough to cooperate, Anarae?" she asked. "I'm talking about something a little deeper than we've gone so far."

"I will listen most attentively to thy proposal, my sister."

"Delphaeic magic is directed primarily inward, isn't it?"

Xanetia nodded.

"That's probably why no one can hear or feel it. Styric magic is just the reverse. We alter things around us, so our magic reaches out. Neither form will work by itself in this particular situation, but if we were to combine them . . ." She left it hanging in the air between them.

"Interesting notion," Aphrael mused.

"I'm not sure I follow," Vanion said.

"The Anarae and I are going to have to experiment a bit," Sephrenia told him, "but if what I've got in mind works, we'll be able to make Berit look so much like Sparhawk that they'll be able to use each other for shaving mirrors."

"As long as each of us knows exactly what the other's doing, it's not too difficult, Sparhawk," Sephrenia assured him later when he and Berit joined her, Vanion, and the Anarae in the room she shared with Vanion.

"Will it really work?" he asked her dubiously.

"They haven't actually tried it yet, Sparhawk," Vanion told him, "so we're not entirely positive."

"That doesn't sound too promising. This isn't much of a face, but it's the only one I've got."

"There will be no danger to thee or to young Sir Berit, Anakha," Xanetia said. "In times past it hath oft been necessary for my people to leave our valley and to go abroad amongst others. This hath been our means of disguising our true identity."

"It works sort of like this, Sparhawk," Sephrenia explained. "Xanetia casts a Delphaeic spell that would normally imprint your features on her own face, but just as she releases *her* spell, *I* release a Styric one that deflects the spell to Berit instead."

"Won't every Styric in Matherion feel it when you release your spell?" Sparhawk asked.

"That's the beauty of it, Sparhawk," Aphrael told him. "The spell itself originates with Xanetia, and others can't feel or hear a Delphaeic spell. Cyrgon himself could be in the next room and he wouldn't hear a thing."

"You're sure it's going to work?"

"There's one way to find out."

Sparhawk, of course, did not feel a thing. He was only the model, after all. It was a bit disconcerting to watch Berit's appearance gradually change, however.

When the combined spell had been completed, Sparhawk carefully inspected his young friend. "Do I really look like that from the side?" he asked Vanion, feeling a bit deflated.

"I can't tell the two of you apart."

"That nose is really crooked, isn't it?"

"We thought you knew."

"I've never looked at myself from the side this way before." Sparhawk looked critically at Berit's eyes. "You should probably try to squint just a little," he suggested. "My eyes aren't as good as they used to be. That's one of the things you have to look forward to as you get older."

"I'll try to remember that." Even Berit's voice was different.

"Do I really sound like that?" Sparhawk was crestfallen.

Vanion nodded.

Sparhawk shook his head. "Seeing and hearing yourself as others do definitely lowers your opinion of yourself," he admitted. He looked at Berit again. "I didn't feel anything, did you?"

Berit nodded, swallowing hard.

"What was it like?"

"I'd really rather not talk about it." Berit gently explored his new face with cringing fingertips, wincing as he did.

"I *still* can't tell them apart," Kalten marveled, staring first at Berit and then at Sparhawk.

"That was sort of the idea," Sparhawk told him.

"Which one are you?"

"Try to be serious, Kalten."

"Now that we know how it's done, we can make some other changes as well," Sephrenia told them. "We'll give you all different faces so that you'll be able to move around freely—and we'll put men wearing *your* faces here in the palace. I think we can all expect to be watched, even after the Harvest Festival, and this should nullify that particular problem."

"We can make more detailed plans later," Vanion said. "Let's get Berit and Khalad on their way first. What's the customary route when someone wants to go overland from here to Beresa?" He unrolled a map and spread it out on the table.

"Most travelers go by sea," Oscagne replied, "but those who don't usually cross the peninsula to Micae and then take a ship across the gulf to the mainland."

"There don't seem to be any roads over there." Vanion frowned, looking at the map.

"It's a relatively uninhabited region, Lord Vanion—" Oscagne shrugged. "—salt marshes and the like. What few tracks there are wouldn't show up on the map."

"Do the best you can," Vanion told the two young men. "Once you get past the Tamul Mountains, you'll hit that road that skirts the western side of the jungle."

"I'd make a special point of staying out of those mountains, Berit," Ulath advised. "There are Trolls there now."

Berit nodded.

"You'd better have a talk with Faran, Sparhawk," Khalad suggested. "I don't think he'll be fooled just because Berit's wearing your face, and Berit's going to have to ride him if this is going to be convincing."

"I'd forgotten that," Sparhawk admitted.

"I thought you might have."

"All right, then," Vanion continued his instructions to the two young men, "follow that road down to Lydros, then take the road around the southern tip of Arjuna to Beresa. That's the logical route, and they'll probably be expecting you to go that way."

"That's going to take quite a while, Lord Vanion," Khalad said.

"I know. Evidently Krager and his friends want it to. If they were in a hurry, they'd have instructed Sparhawk to go by sea."

"Give Berit your wife's ring, Sparhawk," Flute instructed.

"What?"

"Zalasta can sense the ring, and if he can, Cyrgon can, too—and Klæl will *definitely* feel it. If you don't give Berit the ring, changing his face was just a waste of time."

"You're putting Berit and Khalad in a great deal of danger," Sephrenia said critically.

"That's what we get paid for, little mother." Khalad shrugged.

"I'll watch over them," Aphrael assured her sister. She looked critically at Berit. "Call me," she told him.

"Ma'am?"

"Use the spell, Berit," she explained with exaggerated patience. "I want to be sure you're doing it right."

"Oh." Berit carefully enunciated the spell of summoning, his hands moving in the intricate accompanying gestures.

"You mispronounced *'kajerasticon,'*" she corrected him.

Sephrenia was trying without much success to suppress a laugh.

"What's so funny?" Talen asked her.

"Sir Berit's pronunciations raised some questions about his meaning," Stragen explained.

"What did he say?" Talen asked curiously.

"Just never mind what he said," Flute told him primly. "We're not here to repeat off-color jokes about the differences between boys and girls. Practice on that one, Berit. Now try the secret summoning."

"What's that?" Itagne murmured to Vanion.

"It's used to pass messages, your Excellency," Vanion replied. "It summons the awareness of the Child-Goddess, but not her presence. We can give her a message to carry to someone else by using that spell."

"Isn't that just a little demeaning for the Child-Goddess? Do you really make her run errands and carry messages that way?"

"I'm not offended, Itagne." Aphrael smiled. "After all, we live only to serve those we love, don't we?"

Berit's pronunciation of the second spell raised no objections.

"You'll probably want to use that one most of the time anyway, Berit," Vanion instructed. "Krager warned Sparhawk about using magic, so don't be too obvious about things. If you get any further instructions along the road, make some show of following them, but pass the word on to Aphrael."

"There's no real point in decking him out in Sparhawk's armor now, is there, Lord Vanion?" Khalad asked.

"Good point," Vanion agreed. "A mail shirt should do, Berit. We *want* them to see your face now."

"Yes, my Lord."

"Now you'd better get some sleep," Vanion continued. "You'll be starting early tomorrow morning."

"Not *too* early, though," Caalador amended. "We surely wouldn't want th' spies t' oversleep therselfs an' miss seein' y' leave. Gittin' a new face don't mean shucks iffn y' don't git no chance t' show it off, now does it?"

It was chill and damp in the courtyard the following morning, and a thin autumn mist lay over the gleaming city. Sparhawk led Faran out of the stables. "Just be careful," he cautioned the two young men in chain-mail shirts and travelers' cloaks.

"You've said that already, my Lord," Khalad reminded him. "Berit and I aren't deaf, you know."

"You'd better forget that name, Khalad," Sparhawk said critically. "Start thinking of your young friend here as me. A slip of the tongue in the wrong place could give this all away."

"I'll keep that in mind."

"Do you need money?"

"I thought you'd never ask."

"You're as bad as your father was." Sparhawk pulled a purse from under his belt and handed it to his squire. Then he firmly took Faran by the chin and looked straight into the big roan's eyes. "I want you to go with Berit, Faran," he said. "Behave exactly as you would if he were me."

Faran flicked his ears and looked away.

"Pay attention," Sparhawk said sharply. "This is important."

Faran sighed.

"He knows what you're talking about, Sparhawk," Khalad said. "He's not stupid—just bad-tempered."

Sparhawk handed the reins to Berit. Then he remembered something. "We'll need a password," he said. "The rest of us are going to have different faces, so you won't recognize us if we have to contact you. Pick something ordinary."

They all considered it.

"How about *ramshorn*?" Berit suggested. "It shouldn't be too hard to work it into an ordinary conversation, and we've used it before."

Sparhawk suddenly remembered Ulesim, most-favored-disciple-of-holy-Arasham, standing atop a pile of rubble with Kurik's crossbow bolt sticking out of his forehead and the word *ramshorn* still on his lips. "Very good, Berit—ah—Sir Sparhawk, that is. It's a word we all remember. You'd better get started."

They nodded and swung up into their saddles.

"Good luck," Sparhawk said.

"You, too, my Lord," Khalad replied. And then the pair turned and rode slowly toward the drawbridge.

"All we've really got to work with is the name *Beresa*," Sarabian mused, somewhat later. "Krager's note said that Sparhawk would receive further instructions there."

"That could be a ruse, your Majesty," Itagne pointed out. "Actually, the exchange could take place at any time—and any place. That *might* have been the reason for the instructions to go overland."

"That's true," Caalador agreed. "Scarpa and Zalasta might just be waiting on the beach on the west side of the Gulf of Micae wanting to make the trade right there, for all we know."

"We're going to an awful lot of trouble here," Talen said. "Why doesn't Sparhawk just have Bhelliom go rescue the queen? It could pick her up and have her back here before Scarpa even knew she was gone."

"No," Aphrael said, shaking her head. "Bhelliom can't do that any more than I can."

"Why not?"

"Because we don't know where she *is*—and we can't go looking for her, because they'll be able to sense us moving around."

"Oh. I didn't know that."

Aphrael rolled her eyes upward. "Men!" She sighed.

"It was very resourceful of Ehlana to slip her ring to Melidere," Sephrenia said, "but locating her would be much easier if she still had it with her."

"I sort of doubt that, dear," Vanion disagreed. "Zalasta of all people knows that the rings can be traced. If Ehlana had still been wearing it, the first thing Scarpa would have done would have been to send Krager or Elron off in the opposite direction with it."

"You're assuming that Zalasta's involved in this," she disagreed. "There *is* the possibility that Scarpa's acting on his own, you know."

"It's always better to assume the worst." He shrugged. "Our situation is much more perilous if Zalasta and Cyrgon are involved. If it's only Scarpa, he'll be relatively easy to dispose of."

"But *only* after Ehlana and Alean are safe," Sparhawk amended.

"That goes without saying, Sparhawk," Vanion said.

"Everything hinges on the moment of the exchange, then, doesn't it?" Sarabian noted. "We can make some preparations, but we won't be able to do anything at all significant until the moment that Scarpa actually produces Ehlana."

"And that means that we have to stay close to Berit and Khalad," Tynian added.

"No." Aphrael was shaking her head. "You'll give everything away if you all start hovering over those two. Let *me* do the staying close. I don't wear armor, so no one will be able to smell me from a thousand paces off. Itagne's right. The exchange could come at any time. I'll let Sparhawk know the very instant Scarpa shows up with Ehlana and Alean. Then Bhelliom can set him down—with knife—right on top of them. We'll have the ladies back, and we'll be more or less in charge of things again."

"And that brings us right back to a purely military situation," Patriarch Emban mused. "I think we'll want to send word to Komier and Bergsten. We're going to need the Church Knights in Cynesga and Arjuna, not in Edom or Astel—or here in Matherion. Let's have them ride southeast after they come down out of the mountains of Zemoch. We'll have the Atans in Sarna, the eastern Peloi and the Church Knights we've already got in Samar, the Trolls in the Tamul Mountains and Komier and Bergsten on the western side of the Desert of Cynesga. We'll be able to squeeze the land of the Cyrgai like a lemon at that point."

"And see what kind of seeds come popping out," Kalten added bleakly.

Patriarch Emban, First Secretary of the Church of Chyrellos, was a man who absolutely adored lists. The fat little churchman automatically drew up a list when any subject was being discussed. There is a certain point in most discussions when things have all been settled and the participants start going back over the various points. Inevitably, that was the point at which Emban pulled out his list. "All right, then," he said in a tone that clearly said that he was summing up, "Sparhawk will take ship for Beresa, along with Milord Stragen and young master Talen, right?"

"It puts him in place in case Berit and Khalad do, in fact, have to ride all the way down there, your Grace," Vanion said. "And Stragen and Talen have contacts in Beresa, so they'll probably be able to find out just who else is in town."

Emban checked that off his list. "Next: Sir Kalten, Sir Bevier, and Master Caalador will sail south on a different ship and go into the jungles of Arjuna."

Caalador nodded. "I've got a friend in the Delo who has contacts with the robber bands in those jungles," he said. "We'll join one of those bands, so we'll be able to keep an eye on Natayos and pass the word if Scarpa's army starts to move."

"Right." Emban checked *that* off. "Next. Sir Ulath and Sir Tynian will go to the Tamul Mountains to stay in touch with the Trolls." He frowned. "Why is Tynian going there?" he asked. "He doesn't speak Trollish."

"Tynian and I get along well," Ulath rumbled, "and I'll get terribly lonely if there's no one around to talk with but Trolls. You have no idea how depressing it is to be alone with Trolls, your Grace."

"Whatever makes you happy, Sir Ulath." Emban shrugged. "Now then, Sephrenia and Anarae Xanetia will go to Delphaeus to advise Anari Cedon about all these recent developments and to explain what we're doing."

"*And* to see what we can do to make peace between Styricum and the Delphae," Sephrenia added.

Emban checked off another item. He said, "Lord Vanion, Queen Betuana, Ambassador Itagne, and Domi Kring will take the five thousand knights and go to western Tamul proper to join with the forces they have in place in Sarna and Samar."

"Where *is* Domi Kring?" Betuana asked, looking around for the little man.

"He's standing guard over Mirtai," Princess Danae said. "He's still about half-afraid she might try to kill herself."

"We might have a problem there," Bevier observed. "Under those circumstances, Kring might not be willing to leave Matherion."

"We can get along without him if we have to," Vanion said. "I can deal with Tikume directly. Having Kring around would make it easier, but I can make do without him if he really thinks that Mirtai might do something foolish."

Emban nodded. "Emperor Sarabian, Foreign Minister Oscagne, and I will stay here in Matherion to hold down the fort, and the Child-Goddess will keep us all in touch with each other. Have I left anything out?"

"What do you want me to do, Emban?" Danae asked sweetly.

"You'll stay here in Matherion with us, your Royal Highness," Emban replied, "to brighten our gloomy days and nights with the sunshine of your smile."

"Are you making fun of me, your Grace?"

"Of course not, Princess."

To say that Mirtai was unhappy would have been the grossest of understatements. She was in chains when Kring brought her into the council chamber with a hopeless look on his face. "Nothing I say reaches her," the Domi told them. "I think she's even forgotten that we're betrothed."

The golden Atan giantess would not look at any of them, but sank instead to the floor in abject misery.

"She has failed her owner." Betuana shrugged. "She must either avenge her or die."

"Not quite, your Majesty," Sparhawk's daughter said firmly. She slipped down from the chair in the corner from which she had been watching the proceedings. She deposited Rollo in one corner of the chair and Mmrr in the other and crossed the room to Mirtai with a businesslike look on her small face. "Atana Mirtai," she said crisply, "get up off the floor."

Mirtai looked sullenly at her, then slowly rose, her chains clinking.

"In my mother's absence, I am the queen," Danae declared.

Sparhawk blinked.

"You're not Ehlana," Mirtai said.

"I'm not pretending to be. I'm stating a legal fact. Sarabian, isn't that the way it works? Isn't my mother's power mine while she's away?"

"Well—technically, I suppose."

"Technically, my foot. I'm Queen Ehlana's heir. I'm assuming her position until she returns. That means that I temporarily own everything that's hers—her throne, her crown, her jewels, *and* her personal slave."

"I'd hate to have to argue against her in a court of law," Emban admitted.

"Thank you, your Grace," Danae said. "All right, Atana Mirtai, you heard them. You're *my* property now."

Mirtai scowled at her.

"Don't do that," Danae snapped. "Pay attention. I am your owner, and I forbid you to kill yourself. I *also* forbid you to run off. I need you here. You're going to stay here with Melidere and me, and you're going to guard us. You failed my mother. Don't fail me."

Mirtai stiffened, and then she broke her chains with an angry wrench of her arms. "It shall be as you say, Majesty," she snapped, her eyes blazing.

Danae looked around at the rest of them with a smug little smile. "See," she said. "Now that wasn't so hard, was it?"

CHAPTER FOUR

It was a small, single-masted coastal freighter with a leaky bottom and patched sails. It definitely did *not* skim the waves. Berit and Khalad wore their mail shirts and travelers' cloaks and they stood in the bow looking out across the leaden expanse of the Gulf of Micae as the wretched vessel wallowed along. "Is that the coast up ahead?" Berit asked hopefully.

Khalad looked out across the choppy water. "No, just a cloud bank. We're not moving very fast, my Lord. We won't make the coast today, I'm afraid." He looked aft and lowered his voice. "Stay alert after the sun goes down," he instructed. "The crew of this tub is made up of waterfront sweepings, and the captain isn't much better. I think we should take turns sleeping tonight."

Berit glanced back along the deck at the assortment of ruffians loitering on deck. "I wish I had my ax," he muttered.

"Don't say things like that out loud, Berit," Khalad muttered. "*Sparhawk* doesn't use a war ax. Krager knows that, and one of these sailors may be working for him."

"Still? After the Harvest Festival?"

"Nobody's ever figured out a way to kill *all* the rats, my Lord, and it only takes one. Let's both behave as if we're being watched and every word we say is being overheard—just to be on the safe side."

"I'll be a lot happier once we get ashore. Did we really have to make this leg of the trip by sea?"

"It's the custom." Khalad shrugged. "Don't worry. We can hold off these sailors if we have to."

"That's not what's bothering me, Khalad. This scow waddles through the water like a whale with a sprained back. It's making me queasy."

"Eat a piece of dry bread."

"I'd rather not. This is *really* miserable, Khalad."

"But we're having an *adventure,* my Lord," Khalad said brightly. "Doesn't the excitement make up for the discomfort?"

"No. Not really."

"You're the one who wanted to be a knight."

"Yes, I know—and right now I'm trying to remember why."

Patriarch Emban was very displeased. "This is really outrageous, Vanion," he protested as he waddled along with the others toward the chapel in the west wing. "If Dolmant ever finds out that I've permitted the practice of witchcraft in a consecrated place of worship, he'll have me defrocked."

"It's the safest place, Emban," Vanion replied. "The pretense of 'sacred rites' gives us an excuse to chase all the Tamuls out of the west wing. Besides, the chapel's probably never really been consecrated anyway. This is an imitation castle built to make Elenes feel at home. The people who built it couldn't have known the rite of consecration."

"You don't *know* that it hasn't been consecrated."

"And you don't know that it has. If it bothers you all that much, Emban, you can reconsecrate it after we finish."

Emban's face blanched. "Do you know what's involved in that, Vanion?" he protested. "The hours of praying—the prostration before the altar—the fasting?" His chubby face went pale. "Good God, the fasting!"

Sephrenia, Flute, and Xanetia had slipped into the chapel several hours earlier, and they were sitting unobtrusively in one corner listening to a choir of Church Knights singing hymns.

Emban and Vanion were still arguing when they joined the ladies. "What's the problem?" Sephrenia asked.

"Patriarch Emban and Lord Vanion are having a disagreement about whether or not the chapel's been consecrated, little mother," Kalten explained.

"It hasn't," Flute told him with a little shrug.

"How can you tell?" Emban demanded.

She gave him a long-suffering look. "Who am I, your Grace?" she asked him.

He blinked. "Oh. I keep forgetting that for some reason. Is there actually a way you can tell whether or not a place has been consecrated?"

"Well of *course* there is. Believe me, Emban, this chapel's never been consecrated to your Elene God." She paused. "There was a spot not far from here that was consecrated to a tree about eighteen thousand years ago, though."

"A *tree?*"

"It was a very nice tree—an oak. It's always an oak for some reason. Nobody ever seems to want to worship an elm. Lots of people used to worship trees. They're predictable, for one thing."

"How could anybody in his right mind worship a tree?"

"Whoever said that religious people were in their right minds? Sometimes you humans confuse us a great deal, you know."

Since there was an exchange of features involved in most cases here, Sephrenia and Xanetia had experimented a bit to alter the spell that had imprinted Sparhawk's face on Berit. No exchange was necessary for Sparhawk, however, so they modified him first. He sat beside his old friend, Sir Endrik, a veteran with whom he, Kalten, and Martel had endured their novitiates. Xanetia approached them with the color draining from her features and that soft radiance suffusing her face. She examined Endrik meticulously, and then her voice rose as she began to intone the Delphaeic spell in her oddly accented, archaic Tamul. Sephrenia stood at her side simultaneously casting the Styric spell.

Sparhawk felt nothing whatsoever as Xanetia released her spell. Then at the crucial instant, Sephrenia extended her hand, interposing it between Sir Endrik's face and Xanetia's and simultaneously releasing the Styric spell. Sparhawk *definitely* felt that. His features seemed to somehow soften like melting wax, and he could actually feel his face changing, almost as wet clay is changed and molded by the potter's hand. The straightening of his broken nose was a bit painful, and the lengthening of his jaw made his teeth ache as they shifted in the bone.

"What do you think?" Sephrenia asked Vanion when the process had been completed.

"I don't think you could get them any closer," Vanion replied, examining the two men closely. "How does it feel to be twins, Endrik?"

"I didn't feel a thing, my Lord," Endrik replied, staring curiously at Sparhawk.

"*I* did," Sparhawk told him, gingerly touching his reshaped nose. "Does the ache go away eventually, Anarae?" he asked.

"Thou wilt notice it less as time doth accustom thee to the alteration, Anakha. I did warn thee that some discomfort is involved, did I not?"

"You did indeed." Sparhawk shrugged. "It's not unbearable."

"Do I really look like that?" Endrik asked.

"Yes," Vanion replied.

"I should take better care of myself. The years aren't being good to me."

"Nobody stays young and beautiful forever, Endrik." Kalten laughed.

"Is that all that needs to be done to these two, Anarae?" Vanion asked.

"The process is complete, Lord Vanion," Xanetia replied.

"We need to talk, Sparhawk," the preceptor said. "Let's go into the vestry where we'll be out of the way while the ladies modify the others."

Sparhawk nodded, stood up, and followed his friend to the small door to the left of the altar.

Vanion led the way inside and closed the door behind them. "You've made all the arrangements with Sorgi?" he asked.

Sparhawk sat down. "I talked with him yesterday," he replied. "I told him that I had some friends that had to go to Beresa without attracting attention. He's had the usual desertions, so he's holding three berths open. Stragen, Talen, and I'll merge with the crew. We should be able to slip into Beresa without being noticed."

"I imagine that cost you. Sorgi's prices are a little steep sometimes."

Sparhawk massaged the side of his aching jaw. "It wasn't all that bad," he said. "Sorgi owes me a couple of favors, and I gave him time to pick up a cargo to cover most of the cost."

"You'll be going directly to the harbor from here?"

Sparhawk nodded. "We'll use that tunnel Caalador found under the barracks. I told Sorgi that his three new crew members would report to him about midnight."

"You'll sail tomorrow, then?"

Sparhawk shook his head. "The day after. We have to load Sorgi's cargo tomorrow."

"Honest work, Sparhawk?" Vanion smiled.

"You're starting to sound like Khalad."

"He *does* have opinions, doesn't he?"

"So did his father."

"Quit rubbing your face like that, Sparhawk. You'll make your skin raw." Vanion paused. "What was it like?"

"Very strange."

"Painful?"

"The nose was. It feels almost as if somebody broke it again. Be glad you don't have to go through it."

"There wouldn't be much point in that. I won't be sneaking down alleys the way the rest of you will." Vanion looked sympathetically at his friend. "We'll get her back, Sparhawk," he said.

"Of course. Was that all?" Sparhawk's tone was deliberately unemotional. The important thing here was *not* to feel.

"Just be careful, and try to keep a handle on your temper."

Sparhawk nodded. "Let's go see how the others are coming."

The alterations were confusing; there was no question about that. It was hard to tell exactly who was talking, and sometimes Sparhawk was startled by just who answered his questions. They said their good-byes and quietly left the chapel with the main body of the Church Knights. They went out into the torchlit courtyard, crossed the drawbridge, and proceeded across the night-shrouded lawn to the barracks of the knights, where Sparhawk, Stragen, and Talen changed into tar-smeared sailor's smocks while the others also donned the mismatched clothing of commoners. Then they all went down to the cellar.

Caalador, who now wore the blocky face of a middle-aged Deiran knight, led the way into a damp, cobweb-draped tunnel with a smoky torch. When they had gone about a mile, he stopped and raised the torch. "This yere's yer exit, Sparhawk," he said, pointing at a steep, narrow stairway. "You'll come out in an alley—which it is ez don't smell none too sweet, but is good an' dork." He paused. "Sorry, Stragen," he apologized. "I wanted to give you something to remember me by."

"You're too kind," Stragen murmured.

"Good luck, Sparhawk," Caalador said then.

"Thanks, Caalador." The two shook hands, and then Caalador lifted his torch and led the rest of the party down the musty-smelling passageway toward their assorted destinations, leaving Sparhawk, Talen, and Stragen alone in the dark.

"They won't be in any danger, Vanion," Flute assured the preceptor as the ladies were packing. "I'll be going along, after all, and I can take care of them."

"*Ten* knights, then," he amended his suggestion downward.

"They'd just be in our way, love," Sephrenia told him. "I do want you to be careful, though. A body of armed men is far more likely to be attacked than a small party of travelers."

"But it isn't safe for ladies to travel alone," he protested. "There are always robbers and the like lurking in the forest."

"We won't be in one place long enough to attract robbers or anybody else," Flute told him. "We'll be in Delphaeus in two days. I could do it in one, but I'll have to stop and have a long talk with Edaemus before I go into his valley. He might just take a bit of convincing."

"When art thou leaving Matherion, Lord Vanion?" Xanetia asked.

"About the end of the week, Anarae," he replied. "We've got to spend some time on our equipment, and there's always the business of organizing the supply train."

"Take warm clothing," Sephrenia instructed. "The weather could change at any time."

"Yes, love. How long will you be at Delphaeus?"

"We can't be sure. Aphrael will keep you advised. We have a great deal to discuss with Anari Cedon. The fact that Cyrgon has summoned Klæl complicates matters."

"Truly," Xanetia agreed. "We may be obliged to entreat Edaemus to return."

"Would he do that?"

Flute smiled roguishly. "I'll coax him, Vanion," she said, "and you know how good I am at that. If I really want something, I almost always get it."

"You there! Look lively!" Sorgi's bull-necked bo'sun bellowed, popping his whip at Stragen's heels.

Stragen, who now wore the braids and sweeping mustaches of a blond Genidian Knight, dropped the bale he was carrying across the deck and reached for his dagger.

"No!" Sparhawk elbowed him. "Pick up that bale!"

Stragen glared at him for a moment, then bent and lifted the bale again. "This wasn't part of the agreement," he muttered.

"He's not really going to hit you with that whip," Talen assured the fuming Thalesian. "Sailors all complain about it, but the whip's just for show. A bo'sun who really hits his men with his whip usually gets thrown over the side some night during the voyage."

"Maybe," Stragen growled darkly, "but I'll tell you this right now. If that cretin so much as *touches* me with that whip of his, he won't live long enough to go swimming. I'll have his guts in a pile on the deck before he can even blink."

"You new men!" the bo'sun shouted. "Do your talking on your own time! You're here to work, not to discuss the weather!" And he cracked his whip again.

"She *could* do it, Khalad," Berit insisted.

"I think you've been out in the sun too long," Khalad replied. They were riding south along a lonely beach under an overcast sky. The beach was backed by an uninviting salt marsh where dry reeds clattered against each other in the stiff onshore breeze. Khalad rose in his stirrups and looked around. Then he settled back in his saddle again. "It's a ridiculous idea, my Lord."

"Try to keep an open mind, Khalad. Aphrael's a Goddess. She can do *anything.*"

"I'm sure she can, but why would she *want* to?"

"Well—" Berit struggled with it. "She *could* have a reason, couldn't she? Something that you and I wouldn't even understand?"

"Is this what all that Styric training does to a man? You're starting to see Gods under every bush. It was only a coincidence. The two of them look a little bit alike, but that's all."

"You can be as skeptical as you want, Khalad, but I still think that something very strange is going on."

"And I think that what you're suggesting is an absurdity."

"Absurd or not, their mannerisms are the same, their expressions are identical, and they've both got that same air of smug superiority about them."

"Of course they do. Aphrael's a Goddess, and Danae's a Crown Princess. They *are* superior—at least in their own minds—and I think you're overlooking the fact that we saw them both in the same room and at the same time. They even *talked* to each other, for God's sake."

"Khalad, that doesn't mean anything. Aphrael's a Goddess. She can probably be in a dozen different places all at the same time if she really wants to be."

"That still brings us right back to the question of why? What would be the purpose of it? Not even a God does things without any reason."

"We don't *know* that, Khalad. Maybe she's doing it just to amuse herself."

"Are you really all that desperate to witness miracles, Berit?"

"She *could* do it," Berit insisted.

"All right. So what?"

"Aren't you the least bit curious about it?"

"Not particularly." Khalad shrugged.

Ulath and Tynian wore bits and pieces of the uniforms of one of the few units of the Tamul army that accepted volunteers from the Elene kingdoms of western Daresia. The faces they had borrowed were those of grizzled, middle-aged knights, the faces of hard-bitten veterans. The vessel aboard which they sailed was one of those battered, ill-maintained ships that ply coastal waters. The small amount of money they had paid for their passage bought them exactly that—passage, and nothing else. They had brought their own food and drink and their patched blankets, and they ate and slept on the deck. Their destination was a small coastal village some twenty-five leagues east of the foothills of the Tamul Mountains. They lounged on the deck in the daytime, drinking cheap wine and rolling dice for pennies.

The sky was overcast when the ship's longboat deposited them on the rickety wharf of the village. The day was cool, and the Tamul Mountains were little more than a low smudge on the horizon.

"What was that horse trader's name again?" Tynian asked.

"Sablis," Ulath grunted.

"I hope Oscagne was right," Tynian said. "If this Sablis has gone out of business, we'll have to walk to those mountains."

Ulath stepped across the wharf to speak to a pinch-faced fellow who was mending a fishnet. "Tell me, friend," he said politely in Tamul, "where can we find Sablis the horse trader?"

"What if I don't feel like telling you?" the scrawny net-mender replied in a whining, nasal voice that identified him as one of those mean-spirited men who would rather die than be helpful, or even polite.

Tynian had encountered his kind before: small men, usually, with an inflated notion of their own worth, men who delighted in irritating others just for the fun of it. "Let me," he murmured, laying one gently restraining hand on his Thalesian companion's arm. Ulath's bunched muscles clearly spoke of impending violence.

"Nice net," Tynian noted casually, picking up one edge of it. Then he drew his dagger and began cutting the strings.

"What are you *doing*?" the pinch-faced fisherman screamed.

"I'm showing you what," Tynian explained. "You said, 'What if I don't feel like telling you?' *This* is what. Think it over. My friend and I aren't in any hurry, so take your time." He took a fistful of net and sawed through it with his knife.

"*Stop!*" the fellow shrieked in horror.

"Ah—where was it you said we might find Sablis?" Ulath asked innocently.

"His corrals are on the eastern edge of town." The words came tumbling out. Then the scrawny fellow gathered up his net in both arms and held it to his chest, almost like a mother shielding a child from harm.

"Have a pleasant day, neighbor," Tynian said, sheathing his dagger. "I can't *begin* to tell you how much we've appreciated your help." And the two knights turned and walked along the wharf toward the shabby-looking village.

· · ·

Their camp was neat and orderly with a place for everything and everything exactly where it belonged. Berit had noticed that Khalad always set up camp in exactly the same way. He seemed to have some concept of the ideal camp etched in his mind and, since it was perfect, he never altered it. Khalad was very rigid in some ways.

"How far did we come today?" Berit asked as they washed up their supper dishes.

"Ten leagues—" Khalad shrugged. "—the same as always. Ten leagues is standard on level terrain."

"This is going to take *forever*," Berit complained.

"No. It might seem like it, though." Khalad looked around and then lowered his voice until it was hardly more than a whisper. "We're not really in any hurry, Berit," he said. "We might even want to slow down a bit."

"What?"

"Keep your voice down. Sparhawk and the others have a long way to go, and we want to be sure they're in place before Krager—or whoever it is—makes contact with us. We don't know when or where that's going to happen, so the best way to delay it is to slow down." Khalad looked out into the darkness beyond the circle of firelight. "How good are you at magic?"

"Not very," Berit admitted, scrubbing diligently. "I've still got a lot to learn. What did you want me to do?"

"Could you make one of our horses limp—without actually hurting him?"

Berit probed through his memory. Then he shook his head. "I don't think I know any spells that would do that."

"That's too bad. A lame horse would give us a good reason to slow down."

It came without warning: a cold, prickling kind of sensation that seemed to be centered at the back of Berit's neck. "That's good enough," he said in a louder voice. "I'm not getting paid enough to scrub holes in tin plates." He rinsed off the dish he'd been washing, shook most of the water off it, and stowed it back into the pack.

"You felt it, too?" Khalad's whisper came out from between motionless lips. That startled Berit. How could Khalad have known?

Berit buckled the straps on the pack and gave his friend a curt nod. "Let's build up the fire a bit and then get some sleep." He said it loudly enough to be heard out beyond the circle of firelight. The two of them walked toward their pile of firewood. Berit was murmuring the spell and concealing the movements of his hands at the same time.

"Who is it?" Again, Khalad's lips did not move.

"I'm still working on that," Berit whispered back. He released the spell so slowly that it seemed almost to dribble out of the ends of his fingers.

The sense of it came washing back to him. It was something on the order of recognizing an accent—except that it was done when nobody was talking. "It's a Styric," he said quietly.

"Zalasta?"

"No, I don't believe so. I think I'd recognize him. It's somebody I've never been around before."

"Not too much wood, my Lord," Khalad said aloud. "This pile has to get us through breakfast, too, you know."

"Good thinking," Berit approved. He reached out again, very cautiously. "He's moving away," he muttered. "How did you know we were being watched?"

"I could feel it." Khalad shrugged. "I always know when somebody's watching me. How noisy is it when you get in touch with Aphrael?"

"That's one of the good spells. It doesn't make a sound."

"You'd better tell her about this. Let her know that we *are* being watched and that it's a Styric who's doing the watching." Khalad knelt and began carefully to stack his armload of broken-off limbs on their campfire. "Your disguise seems to be working," he noted.

"How did you arrive at that?"

"They wouldn't waste a Styric on us if they knew who you really were."

"Unless they don't have anybody left *except* Styrics. Stragen's celebration of the Harvest Festival might have been more effective than we thought."

"We could probably argue about that all night. Just tell Aphrael about our visitor out there. She'll pass it on to the others, and we'll let *them* get the headache from trying to sort it out with logic."

"Aren't you curious about it?"

"Not so curious that I'm going to lose any sleep over it. That's one of the advantages of being a peasant, my Lord. We're not *required* to come up with the answers to these earthshaking questions. You aristocrats get the pleasure of doing that."

"Thanks," Berit said sourly.

"No charge, my Lord." Khalad grinned.

Sparhawk had never actually worked for a living before and he discovered that he did not like it very much. He quickly grew to hate Captain Sorgi's thick-necked bo'sun. The man was crude, stupid, and spitefully cruel. He fawned outrageously whenever Sorgi appeared on the quarterdeck, but when the captain returned below decks, the bo'sun's natural character reasserted itself. He seemed to take particular delight in tormenting the newest members of the crew, assigning them the most tedious, exhausting, and demeaning tasks aboard ship. Sparhawk found himself quite suddenly in full agreement with Khalad's class prejudices, and sometimes at night he found himself contemplating murder.

"Every man hates his employer, Fron," Stragen told him, using Sparhawk's assumed name. "It's a very natural part of the scheme of things."

"I could stand him if he didn't deliberately go out of his way to be offensive," Sparhawk growled, scrubbing at the deck with his block of pumice-stone.

"He's *paid* to be offensive, my friend. Angry men work harder. Part of your problem is that you always look him right in the eye. He wouldn't single you out the way he does if you'd keep your eyes lowered. If you don't, this is going to be a very long voyage for you."

"Or a short one for him," Sparhawk said darkly.

He considered it that night as he tried, without much success, to sleep in his hammock. He fervently wished that he could get his hands on the idiot who had decided that humans could sleep in hammocks. The roll of the ship made it swing from side to side, and Sparhawk continually felt that he was right on the verge of being thrown out.

Anakha. The voice was only a whisper in his mind.

Sparhawk was stunned. "Blue-Rose?" he said.

Prithee, Anakha, do not speak aloud. Thy voice is as the thunder in mine ears. Speak silently in the halls of thine awareness. I will hear thee.

How is this possible? Sparhawk framed the thought. *Thou art confined.*

Who hath power to confine me, Anakha? When thou art alone and thy mind is clear of other distraction, we may speak thus.

I did not know that.

Until now, it was not needful for thee to know.

I see. But now it is?

Yes.

How dost thou penetrate the barrier of the gold?

It is no barrier to me, Anakha. Others may not sense me within the confines of thine excellent receptacle. I, however, may reach out to thee in this manner. This is particularly true when we are so close.

Sparhawk laid his hand on the leather pouch hanging on a thong about his neck and felt the square outline of the box. *And should it prove needful, may I speak so with thee?*

Even as thou dost now, Anakha.

This is good to know.

I sense thy disquiet, Anakha, and I share thine anxiety for the safety of thy mate.

Thou art kind to say so, Blue-Rose.

Expend thou all thine efforts to securing thy queen's release, Anakha. I will keep watch over our enemies whilst thou art so occupied. The jewel under Sparhawk's hand paused. *Hear me well, my friend,* Bhelliom continued, *should it come to pass that no other course be open to thee, fear not to surrender me up to obtain thy mate's freedom.*

That I will not do—for she hath forbidden it.

Do not be untranquil if it should come to pass, Anakha. I will not submit to Cyrgon, even though mine own child, whom I love even as thou lovest thine, be endangered by my refusal. Be comforted in the knowledge that I will not permit my child—nor thee and all thy kind—to be enslaved by Cyrgon—or worse yet, by Klæl. Thou hast my promise that this will never happen. Should it appear that our task doth verge on failure, I give thee my solemn vow that I shall destroy this child of mine and all who dwell here to prevent such mischance.

Is that supposed to make me feel better?

She was always tired, hovering at times on the verge of exhaustion, and she was nearly always wet and dirty. Her clothes were ripped and tattered, and her hair was a ruin. Those things were unimportant, however. She willingly submitted to discomfort and indignities to keep the madman who was their captor from hurting the terrified Alean.

The realization that Scarpa was mad had come to her slowly. She had known from the first moment she had seen him that he was ruthless and driven, but the evidence of his insanity had become gradually more and more overwhelming as the endless days of her captivity ground on.

He was cruel, but Ehlana had encountered cruel men before. After she and Alean had been hurried through the dank tunnels under the streets of Matherion to the outskirts of the city, they had been roughly shoved into the saddles of waiting horses, bound securely in place, and literally dragged at breakneck speed down the road leading to the port of Micae on the southwestern coast of the peninsula, seventy-five leagues away. A normal man does not mistreat the animals upon which he is totally dependent. That was the first evidence of Scarpa's madness. He drove the horses, flogging them savagely until the poor beasts were staggering with exhaustion, and his only words during those dreadful four days were, "Faster! Faster!"

Ehlana shuddered as she recalled the horror of that endless ride. They had—

Her horse stumbled in the muddy path, and she was jolted forward, bringing her attention back into the immediate present. The cord that tightly bound her wrists to the saddlebow dug into her flesh, and the bleeding started again. She tried to ease into a different position so that the cord would no longer cut into the already open wounds.

"What are you doing?" Scarpa demanded. His voice was harsh, and it came out almost as a scream. Scarpa almost always screamed when he was talking to her.

"I'm just trying to keep the cord from cutting deeper into my wrists, Lord Scarpa," she replied meekly. She had been instructed early in her captivity to address him so and she had quickly found that failure to do so resulted in savage mistreatment of Alean *and* the withholding of food and water.

"You're not here to be comfortable, woman!" he raged at her. "You're here to obey! I see what you're doing there! If you don't stop trying to loosen those cords, I'll use wire!" His eyes bulged, and she saw again that strange, bluish cast to the whites of those eyes and the abnormally large pupils.

"Yes, Lord Scarpa," she said in her most submissive tone.

He glared at her, his face filled with suspicion and his mad eyes looking hungrily for some excuse to punish or humiliate his prisoners further.

She lowered her gaze to stare fixedly at the rough, muddy track that wound deeper and deeper into the rank, vine-choked forest of the southeast coast of Daresia.

The ship they had boarded at the port of Micae had been a sleek, black-hulled corsair that could not have been built for any honest purpose. She and Alean had been unceremoniously dragged below decks and confined in a cramped compartment that smelled of the bilges and was totally dark. After they had been two hours at sea, the compartment door had opened and Krager had entered with two swarthy sailors, one carrying what appeared to be a decent meal, and the other, two pails of hot water, some soap, and a wad of rags for use as towels. Ehlana had resisted an impulse to embrace the fellow.

"I'm really sorry about all this, Ehlana," Krager had apologized, squinting at her nearsightedly, "but I have no control of the situation. Be very careful of what you say to Scarpa. You've probably noticed that he's not entirely rational." He had looked around nervously, then laid a handful of cheap tallow candles on the rough table and left, chaining the door shut behind him.

They had been five days at sea and had reached Anan, a port city on the edge of the jungles of the southeast coast, some time after midnight. Then she and Alean had been hustled into a closed carriage with the pouchy-eyed Baron Parok at the reins. During the transfer from the ship to the carriage, Ehlana had discreetly looked at each of her captors, seeking some weakness. Krager, despite his habitual drunkenness, was too shrewd, and Parok was Scarpa's longtime confederate, a man evidently untroubled by his friend's madness. Then she had coolly appraised Elron. She had noticed that under no circumstances would the foppish Astellian poet look her in the eye. His apparent murder of Melidere had evidently filled him with remorse. Elron was a poseur rather than a man of action, and he clearly had no stomach for blood. She had recalled, moreover, how vain he had been about his long curls when she had first met him and had wondered what form of duress Scarpa had used to force him to shave his head in order to pose as one of Kring's Peloi. She had surmised that the violation of his hair had raised certain strong resentments in him. Elron was clearly reluctant to participate in this affair, and that made *him* the weak link. She kept that fact firmly in mind now. The time might come when she could use it to her advantage.

The carriage had carried them from the waterfront to a large house on the outskirts of Anan. It had been there that Scarpa had spoken with a gaunt Styric with the lumpy features characteristic of the men of his race. The Styric's name was Keska, and his eyes had the look of one hopelessly damned.

"I don't *care* about the discomfort!" Scarpa had half shouted to the gaunt man at one point. "*Time* is important, Keska, time! Just do it! As long as it doesn't kill us, we can endure it!"

The next morning the significance of that command had become all too obvious. Keska was evidently one of those outcast Styric magicians, but not a very good one. He could, with a great deal of clearly exhausting effort, compress the miles that lay between them and Scarpa's intended destination, but only a few miles each time, and the compression was accompanied by a horrid kind of wrenching agony. It seemed almost as if the clumsy magician were jerking them up and hurling them blindly forward with every ounce of his strength, and Ehlana could never be certain after each hideous, bruising jump that she was still intact. She felt torn and battered, but did what she could to conceal her pain from Alean. The gentle girl with the large eyes wept almost continuously now, overcome by her pain and fear and the misery of their circumstances.

Ehlana drew her mind into the present and looked about warily. It was approaching evening again. The overcast sky was gradually darkening, and the time of day Ehlana dreaded the most would soon be upon them.

Scarpa looked with some scorn at Keska, who slumped in his saddle like a wilted flower, obviously near exhaustion. "This is far enough," he said. "Set up some kind of camp and get the women down off those horses." His brittle eyes grew bright as he looked Ehlana full in the face. "It's time for the bedraggled Queen of the Elenes to beg for her supper again. I do hope she'll be more convincing this time. It really distresses me to have to refuse her when her pleas aren't sufficiently sincere."

"Ehlana," Krager whispered, touching her shoulder. The fire had died down to embers, and Ehlana could hear the sound of snores coming from the other side of their rude camp.

"What?" she replied shortly.

"Keep your voice down." He was still wearing the black leather Peloi jerkin, his shaved head was sparsely stubbled, and his wine-reeking breath was nearly overpowering. "I'm doing you a favor. Don't put me in danger. I assume you realize by now that Scarpa's completely insane?"

"Really?" she replied sardonically. "What an amazing thing."

"Please don't make this any more difficult. I seem to have made a small error in judgment here. If I'd fully realized how deranged that half-Styric bastard is, I'd have never agreed to take part in this ridiculous adventure."

"What *is* this strange fascination you have with lunatics, Krager?"

He shrugged. "Maybe it's a character defect. Scarpa actually believes that he can outwit his father—and even Cyrgon. He doesn't really believe that Sparhawk will surrender Bhelliom in exchange for your return, and he's managed to about half convince the others. I'm sure you realize by now how he feels about women."

"He's demonstrated it often enough," she said bitterly. "Does he share Baron Harparin's fondness for little boys instead?"

"Scarpa isn't fond of anything except himself. *He* is his only passion. I've seen him spend hours trimming that beard of his. It gives him the opportunity to adore his reflection in the mirror. You haven't seen his delightful personality in full flower. The details of this trip are keeping what he chooses to call his mind occupied. Wait until we get to Natayos and you hear him start raving. He makes Martel and Annias seem like the very souls of sanity by comparison. I don't dare stay too long, so listen closely. Scarpa believes that Sparhawk will bring Bhelliom with him when he comes, right enough, but he *doesn't* believe he'll bring it to trade for you. Scarpa's absolutely certain that your husband's coming in order to have it out with Cyrgon, *and* he believes that they'll destroy each other in the course of the argument."

"Sparhawk has Bhelliom, you fool, and Bhelliom eats Gods for breakfast."

"I'm not here to argue about that. Maybe Sparhawk will win, and maybe he won't. That's really beside the point. What's important to us is what Scarpa believes. He's convinced himself that Sparhawk and Cyrgon will fight a war of mutual extinction. Then he thinks that Bhelliom will be left lying around free for the taking."

"What about Zalasta?"

"I get the strong feeling that Scarpa doesn't expect Zalasta to be around when the fight's over. Scarpa's more than willing to kill anybody who gets in his way."

"He'd kill his own father?"

Krager shrugged. "Blood ties don't mean anything to Scarpa. When he was younger, he decided that his mother and his half-sisters knew things about him that he didn't want them to share with the authorities, so he killed them. He hated them anyway, so that may not mean all that much. If Sparhawk and Cyrgon *do* kill each other, and if Zalasta's broken out in a sudden rash of mortality during the festivities, Scarpa *might* just be the only one left around to take possession of the Bhelliom. He's got an army in these jungles and, if he has the Bhelliom as well, he might be able to pull it off. He'll march on Matherion, take the city, and slaughter the government. Then he'll crown himself emperor. I'm personally betting against it, though, so for God's sake keep your temper under control. You're not really important to *his* plans, but you're vital to Zalasta's—and mine. If you do anything at all to set Scarpa off, he'll kill you as quickly as he ordered Elron to kill your lady-in-waiting. Zalasta and I believe that Sparhawk *will* trade Bhelliom for you, but only if you're alive. Don't enrage that maniac. If he kills you, all our plans will collapse."

"Why are you telling me this, Krager? There's something else, too, isn't there?"

"Of course. If things go against us, I'd like to have you available to speak out in my behalf when the trials start."

"That wouldn't do any good, I'm afraid," she told him sweetly. "There won't be any trial for you, Krager. Sparhawk's already given you to Khalad, and Khalad's already made up his mind."

"Khalad?" Krager's voice sounded a little weak.

"Kurik's oldest son. He seems to feel that you had some part in his father's death and he feels obliged to do something about it. I suppose you could try to talk him out of it, but I'd advise you to talk fast if you do. Khalad's an abrupt young man, and he'll probably have you hanging from a meat hook before you can get out three words."

Krager didn't answer, but slipped away instead, his shaved scalp pale in the darkness. It wasn't much of a victory, Ehlana privately conceded, but in her situation victories of any kind were very hard to come by.

"They actually do that?" Scarpa's harsh voice was hungry.

"It's an old custom, Lord Scarpa," Ehlana replied in a meek voice, keeping her eyes downcast as they plodded along the muddy path. "Emperor Sarabian is planning to discontinue the practice, however."

"It will be reinstituted immediately following my coronation." Scarpa's eyes were very bright. "It is a proper form of respect." Scarpa had an old purple velvet cloak, shiny with wear, that he had dramatically pulled over one shoulder in a grotesque imitation of an imperial mantle, and he struck absurd poses with each pronouncement.

"As you say, Lord Scarpa." It was tedious to go over the same things again and again, but it kept Scarpa's mind occupied, and when his attention was firmly fixed on the ceremonies and practices of the imperial court in Matherion he was not thinking of ways to make life unbearable for his captives.

"Describe it again," he commanded. "I'll need to know precisely how it's supposed to be done—so that I can punish those who fail to perform it properly."

Ehlana sighed. "At the approach of the imperial person, the members of the court kneel—"

"On both knees?"

"Yes, Lord Scarpa."

"Excellent! Excellent!" His face was exalted. "Go on."

"Then, as the emperor passes, they lean forward, put the palms of their hands on the floor, and touch their foreheads to the tiles."

"Capital!" He suddenly giggled, a high-pitched, almost girlish sound that startled her. She gave him a quick, sidelong glance. His face was grotesquely distorted into an expression of unholy exaltation. And then his eyes grew wide and his expression became one of near-religious ecstasy. "And the Tamuls who rule the world shall be ruled by me!" He intoned in a resonant, declamatory voice. "All power shall be mine! The governance of the world shall be in *my* hands, and disobedience will be death!"

Ehlana shuddered as he raved on.

And he came to her again as humid night settled over their muddy forest encampment, drawn to her by a hunger, a greed that was beyond his ability to control. It was revolting, but Ehlana realized that her knowledge of the particulars of traditional court ceremonies gave her an enormous power over him. His hunger was insatiable, and only she could satisfy it. She grasped that power firmly, drawing strength and confidence from it, actually relishing it even as Krager and the others withdrew with expressions of frightening revulsion.

"Nine wives, you say!" Scarpa's voice was almost pleading. "Why not ninety? Why not nine hundred?"

"It is the custom, Lord Scarpa. The reason for it should be obvious."

"Oh, of course, of course." He brooded darkly over it. "I shall have nine thousand!" he proclaimed. "And each shall be more desirable than the last! And when I have finished with them, they shall be given to my loyal soldiers! Let no woman dare to believe that my favor in any way empowers her! All women are only whores! I shall *buy* them and throw them away when I tire of them!" His mad eyes bulged, and he stared into the campfire. The flickering flames reflected in those eyes seemed to seethe like the madness that lay behind them.

He leaned toward her, laying a confiding hand on her arm. "I have seen that which others are too stupid to see," he told her. "Others look, but they do not see—but *I* see. Oh, yes, I see very well. They are all in it together, you know—all of them. They watch me. They have always watched me. I can never get away from their eyes—watching, watching, watching—and talking, talking behind their hands, breathing their cinnamon-scented breath into each other's faces. All foul and corrupt—scheming, plotting against me, trying to bring me down. Their eyes—all soft and hidden and veiled with the lashes that hide the daggers of their hatred, watching, watching." His voice sank lower and lower. "And talking, talking behind their hands so that I can't hear what they're saying. Whispering. I hear it always. I hear the hissing susurration of their endless whispering. Their eyes following me wherever I go—and their laughing and whispering. I hear the hiss, hiss of their whispering—endless whisper—always my name—Ssscar-pa, Ssscar-pa, Ssscar-pa, again and again, hissing in my ears. Flaunting their rounded limbs and rolling their soot-lined eyes. Plotting, scheming with the endless hissing whispers, always seeking ways to hurt me. Ssscar-pa, Ssscar-pa, trying to humiliate me." His blue-tinged eyeballs were starting from his face, and his lips and beard were flecked with foam. "I was nothing. They made me nothing. They called me Selga's bastard and gave me pennies to lead them to the beds of my mother and my sisters and cuffed me and spat on me and laughed at me when I cried and they lusted after my mother and my sisters and all around me the hissing in my ears—and I smell the sound—that sweet cloying sound of rotten flesh and stale lust all purple and writhing with the liquid hiss of their whispers and—"

Then his mad eyes filled with terror, and he cringed back from her and fell, groveling in the mud. "Please, Mother!" he wailed. "I didn't do it! Silbie did it! Pleasepleaseplease don't lock me in there again! Please not in the dark! Pleasepleaseplease not in the dark! Not in the dark!" And he scrambled to his feet and fled back into the forest with his "Pleasepleaseplease" echoing back in a long, dying fall.

Ehlana was suddenly overcome with a wrenching, unbearable pity, and she bowed her head and wept.

Zalasta was waiting for them in Natayos. The sixteenth and early seventeenth centuries had seen a flowering of Arjuni civilization, a flowering financed largely by the burgeoning slave trade. An ill-advised slave raid into southern Atan, however, coupled with a number of gross policy blunders by the Tamul administrators of that region, had unleashed an uncontrolled Atan punitive expedition. Natayos had been a virtual gem of a city with stately buildings and broad avenues. It was now a forgotten ruin buried in the jungle, its tumbled buildings snarled in ropelike vines, its stately halls now the home of chattering monkeys and brightly colored tropical birds, and its darker recesses inhabited by snakes and the scurrying rats which were their prey.

But now humans had returned to Natayos. Scarpa's army was quartered there, and Arjunis, Cynesgans, and ragtag battalions of Elenes had cleared the quarter near the ancient city's northern gate of vines, trees, monkeys, and reptiles in order to make it semihabitable.

Zalasta stood leaning on his staff at the half-fallen gate, his silvery-bearded face drawn with fatigue and a look of hopeless pain in his eyes. His first reaction when his son arrived with the captives was one of rage. He snarled at Scarpa in Styric, a language that seemed eminently suited for reprimand and one which Ehlana did not understand. She took no small measure of satisfaction, however, in the look of sullen apprehension that crossed Scarpa's face. For all his bluster and airs of pre-eminent superiority, Scarpa still appeared to stand in a certain awe and fear of the ancient Styric who had incidentally sired him.

Once and only once, apparently stung by something Zalasta said to him in a tone loaded with contempt, Scarpa drew himself up and snarled a reply. Zalasta's re-action was immediate and savage. He sent his son reeling with a heavy blow of his staff, then leveled its polished length at him, muttered a few words, and unleashed a fiery spot of light from the tip of the staff. The burning spot struck the still-staggering Scarpa in the belly, and he doubled over sharply, clawing at his stomach and shrieking in agony. He fell onto the muddy earth, kicking and convulsing as Zalasta's spell burned into him. His father, the deadly staff still leveled, watched his writhing son coldly for several endless minutes.

"*Now* do you understand?" he demanded in a deadly voice, speaking in Tamul this time.

"Yes! Yes! Father!" Scarpa shrieked. "Stop! I beg you!"

Zalasta let him writhe and squirm for a while longer. Then he lifted the staff. "You are *not* master here," he declared. "You are no more than a brain-sick incom-petent. Any one of a dozen others here could command this army, so do not try my patience further. Next time, son or no son, I will let the spell follow its natural course. Pain is like a disease, Scarpa. After a few days—or weeks—the body begins to deteriorate. A man can die from pain. Don't force me to prove that to you." And he turned his back on his pale-faced, sweating son. "My apologies, your Majesty," he said to Ehlana. "This was not what I intended."

"And what *did* you intend, Zalasta?" she asked coldly.

"The dispute is between your husband and myself, Ehlana. It was never in my mind to cause you such discomfort. This cretin I must unfortunately acknowledge took it upon himself to mistreat you. I promise you that he will not live to see the sunset of the day in which he does it again."

"I see. The humiliation and pain were not your idea, but the captivity was. Where's the difference, Zalasta?"

He sighed and passed a weary hand over his eyes. "It is necessary," he told her.

"For what reason? Sephrenia will never submit to you, you know. Even if Bhel-liom and the rings fall into your hands, you cannot compel her love."

"There are other considerations as well, Queen Ehlana," he said sorrowfully. "Please bring your maid and come with me. I'll see you to your quarters."

"Some dungeon, I suppose?"

He sighed. "No, Ehlana, the quarters are clean and comfortable. I've seen to that myself. Your ordeal is at an end, I promise you."

"My ordeal, as you call it, will not be at an end until I'm reunited with my hus-band and my daughter."

"That, we may pray, will be very soon. It is, however, in the hands of Prince Sparhawk. All he must do is follow instructions. Your quarters are not far. Follow me, please." He led them to a nearby building and unlocked the door.

Their prison was very nearly luxurious, an apartment of sorts, complete with several bedrooms, a dining hall, a large sitting room, and even a kitchen. The build-ing had evidently been the palace of some nobleman, and, although the upper stories had long since collapsed, the ground-floor rooms, their ceilings supported by great arches, were still intact. The furnishings were ornate, though mismatched, and there were rugs on the floors and drapes to cover the windows—windows, Ehlana noticed, that had recently been fitted with stout iron bars.

The fireplaces were cavernous, and they were all filled with blazing logs, not so much to ward off the minimal chill of the Arjuni winter but to dry out rooms saturated with over a millennium of dank humidity. There were beds and fresh linen and clothing of an Arjuni cut, but most important of all, there was a fair-sized room with a large marble bathtub set into the floor. Ehlana's eyes fixed longingly on that ultimate luxury. It so completely seized her attention that she scarcely heard Zalasta's apologies. After a few vague replies from her, the Styric realized that his continued presence was no longer appreciated, so he politely excused himself and left.

"Alean, dear," Ehlana said in an almost dreamy voice, "that's quite a large tub—certainly large enough for the two of us, wouldn't you say?"

Alean was also gazing at the tub with undisguised longing. "Easily, your Majesty," she replied.

"How long do you think it might take us to heat enough water to fill it?"

"There are plenty of large pots and kettles in that kitchen, my Queen," the gentle girl said, "and all the fireplaces are going. It shouldn't take very long at all."

"Wonderful," Ehlana said enthusiastically. "Why don't we get started?"

"Just exactly who is this Klæl, Zalasta?" Ehlana asked the Styric several days later when he came to call. Zalasta came to their prison often, as if his visits in some way lessened his guilt, and he always talked: long, rambling, sometimes disconnected converse that often revealed far more than he probably intended for her to know.

"Klæl is an eternal being," he replied. Ehlana noted almost absently that the heavily accented Elenic which had so irritated her when they had first met in Sarsos was gone now. Another of his ruses, she concluded. "Klæl is far more eternal than the Gods of this world," he continued. "He's in some way connected to Bhelliom. They're contending principles, or something along those lines. I was a bit distraught when Cyrgon explained the relationship to me, so I didn't fully understand."

"Yes, I can imagine," she murmured. Her relationship with Zalasta was peculiar. The circumstances made ranting and denunciation largely a waste of time, so Ehlana was civil to him. He appeared to be grateful for that, and his gratitude made him more open with her. That civility, which cost her nothing, enabled her to pick up much information from the Styric's rambling conversation.

"Anyway," Zalasta continued, "Cyzada was terrified when Cyrgon commanded him to summon Klæl, and he tried very hard to talk the God out of the notion. Cyrgon was implacable, though, and he was filled with rage when Sparhawk neatly plucked the Trolls right out of his grasp. We'd never even considered the possibility that Sparhawk might release the Troll-Gods from their confinement."

"That was Sir Ulath's idea," Ehlana told him. "Ulath knows a great deal about Trolls."

"Evidently so. At any rate, Cyrgon forced Cyzada to summon Klæl, but Klæl no sooner appeared than he went in search of Bhelliom. That took Cyrgon aback. It had been his intention to hold Klæl in reserve—hiding, so to speak—and to unleash him by surprise. That went out the window when Klæl rushed off to the North Cape to confront Bhelliom. Sparhawk knows that Klæl is here now—although I have no idea what he can do about it. That was what made the summoning of Klæl such idiocy in the first place. Klæl can't be controlled. I tried to explain that to Cyrgon, but he wouldn't listen. Our goal is to gain possession of Bhelliom, and Klæl and Bhelliom are eternal enemies. As soon as Cyrgon takes Bhelliom in his hands, Klæl will attack *him,* and I'm fairly certain that Klæl is infinitely more powerful than he is." Zalasta glanced around cautiously. "The Cyrgai are in many ways a reflection of their God, I'm afraid. Cyrgon abhors any kind of intelligence. He's frighteningly stupid sometimes."

"I hate to point this out, Zalasta," she said insincerely, "but you have this tendency to ally yourself with defectives. Annias was clever enough, I suppose, but his obsession with the Archprelacy distorted his judgment; and Martel's drive for revenge made *his* thinking just as distorted. From what I gather, Otha was as stupid as a stump, and Azash was so elemental that all he had on his mind were his desires. Coherent thought was beyond him."

"You know everything, don't you, Ehlana?" he said. "How on earth did you find all of this out?"

"I'm not really at liberty to discuss it," she replied.

"No matter, I suppose," he said absently. A sudden hunger crossed his face. "How is Sephrenia?" he asked.

"Well enough. She was very upset when she first found out about you, though—and your attempt on Aphrael's life was really ill-conceived, you know. That was the one thing that convinced her of your treachery."

"I lost my head," he confessed. "That cursed Delphaeic woman destroyed three hundred years of patient labor with a toss of her head."

"I suppose it's none of my business, but why didn't you just accept the fact that Sephrenia was wholly committed to Aphrael and let it go at that? There's no way you can compete with the Child-Goddess, you know."

"Could *you* have ever accepted the idea that Sparhawk was committed to another, Ehlana?" His tone was accusing.

"No," she admitted, "I suppose I couldn't have. We do strange things for love, don't we, Zalasta? I was at least direct about it, though. Things might have worked out differently for you if you hadn't tried deceit and deception. Aphrael's not completely unreasonable, you know."

"Perhaps not," he replied. Then he sighed deeply. "But we'll never know, will we?"

"No. It's far too late now."

"The glazier cracked the pane when he was setting it into the frame, my Queen," Alean said quietly, pointing at the defective triangle of bubbled glass in the lower corner of the window. "He was very clumsy."

"How did you come to know so much about this, Alean?" Ehlana asked her.

"My father was apprenticed to a glazier when he was young," the doe-eyed girl replied. "He used to repair windows in our village." She touched the tip of the glowing poker to the bead of lead that held the cracked pane in place. "I'll have to be very careful," she said, frowning in concentration, "but if I do it right, I can fix it so that we can take out this little section of glass and put it back in again. That way, we'll be able to hear what they're talking about out there in the street, and then we'll be able to put the glass back in again so that they'll never know what we've done. I thought you might want to be able to listen to them, and they always seem to gather just outside this window."

"You're an absolute treasure, Alean!" Ehlana exclaimed, impulsively embracing the girl.

"Be careful, my Lady!" Alean cried in alarm. "The hot iron!"

Alean was right. The window with the small defective pane was at the corner of the building, and Zalasta, Scarpa, and the others were quartered in the attached structure. It appeared that whenever they wanted to discuss something out of the hearing of the soldiers, they habitually drifted to the walled-in cul-de-sac just outside the window. The small panes of cheap glass leaded into the window frame were only semitransparent at best, and so, with minimal caution, Alean's modification of the cracked pane permitted Ehlana to listen and even marginally observe without being seen.

On the day following her conversation with Zalasta, she saw the white-robed Styric approaching with a look of bleakest melancholy on his face and with Scarpa and Krager close behind him. "You've got to snap out of this, Father," Scarpa said urgently. "The soldiers are beginning to notice."

"Let them," Zalasta replied shortly.

"No, Father," Scarpa said in his rich, theatrical voice, "we can't do that. These men are animals. They function below the level of thought. If you walk around through these streets with the face of a little boy whose dog just died, they're going to think that something's wrong and they'll start deserting by the regiment. I've spent too much time and effort gathering this army to have you drive them away by feeling sorry for yourself."

"You'd never understand, Scarpa," Zalasta retorted. "You can't even begin to comprehend the meaning of love. You don't love anything."

"Oh, yes I do, Zalasta," Scarpa snapped. "I love me. That's the only kind of love that makes any sense."

Ehlana just happened to be watching Krager. The drunkard's eyes were narrowed, shrewd. He casually moved his ever-present tankard around behind him and poured most of the wine out. Then he raised the tankard and drank off the dregs noisily. Then he belched. "Parn'me," he slurred, reaching out his hand to the wall to steady himself as he weaved back and forth on his feet.

Scarpa gave him a quick, irritated glance, obviously dismissing him. Ehlana, however, rather quickly reassessed Krager. He was not always nearly as drunk as he appeared to be.

"It's all been for nothing, Scarpa," Zalasta groaned. "I've allied myself with the diseased, the degenerate, and the insane for nothing. I had thought that once

Aphrael was gone, Sephrenia might turn to me. But she won't. She'd die before she'll have anything to do with me."

Scarpa's eyes narrowed. "Let her die, then," he said bluntly. "Can't you get it through your head that one woman's the same as any other? Women are a commodity—like bales of hay or barrels of wine. Look at Krager here. How much affection do you think he has for an empty wine barrel? It's the new ones, the full ones, that he loves, right, Krager?"

Krager smirked at him owlishly and then belched again. "Parn'me," he said.

"I can't really see any reason for this obsession of yours anyway." Scarpa continued to grind on his father's most sensitive spot. "Sephrenia's only damaged goods now. Vanion's had her—dozens of times. Are you so poor-spirited that you'd take the leavings of an Elene?"

Zalasta suddenly smashed his fist against the stone wall with a snarl of frustration.

"He's probably so used to having her that he doesn't even waste his time murmuring endearments to her anymore," Scarpa went on. "He just takes what he wants from her, rolls over, and starts to snore. You know how Elenes are when they're in a rut. And she's probably no better. He's made an Elene out of her, Father. She's not a Styric anymore. She's become an Elene—or even worse, a mongrel. I'm really surprised to see you wasting all this pure emotion on a mongrel." He sneered. "She's no better than my mother or my sisters, and you know what *they* were."

Zalasta's face twisted, and he threw back his head and actually howled. "I'd rather see her dead!"

Scarpa's pale, bearded face grew sly. "Why don't you kill her, then, Father?" he asked in an insinuating whisper. "Once a decent woman's been bedded by an Elene, she can never be trusted again, you know. Even if you *did* persuade her to marry you, she'd never be faithful." He laid an insincere hand on his father's arm. "Kill her, Father," he advised. "At least your memories of her will be pure; *she* never will be."

Zalasta howled again and clawed at his beard with his long fingernails. Then he turned quickly and ran off down the street.

Krager straightened, and his seeming drunkenness slid away. "You took an awful chance there, you know," he said in a cautious tone.

Scarpa looked sharply at him. "Very good, Krager," he murmured. "You played the part of a drunkard almost to perfection."

"I've had lots of practice." Krager shrugged. "You're lucky he didn't obliterate you, Scarpa—or tie your guts in knots again."

"He couldn't." Scarpa smirked. "I'm a fair magician myself, you know, and I'm skilled enough to know that you have to have a clear head to work the spells. I kept him in a state of rage. He couldn't have worked up enough magic to break a spiderweb. Let's hope that he *does* kill Sephrenia. That should *really* scatter Sparhawk's wits, not to mention the fact that as soon as the desire of his life is no more than a pile of dead meat, Zalasta's very likely to cut his own throat."

"You really hate him, don't you?"

"Wouldn't you, Krager? He could have taken me with him when I was a child, but he'd come to visit for a while, and he'd show me what it meant to be a Styric, and then he'd go off alone, leaving me behind to be tormented by whores. If he doesn't have the stomach to cut his own throat, I'd be more than happy to lend him a hand." Scarpa's eyes were very bright, and he was smiling broadly. "Where's your wine barrel, Krager?" he asked. "Right now I feel like getting drunk." And he began to laugh, a cackling, insane laugh empty of any mirth or humanity.

"It's no use!" Ehlana said, flinging the comb across the room. "Look at what they've done to my hair!" She buried her face in her hands and wept.

"It's not hopeless, my Lady," Alean said in her soft voice. "There's a style they wear in Cammoria." She lifted the mass of blonde hair on the right side of Ehlana's head and brought it over across the top. "You see," she said. "It covers all the bare places, and it really looks quite chic."

Ehlana looked hopefully into her mirror. "It doesn't look too bad, does it?" she conceded.

"And if we set a flower just behind your right ear, it would really look very stunning."

"Alean, you're wonderful!" the queen exclaimed happily. "What would I ever do without you?"

It took them the better part of an hour, but at last the unsightly bare places were covered, and Ehlana felt that some measure of her dignity had been restored.

That evening, however, Krager came to call. He stood swaying in the doorway, his eyes bleary and a drunken smirk on his face. "Harvest time again, Ehlana," he announced, drawing his dagger. "It seems that I'll need just a bit more of your hair."

CHAPTER SIX

The sky remained overcast, but as luck had it, it had not yet rained. The stiff wind coming in off the Gulf of Micae was raw, however, and they rode with their cloaks wrapped tightly about them. Despite Khalad's belief that it was to their advantage to move slowly, Berit was consumed with impatience. He knew that what they were doing was only a small part of the overall strategy, but the confrontation they all knew was coming loomed ahead, and he desperately wanted to get on with it. "How can you be so patient?" he asked Khalad about midafternoon one day when the on-shore wind was particularly chill and damp.

"I'm a farmer, Sparhawk," Khalad replied, scratching at his short black beard. "Waiting for things to grow teaches you not to expect changes overnight."

"I suppose I've never really thought about what it must be like just sitting still waiting for things to sprout."

"There's not much sitting still when you're a farmer," Khalad told him. "There are always more things to do than there are hours in the day, and if you get bored, you can always keep a close watch on the sky. A whole year's work can be lost in a dry spell or a sudden hailstorm."

"I hadn't thought about that, either." Berit mulled it over. "That's what makes you so good at predicting the weather, isn't it?"

"It helps."

"There's more to it than that, though. You always seem to know about everything that's going on around you. When we were on that log boom, you knew instantly when there was the slightest change in the way it was moving."

"It's called 'paying attention,' my Lord. The world around you is screaming at you all the time, but most people can't seem to hear it. That really baffles me. I can't understand how you can miss so many things."

Berit was just slightly offended by that. "All right, what's the world screaming at you right now that I can't hear?"

"It's telling me that we're going to need some fairly substantial shelter tonight. We've got bad weather coming."

"How did you arrive at that?"

Khalad pointed. "You see those seagulls?" he asked.

"Yes. What's that got to do with it?"

Khalad sighed. "What do seagulls eat, my Lord?"

"Just about everything—fish mostly, I suppose."

"Then why are they flying inland? They aren't going to find very many fish on dry land, are they? They've seen something they don't like out there in the gulf and they're running away from it. Just about the only thing that frightens a seagull is wind—and the high seas that go with it. There's a storm out to sea, and it's coming this way. *That's* what the world's screaming at me right now."

"It's just common sense then, isn't it?"

"Most things are, Sparhawk—common sense and experience." Khalad smiled slightly. "I can still feel Krager's Styric out there watching us. If he isn't paying any more attention than you were just now, he's probably going to spend a very miserable night."

Berit grinned just a bit viciously. "Somehow that information fails to disquiet me," he said.

It was more than a village, but not quite a town. It had three streets, for one thing, and at least six buildings of more than one story, for another. The streets were muddy, and pigs roamed freely. The buildings were made primarily of wood and they were roofed with thatch. There was an inn on what purported to be the main street. It was a substantial-looking building, and there were a pair of rickety wagons with dispirited mules in their traces out front. Ulath reined in the weary old horse he had bought in the fishing village. "What do you think?" he said to his friend.

"I thought you'd never ask," Tynian replied.

"Let's go ahead and take a room as well," Ulath suggested. "The afternoon's wearing on anyway, and I'm getting tired of sleeping on the ground. Besides, I'm a little overdue for a bath."

Tynian looked toward the starkly outlined peaks of the Tamul Mountains lying some leagues to the west. "I'd really hate to keep the Trolls waiting, Ulath," he said with mock seriousness.

"It's not as if we had a definite appointment with them. Trolls wouldn't notice anyway. They've got a very imprecise notion of time."

They rode on into the innyard, tied their horses to a rail outside the stable, and went into the inn.

"We need a room," Ulath told the innkeeper in heavily accented Tamul.

The innkeeper was a small, furtive-looking man. He gave them a quick, appraising glance, noting the bits and pieces of army uniform that made up most of their dress. His expression hardened with distaste. Soldiers were frequently unwelcome in rural communities for any number of very good reasons. "Well," he replied in a whining, singsong sort of voice. "I don't know. It's our busy season—"

"Late autumn?" Tynian broke in skeptically. "*That's* your busy season?"

"Well—there are all the wagoneers who can come by at any time, you know."

Ulath looked beyond the innkeeper's shoulder into the low, smoky taproom. "I count three," he said flatly.

"There are bound to be more along shortly," the fellow replied just a bit too quickly.

"Of *course* there are," Tynian said sarcastically. "But we're here *now,* and we've got money. Are you going to gamble a sure thing against the remote possibility that some wagon might stop here along about midnight?"

"He doesn't want to do business with a couple of pensioned-off veterans, Corporal," Ulath said. "Let's go talk with the local commissioner. I'm sure he'll be interested in the way this fellow treats his Imperial Majesty's soldiers."

"I'm his Imperial Majesty's loyal subject," the innkeeper said quickly, "and I'll be honored to have brave veterans of his army under my roof."

"How much?" Tynian cut him off.

"A half crown?"

"He doesn't seem very certain, does he, Sergeant?" Tynian asked his friend. "I think you misunderstood," he said then to the nervous innkeeper. "We don't want to *buy* the room. We just want to rent it for one night."

Ulath was staring hard at the now-frightened little Tamul. "Eight pence," he countered with a note of finality.

"*Eight?*" the innkeeper objected in a shrill voice.

"Take it or leave it—and don't be all day about it. We'll need a little daylight to find the commissioner."

"You're a hard man, Sergeant."

"Nobody ever promised you that life would be easy, did they?" Ulath counted out some coins and jingled them in his hand. "Do you want these or not?"

After a moment of agonized indecision, the innkeeper reluctantly took the coins.

"You took all the fun out of that, you know," Tynian complained as the two went back out to the stable to see to their horses.

"I'm thirsty." Ulath shrugged. "Besides, a couple of ex-soldiers would know in advance exactly how much they were willing to pay, wouldn't they?" He scratched at his face. "I wonder if Sir Gerda would mind if I shaved off his beard," he mused. "This thing itches."

"It's not *really* his face, Ulath. It's still yours. You've just been modified to look like him."

"Yes, but when the ladies switch our faces back, they'll use *this* one as a model for Gerda, and when they're done, he'll be standing there with a naked face. He might object."

They unsaddled their horses, put them into stalls, and went back into the tap-room. Tamul drinking establishments were arranged differently from those owned by Elenes. The tables were much lower, for one thing, and here the room was heated by a porcelain stove rather than a fireplace. The stove smoked as badly as a fireplace, though. Wine was served in delicate little cups and ale in cheap tin tankards. The smell was much the same, however.

They were just starting on their second tankard of ale when an officious-looking Tamul in a food-spotted wool mantle came into the room and walked directly to their table. "I'll have a look at your release papers, if you don't mind," he told them in a loftily superior tone.

"And if we do?" Ulath asked.

The official blinked. "What?"

"You said if we don't mind. What if we *do* mind?"

"I have the authority to demand to see those documents."

"Why did you ask, then?" Ulath reached inside his red uniform jacket and took out a dog-eared sheet of paper. "In our old regiment, men in authority never asked."

The Tamul read through the documents Oscagne had provided them as a part of their disguise. "These seem to be in order," he said in a more conciliatory tone. "Sorry I was so abrupt. We've been told to keep our eyes out for deserters—all the turmoil, you understand. I guess the army looks a lot less attractive when there's fighting in the wind." He looked at them a bit wistfully. "I see you were stationed in Matherion."

Tynian nodded. "It was good duty—a lot of inspections and polishing, though. Sit down, Commissioner."

The Tamul smiled faintly. "Deputy-Commissioner, I'm afraid, Corporal. This backwater doesn't rate a full commissioner." He slid into a chair. "Where are you men bound?"

"Home," Ulath said, "back to Verel in Daconia."

"You'll forgive my saying so, Sergeant, but you don't look all that much like a Dacite."

Ulath shrugged. "I take after my mother's family. She was an Astel before she married my father. Tell me, Deputy-Commissioner, would we save very much time if we went straight on across the Tamul Mountains to reach Sopal? We thought we'd catch a ferry or some trading ship there, go across the Sea of Arjun to Tiana, and then ride on down to Saras. It's only a short way from there to Verel."

"I'd advise staying out of the Tamul Mountains, my friends."

"Bad weather?" Tynian asked him.

"That's always possible at this time of year, Corporal, but there have been some disturbing reports coming out of those mountains. It seems that the bears up there have been breeding like rabbits. Every traveler who's come through here in the past few weeks reports sighting the brutes. Fortunately they all run away."

"Bears, you say?"

The Tamul smiled. "I'm translating. The ignorant peasants around here use the word *monster,* but we all know what a large, shaggy creature who lives alone in the mountains is, don't we?"

"Peasants are an excitable lot, aren't they?" Ulath laughed, draining his tankard. "We were out on a training exercise once, and this peasant came running up to us claiming that he was being chased by a pack of wolves. When we went out to take a look, it turned out to be one lone fox. The size and number of any wild animal a peasant sees seem to grow with each passing hour."

"Or each tankard of ale," Tynian added.

They talked with the now-polite official for a while longer, and then the man wished them a good journey and left.

"Well, it's nice to know that the Trolls made it this far south," Ulath said. "I'd hate to have to go looking for them."

"Their Gods were guiding them, Ulath," Tynian pointed out.

"You've never talked with the Troll-Gods, I see." Ulath laughed. "Their sense of direction is a little vague—probably because their compass only has two directions on it."

"Oh?"

"North and not-north. It makes finding places a little difficult."

The storm was one of those short, savage gales that seem to come out of nowhere in the late autumn. Khalad had dismissed the possibility of finding any kind of shelter in the salt marshes and had turned instead to the beach. At the head of a shallow inlet he had found the mountain of driftwood he'd been seeking. A couple of hours of fairly intense labor had produced a snug, even cozy little shelter on the leeward side of the pile.

The gale struck just as the last light was fading. The wind screamed through the huge pile of driftwood. The surf crashed and thundered against the beach, and the rain sheeted horizontally across the ground in the driving wind.

Khalad and Berit, however, were warm and dry. They sat with their backs against the huge, bleached-white log that formed the rear wall of their shelter and their feet stretched out toward their crackling fire.

"You always amaze me, Khalad," Berit said. "How did you know that there'd be boards mixed in amongst all this driftwood?"

"There always are." Khalad shrugged. "Anytime you find one of these big heaps of driftwood, you're going to find sawed lumber as well. Men make ships out of boards, and ships get wrecked. The boards float around until the wind and currents and tides push them to the same sheltered places where the sticks and the logs have been accumulating." He reached up and patted the ceiling. "Finding this hatch cover all in one piece was a stroke of luck, though, I'll grant you that." He rose to his feet and went to the front of the shelter. "It's really blowing out there," he noted.

He extended his hands toward the fire. "Cold, too. The rain's probably going to turn to sleet before midnight."

"Yes," Berit agreed pleasantly. "I certainly pity anybody caught out in the open on a night like this." He grinned.

"Me, too." Khalad grinned back. He lowered his voice, although there was no real need. "Can you get any sense of what he's thinking?"

"Nothing specific," Berit replied. "He's seriously uncomfortable, though."

"What a shame."

"There's something else, though. He's going to come and talk with us. He has a message of some kind for us."

"Is he likely to come in here tonight?"

Berit shook his head. "He has orders not to make contact until tomorrow morning. He's very much afraid of whoever told him what to do and when to do it, so he'll obey those orders to the letter. How's that ham coming?"

Khalad drew his dagger and used its point to lift the lid of the iron pot half-buried in embers at the edge of the fire. The steam that came boiling out smelled positively delicious. "It's ready. As soon as the beans are done, we can eat."

"If our friend out there is downwind of us, that smell should add to his misery just a bit." Berit chuckled.

"I sort of doubt it, Sparhawk. He's a Styric, and he's not allowed to eat pork."

"Oh, yes. I'd forgotten about that. He's a renegade, though. Maybe he's discarded his dietary prejudices."

"We'll find out in the morning. When he comes to us tomorrow, I'll offer him a piece. Why don't you saw off a few slices of that loaf of bread? I'll toast them on the pot lid here."

The wind had abated somewhat the following morning, and the rain had slacked off to a few fitful spatters stuttering on the hatch-cover roof. They had more of the ham and beans for breakfast and began to get things ready to pack. "What do you think?" Berit asked.

"Let's make him come to us. Sitting tight until the last of the rain passes wouldn't be all that unusual." Khalad looked speculatively at his friend. "Would you be offended by a bit of advice, my Lord?" he asked.

"Of course not."

"You *look* like Sparhawk, but you don't *sound* very much like him, and your mannerisms aren't quite right. When the Styric comes, make your face colder and harder. Keep your eyes narrow. Sparhawk squints. You'll also want to keep your voice low and level. Sparhawk's voice gets very quiet when he's angry—and he calls people 'neighbor' a lot. He can put all sorts of meaning into that one word."

"That's right, he does call just about everybody 'neighbor,' doesn't he? I'd almost forgotten that. You've got my permission to correct me anytime I start to lose my grip on the real Sparhawk, Khalad."

"*Permission?*"

"Poor choice of words there, I suppose."

"You might say that, yes."

· · ·

"The climate got a little too warm for us back in Matherion," Caalador said, leaning back in his chair. He looked directly at the hard-faced man seated across from him. "I'm sure you take my meaning, Orden."

The hard-faced man laughed. "Oh, yes," he replied. "I've left a few places about one jump ahead of the law a time or two myself." Orden was an Elene from Vardenaise who ran a seedy tavern on the waterfront in Delo. He was a burly ruffian who prospered here because Elene criminals felt comfortable in the familiar surroundings of an Elene tavern *and* because Orden was willing to buy things from them—at about a tenth of their real value—without asking questions.

"What we really need is a new line of work." Caalador gestured at Kalten and Bevier, disguised with new faces and rough, mismatched clothing. "A fairly high personage in the Ministry of the Interior was in charge of the group of policemen who stopped by to ask us some embarrassing questions." He grinned at Bevier, who wore the face of one of his brother Cyrinics, an evil-looking knight who had lost an eye in a skirmish in Rendor and covered the empty socket with a black patch. "My one-eyed friend there didn't care for the fellow's attitude, so he lopped his head off with that funny-looking hatchet of his."

Orden looked at the weapon Bevier had laid on the table beside his ale tankard. "That's a lochaber ax, isn't it?" he asked.

Bevier grunted. Kalten felt that Bevier's flair for dramatics was pushing him a little far. The black eye patch was probably enough, but Bevier's participation in amateur theatricals as a student made him seem to want to go to extremes. His intent was obviously to appear dangerously competent. What he was achieving, however, was the appearance of a homicidal maniac.

"Doesn't a lochaber usually have a longer handle?" Orden asked.

"It wouldn't fit under my tunic," Bevier growled, "so I sawed a couple of feet off the handle. It works well enough—if you keep chopping with it. The screaming and the blood don't bother me all that much, so it suits me just fine."

Orden shuddered and looked slightly sick. "That's the meanest-looking weapon I've ever seen," he confessed.

"Maybe that's why I like it so much," Bevier told him.

Orden looked at Caalador. "What line were you and your friends thinking of taking up, Ezek?" he asked.

"We thought we might try our hand at highway robbery or something along those lines," Caalador said. "You know, fresh air, exercise, wholesome food, no policemen in the neighborhood—that sort of thing. We've got some fairly substantial prices on our heads, and now that the emperor's disbanded Interior, all the policing is being done by the Atans. Did you know that you can't bribe an Atan?"

Orden nodded glumly. "Oh, yes," he said. "It's shocking." He squinted speculatively at "Ezek," who appeared to be a middle-aged Deiran. "Why don't you describe Caalador to me, Ezek? I'm not doubting your word, mind. It's just that things are a little topsy-turvy right now, what with all the policemen we used to bribe either in jail or dead, so we *all* have to be careful."

"No offense taken at all, Orden," Caalador assured him. "I wouldn't trust a man who wasn't careful these days. Caalador's a Cammorian, and he's got curly hair and a red face. He's sort of blocky—you know, big shoulders, thick neck, and a little stout around the middle."

Orden's eyes narrowed shrewdly. "What did he tell you? Repeat his exact words."

"Wal, sir," Caalador replied, exaggerating the dialect just a bit, "Ol' Caalador, he tole us t' come down yere t' Delo an' look up a feller name o' Orden—on accounta this yere Orden, he's th' one ez knows whut's whut in the shadowy world o' crime herebouts."

Orden relaxed and laughed. "That's Caalador, all right," he said. "I knew you were telling me the truth before you'd said three words."

"He certainly mangles the language," Caalador agreed. "He's not as stupid as he sounds, though."

Kalten covered a smile with his hand.

"Not by a dang sight, he ain't," Orden agreed, imitating the dialect. "I think you'll find that highway robbery isn't very profitable around here, Ezek, mainly because there aren't that many highways. It's *safe* enough out in the jungle—not even the Atans can find anybody in all that underbrush—but pickings are slim. Three men alone in the bush won't be able to make ends meet. I think you'll have to join one of the bands out there. They make a fair living robbing isolated estates and raiding various towns and villages. That takes quite a number of men, so there are always job openings." He sat back and tapped one finger thoughtfully against his chin. "Do you want to go a *long* way from town?" he asked.

"The farther out the better," Caalador replied.

"Narstil's operating down by the ruins of Natayos. I can *guarantee* that the police won't bother you *there*. A fellow named Scarpa's got an army stationed in the ruins. He's a crazy revolutionary who wants to overthrow the Tamul government. Narstil has quite a few dealings with him. There's some risk involved, but there's a lot of profit to be made in that neighborhood."

"I think you've found just what we're looking for, Orden," Caalador said eagerly.

Kalten carefully let out a long sigh of relief. Without even being prompted, Orden had come up with the exact answer they'd been looking for. If they joined this particular band of robbers, they'd be close enough to Natayos to smell the smoke from the chimneys, and that was a better stroke of luck than they'd even dared to hope for.

"I'll tell you what, Ezek," Orden said, "why don't I write a letter to Narstil introducing you and your friends?"

"We'd definitely appreciate it, Orden."

"But before I waste all that ink and paper, why don't we have a talk about how much you're going to pay me to write that letter?"

The Styric was wet and muddy and very nearly blue with the cold. He was shivering so violently that his voice quavered as he hailed their camp. "I have a message for you," he called. "Don't get excited and do something foolish." He spoke in

Elenic, and that made Berit quite thankful, since his own Styric was not all that good. It was the one major flaw in his disguise.

"Come on in, neighbor," he called out to the miserable-looking fellow at the upper end of the beach. "Just keep your hands out in plain sight."

"Don't order me around, Elene," the Styric snapped. "I'm the one who's giving the orders here."

"Then deliver your message from right there, neighbor," Berit said coldly. "Take your time, if you want. I'm warm and dry in here, so waiting while you make up your mind won't be all that unpleasant for me."

"It's a *written* message," the man said in Styric. At least Berit *thought* that was what he said.

"Friend," Khalad said, stepping in quickly, "we've got a slightly touchy situation here. There are all sorts of chances for misunderstandings, so don't make me nervous by talking in a language I don't understand. Sir Sparhawk here understands Styric, but *I* don't, and *my* knife in your belly will kill you just as quick as his will. I'll be very sorry afterward, of course, but you'll still be dead."

"Can I come in?" the Styric asked, speaking in Elenic.

"Come ahead, neighbor," Berit told him.

The lumpy-faced messenger approached the front of their shelter, looking longingly at the fire.

"You *really* look uncomfortable, old boy," Berit noted. "Couldn't you think of a spell to keep the rain off?"

The Styric ignored that. "I'm instructed to give you this," he said, reaching inside his homespun smock and drawing out an oilskin-covered packet.

"Tell me what you're going to do before you stick your hand inside your clothes like that, neighbor," Berit cautioned him in a low voice, squinting at him as he said it. "As my friend just pointed out, we've got some wonderful opportunities for misunderstandings here. Startling me when I'm this close to you isn't a good way to keep your guts on the inside."

The Styric swallowed hard and stepped back as soon as Berit took the packet.

"Would you care for a slice of ham while my Lord Sparhawk reads his mail, friend?" Khalad offered. "It's nice and greasy, so it'll lubricate your innards."

The Styric shuddered, and his face took on a faintly nauseated look.

"There's nothing quite like a few gobs of oozy pork fat to slick up a man's gullet," Khalad told him cheerfully. "It must come from all the garbage and half-rotten swill that pigs eat."

The Styric made a retching sound.

"You've delivered your message, neighbor," Berit said coldly. "I'm sure you have someplace important to go, and we certainly wouldn't want to keep you."

"Are you sure you understand the message?"

"I've read it. Elenes read very well. We're not illiterates like you Styrics. The message didn't make me very happy, so it's not going to pay you to stay around."

The Styric messenger backed away, his face apprehensive. Then he turned and fled.

"What does it say?" Khalad asked.

Berit gently held the identifying lock of the queen's hair in his hand. "It says that there's been a change of plans. We're supposed to go down past the Tamul Mountains and then turn west. They want us to go to Sopal now."

"You'd better get word to Aphrael."

There was a sudden, familiar little trill of pipes. The two young men spun around quickly.

The Child-Goddess sat cross-legged on Khalad's blankets, breathing a plaintive Styric melody into her many-chambered pipes. "Why are you staring at me?" she asked them. "I told you I was going to look after you, didn't I?"

"Is this really wise, Divine One?" Berit asked her. "That Styric's no more than a few hundred yards away, you know, and he can probably sense your presence."

"Not right now, he can't." Aphrael smiled. "Right now he's too busy concentrating on keeping his stomach from turning inside out. All that talk about pork fat was really cruel, Khalad."

"Yes. I know."

"Did you have to be so graphic?"

"I didn't know you were around. What do you want us to do?"

"Go to Sopal the way they told you to. I'll get word to the others." She paused. "What *did* you do to that ham, Khalad?" she asked curiously. "You've actually managed to make it smell almost edible."

"It's probably the cloves." He shrugged. "Nobody's really all that fond of the taste of pork, when you get right down to it, but my mother taught me that almost anything can be made edible—if you use enough spices. You might want to keep that in mind the next time you're thinking about serving up a goat."

She stuck her tongue out at him, and then she vanished.

CHAPTER SEVEN

It was snowing in the mountains of Zemoch, a dry, brittle snow that settled like a cloud of feathers in the dead-calm air. It was bitterly cold, and a huge cloud of steam hung like a low-lying fog over the horses of the army of the Knights of the Church as they plodded forward, their hooves sending the powdery snow swirling into the air again. The preceptors of the militant orders rode in the lead, dressed in full armor and bundled in furs. Preceptor Abriel of the Cyrinic Knights, still vigorous despite his advanced age, rode with Darellon, the Alcione preceptor, and with Sir Heldin, a scarred old veteran who was filling in as leader of the Pandions during Sparhawk's absence. Patriarch Bergsten rode somewhat apart. The huge churchman was muffled to the ears in fur, and his Ogre-horned helmet made him look very warlike, an appearance offset to some degree by the small, black-bound prayer book he was reading. Preceptor Komier of the Genidians was off ahead with the scouts.

"I don't think I'll ever be warm again," Abriel groaned, pulling his fur cloak tighter about him. "Old age thins the blood. Don't ever get old, Darellon."

"The alternative isn't very attractive, Lord Abriel." Darellon was a slender Deiran who appeared to have been swallowed up by his massive armor. He lowered his voice. "You didn't really have to come along, my friend," he said. "Sarathi would have understood."

"Oh, no, Darellon. This is probably my last campaign. I wouldn't miss it for the world." Abriel peered ahead. "What's Komier doing out there?"

"Lord Komier said that he wanted to take a look at the ruins of Zemoch," Sir Heldin replied in his rumbling basso. "I guess Thalesians take a certain pleasure in viewing the wreckage after a war's over."

"They're a barbaric people," Abriel muttered sourly. He glanced quickly at Bergsten, who seemed totally immersed in his prayer book. "You don't necessarily have to repeat that, gentlemen," he said to Darellon and Heldin.

"I wouldn't dream of it, Abriel," Bergsten said, not looking up from his prayer book.

"You've got unwholesomely sharp ears, your Grace."

"It comes from listening to confessions. People tend to shout the sins of others from the rooftops, but you can barely hear them when they're describing their own." Bergsten looked up and pointed. "Komier's coming back."

The preceptor of the Genidian Knights was in high spirits as he reined in his horse, swirling up a huge billow of the dustlike snow. "Sparhawk doesn't leave very much standing when he destroys a place," he announced cheerfully. "I didn't entirely believe Ulath when he told me that our broken-nosed friend blew the lid off the Temple of Azash, but I do now. You've never *seen* such a wreck. I doubt if there's a habitable building left in the whole city."

"You really enjoy that sort of thing, don't you, Komier?" Abriel accused.

"That's enough of that, gentlemen!" Bergsten cut in quickly. "We're not going to resurrect *that* worn-out old dispute again. We make war in different ways. Arcians like to build forts and castles, and Thalesians like to knock them down. It's all part of making war, and that's what we get paid for."

"*We*, your Grace?" Heldin rumbled mildly.

"You know what I mean, Heldin. I don't personally get involved in that anymore, of course, but—"

"Why did you bring your ax along, then, Bergsten?" Komier asked him.

Bergsten gave him a flat stare. "For old times' sake—and because you Thalesian brigands pay closer attention to a man who's got an ax in his hands."

"Knights, your Grace," Komier mildly corrected his countryman. "We're called knights now. We used to be brigands, but now we're behaving ourselves."

"The Church appreciates your efforts to mend your ways, my son, even though she knows that you're lying through your teeth."

Abriel carefully covered a smile. Bergsten was a former Genidian Knight himself, and sometimes his cassock slipped a bit. "Who's got the map?" he asked, more to head off the impending argument than out of any real curiosity.

Heldin unbuckled one of his saddlebags, his black armor clinking. "What did you want to know, my Lord?" he asked, taking out his map.

"The usual. How far? How long? What sort of unpleasantness up ahead?"

"It's just over a hundred leagues to the Astellian border, my Lord," Heldin replied, consulting his map, "and nine hundred leagues from there to Matherion."

"A hundred days at least," Bergsten grunted sourly.

"That's if we don't run into any trouble, your Grace," Darellon added.

"Take a look back over your shoulder, Darellon. There are a hundred thousand Church Knights behind us. There's no trouble that we can't deal with. What sort of terrain's up ahead, Heldin?"

"There's some sort of divide about three days east of here, your Grace. All the rivers on this side of it run down into the Gulf of Merjuk. On the other side, they run off into the Astel Marshes. I'd imagine that we'll be going downhill after we cross that divide—unless Otha fixed it so that water runs uphill here in Zemoch."

A Genidian Knight rode forward. "A messenger from Emsat just caught up with us, Lord Komier," he reported. "He says he has important news for you."

Komier nodded, wheeled his horse, and rode back toward the army.

The rest of them pushed on as it started to snow a little harder.

Komier was laughing uproariously when he returned with the travel-stained messenger who had chased them down.

"What's so funny?" Bergsten asked him.

"We have good news from home, your Grace," Komier said gaily. "Tell our beloved Patriarch what you just told me," he instructed the messenger.

"Yes, my Lord," the blond-braided Thalesian said. "It happened a few weeks back, your Grace. One morning the palace servants couldn't find a trace of the Prince Regent anywhere at all. The guards tore the place apart for two straight days, but the little weasel seemed to have vanished entirely."

"Mind your manners, man," Bergsten snapped. "Avin's the Prince Regent, after all—even if he is a little weasel."

"Sorry, your Grace. Anyway, the whole capital was mystified. Avin Wargunsson never went anywhere without taking a brass band along to blow fanfares announcing his coming. Then one of the servants happened to notice a full wine barrel in Avin's study. That seemed odd, because Avin didn't have much stomach for wine, so they got to looking at the barrel a little more closely. It was clear that it had been opened, because quite a bit of wine had been spilled on the floor. Well, your Grace, they'd all worked up quite a thirst looking for Avin, so they decided to open the barrel, but when they tried to pry it open, they found out that it had been nailed shut. Now nobody nails a wine barrel shut in Thalesia, so everybody got suspicious right away. They took some pliers and pulled out the nails and lifted the lid—and there was Avin, stone dead and floating facedown in the barrel."

"You're not serious!"

"Yes, your Grace. Somebody in Emsat's got a very warped sense of humor, I guess. He went to all the trouble of rolling that wine barrel into Avin's study just so that he could stuff him in and nail down the lid. Avin seems to have struggled a bit. He had splinters under his fingernails, and there were claw marks on the underside of the lid. It made an awful mess. I guess the wine drained out of him for a half an hour after they fished him out of the barrel. The palace servants tried to clean him up for the funeral, but you know how hard wine stains are to get out. He was very purple when they laid him out on the bier in the Cathedral of Emsat for his funeral." The messenger rubbed at the side of his face reflectively. "It was the strangest funeral I've ever attended. The Primate of Emsat kept trying to keep from laughing while he was reading the burial service, but he wasn't having much luck, and that got the whole congregation to laughing, too. There was Avin lying on that bier, no bigger than a half-grown goat and as purple as a ripe plum, and there was the whole congregation, roaring with laughter."

"At least everybody noticed him," Komier said. "That was always important to Avin."

"Oh, they noticed him all right, Lord Komier. Every eye in the cathedral was on him. Then, after they put him in the royal crypt, the whole city had a huge party, and we all drank toasts to the memory of Avin Wargunsson. It's hard to find something to laugh about in Thalesia when winter's coming on, but Avin managed to brighten up the whole season."

"What kind of wine was it?" Patriarch Bergsten asked gravely.

"Arcian red, your Grace."

"Any idea of what year?"

"Year before last, I believe it was."

"A vintage year," Bergsten sighed. "There was no way to save it, I suppose?"

"Not after Avin had been soaking in it for two days, your Grace."

Bergsten sighed again. "What a waste," he mourned. And then he collapsed over his saddlebow, howling with laughter.

It was cold in the Tamul Mountains as Ulath and Tynian rode up into the foothills. The Tamul Mountains were one of those geographic anomalies which crop up here and there, a cluster of worn-down, weary-looking peaks with no evident connection to neighboring and more jagged peaks forested by fir and spruce and pine. The gentler slopes of the Tamul Mountains were covered with hardwoods which had been stripped of their leaves by the onset of winter.

The two knights rode carefully, staying in the open and making enough noise to announce their presence. "It's very unwise to startle a Troll," Ulath explained.

"Are you sure they're out there?" Tynian asked as they wound deeper into the mountains.

Ulath nodded. "I've seen tracks—or places where they've tried to brush out their traces—and fresh dirt where they've buried their droppings. Trolls take pains to conceal their presence from humans. It's easier to catch supper if it doesn't know you're around."

"The Troll-Gods promised Aphrael that their creatures wouldn't eat humans anymore."

"It may take a few generations for that notion to sift down into the minds of some of the stupider Trolls—and a Troll can be fearfully stupid when he sets his mind to it. We'd better stay alert. As soon as we get up out of these foothills, I'll perform the ceremony that calls the Troll-Gods. We should be safe after that. It's these foothills that are dangerous."

"Why not just perform the ceremony now?"

Ulath shook his head. "Bad manners. You're not supposed to call on the Troll-Gods until you're up higher—up in *real* Troll country."

"This isn't Troll country, Ulath."

"It is now. Let's find a place to camp for the night."

They built their camp on a kind of stair-stepped bench so that they had a solid cliff to their backs and a steep drop to the front. They took turns standing watch, and as the first faint light of dawn began to wash the darkness out of the overcast sky, Tynian shook Ulath awake. "There's something moving around in the brush at the foot of the cliff," he whispered.

Ulath sat up, his hand going to his ax. He cocked his head to listen. "Troll," he said shortly after a moment.

"How can you tell?"

"Whatever's making all the noise is doing it on purpose. A deer wouldn't crash around like that, and the bears have all denned up for the winter. The Troll wants us to know he's there."

"What do we do?"

"Let's build up the fire a bit—let him know that we're awake. And let's not move too fast." He pushed his blankets aside and rose to his feet as Tynian piled more limbs on the fire.

"Should we invite him in to get warm?" Tynian asked.

"He isn't cold."

"It's freezing, Ulath."

"That's why he's got fur. Trolls build fires for light, not heat. Why don't you go ahead and get started with breakfast? He's not going to do anything until full daylight."

"It's not my turn."

"I have to keep watch."

"I can keep watch as well as you can."

"You wouldn't know what to look for, Tynian." Ulath's tone was reasonable. It usually was when he was talking his way out of doing the cooking.

The light grew gradually stronger. It was a process that was always strange. A man could be looking directly at a dark patch in the surrounding forest and suddenly realize that he could see trees and rocks and bushes where there had been only darkness before.

Tynian brought Ulath a plate of steaming ham and a chunk of leathery-crusted bread. "Leave the ham on the spit," Ulath told him.

Tynian grunted, picked up his own plate, and joined his friend at the front edge of the rocky shelf. They sat and kept watch on the birch forest that ran down the steep slope beneath them as they ate. "There he is," Ulath said gravely, "right beside that big rock."

"Oh, yes," Tynian replied. "I see him now. He blends right in, doesn't he?"

"That's what being a Troll is all about, Tynian. He's a part of the forest."

"Sephrenia says that we're distantly related to them."

"She's probably right. There aren't really all that many differences between us and the Trolls. They're bigger and they have a different diet is about all."

"How long is this likely to take?"

"I have no idea. As far as I know, this has never happened before."

"What'll he do next?"

"As soon as he's sure we know he's there, he'll probably try to communicate in some way."

"Does he know that you speak Trollish?"

"He might. The Troll-Gods are acquainted with me and they know that I run in the same pack with Sparhawk."

"That's an odd way to put it."

"I'm trying to think like a Troll. If I can get it right, I might be able to anticipate what he's going to do next."

Then the Troll shouted up the hill to them.

"What did he say?" Tynian asked nervously.

"He wants to know what he's supposed to do. He's very confused."

"*He's* confused? What about *me*?"

"He's been told to meet us and take us to the Troll-Gods. He doesn't have any idea of our customs or the proper courtesies. We'll have to guide him through this. Put your sword back in its sheath. Let's not make things any worse than they already are." Ulath stood up, being careful not to move too fast. He raised his voice and called to the creature below in Trollish. "Come to this child of Khwaj which we have made. We will take eat together and talk of what we must do."

"What did you tell him?"

"I invited him to join us for breakfast."

"You did *what*? You want a Troll that's no more than a few feet from you to start eating?"

"It's a precaution. It would be discourteous of him to kill us after he's taken food from us."

"Discourteous? That's a *Troll* out there, Ulath."

"Just because he's a Troll doesn't mean that he has bad manners. Oh, I almost forgot. When he comes into camp, he'll want to sniff us. It's polite to sniff him as well. He won't smell very nice, but do it anyway. Trolls do that so that they'll recognize each other if they ever meet again."

"I think you're losing your mind."

"Just follow my lead, and let me do the talking."

"What else *can* I do, you clot? I don't speak Trollish, remember?"

"You *don't*? What an amazing thing. I thought every educated man spoke Trollish."

The Troll approached cautiously, moving smoothly up through the birch forest. He used his arms a great deal as he moved, grasping trees to pull himself along, moving with his whole body. He was about eight and a half feet tall and had glossy brown fur. His face was simian to a degree, though he did not have the protruding muzzle of most apes, and there was a glimmer of intelligence in his deep-sunk eyes. He came up onto the bench where the camp lay, then squatted, resting his forearms on his knees and keeping his paws in plain sight. "I have no club," he half growled.

Ulath made some show of setting his ax aside and held out his empty hands. "I have no club," he repeated the customary greeting. "Undo your sword belt, Tynian," he muttered. "Lay it aside."

Tynian started to object, but decided against it.

"The Child of Khwaj you have made is good," the Troll said, pointing at their fire. "Khwaj will be pleased."

"It is good to please the Gods," Ulath replied.

The Troll suddenly banged his fist on the ground. "This is not how it should be!" he declared in an unhappy voice.

"No," Ulath agreed, dropping down into a squat much like the Troll's, "it is not. The Gods have their reasons for it, though. They have said we must not kill each other. They have also said we must not eat each other."

"I have heard them say it. Could we have misunderstood them?"

"I think we have not."

"Could it be that their minds are sick?"

"It is possible. We must still do as they tell us, though."

"What are you two talking about?" Tynian asked nervously.

"We're discussing philosophy." Ulath shrugged.

Tynian stared at him.

"It's fairly complex. It has to do with whether or not we're morally obliged to obey the Gods if they've gone crazy. I'm saying that we are. Of course my position's a little tainted by self-interest in this particular situation."

"Can it not speak?" the Troll asked, pointing at Tynian. "Are those bird noises the only sounds it can make?"

"The bird noises pass for speech among those of our kind. Will you take some of our eat with us?"

The Troll looked appraisingly at their horses. "Those?" he asked.

"No." Ulath shook his head. "Those are the beasts which carry us."

"Are your legs sick? Is that why you are so short?"

"No. The beasts can run faster than we can. They carry us when we want to go fast."

"What kind of eat do you take?"

"Pig."

"Pig is good. Deer is better."

"Yes."

"Where is the pig? Is it dead? If it is still alive, I will kill it."

"It is dead."

The Troll looked around. "I do not see it."

"We have only brought part of it." Ulath pointed at the large ham spitted over the fire.

"Do you share your eat with the Child of Khwaj?"

Ulath decided not to explain the concept of cooking at that particular moment. "Yes," he said. "It is our custom."

"Does it please Khwaj that you share your eat with his child?"

"It is our thought that it does." Ulath drew his dagger, lifted the spit from off the fire, and sawed off a chunk of ham weighing perhaps three pounds.

"Are your teeth sick?" The Troll even sounded sympathetic. "I had a sick tooth once. It caused me much hurt."

"Our kind does not have sharp teeth," Ulath told him. "Will you take some of our eat?"

"I will." The Troll rose to his feet and came to the fire, towering over them.

"The eat has been near the Child of Khwaj," Ulath warned. "It is hot. It may cause hurt to your mouth."

"I am called Bhlokw," the Troll introduced himself.

"I am called Ulath."

"U-lat? That is a strange thing to be called." Bhlokw pointed at Tynian. "What is it called?"

"Tynian," Ulath replied.

"Tin-in. That is stranger than U-lat."

"The bird noises of our speech make what we are called sound strange."

The Troll leaned forward and snuffled at the top of Ulath's head. Ulath suppressed a strong urge to shriek and run for the nearest tree. He politely sniffed at Bhlokw's fur. The Troll actually didn't smell too bad. Then the monster and Tynian exchanged sniffs. "Now I know you," Bhlokw said.

"It is good that you do." Ulath held out the chunk of steaming ham.

Bhlokw took it from him and stuffed it into his mouth. Then he quickly spat it back out into his hand. "Hot," he explained a little sheepishly.

"We blow on it to make it cool so that we can eat it without causing hurt to our mouths," Ulath instructed.

Bhlokw blew noisily on the piece of ham for a while. Then he crammed it back into his mouth. He chewed reflectively for a moment. Then he swallowed. "It is different," he said diplomatically. Then he sighed. "I do not like this, U-lat," he confided unhappily. "This is not how things should be."

"No," Ulath agreed, "it is not."

"We should be killing each other. I have killed and eaten you man-things since you first came to the Troll-range. *That* is how things should be. It is my thought that the Gods are sick in their minds to make us do this." He sighed a hurricane sort of sigh. "Your thought is right, though. We must do as they tell us to do. Someday their minds will get well. Then they will let us kill and eat each other again." He stood up abruptly. "They want to see you. I will take you to them."

"We will go with you."

They followed Bhlokw up into the mountains all that day and half of the next, and he led them finally to a snow-covered clearing where a fire burned in a large pit. The Troll-Gods were waiting for them there.

"Aphrael came to us," the enormity that was Ghworg told them.

"She said that she would do this," Ulath replied. "She said that when things happened that we should know about, she would come to us and tell us."

"She put her mouth on our faces." Ghworg seemed puzzled.

"She does this. It gives her pleasure."

"It was not painful," Ghworg conceded a bit dubiously, touching the cheek where Aphrael had kissed him.

"What did he say?" Tynian asked quietly.

"Aphrael came here and talked with them," Ulath replied. "She even kissed them a few times. You know Aphrael."

"She actually *kissed* the Troll-Gods?" Tynian's face grew pale.

"What did it say?" Ghworg demanded.

"It wanted me to say what you had said."

"This is not good, Ulath-from-Thalesia. It should not talk to you in words we do not understand. What is its name?"

"It is called Tynian-from-Deira."

"I will make it so that Tynian-from-Deira knows our speech."

"Brace yourself," Ulath warned his friend.

"What? What's happening, Ulath?"

"Ghworg's going to teach you Trollish."

"Now, wait a minute—" Then Tynian suddenly clapped his hands to the sides of his head, cried out, and fell writhing into the snow. The paroxysm passed quickly, but Tynian was pale and shaking as he sat up, and his eyes were wild.

"You are Tynian-from-Deira?" Ghworg demanded in Trollish.

"Y-yes." Tynian's voice trembled as he replied.

"Do you understand my words?"

"They are clear to me."

"It is good. Do not speak the other kind of talk when you are near us. When you do, you make it so that we do not trust you."

"I will remember that."

"It is good that you will. Aphrael came to us. She told us that the one called Berit has been told not to go to the place Beresa. He has been told to go to the place Sopal instead. She said that you would understand what this means." He paused, frowning. "Do you?" he asked.

"Do we?" Tynian asked Ulath, speaking in Trollish.

"I am not sure." Ulath rose, went to his horse, and took a map out of his saddlebag. Then he returned to the fire. "This is a picture of the ground," he explained to the enormous presences. "We make these pictures so that we will know where we are going."

Schlee looked briefly at the map. "The ground does not look like that," he told them. He squatted and thrust his huge fingers down through the snow into the dirt. "This is how the ground looks."

Ulath jumped back as the earth under his feet shuddered slightly. Then he stared down. It was not so much a map as it was a miniaturized version of the continent itself. "This is a *very* good picture of the ground," he marveled.

Schlee shrugged. "I put my hand into the ground and felt its shape. *This* is how it looks."

"Where is Beresa?" Tynian asked Ulath, staring in wonderment at hair-thin little trees bristling like a two-day growth of beard on the sides of tiny mountains.

Ulath checked his map and walked several yards south to a shimmering surface covered with minuscule waves. His feet even sank slightly into Schlee's re-creation of the southern Tamul sea. "It is right here," he replied in Trollish, bending and putting his finger on a spot on the coastline.

"That is where the ones who took Anakha's mate away told him to go," Tynian explained to the Troll-Gods.

"We do not understand," Khwaj said bluntly.

"Anakha is fond of his mate."

"That is how it should be."

"He grows angry when his mate is in danger. The ones who took his mate away know this. They said that they will not give her back to him unless he gives them the flower-gem."

The Troll-Gods all frowned, puzzling their way through it. Then Khwaj suddenly roared, belching out a great, billowing cloud of fire and melting the snow for fifty yards in every direction. "That is wickedness!" he thundered. "It is not right to do this! Their quarrel was with Anakha, not with his mate! I will find these wicked ones! I will turn them into fires that will never go out! They will cry out with hurt forever!"

Tynian shuddered at the enormity of that idea. Then, with a great deal of help from Ulath, he explained their disguises and the subterfuges those disguises made possible.

"Do you in truth look different from how you looked before, Ulath-from-Thalesia?" Ghworg asked, peering curiously at Ulath.

"Much different, Ghworg."

"That is strange. You seem the same to me." The God considered it. "Perhaps it is not so strange," he amended. "Your kind all look the same to me." He clenched his huge fists. "Khwaj is right," he said. "We must cause hurt to the wicked ones. Show us where the one called Berit has been told to go."

Ulath consulted his map again and crossed the miniature world to the edge of the large lake known as the Sea of Arjun. "It is here, Ghworg," he said, bending again and putting his finger to a spot on the coast. Then he bent lower and stared at the shoreline. "It really *is* there!" he gasped. "I can see the tiny little buildings! That is Sopal!"

"Of course," Schlee said as if it were of no particular moment. "It would not be a good picture if I had left things out."

"We have been tricked," Tynian said. "It was our thought that our enemies were in the place Beresa. They are not. They are in the place Sopal instead. The one called Berit does not have the flower-gem. Anakha has the flower-gem. Anakha takes it to Beresa. If the wicked ones meet with Berit in the place Sopal, he will not have the flower-gem with him to give to the wicked ones. They will be angry, and they may cause hurt to Anakha's mate."

"It may be that I taught it too well," Ghworg muttered. "It talks much now."

Schlee, however, had been listening carefully to Tynian's oration. "It has spoken truly, however. Anakha's mate will be in danger. Those who have taken her away may even kill her." The skin on his enormous shoulders flickered, absently shaking off the snowflakes which continually fell on him, and his face twisted as he concentrated. "It is my thought that this will anger Anakha. He may be so angry that he will raise up the flower-gem and make the world go away. We must keep the wicked ones from causing hurt to her."

"Tynian-from-Deira and I will go to the place Sopal," Ulath said. "The wicked ones will not know us because our faces have been changed. We will be nearby when the wicked ones tell the one called Berit that they will give him Anakha's mate if he will give them the flower-gem. We will kill them and take Anakha's mate back when they do this."

"It speaks well," Zoka told the other Troll-Gods. "Its thought is good. Let us help it and the other one—but let us not permit it to kill the wicked ones. Killing them is not enough. The thought of Khwaj is better. Let Khwaj make them into fires that will never go out. Let them burn always. That will be better."

"I will put these man-things into the time which does not move," Ghnomb said. "We will watch them in Schlee's picture of the ground while they go to the place Sopal while the world stands still."

"Can you truly see something as small as a man-thing in Schlee's picture of the ground?" Ulath asked the God of Eat with some surprise.

"Can *you* not?" Ghnomb seemed even more surprised. "We will send Bhlokw with you to help you, and we will watch you in Schlee's picture of the ground. Then, when the wicked ones show Anakha's mate to the one called Berit, to prove to him that they truly have her, you and Tynian-from-Deira will step out of the time which does not move and take her away from them."

"Then *I* will reach into Schlee's picture of the ground and take them up in my hands," Khwaj added grimly. "I will bring them here and make them into fires that will never go out."

"Can you truly reach into Schlee's picture of the ground and pick the wicked ones out of the real world?" Ulath asked in astonishment.

"It is easy." Khwaj shrugged.

Tynian was shaking his head vigorously.

"What?" Schlee demanded.

"The one called Zalasta can also come into the time which does not move. We have seen him do this."

"It will not matter," Khwaj told him. "The one called Zalasta is one of the wicked ones. I will make him into a fire which will never go out as well. I will let him burn forever in the time which does not move. The fire will be just as hot there as it will be here."

The snow was heavier—and wetter—after they crossed the rocky spine that divided the rivers flowing west from those that flowed east. The huge cloud of humid air that hung perpetually above the Astel Marshes lapped against the eastern slopes of the Mountains of Zemoch, unloosing phenomenal snowfalls that buried the forests and clogged the passes. The Church Knights grimly forced their way through sodden drifts as they followed the valley of the south fork on the River Esos toward the Zemoch town of Basne.

Patriarch Abriel of the Cyrinic Knights had begun this campaign with a certain sense of well-being. His health was good, and a lifetime of military training had kept him in peak physical condition. He was, however, fast approaching his seventieth year and he found that starting out each morning was growing harder and harder, though he would never have admitted that.

About midmorning on a snowy day, one of the scouting parties ranging ahead returned with three goatskin-clad Zemochs. The men were thin and dirty, and they had terrified expressions on their faces. Patriarch Bergsten rode ahead to question them. When the rest of the main force caught up to the gigantic churchman, he was having a rather heated discussion with an Arcian Knight.

"But they're Zemochs, your Grace," the knight protested.

"Our quarrel was with Otha, Sir Knight," Bergsten said coldly, "not with these poor, superstitious devils. Give them some food and warm clothing and let them go."

"But—"

"We're not going to have trouble about this, are we, Sir Knight?" Bergsten asked in an ominous tone, swelling even larger.

The knight seemed to consider his situation. He backed up a few paces. "Ah— no, your Grace," he replied, "I don't believe so."

"Our Holy Mother appreciates your obedience, my son," Bergsten told him.

"Did those three have anything useful for us?" Komier asked.

"Not much," Bergsten replied, hauling himself back up into his saddle. "There's an army of some kind moving into place somewhere to the east of Argoch. There was a lot of superstition mixed up in what they told me, so I couldn't get anything very accurate out of them."

"A fight then," Komier said, rubbing his hands together in anticipation.

"I sort of doubt that," Bergsten disagreed. "As closely as I could make out from all the gibberish, the force up ahead is composed largely of irregulars—religious fanatics of some kind. Our Holy Mother in Chyrellos didn't make many friends in this part of the world when she tried to reassimilate the branches of Elene faith in western Daresia during the ninth century."

"That was almost two thousand years ago, Bergsten," Komier objected. "That's a long time to hold a grudge."

Bergsten shrugged. "The old ones are the best. Send your scouts out a little farther, Komier. Let's see if we can get some kind of coherent report on the welcoming committee. A few prisoners might be useful."

"I know how to do this, Bergsten."

"Do it, then. Don't just sit there talking about it."

They passed Argoch, and Komier's scouts brought in several prisoners. Patriarch Bergsten interrogated the poorly clad and ignorant Elene captives briefly, and then he ordered them released.

"Your Grace," Darellon protested, "that was very unwise. Those men will run back to their commanders and report everything they've seen."

"Yes," Bergsten replied, "I know. I *want* them to do that. I *also* want them to tell all their friends that they've seen a hundred thousand Church Knights coming down out of the mountains. I'm encouraging defections, Darellon. We don't want to kill those poor misguided heretics, we just want them to get out of our way."

"I still think it's strategically unsound, your Grace."

"You're entitled to your opinion, my son," Bergsten said. "This isn't an article of the faith, so our Holy Mother encourages disagreement and discussion."

"There isn't much point to discussion after you've already let them go, your Grace."

"You know, that very same thought occurred to me."

They encountered the opposing force in the broad valley of the River Esos just to the south of the Zemoch town of Basne thirty leagues or so to the west of the Astellian border. The reports of the scouts and the information gleaned from the captives proved to be accurate. What faced them was not so much an army as it was a mob, poorly armed and undisciplined.

The preceptors of the four orders gathered around Patriarch Bergsten to consider options. "They're members of our own faith," Bergsten told them. "Our disagreements with them lie in the area of church government, not in the substance of our common beliefs. Those matters aren't settled on the battlefield, so I don't want too many of those people killed."

"I don't see much danger of that, your Grace," Preceptor Abriel said.

"They outnumber us about two to one, Lord Abriel," Sir Heldin pointed out.

"One charge should even things out, Heldin," Abriel replied. "Those people are amateurs, enthusiastic but untrained, and about half of them are only armed with pitchforks. If we all drop our visors, level our lances, and charge them en masse, most of them will still be running a week from now."

And that was the last mistake the venerable Lord Abriel was ever to make. The mounted knights fanned out with crisp precision to form up on a broad front stretching across the entire valley. Rank after rank of Cyrinics, Pandions, Genidians, and Alciones, all clad in steel and mounted on belligerent horses, lined up in what was probably one of the more intimidating displays of organized unfriendliness in the known world.

The preceptors waited in the very center of the front rank as their subalterns formed up the rear ranks and the messengers galloped forward to declare that all was in readiness.

"That should be enough," Komier said impatiently. "I don't think the supply wagons will have to charge, too." He looked around at his friends. "Shall we get started, gentlemen? Let's show that rabble out there how *real* soldiers mount an attack." He made a curt signal to a hulking Genidian Knight, and the huge blond man blew a shattering blast on his Ogre-horn trumpet.

The front rank of the knights clapped down their visors and spurred their horses forward. The perfectly disciplined knights and horses galloped forward in an absolutely straight line like a moving wall of steel.

Midway through the charge the forest of upraised lances came down like a breaking wave, and the defections in the opposing army began. The ill-trained serfs and peasants broke and ran, throwing away their weapons and squealing in terror. Here and there were some better-trained units that held their ground, but the flight of their allies from either side left their flanks dangerously exposed.

The knights struck those few units with a great, resounding crash. Once more Abriel felt the old exulting satisfaction of battle. His lance shattered against a hastily raised shield, and he discarded the broken weapon and drew his sword. He looked around and saw that there were other forces massed behind the wall of peasants that had concealed them from view, and *that* army was like none Abriel had ever seen before. The soldiers were huge, larger than even the Thalesians. They wore breastplates and mail, but their cuirasses were more closely molded to their bodies than was normal. Every muscle seemed starkly outlined under the gleaming steel. Their helmets were exotic steel re-creations of the heads of improbable beasts, and they did not have visors as such but steel masks instead, masks that had been sculpted to bear individualized features—the features, Abriel thought, of the warriors who wore them. The Cyrinic Preceptor was suddenly chilled. The features the masks revealed were not human.

There was a strange domed leather tent in the center of that inhuman army, a ribbed, glossy black tent of gigantic dimensions.

But then it moved, opening, spreading wide—two great wings, curved and batlike. And then, rising up from under the shelter of those wings, was a being huge beyond imagining, a creature of total darkness with a head shaped like an inverted wedge and with flaring, pointed ears. Two slitted eyes blazed in that awful absence of a face, and two enormous arms stretched forth hungrily. Lightning seethed beneath the glossy black skin, and the earth upon which the creature stood smoked and burned.

Abriel was strangely calm. He lifted his visor to look full into the face of Hell. "At last," he murmured, "a fitting opponent." And then he clapped his visor down again, drew his warlike shield before his body, and raised the sword he had carried with honor for over half a century. His unpalsied hand brandished the sword at the enormity still rising before him. "For God and Arcium!" He roared his defiance, set himself, and charged directly into obliteration.

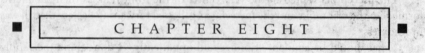

CHAPTER EIGHT

To say that Edaemus was offended would be the grossest of understatements. The blur of white light that was the God of the Delphae was tinged around the edges with flickers of reddish orange, and the dusting of snow that covered the ground in the little swale above the valley of the Delphae fumed tendrils of steam as it melted in the heat of his displeasure. "No!" he said adamantly. "Absolutely not!"

"Oh, be reasonable, cousin," Aphrael coaxed. "The situation has changed. You're holding on to something that no longer has any meaning. There might have been some justification for 'eternal enmity' before. I'll grant you that my family didn't behave very well during the war with the Cyrgai, but that was a long time ago. Clinging to your injured sensibilities now is pure childishness."

"How *couldst* thou, Xanetia?" Edaemus demanded accusingly. "How *couldst* thou do this thing?"

"It was in furtherance of our design, Belovèd," she replied. Sephrenia was more than a little startled by the intensely personal relationship Xanetia had with her God. "Thou didst command me to render assistance unto Anakha, and by reason of his love for Sephrenia, I was obliged to reach accommodation with her. Once she and I did breach the wall of enmity which did stand between us and did learn to trust each other, respect and common purpose did soften our customary despite, and all unbidden, love did gently creep in to replace it. In my heart she is now my dear sister."

"That is an abomination! Thou shalt *not* speak so of this Styric in my presence again!"

"As it please thee, Belovèd," she agreed, submissively bowing her head. But then her chin came up, and her inner light glowed more intensely. "But will ye, nil ye, I will continue to *think* so of her in the hidden silence of my heart."

"Are you ready to listen, Edaemus?" Aphrael asked. "Or would you like to take a century or two to throw a temper tantrum first?"

"Thou art pert, Aphrael," he accused.

"Yes, I know. It's one of the things that makes me so delightful. You *do* know that Cyrgon's trying to get his hands on Bhelliom, don't you? Or have you been so busy playing leapfrog with the stars that you've lost track of what's happening here?"

"Mind your manners," Sephrenia told her crisply.

"He makes me tired. He's been cuddling his hatred to his breast like a sick puppy for ten thousand years." The Child-Goddess looked critically at the incandescent presence of the God of the Delphae. "The light show doesn't impress me, Edaemus. I could do it, too, if I wanted to take the trouble."

Edaemus flared even brighter, and the reddish-orange nimbus around him became sooty.

"How tiresome," Aphrael sighed. "I'm sorry, Xanetia, but we're wasting our time here. Bhelliom and I are going to have to deal with Klæl on our own. Your tedious God wouldn't be any help anyway."

"*Klæl!*" Edaemus gasped.

"Got your attention, didn't I?" She smirked. "Are you ready to listen now?"

"Who hath done this? Who hath unloosed Klæl again upon the earth?"

"Well, it certainly wasn't *me*. Cyrgon had everything going his way, and then Anakha turned things around on him. You know how much Cyrgon hates to lose, so he started breaking the rules. Did you want to help us with this—or would you rather sit around and pout for another hundred eons or so? Quickly, quickly, Edaemus," she said, snapping her fingers at him. "Make up your mind. I don't have all day, you know."

"What makes you think I need any more men?" Narstil demanded. Narstil was a lean, almost cadaverous Arjuni with stringy arms and hollow cheeks. He sat at a table set under a spreading tree in the center of his encampment deep in the jungles of Arjuna.

"You're in a risky kind of business." Caalador shrugged, looking around at the cluttered camp. "You steal furniture and carpets and tapestries. That means that you've been raiding villages and mounting attacks on isolated estates. People fight back when you try that, and that means casualties. About half of your men are wearing bandages right now, and you probably leave a few dead behind you every time you try to steal things. A leader in your line *always* needs more men."

"I don't have any vacancies just now."

"I can arrange some," Bevier told him in a menacing voice, melodramatically drawing his thumb across the edge of his lochaber.

"Look, Narstil," Caalador said in a somewhat less abrasive tone, "we've seen your men. Be honest now. You've gathered up a bunch of local bad-boys who got into trouble for stealing chickens or running off somebody else's goats. You're very light on professionals, and that's what we're offering you—professionalism. Your bad-boys bluster and try to impress each other by looking mean and nasty, but real killing isn't in their nature, and that's why they get hurt when the fighting starts. Killing doesn't bother *us*. We're used to it. Your young bravos have to prove things to each other, but we don't. Orden knows who we are. He wouldn't have sent you that letter otherwise." His eyes narrowed slightly. "Believe me, Narstil, life will be much easier for all of us if we're working *with* you rather than setting up shop across the street."

Narstil looked a little less certain of himself. "I'll think about it," he said.

"Do that. And don't get any ideas about trying to eliminate potential competition in advance. Your bad-boys wouldn't be up to it, and my friends and I would sort of be obliged to take it personally."

"Stop that," Sephrenia chided her sister as the four of them moved through the corridorlike streets of Delphaeus toward the home of Cedon, the Anari of Xanetia's people.

"Edaemus is doing it," Aphrael countered.

"It's his city, and these are his people. It's not polite to do that when you're a guest."

Xanetia gave them a puzzled look.

"My sister's showing off," Sephrenia explained.

"Am not," Aphrael retorted.

"Yes you are, too, Aphrael, and you and I both know it. We've had this argument before. Now stop it."

"I do not understand," Xanetia confessed.

"That's because you've grown accustomed to the sense of her presence, sister," Sephrenia explained wearily. "She's not supposed to flaunt her divinity this way when she's around the worshippers of other Gods. It's the worst form of bad manners, and she knows it. She's only doing it to irritate Edaemus. I'm surprised she hasn't flattened the whole city or set fire to the thatching on the roofs with all that divine personality."

"That's a spiteful thing to say, Sephrenia," Aphrael accused.

"Behave yourself, then."

"I won't unless Edaemus does."

Sephrenia sighed, rolling her eyes upward.

They entered the southern wing of the extended city-building that was Delphaeus and proceeded down a dim hallway to Cedon's door. The Anari was waiting for them, his ancient face filled with wonder. He fell to his knees as the light that was Edaemus approached, but his God dimmed, assumed a human form, and reached out gently to raise him to his feet again. "That is not needful, my old friend," he said.

"Why, Edaemus," Aphrael said, "you're really quite handsome. You shouldn't hide from us in all that light the way you do."

A faint smile touched the ageless face of the Delphaeic God. "Seek not to beguile me with flattery, Aphrael. I know thee, and I know thy ways. Thou shalt not so easily ensnare me."

"Oh, really? Thou art ensnared already, Edaemus. I do but toy with thee now. My hand is already about thine heart. In time, I shall close it and make thee mine." And she laughed a silvery little peal of laughter. "But that's between you and me, cousin. Right now we have other things to do."

Xanetia fondly embraced the ancient Cedon. "As thou canst readily perceive, my dear old friend, momentous changes are afoot. The dire peril which we face doth reshape our entire world. Let us consider that peril first, and then at our leisure may we pause to marvel at how all about us is altered."

Cedon led them down the three worn stone steps into his low-ceilinged chamber with its inwardly curving, white plastered walls, its comfortable furniture, and its cheery fire.

"Tell them what's been going on, Xanetia," Aphrael suggested, climbing up into Sephrenia's lap. "That may explain why it was necessary for me to violate all the rules and come here." She gave Edaemus an arch look. "Regardless of what you may think, cousin, I *do* have good manners, but we've got an emergency on our hands."

Sephrenia leaned back in her chair as Xanetia began her account of the events of the past several months. There was a sense of peace, an unruffled calm about Delphaeus that Sephrenia had not perceived during her last visit. At that time, her mind had been so filled with obsessive hatred that she had scarcely taken note of her surroundings. The Delphae had appealed to Sparhawk to seal their valley away from the rest of the world, but that seemed somehow unnecessary. They were already separate—so separate that they no longer seemed even human. In a peculiar way, Sephrenia envied them.

"Infuriating, aren't they?" the Child-Goddess murmured. "And the word you're looking for is 'serenity.' "

"And you're doing everything in your power to disturb that, aren't you?"

"They're still a part of this world, Sephrenia—for a little while longer, anyway. All I'm doing is reminding them that the rest of us are still out here."

"You're behaving very badly toward Edaemus."

"I'm trying to jerk him back to reality. He's been off by himself for the past hundred centuries and he's forgotten what it's like having the rest of us around. I'm reminding him. Actually, it's good for him. He was starting to get complacent." She slipped down from her sister's lap. "Excuse me," she said. "It's time for me to give him another lesson." She crossed the room and stood directly in front of Edaemus, looking pleadingly into his face with her large, dark eyes.

The God of the Delphae was so engrossed in Xanetia's account that he scarcely noticed Aphrael and, when she held out her arms to him, he absently picked her up and settled her into his lap.

Sephrenia smiled.

"And most recently," Xanetia concluded her report, "young Sir Berit hath been given further instruction. He is to turn aside and go to the town of Sopal on the coast of the Sea of Arjun. He hath advised the Child-Goddess of this alteration of direction, and she in turn hath made the rest of us aware of it. It is the intent of the Troll-Gods to transport Sir Ulath and Sir Tynian to Sopal and to conceal them there in what they call 'No-Time.' It is their thought that when our enemies produce Queen Ehlana to exchange her for Bhelliom, they might leap from their concealment and rescue her."

"No-Time?" Cedon asked, his face puzzled.

"Suspended duration," Aphrael explained. "Trolls are hunters, and their Gods have found a new place of concealment for them so that they're able to stalk their prey unseen. It's clever, but it has its drawbacks."

Edaemus asked her something in that language Sephrenia had tried several times to learn but had never really been able to grasp. Aphrael replied, speaking rapidly in a rather dry, technical tone and making intricate gestures with her hands.

"Ah," he said finally, lapsing back into Tamul and with an expression of comprehension flooding his face. "It is a peculiar notion."

"You know how the Troll-Gods are." She made a little face.

"Didst thou in truth wring acceptance of thine outrageous demands from them?"

"I had something they wanted." She shrugged. "They've been trying to think up some way to escape from Bhelliom for three hundred centuries now. They didn't *like* my conditions very much, but they didn't have much choice."

"Thou are cruel, Aphrael."

"Not really. I was driven by necessity, and necessity's neither cruel nor kindly. It just *is*. I kissed them a few times when I stopped by a couple of days ago, and that made them feel better—it did once they realized that I wasn't going to take a bite out of them, anyway."

"Thou didst *not*!" He seemed aghast.

"They aren't so bad," she defended her action. "I suppose I could have scratched them behind the ears instead, but that might have insulted them, so I kissed them instead." She smiled. "A few more kisses and I'd have had them licking my fingers like puppies."

He straightened, then suddenly blinked as if realizing for the first time where she was sitting.

She gave him another of those mysterious little smiles and patted his cheek. "That's all right, cousin," she told him. "You'll come around eventually. They always do." And she slipped down from his lap and walked back across the room to rejoin her sister.

"That's *my* place!" a burly fellow of indeterminate race asserted threateningly as Kalten dropped his saddlebags and bedroll on a clear spot under a large tree.

"It *was*," Kalten grunted.

"You can't just walk in here and steal a man's place like this."

"Oh? Is it against the law or something?" Kalten straightened. He was at least a head taller than the other man, and he bulked large in his mail shirt. "My friends and I are going to be staying right here," he stated flatly, "so pick up your bed and all this other trash and go someplace else."

"I'm not in the habit of taking orders from Elenes!"

"That's too bad. Now move away. I've got work to do." Kalten was not in a good humor. Alean's peril gnawed at him constantly, and even slight irritations rubbed his temper raw. Some of that must have showed on his face. The other man backed off a few steps.

"Farther," Kalten told him.

"I'll be back," the man blustered, retreating a few more steps. "I'll be back with all my friends."

"I can hardly wait." Kalten deliberately turned his back on the man he had just dispossessed.

Caalador and Bevier joined him. "Trouble?" Caalador asked.

"I wouldn't call it that." Kalten shrugged. "I was just establishing some rank, is all. Anytime you come into a new situation, you have to push a few people around to make everybody else understand that you're not going to put up with any foolishness. Let's get settled in."

They had erected their tent and were gathering leaves and moss for beds when Narstil stopped by. "I see you're getting set up, Ezek," he said to Caalador. His tone was conciliatory, though not quite cordial.

"A few finishing touches are about all that's left," Caalador replied.

"You men make a good camp," Narstil noted. "Tidy."

"A cluttered camp is the sign of a cluttered mind," Caalador declared. "I'm glad you stopped by, Narstil. We hear that there's an army camped out not far from here. Do they cause you any problems?"

"We've got an agreement with them," Narstil replied. "We don't steal from them, and they leave us alone. That's not a real army in Natayos, though. It's more like a large band of rebels. They want to overthrow the government."

"Doesn't everybody?"

Narstil laughed. "Actually, having that mob in Natayos is very good for *my* business. The fact that they're all there keeps the police out of this part of the jungle, and one of the reasons they tolerate *us* is because we rob travelers, and that keeps people from snooping around Natayos. We do a fairly brisk business with them. They're a ready market for just about everything we steal."

"How far is this Natayos place from here?"

"About ten miles. It's an old ruin. Scarpa—he's the one in charge over there—moved in with his rebels a couple of years back. He's fortified it, and he's bringing in more of his followers every day. I don't care much for him, but business is business."

"What's he like?"

"He's crazy. Some days he's so crazy that he bays at the moon. He's convinced that he'll be emperor one day, and I expect it won't be long until he marches his rabble out of those ruins. He's fairly safe in this jungle, but just as soon as he gets out into open country, the Atans will grind him into dog meat right on the spot."

"Are we supposed to care about that?" Bevier asked.

"I personally couldn't care less," Narstil assured the apparently one-eyed ruffian. "It's the loss of his business that concerns me."

"Can just anybody walk in and out of Natayos anytime he feels like it?" Kalten asked as if only mildly curious.

"If you're leading a mule loaded down with food or drink, they'll welcome you with open arms. I send an oxcart loaded down with barrels of ale every few days. You know how soldiers like their ale."

"Oh, yes," Kalten agreed. "I've know a few soldiers in my time, and their whole world stops when somebody opens an ale-barrel."

"It doth derive from our ability to control the light which doth emanate from us," Cedon explained. "What we call sight is profoundly influenced by light. The subterfuge is not perfect. Some faint shimmers do appear, and we must be wary lest our shadows reveal our presence, but with a certain care, we can be unobserved."

"Now *there* are some interesting contrasts," Aphrael said. "The Troll-Gods tamper with time, you tamper with light, and I tamper with the attention of the people I want to hide from, but it's all an attempt to achieve some measure of invisibility."

"Knowest thou of any who can be *truly* invisible, Divine One?" Xanetia asked.

"*I* don't. Do you, cousin?"

Edaemus shook his head.

"We can come close, though," the Child-Goddess said. "The real thing would probably have drawbacks. It's a very good idea, Anari Cedon, but I don't want Xanetia to put herself in any kind of danger. I love her too much for that."

Xanetia flushed slightly, and then she gave Edaemus an almost guilty look. Sephrenia laughed. "I must in honesty warn thee, Edaemus," she said. "Guard well thy worshippers. My Goddess is a notorious thief." She frowned thoughtfully. "If Xanetia could go unobserved into Sopal, it could be very useful. Her ability to reach into the thoughts of others would enable her to discover in short order whether Ehlana's there or not. If she is, we can take steps. If not, we'll know that Sopal's just another diversion."

Cedon looked at Edaemus. "I think, Belovèd One, that we must extend our involvement in the world around us farther than we had earlier planned. Anakha's concern for the safety of his wife doth take precedence in his mind o'er all else, and his promise to us doth stand in peril until she be returned to him safe and whole."

Edaemus sighed. "It may be e'en as thou sayeth, my Anari. Though it doth make me unquiet, it would appear that we must set aside our repugnance and join in the search for Anakha's wife, lending such aid as is within our power."

"Are you *really* sure you want to become involved in this, Edaemus?" Aphrael asked him. "Really, *really* sure?"

"I have said it, Aphrael."

"Aren't you the least bit interested in why I'm so concerned with the fate of a pair of Elenes? Elenes *do* have their own God, you know. Why do you imagine that *I'd* be so interested in them?"

"Why is it ever thy wont to speak circuitously, Aphrael?"

"Because I love to surprise people," she replied sweetly. "I really *do* want to thank you for your concern about the well-being of my mother and father, cousin. You've touched me to the very heart."

He stared at her in stunned astonishment. *"Thou didst not!"* he gasped.

"*Somebody* had to do it." She shrugged. "One of us has to keep an eye on Bhelliom. Anakha is Bhelliom's creature, but as long as I have my hand around his heart, I can more or less control the things he does."

"But they're *Elenes!*"

"Oh, grow up, Edaemus. Elene, Styric, Delphae—what difference does it make? You can love all of them if your heart's not closed."

"But they eat *pigs!*"

"I know." She shuddered. "Believe me, I know. It's one of the things I've been working on."

Senga was a good-natured brigand whose racial origins were so mixed that no one could really tell *what* he was. He grinned a great deal, and he was loud and boisterous and had an infectious laugh. Kalten liked him, and Senga appeared to have found a kindred spirit in the Elene outlaw he knew as Col. He was laughing as he came across Narstil's cluttered compound where furniture and other household goods were stacked in large, untidy heaps on the bare ground. "Ho, Col," he shouted as he approached the tree where Kalten, Caalador, and Bevier had pitched their tent. "You should have come along. An oxcart load of ale opens every door in Natayos."

"Armies make me nervous, Senga," Kalten replied. "The officers are always trying to enlist you—usually at swordpoint—and generals as a group tend to be overly moralistic for my taste. The term *martial law* makes my blood run cold for some reason."

"Scarpa grew up in a tavern, my friend," Senga assured him, "and his mother was a whore, so he's accustomed to the seamier side of human nature."

"How did you make out?" Kalten asked.

Senga grinned, rolled his eyes, and jingled a heavy purse. "Well enough to make me consider giving up crime and opening my own brewery. The only problem with that is the fact that our friends at Natayos probably won't be there all that much longer. If I set up shop as a brewer and my customers all marched off to get killed by the Atans, I'd probably have to drink all that ale by myself, and nobody's *that* thirsty."

"Oh? What makes you think those rebels are getting ready to leave?"

"Nothing very specific," Senga said, sprawling out on the ground and offering Kalten his wineskin. "Scarpa's been gone for the past several weeks. He and two or three Elenes left Natayos last month, and nobody I talked with knew where he was going or why."

Kalten carefully kept his expression disinterested. "I hear that he's crazy. Crazy men don't need reasons for the things they do or the places they go."

"Scarpa's crazy enough, all right, but he can certainly whip those rebels of his into a frenzy. When he decides to make a speech, you'd better find a comfortable place to sit, because you're going to be there for six hours at least. Anyway, he went off a while back, and his army was getting settled in for the winter. That's all changed now that he's back."

Kalten became very alert. "He's come back?"

"That he has, my friend. Here, give us a drink." Senga took the wineskin and tipped it up, squirting a long stream of wine into his mouth. Then he wiped his chin on the back of his hand. "He and those Elene friends of his came riding into Natayos not four days ago. They had a couple of women with them, I hear."

Kalten sank down on the ground and made some show of adjusting his sword belt to cover his sudden excitement. "I thought Scarpa hated women," he said, trying to keep his voice casual.

"Oh, that he does, my friend, but from what I hear, these two women weren't just some playthings he picked up along the way. They had their hands tied, for one thing, and the fellow I talked with said that they were a little bedraggled, but they didn't look like tavern wenches. He didn't get a very good look at them, because Scarpa hustled them into a house that seems to have been fixed up for somebody a little special—fancy furniture and rugs on the floor and all that."

"Was there anything unusual about them?" Kalten almost held his breath.

Senga shrugged and took another drink. "Just the fact that they weren't treated like ordinary camp followers, I suppose." He scratched his head. "There was something else the fellow told me," he said. "What was it now?"

Kalten *did* hold his breath this time.

"Oh, yes," Senga said, "now I remember. The fellow said that these two women Scarpa took all the trouble to invite to Natayos were Elenes. Isn't *that* odd?"

CHAPTER NINE

The town of Beresa on the southeastern Arjuni coast was a low, unlovely place squatting toadlike on the beach lying between the South Tamul Sea and the swampy green jungle behind it. The major industry of the region was the production of charcoal, and acrid smoke hung in the humid air over Beresa like a curse.

Captain Sorgi dropped his anchor some distance out from the wharves and went ashore to consult with the harbormaster.

Sparhawk, Stragen, and Talen, wearing their canvas smocks, leaned on the port rail staring across the smelly water toward their destination. "I have an absolutely splendid idea, Fron," Stragen said to Sparhawk.

"Oh?" Sparhawk replied.

"Why don't we jump ship?"

"Nice try, Vymer." Talen laughed. They were all more or less at ease with the assumed names by now.

Sparhawk looked around carefully to make sure that none of the rest of the crew was near. "An ordinary sailor wouldn't leave without collecting his pay. Let's not do anything to attract attention. All that's really left to do is the unloading of the cargo."

"Under the threat of the bo'sun's whip," Stragen added glumly. "That man *really* tests my self-control. Just the sight of him makes me want to kill him."

"We can endure him this one last time," Sparhawk told him. "This town's going to be full of unfriendly eyes. Krager's bound to have people here to make sure I'm not trying to sneak in reinforcements behind his back."

"That might just be the flaw in this whole plan, Fron," Stragen said. "Sorgi knows that we're not ordinary sailors. Is he the kind to let things slip?"

Sparhawk shook his head. "Sorgi knows how to keep his mouth shut. He was paid to get us to Beresa unnoticed, and Sorgi always does what he's paid to do."

The captain returned late that afternoon, and they raised anchor and eased up to one of the long wharves protruding out into the harbor. They unloaded the cargo the next morning. The bo'sun cracked his whip only sparingly, and the unloading proceeded rapidly.

Then, when the cargo holds were all emptied, the sailors lined up and filed along the quarterdeck where Sorgi sat at a small table with his account book and his stacks of coins. The captain gave each sailor a little speech as he paid him. The speeches varied slightly, but the general message was the same: "Stay out of trouble, and get back to the ship on time. I won't wait for you when the time comes to sail." He did not alter the speech when he paid Sparhawk and his friends, and his face did not in any way betray the fact they were anything other than ordinary crew members.

Sparhawk and his two friends went down the gangway with their seabags on their shoulders and with a certain amount of anticipation. "Now I see why sailors are so rowdy when they reach port," Sparhawk said. "That wasn't really much of a voyage, and I still feel a powerful urge to kick over the traces."

"Where to?" Talen asked when they reached the street.

"There's an inn called the Seaman's Rest," Stragen replied. "It's supposed to be a clean, quiet place out beyond the main battle zone here along the waterfront. It should give us a base of operations to work from."

The sun was just going down as they passed through the noisy, reeking streets of Beresa. The buildings were constructed for the most part of squared-off logs, since stone was rare here on the vast, soggy delta of the Arjun River, and the logs appeared to have been attacked by damp rot almost before they were in place. Moss and fungus grew everywhere, and the air was thick with the chill damp and the acrid wood smoke from the charcoal yards outside of town. The Arjunis in the streets were noticeably more swarthy than their Tamul cousins of the north; their eyes were shifty; and even their most casual gait through the muddy streets of their unlovely town seemed somehow furtive.

Sparhawk muttered the spell under his breath as they passed along the shabby street, and he released it carefully to avoid alerting the watchers he was sure were there.

"Well?" Talen asked. Talen had been around Sparhawk long enough to know the signs that the big Pandion was using magic.

"They're out there," Sparhawk replied. "Three of them that I can pick up."

"Are they concentrating on us?" Stragen asked tensely.

Sparhawk shook his head. "Their attention's sort of generalized. They aren't Styrics, so they won't know I've gone looking for them. Let's just move along. If they start to follow us, I'll let you know."

The Seaman's Rest was a square, tidy inn festooned with fishnets and other nautical decorations. It was run by a burly retired sea captain and his equally burly wife. They brooked no nonsense under their roof and they recited a long list of house rules to each prospective tenant before they would accept his money. Sparhawk had not even heard of some of the things that were prohibited.

"Where to now?" Talen asked after they had stowed their seabags in their room and come back out into the muddy street.

"Back to the waterfront," Stragen replied. "The chief of the local thieves is a man named Estokin. He deals extensively with smugglers and with sailors who pilfer things from cargo holds. I've got a letter from Caalador. Ostensibly, we're here to make sure that he got his money's worth during the Harvest Festival. Arjunis aren't generally trusted, so Estokin won't be too surprised to see us."

Estokin the Arjuni was a man who had clearly been destined for a life of crime from the day he was born. He had what was perhaps the most evil face Sparhawk had ever seen. His left eye peered perpetually off in a northeasterly direction, and he had a pronounced squint. His beard was sparse and straggly, and his skin was blotched with a scaly disease. He scratched at his face almost continually, showering white flakes as if from a winter sky. His high-pitched, nasal voice was very much like the whine of a hungry mosquito, and he reeked of garlic, cheap wine, and pickled herring. "Is Caalador accusing me of cheating him, Vymer?" he demanded with some show of indignation.

"Of course not." Stragen leaned back in the rickety chair in the back room of the smelly waterfront dive. "If he thought that, you'd already be dead. He wants to know if we missed anybody, that's all. Were any local people particularly upset when the bodies started to turn up?"

Estokin squinted at Stragen with his good eye. "What's it worth to him?" he haggled.

"We've been instructed to let you live if you cooperate," Stragen countered in a cool voice.

"You can't threaten me like that, Vymer," Estokin blustered.

"I wasn't threatening you, old boy. I was just letting you know how things stand. Let's get to the point here. Who got excited here in Beresa after the killings?"

"Not very many, really." Stragen's chilly manner had evidently persuaded Estokin to behave himself. "There was a Styric here who was fairly free with his money before the Harvest Festival."

"What was he buying?"

"Information, mostly. He was on the list Caalador gave me, but he managed to get away—rode off into the jungle. I've got a couple of local cutthroats on his trail."

"I'd sort of like to talk with him before they put him to sleep."

"Not much chance, Vymer. They're a long way out in the bush by now." Estokin scratched at his forehead, stirring up another snow flurry. "I'm not sure why

Caalador wanted all those people killed," he said, "and I don't really want to know, but I'm getting a whiff or two of politics, and here in Arjuna that means Scarpa. You might want to warn Caalador to be very careful. I've talked with a few deserters from that rebel army in the jungle. We've all heard stories about how crazy Scarpa is, but let me tell you, my friend, the stories don't even come close. If only half of what I've heard is true, Scarpa's the craziest man who ever lived."

Sparhawk's stomach gave a lurch, and then it settled into a cold knot.

Father?

Sparhawk sat up in bed quickly.

Are you awake? the Child-Goddess asked, her voice roaring in his mind.

"Of course. Please lower your voice a bit. You're jarring my teeth."

I wanted to be sure I had your attention. Some things have happened. Berit and Khalad got some new instructions from Krager. They're supposed to go to Sopal now instead of coming here to Beresa.

Sparhawk swore.

Please don't use that kind of language, Father. I am *just a little girl, you know.*

He ignored that. *Is the trade going to take place in Sopal?*

It's hard to say. Bevier's been in touch with me, too. Kalten talked with an outlaw who's been selling beer to the soldiers in Natayos, and he says that Scarpa's gone back there. Then the outlaw told Kalten that Scarpa had two Elene women with him when he returned.

Sparhawk's heart leapt. *Was he sure?*

Kalten thinks so. The fellow didn't have any reason to lie about it. Of course, Kalten's beer merchant didn't actually see them for himself, so don't get your hopes up too much. It could be a very carefully planted story. Zalasta's in Natayos, and he could be trying to lure you there or trying to trick you into giving away any secrets you might have tucked up your sleeve. He knows you well enough to know that you'll try to do something he doesn't expect.

Is there any way you could find out for sure if your mother's in Natayos?

I'm afraid not. I could slip around Scarpa easily enough, but Zalasta would sense me immediately. It's too risky.

What else is going on?

Ulath and Tynian have reached the Troll-Gods. Ghnomb's going to take them to Sopal in that frozen time he's so fond of, and they'll be there when Berit and Khalad arrive. Ghnomb knows another way to play around with time, so he's going to skip Ulath and Tynian from moment to moment. It's a little complicated, but they'll be there and watching and nobody will be able to see them. If Scarpa and Zalasta try to make the trade in Sopal, Tynian and Ulath will be right on top of them to rescue Mother and Alean.

Zalasta can follow them into that frozen moment, you know.

That wouldn't really pay him, Father. Khwaj was outraged when he heard about Mother, so he's going to be lurking in No-Time. If Zalasta tries to follow Ulath and Tynian, Khwaj will set him on fire—and the fire won't ever go out.

I could learn to grow fond of Khwaj.

Sephrenia and Xanetia are in Delphaeus, Aphrael continued. *Edaemus is being tiresome, but the news about Klæl shook his tree, so I'll probably be able to coax him down out of the branches. He knows that Mother's captivity puts the arrangement you have with Cedon at risk, so he's agreed to help us rescue her. I'll keep working on him. If I can push him just a little farther, he might agree to let the Delphae come out of their valley. They could be enormously helpful to us.*

Why didn't you tell me about all of this earlier?

What would you have done if I had, Sparhawk? Jumped over the side of Sorgi's ship and swum ashore?

I need to know these things when they happen, Aphrael.

Why? Let me take care of the fretting and worrying, Sparhawk. All it does is make you foul-tempered.

He let that pass. *I'll tell this to Bhelliom.*

Absolutely not! We don't dare open that box. Cyrgon or Klæl will feel Bhelliom instantly if we do.

Didn't you know? he asked her mildly. *I don't have to open the box to speak with Bhelliom. We can talk with each other right through the gold.*

Why didn't you tell me?

What would you have done if I had? Jumped into the sea and come swimming after Sorgi's ship?

There was a long moment of silence. *You really enjoy turning my own words around and throwing them back in my teeth like that, don't you, Sparhawk?*

Naturally. Was there anything else you'd like to share with me, Divine One?

But the sense of her presence was gone, leaving only a slightly huffy silence behind.

"Where's—ah—Vymer?" Sparhawk asked Talen as the boy entered the room a few minutes later.

"He's out attending to something," Talen replied evasively.

"Attending to what?"

"He asked me not to tell you."

"All right. *I'm* asking you to ignore him—and I'm right here where I can get my hands on you."

"That's a crude way to put it."

"Nobody's perfect. What's he up to?"

Talen sighed. "One of Estokin's men stopped by—just after you came up to go to bed. He said that there are three Elenes in town who are letting it be known they'll pay good money for information about any strangers who seem to be settling in for a long stay. Vymer decided to look them up." Talen glanced meaningfully at the walls of their small room. "I'd guess that he probably wants to find out just exactly what they mean by 'good money.' You know Vymer when there's some profit to be made."

"He should have told me," Sparhawk said cautiously. "I'm not any more allergic to a quick profit than he is."

"Sharing isn't one of Vymer's strong points, Fron." Talen touched his ear and then laid a finger to his lips. "Why don't we go out and see if we can find him?"

"Good idea." Sparhawk quickly pulled on his clothes, and the two of them clattered down the stairs and out into the street.

"I just had a religious experience," Sparhawk murmured as they walked into the noisy area near the docks.

"Oh?"

"One of those Divine visitations."

"Ah. What did your Divine visitor have to say?"

"A broken-nosed friend of ours got another one of those notes. He's been told to go to Sopal instead of coming here."

Talen muttered a fairly vile oath.

"My feelings exactly. Isn't that Vymer coming up the street?" Sparhawk pointed at a blond man in a tar-smeared smock who was lurching unsteadily toward them.

Talen peered at the fellow. "I think you're right." He made a face. "The ladies who changed things around may have gone a little far. He doesn't even walk the same anymore."

"What are you two doing out this late?" Stragen asked as he joined them.

"We got lonesome," Sparhawk replied in a flat tone of voice.

"For me? I'm touched. Let's go for a walk on the beach, my friends. I find myself yearning for the smell of salt water—and the nice loud sound of waves crashing on the sand."

They walked on past the last of the wharves and then out onto the sand. The clouds had blown off, and there was a bright moon. They reached the water's edge and stood looking out at the long combers rolling in off the South Tamul Sea to hammer noisily on the wet sand.

"What have you been up to, Stragen?" Sparhawk demanded bluntly.

"Business, old boy. I just enlisted us in the intelligence service of the other side."

"You did *what*?"

"The three you sensed when we first got here needed a few good men. I volunteered our services."

"Are you out of your mind?"

"Of course not. Think about it, Sparhawk. What better way is there to gather information? Our celebration of the Harvest Festival thinned their ranks drastically, so they can't afford to be choosy. I paid Estokin to vouch for us, and then I told them a few lies. They're expecting a certain Sir Sparhawk to flood the town with sharp-eyed people. We're supposed to report anybody we see who's acting a little suspicious. I provided them with a prime suspect."

"Oh? Who was that?"

"Captain Sorgi's bo'sun—you know, the fellow with the whip."

Sparhawk suddenly laughed. "That was a truly vicious thing to do, Stragen."

"I rather liked it, myself."

"Aphrael came by to call," Talen said. "She told Sparhawk that Berit and my brother have been ordered to change direction. Now they're supposed to go to Sopal on the coast of the Sea of Arjun."

Stragen swore.

"I already said that," Talen told him.

"We probably should have expected it," Sparhawk said. "Krager's working for the other side and he knows us well enough to anticipate some of the things we might try to do." He suddenly banged his fist into the palm of his hand. "I *wish* I could talk with Sephrenia!" he burst out.

"You *can,* as I recall," Stragen said. "Didn't Aphrael fix it once so that you and Sephrenia talked when she was in Sarsos and you were in Cimmura?"

Sparhawk suddenly felt more than a little foolish. "I'd forgotten about that," he admitted.

"That's all right, old boy," Stragen excused him. "You've got a lot on your mind. Why don't you have a word with her Divine little Whimsicality and see if she can arrange a council of war someplace? I think it might be time for a good, old-fashioned get-together."

Sparhawk knew where he was before he even opened his eyes. The fragrance of wildflowers and tree blossoms immediately identified the eternal spring of Aphrael's own private reality.

"Art thou now awake, Anakha?" the white deer asked him, touching his hand with her nose.

"Yea, gentle creature," he replied, opening his eyes and touching the side of her face. He was in the pavilion again and he looked out through the open flap at the flower-studded meadow, the sparkling azure sea, and the rainbow-colored sky above.

"The others do await thy coming on the eyot," the hind advised him.

"We must hasten, then," he said, rising from his bed. He followed her from the pavilion out into the meadow where the white tigress indulgently watched the awkward play of her large-footed cubs. He rather idly wondered if these were the same cubs she had been tending when he had first visited this enchanted realm a half-dozen years ago.

Well, of course *they are, Sparhawk,* Aphrael's voice murmured in his ear. *Nothing ever changes here.*

He smiled.

The white deer led him to that beautiful, impractical boat, a swan-necked craft with sails like wings, elaborate embellishment, and so much of its main structure above the waterline that a sneeze would have capsized it, had it existed in the real world.

Critic, Aphrael's voice accused him.

It's your dream, Divine One. You can put any impossibility in it that you want.

Oh, thank *you, Sparhawk!* she said with effusive irony.

The emerald green eyot, crowned with ancient oaks and Aphrael's alabaster temple, nestled in the sapphire sea, and the swan-necked boat touched the golden beach in only minutes. Sparhawk looked around as he stepped out onto the sand. The disguises most of them wore in the real world had been discarded, and they all had their own features here in this eternal dream. Some of them had been here before. Those who had not had expressions of bemused wonderment as they all lounged in the lush grass that blanketed the slopes of the enchanted isle.

The Child-Goddess and Sephrenia sat side by side on an alabaster bench in the temple. Aphrael's expression was pensive, and she was playing a complex Styric melody in a minor key on her many-chambered pipes. "What kept you, Sparhawk?" she asked, lowering the rude instrument.

"The person in charge of my travel arrangements took me on a little side trip," he replied. "Are we all here?"

"Everybody who's supposed to be. Come up here, all of you, and let's get started."

They climbed up the slope to the temple.

"Where is this place?" Sarabian asked in an awed voice.

"Aphrael carries it in her mind, your Majesty," Vanion replied. "She invites us here from time to time. She likes to show it off."

"Don't be insulting, Vanion," the Child-Goddess told him.

"Well, don't you?"

"Of course, but it's not nice to come right out and say it like that."

"I feel different here, for some reason," Caalador noted. "Better, somehow."

Vanion smiled. "It's a very healthy place, my friend," he said. "I was seriously ill at the end of the Zemoch war—dying, actually. Aphrael brought me here for a month or so, and I was disgustingly healthy by the time I left."

They all reached the little temple and took seats on the marble benches lining the columned perimeter. Sparhawk looked around, frowning. "Where's Emban?" he asked their hostess.

"It wouldn't have been appropriate for him to be here, Sparhawk. Your Elene God makes exceptions in the case of the Church Knights, but he'd probably throw a fit if I brought one of the Patriarchs of his Church here. I didn't invite the Atans either—or the Peloi." She smiled. "Neither group is comfortable with the idea of religious diversity, and this place would probably confuse them." She rolled her eyes upward. "You wouldn't *believe* how long it took me to persuade Edaemus to permit Xanetia to come. He doesn't approve of me. He thinks I'm frivolous."

"You?" Sparhawk feigned some surprise. "How could he possibly believe something like that?"

"Let's get at this," Sephrenia said. "Why don't you start, Berit? We know generally what happened, but we don't have any details."

"Yes, Lady Sephrenia," the young knight replied. "Khalad and I were coming down the coast, and we'd been watched from almost the moment we came ashore. I used the spell and identified the watcher as a Styric. He came to us after several days and gave us another one of those notes from Krager. This one told us to continue down the coast, but once we get past the Tamul Mountains, we're supposed to cut across-country to Sopal instead of continuing south. We're to get further instructions there. It was definitely from Krager: it had another lock of Queen Ehlana's hair in it."

"I'm going to talk with Krager about that when I catch up with him," Khalad said in a bleak tone of voice. "I want to be sure he understands just how much we resent his touching the queen's hair. Trust me, Sparhawk. Before I'm done with him, he's going to regret it—profoundly."

"I've got enormous confidence in you, Khalad," Sparhawk replied.

"Oh," Khalad said then, "there's something I almost forgot. Does anybody know of a way to make one of our horses limp—without actually hurting him? I think Berit and I might want to be able to slow down from time to time without causing suspicion. An intermittently lame horse should explain it to the people who are watching us."

"I'll talk with Faran," Aphrael promised.

"You won't need to limp on your way to Sopal," Ulath told Khalad. "Ghnomb's going to see to it that Tynian and I are there long before you arrive. You might be able to see us when you get there, but you might not. I'm having a little trouble explaining some things to the Troll-Gods. We'll be able to see you, though. If I can't make Ghnomb understand, I'll slip a note in your pocket."

"If we *do* come out in the open, you'll just *love* our traveling companion." Tynian laughed.

Berit gave him a puzzled look. "Who's that, Sir Tynian?"

"Bhlokw. He's a Troll."

"It's Ghnomb's idea," Ulath explained. "I have to go through a little ceremony before I can talk with the Troll-Gods. Bhlokw doesn't, so having him along speeds up communication. Anyway, we'll be there and out of sight. If Scarpa and Zalasta try to make the trade in Sopal, we'll step out of No-Time, grab the lot of you, and disappear again."

"That's assuming that they're taking Queen Ehlana to Sopal to make the exchange," Itagne said. "We've got some things that don't match up, though. Sir Kalten picked up a rumor that Scarpa's holding the queen and her maid in Natayos."

"I wouldn't want to wager the farm on it, your Excellency," Kalten said. "It's secondhand information at best. The fellow I talked with probably isn't bright enough to make up stories, and he didn't have any reason to lie to me. But he got his information from somebody else, so that makes the whole thing a little wormy."

"You've put your finger on the problem, Sir Kalten," Sarabian said. "Soldiers gossip worse than old women." He tugged at one earlobe and looked up at the rainbow-colored sky. "The other side knows that I wasn't entirely dependent on the Ministry of the Interior for information, so they'll expect me to have ears in Natayos. This story Sir Kalten heard could have been planted for our benefit. Prince Sparhawk, is there any way at all you could use Bhelliom to confirm the rumor?"

"It's too dangerous," Sephrenia said flatly. "Zalasta would know immediately if Sparhawk did that."

"I'm not so sure, little mother," Sparhawk disagreed. "It was just recently that we found out that the gold box doesn't totally isolate Bhelliom. I'm getting a strong feeling that a great deal of what we *think* we know about Bhelliom is pure misdirection. The rings evidently don't really mean anything at all—except possibly as a means of communication, and the gold box doesn't appear to be relevant either. It *could* be an idea Bhelliom planted to keep us from enclosing it in iron. I'm guessing, but I'd say that the touch of iron is still painful to it, but whether it's painful enough to actually confine it isn't all that certain."

"He's right, you know," Aphrael told her sister. "A great deal of what we think we know about Bhelliom came from Ghwerig, and Bhelliom had absolute control of Ghwerig. Our mistake was believing that Ghwerig knew what he was talking about."

"That still doesn't answer the question about using Bhelliom to investigate things in Natayos," Sparhawk said, "and it's not the sort of thing I'd want to experiment with."

"I will go to Natayos," Xanetia said quietly. "It had been mine intent to go unseen to Sopal, but Sir Tynian and Sir Ulath will be there already, and well able to determine if the queen be truly there. I will go to Natayos and seek her there instead."

"Absolutely not!" Sarabian said. "I forbid it."

"I am not subject to thee, Sarabian of Tamuli," she reminded him. "But fear not. There is no peril involved for me. None will know that I am there, and I can reach out to those who are about me and share their thoughts. I will soon be able to determine whether or no the queen and her maidservant are in Natayos. This is precisely the kind of service we offered when we concluded our pact with Anakha."

"It's too dangerous," he said stubbornly.

"It seemeth me that thou hast forgot mine *other* gift, Sarabian of Tamuli," she told him quite firmly. "The curse of Edaemus is still upon me, and my touch is still death, and I choose it so. Fear not for me, Sarabian, for should necessity compel me to it, I can spread death and terror through Natayos. Though it doth cause me pain to confess it, I can make Natayos once more a waste, a weed-choked ruin populated only by the dead."

CHAPTER TEN

The city of Sarna in western Tamul proper lay just to the south of the Atan border in the deep gorge of the river from which it took its name. The surrounding mountains were steep and rugged and were covered with dark evergreens which sighed endlessly in the prevailing wind sweeping down out of the wilderness to the north. The weather was cold, and the leaden sky spat stinging pellets of snow as Vanion's army of Church Knights slowly descended the long, steep road leading down into the gorge. Vanion and Itagne, muffled in their heavy cloaks, rode at the head of the column.

"I'd have much preferred to stay on Aphrael's island," Itagne said, shivering and pulling his cloak tighter. "I've never been particularly fond of this time of year."

"We're almost there, your Excellency," Vanion replied.

"Is it customary to campaign in the wintertime, Lord Vanion?" Itagne asked. "In Eosia, I mean?"

"We try to avoid it, your Excellency," Vanion replied. "The Lamorks attack each other in the winter, but the rest of us usually have better sense."

"It's a miserable time to go to war."

Vanion smiled faintly. "That it is, my friend, but that's not why we avoid it. It's a question of economics, really. It's more expensive to campaign in winter because you have to buy hay for the horses. It's the expense that keeps Elene kings peaceful when there's snow on the ground." Vanion stood up in his stirrups to peer ahead. "Betuana's waiting," he said. "We'd better ride down to meet her."

Itagne nodded, and they pushed their horses into a jolting trot.

The Queen of Atan had left them behind at Dasan on the eastern edge of the mountains, determined to come on ahead. She had several very good reasons, of course, but Vanion privately suspected that her decision had been influenced more by impatience than necessity. Betuana was too polite to speak of it, but she clearly had little use for horses, and she seldom missed an opportunity to outrun them. She and Engessa, both garbed in otter skins, waited at the roadside about a mile outside the city.

"Was there any trouble?" the Atan queen asked.

"No, your Majesty," Vanion replied, his black armor clinking as he swung down out of his saddle. "We were watched, but there's nothing unusual about that. Has anything been happening in Cynesga?"

"They're moving up to the border, Vanion-Preceptor," Engessa replied quietly. "They aren't being very subtle about it. We've been disrupting their supply lines and ambushing their scouting parties just to keep them off balance, but it's fairly obvious that they plan to come across the line in force."

Vanion nodded. "It's more or less what we expected, then. If it's all right with you, your Majesty, I'd like to get my men settled in before we get too involved in discussions. I can always think better after I've seen to all the details."

"Of course," Betuana agreed. "Engessa-Atan and I have arranged quarters for them. When will you be leaving for Samar?"

"Tomorrow or the next day, Betuana-Queen. Tikome's Peloi are probably spread a little thin down there. He has a lot of ground to cover."

"He sent back to Pela for more men, Vanion-Lord," Engessa advised. "You'll have a sizable force in Samar in a week or so."

"Good. Let me go back and hurry the knights along. We have much to discuss."

Night settled early at the bottom of the gorge of the River Sarna, and it was fully dark by the time Vanion joined the others in the headquarters of the city's Atan garrison. Like all Atan structures, the building was severely utilitarian and devoid of any embellishment. The lone exception in the conference room in which they gathered was a very large map covering one entire wall. The map was brightly colored and dotted here and there with fanciful illustrations. Vanion had bathed hurriedly and now wore plain clothing. The years had taught him that armor was impressive and even useful at times, but that no one had yet devised a way to make it comfortable or to eliminate its characteristic smell.

"Are the quarters satisfactory?" Betuana inquired politely.

"Most satisfactory, your Majesty," he replied, settling into a chair. "Have you been advised of the details of our meeting with the Child-Goddess?"

She nodded. "Itagne-Ambassador gave me a report," she replied. She paused. "One is curious to know why one was excluded," she added.

"Theological considerations, your Majesty," Vanion explained. "As I understand it, the Gods have an exquisitely complex etiquette in these situations. Aphrael didn't want to offend your God by inviting his children to her island. There were some other rather conspicuous absences as well. Emperor Sarabian was there and Ambassador Itagne, but Foreign Minister Oscagne wasn't."

Itagne frowned slightly. "The emperor and I are skeptics—agnostics, I suppose you could call us—but Oscagne's an out-and-out atheist. Would that account for it?"

"It might. I'll ask Aphrael the next time I talk with her."

Engessa looked around. "I didn't see Kring-Domi when we met you, Vanion-Preceptor," he noted.

"Kring took his men and veered off toward Samar not long after you and her Majesty left. He thought he'd be more useful there than he would here in Sarna—and you know how the western Peloi feel about mountains and forests. Have the Cynesgans made any forays across the border as yet?"

"No, Vanion-Preceptor," Engessa replied. "They're massing in staging areas and bringing up supplies." He rose and went to the map. "A large force moved out of Cynestra a while back," he said, pointing at the Cynesgan capital. "They're positioned near the border more or less opposite us here. Another force has taken up a similar position just across the line from Samar."

Vanion nodded. "Cyrgon's more like a general than a God in most ways. He's not going to leave fortified positions to his rear. He'll have to neutralize Samar and Sarna before he can strike any deeper into Tamul proper. I'd say that the force you're facing here has been ordered to take Sarna, seal the southern border of Atan, and then swing northeast toward Tualas. I'm sure they'd rather not have the entire Atan nation come swarming down out of these mountains."

"There aren't enough Cynesgans living to keep my people hemmed in," Betuana told him.

"I'm sure of it, your Majesty, but there probably are enough to slow you down, and Cyrgon can recruit armies from the past to hinder you all the more." He studied the map, his lips pursed. "I think I see where he's going," he said. "Matherion's on a peninsula, and that narrow neck of land at Tosa is the key to that. If I had to wager anything on it, I'd say that the main battle's going to take place there. Scarpa will move north out of Natayos. Probably the southern Cynesgans are planning to capture Samar and then swing around the north shore of the Sea of Arjun to join him somewhere in the vicinity of the Tamul Mountains. From there the combined army can march up the west shore of the Gulf of Micae to Tosa." He smiled faintly. "Of course, there's a very nasty surprise waiting for them in the Tamul Mountains. I'd imagine that before this is over, Cyrgon will wish that he'd never *heard* of the Trolls."

"I will send an army out of northern Atan to Tosa, Vanion-Preceptor," Betuana said, "but I'll leave enough of my people along the southern and eastern borders to tie up half of the Cynesgans."

"In the meantime I think we can disrupt their preparations," Engessa added. "Raids in force across that border will delay their main attack."

"And that's all we really need." Vanion chuckled. "If we can delay them long enough, Cyrgon's going to have a hundred thousand Church Knights swarming across his western frontier. I think he'll forget about Tosa at that point."

· · ·

"Don't worry about him, Fron," Stragen told Sparhawk. "He can take care of himself."

"I think we sometimes forget that he's only a boy, Vymer. He doesn't even shave regularly yet."

"Reldin stopped being a boy before his voice started to change." Stragen leaned back on his bed reflectively. "Those of us in our particular line of work tend to lose our childhoods," he said. "It might have been nice to roll hoops and catch polliwogs, but . . ." He shrugged.

"What are you going to do when this is all over?" Sparhawk asked him. "Assuming that we survive?"

"There's a certain lady of our acquaintance who proposed marriage to me a while back. It's part of a business arrangement that's very attractive. The notion of marriage never really appealed to me, but the business proposition's just too good to pass up."

"There's more, too, isn't there?"

"Yes," Stragen admitted. "After what she did back in Matherion that night, I'm not about to let her get away from me. She's one of the coolest and most courageous people I've ever met."

"Pretty, too."

"You noticed." Stragen sighed. "I'm afraid I'm going to end up being at least semi-respectable, my friend."

"Shocking."

"Isn't it? First, though, there's this other little matter I want to deal with. I think I'll present my beloved with the head of a certain Astellian poet of our acquaintance. If I can find a good taxidermist, I may even have it stuffed and mounted for her."

"It's the kind of wedding present every girl dreams of."

"Maybe not *every* girl—" Stragen grinned. "—but I'm in love with a very special lady."

"But there are so *many* of them, U-lat," Bhlokw said plaintively. "They would not miss just one, would they?"

"I am certain they would, Bhlokw," Ulath told the huge, brown-furred Troll. "The man-things are not like the deer. They pay very close attention to the other members of the herd. If you eat one of them, they will know that we are here. Catch and eat one of their dogs instead."

"Is dog good-to-eat?"

"I am not sure. Eat one and tell me if it is good."

Bhlokw grumbled and squatted down on his haunches.

The process Ghnomb had called "breaking the moments in two pieces" produced some rather strange effects. The brightness of noon was dimmed to twilight, for one thing, and the citizens of Sopal seemed to walk about their town with a fast, jerky kind of movement, for another. The God of Eat had assured them that because they were present in only a small part of each instant, they had been rendered effectively invisible. Ulath could see a rather large logical flaw in the explanation, but the spell did work.

Tynian came back up the street shaking his head. "It's impossible to understand them," he reported. "I can pick up a word or two now and then, but the rest is pure gibberish."

"It is talking in bird-noises again," Bhlokw complained.

"You'd better speak in Trollish, Tynian," Ulath said. "You're making Bhlokw nervous."

"I forgot," Tynian admitted, reverting to the hideous language of the Trolls. "I am—" he groped. "What is the word that means that you want it that you had not done something?" he asked their shaggy companion.

"There is no such word, Tin-in," Bhlokw replied.

"Can you ask Ghnomb to make it so that we can understand what the man-things are saying?" Ulath asked.

"Why? What does it matter?" Bhlokw's face was puzzled.

"If we can know what they are saying, we will know which ones of the herd we should follow," Tynian explained. "They will be the ones who will know about the wicked ones."

"They do not *all* know?" Bhlokw asked with some amazement.

"No. Only some know."

"The man-things are very strange. I will talk with Ghnomb. He may understand this." He rose to his feet, towering over them. "I will do it as soon as I come back."

"Where are you going?" Tynian asked politely.

"I am hungry. I will go eat a dog. Then I will come back and talk with Ghnomb." He paused. "I can bring a dog back for you as well, if you are also hungry."

"Ah—no, Bhlokw," Tynian replied. "I do not think I am hungry right now. It was good of you to ask, though."

"We are pack-mates now." Bhlokw shrugged. "It is right to do this." And he shambled off down the street.

"It's not really all that far," Aphrael told her sister as they rode with Xanetia out of the valley of Delphaeus toward the town of Dirgis in southern Atan, "but Edaemus is still reluctant to help us, so I think I'd better mind my manners. He might be offended if I start 'tampering' in the home of his children."

"You've never used that word to describe it before," Sephrenia noted.

"Sparhawk's influence, I guess," the Child-Goddess replied. "It's a useful sort of term: it glosses over things that we don't want to discuss in front of strangers. After we get to Dirgis, we'll be well clear of the home of the Delphae. Then I'll be able to tamper to my heart's content."

"How long dost thou think it will take us to reach Natayos, Goddess?" Xanetia asked. She had once again altered her coloration and suppressed her inner radiance to conceal her racial characteristics.

"No more than a few hours—in real time." Aphrael shrugged. "I can't *quite* jump us around the way Bhelliom does, but I can cover a lot of ground in a hurry when there's an emergency. If things were really desperate, I could fly us there."

Sephrenia shuddered. "It's not *that* desperate, Aphrael."

Xanetia gave her Styric sister a puzzled look.

"It makes her queasy," Aphrael explained.

"No, Aphrael," Sephrenia corrected, "not queasy—terrified. It's a horrible experience, Xanetia. She's done it to me about five times in the past three hundred years. I'm an absolute wreck for weeks afterward."

"I keep telling you not to look down, Sephrenia," Aphrael told her. "If you'd just look at the clouds instead of down at the ground, it wouldn't bother you so much."

"I can't help myself, Aphrael," Sephrenia told her.

"Is it truly so disturbing, sister mine?" Xanetia asked.

"You couldn't even begin to imagine it, Xanetia. You skim along with nothing but about five thousand feet of empty air between you and the ground. It's *awful!*"

"We'll do it the other way," Aphrael assured her.

"I'll start composing a prayer of thanksgiving immediately."

"We'll stay the night in Dirgis," Aphrael told them, "and then tomorrow morning we'll run down to Natayos. Sephrenia and I'll stay out in the woods, Xanetia, and you can go into town and have a look around. If Mother's really being held there, we should be able to bring this little crisis to an end in short order. Once Sparhawk knows exactly where she is, he'll fall on Scarpa and his father like a vengeful mountain. Natayos won't even be a ruin anymore when he's done. It'll just be a big hole in the ground."

"He actually saw them," Talen reported. "He described them too well to have just been making it up." The young thief had just returned from his foray into the seamier parts of Beresa.

"What sort of fellow was he?" Sparhawk asked. "This is too important for us to be taken in by random gossip."

"He's a Dacite," Talen replied, "a guttersnipe from Jura. His politics go about as far as his purse. His main reason for joining Scarpa's army in the first place was his enthusiasm for the idea of taking part in the looting of Matherion. We're not talking about a man with high ideals here. When he got to Natayos and found out that there might be actual fighting involved, he started to lose interest. Anyway, I found him in one of the shabbiest taverns I've ever seen, and he was roaring drunk. Believe me, Fron, he was in no condition to lie to me. I told him that I was thinking of joining Scarpa's army, and he turned all fatherly on me—'Don' even *shink* about it, boy. It's tur'ble there'—that sort of thing. He said that Scarpa's a raving lunatic with delusions of invincibility who thinks he can just blow on the Atans and make them go away. He said he'd just about decided to desert anyway, and then Scarpa came back to Natayos—along with Krager, Elron, and Baron Parok. They had the queen and Alean with them, and Zalasta met them at the gate. The Dacite happened to be nearby, so he could hear what they were saying. Evidently, Zalasta's still got a *few* good manners, so he wasn't very happy about the way Scarpa had been treating his prisoners. The two of them had an argument about it, and Zalasta tied his son into a very complicated knot with magic. I guess Scarpa was squirming around like a worm on a hot rock for a while. Then Zalasta took the ladies to a large house that had been fixed up for them. From what my deserter said, the house comes fairly close to being luxurious—if you discount the bars on the windows."

"He could have been coached," Sparhawk fretted. "Maybe he wasn't as drunk as he appeared to be."

"Believe me, Fron, he was drunk," Talen assured him. "I cut a purse on my way to that tavern—just to keep in practice—so I had plenty of money. I poured enough strong drink into him to stun a regiment."

"I think he's right, Fron," Stragen said. "There are just too many details for this to be a contrived story."

"And if this deserter had been sent to spin cobwebs for our benefit, why would he waste time and effort entertaining a young pickpocket?" Talen added. "None of us look the way we did the last time Zalasta saw us, and I doubt that even he could have guessed how Sephrenia and Xanetia put their heads together to modify us."

"I still think we should hold off," Sparhawk said. "Aphrael's going to put Xanetia into Natayos in a day or so, and Xanetia can find out for sure if it's really Ehlana who's locked up in that house."

"We could at least get closer," Stragen said.

"Why? Distance doesn't mean anything to my blue friend here." Sparhawk touched the bulge under the front of his tunic. "Just as soon as I know for certain that Ehlana's there, we'll go pay Zalasta and his bastard a call. I might even invite Khwaj to come along. He has some plans for them that sort of interest me."

The light was suddenly very bright, and the citizens of Sopal suddenly stopped jerking around like marionettes on strings and started to walk like normal humans. It had taken a half a day to explain to Ghnomb why it was necessary for them to return to real time, and the God of Eat still had some serious reservations about the whole idea.

"I'll wait in that tavern just up the street," Tynian said to Ulath as the two of them stepped out of the narrow alley. "Do you remember the password?"

Ulath grunted. "I shouldn't be long," he said. He walked across the street toward the pair of travelers who had just come into town. "That's an interesting looking saddlebow you've got there, neighbor," he said to one of them, a broken-nosed man on a roan horse. "What's it made of? Ramshorn?"

Berit gave him a startled look, then glanced quickly around the narrow street near the east gate of Sopal. "I didn't think to ask the saddlemaker, Sergeant," he replied, noticing the blond Elene's tattered-looking uniform jacket. "Ah—maybe you could give my young friend and me some advice."

"Advice is free. Go ahead and ask."

"Do you happen to know of a good inn here in Sopal?"

"The one my friend and I are staying at isn't too bad. It's about three streets over." Ulath pointed. "It's got the sign of a boar hanging out front—although the picture doesn't look very much like any boar *I've* ever seen."

"We'll look into it."

"Maybe my friend and I'll see you there. We're usually in the taproom after supper."

"We'll stop by—if we decide to stay there."

Ulath nodded and walked up the street to a tavern and went inside, where he joined Tynian at a table near the fire. "What did you do with our shaggy friend?" he asked.

"He went out looking for another dog," Tynian replied. "You might have made a mistake there, Sergeant. He seems to be developing a taste for them. There won't be a dog left in the whole town if we stay much longer."

Ulath sat down and leaned back. "Ran into an Elene fellow out there in the street," he said, loudly enough to be heard by the other tavern patrons.

"Oh?" Tynian said casually. "Astellian or Edomish?"

"It was sort of hard to say. He'd had his nose broken at one time or another, so it was a little hard to determine his race. He was looking for a good inn, so I recommended the one where we're staying. We might see him there. It's good to hear somebody talking Elenic for a change. I get tired of listening to people babbling at me in Tamul. If you're about finished here, why don't we drift on down to the harbor and see if we can find somebody to ferry us on across the lake to Tiana."

Tynian drained his tankard. "Let's go," he said, standing up.

The two of them left the tavern and strolled back to their inn, talking casually and moving at the leisurely pace of men with nothing really pressing to do.

"I want to have a look at that shoe on my horse's left forehoof," Ulath said when they arrived. "Go on ahead. I'll meet you in the taproom."

"Where else?" Tynian laughed.

Khalad was in the stable as Ulath had expected. He was making some show of currying Faran. "I see that you and your friend decided to stay here," the big Thalesian said in a casual tone.

"It was handy." Khalad shrugged.

"Listen carefully," Ulath said in a voice hardly more than a whisper. "We were able to pick up some information. Nothing's going to happen here. You'll get another one of those messages."

Khalad nodded.

"It's going to tell you to go on across the lake to Tiana. Be careful of what you say on the boat, because there'll be a fellow on board who's working for the other side—an Arjuni with a long scar on his cheek."

"I'll keep an eye out for him," Khalad said.

"You'll get another message in Tiana," Ulath continued. "You'll be told to go on around the lake to Arjun."

"That's the long way around," Khalad objected. "We could take the road from here and be in Arjun in less than half the time."

"Evidently they don't want you to get there that soon. They've probably got some other irons in the fire. I won't swear to this, but I *think* they'll send you on to Deral from Arjun. If Kalten's right and Ehlana's being held in Natayos, that would be the next logical step."

Khalad nodded again. "I'll tell Berit. I think we'd better stay out of that taproom. I'm sure we're being watched, and if we start talking with other Elenes, we'll just put the other side on their guard."

The horses in the stable suddenly began to squeal and kick at the sides of their stalls.

"What's wrong with the horses?" Khalad demanded. "And what's that odd smell?"

Ulath muttered an oath. Then he raised his voice and spoke in Trollish. "Bhlokw, it is not good that you come into the dens of the man-things this way. You have been eating dog, and the man-things and their beasts can smell you."

There was an injured silence as Ulath's unseen traveling companion withdrew from the stable.

Betuana and Engessa, dressed in sleek otter skins, accompanied Vanion and the knights south from Sarna. At Engessa's suggestion they proceeded due west to come down out of the mountains in eastern Cynesga.

"We've been watching them, Vanion-Preceptor," the towering Atan said as he loped along beside Vanion's horse. "Their main supply dump is about five leagues west of the frontier."

"Did you have anything pressing to attend to, your Majesty?" Vanion asked Betuana, who was running along on the other side.

"Nothing that can't wait. What did you have in mind?"

"Since we're here anyway, we might as well swing over and burn their supply dump. My knights are getting restless, and a little exercise might do them some good."

"It is rather chilly," she observed with just the hint of a smile. "A fire *would* be nice."

"Shall we, then?"

"Why don't we?"

The Cynesgan supply dump covered about five acres. It lay in a rocky, treeless basin, and it was defended by a regiment of Cynesgan troops in flowing robes. As the column of armored knights approached, the defenders galloped forth to meet them. That particular maneuver might best be described as a tactical blunder. The gravel-covered floor of the Desert of Cynesga was flat and clear of obstructions, so the charge of the Church Knights was unimpeded. There was an enormous crash as the two forces collided, and the knights, after only a momentary hesitation, rode on, trampling the bodies of the wounded and slain under the steel-shod hooves of their mounts while the squealing horses of the Cynesgans fled in terror.

"Impressive," Betuana conceded as she ran along beside Vanion's mount. "But isn't it tedious to endure the weight—and the smell—of the armor for months on end for the sake of two minutes of entertainment?"

"There are drawbacks to any style of warfare, your Majesty," Vanion said, raising his visor. "A part of the idea behind armored charges is to persuade others to avoid confrontations. It holds down the casualties in the long run."

"A reputation for extreme severity *is* a good weapon, Vanion-Preceptor," she agreed.

"We like it." He smiled. "Let's go build that bonfire so that your Majesty can warm her toes."

"That would be nice." She smiled.

There was a dust-covered hill directly ahead, rising like a slightly rounded pyramid to block the way to the supply dump. With simple arm gestures, Vanion directed his knights to diverge and sweep around both sides of the hill to swarm over the accumulated supplies of Cyrgon's army. They galloped forward with that vast, steely, clinking thunder that proclaims implacable invincibility.

And then the hill moved. The dust which had covered it shuddered away in a great billowing cloud, and the two enormous wings unfurled their glossy blackness to reveal the wedge-shaped face of Klæl. The beast of ultimate darkness roared, and the fangs of lightning, jagged and flickering, emerged from behind snarling lips.

And out from beneath the shelter of those two great wings came an army like no army Vanion had ever seen.

They were as tall as the Atans and more bulky. Their bare arms were huge, and their steel breastplates fit them like a second skin, revealing every knotted muscle. Their helmets bore exotic-looking embellishments—horns or antlers or stiff steel wings—and, like their breastplates, their visors fit tightly over their faces, exactly duplicating the features of each individual warrior. There was no humanity in those polished faces. The brows were impossibly wide, and, like the face of Klæl himself, they narrowed down to almost delicately pointed chins. The eye-slits blazed, and there were twin holes in place of noses. The mouths of those masks were open, and they were filled with cruelly pointed teeth.

They swarmed out from beneath Klæl's wings with his lightning playing around them. They brandished weapons that appeared to be part mace and part ax—steel atrocities dredged from a nightmare.

They were too close to permit any kind of orderly withdrawal, and the knights, still moving at a thunderous gallop, were committed before they could fully comprehend the nature of the enemy.

The impact as the two armies came together shook the earth, and that solid, steely crash shattered into a chaos of sound—blows, shrieks, the agonized squeals of horses, and the tearing of metal.

"Sound a withdrawal!" Vanion bellowed to the leader of the Genidians. "Blow your heart into that Ogre-horn, man! Get our people clear!"

The carnage was ghastly. Horses and men were being ripped to pieces by Klæl's inhuman army. Vanion drove his spurs home, and his horse leapt forward. The Pandion Preceptor drove his lance through the steel breastplate of one of the aliens and saw blood—at least he thought it might be blood, thick yellow blood—gushing from the steel-lipped mask. The creature fell back, but still swung its cruel weapon. Vanion pulled his hand clear of the butt of the lance, leaving the beast transfixed, skewered, as it were, and drew his sword.

It took a long time. The thing absorbed blows that would have dismembered a human. Eventually, however, Vanion chopped it down—almost like a peasant chopping at a tough, stringy thornbush.

"Engessa!" Betuana's shriek of rage and despair rang out above the other sounds of the battle.

Vanion wheeled his horse and saw the Atan queen rushing to the aid of her stricken general. Even the monstrous creatures Klæl had unleashed quailed in the face of her fury as she cut her way to Engessa's side.

Vanion smashed his way through to her, his sword flickering in the chill light, spraying yellow blood in gushing fountains. "Can you carry him?" he shouted to Betuana.

She bent and with no apparent effort lifted her fallen friend in her arms.

"Pull back!" Vanion shouted. "I'll cover you!" And he hurled his horse into the path of the monsters who were rushing to attack her.

There was no hope in Betuana's face as she ran toward the rear, cradling Engessa's limp body in her arms, and her eyes were streaming tears.

Vanion ground his teeth together, raised his sword, and charged.

Sephrenia was very tired when they reached Dirgis. "I'm not really hungry," she told Xanetia and Aphrael after they had taken a room in a respectable inn near the center of the city. "All I want is a nice hot bath and about twelve hours of sleep."

"Art thou unwell, sister mine?" Xanetia's voice was concerned.

Sephrenia smiled wearily. "No, dear," she said, laying one hand on the Anarae's arm, "just a little tired. All this rushing around is starting to wear on me. You two go ahead and have some supper. Just ask someone to bring a small pot of tea up to the room. That'll be enough for right now. I'll make up for it at breakfast time. Just don't make too much noise when you come up to bed."

She spent a pleasant half hour immersed to her ears in steaming water in the bathhouse and returned to their room tightly wrapped in her Styric robe and carrying a candle to light her way.

Their room was not large, but it was warm and cozy, heated by one of the porcelain stoves common in Tamuli. Sephrenia rather liked the concept of a stove, since it kept the ashes and cinders off the floor. She drew a chair close to the fire and began to brush her long, black hair.

"Vanity, Sephrenia? After all these years?"

She started half to her feet at the sound of the familiar voice. Zalasta scarcely looked the same. He no longer wore his Styric robe, but rather a leather jerkin of an Arjuni cut, stout canvas trousers, and thick-soled boots. He had even so far discarded his heritage that he wore a short sword at his waist. His white hair and beard were tangled, and his face was haggard. "Please don't make a scene, love," he told her. His voice was weary and devoid of any emotion beyond a kind of profound regret. He sighed. "Where did we go wrong, Sephrenia?" he asked sadly. "What tore us apart and brought us to this sorry state?"

"You don't really want me to tell you, do you, Zalasta?" she replied. "Why couldn't you just let it go? I *did* love you—not *that* way, of course, but it was love. Couldn't you accept that and forget about the other?"

"Evidently not. It didn't even occur to me."

"Sparhawk's going to kill you, you know."

"Perhaps. To be honest with you, though, I no longer really care."

"What's the point of this, then? Why have you come here?"

"I wanted to see you one last time—hear the sound of your voice." He rose from the chair in the corner where he had been sitting. "It all could have been so different—if it hadn't been for Aphrael. *She* was the one who took you into the lands of the Elenes and corrupted you. You're Styric, Sephrenia. We Styrics have no business consorting with the Elene barbarians."

"You're wrong, Zalasta. Anakha's an Elene. *That's* our business with them. You'd better leave. Aphrael's downstairs eating supper right now. If she finds you here, she'll have your heart for dessert."

"In a moment. There's something I have to do first. After that, she can do anything to me she wants to do." His face suddenly twisted into an expression of anguish. "Why, Sephrenia? Why? How could you *bear* the unclean touch of that Elene savage?"

"Vanion? You wouldn't understand. You couldn't even begin to comprehend it." She stood, her face defiant. "Do whatever it is you have to do and leave. The very sight of you sickens me."

"Very well." His face was suddenly as cold as stone.

She was not really surprised when he drew a long bronze dagger out from under his jerkin. In spite of everything, he was still Styric enough to loathe the touch of steel. "You have no idea of how much I regret this," he told her as he came closer.

She tried to struggle, clawing at his face and eyes as she called out for help. She even felt a momentary sense of triumph when she seized his beard and saw him wince with pain. She jerked at his beard, sawing his face this way and that, but then he jerked free, roughly shoving her back from him. She stumbled back and half fell over a chair, and that was what ultimately defeated her. Even as she struggled to regain her feet, he caught her by the hair, and she knew that she was lost. Despairing, she drew Vanion's face from her memory, filling her eyes and heart with his features even as she attempted again to claw at Zalasta's eyes.

And then he drove the dagger directly into her breast and wrenched it free again.

She cried out, falling back and clutching at the wound, feeling the blood spurting out between her fingers.

He caught her in his arms. "I love you, Sephrenia," he said in a broken voice as the light faded from her eyes.

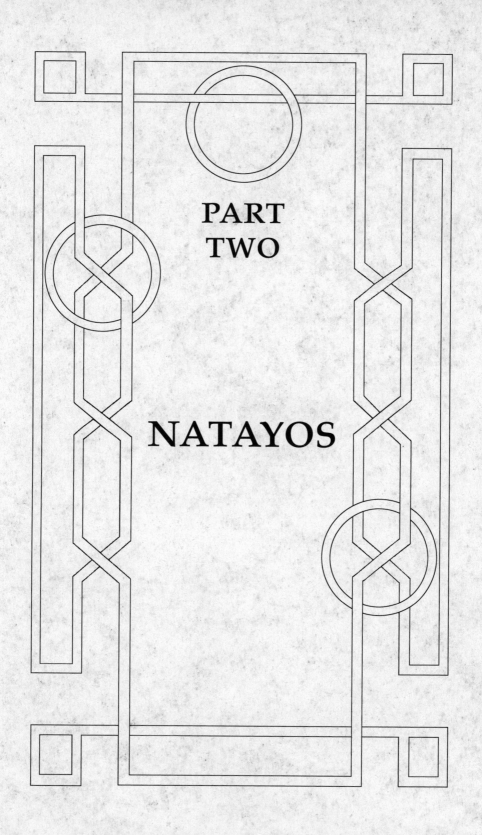

PART TWO

NATAYOS

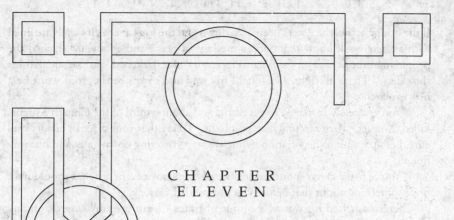

I can't find anybody willing to stay in one place long enough for me to ask him any questions," Komier growled when he returned late one cloudy afternoon with his scouts. He looked sourly back across the empty, winter-fallow fields all neatly bordered with low stone walls, carefully shifting his broken right arm. "These Astellian serfs all take one look at us and bolt for the woods like frightened deer."

"What's ahead?" Darellon asked him. Darellon's helmet hung from his saddle-bow, one side so crushed in that it no longer fit his bandaged head. His eyes were unfocused, and his bandage was bloodsoaked.

Komier took out his map and studied it. "We're coming to the River Astel," he replied. "We saw a city over on the other side—Darsas, most likely. I couldn't catch anybody to tell me for sure, though. I'm not the prettiest fellow in the world, but I've never had people flee from me in terror like this before."

"Emban warned us about that," Bergsten said. "The countryside's crawling with agitators. They're telling the serfs that we've all got horns and tails and that we're coming here to burn down their churches and ram assorted heresies down their throats at swordpoint. This fellow called Sabre seems to be the one behind it all."

"He's the one I want," Komier muttered darkly. "I think I'll run him down and set him up as the centerpiece in a bonfire."

"Let's not stir up the locals any more than they already are, Komier," Darellon cautioned. "We're not in any condition for confrontations at the moment." He glanced back at the battered column and the long string of wagons bearing the gravely wounded.

"Did you see any signs of organized resistance?" Heldin asked Komier.

"Not yet. I expect we'll find out how things really stand when we get to Darsas.

If the bridge across the Astel's been torn down and the tops of the city walls are lined with archers, we'll know that Sabre's message of peace and goodwill's reached the people in authority." The Genidian Preceptor's face darkened, and he squared his shoulders. "That's all right. I've fought my way into towns before, so it won't be a new experience."

"You've already managed to get Abriel and about a third of the Church Knights killed, Komier," Bergsten told him pointedly. "I'd say that your place in history's secure. Let's try a bit of negotiation before we start battering down gates and burning houses."

"You've had a clever mouth ever since we were novices, Bergsten. I should have done something about that before you put on that cassock."

Bergsten hefted his war ax a couple of times. "I can take my cassock off any time it suits you, old friend," he offered.

"You're getting sidetracked, gentlemen," Darellon said, his speech slightly slurred. "Our wounded need attention. This isn't the time to pick fights—either with the local population or with each other. I think the four of us should ride on ahead under a flag of truce and find out which way the wind's blowing before we start building siege engines."

"Am I hearing the voice of reason here?" Heldin rumbled mildly.

They tied a gleaming white Cyrinic cape to Sir Heldin's lance and rode ahead through the cheerless afternoon to the west bank of the River Astel.

The city beyond the river was clearly Elene, an ancient town with soaring towers and spires. It stood proudly and solidly on the far shore of the river under its snapping pennons of red and blue and gold proclaiming, or so it seemed, that it had always been there and always would be. It had high, thick walls and massive, closed gates. The bridge across the Astel was blocked by towering, bronze-faced warriors wearing minimal armor and carrying very unpleasant looking weapons. "Atans," Sir Heldin identified them. "We definitely don't want to fight those people."

The ranks of bleak-faced infantry parted, and an ancient, wrinkled Tamul in a gold-colored mantle came forward to meet them flanked by a vastly bearded Astellian clergyman all in black. "Well met, Sir Knights," the hairless old Tamul greeted the armored men in a dry, dusty voice. "King Alberen's a trifle curious as to your intentions. We don't see Church Knights in this part of the world very often."

"You would be Ambassador Fontan," Bergsten said. "Emban described you very well."

"I thought he had better manners," Fontan murmured.

Bergsten flashed him a brief smile. "You might want to send word back to the city, your Excellency. Assure his Majesty that our intentions are entirely peaceful."

"I'm sure he'll be happy to hear that."

"Emban and Sir Tynian came back to Chyrellos a couple of months ago," Bergsten continued. "Sparhawk sent word that things were getting out of hand here. Dolmant dispatched us to help restore order." The huge Patriarch made a sour face. "We didn't get off to a very good start, I'm afraid. We had an unfortunate encounter near Basne and we have many wounded in need of medical attention."

"I'll send word to the nearby monasteries, Sir Knight," the bearded clergyman standing at Fontan's elbow offered.

"Bergsten's not a knight anymore, your Reverence," Komier corrected him. "He *used* to be, but God had other plans for him. He's a Patriarch of the Church now. He prays well enough, I suppose, but we haven't been able to get his ax away from him yet."

"My manners must be slipping," Fontan apologized. "My friend here is Archimandrite Monsel, the duly anointed head of the Church of Astel."

"Your Grace." Bergsten inclined his head politely.

"Your Grace," Monsel replied, looking curiously at the warlike clergyman. "Your friend Emban and I had some very stimulating discussions about our doctrinal differences. You and I might want to continue those, but let's see to your wounded first. How many injured men do you have?"

"Roughly twenty thousand, your Grace," Komier answered bleakly. "It's a little hard to keep an exact count. A few score die on us every hour or so."

"What in God's name did you encounter up in those mountains?" Monsel gasped.

"The King of Hell, as closely as we can determine, your Grace," Darellon replied. "We left thirty thousand dead on the field—mostly Cyrinics. Lord Abriel, their preceptor, led the charge, and his knights followed close behind him. They were fully engaged before they realized what they were up against." He sighed. "Abriel was nearing seventy, and he seemed to think he was leading his last charge."

"He was right about that," Komier grunted sourly. "There wasn't enough of him left to bury."

"He died well, though," Heldin added. "Do you have any fast messengers available, your Excellency? Sparhawk and Vanion are counting on us to reach Matherion as soon as possible, so we'd probably better let them know that we're going to be delayed."

"His name's Valash," Stragen told Sparhawk and Talen as the three of them, still wearing their tar-smeared sailor's smocks, stepped out of the noisy torchlit street into a dark, foul-smelling alley. "He and his two friends are Dacites from Verel."

"Have you been able to find out who they're working for?" Sparhawk asked him as they stopped to let their eyes adjust to the darkness and their noses to the smell. The alleys of Beresa were particularly unpleasant.

"I heard one of them mention Ogerajin," Stragen replied. "It makes sense, I guess. Ogerajin and Zalasta seem to be old friends."

"I thought Ogerajin's brains were rotting out," Talen objected.

"Maybe he has lucid moments. It doesn't really matter who sent them, though. While they're here, they're reporting to Krager. As near as I can make out, they've been sent to assess the damage we did to them during the Harvest Festival and to pick up any bits of information that fall to hand. They've got money, but they don't want to turn much of it loose. They're in this strictly for gain—and for the chance to seem important."

"Does Krager come here to get their reports?" Sparhawk asked.

"He hasn't recently. Valash communicates with him by messenger. These three

Dacites are seriously out of their depth here. They want to hold on to as much of the money Ogerajin gave them as they can, but they don't want to miss anything important. They aren't professionals by any stretch of the imagination. They spend most of their time trying to figure out some way to get information without paying for it."

"A swindler's dream," Talen noted. "What did they do for a living back in Verel?"

"They sold children to people whose tastes run in that direction," Stragen replied in a disgusted tone. "As I understand it, Ogerajin used to be one of their best customers."

"That puts them right at the bottom, doesn't it?"

"Probably even lower than that." Stragen glanced around to make sure they were alone. "Valash wants to meet you two." Stragen pointed toward the end of the alley. "He's just up those stairs. He's renting a corner in the loft from a fellow who deals in stolen goods."

Talen smiled a rather nasty little smile. "If these Dacites just happened to pass too much erroneous information and false rumors on to Krager, he might just decide that they've outlived their usefulness, wouldn't you say?"

"Probably." Stragen shrugged.

"That sort of stirs my creativity."

"Oh? Why's that?"

"I don't like people who sell children. It's a personal sort of thing. Let's go meet this Valash. I'd like to find out if he's as gullible as you say."

They climbed a rickety outside stairway to a door that was flimsy and patched and showed some signs of having been kicked in a few times. The loft beyond the door was incredibly cluttered with all manner of worn clothing, battered furniture, and dented kitchen utensils. There were even broken farm tools gathering dust in the corners. "Some people will steal anything," Talen sniffed.

A lone candle guttered on the far side of the room, and a bony Elene sat drowsing at a table by its uncertain light. He wore a short green brocade jacket of a Daconian cut, and his sparse mud-colored hair stood almost straight up, looking much like a thin, dirty halo around his gaunt head. As they crossed the loft toward him, he stirred himself and quickly picked up some papers and began to shuffle them in a self-important manner. He looked up with feigned impatience as they approached. "You're late, Vymer," he accused in a high-pitched, nasal voice.

"Sorry, Master Valash," Stragen apologized in a servile tone. "Fron and I were busy extricating young Reldin here from a tense situation. Reldin's very good, but he overextends himself sometimes. Anyway, you wanted to meet my associates." He laid one hand on Sparhawk's shoulder. "This is Fron. He's a tavern brawler, so we let him deal with any situation that can be settled with a few quick punches or a kick in the belly. The boy there is Reldin, the nimblest sneak thief I've ever known. He can wriggle through mouseholes, and his ears are sharp enough to hear ants crossing the street on the other side of town."

"I just want to hire him, Vymer," Valash said. "I don't want to buy him." He giggled at his own joke. He smirked at them, clearly expecting them to join in his laughter. Talen, however, did not laugh. His eyes took on an icy glitter.

Valash seemed a bit abashed by their reception of his feeble joke. "Why are you all dressed as sailors?" he asked, more for something to say than out of any real curiosity.

Stragen shrugged. "It's a port city, Master Valash. The streets are crawling with sailors, so three more won't attract any particular attention."

Valash grunted. "Have you anything for me that I might find worth my while?" he asked in a superior, bored tone of voice.

Talen snatched off his cap. "You'll have to decide that for yourself, Master Valash," he whined, as he bowed awkwardly. "I *did* come across something, if you'd care to hear it."

"Go on," Valash told him.

"Well, sir, there's this rich Tamul merchant who owns a big house over in the fancy part of town. He's got a tapestry on the wall of his study that I've had my eye on for quite some time now. It's a very good one—lots of tiny stitches, and the color hasn't faded very much. The only trouble is that it covers the whole wall. You can get a fortune for really good tapestry, but only if you can get it all out in one piece. It's not worth much if you have to cut it up to carry it out. Anyway, I went into his house the other night to try and come up with some way to get it out without butchering it. The merchant was in the study, though, and he had a friend with him—some noble from the imperial court at Matherion. I listened at the door, and the noble was telling the merchant about some of the rumors running around the imperial palace. Everybody's saying that the emperor's very unhappy with these people from Eosia. That attempt to overthrow the government last fall really frightened him, and he'd like to come to some kind of agreement with his enemies, but this Sparhawk person won't let him. Sarabian's convinced that they're going to lose, so he's secretly outfitted a fleet of ships all loaded down with treasure and as soon as trouble shows up on the horizon, he's going to make a run for it. The courtiers all know about his plans, so they're secretly making arrangements for their own escapes when the fighting starts. Some morning very soon this Sparhawk's going to wake up and find an unfriendly army at his gates and nobody around to help hold them off." He paused. "Was that the sort of information you wanted?"

The Dacite made some effort to conceal his excited interest. He put on a deprecating expression. "It's nothing we haven't heard before. About all it does is help to confirm what we've already picked up." He tentatively pushed a couple of small silver coins across the table. "I'll pass it on to Panem-Dea and see what they think about it."

Talen looked at the coins and then at Valash. Then he crammed his cap back on. "I'll be leaving now, Vymer," he said in a flat tone, "and don't waste my time on this cheapskate again."

"Don't be in such a rush," Stragen said placatingly. "Let me talk with him first."

"You're making a mistake, Valash," Sparhawk told the Dacite. "You've got a heavy purse hanging off your belt. If you try to cheat Reldin, he'll come back some night and slice open the bottom of it. He won't leave you enough to buy breakfast."

Valash put his hand protectively over his purse. Then he opened it with what appeared to be extreme reluctance.

"I thought Lord Scarpa was at Natayos," Stragen said casually. "Has he moved his operations to Panem-Dea?"

Valash was sweating as he counted out coins, his fingers lingering on each one as if he were parting with an old friend. "There are a lot of things you don't know about our operation, Vymer," he replied. He gave Talen a pleading look as he tentatively pushed the money across the table.

Talen made no move to accept the coins.

Valash made a whimpering sound and added more coins.

"That's a little better," Talen told him, scooping up the money.

"Then Scarpa's moved?" Stragen asked.

"Of course not," Valash retorted. "You didn't think his *whole* army's at Natayos, did you?"

"That's what I'd heard. He has other strongholds as well, I take it?"

"Of course. Only a fool puts his entire force in one place, and Scarpa's far from being a fool, I'll tell the world. He's been recruiting men in the Elene kingdoms of western Tamuli for years now, and he sends them all to Lydros and then on to Panem-Dea for training. After that, they go on to either Synaqua or Norenja. Only his crack troops are at Natayos. His army's at least five times larger than most people believe. These jungles positively seethe with his men."

Sparhawk carefully concealed a smile. Valash obviously had a great need to appear important, and that need made him reveal things he shouldn't be talking about.

"I didn't know Scarpa's army was so big," Stragen admitted. "It makes me feel better. It might be nice to be on the winning side for a change."

"It's about time," Sparhawk growled. "I'm getting a little tired of being chased out of every town we visit before I've even had the time to unpack my seabag." He squinted at Valash. "As long as the subject's come up anyway, could we expect Scarpa's people out there in the brush to take us in if things turn sour and we make a run for it?"

"What could possibly go wrong?"

"Have you ever taken a good look at an Atan, Valash? They're as tall as trees and they've got shoulders like bulls. They do unpleasant things to people, so I want a friendly place to come down if I suddenly have to take flight. Are there any other safe places out there in the woods?"

Valash's expression grew wary as if he had suddenly realized that he'd said too much already.

"Ah—I think we know what we need to, Fron," Stragen interposed smoothly. "There *are* safe places out there if we really need to find them. I'm sure there are many things Master Valash knows that he's not supposed to talk about."

Valash puffed himself up slightly, and his expression took on a knowing, secretive cast. "You understand the situation perfectly, Vymer," he said. "It wouldn't be proper for me to reveal things Lord Scarpa's told me in strictest confidence." He pointedly picked up his papers again.

"We won't keep you from important matters, Master Valash," Stragen said, backing away. "We'll nose around town some more and let you know if we find out anything else."

"I'd appreciate that, Vymer," Valash replied, shuffling his papers as his visitors departed.

"What an ass," Talen muttered as the three of them carefully descended the rickety staircase to the alley again.

"Where did you learn so much about tapestry?" Sparhawk asked him.

"I don't know anything about tapestry."

"You were talking as if you did."

"I talk about a lot of things I don't know anything about. It fills in the gaps when you're trying to peddle something that's worthless. I could tell by the way Valash's eyes glazed over when I mentioned the word *tapestry* that he didn't know any more about it than I did. He was too busy trying to make us think that he's important to pay any real attention. I could get rich from that one. I could sell him blue butter."

Sparhawk gave him a puzzled look.

"It's a swindler's term," Stragen explained. "The meaning's a little obscure."

"I'm sure it is."

"Did you want me to explain it?"

"Not particularly, no."

"Is it a family custom? Or just a way to honor your father?" Berit asked Khalad as the two of them, wearing mail shirts and grey cloaks, lounged against the forward rail of the scruffy lake freighter plodding across the Sea of Arjun from Sopal to Tiana.

Khalad shrugged. "No, it's nothing like that. It's just that the men in our family all have heavy beards—except for Talen. If I decided not to wear a beard, I'd have to shave twice a day. I clip it close with scissors once a week and let it go at that. It saves time."

Berit rubbed at his altered cheek. "I wonder what Sparhawk would do if I let his beard grow," he mused.

"*He* might not do anything, but Queen Ehlana would probably peel you like an apple. She likes his face just the way it is. She's even fond of that crooked nose."

"It looks as if we've got weather up ahead." Berit pointed toward the west.

Khalad frowned. "Where did *that* come from? The sky was clear just a minute ago. It's funny I didn't smell it coming."

The cloud bank hovering low on the western horizon was purplish black, and it roiled ominously, swelling upward with surprising speed. There were flickers of lightning deep inside the cloud, and the sullen rumble of thunder came to them across the dark, choppy waters of the lake.

"I hope these sailors know what they're doing," Berit said. "That has the earmarks of a very nasty squall."

They continued to watch the inky cloud as it boiled higher and higher, covering more and more of the western sky.

"That's not a natural storm, Berit," Khalad said tensely. "It's building too fast."

Then there was a shocking crash of thunder, and the cloud blanched and shuddered as the lightning seethed within it. Both the young men saw the shadowy shape in the instant that the bluish lightning thrust back the darkness to reveal what lay hidden in the cloud. "Klæl!" Berit gasped, staring at the monstrous, winged shape half-concealed in the churning stormfront.

The next crash of thunder ripped the sky, and the shabby vessel shuddered in the overwhelming sound. The inverted wedge of Klæl's face seemed to ripple and change in the midst of its veiling cloud, and the slitted eyes flamed in sudden rage. The great, batlike wings began to claw at the approaching storm, and the awful mouth opened to roar forth the thunder of Klæl's frustration. He howled in vast fury, and his enormous arms stretched up into the murky air, reaching hungrily to clutch at something that was not there.

And then the thing was gone, and the unnatural cloud tattered and streamed harmlessly off to the southeast to become no more than a dirty smudge on the horizon. The air, however, was filled with a sulfurous reek.

"You'd better pass the word to Aphrael," Khalad said grimly. "Klæl's loose again. He was looking for something, and he didn't find it. God knows where he'll look next."

"Komier's arm is broken in three places," Sir Heldin rumbled when he joined the mail-shirted Patriarch Bergsten, Ambassador Fontan, and Archimandrite Monsel in Monsel's book-littered study in the east wing of the palace, "and Darellon's still seeing two of everything. Komier can travel if he has to, but I think we'd better leave Darellon here until he recovers."

"How many knights are fit to ride?" Bergsten asked.

"Forty thousand at most, your Grace."

"We'll just have to make do with what we've got. Emban knew that we'd probably come this way; he's been sending messengers by the platoon. Things are coming to a head in southeastern Tamuli. Sparhawk's wife has been taken hostage, and our enemies are offering to trade her for Bhelliom. There's a rebel army in the Arjuni jungles preparing to march on Matherion, and two more armies massing on the eastern frontier of Cynesga. If those armies all join up, the game's over. Emban wants us to ride east across the steppes until we're past the Astel Marshes and then turn south and lay siege to the Cynesgan capital. He needs a diversion of some kind to pull those armies back from the border."

Sir Heldin pulled out his map. "It's workable," he said after a moment's study, "but we're going to be a little light for that kind of job."

"We'll get by. Vanion's in the field, but he's badly outnumbered along that Cynesgan frontier. If we don't create enough of a disturbance to relieve some of the pressure on him, he'll be swarmed under."

Heldin looked speculatively at the huge Thalesian Patriarch. "You're not going to like this, your Grace," he said, "but there's not much choice in the matter."

"Go ahead," Bergsten told him.

"You're going to have to lay your cassock aside and take command. Abriel's been killed, Darellon's incapacitated, and if Komier gets into a fight, the weight of his ax will cripple him."

"*You're* still here, Heldin. You can take charge."

Heldin shook his head. "I'm not a preceptor, your Grace, and everybody in the army knows it. I'm also a Pandion, and the other orders have strong feelings about us. We haven't made very many friends in the past couple of centuries. The other orders won't accept me as commander. You're a patriarch, and you speak for Sarathi—and the Church. They'll accept you with no argument."

"It's out of the question."

"Then we'll have to sit here until Dolmant sends us a new commander."

"We *can't* wait!"

"My point exactly. Do I have your permission to tell the knights that you're taking command?"

"I can't, Heldin. You know that I'm forbidden to use magic."

"We can work our way around that, your Grace. There are plenty of accomplished magicians in the ranks. Just tell us what you want done, and we'll see to it."

"I've taken an oath."

"You took another one earlier, Lord Bergsten. You promised to defend the Church. *That* oath takes precedence in this situation."

The hugely bearded and black-robed Archimandrite Monsel looked speculatively at the reluctant Thalesian. Then he spoke in a neutral sort of way. "Would you like an independent opinion, Bergsten?"

Bergsten scowled at him.

"You're going to get it anyway," the Astellian churchman said with unruffled calm. "Given the nature of our opponent, we're face-to-face with a 'Crisis of the Faith,' and that suspends all the other rules. God needs your ax, Bergsten, not your theology." He squinted at the Thalesian Patriarch. "You don't seem convinced," he said.

"I'm not trying to be offensive, Monsel, but 'Crisis of the Faith' can't just be pulled out and dusted off whenever we want to bend some rules."

"All right, let's try this one, then. This is Astel, and your Church at Chyrellos recognizes *my* authority here. As long as we're in Astel, *I* speak for God."

Bergsten pulled off his helmet and absently polished the glossy black Ogrehorns on his sleeve. "Technically, I suppose," he conceded.

"Technicalities are the very soul of doctrine, your Grace." Monsel's huge beard bristled with disputational fervor. "Do you agree that I speak for God here in Astel?"

"All right, for the sake of argument, yes."

"I'm glad you agree; I'd hate to have to excommunicate you. Now then, I speak for God here, and God wants you to take command of the Church Knights. Go forth and smite God's enemies, my son, and may heaven strengthen your arm."

Bergsten squinted out the window at the dirty-looking sky for a long moment, mulling the clearly specious argument over in his mind. "You take full responsibility, Monsel?" he asked.

"I do."

"That's good enough for me, then." Bergsten crammed his helmet back on his head. "Sir Heldin, go tell the knights that I'm assuming command of the four orders. Instruct them to make all the necessary preparations. We march first thing in the morning."

"At once, General Bergsten," Heldin replied, coming to attention.

· · ·

Anakha, Bhelliom's voice echoed in the vaults of Sparhawk's mind, *thou must awaken.*

Even before he opened his eyes, Sparhawk could feel a light touch on the thong about his neck. He caught the little hand and opened his eyes. "What do you think you're doing?" he demanded of the Child-Goddess.

"I *have* to have the Bhelliom, Sparhawk!" Her voice was desperate, and her eyes were streaming tears.

"What's going on, Aphrael? Calm down and tell me what's happened."

"Sephrenia's been stabbed! She's dying! Please, Sparhawk! Give me the Bhelliom!"

He came to his feet all in one motion. "Where did this happen?"

"In Dirgis. She was getting ready for bed, and Zalasta came into her room. He stabbed her in the *heart,* Sparhawk! Please, Father, give me the Bhelliom! I've got to have it to save her!"

"She's still alive?"

"Yes, but I don't know for how long! Xanetia's with her. She's using a Delphaeic spell to keep her breathing, but she's dying, my sister's dying!" She wailed and hurled herself into his arms, weeping uncontrollably.

"Stop that, Aphrael! This isn't helping. When did this happen?"

"A couple of hours ago. Please, Sparhawk! Only Bhelliom can save her!"

"We *can't,* Aphrael! If we take Bhelliom out of that box, Cyrgon will know immediately that we're trying to trick him, and Scarpa will kill your mother!"

The Child-Goddess clung to him, sobbing uncontrollably. "I *know!*" she wailed. "What are we going to do, Father? We *can't* just let her die!"

"Can't *you* do something?"

"The knife touched her heart, Sparhawk! I can't reverse that! Only Bhelliom has that kind of power!"

Sparhawk's soul seemed to shrivel, and he smashed at the wall with his fist. He lifted his face. "What can I do?" he hurled his voice upward. "What in God's name can I do?"

Compose thyself, Anakha! Bhelliom's voice was sharp in his mind. *Thou wilt serve neither Sephrenia nor thy mate by this unseemly display!*

We have to do something, Blue-Rose!

Thou art not at this moment fit to decide. Thou must therefore be ruled by me. Go at once and do as the Child-Goddess doth entreat thee.

Thou wilt condemn my wife!

That is not certain, Anakha. Sephrenia, however, doth linger on the brink of death. That much is certain. It is her need that is most pressing.

No! I can't do that!

Thou wilt obey me, Anakha! Thou art my creature, and therefore subject to my will! Go thou and do as I have commanded thee!

CHAPTER TWELVE

Sparhawk dug into his seabag, throwing clothes on the floor.

"What are you *doing*?" Aphrael demanded urgently. "We have to hurry!"

"I've got to leave a note for Stragen, but I can't find any paper."

"Here." She held out her hand, and a sheet of parchment appeared in it.

"Thank you." He took the parchment and continued to rummage in the bag.

"Get *on* with it, Sparhawk."

"I need something to write with."

She muttered something in Styric and handed him a quill and a small inkpot.

Vymer, Sparhawk scribbled, *something's come up, and I'll be gone for a while. Keep Reldin out of trouble.* And he signed it, *Fron.* Then he laid it in the center of Stragen's bed.

"*Now* can we go?" she asked impatiently.

"How are you going to do this?" He picked up his cloak.

"We have to get out of town first. I don't want anybody to see us. What's the quickest way to the woods?"

"East. It's about a mile to the edge of the forest."

"Let's go."

They left the room, hurrying down the stairs and out into the street. Sparhawk picked her up and half enfolded her in his cloak.

"I can walk," she protested.

"Not without attracting attention, you can't. You're a Styric, and people would notice that." He started off down the street, carrying her in his arms.

"Can't you go any faster?"

"Just let me handle this part of it, Aphrael. If I start running, people will think I've stolen you." He looked around to make sure no one on the muddy street was close enough to hear. "How are you going to manage this?" he asked her. "There *are* people out there who can feel it when you tamper with things, you know. We don't want to attract attention."

She frowned. "I'm not sure. I was upset when I came here."

"Are you *trying* to get your mother killed?"

"That's a hateful thing to say." She pursed her little mouth in thought. "There's always a certain amount of noise," she mused.

"I didn't quite follow that."

"It's one of the disadvantages of having our two worlds overlap the way they do. The sounds of one spill over into the other. Most humans can't hear us—or feel us—when we move around, but *we* can definitely hear and feel each other."

Sparhawk crossed the street to avoid a noisy brawl that had just erupted from a sailors' tavern. "If the others can hear you, how are you going to hide what you're doing?"

"You didn't let me finish, Sparhawk. We're not alone here. There are others all around us—my family, the Tamul Gods, your Elene God, various spirits and ghosts, and the air's positively littered with the Powerless Ones. Sometimes they flock up like migrating birds."

He stopped and stepped back to let a rickety charcoal wagon creak past. "Who are these 'Powerless Ones'?" he asked her. "Are they dangerous?"

"Hardly. They don't even really exist anymore. They're nothing but memories—old myths and legends."

"Are they real? Could I see them?"

"Not unless you believe in them. They were Gods once, but their worshippers either died out or were converted to the worship of other Gods. They wail and flutter around the edges of reality without substance or even thought. All they have is need." She sighed. "We go out of fashion, Sparhawk—like last year's gowns or old shoes and hats. The Powerless Ones are discarded Gods who shrink and shrink as the years go by until they're finally nothing at all but a kind of anguished wailing." She sighed again. "Anyway," she went on, "there's all this noise in the background, and it sometimes makes it hard to concentrate or pick out specifics."

They passed another smelly tavern loud with drunken song. "Is this noise something like that?" Sparhawk asked, jerking his head toward the singing. "Meaningless sound that fills up your ears and keeps you from hearing what you're really listening for?"

"More or less. We have a couple of senses that you don't, though, so we know when others are around, for one thing, and we know when they're doing things—tampering, if you want to call it that—for another. Maybe I can hide what I'm doing in all that other noise. How much farther do we have to go?"

He turned a corner into a quiet street. "We're coming to the edge of town now." He shifted her in his arms and continued on up the street, walking a little faster now. The houses here on the outskirts of Beresa were more substantial, and they were set back from the streets in aloof, self-important pride. "After we go through the charcoal yards, we'll come to the woods," he told her. "Are you sure this noise that I can't hear will be loud enough to hide your spells?"

"I'll see if I can get some help. I just thought of something. Cyrgon doesn't know exactly where I am, and it'll take him a little while to identify me and pinpoint my exact location. I'll ask some of the others to come here and have a party or something. If they're loud enough, and if I move fast enough, he won't even know that I've been here."

There were only a few workmen tending the sullen fires in the charcoal yards that ringed Beresa, incurious men, blackened by their tasks and far gone with drink, who lurched around the smoky flames like hellish imps dancing on eternal coals. Sparhawk walked even faster now, carrying the distraught Child-Goddess toward the shadowy edge of the tangled forest.

"I'll need to be able to see the sky," she told him. "I don't want any tree limbs in my way." She paused. "Are you afraid of heights?" she asked.

"Not particularly, why?"

"Just asking. Don't get excited when we start. I won't let anything happen to you. You'll be perfectly safe as long as I'm holding your hand." She paused again. "Oh, dear," she murmured. "I just remembered something."

"What?" He pushed aside a branch and slipped past it into the darkness of the forest.

"I have to be real when I do this."

"What do you mean 'real'? You're real now, aren't you?"

"Not exactly. Don't ask questions, Sparhawk. Just find me a patch of open sky and don't bother me for a while. I have to appeal for some help—if I can find them."

He pushed through the tangled brush, a cold knot in his stomach and his heart like a stone in his chest. The hideous dilemma they faced tore at him, seeming almost to rip him apart. Sephrenia was dying, but he must endanger Ehlana in order to save her life. It was only the force of Bhelliom's will that kept him moving at all. His own will was paralyzed by the conflicting needs of the two he loved most in all the world. He pushed at the tangle surrounding him in a kind of hopeless frustration.

Then he broke through the screen of brush into a small clearing carpeted by deep moss where a pool of water fed by a gurgling spring winked back at the stars strewn like bright grain across the velvet night. It was a quiet place, almost enchanted, but his eyes refused to accept its beauty. He stopped and set Aphrael down. Her small face was devoid of expression, and her eyes were blank, unseeing. Sparhawk waited tensely.

"Well, *finally!*" she said at last in an exasperated tone of voice. "It's so hard to explain anything to them. They never stop babbling long enough to listen."

"Who's this we're talking about?"

"The Tamul Gods. Now I can see why Oscagne's an atheist. I finally persuaded them to come *here* to do their playing. That should help to hide you and me from Cyrgon."

"Playing?"

"They're children, Sparhawk, babies who run and play and squeal and chase each other for months on end. Cyrgon absolutely hates them, so he won't go anywhere near them. That should help. They'll be here in a few minutes, and then we'll be able to start. Turn your back, Father. I don't like having people watch me change."

"I've seen you before—your reflection, anyway."

"That part doesn't bother me. The process of the changeover's a little degrading, though. Just turn your back, Father. You wouldn't understand."

He obediently turned and gazed up at the night sky. Several familiar constellations were either missing or in the wrong places.

"All right, Father, you can turn around now." Her voice was richer and more vibrant.

He turned. "Would you *please* put some clothes on?"

"Why?"

"Just do it, Aphrael. Humor my quirks."

"This is so tedious." She reached out and took hold of a gauzy kind of veil she had spun out of nothing and wrapped herself in it. "Better?" she asked.

"Not much. Can we leave now?"

"I'll check." Her eyes went distant for a moment. "They're coming," she reported. "They got sidetracked. It doesn't take much to distract them. Now, listen very carefully. Try to stay calm when we do this. Just keep the fact firmly in mind that I'm not going to let you get hurt. You won't fall."

"Fall? Fall from where? What are you talking about?"

"You'll see. I'd do it differently, but we have to get to Dirgis in a hurry, and I don't want Cyrgon to have time to locate me. We'll take it in easy stages at first, so you'll have time to get used to the idea." She turned her head slightly. "They're here," she said. "We can start now."

Sparhawk cocked his head slightly. He seemed to hear the distant sound of childish laughter, though it might have been only the sound of an errant breeze rustling the leaves in the treetops.

"Give me your hand," she instructed.

He reached out and took her by the hand. It seemed very warm and somehow comforting.

"Just look up at the sky, Sparhawk," the heartbreakingly beautiful young woman instructed.

He raised his face and saw the upper edge of the moon come creeping pale and luminous up above the treetops.

"You can look down now."

They were standing some ten feet above the rippled waters of the pool. Sparhawk's muscles tensed.

"Don't do that!" she said sharply. "Just relax. You'll slow us down if I have to drag you through the air like a waterlogged canoe."

He tried, but he didn't have much success. He was certain that his eyes were lying to him, though. He could *feel* solidity under his feet. He stamped on it, and it was as firm as earth ought to be.

"That's just for now," the Goddess told him. "In a little while you won't need it anymore. I always have to put something solid down for Sephrenia—" Her voice broke off with a strange little sob. "*Please* get control of yourself, Sparhawk," she pleaded. "We *must* hurry. Look at the sky again. We're going a little higher."

He felt nothing at all, no rush of air, no sinking in the pit of his stomach, but when he looked down again, the clearing and its enchanted pool had shrunken to a dot. The tiny lights of Beresa twinkled from minuscule windows, and the moon had laid a long, glowing path out across the Tamul Sea.

"Are you all right?" Her inflections were still Aphrael's, but her voice, and most definitely her appearance, were totally different. Her face peculiarly combined Flute's features with Danae's, making her the adult who had somehow been both little girls. Sparhawk didn't answer, but stood instead stamping one foot on the solid nothing under him.

"I won't be able to keep that there when we start," she warned. "We'll be going too fast. Just hold on to my hand, but don't get excited and break my fingers."

"Don't do anything to surprise me, then. Are you going to sprout wings?"

"What an absurd idea. I'm not a bird, Sparhawk. Wings would only get in my way. Just lean back and relax." She looked intently at him. "You're really handling this well. Sephrenia's usually in hysterics at this point. Would you be more at ease if you sat down?"

"On what?"

"Never mind. Maybe we'd better stand. Take a couple of deep breaths, and let's get started."

He found that looking up helped. When he was looking at the stars and the newly risen moon, he could not see the awful emptiness under him.

There was no sense of movement, no whistle of the wind in his ears, no flapping of his cloak. He stood holding Aphrael's hand and looking intently at the moon as it receded ponderously southward.

Then there was a pale luminosity coming up from beneath.

"Oh, bother," the Goddess said.

"What's wrong?" His voice was a little shrill.

"Clouds."

He looked down and saw a fairy-tale world under them. Tumbled white cloud, glowing in the moonlight, stretched out as if forever. Mountains of airy mist swelled up from a folded, insubstantial plain, and pillars and castles of curded cloud stood sentinel-like between. Sparhawk's mind filled with wonder as the soft, moonlit cloudscape flowed smoothly back below them. "Beautiful," he murmured.

"Maybe, but I can't see the ground."

"I think I prefer it that way."

"I need reference points, Sparhawk. I can't see where I am, so I can't tell where I'm going. Bhelliom can find a place with nothing but a name to work with, but I can't. I need landmarks, and I can't see them with all these clouds in the way."

"Why don't you use the stars?"

"What?"

"That's what sailors do when they're out at sea. The stars don't move, so the sailors pick out a certain star or constellation and steer toward it."

There was a long silence while the swiftly receding rush of cloud beneath them slowed and finally stopped. "Sometimes you're so clever that I can't stand you, Sparhawk," the Goddess holding his hand said tartly.

"Do you mean you've never even thought of it?" he asked her incredulously.

"I don't fly at night very often." Her tone was defensive. "We're going down. I have to find a landmark."

They sank downward, the clouds rushing up to meet them, and then they were immersed in a dense, clinging mist. "They're made out of fog, aren't they? Clouds, I mean." Sparhawk was surprised.

"What did you think they were?"

"I don't know. I've never thought of it before. It just seems strange for some reason."

They broke out of the underside of the cloud—clouds no longer bathed in moonglow, now hanging close over their heads like a dirty ceiling that closed off the light. The earth beneath them was enveloped in almost total darkness. They drifted along, standing in air and veering this way and that, peering down and searching for something recognizable.

"Over there." Sparhawk pointed. "It must be a fair-sized town. There's quite a lot of light."

They moved in that direction, drawn toward the light like mindless insects. There was a sense of unreality as Sparhawk looked down. The town lying beneath them seemed tiny. It huddled like some child's toy on the edge of a large body of water. Sparhawk scratched at his cheek, trying to remember the details of his map. "It's probably Sopal," he said. "That lake almost has to be the Sea of Arjun." He stopped, his mind suddenly reeling. "That's over three hundred leagues from where we started, Aphrael!" he exclaimed. "Almost a thousand miles!"

"Yes—if that town really *is* Sopal."

"It has to be. The Sea of Arjun's the only large body of water on this part of the continent, and Sopal's on the east side of it. Arjun's on the south side, and Tiana's on the west." He stared at her incredulously. "A thousand miles! And we only left Beresa a half an hour ago! Just how fast are we going?"

"What difference does it make? We got here. That's all that matters." The young woman holding his hand looked speculatively down at the miniature town on the lakeshore. "Dirgis is off to the west a little way, so we won't want to go straight north." She shifted them around in midair until they were facing in a slightly northwesterly direction. "That should be fairly close. Don't move your head, Sparhawk. Keep looking in that direction. We'll go back up, and you pick out a star."

They rose swiftly through the clouds, and Sparhawk saw the familiar constellation of the wolf lying above the misty horizon ahead. "There." He pointed. "The five stars clustered in the shape of a dog's head."

"It doesn't look like any dog *I've* ever seen."

"You have to use your imagination. How is it you've never thought of steering by the stars before?"

She shrugged. "Probably because I can see farther than you can. You see the sky as a surface—a kind of overturned bowl with the stars painted on it all at the same distance from you. That's why you can see that cluster of stars as a dog's head. I can't, because I can see the difference in distances. Keep an eye on your dog, Sparhawk. Let me know if we start to drift off course."

The moon-bathed cloud beneath them began to flow smoothly back again, and they flew on in silence for a while. "This isn't so bad," Sparhawk said, "at least not when you get used to it."

"It's better than walking," the gauze-clad Goddess replied.

"It made my hair stand on end right at first, though."

"Sephrenia's never gotten past that stage. She starts gibbering in panic as soon as her feet come up off the ground."

Sparhawk remembered something. "Wait a minute," he objected. "When we killed Ghwerig and stole the Bhelliom, you came floating up out of that chasm in his cave, and she walked out across the air to meet you. She wasn't gibbering in panic then."

"No. It was probably the bravest thing she's ever done. I was so proud of her that I almost burst."

"Was she conscious at all? When you found her, I mean?"

"Off and on. She was able to tell us who'd attacked her. I managed to slow her heartbeat and take away the pain. She's very calm now." Aphrael's voice quavered. "She expects to die, Sparhawk. She can feel the wound in her heart, and she knows what that means. She was giving Xanetia a last message for Vanion when I left." The young Goddess choked back a sob. "Can we talk about something else?"

"Of course." Sparhawk's eyes flickered away from the constellation in the night sky. "There are mountains sticking up out of the clouds just ahead."

"We're almost there, then. Dirgis is in the big basin lying beyond that first ridge."

Their rapid flight began to slow. They passed over the snowy peaks of the southernmost expanse of the mountains of Atan, peaks that rose out of the clouds like frozen islands, and found that there was only thin cloud-cover over the basin lying beyond.

They descended, drifting down like dandelion puffs toward the forest-covered hills and valleys of the basin, a landscape sharply etched in the moonlight that leached out all color. There was another cluster of lights some distance to the left— ruddy torches in narrow streets and golden candlelight in little windows. "That's Dirgis," Aphrael said. "We'll set down outside of town. I should probably change back before we go on in."

"Either that or put on some more clothes."

"That really bothers you, doesn't it, Sparhawk? Am I ugly or something?"

"No. Quite the opposite—and that bothers me all the more. I can't think while you're standing around naked, Aphrael."

"I'm not really a woman, Sparhawk—not in the sense that seems to bother you so much, anyway. Can't you think of me as a mare—or a doe?"

"No, I can't. Just do whatever you have to do, Aphrael. I don't really think we need to talk about how I think of you."

"Are you blushing, Sparhawk?"

"Yes, as a matter of fact, I am. Now can we drop it?"

"That's really rather sweet, you know?"

"Will you stop?"

They came down in a secluded little glen about a half mile from the outskirts of Dirgis, and Sparhawk turned his back while the Child-Goddess once again assumed the more familiar form of the Styric waif they all knew as Flute. "Better?" she asked when he turned around.

"Much." He picked her up and started toward town, his long legs stretching out in a rapid stride. He concentrated on that. It seemed to help him avoid thinking.

They went directly into town, made one turn off the main street, and came to a large, two-story building. "This is it," Aphrael said. "We'll just go in and up the stairs. I'll make the innkeeper look the other way."

Sparhawk pushed open the door, crossed the common room on the main floor, and went up the stairs.

They found Xanetia all aglow and cradling Sephrenia in her arms. The two women were on a narrow bed in a small room with roughly squared-off log walls. It was one of those snug, comfortable rooms such as one finds in mountain inns the world over. It had a porcelain stove, a couple of chairs, and a nightstand beside each bed. A pair of candles cast a golden light on the pair on the bed. The front of Sephrenia's robe was covered with blood, and her face was deathly pale, tinged slightly with that fatal grey. Sparhawk looked at her, and his mind suddenly filled with flames. "I will cause hurt to Zalasta for this," he growled in Trollish.

Aphrael gave him a startled look. Then she also spoke in the guttural language of the Trolls. "Your thought is good, Anakha," she agreed fiercely. "Cause much hurt to him." The rending sound of the Trollish word for *hurt* seemed very satisfying to both of them. "His heart still belongs to me, though," she added. "Has there been any change?" she asked Xanetia, lapsing into Tamul.

"None, Divine One," Xanetia replied in a voice near to exhaustion. "I am lending our dear sister of mine own strength to sustain her, but I am nearly spent. Soon both she and I will die."

"Nay, gentle Xanetia," Aphrael said. "I will not lose you both. Fear not, however. Anakha hath come with Bhelliom to restore ye both."

"But that must not be," Xanetia protested. "To do so would put the life of Anakha's queen in peril. Better that thy sister and I both perish than that."

"Don't be noble, Xanetia," Aphrael told her tartly. "It makes my hair hurt. Talk to Bhelliom, Sparhawk. Find out how we're supposed to do this."

"Blue-Rose," Sparhawk said, touching his fingers to the bulge under his smock. *I hear thee, Anakha.* The voice in Sparhawk's mind was a whisper.

"We have come unto the place where Sephrenia lies stricken."

Yes.

"What must we now do? I implore thee, Blue-Rose, do not increase the peril of my mate."

Thine admonition is unseemly, Anakha. It doth bespeak a lack of trust. Let us proceed. Surrender thy will to me. It is through thy lips that I must speak with Anarae Xanetia.

A strange, detached lassitude came over Sparhawk, and he felt himself somehow separating, his awareness sliding away from his body.

"Attend to me, Xanetia." It was Sparhawk's altered voice, but he had no consciousness of having spoken.

"Most closely, World-Maker," the Anarae replied in her exhausted voice.

"Let the Child-Goddess assume the burden of supporting her sister. I have need of thy hands."

Aphrael slipped onto the bed and took Sephrenia from Xanetia's arms and held her in a tender embrace.

Take forth the box, Anakha, Bhelliom instructed, *and surrender it up unto Xanetia.*

Sparhawk's movements were jerky as he pulled the golden box out from under his tunic and lifted the thong upon which it was suspended up over his head.

"Gather about thee that serenity which the curse of Edaemus hath bestowed upon thee, Xanetia," Bhelliom instructed the Anarae in Sparhawk's voice, "and enfold the box—and mine essence—in thy hands, letting thy peace infuse that which thou dost hold."

Xanetia nodded and extended her glowing hands to take the box from Sparhawk's grasp.

"Very good. Now, take the Child-Goddess in thine arms. Embrace her and deliver me up unto her."

Xanetia clasped both Aphrael and Sephrenia in her arms.

"Excellent. Thy mind is quick, Xanetia. This is even better. Aphrael, open thou
the box and draw me forth." Bhelliom paused. "No tricks," it admonished her with
uncharacteristic colloquialism. "Seek not to ensnare me with thy wiles and thy soft
touch."

"Don't be absurd, World-Maker."

"I know thee, Aphrael, and I know that thou art more dangerous than ever
Azash was or Cyrgon could be. Let us both concentrate all our attention upon the
cure of thy sister."

The Child-Goddess opened the lid of the box and lifted out the glowing sapphire rose. Sparhawk, all bemused, saw the steady white glow which emanated from
Xanetia take on a faint bluish flush as Bhelliom's radiance joined her own.

"Apply me, poulticelike, to her wound, that I may heal that injury which Zalasta hath inflicted."

Sparhawk was a soldier and he knew a great deal about wounds. His stomach
knotted when he saw the deep, seeping gash in the upper swell of Sephrenia's left
breast.

Aphrael reached out with Bhelliom and gently touched it to the bleeding
wound.

Sephrenia started to glow with an azure radiance. She half raised her head.
"No," she said weakly, trying to push Aphrael's hand away.

Sparhawk took both her hands in his and held them. "It's all right, little
mother," he lied softly. "Everything's been taken care of."

The wound in Sephrenia's breast had closed, leaving an ugly purple scar. Then,
even as they watched, the sapphire rose continued its work. The scar shrank down
to a thin white line that became fainter and fainter and finally disappeared entirely.

Sephrenia began to cough. It was a gurgling, liquid kind of cough such as a
nearly drowned man might make.

"Hand me that basin, Sparhawk," Aphrael instructed. "She has to clear the
blood out of her lungs."

Sparhawk reached out and took the large, shallow basin from the nightstand
and handed it to her.

"Here," she said. "You can have this back now." She gave him the closed box,
took the basin, and held it under Sephrenia's chin. "That's right," she said encour-
agingly to her sister as the small woman began coughing up chunks of clotted
blood. "Get it all out."

Sparhawk looked away. The procedure was not pretty.

Put thy mind at rest, Anakha, Bhelliom's voice told him softly. *Thine enemies are
unaware of what hath come to pass.* The jewel paused. *I have not given Edaemus his
due, for he is very shrewd. Methinks none other could have perceived the true import of
what he hath done. To curse his children as he hath was the only true way to conceal
them. I shudder to imagine the pain it must have caused him.*

I do not understand, Sparhawk confessed.

A blessing rings and shimmers in the lucid air like bell-sound, Anakha, but a curse is dark and silent. Were the light which doth emanate from Anarae Xanetia a blessing, all the world would hear and feel its o'erwhelming love, but Edaemus hath made it a curse instead. Therein lay his wisdom. The accursèd are cast out and hidden, and no one—man or God—can hear or feel their comings and goings up and down in the land. When she did take the box in her hands, Anarae Xanetia did smother all sound and sense of my presence, and when she did embrace Aphrael and Sephrenia and enfold them in her luminous darkness, none living could detect me. Thy mate is safe—for now. Thine enemies have no knowledge of what hath come to pass.

Sparhawk's heart soared. *I do sorely repent my lack of trust, Blue-Rose,* he apologized.

Thou wert distraught, Anakha. I do freely forgive thee.

"Sparhawk." Sephrenia's voice was little more than a whisper.

"Yes, little mother?" He went quickly to the side of the bed.

"You shouldn't have agreed to this. You've put Ehlana in terrible danger. I thought you were stronger."

"Everything's all right, Sephrenia," he assured her. "Bhelliom just explained it to me. Nobody heard or felt a thing while you were being healed."

"How is that possible?"

"It was Xanetia's presence—and her touch. Bhelliom says she completely muffled what was going on. It has to do with the difference between a blessing and a curse, as I understand it. However it works, what just happened didn't put Ehlana in any danger. How are you feeling?"

"Like a half-drowned kitten, if you really want to know." She smiled weakly. Then she sighed. "I would never have believed that Zalasta could be capable of what he did."

"I'll make him wish he'd never thought of it," Sparhawk said grimly. "I'm going to tear out his heart, roast it on a spit, and then serve it up to Aphrael on a silver plate."

"Isn't he a nice boy?" Aphrael said fondly.

"No." Sephrenia's voice was surprisingly firm. "I appreciate the thought, dear ones, but I don't want either of you to do anything to Zalasta. I'm the one he stabbed, so I want to be the one who decides who gets him."

"I suppose that's fair," Sparhawk conceded.

"What have you got in mind, Sephrenia?" Aphrael asked.

"Vanion's going to be dreadfully upset when he hears about this. I don't want him raging and breaking up the furniture, so I'm going to give Zalasta to him—all tied up in a bright red ribbon."

"I still get his heart, though," Aphrael insisted.

CHAPTER THIRTEEN

The sky was overcast with sullen cloud, and a chill, arid wind scoured the empty floor of the Desert of Cynesga as Vanion led the retreat eastward. Fully half of his armored knights had perished in the encounter with Klæl's soldiers, and very few of the survivors had escaped serious injury. Vanion had ridden forth from Sarna with an army. He was returning at the head of a column of groaning invalids, battered and dented, after what had really been no more than a skirmish.

Four Atans carried Engessa on a litter, and Queen Betuana strode along at his side, her face ravaged with grief. Vanion sighed. Engessa was still breathing, but only barely.

The preceptor straightened in his saddle, trying to shake off his shock and dismay and to think rationally. The fight with Klæl's warriors had decimated his force of Church Knights, and they had been central to the strategy of containment. Without those armored horsemen, the eastern frontier of Tamul proper was no longer secure.

Vanion muttered a sour oath. The only thing he could really do now was to warn the others about the change in the situation. "Sir Endrik," he called to the old veteran riding some distance behind, "take over here. I've got something to take care of."

Endrik came forward.

"Keep them going east," Vanion instructed. "I'll be back in a little bit." He spurred his tired horse into a loping canter and rode on ahead.

When he was about a mile ahead of the column, he reined in and cast the spell of summoning.

Nothing happened.

He cast it again, more urgently this time.

What? Aphrael's voice in his ear was irritably impatient.

I've got some bad news, Divine One, he told her.

What else can go wrong? Hurry up, Vanion. I'm very busy right now.

We ran into Klæl out in the desert. He had an army of giants, and we got mauled. Tell Sparhawk that I probably won't be able to hold Samar if the Cynesgans lay siege to it. I've lost half the knights, and the ones I've got left aren't in any condition for a fight. Tikume's Peloi are brave men, but they don't have any experience with sieges.

When did this happen?

About four hours ago. Can you find Abriel and the other preceptors? They should be in Zemoch or western Astel by now. They have to be warned about Klæl. Tell them that under no circumstances should they engage in any pitched battles with Klæl's troops. We're no match for them. If the main body of the Church Knights gets waylaid and wiped out, we'll lose this war.

Who are these giants you're talking about, Vanion?

We didn't have time for introductions. They're bigger than the Atans, though—

almost as big as Trolls. They wear very close-fitting armor and steel face masks. Their weapons aren't like anything I've ever seen, and they've got yellow blood.

Yellow? That's impossible!

It's yellow all the same. You can come here and look at my sword-blade, if you'd like. I managed to kill a couple of them while I was covering Betuana's retreat.

Retreat? Betuana?

She was carrying Engessa.

What's wrong with Engessa?

He was out front a little ways, and Klæl's soldiers attacked him. He fought well, but they swarmed him under. We charged into them, and Betuana cut her way through to Engessa. I ordered a retreat and covered Betuana while she carried Engessa to the rear. We're taking him back to Sarna, but I think it's a waste of effort. The side of his head's been bashed in, and I'm afraid we're going to lose him.

Don't say that, Vanion. Don't ever say that. There's always hope.

Not much this time, Divine One. When somebody breaks into a man's brain, about all you can do for him is dig a grave.

I'm not going to lose him, Vanion! How fast can you get him back to Sarna?

Two days, Aphrael. It took us two days to get here, and two days out means two days back.

Can he hold on that long?

I doubt it.

She said a short, ugly word in Styric. *Where are you?*

Twenty leagues south of Sarna and about five leagues out into the desert.

Stay there. I'll come and find you.

Be a little careful when you approach Betuana. She's behaving very strangely.

Say what you mean, Vanion. I don't have time for riddles.

I'm not sure what I mean, Aphrael. Betuana's a soldier, and she knows that people sometimes get killed in battle. Her reaction to what's happened to Engessa is—well—excessive. She's broken down completely.

She's an Atan, Vanion. They're a very emotional people. Go back and halt your column. I'll be there in a little while.

Vanion nodded, although there was no one there to nod to, turned his horse, and rode back to rejoin his knights. "Any change?" he asked Queen Betuana.

She lifted her tear-streaked face. "He opened his eyes once, Vanion-Preceptor," she replied. "I don't think he saw me, though." She was holding Engessa's hand.

"I talked with Aphrael," he advised her. "She's coming here to have a look at him. Don't give up hope yet, Betuana. Aphrael cured *me,* and I was closer to being dead than Engessa is."

"He *is* fairly strong," she said. "If the Child-Goddess can heal his wound before it carries him off—" Her voice caught with an odd little note.

"He'll be all right, your Majesty," he said, trying to sound more certain than he really was. "Can you get word to your husband—about Klæl, I mean? He should know about those soldiers Klæl hides under his wings."

"I'll send a runner. Should I tell Androl to come to Sarna instead of going to Tosa? Klæl is here *now,* and Scarpa's army won't reach Tosa for quite some time—and that's only if they can evade the Trolls."

"Let's wait until I've had the chance to talk with the others first. Is King Androl already on the march?"

"He should be. Androl always jumps when I suggest something. He's a good man—and very, very brave." She said it almost as if defending her husband from some unspoken criticism, but Vanion noticed that she absently stroked Engessa's ashen face even as she spoke.

"He must have been in a hurry," Stragen said, still puzzling over Sparhawk's terse note.

"He's never been very good at writing letters—" Talen shrugged. "—except for that one time when he spent days composing lies about what we were supposedly doing on the Isle of Tega."

"Maybe that took it all out of him." Stragen folded the note and looked closely at it. "Parchment," he said. "Where did he get his hands on parchment?"

"Who knows? Maybe he'll tell us when he comes back. Let's go take a walk on the beach. I need some exercise."

"All right." Stragen picked up his cloak, and he and the younger thief went downstairs and out into the street.

The southern Tamul Sea was calm, and the moon-path across its dark surface was unbroken and very bright. "Pretty," Talen murmured when the two reached the damp sand at the edge of the water.

"Yes," Stragen agreed.

"I think I've come up with something," Talen said.

"So have I," Stragen replied.

"Go ahead."

"No, let's hear yours first."

"All right. The Cynesgans are massing on the border, right?"

"Yes."

"A good story could unmass them."

"I don't think there is such a word."

"Did we come here to discuss vocabulary? What will the Cynesgans do if they hear that the Church Knights are coming? Wouldn't they almost have to send an army to meet them?"

"I think Sparhawk and Vanion want to keep the fact that the knights are coming more or less a secret."

"Stragen, how are you going to keep a hundred thousand men a secret? Let's say that I tell Valash that I've picked up a very reliable report that a fleet of ships flying church banners has rounded the southern tip of Daconia bound for Kaftal. Wouldn't that cause the other side some concern? Even if they know about the knights coming across Zemoch, they'd *still* have to send troops to meet that fleet. They couldn't ignore the possibility that the knights are coming at them from two different directions."

Stragen suddenly laughed.

"What's so funny?"

"You and I have been running together for too long, Talen. We're starting to think alike. I came up with the idea of telling Valash that the Atans are going to cross the steppes of eastern Astel and strike down into northern Cynesga toward the capital."

"Nice plan," Talen said.

"So's yours." Stragen squinted out across the moon-bathed water. "Either story's strategically credible," he mused. "They're exactly the kind of moves a military man *would* come up with. What we're *really* planning is a simultaneous strike from the east and the west. If we can make Cyrgon believe that we're going to hit him from the north and south instead, we'll pull him so far out of position that he'll never be able to get his armies back to meet our real attacks."

"Not to mention the fact that we'll cut his army in two."

"We'll have to be careful, though," Stragen cautioned. "I don't think even Valash is gullible enough to swallow these stories if we drop them both on him at the same time. We'll have to spread them out and dribble them to him a bit at a time. What I'd *really* like to do is let the fairy tale about the Atans come from someone other than me."

"Sparhawk could probably get Aphrael to arrange that," Talen suggested.

"If he ever comes back. His note was a little vague. Let's get things rolling, though. We can modify your story a bit. Push your make-believe fleet back to Valesia. Give Cyrgon some time to worry about it before we pinpoint Kaftal as the final destination. I'll plant a couple of hints about the Atans massing up near their northwestern frontier. We'll let things stand that way until Sparhawk comes back."

Talen sighed.

"What's wrong?"

"This is almost legal, isn't it?"

"I suppose you could say so, yes. Is there some problem with that?"

"If it's legal, why am I having so much fun?"

"Nothing?" Ulath asked, opening the neck of his red uniform jacket.

"Not a peep," Tynian replied. "I cast the spell four times, and I still can't raise her."

"Maybe she's busy."

"It's possible, I guess."

Ulath rubbed at his cheek reflectively. "I definitely think I'll shave off Sir Gerda's beard," he muttered. "You know, it *could* be that it's because we're in No-Time. When we did this the first time—back in Pelosia—none of our spells worked."

"I think this spell's different, Ulath. I'm not really trying to *do* anything. I just want to talk with Aphrael."

"Yes, but you're mixing magic. You're trying to use a Styric spell when you're up to your ears in a Trollish one."

"Maybe that's it. I'll try again when we get to Arjun and go back into real time."

Bhlokw came shambling back through the grey light of Ghnomb's frozen moment, passing a flock of stationary birds hanging in the air. "There are some of the dens of the man-things in the next valley," he reported.

"Many or few?" Ulath asked him.

"Many," Bhlokw replied. "Will the man-things have dogs there?"

"There are always dogs near the dens of the man-things, Bhlokw."

"We should hurry, then." The shaggy Troll paused. "What do the man-things call this place?"

"It is the place Arjun—I think."

"That is the place where we want to go, is it not?"

"Yes."

"Why?"

"The wicked ones have told the one called Berit to go there. It is our thought that we should go there in Ghnomb's broken moment and listen to the bird-talk of the man-things. One of the wicked ones may say where the one called Berit is to go next. The next place may be the place where Anakha's mate is. It would be good to know this."

Bhlokw's shaggy brow furrowed as he struggled his way through that. "Are the hunts of the man-things always so not-simple?" he asked.

"It is the nature of our kind to be not-simple."

"Does it not make your head hurt?"

Ulath smiled, being careful not to show his teeth. "Sometimes it does," he admitted.

"It is my thought that a simple hunt is better than a not-simple hunt. The hunts of the man-things are so not-simple that sometimes I forget why I am hunting. Trolls hunt things-to-eat. The man-things hunt thought."

Ulath was a bit startled at the Troll's perception. "Your thought may be good," he admitted. "The man-things do hunt thought. We put much value on it."

"Thought is good, U-lat, but you cannot eat it."

"We hunt thought after our bellies are full."

"That is how Trolls and the man-things are different, U-lat. I am a Troll. My belly is never full. Let us hurry. It is my thought that it will be good to know if the dogs of this place are as good-to-eat as the dogs of the other place." He paused. "I do not wish to cause you anger, U-lat, but it is my thought that the dogs of the man-things are more good-to-eat than the man-things themselves." He scratched at his cheek with one shaggy paw. "I would still eat a man-thing if my belly was empty, but I would like a dog better."

"Let us go find you a dog, then."

"Your thought is good, U-lat." The huge beast reached out and affectionately patted Ulath on the head, nearly driving him to his knees.

The Child-Goddess touched her fingertips lightly to the sides of Engessa's broken head, and her eyes became distant.

"Well?" Vanion asked, his tone urgent.

"Don't rush me, Vanion. The brain is very complicated." She continued her gentle probing. "Impossible," she said finally, withdrawing her fingers.

Betuana groaned.

"Please don't do that, Betuana," Aphrael said. "All I meant was that I can't do it here. I'll have to take him someplace else to repair him."

"The island?" Vanion guessed.

She nodded. "I can control things there. This is still Cynesga—Cyrgon's place. I don't think he'd give me permission no matter how sweetly I asked him. Can you pray here, Betuana?"

The Atan queen shook her head. "Only in Atan itself."

"I'm going to talk to your God about that. It's really *very* inconvenient." She bent again and put her hand on Engessa's chest.

The Atan general appeared to stop breathing, and his face and body were suddenly covered with frost.

"You've killed him!" Betuana shrieked at her.

"Oh, hush! I just froze him to stop the bleeding until I can get him to the island. The injury itself isn't so bad, but the bleeding's tearing up the rest of his brain. The freezing slows it down to a trickle. That's all I can do for right now, but it should be enough to keep his body from doing any more damage to itself while you're taking him back to Sarna."

"There's no hope," Betuana said with a look of anguish.

"What are you talking about? I can have him back on his feet in a day or two—but I have to take him to the island where I can control time. The brain is easy. It's the heart that's so—well, never mind that. Listen closely, Betuana. As soon as you and Vanion get him to Sarna, I want you to go to the Atan border as fast as you can run. As soon as you get across that line, fall on your knees and start praying to your God. He'll be stubborn—he always is—but keep after him. Make a pest of yourself until he gives in. I need his permission to take Engessa to my island. If nothing else works, promise him that I'll do something nice for him someday. Don't be too specific, though. Keep bearing down on the fact that I can save Engessa, and *he* can't."

"I will do as you have commanded, Divine One," Betuana declared.

"I didn't *command*, Betuana. I only suggested. I don't have the authority to command you." The Child-Goddess turned to Vanion. "Let me see your sword," she said. "I want to have a look at this yellow blood."

Vanion drew his sword and offered it to her hilt-first.

She shuddered. "*You* hold it, dear one. Steel makes me nauseous." She squinted at the stains on the blade. "Astonishing," she murmured. "That isn't blood at all."

"It's what came out of them when we cut them."

"Perhaps, but it's still not blood. It's some kind of bile. Klæl's going a little far afield for allies. Those giants you ran across don't come from here, Vanion. They aren't like any creatures on *this* world."

"We noticed that almost immediately, Divine One."

"I'm not talking about their size or shape, Vanion. They don't even seem to have the same kind of internal organs as the humans and animals. I'd guess that they don't even have lungs."

"*Everything* has lungs, Aphrael—except maybe fish."

"That's *here*, dear one. If these creatures have bile in their veins instead of blood, then they're relying on their livers for—" She broke off, frowning. "I guess it *is* possible," she said a little dubiously. "I'd hate to smell the air on their world, though."

"You *do* know that I haven't got the foggiest idea of what you're talking about, don't you?"

She smiled. "That's all right, dear one. I love you anyway."

"Thank you."

"Don't mention it."

"It *could* be good country, friend Tikume," Kring said, adjusting his black leather jerkin and looking around at the rocky desert. "It's open and not too rugged. All it needs is water—and a few good people." The two of them rode at the front of their disorganized mob of Peloi.

Tikume grinned. "When you get right down to it, friend Kring, that's all Hell really needs."

Kring laughed. "How far is it to this Cynesgan camp?" he asked.

"Another five leagues. It's easy fighting, Domi Kring. The Cynesgans ride horses and carry curved swords much like your sabers, but their horses are scrubby and not very good, and the Cynesgans are too lazy to practice their swordsmanship. To make it even better, they wear flowing robes with big, floppy sleeves. Half the time they get tangled up in their own clothing."

Kring's grin was wolfish.

"They run fairly well, though," Tikume added, "but they always come back."

"To the same camps?" Kring asked incredulously.

Tikume nodded. "It makes it even easier. We don't even have to go looking for them."

"Incredible. Are they using rotten tree stumps for leaders?"

"From what I've heard, they're getting their orders from Cyrgon." Tikume rubbed his shaved scalp. "Do you think it might be heresy to suggest that even a God can be stupid?"

"As long as you don't say it about *our* God, I think you're safe."

"I wouldn't want to get in trouble with the Church."

"Patriarch Emban's a reasonable man, Domi Tikume. He won't denounce you if you say unflattering things about our enemy." Kring raised up in his stirrups to peer across the brown, gravel-strewn expanse of the Desert of Cynesga. "I'm looking forward to this," he said. "I haven't been in a real fight for a long time." He sank back into his saddle. "Oh, I almost forgot. I talked with friend Oscagne about the possibility of a bounty on Cynesgan ears. He said no."

"That's a shame. Men fight better if they've got an incentive of some kind."

"It even gets to be a habit. We had a fight with the Trolls up in northern Atan, and I had a dead Troll's ear half sawed off before I remembered nobody was around to buy it from me. That's a funny-looking hill up there, isn't it?" He pointed ahead at an almost perfectly shaped dome rearing up out of the desert floor.

"It *is* a little odd," Tikume agreed. "There aren't any rocks on its sides—just dust."

"Probably some kind of dust dune. They have sand dunes down in Rendor that look like that. The wind whirls the sand around and leaves it in round hills."

"Would dust behave like sand?"

"Evidently so. There's the proof just up ahead."

And then, even as they watched, the hill split down the middle and its sides fanned out. They stared at the triangular face of Klæl as he rose ponderously to his feet, shedding great waterfalls of dust from his gleaming black wings.

Kring reined in sharply. "I *knew* something wasn't right about that hill!" he exclaimed, cursing his own inattention, as their men surged around them.

"He didn't come alone this time!" Tikume shouted. "He had soldiers hidden under his wings! Hold!"

"Big devils, aren't they?" Kring squinted at the armored warriors rushing toward them. "Big or little, though, they're still infantry, and that's all the advantage we need, isn't it?"

"Right!" Tikume chortled. "This should be more fun than chasing Cynesgans."

"I wonder if they've got ears," Kring said, drawing his saber. "If they do, we might just want to gather them up. I still haven't given up on friend Oscagne yet."

"There's one way to find out," Tikume said, hefting his javelin and leading the charge.

The standard Peloi tactics seemed to baffle Klæl's soldiers. The superb horses of the nomads were as swift as deer, and the eastern Peloi's preference for the javelin over the saber was an additional advantage. The horsemen split up into small groups and began their attack. They slashed forward in long files, each group concentrating on one of the steel-masked monsters and each Peloi hurling his javelin into the huge bodies at close range and then swerving away to safety. After a few such attacks, the front ranks of the enemy warriors bristled like hedgehogs with the short spears protruding from their bodies.

The armored soldiers grew increasingly desperate, and they flailed ineffectually at their swift-charging tormentors with their brutal maces, savaging the unoffending air and almost never striking a solid blow.

"Good fight!" Kring panted to his friend after several charges. "They're big, but they're not quite fast enough."

"And not in very good condition either," Tikume added. "That last one I skewered was puffing and wheezing like a leaky bellows."

"They *do* seem to be having some trouble getting their breath, don't they?" Kring agreed. His eyes suddenly narrowed. "Wait a minute, let's try something. Tell your children to just ride in and then wheel and ride out again. Don't waste any more javelins."

"I don't quite follow, Domi."

"Have you ever gone up into the high mountains?"

"A few times. Why?"

"Do you remember how hard it was to get your breath?"

"Right at first, I suppose. I remember getting a little light-headed."

"Exactly. I don't know where Klæl went to recruit these soldiers, but it wasn't from around here. I think they're used to thicker air. Let's make them chase us. Why go to all the trouble of killing somebody if the air's going to do the job for you?"

"It's worth a try." Tikume shrugged. "It takes a lot of the fun out of it, though."

"We can have fun with the Cynesgans later," Kring told him. "Let's run Klæl's infantry to death first. *Then* we can go slaughter Cyrgon's cavalry."

"Sort of follow my lead on this," Stragen told Talen as the two mounted the rickety stairs leading up to the loft. "I've gotten to know Valash fairly well, so I can gauge his reactions a little better than you can."

"All right." Talen shrugged. "He's your fish. I'll let you play him."

Stragen opened the door to the stale-smelling loft, and the two of them threaded their way through the clutter to Valash's corner.

The bony Dacite in the brocade jacket was not alone. A gaunt Styric with open, seeping sores on his face slumped in a chair at the table. The Styric's right arm hung limply at his side, the right side of his ulcerated face sagged, and his right eyelid drooped down to almost totally cover the eye. He was mumbling to himself, evidently completely unaware of his surroundings.

"This isn't a good time, Vymer," Valash said.

"It's quite important, Master Valash," Stragen said quickly.

"All right, but don't take too long."

As they approached the table, Talen's stomach suddenly churned. An overpowering odor of putrefying flesh emanated from the comatose Styric.

"This is my master," Valash said shortly.

"Ogerajin?" Stragen asked.

"How did you know his name?"

"You mentioned it to me once, I think—or maybe it was one of your friends. Isn't he a little sick to be out and about?"

"That's none of your concern, Vymer. What's this important information you have for me?"

"Not me, Master Valash. Reldin here picked up something."

"Speak up, then, boy."

"Yes, Master Valash," Talen said, ducking his head in a sort of half bow. "I went into a waterfront tavern earlier today, and I heard a couple of Edomish sailors talking. They seemed excited about something, so I slipped a little closer to find out why they were so worked up. Well, you know how Edomishmen feel about the Church of Chyrellos."

"Get on with it, Reldin."

"Yes, sir. I was only trying to explain. Anyway, one of the sailors had just reached port, and he was telling the other one to get word to somebody in Edom— Rebal, I think his name is. It seems that the first sailor had just come in from Valesia, and when he'd been leaving port there, his ship passed a fleet coming into the harbor at Valles."

"What's so significant about that?" Valash demanded.

"I was just coming to that. What made the first sailor so excited was the fact that the ships he saw were all flying the banners of the Church of Chyrellos and the rails were lined with men wearing armor. He kept babbling something about Church Knights coming to impose heresies on the people of Tamuli."

Valash was staring at him in openmouthed horror.

"As soon as I heard that part, I slipped away. Vymer here thought you might want to know about it, but I wasn't so sure. What difference should it make to us that the Elenes are arguing about religion? It doesn't involve us, does it?"

"How many ships?" Valash demanded in a half-strangled tone. His eyes were bulging.

"The sailor wasn't too specific, Master Valash." Talen smiled. "I sort of got the impression that he ran out of the numbers that he knew the names of. I guess that fleet stretched from horizon to horizon. If those men in armor *are* Church Knights, I'd say that *all* of them are on board these ships. I've heard things about those people. *I* certainly wouldn't want to be the one they're coming after. How much would you say this information's worth, Master Valash?"

Valash reached for his purse without any protest.

"Have any messengers from those camps out in the woods come by lately, Master Valash?" Stragen asked suddenly.

"That's none of your concern, Vymer."

"Whatever you say, Master Valash. All I was getting at is that you ought to warn them about talking in public. I came across a couple of men who looked as if they've been living in the woods. One of them was telling the other that they couldn't do anything until Scarpa got instructions from Cyrga. Who's Cyrga? I've never heard of him."

"It's not a who, Vymer," Talen said. "It's a where. Cyrga's a town over in Cynesga."

"Really?" Stragen's expression grew curious. "This is the first time I've ever heard the name. Where is it? What route would you take to get to Cyrga?"

"The pathway lies close by the Well of Vigay," the diseased Ogerajin announced in a loud, declamatory voice.

Valash made a slightly strangled noise and ineffectually tried to wave his hands warningly in front of his master's face, but Ogerajin brushed him aside. "Keep morning at thy back," the Styric continued.

"Master Ogerajin," Valash protested in a squeaky tone.

"Silence, knave," Ogerajin thundered at him. "I will answer this traveler's question. If it is his intent to present himself and bow down to Cyrgon, he must know the way. Proceed, traveler, past the Well of Vigay and trek northwesterly into the desert. Thy destination shall be the Forbidden Mountains where none may go without Cyrgon's leave except at their peril. When thou dost reach those black, forbidding heights, seek ye the Pillars of Cyrgon, for without them to guide thee, Cyrga will remain forever hidden."

"Please, Master." Valash was helplessly wringing his hands as he stared in chagrin at the raving old lunatic.

"I have commanded thy silence, knave. Speak once more and thou shalt surely die." He turned back to fix Stragen with his single wild eye. "Be not dismayed, traveler, by the Plains of Salt which nomads fear to cross. Ride, boldly ride across the dead whiteness, empty of life save only where miscreants labor in the quarries to mine the precious salt.

"From the verge of the Plains of Salt wilt thou behold low on the horizon before thee the dark shapes of the Forbidden Mountains, and, if it please Cyrgon, his fiery white pillars will guide thee to his Hidden City.

"Let not the Plain of Bones disquiet thee. The bones are those of the nameless slaves who toil until death for Cyrgon's chosen, and, having served their purpose, are then given to the desert.

"Beyond the Plain of Bones wilt thou come to the Gates of Illusion behind which lies concealed the Hidden City of Cyrga. The eye of mortal man cannot perceive those gates. Stark they stand as a fractured wall at the verge of the Forbidden Mountains to bar thy way. Bend thine eye, however, upon Cyrgon's two white pillars and direct thy steps toward the emptiness which doth lie between them. Trust not the evidence which thine eye doth present unto thee, for the solid-seeming wall is as mist and will not bar thy way. Pass through it and proceed along the dark corridor to the Glen of Heroes where lie the unnumbered regiments of Cyrgon in restless sleep, awaiting the trumpet call of his mighty voice summoning them forth once more to smite his enemies."

Valash stepped back a pace and urgently beckoned to Talen to follow him.

Curious, Talen followed the Dacite. "Don't pay any attention to Master Ogerajin, boy," Valash said urgently. "He hasn't been well lately, and he has these spells quite often."

"I'd already guessed that, Master Valash. Shouldn't you get him to a physician? He's really raving, you know."

"There's nothing a physician could do for him." Valash shrugged. "Just make sure that Vymer understands that the old man doesn't know what he's talking about." Valash seemed unusually concerned about Ogerajin's ravings.

"He already knows, Master Valash. Anytime somebody starts throwing the 'thees' and 'thous' around, you can be fairly sure that his saddle's starting to slip."

The diseased Styric was still raving in that hollow, declamatory voice. "Beyond the Glen of Heroes wilt thou see the Well of Cyrgon, sparkling in the sun and sustaining the Hidden City.

"Close by the well in fields laced with channels thou wilt see black Cyrga rising like a mountain within its walls of night. Go boldly there and into the city of the Blessed Cyrgai. Mount the steep streets to the summit of that enclosèd peak, and there at the crown of the known world thou wilt find amid that blackness the white, where columns of chalk bear the lintels and roof of the Holy of Holies wherein Cyrgon burns eternal upon the sacred altar.

"Fall upon thy face in that awful presence, crying *'Vanet, tyek Alcor! Yala Cyrgon!'* and, should it please him, he will hear thee. And should it please him not, he will destroy thee.

"Thus, traveler, is the way to the Hidden City which lieth at the heart of Mighty Cyrgon, King and God of all that was, all that is, and all that shall ever be."

Then the crazed Styric's face contorted into a grotesque mask of glee, and he began to cackle in a shrill, meaningless giggle.

CHAPTER FOURTEEN

"All right, Sparhawk, you can turn around now."

"Are you dressed?"

She sighed. "Just a minute." There was a satiny rustle. "Will *this* do?" she asked tartly.

He turned. The Goddess was wrapped in a shimmering white robe. "That's a little better," he told her.

"Prude. Give me your hand."

He took her slender hand in his and they drifted upward, rising out of the forested hills just east of Dirgis. "Sarna's somewhat to the west of due south," he told her.

"I know where it is." Her tone was crisp.

"I was just trying to be helpful."

The ground beneath them began to flow back as they sped southwesterly.

"Can people see us from the ground?" he asked curiously.

"Of course not. Why?"

"Just wondering. It occurred to me that if they can it might explain a lot of the wild stories that crop up in folklore."

"You humans are very creative. You can invent wild stories without any help from us."

"You're in a disagreeable frame of mind today. How long is it going to take us to get there?"

"Just a few minutes."

"It's an interesting way to travel."

"It's overrated."

They drifted on in silence for a while. "That's Sarna just ahead," Aphrael said.

"Do you think Vanion's reached here by now?"

"I doubt it. Later today, probably. We're going down." They settled gently to earth in a clearing a mile or so from the northern edge of the city, and Aphrael returned to the more familiar form of Flute. "Carry me," she said, reaching up to him.

"You know how to walk."

"I just carried you all the way from Dirgis. Fair *is* fair, Sparhawk."

He smiled. "Only teasing, Aphrael." He lifted her into his arms and started through the forest toward town. "Where to?" he asked her.

"The Atan barracks. Vanion says that Itagne's there." She frowned. "Oh, that's *really* impossible!" she burst out.

"What's wrong?"

"Sir Anosian's hopelessly inept. I can't make any sense out of what he's saying."

"Where is he?"

"At Samar. He's trying to tell me about something Kring and Tikume just discovered, but I'm only getting about every third word. Why *won't* the man concentrate on his studies?"

"Anosian's sort of—ah—"

"The word you're looking for is *lazy*, Sparhawk."

"He likes to conserve his energy," Sparhawk defended his fellow Pandion.

"Of *course* he does." She frowned. "Stop a minute," she said.

"What's the matter?"

"I just thought of something."

"What now?"

"It just occurred to me that Tynian may have been a little unselective when he was gathering those knights he brought back from Chyrellos."

"He brought the best men he could lay his hands on."

"I think that's the problem. I've been wondering why I haven't been getting any reports from Komier. I don't think Tynian left him a single Pandion who has any more skill than Anosian does. There aren't all that many of you who can reach out more than a few leagues, and Tynian seems to have inadvertently commandeered them all."

"Could you make any sense at all about what Anosian was trying to tell you?"

"It's something about breathing. Somebody's having problems with it. I'll run on down there after we talk with Itagne. Maybe Anosian can be coherent if I'm in the same room with him."

"Be nice."

They passed through the city gates and entered Sarna. Sparhawk carried the Child-Goddess through the narrow streets to the bleak stone fortress that housed the local Atan garrison.

They found the red-mantled Itagne in a large conference room examining the map that covered one entire wall. "Ah, Itagne," Sparhawk said, "there you are." He set Flute down on her feet.

"I'm afraid you have the advantage of me, Sir—?"

"It's me, Itagne—Sparhawk."

"I'll *never* get used to that," Itagne said. "I thought you were in Beresa."

"I *was*—until yesterday."

"How did you get here so fast?"

Sparhawk laid his hand on Flute's little shoulder. "Need you ask?"

"Oh. What brings you to Sarna?"

"Vanion ran into trouble out in the desert. He's coming back. He and Betuana are bringing Engessa in on a litter."

"Do you mean there's somebody in this world big enough to hurt Engessa?"

"Perhaps not in *this* world, Itagne," Aphrael told him. "Klæl's brought in an army from someplace else. They're very strange. Vanion and Betuana should get here this afternoon. Then Betuana has to go to Atan. How far is that?"

Itagne looked at the map. "Fifteen leagues."

"Good. It shouldn't take her long, then. She has to get her God's permission for me to take Engessa to the island. The side of his head's been bashed in, and I can't fix that here."

"Good God!" Itagne exclaimed.

"How nice of you to notice."

He smiled faintly. "What else is going on?" he asked.

"Quite a bit," Sparhawk told him. "Zalasta tried to kill Sephrenia."

"You're not serious!"

"I'm afraid so. We had to use Bhelliom to save her life."

"Sparhawk!" Itagne's eyes widened.

"It's all right, Itagne," Aphrael assured him, going across the room to him and holding out her hands.

"Didn't that endanger Queen Ehlana?" he asked, lifting her into his lap.

Sparhawk shook his head. "Xanetia can muffle those telltale noises, I guess. Ehlana's still safe—or so Bhelliom tells me." His face, however, was worried.

"Thank God!"

"You're welcome," Aphrael said, "but it was really Bhelliom's idea. We still have some problems, though. Vanion's encounter with Klæl's army cost him about half of his knights."

"That's disastrous! We won't be able to hold Samar without those knights!"

"Don't be quite so sure, Itagne," she said. "I just received a garbled message from a Pandion named Anosian. He's in Samar, and Kring and Tikume have discovered something about Klæl's soldiers. I'll run down there and find out what's going on."

"Klæl's keeping an eye on Berit and Khalad," Sparhawk continued. "They saw him while they were crossing the Sea of Arjun." He rubbed at the side of his face. "Can you think of anything else, Aphrael?"

"Lots of things," she replied, "but they don't have much to do with what we're doing here." She kissed Itagne and slipped down out of his lap. "I shouldn't be too long," she told them. "If Vanion gets here before I come back, break the news about Sephrenia to him gently and tell him that she's all right now. Keep a grip on him, gentlemen. It's wintertime, and you need the roof on this building." She went to the door, opened it, and vanished as she stepped through.

Tiana lay on the north shore of the large lake known as the Sea of Arjun. It was a bustling Tamul town with an extensive harbor. As soon as the scruffy lake freighter docked, Berit and Khalad led their horses ashore and mounted. "What was the name of that inn again?" Khalad asked.

"The White Gull," Berit replied.

"Poetic," Khalad noted.

"The other names had probably already been used up. You can only have so many lions and dragons and boars in one town before people start to get confused."

"Krager's starting to give us more specific instructions in those notes," Khalad said. "When he sent us to Sopal, he just gave us the name of the town. Now he's picking our accommodations for us. That *might* mean that we're getting closer to the end of this little excursion."

"Sir Ulath said that they're going to send us to Arjuna from here."

"If I'd known we were going to spend so much time wandering around this lake, I'd have brought a fishing line."

"I'm not really all that fond of fish, myself."

"Who is? It's an excuse to get outside. My brothers and I have found that if we lay around the house too long, our mothers start finding things for us to do."

"You've got a strange family, Khalad. Most men only have one mother."

"It was Father's idea. There's the White Gull." Khalad pointed up the street.

The inn was surprisingly clean and substantial. It had a well-maintained stable, and the rooms were neat almost to the point of fussiness. The two young men saw to their horses, dropped their saddlebags off in their room, and took advantage of the bathhouse adjoining the rear of the inn. Then, feeling much improved, they adjourned to the taproom to pass the time until supper. Khalad rose and closely examined the porcelain stove. "It's an interesting idea," he told Berit. "I wonder if it'd catch on in Eosia."

"I sort of like looking at the fire myself," Berit replied.

"You can stare at the candles, if that's all you want. A fireplace isn't very efficient, and it makes an awful mess. A stove's a lot more practical—and you can cook on it. When we get home, I think I'll build one for my mothers."

Berit laughed. "If you start tearing up their kitchen, they'll take their brooms to you."

"I don't think so. The notion of a stew that doesn't have cinders floating in it might appeal to them."

The man who approached their table wore a hooded smock, and the hood partially concealed his face. "You don't mind if I join you, do you?" he asked, sitting down and pushing the hood back slightly.

It was the same Styric they had last seen on the shore of the Gulf of Micae.

"You made good time, neighbor," Berit said. "Of course, you knew where you were going, and we didn't."

"How long did it take you to get dry?" Khalad asked him.

"Shall we skip the pleasantries?" the Styric said coldly. "I have further instructions for you."

"You mean you didn't stop by just to renew our acquaintance?" Khalad said. "I'm crushed."

"Very funny." The Styric hesitated. "I'm going to reach into my pocket for the note, so don't start drawing your knives."

"Wouldn't dream of it, old boy," Khalad drawled.

"This is for you, Sparhawk." The Styric handed Berit the sealed parchment.

Berit took the parchment and broke the seal. He carefully lifted out the identifying lock of the queen's hair and read aloud, " 'Sparhawk. Go overland to Arjun. You'll receive further instructions there. Krager.' "

"He must have been drunker than usual," Khalad observed. "He didn't bother with all the snide little comments this time. Just out of curiosity, friend, why didn't he send us straight on to Arjun from Sopal? He could have saved everybody a great deal of time."

"That's really none of your business, Elene. Just do as you're told."

"I'm a peasant, Styric, so I'm used to doing that. Prince Sparhawk here might get a little impatient, though, and that makes him bad-tempered." Khalad squinted at the lumpy-faced messenger. "Since the subject's come up anyway, I've got a word of friendly advice for you, old boy. It's about twenty days on horseback from here to Arjun. He's going to be very unpleasant by the time he gets there. If you should happen to be the one who delivers the next message, I wouldn't get too close to him."

"I think we can come up with a way for him to work off his bad temper," the Styric sneered. "You don't *have* twenty days to get to Arjun. You have fourteen." He stood up. "Don't be late." He turned and started toward the door.

"Let's go," Khalad said.

"Where?"

"After him."

"What for?"

Khalad sighed. "To shake him down, Berit," he explained with exaggerated patience. "I want to strip him and go through his clothes. He just *might* have the next message on him."

"Are you mad? They'll kill the queen if we do that."

"Just because we rough up their messenger boy? Don't be silly. They want the Bhelliom, and the queen's the only thing they've got to trade for it. We could routinely kill every single one of their messengers, and they wouldn't do a thing to her. Let's go shake that Styric up a little bit and go through his pockets. If we can get hold of the next message, we might be able to get the jump on them."

"You know, I think you're right. They won't do anything to the queen, will they?"

"Not a chance, my Lord. Let's go teach that Styric some manners. It's exactly the sort of thing Sparhawk would do."

"He *would,* wouldn't he?" Berit looked closely at his friend. "That fellow really irritates you, doesn't he?"

"Yes, as a matter of fact, he does. I don't like his attitude."

"Well, let's go change it, then."

"I'm not going to do anything foolish," Kalten said. "I just want to have a look around." The three of them were sitting under their tree in Narstil's cluttered jungle camp. They had a fire going, and three stolen chickens were spitted over it, dripping grease into the flames.

"It won't hurt," Caalador said to Bevier. "If the time ever comes when we have to go in there, we should probably know the lay of the land."

"Are you sure you can keep a handle on your temper?" Bevier asked Kalten. "You'll be all alone there, you know."

"I'm all grown up now, Bevier," Kalten assured him. "I'm not going to do anything noisy until *after* things are back the way they should be. We may not get a chance like this again. Senga's invited me to go along to help him sell beer. It's the most natural thing in the world, and nobody's going to recognize me. I can pick up some very valuable information in Natayos, and if I happen to see somebody I recognize standing in a window or something, we'll know for sure exactly where those two friends of ours are located. Then the fellow with the broken nose can have a word with his blue friend and they can lift them out before anybody can even blink.

Then we can all go down there and explain to certain people just how unhappy we are."

"I'm in favor of it, myself," Caalador said to Bevier.

"It's tactically sound," Bevier admitted, "but—uh—Col here doesn't have any way to call for help if he gets in trouble."

"I won't need any help, because I'm not going to do anything out of the ordinary. I'm going anyway, Shallag, so don't waste your breath trying to talk me out of it."

Senga came across the littered camp. "The cart's all loaded, Col," he called. "Are you about ready?"

Kalten stood up. "Anytime you are, Senga," he replied, pulling his half-cooked chicken off the spit and going to join his newfound friend. "I'm getting bored just sitting here counting trees."

It took the two of them about three hours to reach Natayos, since there is no real way to hurry an ox. The trail was fairly well traveled, and it wound around through the jungle, following the course of least resistance.

"There it is," Senga said as the cart jolted through a ford that crossed a narrow stream. He pointed across the stump-dotted clearing at an ancient city, a ruin so old that the passage of centuries had rounded down the very stones. "Stay close to me when we get there, Col. There are a couple of places we have to keep away from. There's one building right near the gate that they *really* don't want anybody to go near."

"Oh?" Kalten said, squinting at the mossy ruin ahead. "What's inside that makes them so touchy?"

"I haven't the faintest idea, and I'm not curious enough to risk my health by asking."

"Maybe it's their treasure house," Kalten speculated. "If this army's as big as you say, they've probably picked up quite a bit of loot."

Senga shrugged. "It could be, I suppose, but I'm not going to fight all those guards just to find out. We're here to sell beer, Col. We'll get a goodly share of their treasure that way, and it's not as risky."

"But it's so *honest*," Kalten objected, grinning. "Isn't honest work immoral for people like us?"

Senga laughed and tapped the ox's rump with the long, slender stick he carried. The creaking cart jolted over the uneven ground toward the moldering walls.

"Ho, Senga!" one of the slovenly guards at the gate greeted Kalten's friend. "What kept you? It's been as dry as a plate of sand since the last time you left."

"You fellows are overworking my brewer," Senga replied. "He can't keep up with the demand. We have to let the beer age a *little* while before you drink it. Green beer does funny things to a man's guts."

"You haven't raised your prices again, have you?"

"No. Same price as before."

"Ten times what you paid for the beer in the first place, I'll wager."

"Oh, not quite *that* much. Where do you want me to set up?"

"Same place as last time. I'll pass the word, and they'll start lining up."

"I want some guards this time, Mondra," Senga told him. "I don't want another riot when the last cask runs dry, the way there was last week."

"I'll see to it. Save some for me."

The oxcart clattered through the gate and into a wide street where most of the moss had been worn off the cobblestones. A great deal of work had clearly taken place here in Natayos in the past few years. The squared-off stones of the broken walls had been rather carelessly restacked and then shored up with peeled log braces. Long-vanished roofs had been replaced with crude thatching made of tree limbs, providing nesting sites for raucous tropical birds, and here and there blackened piles of half-burned trees and bushes marked the places where indifferent workmen had attempted to dispose of the mountains of brush that had been cleared from the streets and houses. The men living here lounged idly in the streets. There were Elenes from Astel, Edom, and Daconia, as well as Arjunis and Cynesgans. They were a roughly dressed, unshaven lot who showed no signs that they even knew the meaning of the word *discipline*.

"What price are you getting for this?" Kalten asked, patting one of the beer barrels in the cart.

"A penny a gill," Senga replied.

"That's outrageous!"

"They don't *have* to buy it." Senga shrugged. "Get the money *before* you start to pour. Don't take promises."

"You've put my moral qualms to rest, Senga." Kalten laughed. "At *that* price, this is hardly honest."

"There's that building I was telling you about."

Kalten tried to look casual as he turned to stare at the substantial-looking ruin. "They *really* don't want anybody to look into that place," he said. "Those bars on the windows make it look like a jail."

"Not quite, Col. Those bars are there to keep people *out*, not in."

Kalten grunted, still staring intently at the building. The barred windows had panes of glass in them, cheap, cloudy glass that had been poorly installed. Drapes on the inside cut off any possibility of seeing anything or anyone who might be in there. There were guards at the door, and other guards stationed at every corner. Kalten wanted to howl with frustration. The gentle girl who had become the center of his life was possibly no more than twenty yards away, but she might as well have been on the other side of the moon; and even if she were to look out through that clouded glass she would not recognize his altered features.

Senga paid the guards in the square with beer, and then he and his friend got down to work. Scarpa's rebels were rowdy, shouting and laughing, but they were generally in a good humor. They lined up in an orderly fashion and came to the rear of the cart two by two, where Senga and Kalten filled their containers with the amber beer. There were a few arguments about the capacity of the assorted tankards, jugs, and pails, but Senga's word on the subject was final, and anyone who objected too loudly was sent back to the end of the line to think things over for an hour or so while he worked his way back to the front again.

It was after the two entrepreneurs had drained the last barrel and sent the disappointed latecomers away that Kalten saw a familiar figure come weaving across the mossy square toward the oxcart. Krager was not wearing well. His head was shaved and as pale as a fish-belly, and his dissipated face was eroded by decades of hard drinking. His clothing, though obviously expensive, was wrinkled and filthy. He shook continually with a palsied tremor that ran through him in waves.

"I don't suppose you brought any wine," he asked Senga hopefully.

"Not much call for it," Senga told him, refastening the tailgate of the cart. "Most of these fellows want beer."

"Do you know any place where you can *get* wine?"

"I can ask around. What's your preference?"

"Arcian red, if you can find any."

Senga whistled. "*That* will cost you, my friend. I could probably chase down some of the local reds for you, but the imported stuff—that's going to take a *big* bite out of your purse."

Krager smirked at him. "It's no problem," he said in his slurred voice. "I'm what you might call independently wealthy at the moment. These local reds taste like pig swill. I want *real* wine."

"It might take a while," Senga told him dubiously. "I've got contacts in Delo that might be able to find some for you, but Delo's a long way off."

"When are you coming back?"

"A couple of days. The brewery where I buy this slop's running day and night, but I still can't keep up."

"Bring me a couple of barrels of the local pig swill then—enough to tide me over until you can find me some Arcian red."

"You can count on me," Senga assured him. He gave Krager a hard look. "I'll need something in advance, though. I'll have to buy the Arcian red before I can sell it to you. I'm doing fairly well, but I'm not *that* rich yet."

Krager fumbled for his purse.

Kalten was suddenly gripped by an almost intolerable impatience. He was sure now that Alean was here. Krager's presence virtually confirmed it. The prisoners were almost certainly being held in the building with barred windows. He absolutely *had* to get back to Narstil's camp so that Bevier could pass the word on to Aphrael. If Xanetia *could* enter Natayos unseen, she could either penetrate the prison walls or reach into Krager's wine-sodden mind to verify what was almost a certainty now. If all went well, it would be no more than a few days until he and Sparhawk were reunited with the women they loved. *Then* they could all come here and do unpleasant things to the people responsible.

Vanion and Betuana reached Sarna late that afternoon, and the Atan queen scarcely paused before setting out for the border.

"It was ghastly, Sparhawk," Vanion said, leaning wearily back in his chair and putting his visored helmet on the table. "They're like no soldiers I've ever seen before. They're big, and they're fast, and their hides are so tough that most of the time my sword just bounced off them. I don't know where Klæl found them, but they've got yellow blood, and they made mincemeat out of my knights."

"Kring and Tikume ran into them as well, I guess," Sparhawk told him.

"Anosian tried to pass word to Aphrael, but he garbled the spell so badly that she couldn't make any sense out of it. She's a little unhappy with Tynian. When he was gathering up the knights he brought back to Matherion, he accidentally picked every Pandion who has the least bit of skill with the spells. That's why she can't get any reports from Komier."

"We might have to send somebody to join him and handle communications—except that it'd take weeks for him to get there."

"Not if Aphrael takes him, it won't," Sparhawk disagreed. "She carried me from Beresa to Sopal—almost a thousand miles—in about a half an hour."

"You're not serious!"

"You'll *love* flying, Vanion."

"You're carrying tales, Sparhawk."

They turned quickly.

The Child-Goddess was sitting in a chair at the far end of the room with her grass-stained little feet up on the table.

"I wish you wouldn't do that," Sparhawk told her.

"Would you prefer some kind of announcement, Sparhawk? Multitudes of spirits bawling hymns of praise to introduce me? It's a little ostentatious, but I can arrange it."

"Just forget I said anything."

"I'll do that. I had a chat with Anosian, and he's practicing now—very hard. Kring and Tikume ran across Klæl and his soldiers out in the desert, and they discovered something you gentlemen should know. I was right, Vanion. Klæl's soldiers have bile in their veins instead of blood because they breathe with their livers. That means that the air where they come from isn't anything like the air here—probably something like marsh gas. There's something in it that they need, and they can't get it out of our air. The Peloi used their standard cut-and-run tactics, and after a little while those monsters started to collapse. Next time you come up against them, just turn around and run away. If they try to chase you, they'll choke to death. Did Betuana leave?"

"Yes, Divine One," Itagne replied.

"Good. The quicker I can get Engessa to my island, the quicker I'll have him back on his feet."

"I've been meaning to ask you about that," Sparhawk said. "You said that his brain's been injured."

"Yes."

"The brain's very complicated, isn't it?"

"Yours aren't quite as complex as ours, but they aren't simple, by any means."

"And you can heal Engessa's brain on your island?"

"Of course."

"If you can fix a brain, you should be able to fix somebody's heart. Why didn't you just take Sephrenia to your island and heal her there? Why did you come to Beresa and try to steal Bhelliom?"

"*What's this?*" Vanion exclaimed, coming to his feet.

"Wonderful, Sparhawk," Aphrael said dryly. "I'm awed by your subtlety. She's all right, Vanion. Bhelliom brought her back."

Vanion smashed his fist down on the table and then controlled himself with an obvious effort. "Would it inconvenience anybody to tell me what happened?" he asked them in an icy voice.

"We were in Dirgis." Aphrael shrugged. "Sephrenia was alone in the room, and Zalasta came in and stabbed her in the heart."

"Good God!"

"She's fine, Vanion. Bhelliom took care of it. She's coming along very well. Xanetia's with her."

Vanion started toward the door.

"Oh, come back here," the Child-Goddess told him. "As soon as I get Engessa to the island and deal with his injury, I'll take you to Dirgis. She's asleep now anyway, and you've seen her sleep before—lots of times."

Vanion flushed slightly and then looked a bit sheepish.

"You still haven't answered my question," Sparhawk said. "If you can fix a brain, why can't you fix a heart?"

"Because I can shut a brain down to work on it, Sparhawk," she replied in a long-suffering tone. "The heart has to keep on beating, and I can't work on it while it's jumping around like that."

"Oh, I guess that makes sense."

"Do you happen to know where I could find Zalasta?" Vanion asked in a dreadful voice.

"He's probably gone back to Natayos," Aphrael replied.

"After I visit Sephrenia, do you suppose you could take me there? I'd *really* like to have a talk with him."

"I get his heart," the Child-Goddess said.

Vanion gave her a strange look.

"It's an ongoing joke," Sparhawk told him.

"I'm not joking, Sparhawk," Aphrael said bleakly.

"We can't go to Natayos," Sparhawk said. "Ehlana might be there, and Scarpa will kill her if we come pounding on the gate. Besides, I think you'll have to talk with Khwaj before you do anything to Zalasta."

"Khwaj?" Vanion asked.

"Tynian told Aphrael that Khwaj has his own plans for our Styric friend. He wants to set him on fire."

"I've got some more interesting ideas," Vanion said grimly.

"I wouldn't be so sure, my Lord. Khwaj wants to set Zalasta on fire, but he doesn't want to burn him to death. He's talking about an eternal flame—with Zalasta screaming in the middle of it—forever."

Vanion considered that. "What a merry idea," he said finally.

"My lady," Alean whispered urgently, "come quickly. Zalasta's returned."

Ehlana drew the linen headcloth down over her forehead and joined her maid at the defective window. The wimple had been Alean's idea. It fit snugly over the queen's ravaged scalp, and covered her throat and the underside of her chin as well. It was uncomfortable, but it concealed the horror Krager's knife had made of her hair. She bent and looked out through the small triangular opening in the window.

Zalasta's gaunt face was twisted with grief, and his eyes were dead. Scarpa came hurrying up, his face eager. "Well?" he demanded.

"Go away, Scarpa," Zalasta told him.

"I only wanted to be sure you were all right, Father," Scarpa replied with obvious insincerity. Scarpa had fashioned a crude crown for himself out of a serving bowl made of hammered gold. He was evidently unaware of how absurd he looked with the lopsided adornment perched on his shaved head.

"Leave me!" Zalasta thundered. "Get out of my sight!"

"Is she dead?" Scarpa ignored the dreadful threat implicit in his father's voice.

Zalasta's face hardened. "Yes," he replied in a strangely neutral tone. "I drove my knife straight into her heart. I'm deciding right now whether or not I can live with what I've done. Please stay, Scarpa, by all means. This was your idea, after all. It was such a marvelous notion that I may want to reward you for it."

Scarpa backed away, his suddenly rational eyes now filled with fear.

Zalasta barked two words in Styric and reached out his hand, his fingers curved like hooks. Scarpa clutched at his belly and screeched. His makeshift crown fell unnoticed as Zalasta implacably dragged him back.

"You're pathetically obvious, Scarpa," Zalasta grated, his face only inches from his son's, "but your plan had one minor flaw. I may very well kill myself for what I did to Sephrenia, but I'll kill you first—just as unpleasantly as I possibly can. I may just kill you anyway. I don't really like you, Scarpa. I felt a certain responsibility for you, but that's a word you wouldn't understand." His eyes suddenly burned. "Your madness must be contagious, my son. I'm starting to lose my grip on sanity myself. You talked me into killing Sephrenia, and I loved her far more than I could ever love you." He unhooked his fingers. "Run away, Scarpa. Pick up your cheap toy crown and run. I'll be able to find you when I decide to kill you."

Scarpa fled, but Ehlana did not see him leave. Her eyes were filled with tears, and she turned from the window with a grief-stricken wail.

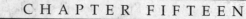

CHAPTER FIFTEEN

It was snowing in Sarna when Sparhawk woke the following morning, a thick, heavy snow that swirled and danced in the driving wind coming down out of the Atan mountains lying to the north. Sparhawk looked sourly out of the window of his barracks room, then pulled on his clothes and went looking for the others.

He found Itagne sitting by the stove in the war room with a sheaf of documents in his lap. "Something important?" he asked as he entered.

"Hardly," Itagne replied. He made a face and put the papers away. "I made a serious blunder last spring before Oscagne uprooted me and sent me to Cynestra. I was teaching a class in foreign relations at the university, and I slipped and said the fatal words, 'write a paper.' Now I've got a bale of these things to plow through." He shuddered.

"Bad?"

"Unbelievably so. Undergraduates should never be allowed to touch a quill pen. So far I've encountered fifteen different versions of my own lecture notes—all couched in graceless, semiliterate prose."

"Where's Vanion?"

"He's checking on his wounded. Have you seen Aphrael yet this morning?"

Sparhawk shook his head. "She could be anywhere."

"Did she actually fly you here from Dirgis?"

"Oh, yes—and up from Beresa before that. It's an unusual experience, and it always starts with the same argument."

Itagne gave him a questioning look.

"She has to revert to her real form when she does it."

"Blazing light? Trailing clouds of glory, and all that?"

"No, nothing like that. It's just that, with us, she always poses as a little girl, but actually, she's a young woman."

"What do you argue with her about?"

"Whether or not she's going to wear clothes. The Gods evidently don't need them, and they haven't quite grasped the concept of modesty yet. She's a bit distracting when she first appears."

"I can imagine."

The door opened, and Vanion came in, brushing the snow off the shoulders of his cloak.

"How are the men?" Sparhawk asked him.

"Not good," the preceptor replied. "I wish we'd known more about Klæl's soldiers before we closed with them. I lost a lot of good knights needlessly during that skirmish. If I'd had my wits about me, I'd have suspected something when they didn't pursue us after we broke off our attack."

"How long were you engaged?"

"It seemed like hours, but it was probably no longer than ten minutes."

"When you get to Samar, you might want to talk with Kring and Tikume. We should try to get some idea of just how long those soldiers can function in our air before they start to collapse."

Vanion nodded.

There was really nothing for them to do, and the morning dragged sluggishly by.

It was shortly before noon when Betuana, clad in close-fitting otterskin clothing, came running effortlessly out of the swirling snow. Her almost-inhuman stamina was somehow unnerving. She seemed hardly winded and not even flushed as she entered the room where they waited. "Invigorating," she noted absently as she peeled off her outer garment. She took one lock of her night-dark hair and stretched it out to look critically at its sodden length. "Does anyone have a comb?" she asked.

They all started at the sound of a blaring trumpet fanfare from the other end of the room. They spun around and saw the Child-Goddess. She was surrounded by a nimbus of pure light, she sat sedately in midair, and she was smiling sweetly at Sparhawk. "Is that sort of what you had in mind?" she asked him.

He cast his eyes upward. "Why me?" he groaned. Then he looked at her smiling little face. "I give up, Aphrael," he said. "You win."

"Of course. I always win." She gently settled to the floor, and her light dimmed. "Come here, Betuana. Let me comb that out for you." She held out her hands, and a comb appeared in one and a towel in the other.

The Queen of the Atans went to her and sat in a chair.

"What did he say?" Aphrael asked as she began to wrap Betuana's dripping hair in the length of cloth.

"He said 'no' right at first," the queen replied, "and 'no' the second and third times as well. He started to weaken about the twelfth time, as I remember it."

"I knew it would work." Aphrael smiled, working the towel through Betuana's locks.

"Are we missing something?" Vanion asked her.

"The Atans don't call on their God very often, so he almost *has* to respond when they do. He was probably concentrating on something else and each time Betuana called him, he had to put it down and go see what she wanted."

"I was very polite." Betuana smiled. "But I did keep asking. He's afraid of you, Divine One."

"I know." Aphrael laid down her towel and picked up the comb. "He thinks I'm going to steal his soul or something. He won't come anywhere near me."

"I let him know that I was going to keep on calling him until he gave me permission," Betuana went on, "and he finally gave in."

"They always do." Aphrael shrugged. "You'll get what you want eventually if you just keep asking."

"It's called *nagging,* Divine One," Sparhawk told her.

"How would you like to listen to a few days of trumpet fanfares, Sparhawk?" she asked.

"Ah—no, thanks. It was good of you to ask, though."

"He *definitely* gave his permission?" Aphrael asked the queen.

Betuana smiled. "Very definitely. He said, 'Tell her she can do anything she wants! Just leave me alone!' "

"Good. I'll take Engessa to the island, then." Aphrael pursed her lips. "Maybe you'd better send a runner to your husband. Tell him about Klæl's soldiers. I know your husband, so you'll have to *order* him not to attack them. I've never known *anyone* so totally incapable of turning around as he is."

"I'll *try* to explain it to him," Betuana said a little dubiously.

"Good luck. Here." Aphrael handed over the comb. "I'll take Engessa to the island, thaw him out, and get started."

Ulath called a halt on the outskirts of town, and Bhlokw summoned Ghnomb. The God of Eat appeared holding the half-eaten hindquarter of some large animal in one huge paw.

"We have reached the place where the one called Berit has been told to come," Ulath told the huge Troll-God. "It would be well now if we come out of No-Time and go into the time of broken moments."

Ghnomb gave him a baffled look, clearly not understanding what they were doing.

"U-lat and Tin-in hunt thought," Bhlokw explained. "The man-things have bellies in their minds as well as the bellies in their bellies. They have to fill both bellies. Their belly-bellies are full now. That is why they ask this. It is their wish to now fill their mind-bellies."

A slow look of comprehension began to dawn on Ghnomb's brutish face. "Why did you not say this before, Ulath-from-Thalesia?"

Ulath groped for an answer.

"It was Bhlokw who found that we have mind-bellies." Tynian stepped in. "We did not know this. We only knew that our minds were hungry. It is good that Ghworg sent Bhlokw to hunt with us. Bhlokw is a very good hunter."

Bhlokw beamed.

Ulath quickly expanded the metaphor. "Our mind-bellies hunger for thoughts about the wicked ones," he explained. "We can track those thoughts in the bird-noises the man-things make when they speak. We will stand on one side of the broken moment where they can not see us, and listen to the bird-noises they are making. We will follow those tracks to the ones we hunt, and they will not know we are there. Then we will listen to the bird-noises they make and learn where they have hidden Anakha's mate."

"You hunt well," Ghnomb approved. "I had not thought of this kind of hunting before. It is almost as good as hunting things-to-eat. I will help you in your hunt."

"It makes us glad that you will," Tynian thanked him.

Arjun was the capital of the Kingdom of Arjuna, a substantial city on the south shore of the lake. The royal palace and the stately homes of the noble families of the kingdom lay in the hills on the southern edge of town, and the commercial center was near the lakefront.

Ulath and Tynian concealed their horses and proceeded on foot through the grey half-light of Ghnomb's broken moments into the city itself. Then they split up and began to search for the food their mind-bellies craved. Bhlokw went looking for dogs.

It was almost evening when Ulath came out of another of the seedy taverns near the docks on the east side of town. "This is going to take all month," he muttered to himself. The name *Scarpa* had cropped up in a few of the conversations he had overheard, and each time he heard it, he had eagerly drawn closer to listen. Unfortunately, however, Scarpa and his army were general topics of conversation here, and Ulath had not been able to pick up anything that was at all useful.

"Get out of my way!" The voice was harsh, peremptory. Ulath turned to see who was being so offensive.

The man was a richly dressed Dacite. He was riding a spirited black horse, and his face bore the marks of habitual dissipation.

Though he had never seen the fellow before, Ulath recognized him immediately. Talen's pencil had captured that face almost perfectly. Ulath smiled. "Well, now," he murmured, "that's a little better." He stepped out into the street and followed the prancing black horse.

Their destination was one of the grand houses near the royal palace. A liveried servant rushed from the house to greet the sneering Elene. "We've been eagerly awaiting your arrival, my Lord," he declared, bowing obsequiously.

"Get somebody to take care of my horse," the Elene snapped as he dismounted. "Is everybody here?"

"Yes, Baron Parok."

"Astonishing. Don't just stand there, fool. Take me to them at once."

"Yes, my Lord Baron."

Ulath smiled again and followed them into the house.

The room to which the servant led them appeared to be a study of some kind. The walls were lined with bookcases, though the books shelved there showed no signs of ever having been opened. There were about a dozen men in the room: some Elene, some Arjuni, and even one Styric.

"Let's get down to business," Baron Parok told them, negligently tossing his plumed hat and his gloves down on the table. "What have you to report?"

"Prince Sparhawk has reached Tiana, Baron Parok," the lone Styric told him.

"We expected that."

"We did not, however, expect his treatment of my kinsman. He and that brute he calls his squire followed our messenger and assaulted him. They tore off all his clothes and turned all his pockets inside out."

Parok laughed harshly. "I've met your cousin, Zorek," he said. "I'm sure he richly deserved it. What did he say to the prince to merit such treatment?"

"He gave them the note, my Lord, and that ruffian of a squire made some insulting remark about a twenty-day journey on horseback. My cousin took offense at that and told them that they only had fourteen days to make the journey."

"That was *not* in the instructions," Parok snapped. "Did Sparhawk kill him?"

"No, my lord." Zorek's tone was sullen.

"Pity," Parok said darkly. "Now I'll have to attend to it myself. You Styrics get above yourselves at times. When I have leisure, I'm going to run your cousin down and hang his guts on a fence as an example to the rest of you. You're being paid to do as you're told, not to get creative." He looked around. "Who's got the next note?" he asked.

"I have, my Lord," a rather prosperous-looking Edomishman replied.

"You'd better hold off on delivering it. Zorek's cousin upset our timetable with his excursion into constructive creativity. Let Sparhawk cool his heels here for a week or so. Then give him the note that tells him to go on to Deral. Lord Scarpa wants his army to start moving north before we send Sparhawk on to Natayos for the exchange."

"Baron Parok," a baggy-eyed Arjuni in a brocade doublet said arrogantly, "this delay—particularly here in the capital—poses some threat to my king. This Sparhawk person is notoriously irrational, and he *does* still have the jewel of power in his possession. His Majesty does *not* want that Elene barbarian lingering here in Arjun with spare time on his hands. Send him on to Deral immediately. If he's going to destroy some place, let it be Deral instead of Arjun."

"You have amazingly sharp ears, Duke Milanis," Parok said sardonically. "Can you *really* hear what King Rakya is saying when you're a mile from the palace?"

"I'm here to protect his Majesty's interests, Baron. I have full authority to speak for him. His Majesty's alliance with Lord Scarpa is *not* etched on a diamond. Keep Prince Sparhawk moving. We don't want him here in Arjun."

"And if I don't?"

Milanis shrugged. "His Majesty will abrogate the alliance and make a full report of what you people have been doing—and what you're planning to do—to the Tamul ambassador."

"I see that the old saw about the stupidity of trusting an Arjuni is still true."

"Just do as you're told, Parok," Milanis snapped. "Don't bore me with all these tedious protests and racial slurs. His Majesty's report to the ambassador has already been written. All he requires is an excuse to send it across town."

A servant entered with a flagon and a tray of wineglasses, and Ulath took advantage of the open door to slip from the room. It was going to take a while to round up Tynian and Bhlokw, and then they were going to have to compose a fairly extensive message to Aphrael.

After he had slipped out of the house, however, Sir Ulath very briefly indulged himself. He leapt high into the air with a triumphant bellow, smacking his hands together with glee. Then he composed himself and went looking for his friends.

The black-armored Sir Heldin returned to rejoin Patriarch Bergsten at the head of the column.

"Any luck?" Bergsten asked him.

Heldin shook his head. "Sir Tynian was very thorough," he rumbled in his deep basso. "He winnowed through the ranks of the Pandion Order like a man panning for gold. I think he took just about everybody who can even pronounce the Styric language."

"*You* know the spells."

"Yes, but Aphrael can't hear me. My voice is pitched too low for her ears."

"That raises some very interesting theological points," Bergsten mused.

"Could we ponder them some other time, your Grace? Right now we have to get word of what happened in Zemoch to Sparhawk and Vanion. The war could be over by the time Ambassador Fontan's messengers reach them."

"Talk with the other orders, Heldin," Bergsten suggested.

"I don't think it would work, your Grace. Each order works through the personal God of the Styric who taught them the secrets. We have to get word to Aphrael. *She's* the one who's perched on Sparhawk's shoulder."

"Heldin, you spent too much time practicing with your weapons during your novitiate. Theology *does* have a purpose, you know."

"Yes, your Grace," Heldin sighed, rolling his eyes upward and bracing himself for a sermon.

"Don't do that," Bergsten told him. "I'm not talking about *Elene* theology. I'm talking about the misguided beliefs of the Styrics. How many Styric Gods are there?"

"A thousand, your Grace," Heldin replied promptly. "Sephrenia always made some issue of that."

"Do these thousand Younger Gods exist independently of each other?"

"As I understand it, they're all related—sort of like a family."

"Amazing. You *did* listen when Sephrenia was talking to you. You Pandions all worship Aphrael, right?"

"*Worship* would be too strong a term, your Grace."

"I've heard stories about Aphrael, Heldin." Bergsten smiled. "She has a private agenda. She's trying to steal the whole of humankind. Now then, I'm a member of the Genidian Order." He paused. "I *was*," he corrected himself. "We make our appeals to Hanka; the Cyrinics work through Romalic; and the Alciones deal with Setras. Do you imagine that in their misty heaven somewhere above the clouds these Styric Gods might now and then talk with each other?"

"Please don't beat me over the head, Bergsten. I overlooked something, that's all. I'm not stupid."

"Never said you were, old boy." Bergsten smiled. "You just needed spiritual guidance, that's all. That's the purpose of our Holy Mother. Come to *me* with your spiritual problems, my son. I will gently guide you—and if guidance doesn't work, I'll take my ax and drive you."

"I see that your Grace adheres to the notion of the Church Muscular," Heldin said sourly.

"That's *my* spiritual problem, my son, not yours. Now go find an Alcione. Legend has it that Aphrael and Setras are particularly close. I think we can count on Setras to pass things along to his thieving little cousin."

"*Your Grace!*" Heldin protested.

"The Church has had her eye on Aphrael for centuries, Heldin. We know all about your precious little Child-Goddess and her tricks. Don't let her kiss you, my friend. If you do, she'll pinch your soul while you're not looking."

There were a dozen wobbly oxcarts this time, all heavily laden with beer barrels, and Senga had recruited several dozen of Narstil's shabby outlaws to assist him in guarding and dispensing his product. Kalten had rather smoothly insinuated Caalador and Bevier into the company.

"I still think you're making a mistake, Senga," Kalten told his good-natured employer as their rickety cart jolted along the rough jungle path toward Natayos. "You've got a complete lock on the market. Why lower your prices?"

"Because I'll make more money if I do."

"That doesn't make sense."

"Look, Col," Senga explained patiently, "when I came here before, I only had one cartload of beer. I could get any price I asked, because my beer was so scarce."

"I guess that makes sense."

"I've got an almost unlimited supply now, though, so I'm making my profit on volume instead of price."

"That's what doesn't make sense."

"Let me put it this way. Which would you rather do—steal ten crowns from one man or a penny from each of ten thousand men?"

Kalten did some quick counting on his fingers. "Oh," he said. "Now I see what you're driving at. Very shrewd, Senga."

Senga puffed himself up a little. "It never hurts to think long-range, Col. My *real* concern is the fact that it's not really all that hard to make beer. If some clever fellow's got a recipe, he could set up his own brewery right here. I don't want to get involved in a price war just when things are starting to go well for me."

They had left Narstil's camp at daybreak, and so it was midmorning when they reached Natayos. They passed unchallenged through the gates, rumbled by the house with barred windows, and set up shop again in the same square as before. As Senga's closest associate, Kalten had been promoted to the position of Chief of Security. The reputation for unpleasantness he had established early on in Narstil's camp ensured that none of the outlaws would question his orders, and the presence of Bevier, patch-eyed, lochaber-armed, and obviously homicidal, added to his authority.

"We ain't likely t' accomplish too much here, Col," Caalador muttered to Kalten as the two of them stood guard near one of the busy beer carts. "Ol' Senga's so worried 'bout some feller slippin' by 'thout payin' that me'n you is tied down tighter'n a couple o' dawgs on short leashes."

"Wait until later, Ezek," Kalten advised. "We'll be able to move around a little more freely after everybody gets drunk."

Bevier slouched over to join them, his short-handled lochaber in his fist. People automatically got out of his way for some reason. "I just had a thought," he said.

"You want to kill somebody?" Kalten suggested.

"Be serious, Col. Why don't you take your friend Senga aside and suggest that he set up a permanent establishment here in Natayos? It's the logical thing to do, and it'd give the three of us an excuse to stay here. If we cleaned out one of these ruined buildings and opened a tavern, we could stay here and run it. It makes more sense than selling beer off the tailgate of an oxcart."

"He's got hisself a point there, Col," Caalador said. "Ol' Shallag here, he *looks* like he drinks blood for breakfast, but his head's still a-workin' in back o' that there eye patch."

Kalten thought about it. "It *would* set us up right here in Natayos, wouldn't it? We'd be able to keep an eye on things." He looked around. "Senga's a little worried that somebody here might start his own brewery," he said for the benefit of nearby soldiers. "If the three of us are right here, we could probably persuade anybody who does that to take up another hobby. I'll go talk with Senga and see what he thinks of the notion."

He found his good-natured friend sitting at a makeshift table behind one of the oxcarts. The outlaw was counting money with an almost dreamy expression on his face. "Oh, this is just *fine*, Col," he almost crooned.

"They're only pennies."

"I know, but there are so *many* of them."

"Shallag came up with an idea."

"He wants to thin out the crowd by hacking the head off every third man in line?"

"Shallag's not really *that* bad."

"Oh, really? Every man in camp has nightmares about him."

"He hasn't killed a single man since he came to Arjuna."

"He's saving up. He's just biding his time until he can gather up a few dozen of us all together and kill all of us at once."

"Do you want to listen to his idea, or haven't you finished making bad jokes yet?"

"Sorry. Go ahead."

"He thinks we ought to clean out one of these empty ruins and set up a permanent tavern."

"You mean like a real business? With a counter and tables and chairs and all that?"

"Why not? Now that your brewer's working full-time, you've got access to a steady supply, and this is where your customers are. If you set up shop here, you can sell beer all day every day instead of just coming here once a week. Then your customers would come to you in manageable numbers instead of by the regiment."

"I never thought of it," Senga admitted. "I just thought I'd make a quick profit and then run for the border. I could set up a real tavern here, Col—a real, honest-to-God legitimate business. I wouldn't have to steal anymore."

"I've seen your price list, Senga. Don't worry. You're still stealing."

Senga ignored him. "Maybe I could call it 'Senga's Palace,' " he said in a dreamy tone of voice. He frowned. "No," he decided. "That's a little too flashy for a beer tavern. I think I'll just call it 'Senga's.' That'd definitely be a more lasting memorial than just a grave marker with the date when I got hung carved on it." Then he shook his head and sighed. "No, Col," he said regretfully. "It wouldn't work. If I took you and my other guards out of here, Scarpa's soldiers would just march in and drink up all my beer without paying."

"Why take us out, then? We can stay right here and make sure they pay."

"I'm not sure Narstil would like it if we didn't go back to camp at night."

"Senga," Kalten said gently, "do you really need Narstil anymore? You're an honest businessman now. You shouldn't be associating with bandits."

Senga laughed. "You're coming at me a little too fast, Col. Give me some time to adjust my thinking." Then he suddenly swore.

"What's wrong?"

"It's a beautiful idea, Col, but it won't work."

"Why not?"

"Because I'll need Scarpa's permission to set up shop here, and I'm not going to go anywhere near him to ask for it."

"I don't think you'll have to, my friend. I went rummaging around through those heaps of trash in Narstil's camp yesterday, and guess what I found?"

"What?"

"A very fancy, silver-mounted cask of Arcian red. It's even equipped with a silver spigot. The fellow who stole it didn't know how much it was worth—he's a beer man. I got it off him for half a crown. I'll sell it to you, and you can make a present of it to that Krager fellow. Why don't we let *him* persuade Scarpa to give you permission to go into business here?"

"Col, you're a genius! What'll you take for that cask of Arcian red?"

"Oh—five crowns, I guess."

"*Five crowns?* Ten times what you paid for it? That's robbery!"

"You ought to know, Senga. You're my friend, but business is business, after all."

They found the bleary-eyed Krager sitting on a broken wall watching the crowd of thirsty soldiers in the square without much interest. He held a tankard in one hand and he drank from it occasionally with obvious distaste.

"Ah, there you are, Master Krager," Senga said jovially. "Why don't you dump out that slop and try a sup of this?" He patted the ornate wine cask he was carrying under one arm.

"More local swill?" Krager asked.

"Try it and see what you think," Senga suggested.

Krager emptied his wine out on the ground and held out his pewter tankard. Senga turned the handle of the silver spigot and dribbled about a half cupful of Arcian red into it.

Krager squinted into his mug and sniffed at it suspiciously. Then his eyes rolled up ecstatically. "Oh, dearie, dearie me!" he breathed in a reverent tone of voice. He took a small sip and actually seemed to quiver with delight.

"I thought you might like it," Senga said. "Now that I've got your attention, I've got a business proposition for you. I'd like to set up a permanent tavern here in Natayos, but I'll need permission to do that. I'd take it as a real favor if you could see your way clear to put in a good word for me with Lord Scarpa. I'd be very grateful to you if you can get his approval."

"*How* grateful?" Krager asked quickly.

"Probably about *this* grateful." Senga patted the silver-mounted cask again. "Tell Lord Scarpa that I won't cause any problems. I'll pick one of these empty buildings a little way off from his main camp and clean it out and fix the roof my very own self. I'll provide my own security and make sure that none of his soldiers gets *too* drunk."

"Go ahead and get started, Master Senga," Krager said, eyeing the cask. "You've got my personal guarantee that Lord Scarpa will agree." He reached out for the wine.

Senga stepped back. "*After*, Master Krager," he said firmly. "At the moment, I'm filled with appreciation. The gratitude comes *after* Scarpa gives his permission."

Then Elron came hurrying across the crowded square. "Krager!" he said in a shrill voice. "Come at once! Lord Scarpa's in a rage! He's commanded us all to meet him at headquarters immediately!"

"What's the matter?" Krager rose to his feet.

"Cyzada just came in from Cynesga. He told Zalasta and Lord Scarpa that Klæl went to have a look at the fellow we've been following all this time! It's not Sparhawk, Krager! Whoever it is *looks* like Sparhawk, but Klæl knew immediately that it's somebody else!"

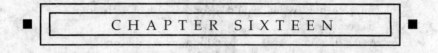

CHAPTER SIXTEEN

"I *know* it's him, my Lady," Alean insisted.

"Alean, dear," Ehlana said gently, "he doesn't look the least bit like Sir Kalten."

"I don't know how they've done it, but that's Kalten out there in the street," the girl replied. "My heart sings every time he walks by."

Ehlana peered through the little opening in the window. The man *looked* like an Elene, there was no question about that, and Sephrenia *was* a magician, after all.

The thought of Sephrenia filled the queen's eyes with tears again. She straightened, quickly wiping her eyes. "He's gone by," she said. "What makes you so sure, dear?"

"A thousand things, my Lady—little things. It's the way he holds his head, that funny way he rolls his shoulders when he walks, his laugh, the way he hitches up his sword belt. They've changed his face somehow, but I know it's him."

"You *could* be right, Alean," Ehlana concluded a bit dubiously. "I could probably pick Sparhawk out of a crowd no matter *whose* face he happened to be wearing."

"Exactly, my Lady. Our hearts know the men we love."

Ehlana began to pace the floor, her fingers absently adjusting the wimple that covered her head. "It's not impossible," she conceded. "Sparhawk's told me about all the times he disguised himself when he was in Rendor, and Styric magic might very well be able to change people's faces. And of course, if Sephrenia hadn't been able to do it, Bhelliom certainly could have. Let's trust your heart and say that it is Sir Kalten out there."

"I *know* it is, my Lady."

"It *does* stand to reason," Ehlana mused. "If Sparhawk's somehow found out that we're here, he'd most *definitely* want to have some of our friends close by when the rest of them come to rescue us." She frowned as a thought came to her. "Maybe he *doesn't* know for sure, though. Kalten *might* just be here to look around. We have to come up with some way to let him know that we're here before he gives up and moves on."

"But, my Lady," the girl with the huge eyes protested, "if we try to call out to him, we'll put him in terrible danger." She bent and looked out at the street again. "He's coming back," she said.

"Sing, Alean!" Ehlana exclaimed suddenly.

"What?"

"Sing! If anyone in the whole world would recognize your voice, Kalten would!"

Alean's eyes suddenly widened. "He *would*!" she exclaimed.

"Here. Let me watch his face. Sing your soul out, Alean! Break his heart!"

Alean's voice throbbed as her clear soprano reached effortlessly up in aching song. She sang "My Bonnie Blue-Eyed Boy," a very old ballad which Ehlana knew held special significance for her maid and the blond Pandion. The queen looked out the window again. The roughly dressed man in the street was standing stock-still, frozen in place by Alean's soaring voice.

All doubt vanished from Ehlana's mind. It was Kalten! His eyes streamed tears, and his expression had become exalted, adoring.

And then he did something so unexpected that Ehlana was forced to revise her long-held opinion about his intelligence. He sat down on the mossy cobblestones, removed one shoe, and began to whistle an accompaniment to Alean's song. He *knew*! And he was whistling to let them know that he knew! Not even Sparhawk could have responded so quickly, or come up with so perfect a way to convey his understanding of the situation.

"That's enough, Alean," Ehlana hissed. "He got our message."

Alean stopped singing.

"What are you doing there?" one of the Arjunis who guarded the door demanded, coming into view.

"Stone in my shoe," Kalten explained, shaking the shoe he'd just removed. "It felt like a boulder."

"All right, move on."

Kalten's altered features took on a truculent look. He pulled his shoe back on and stood up. "Friend," he said in a pointed sort of way, "you'll be getting off duty before very long, and you might just decide to stop by Senga's tavern for a few tankards of beer. I'm in charge of security there, and if you start pushing me around *here*, I might just decide that you're too rowdy to be served when you get *there*. Understand?"

"I'm supposed to keep people away from this building," the guard explained, quickly modifying his tone.

"But politely, friend, politely. Every man in this whole place is armed to the teeth, so we all have to be polite to each other." Kalten threw a guarded glance at the barred window from which Ehlana watched. "I learned politeness when I took up with Shallag—you know him, don't you? The one-eyed fellow with the lochaber ax?"

The guard shuddered. "Is he as bad as he looks?" he asked.

"Worse. He'll hack your head off if you even sneeze on him." Kalten squared his shoulders. "Well, I guess I'd better be getting back to the tavern. As my friend Ezek says, ' 'Tain't hordly likely that I'll make no profit lollygaggin' around in the street.' Come on by the tavern when you get off work, friend. I'll buy you a tankard of beer." And he went off down the street, still whistling "My Bonnie Blue-Eyed Boy."

"Treasure him, Alean," Ehlana said, her heart still soaring, "and don't let that face deceive you. He gave me more information in two minutes than Sparhawk could have in an hour."

"My Lady?" Alean looked baffled.

"He knows that we're here. He started to whistle along while you were singing. He also told me that Sir Bevier and Caalador are here with him."

"How did he do that?"

"He was talking with the guard. Bevier's probably the only man in Daresia right now with a lochaber ax, and his other friend sounds just like Caalador. They know we're here, Alean, and if they know, Sparhawk knows. We might as well start packing. We'll be leaving here shortly and going back to Matherion." She laughed delightedly and threw her arms around her maid.

Kalten tried very hard to keep his face expressionless as he walked back along the moss-covered streets toward Senga's tavern, but the excitement kept bubbling up in him, and it was very difficult to keep from laughing out loud.

Scarpa's army had cleared the northern quarters of Natayos and restored the buildings there to some degree of habitability when they had first arrived, but most of the city was still a vine-choked ruin. Senga had considered several possible sites for his tavern and had rather shrewdly decided to set up operations some distance deeper into the old city to avoid interference from officious sergeants or junior Elene officers with deep convictions and not much sense. He had chosen a low, squat building with thick walls but no roof, a deficiency easily overcome with tent canvas. He had considered hiring off-duty soldiers to clear the brush out of the street leading from Scarpa's main camp to the tavern door, but Caalador had per-suaded him to save his money. "Ther ain't no need, Senga," the disguised Cammo-rian had told the harried businessman, reverting to his dialect. "Them thirsty soldiers'll clear the street fer us ther very own-selfs 'thout no money changin' hands a-tall." The tavern crouched in the ruins, indistinguishable from nearby buildings except for its canvas roof and the crudely lettered sign reading SENGA'S out front.

Kalten entered the tavern through the side door and paused to let his eyes ad-just to the dimmer light. The place was moderately crowded, even at midday, and the six aproned outlaws from Narstil's camp hustled back and forth behind a rough plank counter, drawing foamy beer and collecting money.

Kalten pushed through the noisy crowd, looking for Bevier and Caalador. He found them sitting at a table on the near side of the room. Bevier's sawed-off locha-ber and Caalador's stout cudgel lay in plain sight on the table as a sort of constant reminder to the assembled revelers that while having a good time was encouraged, there *were* strictly enforced limits.

Kalten carefully lowered himself onto the bench, keeping his exuberance tightly bottled in. He leaned forward, motioning his friends closer. "They're here," he said quietly.

Caalador looked around the tavern. "Wal," he drawled, "not quite *all* of 'em, but most likely ever'body who's off duty."

"I'm not talking about this crowd, Ezek. I'm talking about the house with the barred windows. The people we've been looking for are definitely inside that house."

"How do you know?" Bevier demanded in an intense whisper. "Did you see them?"

"I didn't have to. One of them is a very special friend of mine, and this friend recognized me—even with this face. Don't ask me how."

"Are you sure?" Bevier pressed.

"Oh, yes. This friend started to sing in a voice I'd recognize in the middle of a thunderstorm. It was a very old song that has a personal meaning for the two of us. Our friends inside recognized me, there's no question about it. This friend I was just talking about only sings that song for me."

"I don't suppose there was any way you could let them know that you'd received their message?" Caalador asked. "Short of tearing down the door, I mean?"

"No, I didn't have to tear down the door. I whistled along. I've done that before, so my friend knew what I was trying to say. Then I struck up a conversation with one of the guards, and I slipped in enough hints to let our friends inside know the things they ought to be aware of."

Caalador leaned back in his chair. "Yer idee 'bout this yere tavern's workin' out real good, Shallag. We bin a-pickin' up all sorts o' useful information since we settled in."

Kalten looked around the tavern. "Things are quiet right now," he said quietly. "The fights probably won't start until the sun goes down. Why don't we take a stroll back into the ruins? I think we'd better have another chat with that certain little girl. This time we've got some *good* news for her."

"Let's get at it," Caalador said, rising to his feet. He pushed his way through to the counter, spoke briefly with one of the foam-soaked outlaws, and then led the way outside. They went around behind the tavern and pushed their way along a vine-choked side street that ran past some fallen buildings where bright-colored birds perched, squawking raucously. They went into a partially collapsed ruin, and Kalten and Caalador stood watch while Bevier cast the spell.

The Cyrinic was grinning when he came out. "You'd better brace yourself, Kalten," he said.

"What for?"

"Aphrael plans to kiss you into insensibility the next time she sees you."

"I suppose I can live with that. I gather she was pleased?"

"She almost ruptured my eardrums."

"Well, as she always says, 'We only live to please those we love.' "

Scarpa was screaming even before he came through the door. His voice was high and shrill, his eyes bulged, and his makeshift crown was askew. He was clearly in the throes of hysterical rage. His lips and beard were flecked with foam as he burst into the room. "Your husband has betrayed you, woman!" he shrieked at Ehlana. "You will pay for his perfidy! I will have your life for this!" He started toward her, his hands extended like claws.

Then Zalasta was in the doorway. "No!" he barked in an icy tone.

Scarpa spun on his father. "Stay out of this!" he shrieked. "She is *my* prisoner! I will punish her for Sparhawk's treachery!"

"No, actually you won't. You'll do as I tell you to do." Zalasta spoke in Elenic, and all traces of his accent were gone now.

"He disobeyed my orders! I will make him pay!"

"Are you so stupid that you didn't expect this? I *told* you how devious the man was, but your mind's so clogged with cobwebs that you wouldn't listen."

"I gave him an *order!*" Scarpa's voice had risen to a squeal. He stamped his foot. Then he stamped the other. Then he began jumping up and down on the floor, quite literally dancing with fury. "I am the *emperor!* He *must* obey me!"

Zalasta did not even bother to use magic this time. He simply swung his staff and knocked his hysterical son to the floor, sending his crown rolling. "You sicken me," he said in a voice loaded with contempt. "I have no patience with these temper tantrums. You are *not* the emperor. When you're in this condition, you're not even meaningful." His face was unemotional, and his eyes were remote. "Have a care, Scarpa," he said in a dreadful voice. "There's nothing in this world that I love now. You have freed me from all human attachments. If you annoy me, I'll squash you like a bug."

Scarpa scrambled away from the terrible old man, flecks of foam speckling his face.

"What's happened?" Ehlana asked anxiously.

"One of my associates—Cyzada of Esos—just arrived from Cynesga," Zalasta replied calmly. "He brought us some news that we probably should have expected. Your husband's a devious man, Ehlana. We thought that we had him, but he managed to wriggle free."

"I don't understand."

"We left him instructions when we abducted you. He was supposed to take his squire and set out on horseback for the town of Beresa in southern Arjuna. We had people watching, and he *seemed* to be obeying. He was *not,* however. Evidently he's not as fond of you as we'd thought he was."

"He was simply following my orders, Zalasta. I told him that under no circumstances was he to give up the Bhelliom."

"How did you manage that?" Zalasta seemed actually startled.

"Your lunatic son here told Elron to kill Baroness Melidere. Elron's a hopeless incompetent, so Melidere was able to deflect his sword thrust. I have some remarkable people working for me, Zalasta. Melidere was able to play dead very convincingly. I feigned hysteria and managed to whisper instructions to her while I covered her with a blanket." She gave him a rather malicious sidelong glance. "Your mind must be slipping, Zalasta. You didn't even notice that I no longer had my ring. I left *that* with Melidere as well."

"Very resourceful, Ehlana," he murmured. "You and your husband are stimulating opponents."

"I'm so glad you approve. How did Sparhawk trick you?"

"We're not entirely sure. We had people watching him from the moment he left the imperial compound in Matherion, and he followed our orders to the letter. We even diverted him a couple of times to prevent any tricks. Then Klæl escaped again and went looking for Bhelliom. The man we *thought* was Sparhawk was on a ship crossing the Sea of Arjun with his squire, Khalad. Klæl took one look and instantly knew that the man who *appeared* to be your husband was *not* Anakha. That's the news that Cyzada just brought to us."

She smiled almost beatifically at him. "And so now Sparhawk's out there some-where—with Bhelliom in his fist and murder in his heart—and you haven't the faintest idea of where he might be, and quite probably not even what he looks like. You've got a big problem, Zalasta."

"You're very quick, your Majesty. You think even faster than my colleagues."

"That isn't very difficult. You're surrounded with defectives. Which particular stroke of my genius is it that you admire?"

He smiled faintly. "I rather like you, Ehlana," he told her. "You have spirit. My assorted defectives haven't yet fully grasped the implications of your husband's ploy. If he's somehow managed to make someone resemble him, he's surely able to alter his own features as well."

"He does it all the time, Zalasta. He had a great deal of experience with dis-guises when he was in Rendor. It's all falling apart on you, isn't it? I'd suggest that you start running immediately."

"I'll be leaving shortly, right enough, but *you'll* be going with me. Tell your maid to start making preparations for a journey."

"What are you saying?" Scarpa scrambled to his feet. "She *can't* leave here!" he shrieked. "We're going to make the exchange here!"

"You imbecile," Zalasta sneered. "You didn't *really* think I was going to let you go through with that, did you? I never had any intention of letting you get within five miles of Bhelliom."

Scarpa gaped at him.

"It was a misguided attempt to save your life, idiot. Bhelliom would have de-stroyed you in the instant that you touched it."

"Not if I had the rings. They would have protected me." Scarpa's eyes were wild again.

"The rings are a fraud." Zalasta sneered. "They have no power over Bhelliom whatsoever."

"You're lying!"

"You desperately want to believe that, don't you, Scarpa? You thought that all you had to do to gain control of the most powerful force in the universe was to put on a pair of rings. Ghwerig the Troll-Dwarf made the rings at Bhelliom's instruc-tion. They were designed to deceive a *Troll* into thinking he had some power over the jewel. *Bhelliom* induced Ghwerig to make the rings, and then it tricked Aphrael into stealing them. Everyone's attention was so fixed on the rings that we didn't even bother trying to steal Bhelliom from the royal crown of Thalesia."

Scarpa suddenly sneered. "You just outsmarted yourself, old man. If Bhelliom's so deadly, how is it that the kings of Thalesia could touch it and not die?"

"Because Bhelliom's *alive*, you dolt. It has an awareness. It kills only those it *wants* to kill—and that would certainly include you. You're my son, and even *I* want to kill you most of the time. You had some deranged, half-formed notion that you could just pick up Bhelliom and start giving it commands, didn't you?"

Scarpa flushed guiltily.

"Can't you get it through your sick head that only a God—or Anakha—can safely take up Bhelliom and start giving it orders? I realized that over a century ago. Why do you think I made an alliance with Azash—or with Cyrgon? Did you think

I was having religious yearnings?" He smiled a cruel smile. "Did you really think Bhelliom would have made you a match for me, Scarpa? You were going to put on the rings, snatch up the Bhelliom, and order it to kill me, weren't you? I almost wish the situation were different. I'd have loved to have seen the expression on your face as Bhelliom slowly turned you to stone." Zalasta straightened. "Enough of this," he said. He went to the door. "Come in here," he barked, "all of you."

The men who entered were fearful and hesitant as they sidled through the door. Krager appeared to have been frightened to the point that he was sober, and Elron was actually cringing. The third man was a stringy-looking Styric with a long beard, shaggy eyebrows, and sunken, burning eyes.

"All right, gentlemen," Zalasta said, "this new development calls for a change of plans. My son and I have discussed the matter, and he's evidently decided that he wants to go on living, because he's agreed to follow my instructions. I'm going to take the queen and her maid to a safe place. Natayos is no longer secure. Sparhawk could literally be anywhere. For all I know, he's already here. I want you three to stay here with Scarpa. Keep sending those letters of instruction to this counterfeit Sparhawk. Don't let our enemies know that we're onto them. Give me a couple of days and then send instructions to Panem-Dea. Tell them to prepare suitable quarters for two very important ladies. Then wait two more days and send a closed carriage down there. Security's an alien concept to those cretins at Panem-Dea, so word of your message will be all over southern Arjuna almost before your messenger arrives. Cyzada, I want you to keep a close watch over my deranged son here. If he doesn't follow my instructions to the letter, I want you to summon one of the servants of Azash from the netherworld to kill him. Be creative, old boy. Pick the cruelest and most hideous demon you can find. If Scarpa disobeys me again, I want him to take a long, long time to die, and I want them to be able to hear him screaming all the way from here to Matherion."

Cyzada's dead eyes came alight with a sudden cruel anticipation. He fixed a ghastly smile on the now totally rational Scarpa. "I'll see to it, Zalasta," he promised in a hollow voice. "I know just the one to call on."

Scarpa shrank back fearfully.

"Where are you going to take the prisoners, Lord Zalasta?" Elron quavered. "Where can you be safe from that vengeful monster they call Anakha?"

"You don't need to know that, Elron," Zalastra replied. "The Pandions have a reputation for severity when they interrogate prisoners. You won't be able to tell them what you don't know—even when they start to torture you."

"Torture?" Elron's eyes widened, and his voice came out in a terrified squeak.

"This is the real world, Elron, not some romanticized daydream. The posturing and play-acting are over now, but I'm sure we'll all be impressed by how heroically you endure the agonies they'll surely inflict on you when they catch you."

Elron fell back in a near faint.

Her Royal Highness, Crown Princess Danae of Elenia, sat pensively on an out-of-the-way window seat on one of the upper floors of her mother's castle. The weather outside was unsettled, and a blustery wind skipped the dead leaves across the lawns below like scurrying brown mice. Danae absently stroked her purring cat as she considered options, alternatives, and possibilities.

Mirtai, grim, implacable, and wearing an Atan breastplate of polished steel and black leather, stood several yards down the corridor, her face set in an expression of sullen obedience and her hand on her sword hilt.

"You're still angry with me, aren't you?" Danae asked the golden giantess, not even bothering to turn around.

"It's not my place to either approve or disapprove of my owner." Mirtai was being stubborn about it.

"Oh, stop that. Come here."

Mirtai marched up the hall to where her capricious little owner was sitting. "Yes?"

"I'm going to try again. Please listen to me this time."

"As your Majesty commands."

"That's getting very tiresome, you know. We love you, Mirtai."

"Is your Majesty speaking in the royal plural?"

"You're starting to make me cross. I've got a name, and you know what it is. We all love you, and it would have broken our hearts if you'd decided to kill yourself. I spoke to you the way I did to bring you to your senses, you ninny."

"I know why you did it, Danae, but did you have to humiliate me in front of the others?"

"I apologize."

"You can't do that. You're a queen, and queens can't apologize."

"I can if I want." Danae paused. "So there," she added.

Mirtai laughed and suddenly embraced the little girl. "You're never going to learn how to be a queen, Danae."

"Oh, I don't know. Being the queen just means that you get what you want. I do that all the time anyway. I don't need a crown or an army for something as simple as that."

"You're a very spoiled little girl, your Majesty."

"I know, and I love every minute of it."

Then the princess heard a faint, faraway murmur, a murmur that Mirtai could not, of course, even sense. "Why don't you go find Melidere?" she suggested. She sighed and rolled her eyes upward. "I'm sure she's looking for me anyway. It's probably time for another one of those girl lessons."

"She's giving you instruction in courtly manners and traditional courtesies, Danae," Mirtai reproved her. "If you're going to be a queen, you'll need to know those things."

"I think it's silly, myself. Go on ahead, Mirtai. I'll be along in a minute."

The giantess went off down the hall, and Princess Danae spoke very quietly. "What is it, Setras?" she asked the empty air.

"You already know the courtesies, Aphrael," her curly-haired cousin said, appearing suddenly beside her. "Why are you taking lessons?"

"It gives Melidere something to occupy her mind with and keeps her out of mischief. I spent a great deal of time and effort getting her and Stragen together. I don't want her to spoil it by getting bored and starting to look for outside entertainment."

"That's very important to you, isn't it?" Setras sounded a little puzzled. "Why should the things they do to perpetuate themselves interest you at all?"

"You probably wouldn't understand, Setras. You're too young."

"I'm as old as you are."

"Yes, but you don't pay any attention to what your worshippers are doing when they're alone together."

"I know what they're doing. It's ridiculous."

"*They* seem to like it."

"Flowers are much more dignified about it," he sniffed.

"Is this what you wanted to talk to me about?"

"Oh, I almost forgot. I have a message for you. There's an Alcione Knight— one of the ones who serve *me*. I think you know him. He's a moon-faced fellow named Tynian."

"Yes."

"He went back to Chyrellos to pick up some help, and it seems that he inadvertently chose every Pandion skilled enough to pass messages on to you and brought them all to this part of the world, so there wasn't anybody with the Church Knights to tell you what happened in Zemoch."

"Yes, I already know about that. Anakha's going to talk with Tynian about that. What happened in Zemoch?"

"The Church Knights had an encounter with Klæl. A third of them were killed."

Aphrael unleashed a blistering string of curses.

"Aphrael!" he gasped. "You're not supposed to talk that way!"

"Oh, go bury it, Setras! Why didn't you tell me about this as soon as you got here?"

"I was curious about the other thing," he confessed. "It's not as if they *all* got killed, Aphrael. There are still plenty of them left. In a little while there'll be as many as before. They're ferociously prolific."

"I love them *all,* you dolt! I don't want to lose any of them."

"You're greedy. That's one of your shortcomings, cousin. You can't keep them *all,* you know."

"Don't make any wagers on that, Setras. I'm only just getting started." She threw her hands in the air. "This is impossible! You don't even understand the message you're trying to give me. Where are the Church Knights now?"

"They're coming across the steppes of central Astel to invade Cynesga. They'll probably run into Klæl again when they get there. I hope they don't *all* get killed."

"Who's in command?"

"One of Romalic's servants—an old man called Abriel—was in charge when they left Chyrellos, but he got killed in Zemoch, so one of the high priests of the Church of the Elene God—a Thalesian named Bergsten—is giving orders now."

"I should have guessed," she said. "I have a few things to take care of first. Then I'll go find Bergsten and get a true account of what happened."

"I was *only* trying to help." Setras sounded a little injured.

"You did just fine, cousin." Aphrael forgave him. "It's not your fault that you haven't been keeping abreast of things here."

"I have important things on my mind, Aphrael," he said defensively. "Come by my studio sometime," he added brightly. "I made a sunset the other day that's probably one of the best pieces I've ever done. It's so lovely that I've decided to keep it."

"Setras! You can't just stop the sun that way!"

"There's nobody living there, Aphrael. They won't notice."

"Oh, dear!" She buried her face in her hands.

"You're disappointed in me, aren't you?" His lower lip trembled slightly, and his large, luminous eyes filled with sudden tears. "And I try so hard to make you and the others proud of me."

"No, Setras," she said. "I still love you."

He brightened. "Everything's all right, then, isn't it?"

"You're a dear, Setras." She kissed him. "Run along now. I have to talk with these others."

"You *will* come and look at my sunset, won't you?"

"Of course, cousin. Go along now." She lifted her drowsing cat and blew into the furry creature's ear. "Wake up, Mmrr," she said.

The yellow eyes opened.

"Go back to the place where we nest," the little princess said, speaking in cat. "I have to do something." She set Mmrr down on the floor, and the cat arched her back, hooking her tail into a sinuous question mark, and yawned. Then she padded off down the corridor.

Danae looked around, probing with eyes and mind to make certain she was alone. There were human males knocking around the halls of this castle, and the appearance of a naked Goddess always excited the males. It was flattering, of course, but it was also a little confusing for a being with a total lack of any reproductive urges. No matter how hard she tried, Aphrael had never been able to understand how the mating impulse of human males could be so indiscriminate.

The Child-Goddess briefly resumed her true person and then divided, becoming both little girls.

"You're starting to get older, Danae," Flute noted.

"Does it show? Already?"

"It's noticeable. You still have a way to go before you're fully mature, though. Are you really sure you want to go through with this?"

"It might help us all to understand them a little better. I don't think Setras even knows that it takes a male and a female to—well, you know." Danae blushed.

"Setras isn't overly bright. Can I borrow Mirtai?" Flute asked.

"What for?"

"You don't really need her here, and after what happened in Dirgis, I'd like to have somebody I trust to stand guard over Sephrenia."

"Good idea. Let's go talk with Sarabian and the others. They'll be able to send messengers to people we don't have any contacts with."

Flute nodded. "It would be *so* much more convenient if they were *all* ours."

Danae laughed. "I think Setras was right. We *are* greedy, aren't we?"

"We love them all, Danae. I don't see any reason why they can't love us."

The two little girls started off down the corridor hand in hand. "Danae," Flute said, "do you think Mirtai might be afraid of heights?"

"He *does* look a lot like that picture Talen drew, doesn't he?" Tynian murmured to Ulath.

"Very close," Ulath agreed. "That boy has a tremendous talent."

"Yes. He draws well, too."

Ulath laughed shortly. Then he looked at the men clustered around Parok and drew Tynian a little farther away from them. "Parok's giving all the orders," he whispered, "but the Arjuni in the flamboyant doublet speaks for King Rakya."

"Sarabian's going to be very put out with the King of Arjun."

Ulath nodded. "I wouldn't be at all surprised to see a new king on the throne before long."

"What exactly did Parok say about Natayos? You couldn't have mistaken his meaning, could you?"

"Not a chance, Tynian. Just before he got into the argument with Duke Milanis, Parok said that Scarpa wanted to move his army out of Natayos before they gave Sparhawk the last note. I almost started cheering when he said that they were going to tell Sparhawk to go to Natayos for the exchange."

"We'll have to be careful, though. They *could* be holding Ehlana someplace else. They may not take her to Natayos until the last minute."

"We'll find out for sure once Xanetia goes there." Ulath shrugged.

The door to the book-lined room opened, and a liveried servant hurried in. "An important message has arrived from Natayos, Baron," he told Parok. "The messenger rode his horse half to death."

"Horses are cheap. Send the fellow in."

"I could learn to dislike that man," Tynian murmured.

"I already do," Ulath replied. He looked up speculatively. "We're sort of invisible, aren't we?" he asked.

"That's what Ghnomb says."

"Can you imagine the expression Parok would get on his face if he suddenly got ripped up the front with an invisible knife?"

"Slowly," Tynian added. "Very, very slowly."

The messenger from Natayos was a shabbily dressed Dacite, and he was reeling with exhaustion as he staggered into the room. "Baron," he gasped. "Thank God I found you."

"Speak up, man!"

"Could I have a drink of water?"

"Talk first. Then you can drink anything you want."

"Lord Scarpa ordered me to tell you that the man you've been watching *isn't* Sparhawk."

"I see that Scarpa's finally gone completely mad."

"No, Baron. Zalasta confirmed it. Somebody they call Klæl went and had a look at this man you've been giving the notes to. They seemed to think you'd know who this Klæl fellow is. Anyway, he sent word that the man with the broken nose *looks* like Sparhawk, but it's not really him. This Klæl must have some way to know for sure."

Parok began to swear sulfurously.

"That tears it," Tynian growled. "I'll pass this on to Aphrael. We'd better get Berit and Khalad to safety."

"Did Scarpa kill Sparhawk's wife?" Baron Parok asked the messenger.

"No, my Lord Baron. He was going to, but Zalasta stopped him. I'm supposed to tell you not to do anything to let the imposter know that we're onto him. Zalasta needs some time to move the prisoners to someplace that's safe. He wants you to continue as if nothing had happened. After he has those two women clear, he'll get word to you that it's all right to kill the man who's posing as Sparhawk."

"Zalasta's in full command then?"

"Yes, Baron Parok. Lord Scarpa's a bit—ah—distraught, I suppose you might say."

"You might say crazy, too. That'd be more accurate." Parok started to pace the floor. "I wondered how much it would take to push Scarpa over the edge," he muttered. "It's probably better this way. Zalasta's a Styric, but at least his head's on straight. Go back and tell him that I've received his message and that I won't do anything to upset his plans. Let him know that I have no real fondness for Scarpa and that I'll be completely loyal to him."

"I will, my Lord Baron."

Duke Milanis rose and crossed the room to close the window. "What in God's name is that awful smell?" he exclaimed.

Tynian turned and saw the hulking Troll standing just behind them. "Bhlokw," he said, "it is not good that you come into the dens of the man-things this way."

"I was sent by Khwaj, Tin-in," Bhlokw explained. "Khwaj grows tired of waiting. He wants to burn the wicked ones always."

Then their dim half moment suddenly filled with smoke, and the enormous presence of the Fire-God was there. "Your hunt takes too long, Ulath-from-Thalesia. Have you found any of the wicked ones yet? If you have, point out which one it is. I will make it burn forever."

Tynian and Ulath exchanged a long look. Then Tynian grinned wolfishly. "Let's," he said.

"Why don't we?" Ulath agreed. He looked at the flickering God of Fire. "Our hunt has been successful, Khwaj," he declared. "We have found one of the ones who stole Anakha's mate. You can make it burn forever now." He paused. "There are others we also hunt, though," he added. "We do not want to frighten them away so that they will be harder to hunt. Can Ghnomb put the one we have found into No-

Time? You can burn it always there. When it burns in No-Time, the others of its herd will not smell the smoke or hear the crying-out with hurt, and so they will not run away."

"Your thought is good, Ulath-from-Thalesia," Khwaj agreed. "I will talk with Ghnomb about this. He will make it so that the one who burns always burns in the time which does not move. Which one of these should I burn?"

"That one," Ulath replied, pointing at Baron Parok.

Duke Milanis was turning from the window when he suddenly stopped, becoming a statue in midstride.

Baron Parok continued his restless pacing. "We're going to have to start taking extra precautions," he said, not yet realizing that the men around him were no longer moving. Then he turned and almost bumped into the exhausted messenger from Natayos. "Get out of my way, idiot!" he snapped.

The man did not move.

"I told you to take a message to Zalasta," Parok raged. "Why are you still here?" He struck the messenger across the face and cried out in pain as his hand hit something harder than stone. He looked around wildly. "What's the matter with all of you?" he demanded in a shrill voice.

"What did it say?" Khwaj's voice was dreadful.

Parok gaped at the vast Troll-God, shrieked, and ran for the door.

"It does not understand that it is now in No-Time," Ulath replied in Trollish.

"It should know why it is being punished," Khwaj decided. "Will it understand if you talk to it in the bird-noises of the man-things?"

"I will *make* it understand," Ulath promised.

"It is good that you will. Speak to it."

Parok was hammering futilely on the immovable door.

"That won't do you any good, old boy," Ulath urbanely advised the terrified Dacite nobleman. "Things have definitely taken a turn for the worse for you, Baron. This large fellow with the smoke coming out of his ears is the Troll-God Khwaj. He disapproves of your abduction of Queen Ehlana."

"Who are you?" Parok half screamed. "What's going on here?"

"You've been brought to the place of punishment, Baron," Tynian advised him. "As my friend here just explained, Khwaj is quite put out with you. Trolls are very moralistic. Things that we've come to take in stride—abductions, poisonings, and holding people for ransom—upset them enormously. There is one small advantage, though. You're going to live forever, Baron Parok. You'll never, ever die."

"What are you talking about?"

"You'll see."

"Does it understand now?" Khwaj demanded impatiently.

"It is our thought that it does," Ulath replied in Trollish.

"Good." Khwaj implacably advanced on the cringing Dacite, extending one vast paw. Then he clapped it down on top of Parok's head. "Burn!" he growled.

Baron Parok shrieked.

Then his face seemed to split, and incandescent fire came spurting out through his skin. His doublet smoked for an instant and then flashed into ashes.

He shrieked again.

His form was still the form of a man, but it was a form etched in flame. The baron burned, unconsumed, and he danced and howled in agony.

Khwaj struck the immovable door with one huge paw, and the door burst outward in flaming chunks. "Go!" he roared. "Run! Run forever, and burn always!"

The flaming Dacite fled shrieking.

The town of Arjun stood frozen in that eternal instant of perpetual now. The citizens, like statues, stood frozen stock-still, unaware of the burning wraith that ran through their silent streets. They did not hear its agonized screams. They did not see it flee toward the lakeshore.

Baron Parok ran, all ablaze, trailing greasy smoke. He reached the docks and fled in flames out a long pier stretching into the dark waters of the sea of Arjun. He did not pause when he reached the end of the pier, but plunged off, yearning toward the quenching water. But, like the moment itself, the surface of the lake was unyielding and as hard as diamond. The wraith of flame howled in frustration, kneeling on the glittering surface and hammering on it, pleading to be let in, begging to drown in the blessed coolness just beyond reach. Then Parok leapt to his feet, driven by the Troll-God's awful command. Shrieking still in agony, the man-shape of eternal flame ran out across the dark crystal surface, receding incandescent until it was no more than a single bright spark far out on the night-darkened lake. And its lost wail of pain and endless solitude came echoing back to the incurious shore.

"I wish Sparhawk would find his way home again," Talen muttered as he and Stragen once again climbed the rickety stairs to the loft. "We've got some fairly important information, and there's no way to pass it on to the others."

"There's nothing we can do about it right now," Stragen told him. "Let's see how Valash reacts to this story you cooked up. Keep it sort of vague until we see which way he jumps."

"And then will you teach me how to pick a pocket?" Talen asked with overly feigned enthusiasm.

"All right." Stragen sighed. "I apologize. I'll concede that you know what you're doing."

"Oh, *thank* you, Vymer!" Talen gushed. "Thank you, thank you!"

"You've been spending too much time with Princess Danae," Stragen muttered sourly. "I hope she *does* marry you. You deserve it."

"Bite your tongue, Stragen. I can still run faster than she can."

"Running doesn't always help, Reldin. I thought I could run, too, but Melidere cut my legs out from under me with a single word."

"Oh? Which word was that?"

"Profit, my young friend. She waved unlimited amounts of gold in front of my face."

"You sold out, Stragen," Talen accused. "You betrayed every bachelor in the world for money."

"Wouldn't you have? We're not talking about a few farthings here."

"It's the principle of the thing," Talen replied loftily. "*I* wouldn't sell out for money."

"I don't think it'll be money that Danae's going to offer you, my innocent young friend. If you start running right now, you *might* escape, but I sort of doubt it. I knew your father, and there's a certain weakness in your family. Danae's going to get you, Talen. You don't have a chance."

"Could we talk about something else? This is a very distressing sort of subject."

Stragen laughed, and they went through the patched door at the top of the stairs.

Valash sat in the faint light of his single candle, listening with a look of pained resignation on his face as Ogerajin babbled and drooled a long, strung-out series of disconnected phrases.

"He doesn't seem to be getting any better," Stragen observed quietly when he and Talen joined the two at the table.

"He won't get better, Vymer." Valash sighed. "I've seen this particular disease run its course before. Don't get too close to him. He's virulently infectious at this stage."

"I certainly wouldn't want to catch what he's got." Talen shuddered.

"Do you have something for me?" Valash asked.

"I'm not going to swear to this, Master Valash," Talen said cautiously. "The fellows I picked it up from weren't any too reliable. You might want to pass it on to Panem-Dea, though. It concerns them rather directly, so they might want to take a few extra precautions."

"Go on," Valash said.

"Well, I overheard a couple of Arjuni soldiers talking in a tavern down by the waterfront—*real* Arjuni soldiers, I mean, not the ones Lord Scarpa's recruited. They were talking about some orders that just came in from the capital of Arjuna. From what I was able to gather, they've been ordered to prepare for an extended campaign out in the jungle. They *think* they're going to be mounting an attack on Lord Scarpa's camp at Panem-Dea."

"Impossible!" Valash snorted.

"They were saying that the orders came from King Rakya himself. The message had been sent to their officers, of course, so they probably garbled it, but they're convinced that the Arjuni army's going to attack Scarpa's forces. I just thought you ought to know."

"Those soldiers were drunk, Reldin. King Rakya is our ally."

"Really? What an amazing thing. He ought to let his troops know about it, then. The two I was listening to were positively drooling about all the loot they thought they were going to carry out of Panem-Dea."

"The queen is coming to Panem-Dea," Ogerajin suddenly sang in a wheezy voice to the tune of an old nursery song, "the queen is coming to Panem-Dea." Then he began to cackle in a high-pitched laugh.

A look of sudden chagrin crossed Valash's face. "Calm yourself, Master Ogerajin," he said, giving Stragen and Talen a worried look.

"The queen is coming to Panem-Dea, riding in a carriage," Ogerajin sang in his cracked voice.

"Don't pay any attention to him," Valash said rather too quickly. "He's only babbling."

"His mind really *is* slipping, isn't it?" Stragen noted.

"Six white horses and silver wheels—" Ogerajin sang on.

"Have you ever *heard* such gibberish?" Valash asked with a weak laugh.

"Our presence must be disturbing him," Stragen said. "Does he generally drift off to sleep later in the evening?"

"Usually."

"Good. From now on, Reldin and I'll come by after midnight, when he's asleep."

"I'd appreciate it, Vymer." Valash looked at them, his face still worried. "He wasn't always like this, you know. It's the disease."

"I'm sure of it. He's probably not even aware of what he's saying."

"Exactly, exactly. He's completely out of his head. Why don't you two just forget his crazy singing?" Valash snatched his purse from his belt and dug out several coins. "Here. Come by again after he's gone to sleep."

The two thieves bowed and quietly left.

"Nervous, wasn't he?" Talen said as they went back down the stairs.

"You noticed. He even forgot himself and opened his purse."

They reached the bottom of the stairs. "Where to?" Talen asked.

"No place for the moment. Keep this to yourself, Talen."

"Keep what?"

But Stragen was already speaking in sonorous Styric, weaving his fingers intricately in the air in front of him.

Talen stared as Stragen opened his hands palm up and made a sort of tossing gesture rather like a man releasing a pigeon. His eyes became distant, and his lips moved silently for a time. Then he smiled. "Surprised her," he said. "Let's go."

"What's going on here?" Talen demanded.

"I passed the things we just discovered along to Aphrael." Stragen shrugged.

"*You?* When did you learn Styric magic?"

"It's not really all that difficult, Talen." Stragen grinned. "I've seen Sparhawk do it often enough, and I *do* speak Styric, after all. The gestures were a little tricky, but Aphrael gave me some instructions. I'll do it better next time."

"How did you know it would work?"

"I didn't. I thought it was time I gave it a try, though. Aphrael's very pleased with me."

"You *do* know that you just volunteered to serve her, don't you? I know *that* much about her. You're her slave now, Stragen. She's got you."

"Oh, well." Stragen shrugged. "I suppose a man could do worse. Aphrael's a thief herself, so I'm sure we'll get along." He squared his shoulders. "Shall we go?" he suggested.

CHAPTER EIGHTEEN

"You're absolutely certain?" Sparhawk eagerly asked the Child-Goddess.

"Kalten is," she replied. "He was walking past the building, and Alean started to sing. He'd recognize her voice, wouldn't he?"

Sparhawk nodded. "She could raise him from the dead by singing to him. How fast can you get me to Natayos?"

"Let's take the others to Dirgis first. I want to fill Xanetia and Sephrenia in on what's been happening."

"I already know about all that. I need to get to Natayos, Aphrael."

"All in good time, Sparhawk. It's not going to take us long to get to Dirgis, and the others might have some useful ideas."

"Aphrael—" he began to protest.

"We'll do it my way, Sparhawk," she told him firmly. "It won't take all that long, and it might give you enough time to get your temper under control. The others are waiting in the room with the map on the wall. Let's get them and go to Dirgis."

There was one brief argument before they started. "I have no need of a horse," Betuana insisted, tightening the lace on one of her half boots.

Aphrael sighed. "Please do it my way, Betuana," she said.

"I can run faster than a horse. Why burden myself with one?"

"Because you know how far it is from here to Dirgis, and the horse doesn't. It's easier for me that way. Please, Betuana, just for me." The Child-Goddess looked appealingly at the armored Atan queen.

Betuana laughed and gave in.

And so they went out into the snowy courtyard, mounted, and rode out into the streets of Sarna. The sky was heavy with clouds that obscured the surrounding mountains, and it was spitting snow. They left town by way of the east gate and slogged their way up the steep slope to the top of the gorge. Sparhawk, Itagne, and Vanion rode in the lead, breaking trail for the Queen of Atan, who rode wrapped in her heavy cloak, with the Child-Goddess nestled in her arms. There was a strange dichotomy in the personality of the little divinity that troubled Sparhawk. He knew that she was wise beyond his ability to comprehend it, and yet she was still in most ways a little girl. Then he remembered the naked reality of the *true* Goddess, and all hope of ever understanding her vanished.

"Can't we go any faster?" Vanion demanded.

Sparhawk's friend had been in an agony of impatience ever since he had learned of the attack on Sephrenia, and Sparhawk had at times feared that he might have to physically restrain him. "Fast or slow doesn't matter, Vanion," he said. "We can run or crawl, and we'll still get there at just about the same time."

"How can you be so calm?"

"You get numb after a while." Sparhawk laughed wryly.

It was perhaps a quarter of an hour later when they crested the top of that long hill and looked down at the town of Dirgis—where the sun was shining brightly.

"That's incredible!" Itagne exclaimed. Then he turned to look back down the trail they had just climbed, and his eyes suddenly went very wide.

"I asked you not to do that, Itagne," Aphrael reminded him.

"It's still snowing there," he choked, "but—" He stared at the sun-drenched snowfield just ahead again.

"Why do people *always* want to stop right there?" the little girl said irritably. "Just move along, Itagne. Once you've passed the crossover between the two places, it won't bother you anymore."

Itagne resolutely set his face forward and rode on into the bright sunlight. "Did you understand that, Sparhawk?" he asked in a strained voice.

"Sort of. Do you really want to hear about what happens to you when you step through the place where two hundred miles have just been abolished?"

Itagne shuddered.

They rode down the hill and entered the city.

"How much farther?" Vanion demanded.

"Just a little way," Sparhawk replied. "It's not all that big a town."

They rode through the narrow streets where the snow lay thickly piled against the sides of the buildings. They reached the inn, rode into the courtyard just behind it, and dismounted.

"Everything's been fixed now, Betuana," Aphrael was assuring the Atan queen. "I'm keeping him in a deep sleep so that everything has a chance to knit back together again."

"Who's watching over him? Perhaps I should go there."

"No, Betuana," Aphrael said firmly. "I don't have permission to take you there—yet."

"But he's alone."

"Of course he's not alone. I'm right there beside him."

"But—" Betuana stared at the little girl.

"Try not to think about it." The Child-Goddess pursed her lips thoughtfully. "Engessa-Atan's a deceptive man, you know—probably because he's so quiet. I didn't realize how remarkable he really is until I got into his mind."

"I have always known," Betuana said. "How long will it be necessary to keep him away from me—us."

Aphrael let the queen's slip pass without comment. "A few weeks. I want to be sure that everything's healed. Let's go inside before Vanion has apoplexy."

Sparhawk led them into the inn where the innkeeper seemed to be so engrossed in wiping off a table that he was totally oblivious to anything else. They went up the stairs, and Sparhawk was startled to see Mirtai standing guard at Sephrenia's door. "What are you doing here?" he asked her. "I thought you were back in Matherion."

"I've been lent out," she replied, "like an old cloak."

"You know that's not true, Mirtai," Aphrael said. "Danae's perfectly safe where she is, but I needed someone I could count on to guard Sephrenia. Let's go inside."

Sephrenia was sitting up in bed when they entered, and Xanetia was hovering protectively over her. The room was flooded with sunlight.

Vanion went directly to the woman he loved, knelt at her bedside, and gently put his arms around her. "I'm never going to let you out of my sight again," he told her in a thick voice.

Sephrenia took his face between her hands and kissed him.

"You'll hurt yourself."

"Hush, Vanion," she told him, embracing his head and holding his face fiercely against her body.

Aphrael's huge eyes were luminous with tears. Then she seemed to shake off her sudden emotion. "Let's get started," she said crisply. "A great deal has happened since the last time we were all together like this."

"And all of it bad," Itagne added in a gloomy voice.

"Not entirely," she said. "The worst of it is that Klæl ambushed the Church Knights in the mountains of Zemoch. He had those strange soldiers with him, and our friends lost almost half their number in killed and wounded."

"Good God!" Itagne groaned.

Since Sparhawk already knew the details of recent events, his mind turned to the mystery of Klæl's soldiers. He touched his fingertips to the bulge under his tunic. Blue-Rose, he said in the silence of his mind.

I hear thee, Anakha.

Our friends have encountered Klæl again. He hath brought warriors here from some other place.

It was not unexpected. Klæl is unsuited to direct engagement with humans by reason of his size.

We are like mice in his eyes? Sparhawk surmised.

Thou dost wrong thyself, Anakha.

Perhaps. These soldiers are not of this world, methinks. Their blood is yellow and their faces are much like Klæl's face.

Ah, the voice said. *Thou wilt recall that I once told thee that it is customary for Klæl and me to contest with each other for possession of the various worlds I have caused to be?*

Yes.

It pains me to admit this, Anakha, but I have not always prevailed in these contests. Klæl hath wrested some of my worlds from me. It is from one of those worlds—Arcera would be my surmise—that he hath brought these creatures which thou and thy companions have met.

They are fearsome, Blue-Rose, but not invincible. We have noted some evidence of distress in them during prolonged sojourns here.

I would be surprised hadst thou not. The air of Arcera would sear thy lungs shouldst thou take but one breath of it. The air of this world is so sweet and wholesome that it may be most simply assimilated by thy kind and other creatures here. The creatures of Arcera are not so fortunate. Their means of assimilating the noxious miasmas of their home are far more complex than thy simple means of suspiration. Moreover, that which would be lethal to thee hath become necessary for them. I am certain that they find thine air thin and unsatisfying by comparison.

And deadly? Sparhawk pressed.

In time, most certainly.

Wouldst thou venture a surmise as to how much time it might take our air to kill them?

Thou art savage, Anakha.

I am outnumbered, Blue-Rose. The warriors of Klæl put our cause in direst peril. We must know *how long they can survive here.*

That will vary from warrior to warrior. No more than a day, certainly, and exertion will hasten the process.

I thank thee, Blue-Rose. My companions and I will devise tactics to use this information to best advantage.

"Pay attention, Sparhawk," Aphrael told him.

"Sorry," he apologized. "I was conferring with our friend." He patted the bulge at his front. He looked at Vanion. "I picked up some more information about the weakness of Klæl's soldiers," he said. "You and I need to work out some tactics."

Vanion nodded.

"Are you sure Berit and Khalad are all right?" Sephrenia asked the little girl.

Aphrael nodded. "Zalasta doesn't want us to know that he's found out that we were deceiving him. He's given orders to everyone to behave as if nothing's happened." She thought a moment. "I guess that's about all," she said. "Bergsten's coming across the steppes; Kalten, Bevier, and Caalador are already in Natayos; and Ulath, Tynian, and their pet Troll will be there before long."

"Can you get word to the emperor?" Itagne asked her. "He should know that the King of Arjuna's in league with Scarpa."

"I'll take care of it," she promised. Then she frowned slightly. "Sephrenia," she said, "have you been giving Stragen instruction in the secrets?"

"No, why?"

"He cast the spell of the secret summoning. He didn't do it very well, but he got my attention."

"How in God's name did he learn that?" Vanion exclaimed, still holding Sephrenia in his arms.

"Probably from watching the rest of you. Stragen's very quick, and he *does* speak Styric. Stealing secrets is almost the same as picking pockets, I guess. Anyway, it was Stragen who told me about Scarpa's other forts. He and Talen are planting false stories with that Dacite in order to confuse the other side."

"Methinks it is time for me to go to Natayos," Xanetia said. "We must verify the presence there of Anakha's queen and make preparations for her rescue."

"*Before* Zalasta tries to move her," Sparhawk added. "I'd better go along as well. The others are there already, and Kalten might need a firm hand to keep him from doing anything rash. Besides, if Ehlana and Alean are there, we might just as well pull them out of danger. Then I'll disperse Scarpa's army and we'll go have a talk with Cyrgon."

"And Zalasta," Vanion added bleakly.

"Oh, by the way," Aphrael said, "is anybody keeping a list of the people we want to do things about? If you are, you can scratch off Baron Parok's name."

"Did Ulath kill him?" Sparhawk guessed.

"Oh, he isn't dead, Sparhawk. You see, when Khwaj started pushing Ulath and

Tynian for information about the people who'd abducted Ehlana, they gave him Parok."

"What happened?" Itagne asked.

"Ghnomb froze time." She shrugged. "Then Khwaj set fire to Parok. He's completely engulfed in flame. He's still running, and he'll run—and burn—in that empty, unmoving instant for all eternity."

"Dear God!" Itagne choked in horror.

"I'll pass that on to Khwaj, Itagne," the Child-Goddess promised. "I'm sure he'll be pleased that you approve."

The air was cool and dry and the sky was peculiarly grey. Tynian and Ulath rode out of Arjun in frozen time with Bhlokw shambling along between their horses. "How long would you say it's going to take us to reach Natayos?" Tynian asked.

"Oh," Ulath replied, "I don't know—a couple of seconds, probably."

"Very funny."

"I rather liked it." Ulath looked up at the flock of birds hanging in midair overhead. "I wonder if a man ages at all when he's walking around in this No-Time."

"I don't know. You could go ask Baron Parok, I suppose."

"I doubt that he'd be very coherent." Ulath scratched at one bearded cheek. "I'm definitely going to shave this thing off, and if Gerda doesn't like it, that's just too bad." Then he thought of something he had been meaning to ask their shaggy friend. "Bhlokw," he said.

"Yes, U-lat?"

"It makes us sad that our hunt takes us to the lands of the sun where the heat causes hurt to you."

"It causes no hurt to me, U-lat. There is no heat or cold in No-Time."

Ulath stared at him. "You are sure?" he asked incredulously.

"Do you feel heat?" Bhlokw asked simply.

"No," Ulath admitted, "I do not. It had been my thought—" He broke off, frowning and trying to frame his next question in coherent Trollish. "We were far to the north when you and your pack-mates ate the children of Cyrgon who were both dead and not dead."

"Yes. It was north from where we are now."

"Then Ghnomb took you and your pack-mates into No-Time."

"Yes."

"Then Ghworg led you to the lands of the sun."

"Yes."

"There was no hurt caused to you when he did this?"

"No. The hurt was caused by the things that were not how they should be."

"Which things were not how they should be?"

"All of the Trolls were one pack. This is not how it should be. Troll-packs do not have so many. It is not a good way to hunt." Bhlokw rubbed at his shaggy face with one massive paw. "We did not hunt this way when we were in the Troll-range where we are supposed to be. My thought was that Ghworg's mind was sick when he came to us and told us to cross the ice-which-never-melts to come to this place. It was not Ghworg who did this. It was Cyrgon. Cyrgon had made himself to look like Ghworg and spoke in Ghworg's voice. It was my mind which was sick. My thought should have told me that it was not Ghworg."

"Does it cause hurt to you that the Trolls are all one pack?"

"Much hurt, U-lat. I do not like it when things are not how they should be. I have known Grek for many snows. His pack hunts near my pack in the Troll-range. I do not like Grek. It has been in my thought for the past two snows to kill him. Ghworg will not let me kill him. This causes hurt to me."

"It will not be this way always, Bhlokw," Ulath said consolingly. "After we have killed all of Cyrgon's children, the Gods will take the Trolls back to the Troll-range. Then things will be how they should be again."

"It will make me glad when they are. I would really like to kill Grek." Bhlokw shambled away mournfully.

"What was that all about?" Tynian asked.

"I'm not sure," Ulath admitted. "I'm groping around the edges of something here. I know it's right in front of me, but I can't put my finger on it."

"For the moment, let's just hope that the Troll-Gods can control the homicidal impulses of their children," Tynian said fervently.

"Trollicidal," Ulath corrected.

"What?"

"You said *homicidal*. Bhlokw wants to kill Grek. Grek's a Troll. The right word would be *Trollicidal*."

"That's petty quibbling, Ulath."

"Right is right, Tynian," Ulath replied in a faintly injured tone.

It was still quite early the next morning when Aphrael returned from Sarna. The sky to the east was lighted with the pale approach of day, even though the moon still held sway above the western horizon.

Sparhawk and Xanetia had been waiting for no more than half an hour when they heard the familiar trill of Flute's pipes coming from back in the dark forest.

"That was quick," Sparhawk said as the Child-Goddess joined them.

"It's not as if Sarna were on the other side of the continent, Sparhawk," she replied. "I got them all settled in." She smiled. "Vanion's being a pest. He was trying to make Sephrenia go to bed when I left."

"She *has* been very weak, Aphrael," he reminded her.

"But she isn't now. She needs to be up and moving about. Turn your backs." Xanetia looked puzzled.

"It's one of her quirks," Sparhawk explained. "She doesn't want people watching while she changes." He looked at the Child-Goddess. "Don't forget the clothes this time, Aphrael," he told her. "Let's not offend the Anarae."

"You're so tiresome about that, Sparhawk. Now please turn around."

It only took a few moments. "All right," Aphrael said. They turned. Sparhawk noted the Goddess was once again garbed in that satiny white robe.

"Thou art fair beyond description, Divine One," Xanetia said.

Aphrael shrugged. "I cheat a lot. Do you trust me, Anarae?"

"With my life, Divine Aphrael."

"I hope you're taking notes, Sparhawk."

"Have you arranged for some noise to hide what you're doing from Zalasta?"

"I don't have to. Xanetia's coming along, and her presence will conceal every-thing."

"I suppose I hadn't thought of that," he admitted.

"Now then, Anarae," Aphrael explained, "we're all going to hold hands. Then we'll rise up into the air. It's really better if you don't look down. As soon as we get above the tops of these mountains, we'll start moving. You won't feel any wind or cold or sense of movement. Just hold on to my hand and try to think of something else. It won't take very long." She squinted toward the eastern horizon. "We'd bet-ter get started. I'd like to get us to Natayos and into a good hiding place before Scarpa's soldiers start stirring around." She held out her hands, and Sparhawk and Xanetia took them.

Sparhawk steeled himself and watched the ground rapidly receding as they rose swiftly toward the dawn sky.

"You're squeezing, Sparhawk," Aphrael told him.

"Sorry. I'm still not entirely used to this." He looked at Xanetia. The Anarae, all aglow, was a picture of absolute serenity as they rose higher and higher.

"The world is fair," she said softly with a note of wonder in her voice.

"*If* you get high so that you can't see the ugliness." Aphrael smiled. "I come up here to think now and then. It's one place where I can be fairly sure I won't be in-terrupted." She took a bearing on the newly risen sun, which had seemed almost to rush up into the sky as they rose, set her face resolutely toward the southeast, and gave a peculiar little nod.

The earth beneath began to flow smoothly, rushing toward them from the front and receding just as rapidly behind.

"It seemeth me a merry way to travel," Xanetia observed.

"I've always rather liked it," Aphrael agreed. "It's certainly faster than plodding along on horseback."

They fled southeasterly with an eerie kind of silence around them.

"The Sea of Arjun," Sparhawk said, pointing toward a large body of water off to the right.

"So small?" Xanetia said. "I had thought it larger."

"We're up quite a ways," Aphrael explained. "Everything looks small from a distance."

They sped on and were soon over the dense green jungle that covered the southeastern coast of the continent.

"We'll go down a bit now," Aphrael warned. "I'll take a bearing on Delo, and then we'll swerve toward the southwest to reach Natayos."

"Will we not be seen from the ground?" Xanetia asked.

"No—although it's an interesting idea. Your light would definitely startle peo-ple. Whole new religions could be born if people on the ground started seeing an-gels flying over their heads. There's Delo."

The port city looked like a child's toy carelessly left on the shore of the deep

blue Tamul Sea. They veered to the southwest, following the coastline and gradually descending.

Aphrael was peering intently down at the jungle rushing back beneath them.
"There," she said triumphantly.

The ruin might have been more difficult to find had not the northern quarter
been cleared of the brush and trees which covered the rest of the ancient city. The
tumbled grey stones of the half-fallen buildings stood out sharply in the light of the
sunrise, and the newly cleared road stretching toward the north was a yellow scar
cut deeply into the face of the dark green of the jungle.

They settled gently to earth on the road about a quarter of a mile north of the
ruins, and Sparhawk immediately led them back a hundred paces into the thick un-
dergrowth. He was tense with excitement. If Kalten was right, he was less than a
mile from the place where Ehlana was being held captive.

"Go ahead, Xanetia," Aphrael suggested. "I want to look you over before you
go into the city. This is important, but I don't want to put you in any danger. Let's
be sure nobody can see you."

"Thou art overly concerned, Divine One. Over the centuries, we of the Delphae have perfected this particular subterfuge." She straightened, and her face assumed an expression of almost unnatural calm. Her form seemed to shimmer, and
little rainbow flickers of light seethed beneath her plain homespun robe. She
blurred and wavered, her form becoming indistinct.

Then she was only an outline, and Sparhawk could clearly see the trunk of the
tree behind her.

"How do you make the things on the other side of you visible?" Aphrael asked
curiously.

"We bend the light, Divine One. That is at the core of this deception. The
light flows around us like a swift-moving stream, carrying with it the images of such
objects as our bodies would normally obscure."

"Very interesting," Aphrael mused. "I hadn't even thought of that possibility."

"We must be wary, however," Xanetia told the Goddess. "Our shadows, like
telltale ghosts, can betray us."

"That's simple. Stay out of the sunlight."

Sparhawk concealed a faint smile. Even a Goddess could give blatantly obvious
instructions sometimes.

"I shall most carefully adhere to thine advice, Divine One," Xanetia replied
with exaggerated calm.

"You're making fun of me, aren't you, Xanetia?"

"Of course not, Divine Aphrael." Even the outline was gone now, and Xanetia's
voice seemed to come out of nowhere. "To work, withal," she said, her sourceless
voice receding in the direction of the road. "I shall return anon."

"I'll have to compliment Edaemus," Aphrael said. "That's a very clever means
of concealment. Turn around, Sparhawk. I'm going to change back."

After the Child-Goddess had resumed the familiar form of Flute, she and Sparhawk made themselves comfortable and waited as the sun gradually rose. The jungle steamed, and the air was alive with the chattering of birds and the buzzing of
insects. The moments seemed to drag. They were so close to Ehlana that Sparhawk

almost imagined that he could smell her familiar fragrance. "Are Ulath and Tynian here yet?" he asked, more to get his mind away from his anxious concern than out of any real curiosity.

"Probably," Flute replied. "They set out from Arjun yesterday morning. It probably seemed like three weeks to them, but it was no more than a heartbeat for everybody else."

"I wonder if they stayed in No-Time or just merged into Scarpa's army."

"It's hard to say. Maybe I should have checked before Xanetia left."

Then they heard several men talking on the road. Sparhawk crept closer, with Aphrael just behind him.

"Because I don't trust these soldiers, Col," a rough-looking fellow was saying to a blond Elene.

"It's daytime, Senga. Nobody's going to ambush your beer wagons in broad daylight."

"You can't be too careful. Money's running short here in Natayos, and that beer's the lifeblood of my business. A thirsty man who's running short of money might do anything."

"Have you considered lowering your prices?" an evil-looking fellow with a black eye patch asked.

"Bite your tongue, Shallag," Senga replied.

"Just a suggestion." The patch-eyed man shrugged as the dozen or so heavily armed men moved on out of earshot.

"You recognized them, of course," Aphrael murmured to Sparhawk.

"Kalten and Bevier, yes. I didn't see Caalador, though." He thought for a moment. "Will you be all right here? Alone, I mean?"

"Well, it's *awfully* dangerous, Sparhawk—lions and tigers and bears, you know."

"It was a silly question, wasn't it?"

"I'd say so, yes. What have you got in mind?"

"Kalten and Bevier are obviously working for that fellow they called Senga. I think I can get them to vouch for me. They seem to have the run of Natayos, so hiring on as a beer guard would give me a way to get into the city without attracting attention."

"Will you be able to restrain yourself when you're that close to Mother?"

"I'm not going to do anything foolish, Aphrael."

"Well, I suppose it's all right. You have my permission."

"Oh, *thank* you, Divine Aphrael," he said. "Thank you, thank you, thank you."

"You have a very clever mouth, Sparhawk," she said tartly.

"It's probably the clever company I've been keeping lately." He shrugged.

"I have to run back to Sarna for a little while," Aphrael told him. "Try to stay out of trouble when you get into the city."

"I'll miss you desperately." He grinned.

"You're in an odd humor today."

"I feel good. If all goes well, I'll have your mother out of there before the sun goes down."

"We'll see."

They waited as the sun crept farther up in the eastern sky. Then from off to the north they heard the approach of several heavily laden wagons. "I'll keep you posted," Sparhawk promised, and he stepped out of the bushes to stand at the side of the muddy road.

The first wagon, drawn by four patient oxen, came creaking around a bend. The wagonbed was piled high with barrels, and the one known as Senga sat on the seat beside the villainous-looking driver. Kalten, his expression oddly familiar on his altered face, was perched on top of the barrels.

"Ho, Col," Sparhawk called from the roadside. "I *thought* I recognized your voice when you passed here a little while ago."

"Well, strike me blind if it isn't Fron!" Kalten exclaimed with a broad grin. Sparhawk suddenly wondered what might have happened if Kalten hadn't recognized him. Kalten was laughing now with genuine delight. "We all thought you'd run away to sea when things came apart on us back in Matherion."

"It didn't work out." Sparhawk shrugged. "There was a bo'sun on board who was a little too free with his whip. He decided to swim for shore one dark night. I can't imagine what came over him. We were twenty leagues out to sea when I helped him over the side."

"People do strange things sometimes. What are you doing here?"

"I heard about this army, and I thought it might be a good place to hide. Word's going about that this Scarpa fellow plans to attack Matherion. I've got a few old scores to settle there, so I decided to tag along for fun and profit."

"I think we can find a better spot for you than back in the rear ranks of Scarpa's army." Kalten nudged Senga's shoulder with his foot. "The fellow standing ankle-deep in the mud there is an old friend of ours from Matherion," he told the tavern-keeper. "His name's Fron, and he's a very good man in a fight. When the police jumped on us back in Matherion, he stood shoulder to shoulder with Shallag, holding them off while the rest of us got away. Do you think there might be a spot for him in your operation here in Natayos?"

"Do you vouch for him, Col?" Senga asked.

"I couldn't ask for better help if trouble crops up."

"You're in charge of security." Senga shrugged. "Hire anybody you want."

"I was hoping you'd see it that way." Kalten beckoned to Sparhawk. "Climb on up, Fron," he said. "I'll show you the wonders of Natayos."

"From the top of a beer wagon?"

"Can you think of a better place?"

Kring arrived in Sarna late in the afternoon of the same day in which Aphrael had transported Sephrenia and the others there from Dirgis. Mirtai calmly went down into the courtyard of the Atan garrison to meet her bandy-legged betrothed. The two of them embraced rather formally and then came into the building.

"She seems very restrained," Vanion observed quietly to Betuana as the two watched from the window of the conference room.

"It is not seemly to openly display affection in public, Vanion-Preceptor," the queen replied. "Decorum must be maintained, even though the heart might prefer it otherwise."

"Ah."

"Ho, friend Vanion," Kring said as he and his tall beloved entered, "you're just the man I was looking for."

"It's good to see you, too, friend Kring. How are things going in Samar?"

"It's quiet. The Cynesgans have pulled back from the border. Is there something going on to the south that I haven't been told about?"

"Not that I know of. Why do you ask?"

"The Cynesgans were massing just across the border, and we were expecting them to come across to lay siege to Samar almost anytime. Then several days ago they pulled back and left only a few units in place. The rest of their army marched south."

"Why would they do that?" Vanion asked, frowning.

"Probably to meet the Church Knights," Aphrael replied.

Vanion turned to see the Child-Goddess calmly sitting in her usual place on Sephrenia's lap. She had not been there a moment before. There was no point to making an issue of it. Aphrael would never change. "The Church Knights aren't coming from that direction, Divine One," he said.

"*We* know that, Vanion," she replied, "but Stragen and Talen have been busy in Beresa. They've managed to convince that Dacite spy that there's a huge fleet of ships flying Church flags knocking about in the Gulf of Daconia. Evidently the Dacite passed the word on, and the Cynesgan high command took it seriously enough to send their main force south to defend southern Cynesga."

"But they *know* that the Church Knights are coming overland through Astel."

"They know about *that* force, Lord Vanion," Itagne said, "but they must have been convinced that there's another coming by sea."

"There aren't that many of us, Itagne."

"You and I know that, Lord Vanion, but it's generally believed here in Tamuli that there are at least a million of you fellows. The term *Church Knights* conjures up visions of armies stretching from horizon to horizon."

Vanion frowned. "Oh," he said finally. "I think I understand. During the Zemoch wars, we joined forces with the armies of the kings of Eosia. The Tamul observers must have thought that everyone in armor was a Church Knight."

"I think I'll have a talk with the emperor," Itagne mused. "Titles of nobility might be in order for your pair of thieves. This imaginary fleet of theirs seems to have pulled half the Cynesgan army off the border and most likely pinned down the Arjunis as well."

"It's a great little fleet—" Vanion grinned. "—and you don't even have to feed the sailors. Let's keep the stories alive." He looked at Aphrael. "Could you arrange some illusions, Divine One?"

"Dragons? Flights of angels?"

"How about a thousand ships hull-down on the horizon instead?"

"What do I get in return?"

"Stop teasing," Sephrenia told her with a gentle smile.

"Where would you like your make-believe boats, Vanion?"

He thought about it. "Why don't you just bounce them up and down the coastline of Daconia and western Arjuna?" he suggested. "Let's run the Cynesgans and Arjunis ragged trying to position themselves to defend against landings."

"I'll go take care of it right now," she said, slipping down from her sister's lap, "before I forget."

"When did you ever forget anything?" Sephrenia smiled.

"I don't know. I must have at some time, though. I've probably forgotten exactly when." She gave them all an impish little smile, and then she vanished.

Kring was sitting at Mirtai's side, and he had been squinting speculatively at the ceiling, absently running one hand over his stubbled scalp. He was not free to use the other, since Mirtai had taken possession of it. Her contented, almost placid, expression clearly said that she did not intend to release his hand in the foreseeable future.

"If Divine Aphrael can keep those Cynesgan troops more or less permanently distracted, Tikume and I'll be able to hold Samar without any help," the Domi said, "particularly now that we know how to deal with Klæl's soldiers." He rubbed even more briskly at his scalp.

"Quit worrying at it," Mirtai told him. "I'll shave you just as soon as we finish here."

"Yes, love," he agreed immediately.

"Oh, that reminds me," Vanion said. "Sparhawk had a talk with Bhelliom. Klæl's soldiers can only breathe our air for about a day before they start dying, and exertion speeds up the process. If you come across them again, keep them running."

Kring nodded.

A tall Atan came in and murmured something to Itagne.

"I'm really awfully busy right now, old boy," Itagne objected.

"He's most insistent, Itagne-Ambassador."

"Oh, very well." Itagne rose to his feet. "I'll be right back, Lord Vanion," he said, and followed the Atan from the room.

"Did Sparhawk find out what country Klæl's soldiers come from, friend Vanion?" Kring asked. "I'd sort of like to avoid that place."

"I don't think you need to worry, Domi Kring." Sephrenia smiled. "Klæl's soldiers were brought here from someplace beyond the stars."

Kring frowned. "You might want to have a talk with Sparhawk, friend Vanion," he said. "I enjoy a good fight as much as the next man, but if he's going to declare war on the whole universe, he ought to let the rest of us in on his plans."

"I'll definitely speak with him about it, Domi Kring," Vanion said. Then he sighed. "I wish we'd known more about Klæl's soldiers earlier. The Church Knights encountered them in the mountains of Zemoch and lost half their number in killed and wounded."

"I'm sorry, friend Vanion. Did you lose many old comrades?"

"Many, Domi Kring," Vanion replied sadly, "many."

"How's friend Engessa coming along?" Kring asked Betuana.

"Aphrael says that he's recovering, Domi," she replied. "I'd like to see that for myself, though."

Itagne returned, accompanied by a Tamul wearing slightly out-of-date clothing. "Would you please see to it that we're not disturbed?" he said to the Atan guard in the hall. Then he closed and bolted the door. "I have some good news for a change," he said then. He put his hand on the stranger's shoulder. "This is my very dear—though newfound—friend, Ekrasios," he said.

Betuana frowned. "That is not a Tamul name," she said.

"No, your Majesty," Itagne agreed, "it's not. Actually, it's Delphaeic. The Delphae are such a musical people. It probably derives from the fact that they still speak classical Tamul. My friend here just stopped by to advise us that the Delphae have decided to come out of their splendid seclusion. Ekrasios, this is Preceptor Vanion, the close friend of Anakha. The regal lady is Betuana, Queen of the Atans. The short fellow is Domi Kring of the western Peloi. The tall, pretty girl with the death grip on his hand is Mirtai, his betrothed, and the exquisite Styric lady is Sephrenia, High Priestess of the Goddess Aphrael."

"Nobles all," Ekrasios greeted them with a formal bow. "I bring greetings from Belovèd Edaemus. Divine Aphrael hath persuaded him that we have common cause in the current situation, and he hath thus relaxed his centuries-old prohibition upon us. I am sent to thee, Lord Vanion, to advise thee that I and diverse companions are at thine immediate disposal. Where might we best be deployed to further our cause?"

"If I may, Lord Vanion?" Itagne interposed. "It just occurred to me that the Delphae might be best suited to empty those ruins in the Arjuni jungles. If Ekrasios and his friends were to appear in all their glowing splendor at the gates of Scarpa's camps down there, the rebels would probably go back home and take up peaceful pursuits—just as fast as they possibly could."

"Well said," Mirtai murmured her agreement.

"He certainly moves around, doesn't he?" Ulath said to Tynian as the beer wagon with Sparhawk and Kalten perched atop the barrels rumbled past on the ancient street. "Last I heard, he was in Dirgis."

"The natcherl rules don't seem t' apply t' ol' Sporhawk," Tynian replied in a bad imitation of Caalador's dialect. "What do you think? Should we slip back into real time? Or should we stay where we are?"

"I think we'll be more useful if we stay out of sight," Ulath replied.

"That's fine with me, but how are we going to get word to Sparhawk and the others that we're here?"

"I'll slip a note in his pocket—or blow in his ear."

"That ought to get his attention."

Bhlowk came shambling back up the street with a mournful expression on his apelike face. "There are no dogs here," he reported in Trollish.

"Soldiers don't usually keep dogs, Bhlowk," Tynian explained.

"I have hunger, Tin-in. Would the man-things here miss one of their herd—a small one?"

"We might have a problem here," Tynian muttered to Ulath. "It's definitely in our best interests to keep our friend here well fed."

Ulath scratched at his now-clean-shaven cheek. "We can't just turn him loose," he noted. "He'll attract attention if he starts grabbing people and jerking them into these broken moments."

"He's invisible, Ulath."

"Yes, but if some Arjuni suddenly vanishes and his bones start getting tossed back out of nowhere, it's bound to attract attention." He turned back to the Troll. "It is our thought that it would not be good for you to kill and eat the man-things here, Bhlokw. We hunt thought here, and if you kill and eat the man-things, you will frighten the thought away."

"I do not like this hunting of thought, U-lat," Bhlowk complained. "It makes things not-simple."

"The forest is near, Bhlokw," Tynian said. "There must be many good-to-eat things there."

"I am not an Ogre, Tin-in," Bhlokw protested in a slightly offended tone. "I do not eat trees."

"There should be creatures that are good-to-eat among the trees, Bhlokw," Ulath said. "That is what Tin-in was trying to say. It was not his thought to insult you."

Bhlokw glowered at Tynian for a moment. "I will go hunt now," he said abruptly. Then he turned and shambled off.

"You have to be careful, Tynian," Ulath warned his friend. "If you want to get into a fight almost immediately, all you have to do is suggest to a Troll that he might be an Ogre."

"They're actually prejudiced?" Tynian asked in amazement.

"You wouldn't *believe* how prejudiced," Ulath replied. "Trolls and Ogres have hated each other since the beginning of time."

"I thought that prejudice was a human failing."

"Some things are just too good to stay private, I guess. Let's follow Sparhawk and let him know that we're here. He might have something for us to do."

They trailed along behind the beer caravan winding through the cleared streets toward that part of Natayos that was still choked in brush and vines. The wagons trundled along a recently cleared street and then went around behind a canvas-roofed building identified by a crudely lettered sign that read SENGA'S.

"Trust Kalten to get close to the beer," Tynian said.

"Truly," Ulath agreed. "Wait here. I'll go let Sparhawk know that we're in Natayos." He walked over to where Sparhawk, Kalten, and Bevier, looking strange with their altered features, stood off to one side while Senga supervised the unloading of the barrels. "Ramshorn," he said quietly. "Don't get excited and start looking around," he added. "You won't be able to see me."

"Ulath?" Kalten asked incredulously.

"Right. Tynian, Bhlokw, and I got here yesterday. We've been nosing around."

"How have you managed to become invisible?" the patch-eyed Bevier asked.

"We aren't actually. Ghnomb's breaking the seconds into two pieces. We're only present during the smaller piece. That's why you can't see us."

"But you can see *us*?"

"Yes."

"Ulath, that's logically inconsistent."

"I know, but Ghnomb *believes* that it works, and I guess his belief is strong enough to override logic. Tynian and I are here, and nobody can see us. Is there anything you want us to do?"

"Can you get into that building near the gate?" Sparhawk asked quickly. "The one with the barred windows?"

"Not a chance. We already looked into the possibility. Too many guards on the doors. Bhlokw even tried going in through the roof, but it's all sealed up."

"That's my *wife* in there, Ulath!" Sparhawk exclaimed. "Are you saying that you tried to send a *Troll* into the same building with her?"

"Bhlokw wouldn't have hurt her, Sparhawk—frightened her a little, maybe, but he wouldn't have hurt her. We sort of thought he might be able to go in through the roof, pick Ehlana and Alean up, and carry them out." Ulath paused. "It wasn't really our idea, Sparhawk. Bhlokw volunteered—well, actually he didn't even volunteer. He just started climbing up the wall before we could stop him. He said, 'I will go get them. I will bring Anakha's mate and her friend out so that we can kill all these children of Cyrgon and eat them.' Bhlokw's a little elemental, but his heart's in the right place. I hate to admit it, but I'm actually starting to like him."

Kalten looked around nervously. "Where is he now?" he asked.

"He's out hunting. When we were knocking around those cities by the lake, we persuaded him not to eat people. We got him started on dogs instead. He really likes them, but there aren't any dogs here in Natayos, so he's out in the woods—probably chasing elephants or something." Then something flickered at the corner of Ulath's eye. "What in God's name is that?" he exclaimed.

"What?" Kalten asked, looking around in bafflement.

"There's somebody made out of rainbows coming around the side of the building!" Ulath gaped at the clearly defined shape approaching. The many-colored light was dazzling.

"That's Xanetia," Sparhawk explained. "Can you actually *see* her?"

"Are you saying that you can't?"

"She's invisible, Ulath."

"Not to *me*, she isn't."

"It must have something to do with the peculiar time you're in, my friend,"

Bevier suggested. "You'd better let her know that you can see her. It might be important someday."

The shimmering rainbow stopped a few paces away. "Anakha," Xanetia said softly.

"I hear thee, Anarae," Sparhawk replied.

"It pains me to tell thee that I have failed," she confessed. "The mind of Scarpa is so twisted that I cannot wring coherence from his thought. I did gently probe the minds of some of his followers, however, and I must sadly advise thee that thy queen is no longer here in Natayos. When our enemies did discover the subterfuge involving young Sir Berit, Zalasta did spirit thy wife and her handmaiden away under cover of darkness. I shall endeavor to glean their destination from the thoughts of others here, and it please thee."

Ulath's heart twisted with sympathy at the look of sudden despair that came over Sparhawk's face.

They ran easily in their endless regiments, tall and lightly armored, with their bronze limbs glowing in the cool grey light. The towering King Androl ran smoothly at the front of his army. It was good to be on the move again, and the prospect of battle was exhilarating. Battle was meaningful, and one could actually *see* results. The absence of his wife had thrust a thousand petty administrative chores on Androl's unprepared shoulders. It was so frustrating to make decisions about things he didn't really understand and even more frustrating not to see any immediate results that would have told him whether or not his decisions had been correct. Once again the King of Atan thanked his God for giving him Betuana to wife. They made a good team, actually. The queen was very skilled with details. Her mind was quick, and she could pick out subtleties and nuances that frequently escaped her husband. Androl, on the other hand, was made for action. He gladly let his wife make all the tiresome decisions, and then, when it was all settled and they knew what they were going to do, *he* took charge of carrying her decisions out. It was better that way, actually. The King of Atan was fully aware of his limitations and he knew that his wife forgave him when he occasionally overlooked something. He hoped that he didn't disappoint her too much.

Her suggestion—she never gave him orders—that he take the bulk of their people to the south end of Lake Sarna in preparation for a grand battle at Tosa was exactly the sort of thing Androl truly loved. Here was action, simple and uncomplicated. The troublesome decisions had all been made, the enemy had been identified, and all the boring details had been swept out of the way. He smiled as he led his army into the last outcropping of mountains some fifty leagues to the southeast of Tualas. Betuana's message had hinted that the battle at Tosa would be a titanic one, a grand clash at arms with struggling armies stretching for miles and the ring of sword against sword reaching to the skies. He would make her proud of him.

The route through the outcropping mountains led up a long ridgeline, through a narrow notch, and then down into the deep gorge of a turbulent stream that had gnawed at the rock for eons.

King Androl was breathing a bit heavily when he crested the ridgeline and led his forces through the notch. The wasted hours spent conferring with Ambassador Norkan had taken off Androl's edge. A warrior should never permit himself to be lured away from the practice field or the exercise yard. He picked up the pace as he led his army down into the narrow gorge, running smoothly along the south bank of the rushing mountain river. If *he* was out of shape, his soldiers probably were as well. He hoped that he could find a suitable place for an encampment at Lake Sarna, a proper encampment with enough space for training and practice and those necessary calisthenics that honed warriors to the peak of fitness. Androl was sublimely confident that *any* opposing force could be overcome if only his army were fully trained and fit.

"Androl-King!" General Pemaas shouted over the sound of the turbulent stream. "Look!"

"Where?" Androl demanded, half turning and reaching for his sword.

"At the top of the gorge—on the right!"

The Atan king craned his neck to peer up the sheer cliff-face to the rocky brink high above.

The King of Atan had seen many things in his life, but nothing to compare with the vast, monstrous form rearing suddenly above them on the rim of the gorge.

The thing was glossy black, like polished leather, and it had enormously outspreading wings, jointed and batlike. Its wedge-shaped head was accentuated by blazing eye-slits and a gaping mouth that dripped flame.

King Androl considered it. The problem, of course, was the fact that the towering creature was at the top of the gorge while he stood at the bottom. He could turn and retrace his steps, running back up the gorge to the notch and scrambling around the rocks to reach the rim; but that would give the thing plenty of opportunity to run away, and then he would have to chase it down in order to kill it. In his present less-than-perfect condition, that would be very tedious. He could always climb up the cliff, but that would still take time, and the creature might very well see him coming and try to flee.

Then, amazingly, the large being at the top of the gorge provided the solution. It raised its enormous arms and began to slash at the top of the cliff with what appeared to be fire of some kind.

Androl smiled as the cliff-face began to topple outward, tumbling and roaring down into the gorge. The silly beast was accommodatingly providing the means for its own destruction. How could it *be* so stupid?

King Androl adroitly dodged a tumbling, house-sized boulder, carefully assessing the rapidly growing slope of rubble piling up at the base of the cliff.

The beast actually intended to attack! Androl laughed with delight. The creature was stupid beyond imagining, but he did have to give it credit for courage— foolish courage, of course, but courage nonetheless. All the universe knew that Androl of Atan was invincible, and yet this poor dumb brute meant to pit its puny strength against the greatest warrior since the beginning of time.

Androl looked speculatively at the steep, growing slope of rubble, ignoring the cries of those of his soldiers not nimble enough to avoid being crushed in the avalanche rumbling down upon them. Almost high enough now. Just a few more feet.

And then he judged that the steep slope had grown high enough to give him access to the stupid creature roaring and flapping its wings high above. He dodged another boulder and began his rush, scrambling, dodging, leaping, as he swiftly mounted toward the doomed beast above him.

When he was almost to the top, he paused, drew his sword, and set himself.

And then with a savage war cry he rushed up the remaining slope, ignoring the momentary flicker of sympathy he felt for the brave, misguided creature he was about to kill.

"Where do you think you're going?" a burly Dacite wearing a shabby uniform tunic and holding a long pike demanded as Sparhawk and Kalten pulled the wobbly cart with two large barrels in it around the corner of the building.

"We've got a delivery from Senga for Master Krager," Kalten replied.

"Anybody could say that."

"Go ask him," Kalten suggested.

"I wouldn't want to disturb him."

"Then you'd better let us past. He's been waiting for this wine for quite some time now. If you keep us from delivering it, he'll *really* be disturbed. He might even be disturbed enough to take the matter to Lord Scarpa."

The guard's face grew apprehensive. "Wait here," he said, then turned and went along the back of the building to the heavy door.

"I'll stay in the background when we get inside," Sparhawk quietly told his friend. "If he asks, just tell him that I'm a strong back you commandeered to help pull the cart."

Kalten nodded.

"Are you here, Anarae?" Sparhawk asked, looking around in spite of the fact that he knew he wouldn't be able to see her.

"Right at thy side, Anakha," her voice replied softly.

"We'll keep him talking for as long as we can. He'll probably be a little drunk. Will that make it difficult for you?"

"I have shared the thoughts of this Krager before," she told him. "He is coherent unless he is far gone with drink. If it be convenient, direct his attention toward the house where thy queen was late held captive. That may prod his mind toward thoughts of interest to us."

"I'll see what I can do, Anarae," Kalten promised.

The Dacite guard came back. "He'll receive you," he announced.

"Somehow I was almost sure he would." Kalten smirked. "Master Krager's very fond of this particular wine." He and Sparhawk lifted the shafts of the cart and pulled it along over the rough, littered ground at the back of the semirestored ruin that appeared to be Scarpa's main headquarters.

Krager was eagerly waiting in the doorway. His head was shaved, but he still looked much the same. He was dishevelled and unshaven, his nearsighted, watery eyes were bloodshot, and his hands were visibly shaking. "Bring it inside," he ordered in his familiar, rusty-sounding voice.

Kalten and Sparhawk set the shafts of the cart down, untied the ropes that had held the two barrels in place, and carefully eased one of them out onto the ground. Kalten measured the height of the barrel with a length of the rope and then checked the width of the doorway. "Just barely," he said. "Tip it over, Fron. We'll be able to roll it in."

Sparhawk heaved the barrel over onto its side, and he and his friend rolled it through the doorway into the cluttered room beyond. There was an unmade bed against one wall, and clothes littered the floor. The place was permeated with the acrid smell of Krager's unwashed, wine-sodden body, and there was a heap of empty casks and broken earthenware bottles in one corner.

"Where did you want these, Master Krager?" Kalten asked.

"Anyplace," Krager said impatiently.

"That's not thinking ahead," Kalten said critically. "They're too heavy for you to move by yourself. Pick a spot that'll be convenient."

"You might be right." Krager squinted around the room. Then he went to a place near the head of the bed and kicked some clothes out of the way. "Put them right here," he instructed.

"Ah—before we go any further, why don't we settle up? These are very expensive, Master Krager."

"How much?"

"Senga told me that he had to have fifty crowns a barrel. Arcian red's very hard to come by this far away from Arcium."

"Fifty crowns?" Krager exclaimed.

"Each," Kalten insisted. "He told me to open the barrels for you, too."

"I know how to open a wine barrel, Col."

"I'm sure of it, but Senga's an honest businessman and he wants me to make sure you're satisfied before I take your money." He rolled the barrel over against the wall. "Help me set it up, Fron," he told Sparhawk. They righted the barrel, and Kalten took a pry-bar out from under his belt. "Beer's a lot easier to deal with," he noted. "Somebody ought to tell those Arcian vintners about the advantages of putting a bunghole in the side of a barrel." He carefully pried up the lid as Krager, cup in hand, eagerly waited at his elbow.

"Give it a try, Master Krager," Kalten said then, lifting off the lid and stepping aside.

Krager dipped his cup into the deep red liquid, lifted it with a trembling hand, and drank deeply. "Marvelous!" He sighed happily.

"I'll tell Senga that it meets with your approval," Kalten said. He laughed. "You wouldn't expect it of a highway robber, but Senga's very concerned about satisfying his customers. Would you believe that he even had us pour out a barrel of beer that had gone sour? Come on, Fron, let's get the other barrel. We'll have Master Krager test that one and then we'll settle accounts."

The two of them went back outside and manhandled the second barrel out of the cart.

"Ask him why they've taken the guards off the doors of the house where they were holding Ehlana and Alean," Sparhawk muttered.

"Right." Kalten grunted as they lowered the wine barrel to the ground.

They put the second barrel beside the first, Kalten pried open the lid, and Krager sampled it.

"Satisfactory?" Kalten asked.

"Just fine," Krager said. He dipped out another cup and sank back happily on his bed. "Absolutely splendid."

"That'll be a hundred crowns, then."

Krager pulled a heavy purse out from under his belt and negligently tossed it to Kalten. "Here," he said. "Count it out yourself. Don't steal too much."

"This is business, Master Krager," Kalten told him. "If I was robbing you, I'd have my knife against your throat." He swept some clothing and a few dried crusts of bread off the top of a table with his forearm, opened the purse, and started counting out coins. "We noticed that all the guards have been pulled away from the house with the bars on the windows," he said. "A couple of days ago a man couldn't get within twenty paces of that place, but this morning Fron and I wheeled that cart right past the front door, and nobody paid any attention to us. Has Lord Scarpa moved whatever was so valuable out of there?"

Krager's puffy face became suddenly alert. "That's none of your business, Col."

"I didn't say it was. You might just make a suggestion to Lord Scarpa, though. If he doesn't want people to notice things like that, he shouldn't change anything. He should have kept all the guards right where they were. Senga and the rest of us are all robbers, you know, and we all more or less believed that Lord Scarpa was keeping his treasure in that house. The word *treasure* makes men like us prick up our ears."

Krager stared at him and then he began to laugh.

"What's so funny?" Kalten looked up from his counting.

"It was a treasure all right, Col—" Krager smirked. "—but not the kind you can count."

"Like you say, it's none of my business, but every man who works in Senga's tavern knows that it's been moved. I'm sure they'll all be poking around in these ruins looking for the new storehouse."

"Let them look." Krager shrugged. "The treasure's a long, long way from here by now."

"I hope you've still got guards on it. Those woods out there are crawling with fellows like Fron and me. Would you come here and check my count?"

"I trust you, Col."

"You're a fool, then."

"Take another ten crowns for yourself and your man," Krager said expansively, "and then if you don't mind, I'd like to be alone with my two new friends here."

"You're very generous, Master Krager." Kalten took some more coins from the purse, scooped up all the ones he had previously counted out, and dumped them into the side pocket of his smock. "Let's go, Fron," he said to Sparhawk. "Master Krager wants to be alone."

"Tell Senga that I'm grateful to him," Krager said, dipping out more wine, "and tell him to keep his eye out for more of this excellent vintage. I'll buy all he can find."

"I'll tell him, Master Krager. Enjoy yourself." And Kalten led the way out of the reeking room.

Sparhawk closed the door and held out his hand.

"What?" Kalten asked.

"My five crowns, if you don't mind," Sparhawk said firmly. "Let's keep accounts current, shall we?"

"Thou art shrewd, Sir Kalten," Xanetia's whispered voice came to them. "Thou didst most skillfully guide his thought in precisely the direction most useful to us."

Kalten made some show of counting coins into Sparhawk's hand. "What did you find out, Anarae?" he asked in a tense voice.

"Some day or two ago, a closed carriage did depart from this place after making some show of stopping—under heavy guard—at the door to the house upon which all our attention hath been fixed. The carriage, which was but a ploy, is bound for Panem-Dea. Those we seek are not inside, however. They had long since departed from Natayos with Zalasta."

"Did Krager know where Zalasta was taking them?" Sparhawk asked.

"It was evidently in Zalasta's mind that none here should know," Xanetia replied, "but Krager, ever alert to the main chance, was well aware that news of Zalasta's destination might well save his life should things go awry, and he did strive most assiduously to learn the Styric's plans. By feigning drunken stupor, he was able to be present when Zalasta did speak with his comrade, Cyzada. The twain spake in Styric, but Krager, unbeknownst to us all, hath a smattering of that tongue, and he was thus able to glean from their hurried conversation the very information which he—and we—are most curious about."

"That's a surprise," Kalten muttered. "Drunk or sober, Krager's a shrewd one, all right. Where's Zalasta taking the ladies, Anarae?"

Xanetia sighed. "The information is melancholy, Sir Kalten," she told him. "I do fear me that it is Zalasta's intent to take the queen and her handmaiden to the Hidden City of Cyrga, where Cyrgon himself doth hold sway, and by his power there can deny us all access to those we love."

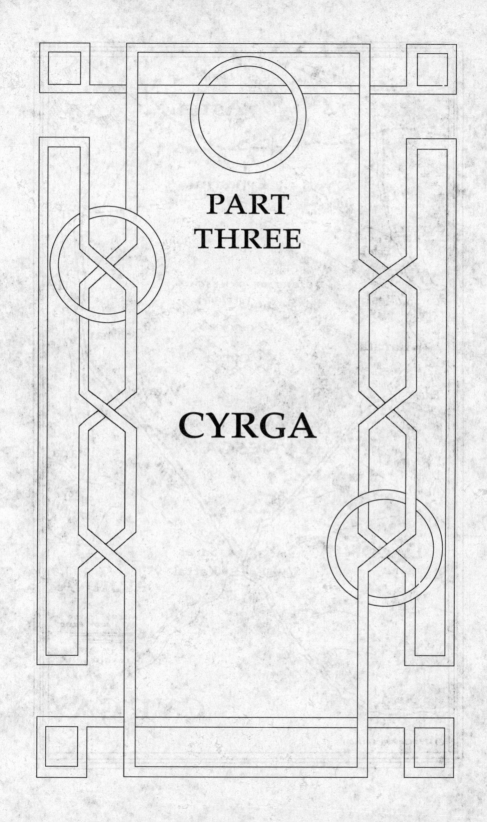

PART THREE

CYRGA

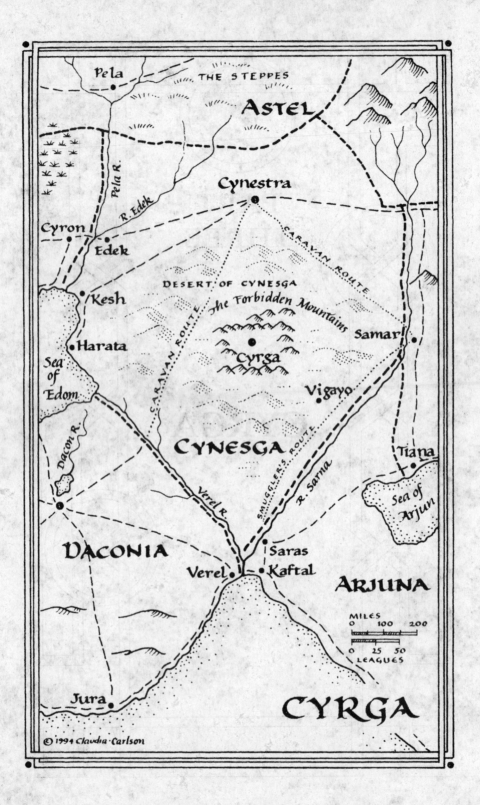

Pela

THE STEPPES

ASTEL

Pela R.

R. Edek

Cynestra

Cyron

Edek

CARAVAN ROUTE

DESERT OF CYNESGA

Kesh

The Forbidden Mountains

Samar

CARAVAN ROUTE

Harata

Cyrga

Sea of Edom

Vigayo

Dacon R.

CYNESGA

SMUGGLER'S ROUTE

Tiana

R. Sarna

Sea of Arjun

Verel R.

VACONIA

Saras

Verel

Kaftal

ARJUNA

MILES
0   100   200

0   25   50
LEAGUES

Jura

CYRGA

© 1994 Claudia Carlson

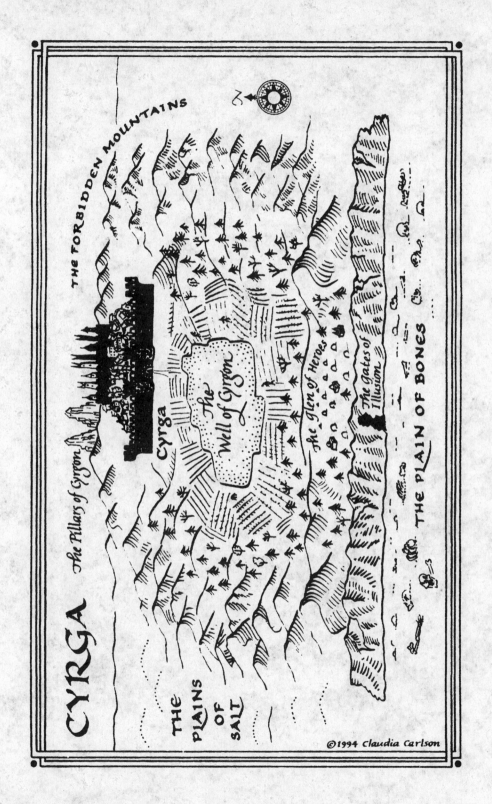

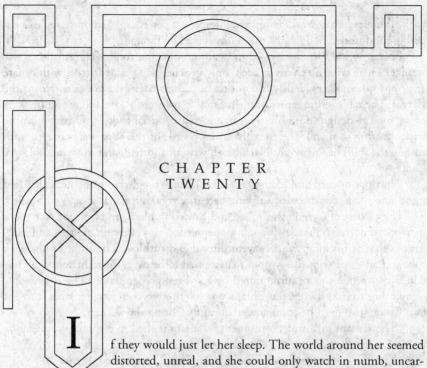

CHAPTER
TWENTY

I
f they would just let her sleep. The world around her seemed distorted, unreal, and she could only watch in numb, uncaring bemusement as her exhausted body screamed for sleep— or even for death. She stood exhausted at the window. The slaves toiling in the fields around the lake below looked almost like ants crawling across the winter-fallow fields as they grubbed at the soil with crude implements. Other slaves gathered firewood among the trees on the sloping sides of the basin, and the puny sounds of their axes drifted up to the dark tower from which she watched.

Alean lay on an unpadded bench—sleeping or dead, Ehlana could no longer tell which, but she envied her gentle maid in either case.

They were not alone, of course. They were never alone. Zalasta, his own face gaunt with weariness, talked on and on with King Santheocles. Ehlana was too tired to make any sense of the haggard Styric's droning words. She absently looked at the King of the Cyrgai, a man in a close-fitting steel breastplate, a short leather kirtle, and ornate steel wristguards. Santheocles was of a race apart, and generations of selective breeding had heightened those features most admired by his people. He was tall and superbly muscled. His skin was very fair, although his carefully curled and oiled hair and beard were glossy black. His nose was straight, continuing the unbroken line of his forehead. His eyes were very large and very dark—and totally empty. His expression was haughty, cruel. His was the face of a stupid, arrogant man devoid of compassion or even simple decency.

His ornate breastplate left his upper arms and shoulders bare, and as he listened, he absently clenched and relaxed his fists, setting his muscles to writhing and dancing under his pale skin. He was obviously not paying much attention to Zalasta's words, but sat instead totally engrossed in the rhythmic flexing and relaxing of the muscles in his arms. He was in all respects a perfect soldier, possessed of a superbly conditioned body and a mind unviolated by thought.

Ehlana wearily let her eyes drift again around the room. The furniture was strange. There were no chairs as such, only benches and padded stools with ornate arms but no backs. Evidently the notion of a chair-back had not occurred to the Cyrgai. The table in the center of the room was awkwardly low, and the lamps were of an ancient design, no more than hammered copper bowls of oil with burning wicks floating in them. The roughly sawed boards of the floor were covered with rushes, the walls of square-cut black basalt were unadorned, and the windows were undraped.

The door opened and Ekatas entered. Ehlana struggled to bring her exhausted mind into focus. Santheocles was king here in Cyrga, but it was Ekatas who ruled. The High Priest of Cyrgon was robed and cowled in black, and his aged face was a network of deep wrinkles. Although his expression was every bit as cruel and arrogant as that of his king, *his* eyes were shrewd and ruthless. The front of his black robe was adorned with the symbol that seemed to be everywhere here in the Hidden City, a white square surmounted by a stylized golden flame. There was some significance to it, certainly, but Ehlana was too tired to even wonder what it might be. "Come with me," he commanded abruptly. "Bring the women."

"The servant girl is of no moment," Zalasta replied in a slightly challenging tone. "Let her sleep."

"I am not accustomed to having my commands questioned, Styric."

"*Get* accustomed, Cyrg. The women are *my* prisoners. My arrangement is with Cyrgon, and you're no more than an appendage to that arrangement. Your arrogance is beginning to annoy me. Leave the girl alone."

Their eyes locked, and a sudden tension filled the room. "Well, Ekatas?" Zalasta said very quietly, "Has the time come? Have you finally worked up enough courage to challenge me? Anytime, Ekatas. Anytime at all."

Ehlana, now fully alert, saw the flicker of fear in the eyes of Cyrgon's priest. "Bring the queen, then," he said sullenly. "It is *she* whom Cyrgon would behold."

"Wise decision, Ekatas," Zalasta said sardonically. "If you keep making the right choices, you might even live for a little while longer."

Ehlana took her cloak and gently covered Alean with it. Then she turned to face the three men. "Let's get on with this," she told them, mustering some remnant of her royal manner.

Santheocles rose woodenly to his feet and put on his high-crested helmet, taking great paints to avoid mussing his carefully arranged hair. He spent several moments buckling on his large round shield, and then he drew his sword.

"What an ass," Ehlana noted scornfully. "Are you really sure you should trust his Majesty with anything sharp? He might hurt himself with it, you know."

"It is customary, woman," Ekatas replied stiffly. "Prisoners are always kept under close guard."

"Ah," she murmured, "and we *must* obey the dictates of custom, mustn't we, Ekatas? When custom rules, thought is unnecessary."

Zalasta smiled faintly. "I believe you wanted to take us to the temple, Ekatas. Let's not keep Cyrgon waiting."

Ekatas choked back a retort, jerked the door open, and led them out into the chilly hallway.

The stairs that descended from the topmost tower of the royal palace were narrow and steep, endless stairs winding down and down. Ehlana was trembling by the time they reached the courtyard below.

The winter sun was very bright in that broad courtyard, but there was not much heat to it.

They crossed the flagstoned courtyard to the pale temple, a building constructed not of marble but of chalky limestone. Unlike marble, the limestone had a dull, unreflective surface, and the temple looked somehow diseased, leprous.

They mounted the stairs to the portico and entered through a wide doorway. Ehlana had expected it to be dark inside this Holy of Holies, but it was not. She stared with a certain apprehensive astonishment at the source of the light even as Ekatas and Santheocles prostrated themselves, crying in unison, *"Vanet, tyek Alcor! Yala Cyrgon!"*

And then it was that the queen understood the significance of that ubiquitous emblem that marked virtually everything here in the Hidden City. The white square represented the blocky altar set in the precise center of the temple, but the flame that burned atop that altar was no stylized representation. It was instead an actual fire that twisted and flared, reaching hungrily upward.

Ehlana was suddenly afraid. The fire burning on the altar was not some votive offering, but a living flame, conscious, aware, and possessed of an unquenchable will. Bright as the sun, Cyrgon himself burned eternal on his pale altar.

"No," Sparhawk decided, "we'd better not. Let's just sit tight—at least until Xanetia has the chance to winnow through a few minds. We can always come back and deal with Scarpa and his friends later. Right now we need to know where Zalasta's taking Ehlana and Alean."

"We already know," Kalten said. "They're going to Cyrga."

"That's the whole point," the now-visible Ulath told him. "We don't know where Cyrga is."

They had gone back into the vine-choked ruins and had gathered on the second floor of a semi-intact palace to consider options.

"Aphrael has a general idea," Kalten said. "Can't we just start out for central Cynesga and do some poking around when we get there?"

"I don't think that'd do much good," Bevier pointed out. "Cyrgon's been concealing the place with illusions for the past ten eons. We could probably walk right through the streets of the city and not even see it."

"He's not hiding it from *everybody*," Caalador mused. "There are messages going back and forth, so *somebody* here in Natayos has to know the way. Sparhawk's right. Why don't we let Xanetia do the poking around *here,* instead of the lot of us going off into the desert to dodge scorpions and snakes while we turn over pebbles and grains of sand?"

"We stay here, then?" Tynian asked.

"For the time being," Sparhawk replied. "Let's not do anything to attract attention until we find out what Xanetia can discover. That's our best option at the moment."

"We were so *close*!" Kalten fumed. "If we'd just gotten here a day or two earlier."

"Well, we didn't," Sparhawk said flatly, forcing back his own disappointment and frustration, "so let's salvage what we can."

"With Zalasta getting farther and farther away with every minute," Kalten added bitterly.

"Don't worry, Kalten," Sparhawk told him in a tone as cold as death. "Zalasta can't run far enough or fast enough to get away from me when I decide to go after him."

"Are you busy, Sarabian?" Empress Elysoun asked tentatively from the doorway of the blue-draped room.

"Not really, Elysoun," he sighed, "just brooding. I've had a great deal of bad news in the last day or so."

"I'll come back some other time. You're not much fun when you've got things on your mind."

"Is that all there is in the world, Elysoun?" he asked her sadly. "Only fun?"

Her sunny expression tightened slightly, and she stepped into the room. "That's what you married us for in the first place, wasn't it, Sarabian?" She spoke in crisp Tamul that was not at all like her usual relaxed Valesian dialect. "Our marriages to you were to cement political alliances, so we're here as symbols, playthings, and ornaments. We're certainly not a part of the government."

He was rather startled by her perception and by the sudden change in her. It was easy to underestimate Elysoun. Her single-minded pursuit of pleasure and the aggressively revealing nature of her native dress proclaimed her to be an empty-headed sensualist, but this was a completely different Elysoun. He looked at her with new interest. "What have you been up to lately, my love?" he asked her fondly.

"The usual." She shrugged.

He averted his eyes. "Please don't do that."

"Do what?"

"Bounce that way. It's very distracting."

"It's supposed to be. You didn't think I dress this way because I'm too lazy to put on clothes, did you?"

"Is that why you came by, for fun? Or was there something more tedious?" They had never talked this way before, and her sudden frankness intrigued him.

"Let's talk about the tedious things first," she said. She looked at him critically. "You need to get more sleep," she chided.

"I wish I could. I've got too much on my mind."

"I'll have to see what I can do about that." She paused. "There's something going on in the women's palace, Sarabian."

"Oh?"

"A lot of strangers have been mingling with the assorted lapdogs and toadies that litter the halls."

He laughed. "That's a blunt way to describe courtiers."

"Aren't they? There's not a real man among them. They're in the palace to help us with our schemes. You *did* know that we spend our days plotting against each other, didn't you?"

He shrugged. "It gives you all something to do in your spare time."

"That's the only kind of time we have, my husband. *All* of our time is spare time, Sarabian, that's what's wrong with us. Anyway, these strangers aren't attached to any of the established courts."

"Are you sure?"

Her answering smile was wicked. "Trust me. I've had dealings with all the regular ones. They're all little more than butterflies. These strangers are wasps."

He gave her an amused look. "Have you actually winnowed your way through *all* the courtiers in the women's palace?"

"More or less." She shrugged again—quite deliberately, he thought. "Actually it was rather boring. Courtiers are a tepid lot, but it was a way to keep track of what was going on."

"Then it wasn't entirely—?"

"A little, perhaps, but I have to take steps to protect myself. Our politics are subtle, but they're savage."

"Are these strangers Tamuls?"

"Some are. Some aren't."

"How long has this been going on?"

"Since we all moved back to the women's palace. I didn't see any of these wasps when we were all living here with the Elenes."

"Just the past few weeks, then?"

She nodded. "I thought you should know. It could be just more of the same kind of thing that's been going on for years, but I don't really think so. It *feels* different somehow. Our politics are more indirect than yours, and what's happening in the women's palace is men's politics."

"Do you suppose you could keep an eye on it for me? I'd be grateful."

"Of course, my husband. I *am* loyal, after all."

"Oh, really?"

"Don't make that mistake, Sarabian. Loyalty shouldn't be confused with that other business. That doesn't mean anything. Loyalty does."

"There's a lot more to you than meets the eye, Elysoun."

"Oh? I've never tried to conceal anything." She inhaled deeply.

He laughed again. "Do you have plans for this evening?"

"Nothing that can't be put off until some other time. What did you have in mind?"

"I thought we might talk a while."

"Talk?"

"Among other things."

"Let me send a message first. Then we can talk for as long as you like—among those other things you mentioned."

· · ·

They were two days out of Tiana on their way around the west end of the lake on the road to Arjuna. They had camped on the lakeshore some distance from the road, and Khalad had shot a deer with his crossbow. "Camp meat," he explained to Berit as he skinned the animal. "It saves time and money."

"You're really very good with that crossbow," Berit said.

Khalad shrugged. "Practice," he replied. Then his head came up sharply. "Company coming." He pointed toward the road with his knife.

"Arjuni," Berit noted, squinting at the approaching riders.

"Not all of them," Khalad disagreed. "The one in front's an Elene—an Edomishman, judging from his clothes." Khalad wiped his bloody hands on the long grass, picked up his crossbow, and recocked it. "Just to be on the safe side," he explained. "They *do* know who we really are, after all."

Berit nodded bleakly and loosened his sword in its scabbard.

The riders reined in about fifty yards away. "Sir Sparhawk?" the Edomishman called out in Elenic.

"Maybe," Berit called back. "What can I do for you, neighbor?"

"I have a message for you."

"I'm touched. Bring it on in."

"Come alone," Khalad added. "You won't need your bodyguards."

"I've heard about what you did to the last messenger."

"Good," Khalad replied. "We sort of intended for word of that to get around. The fellow had a little trouble being civil, but I'm sure you have better manners. Come ahead. You're safe—as long as you're polite."

The Edomishman still hesitated.

"Friend," Khalad said pointedly, "you're well within range of my crossbow, so you'd better do as I tell you. Just come on in alone. We'll conduct our business, and then you and your Arjuni friends can be on your way. Otherwise, this might turn unpleasant."

The Edomishman conferred briefly with his bodyguards and then rode cautiously forward, holding a folded parchment above his head. "I'm not armed," he announced.

"That's not very prudent, neighbor," Berit told him. "These are troubled times. Let's have the note."

The messenger lowered his arm slowly and extended the parchment. "The plans have changed, Sir Sparhawk," he said politely.

"Astonishing." Berit opened the parchment and gently took out the lock of identifying hair. "This is only about the third time. You fellows seem to be having some difficulty making up your minds." He looked at the parchment. "That's accommodating. Somebody even drew a map this time."

"The village isn't really very well known," the Edomishman explained. "It's a tiny place that wouldn't even be there if it weren't for the slave trade."

"You're a very good messenger, friend," Khalad told him. "Would you like to carry a word back to Krager for me?"

"I'll try, young Master."

"Good. Tell him that I'm coming after him. He should probably start looking back over his shoulder, because no matter how this turns out, one day I'll be there."

The Edomishman swallowed hard. "I'll tell him, young Master."

"I'd appreciate it."

The messenger carefully backed his horse off a few yards and then rode back to rejoin his Arjuni escort.

"Well?" Khalad asked.

"Vigayo—over in Cynesga."

"It's not much of a town."

"You've been there?"

"Briefly. Bhelliom took us there by mistake when Sparhawk was practicing with it."

"How far is it from here?"

"About a hundred leagues. It's in the right direction, though. Aphrael said that Zalasta's taking the queen to Cyrga, so Vigayo's got to be closer than Arjun. Pass the word, Berit. Tell Aphrael that we'll start out first thing in the morning. Then you can come and help me cut up this deer. It's ten days to Vigayo, so we're probably going to need the meat."

"He hath been there," Xanetia told them. "His memories of the Hidden City are vivid, but his recollection of the route is imprecise. I could glean no more than disconnected impressions of the journey. His madness hath bereft his thought of coherence, and his mind doth flit from reality to illusion and back without purpose or direction."

"I'd say we got us a problem," Caalador drawled. "Ol' Krager, he don't know th' way on accounta he wuz too drunk t' pay attention when Zalasta wuz a-talkin' 'bout how t' git t' Cyrga, an' Scarpa's too crazy t' remember how he got thar." His eyes narrowed, and he discarded the dialect. "What about Cyzada?" he asked Xanetia.

She shuddered. "It is not madness nor drunkenness which doth bar my way into the thought of Cyzada of Esos," she replied in a voice filled with revulsion. "Deeply hath he reached into the darkness that was Azash, and the creatures of the netherworld have possessed him so utterly that his thought is no longer human. His spells at first did in some measure control those horrid demons, but then he did summon Klæl, and in that act was all unloosed. Prithee, do not send me again into that seething chaos. He doth indeed know a route to Cyrga, but we could in no wise follow *that* path, for it doth lie through the realm of flame and darkness and unspeakable horror."

"That more or less exhausts the possibilities of this place, then, doesn't it?" They all turned quickly at the sound of the familiar voice. The Child-Goddess sat demurely on a window ledge holding her pipes in her hands.

"Is this wise, Divine One?" Bevier asked her. "Won't our enemies sense your presence?"

"There's no one left here who can do that, Bevier," she replied. "Zalasta's gone. I just stopped by to tell you that Berit's received new instructions. He and Khalad are going to Vigayo, a village just on the other side of the Cynesgan border. As soon as you're ready, I'll take you there."

"What good will that do?" Kalten asked.

"I need to get Xanetia close to the next messenger," she replied. "Cyrga's completely concealed—even from me. There's a key to that illusion and *that's* what we have to find. Without that key, we could all grow old wandering around out in that wasteland and still not find the city."

"I suppose you're right," Sparhawk conceded. He looked directly at her. "Can you arrange another meeting? We're getting close to the end of this, and I need to talk with the others—Vanion and Bergsten in particular, and probably with Betuana and Kring as well. We've got armies at our disposal, but they won't be much use if they're running off in three different directions or attacking Cyrga piecemeal. We've got a general idea of where the place is, and I'd like to put a ring of steel around it, but I *don't* want anybody to go blundering in there until we get Ehlana and Alean safely out."

"You're going to get me in trouble, Sparhawk," she said tartly. "Do you have any idea of the kinds of promises I'll have to make to get permission for that kind of gathering? And I'll have to *keep* all those promises, too."

"It's really very important, Aphrael."

She stuck her tongue out at him, and then she wavered and vanished.

"Domi Tikume sent orders, your Reverence," the shaved-headed Peloi advised Patriarch Bergsten when they met in the churchman's tent just outside the town of Pela in central Astel. "We're to provide whatever assistance we can."

"Your Domi's a good man, friend Daiya," the armored Patriarch replied.

"His orders stirred up a hornet's nest," Daiya said wryly. "The idea of an alliance with the Church Knights set off a theological debate that went on for days. Most people here in Astel believe that the Church Knights were born and raised in Hell. A fair number of the debaters are currently taking the matter up with God in person."

"I gather that religious disputes among the Peloi are quite spirited."

"Oh, yes," Daiya agreed. "The message from Archimandrite Monsel helped to quiet things, though. Peloi religious thought isn't really all that profound, your Reverence. We trust God and leave the theology to the churchmen. If the Archimandrite approves, that's good enough for us. If he's wrong, he's the one who'll burn in Hell for it."

"How far is it from here to Cynestra?" Bergsten asked him.

"About a hundred and seventy-five leagues, your Reverence."

"Three weeks," Bergsten muttered sourly. "Well, there's not much we can do about that, I suppose. We'll start out first thing in the morning. Tell your men to get some sleep, friend Daiya. It's probably going to be in short supply for the next month or so."

"Bergsten." The voice crooning his name was light and musical.

The Thalesian Patriarch sat up quickly, reaching for his ax.

"Oh, don't do that, Bergsten. I'm not going to hurt you."

"Who's there?" he demanded, fumbling for his candle and his flint and steel.

"Here." A small hand emerged from the darkness with a tongue of flame dancing on its palm.

Bergsten blinked. His midnight visitor was a little girl—Styric, he guessed. She was a beautiful child with long hair and large eyes as dark as night. Bergsten's hands started to tremble. "You're Aphrael, aren't you?" he choked.

"Keen observation, your Grace. Sparhawk wants to see you."

He drew back from this personage that standard Church doctrine told him did not—could not—exist.

"You're being silly, your Grace," she told him. "You know that I couldn't even be talking to you if I didn't have permission from your God, don't you? I can't even come near you without permission."

"Well, theoretically," he reluctantly conceded. "You *could* be a demon, though, and the rules don't apply to them."

"Do I *look* like a demon?"

"Appearance and reality are two different things," he insisted.

She looked into his eyes and pronounced the true name of the Elene God, one of the most closely kept secrets of the Church. "A demon couldn't say that name, could it, your Grace?"

"Well, I suppose not."

"We'll get along well, Bergsten." She smiled, kissing him lightly on the cheek. "Ortzel would have argued that point for weeks. Leave your ax here, please. Steel makes my flesh crawl."

"Where are we going?"

"To meet with Sparhawk. I already told you that."

"Is it far?"

"Not really." She smiled, opening the tent flap.

It was still night in Pela, but it was broad daylight beyond the tent flap—a strange sort of daylight. A pristine white beach stretched down to a sapphire sea all under a rainbow-colored sky, and a small green eyot surmounted by a gleaming alabaster temple rose from that incredibly blue sea about a half mile from the beach.

"What place is this?" Bergsten asked, poking his head out of the tent and looking around in amazement.

"I suppose you could call it Heaven, your Grace," the Child-Goddess replied, blowing out the flame dancing on her palm. "It's mine, anyway. There are others, but this one's mine."

"Where is it?"

"Everywhere and anywhere. All the Heavens are everyplace all at once. So are all the Hells, of course—but that's another story. Shall we go?"

Cordz of Nelan was the perfect man. That realization had not come easily to the devout Edomishman. It had only been after extended soul-searching and a meticulous examination of the sacred texts of his faith that he had arrived at the inescapable conclusion. He was perfect. He obeyed all of God's commandments, he did what he was supposed to do, and he did not do the things that were forbidden. Isn't that what perfection is all about?

It was a comfort to be perfect, but Cordz was not one to rest on his laurels. Now that *he* had achieved perfection in the eyes of God, it was time to turn his attention to the faults of his neighbors. Sinners, however, seldom sin openly, so Cordz was obliged to resort to subterfuge. He peeked through windows late at night; he eavesdropped on private conversations; and, when his sinful neighbors cleverly concealed their wrongdoing from him, he imagined the sins they *might* be committing. The Sabbath was a very special day for Cordz, but not for the sermons. After all, what need had a perfect man for sermons? It was on the Sabbath that he was able to rise to his feet and denounce the sins of his neighbors, both the sins they *had* committed and the sins they *might* be committing.

He probably irritated the Devil. God knows he irritated his neighbors.

But then a crisis had arisen in Edom. The debauched and heretical Church of Chyrellos, after two eons of plotting and scheming, was finally preparing to make her move against the righteous. The Church Knights were on the march, and horrors beyond imagining marched with them.

Cordz was among the first to enlist in Rebal's army; the perfect man abandoned his neighbors to their sinful ways to join a holier cause. He became Rebal's most trusted messenger, killing horses by the dozen as he rushed about the Elene kingdoms of western Tamuli carrying the dispatches so vital to the cause.

On this particular day Cordz was flogging his exhausted horse southward toward the corrupt cities of southern Daconia, cesspools of sin and licentiousness, if the truth were to be known, where the citizens not only did not *know* that they were sinners, they did not even care. Worse yet, an obscure and probably heretical tradition of the Dacite Church prevented laymen from speaking aloud during Sabbath services. Thus, God's very own spokesman, the perfect man, was not permitted to expose and denounce the sins he saw all around him. The frustration of it sometimes made him want to scream.

He had been riding hard for the past week and he was very tired. Thus it was with some relief that he finally crested the hill that overlooked the port city of Melek.

Then all thoughts of the sins of others vanished. Cordz reined in his staggering horse and gaped in horror at what he saw.

There on a sea sparkling in the winter sun was a vast armada, ships beyond counting, sailing majestically down the coast under the red and gold banners of the Church of Chyrellos!

The perfect man was so overcome with horror that he did not even hear the plaintive sound of a shepherd's rude pipe playing a Styric air in a minor key somewhere off to his left. He gaped for a time at his worst nightmare, and then he desperately drove his spurs into his horse's flanks, rushing to spread the alarm.

General Sirada was the younger brother of Duke Milanis, and he commanded the rebel forces in Panem-Dea. King Rakya had so arranged it that most of Scarpa's generals were Arjuni. Sirada knew that there were risks involved, but the younger sons of noble families were obliged to take risks if they wanted to get ahead in the world. For them, rank and position had to be won. Sirada had endured the years of association with the crazy bastard son of a tavern wench and the discomfort of camping out in the jungle waiting for his chance.

And now it had come. The madman in Natayos had finally sent the order to march. The campaign had begun. There was no sleep in Panem-Dea that night. The preparations for the march went on through the hours of darkness, and the undisciplined rabble Sirada commanded was incapable of doing *anything* quietly. The general spent the night poring over his maps.

The strategy was sound; he was forced to admit that. He was to join forces with Scarpa and the other rebels near Deral. Then they would march north to the Tamul Mountains to be reinforced by Cynesgans. From there, they would march on Tosa in preparation for the final assault on Matherion.

General Sirada's own strategy was much simpler. Scarpa would crush any resistance at Tosa, but he would not live to see the gleaming domes of the imperial capital. Sirada smiled thinly and patted the little vial of poison he carried in his inside pocket. The army would capture Matherion, but it would be General Sirada who would lead the final assault and personally run his sword through Emperor Sarabian. The younger brother of Duke Milanis expected an earldom at the very least to come out of this campaign.

The door banged open, and his adjutant burst into the room, his eyes starting from his head and his face a pasty white. "Good God, my General!" he shrieked.

"What do you think you're doing?" Sirada demanded. "How *dare* you? I'll have you flogged for this!"

"We're being attacked, my General!"

Sirada could hear the squeals of terror now. He rose quickly and went out the door.

It was not yet daylight, and a clinging mist had crept out of the tangled forest to blur the ruined walls and houses of Panem-Dea. There were fires and flaring torches pushing back the darkness with their ruddy light, but there were other lights in the weed-choked streets as well: pale, cold lights that did not burn or flicker. Creatures of light, pale as wandering moons, stalked the streets of Panem-Dea. The general's heart filled with terror. It was impossible! The Shining Ones were a myth! There were no such creatures!

Sirada shook off his fright and drew his sword. "Stand fast!" he roared at his demoralized men. "Form up! Pikemen to the front!" He bulled his way into the milling mob of terrified troops, flailing about him with the flat of his sword. "Form up! Make a line!"

But there was no rationality nor fear of authority in the panic-stricken faces of his poorly trained men. The screaming mob simply diverged and bypassed him on either side. He ran at them again, swinging great strokes with his sword, cutting down his own men.

He was so desperate to restore order that he did not even feel the knife-stroke that went in just below his ribs on the left side. He could not even understand why his knees buckled or why he fell under the trampling feet of his soldiers as they fled screaming into the trackless forest.

"Are you sure this map's accurate, Tynian?" Patriarch Bergsten demanded, peering at the miniature world under his feet.

"It's the most accurate map you'll ever see, your Grace," Tynian assured him. "Bhlokw cast the spell, and the Troll-Gods put their hands into the ground and felt the shape of the continent. This is it—down to the last tree and bush. Everything's here."

"Except for Cyrga, Tynian-Knight," Engessa amended. The Atan general was completely healed now, and he looked as fit as ever. His face, however, was troubled. His queen had greeted him almost abruptly when she had first arrived, and she was quite obviously avoiding him.

Sephrenia was seated on one of the benches in Aphrael's alabaster temple with the rainbow light from the impossible sky playing over her face. "We'd hoped that Schlee might be able to feel Cyrga when he re-created the continent, your Grace," she said, "but Cyrgon's illusion seems to be absolute. Not even a Trollish spell can break it."

"What's the best guess we can come up with?" Bergsten asked.

Aphrael walked lightly across the tiny world Bhlokw had conjured up for them. She stepped over the minuscule city of Cynestra and continued south to a mountainous region in the center of the desert. "It used to be somewhere in this general vicinity," she said, gesturing vaguely over the mountains.

"Used to be?" Bergsten asked her sharply.

She shrugged. "Sometimes we move things."

"Whole cities?"

"It's possible—but it's a reflection of bad planning."

Bergsten shuddered and began marking off distances on the miniature continent with a long piece of string. "I'm up here at Pela," he told them, pointing at a spot in central Astel. "That's almost three hundred leagues from the general vicinity of Cyrga, and I'll have to stop to capture Cynestra along the way. The rest of you are much closer, so you're going to have to hold off a bit if we all want to get there at approximately the same time."

Aphrael shrugged. "I'll tamper," she said.

Bergsten gave her a puzzled look.

"Divine Aphrael has ways of compressing time and distance, your Grace," Sparhawk explained. "She can—"

"I don't want to hear about it, Sparhawk!" Bergsten said sharply, putting his hands over his ears. "You've already put my soul in danger just by bringing me here. Please don't make it any worse by telling me things I don't need to know about."

"Whatever you say, your Grace," Sparhawk agreed.

Emban was pacing around the cluster of upthrusting mountains in the center of the Cynesgan desert. "We're all going to be converging on these mountains," he said. "I'm no expert, but wouldn't our best move be just to stop in the foothills and wait until everyone's in place before we make the final assault?"

"No, your Grace," Vanion said firmly. "Let's stay out a bit from the foothills—at least a day's ride. If we run into Klæl's creatures, we'll need room to maneuver. I want a lot of flat ground around me when that happens."

The fat little churchman shrugged. "You're the soldier, Vanion." He pointed toward the south. "There's our weakness," he said. "We've got a good concentration of forces coming out of the east, the northeast, and the north, but we don't have anybody covering the south."

"Or the west," Sarabian added.

"I'll cover the west, your Majesty," Bergsten told him. "I can position my knights and the Peloi to block off that entire quadrant."

"That still leaves the south," Emban mused.

"It's already been taken care of, Emban," Aphrael assured him. "Stragen's been spinning stories about a vast Church fleet off the southern coast, and I've been weaving illusions to back him up. How long is it going to take the Trolls to get into position north of Zhubay, Ulath?"

"Just as long as it takes to persuade the Troll-Gods that we need their children there instead of in the Tamul Mountains," the big Thalesian replied, "—a day or so probably. Once they're convinced, they'll put their children into No-Time. If we didn't have to stop now and then to feed the Trolls, we could be in Zhubay before you could even blink. If I knew where Cyrga was, I could have fifteen hundred Trolls on the doorstep by morning."

"There's no need to rush." The Child-Goddess looked around with steely eyes. "Nobody—and I mean *nobody*—is going to move on Cyrga until I know that Ehlana and Alean are safe. If I have to, I can keep you running around in circles out there in that desert for generations, so don't try to get creative on me."

"Is the Queen of Elenia so very important to you, Divine One?" Betuana asked mildly. "War is hard, and we must accept our losses."

"It's a personal matter, Betuana," Aphrael said shortly. "These are your positions." She gestured over the miniature continent. "Bergsten will come in from the north and west to cover that side of the city; Ulath, Tynian, and Bhlokw will bring the Trolls down from Zhubay and join with Betuana's Atans on their left flank; Vanion will come in from the east and be joined on *his* left by Kring and the Peloi; Stragen's persuaded that disgusting Dacite in Beresa that there are a million or so Church Knights landing on the coast around Verel and Kaftal, and that should divert most of the armies of Cynesga. We'll all converge on Cyrga. There are some discrepancies in the distances, but I'll take care of those. When the time comes, you *will* all be in place—even if I have to pick you up one by one and carry you." She stopped abruptly. "What *is* your problem, Bergsten? Don't laugh at me, or I'll take you by the nose and shake you."

"I wasn't laughing, Divine One," he assured her. "I was only smiling in approval. Where *did* you learn so much about strategy and tactics?"

"I've been watching you Elenes make war since shortly after you discovered fire, your Grace. I was bound to learn a *few* of the tricks of the trade." She turned suddenly on Bhlokw. "What?" she asked irritably in Trollish.

"U-lat has said to me what you have said, Child-Goddess. Why are we doing this?"

"To punish the wicked ones, Priest of the Troll-Gods."

"*What?*" Sparhawk said to Ulath in stunned amazement. "What did she call him?"

"Oh?" Ulath said mildly. "Didn't you know? Our shaggy friend has a certain eminence."

"They actually have priests?"

"Of course. Doesn't everybody?"

"It is good to punish the wicked ones who have taken Anakha's mate away," Bhlokw was saying, "but do we need to take so many? Khwaj will punish the wicked ones. This is the season of Schlee, and we should be following the way of the hunt. The young must be fed or they will die, and that is not a good thing."

"Oh, dear," Aphrael murmured.

"What's happening here, Sir Ulath?" Sarabian asked.

"The Trolls are hunters, your Majesty," Ulath explained, "not warriors. They have no real understanding of warfare. They eat what they kill."

Sarabian shuddered.

"It *is* very moral, your Majesty," Ulath pointed out. "From a Troll's point of view, wasting the meat is criminal."

Aphrael was squinting at the priest of the Troll-Gods. "It is a good thing to do that which follows the way of the hunt *and* punishes the wicked ones at the same time," she said. "If we hunt this way, we will cause hurt to the wicked ones *and* bring much meat to the young during the season of Schlee."

Bhlokw considered that. "The hunts of the man-things are not-simple," he said dubiously, "but it is my thought that the hunts of the God-things are even *more* not-simple." He reflected on it. "It is good, though. A hunt that gathers more than meat is a good hunt. You hunt very well, Child-Goddess. Sometime we might take eat together and talk of old hunts. It is good to do this. It makes pack-mates closer so that they hunt together better."

"It would make me glad if we did this, Bhlokw."

"Then we will do it. I will kill a dog for us to eat. Dog is even more good-to-eat than pig."

Aphrael made a slight gagging sound.

"Will it cause anger to you if I speak to our pack-mates in bird-noises, Bhlokw?" Sparhawk stepped in. "It will soon be time for the hunt to begin, and all must be made ready."

"It will not cause anger to me, Anakha. U-lat can say to me what you are saying."

"All right, then," Sparhawk said to the rest of them. "We all know how we're going to converge on Cyrga, but there are several of us who have to go in first. Please hold off on your attack until we're in position. Don't crowd us by trampling on our heels."

"Who are you taking in with you, Sparhawk?" Vanion asked.

"Kalten, Bevier, Talen, Xanetia, and Mirtai."

"I don't quite—"

Sparhawk held up one hand. "Aphrael made the choices, my Lord," he said. "If there are any objections, take them up with her."

"You have to have those people with you, Sparhawk," Aphrael explained patiently. "If you don't, you'll fail."

"Whatever you say, Divine One," he surrendered.

"You'll be out in front of Berit and me then?" Khalad asked.

Sparhawk nodded. "The people on the other side will expect us to trail along behind you. If we're in front, it might confuse them—at least that's what we're hoping. Aphrael will take us directly to Vigayo and we'll nose around a bit. If the fellow with the next message is already there, Xanetia should be able to pick up your next destination. Sooner or later, somebody's going to have to give you the key to the illusion that's hiding Cyrga, and *that's* the one piece of information we have to have. Once we've got that, the rest is easy."

"I like his definition of easy," Caalador murmured to Stragen.

Emban jotted another note on his inevitable list. Then he cleared his throat.

"*Must* you, Emban?" Bergsten sighed.

"It helps me to think, Bergsten, and it makes sure that we haven't left anything out. If it bores you so much, don't listen."

"The man-things talk much when they decide how they will hunt, U-lat," Bhlokw complained.

"It is the nature of the man-things to do this."

"It is because the hunts of the man-things are too much not-simple. It is my thought that their hunts are not-simple because they do not eat the ones they kill. They hunt and kill for reasons which I do not understand. It is my thought that this thing the man-things call 'war' is a very great wickedness."

"It is not in our thought to cause anger to the priest of the Troll-Gods," Patriarch Bergsten said in flawless Trollish. "The thing which the man-things call 'war' is like the thing which happens when two Troll-packs come to hunt on the same range."

Bhlokw considered that. Then he grunted as comprehension came over his shaggy face. "Now it is clear to me," he said. "This thing the man-things call 'war' is like the hunting of thought. That is why it is not-simple. But you still talk much." The Troll squinted at Emban. "That one is the worst," he added. "His mind-belly is as big as his belly-belly."

"What did he say?" Emban asked curiously.

"It wouldn't translate very well, your Grace," Ulath replied blandly.

Patriarch Emban gave him a slightly suspicious look and then meticulously laid out their deployment once again, checking items off his list as he went. When he had finished, he looked around. "Can anybody think of anything else?"

"Perhaps," Sephrenia said, frowning slightly. "Our enemies know that Berit's not really Sparhawk, but they're going to think that Sparhawk won't have any choice but to follow along behind. It might help to confirm that belief. I think I know a way to duplicate the sound and sense of Bhelliom. If it works, our enemies will think that Sparhawk's somewhere in the column of knights Vanion's going to lead out into the desert. They'll concentrate on us rather than looking for him."

"You're putting yourself in danger, Sephrenia," Aphrael objected.

"There's nothing particularly new about that." Sephrenia smiled. "And when you consider what we're trying to do, no place is really safe."

"Is that it, then?" Engessa asked, standing up.

"Probably, friend Engessa," Kring replied, "except for the hour or so we'll all spend telling each other to be careful."

Engessa squared his shoulders, turned, and faced his queen directly. "What are your orders, Betuana-Queen," he asked her with military formality.

She drew herself up with a regal stiffness. "It is our instruction that you return with us to Sarna, Engessa-Atan. There you will resume command of our armies."

"It shall be as you say, Betuana-Queen."

"Directly upon our return, you will send runners to my husband, the king. Tell him that there is no longer a threat to Tosa. The Shining Ones will deal with Scarpa."

He nodded stiffly.

"Further, tell him that I have need of his forces in Sarna. That is where we will prepare for the main battle, and he should be there to take command." She paused. "This is not because we are dissatisfied with *your* leadership, Engessa-Atan, but Androl *is* the king. You have served well. The royal house of Atan is grateful."

"It is my duty, Betuana-Queen," he replied, clashing his fist against his breastplate in salute. "No gratitude is necessary."

"Oh, dear," Aphrael murmured.

"What's wrong?" Sephrenia asked her.

"Nothing."

CHAPTER TWENTY-TWO

"It's definitely Chacole and Torellia, Sarabian," Elysoun insisted several days later. "Chacole's more or less running things. She's older and shrewder. The strangers usually go directly to her. They talk privately for a while, and then she sends for Torellia. They weren't really all that fond of each other before, but now they've got their heads together all the time."

"They're probably getting orders from home," Sarabian mused. "King Jaluah of Cynesga is Chacole's brother, and Torellia's the daughter of King Rakya of Arjuna. Can you get any sense at all of what they might be up to?"

She shook her head. "It's too early."

"Early?"

"Women's politics again. We're more devious than men. Chacole will want everything in place before she starts to form other alliances. She's got Torellia under control, but she's not quite ready to start trying to expand yet."

"You're sure that Torellia's the subordinate one?"

She nodded. "Chacole's servants are lording it over hers. That's the first sign of dominance in the women's palace. Cieronna's servants are all insufferable because she's the first wife, and we're all subordinate to her—except for Liatris, of course."

"Of course." Sarabian smiled. "No one in his right mind is impertinent to Liatris. Has she killed anybody lately?"

"Not since she butchered Cieronna's footman last year."

"There's a thought. Should we bring Liatris into this?"

Elysoun shook her head. "Maybe later, but not at this stage. Atana Liatris is too direct. If I approached her with this, she'd simply kill Chacole and Torellia. Let's wait until Chacole approaches me before we involve Liatris."

"Are you sure Chacole *will* approach you?"

"It's almost certain. My servants have greater freedom of movement than hers—because of my social activities."

"That's a delicate way to put it."

"You knew I was a Valesian when you married me, Sarabian, and you know about our customs. That's why my servants have the run of the compound. It's always been a tradition."

He sighed. "How many are there currently, Elysoun?"

"None, actually." She smiled at him. "You don't really understand, do you, Sarabian? The biggest part of the fun of those little adventures has always been the intrigue, and I'm getting plenty of that playing politics."

"Aren't you feeling a little—deprived?"

"I can endure it—" She shrugged. "—and if I get desperate, I always have you to fall back on, don't I?" And she gave him an arch little smile.

"Wal, sir, Master Valash," Caalador drawled, leaning back in his chair in the cluttered loft, "Ol' Vymer here, he done tole me that yer a' willin' t' pay good money fer infermation, an' he sorta figgered ez how y' might want t' hear 'bout the stuff I seen in southwest Atan fer yer very ownself."

"You two have known each other for quite some time then?" Valash asked.

"Oh, gorsh yes, Master Valash. Me'n Vymer goes way back. We wuz all t'gether durin' that fracas in Matherion—him an' me an' Fron an' Reldin—along with a couple others—when the fellers from Interior come a-bustin' in on us. They wuz hull bunches o' excitement that night, let me tell yew. Anyway, after we shuck off the po-lice, we all split up an' scattered t' th' winds. 'Tain't a *real* good idee t' stay all bunched up whin yer a-runnin' from th' law."

Stragen sat back from the table out of the circle of light from the single candle, carefully watching Valash's face. Caalador had just arrived to replace Sparhawk and Talen in the ongoing deception of Valash, and Stragen was once again impressed by how smooth his friend really was. Valash seemed lulled by the easy, folksy charm of Caalador's dialect. Stragen despised the slovenly speech, but he was forced to admit its utility. It always seemed so genuine, so innocently artless.

"Where *is* Fron, anyway?" Valash asked.

"Him an' Reldin tuk off 'bout a week ago." Caalador shrugged. "I happened t' stop off in a tavern up in Delo whilst I wuz a-comin' on down yere, an' they wuz a feller what had *policeman* wrote all over him who wuz describin' ol' Fron an' the boy right down t' th' warts. Soon's I got yere, I tole 'em 'bout it, an' they figgered that it might just be time t' move on. Anyhow, Vymer here sez as how yer innerested in whut's a-goin' on here an' thar, an' I seen a few things after we all got run outta Matherion that he's a-thankin' might be worth somethin' to ya."

"I'll certainly listen, Ezek." Valash raised his head sharply as the comatose Ogerajin began to mumble in his sleep.

"Is he all right?" Stragen asked.

"It's nothing," Valash said shortly. "He does that all the time. Go ahead, Ezek."

"Wal, sir, she wuz a couple weeks ago, I guess, an' I wuz a-hot-footin' it across Atan, figgerin' t' make m' way on acrost Astel t' Darsos—on accounta the law bein' hot on m' heels an' all. I wuz a-comin' on down outten th' mountings when I pult up short, cuz I seen more gol-dang Atans than I thought they wuz in the hull world—I mean, they wint on fer *miles*! They wuz *multitudes* o' them big rascals— all geared up fer war an a-lookin' real mean an' on-friendly-like."

"The entire Atan army?" Valash exclaimed.

"It lookt t' me more like a gineral my-grashun of the hull dang race, Master Valash. Y' ain't niver *seen* s' miny of 'em!"

"Where exactly were they?" Valash asked excitedly.

"Wal, sir, close ez I could make out, they wuz right close t' the Cynesgan border—up thar close by a little town calt Zhubay. Iff'n y' happen t' have a map handy, I could point out th' egg-zact spot fer ya." Caalador squinted at the Dacite. "Whut would y' say this infermaytion's worth, Master Valash?"

Valash didn't even hesitate when he reached for his purse.

"It was very strange, Domi Tikume," Kring told his friend as they rode at the head of their massed tribesmen out into the Cynesgan desert the morning after the conference on Aphrael's island. "The Child-Goddess said that we were all dream- ing, but everything seemed so real. I could actually smell the flowers and the grass. I've never smelled anything in a dream before."

Tikume looked dubious. "Are you sure it wasn't heresy to go there, Domi Kring?"

Kring laughed wryly. "Well, if it was, I was in good company. Patriarch Emban was there, and so was Patriarch Bergsten. Anyway, you and I are supposed to con- tinue making these raids into Cynesga. Then we're supposed to go ahead and ride in toward those mountains out in the middle of the desert. We're hoping that Prince Sparhawk will have pinpointed the exact location of Cyrga by the time we get there."

One of the scouts who had been ranging the burnt brown desert ahead came galloping back. "Domi Tikume," he said as he reined in. "We've found them."

"Where?" Tikume demanded.

"There's a dry watercourse about two miles ahead, Domi. They're crouched down in there. I'd say they're planning to ambush us."

"What sort of soldiers are they?" Kring asked.

"There was Cynesgan cavalry and more of those big ones with the steel masks that we've been running to death lately. There was some other infantry as well, but I didn't recognize them."

"Breastplates? Short kirtles? Helmets with high crests, and big round shields?"

"Those are the ones, Domi Kring."

Kring rubbed one hand across his shaved scalp. "How wide is the watercourse?" he asked.

"Fifty paces or so, Domi."

"Crooked? Fairly deep?"

The scout nodded.

"It's an ambush, all right," Kring said. "The cavalry probably intends to let us see them and then retreat into the gully. If we follow them, we'll run right into the infantry. We've been running Klæl's soldiers to death in open country, so they want to get us into tight quarters."

"What do we do?" Tikume asked.

"We stay out of that streambed, friend Tikume. Send out flankers to cut off their cavalry after they ride out. We'll slaughter them, and that should bring Klæl's soldiers out into the open."

"What about the Cyrgai? Are they more of those ones out of the past that we keep coming across?"

"I don't think so. This is inside the borders of Cynesga, so they're probably live ones from Cyrga itself." Kring stopped suddenly, and a slow grin crossed his face. "I just thought of something. Send out your flankers, friend Tikume. Give me some time to think my way through this."

"That's a particularly nasty grin there, friend Kring."

"I'm a particularly nasty fellow sometimes, friend Tikume," Kring replied, his grin growing even wider.

"Slavers," Mirtai said shortly after she had peered down the rocky hill at the column creeping slowly across the barren brown gravel toward the village clustered around the oasis. The almost instantaneous change from the humidity of the Arjuni jungle to the arid Cynesgan desert had given Sparhawk a slight headache.

"How can you tell at this distance?" Bevier asked her.

"Those hooded black robes," she replied, peering again over the boulder which concealed them. "Slavers wear them when they come into Cynesga so that the local authorities won't interfere with them. Cynesga's about the only place left where slavery's openly legal. The other kingdoms frown on it."

"There's a thought, Sparhawk," Bevier said. "If we could get our hands on some of those black robes, we'd be able to move around out in the desert without attracting attention."

"We don't look very much like Arjuni, Bevier," Kalten objected.

"We don't have to," Talen told him. "From what I heard back in Beresa, there are bands of raiders out in the desert who ambush the caravans in order to steal the slaves, so the Arjuni slavers hire lots of fighting men of all races to help protect the merchandise."

"Oh," Kalten said. "I wonder where we could lay our hands on black robes."

"I see a hundred or so of them right out there," Bevier said, pointing at the caravan.

"Elenes," Xanetia sighed, rolling her eyes upward.

"You're even starting to *sound* like Sephrenia, Anarae," Sparhawk said with a faint smile. "What are we overlooking?"

"Robes of any shade or hue will serve, Anakha," she explained patiently, "and doubtless may be obtained in Vigayo close by yon oasis."

"They have to be black, Anarae," Bevier objected.

"Color is an aspect of light, Sir Bevier, and I am most skilled at controlling light."

"Oh," he said. "I guess I didn't think of that."

"I had noticed that myself—almost immediately."

"Be nice," he murmured.

Bergsten's knights and their Peloi allies crossed the Cynesgan border on a cloudy, chill afternoon after what *seemed* to be several days of hard riding, and headed southeasterly toward the capital at Cynestra. Peloi scouts ranged out in front, but they encountered no resistance that day. They made camp, put out guards, and bedded down early.

It was not long after they had broken camp and set out on what was ostensibly the next morning that Daiya came riding back to join Bergsten and Heldin at the head of the column. "My scouts report that there are soldiers massing about a mile ahead, your Reverence," he reported.

"Cynesgans?" Bergsten asked quickly.

"It does not appear so, your Reverence."

"Go have a look, Heldin," Bergsten ordered.

The Pandion nodded and spurred his horse to the top of a rocky hill a quarter mile to the front. His face was bleak when he returned. "We've got trouble, your Grace," he rumbled. "They're more of those monsters we came up against in eastern Zemoch."

Bergsten muttered a fairly savage oath. "I knew things were going too well."

"Domi Tikume has warned us about these foreign soldiers," Daiya said. "Would it offend your Reverence if I suggested that you let *us* deal with them? Domi Tikume and Domi Kring have devised certain tactics that seem to work."

"I'm not offended in the slightest, friend Daiya," Bergsten replied. "*We* didn't exactly cover ourselves with glory the last time we encountered those brutes, so I'd be very interested in seeing something that's a little more effective than *our* tactics were."

Daiya conferred briefly with his clan-chiefs, and then he led Bergsten, Heldin, and several other knights up to the top of the hill to watch.

Bergsten immediately saw the advantages of light cavalry as opposed to armored knights mounted on heavy warhorses. The huge soldiers in their tight-fitting armor seemed baffled by the slashing attacks of the Peloi armed with javelins. They floundered forward, desperately trying to close with their tormentors, but the cat-footed horses of the Peloi were simply too quick. The javelins began to take their toll, and more and more of the hulking monsters fell in that deadly rain.

"The idea is to force them to run, your Reverence," Daiya explained. "They're very dangerous in close quarters, but they don't seem to have much endurance, so they aren't nearly as much a threat in a running fight."

"Vanion told me about that," Bergsten said. "Did Domi Tikume give you any idea of how long it takes them to run out of breath?"

"Nothing very specific, your Reverence."

Bergsten shrugged. "That's all right, friend Daiya. We've got plenty of open ground, and it's still morning. We can run them all day if we have to."

Stung by the repeated attacks, the huge soldiers began to lumber forward in a kind of shuffling trot, brandishing their horrid weapons and bellowing hoarse war cries.

The Peloi, however, refused those challenges and continued their slash-and-run tactics.

Then, driven and stung beyond endurance, the creatures broke into a shambling run.

"It's feasible," Sir Heldin mused in his deep, rumbling basso. "We'd need different equipment, though."

"What are you talking about, Heldin?" Bergsten demanded.

"Looking to the future, your Grace," Heldin replied. "If those beasts become a standard fixture, we'll have to modify a few things. It might not be a bad idea to train and equip a few squadrons of Church Knights to serve as light cavalry."

"Heldin," Bergsten said acidly, "if those things become a standard fixture, it'll be because we've lost this war. What makes you think there'll *be* any Church Knights at that point?"

"They're breaking off, your Reverence!" Daiya cried excitedly. "They're running away!"

"But where are they running to, Daiya?" Bergsten demanded. "It's the air that's killing them, and the air's everywhere. Where can they go, Daiya? Where can they go?"

"Where can they go?" Kring asked in bafflement as Klæl's soldiers broke off from their clumsy pursuit of the Peloi horsemen and fled into the desert.

"Who cares?" Tikume laughed. "Let them run. We've still got those Cyrgai penned up in that gully. We'd better get them to moving before some clever subaltern in the rear ranks has time to take his bearings."

The Cyrgai were following a strategy from the dawn of time. They advanced steadily, marching in step, with their large round shields protecting their bodies and with their long spears leveled to the front. As the Peloi slashed in on them, they would stop and close ranks. The front rank would kneel with overlapping shields and leveled spears. The ranks behind would close up, their shields also overlapping and spears also to the front.

It was absolutely beautiful—but it didn't accomplish anything at all against cavalry.

"We have to get them to run, Domi Tikume!" Kring shouted to his friend as they galloped clear of the massed Cyrgai regiments again. "Pull your children back a little farther after the next attack! This won't work if those antiques just keep plodding! Make them run!"

Tikume shouted some orders, and his horsemen altered their tactics, pulling back several hundred yards and forcing the Cyrgai to come to them.

A brazen trumpet sounded from the center of one of the advancing regimental squares, and the Cyrgai broke into a jingling trot, their ranks still perfectly straight.

"They look good, don't they?" Tikume laughed.

"They would if this was a parade ground," Kring replied. "Let's sting them again and then pull back even farther."

"How far is it to the border?" Tikume asked.

"Who knows? Nobody I've talked with is really sure. We're close, though. Make them run, Tikume! Make them run!"

Tikume rose in his stirrups. "Pass the word!" he bellowed. "Full retreat!"

The Peloi turned tail and galloped to the east across the rattling brown gravel.

A thin cheer went up from the massed regiments of the Cyrgai, and the trumpet sounded again. The ancient soldiers, still in perfect step and with their ranks still perfectly straight, broke into a running charge. Sergeants barked the staccato cadence, and the sound of the half boots of the Cyrgai beating on the barren ground was like the pounding of some huge drum.

And then the full light of a winter midday dimmed as if some giant, silent wings had somehow blotted out the sun. A chill wind swept across the desert, and there was a wailing sound like the sum of human woe.

The suddenly stricken Cyrgai, rank upon rank, died soundlessly in midstride, falling limply to earth to be trampled by their blindly advancing comrades, who also fell, astonished, on top of them.

Kring and Tikume, both pale and trembling, watched in awestruck wonder as the ancient Styric curse did its dreadful work. Then, sickened, they wheeled and rode back eastward, turning their backs on the heaped reminder of those perfect soldiers rushing blindly into chill, wailing obliteration.

"These clothes are good enough for Arjuna and Tamul proper, neighbor," Sparhawk told the shopkeeper later that same day, "but they don't exactly turn the trick in a dust storm. I think that last one put about four pounds of dirt down my back."

The shopkeeper nodded sagely. "Other races laugh at our customary garb, good Master," he observed. "They usually keep laughing right up until the time when they ride through their first dust storm."

"Does the wind blow all the time out there?" Talen asked him.

"Not quite *all* the time, young Master. The afternoons are usually the worst." He looked at Sparhawk. "How many robes will you be needing, good Master?"

"There are six of us, neighbor, and none of us are so fond of each other that we'd care to share a robe."

"Have you any preferences in colors?"

"Does one color keep the dust out better than the others?"

"Not that I've noticed."

"Then any color will do, I guess."

The shopkeeper hustled into his storeroom and returned with a pile of neatly folded garments. Then he smiled, rubbed his hands together, and broached the subject of the price.

"He overcharged you, you know," Talen said as they emerged from the cluttered shop into the dusty street.

Sparhawk shrugged. "Perhaps," he said.

"Someday I'm going to have to teach you about the finer points of haggling."

"Does it really matter?" Sparhawk asked, tying the bundle of Cynesgan robes to the back of his saddle. He looked around. "Anarae?"

"I am here, Anakha," her whispered voice responded.

"Were you able to find anything?"

"Nay, Anakha. Clearly the messenger hath not yet arrived."

"Berit and Khalad are still several days away, Sparhawk," Talen said quietly, "and this isn't such an attractive place that the messenger would want to get here early to enjoy the scenery." He looked around at the winter-dispirited palm trees and the muddy pond that lay at the center of the cluster of white houses.

"Attractive or not, we're going to have to come up with some reason for staying," Sparhawk said. "We can't leave until the messenger gets here and Anarae Xanetia can listen to what he's thinking."

"I can remain here alone, Anakha," Xanetia told him. "None here can detect my presence, so I do not need protection."

"We'll stay all the same, Anarae," Sparhawk told her. "Courtesy and all that, you understand. An Elene gentleman will *not* permit a lady to go about unescorted."

An argument had broken out on the shaded porch of what appeared to be a tavern or a wineshop of some kind. "You don't know what you're talking about, Echon!" a wheezy-voiced old man in a patched and filthy robe declared loudly. "It's a good hundred miles from here to the River Sarna, and there's no water at all between here and there."

"You either drink too much or you've been out in the sun too long, Zagorri," Echon, a thin, sun-dried man in a dark blue robe, scoffed. "My map says that it's sixty miles—no more."

"How well do you know the man who drew the map? I've been here all my life, and I know how far it is to the Sarna. Go ahead, though. Take only enough water for sixty miles. Your mules will die, and you'll be drinking sand for that last forty miles. It's all right with me, though, because I've never liked you all that much anyway. But, mark my words, Echon. It's one hundred miles from the Well of Vigay there to the banks of the Sarna." And the old man spat in the direction of the pale brown pond.

Talen suddenly began to laugh.

"What's so funny?" Sparhawk asked him.

"We just had a stroke of luck, revered leader," the boy replied gaily. "If we're all finished up here, why don't we go back to where the others are waiting? We'll all want to get a good night's sleep—since we'll probably be leaving first thing in the morning."

"Oh? For where?"

"Cyrga, of course. Wasn't that where we wanted to go?"

"Yes, but we don't know where Cyrga is."

"That's where you're wrong, Sparhawk. We *do* know the way to Cyrga—at least *I* do."

CHAPTER TWENTY-THREE

"Did he die well?" Betuana asked. Her face was very pale, but she gave no other outward sign of distress.

"It was a suitable death, Betuana-Queen," the messenger replied. "We were at the bottom of a gorge and the Klæl-beast was hurling the sides of it down upon us. Androl-King attacked the beast, and many escaped that would have died if he had not."

She considered it. "Yes," she agreed finally. "It was suitable. It will be remembered. Is the army fit to travel?"

"We have many injured, Betuana-Queen, and thousands are buried in the gorge. We withdrew to Tualas to await your commands."

"Leave some few to care for the injured, and bring the army here," she told him. "Tosa is no longer in danger. The danger is here."

"It shall be as you say, my Queen." He clashed his fist against his breastplate in salute.

The Queen of Atan rose to her feet, her still-pale face betraying no emotion. "I must go apart and consider this, Itagne-Ambassador," she said formally.

"It is proper, Betuana-Queen," he responded. "I share your grief."

"But not my guilt." She turned and slowly left the room.

Itagne looked at the stony-faced Engessa. "I'd better pass the word to the others," he said.

Engessa nodded shortly.

"Could you speak with the messenger before he leaves, Engessa?" Itagne asked. "Lord Vanion will need casualty figures before he can change his strategy."

"I will obtain them for you, Itagne-Ambassador." Engessa inclined his head shortly and went out.

Itagne swore and banged his fist on the table. "Of all the times for *this* to happen!" he fumed. "If that idiot had only *waited* before he got himself killed!"

Betuana had done nothing wrong. There had been no stain of dishonor in her concern for Engessa, and if she had only had a week or two to put it behind her, it would probably have been forgotten—along with the personal feelings which caused it. But Androl's death, coming as it did at this particular time—Itagne swore

again. The Atan queen had to be able to function, and this crisis might well inca-
pacitate her. For all Itagne knew, she was in her room right now preparing to fall on
her sword. He rose and went looking for paper and pen. Vanion had to be warned
about this before everything here in Sarna flew apart.

"It all fell into place when I heard that old man call their little pond 'the Well
of Vigay,' " Talen explained. "Ogerajin used exactly the same term."

"I don't know that it means very much," Mirtai said dubiously. "Cynesgans call
all these desert springs wells. Vigay was probably the one who discovered it."

"But the important thing is that *this* is one of the landmarks Ogerajin mentioned," Bevier said. "How did the subject come up?" he asked Talen.

"Stragen and I were spinning moonbeams for Valash," the boy replied. "Ogerajin had just arrived from Verel, and he was sitting in a chair with his brains quietly
rotting. Stragen was telling Valash about something he'd supposedly overheard—
some fellow telling another that Scarpa was waiting for instructions from Cyrga. He
was fishing for information, and he casually asked Valash what route a man would
have to follow to get to Cyrga. That's when Ogerajin jumped in. He started rambling about the 'Well of Vigay' and the 'Plains of Salt' and other places with names
that sounded as if they'd come right out of a storybook. I thought he was just raving, but Valash got really excited and tried to hush him up. That's what made me
pay attention—I got the feeling that Ogerajin was giving Stragen very specific directions to Cyrga, but that the directions were all clouded over with those storybook
names. This 'Well of Vigay' business makes me start to wonder if the directions
were as cloudy and garbled as I thought they were right at first."

"What were his exact words, young Talen?" Xanetia asked.

"He said, 'The pathway lies close by the Well of Vigay.' That's when Valash
tried to shut him up, but he kept right on. He said something about wanting to give
Stragen directions so that he could go to Cyrga and bow down to Cyrgon. He told
him to go northwest from the 'Well of Vigay' to the 'Forbidden Mountains.' "

"There *are* several clusters of mountains in central Cynesga, and that's the general region Aphrael pointed out back on the island. What else did he say, Talen?"

"He sort of jumped around. He talked about the 'Forbidden Mountains'
and the 'Pillars of Cyrgon.' Then he doubled back on himself and started talking
about the 'Plains of Salt.' From what he told Stragen, you're supposed to be able to
see these 'Forbidden Mountains' from those salt plains. Then there was something
about 'Fiery White Pillars' and 'The Plain of Bones.' He said that the bones are 'the
nameless slaves who toil until death for Cyrgon's Chosen.' Evidently when a slave
dies in Cyrga, he's taken out and dumped in the desert."

"That boneyard wouldn't be very far from the city, then," Kalten mused.

"It *does* all sort of fit together, Sparhawk," Bevier said seriously. "The Cynesgans themselves are largely nomads, so they wouldn't have any real need for large
numbers of slaves. Ogerajin spoke of 'Cyrgon's Chosen.' That would be the Cyrgai,
and *they're* probably the ones who buy slaves."

"And that would mean that the caravan of slavers we saw is going to Cyrga,
wouldn't it?" Talen added excitedly.

"*And* they were going northwest," Mirtai said, "the exact direction Ogerajin was raving about."

Sparhawk went to his saddlebags and took out his map. He sat down again and opened it, holding it firmly as the desert wind started to flap its corners. "We know that Cyrga's somewhere in these mountains in central Cynesga," he mused, "so we'll be going in that direction anyway. If Ogerajin was just raving and his directions don't go anyplace, we'll still be in the right vicinity if we follow them."

"It's better than just sitting here waiting for Berit and Khalad," Kalten said impatiently. "I have to be doing *something*—even if it's only riding around in circles out there in the desert."

Sparhawk wordlessly put a comforting hand on his old friend's shoulder. His own desperate concern was at least as driving as Kalten's, but he knew that he had to keep it separate, remote. Desperate men make mistakes, and a mistake here could put Ehlana in even greater peril. His emotions screamed at him, but he grimly, implacably, pushed them into a separate compartment of his mind and firmly closed the door.

"Anakha would be made glad if we would do this," Ulath said in Trollish to the enormous presences.

Ghworg, God of Kill, rumbled ominously. "Anakha's thought is like the wind," he complained. "One time he said to us, 'Go to the place the man-things call the Tamul Mountains to kill the children of Cyrgon.' Now he says to us, 'Go to the place the man-things call Zhubay to kill the children of Cyrgon.' Can he not decide which children of Cyrgon he wants us to kill?"

"It is the way of the hunt, Ghworg," Tynian explained. "The children of Cyrgon are not like the red-deer, which feed always in the same range. The children of Cyrgon are like the reindeer, which go from this place to that place as the seasons change to find better food. Before, they were going to this place, Tamul Mountains, to feed, but now they go to the place Zhubay to feed. If we hunt in the Tamul Mountains, we will find no game to kill and eat."

"It speaks well," Ghnomb, God of Eat, said. "It is not Anakha's thought which changes, it is the path of the creatures we hunt which changes. The way of the hunt tells us that we must go where they graze if we would find them and kill them and eat them."

"This hunt becomes more and more not-simple," Ghworg grumbled.

"That is because the man-things are more not-simple than the deer-things," Khwaj, God of Fire, told him. "The thought of Tynian-from-Deira is good. The one who hunts where there is no game does not eat."

Ghworg pondered it. "We must follow the way of the hunt," he decided. "We will take our children to the place Zhubay to hunt the children of Cyrgon. When they come there to graze, our children will kill them and eat them."

"It would make us glad if you would," Tynian said politely.

"I will take our children into the Time-Which-Does-Not-Move," Ghnomb said. "They will be in the place Zhubay before the children of Cyrgon come there."

Schlee, God of Ice, stuck his huge fingers into the dirt. The earth shuddered slightly and contorted itself into his picture of the continent. "Show us where, Ulath-from-Thalesia," he said. "Where is the place Zhubay?"

Ulath walked some distance along the southwestern edge of the tiny mountains of Atan, peering intently at the ground. Then he stopped, bent, and touched a spot a short way out into the northern end of the Desert of Cynesga. "It is here, Schlee," he said.

Ghworg, God of Kill, stood up. "We will take our children there," he declared. "Let us make Anakha glad."

"They're watching us, Vanion," Sephrenia said quietly.

He pulled his horse in closer to hers. "Styrics?" he asked quietly.

"One of them is," she replied. "He's not particularly skilled." She smiled faintly. "I may have to hit him over the head to get his attention."

"Whatever it takes, love," he said. He glanced back over his shoulder at the column of knights and then on ahead. They were coming down out of the mountains, and the Valley of the Sarna was beginning to broaden. "We should reach that bridge tomorrow," he told her. "After we cross the river, we'll be in Cynesga."

"Yes, dear one," she said, "I've seen the map."

"Why don't you cast the spell?" he suggested. "Let's give our inept Styric out there a chance to earn his keep." He looked at her gravely. "I'm having some second thoughts about this, Sephrenia. Klæl's still out there, and if he thinks Sparhawk's somewhere in this column with Bhelliom, he'll be all over us."

"You can't have it both ways, Vanion," she said with a fond smile. "You said that you were never going to let me out of your sight, so if you insist on going into dangerous places, I'm sort of obliged to go along. Now if you'll excuse me, I'll wake up that Styric." She began to speak softly in Styric, her fingers weaving the spell as she did so.

Vanion was puzzled. He took a certain pride in his familiarity with most of the spells, but this was one he had never seen or heard before. He watched more closely.

"Never mind," she told him crisply, breaking off the spell. "You don't need to know this one."

"But—"

"Just look over there, Vanion," she said. "I can do this without any help." She paused. "Humor me, dear one. A girl needs a *few* secrets, after all."

He smiled and turned his head.

There was a kind of vague blurring in the air about ten yards away, and then, as surely as if he were really there, Vanion saw Sparhawk appear, mounted as always on his evil-tempered roan. So real was the image that flies were attracted to the horse. "Brilliant!" Vanion exclaimed. He sent out a probing thought and even encountered the familiar sense of Sparhawk's presence. "If I didn't know better, I'd swear that he was really here. Can you sustain this illusion?"

"Naturally," she said in an infuriatingly offhand way. And then she laughed, reached out, and fondly touched his cheek.

·　·　·

"What took you so long?" Talen asked the Child-Goddess when she appeared on the edge of their camp outside Vigayo the following morning.

"I've been busy," she replied with a little shrug. "This is a fairly complex business, you know. We all *do* want to get there at approximately the same time, don't we? What's the problem here, Sparhawk?"

"We might have just had a bit of good luck for a change, Divine One," he replied. "Talen and I were in the village yesterday, and we heard one of the villagers refer to their oasis as 'the Well of Vigay.' "

"So?"

"Why don't you tell her about it, Talen?"

The young thief quickly repeated the conversations between Ogerajin and Stragen back in Beresa.

"What do you think?" Kalten asked the Child-Goddess.

"Does somebody have a map?" she asked.

Sparhawk went to his saddlebags, took out his tightly rolled map, and brought it to her.

She spread it out on the ground, knelt in front of it, and studied it for several moments. "There *are* some salt flats out there," she conceded.

"And they *are* in the right direction," Bevier pointed out.

"Ogerajin's been there," Talen added, "at least he *says* he has, so he'd almost have to know the way, wouldn't he?"

"There's also a slaver's route that runs off to the northwest," Mirtai said. "We saw a caravan following it when we first got here, and Ogerajin mentioned the fact that the Cyrgai keep slaves. It sort of stands to reason that the slave caravan's bound for Cyrga, doesn't it?"

"You're hanging all this speculation on the ravings of a madman, you know," Flute said critically.

"You said yourself that Cyrga's somewhere in central Cynesga," Kalten reminded her, "and that's where all of this points. Even if Ogerajin left some things out, we'll still end up in the general vicinity of Cyrga. We'll be a lot closer than we are right now, anyway."

"Since you've all made up your minds, why did you bother me with it?" Her tone was just a bit petulant.

Talen grinned at her. "We didn't think it'd be polite to run off without telling you, Divine One."

"I'll get you for that, Talen," she threatened.

"How far ahead of us would you say that caravan is by now?" Sparhawk asked Mirtai.

"Ten leagues," she replied, "twelve at the most. Slave caravans don't move very fast."

"I think that's our best bet, then," he decided. "Let's put on those black robes and get started. We'll trail along a couple of leagues behind that caravan, and anybody who happens to see us will think we're stragglers."

"Anything's better than just sitting still," Kalten said.

"Somehow I was sure you'd feel that way about it," Sparhawk replied.

"We're little more than prisoners here," Empress Chacole declared, waving her hand at the luxurious furnishings of the women's palace. Chacole was a ripe-figured Cynesgan lady in her thirties. Her tone was one of only idle discontent, but her eyes were hard and shrewd as she looked at Elysoun.

Elysoun shrugged. "*I've* never had any trouble coming and going as I choose."

"That's because you're a Valesian," Empress Torel!ia told her with just a touch of resentment. "They make allowances for you they don't make for the rest of us. I don't think it's very fair."

Elysoun shrugged again. "Fair or not, it's the custom."

"Why should you have more freedom than the rest of us?"

"Because I have a more active social life."

"Aren't there enough men in the women's palace for you?"

"Don't be catty, Torellia. You're not old enough to make it convincing." Elysoun looked appraisingly at the Arjuni empress. Torellia was a slender girl in her midtwenties, and, like all Arjuni women, she was quite subservient. Chacole was obviously taking advantage of that.

"You don't see anybody restricting Cieronna's movements," Chacole said.

"Cieronna's the first wife," Elysoun replied, "and she's the oldest. We should respect her age if nothing else."

"I will *not* be a servant to an aging Tamul hag!" Chacole flared.

"She doesn't *want* you as a servant, Chacole," Elysoun told her. "She already has more servants than she can count—unless Liatris has thinned them out some more. All Cieronna really wants is a fancier crown than the rest of us have and the right to walk in front of us in formal processions. It doesn't take much to make her happy. She's not the brightest person in Matherion."

Torellia giggled.

"Here comes Gahenas," Chacole hissed.

The jug-eared Tegan empress, covered to the chin in scratchy wool, approached with a disapproving expression, an expression that came over her face every time she so much as looked at the barely dressed Elysoun. "Ladies," she greeted them with a stiff little nod.

"Join us, Gahenas," Chacole invited. "We're discussing politics."

Gahenas' bulging eyes brightened. Tegans lived and breathed politics.

"Chacole and Torellia want to get up a petition to our husband," Elysoun said. She raised her arms and yawned deeply, stretching back and literally thrusting her bare breasts at Gahenas.

Gahenas quickly averted her eyes.

"I'm sorry, ladies," Elysoun apologized. "I didn't get much sleep last night."

"How do you find enough hours in the day?" Gahenas asked spitefully.

"It's only a matter of scheduling, Gahenas." Elysoun shrugged. "You can get all sorts of things accomplished if you budget your time. Why don't we just drop it, dear? You don't approve of me, and I don't really care. We'll never understand each other, so why waste our time trying?"

"You can go anywhere in the imperial compound you want to, can't you, Elysoun?" Chacole asked rather tentatively.

Elysoun feigned another yawn to conceal her smile. Chacole had finally gotten to the point. Elysoun had wondered how long it was going to take. "I can come and go more or less as I choose," she replied. "I guess all the spies got tired of trying to keep up with me."

"Do you suppose I could ask a favor of you?"

"Of course, dear. What do you need?"

"Cieronna doesn't like me, and her spies follow me everywhere I go. I'm involved in something at the moment I'd rather she didn't find out about."

"Why, Chacole! Are you saying that you've finally decided to go a little farther afield for entertainment?"

The Cynesgan empress gave her a blank stare, obviously missing her point.

"Oh, come now, dear," Elysoun said slyly. "We all have our little private amusements here inside the women's palace—even Gahenas here."

"I most certainly do *not*!" the Tegan protested.

"Oh, *really*, Gahenas? I've seen that new page boy of yours. He's absolutely luscious. Who's *your* new lover, Chacole? Some husky young lieutenant in the guards? Did you want me to smuggle him into the palace for you?"

"It's nothing like that, Elysoun."

"Of *course* it isn't," Elysoun agreed with heavy sarcasm. "All right, Chacole. I'll carry your love notes for you—if you're really sure you trust me that close to him. But why go so far afield, sister dear? Gahenas has this lovely young page boy, and I'm sure she's trained him very well—haven't you, Gahenas?" She raised one mocking eyebrow. "Tell me, dear," she added, "was he a virgin? Before you got your hands on him, I mean?"

Gahenas fled with Elysoun's mocking laughter following after her.

CHAPTER TWENTY-FOUR

"It's supposed to be two words," Kalten insisted that afternoon some miles outside Vigayo. "Ram's. Horn. Two words."

"It's a password, Sir Kalten," Talen tried to explain. "*Ramshorn.* Like that."

"What do you say, Sparhawk?" Kalten asked his friend. "Is it one word or two?" The three of them had just finished piling rocks in a rough approximation of a grave at the side of the trail, and Talen and Kalten were arguing about the crude marker the boy had prepared.

"What difference does it make?" Sparhawk shrugged.

"If it's spelled wrong, Berit might not recognize it when he rides by," Talen said.

"He'll recognize it," Sparhawk disagreed. "Berit's quick. Just don't disturb the arrangement of those yellow rocks on the top of the grave."

"Are you sure Khalad will understand what those rocks mean?" Talen asked skeptically.

"Your father would have," Sparhawk replied, "and I'm sure he taught Khalad all the usual signals."

"I still say it's supposed to be two words," Kalten insisted.

"Bevier!" Sparhawk called.

The Cyrinic Knight walked back to the imitation grave with an inquiring expression.

"These two are arguing about how to spell *ramshorn*," Sparhawk told him. "You're the scholar. *You* settle it."

"I say he spelled it wrong," Kalten said truculently. "It's supposed to be two words, isn't it?"

"Ah—" Bevier said evasively, "there are two schools of thought on that."

"Why don't you tell them about it as we ride along?" Mirtai suggested.

Sparhawk looked at Xanetia. "Don't," he warned her quietly.

"What wouldst thou not have me do, Anakha?" she asked innocently.

"Don't laugh. Don't even smile. You'll only make it worse."

It may or may not have been three weeks later. Patriarch Bergsten had given up on trying to keep track of actual time. Instead he glared in sullen theological discontent at the mud-walled city of Cynestra and at the disgustingly young and well-conditioned person coming toward him. Bergsten believed in an orderly world, and violations of order made him nervous.

She was very tall and she had golden skin and night-dark hair, she was also extremely pretty and superbly muscled. She emerged from the main gate of Cynestra under a flag of truce, running easily out to meet them. She stopped some distance to their front, and Bergsten, Sir Heldin, Daiya, and Neran, their Tamul translator, rode forward to confer with her. She spoke at some length with Neran.

"Keep your eyes where they belong, Heldin," Bergsten muttered.

"I was just—"

"I know what you were doing. Stop it." Bergsten paused. "I wonder why they sent a woman."

Neran, a slender Tamul who had been sent along by Ambassador Fontan, returned. "She's Atana Maris," he told them, "commander of the Atan garrison here in Cynestra."

"A *woman*?" Bergsten was startled.

"It's not uncommon among the Atans, your Grace. She's been expecting us. Foreign Minister Oscagne sent word that we were coming."

"What's the situation in the city?" Heldin asked.

"King Jaluah's been quietly dribbling troops into Cynestra for the past month or so," Neran replied. "Atana Maris has a thousand Atans in her garrison, and the Cynesgans have been trying to restrict their movements. She's been growing impatient with all of that. She probably would have moved against the royal palace a week ago, but Oscagne instructed her to wait until we arrived."

"How did she get out of the city?" Heldin rumbled.

"I didn't ask her, Sir Heldin. I didn't want to insult her."

"What I meant was, didn't they try to stop her?"

"They're dead if they did."

"But she's a *woman!*" Bergsten objected.

"You're not really familiar with the Atans, are you, your Reverence?" Daiya asked.

"I've heard of them, friend Daiya. The stories all seem wildly exaggerated to me."

"No, your Reverence, they aren't," Daiya said firmly. "I know of this girl's reputation. She's the youngest garrison commander in the entire Atan army, and she didn't get to where she is by being sweet and ladylike. From what I've heard, she's an absolute savage."

"But she's so pretty," Heldin protested.

"Sir Heldin," Neran said firmly to him, "while you're admiring her, pay particular attention to the development of her arms and shoulders. She's as strong as a bull, and if you offend her in any way at all, she'll tear you to pieces. She almost killed Itagne—or so the rumor has it."

"The foreign minister's brother?" Bergsten asked.

Neran nodded. "He was here on a mission and he decided to place the city under martial law. He needed Atana Maris' help with that, so he seduced her. Her response was enthusiastic—but very muscular. Be very careful around her, gentlemen. She's almost as dangerous to have as a friend as an enemy. She asked me to give you your instructions."

"*Instructions?*" Bergsten erupted. "I don't take orders from women!"

"Your Grace," Neran said, "Cynestra's technically still under martial law, and that puts Atana Maris in charge. She's been ordered to deliver the city to you, but she's instructed you to wait outside the walls until she's crushed all the resistance. She wants to present the city to you as a gift—all neat and tidy. Please don't spoil it for her. Smile at her, thank her politely, and wait right here until she's finished cleaning the streets. After she's got all the bodies stacked in neat piles, she'll invite you in and turn the city over to you—along with King Jaluah's head, more than likely. I know that the situation seems unnatural to you, but for God's sake don't do anything to offend her. She'll go to war with you just as quickly as with anybody else."

"But she's so pretty," Heldin objected again.

Berit and Khalad dismounted and led their horses down to the oasis to water them. In theory, they *might* have reached Vigayo this soon. "Can you tell if he's here?" Khalad muttered.

Berit shook his head. "I *think* that means that he's not a Styric. We'll just have to wait for him to come to us." He looked around at the few white-walled houses shaded by low palm trees. "Is there any kind of inn here?"

"Not very likely. I see a lot of tents on the other side of the oasis. I'll ask around, but don't get your hopes up."

Berit shrugged. "Oh, well. We've lived in tents before. Find out where we're permitted to set up."

The village of Vigayo itself was clustered along the eastern side of the oasis, and the informal encampment of nomads and merchants stretched along the west shore of what was actually a fair-sized pool of artesian water. Berit and Khalad picketed their horses, erected their tent near the water, and sat down in the shade to wait. "Can you tell if Sparhawk's around anyplace?" Khalad asked.

Berit shook his head. "He may have already passed through. Or he could be watching from one of the hills outside of town. He might not want people to know that he's here."

It was an hour or so past sunset, and twilight was descending when a Cynesgan in a loose-fitting striped robe approached their tent. "I'm supposed to ask if one of you might be named Sparhawk," he said in a slightly accented voice.

Berit rose to his feet. "I might be named Sparhawk, neighbor."

"Might be?"

"That's the way you phrased your question, friend. You've got a note for me. Why don't you just hand it over and be on your way? We don't really have anything else to talk about, do we?"

The messenger's face hardened. He reached inside his robe, took out a folded and sealed parchment, and negligently tossed it at Berit's feet. Then he turned and walked away.

"You know, Berit," Khalad said mildly, "sometimes you're even more abrasive than Sparhawk himself."

Berit grinned. "I know. I'm trying to maintain his reputation." He bent, picked up the parchment, and broke the seal. He removed the identifying lock of hair and quickly read the brief message.

"Well?" Khalad asked.

"Nothing very specific. It says that there's a caravan route running off to the northwest. We're supposed to follow that. We'll get further instructions along the way."

"Will it be safe to use the spell and talk with Aphrael once we get out of town?"

"I think so. I'm sure she'd have told me if I wasn't supposed to use it here in Cynesga."

"We don't have much choice," Khalad said. "We can't tell if Sparhawk's already been here, if he's here now, or if he's still on the way, and we've got to let him know about these new instructions."

"Do you think we ought to start out tonight?"

"No, let's not start floundering around in the dark. We might miss the trail, and there's nothing out in that desert but empty."

"I won't do anything to put Berit in any kind of danger," Elysoun insisted a few days later. "I'm very fond of him."

"They found out that he was posing as Sparhawk quite some time ago, Elysoun," Baroness Melidere told her. "You won't be putting him in any more danger than he's already in. Telling Chacole about his disguise will convince her that you've gone over to her side—*and* that you have access to important information."

"You might want to make them believe that your husband's totally smitten with you, Empress Elysoun," Patriarch Emban added. "Let them think that he tells you everything."

"*Are* you smitten with me, Sarabian?" Elysoun asked archly.

"Oh, absolutely, my dear." He smiled. "I adore you."

"What a nice thing to say." She smiled warmly.

"Later, children," Melidere told them absently, her forehead furrowed with concentration. "At the same time you tell Chacole about Berit's disguise, drop a few hints about a fleet of Church ships in the Gulf of Daconia. Stragen's been very carefully planting that particular lie, so let's give them some confirmation. After you tell them about Berit, they'll be inclined to believe your story about the fleet." She looked at the emperor. "Is there anything else we can give them that won't hurt us? Something they can verify?"

"Does it have to be important?"

"Not really, just something that's true. We need another truth to get the mix right."

"The mix?"

"It's like a recipe, your Majesty." She smiled. "Two parts truth to one part lie; stir well and serve. If you get the mix right, they'll swallow the whole thing."

They had set out at first light, and the sun had not yet risen when they topped a low ridge and saw a vast, flat expanse of dead whiteness lying ahead. Time, like climate, had lost all meaning.

"I'd hate to have to cross *that* in the summertime," Kalten said.

"Truly," Sparhawk agreed.

"The slavers' trail swings north here," Bevier noted, "probably to go around those flats. If a Cynesgan patrol stumbles across us out there, we might have trouble convincing them that we're attached to that caravan we've been following."

"We'll just say that we got lost," Kalten said with a shrug. "Let me do the talking, Bevier. I get lost all the time anyway, so I can be fairly convincing. How far is it to the other side, Sparhawk?"

"About twenty-five leagues, according to my map."

"Two days—even if we push," Kalten calculated.

"And no cover," Bevier added. "You couldn't hide a spider out—" He broke off. "What's that?" he asked, pointing at an intensely bright spot of light on the mountainous western horizon.

Talen squinted at the light. "I think it might be the landmark we've been looking for," he said.

"How did you arrive at that?" Kalten asked skeptically.

"It's in the right direction, isn't it? Ogerajin said that we were supposed to go northwest from Vigayo to the Plains of Salt. Then he said, 'From the verge of the

Plains of Salt wilt thou behold low on the horizon before thee the dark shapes of the Forbidden Mountains, and, if it please Cyrgon, his fiery white pillars will guide thee to his Hidden City.' There *are* mountains there, and that light's coming from right in the middle of them. Wouldn't it almost *have* to be coming from the pillars?"

"The man was crazy, Talen," Kalten objected.

"Maybe," Sparhawk disagreed, "but so far, everything he described is right where he said it would be. Let's chance it. It's still the right direction."

"About the only thing that might cause us any trouble would be if we stumbled across a helpful Cynesgan patrol and they decided to escort us back to that caravan we've been following for the last few days," Mirtai observed.

"Logically, our chances of coming across a patrol out there on the flats are very slim," Bevier suggested. "Cynesgans would normally avoid that waste in the first place, and the war's probably pulled almost everybody off patrol duty in the second."

"And any patrols unlucky enough to cross us won't be making any reports in the third," Mirtai added, her hand on her sword hilt.

"We've tentatively located the pillars," Sparhawk said, "and if Ogerajin knew what he was talking about, we'll have to take a line of sight on them to penetrate the illusion. Now that we've found them, let's not lose them. We'll just have to take our chances out there on the flats. If we're lucky, nobody will even notice us. If not, we'll try lying to them, and if that doesn't work, we still have our swords." He looked around at them. "Does anybody have anything else to add?"

"I think that covers it," Kalten said, still somewhat dubious.

"Let's get started, then."

"They just broke off and ran away, friend Vanion," Kring said a day or so later. Kring's face was baffled. "We were using those tactics Tikume and I came up with, and everything was going more or less the way we expected, and then somebody blew a horn or something, and they turned tail and ran—but where? If what we've been told is true, there's no place in the whole world they can go to catch their breath."

"Did you have anybody follow them?" Vanion asked.

"I probably should have, I suppose, but I was concentrating on luring the Cyrgai across the border." Kring smiled at Sephrenia. "That Styric curse doesn't seem to have worn thin in the last ten thousand years, Lady. Three full regiments of Cyrgai went down like newly mown wheat when they crossed the border." He paused. "They're not really very bright, are they?"

"The Cyrgai? No. It's against their religion."

"You'd think that at least a *few* of them would have realized that something was wrong, but they just kept running across the border and falling over dead."

"Independent thinking isn't encouraged among them. They're trained to follow orders—even bad ones."

Kring looked at the bridge crossing the Sarna. "You'll be operating from here, friend Vanion?" he asked.

"I'll put a force on the other side of the bridge," Vanion replied, "but our main camp will be on this side. The river marks the boundary between Tamul proper and Cynesga, doesn't it?"

"Technically, I suppose." The Domi shrugged. "The curse line's a couple of miles farther west, though."

"The boundary's changed several times over the years," Sephrenia explained.

"Tikume thought I should come up here and talk things over with you, friend Vanion," Kring said then. "We don't want to interfere with Sparhawk, so we haven't been going too far into Cynesga, but we're running out of people to chase."

"How far in have you been going?" Vanion asked.

"Six or seven leagues," Kring replied. "We come back to Samar every night—although there's no real reason for it now. I don't think there's any danger of a siege anymore."

"No," Vanion agreed. "We've pushed them enough so that they can't really concentrate on Samar now." He opened his map and frowned at it for a few moments, then he dropped to one knee and spread it out on the winter-brown grass. "Step on that corner, please," he said to Sephrenia. "I don't want to have to chase it again."

Kring looked puzzled.

"Household joke," Sephrenia explained, putting one small foot on the corner of Vanion's map. "Vanion's fond of maps, and an errant breeze turned his current favorite into a kite two days ago."

Vanion let that pass. "I'll agree that we don't want to crowd Sparhawk, Domi, but I think we'll want to build some fortified positions out there in the desert. They'll give us jumping-off places when we start our advance on Cyrga."

"I had the same thought, friend Vanion."

"Let's establish a presence across that border," Vanion decided. "I'll send word to Betuana, and she'll do the same."

"How deep in should we go?" Kring asked.

Vanion looked at Sephrenia. "Ten leagues?" he suggested. "That's not so deep that we'll be stepping on Sparhawk's heels, but we'll have room to maneuver, and it'll give you some elbow room for that spell of yours."

"Using the spell's a good plan, friend Vanion," Kring said a bit dubiously, "but you're deliberately drawing the best our enemies can throw at us to yourself—and to Lady Sephrenia. Is that what you want? I don't mean to be offensive, but your fight with Klæl's soldiers seriously reduced your ranks."

"That's one of the reasons I want forts out there in the desert, Domi," Vanion said wryly. "If worse comes to worst, I'll pull back into those positions. I'm almost sure I can count on some dear friends on my flanks to come to my rescue."

"Well said," Sephrenia murmured.

"Stop," Khalad said sharply, reining in his horse when they were perhaps five miles outside Vigayo.

"What is it?" Berit asked tensely.

"Somebody named Ramshorn died," Khalad said, pointing. "I think we should stop and pay our respects."

Berit looked at the crude grave beside the trail. "I looked right through it," he confessed. "Sorry, Khalad."

"Pay attention, my Lord."

"It seems you've said that before."

They dismounted and approached the rude "grave."

"Clever," Berit murmured quietly. It was probably not necessary to lower his voice, but it had gotten to be a habit.

"Talen's idea, probably," Khalad said as they both knelt beside the mound. "It's a little subtle for Sparhawk."

"Isn't that supposed to be two words?" Berit asked, pointing at the weathered plank with *Ramshorn* roughly carved into its face.

"You're the educated one, my Lord. Don't touch those rocks."

"Which rocks?"

"The yellow ones. We'll mix them up as soon as I read them."

"You read rocks? Is that like reading seagulls?"

"Not exactly. It's a message from Sparhawk. He and my father worked this out a long time ago." The short-bearded young man leaned first this way and then that, squinting at the mound. "Naturally," he said finally with a certain resignation. He rose and moved to the head of the grave.

"What?"

"Sparhawk wrote it upside down. Now it makes sense." Khalad studied the apparently random placement of the yellowish rocks on the top of the predominantly brown mound. "Pray, Berit," he said. "Offer up a prayer for the soul of our departed brother, Ramshorn."

"You're not making any sense, Khalad."

"Somebody might be watching. Act religious." The husky young squire took the reins of their horses and led them several yards away from the ill-defined trail. Then he bent, took Faran's left foreleg in both hands, and carefully inspected the hoof.

Faran gave him an unfriendly stare.

"Sorry," Khalad apologized to the bad-tempered brute, "it's nothing important." He lowered the hoof to the gravel again. "All right, Berit," he said then, "say 'Amen,' and we'll get going again."

"What was that all about?" Berit's tone was surly as he remounted.

"Sparhawk left a message for us," Khalad replied, swinging up into his saddle. "The arrangement of the yellow rocks told me where to find it."

"Where is it?" Berit asked eagerly.

"Right now? It's in my left boot. I picked it up when I was checking Faran's hoof."

"I didn't see you pick up a thing."

"You weren't supposed to, my Lord."

Krager awoke with the horrors to the sound of distant screaming. Days and nights had long since blurred in Krager's awareness, but the sun shattering against his eyes told him that it was full and awful morning. He had certainly not intended to drink so much the previous night, but the knowledge that he was reaching the bottom of his last cask of Arcian red had somehow worried at him as he had grown progressively drunker, and the knowledge that it would soon be all gone had somehow translated itself in his fuddled mind into a compulsion to drink it all before it somehow got away from him.

Now he was paying for that foolishness. His head was throbbing, his stomach was on fire, and his mouth tasted as if something had crawled in there and died. He was shaking violently, and there were sharp stabbing pains in his liver. He sat on the edge of his tangled bed with his head in his hands. There was a sense of dread hanging over him, a shadowy feeling of horror. He kept his burning eyes closed and groped under the bed with one shaking hand for the emergency bottle he always kept there. The liquid it contained was neither wine nor beer but a dreadful concoction of Lamork origin that was obtained by setting certain inferior wines out in the winter and allowing them to freeze. The liquid that rose to the top and remained unfrozen was almost pure spirits. It tasted foul, and it burned like fire going down, but it put the horrors to sleep. Shuddering, Krager drank off about a pint of the awful stuff and lurched to his feet.

The sun was painfully bright when he stumbled out into the streets of Natayos and went looking for the source of the screams that had awakened him. He reached a central square and recoiled in horror. Several men were being systematically tortured to death while Scarpa, dressed in his shabby imitation royal robe and his makeshift crown, sat in an ornate chair watching with approval.

"What's going on?" Krager asked Cabah, a shabby Dacite brigand with whom he had frequently gotten drunk.

Cabah turned quickly. "Oh, it's you, Krager," he said. "As closely as I can gather, the Shining Ones descended on Panem-Dea."

"That's impossible," Krager said shortly. "Ptaga's dead. There aren't any more of those illusions to keep the Tamuls running around in circles."

"If we can believe what some of those dying fellows said, the ones who went into Panem-Dea weren't illusions," Cabah replied. "A fair number of the officers there got themselves dissolved when they tried to stand and fight."

"What's happening here?" Krager asked, pointing at the screaming men bound to poles set up in the middle of the square.

"Scarpa's making examples of the ones who ran away. He's having them cut to pieces. Here comes Cyzada." Cabah pointed at the Styric hurrying out of Scarpa's headquarters.

"What are you *doing*?" the hollow-eyed Cyzada bellowed at the madman sitting on his cheap throne.

"They deserted their posts," Scarpa replied. "They're being punished."

"You need every man, you idiot!"

"I ordered them to march to the north to join my loyal armies." Scarpa shrugged. "They concocted lies to excuse their failure to obey. They must be punished. I *will* have obedience!"

"You will *not* kill your own soldiers! Order your butchers to stop!"

"That's quite impossible, Cyzada. An imperial order, once given, cannot be rescinded. I have commanded that every deserter from Panem-Dea be tortured to death. It's out of my hands now."

"You maniac! You won't have a soldier left by tomorrow morning! They'll *all* desert!"

"Then I will recruit more and hunt them all down. I *will* be obeyed!"

Cyzada of Esos controlled his fury with an obvious effort. Krager saw his lips moving and his fingers weaving intricate patterns in the air. "Let's get out of here, Cabah!" he said urgently.

"What? The crazy man ordered us all to watch."

"You don't want to watch what's going to happen next," Krager told him. "Cyzada's casting a spell—Zemoch, most likely. He's summoning a demon to teach our 'emperor' the real meaning of the word *obedience*."

"He can't do that. Zalasta left his son in charge here."

"No, actually Cyzada's in charge. I personally heard Zalasta tell that Styric who's wriggling his fingers right now to kill Scarpa the minute he stepped out of line. 'Course Cyzada might have something else in mind, but either way, it won't be pretty. I don't know about you, my friend, but *I'm* going to find someplace to hide. I've seen the kind of creatures that were subject to Azash before, and I'm feeling a little delicate this morning, so I don't want to see one again."

"We'll get into trouble, Krager."

"Not if the demon Cyzada's summoning right now eats Scarpa alive, we won't." Krager drew in a deep breath. "It's up to you, Cabah. Stay if you want, but I think I've seen as much as I want to of Natayos."

"You're going to desert?" Cabah was aghast.

"The situation's changed. If Sparhawk's allied himself with the Delphae, I want to be a long way from here when they come glowing out of that jungle. I find that I'm suddenly homesick for Eosia. Come or stay, Cabah, but *I'm* leaving—now."

■ CHAPTER TWENTY-FIVE ■

Zalasta's face was strangely altered when Ekatas unlocked and opened the door to the small, dank cell at the top of the tower. The doubt and remorse which had filled it when he had brought Ehlana and Alean to Cyrga were gone, and the Styric's expression was now one of calm detachment. He took in the horrid little room at a glance. Ehlana and Alean were chained to the wall, and they were sitting on heaps of moldy straw that were supposed to serve as beds. Crude earthenware bowls filled with cold gruel sat untouched on the floor. "This won't do, Ekatas," Zalasta said in a remote kind of voice.

"It's really none of your concern," the high priest replied. "Prisoners are kept closely confined here in Cyrga." As always, Ekatas sneered when he spoke to Zalasta.

"Not *these* prisoners." Zalasta stepped into the cell and took up the chains that bound the two women to the wall. Then, showing no emotion, he crushed them into powdery rust. "The situation here has changed, Ekatas," he snapped, helping Ehlana to her feet. "Get this mess cleaned up."

Ekatas drew himself up. "I don't take orders from Styrics. I am the High Priest of Cyrgon."

"I'm truly sorry about this, your Majesty," Zalasta apologized to Ehlana. "My attention's been diverted for the past week or so. Evidently I didn't make my wishes clear to the Cyrgai. Please excuse me for a moment, and I'll correct that oversight." He turned back to Ekatas. "I told you to do something," he said in a dreadful voice. "Why haven't you started?"

"Come out of there, Zalasta, or I'll lock you in with them."

"Oh, really?" Zalasta said with a thin smile. "I thought you had better sense. I don't have time for this, Ekatas. Get this room cleaned up. I have to take our guests to the temple again."

"I've received no such instructions."

"Why should you have?"

"Cyrgon speaks through me."

"Precisely. The instructions didn't come from Cyrgon."

"Cyrgon is God here."

"Not anymore, he isn't." Zalasta gave him an almost pitying look. "You didn't even feel it, did you, Ekatas? The world heaved and convulsed all around you, and you didn't even notice. How can you possibly be so dense? Cyrgon has been supplanted. Klæl rules in Cyrga now—and I speak for Klæl."

"That's not possible! You're lying!"

Zalasta walked out of the cell and took hold of the front of the high priest's robe. "Look at me, Ekatas," he commanded. "Take a long, hard look, and then tell me that I'm lying."

Ekatas struggled momentarily, and then, unable to help himself, he looked into Zalasta's eyes. The blood slowly drained from his face, and then he screamed. He screamed again, trying to tear himself free from the Styric's iron grasp. "I beg of you!" he cried out in a voice filled with horror, "No more! No more!" Then he sagged, covering his eyes with his hands.

Zalasta contemptuously let go of the front of his black robe, and he fell to the floor, weeping uncontrollably.

"Now do you understand?" Zalasta asked him, almost gently. "Cyzada and I tried to warn you and our petty Godling about the dangers involved in summoning Klæl, but you wouldn't listen. Cyrgon wanted to enslave Bhelliom, and now he's the slave of Bhelliom's opposite. And, since I speak for Klæl, I guess that makes you *my* slave." He prodded the weeping priest with one foot. "Get up, Ekatas! Get on your feet when your master speaks!"

The groveling priest scrambled to his feet, his tear-streaked face still filled with unspeakable horror.

"Say it, Ekatas," Zalasta said in a cruel voice. "I want to hear you say it—or would you like to witness the death of another star?"

"M-M-Master," the high priest choked.

"Again—a little louder, if you don't mind."

"Master!" It came out almost as a shriek.

"Much better, Ekatas. Now wake up those lazy cretins in the guardroom next door and put them to work cleaning this cell. We have preparations to make when I come back from the temple. Anakha's bringing Bhelliom to Cyrga, and we'll want to be ready when he arrives." He turned. "Bring your maid, Ehlana. Klæl wants to look at you." Zalasta paused, surveying her critically. "I know that we've treated you badly," he half apologized, "but don't let our bad manners break your spirit. Remember who you are and draw that about you. Klæl respects power and those who wield it."

"What do I say to him?"

"Nothing. He'll find out what he wants to know just by looking at you. He doesn't understand your husband, and seeing you will give him some hints about Anakha's nature. Anakha's the unknown element in this business. He always has been, I suppose. Klæl understands Bhelliom. It's Bhelliom's creature who baffles him."

"You've changed, Zalasta."

"I suppose I have," he admitted. "I have a feeling that I won't live much longer. Klæl's touch does peculiar things to people. We'd better not keep him waiting." He looked at Ekatas, who stood trembling violently. "I want this room clean when we come back."

"I'll see to it, Master," Ekatas promised in a grotesquely servile tone.

"How do you find them again?" Itagne asked curiously. "What I'm trying to get at is that the Trolls are in this 'No-Time,' but you and Tynian had to come out into real time in order to come into Sarna, so time started moving for you. How do you get back to the moment when you left the Trolls?"

"Please don't ask metaphysical questions, Itagne," Ulath replied with a pained expression. "We just go back to the spot where we left the Trolls, and there they are. We deal with where and let the Troll-Gods deal with *when*. They seem to be able to jump around in time without paying much attention to the rules."

"Where are the Trolls right now?"

"Just outside of town," Tynian replied. "We didn't think it was a good idea to bring them into Sarna with us. They're starting to get a little out of hand."

"Is it something we should know about, Tynian-Knight?" Engessa asked.

Ulath leaned back in his chair. "Cyrgon disrupted Trollish behavior rather profoundly when he went to Thalesia and posed as Ghworg," he explained somberly. "Zalasta told him about the Trolls, but Cyrgon's been a little out of touch, so he mistook the Trolls for the Dawn-men. The Dawn-men were herd animals, but the Trolls sort of run in packs. Herd animals will accept any member of their species, but pack animals are a little more selective. It's to our advantage right now to have the Trolls behave like a herd. At least we can keep them all going in the same direction, but some problems are starting to crop up. The packs are beginning to separate, and there's a great deal of snapping and snarling going on."

Tynian glanced at Queen Betuana, who, gowned all in black, was sitting somewhat apart from them. He motioned Engessa slightly to one side. "Is she all right?" he asked very quietly.

"Betuana-Queen is in ritual mourning," Engessa replied, also in a half whisper. "The loss of her husband has touched her very deeply."

"Were they really that close?"

"It did not seem so," Engessa admitted. His eyes were troubled as he looked at his melancholy queen. "The mourning ritual is seldom observed now. I am keeping careful watch over her. She must not be allowed to do herself injury." Engessa's shoulder muscles bunched.

Tynian was startled. "Is there any real danger of that?"

"It was not uncommon a few centuries ago," Engessa replied.

"We'd been expecting you earlier," Itagne was saying to Ulath. "As I understand it, *No-Time* means that the Trolls can go from one place to another almost instantaneously."

"Not quite instantaneously, Itagne. We've been a week or so getting here from the Tamul Mountains. We have to stop and go back into real time every so often so that they can hunt. Hungry Trolls aren't the best of traveling companions. So now, tell us, what's been happening? We can't make contact with Aphrael when we're in No-Time."

"Sparhawk's found some clues about the location of Cyrga," Itagne replied. "They aren't too precise, but he's going to try to follow them."

"How's Patriarch Bergsten coming?"

"He's captured Cynestra—had it handed to him on a plate, actually."

"Oh?"

"Do you remember Atana Maris?"

"The pretty girl who commanded the garrison in Cynestra? The one who liked you?"

Itagne smiled. "That's the one. She's an abrupt sort of girl, and I'm quite fond of her, and when she saw Bergsten and the Church Knights approaching, she decided to present him with the city. She swept the streets clean of Cynesgan troops and opened the gates for Bergsten. She was going to give him King Jaluah's head as well, but he persuaded her not to."

"Pity," Ulath murmured, "but that's the sort of thing you have to expect when a good man gets religion."

"Vanion's in place," Itagne continued, "and he and Kring are establishing strongholds about a day's ride out into Cynesga. We're going to do the same here, but we thought we'd wait until you arrived first."

"Is anybody encountering any significant opposition?" Tynian asked.

"It's hard to say exactly," Itagne mused. "We're moving on central Cynesga, but Klæl's soldiers pop out of every crack between two rocks. The farther back we push them, the tighter they'll be concentrated. If we don't come up with a way to neutralize them, we'll have to carve our way through them, and from what Vanion tells me, they don't carve very well. Kring's tactics are working smoothly enough now, but when we get closer to Cyrga . . ." He spread his hands helplessly.

"We'll work something out," Ulath said. "Anything else?"

"It's all still sort of up in the air, Sir Ulath," Itagne replied. "The fairy stories

Stragen and Caalador are hatching in Beressa are diverting most of the Cynesgan cavalry away from the eastern border. Half of them are running south toward the coast around Kaftal, and the other half are running north toward a little village called Zhubay. Caalador added an imaginary massing of the Atans up there to Stragen's illusory fleet off the southern coast. Between them, they've split the entire Cynesgan army in two and sent them off to chase moonbeams."

"You say that half of them are going north?" Tynian asked innocently.

"Toward Zhubay, yes. They seem to think the Atans are massing there for some reason."

"What an amazing thing," Ulath said with a straight face. "It just so happens that Tynian and I have been sort of drifting in that general direction anyway. Do you think the Cynesgans would be *too* disappointed if they came up against Trolls instead of Atans?"

"You could go up there and ask them, I suppose," Itagne replied, also with no hint of a smile. They all knew what was going to happen at Zhubay.

"Convey our apologies to them, Ulath-Knight," Betuana said with a sad little smile.

"Oh, we *will*, your Majesty," Ulath assured her, "if we can find any of them still in one piece after they've frolicked around with the Trolls for a couple of hours."

"Get out of there!" Kalten shouted, galloping his horse toward the doglike creatures clustered around something lying on the gravel floor of the desert. The beasts scampered away, hooting with soulless laughter.

"Are they dogs?" Talen asked in a sick voice.

"No," Mirtai replied shortly. "Hyenas."

Kalten rode back. "It's a man," he reported bleakly, "or what's left of one."

"We must bury him," Bevier said.

"They'd only dig him up again," Sparhawk told him. "Besides," he added, "if you start trying to bury them all, we'll be here for several lifetimes." He gestured at the bone-littered plain stretching off to the low range of black mountains lying to the west. He looked at Xanetia. "It was a mistake to bring you along, Anarae," he apologized. "This is going to get worse before it gets any better."

"It was not unexpected, Anakha," she replied.

Kalten looked up at the flock of vultures circling overhead. "Filthy brutes," he muttered.

Sparhawk raised up in his stirrups to peer ahead. "We've got a couple more hours until the sun goes down, but maybe we'd better pull back a mile or two and set up camp a little early. We'll have to spend *one* night out there. Let's not spend two."

"We need those pillars for landmarks anyway," Talen added, "and they're a lot brighter when the sun first comes up."

"That's *if* that bright spot we've been following really comes from those pillars," Kalten said dubiously.

"They got us here, didn't they? This *has* to be what Ogerajin called 'the Plain of Bones,' doesn't it? I admit, I had my own doubts right at first. Ogerajin was raving so much of the time that I was sure that he'd garbled at least some of the directions, but he hasn't led us astray yet."

"We still haven't seen the city, Talen," Kalten reminded him, "so I'd sort of hold off on composing the letter of thanks."

"I've got all the money I'll ever need, Orden," Krager said expansively, leaning back in his chair and looking out through the window at the buildings and the harbor of the port city of Delo. He took another drink of wine.

"I wouldn't go around announcing that, Krager," the burly Orden advised, "particularly not here on the waterfront."

"I've hired some bodyguards, Orden. Can you ask around and find out if there's a fast ship leaving for Zenga in Cammoria in the next week or so?"

"Why would anybody want to go to Zenga?"

"I grew up there, and I'm homesick," Krager replied with a shrug. "Besides, I'd sort of like to grind a few faces—all the people who said that I'd come to no good end while I was growing up."

"Did you happen to come across a fellow named Ezek while you were in Natayos?" Orden asked. "I think he's a Deiran."

"The name rings a bell. I think he was working for the fellow who ran the tavern."

"I sent him down there," Orden explained, "him and the other two—Col and Shallag. They were going to see if they could join Narstil's band of outlaws."

"They may have, but they were working in the tavern when I left."

"It's none of my business, but if you were doing so well in Natayos, why did you leave?"

"Instincts, Orden," Krager replied owlishly. "I get this cold little feeling at the base of my skull, and I know that it's time to run. Have you ever heard of a man named Sparhawk?"

"You mean Prince Sparhawk? Everybody's heard of him. He's got quite a reputation."

"Oh, yes. That he does. Anyway, Sparhawk's been looking for an opportunity to kill me for twenty years or so, and that's the sort of thing that puts a very fine edge on a man's instincts." Krager took another long drink.

"You might want to give some thought to drying out for a while," Orden advised, looking meaningfully at Krager's tankard of Arcian red. "I run a tavern, and I've learned to recognize the signs. Your liver's starting to go on you, my friend. Your eyeballs are turning yellow."

"I'll cut down once I get out to sea."

"I think you'll have to do more than just cut down, Krager. You're going to have to give it up entirely if you want to go on living. Believe me, you *don't* want to die the way most drunkards do. I knew one who screamed for three straight weeks before he finally died. It was awful."

"There's nothing wrong with my liver," Krager said truculently. "It's just the funny light in here. When I get out to sea, I'll space out my drinks. I'll be all right."

His face had a haunted expression, however, and the mere mention of giving up strong drink had set his hands to trembling violently.

Orden shrugged. He *had* tried to warn the man. "It's up to you, Krager," he said. "I'll ask around and see if I can find a ship that'll get you out of Prince Sparhawk's reach."

"Soon, Orden. Soon." Krager held out his tankard. "In the meantime, why don't we have another?"

Ekrasios and his party of Delphae reached Norenja late in the afternoon on a murky day when heavy clouds hung low over the treetops and there was not a breath of air moving. Ekrasios took his boyhood friend, Adras, and crept forward through the tangle of brush and vines to the edge of the clearing to survey the ruin.

"Thinkest thou that they will offer resistance?" Adras asked quietly.

"That is difficult to predict," Ekrasios replied. "Anakha and his companions have advised that these rebels are but poorly trained. Methinks their response to our sudden appearance will depend on the character of their officers. Better that we leave them a clear path to the surrounding forest. Should we encircle them, desperation will impel them to fight."

Adras nodded. "They have made some effort to repair the gates," he said, pointing at the entrance to the city.

"The gates will pose no problem. I will instruct thee and our companions in the spell which doth modify the curse of Edaemus. Those newly made gates are constructed of wood, and wood is as susceptible to decay as is flesh." He looked up at the dirty grey clouds. "Canst thou make any estimate as to the time of day?"

"No more than two hours until dusk," Adras replied.

"Let us proceed, then. We must find yet another gate to provide means of escape for those whom we would confront this night."

"And if there be none other?"

"Then those who would escape must find their own way. I am reluctant to unleash the full force of the curse of Edaemus. Should necessity compel me to it, however, I will not shrink from that stern duty. Should they flee, well and good. Should they choose to stay and fight, we will do what we must. I do assure thee, Adras, that when tomorrow's sun rises, none living shall remain within the walls of Norenja."

"Good God!" Berit exclaimed, peering over the edge of the dry gully at the huge soldiers in close-fitting armor running westward across the sun-baked gravel. "They're *monsters*!"

"Keep your voice down," Khalad cautioned. "There's no way of knowing how good their ears are."

The strange, bestial soldiers were larger than Atans, and their burnished steel breastplates fit their torsos snugly, outlining each muscle. They wore helmets adorned with fanciful horns or wings, and the visors of those helmets were individualized, evidently forged to fit each warrior's face. They ran westward in a sort of ragged formation, and their hoarse gasping was clearly audible even at this distance.

"Where are they going?" Berit demanded. "The border's off in the other direction."

"That one who's trailing along behind the others has a broken-off javelin sticking out of him," Khalad replied. "I'd say that means that they've come up against Tikume's Peloi. They've already been to the border, and now they're coming back."

"Back to where?" Berit was baffled. "Where can they go? They can't breathe here."

Khalad cautiously poked his head above the rim of the gully and squinted out across the rocky desert. "They seem to be going toward that cluster of hills about a mile to the west." He paused. "Just how curious are we feeling today, Berit?"

"What have you got in mind?"

"This gully comes down out of those hills, and if we follow it and keep our heads down, they won't see us. Why don't we drift off toward the west? We might find out something useful if we tag along behind those fellows."

Berit shrugged. "Why not?"

"That's really not a very logical answer, Berit. I can think of a half-dozen reasons why not." Khalad squinted at the panting soldiers lurching across the desert. "Let's do it anyway, though."

They slid back down into the gully and led their horses along the dry watercourse toward the west.

They moved quietly along the bottom of the wash for about a quarter of an hour. "Are they still out there?" Berit whispered.

"I'll look." Khalad carefully climbed back up the steep bank to the rim of the gully and eased his head up far enough to look. Then he slid back down again. "They're still staggering toward the hills," he reported. "This gully starts getting shallower up ahead. Let's leave the horses here."

They crept along, crouched over to stay out of sight, and as the gully started to run uphill, they found that they were forced to crawl on their hands and knees.

Khalad rose slightly to look again. "They seem to be swinging around behind that other hill," he said quietly. "Let's slip up to the top of this ridge and see what's back there."

The two of them crawled out of the now-shallow wash and slanted their way up the ridgeline to a point from which they could see what lay behind the hill Khalad had pointed out.

It was a kind of shallow basin nestled down among the three hills that heaved up out of the surrounding desert. The basin was empty. "Where did they go?" Berit whispered.

"That basin was the place they were making for," Khalad insisted with a puzzled frown. "Wait. Here comes that one with the javelin in his belly."

They watched the wounded soldier stumble into the basin, half falling, then rising again to drag himself along. He raised his masked face and bellowed something.

Khalad and Berit waited tensely.

Then two other soldiers emerged from a narrow opening in the side of one of the hills, descended to the floor of the basin, and half dragged their injured comrade back up the hill and through the mouth of the cave.

"That answers that," Khalad said. "They ran across miles of open desert to get to that cave."

"Why? What good will it do them?"

"I haven't got a clue, Berit, but I think it's important." Khalad stood up. "Let's go back to where we left the horses. We can still cover a few more miles before the sun goes down."

Ekrasios crouched at the edge of the forest waiting for the torches inside the walls of Norenja to burn down and for the sounds of human activity to subside. The events at Panem-Dea had confirmed the assessment of these rebels Lord Vanion had given him at Sarna. Given the slightest opportunity, these poorly trained soldiers would flee, and that suited Ekrasios very well. He was still somewhat reluctant to unleash the curse of Edaemus, and people who ran away did not have to be destroyed.

Adras returned, ghosting back to the edge of the jungle through the night mist. "All is in readiness, Ekrasios," he reported quietly. "The gates will crumble at the merest touch."

"Let us then proceed," Ekrasios replied, standing up and relaxing the rigid control that dimmed his inner light. "Let us pray that all within yon walls may flee."

"And if they do not?"

"Then they must surely die. Our promise to Anakha binds us. We will empty yon ruin—in one fashion or the other."

"It's not so bad here," Kalten said as they dismounted. "The bones are older, for one thing." Necessity had compelled them to camp in the hideous boneyard the previous night, and they were all eager to reach the end of the horror.

Sparhawk grunted, looking across the intervening stretch of desert at the fractured basalt cliff that seemed to mark the eastern edge of the Forbidden Mountains. The sun had just come up above the eastern horizon, and its brilliant light reflected back from the pair of quartz-laced peaks rearing up out of the rusty black mountains just to the west.

"Why are we stopping here?" Mirtai asked. "That cliff's still a quarter of a mile away."

"I think we're supposed to line up on those two peaks," Sparhawk replied. "Talen, can you remember Ogerajin's exact words?"

"Let's see." The boy frowned in concentration. Then he nodded shortly. "I've got it now," he said.

"How do you do that?" Bevier asked him curiously.

Talen shrugged. "There's a trick to it. You don't think about the words. You just concentrate on where you were when you heard them." He lifted his face slightly, closed his eyes, and began to recite. " 'Beyond the Plain of Bones wilt thou come to the Gates of Illusion behind which lies concealed the Hidden City of Cyrga. The eye of mortal man cannot perceive those gates. Stark they stand as a fractured wall at the verge of the Forbidden Mountains to bar thy way. Bend thine eye, however, upon Cyrgon's two white pillars and direct thy steps toward the emptiness which doth lie between them. Trust not the evidence which thine eye doth present unto thee, for the solid-seeming wall is as mist and will not bar thy way.' "

"That didn't even sound like your own voice," Bevier said.

"That's part of the trick," Talen explained. "That was Ogerajin's voice—sort of."

"All right, then," Sparhawk said. "Let's see if he really knew what he was talking about." He squinted at the two brilliant points of reflected light. "There are the pillars." He took a few steps to the right and shook his head. "From here they merge into one light." Then he walked to the left. "It does the same thing here." Then he went back to his original location. "This is the spot," he said with a certain amount of excitement. "Those two peaks are very close together. If you move a few feet either way, you can't even see that gap between them. Unless you're really looking for it, you could miss it altogether."

"Oh, that's just fine, Talen," Kalten said sarcastically. "If we go any closer, the cliff will block off our view of the peaks."

Talen rolled his eyes upward.

"What?" Kalten asked.

"Just start walking toward the cliff, Kalten. Sparhawk can stand here and keep his eyes on the gap. He'll tell you whether to go to the right or the left."

"Oh." Kalten looked around at the others. "Don't make an issue of it," he told them. Then he started off toward the cliff.

"Veer to the right," Sparhawk told him.

Kalten nodded and changed direction.

"Too far. Back to the left a little."

The blond Pandion continued toward the cliff, altering his direction in response to Sparhawk's shouted commands. When he reached the cliff, he went along slapping his hands on the face of the rock. Then he drew his heavy dagger, stuck it into the ground, and started back.

"Well?" Sparhawk called when he had covered half the distance.

"Ogerajin didn't know what he was talking about," Kalten shouted.

Sparhawk swore.

"Do you mean there's no opening?" Talen called.

"Oh, the opening's there, all right," Kalten replied, "but it's at least five feet to the left of where your crazy man said it would be."

"Please don't do that, Talen," Bevier said. "Either go all the way in or stay outside. It's very disturbing to see the bottom half of you sticking out of solid rock that way."

"It's not solid, Bevier." The boy stuck his hand into the rock and pulled it out again to demonstrate.

"Well, it *looks* solid. Please, Talen, in or out. Don't hover in between."

"Can you feel anything at all when you poke your head through?" Mirtai asked.

"It's a little cooler in there," Talen replied. "It's a sort of cave or tunnel. There's a light at the far end."

"Can we get the horses through?" Sparhawk asked.

Talen nodded. "It's big enough for that—if we go through in single file. I guess Cyrgon wanted to keep down the chances of anybody accidentally discovering the opening."

"You'd better let me go first," Sparhawk said. "There might be guards at the other end."

"I'll be right behind you," Kalten said, retrieving his dagger and drawing his sword.

" 'Tis a most clever illusion," Xanetia observed, touching the rock face on the left of the gate. "Seamless and indistinguishable from reality."

"It's been good enough to hide Cyrga for ten thousand years, I guess," Talen said.

"Let's go in," Sparhawk said. "I want to have a look at this place."

There was difficulty with the horses, of course. No matter how reasonably one explains something to a horse, he will not willingly walk into a stone wall. Bevier solved the problem by wrapping cloth around their heads, and, with Sparhawk in the lead, the party led their mounts into the tunnel.

It was perhaps a hundred feet long, and since the opening at the far end was still in shade, the light from it was not blinding. "Hold my horse," Sparhawk muttered to Kalten. Then, his sword held low, he moved quietly toward the opening. When he reached it, he tensed himself and then stepped through quickly, whirling to fend off an attack from either side.

"Anything?" Kalten demanded in a hoarse whisper.

"No. There's nobody here."

The rest of them cautiously led their horses out of the tunnel.

They had emerged into a tree-shaded swale carpeted with dry grass and dotted with white stone markers. "The Glen of Heroes," Talen murmured.

"What?" Kalten asked.

"That's what Ogerajin called it. I guess it sounds nicer than 'graveyard.' The Cyrgai seem to treat their own dead a little better than they do the slaves."

Sparhawk looked across the extensive cemetery. He pointed to the western side where a slight rise marked the edge of the burial ground. "Let's go," he told his friends. "I want to see just exactly what we're up against."

They crossed the cemetery to the bottom of the rise, tied their horses to the trees growing there, and carefully crept to the top.

The basin was significantly lower than the floor of the surrounding desert, and there was a fair-sized lake nestled in the center, dark and unreflective in the morning shadows. The lake was surrounded by winter-fallow fields, and a forest of dark trees stretched up the slopes of the basin. There was a sort of rigid tidiness about it all, as if nature itself had been coerced into straight lines and precise angles. Centuries of brutal labor had been devoted to hammering what might have been a place of beauty into a stern reflection of the mind of Cyrgon himself.

The hidden valley was perhaps five miles across, and on the far side stood the city that had remained concealed for ten eons. The surrounding mountains had provided the building materials, and the city wall and the buildings within were constructed of that same brownish-black volcanic basalt. The exterior walls were high and massive, and a steep, conelike hill, its sides thickly covered with buildings, rose inside those walls. Surmounting that hill was yet another walled enclosure with black spires rising on one side and, in startling contrast to the rest of the city, white spires on the other.

"It's not particularly creative," Bevier observed critically. "The architect doesn't seem to have had much imagination."

"Imagination was not a trait encouraged amongst the Cyrgai, Sir Knight," Xanetia told him.

"We could swing around the sides of the basin and get closer," Kalten suggested. "The trees would hide us. The ground around the lake doesn't offer much concealment."

"We've got some time," Sparhawk said. "Let's get away from the mouth of this tunnel. If it's the only way in or out of the valley, there's bound to be traffic going through here. I can see people working in those fields down there—slaves, most likely. There'll be Cyrgai watching them, and there may be patrols as well. Let's see if we can pick up some kind of routine before we blunder into anything."

Berit and Khalad made a dry camp in another cluster of jumbled boulders two days west of the place where they had seen the strange soldiers. They watered their horses sparingly, built no fire, and ate cold rations. Khalad spoke very little, but sat instead staring moodily out at the desert.

"Quit worrying at it, Khalad," Berit told him.

"It's right in front of my face, Berit. I know it is, but I just can't put my finger on it."

"Do you want to talk it out? Neither one of us is going to get any sleep if you spend the whole night wrestling with it."

"I can brood quietly."

"No, actually you can't. We've been together too long, my friend. I can hear you thinking."

Khalad smiled faintly. "It has to do with those creatures," he said.

"Really? I never would have guessed. That's all you've been thinking about for the past two days. What did you want to know about them—aside from the fact that they're big, ugly, savage, and they've got yellow blood?"

"That's the part that's nagging at me—that yellow blood. Aphrael says that it's because they breathe with their livers. They do that because what they're used to breathing isn't air. They can get along here for a little while, but when they start exerting themselves, they start to fall apart. The ones we saw the other day weren't just running around aimlessly out there in the desert. They had a specific destination in mind."

"That cave? You think it might be a haven for them?"

"*Now* we're starting to get somewhere," Khalad said, his face growing intent. "The Peloi are probably the best light cavalry in the world, but Klæl's soldiers are almost as big as Trolls, and they seem to be able to ignore wounds that would kill one of us. I don't think they're running from the Peloi."

"No. They're trying to run away from the air."

Khalad snapped his fingers. *"That's it!"* he exclaimed. *"That's* why they break off and run back to those caves. They aren't hiding from the Peloi. They're hiding from the air."

"Air is air, Khalad—whether it's out in the open or inside a cave."

"I don't think so, Berit. I think Klæl has filled that cave with the kind of air his soldiers are used to breathing. He can't change all the air on the whole world, because it would kill the Cyrgai as well as all the rest of us, and Cyrgon won't let him do that. He *can* fill a cave with that other kind of air, though. It'd be the perfect place. It's closed-in and more or less airtight. It gives those monsters a place to go when they start to get winded. They can rest up in there and then come back out and fight some more. You'd better pass this on, Berit. Aphrael can let the others know that Klæl's soldiers are hiding out in caves because they can breathe there."

"I'll tell her," Berit said dubiously. "I'm not sure what good it's going to do us, but I'll tell her."

Khalad leaned back on his elbows with a broad grin. "You're not thinking, Berit. If something's giving you problems, and it's hiding out in a cave, you don't have to go in after it. All you have to do is collapse the entrance. Once it's trapped inside, you can forget about it. Why don't you pass this on to Aphrael? Suggest that she tell the others to collapse every cave they come across. She won't even have to do it herself." Then he frowned again.

"What's wrong now?"

"That was too easy," Khalad told him, "and it doesn't really help all that much. As big as those beasts are, you could collapse a whole mountain on them, and they could still dig their way out. There's something else that hasn't quite come together yet." He held up one hand. "I'll get it," he promised. "I'll get it if it takes me all night."

Berit groaned.

"I have decided to go with you, Bergsten-Priest," Atana Maris replied haltingly in heavily accented Elenic. She had come up from behind their column when they were five days south of Cynestra.

Bergsten suppressed an oath. "We're an army on the move, Atana Maris," he tried to explain diplomatically. "We wouldn't be able to make suitable arrangements for your comfort or safety when we stop for the night."

"Arrangements?" She looked at Neran, the translator, with a puzzled expression.

Neran spoke at some length in Tamul, and the tall girl burst out laughing.

"What's so funny, Atana?" Bergsten asked suspiciously.

"That you would worry about *that*, Bergsten-Priest. I am a soldier. I can defend myself against any of your men who admire me too much."

"Why have you decided to come along with us, Atana Maris?" Heldin stepped in.

"I had a thought after you left Cynestra, Heldin-Knight," she replied. "It has been in my mind for much weeks now to go find Itagne-Ambassador. You are going to the place where he will be, so I will go with you."

"We could carry a message to him for you, Atana. You don't really have to go along."

She shook her head. "No, Heldin-Knight. It is a personal matter between Itagne-Ambassador and me. He was friendly to me when he was in Cynestra. Then he had to go away, but he said to me that he would write letters to me. He did not do that. Now I must go find him to make sure that he is well." Her eyes went hard. "If he is well, I must know if he does not want to be friendly to me anymore." She sighed. "I hope much that his feelings have not changed. I would not want to have to kill him."

"I want no part of this," Gahenas said abruptly, standing up and giving the rest of them a reproving look. "I was willing to join with you if it meant tweaking Cieronna's nose, but I'm not going to involve myself in treason."

"Who said anything about treason, Gahenas?" Chacole asked her. "There won't be any *real* danger to our husband. We're just going to make it *appear* that there's a plot against him—and we're going to plant enough evidence to lay the plot at Cieronna's door. If something *were* to happen to Sarabian, the crown prince would be elevated to the imperial throne, and Cieronna would be regent—which none of us want to happen. No, we'll expose her plot before anything really happens, so she'll be discredited—probably imprisoned—and we won't have to kowtow to her anymore."

"I don't care what you say, Chacole," the jug-eared Tegan empress declared flatly. "You're putting something in motion that's treasonous, and I won't be a party to it. I'm going to keep an eye on you, Chacole. Dismiss your spies and drop this wild scheme at once, because if you don't . . ." Gahenas left it hanging ominously in the air as she turned on her heel and stalked away.

"That was very clumsy, Chacole," Elysoun drawled, carefully selecting a piece of fruit from the silver platter on the table. "She might have gone along if you hadn't gone into such detail. She didn't *have* to know that you were actually going to send out your assassins. You weren't really sure of her yet, and you went too fast."

"I'm running out of time, Elysoun." Chacole's tone was desperate.

"I don't see the need for all this urgency," Elysoun replied, "and how much time did you save today? That Tegan hag's going to be watching your every move now. You blundered, Chacole. Now you're going to have to kill her."

"*Kill?*" Chacole's face went white.

"Unless you don't mind losing your head. One word from Gahenas can send you to the block. You aren't really cut out for men's politics, dear. You talk too much." Elysoun rose lazily to her feet. "We can discuss this later," she said. "I have an enthusiastic young guardsman waiting for me, and I wouldn't want him to cool off." She sauntered away.

Elysoun's casual attitude concealed a great deal of urgency. Chacole's Cynesgan upbringing had made her painfully obvious. She had drawn on the hatred of Sarabian's other wives for Empress Cieronna. That part was clever enough, but the elaborate, involved story of staging an imitation assassination attempt was ridiculously excessive. Very clearly the attempt was not designed to fail, as Chacole and Torellia so piously proclaimed. Elysoun began to walk faster. She had to get to her husband in order to warn him that his life was in immediate danger.

"Xanetia!" Kalten said, starting back in surprise as the Anarae suddenly appeared in their midst that evening. "Can't you cough or something before you do that?"

"It was not mine intent to startle thee, my protector," she apologized.

"My nerves are strung a little tight right now," he said.

"Did you have any luck?" Mirtai asked.

"I gleaned much, Atana Mirtai." Xanetia paused, collecting her thoughts. "The slaves are not closely watched," she began, "and their supervision is given over to Cynesgan overseers, for such menial tasks are beneath the dignity of the Cyrgai. The desert itself doth confine the slaves. Those foolish enough to attempt escape inevitably perish in that barren waste."

"What's the customary routine, Anarae?" Bevier asked her.

"The slaves emerge from their pens at dawn," she replied, "and, unbidden and unguarded, leave the city to take up their tasks. Then, at sunset, still uncommanded and scarce noticed, they return to the city and to the slave pens for feeding. They are then chained and locked in their pens for the night, to be released again at first light of day."

"Some of them are up here in these woods," Mirtai noted, peering out through the trees that concealed them. "What are they supposed to be doing?"

"They cut firewood for their masters in this extensive forest. The Cyrgai warm themselves with fires in the chill of winter. The kenneled slaves must endure the weather."

"Were you able to get any sense of how the city's laid out, Anarae?" Bevier asked her.

"Some, Sir Knight." She beckoned them to the edge of the trees so that they could look across the valley at the black-walled city. "The Cyrgai themselves live on the slopes of the hill which doth rise within the walls," she explained, "and they do hold themselves aloof from the more mundane portion of the city below. There is yet another wall within the outer one, and that inner wall doth protect Cyrgon's Chosen from contact with inferior races. The lower city doth contain the slave pens, the warehouses for foodstuffs, and the barracks of the Cynesgans who oversee the slaves and man the outer wall. As thou canst see, there is yet that final wall which doth enclose the summit of the hill. Within *that* ultimate wall lieth the palace of King Santheocles and the Temple of Cyrgon."

Bevier nodded. "It's fairly standard for a fortified town, then."

"If thou wert aware of all this, why didst thou ask, Sir Knight?" she asked tartly.

"Confirmation, dear lady," he replied, smiling. "The city's ten thousand years old. They might have had different ideas about how to build a fort before the invention of modern weapons." He squinted across the valley at walled Cyrga. "They're obviously willing to sacrifice the lower city," he said. "Otherwise that outer wall would be defended by Cyrgai. The fact that they've turned that chore over to the Cynesgans means that they don't place much value on those warehouses and slave pens. The wall at the foot of 'Mount Cyrgon' will be more fiercely defended, and if necessary, they'll pull back up the hill to that last wall that encloses the palace and the temple."

"All of this is well and good, Bevier," Kalten interrupted him, "but where are Ehlana and Alean?"

Bevier gave him a surprised look. "Up on top, of course," he replied, "either in the palace or in the temple."

"How did you arrive at that?"

"They're hostages, Kalten. When you're holding hostages, you have to keep them close enough to threaten them when your enemies get too close. *Our* problem is how to get into the city."

"We'll come up with something," Sparhawk said confidently. "Let's go back into the woods a ways and set up for the night."

They moved back among the trees and ate cold rations, since a fire was out of the question.

"The problem's still there, Sparhawk," Kalten said as evening settled over the hidden valley. "How are we going to get inside all those walls?"

"The first wall's easy," Talen said. "We just walk in through the gate."

"How do you propose to do that without being challenged?" Kalten demanded.

"People walk out of the city every morning and back again every evening, don't they?"

"Those are slaves."

"Exactly."

Kalten stared at him.

"We want to get into the city, don't we? That's the easiest way."

"What about the other walls?" Bevier objected.

"One wall at a time, Sir Knight," Talen said gaily, "one wall at a time. Let's get through the outer one first. *Then* we'll worry about the other two."

·   ·   ·

Daiya the Peloi came riding hard back across the gravelly desert about mid-morning the next day. "We've found them, your Reverence," he reported to Bergsten as he reined in. "The Cynesgan cavalry tried to lead us away from where they're hiding, but we found them anyway. They're in those hills just ahead of us."

"More of those big ones with masks on their faces?" Heldin asked.

"Some of those, friend Heldin," Daiya replied, "but there are others as well—wearing old-fashioned helmets and carrying spears."

"Cyrgai," Bergsten grunted. "Vanion mentioned them. Their tactics are so archaic that they won't be much of a problem."

"Where exactly are they, friend Daiya?" Heldin asked.

"They're in a large canyon on the east side of those hills, friend Heldin. My scouts saw them from the canyon rim."

"We definitely don't want to go into that canyon after them, your Grace," Heldin cautioned. "They're infantry, and close quarters are made-to-order for their tactics. We'll have to devise some way to get them to come out into the open."

Atana Maris asked Neran a question in Tamul, and he replied at some length. She nodded, spoke briefly to him, and then she ran off toward the south.

"Where's she going?" Bergsten demanded.

"She said that your enemies have laid a trap for you, your Grace," Neran replied with a shrug. "She's going to go spring it."

"Stop her, Heldin!" Bergsten said sharply.

It must be said in Sir Heldin's defense that he *did* try to catch up to the lithe, fleet-footed Atan girl, but she merely glanced back over her shoulder, laughed, and ran even faster, leaving him far behind, flogging at his horse and muttering curses.

Bergsten's curses were *not* muttered. He blistered the air around him. "What is she *doing*?" he demanded of Neran.

"They're planning an ambush, your Grace," Neran replied calmly. "It won't work if somebody sees them hiding in that canyon. Atana Maris is going to run into the canyon, let them see her, and then run out again. They'll have to try to catch her. That'll bring them out into the open. You might want to give some thought to picking up your pace just a bit. She'll be terribly disappointed in you if you're not in position when she leads them out."

Patriarch Bergsten looked out across the desert at the golden Atana running smoothly to the south with her long black hair flying behind her. Then he swore again, rose up in his stirrups, and bellowed, "Charge!"

Ekrasios and his comrades reached Synaqua late in the afternoon just as the sun broke through the heavy cloud cover that had obscured the sky for the past several days.

The ruins of Synaqua were in much greater disrepair than had been the case with Panem-Dea and Norenja. The entire east wall had been undercut by one of the numerous streams that flowed sluggishly through the soggy delta of the Arjun River, and it had collapsed at some unknown time in the past. When Scarpa's rebels had moved in to occupy the ruin, they had replaced it with a log palisade. The construction was shoddy, and the palisade was not particularly imposing.

Ekrasios considered that as he sat alone moodily watching the sun sinking into a cloud bank off to the west. A serious problem had arisen following their disastrous assault on Norenja. It had *seemed* that there were many gates through which the panic-stricken rebels could flee, but their commander had blocked off those gates with heaps of rubble as a part of his defenses. The terrified soldiers had been trapped inside the walls, and had therefore had no choice but to turn and fight. Hundreds had died in unspeakable agony before Ekrasios had been able to divert his men into the uninhabited parts of the ruin so that the escape route through the main gate was open. Many of the Delphae had wept openly at the horror they had been forced to inflict on men who were essentially no more than misguided peasants. It had taken Ekrasios two days and all of his eloquence to keep half his men from abandoning the cause and returning immediately to Delphaeus.

Adras, Ekrasios' boyhood friend and his second-in-command, was among the most profoundly disturbed. Adras now avoided his leader whenever possible, and what few communications that passed between them were abrupt and official. And so it was that Ekrasios was somewhat surprised when Adras came to him unsummoned in the ruddy glow of that fiery sunset.

"A word with thee, Ekrasios?" he asked tentatively.

"Of course, Adras. Thou knowest that it is not needful for thee to ask."

"I must advise thee that I will not participate in this night's work."

"We are bound by our pledge to Anakha, Adras," Ekrasios reminded him. "Our Anari hath sworn to this, and we are obliged to honor his oath."

"I cannot, Ekrasios!" Adras cried, sudden tears streaming down his face. "I cannot *bear* what I have done and must do again should I enter yon city. Surely Edaemus did not intend for us so to use his dreadful gift."

There were a dozen arguments Ekrasios might have raised, but he knew in his heart that they were all spurious. "I will not insist, Adras. That would not be the act of a friend." He sighed. "I am no less unquiet than thou, I do confess. We are not suited for war, Adras, and the curse of Edaemus makes *our* way of making war more horrible than the casual bloodletting of other races. Since we are not fiends, the horror doth tear at our souls." He paused. "Thou art not alone in this resolve, art thou, Adras? There are others as well, are there not?"

Adras nodded mutely.

"How many?"

"Close on to a hundred and fifty, my friend."

Ekrasios was shaken. Quite nearly a third of his force had literally defected. "You trouble me, Adras," he said. "I *will* not command thee to forswear the dictates of thy conscience, but thine absence and that of they who feel similarly constrained do raise doubts about our possible success this night. Let me think on't." He began to pace up and down in the muddy forest clearing, considering various possibilities. "We may yet salvage some measure of victory this night," he said finally. "Let me probe the extent of thy reluctance, my friend. I do concede that thou canst not in conscience enter the ruin which doth lie before us, but wilt thou abandon me utterly?"

"Never, Ekrasios."

"I thank thee, Adras. Yet mayest thou and thy fellows further our design without injury to thy sensibilities. As we discovered at Norenja, the curse of Edaemus extends its effects to things other than flesh."

"Truly," Adras agreed. "The gates of that mournful ruin did collapse in decay at our merest touch."

"The east wall of Synaqua is constructed of logs. Might I prevail upon thee and thy fellows to pull it down whilst I and the remainder of our force do enter the city?"

The mind of Adras was quick. His sudden grin erased the estrangement that had marred their friendship for the past several days. "Thou wert born to command, Ekrasios," he said warmly. "My friends and I will most happily perform this task. Do thou and thy cohorts enter Synaqua by the front gate whilst I and mine do open a huge back gate to the east, that they who reside within yon city may freely depart. Both ends are thus served."

"Well said, Adras," Ekrasios approved. "Well said."

CHAPTER TWENTY-SEVEN

"They're out of sight now," Talen hissed. "Go grab their cart."

Kalten and Sparhawk rose from the bushes, expropriated the half-full wood cart, and pulled it back out of sight. It was about noon.

"I still think this is a really stupid idea," Kalten grumbled. "Assuming that we don't get stopped when we try to go through the gate, how are we going to unload our weapons and mail shirts without being seen? And how are we going to get out of the slave pen to pick them up?"

"Trust me."

"This boy's making me old, Sparhawk," Kalten complained.

"We might be able to pull it off, Kalten," Bevier said. "Xanetia told us that the Cynesgan overseers don't pay much attention to the slaves. Right now, though, we'd better get this cart away from here before the fellows it belongs to come back and find that it's gone."

They pulled the wobbly, two-wheeled cart along the narrow track toward the spot where Xanetia and Mirtai were concealed in the bushes. "Lo," Mirtai said dryly from her hiding place, "our heroes return with the spoils of war."

"I love you, little sister," Sparhawk retorted, "but you've got an overly clever mouth. Kalten's got a point, Talen. The Cynesgan overseers themselves might be too stupid to notice what we're doing, but the other slaves probably will, and the first one to open his mouth about it will probably get a lot of attention."

"I'm a-workin' on that port, Sporhawk," the boy replied. He dropped to his knees and scrutinized the underside of the cart. "No problem," he said confidently, rising and brushing dirt off his bare knees. They had modified the Cynesgan robes they had bought in Vigayo by removing the sleeves and hoods and cutting the tails off just above the knees. The resulting garments now resembled the smocks worn by the slaves who labored in the fields and woods surrounding Cyrga.

While the rest of them fanned out through the woods to pilfer firewood from the stacks cut by the slaves, Talen remained behind, working at something on the underside of the cart. They had amassed a sizable pile by the time he had finished. Sparhawk returned once more with an armload of wood to find the boy just finishing up. "Do you want to take a look at this, Sparhawk?" he asked from under the cart.

Sparhawk knelt to examine the young thief's handiwork. Talen had wedged the ends of slender tree limbs between the floorboards of the cart, then had woven them into a shallow basket that fit snugly under the bottom of the stolen conveyance. "Are you sure it won't come apart if we hit a bump?" he asked dubiously. "It might be a little embarrassing to have all our weapons and our mail come spilling out just as we're passing through the gate."

"I'll ride in it myself, if you want," Talen replied.

Sparhawk grunted. "Tie the swords together so that they won't rattle, and stuff grass in around the shirts to muffle the clinking."

"Yes, O Glorious Leader. And how many other things that I already know did you want to tell me?"

"Just do it, Talen. Don't make clever speeches."

"I'm not trying to be offensive, Mirtai," Kalten was saying. "It's just that your legs are prettier than mine."

Mirtai lifted the bottom of her smock a little and looked critically at her long, golden legs. Then she squinted at Kalten's. "They are rather, aren't they?"

"What I'm getting at is that they won't be quite as noticeable if you smear some mud on them. I don't think the gate guards are blind, and if one of them sees the dimples on your knees, he'll probably realize that you aren't a man, and he might decide to investigate further."

"He'd better not," she replied in a chill tone.

"There are not so many dens of the man-things in this place as there were in the place Sopal or the place Arjun," Bhlokw noted as he and Ulath looked down at the village at Zhubay. It had *seemed* that they had been traveling for several days, but they all knew better.

"No," Ulath agreed. "It is a smaller place, with fewer of the man-things."

"But there are many of the dens-of-cloth on the other side of the water hole," the Troll added, pointing at the large tent city on the far side of the oasis.

"Those are the ones we hunt," Ulath told him.

"Are you certain that we are permitted to kill and eat those?" Bhlokw asked. "You and Tin-in would not let me do that in the place Sopal or the place Arjun or even in the place Nat-os."

"It is permitted here. We have put bait out to bring them to this place so that we can hunt them for food."

"What bait do you use to lure the man-things?" Bhlokw asked curiously. "If the minds of the Gods ever get well again and they let us go back to hunting the man-things, it would be good to know this."

"The bait is thought, Bhlokw. The man-things in the dens-of-cloth have come to this place because certain of our pack-mates put it in their thought that the tall man-things with the yellow skin will be here. The ones in the dens-of-cloth have come here to fight with the tall ones with yellow skin."

Bhlokw's face contorted into a hideous approximation of a grin. "That is good bait, U-lat," he said. "I will summon Ghworg and Ghnomb and tell them that we will hunt now. How many of them may we kill and eat?"

"All, Bhlokw. All."

"That is not a good thought, U-lat. If we kill and eat them all, they will not breed, and there will not be new ones to hunt in the next season. The good thought is always to let enough run away so that they can breed to keep the numbers of their herd the same. If we eat them all now, there will be none to eat by-and-by."

Ulath considered that as Bhlokw cast the brief Troll-spell that summoned Ghworg and the others. He decided not to make an issue of it. The Trolls were hunters, not warriors, and it would take far too long to explain the concept of total war to them.

Bhlokw conferred at some length with the enormous presences of his Gods in the grey light of No-Time, and then he raised his brutish face and bellowed his summons to the Trolls.

The great shaggy mass flowed down the hill toward the village and the forest of tents beyond the oasis in the steely light of frozen time as Ulath and Tynian watched from the hilltop. The Trolls divided, went around the village, and moved in among the Cynesgan tents, fanning out as each of the great beasts selected its prey. Then, evidently at a signal from Bhlokw, the chill light flickered and the sunlight returned.

There were screams, of course, but that was to be expected. Scarcely a man in the entire world would *not* scream when a full-grown Troll suddenly stepped out of nowhere immediately in front of him.

The carnage in that vast slaughtering ground beyond the oasis was ghastly, since the Trolls were bent not on fighting the Cynesgans but on tearing them to pieces in preparation for the feast to follow.

"Some of them are getting away," Tynian observed, pointing at a sizable number of panic-stricken Cynesgans desperately flogging their horses southward.

Ulath shrugged. "Breeding stock," he said.

"What?"

"It's a Trollish concept, Tynian. It's a way to guarantee a continuing food supply. If the Trolls eat them all today, there won't be any left when suppertime rolls around tomorrow."

Tynian shuddered with revulsion. "That's a *horrible* thought, Ulath!" he exclaimed.

"Yes," Ulath agreed, "moderately horrible, but one should always respect the customs and traditions of one's allies, wouldn't you say?"

At the end of a half hour, the tents were all flattened, the breeding stock had been permitted to escape, and the Trolls settled down to eat. The Cynesgan threat in the north had been effectively eliminated, and now the Trolls were free to join the march on Cyrga.

Khalad sat up suddenly, throwing off his blankets. "Berit," he said sharply.

Berit came awake instantly, reaching for his sword.

"No," Khalad told him. "It's nothing like that. Do you know what fire-damp is?"

"I've never heard of it." Berit yawned and rubbed at his eyes.

"I'm going to have to talk with Aphrael, then—personally. How long will it take you to teach me the spell?"

"That depends, I guess. Can't you pass what you have to tell her through me?"

"No. I need to ask her some questions, and you wouldn't understand what I'm talking about. I've got to talk with her myself. It's very important, Berit. I don't have to understand the language to just repeat the words, do I?"

Berit frowned. "I'm not sure. Sephrenia and the Styric who replaced her at Demos wouldn't let us do it that way, because they said we had to think in Styric."

"That could just be *their* peculiarity, not Aphrael's. Let's try it and find out if I can reach her."

It took them almost two hours, and Berit, sandy-eyed and definitely in need of more sleep, began to grow grouchy toward the end.

"I'm going to be mispronouncing words," Khalad said finally. "There's no way I'll ever be able to twist my mouth around to make some of those sounds. Let's try it and see what happens."

"You'll make her angry," Berit warned.

"She'll get over it. Here goes." Khalad began haltingly to pronounce the spell, and his fingers faltered as he moved them in the accompanying gestures.

"What on *earth* are you doing, Khalad?" Her voice almost crackled in his ears.

"I'm sorry, Flute," he apologized, "but this is urgent."

"Berit's not hurt, is he?" she demanded with a note of concern.

"No. He's fine. It's just that I need to talk with you personally. Do you know what firedamp is?"

"Yes. It sometimes kills coal miners."

"You said that Klæl's soldiers breathe something like marsh gas."

"Yes. Where are we going with this? I'm sort of busy just now."

"Please be patient, Divine One. I'm still groping my way toward this. Berit told you that we saw some of those aliens run into a cave, didn't he?"

"Yes, but I still don't—"

"I thought that Klæl might have filled the cave with marsh gas so that his soldiers could go there to breathe, but now I'm not so sure. Maybe the gas was already there."

"Would you *please* get to the point?"

"Is it possible that firedamp and marsh gas are anything at all alike?"

She sighed one of those infuriating, long-suffering sighs. "Very much alike, Khalad—which sort of stands to reason, since they're the same thing."

"I *do* love you, Aphrael," he said with a delighted laugh.

"What brought that on?"

"I *knew* there had to be a connection of some kind. This is a desert, and there aren't any swamps here. I couldn't for the life of me figure out where Klæl might be getting marsh gas to fill that cave. But he didn't have to, did he? If marsh gas is the same thing as firedamp, all he had to do was find a cave with a seam of coal in it."

"All right, now that I've answered your question and satisfied your scientific curiosity, can I go?"

"In a minute, Divine Aphrael," he said, rubbing his hands together gleefully. "Is there some way that you can blow some of *our* air into that cave so that it'll mix with the firedamp those soldiers are breathing?"

There was another of those long pauses. "That's *dreadful*, Khalad!" she exclaimed.

"And what happened to Lord Abriel and Lord Vanion's knights *wasn't?*" he demanded. "This is war, Aphrael, and it's a war we absolutely *have* to win. If Klæl's soldiers can run into those caves to catch their breath, they'll be coming out and attacking our friends every time we turn around. We have to come up with a way to neutralize them, and I think this is it. Can you take us back to that cave where we saw those soldiers?"

"All right." Her tone was a little sulky.

"What were you talking with her about?" Berit asked.

"A way to win the war, Berit. Let's gather up our things. Aphrael's going to take us back to that cave."

"Are they still coming?" Vanion called back to Sir Endrik, who was trailing behind the other knights.

"Yes, my Lord," Endrik shouted. "Some of them are starting to fall behind, though."

"Good. They're starting to weaken." Vanion looked out across the rocky barrens lying ahead. "We've got plenty of room," he told Sephrenia. "We'll lead them out onto those flats and run them around for a while."

"This is cruel, Vanion," she reproved him.

"They don't *have* to follow us, love." He rose up in his stirrups. "Let's pick up the pace, gentlemen," he called to his knights. "I want those monsters to really run."

The knights pushed their horses into a gallop and moved out onto the barren flats with a vast, steely jingling sound.

"They're breaking off!" Endrik called from behind after about a half an hour.

Vanion raised his steel-clad arm to call a halt. Then he reined in and looked back.

The masked giants had given up their pursuit and were running due west now, staggering toward an outcropping of rocky hills several miles away.

"*That's* the part that has everybody baffled," he told Sephrenia. "From what Aphrael told me, the others have encountered the same thing. Klæl's soldiers chase after us for a while, and then they break off and run toward the nearest cluster of hills. What can they possibly hope to find that's going to do them any good?"

"I have no idea, dear one," she replied.

"This is all very fine, I suppose," Vanion said with a worried frown, "but when we begin our final advance on Cyrga, we won't have time to run those brutes into exhaustion. Not only that, Klæl will probably start massing them in units larger than these regiments we've been coming across out here in the open. If we don't come up with some way to neutralize them permanently, our chances of getting to Cyrga alive aren't very good."

"Lord Vanion!" one of the knights cried out in alarm. "There are more of them coming!"

"Where?" Vanion looked around.

"From the west!"

Vanion peered after the fleeing monsters. And then he saw them. There were *two* regiments of Klæl's soldiers out there on the flats. The one they had encountered earlier was reeling and staggering toward the hills jutting up from the horizon. The other was coming toward them *from* the hills, and the second regiment showed no signs of the exhaustion which had incapacitated their fellows.

"This is ridiculous," Talen muttered, examining the lock on his chain with sensitive fingertips.

"You said you could unlock them," Kalten accused in a hoarse whisper.

"Kalten, you could unlock these. They're the worst locks I've ever seen."

"Just open them, Talen," Sparhawk told him quietly. "Don't give lectures. We still have to get out of this pen."

They had merged with the other woodcutters and had passed unchallenged through the gates of Cyrga just as the sun was setting. Then they had followed the slaves to an open square near the gate, unloaded their cart onto one of the stacks of wood piled there, and leaned the cart against a rough stone wall with the others. Then, like docile cattle, they had gone into the large slave pen and allowed the Cynesgan overseers to chain them to rusty iron rings protruding from the rear wall of the pen.

They had been fed a thin, watery soup and had then bedded down in piles of filthy straw heaped against the wall to wait for nightfall. Xanetia was not with them. Silent and unseen, she roamed the streets outside the pen instead.

"Hold your leg still, Kalten," Talen hissed. "I can't get the chain off when you're flopping around like that."

"Sorry."

The boy concentrated for a moment, and the lock snapped open. Then he moved on, crawling through the rustling straw.

"Don't get so familiar," Mirtai's voice muttered in the darkness.

"Sorry. I was looking for your ankle."

"It's on the other end of the leg."

"Yes. I noticed that myself. It's dark, Atana. I can't see what I'm doing."

"What are you men doing there?" It was a whining, servile kind of voice coming from somewhere in the straw beyond where Kalten lay.

"It's none of your business," Kalten rasped. "Go back to sleep."

"I want to know what you're doing. If you don't tell me, I'll call the overseers."

"You'd better shut him up, Kalten," Mirtai muttered. "He's an informer."

"I'll deal with it," Kalten replied darkly. He slipped away through the rustling straw.

"What are you doing?" the slave with the whining voice demanded. "How did you—" The voice broke off, and there was a sudden thrashing in the straw and a kind of wheezy gurgling.

"What's going on out there?" a harsh voice called from the overseer's barracks. The barracks doorway poured light out into the yard.

There was no answer, only a few spasmodic rustles in the straw. Kalten was breathing a little hard when he returned to his place, quickly wrapped his chain around his ankle again, and covered it with straw.

They waited tensely, but the Cynesgan overseer evidently decided not to investigate. He went back inside, closing the door behind him and plunging the yard into darkness again.

"Does that happen often—among slaves, I mean?" Bevier whispered to Mirtai as Talen was unchaining him.

"All the time," she murmured. "There's no loyalty among slaves. One slave will betray another for an extra crust of bread."

"How sad."

"Slavery? I could find harsher words than sad."

"Let's go," Sparhawk told them.

"How are we going to find Xanetia?" Kalten whispered as they crossed the pen.

"We can't. She's going to have to find us."

It took Talen only a moment to unlock the gate, and they all slipped out into the dark street beyond. They crept along that street to the large square where the firewood was stacked and stopped before stepping out into the open.

"Take a look, Talen," Sparhawk suggested.

"Right." The young thief melted away into the darkness. The rest of them waited tensely.

"It's all clear," Talen's whisper came to them after a few minutes. "The carts are over here."

They followed the sound of his hushed voice and soon reached the line of wood carts leaning against the wall.

"Did you see any guards?" Kalten asked.

"Who's going to stay up all night to guard a woodpile?" Talen dropped down onto his stomach and wormed his way under the cart. There was a faint creaking of the tightly woven limbs of the makeshift basket. "Here," Talen said. A sword-tip banged against Sparhawk's shin.

Sparhawk took the sword, handed it to Kalten, and then leaned down. "Pass them out hilt-first," he instructed. "Don't poke me with the sharp end of a sword that way."

"Sorry." Talen continued to pass out weapons and then followed them with their mail shirts and tunics. They all felt better once they were armed again.

"Anakha?" The voice was soft and very light.

"Is that you, Xanetia?" Sparhawk realized how foolish the question was almost before it left his lips.

"Verily," she replied. "Come away, I prithee. The whisper is the natural voice of stealth, and it doth carry far by night. Let us away 'ere they who watch this sleeping city come hither in search of the source of our incautious conversation."

"We're going to have to wait a bit," Khalad said. "Aphrael has to blow air into that cave."

"Are you sure this is going to work?" Berit asked dubiously.

"No, not really, but it's worth a try, isn't it?"

"You don't even know for sure that they're still inside the cave."

"That doesn't really matter. Either way they won't be able to hide in the cave anymore." Khalad began to carefully wrap a length of oil-soaked rag around one of his crossbow bolts. Then, being careful to conceal the sparks with his body, he began striking his flint and steel together. After a moment, his tinder caught; he lit his stub of a candle and brushed the fire out of his tinder. Then he carefully put the candle behind a fair-sized rock.

"Aphrael seems to be unhappy about this, Khalad," Berit said as a chill breeze came up.

"I wasn't too happy about what happened to Lord Abriel," Khalad replied bleakly. "I had a good deal of respect for that old man, and these monsters with yellow blood tore him to pieces."

"Then you're doing this for revenge?"

"No. Not really. This is just the most practical way to get rid of them. Ask Aphrael to let me know when there's enough air in the cave."

"How long is that likely to take?"

"I have no idea. All the coal miners who've ever seen it up close are dead." Khalad scratched at his beard. "I'm not entirely sure what's going to happen here, Berit. When marsh gas catches on fire, it just burns off and goes out. Firedamp's a little more spectacular."

"What's all this business about blowing air into the cave?" Berit demanded.

Khalad shrugged. "Fire's a living thing. It has to be able to breathe."

"You're just guessing about this, aren't you? You don't have any idea at all whether or not it's going to work—or if it does, what's going to happen."

Khalad gave him a tight grin. "I've got a good working theory."

"I think you're insane. You could set the whole desert on fire with this silly experiment of yours."

"Oh, that probably won't happen."

"Probably?"

"It's very unlikely. I can just make out that cave mouth. Why don't I try it?"

"What happens if you miss?"

Khalad shrugged. "I'll shoot again."

"That's not what I meant. I was—" Berit broke off, listening intently. "Aphrael says that the mixture's right now. You can shoot whenever you're ready."

Khalad held the point of his crossbow bolt in the candle flame, turning it slowly to make certain that the oily rag was evenly ablaze. Then he set the burning bolt in place, laid the forestock of his crossbow on a rock, and took careful aim. "Here goes," he said, slowly pressing the lever.

The crossbow gave a ringing thud, and the burning arrow streaked through the darkness and disappeared into the narrow cave mouth.

Nothing happened.

"So much for your good working theory," Berit said sardonically.

Khalad swore, banging his fist on the gravel. "It *has* to work, Berit. I did everything exactly—"

The sound was beyond noise when the hill exploded, and a ball of fire hundreds of feet across seethed skyward out of the crater that had suddenly replaced the hill. Without thinking, Khalad threw himself across Berit's head, covering the back of his own neck with his hands.

Fortunately, what fell on them was small gravel for the most part. The larger rocks fell much farther out into the desert.

It continued to rain gravel for several minutes, and the two young men, battered and shaken, lay tensely clenched, enduring the cataclysmic results of Khalad's experiment.

Gradually, the stinging rain subsided.

"*You idiot!*" Berit screamed. "You could have killed us both!"

"I must have miscalculated just a little," Khalad conceded, shaking the dirt out of his hair. "I'll have to work on it a bit before we try it again."

"*Try it again? What are you talking about?*"

"It *does* work, Berit," Khalad said in his most reasonable tone of voice. "All I have to do is fine-tune it a little bit. Every experiment's got a few rough places around the edges." He stood up, banging the side of his head with the heel of his hand to shake the ringing out of his ears. "I'll get it perfected, my Lord," he promised, helping Berit to his feet. "The next time won't be nearly so bad. Now, why don't you ask Aphrael to take us back to camp? We're probably being watched, so let's not arouse any suspicions."

CHAPTER TWENTY-EIGHT

We're inside the city, Aphrael, Sparhawk announced silently after he had cast the spell.

How did you manage that? She sounded surprised.

It's a long story. Tell Khalad that I've marked the passageway that leads into the valley. He'll know what to look for.

Have you found out where they're keeping Mother yet?

Speculatively.

There was a long pause. *I'd better come there,* she decided.

How will you find us?

I'll use you as a beacon. Just keep talking to me.

I don't think it's a good idea. We're right in Cyrgon's lap here. Won't he be able to sense you?

Xanetia's there, isn't she?

Yes.

Then Cyrgon won't feel a thing. That's why I sent her along. She paused again. *Who came up with a way to get you inside the city?*

It was Talen's idea.

You see? And you wanted to argue with me about taking him with you. When will you learn to trust me, Father? Keep talking. I've almost got you located. Tell me how Talen managed to get you inside the walls of Cyrga.

He described the subterfuge at some length.

"All right," she said from just behind him. "That's enough. I get the general drift." He turned and saw her in Xanetia's arms. She looked around. "I see that the Cyrgai haven't discovered fire yet. It's darker than the inside of an old boot here. Exactly where are we?"

"In the outer city, Divine One," Bevier said softly. "I suppose you could call it the commercial district. The slave pens are here, and various warehouses. It's guarded by Cynesgans, and they're not particularly alert."

"Good. Let's get out of the street."

Talen groped his way along one of the barnlike storehouses until he found a door. "Over here," he whispered.

"Isn't it locked?" Kalten asked.

"Not anymore."

They joined him and went inside.

"Would you mind, dear?" Aphrael asked Xanetia. "I can't see a thing in this place."

Xanetia's face began to glow, a soft light that faintly illuminated the area around them.

"What do they keep in here?" Kalten asked, peering into the dimness. "Food maybe?" His tone was hopeful. "That slop they fed us in the slave pens wasn't very filling."

"I don't think it's a food warehouse," Talen told him. "It doesn't smell quite right."

"You can go exploring some other time," Aphrael told him crisply. "We have other things to do now."

"How are the others making out?" Sparhawk asked her.

"Bergsten's captured Cynestra," she reported, "and he's coming south with the Church Knights. Ulath and Tynian took the Trolls to Zhubay, and the Trolls ate about half of the Cynesgan cavalry. Betuana and Engessa are marching southwest with the Atans. Vanion and Sephrenia are out in the desert laying down false hints that you're with them. Kring and Tikume are allowing themselves to be chased all over the desert west of Sarna by Cyrgai, Cynesgan calvary, and Klæl's overgrown soldiers—although I don't think *those* brutes are going to be a problem for much longer; Khalad's devised a way to neutralize them."

"All by himself?" Talen sounded surprised.

"Klæl outsmarted himself. He found caves where his soldiers could breathe, and they were hiding in the caves and then coming out to attack us. Khalad's come up with a way to set the caves on fire. The results are fairly noisy."

"That's my brother for you," Talen said proudly.

"Yes," the Child-Goddess said critically. "He's inventing new horrors at every turn. Stragen and Caalador have managed to convince that Dacite in Beresa that we've got an invasion force off the south coast and—" She stopped. "You know about all this already, Sparhawk. Why am I wasting time describing it to you?"

"It's all going according to plan, then?" he asked her. "No setbacks? No new surprises?"

"Not for *us*. Cyrgon's not having such a good time, though. The Delphae have almost completely dispersed Scarpa's army, so the danger to Matherion's pretty much evaporated. I've enlisted some of my family to lend a hand. They're compressing time and distance. As soon as Ehlana's safe, I'll pass the word, and we'll have whole armies knocking at the gates of Cyrga."

"Did you get word of Khalad's invention to the others?" Talen asked her.

"My cousin Setras is taking care of it for me. Setras is a little vague sometimes, but I went over it with him several times. I don't think he'll garble it *too* badly. Everything's in place. The others are simply waiting for word from us to start moving, so let's get down to business. Has anyone had a chance to look around here at all?"

"I have explored the outer city to some degree, Divine Aphrael," Xanetia replied. "Anakha deemed it unwise for me to share their captivity in the slave pens."

The Child-Goddess handed Talen a large sheet of stiff, crackling parchment and a pencil. "Here," she said to him, "earn your keep."

"Where did you get these?" he asked curiously.

"I had them in one of my pockets."

"You don't *have* any pockets, Flute."

She gave him one of those long-suffering looks.

"Oh," he said. "I keep forgetting that for some reason. All right, Anarae, you describe the city, and I'll draw it."

The sketch that emerged was fairly detailed—as far as it went. "I was not able to penetrate the wall which doth encircle the inner city," Xanetia apologized. "The gates are perpetually locked, for the Cyrgai do hold themselves aloof from their Cynesgan hirelings and from the slaves whose toil supports them."

"This should be enough to work with for now," Flute said, pursing her lips as she examined Talen's drawing. "All right, Bevier, you're the expert on fortifications. Where's the weak spot?"

The Cyrinic studied the sketch for several minutes. "Did you see any wells, Anarae?" he asked.

"Nay, Sir Knight."

"They've got a lake right outside the front gate, Bevier," Kalten reminded him.

"That wouldn't do much good if the city were under siege," Bevier replied. "There has to be some source of water inside the walls—either a well or some kind of a cistern. A siege ends rather quickly when the defenders run out of water."

"What makes you think that the place was built to hold off a siege?" Mirtai asked. "Nobody's supposed to be able to find it."

"The walls are a little too high and thick to be purely ornamental, Atana. Cyrga's a fortified city, and that means that it was built to withstand a siege. The Cyrgai aren't very bright, but *nobody's* stupid enough to build a fort without water inside. That's my best guess, Divine Aphrael. Find out how they're getting water— both here in the outer city and in the inner city as well. There might be a weakness there. If not, we may have to tunnel under the inner wall or try to scale it."

"Let's hope it doesn't come to that," Aphrael said. "We're inside the enemy city, and the longer we putter around, the more chance there is of being discovered. If it's in any way possible, we want to free Ehlana and Alean tonight. I'll send out word and start the others moving. Nobody's going to get much sleep tonight, but that can't be helped. All right, then, Xanetia, let's go look for water. The rest of you stay here. We don't want to have to go looking for you when we come back."

"Are you mad, Gardas?" Bergsten demanded of the massively armored Alcione Knight. The Thalesian Patriarch refused to look at the pleasant-faced young man standing beside the knight. "I'm not even supposed to admit that he exists, much less sit down and talk with him."

"Aphrael said you might be tedious about this, Bergsten," noted the person whom Gardas had escorted into the Patriarch's tent. "Would it help at all if I did something miraculous?"

"God!" Bergsten said. "Please don't do that! I'm probably in trouble already!"

"Dolmant had some problems when I visited him, too," Aphrael's cousin observed. "You servants of the Elene God have some strange ideas. *He* doesn't get excited about us, so why should you? Anyway, the normal rules are all more or less suspended until this crisis is over. We've even enlisted Edaemus and the Atan God—and they haven't spoken to any of the rest of us for eons. Aphrael wants me to tell you about something having to do with the soldiers Klæl brought with him. Somebody named Khalad has devised a means of destroying them."

"Tell Gardas about it," Bergsten suggested. "He can pass it on to me, and I won't get into trouble."

"I'm sorry, Bergsten, but Aphrael insisted that I say it directly to you. Just pretend that I'm a dream or something." Setras' face grew slightly puzzled, and his large, luminous eyes revealed a frightening lack of comprehension. "I don't entirely understand this," he confessed. "Aphrael's much more clever than I am—but we love each other, so she doesn't throw my stupidity into my face very often. She's terribly polite. She's even nice to *your* God, and he can be terribly tedious sometimes— where was I?"

"Ah," Sir Gardas said gently, "you were going to tell his Grace about Klæl's soldiers, Divine Setras."

"I was?" The large eyes were blank. "Oh, yes. I was, wasn't I? You mustn't let me ramble on like that, Gardas. You *know* how easily I get distracted."

"Yes, Divine Setras. That *had* occurred to me."

"Anyway," Setras pushed on, "this Khalad person—a frightfully clever young man, I gather—realized that there might be some similarity between the awful stuff Klæl's soldiers breathe and something he calls 'firedamp.' Have you any idea at all of what he was talking about, Bergsten?" Setras hesitated. "Am I supposed to call you 'your Grace' the way Gardas did? Are you really that graceful? You look awfully large and clumsy to me."

"It's a formal mode of address, Divine One," Sir Gardas explained.

"Oh. We don't have to be formal with each other, do we, Bergsten? We're almost old friends now, aren't we?"

The Patriarch of Emsat swallowed very hard. Then he sighed. "Yes, Divine Setras," he said. "I suppose we are. Why don't you go ahead and tell me about this strategy Sparhawk's squire has devised?"

"Of course. Oh, there's one other thing, too. We have to be at the gates of Cyrga by morning."

"Please, Atana Liatris," Baroness Melidere said patiently to Sarabian's Atan wife, "we *want* them to make the attempt."

"It is too dangerous," Liatris said stubbornly. "If I go ahead and kill Chacole and Torellia, the others will run away and that will be the end of it."

"Except that we'll never find out who else is involved," Patriarch Emban explained, "and we won't know for certain that they won't try again."

Princess Danae sat a little apart from them with Mmrr curled up in her lap. Her vision was strangely doubled with one image superimposed on the other. It seemed that the dark streets of Cyrga lay just behind the people speaking here in the sitting room.

"I'm touched by your concern, Liatris," Sarabian was saying, "but I'm not nearly as helpless as I seem." He flourished his rapier.

"And we *will* have guards nearby," Foreign Minister Oscagne added. "Chacole and Torellia almost *have* to be getting help from somebody inside the government—some leftover from that coup attempt, most likely."

"I will wring his identity from them before I kill them," Liatris declared.

Sarabian winced at the word *wring*.

"We are near, Divine Aphrael." Xanetia's voice seemed at once a long way away and very close. "Methinks I do smell water." The dark, narrow street they followed opened out into some kind of square a hundred feet farther on.

"Let's catch them all, Liatris," Elysoun urged her sister-empress. "You might be able to beat one or two names out of Chacole and Torellia, but if we can catch the assassins in the actual attempt, we'll be able to sweep the palace compound clean. If we don't, our husband's going to have to go through the rest of his life with a drawn rapier."

"Hark!" Xanetia whispered in that other city. "I do hear the sound of running water."

Danae concentrated very hard. It was exhausting to keep things separate.

"I really hate to have to put it this way, Liatris," Sarabian said regretfully, "but I forbid you to kill either Chacole or Torellia. We'll deal with them *after* their assassins try to kill me."

"As my husband commands," Liatris responded automatically.

"What I want you to do is to protect Elysoun and Gahenas," he continued. "Gahenas is probably in the greater danger right now. Elysoun's still useful to the people involved in this, but Gahenas knows more than they want her to. I'm sure they'll try to kill her, so let's get her out of the women's palace tonight."

"It is beneath the street, Divine One," Xanetia said. "Methinks there is some volume of water passing under our feet."

"Truly," the Child-Goddess replied. "Let's follow the sound back to its source. There has to be *some* way to get to the water here in the outer city."

"How did you become involved in this, Elysoun?" Liatris was asking.

Elysoun shrugged. "I have more freedom of movement than the rest of you," she replied. "Chacole needed somebody she trusted to carry messages out of the women's palace. I pretended to fall in with her plan. It wasn't too hard to deceive Chacole. She *is* a Cynesgan, after all."

"It is here, Divine One," Xanetia whispered, laying her hand on a large iron plate set into the cobblestones. "Thou canst feel the urgent rush of water through the very iron."

"I'll take your word for it, Anarae," Aphrael replied, cringing back from the notion of touching iron. "How do they get it open?"

"These rings do suggest that the plate can be lifted."

"Let's go back and get the others. I think this might be the weakness Bevier was looking for."

Danae yawned. Everything seemed to be under control here, so she curled up in her chair, nestled Mmrr in her arms, and promptly fell asleep.

"Couldn't you have just—well—?" Talen wiggled his fingers.

"It's iron, Talen," Flute said with exaggerated patience.

"So? What's that got to do with it?"

She shuddered. "I can't bear the touch of iron."

Bevier looked intently at her. "Bhelliom suffers from the same affliction," he observed.

"Yes. So what?"

"That would suggest a certain kinship."

"Your grasp of the obvious is positively dazzling, Bevier."

"Behave yourself," Sparhawk chided.

"What's so unpleasant about iron?" Talen asked. "It's cold, it's hard, you can pound it into various shapes, and it gets rusty."

"That's a nice scholarly description. Do you know what a lodestone is?"

"It's a piece of iron ore that sticks to other iron, isn't it? I seem to remember Platime talking about something called magnetism once."

"And you actually listened? Amazing."

"*That's* why Bhelliom had to congeal itself into a sapphire!" Bevier exclaimed. "It's the magnetism of iron, isn't it? Bhelliom can't bear it—and neither can *you*, can you?"

"Please, Bevier," Aphrael said weakly. "Just thinking about it makes my flesh crawl. Right now we don't want to talk about iron. We want to talk about water. There's a stream or river of some kind running under the streets here in the outer city, and it's flowing in the direction of the inner wall. There's a large iron plate set in the middle of the street not far from here, and you can hear the water running beneath it. I think that's the weakness you were looking for. The water's running through a tunnel of some kind, and that tunnel goes under the wall of the inner fortress—at least I hope so. I'll go find out as soon as you gentlemen lift off that iron plate for me."

"Did you see any patrols in the streets?" Kalten asked.

"Nay, Sir Knight," Xanetia replied. "Centuries of custom have clearly dulled the alertness of the Cynesgans responsible for the defense of the outer city."

"A burglar's dream," Talen murmured. "I could get rich in this town."

"What would you steal?" Aphrael asked him. "The Cyrgai don't believe in gold and silver."

"What do they use for money?"

"They don't. They don't need money. The Cynesgans provide them with everything they need, so they don't even think about money."

"That's monstrous!"

"We can discuss economics some other time. Right now I want to investigate their water supply."

"You idiot!" Queen Betuana raged at her general.

"We had to find out, Betuana-Queen," Engessa explained, "and I will not send another where I will not go."

"I am most displeased with you, Engessa-Atan!" Betuana's retreat into ritualized mourning had vanished. "Did your last encounter with the Klæl-beasts teach you nothing? They could have been lurking just inside the cave, and you would have faced them alone again."

"It is not reasonable to suppose that they would have," he replied stiffly. "Aphrael's messenger told us that the Klæl-beasts take shelter in caves that they might breathe a different air. The air at the entrance to this cave will be the same as the air outside. It is of no moment, however. It is done, and no harm came from it."

She controlled her anger with an obvious effort. "And what did you prove by your foolish venture, Engessa-Atan?"

"The Klæl-beasts have sealed the cave, Betuana-Queen," he replied. "Some hundred paces within stands a steel wall. It is reasonable to suppose that it may in some fashion be opened. The Klæl-beasts retreat beyond the barrier, close it behind them, and are then able to breathe freely for a time. Then they emerge again and attack us once more."

"Was this information worth the risk of your life?"

"We have yet to discover that, my Queen. The tactics devised by Kring-Domi keep us out of the reach of the Klæl-beasts, but I do not like this running away."

Betuana's eyes hardened. "Nor do I," she conceded. "I dishonor my husband's memory each time I turn and flee."

"Aphrael's cousin told us that Khalad-squire had found that the air which the Klæl-beasts breathe will burn when it mixes with *our* air."

"I have not seen air burn before."

"Nor have I. If the trap that I have set for the Klæl-beasts works, we may both see it happen."

"What sort of trap, Engessa-Atan?"

"A lantern, my Queen—well hidden."

"A lantern? That's all?"

"If Khalad-squire was right, it should be enough. I closed the lantern so that the Klæl-beasts will see no light when they open their steel door to come out again. All unseen, their air will join with ours and the mix will find its way to the candle burning inside my lantern. Then we will discover if Khalad-squire was right."

"Then we must wait until they open that door. I will not leave them behind us until I know without any doubt that this burning of air will kill them. As Ulath-Knight says, only a fool leaves live enemies behind him."

They concealed themselves behind an outcropping of rock and waited, intently watching the cave mouth faintly visible in the light of the stars. "It may be some time before they open their door, my Queen," Engessa noted.

"Engessa-Atan," Betuana said firmly, "I have long thought that this formality of yours is out of place. We are soldiers, and comrades. Please address me as such."

"As you wish, Betuana-Atan."

They waited patiently, watching the sizable peak and the dark mouth of the cave. Then, like a deep, subterranean thunder, a stunning sound shattered the silence, shaking the ground, and a great billow of boiling fire blasted out of the cave mouth, searing the few scrubby thornbushes growing nearby. The fire spewed out of the cave, roaring on and on, until it gradually subsided.

Engessa and his queen, shocked by that violent eruption, could only stare in wonder. Finally, Betuana rose to her feet. "Now I have seen air burn," she noted in a cool sort of way. "It was worth the wait, I suppose." Then she smiled at her still-shaken comrade. "You lay good traps, Engessa-Atan, but now we must hurry to rejoin the Trolls. Ulath-Knight says that we must reach Cyrga by morning."

"Whatever you say, Betuana-Atan," he replied.

"All together, when I say 'lift,' " Sparhawk instructed, settling his hands into place around the ring, "and don't let it clank when we set it down. All right, lift."

Kalten, Bevier, Mirtai, and Sparhawk all rose slowly, straining to lift the rusty iron plate up out of its place among the worn cobblestones.

"Be careful," Talen said to Mirtai. "Don't fall in."

"Do you want to do this?" she asked.

The four of them shuffled around slightly and moved the ponderous weight to one side so that the large square hole was partially uncovered. "Set it down," Sparhawk said from between his clenched teeth. "Easy," he added.

They slowly lowered the cover to the stones.

"It'd be easier to pick up a house," Kalten wheezed.

"Turn your backs," Flute instructed.

"Do you have to do that?" Talen asked. "Is it like flying?"

"Just turn around, Talen."

"Don't forget the clothes," Sparhawk told her.

"They'd just be in my way. If you don't like it, don't look." Her voice was already richer.

Bevier had his eyes tightly closed, and his lips were moving. He obviously was praying—very hard.

"I'll be right back," the Goddess promised. "Don't go away."

They waited for what seemed to be hours. Then they heard a faint splashing down below. The splashing was accompanied by muffled laughter.

Talen knelt at the edge of the rectangular shaft. "Are you all right?" he whispered.

"I'm fine."

"What's so funny?"

"The Cyrgai. You wouldn't *believe* how stupid they are."

"What did they do now?"

"The water comes from a large artesian spring right near the outer wall. The Cyrgai built a sort of cistern around it. Then they built a tunnel that goes under the inner wall to carry water to a very large pool that lies underneath the mountain they've built their main city on."

"What's wrong with that?"

"Nothing—as far as it goes. They seem to have realized the same thing that Bevier did. Their water source is a weakness. They very carefully built a stone lattice at the mouth of the tunnel. Nobody can get into the tunnel from the cistern."

"I still don't see anything to laugh about."

"I'm just coming to that. This shaft that leads down to the tunnel seems to have been added later—probably so that they could get into the tunnel to clean it."

"That doesn't sound like such a bad idea. It is supposed to be drinking water, after all."

"Yes, but when they dug the shaft, they forgot something. The other end of the tunnel—the one that's inside their second wall—is completely open. There aren't any bars, no lattice, no chains, nothing."

"You're not serious!"

"May muh tongue turn green iff'n I ain't."

"This is going to be easier than I thought," Kalten said. He leaned over and peered down into the darkness. "Is that current very swift?" he called down softly.

"Swift enough," Aphrael replied. "But that's all right. It speeds you right straight through, so you won't have to hold your breath so long."

"Do what?" His voice was choked.

"Hold your breath. You have to swim underwater."

"Not me," he said flatly.

"You *do* know how to swim, don't you?"

"I can swim in full armor if I have to."

"What's the problem, then?"

"I *don't* swim underwater. It sends me into a panic."

"He's right, Aphrael," Sparhawk called down softly. "As soon as Kalten's head goes underwater, he starts screaming."

"He can't do that. He'll drown."

"Exactly. I used to have to stand on his chest to squeeze the water out of him. It happened all the time when we were boys."

"Oh, dear," she said. "I hadn't counted on this."

CHAPTER TWENTY-NINE

The moon would be almost full; already it stained the eastern horizon in a pallid imitation of dawn. It slid slowly into view, rising ponderously above the brittle white salt flats.

"Good God!" Berit exclaimed, staring at the horror all around them. What had seemed to be round white rocks by the faint light of the stars were revealed as bleached skulls, nesting in jumbles of bones and staring in mute accusation at the heavens.

"It looks as if we've come to the right place," Khalad observed. "The note Sparhawk left us talked about a 'Plain of Bones.'"

"It goes on forever!" Berit gasped, looking off toward the west.

"Let's hope not. We have to cross it." Khalad stopped, peering intently toward the west. "There it is," he said, pointing toward a gleaming spot of reflected light in the center of a low range of dark hills some distance beyond the ghastly plain.

"There what is?"

"Our landmark. Sparhawk called it the 'Pillars of Cyrgon.' Something out there's catching the moonlight. We're supposed to ride toward that spot."

"Who's that?" Berit hissed, pointing at a figure walking toward them out of the bone-littered desert.

Khalad loosened his sword in its sheath. "Another note from Krager, maybe," he muttered. "Let's start being a little careful, my Lord. I think we're getting very close to the place where we'll have outlived our usefulness."

The figure coming out of the desert seemed to be moving at no more than a casual stroll, and as he came closer, they were able to make out his features.

"Watch yourself, Khalad!" Berit hissed sharply. "He's not human!"

Khalad felt it as well. It was nothing really definable, just an overpowering sense of presence, an aura that no human had. The figure appeared to be that of an extraordinarily handsome young man. He had tightly curled hair, classic features, and very large, almost luminous eyes. "Ah, there you are, gentlemen," he said urbanely in flawless Elenic. "I've been looking all over for you." He glanced around. "This is a really *wretched* place, don't you think? Exactly the sort of place you'd expect the Cyrgai to inhabit. Cyrgon's terribly warped. He adores ugliness. Have you ever met him? Frightful fellow. No sense of beauty whatsoever." He smiled, a radiant, slightly vague smile. "My cousin Aphrael sent me. She'd have come herself, but she's a little busy right now—but then, Aphrael's *always* busy, isn't she? She can't stand to sit quietly." He frowned. "She wanted me to tell you something." His frown intensified. "What was it, now? I have the worst memory lately." He held up one hand. "No," he said, "don't tell me. It'll come to me in a moment. It's terribly important, though, and we're supposed to hurry. I'll probably think of it as we go along." He looked around. "Do you gentlemen by any chance happen to know which way we're supposed to go?"

"It won't work, Aphrael," Kalten said morosely. "I've tried it when I was dead drunk and the same thing happens. I go crazy when I feel the water closing over my head."

"Just try it, Kalten," the minimally dressed Goddess urged. "It really will relax you." She pushed the tankard into his hand.

He sniffed suspiciously. "It *smells* good. What is it?"

"We drink it at parties."

"The beer of the Gods?" His eyes brightened. "Well, now." He took a cautious sip. "*Well* now," he said enthusiastically. "That's the way it's *supposed* to taste."

"Drink it all," she instructed, watching him intently.

"Gladly." He drained the tankard and wiped his lips. "That's *really* good. If a man had the recipe for *that,* he could—" He broke off, his eyes glazed.

"Lay him down," Aphrael instructed, "quickly, before he stiffens up. I don't want him all twisted into a pretzel when I drag him through the tunnel."

Talen was doubled over with both hands tightly over his mouth to stifle his laughter.

"What's *your* problem?" the Goddess demanded tartly.

"Nothing," he gasped. "Nothing at all."

"I've got a long way to go with that one," Aphrael muttered to Sparhawk.

"Is this going to work?" Sparhawk asked her. "Kalten, I mean? Can you really drag an unconscious man underwater for any distance without drowning him?"

"I'll stop his breathing." She looked around at the others. "I don't want any of you to try to help me," she cautioned. "You just concentrate on getting through yourselves. I don't have to breathe, but you do, and I don't want to have to spend an hour fishing you out of that pool one by one after we get there. Now, does anybody *else* have any problems you haven't told me about? This is the time to talk about them—*before* we're all underwater." She looked pointedly at Bevier. "Is there something *you'd* like to tell me, Sir Knight? You seem to be having a crisis of some sort."

"It's nothing, Divine One," he mumbled. "I'll be fine. I swim like a fish." He deliberately avoided looking at her.

"What's bothering you, then?"

"I'd really rather not say."

She sighed. "Men." Then she climbed into the shaft leading down toward the unseen water rushing toward the inner wall. "Bring Kalten," she ordered, "and let's get at this."

· · ·

"I'd really like to do something about that," Sephrenia murmured to Vanion as they peered over the top of the gravel mound at the encampment of the slavers.

"So would I, love," Vanion replied, "but I think we'd better wait until later. If everything goes the way it's supposed to, we'll be waiting for them when they reach Cyrga." He raised himself a bit higher. "I think that's the salt flats just beyond that trail they're following."

"We'll be able to tell for certain when the moon rises," she replied.

"Have you heard anything at all from Aphrael?"

"Nothing I can make any sense of. The echoes are very confusing when she's in two places at the same time. I gather that things are coming to a head in Matherion, and she and Sparhawk are swimming."

"Swimming? This is a desert, Sephrenia."

"Yes, I noticed that. They've found *something* to swim in, though." She paused. "Does Kalten know how to swim?" she asked.

"He splashes a great deal, but he manages to drag himself through the water. I wouldn't call him graceful, by any means. Why do you ask?"

"She's having some sort of problem with him, and it has to do with the swimming. Let's go back and join the others, dear one. Just the sight of those slavers is setting my blood to boiling."

They slid back down the gravel-strewn mound and walked along a shallow gully toward their armored soldiers.

The Cyrinic Knight, Sir Launesse, stood somewhat diffidently beside a burly, intricately curled, and massively eyebrowed personage with heavy shoulders and a classical demeanor. "Sephrenia!" the clearly nonhuman being said in a voice that could probably have been heard in Thalesia. "Well met!"

"Well met indeed, Divine Romalic," she replied with just a trace of a weary sigh.

"Please, dear," Vanion murmured, "ask him to lower his voice."

"Nobody else can hear him," she assured him. "The Gods speak loudly—but only to certain ears."

"Thy sister bids me give thee greetings," Romalic announced in a voice of thunder.

"Thou art kind to bear those greetings, Divine One."

"Kindness and courtesy aside, Sephrenia," the huge God declaimed, combing his beard with enormous fingers, "art thou yet prepared to serve us all and to assume thy proper place?"

"I am unworthy, Divine One," she replied modestly. "Surely there are others wiser and better suited."

"What's this?" Vanion asked.

"It's been going on for a long time, dear one," she explained. "I've been avoiding it for centuries. Romalic always has to bring it up, though."

It all fell into place in Vanion's mind. "Sephrenia!" he gasped. "They want you to be Over-Priestess, don't they?"

"It's Aphrael, Vanion, not me. They think they can get around her by offering this to me. I don't really want it, and they don't really want to give it to me, but they're afraid of her, and this is their way to placate her."

"Aphrael bids thee to make haste," Romalic proclaimed. "Ye must all be at the gates of Cyrga 'ere dawn, for this is the night of decision, when Cyrgon and, yea, even Klæl, must be confronted and, we may hope, confounded. E'en now doth Anakha move ghostlike through the streets of the Hidden City toward his design. Let us hasten." He lifted his voice and thundered, "On to Cyrga!"

"Is he always like this?" Vanion murmured.

"Romalic?" Sephrenia said. "Oh, yes. He's perfectly suited to the Cyrinic Knights. Come along, dear one. Let's go to Cyrga."

There were dim, flickering lights far above, but the pool was sunk in inky blackness when Sparhawk surfaced and explosively blew out the breath he had been holding.

"Kalten," he heard Aphrael saying, "wake up."

There was a startled cry and a great deal of splashing.

"Oh, stop that," the Goddess told Sparhawk's friend. "It's all over, and you came through it just fine. Xanetia, dear, could we have a little light?"

"Of a certainty, Divine One," the Anarae replied, and her face began to glow.

"Are we all here?" Aphrael asked quietly, looking around. As Xanetia's light gradually increased, Sparhawk saw that the Goddess appeared to be no more than waist-deep in the pool, and she was holding Kalten up by the back of his tunic.

"Do you want to give me a hand with this, Sparhawk?" Bevier said.

"Right." Sparhawk swam over to join the Cyrinic, and together they hauled in the slender rope Bevier had trailed behind him as they had come through the tunnel. At the other end of the rope were their tightly bundled mail shirts and swords.

"Wait a minute," Bevier said when the rope suddenly went taut. "It's caught on something." He drew in several deep breaths, plunged under the surface, and went hand-over-hand back along the rope.

Sparhawk waited, unconsciously holding his own breath. Then the rope came free, and he hauled it in quickly. Bevier popped to the surface again, blowing out air.

"Are you sure you aren't part fish?" Sparhawk asked him.

"I've always had good lungs," Bevier replied. "Do you think we should get out our swords?"

"Let's see what Aphrael says first," Sparhawk decided, peering around. "I don't see any place to climb up out of the water yet."

"Now what?" Talen was asking the Goddess. "We're swimming around at the bottom of a well here." He looked up at the sheer sides of the shaft rising from the pool. "There are some openings up there, but there's no way to get to them."

"Did you bring it, Mirtai?" Aphrael asked.

The giantess nodded. "Excuse me a moment," she said, and she sank beneath the surface and began to pull off her tunic.

"What's she doing?" Talen asked, peering down through the clear water.

"She's taking off her clothes," Aphrael replied, "and she doesn't need any help from you. Keep your eyes where they belong."

"*You* run around naked all the time," he protested. "Why should you care if we watch Mirtai get undressed?"

"It's entirely different," she replied in a lofty tone. "Now do as you're told."

Talen thrust himself around in the water until he had his back to Mirtai. "I'm never going to understand her," he grumbled.

"Oh, yes you will, Talen," she told him in a mysterious little voice, "but not quite yet. I'll explain it all to you in a few more years."

Then Mirtai rose to the surface holding the coil of rope that had been slung over her shoulder under her tunic. "I'll need something to stand on, Aphrael," she said, hefting the grappling hook attached to one end of the rope. "I won't be able to throw this while I'm treading water."

"All right, gentlemen," Aphrael said primly, "eyes front."

Sparhawk's smile was concealed in the dimness. Talen was right. Aphrael seemed almost unaware of her own nakedness, but Mirtai's was an entirely different matter. He heard the sound of water trickling off the sleek limbs of the golden giantess as she rose to stand, he surmised, on its very surface.

Then he heard the whistling sound of the grappling hook as Mirtai swung it in wider and wider circles. Then the whistling stopped for an interminable, breathless moment. There was the clink of steel on stone high above, followed by a grating sound as the points dug in.

"Good cast," Aphrael said.

"Lucky," Mirtai replied. "It usually takes two or three throws."

Sparhawk felt a touch on his shoulder. "Here," Mirtai said, handing him the rope. "Hold this while I get dressed. Then we'll climb up and go find your wife."

"What on *earth* are you doing, Bergsten?"

The Patriarch of Emsat started violently and jerked his head around to stare at the God who had just walked up behind him.

"You're supposed to be hurrying, you know," Setras chided him. "Aphrael wants everybody to be in place by morning."

"We came across some of Klæl's soldiers, Divine One," Sir Heldin rumbled. "They're inside that cave." He pointed at a barely visible opening in the hillside across the shallow gully.

"Why didn't you deal with them? I told you how to do it."

"We put a lantern in there, but there's a door inside the cave, Setras-God," Atana Maris advised him.

"Well, *open* it, dear lady," Setras said. "We really *must* reach Cyrga by morning. Aphrael will be terribly vexed with me if we're late."

"We'd gladly open it if we knew how, Divine One," Bergsten told him, "but late or not, I *won't* ride away from here and leave those monsters behind me, and if that vexes Aphrael, that's just too bad." The handsome, stupid God irritated Bergsten for some reason.

"Why do I have to do everything myself?" Setras sighed. "Wait here. I'll deal with this, and then we'll be able to move on. We're terribly behind schedule, you know. We'll have to get cracking if we're going to make it by morning." He strolled on across the rocky gully and entered the cave.

"That young fellow's *really* trying my patience," Bergsten muttered. "Trying to explain something to him is like talking to a brick. How *can* he be so—" Bergsten pulled up short just this side of heresy.

"He's coming back out," Atana Maris said.

"I thought he might," Bergsten said with some satisfaction. "Apparently he didn't have any better luck with that door than we did."

Setras was strolling toward them humming a Styric melody when the entire hill vanished in a great, fiery explosion that shook the very earth. The fire billowed out with a dreadful, seething roar, hurling Bergsten and the others to the ground and engulfing Aphrael's cousin.

"Dear God!" Bergsten gasped, staring at the boiling fire.

Then Setras, with not so much as a hair out of place, came sauntering out of the fire. "There now," he said mildly, "that wasn't so difficult, was it?"

"How did you get the door open, Divine One?" Heldin asked curiously.

"I didn't, old boy." Setras smiled. "Actually, they opened it for me."

"Why would they do that?"

"I knocked, dear boy. I knocked. Even creatures like that have *some* manners. Shall we be going, then?"

"They are much feared by the other Cyrgai," Xanetia reported, "and all do give way to them."

"That would be useful—if it weren't for the racial differences," Bevier noted.

"Such differences do not pose an insurmountable obstacle, Sir Knight," Xanetia assured him. "Should it prove needful, thy features and those of thy companions may once more be altered. Divine Aphrael can doubtless serve in her sister's stead in the combining of the two spells which do yet disguise ye."

"We can talk about that in a moment," Flute said. "First, though, I think we should all get some idea of how this part of the city's laid out." The Goddess had resumed her more familiar form, and Bevier for one seemed much relieved.

"Methinks this mount is not of natural origin, Divine One," Xanetia told her. "The sides are of uniform steepness, and the avenues which do ascend to the top are more stairways than streets. Cross-streets, however, do encircle the hill at regular intervals."

"Unimaginative, aren't they?" Mirtai observed. "Are there many of them wandering around out there?"

"Nay, Atana. 'Tis late, and most have long since sought their beds."

"We *could* chance it," Kalten mused. "If Flute and Xanetia can make us look like Cyrgai, we could just march right up the hill."

"Not in *these* clothes we can't," Sparhawk disagreed.

Talen slipped out of the shadows to reenter the passageway leading back to the central shaft of the well. In many ways the agile young thief could be nearly as invisible as Xanetia. "More soldiers coming," he whispered.

"Those patrols could get to be a nuisance," Kalten said.

"These aren't like those others," Talen told him. "They aren't patrolling the side streets. They're just climbing the stairs toward the top of the city. They aren't wearing the same kind of armor either."

"Describe them, young Master Talen," Xanetia said intently.

"They're wearing cloaks, for one thing," Talen replied, "and they've got a sort of emblem on their breastplates. Their helmets are different, too."

"Temple Guards, then," Xanetia said, "the ones of which I spake earlier. I did glean from the thought of such few as I encountered that other Cyrgai do avoid them insofar as they might, and that all are obliged to bow down when they pass."

Sparhawk and Bevier exchanged a long look. "There are the clothes you wanted, Sparhawk." Bevier said.

"How many are there?" Sparhawk asked Talen.

"I counted ten."

Sparhawk considered it. "Let's do it," he decided, "but try to keep the noise down." And he led them out of the passageway into the street.

"Good God, Ulath!" Itagne exclaimed, "don't do that! My heart almost stopped!"

"Sorry, Itagne," the big Thalesian apologized. "There's no really graceful way to come out of No-Time. Let's go talk with Betuana and Engessa."

They rode back to join the queen and her general.

"Sir Ulath just arrived with news, your Majesty," Itagne said politely.

"Ah," she said. "Good news or bad news, Ulath-Knight?"

"A little of each, your Majesty," he replied. "The Trolls are a couple of miles east of here."

"And what's the good news?"

He smiled slightly. "That *is* the good news. The bad news is that there's another large force of Klæl's soldiers waiting in ambush just south of here. They'll probably hit you within the hour. They're in our way, and we have to hurry. Sparhawk and the others are going to rescue Ehlana and her maid tonight, and he wants us all to converge on the city by morning."

"We must fight the Klæl-beasts then," she said.

"That could be troublesome," Itagne murmured.

"Tynian and I have worked out a solution of sorts," Ulath continued, "but we don't want to offend you, your Majesty, so we thought I should stop by and talk it over first. Klæl's troops are preparing to ambush *you.* I know you'd prefer to deal with that yourself, but in the interests of expediency, would you be willing to forgo the pleasure?"

"I'd be willing to *listen,* Ulath-Knight," she said.

"There are ways we could just slip around that ambush, but Klæl can probably do the same kinds of things to time and distance that Aphrael and her cousins can, and I don't think we want those brutes coming up behind us."

"What's your solution then, Ulath-Knight?"

"I've got a sizable force at my disposal, your Majesty," he replied, "and they're hungry. Since we're too busy right now for an extended romp through the desert, why don't we just let the Trolls have Klæl's soldiers for breakfast?"

Sir Anosian looked a little shaken as he rode forward to speak with Kring and Tikume.

"What's the matter, friend Anosian?" Tikume asked the black-armored Pandion. "You look as if you just saw a ghost."

"Worse, friend Tikume," Anosian replied. "I've just been reprimanded by a God. Most men don't survive that experience."

"Aphrael again?" Kring guessed.

"No, friend Kring. This time it was her cousin Hanka. He's very abrupt. The Genidian Knights rely on him for assistance with their spells."

"He was unhappy with you?" Tikume asked. "What did you do this time?"

Anosian made a sour face. "Sometimes my spells are a little sloppy," he admitted. "Aphrael's generous enough to forgive me. Her cousin isn't." He shuddered. "Divine Hanka's going to hurry us along just a bit."

"Oh?"

"We have to be at the gates of Cyrga by morning."

"How far is it?" Kring asked him.

"I have no idea," Anosian admitted, "and under the circumstances, I didn't think it would be prudent to ask. Hanka wants us to ride west from here."

Tikume frowned. "If we don't know how far it is, how can we be sure we'll get there by morning?"

"Oh, we'll get there all right, friend Tikume," Anosian assured him. "I think we'd better start moving, though. Divine Hanka's notoriously short-tempered. If we don't start riding west very soon, he might just decide to pick us up and *throw* us from here to Cyrga."

The Temple Guardsman assumed a warlike posture—a rather stiff, formalized pose such as one occasionally sees on a frieze carved by an indifferently talented sculptor. Kalten brushed the man's sword aside and slammed his fist against the side of his helmet. The guardsman reeled away and fell heavily onto the cobblestones. He was struggling to rise again when Kalten kicked him solidly in the face.

"Quietly, Kalten!" Sparhawk said in a hoarse whisper.

"Sorry. I guess I got carried away." Kalten bent and peeled back the fallen guardsman's eyelid. "He'll sleep till noon," he said. He straightened and looked around. "Is that all of them?"

"That was the last," Bevier whispered. "Let's get them out of the middle of the street. The moon's going to make it up over those mountains soon, and it'll be as bright as day down in this basin in just a little while."

It had been a short, ugly little fight. Sparhawk and his friends had rushed out of a dark side street and had fallen on the detachment from the rear. Surprise had accounted for much of their success, and what surprise had not accomplished had been more than made up for by the ineptitude of the ceremonial troops. Sparhawk concluded that the Cyrgai *looked* impressive, but that their training over the centuries had grown so formalized and detached from reality that it had almost become more a form of dance than a preparation for real combat. Since the Cyrgai could not cross the Styric curse line, they had not been involved in any real fights for ten thousand years, and so they were hopelessly unprepared for all the nasty little tricks that crop up from time to time in close, hand-to-hand fighting.

"I still don't see how we're going to pull this off," Talen puffed as he dragged an inert guardsman back into the shadows. "One look will tell the gate guards that we're not Cyrgai."

"We've already discussed that," Sparhawk told him, "while you were out scouting. Xanetia and Aphrael are going to mix spells again—the way the Anarae and Sephrenia did back in Matherion. We'll look enough like Cyrgai to get us through the gate—particularly if the rest of the Cyrgai are as much afraid of these Temple Guardsmen as Xanetia says they are."

"As long as the subject's come up," Kalten said, "after we've bluffed our way past those gate guards, I want my own face back. We stand a fair chance of getting killed tonight, and I'd like to have my own name on my tombstone. Besides, if by some remote chance we succeed, I don't want to startle Alean by coming at her with a stranger's face. After what she's been through, she's entitled to see the real me."

"I don't have any problem with that," Sparhawk agreed.

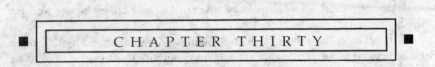

CHAPTER THIRTY

Captain Jodral returned just after dark, his loose robe flapping and his eyes wide as he desperately flogged at his horse. "We're doomed, my General," he shrieked.

"Get control of yourself, Jodral!" General Piras snapped. "What did you see?"

"There are millions of them, General!" Jodral was still on the verge of hysteria.

"Jodral, you've never seen a million of anything! Now, what's out there?"

"They're coming across the Sarna, General," Jodral replied, trying his best to control his quavering voice. "The reports about that fleet are true. I saw the ships."

"Where? We're ten leagues from the coast."

"They've sailed up the River Sarna, General Piras, and they've lashed their ships together side by side to form bridges."

"Absurd! The Sarna's five miles wide down here! Talk sense, man!"

"I know what I saw, General. The other scouts will be along shortly to confirm it. Kaftal's in flames. You can see the light of the fire from here." Jodral turned and pointed south toward a huge, flickering orange glow in the sky above the low coastal hills standing between the Cynesgan forces and the sea.

General Piras swore. This was the third time this week that his scouts had reported a crossing of the lower Sarna or the Verel River, and he had not thus far seen any sign of hostile forces. Under normal circumstances, he'd have simply had his scouts flogged or worse, but these were not normal circumstances. The enemy force that had been harrying the southern coast was made up of the Knights of the Church of Chyrellos—sorcerers to a man—who were quite capable of vanishing and then reappearing miles to his rear. Still muttering curses, he summoned his adjutant. "Sallat!" he snapped, "Wake up the troops. Tell them to prepare themselves! If those accursed knights *are* crossing the Sarna here, we'll have to engage them before they can establish a foothold on this side of the river."

"It's just another ruse, my General," his adjutant said, looking at Captain Jodral with contempt. "Every time some idiot sees three fishermen in a boat, we get a report of a crossing."

"I *know*, Sallat," Piras replied, "but I *have* to respond. King Jaluah will have my head if I let the knights get across those rivers." The general spread his hands helplessly. "What else can I do?" He swore again. "Sound the charge, Sallat. Maybe *this* time we'll find somebody real when we reach the river."

Alean was trembling violently when Zalasta returned the two captives to the small but now scrupulously clean cell following yet another of those hideous, silent interviews with the bat-winged Klæl, but Ehlana felt drained of all emotion. There was a perverse seductiveness to the strangely gentle probing of that infinite mind, and Ehlana always felt violated and befouled when it was over.

"That will be the last time, Ehlana," Zalasta told her apologetically. "If it's any comfort to you, he's still baffled by your husband. He cannot understand how any creature with such power would willingly subordinate himself to—" He hesitated.

"To a mere woman, Zalasta?" she suggested wearily.

"No, Ehlana, that's not it. Some of the worlds Klæl dominates are wholly ruled by females, and males are kept for breeding purposes only. No, Klæl simply cannot understand the relationship between you and Sparhawk."

"You might explain the meaning of love to him, Zalasta." She paused. "But you don't understand it yourself, do you?"

His face went cold. "Good night, your Majesty," he said in an unemotional tone. Then he turned and left the cell, closing and locking the door behind him.

Ehlana had her ear pressed to the door before the clanging echo of its closing had subsided.

"I do not fear them," she heard King Santheocles declare.

"Then you're a bigger fool than I thought," Zalasta told him bluntly. "All of your allies have been systematically neutralized, and your enemies have you surrounded."

"We are Cyrgai," Santheocles insisted. "No one can stand against us."

"That may have been true ten thousand years ago when your enemies dressed in furs and charged your lines with flint-tipped spears. Now you face Church Knights armed with steel; you face Atan warriors who can kill your soldiers with their fingertips; you face Peloi who ride through your ranks like the wind; you face Trolls, who not only kill your soldiers, but also eat them. If that weren't bad enough, you face Aphrael, who can stop the sun or turn you to stone. Worst of all, you face Anakha and Bhelliom, and that means that you face obliteration."

"Mighty Cyrgon will protect us." Santheocles' voice was set in a willful note of stubborn imbecility.

"Why don't you go talk with Otha of Zemoch, Santheocles?" There was a sneer in Zalasta's voice. "He'll tell you how the Elder God Azash squealed when Anakha destroyed him." Zalasta suddenly broke off. *"He comes!"* he choked. "Closer than we'd ever thought possible!"

"What are you talking about?" Ekatas demanded.

"Anakha is here!" Zalasta exclaimed. "Go to your generals, Santheocles! Tell them to call out their troops and order them to scour the streets of Cyrga, for Anakha is within your walls! Hurry, man! Anakha is here, and our deaths stalk the streets with him! Come with me, Ekatas! Cyrgon must be warned, and eternal Klæl! The night of decision is upon us!"

And thou, O Blue, all cares and griefs shall ban
And lift our hearts to heights unknown to mortal man

Elron ticked off the count on his fingers and swore. No matter how he slurred or compressed the words of that last line, it still had one beat too many. He hurled his quill pen across the room and sank his face into his hands in an artful pose of poetic despair. Elron did that frequently when composing verse.

Then he hopefully raised his face as a thought came to him. He *was* nearing the final stanzas of his masterpiece, after all, and an alexandrine *would* add emphasis. What would the critics say?

Elron agonized over the decision. He cursed the day when he had chosen to cast the most important work of his career in heroic couplets. He *hated* iambics. They were so mercilessly regular and unforgiving, and pentameter was like a chain around his neck, jerking him up short at the end of every line. "Ode to Blue" hung in the balance while her creator struggled with the sullen intransigences of form and meter.

Elron could not be sure how long the screaming had been going on or exactly when it had started. His mind, caught up in a creative frenzy, had blotted out everything external to that one maddeningly recalcitrant line. The poet rose irritably to his feet and went to the window to look out at the torchlit streets of Natayos. What *were* they screaming about?

Scarpa's soldiers—ignorant, unwashed serfs for the most part—were running, bawling in terror like so many bleating sheep. What had set them off *this* time?

Elron leaned slightly out to look up the street. There seemed to be a different kind of light coming from the part of the ruined city that was still buried in tangled brush and creeping vines. Elron frowned. It was most definitely not torchlight. It seemed to be a pale white glow instead, steady, unwavering, and coming from dozens of places at the same time.

Then Elron heard Scarpa's voice rising over the screams. The crazy charlatan was shouting orders of some kind in his most imperial voice. The rabble in the streets, however, were ignoring him. The army was streaming along the cobbled streets of ruined Natayos toward the main gate, pushing, howling, jamming together and struggling to get through that hopelessly clogged gateway. Beyond the gate, Elron saw winking torches streaming off into the surrounding jungle. What in God's name was going on here?

Then his blood suddenly froze. He gaped in horror at the glowing figures emerging from the side streets of the ruin to stalk implacably along the broad avenue that led to the gate. The Shining Ones who had depopulated Panem-Dea, Norenja, and Synaqua had finally descended on Natayos!

The poet stood frozen for only a moment, and then his mind moved more quickly than he'd have thought possible. Flight was clearly out of the question. The gate was so completely jammed that even those who had already reached it had little chance of forcing their way through. Elron dashed to his writing table and swatted his candle with the flat of his hand, plunging the room into darkness. If there were no lights in the windows of this upper floor, the horrors that stalked the streets would have no reason to search. Frantically, stumbling in the darkness, he ran from room to room, desperately searching for any other burning candles that might betray his location.

Then, certain that he was safe for the moment at least, the one known throughout Astel as Sabre crept back to his room to peer fearfully around the edge of the windowframe at the street below.

Scarpa stood atop a partially collapsed wall issuing contradictory commands to regiments that evidently only he could see. His threadbare velvet cloak was draped over his shoulders and his makeshift crown was slightly askew.

Not far from where he stood, Cyzada was saying something in his hollow voice—an incantation of some kind, Elron guessed—and his fingers were weaving intricate designs in the air. Louder and louder he spoke in guttural Styric, summoning God only knew what horrors to face the silent, glowing figures advancing on him. His voice rose to a screech, and he pawed at the air, frantically exaggerating the gestures.

And then one of the incandescent intruders reached him. Cyzada screamed and flinched back violently, but it was too late. The glowing hand had already touched him. He reeled back as if that almost gentle touch had been some massive blow. Staggering, he turned as if to flee, and Elron saw his face.

The poet retched, clamping his hands over his mouth to hold in any sound that might give away his presence. Cyzada of Esos was dissolving. His already unrecognizable face was sliding down the front of his head as if it were melted wax, and a rapidly spreading stain was discoloring the front of his white Styric robe. He staggered a few steps toward the still-raving Scarpa, his arms reaching hungrily out toward the madman even as the flesh slid away from those skeletal, outstretched hands. Then the Styric slowly collapsed to the stones, bubbling and seething, his decaying body oozing out through the fabric of his robe.

"Archers to the front!" Scarpa commanded in his rich, theatrical voice. "Sweep them with arrows!"

Elron fell to the floor and scrambled away from the window.

"Cavalry to the flanks!" he heard Scarpa command. "Sabers at the ready!"

Elron crawled toward his writing table, groping in the dark.

"Imperial guardsmen!" Scarpa bellowed. "Quicktime, march!"

Elron found the leg of the table, reached up, and frantically began grabbing at the sheets of paper lying on the tabletop.

"First Regiment—charge!" Scarpa commanded in a great voice.

Elron knocked over the table, whimpering in his desperate haste.

"Second Regiment—" Scarpa's voice broke off suddenly, and Elron heard him scream.

The poet spread his arms, trying to gather the priceless pages of "Ode to Blue" out of the darkness.

Scarpa's voice was shrill now. "Mother!" he shrieked. "Please please please!" The resonant voice had become a kind of liquid screech. "Pleasepleaseplease!" It sounded almost like a man trying to cry out from underwater. "Pleasepleaseplease!" And then the voice wheezed off into a dreadful gurgling silence.

Clutching the pages he had found, Sabre abandoned his search for any others, scurried across the room on his hands and knees, and hid under the bed.

Bhlokw's expression was reproachful as he shambled back across the night-shrouded gravel. "Wickedness, U-lat," he accused. "We are pack-mates, and you said a thing to me that was not so."

"I would not do that, Bhlokw," Ulath protested.

"You put the thought into my mind-belly that the big things with iron on their faces were good-to-eat. They are *not* good-to-eat."

"Were they bad-to-eat, Bhlokw?" Tynian asked sympathetically.

"*Very* bad-to-eat, Tin-in. I have not tasted anything so bad-to-eat before."

"I did not know this, Bhlokw," Ulath tried to apologize. "It was my thought that they were big enough that one or two might fill your belly."

"I only ate one," Bhlokw replied. "It was so bad-to-eat that I did not want to eat another. Not even Ogres would eat those, and Ogres will eat anything. It makes me not-glad that you said the thing that was not so to me, U-lat."

"It makes me not-glad as well," Ulath confessed. "I said a thing which I did not know. It was wicked of me to do this."

Queen Betuana drew Tynian aside. "How long will it take us to reach the Hidden City, Tynian-Knight?" she asked.

"Is your Majesty talking about how long it's really going to take or how long it's going to seem."

"Both."

"It's going to *seem* like weeks, Betuana-Queen, but in actual time, it'll be instantaneous. Ulath and I left Matherion just a few weeks ago in real time, but it seems that we've been on the road for nearly a year. It's very strange, but you get used to it after a while."

"We must start soon if we are to reach Cyrga by morning."

"Ulath and I'll have to talk with Ghnomb about that. He's the one who stops time, but he's also the God of Eat. He may not be happy with us. The idea of letting the Trolls kill Klæl's soldiers was a good one, but Ghnomb expects them to eat what they kill, and they don't like the taste."

She shuddered. "How can you stand to be around the Troll-beasts, Tynian-Knight? They're horrible creatures."

"They aren't really so bad, your Majesty," Tynian defended them. "They're very moral, you know. They're fiercely loyal to their own packs; they don't even know how to lie; and they won't kill anything unless they intend to eat it—or unless it attacks them. As soon as Ulath finishes apologizing to Bhlokw, we'll summon Ghnomb and talk with him about stopping time so that we can get to Cyrga." Tynian made a face. "*That's* what's going to take a while. You have to be patient when you're trying to explain something to the Troll-Gods."

"Is that what Ulath-Knight is doing?" she asked curiously, "Apologizing?"

Tynian nodded. "It's not as easy as it sounds, your Majesty. There's nothing in Trollish that even comes close to 'I'm sorry,' probably because Trolls never do anything that they're ashamed of."

"*Will* you be still?" Liatris hissed at the protesting Gahenas. "They're in the next room right now."

The three empresses were hiding in a dark antechamber adjoining the Tegan's private quarters. Liatris stood at the door with her dagger in her hand.

They waited in tense apprehension.

"They're gone now," Liatris said. "We'd better wait for a little while, though."

"Will you *please* tell me what's going on?" Gahenas asked.

"Chacole sent some people to kill you," Elysoun told her. "Liatris and I found out about it, and came to rescue you."

"Why would Chacole do that?"

"Because you know too much about what she's planning."

"That silly plan to implicate Cieronna in a spurious assassination plot?"

"The plot wasn't spurious, and Cieronna wasn't even remotely connected with it. Chacole and Torellia are planning to kill our husband."

"Treason!" Gahenas gasped.

"Probably not. Chacole and Torellia are members of royal houses currently at war with the Tamul Empire, and they're getting orders from home. The assassination of Sarabian could technically be called an act of war." Elysoun stopped as a wave of nausea swept over her. "Oh, dear," she said in a sick little voice.

"What's wrong?" Liatris demanded.

"It's nothing. It'll pass."

"Are you sick?"

"Sort of. It's nothing to worry about. I should have eaten something when you woke me up, that's all."

"You're white as a sheet. What's wrong with you?"

"I'm pregnant, if you really have to know."

"It was *bound* to happen eventually, Elysoun," Gahenas said smugly. "I'm surprised it didn't happen earlier, the way you carry on. Have you any idea at all of who the father is?"

"Sarabian," Elysoun replied with a shrug of her shoulders. "Do you think it's safe to leave now, Liatris? I think we'd better get to our husband as quickly as we can. Chacole wouldn't have sent people to kill Gahenas unless this was the night when she was planning her attempt on Sarabian."

"She'll have people watching all the doors," Liatris said.

"Not *all* the doors, dear." Elysoun smiled. "I know of at least three that she's not aware of. You see, Gahenas, there are *some* advantages to having an active social life. Check the hallway, Liatris. Let's get Gahenas out of here before Chacole's assassins come back."

The Cyrgai at the bronze gate stood back fearfully as Sparhawk led the others up the last few steps. "*Yala Cyrgon!*" the officer in charge said, smashing his fist against his breastplate in a kind of formal salute.

"Respond, Anakha," Xanetia's voice murmured in Sparhawk's ear. " 'Tis customary."

"*Yala Cyrgon!*" Sparhawk said, also banging on his chest and being careful not to allow the cloak he'd removed from the unconscious Temple Guardsman to open and reveal the fact that he was wearing his mail shirt rather than an ornate breastplate.

The officer seemed not to notice. Sparhawk and the others marched through the gate and moved along a broad street toward a kind of central square. "Is he still watching?" Sparhawk muttered.

"Nay, Anakha," Xanetia replied. "He and his men have returned to the guardroom beside the gate."

It had appeared from below that the only buildings within the walls at the summit of Cyrga were the fortress-palace and the temple, but that was not entirely true. There were other structures as well, low, utilitarian-looking buildings—storehouses for the most part, Sparhawk guessed. "Talen," he said over his shoulder, "ease over to the side of the street. Find a door you get open in a hurry. Let's get out of sight while Xanetia scouts around."

"Right," Talen replied. He ducked into the shadows, and a moment later they heard his whisper and quickly moved to the door he was holding open for them.

"Now what?" Kalten asked.

"Xanetia and I go looking for Ehlana and Alean," Aphrael's voice replied out of the darkness.

"Where were you?" Talen asked curiously, "when we were coming up the hill, I mean?"

"Here and there," she replied. "My family's moving all the others into position, and I wanted to be sure everything's going according to schedule."

"Is it?"

"It is now. There were a couple of problems, but I took care of them. Let's get at this, Xanetia. We still have a lot to do before morning."

"Ah, *there* they are," Setras said. "I wasn't really all that far off, now was I?"

"Are you *sure* this time?" Bergsten demanded.

"You're cross with me, aren't you, Bergsten?"

Bergsten sighed, and decided to let it pass. "No, Divine One," he replied. "We all make mistakes, I guess."

"That's frightfully decent of you, old boy," Setras thanked him. "We were moving in *generally* the right direction. I was just off a few degrees, that's all."

"Are you *certain* those are the right peaks this time, Divine One?" Heldin rumbled.

"Oh, absolutely," Setras said happily. "They're exactly as Aphrael described them. You notice how they glow in the moonlight?"

Heldin squinted across the desert at the two glowing spires rearing up out of the dark jumble of broken rock. "They *look* about right," he said dubiously.

"I have to go find the gate," Setras told them. "It's supposed to be exactly on a line from the gap between the two peaks."

"Are you *sure*, Divine One?" Bergsten asked. "It's that way on the south side, but do we know for certain that it's the same here on the north?"

"You've never met Cyrgon, have you, old boy? He's the most rigid creature you've ever seen. If there's a gate on the south, there'll be one on the north as well, believe me. Don't go away. I'll be right back." He turned and strolled off across the desert toward the two peaks glowing in the moonlight.

Atana Maris was standing to one side of Bergsten and Heldin with a slightly troubled look on her face.

"What's the matter, Atana?" Heldin asked her.

"I think there is something I do not understand, Heldin-Knight," she replied, struggling to put her thought into Elenic. "The Setras person is a God?"

"A Styric God, yes."

"If he is a God, how did he get lost?"

"We're not certain, Atana Maris."

"That is what I do not understand. If Setras-God were a human, I would say that he is stupid. But he is a God, so he cannot be stupid, can he?"

"I think you'd better take that up with his Grace here," Heldin replied. "I'm only a soldier. He's the expert on theology."

"Thanks, Heldin," Bergsten said in a flat tone of voice.

"If he is stupid, Bergsten-Priest, how can we be certain that he's brought us to the right place?"

"We have to trust Aphrael, Atana. Setras may be a little uncertain about things, but Aphrael isn't, and she talked with him for quite some time, as I recall."

"Speaking slowly," Heldin added, "and using short, simple words."

"Is it possible, Bergsten-Priest?" Maris asked insistently. "Can a God be stupid?"

Bergsten looked at her helplessly. "*Ours* isn't," he evaded, "and I'm sure yours isn't either."

"You didn't answer my question, Bergsten."

"You're right, Atana," he replied, "I didn't—and I'm not going to. If you're really curious, I'll take you to Chyrellos when this is all over, and you can ask Dolmant."

"Bravely spoken, Lord Bergsten," Heldin murmured.

"Shut up, Heldin."

"Yes, your Grace."

Sparhawk, Bevier, and Kalten stood at a small, barred window in the musty-smelling warehouse looking out at the fortresslike palace rearing above the rest of the city. "That's really archaic," Bevier said critically.

"It looks strong enough to me," Kalten said.

"They've built the main structure of the palace right up against the outer wall, Kalten. It saves building two walls, but it compromises the structural integrity of the fortress. Give me a couple of months and some good catapults, and I could pound the whole thing to pieces."

"I don't think catapults had been invented when they built it, Bevier," Sparhawk said. "It was probably the strongest fort in the world ten thousand years ago." He looked out at the gloomy, rearing pile. As Bevier had noted, the main structure was backed up against the wall that separated this part of Cyrga from the rest of the city. Shorter towers stair-stepped up to the large central tower that shouldered high above the rest of the palace and grew, or so it seemed, out of the wall itself. It appeared that the palace had not been built to look out over the city, but rather to face the white limestone temple. The Cyrgai clearly looked at their God, and turned their backs on the rest of the world.

The door that Talen had unlocked to provide them entry into this storehouse creaked as it opened and then closed again. Then the soft glow of Xanetia's face once again dimly illuminated the area around her.

"We've found them," the Child-Goddess said as the Anarae set her down on the flagstoned floor.

Sparhawk's heart leapt. "Are they all right?"

"They haven't been treated very well. They're tired and hungry and very much afraid. Zalasta took them to see Klæl, and that's enough to frighten anybody."

"Where are they?" Mirtai demanded intently.

"At the very top of that highest tower at the back of the palace."

"Did you talk with them?" Kalten asked intently.

Aphrael shook her head. "I didn't think it was a good idea. What they don't know about, they can't talk about."

"Anarae," Bevier said thoughtfully, "would the soldiers in the palace let Temple Guardsmen move around freely in there?"

"Nay, Sir Knight. The Cyrgai are much driven by custom, and Temple Guardsmen have little cause to enter the palace."

"I guess we can discard these, then," Kalten said, pulling off the ornate bronze helmet and dark cloak he had purloined in the lower city. He touched his cheek. "We still look like Cyrgai. We could steal some different uniforms and then just march in, couldn't we?"

Xanetia shook her head. "The soldiers within the palace are all kinsmen, members of the royal clan, and are all known to one another. Subterfuge would be far too perilous."

"We've *got* to come up with a way to get into that tower!" Kalten said desperately.

"I already have," Mirtai told him calmly. "It's dangerous, but I think it's the only way."

"Go ahead," Sparhawk told her.

"We might be able to sneak up through the palace, but if we're discovered, we'd have to fight, and that'd put Ehlana and Alean in immediate danger."

Sparhawk nodded bleakly. "It's just too dangerous to risk," he agreed.

"All right, then. If we can't go *through* the palace, we'll have to go up the outside."

"You mean climb the tower?" Kalten asked incredulously.

"It's not as difficult as it sounds, Kalten. Those walls aren't built of marble, so they aren't smooth. They're rough stone blocks, and there are plenty of handholds and places to put your feet. I could climb that back wall like a ladder, if I had to."

"I'm not really very graceful, Mirtai," he said dubiously. "I'll do anything at all to rescue Alean, but I won't be much good to her if I make a misstep and fall five hundred feet into the lower city."

"We have ropes, Kalten. I'll keep you from falling. Talen can scamper up a wall like a squirrel, and I can climb almost as well. If we had Stragen and Caalador along, they'd be halfway up the side of that tower by now."

"Mirtai," Bevier said in a pained voice, "we're wearing mail shirts. Climbing a sheer wall with seventy pounds of steel hanging from your shoulders might be a little challenging."

"Then take it off, Bevier."

"I might need it when I get up on top."

"No problem," Talen assured him. "We'll bundle them all together and pull them up behind us. I *do* sort of like it, Sparhawk. It's quiet; it's fairly fast; and there probably won't be any guards going hand-over-hand around the outside of the tower looking for intruders. Mirtai's had training from Stragen and Caalador, and I was born for burglary. She and I can do the real climbing. We'll drop ropes down to the rest of you at various stages along the way, and you can haul up the mail and swords behind you. We can get to the top of that tower in no time at all. We can do it, Sparhawk. It'll be easy."

"I can't really think of any alternatives," Sparhawk conceded dubiously.

"Let's do it, then," Mirtai said abruptly. "Let's get Ehlana and Alean out of there, and once they're safe, we can start to take this place apart."

"*After* I get my real face back," Kalten added adamantly. "Alean's entitled to *that* much consideration."

"Let's do that right now, Xanetia," Aphrael said. "Kalten will nag us about it all night if we don't."

"Nag?" Kalten objected.

"What color was your hair again, Kalten? Purple, wasn't it?" she asked him with an impish little smile.

There were deep shadows along the western side of the women's palace when Elysoun, Liatris, and Gahenas emerged through the little-used door and moved quickly through the darkness to take cover in a nearby grove of ornamental ever-greens. "This is going to be the dangerous part," Liatris cautioned in a low voice. "Chacole knows by now that her assassins weren't able to find Gahenas, and she's certain to have her people out to try to prevent us from reaching Ehlana's castle."

Elysoun looked out at the moon-drenched lawn. "That's impossible," she said. "It's just too bright. There's a path that goes on through this grove. It comes out near the Ministry of the Interior."

"That's the wrong direction, Elysoun," Gahenas protested. "The Elene castle's the other way."

"Yes, I know, but there's no cover. There's nothing between here and the castle but open lawn. We'd better stick to the shadows. If we go around on the other side of Interior, we'll be able to go through the grounds of the Foreign Ministry. It's only about fifty yards from there to the drawbridge of the castle."

"What if the drawbridge has been raised?"

"We'll worry about that when we get there, Gahenas. Let's get into the gardens around the Foreign Ministry first."

"Let's go, then, ladies," Liatris said abruptly. "We're not accomplishing any-thing by standing around talking. Let's go find out what we're up against."

"Back here," Talen whispered to them, coming out of a narrow alleyway. "The palace wall runs back to the place where it joins the outer fortifications at the end of this alley. The right angle where the two walls meet is perfect for climbing."

"Will you need this?" Mirtai asked, holding her grappling hook out to him.

"No. I can make it to the top without it, and we'd better not risk having some sentry up there hear the hook banging on the stones." He led them back along the alley to the cul-de-sac where the palace wall butted up against the imposing fortifi-cations separating the compound from the rest of the city.

"How high would you say it is?" Kalten asked, squinting upward. It was strange to see Kalten's face again after all the weeks it had been disguised. Sparhawk tenta-tively touched his own face and immediately recognized the familiar contours of his broken nose.

"Thirty feet or so," Bevier replied softly to Kalten's question.

Mirtai was examining the angle formed by the joining of the two walls. "This won't be very difficult," she whispered.

"The whole structure's poorly designed," Bevier agreed critically.

"I'll go up first," Talen said.

"Don't do anything foolish up there," Mirtai cautioned.

"Trust me." He set his foot up on one of the protruding stones of the outer wall and reached for a handhold on the palace wall. He went up quickly.

"We'll check for sentries when we get up there," Mirtai quietly told the others. "Then we'll drop a rope down to you." She reached up and began to follow the young thief up the angle between the two walls.

Bevier leaned back and looked upward. "The moon's up now," he said.

"Thinkest thou that it might reveal us?" Xanetia asked him.

"No, Anarae. We'll be climbing the north side of the tower, so we'll be in shadow the whole way to the top."

They waited tensely, craning their necks to watch the climbers creeping upward.

"Somebody's coming!" Kalten hissed. "Up there—along the battlements!"

The climbers stopped, pulling back into the shadows of the sharp angle between the two walls.

"He's got a torch," Kalten whispered. "If he holds it out over those battlements . . ." He left it hanging.

Sparhawk held his breath.

"It's all right now," Bevier said. "He's going back."

"We might want to deal with him when we get up there," Kalten noted.

"Not if we can avoid it," Sparhawk disagreed. "We don't want somebody else to come looking for him."

Talen had reached the battlements. He clung to the rough stones for a moment, listening. Then he slipped over the top and out of sight. After several interminable moments, Mirtai followed him.

Sparhawk and the others waited in the darkness.

Then Mirtai's rope came slithering down the wall.

"Let's go," Sparhawk said tensely, "one at a time."

The building blocks were of rough, square-fractured basalt, and they protruded unevenly from the walls, making climbing much simpler than it appeared. Sparhawk didn't even bother to use the rope. He reached the top and clambered over the battlements. "Do the sentries have any kind of set routine up here?" he asked Mirtai.

"It seems that each one has his own section of wall," she replied. "The one at this end doesn't walk very fast. I'm guessing, but I'd say that it'll be a quarter of an hour before he comes back."

"Is there any place where we can take cover before then?"

"There's a door in that first tower," Talen said, pointing at the squat structure rising at the end of the parapet. "It opens onto a stairwell."

"Have you taken a look at the back wall yet?"

Talen nodded. "There's no parapet along that side, but there's a ledge a couple of feet wide where the outer wall joins the back of the palace. We'll be able to make our way along that until we get on that central tower. Then we get to start climbing."

"Does the sentry look back there when he reaches this end of the parapet?"

"He didn't last time," Mirtai said.

"Let's look at that stairwell, then," Sparhawk decided. "As soon as the others are up, we'll hide in there until the sentry reaches this end and starts back. That should give us a half hour to crawl along that ledge to the central tower. Even if he looks around the corner next time, we should be out of the range of his torch by then."

"He's right on top of these things, isn't he?" Talen said gaily to Mirtai.

"What *is* this boy's problem?" Sparhawk demanded of the golden giantess.

"There's a certain kind of excitement involved in this, Dorlin' " Mirtai replied. "It sets the blood to pounding."

"Dorlin'?"

"Professional joke, Sparhawk. You probably wouldn't understand."

Vanion's scouts had returned about sunset to report contact with Kring to the south and Queen Betuana's Atans to the north. The ring of steel around the Forbidden Mountains was drawing inexorably tighter. The moon was rising over the desert when Betuana and Engessa came running in from Vanion's right flank and Kring and Tikume rode in from the left.

"Tynian-Knight will be along soon, Vanion-Preceptor," Engessa reported. "He and Ulath-Knight have spoken with Bergsten-Priest on *their* right. Ulath-Knight has remained with the Trolls to try to prevent incidents."

"Incidents?" Sephrenia asked.

"The Trolls are hungry. Ulath-Knight gave them a regiment of the Klæl-beasts to eat, but the flavor did not please the Trolls. Ulath-Knight tried to apologize, but I am not sure if the Trolls understood."

"Have you seen Berit and Khalad yet, friend Vanion?" Kring asked.

"No, but Aphrael said that they're just ahead of us. Her cousin guided them to the spot where that hidden gate's supposed to be."

"If they know where the gate is, we could go on in," Betuana suggested.

"We'd better wait, dear," Sephrenia replied. "Aphrael will let me know as soon as Sparhawk rescues Ehlana and Alean."

Tynian came riding across the vast open graveyard. "Bergsten's in place," he reported, swinging down out of his saddle. He looked at Itagne. "I have a message for you, your Excellency."

"Oh? From whom?"

"Atana Maris is with Bergsten. She wants to talk with you."

Itagne's eyes widened. "What's *she* doing here?" he exclaimed.

"She said that your letters must have gone astray. Not a single one of them reached her. You *did* write to her, didn't you, your Excellency?"

"Well—I was intending to." Itagne looked slightly embarrassed. "Something always seemed to come up, though."

"I'm sure she'll understand." Tynian's face was blandly expressionless. "Anyway, after she handed the city of Cynestra over to Bergsten, she decided to come looking for you."

Itagne's expression was slightly worried. "I hadn't counted on that," he confessed.

"What's this?" Betuana asked curiously.

"Ambassador Itagne and Atana Maris became good friends while he was in Cynestra, your Majesty," Sephrenia explained, "*very* good friends, actually."

"Ah," Betuana said. "It's a little unusual, but it's not unheard of, and Maris has always been an impulsive girl." Although the Atan queen still wore deep mourning, she seemed to have abandoned her ritual silence. "A word of advice, Itagne-Ambassador—if you'd care to hear it."

"Of course, your Majesty."

"It's not at all wise to toy with the affections of an Atan woman. It might not seem so, but we're very emotional. Sometimes we form attachments that aren't really appropriate." She did not look at Engessa as she said it. "Appropriate or not, however, those emotions are extremely powerful, and once the attachment is formed, there's very little we can do about it."

"I see," he said. "I'll definitely keep that in mind, your Majesty."

"Do you want me to go find Berit and Khalad and bring them back here, friend Vanion?" Kring asked.

Vanion considered it. "We'd better stay away from that gate," he decided. "The Cyrgai might be watching. Berit and Khalad are *supposed* to be there, but we aren't. Let's not stir anything up until Sparhawk sends word that his wife's safe. Then we'll *all* go in. There are a number of accounts that are long past due, and I think the time's coming when we'll want to settle up."

The ledge that ran along the back of the palace made reaching the central tower a matter of hardly more than a casual stroll. It still took time, however, and Sparhawk was acutely aware of the fact that the night was already more than half over. Mirtai and Talen moved up the side of the tower quickly, but the rest of them, roped together for safety, made much slower progress.

Sparhawk was peering upward when Kalten joined him. "Sparhawk, where's Aphrael?" the blond Pandion asked quietly.

"Everywhere. Didn't she tell you?"

"Very funny." Kalten looked off toward the east. "Are we going to make it before it starts getting light?"

"It could be close. There seems to be some kind of balcony just above us—and lighted windows."

"Are we going around them?"

"I'll have Talen take a look. If there aren't too many Cyrgai in the room, we might be able to finish this climb inside."

"Let's not take chances, Sparhawk. I'll climb all the way to the moon if I have to. Go ahead on up. I've got the rope tied off."

"Right." Sparhawk started to climb again. A slight breeze had come up, brushing the basalt wall with tenuous fingers. It was not strong enough to pose any dangers as yet, but Sparhawk definitely didn't want it getting any stronger.

"You're out of condition, Sparhawk," Mirtai told him critically when he reached the spot just below where she and Talen clung to the wall.

"Nobody's perfect. Can you make out any details of that balcony yet?"

"I was just going to swing over and have a look," Talen replied. He untied the rope from about his waist and began working his way across the wall toward the balcony.

You're making me cross, Sparhawk. Aphrael's voice seemed very loud in the silence of his mind. *I have plans for that young man, and they don't include scraping him up off a street five hundred feet below.*

He knows what he's doing. You worry too much. As long as you're here, could you give me a few details about the top of this tower?

There's a separate building up there—probably an afterthought of some kind. It's got the three rooms, a guardroom for the platoon or so of ceremonial troops, the cell where Mother and Alean are being held, and a large room across the front. Santheocles spends most of his time there.

Santheocles?

The King of the Cyrgai. He's an idiot. They all are, but he's worse than most.

Is there a window in Ehlana's cell?

A small one. It's barred, but you couldn't get through it anyway. The building up there is smaller than the rest of this tower, so there's a kind of parapet that runs all the way around it.

Do those guards patrol it?

No. There's no real need for that. It's the highest place in the city, and the notion that somebody might scale the tower has never occurred to the Cyrgai.

Is Santheocles up there right now?

He was, but I think he might have left since I looked in through the window. Zalasta was with him—and Ekatas. There was some sort of gathering they were planning to attend.

There was a low whistle, and Sparhawk looked toward the balcony. Talen was motioning to him. "I'm going to go have a look," Sparhawk told Mirtai.

"Don't be too long," she cautioned. "The night's starting to run out on us."

He grunted and started across toward the balcony.

The drawbridge was down, and no one was standing watch. "How very convenient," Elysoun said as she, Liatris, and Gahenas crossed the bridge into the courtyard of the castle. "Chacole thinks of everything, doesn't she?"

"I thought there were supposed to be Church Knights on guard here," Gahenas said. "Chacole couldn't bribe *them*, could she?"

"Lord Vanion took his knights with him," Liatris replied. "The responsibility for guarding the castle's been turned over to ceremonial troops from the main garrison. Some officer is probably quite a bit richer than he was yesterday. You've been here before, Elysoun. Where can we find our husband?"

"He's usually up on the second floor. There are royal apartments there."

"We'd better get up there in a hurry. That unguarded gate makes me very nervous. I doubt that we'd be able to find a guard anywhere in the castle, and that means that Chacole's assassins have free access to Sarabian."

· · ·

The balcony appeared not to have been used for at least a generation. Dust lay deep in the corners, and the thick crust of bird droppings on the floor was undisturbed. Talen was crouched beside the window, peering around the edge, when Sparhawk came up over the stone balustrade. "Is there anybody in there?" the big Pandion whispered.

"A whole crowd," Talen whispered back. "Zalasta just came in with a couple of Cyrgai."

Sparhawk joined his young friend and looked in.

The room appeared to be some kind of torchlit throne room. The balcony where Sparhawk and Talen crouched was above the level of the floor and was reached from the inside by a flight of stone stairs. There was a slightly raised dais at the far end of the room with a throne carved from a single rock at the back of it. A well-muscled, handsome man in an ornate breastplate and a short leather kirtle sat there, surveying the men around him with an imperious expression. Zalasta stood to one side of the man on the throne, and a wrinkled man in an ornamented black robe was at the front of the dais speaking in his own language. Sparhawk swore and quickly cast the spell that would attract the notice of the Child-Goddess.

Now what? Aphrael's voice sounded in his mind.

Can you translate for me?

I can do better than that.

He seemed to hear a faint buzzing sound and felt a momentary giddiness.

"—and even now those forces do surround the sacred city," the wrinkled man was saying in a language Sparhawk now understood.

A man with iron-grey hair and powerfully muscled arms stepped forward from the gathering before the dais. "What is there to fear, Ekatas?" he asked in a booming voice. "Mighty Cyrgon clouds the eyes of our enemies as he has for a hundred centuries. Let them crouch among the bones beyond our valley and seek vainly the Gates of Illusion. They are as blind men and pose no danger to the Hidden City."

There was a murmur of agreement from the others standing before the dais.

"General Ospados speaks truth," another armored man declared, also stepping forward. "Let us, as we have always, ignore these puny foreigners at our gates."

"Shameful!" another bellowed, stepping to the front some distance from the two who had already spoken. "Will we hide from inferior races? Their presence at our gates is an affront that must be punished!"

"Can you make out what they're saying?" Talen whispered.

"They're arguing," Sparhawk replied.

"Really?" Talen's tone was sardonic. "Could you be a little more specific, Sparhawk?"

"Evidently Aphrael's cousins have managed to get everybody here. From what the fellow in the black robe was saying, the city's surrounded."

"It's a comfort to have friends nearby. What do these people plan to do about it?"

"That's what they're arguing about. Some of them want to just sit tight. Others want to attack."

Then Zalasta came to the front of the dais. "Thus says Eternal Klæl," he declared. "The forces beyond the Gates of Illusion are as nothing. The danger is here within the walls of the Hidden City. Anakha is even now within the sound of my voice."

Sparhawk swore.

"What's wrong?" Talen demanded.

"Zalasta knows we're here."

"How did he find *that* out?"

"I have no idea. He says that he's speaking for Klæl, and Klæl can probably feel Bhelliom."

"Even through the gold?"

"The gold might hide Bhelliom from Cyrgon, but Bhelliom and Klæl are brothers. They can probably feel each other halfway across the universe—even when there are whole suns burning between them." Sparhawk held up his hand. "He's saying something else." He leaned closer to the window.

"I know you can hear me, Sparhawk!" Zalasta said in a loud voice, speaking in Elenic. "You're Bhelliom's creature, and that gives you a certain amount of power. But I am Klæl's now, and that gives me just as much as you have." Zalasta sneered. "The disguises were very clever, but Klæl saw through them immediately. You should have done as you were told, Sparhawk. You've doomed your two young friends, and there's not a single thing you can do about it."

There were a half-dozen men in nondescript clothing in the hallway outside the door to the room where the emperor had been the last time Elysoun had visited him. Elysoun did not even think. "Sarabian!" she shouted. "Lock your door!"

The emperor, of course, did not. After a momentary shocked pause while the assassins froze in their tracks and Liatris blistered the air around her with curses even as she drew her daggers, the door burst open and Sarabian, dressed in Elene hose, a full-sleeved linen shirt, and with his long black hair tied back, lunged out into the hallway, rapier in hand.

Sarabian was tall for a Tamul, and his first lunge pinned an assassin to the wall opposite the door. The emperor whipped his sword free of the suddenly collapsing body with a dramatic flourish.

"Quit showing off!" Liatris snapped at her husband as she neatly ripped one of the assassins up the middle. "Pay attention!"

"Yes, my love," Sarabian said gaily, crouching again into *en garde*.

Elysoun had only a small, neat dagger with a five-inch blade. It was long enough, though. An Arjuni assassin with a foot-long poniard parried Sarabian's next thrust and, snarling spitefully, plunged his needlelike dagger at the emperor's very eyes. Then he arched back with a choked cry. Elysoun's little knife, sharp as any razor, had plunged smoothly into the small of his back, ripping into his kidneys.

It was Gahenas, however, who shocked them all. Her weapon was a slim curved knife. With a shrill scream, the jug-eared Tegan empress flew into the middle of the fray, slashing at the faces of Chacole's hired killers. Screeching, Gahenas hacked at the startled assailants, and Sarabian took advantage of every lapse. His thin blade whistled as he danced the deadly dance of thrust and recover. This is not to say that the Emperor of Tamuli was a master swordsman. He *was* fairly skilled, but Stragen might have found room for criticism. In truth, it was the wives who carried the day—or night, in this case.

"Inside, my dear ones," Sarabian said, thrusting his savage women toward the door while he slashed at the empty air over the fallen assassins. "I'll cover your backs."

"Oh, dear," Liatris murmured to Elysoun and Gahenas, "he's such a baby."

"Yes, Liatris," Elysoun replied, wrapping one arm affectionately about her ugly Tegan sister, "but he's ours."

"Kring's coming," Khalad said quietly, pointing at the shadowy horseman galloping across the bone-littered gravel in the moonlight.

"That's not a good idea," Berit said, frowning. "Somebody might be watching."

The Domi reached them and reined in sharply. "Come away!" he urged.

"What's wrong?" Berit demanded.

"The Child-Goddess says for you to come back to where the others are! The Cyrgai are coming out to kill you."

"I was wondering how long it was going to take them to decide to try that," Khalad said, swinging up into his saddle. "Let's go, Berit."

Berit nodded, reaching for Faran's reins. "Is Lord Vanion going to do anything when the Cyrgai come out?" he asked Kring.

Kring's answering grin was wolfish. "Friend Ulath has a little surprise for them when they come through the gate," he replied.

Berit looked around. "Where is he?" he asked. "I don't see him."

"Neither will the Cyrgai—until it's too late. Let's get back away from this cliff. We'll let them see us when they come out. They've been ordered to kill you, so they'll come running after us. Friend Ulath has six or eight very hungry Trolls with him, and they'll be right on top of the Cyrgai when they come out."

"Did he know where you were?" Kalten asked tensely as they clung to the wall.

"I don't think so," Sparhawk replied. "He knows that I'm somewhere in the city, but there are several ways I could be listening to him. I don't think he realized just how close I was when he started making threats."

"Are Berit and Khalad going to be all right?"

Sparhawk nodded. "Aphrael was with me when Zalasta made his little speech. She's taking care of it."

"All right, Sparhawk," Mirtai called from above them, "here comes the rope."

The free end of the rope came slithering down out of the dimness above them, and Sparhawk quickly climbed up. "How much farther?" he asked quietly when he reached Mirtai's side.

"About one more climb," she replied. "Talen's already up there."

"He should have waited," Sparhawk fumed. "I'm going to have a talk with that boy."

"It won't do any good. Talen likes to take chances. Is Kalten still dragging our equipment behind him? I'd hate to get up there and have to deal with things with just my fingernails."

"He's hauling it up—stage by stage." Sparhawk peered up the wall. "Why don't you let me go on ahead this time? Get the others up there as quickly as you can. We've still got a lot left to do, and this night won't last forever."

She gestured up the rough stone wall. "Feel free," she said.

"I don't know if I've ever said this," he told her, "but I'm glad you came along. You're probably the best soldier I've ever known."

"Don't get emotional, Sparhawk. It's embarrassing. Are you going to go up the wall? Or did you want to wait for the sun to come up?"

He started up, moving carefully. It was to their advantage that the north side of the tower was in shade, but the deep shadows made it necessary to feel for each handhold and to probe carefully with his toes for places to put his feet. He concentrated on the climbing and resisted the impulse to lean back to look at the wall above and the sharp line of the edge of the parapet some fifty feet farther up.

"What kept you?" Talen whispered as the big Pandion clambered over the top of the balustrade marking the edge of the parapet.

"I stopped to smell the flowers," Sparhawk replied acidly. He looked quickly toward the east and saw the faint light of false dawn outlining the mountains. They had at most one more hour of darkness left. "No sentries, I gather?" he whispered.

"No," Talen replied quietly. "The Cyrgai evidently feel that they need their sleep."

"Sparhawk?" Kalten's whisper came from below.

"Up here."

"Take the baggage." A coil of rope came unwinding up out of the darkness.

"Give me a hand with this, Talen." He leaned over the stone railing. "Get clear of it," he called down softly to Kalten. "We're going to pull it up."

Kalten grunted, and they could hear him moving across the wall to one side. Then Sparhawk and Talen slowly pulled the awkward, bulky bundle up to the top of the tower, being careful not to let it bang against the stones of the wall. Sparhawk quickly retrieved his sword and then fumbled through the mail shirts, searching for his own.

Kalten was puffing as he climbed up over the railing. "Why did you let me get so badly out of shape, Sparhawk?" he asked accusingly.

Sparhawk shrugged. "Careless, I guess. Ah, here it is." He lifted his own shirt free of the others.

"How can you tell?" Talen asked curiously. "In the dark, I mean?"

"I've worn it for over twenty years. Believe me, I recognize it. See how the others are coming."

Talen went to the rail and helped Xanetia onto the parapet while Bevier and Mirtai clambered over on their own.

It took only a couple of minutes for the knights to re-arm themselves. "Where did Talen go?" Kalten whispered, looking around.

"He's snooping," Mirtai replied, settling her sword belt into place.

"I think it's called scouting," Bevier corrected her.

She shrugged. "Whatever."

Then Talen came back. "I think I found what we're looking for," he said softly. "There's a small window with a sort of iron grate over it. It's up high, so I didn't look in."

"Is Aphrael coming back?" Bevier asked. "Should we wait for her?"

Sparhawk shook his head. "It's going to start getting light before long. Aphrael knows what we're doing. She's making sure the others are all in place."

Talen led them around to the east side of the tower. "Up there," he whispered, pointing at a small, barred window about ten feet up the side of the rough wall.

"Do any of the windows on the front side have bars?" Sparhawk asked him.

"No, and they're bigger and closer to the floor."

"That's it, then." Sparhawk fought back an urge to shout with exultation. "Aphrael described that window to me."

Kalten squinted up at the iron-grated window high in the wall. "Let's make sure of this before we start to celebrate." He braced his hands on the wall and set his feet wide apart. "Climb up and take a look, Sparhawk."

"Right." Sparhawk put his hands on his friend's arms and climbed up his broad back. He set his feet carefully on Kalten's shoulders and slowly straightened, reaching up to grasp the rusty grating that covered the window. He pulled his face up and peered into the darkness. "Ehlana?" he called softly.

"Sparhawk?" Her voice was startled.

"Please keep your voice down. Are you all right?"

"I am now. How did you get here?"

"It's a long story. Is Alean there, too?"

"Right here, Prince Sparhawk," the girl's silvery voice replied. "Is Kalten with you?"

"I'm standing on his shoulders right now. Can you make a light of any kind?"

"Absolutely not!" Ehlana's voice was stricken.

"What's wrong?"

"They've cut off all my hair, Sparhawk!" she moaned. "I don't want you to look at me!"

CHAPTER THIRTY-TWO

Talen dropped back to the parapet from the small window. "I can get through it," he whispered confidently.

"What about that iron grate?" Kalten demanded.

"It's ornamental. It wasn't very good to begin with, and it's been there for at least a couple of centuries. It won't take long to work it loose."

"Let's hold off until Xanetia gets back," Sparhawk decided. "I want to know what we're up against before we start crashing around."

"I'm not trying to be offensive," Mirtai said softly to Talen, "but I don't see what good it's going to do us to have you inside the cell when the fighting starts and a half-dozen Cyrgai rush into the cell to kill Ehlana and Alean."

"It's on accounta the fact that they ain't a-gonna *git* in the cell, Dorlin'," he said with an outrageous grin. "The door's locked."

"They've got a key."

"Give me about a half a minute with the lock, and their key won't fit. They won't get in; trust me."

"Are there alternatives?" Bevier asked.

"Not in the amount of time we've got left before it starts getting light," Sparhawk replied with a worried glance at the eastern horizon. "Kalten, go up and have a look at that grating."

"Right." The blond Pandion climbed up to the small window, took hold of the ancient iron lattice in both hands, and began to heave on it. Crumbs and fragments of mortar began to shower down on the rest of them.

"Quietly!" Mirtai whispered urgently at him.

"It's already loose," he reported in a hoarse whisper. "The mortar's rotten." He stopped wrenching at the bars and leaned closer to the window. "Ehlana wants to talk to you, Sparhawk," he called down softly.

Sparhawk climbed back up to the window. "Yes, love?" he whispered into the darkness.

"What are you planning, Sparhawk?" she murmured, her voice so near that it seemed he could almost touch her.

"We're going to pull the bars loose, and then Talen's going to crawl through the window. He'll jam the lock so the people outside can't get into the cell. Then the rest of us will rush the guards. Is Zalasta out there anywhere?"

"No. He and Ekatas went to the temple. He knows that you're here, Sparhawk. He sensed you somehow. Santheocles has men searching the city for you right now."

"I think we're ahead of them. I don't believe they realize that we're already up here."

"How *did* you get up here, Sparhawk? All the stairways are guarded."

"We climbed up the outside of the tower. When do those guards out there start stirring around?"

"When it begins to get light, usually. They cook what passes for food around here in the guardroom. Then a couple of them bring breakfast to Alean and me."

"Your breakfast might be a little late this morning, love," he whispered with a tight grin. "I think the cooks might have other things on their minds before long."

"Be careful, Sparhawk."

"Of course, my Queen."

"Sparhawk," Mirtai called up softly. "Xanetia's back."

"I have to run now, dear," he whispered into the darkness. "We'll have you out of there shortly. I love you."

"What a lovely thing to say."

Sparhawk quickly climbed back down to the parapet. "Welcome back, Anarae," he greeted Xanetia.

"Thou art in a peculiar humor, Anakha," she replied in a slightly puzzled tone.

"I just had a chat with my wife, Anarae," he said. "That always brightens my day. How many guards will we have to deal with?"

"I do fear me that they number some score or more, Anakha."

"That could be a problem, Sparhawk," Bevier noted. "They're Cyrgai and none too bright, but twenty of them might give us some trouble."

"Maybe not," Sparhawk disagreed. "Aphrael said that there are only three rooms up here—the main room, the cell where Ehlana and Alean are, and the guardroom. Was she right, Anarae?"

"Indeed," she replied. "The cell and the guardroom are here on this north side. The main room is on the south, overlooking the Temple of Cyrgon. I did glean from the sleepy thought of such Cyrgai who were awake that this ultimate tower is the customary retreat of King Santheocles, for he doth take some pleasure in surveying his domain from the parapet—and above all in receiving the adulation of his subjects in the city below."

"Stupid," Mirtai muttered. "Doesn't he have anything better to do?"

Xanetia smiled faintly. "Much else would be quite beyond him, Atana. His guardsmen, limited though they themselves are, do hold their king's understanding in low regard. But his wits, or lack thereof, are of little moment. Santheocles is the descendant of the royal house, and his sole function is to wear the crown."

"A hat rack could do that," Talen noted.

"Truly."

"Do the guardsmen have any kind of set routine?" Bevier asked.

"Nay, Sir Knight. They do but hold themselves in readiness to respond to the commands of their king, nothing more. In truth, they are trumpeteers rather than warriors. Their primary duty is to announce with brazen notes to their fellow citizens that Santheocles will appear on the parapet to accept the adulation of the Cyrgai."

"And they do their waiting in the guardroom?" Sparhawk pressed.

"Save only for the pair who stand guard at the door to thy queen's prison and the other pair who bar the stairway which doth lead down into the lower levels of this tower."

"Can they get into the queen's cell from the guardroom?" Bevier asked intently.

"Nay. There is but one door."

"And how wide is the doorway between the guardroom and the main room?"

"Wide enough for one man only, Sir Bevier."

"Kalten and I can hold that one, Sparhawk."

"Are there any other doors to the guardroom?" Kalten asked.

Xanetia shook her head.

"Any large windows?"

"One window only—the mate to this one above us—though it is not barred."

"That narrows the opposition down to just those four guards in the main room," Kalten said. "Bevier and I can keep the rest of them penned in for a week, if we have to."

"And Sparhawk and I can deal with the ones at the cell door and the top of the stairs," Mirtai added.

"Let's get Talen inside that cell," Sparhawk said, looking again toward the east where a faint lessening of the darkness had begun.

Kalten scrambled back up the wall to the window and began digging at the mortar with his heavy dagger.

"Slip around and keep watch, Anarae," Sparhawk whispered. "Let us know if anybody comes up those stairs."

She nodded and went back around the corner of the tower.

Sparhawk climbed up and attacked the mortar on the left side of the iron lattice while his friend continued to dig at the right. After a few moments Kalten took hold of the rusty iron and pulled. "The bottom's loose," he muttered. "Let's get the top."

"Right." The two of them went to the top of the window and began to chip away the mortar there. "Be careful when it breaks away," Sparhawk cautioned. "We don't want it clanging down on that parapet."

"This side's free," Kalten whispered. "I'll hold it while you dig your side loose." He reached inside, found a secure handhold with his right hand, and grasped the grating with his left.

Sparhawk dug harder, sending a shower of chunks and dust to the parapet below. "I think that's got it," he whispered.

"We'll see." Kalten's shoulders heaved and there was a grinding sound as the ancient grate tore loose from the wall. Then, with the same movement, Sparhawk's burly friend hurled the heavy obstruction out beyond the balustrade.

"What are you *doing*?" Sparhawk choked.

"Getting rid of it."

"Do you know how much noise that thing's going to make when it hits the ground?"

"So what? It's five hundred feet down. Let it make all the noise it wants to. If some Cyrgai or Cynesgan slave driver's standing under it, he's in for a nasty surprise, but we can live with that, can't we?"

Sparhawk pushed his head through the now-unobstructed opening. "Ehlana?" he whispered. "Are you there?"

"Where else *would* I be, Sparhawk?"

"Sorry. Stupid question, I suppose. The bars are out of the way now. We're sending Talen in. Shout or something as soon as he gets the lock jammed so that the guards can't get through the door."

"Get out of the way, Sparhawk," Talen said abruptly from just below. "I can't get in there with you filling up the whole window."

Sparhawk swung himself clear of the opening, and the agile boy began to wriggle his way through. Suddenly he stopped. "It's not working," he muttered. "Pull me back out."

"What's wrong?" Kalten demanded.

"Just pull me back out, Kalten. I don't have time to explain."

Sparhawk's heart sank as he and Kalten hauled the young thief back.

"Hold on for a minute." Talen turned until he was on his side, and then he extended his arms until they were stretched out above his head. "All right, push."

"You'll just get stuck again," Kalten objected.

"Then you'll have to push harder. This is what comes of all that wholesome food, exercise, and clean living you keep pushing on me, Sparhawk. I've grown so much that I can't get my shoulders through." He began to wriggle through the opening again. "Push, gentlemen!" he instructed.

The two of them pushed their hands against the soles of his feet.

"Harder!" he grunted.

"You'll tear all your skin off," Kalten warned.

"I'm young. I heal fast. Push!"

The two shoved at his feet, and, with a great deal of squirming and a few muttered oaths, he was through.

"Is he all right?" Sparhawk whispered hoarsely through the window.

"I'm fine, Sparhawk," Talen whispered back. "You'd better get moving. This won't take me very long."

Sparhawk and Kalten dropped back to the parapet. "Let's go," Sparhawk said shortly, and the three knights and the Atan giantess moved quickly around the narrow parapet to the south side of the tower.

"Quietly, Anakha." Xanetia's voice seemed to come out of nowhere.

"Are they stirring yet, Anarae?" Bevier whispered.

"Some few sounds do emanate from the guardroom," her voice replied.

There were two large unglazed windows at the front of the tower, one on each side of the broad door. Sparhawk cautiously raised his head above the lower edge of one of them and peered inside. The room, as Aphrael had reported, was fairly large. It was sparsely furnished with benches, a few backless chairs, and a couple of low tables, and it was lighted with primitive oil lamps. There was a narrow door on the right side of the rear wall with two statuelike Cyrgai, one on each side, guarding it. The stairway on the left side of the room, also guarded, was enclosed on three sides by a low wall. The second doorway, the one leading into the guardroom, was also on the left side, not far from the top of the stairs.

Sparhawk looked intently at the guards, closely studying their weapons and equipment. They were well-muscled men in archaic breastplates, crested helmets, and short leather kilts. Each had a large round shield strapped to his left arm, and each grasped an eight-foot spear in his right. They all had swords and heavy daggers belted at their waists.

Sparhawk moved his head away from the window. "You'd all better take a look," he whispered to his friends.

One by one, Kalten, Bevier, and Mirtai raised up slightly to peer into the room.

"Is this locked, Anarae?" Sparhawk whispered, pointing at the door leading out onto the parapet.

"I did not think it wise to try it, Anakha. Cyrgai construction is crude, and methinks no doorlatch in the city may be attempted soundlessly."

"You're probably right," he breathed. "Let's pull back around the corner," he told the others, leading them around to the east side.

"It's getting lighter," Kalten noted, pointing toward the horizon.

Sparhawk grunted. "We'll go in through the windows," he told them. "We'd just jam up if we tried to go through the doorway anyhow. Bevier, you and Mirtai go through the one on the far side of the door. Kalten and I'll go through the one on this side. Be careful. Those spears seem to be their primary weapon, so they've probably had lots of training with them. Get in close and fast. Take them down in a hurry and then block that door to the guardroom. We're going to have to hold those stairs, too."

"I'll do that, Sparhawk," Mirtai assured him. "You concentrate on getting our friends out of that cell."

"Right," he agreed. "As soon as they're free, I'll unleash the Bhelliom. That should change the odds up here significantly."

And then there was a clear voice raised in aching song that soared out above the sleeping city.

"That's the signal!" Kalten told them. "That's Alean! Talen's finished up! Let's go!"

"You heard him!" Sparhawk said, stepping back so that Bevier and Mirtai could get past. "I'll give the word, and we'll all go in at the same time!"

Bevier and Mirtai crouched low as they ran past the window on the near side to take positions under the window beyond the door. "Stay clear of this, Anarae," Sparhawk murmured to the invisible Xanetia. "It's not your kind of fight." He frowned. There was no sense of her presence nearby. "All right, Kalten," he said then, "let's get to work."

The two of them silently crept forward, swords in hand, to crouch beneath the broad window. Sparhawk raised slightly to look along the parapet. Bevier and Mirtai waited tensely under the far window. He drew in a deep breath and set himself. "Now!" he shouted, setting his hand on the windowledge and vaulting through into the room.

There had been four Cyrgai inside before. Now there were ten.

"They're changing the guard, Sparhawk!" Bevier shouted, swinging his deadly lochaber in both hands.

They still had the element of surprise, but the situation had drastically changed. Sparhawk swore and cut down a Cyrgai carrying a pail of some kind—the captives' breakfast, most likely. Then he rushed the four confused guards milling in front of the cell door. One of them was fighting with the lock while the other three tried to get into position. They were disciplined, there was no question about that, and their long spears *did* raise deadly problems.

Sparhawk swore a savage oath and swung his heavy broadsword, chopping at the spears. Kalten had moved to one side, and he was also swinging massive blows at the spears. There were sounds of fighting coming from the other side of the room, but Sparhawk was too intent on breaking through to the guard who was trying to force the cell door to turn and look.

Two of the spears were broken now, and the Cyrgai had discarded them and drawn their swords. The third soldier, his spear still intact, had stepped back to protect the one still feverishly struggling with the lock.

Sparhawk risked a quick glance at the other side of the room, just in time to see Mirtai lift a struggling guard over her head and hurl him bodily down the stairs with a great clattering sound. Two other Cyrgai lay dead or dying nearby. Bevier, even as he had in Otha's throne room in Zemoch, held the door to the guardroom while Mirtai, like some great, golden cat, savaged the remaining guards at the top of the stairs. Sparhawk quickly turned his attention back to the men he faced.

The Cyrgai were indifferent swordsmen, and their oversized shields seriously hindered their movements. Sparhawk made a quick feint at the head of one, and the man instinctively raised his shield. Sparhawk instantly recovered and, ducking low, drove his sword up into the gleaming breastplate. The Cyrgai cried out and fell back with blood gushing from the sheared gash in his armor.

It was not enough. The Cyrgai at the cell door had abandoned his efforts to unlock it and had begun slamming his shoulder against it. Sparhawk could clearly hear the splintering of wood. Desperately, he renewed his attack. Once the Cyrgai broke through that door—

And then, without even being forced, the door swung inward. With a triumphant shout, the Cyrgai who had been battering at the door drew his sword.

And then he screamed as a new light flooded the room.

Xanetia, blazing like the sun, stood in the doorway with one deadly hand extended.

The Cyrgai screamed again, falling back, tangling himself in the struggles of his two comrades. Then he broke free, ran to the window, and plunged through.

He was still running when he went over the balustrade with a long despairing scream.

The two other Cyrgai at the cell door also fled, scurrying around the room like frightened mice. "Mirtai!" Sparhawk roared. "Stand clear! Let them go!"

The Atana had just raised another struggling warrior over her head. She threw him down the stairs and turned sharply. Then she dodged clear to allow the demoralized Cyrgai to escape.

"Stand aside, Sir Knight!" Xanetia commanded Bevier. "*I* will bar that door, and I do vouchsafe that none shall pass!"

Bevier took one look at her glowing face and stepped away from the guardroom door.

The Cyrgai inside the room also looked at her, and then they slammed the door shut.

"It's all right now, Ehlana," Sparhawk called.

Talen came out first, and his face was pale and shaken. The boy's tunic was ripped in several places, and a long, bleeding scrape on one arm spoke of his struggle to get through the narrow window. He was staring in awe at Xanetia. "She came through the window in a puff of smoke, Sparhawk!" he choked.

"Mist, young Talen," Xanetia corrected in a clinical tone. She was still all aglow and facing the guardroom door. "Smoke would be impractical for human flesh."

There was a great deal of noise coming from the guardroom. "They seem to be moving furniture in there, Sparhawk," Bevier laughed. "Piling it against the door, I think."

Then Alean came running out of the cell to hurl herself into Kalten's arms, and, immediately behind her, Ehlana emerged from her prison. She was even more pale than usual, and there were dark circles under her eyes. Her clothing was tattered, and her head was tightly bound in a bandagelike wimple. "Oh, Sparhawk!"

she cried in a low voice, holding her arms out to him. He went to her and enfolded her in a rough embrace.

From far below there came a savage bellow.

"Anakha!" Bhelliom's voice roared in Sparhawk's mind. "Cyrgon hath awakened to his peril! Release me."

Sparhawk jerked the pouch out from under his tunic and fumbled with the drawstring.

"What's that shouting?" Talen demanded.

"Cyrgon knows that we've released Ehlana!" Sparhawk replied tensely, drawing Kurik's box out of the pouch. "Open!" he commanded.

The lid raised, and the blue radiance of the Bhelliom blazed forth. Sparhawk carefully lifted out the jewel.

"They're coming up the stairs, Sparhawk!" Mirtai warned.

"Get clear!" he said sharply. "Blue-Rose!" he said then. "Canst thou bar the way to our enemies, who even now rush up yon stairway?"

The Bhelliom did not answer, but the waist-high wall surrounding the head of the stairs collapsed, crashing down into the stairwell with a great clattering and a billowing cloud of dust.

Advise Aphrael that her mother is safe. Bhelliom's voice was crisp. *Let the attack begin.*

Sparhawk cast the spell. *Aphrael!* he said sharply. *We've got Ehlana! Tell the others to move in!*

Can Bhelliom break Cyrgon's illusion? she asked in a tone every bit as crisp as the sapphire rose's had been.

Blue-Rose, Sparhawk said silently, *the illusion of Cyrgon doth still impede the advance of our friends upon the city. Canst thou dispel it that they may bring their forces to bear upon this accursed place?*

It shall be as thou wouldst have it, my son.

There was a momentary pause, and then the earth seemed to shudder slightly, and a vast shimmer ran in waves across the sky.

From the leprous white temple far below there came a shrill screech of pain.

"My goodness," Flute said mildly as she suddenly appeared in the center of the room. "I've never had a ten-thousand-year-old spell broken. I'll bet it hurts like anything. Poor Cyrgon's having an absolutely *dreadful* night."

"The night is not yet over, Child-Goddess," Bhelliom spoke through Kalten's lips. "Save thine unseemly gloating until all danger is past."

"Well, *really!*"

"Hush, Aphrael. We must look to our defenses, Anakha. What Cyrgon knoweth, Klæl doth also know. The contest is at hand. We must make ready."

"Truly," Sparhawk agreed. He looked around at his friends. "Let's go," he told them. "We'll spread out along the parapet, and keep your eyes open. Klæl's coming, and I don't want him creeping up behind me. Is that stairway completely blocked?"

"A mouse couldn't get through all that rubble," Mirtai told him.

"We can forget about the guards," Bevier announced, removing his ear from the guardroom door. "They're still rearranging the furniture."

"Good." Sparhawk went to the door leading out to the parapet. It opened with a shrill protest of rusty hinges. "Don't start getting brave," he cautioned his friends. "The fight's between Bhelliom and Klæl. Spread out and keep watch."

The eastern sky was pale with the approach of day as they came out onto the parapet, and Cyrgon's agonized shrieking still echoed through the Hidden City.

"There," Talen said, pointing toward the basalt escarpment beyond the lake to the south.

A mass of figures, tiny in the distance and still dark in the dawn light, were streaming out of "the Glen of Heroes," moving into the basin before the gates of Cyrga.

"Who are they?" Ehlana cried, suddenly gripping Sparhawk's arm.

"Vanion," Sparhawk told her, "along with just about everybody else—Betuana, Kring, Ulath and the Trolls, Sephrenia—"

"Sephrenia?" Ehlana exclaimed. "She's dead!"

"You didn't really think I'd let Zalasta kill my sister, did you, Ehlana?" Flute said.

"But, he said that he'd stabbed her in the heart!"

The Child-Goddess shrugged. "He did, but Bhelliom cured it. And don't worry, Vanion's going to take steps."

Talen came running around the parapet from the back of the tower. "Bergsten's coming in from the other side," he reported. "His knights just trampled about three regiments of Cyrgai underfoot without even slowing down."

"Are we going to be caught in the middle of a siege here?" Kalten asked with a worried expression.

"Not too likely," Bevier replied. "The defenses of this place are pitifully inadequate, and Patriarch Bergsten tends to be a very abrupt sort of man."

There was a sudden eruption far below, and the roof of the pale temple exploded, hurling chunks of limestone in all directions as the infinite darkness of Klæl shouldered his way up out of the House of Cyrgon. His vast, leathery wings spread wide, and his blazing, slitted eyes looked about wildly.

"Prithee, Anakha, hold me aloft that my brother may behold me." The voice coming from Kalten's lips was detached.

Sparhawk's hand was shaking as he raised the sapphire rose over his head.

Kalten, moving somewhat woodenly, gently put Alean's clinging arms aside and stepped to the stone rail at the front of the parapet. He spoke in a tongue no human mouth could have produced, and his words could quite probably have been heard in Chyrellos, half a world away.

Enormous Klæl, waist-deep in the ruins of Cyrgon's Temple, raised his triangular face and roared his reply, his fanged mouth dripping flame.

Attend closely, Anakha. Bhelliom's voice in Sparhawk's mind was very quiet. *I will continue to taunt mine errant brother, and, all enraged, will he come to do battle with me. Be thou steadfast in the face of that approaching horror, for our success or failure does hang entire upon thy courage and the strength of thine arm.*

I do not take thy meaning, Blue-Rose. Am I to smite Klæl?

Nay, Anakha. Thy task is to free me.

The beast of darkness below savagely kicked aside the limestone rubble and advanced on the palace with hungry arms outstretched. When he reached the massive gates, he brushed them from his path with a whip of lightning clutched in one enormous fist.

Kalten continued his deafening taunts, and Klæl continued to howl his fury as he crushed his way through the lower wings of the palace, destroying everything that lay in the path of his relentless drive toward the tower.

And then he reached it, and, seizing its rough stones in his two huge hands, he began to climb, his wings clawing at the morning air as he mounted up and up.

How am I to free thee, Blue-Rose? Sparhawk asked urgently.

My brother and I must be briefly recombined, my son, Bhelliom replied, *to become one again, as we once were, else must I forever be imprisoned within this azure crystal—even as Klæl must remain in his present monstrous form. In our temporary combination will we both be freed.*

Combine? How?

When he doth reach this not-inconsiderable height and doth exult with resounding bellow of victory, must thou hurl me straightway into his gaping maw.

Do what?

He would with all his soul devour me. Make it so. In the moment of our union shall Klæl and I both be freed of our present forms, and then shall our contest begin. Fail not, my son, for this is thy purpose and the destiny for which I made thee.

Sparhawk drew in a deep breath. *I will not fail thee, Father,* he pledged with all his heart.

Still raging and with his leathery wings straining for purchase on the wind, Klæl mounted higher and higher up the front of the palace tower. Sparhawk felt a sense of odd, undismayed detachment come over him. He looked full into the face of the King of Hell and felt no fear. His task was simplicity in itself. He had only to hurl the sapphire rose into that gaping maw and, should a suitable opportunity for that not present itself, to hurl himself—with Bhelliom in his outstretched fist instead. He felt no regret nor even sadness as the unalterable resolve settled over him. Better this than to die in a meaningless, unremembered skirmish on some disputed frontier as so many of his friends had. This had significance, and for a soldier, that was the best one could hope for.

And still Klæl came, climbing higher and higher, reaching hungrily for his hated brother. No more than a few yards below now, his slitted eyes blazed in cruel triumph and his jagged fangs dripped fire as he roared his challenge.

And then Sparhawk leapt atop the ancient battlement to stand poised with Bhelliom aloft in his fist. "For God and my Queen!" he bellowed his defiance.

Klæl reached up with one awesome hand.

Then, like the sudden uncoiling of some tight-wound spring, Sparhawk struck. His arm snapped down like a whip. "Go!" he shouted as he released the blazing jewel.

As true as an arrow the sapphire rose flew from his hand even as Klæl's mouth gaped wider. Straight it went to vanish in the flaming maw.

The tower trembled as a shudder ran through the glossy blackness of the enormity clinging to its side, and Sparhawk struggled to keep his balance on his precarious perch even as Kalten fell backward to the parapet.

Klæl's wings stiffened to their fullest extent, quivering with awful tension. The great beast swelled, growing even more enormous. Then he contracted, shriveling.

And then he exploded.

The detonation shook the very earth, and Sparhawk was hurled back from the battlement to fall heavily on the parapet. He rolled quickly, came to his feet, and rushed back to the battlements.

Two beings of light, one a glowing blue, the other sooty red, grappled with each other on insubstantial air not ten feet away. Their struggle was elemental, a savage contesting of will and strength. They were featureless beings, and their shapes were only vaguely human. Heaving back and forth, they clung to each other like wrestlers in some rude village square, each bending all his will and force to subdue his perfectly matched opponent.

Sparhawk and his friends lined the battlements, frozen, awed, able only to watch that primeval struggle.

And then the two broke free of each other and stood, backs bowed and arms half-extended, each facing his immortal brother in some inconceivable communion.

It falls to thee, Anakha, Bhelliom's voice in Sparhawk's mind was calm. *Should Klæl and I continue, this world shall surely be destroyed, as hath oft-time come to pass before. Thou art of this world and must therefore be my champion. Constraints are upon thee which do not limit me. Klæl's champion is also of this world and is similarly constrained.*

It shall be even as thou hath said, my father, Sparhawk replied. *I will serve as thy champion if need be. With whom must I contend?*

A great roar of rage came from far below, and a living flame surged up out of the shattered ruins of the chalk-white temple.

There is thine opponent, my son, the azure spirit replied. *Klæl hath called him forth to do battle with thee.*

Cyrgon!

Even so.

But he is a God!

And art thou not?

Sparhawk's mind reeled.

Look within thyself, Anakha. Thou art my son, and I made thee to be the receptacle of my will. I now release that will to thee that thou mayest be the champion of this world. Feel its power infuse thee.

It was like the opening of a door that had always been closed. Sparhawk felt his mind and will expanding infinitely as the barrier went down, and with that expansion there came an unutterable calm.

Now art thou truly Anakha, my son! Bhelliom exulted. *Thy will is now my will. All things are now possible for thee. It was thy will which vanquished Azash. I was but thine instrument. In this occasion, however, shalt thou be mine. Bend thine invincible will to the task. Seize it in thine hands and mold it. Forge weapons with thy mind and confront Cyrgon. If thine heart be true, he cannot prevail against thee. Now go. Cyrgon awaits thee.*

Sparhawk drew in a deep breath and looked down at the rubble-littered square far below. The flame which had emerged from the ruins had coalesced into a blazing man-shape standing before the wreck of the temple. "Come, Anakha!" it roared. "Our meeting hath been foretold since before time began! *This* is thy destiny! Thou art honored above all others to fall by *my* hand."

Sparhawk deliberately pushed aside the windy pomposity of archaic expression. "Don't start celebrating until after you've won, Cyrgon!" he shouted his reply. "Don't go away! I'll be right down!" Then he set one hand atop the battlement and lightly vaulted over it.

He stopped, hanging in midair. "Let go, Aphrael," he said.

"What are you *doing*?" she exclaimed.

"Just do as you're told. Let me go."

"You'll fall."

"No, I won't. I can handle this. Don't interfere. Cyrgon's waiting for me, so please let go."

It was not actually flying, although Sparhawk was certain that he *could* fly if he needed to. He felt a peculiar lightness as he drifted down toward the ruins of the House of Cyrgon. It was not that he had no weight; it was more that his weight had no meaning. His will was somehow stronger than gravity. Sword in hand, he settled down and down like a fearsome, drifting feather.

Cyrgon waited below. The burning figure of the ancient God drew his fire about him, congealing the incandescent flame into the antique armor customarily worn by those who worshipped him—a burnished steel cuirass, a crested helmet, a large round shield, and a sword in his fist.

A peculiar insight came to Sparhawk as he slid down through the dawn-cool air. Cyrgon was not so much stupid as he was conservative. It was change that he hated, change that he feared. Thus he had frozen his Cyrgai eternally in time and had erased any potential for change or innovation from their minds. The Cyrgai, unmoved by the winds of time, would remain forever as they had been when their God had first conceived of them. He had wrought an ideal and fenced it all about with law and custom and an innate hatred of change, and frozen thus, they were doomed—and had been since the first of them had placed one sandaled foot on the face of the ever-changing world.

Sparhawk smiled faintly. Cyrgon, it appeared, needed instruction in the benefits of change, and his first lesson would be in the advantages of modern equipment, weaponry, and tactics. Sparhawk thought, *Armor,* and he was immediately encased in black-enameled steel. He almost casually discarded his plain working sword and filled his hand with his heavier and longer ceremonial blade. Now he was a fully armed Pandion Knight, a soldier of God—of several Gods, he rather ruefully amended that thought. And he was, almost by default, the champion not only of his queen, his Church, and his God, but also, if he read Bhelliom's thought correctly, of his fair and sometimes vain sister, the world.

He drifted down and settled to earth amidst the wreck of the destroyed temple. "Well met, Cyrgon," he said with profoundest formality.

"Well met, Anakha," the God replied. "I had misjudged thee. Thou art suitable now. I had despaired of thee, fearing that thou wouldst never have realized thy true significance. Thine apprenticeship hath been long and methinks, hindered by thine inappropriate affiliation with Aphrael."

"We're wasting time, Cyrgon," Sparhawk cut through the flowery courtesies. "Let's get at this. I'm already late for breakfast."

"So be it, Anakha!" Cyrgon's classic features were set in an expression of approval. "Defend thyself!" And he swung a huge sword-stroke at Sparhawk's head.

But Sparhawk had already begun his stroke, and so their swords clashed harmlessly in the air between them.

It was good to be fighting again. There were no politics here, no confusion of dissembling words or false promises, just the clean, sharp ring of steel on steel and the smooth flow of muscle and sinew over bone.

Cyrgon was quick, as quick as Martel had been in his youth, and, despite his hatred of innovation, he learned quickly. The intricate moves of wrist and arm and shoulder that marked the master swordsman seemed to come unbidden, almost in spite of himself, to the ancient God. "Invigorating, isn't it?" Sparhawk panted through a wolflike grin, lashing a stinging cut at the God's shoulder. "Open your mind, Cyrgon. Nothing is set in stone—not even something as simple as this." And he lashed out with his sword again, flicking another cut onto Cyrgon's sword arm.

The immortal rushed at him, forcing the oversized round shield against him, trying with will and main strength to overcome his better-trained opponent.

Sparhawk looked into that flawless face and saw regret and desperation there. He bunched his shoulder, as Kurik had taught him, and locked his shield arm, forming an impenetrable barrier against the ineffectual flailing of his opponent. He parried only with his lightly held sword. "Yield, Cyrgon," he said, "and live. Yield, and Klæl will be banished. We are of *this* world, Cyrgon. Let Klæl and Bhelliom contend for other worlds. Take thy life and thy people and go. I would not slay even thee."

"I spurn thine insulting offer, Anakha!" Cyrgon half shrieked.

"I guess that satisfies the demands of knightly honor," Sparhawk muttered to himself with a certain amount of relief. "God knows what I'd have done if you'd accepted." He raised his sword again. "So be it, then, brother," he said. "We weren't meant to live in the same world together anyway." He felt his body and will seem to swell inside his armor. "Watch, brother," he grated through clenched teeth. "Watch and learn."

And then he unleashed five hundred years of training, coupled with his towering anger, at this poor, impotent Godling, who had ripped asunder the peace of the world, a peace toward which Sparhawk had yearned since his return from exile in Rendor. He ripped Cyrgon's thigh with the classic *pas-four*. He slashed that perfect face with Martel's innovative *parry-pas-nine*. He cut away the upper half of Cyrgon's oversized round shield with Vanion's third-feint-and-slash. Of all the Church Knights, the Pandions were the most skilled swordsmen, and of all the Pandions, Sparhawk stood supreme. Bhelliom had called him the equal of a God, but Sparhawk fought as a man—superbly trained, a little out of condition, and really too old for this kind of thing—but with an absolute confidence that if the fate of the world rested in his hands, he was good for at least one more fight.

His sword blurred in the light of the new-risen sun, flickering, weaving, darting. Baffled, the ancient Cyrgon tried to respond.

The opportunity presented itself, and Sparhawk felt the perfect symmetry of it. Cyrgon, untaught, had provided the black-armored Pandion precisely the same opening Martel had given him in the Temple of Azash. Martel had fully understood the significance of the series of strokes. Cyrgon, however, did not. And so it was that the thrust which pierced him through came as an absolute surprise. The God stiffened and his sword fell from his nerveless fingers as he lurched back from that fatal thrust.

Sparhawk recovered from the thrust and swept his bloody sword up in front of his face in salute. "An innovation, Cyrgon," he said in a detached sort of voice. "You're really very good, you know, but you ought to try to stay abreast of things."

Cyrgon sagged to the flagstoned court, his immortal life spilling out through the gash in his breastplate. "And wilt thou take the world now, Anakha?" he gasped.

Sparhawk dropped to his haunches beside the stricken God. "No, Cyrgon," he replied wearily. "I don't want the world—just a quiet little corner of it."

"Then why camest thou against me?"

"I didn't want you to have it either, because if you had, my little part wouldn't have been safe." He reached out and took the pallid hand. "You fought well, Cyrgon. I have respect for you. Hail and farewell."

Cyrgon's voice was only a whisper as he replied, "Hail and farewell, Anakha."

There was a great despairing howl of frustration and rage. Sparhawk looked up and saw a man-shape of sooty red streaking upward into the dawn sky as Klæl resumed his endless journey toward and beyond the farthest star.

CHAPTER THIRTY-THREE

There was fighting somewhere—the ring of steel on steel and shouts and cries—but Ehlana scarcely heard the sounds as she stared down at the square lying between the ruins of the temple and the only slightly less ruined palace.

The sun was fully above the eastern horizon now, and it filled the ancient streets of Cyrga with harsh, unforgiving light. The Queen of Elenia was exhausted, but the ordeal of her captivity was over, and she yearned only to lose herself in her husband's embrace. She did not understand much of what she had just witnessed, but that was not really important. She stood at the battlements holding the Child-Goddess in her arms, gazing down at her invincible champion far below.

"Do you think it might be safe for us to go down?" she asked the small divinity in her arms.

"The stairway's blocked, Ehlana," Mirtai reminded her.

"I can take care of that," Flute said.

"Maybe we'd better stay up here," Bevier said with a worried frown. "Cyrgon and Klæl are gone, but Zalasta's still out there somewhere. He might try to seize the queen again so that he can use her to bargain his way out of here."

"He'd better not," the Child-Goddess said ominously. "Ehlana's right. Let's go down."

They went back inside, reached the head of the stairs, and peered down through billowing clouds of dust. "What did you do?" Talen asked Flute. "Where did all the rocks go?"

She shrugged. "I turned them into sand," she replied.

The stairway wound downward along the inside of the tower walls. Kalten and Bevier, swords in hand, led the way, prudently investigating each level as they reached it. The top three or four levels were empty, but as they began the descent to a level about midway down the inside of the tower, Xanetia hissed sharply. "Someone approaches!"

"Where?" Kalten demanded. "How many?"

"Two, and they do mount the stairs toward us."

"I'll deal with them," he muttered, gripping his sword hilt even more tightly.

"Don't do anything foolish," Alean cautioned.

"It's the fellows coming up the stairs who are being foolish, love. Stay with the queen." He started on ahead.

"I'll go with him," Mirtai said. "Bevier, it's your turn to guard Ehlana."

"But—"

"Hush!" she commanded. "Do as you're told."

"Yes, ma'am," he surrendered with a faint smile.

A murmured sound of voices came echoing up the stairs.

"Santheocles!" Ehlana identified one of the speakers in a short, urgent whisper.

"And the other?" Xanetia asked.

"Ekatas."

"Ah," Xanetia said. Her pale brow furrowed in concentration. "This is not exact," she apologized, "but it seemeth me that they are unaware of thy release, Queen of Elenia, and they do rush to thy former prison, hoping that by threatening thy life might they gain safe conduct through the ranks of their enemies."

There was a landing perhaps twenty steps down the narrow stairway, and Kalten and Mirtai stopped there, stepping somewhat apart to give themselves room.

Santheocles, wearing his gleaming breastplate and crested helmet, came bounding up the stairs two at a time with his sword in his hand. He stopped suddenly when he reached the landing, staring at Kalten and Mirtai in stupefied disbelief. He waved his sword at them and issued a peremptory command in his own language.

"What did he say?" Talen demanded.

"He ordered them to get out of his way," Aphrael replied.

"Doesn't he realize that they're his enemies?"

"*Enemy* is a difficult concept for someone like Santheocles," Ehlana told him. "He's never been outside the walls of Cyrga, and I doubt that he's seen more than ten people who weren't Cyrgai in his entire life. The Cyrgai obey him automatically, so he hasn't had much experience with open hostility."

Ekatas came puffing up the stairs behind Santheocles. His eyes were wide with shock and his wrinkled face ashen. He spoke sharply to his king, and Santheocles placidly stepped aside. Ekatas drew himself up and began speaking sonorously, his hands moving in the air before him.

"Stop him!" Bevier cried. "He's casting a spell!"

"He's *trying* to cast a spell," Aphrael corrected. "I think he's in for a nasty surprise."

The high priest's voice rose in a long, slow crescendo and he suddenly leveled one arm at Kalten and Mirtai.

Nothing happened.

Ekatas held his empty hand up in front of his face, gaping at it in utter astonishment.

"Ekatas," Aphrael called sweetly to him, "I hate to be the bearer of bad tidings, but now that Cyrgon's dead, your spells won't work anymore."

He stared up at her, comprehension and recognition slowly dawning on his face. Then he spun and bolted through the door on the left side of the landing and slammed it behind him.

Mirtai moved quickly after him. She briefly tried the door, then stepped back and kicked it to pieces.

Kalten advanced on the sneering King of the Cyrgai. Santheocles struck a heroic pose, his oversized shield extended, his sword raised, and his head held high.

"He's no match for Kalten," Bevier said. "Why doesn't he run?"

"He doth believe himself invincible, Sir Bevier," Xanetia replied. "He hath slain many of his own soldiers on the practice field, and thus considers himself the paramount warrior in all the world. In truth, however, his subordinates would not strike back or even defend themselves, because he was their king."

Kalten, grim-faced and vengeful, fell on the feebleminded monarch like an avalanche. The face of Santheocles was filled with shock and outrage as, for the first time in his life, someone actually raised a weapon against him.

It was a short, ugly fight, and the outcome was quite predictable. Kalten battered down the oversized shield, parried a couple of stiffly formal swings at his head, and then buried his sword up to the hilt in the precise center of the burnished breastplate. Santheocles stared at him in sheer astonishment. Then he sighed, toppled backward off the blade, and clattered limply down the stairs.

"*Yes!*" Ehlana exulted in a savage voice as the most offensive of her persecutors died.

From beyond the splintered door came a long, despairing scream fading horribly away, and Mirtai emerged with an expression of bleak satisfaction.

"What did you do to him?" Kalten asked curiously.

"I defenestrated him," she replied with a shrug.

"*Mirtai!*" he gasped. "That's *awful!*"

She gave him a baffled look. "What are you talking about?"

"That's a *terrible* thing to do to a man!"

"Throw him out a window? I can think of much worse things to do to somebody."

"Is *that* what that word means?"

"Of course. Stragen used to talk about it back in Matherion."

"Oh." Kalten flushed slightly.

"What did you think it meant?"

"Ah—never mind, Mirtai. Just forget I said anything."

"You must have thought it meant *something*."

"Let's just drop it, shall we? I misunderstood, that's all." He looked up at the others. "Let's go on down," he suggested. "I don't think there'll be anybody else in our way."

Ehlana suddenly burst into tears. "I *can't*!" she wailed. "I can't face Sparhawk like this!" She put one hand on the wimple that covered her violated scalp.

"Are you still worrying about that?" Aphrael asked.

"I look so *awful*!"

Aphrael rolled her eyes upward. "Let's go into that room," she suggested. "I'll fix it for you—if it's so important."

"Could you?" Ehlana asked eagerly.

"Of course." The Child-Goddess squinted at her. "Would you like to have me change the color?" she asked. "Or maybe make it curly?"

The queen pursed her lips. "Why don't we talk about that a little?" she said.

The Cynesgans who manned the outer wall of the Hidden City were not particularly good troops in the first place, and when the Trolls came leaping out of No-Time to scramble up the walls toward them, they broke and ran.

"Did you tell the Trolls to open the gates for us?" Vanion asked Ulath.

"Yes, my Lord," the Genidian replied, "but it might be a little while before they remember. They're hungry right now. They'll eat breakfast first."

"We *have* to get inside, Ulath," Sephrenia said urgently. "We have to protect the slave pens."

"Oh, Lord," he said. "I forgot about that. The Trolls won't be able to distinguish slaves from Cynesgans."

"I'll go have a look," Khalad volunteered. He swung down from his horse and ran forward to the massively timbered gates. After a couple of moments he came back. "It's no particular problem, Lady Sephrenia," he reported. "Those gates would fall apart if you sneezed on them."

"What?"

"The timbers are very old, my Lady, and they're riddled with dry rot. With your permission, Lord Vanion, I'll take some men and rig up a battering ram. We'll knock down the gate so that we can get inside."

"Of course," Vanion replied.

"Come along, then, Berit," Khalad told his friend.

"That young man always manages to make me feel inadequate," Vanion muttered as they watched the pair ride back to rejoin the knights massed some yards to the rear.

"As I remember, his father had the same effect on you," Sephrenia said.

Kring came galloping back around the wall. "Friend Bergsten's preparing to assault the north gate," he reported.

"Send word to him to be careful, friend Kring," Betuana advised. "The Trolls are already inside the city—and they're hungry. It might be better if he delayed his attack just a little."

Kring nodded his agreement. "Working with Trolls changes the complexion of things, doesn't it, Betuana-Queen? They're very good allies in a fight, but you don't want to let them get hungry."

About ten minutes later, Khalad and a few dozen knights dragged a large log into place before the gate, suspended it on ropes attached to several makeshift tripods, and began to pound on the rotting timbers. The gate shuddered out billows of powdery red dust and began to crumble and fall apart.

"Let's go!" Vanion called tersely to his oddly assorted army, and led the way into the city. At Sephrenia's insistence, the knights went straight to the pens, freed the shackled slaves, and escorted them to safety outside the walls. Then Vanion's force moved directly to the inner wall that protected the steep hill rising in the middle of Cyrga.

"How long is that likely to last, Sir Ulath?" Vanion said, gesturing toward a cluster of ravening Trolls.

"It's a little hard to say, Lord Vanion," Ulath replied. "I don't think we'll get much cooperation from them as long as there are still Cynesgans running up and down the streets here in the outer city, though."

"Maybe it's just as well," Vanion decided. "I think *we* want to get to Sparhawk and the others before the Trolls do." He looked around. "Khalad," he called, "tell your men to drag that battering ram up here. Let's pound down the gate to the inner city and go find Sparhawk."

"Yes, my Lord," Khalad replied.

The gates to the inner wall were more substantial, and Khalad's ram was pounding out great booming sounds when Patriarch Bergsten came riding along the wall, accompanied by the veteran Pandion Sir Heldin, a Peloi whom Vanion did not recognize, and a tall, lithe Atan girl. Vanion was a bit startled to see that the Styric God Setras was also with them. "What do you think you're doing, Vanion?" Bergsten roared.

"Knocking down this gate, your Grace," Vanion replied.

"That's not what I'm talking about. What in God's name possessed you to let the Trolls make the initial assault?"

"It wasn't really a question of *let*, your Grace. They didn't exactly ask for permission."

"We've got absolute chaos here in the outer city. My knights can't concentrate on this inner wall because they keep running into Trolls. They're in a feeding frenzy, you know. Right now they'll eat anything that moves."

"Must you?" Sephrenia murmured with a shudder.

"Hello, Sephrenia," Bergsten said. "You're looking well. How much longer are you going to be with this gate, Vanion? Let's get our people into the inner city where all we have to worry about are the Cyrgai. Your allies are making my men very nervous." He looked up at the top of the inner wall, sharply outlined against the dawn sky. "I thought the Cyrgai were supposed to be soldiers. Why aren't they manning this wall?"

"They're a little demoralized right now," Sephrenia explained. "Sparhawk just killed their God."

"He *did*? I thought Bhelliom was going to do that."

She sighed. "In a certain sense it did," she said. "It's a little hard to separate the two of them at this point. Aphrael isn't entirely sure where Bhelliom leaves off and Sparhawk begins right now."

Bergsten shuddered. "I don't think I want to know about that," he confessed. "I'm in enough theological trouble already. What about Klæl?"

"He's gone. He was banished as soon as Sparhawk killed Cyrgon."

"Oh, fine, Vanion," Bergsten said with heavy sarcasm. "You make me ride a thousand leagues in the dead of winter, and the fighting's all over before I even get here."

"The exercise was probably good for you, your Grace." Vanion raised his voice. "How much longer, Khalad?" he called.

"Just a few more minutes, my Lord," Sparhawk's squire replied. "The timbers are starting to crack."

"Good," Vanion said bleakly. "I want to locate Zalasta. He and I have some things to talk about—at great length."

"They've all bolted, Sparhawk," Talen reported, returning from his quick survey of the ruined palace. "The gates are standing wide open, and we're the only people up here."

Sparhawk nodded wearily. It had been a long night, and he was emotionally as well as physically drained. He could still, however, feel that enormous calm that had settled over him when he had at last understood the true significance of his strange relationship with Bhelliom. There were some fleeting temptations—curiosity perhaps more than anything else—the desire to experiment and test the limits of newly recognized capabilities. He deliberately repressed them.

Go ahead, Sparhawk. Flute's voice in his mind had a slight challenge in it. He turned his head slightly to look quizzically at the ageless child standing beside his wife. Ehlana's face was serene as she ran her fingers through her long pale-blonde hair. *What did you want me to do?* he sent the thought back.

Anything that comes into your mind.

Why?

Aren't you just the least bit curious? Wouldn't you like to find out if you can turn a mountain inside out?

I can, he replied, *I don't see any reason to do something like that, though.*

You're hateful, Sparhawk! she suddenly flared.

What's your problem, Aphrael?

You're such a lump!

He smiled gently at her. *I know, but you love me anyway, don't you?*

"Sparhawk," Kalten called from the ornate bronze gate, "Vanion's coming up the hill. He's got Bergsten with him."

Vanion had known Sparhawk since his novitiate, but the weary-looking man in black armor seemed to be almost a stranger. There was something about his face and in his eyes that had never been there before. The preceptor approached his old friend with Patriarch Bergsten and Sephrenia with a sense of something very close to awe.

As soon as Ehlana saw Sephrenia, she ran to her with a low cry and embraced her fiercely.

"I see that you've wrecked another city, Sparhawk," Bergsten said with a broad grin. "That's getting to be a habit, you know."

"Good morning, your Grace," Sparhawk replied. "It's good to see you again."

"Did you do all this?" Bergsten gestured at the ruined temple and the half-collapsed palace.

"Klæl did most of it, your Grace."

The hulking churchman squared his shoulders. "I've got orders for you from Dolmant," he said. "You're supposed to turn the Bhelliom over to me. Why don't you do that now—before we both forget?"

"I'm afraid that isn't possible, your Grace," Sparhawk sighed. "I don't have it anymore."

"What did you do with it?"

"It no longer exists—at least not in the shape it was before. It's been freed from its confinement to continue its journey."

"You released it without consulting the Church? You're in trouble, Sparhawk."

"Oh, *do* be serious, Bergsten," Aphrael told him. "Sparhawk did what had to be done. I'll explain to Dolmant later."

Vanion, however, had something else on his mind. "This is all very interesting," he said bleakly, "but right now I'm far more concerned about finding Zalasta. Does anybody have any idea of where he went?"

"He might be under all that, Vanion," Ehlana told him, pointing at the ruined temple. "He and Ekatas were going there when they discovered that Sparhawk was here inside the walls of Cyrga. Ekatas escaped, and Mirtai killed him, but Zalasta might have been crushed when Klæl exploded the place."

"No," Aphrael said shortly. "He's nowhere in the city."

"I *really* want to find him, Divine One," Vanion said.

"Setras, dear," Aphrael said sweetly to her cousin, "would you see if you can find Zalasta for me? He has a great deal to answer for."

"I'll see what I can do, Aphrael," the handsome God promised, "but I really ought to get back to my studio. I've been letting my own work slide during all this."

"Please, Setras," she wheedled, unleashing that devastating little smile.

He laughed helplessly. "Do you see what I was talking about, Bergsten?" he said to the towering Patriarch. "She's the most dangerous creature in the universe."

"So I've heard," Bergsten replied. "You'd probably better go ahead and do as she asks, Setras. You'll do it in the end anyway."

"Ah, there you are, Itagne-Ambassador," Vanion heard Atana Maris say in a deceptively pleasant tone of voice. He turned and saw the lithe young commander of the garrison at Cynestra descending on the clearly apprehensive Tamul diplomat. "I've been looking all over for you," she continued. "We have a great deal to talk about. Somehow, not one of your letters reached me. I think you should reprimand your messenger."

Itagne's face took on a trapped expression.

Betuana dispatched runners to Matherion just before noon, when the last of the demoralized Cyrgai capitulated. Sir Ulath made some issue of the fact that what had happened to the Cynesgans in the outer city might have influenced their decision to surrender to some degree. Patriarch Bergsten had taken to looking at his countryman with a critical and speculative eye. Bergsten was a rough-and-ready churchman, willing to bend all sorts of rules in the name of expediency, but he choked just a bit on Ulath's unbridled ecumenicism. "He's just a little too enthusiastic, Sparhawk," the huge Patriarch declared. "All right, I'll grant you that the Trolls were sort of useful, but—" He groped for a way to express his innate prejudices.

"There's a rather special kinship between Ulath and Bhlokw, your Grace." Sparhawk sidestepped the issue. "How much have we got left to do here? I'd sort of like to get my wife back to civilization."

"You can leave now, Sparhawk," Bergsten said with a shrug. "We can take care of cleaning up here. You didn't leave very much for the rest of us to worry about. I'll stay here with the knights to finish rounding up the Cyrgai; Tikume will take his Peloi back to Cynestra to help Itagne and Atana Maris set up the occupation; and Betuana's going to send her Atans into Arjuna to reestablish imperial authority." He made a sour face. "There's nothing really left but all the niggling little administrative details. You've robbed me of a very good fight, Sparhawk."

"I can send for more of Klæl's soldiers if you want, your Grace."

"No. That's all right, Sparhawk," Bergsten replied quickly. "I can live without any more of *those* fights. You'll be going straight back to Matherion?"

"Not straight back, your Grace. Courtesy obliges us to escort Anarae Xanetia back to Delphaeus."

"She's a very strange lady," Bergsten mused. "I keep catching myself just on the verge of genuflection every time she enters a room."

"She has that effect on people, your Grace. If you really don't need us here, I'll talk with the others, and we'll get ready to leave."

"What actually happened, Sparhawk?" Bergsten asked directly. "I have to make a report to Dolmant, and I can't make much sense out of what the others have been telling me."

"I'm not sure I can explain it, your Grace," Sparhawk replied. "Bhelliom and I were sort of combined for a while. It needed my arm, I guess." It was an easy answer, and it evaded a central issue that Sparhawk was not yet fully prepared to even think about.

"You were just a tool, then?" Bergsten's look was intent.

Sparhawk shrugged. "Aren't we all, your Grace? We're the instruments of God. That's what we get paid for."

"Sparhawk, you're right on the verge of heresy here. Don't throw the word *God* around like that."

"No, your Grace," Sparhawk agreed. "It's just a reflection of the limitations of language. There are things that we don't understand and don't have names for. We just lump them all together, call it *God,* and let it go at that. You and I are soldiers, Patriarch Bergsten. We get paid to hit the ground running when somebody blows a trumpet. Let Dolmant sort it out. That's what *he* gets paid for."

Sparhawk and his friends, accompanied by Kring, Betuana, and Engessa, rode out of shattered Cyrga shortly after dawn the following morning, bound for Sarna. Sparhawk had neither seen nor heard from Bhelliom since his encounter with Cyrgon, and he felt a peculiar sense of disappointment about that. The Troll-Gods had also departed with their children—all except for Bhlokw, who shambled along between Ulath and Tynian. Bhlokw was evasive about his reasons for accompanying them.

They rode northeast across the barren wastes of Cynesga, traveling in easy stages. The urgent need for haste was gone now. Sephrenia and Xanetia, once again working in concert, had returned all the faces to their rightful owners, and things were slowly settling back to normal.

It was about midmorning ten days after they had left Cyrga and when they were but a few leagues from Sarna that Vanion rode forward to join Sparhawk at the head of the column. "A word with you, Sparhawk?" he said.

"Of course."

"It's sort of private."

Sparhawk nodded, turned the column over to Bevier, and nudged Faran into a rolling canter. He and Vanion slowed again when they were about a quarter of a mile ahead of the others. "Sephrenia wants us to get married," Vanion said, cutting past any preamble.

"You're asking my permission?"

Vanion gave him a long, steady look.

"Sorry," Sparhawk apologized. "You took me by surprise. There are problems with that, you know. The Church will never approve, and neither will the Thousand of Styricum. We're not quite as hidebound as we used to be, but the notion of interracial or interfaith marriage still raises some hackles."

"I know," Vanion said glumly. "Dolmant probably wouldn't have any personal objections, but his hands are tied by Church law and doctrine."

"Who are you going to get to officiate, then?"

"Sephrenia's already solved that problem. Xanetia's going to perform the ceremony."

Sparhawk nearly choked on that.

"She *is* a priestess, Sparhawk."

"Well—technically, I suppose." Then Sparhawk suddenly broke out laughing.

"What's so funny?" Vanion demanded truculently.

"Can you imagine the look on Ortzel's face when he hears that a preceptor of one of the four orders, a Patriarch of the Church, has been married to one of the Thousand of Styricum by a Delphaeic priestess?"

"It *does* violate a few rules, doesn't it?" Vanion conceded with a wry smile.

"A *few*? Vanion, I doubt that you could find any single act that'd violate more."

"Do you object, too?"

"Not me, old friend. If this is what you and Sephrenia want, I'll back the two of you all the way up to the Hierocracy."

"Would you stand up with me, then? During the ceremony, I mean?"

Sparhawk clapped him on the shoulder. "I'd be honored, my friend."

"Good. That'll keep it all in the family. Sephrenia's already spoken to your wife about it. Ehlana's going to stand with her."

"Somehow I almost knew that was coming." Sparhawk laughed.

They passed through Sarna and proceeded north along a snow-clogged mountain trail toward Dirgis in southern Atan. After they left Dirgis, they turned westward again and rode higher into the mountains.

"We're leaving a very wide trail behind us, Sparhawk," Bevier said late one snowy afternoon, "and the trail's leading directly to Delphaeus."

Sparhawk turned and looked back. "You've got a point," he conceded. "Maybe I'd better have a talk with Aphrael. Things have changed a bit, but I don't think the Delphae are *quite* ready to welcome crowds of sightseers." He turned Faran around and rode back to join the ladies. Aphrael, as usual, rode with Sephrenia. "A suggestion, Divine One?" Sparhawk said tentatively.

"You sound just like Tynian."

He ignored that. "How good are you with weather?" he asked.

"Did you want it to be summer?"

"No. Actually I want a moderate-sized blizzard. We're leaving tracks in the snow behind us, and the tracks are pointing right straight at Delphaeus."

"What difference does that make?"

"The Delphae might not want unannounced visitors."

"There won't be any—announced or otherwise. You promised to seal their valley, didn't you?"

"Oh, God!" he said. "I'd forgotten about that! This is going to be a problem. I don't have Bhelliom anymore."

"Then you'd better try to get in touch with it, Sparhawk. A promise is a promise, after all. Xanetia's kept her part of the bargain, so you're morally obliged to keep yours."

Sparhawk was troubled. He rode off some distance into a thick grove of spindly sapling pines and dismounted. "Blue-Rose," he said aloud, not really expecting an answer. "Blue-Rose."

I hear thee, Anakha, the voice in his mind responded immediately. *I had thought thou might be in some way discontent with me.*

Never that, Blue-Rose. Thou hast fulfilled—or exceeded—all that I did require of thee. Our enemies are overthrown, and I am content. I did, however, pledge mine honor to the Delphae in exchange for their aid. I am obliged to seal up their valley that none of this world may come upon them.

I do recall thy pledge, Anakha. It was well given. Soon, however, it will not be needful.

Thy meaning escapes me.

Watch then, my son, and learn. There was a lengthy pause. *It is not mine intent to offend, but why hast thou brought this to me?*

I gave my word that I would seal their valley, Father.

Then seal it.

I was not certain that I could still speak with thee to entreat thine aid.

Thou hast no need of aid, Anakha—not mine nor that of any other. Did not thine encounter with Cyrgon convince thee that all things are possible for thee? Thou are Anakha and my son, and there is none other like thee in all the starry universe. It was needful to make thee so, that my design might be accomplished. Whatsoever thou couldst do through me, thou couldst as easily have done with thine own hand. The voice paused. *I am, however, somewhat pleased that thou wert unaware of thine ability, for it did give me some opportunity to come to know thee. I shall think often of thee in my continuing journey. Let us then proceed to Delphaeus, where thy comrade Vanion and our dearly loved Sephrenia will be joined, and where thou wilt behold a wonder.*

Which particular wonder is that, Blue-Rose?

'Twould hardly be a wonder for thee shouldst thou know of it in advance, my son. There were faint traces of amusement in the voice as the sense of Bhelliom's presence faded.

It was early on a snowy evening when they crested a ridge and looked down into the valley where the glowing lake, misty in the swirling snowflakes, shone with a light almost like that of the moon. Ancient Cedon awaited them at the rude gate to this other hidden city, and standing beside him was Itagne's friend, Ekrasios.

They talked until quite late, for there was much to share. It was midmorning of the following day before Sparhawk awoke in the oddly sunken bedroom he shared with his wife. It was one of the peculiarities of Delphaeic construction that the floors of most of their rooms were below ground-level. Sparhawk didn't give it much thought, but Khalad had seemed quite intrigued by the notion.

Sparhawk gently kissed his still-sleeping wife, slipped quietly from their bed, and went looking for Vanion. He remembered his own wedding day, and he was quite sure that his friend was going to need some support.

He found the silvery-haired preceptor talking with Talen and Khalad in the makeshift stable. Khalad's face was bleak. "What's the problem?" Sparhawk asked as he joined them.

"My brother's a little unhappy," Talen explained. "He talked with Ekrasios and the other Delphae who dispersed Scarpa's army down in Arjuna, and nobody could tell him one way or the other about what happened to Krager."

"I'm going to operate on the theory that he's still alive," Khalad declared. "He's just too slippery not to have escaped."

"We have plans for you, Khalad," Vanion told him. "You're too valuable to spend your whole life trying to chase down a weaselly drunkard who may or may not have gotten out of Natayos alive."

"It won't take him all that long, Lord Vanion," Talen said. "As soon as Stragen and I get back to Cimmura, we'll talk with Platime, and he'll put out the word. If Krager's still alive—anywhere in the world—we'll find out about it."

"What are the ladies doing?" Vanion asked nervously.

"Ehlana's still asleep," Sparhawk replied. "Are you and Sephrenia going back to Matherion with us when we leave here?"

"Briefly," Vanion replied. "Sephrenia wants to speak with Sarabian about a few things. Then we'll go back to Atan with Betuana and Engessa. It's only a short trip from there to Sarsos. Have you noticed what's going on between Betuana and Engessa, by the way?"

Sparhawk nodded. "Evidently Betuana's decided that the Atans need a king. Engessa's suitable, and he's probably a great deal more intelligent than Androl was."

"That's not saying too much for him, Sparhawk," Talen said with a broad grin. "Androl was hardly any more intelligent than a brick."

The day wore on. The ladies, of course, made extended preparations. The knights, on the other hand, did what they could to keep Vanion's mind occupied.

An obscure tenet of the Delphaeic faith dictated that the ceremony take place on the shore of the glowing lake just at dusk. Sparhawk dimly perceived why this might be appropriate for the Shining Ones, but the wedding of Vanion and Sephrenia had little if anything to do with the covenant between the Delphae and their God. Courtesy, however, dictated that he keep his opinions to himself. He *did* offer to clothe Vanion in traditional black Pandion armor, but the preceptor chose instead to wear a white Styric robe. "I've fought my last war, Sparhawk," he said a bit sadly. "Dolmant won't have any choice but to excommunicate me and strip me of my knighthood after this. That makes me a civilian again. I never really enjoyed wearing armor all that much anyway." He looked curiously at Ulath and Tynian, who were talking earnestly with Bhlokw just outside the stable door. "What's going on there?"

"They're trying to explain the concept of a wedding to their friend. They aren't making very much headway."

"I don't imagine that Trolls set much store in ceremonies."

"Not really. When a male feels that way about a female, he takes her something—or somebody—to eat. If she eats it, they're married."

"And if she doesn't?"

Sparhawk shrugged. "They usually try to kill each other."

"Do you have any idea of why Bhlokw didn't go off with the rest of the Trolls?"

"Not a clue, Vanion. We haven't been able to get a straight answer out of him. Evidently there's something the Troll-Gods want him to do."

The afternoon dragged on, and Vanion grew more and more edgy with each passing moment. Inevitably, however, the grey day slid into a greyer evening, and dusk settled over the hidden valley of Delphaeus.

The path from the city gate to the edge of the lake had been carefully cleared, and Aphrael, who was not above cheating on occasion, had strewn it with flower petals. The Delphae, all aglow and singing an ancient hymn, lined the sides of the path. Vanion waited at the edge of the lake with Sparhawk, and the other members of their party stood in smiling anticipation as Sephrenia, with Ehlana at her side, emerged from the city to walk down to the shore.

"Courage, my son," Sparhawk murmured to his old friend.

"Are you trying to be funny?"

"Getting married doesn't really hurt, Vanion."

It happened when the bride and her attendant were perhaps halfway to the lakeshore. A sudden cloud of inky darkness appeared at the edge of the snow-covered meadow, and a great voice bellowed, *"NO!"* Then a spark of incandescent light emerged from the center of the cloud and began to swell ominously, surging and surrounded by a blazing halo of purplish light. Sparhawk recognized the phenomenon.

"I forbid this abomination!" the great voice roared.

"Zalasta!" Kalten exclaimed, staring at the rapidly expanding sphere.

The Styric was haggard and his hair and beard were matted. He wore his customary white robe and held his polished staff in his trembling hands. He stood inside the glowing sphere, surrounded by its protective nimbus. Sparhawk felt an icy calm descending over him as he prepared his mind and spirit for the inevitable confrontation.

"I have lost you, Sephrenia!" Zalasta declared, "but I *will* not permit you to wed this Elene!"

Aphrael dashed to her sister, her long black hair flying and a look of implacable determination on her small face.

"Fear not, Aphrael," Zalasta said, speaking in formal Styric. "I have not come to this accursed place to pit myself against thee or thine errant sister. I speak for Styricum in this matter, and I have come to prevent this obscene sham of a ceremony which will befoul our entire race." He straightened and pointed an accusing finger at Sephrenia. "I abjure thee, woman. Turn away from this unnatural act! Go out from here, Sephrenia of Ylara! This wedding shall not take place!"

"It *will*!" Sephrenia's voice rang out. "You cannot prevent it! Go away, Zalasta! You lost all claim on me when you tried to kill me!" She raised her chin. "And have you come to try again?"

"No, Sephrenia of Ylara. That was the result of a madness that came over me. There is yet another way to prevent this abomination." And he quickly turned, leveling his deadly staff at Vanion. A brilliant spark shot from the tip of the staff, sizzling in the pale evening light, straight as an arrow it flew, carrying death and all Zalasta's hatred.

But vigilant Anakha was ready, having already surmised at whom Zalasta would direct his attack. The deadly bolt flew straight, but agile Anakha stretched forth his hand to subdue it. He grasped the spark and saw its fury spurting out between his fingers. Then, like a small boy throwing a stone at a bird, he hurled it back to explode against the surface of the blazing sphere.

Well done, my son, Bhelliom's voice applauded.

Zalasta flinched violently within his protective sphere. Pale and shaken, he stared at the dreadful form of Bhelliom's Child.

Methodical Anakha raised his hand, palm outward, and began to chip away at the blazing envelope that protected the desperate Styric with bolt after bolt of the kind of force that creates suns, noting almost absently as he did that the wedding guests were scattering and that Sephrenia was rushing to Vanion's side. As he whipped out that force again and again, curious Anakha studied it, testing its power, probing for its limits.

He found none.

Implacable Anakha advanced on the deceitful Styric who had been ultimately the cause of a lifetime of suffering and woe. He knew that he could obliterate the now-terrified sorcerer with a single thought.

He chose not to.

Vengeful Anakha moved forward, savaging the Styric's last desperately erected defenses, cutting them away bit by bit and brushing aside Zalasta's pitiful efforts to respond.

"Anakha! It is not right!" The voice spoke in Trollish.

Puzzled Anakha turned to look.

It was Bhlokw, and Bhelliom's Child had respect for the shaggy priest of the Troll-Gods.

"This is the last of the wicked ones!" Bhlokw declared. "It is the wish of Khwaj to cause hurt to it! Will the Child of the flower-gem hear the words of Khwaj?"

Troubled Anakha considered the words of the priest of the Troll-Gods. "I will hear the words of Khwaj," he said. "It is right that I should do this, for Khwaj and I are pack-mates."

The enormity of the Fire-God appeared, steaming away the snow covering the meadow around him. "Will Bhelliom's Child be bound by the word of his pack-mate, Ulath-from-Thalesia?" he demanded in a voice that roared like a furnace.

"The word of Ulath-from-Thalesia is my word, Khwaj," honorable Anakha conceded.

"Then the wicked one is mine!"

Regretful Anakha curbed his wrath. "The words of Khwaj are right words," he agreed. "If Ulath-from-Thalesia has given the wicked one to Khwaj, then I will not say that it shall not be so." He looked at the terrified Styric, who was struggling desperately to retain some small measure of defense. "It is yours, Khwaj. It has caused me much hurt, and I would cause hurt to it in return, but if Ulath-from-Thalesia has said that it is the place of Khwaj to cause hurt to it, then so be it."

"Bhelliom's Child speaks well. You have honor, Anakha." The Fire-God looked accusingly at Zalasta. "You have done great wickedness, one-called-Zalasta."

Zalasta stared at Khwaj in terrified incomprehension.

"Say to it what I have said, Anakha," Khwaj requested. "It must know why it is being punished."

Courteous Anakha said, "I will, Khwaj." He looked sternly at the disheveled Styric. "You have caused me much pain, Zalasta," he said in a dreadful voice, speaking in Styric. "I was going to repay you for all those friends of mine you destroyed or corrupted, but Khwaj here has laid claim to you, and I'm going to honor his claim. You should have stayed away, Zalasta. Vanion would have hunted you down eventually, but death is a little thing, and once it's over, it's over. What Khwaj is going to do to you will last for eternity."

"Does it understand?" Khwaj demanded.

"In some measure, Khwaj."

"In time it will understand more, and it has much time. It has always." And the dreadful Fire-God moved forward, blew away Zalasta's last pitiful defenses, and laid a strangely gentle hand on the cringing Styric's head. "Burn!" he commanded. "Run and burn until the end of days!"

And, all aflame, Zalasta of Styricum went out from that place shrieking and engulfed in endless fire.

Compassionate Anakha sighed as he watched the burning man run out across the snowy meadow, growing smaller and smaller in the distance and with his cries of agony and woe and unspeakable loneliness receding with him as he began the first hour of his eternal punishment.

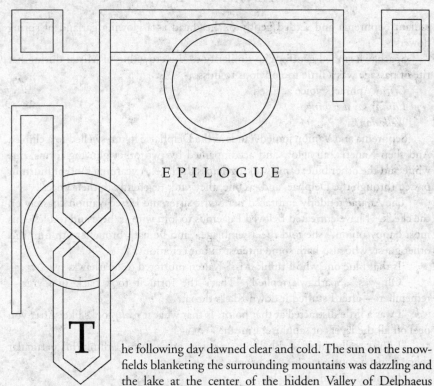

EPILOGUE

The following day dawned clear and cold. The sun on the snow-fields blanketing the surrounding mountains was dazzling and the lake at the center of the hidden Valley of Delphaeus steamed. The wedding had been postponed, of course, and was now to take place this evening.

There had been questions, naturally, but Sparhawk had put them to rest by explaining that everything that had happened had been Bhelliom's doing, and that he had only been its instrument—which was not *exactly* a lie.

They spent the day quietly and gathered again as the sun went down and the shadows of evening settled over the valley. A strange sense of anticipation had nagged at Sparhawk all afternoon. Something was going to happen here. Bhelliom had told him that he would behold a wonder, and that was not the kind of word Bhelliom would use lightly.

The shadows of evening deepened, and Sparhawk and the other men escorted Vanion down to the shore of the glowing lake to await the bride's party while the Shining Ones once again sang the ancient hymn which had been so abruptly broken off the previous evening.

Then the bride appeared at the gate with the Queen of Elenia at her side and the other ladies close behind them. The Child-Goddess, whirling and dancing in the air and with her clear voice raised in flute-song, preceded them, again strewing their path with flower petals.

Sephrenia's face was serene as she came down the path to the lake. As the small Styric bride approached the man whom two major religions had forbidden her to marry, her personal Goddess provided a visible symbol that *she*, at least, approved. The stars had just begun to appear overhead, and one of them seemed to have lost its way. Like a tiny comet, a brilliant spark of light descended over the radiant Sephrenia and settled gently on her head as a glowing garland of spring flowers.

Sparhawk smiled gently. The similarity to the crowning of Mirtai during her rite of passage was a little too obvious to miss.

Critic, Aphrael's voice accused.

I didn't say anything.

Well, don't.

Sephrenia and Vanion joined hands as the Delphaeic hymn swelled to a climax. And then Xanetia, all aglow and accompanied by two other glowing forms, one white and the other blue, came walking across the lake. A yearning kind of murmur passed through the Delphae, and, as one, they sank reverently to their knees.

The Anarae tenderly embraced her Styric sister and kissed Vanion chastely on the cheek. "I have entreated Belovèd Edaemus to join with us here and to bless this most happy union," she told the assemblage, "and he hath brought with him this other guest, who also hath some interest in our ceremony."

"Is that blue one who I think it is?" Kalten muttered to Sparhawk.

"Oh, yes," Sparhawk replied. "That's the form it took back in Cyrga—remember?—after I stuffed it down Klæl's throat."

"I was a little distracted at that point. Is that what it *really* looks like? After you peel off all the layers of sapphire, I mean?"

"I don't really think so. Bhelliom's a spirit, not a form. I think this particular shape is just a courtesy—for our benefit."

"I thought it had already left."

"No, not quite yet."

The glowing form of Edaemus straightened, somehow managing to look uncomfortable. Xanetia's face hardened and her eyes narrowed.

"I had thought ill of thee, Sephrenia of Ylara," the God of the Delphae admitted. "Mine Anarae hath persuaded me that my thought was in error. I do entreat thee to forgive me." Gentle Xanetia, it appeared, was not above a certain amount of bullying.

Sephrenia smiled benignly. "Of course I forgive thee, Divine Edaemus. I was not entirely blameless myself, I do confess."

"Let us all then pray to our separate Gods to bless the union of this man and this woman," Xanetia said in formal tones, "for methinks it doth presage a new birth of understanding and trust for all of mankind."

Sparhawk was a little dubious about that, but like the others, he bowed his head. He did not, however, direct his words to his Elene God. *Blue-Rose,* he sent out his thought.

Art thou praying, my son? The answering voice sounded slightly amused.

Consulting, Blue-Rose, Sparhawk corrected. *Others will direct our entreaty to our Elene God, and I do perceive that the time fast approaches when thou and I must part.*

Truly.

I thought to take this opportunity to ask a boon of thee.

If it be within my power.

I have seen the extent of thy power, Blue-Rose—and in some measure shared it. It is uncandid of thee to suggest that there are any limits to what thou canst do.

Be nice, Bhelliom murmured. It seemed to have become quite fond of that particular phrase. *What is this boon, my son?*

I do entreat thee to take all *thy power with thee when thou dost depart. It is a burden I am unprepared to accept. I am thy son, Blue-Rose, but I am also a man. I have neither the patience nor the wisdom to accept responsibility for what thou hast bestowed upon me. This world which thou hast made hath Gods in plenty. She doth not need another.*

Think, my son. Think of what thou dost propose to surrender.

I have, my father. I have been Anakha, for it was needful. Sparhawk struggled for a way to put his feelings into archaic Elenic. *When I did as Anakha confront the Styric Zalasta, I did feel a great detachment within myself, and that detachment abideth within me still. It seemeth me that thy gift hath altered me, making me more—or less— than a man. I would, an it please thee, no longer be "patient Anakha" or "curious Anakha" or "implacable Anakha." Anakha's task is finished. Now, with all my heart, I would be Sparhawk again. To be "loving Sparhawk" or even "irritated Sparhawk" would please me far more than the dreadful emptiness which is Anakha.*

There was a long pause. *Know that I am well pleased with thee, my son.* There was pride in the silent voice in Sparhawk's mind. *I find more merit in thee in this moment than in any other. Be well, Sparhawk.* And the voice was gone.

The wedding ceremony was strange in some ways and very familiar in others. The celebration of the love that existed between Vanion and Sephrenia was there, but the preaching that distinguished the Elene ritual was not. At the conclusion, Xanetia gently laid her hands in loving benediction upon the heads of the two she had just joined. The gesture seemed to proclaim that the ceremony was at an end.

But it was not.

The second of the two figures that had accompanied Xanetia across the luminous waters of the lake stepped forward, all glowing blue, to add its own benediction. It raised its hands over the man and the woman, and for a brief moment they shared its azure incandescence. And when the light faded, Sephrenia had subtly changed. The cares and weariness which had marked her face in a dozen tiny ways were gone, and she appeared to be no older than Alean. The changes Bhelliom's glowing touch had wrought on Vanion were more visible and pronounced. His shoulders, which had imperceptibly slumped over the years, were straight again. His face was unlined, and his silvery hair and beard were now the dark auburn Sparhawk dimly remembered from the days of his novitiate. It was Bhelliom's final gift, and nothing could have pleased Sparhawk more.

Aphrael clapped her hands together with a squeal of delight and flew into the arms of the nebulous, glowing figure that had just rejuvenated her sister and Vanion.

Sparhawk rather carefully concealed a smile. The Child-Goddess had finally maneuvered Bhelliom into a position where she could unleash the devastating effects of her kisses upon it. The kisses *could,* of course, have been pure, effusive gratitude—but they probably weren't.

The wedding was at an end, but the glowing Delphae did not return to their empty city. Xanetia placed one supporting arm around Anari Cedon's frail old shoulders and guided him instead out onto the radiant surface of the lake, and the

Shining Ones followed, raising a different hymn as incandescent Edaemus hovered in the air above them. The light of the lake grew brighter and brighter, and the ethereal glow of the Delphae seemed to merge, and individual figures were no longer distinguishable. Then, like the point of a spear, Edaemus streaked skyward, and all of his children streamed upward behind him. When Sparhawk and his friends had first come to Delphaeus, Anari Cedon had told them that the Delphae journeyed toward the light and that they would *become* the light, but that there were yet impediments. Bhelliom had evidently removed those barriers. The Delphae marked the starry sky like a comet as they rose together on the first step of their inconceivable journey.

The pale, clear radiance of the lake was gone, but it was not dark. An azure spark hung over it as Bhelliom surveyed what it had wrought and found that it was good. Then it, too, rose from the earth to rejoin the eternal stars.

They stayed that night in deserted Delphaeus, and Sparhawk awoke early as usual. He dressed himself quietly and left the simple bedroom and his tousled, sleeping wife to go outside to check the weather.

Flute joined him when he reached the city gate. "Why don't you put some shoes on?" he asked her, noting that her bare, grass-stained little feet were sunk in the snow.

"What do I need with shoes, Father?" She held out her arms, and he picked her up.

"It was quite a night, wasn't it?" he said, looking up at the cloudy sky.

"Why did you do that, Sparhawk?"

"Do what?"

"You know what I mean. Do you realize what you could have done? You could have turned this world into a paradise, but you threw it all away."

"I don't think that would have been a good idea, Aphrael. My idea of paradise would probably have been different from other people's." He sniffed at the chill air. "I think we've got weather coming," he observed.

"Don't change the subject. You had ultimate power. Why did you give it up?"

He sighed. "I didn't really like it all that much. There wasn't any effort involved in it, and when you get something without working for it, it doesn't really have any value. Besides, there are people who have claims on me."

"What's that got to do with it?"

"What could I have done if Ehlana had decided that she wanted Arcium? Or if Dolmant had decided that he wanted to convert Styricum, or all of Tamuli? I have loyalties and obligations, Aphrael, and sooner or later, I'd have made bad decisions because of them. Trust me. I made the right choice."

"I think you're going to regret it."

"I've regretted lots of things. You learn to live with it. Can you get us to Matherion?"

"You could have done it yourself, you know."

"Don't beat it into the ground, Aphrael. If you don't want to, then we'll just plow our way through the snow. We've done it before."

"You're hateful, Sparhawk. You *know* I won't let you do that."

"*Now* do you see what I mean about the power of loyalties and obligations?"

"Don't start lecturing me. I'm in no mood for it. Go wake up the others, and let's get started."

"Whatever you say, Divine One."

They located the rather large communal kitchen in which the Delphae had prepared all their meals and the storerooms where the food was kept. Despite their eons of enmity, the dietary prejudices of the Styrics and Delphae were remarkably similar. Sephrenia found the breakfast much to her liking, but Kalten grumbled a great deal. He *did* eat three helpings, however.

"Whatever happened to friend Bhlokw?" Kring asked, pushing back his plate. "I just realized that I haven't seen him since Zalasta took fire."

"He went off with his Gods, Domi," Tynian replied. "He did what they sent him to do, and now he and the rest of the Trolls are on their way back to Thalesia. He wished us all good hunting. That's about as close as a Troll can come to saying good-bye."

"It might sound a little strange," Kring admitted, "but I liked him."

"He's a good pack-mate," Ulath said. "He hunts well, and he's willing to share what he kills with the others in the pack."

"Oh, yes," Tynian agreed with a shudder. "If it wasn't a freshly killed dog, it was a haunch of raw Cyrgai."

"It was what he had, Tynian," Ulath defended his shaggy friend, "and he was ready to share it. You can't ask more than that, can you?"

"Sir Ulath," Talen said, "I've just eaten. Do you suppose we could talk about something else?"

They saddled their horses and rode out of Delphaeus.

As he left, Khalad reined in, dismounted, and closed the gate. "Why did you do that?" Talen asked him. "The Delphae aren't coming back, you know."

"It's the proper thing to do," Khalad said as he remounted. "Leaving it open would have been disrespectful."

Since they all knew who she really was, Flute made no attempt to conceal her tampering this time. The horses plodded along, as horses will if they aren't being pushed, but every few minutes the horizon flickered and changed. Once, somewhat east of Dirgis, Sparhawk rose in his stirrups to look to the rear. Their clearly visible trail stretched back to the middle of an open meadow where it stopped abruptly, almost as if the horses and riders had been dropped there out of the sky.

They reached the now-familiar hilltop overlooking fire-domed Matherion and its harbor just as evening was approaching, and they rode down to the city gratefully. They had all been long on the road, and it was good to be home again. Sparhawk rather quickly amended that thought in his mind. Matherion was not really home. Home was a dank, unlovely city on the Cimmura River, half a world away.

There were some startled looks at the gate of the imperial compound, and some that were even more startled at the drawbridge to Ehlana's castle. Vanion had stubbornly rejected his wife's urgings to conceal his head and face with the hood of his cloak and quite literally flaunted the fact that thirty-odd years had somehow fallen away. Vanion was like that sometimes.

There were some visible changes inside the castle as well. They found the emperor in the blue-draped sitting room on the second floor, and in addition to Baroness Melidere, Emban, and Oscagne, three of his wives, Elysoun, Gahenas, and Liatris, were also present. Elysoun was probably the most notable, since she was now modestly dressed.

"Good God, Vanion!" Emban exclaimed when he saw the Pandion Preceptor. "What's happened to you?"

"I got married, your Grace," Vanion replied. He smoothed back his mahogany-colored hair. "This was one of the wedding presents. Do you like it?"

"You look ridiculous!"

"Oh, I wouldn't say that," Sephrenia disagreed. "*I* rather like it."

"I gather that congratulations are in order," Sarabian said urbanely. There was a marked difference in the Tamul emperor. He had a self-confidence and a commanding presence that had not been there before. "Considering the enormous religious barriers, who performed the ceremony?"

"Xanetia did, your Majesty," Vanion replied. "Delphaeic doctrine didn't have any objections."

Sarabian looked around. "Where *is* Xanetia?" he asked.

Sephrenia pointed upward with one finger. "Out there," she replied rather sadly, "with the rest of the Delphae."

"What?" The emperor's expression was baffled.

"Edaemus took them, Sarabian," Flute explained. "Evidently he and Bhelliom made some sort of arrangement." She looked around. "Where's Danae?"

"She's in her room, Divine One," Baroness Melidere said. "She was a little tired, so she went to bed early."

"I'd better go tell her that her mother's home," the Child-Goddess said, going toward the door leading back into the rest of the apartment.

"We've received any number of reports," Foreign Minister Oscagne said, "but they were all couched in generalities—'the war's over, and we won,' that sort of thing. No offense intended, Queen Betuana. Your Atans are excellent messengers, but it's hard to get details out of them."

She shrugged. "Perhaps it's a racial flaw, Oscagne-Excellency." As she always did now, Betuana stood very close to the silent Engessa. She seemed reluctant to let him get very far away from her side.

"The thing that puzzles me the most is the rather garbled message I got from my brother," Oscagne confessed.

"Itagne-Ambassador has a great deal on his mind just now," Betuana said blandly.

"Oh?"

"He and Atana Maris became quite friendly when he was posted to Cynestra last fall. *He* didn't take it too seriously, but *she* did. She came looking for him. She found him in Cyrga and took him back with her to Cynestra."

"Really?" Oscagne said, his face betraying no hint of a smile. Then he shrugged. "Oh, well," he added, "it's time that Itagne settled down anyway. As I recall, Atana Maris is a very vigorous young woman."

"Yes, Oscagne-Excellency, and very determined. I think your clever brother's days as a bachelor are numbered."

"What a shame," Oscagne sighed. "Pardon me a moment." He went rather quickly into the next room, and they all heard the sounds of muffled laughter coming from there.

And then Danae, her black hair flying, came running into the room to hurl herself into her mother's arms.

Sarabian's face went bleak. "Who finally killed Zalasta?" he asked. "He was at the bottom of all this, when you get right down to it."

"Zalasta isn't dead," Sephrenia said sorrowfully, lifting Flute into her lap.

"He *isn't*? How did he manage to get away?"

"We let him go, your Majesty," Ulath replied.

"Are you mad? You *know* the kind of trouble he can stir up."

"He won't be causing any more trouble, your Majesty," Vanion said, "unless he happens to start a few grass fires."

"He won't do that, Vanion," Flute said. "It's a spiritual fire, not a real one."

"Will somebody *please* tell me what happened?" Sarabian said.

"Zalasta showed up at Sephrenia's wedding, your Majesty," Ulath told him. "He tried to kill Vanion, but Sparhawk stopped him. Then our friend here was just about to do something fairly permanent about Zalasta, but Khwaj asserted a prior claim. Sparhawk considered the politics of the situation and agreed. Then Khwaj set Zalasta on fire."

"What a gruesome idea." Sarabian shuddered. Then he looked at Sephrenia. "I thought you said that he isn't dead. But Sir Ulath just told me that he'd been burned to death."

"No, your Majesty," Ulath corrected. "I just said that Khwaj set fire to him. The same thing happened to Baron Parok."

"The Trollish notion of justice sort of appeals to me," Sarabian said with a bleak smile. "How long will they burn?"

"Forever, your Majesty," Tynian replied somberly. "The fire is eternal."

"Good God!"

"It's further than I'd have gone," Sparhawk conceded, "but as Ulath said, there were political considerations involved."

They talked until quite late, providing details of the campaign, the rescue of Ehlana and Alean, the freeing of Bhelliom, and the final confrontation between Sparhawk and Cyrgon. Sparhawk rather carefully stressed his surrogacy in that particular event and made some issue of the fact that he was no longer Anakha. He wanted that particular book permanently closed with no doubts remaining in anyone's mind that there was absolutely no way to reopen it.

Also during the course of that long conversation, Sarabian told them of the attempt on his life by Chacole and Torellia. "They might have actually pulled it off if it hadn't been for Elysoun," he concluded, looking fondly at his now-demure Valesian wife.

Mirtai looked at Elysoun with one questioningly raised eyebrow. "Why the change of costume?" she asked bluntly.

Elysoun shrugged. "I'm with child," she replied. "I guess my days of adventuring are over." She looked at Mirtai's puzzled expression. "It's a Valesian custom," she explained. "We're allowed a certain amount of freedom until our first pregnancy. After that, we're supposed to behave ourselves." She smiled. "I'd more or less exhausted the potentials of the imperial compound anyway," she added. "Now it's time to settle down—and catch up on my sleep."

"Has anybody heard from Stragen and Caalador?" Talen asked.

"Viscount Stragen and Duke Caalador came back to Matherion a week ago," Sarabian replied.

"New embellishments?" Ehlana asked with some surprise.

"Rewards for services rendered, Ehlana." Sarabian smiled. "It seemed appropriate. Duke Caalador's accepted a position in the Ministry of the Interior, so he's gone back to Lebas to settle up his affairs there."

"And Stragen?"

"He's on his way to Astel, your Majesty," Baroness Melidere replied with a bleak smile. "He said that he wants to have a few words with Elron."

"Did Elron manage to get out of Natayos alive?" Kalten sounded surprised. "Ekrasios said that the Shining Ones had obliterated the place."

"The word Caalador picked up was that Elron hid out somewhere while the Shining Ones were dissolving Scarpa and Cyzada. Then, after they were gone, he crept out of the ruins and bolted for home. Stragen's going to look him up." The Baroness looked at Khalad. "Krager got out as well," she told him. "Caalador found out that he was bound for Zenga in eastern Cammoria. There's something you should know about Krager, though."

"Oh?"

"Do you remember how King Wargun died?"

"His liver finally gave out on him, didn't it?"

She nodded. "The same thing's happening to Krager. Caalador talked with a man named Orden in the town of Delo. Krager was completely out of his head when they put him on the ship bound for Zenga."

"He's still alive, though, isn't he?" Khalad asked bleakly.

"If you can call it that." She sighed. "Let it go, Khalad. He wouldn't even feel it if you ran your sword through him. He wouldn't know who you were or why you were killing him."

"Thank you, Baroness," Khalad said, "but I think that when we get back to Eosia, Berit and I'll run on down to Zenga just to make sure. Krager's gotten away from us just a few too many times to take any chances. I want to see him in the ground."

"Can I come, too?" Talen asked eagerly.

"No," Khalad replied.

"What do you mean, no?"

"It's time for you to start your novitiate."

"That can wait."

"No, it can't. You're already a half a year late. If you don't start training now, you'll never become proficient."

Vanion looked approvingly at Sparhawk's squire. "Don't forget what we talked about earlier, Sparhawk," he said. "And pass my recommendation on to Dolmant."

"What's this?" Khalad asked.

"I'll tell you about it later," Sparhawk replied.

"Oh, by the way, Ehlana," Sarabian said, "as long as the subject's come up anyway, would you be put out with me if I bestowed a title on your little songbird here?" He smiled fondly at Alean. "I certainly hope not, dear heart, because I'm going to do it anyway—for outstanding service to the empire, if nothing else."

"What a splendid idea, Sarabian!" Ehlana exclaimed.

"I can't really take much credit for the notion of the titles, I'm afraid," he admitted a bit ruefully. "Actually, they were your daughter's idea. Her Royal Highness is a very strong-minded little girl."

Sparhawk glanced briefly at his daughter and then at Flute. They wore identical expressions of smug self-satisfaction. Divine Aphrael clearly would not let anything stand in the way of her matchmaking. Sparhawk smiled briefly and then cleared his throat. "Ah—your Majesty," he said to the emperor, "it's growing rather late, and we're all tired. I'd suggest that we continue this tomorrow."

"Of course, Prince Sparhawk," Sarabian agreed, rising to his feet.

"A word with you, Sparhawk?" Patriarch Emban said as the others started to file out.

"Of course." They waited until they were alone in the room.

"What are we going to do about Vanion and Sephrenia?" Emban asked.

"I don't exactly follow you, your Grace."

"This so-called marriage is going to put Dolmant in a very difficult position, you know."

"It's not a 'so-called marriage,' Emban," Sparhawk said firmly, cutting across the formalities.

"You know what I mean. The conservatives in the Hierocracy will probably try to use it to weaken Sarathi's position."

"Why tell them, then? It's none of their business. A lot of things that our theology can't explain have happened here in Tamuli, your Grace. The empire's outside the jurisdiction of our Church, so why tell the Hierocracy anything about them?"

"I can't just lie to them, Sparhawk."

"I didn't suggest that. Just don't talk about it."

"I *have* to report to Dolmant."

"That's all right. He's flexible." Sparhawk considered it. "That's probably your best course anyway. We'll take Dolmant off to one side and tell him about everything that's happened here. We'll let *him* decide how much to tell the Hierocracy."

"You're putting an awful burden on him, Sparhawk."

Sparhawk shrugged. "That's what he gets paid for, isn't it? Now if you'll excuse me, your Grace, there's a family reunion going on that I should probably attend."

There was a melancholy sense of endings for the next several weeks. They were all fully aware of the fact that once the weather broke, most of them would be leaving Matherion. The likelihood that they would ever gather again was very slight. They savored their moments together, and there were frequent private little inter-

ludes when two or perhaps three of them would gather in out-of-the-way places, ostensibly to talk at great length about inconsequential matters, but in fact to try to
cement faces, the sounds of voices, and very personal connections forever in their
memories.

Sparhawk entered the sitting room one blustery morning to find Sarabian and
Oscagne with their heads together over a bound book of some kind. There was a
certain outrage in their expressions. "Trouble?" Sparhawk asked.

"Politics," Sarabian said sourly. "That's always trouble."

"The Contemporary History Department at the university has just published
their version of recent events, Prince Sparhawk," Oscagne explained. "There's very
little truth in it—particularly in light of the fact that Pondia Subat, our esteemed
prime minister, turns out to be a hero."

"I should have deleted Subat as soon as I found out about his activities," Sarabian said moodily. "Who would be the best one to answer this tripe, Oscagne?"

"My brother, your Majesty," the foreign minister replied promptly. "He *is* a
member of the faculty, and he has a certain reputation. Unfortunately, he's in
Cynestra just now."

"Send for him, Oscagne. Get him back here before Contemporary History
contaminates the thinking of a whole generation."

"Maris will want to come, too, your Majesty."

"Fine. Your brother's too clever by half. Let's keep Atana Maris nice and close
to him. She might be able to teach him humility."

"What are we going to do with the Cyrgai, your Majesty?" Sparhawk asked.
"Sephrenia says that the curse that confined them was lifted when Cyrgon died, and
even though it's not actually their fault, there really isn't any place for them in the
modern world."

"I've been brooding about that myself," the emperor admitted. "I think we'll
want to keep them away from normal human beings. There's an island about five
hundred leagues east of Tega. It's fairly fertile and it has a more or less acceptable climate. Since the Cyrgai are so fond of isolation, it should turn the trick. How long
do you think it might take them to invent boats?"

"Several thousand years, your Majesty. The Cyrgai aren't very creative."

Sarabian grinned at him. "I'd say that's the perfect place, then."

Sparhawk grinned back. "Sounds good to me," he agreed.

Spring came to eastern Tamuli in a rush that year. A sudden warm, wet wind
blew in off the Tamul Sea, cutting the snow off the sides of nearby mountains in a
single night. The streams ran bank-full, of course, so it was still too early for travel.
Sparhawk's impatience grew with each lingering day. It was not so much that he had
anything pressing to attend to, but more that this prolonged farewell was extremely
painful.

There *was* one fairly extended argument. Ehlana insisted at first that they
should all journey to Atan to celebrate the wedding of Mirtai and Kring.

"You're being ignorant again, Ehlana," Mirtai finally told her with characteristic bluntness. "You've seen weddings before, and you've got a kingdom to run. Go
back to Cimmura where you belong."

"Don't you want me to be present?" Ehlana's eyes filled with tears.

Mirtai embraced her. "You *will* be, Ehlana," she said. "You're in my heart forever now. Go back to Cimmura. I'll come by after Kring and I get settled in Pela—or wherever we decide to live."

Vanion and Sephrenia decided to accompany Queen Betuana's party as far as Atan and then to proceed on to Sarsos. "It's probably the best place for us, dear one," Sephrenia told Sparhawk. "I have a certain status there, and I can shout down the fanatics who'll try to object to the fact that Vanion and I are married now."

"Well put," Sparhawk said. Then he sighed. "I'm going to miss you, little mother," he told her. "You and Vanion won't ever be able to come back to Eosia, you know."

"Don't be absurd, Sparhawk." She laughed. "I've always gone anyplace I wanted to go, and I always will. There are ways I can disguise Vanion's face—and mine—so we'll stop by from time to time. I want to keep an eye on your daughter, if nothing else." Then she kissed him. "Run along now, dear one. I have to go talk with Sarabian about Betuana."

"Oh?"

"She's been muttering some nonsense about abdicating so that she can marry Engessa. The Atans are subject to the imperial crown, so I have to persuade Sarabian to keep her from doing something foolish. Engessa will make a very good co-ruler, and Sarabian needs stability in Atan."

As the spring runoff began to recede and the soggy fields around the capital began to dry out, Sparhawk went down to the harbor looking for Captain Sorgi. There were less battered and more luxurious ships swinging at anchor in the crowded harbor, but Sparhawk trusted Sorgi, and to sail home with him would provide a comforting sense of continuity to the conclusion of this whole business. He found the curly-haired sea captain in a neat, well-lighted wharfside tavern that was quite obviously run by an Elene proprietor.

"There'll be thirteen of us, Captain," Sparhawk said, "and seven horses."

"We'll be a bit crowded, Master Cluff," Sorgi replied, squinting at the ceiling, "but I think we can manage. Are you going to be covering the cost of the passage yourself?"

Sparhawk grinned. "The emperor has graciously offered to defray the expense," he said. "He's a friend, so please don't bankrupt him."

Sorgi grinned back. "I wouldn't think of it, Master Cluff." He leaned back in his chair. "It's been an interesting time, and the Tamul Empire's an interesting place, but it'll be good to get back home again."

"Yes," Sparhawk agreed. "Sometimes it seems that I've spent my whole life trying to get back home."

"I'll reckon up the cost of the voyage and have my bo'sun bring it up to the imperial compound to you. I almost lost him down in Beresa, you know."

"Your bo'sun?"

Sorgi nodded. "A couple of rascals waylaid him in an alleyway. He barely got out alive."

"Imagine that," Sparhawk said blandly. Evidently Valash had tried to cut some corners on the hiring of assassins as well as on everything else.

"When exactly did you want to sail, Master Cluff?"

"We haven't quite decided yet—sometime in the next week or so. I'll let you know. Some of our friends are leaving to go overland to Atan. It might be best if we sailed on the same day."

"Good idea," Sorgi approved. "It's always best not to drag out the farewells. Sailors have learned how to say good-bye in a hurry. When the time comes to leave, we always have to catch the tide, and it won't wait."

"Well put, Sorgi." Sparhawk smiled.

Not surprisingly it was Betuana who made the decision. "We'll leave tomorrow," she declared flatly at the dinner table a week later.

"So soon?" Sarabian's voice sounded slightly stricken.

"The streams are down and the fields are dry, Sarabian-Emperor," she pointed out. "Why should we linger?"

"Well . . ." He let it trail off.

"You're too sentimental, Sarabian," she told him bluntly. "You know that we're going to leave. Why prolong it? Come to Atan next fall, and we'll go boar hunting. You spend too much time penned up here in Matherion."

"It's pretty hard for me to get away," he said dubiously. "Somebody has to stay here and mind the store."

"Let Oscagne do it. He's honorable, so he won't steal too much."

"Your Majesty!" Oscagne protested.

She smiled at him. "I was only teasing you, Oscagne," she told him. "Friends can do that without giving offense."

There was little sleep for any of them that night. There was packing, of course, and a myriad of other preparations, but the bulk of the night was spent running up and down the hallways with urgent messages that were all basically the same: "Promise that we'll keep in touch."

And they all did promise, of course, and they all really meant it. The fading of that resolve would not begin for at least a year—or maybe even two.

They gathered in the castle courtyard just as dawn was breaking over the Tamul Sea. There were all the customary kisses and embraces and gruff handshakes.

It was finally Khalad, good, solid, dependable Khalad, who looked appraisingly at the eastern sky, cleared his throat, and said, "We'd better get started, Sparhawk. Sorgi'll charge you for an extra day if you make him miss the morning tide."

"Right," Sparhawk agreed. He lifted Ehlana up into the open carriage Sarabian had provided and in which Emban, Talen, Alean, and Melidere were already seated. Then he looked around and saw Danae and Flute speaking quietly together. "Danae," he called his daughter, "time to go."

The Crown Princess of Elenia kissed the Child-Goddess of Styricum one last time and obediently came across the courtyard to her father.

"Thanks for stopping by, Sparhawk," Sarabian said simply, holding out his hand.

Sparhawk took the hand in his own. "My pleasure, Sarabian," he replied. Then he swung himself up into Faran's saddle and led the way across the drawbridge and out onto the still-shadowy lawns.

It took perhaps a quarter of an hour to reach the harbor, and another half hour to load the horses in the forward hold. Sparhawk came back up on deck where the others waited and looked toward the east, where the sun had not yet risen.

"All ready, Master Cluff?" Sorgi called from the quarterdeck at the stern of his ship.

"That's it, Captain Sorgi," Sparhawk called back. "We've done what we came to do. Let's go home."

The self-important bo'sun strutted up and down the deck unnecessarily supervising the casting off of all lines and the raising of the sails.

The tide was moving quite rapidly, and there was a good following breeze. Sorgi skillfully maneuvered his battered old ship out through the harbor to the open sea.

Sparhawk lifted Danae in one arm and put the other about Ehlana's shoulders, and they stood at the port rail looking back at the city the Tamuls called the center of the world. Sorgi swung his tiller over to take a southeasterly course to round the peninsula, and just as the sails bellied out in the breeze, the sun slid above the eastern horizon.

Matherion had been pale in the shadows of dawn, but as the sun rose, the opalescent domes took fire, and shimmering, rainbow-colored light played across the gleaming surfaces. Sparhawk and his wife and daughter stood at the rail, their eyes filled with the wonder of the glowing city that seemed somehow to be bidding them its own farewell and wishing them a safe voyage home.

ABOUT THE AUTHOR

David Eddings (1931-2009) published his first novel, *High Hunt*, in 1973, before turning to the field of fantasy with the Belgariad series, soon followed by the Malloreon. Born in Spokane, Washington, and raised in the Puget Sound area north of Seattle, he received his bachelor of arts degree from Reed College in Portland, Oregon, and a master of arts degree from the University of Washington. He served in the US Army, worked as a buyer for the Boeing Company, and was both a grocery clerk and a college English teacher. He lived in Nevada with his wife and frequent collaborator, Leigh Williams, until his death at the age of 77.